PENGUIN BOOKS

LES MISÉRABLES

VICTOR HUGO (1802–85) was the most forceful, prolific and versatile of the French nineteenth-century writers. He wrote Romantic costume dramas, many volumes of lyrical and satirical verse, political and other journalism, criticism and several novels, the best known of which was *Les Misérables* (1862) and the youthful *Notre Dame de Paris* (1831). A royalist and conservative as a young man, Hugo later became a committed social democrat and during the Second Empire of Napoleon III was exiled from France, living in the Channel Islands. He returned to Paris in 1870 and remained a great public figure until his death: his body lay in state under the Arc de Triomphe before being buried in the Panthéon.

NORMAN DENNY was educated at Radley College, and in Vienna and Paris. He has written a great many short stories under different names and several novels. Among his many translations are *Prometheus: A Life of Balzac* by André Maurois, *My Life and Films* by Jean Renoir and *The Future of Man* by Teilhard de Chardin.

VICTOR HUGO

Les Misérables

Translated and with an Introduction by
NORMAN DENNY

PENGUIN BOOKS

PENGUIN BOOKS

Published by the Penguin Group
Penguin Group (USA) Inc., 375 Hudson Street, New York, New York 10014, USA
Penguin Group (Canada), 90 Eglinton Avenue East, Suite 700, Toronto,
Ontario M4P 2Y3, Canada (a division of Pearson Penguin Canada Inc.)
Penguin Books Ltd, 80 Strand, London WC2R 0RL, England
Penguin Ireland, 25 St Stephen's Green, Dublin 2, Ireland (a division of Penguin Books Ltd)
Penguin Group (Australia), 707 Collins Street, Melbourne, Victoria 3008, Australia
(a division of Pearson Australia Group Pty Ltd)
Penguin Books India Pvt Ltd, 11 Community Centre, Panchsheel Park, New Delhi – 110 017, India
Penguin Group (NZ), 67 Apollo Drive, Rosedale, Auckland 0632,
New Zealand (a division of Pearson New Zealand Ltd)
Penguin Books (South Africa), Rosebank Office Park,
181 Jan Smuts Avenue, Parktown North 2193, South Africa
Penguin China, B7 Jiaming Center, 27 East Third Ring Road North,
Chaoyang District, Beijing 100020, China

Penguin Books Ltd, Registered Offices:
80 Strand, London WC2R 0RL, England

First published 1862
This translation first published by the Folio Press 1976
Published in Penguin Books in two volumes 1980
Reprinted in a one-volume edition 1982
This edition published 2012
Published in Penguin Books (USA) 2012

1 3 5 7 9 10 8 6 4 2

Translation copyright © The Folio Society Limited, 1976
All rights reserved

The footnotes by Professor Marius-François Guyard are used
by kind permission of Éditions Garnier Frères

CIP data available
ISBN 978-0-14-312359-0

Printed in the United States of America

CONTENTS

INTRODUCTION 7

Part One: Fantine

I.	AN UPRIGHT MAN	19
II.	THE OUTCAST	71
III.	IN THE YEAR 1817	119
IV.	TO TRUST IS SOMETIMES TO SURRENDER	144
V.	DEGRADATION	155
VI.	JAVERT	191
VII.	THE CHAMPMATHIEU AFFAIR	202
VIII.	COUNTER-STROKE	260

Part Two: Cosette

I.	WATERLOO	279
II.	THE SHIP *ORION*	325
III.	FULFILMENT OF A PROMISE	338
IV.	THE GORBEAU TENEMENT	385
V.	HUNT IN DARKNESS	399
VI.	LE PETIT-PICPUS	425
VIII.	CEMETERIES TAKE WHAT THEY ARE GIVEN	451

Part Three: Marius

I.	PARIS IN MICROCOSM	495
II.	A GRAND BOURGEOIS	512
III.	GRANDFATHER AND GRANDSON	522
IV.	THE A B C SOCIETY	555
V.	THE VIRTUES OF MISFORTUNE	584
VI.	CONJUNCTION OF TWO STARS	603
VII.	PATRON-MINETTE	619
VIII.	THE NOXIOUS POOR	627

Part Four: The Idyll in the Rue Plumet and the Epic of the Rue Saint-Denis

I.	A FEW PAGES OF HISTORY	705
II.	ÉPONINE	739
III.	THE HOUSE IN THE RUE PLUMET	756
IV.	HELP FROM BELOW MAY BE HELP FROM ABOVE	788
V.	OF WHICH THE END DOES NOT RESEMBLE THE BEGINNING	797
VI.	THE BOY GAVROCHE	812
VIII.	ENCHANTMENT AND DESPAIR	844
IX.	WHERE ARE THEY GOING?	876
X.	5 JUNE 1832	883
XI.	THE STRAW IN THE WIND	904
XII.	CORINTH	915
XIII.	MARIUS ENTERS THE DARKNESS	943
XIV.	THE GREATNESS OF DESPAIR	953
XV.	IN THE RUE DE L'HOMME-ARMÉ	970

Part Five: Jean Valjean

I.	WAR WITHIN FOUR WALLS	987
II.	THE ENTRAILS OF THE MONSTER	1061
III.	MIRE, BUT THE SOUL	1076
IV.	JAVERT IN DISARRAY	1104
V.	GRANDSON AND GRANDFATHER	1110
VI.	THE SLEEPLESS NIGHT	1129
VII.	THE BITTER CUP	1145
VIII.	THE FADING LIGHT	1162
IX.	SUPREME SHADOW, SUPREME DAWN	1173

APPENDIX A: The Convent as an Abstract Idea (Part Two, Book VII)	1202
APPENDIX B: Argot (Part Four, Book VII)	1214

I

VICTOR HUGO was born in 1802 at Besançon, now capital of the department of Doubs in eastern France. His father, a career officer in Napoleon's army, was at that time a major, but he rose eventually to the rank of general and was created a count. His various garrison appointments occasioned a number of removals, and the education of the youthful Victor-Marie was in consequence diversified, taking place in Italy and Spain as well as in Paris, at the Maison des Feuillantines. This was certainly good for him. There may be some doubt as to whether he could really read Tacitus at the age of seven, as he claimed, but he received a very thorough grounding in the humanities.

Hugo was, in short, the precocious son (the youngest of three brothers) of well-to-do middle-class parents. His literary vocation was very soon manifest. A poem written while he was still at school won a literary prize, and in 1819, with his brother Abel, he launched the *Conservateur Littéraire*, a review which, although it survived for only two years, achieved some prominence as a mouthpiece of the Romantic movement.

He shared with nearly all major writers the quality of abundance. The works poured out in an uneven flood, good, bad and indifferent, splendid at their best and, at their worst, lamentable: some twenty volumes of poetry, of which the best known are *Les Châtiments* (1853) and *Les Contemplations* (1856), nine novels, ten plays, mostly in verse (*Hernani*, *Ruy Blas*) and a huge amount of general writing, literary, sociological and political. Hugo was always, in the French word, *engagé*, deeply concerned with the social and political developments of his time. His politics might change in the light of events and as a reflection of his own growth, but his essential position remained unchanged. He was first and foremost, by nature as well as by conviction, a romantic. It was an attitude to life expressing itself in all life's activities, above all in the arts but also in politics, where it bore the name of liberalism. As time went on and he outgrew the Bonapartism inherited from his father and the royalism inherited from his mother, this liberalism took the form of outspoken republicanism. Universal suffrage and free (compulsory) education were to become the basic tenets of his political creed.

He was greatly afflicted by the death, in 1843, of his daughter, Léopoldine, and for some years there was a pause in the flow of purely literary work; but his political career and his growth as a national figure both continued to progress. Although he was becoming increasingly disenchanted with monarchism he contrived to be on good terms with Louis-Philippe, for whom, as his account in *Les Misérables* shows, he had both liking and respect. He was awarded the Légion d'honneur in 1837, was elected to the Académie Française in 1841 and created a *pair de France* (a life peer and member of the Upper House) in 1845.

Three years later, when the revolution of 1848 drove Louis-Philippe from the throne, he became a member of the Constituent Assembly of the newly formed republic; but he could not stomach Louis Napoleon's Second Empire (1851), and since his condemnation of it was too loud to be overlooked he was forced to leave France. After staying for a time in Brussels, he moved to the Channel Islands, first to Jersey and then to Guernsey, where he lived with his wife and family for fourteen years, with the actress Juliette Drouet, his lifelong mistress, close at hand. It was here that he wrote, among other things, *Les Travailleurs de la mer* (1866) and completed the novel which is generally considered to be his masterpiece, *Les Misérables*, published in 1862.

II

The brothers Goncourt, at that time the high priests of literature in France, were not impressed by *Les Misérables*. 'The lack of first-hand observation,' they wrote, 'is everywhere painfully manifest. Hugo has built his book, situation and characters alike, on the appearance of reality, not on reality itself.' This was their conclusion after reading the first volume. Having read the whole book they likened the author to 'those English preachers who harangue strollers in the parks on a Sunday'.

Professor Marius-François Guyard, from whose meticulously edited and annotated text (Garnier Frères, 1963) this translation has been made, and to whom the present translator is immensely indebted, answers the Goncourts by citing some of the novel's more unforgettable characters – Jean Valjean, the Thénardiers, Fantine, Javert and, above all, the splendid street-urchin Gavroche. He is silent however on the subject of Marius, that singularly lacklustre young man who is supposedly a portrait of the youthful Victor Hugo himself.

The Goncourts were both right and wrong, right in the narrow sense but not in the large one. They were right about the realism which Hugo strove so laboriously and, on the whole, so unsuccessfully to achieve. No one could have worked harder at it. He read and read, he pored endlessly over maps and documents, and the fruits of his researches so encumber his book that many readers beside the Goncourts must have found themselves unequal to the effort of pursuing it. But this factual realism is constantly at war with the poet. Imaginative realism is another matter. *Les Misérables*, with its depth of vision and underlying truth, its moments of lyrical quality and of moving compassion, is a novel of towering stature, one of the great works of western literature, a melodrama that is also a morality and a social document embracing a wider field than any other novel of its time, conceived on the scale of *War and Peace* but even more ambitious.

That is the trouble. The defects which the Goncourts saw, and which no one can fail to see, since they are as monumental as the book itself, may be summed up in the single word, extravagance. Hugo, although as the final result shows he was masterly in the construction of his novel, had little or no regard for the discipline of novel-writing. He was wholly unrestrained and unsparing of his reader. He had to say everything and more than everything; he was incapable of leaving anything out. The book is loaded down with digressions, interpolated discourses, passages of moralizing rhetoric and pedagogic disquisitions.

One reason for this is that it was written over a period of nearly twenty years. A first unfinished novel entitled *Misères* was written during the three years from 1845 to 1848; it was then put aside for twelve years, to be completed in 1860–62 as *Les Misérables*. (An untranslatable title: the first meaning of the French *misère* is simply misery; the second meaning is utmost poverty, destitution; but Hugo's *misérables* are not merely the poor and wretched, they are the outcasts, the underdogs, the rejected of society and the rebels against society.)

As to the digressions, many of them are in fact interpolations.

Much had happened in the world during the twelve years that the book was laid aside and much had happened to Hugo himself. He had moved steadily away from his right-wing bourgeois origins to the point where he was not only an avowed republican but could openly proclaim himself a socialist. It is not surprising that that earlier work required considerable amendment if it was to conform to the changed viewpoint of the Hugo who returned to it in 1860.

But some of the digressions, or interpolations, are still indefensible, the most flagrant being the account of the Battle of Waterloo, which occupies the third book of Part Two. It is subdivided into nineteen chapters filling sixty-nine pages of the closely printed French text, and only the last chapter, seven pages long, has any real bearing on Hugo's story. The rest is entirely concerned with the battle. Hugo, as he tells us, had tramped over the battlefield, presumably when he was living in Brussels in 1853; he had studied maps and army-lists and such professional records as were available to him, and out of this he concocted his own elaborate and poeticized layman's version of an event which, tremendous though it was, had no more to do with the story of *Les Misérables* than any other major historical event that had occurred during the century.

This is the largest of the digressions, and it is reasonable to assume that the bulk of it was written long before Hugo returned to his novel. The present English version has retained it, very slightly abridged, in the place it occupies in the novel, partly because it is a magnificent piece of writing and also because the episode described in that final chapter is crucial to the story.

Two other long digressions, however, have been treated with less respect. The first is in the seventh book of Part Two, entitled *Parenthèse*, in which Hugo discourses upon the subject of strictly enclosed religious orders, of which he disapproved (he himself, although he was broadly and sincerely religious, subscribed to no particular orthodoxy). This parenthesis follows immediately upon another, the meticulous (and fascinating) account of life in the Petit-Picpus convent, so that the story, at a highly dramatic point, is left in mid-air for some fifty pages. Hugo's publisher, Lacroix, feeling that this would be trying the reader's patience altogether too high, urged him to take it out; but Hugo refused, as it seems for purely personal reasons: his cousin Marie, to whom he was attached, had taken the veil in 1848. This section has accordingly been removed from the body of the book and transferred to the end as Appendix A.

The discourse on *argot* (Book Seven, Part Four) has been similarly treated and is relegated to Appendix B in Volume II. Here little explanation is needed. In so far as it related directly to the *argot* (Paris underworld slang) of Hugo's day, his discourse, with its numerous examples, can be of interest only to specialists; where it spreads into the wider field of the general significance of thieves' cant (a digression within a digression!) it is more interesting; but in any event it does nothing to advance the story.

The other digressions, homilies and disquisitions, or simply over-large elaborations, have been left where they were, but in some cases, particularly those of over-elaboration, they have been somewhat abridged. And here I must abandon any suggestion of the editorial 'we' and state as plainly as I can my personal approach to the translation of *Les Misérables* and the liberties I have felt justified in taking with Hugo's text.

III

There are three earlier English renderings of Hugo's novel, of which I have seen only one. I shall not disclose which one, or make any comment except to say that I found it very heavy going. It was made at the turn of the century and the translator, conscientiously observing the principles of translation at that time, has made a brave attempt to follow Hugo in the smallest detail, almost literally word for word. The result is something that is not English, not Hugo and, it seems to me, scarcely readable. It reads, in short, like a translation and it does no service to Hugo. I am told that the other English versions, which I have not seen, are not very different.

The principles of translation have greatly changed in the past twenty or thirty years. It is now generally recognized that the translator's first concern must be with his author's *intention*; not with the words he uses or with the way he uses them, if they have a different impact when they are rendered too faithfully into English, but with what he is seeking to convey to the reader. This, of course, embraces a great deal more than literal meaning or the plain statement of fact: feeling, colour, poetry, humour, irony, all these are elements which the translator may on no account ignore; he must catch them as best he can. But there is an overriding intention, larger than all others. The author – each and every author – writes because he wants to be *read*. Readability must be the translator's first concern. Sometimes he is set an impossible task. There are writers who may fairly be termed unreadable. But Victor Hugo is not one of them. He is in many ways the most exasperating of writers – long-winded, extravagant in his use of words (it is not uncommon to find eight or ten adjectives appended to a single noun), sprawling and self-indulgent. At times (the vanity for which he was famous may account for it) he was, with all his high-minded earnestness, extraordinarily lacking in self-criticism. There are passages of mediocrity and banality in *Les Misérables*, as in all his work, which may cause the reader to lose all patience with him and put the book aside, without having ever reached the nobility of spirit that inspired it.

The translator (and here I am referring specifically to myself and *Les Misérables*) can, I maintain, do something to remedy these defects without falsifying the book, if he will nerve himself to treat Hugo not as a museum piece or a sacred cow but as the author of a very great novel which is still living, still relevant to life, and which deserves to be read. He can 'edit' – that is to say abridge, tone down the rhetoric, even delete where the passage in question is merely an elaboration of what has already been said.

I have edited in this sense throughout the book, as a rule only to a minor degree, and never, I hope, so drastically as to be unfaithful to Hugo's intention. I must cite the most extreme case in illustration of what I mean. This is the third book of Part One entitled 'In the year 1817'. Hugo has sought to convey the social climate of that particular year by compiling a lengthy catalogue of personalities and events, most of them of no great importance – people and happenings, in short, that got into the news at the time. One has the impression that he did it by skimming through the newspaper headlines. What is certain is that most of his allusions would have meant nothing to any except his oldest readers even when the book was published in 1862. As for the present day, Professor Guyard has found it necessary to append sixty-two footnotes for the enlightenment of contemporary French readers – incidentally pointing out, not infrequently, that Hugo got his facts wrong. I have dealt with this section by drastically reducing it, cutting out references that would be meaningless to English readers and including only those that serve Hugo's purpose of conveying the atmosphere of Paris in that year. The footnotes have either been incorporated in the text or abolished where they no longer applied, except in the case of a very few which had to go at the bottom of the page. I may mention incidentally that the footnotes throughout the book are to be attributed to Professor Guyard except where I specifically acknowledge them – 'trs.'.

This foreword is unavoidable if the reader is to know exactly what he is getting – not a photograph but a slightly modified version of Hugo's novel designed to bring its great qualities into clearer relief by thinning out, but never completely eliminating, its lapses. It must stand or fall not by its literal accuracy, although I profoundly hope that I have been guilty of no major solecisms, but by its faithfulness to the spirit of Victor Hugo. He was above all things, and at all times, a poet. If the fact is not apparent to the English reader then this rendering of his work must be said to have failed.

NORMAN DENNY

While through the working of laws and customs there continues to exist a condition of social condemnation which artificially creates a human hell within civilization, and complicates with human fatality a destiny that is divine; while the three great problems of this century, the degradation of man in the proletariat, the subjection of women through hunger, the atrophy of the child by darkness, continue unresolved; while in some regions social asphyxia remains possible; in other words, and in still wider terms, while ignorance and poverty persist on earth, books such as this cannot fail to be of value.

Hauteville House, 1 January 1862

PART ONE
FANTINE

BOOK ONE

AN UPRIGHT MAN

I

Monseigneur Myriel

IN THE year 1815 Monseigneur Charles-François-Bienvenu Myriel was Bishop of Digne. He was then about seventy-five, having held the bishopric since 1806.

Although it has no direct bearing on the tale we have to tell, we must nevertheless give some account of the rumours and gossip concerning him which were in circulation when he came to occupy the diocese. What is reported of men, whether it be true or false, may play as large a part in their lives, and above all in their destiny, as the things they do. Monseigneur Myriel was the son of a coun-sellor of the Parliament of Aix, a member of the *noblesse de robe*. It was said of him that his father, intending him to inherit his office, had arranged for him to marry at a very early age, about eighteen or twenty, following the custom that was fairly widespread in parlia-mentary families. Charles Myriel, it was said, had attracted much gossip despite this marriage. He was good-looking although of small stature, elegant, graceful, and entertaining; his early life was wholly devoted to worldly matters and affairs of gallantry. Then had come the revolution, and in the rush of those events the decimated and persecuted parliamentary families had been scattered. Charles Myriel emigrated to Italy, and here his wife died of the chest complaint that had long afflicted her. There were no children. What happened after this to Monseigneur Myriel? Did the collapse of the old French social order, the downfall of his own family, the tragic events of '93 – perhaps even more fearful to an *émigré* witnessing them at a distance – inspire in him thoughts of renunciation and solitude? Amid the distractions and frivolities that occupied his life, did it happen that he was suddenly overtaken by one of those mysterious and awful revulsions which, striking to the heart, change the nature of a man who cannot be broken by outward disasters affecting his life and fortune? No one can say. All that is known is that when he returned from Italy he was a priest.

In 1804 M. Myriel was curé of Brignolles, where, already elderly, he lived in profound seclusion.

At the time of the Emperor's coronation, some small matter of parish business took him to Paris. Among the influential personages whom he had occasion to visit was Cardinal Fesch, the uncle of Napoleon, and it happened one day, when he was waiting in the cardinal's antechamber, that the Emperor passed through on his way to call on his uncle. Seeing the old priest intently regarding him, he turned to him and asked sharply:

'Who is the gentleman who is staring at me?'

'Sire,' replied M. Myriel, 'you are looking at a plain man and I am looking at a great man. Each of us may benefit.'

That evening the Emperor asked the cardinal the priest's name, and shortly afterwards M. Myriel learned to his great surprise that he had been appointed Bishop of Digne.

As to the truth in general of the tales that were told about the early life of M. Myriel, no one could vouch for it. Few people remained who had known his family before the revolution. He had to accept the fate of every newcomer to a small town where there are plenty of tongues that gossip and few minds that think. He had to bear with this in spite of being a bishop and because he was a bishop. And after all, these tales were perhaps only tales, rumour and fabrication and nothing more.

However that may be, by the ninth year of his residence as Bishop of Digne all the chatter that at first occupies small people in small places had died down and been forgotten. No one would have presumed to refer to it or even to remember it.

M. Myriel had come to Digne accompanied by his sister, Mademoiselle Baptistine, an unmarried woman ten years younger than himself. Their only servant was Madame Magloire, a woman of the same age as Mlle Baptistine, who, from having been the servant of M. le Curé, now assumed the twofold office of personal maid to Mademoiselle and housekeeper to Monseigneur.

Mlle Baptistine was tall, pale, thin and gentle, a perfect expression of all that is implied by the word 'respectable': for it seems that a woman must become a mother before she can be termed 'venerable'. She had never been pretty. Her life, which had been wholly occupied with good works, had endowed her with a kind of pallor and luminosity, and as she grew older she had acquired what may be called the beauty of goodness. What had been skinniness in her youth had become, as she matured, a quality of transparency through which her saintly nature could be seen to shine. She was a spirit more than she was a virgin. Her being seemed composed of shadow, with too little substance for it to possess sex. It was a shred of matter harbouring a light, with large eyes that were always cast down; a pretext for a soul to linger on earth.

Mme Magloire was a small, plump, white-haired old woman, always busy and always breathless, partly because of her incessant activity and also because she suffered from asthma.

Upon his arrival in Digne M. Myriel was installed in the bishop's palace with the honours prescribed by the imperial decree, which ranked a bishop immediately below a Marshal of France. The Mayor and the President of the Council were the first dignitaries to call upon him, and his own first visits were paid to the General and the prefect.

His installation over, the town waited to see their new bishop at work.

II

Monseigneur Myriel becomes Monseigneur Bienvenu

The bishop's palace in Digne was next door to the hospital. It was a large and handsome stone mansion built at the beginning of the previous century by Henri Puget, Doctor of Theology at the University of Paris and Abbot of Simore, who became Bishop of Digne in 1712. Everything in the palace was on the grand scale, the bishop's personal apartments, the drawing-rooms and bedrooms, the broad courtyard flanked by arcades in the old Florentine manner and the gardens planted with splendid trees. The dining-room was a long and magnificent gallery on the ground floor, giving on to the garden. It was here, on 29 July 1714, that Monseigneur Puget had entertained at a ceremonial dinner seven high dignitaries of the Church, among them Philippe de Vendôme, Grand Prior of France and the great-grandson of Henri IV and Gabrielle d'Estrées. The portraits of the seven reverend gentlemen now hung in the dining-room, together with a white marble tablet carrying the date inscribed in letters of gold.

The hospital was a narrow, two-storeyed house with a small garden.

The bishop called at the hospital on the third day after his arrival. Having concluded his visit he asked the director to accompany him to the palace.

'Monsieur le Directeur,' he said, 'how many patients have you at present?'

'Twenty-six, Monseigneur.'

'That is a large number.'

'The beds,' said the director, 'are very close together.'

'As I noticed.'

'The wards are no bigger than single rooms. They get very stuffy.'

'That seems to be the case.'

'And when we get a little sunshine there is scarcely room in the garden for the convalescents.'

'So I imagine.'

'And when there's an epidemic – we had typhus this year and an outbreak of military fever two years ago, sometimes as many as a hundred patients – we don't know where to turn.'

'That thought also occurred to me.'

'But it can't be helped, Monseigneur,' said the director. 'We have to make the best of things.'

This conversation took place in the ground-floor banqueting-hall. The bishop was silent for some moments, and then he turned abruptly to the director.

'Tell me,' he said, 'how many beds do you think could be put in this room?'

'In the bishop's dining-room?' exclaimed the director in astonishment.

The bishop was gazing round the room, apparently making calculations of his own.

'At least twenty beds,' he murmured as though to himself. Then he said more loudly: 'Monsieur le Directeur, I will tell you what has happened. There has been a mistake. You have twenty-six persons in five or six small rooms, while in this house there are three of us and room for sixty. We must change places. Let me have the house that suits me, and this one will be yours.'

On the following day the twenty-six paupers were moved into the palace and the bishop took up residence in the hospital.

M. Myriel had no private means; his family had been ruined by the revolution. His sister's annuity of five hundred francs had sufficed for their personal needs during his curacy. As bishop he received a stipend of fifteen thousand francs. On the day of his removal to the hospital he laid down, once and for all, how this money was to be used. The note, written in his own hand, reads as follows:

Note on the Disposal of my Household Expenses

For the small seminary	1500 francs
Missionary congregation	100 francs
Lazarists of Montdidier	100 francs
Seminary of foreign missions in Paris	200 francs
Congregation of the Saint-Esprit	150 francs
Religious establishments in the Holy Land	100 francs
Maternity societies	300 francs
In addition, for that of Arles	50 francs
For the improvement of prisons	400 francs
For the relief and deliverance of prisoners	500 francs
For the release of fathers of families imprisoned for debt	1000 francs
To supplement the salaries of underpaid schoolmasters in the diocese	2000 francs
Grain reserve in the Hautes-Alpes	100 francs
Ladies' Association of Digne, Manosque, and Sisteron for the free education of poor girls	1500 francs
For the poor	6000 francs
Personal expenses	1000 francs
Total	15,000 francs

During the time he occupied the see of Digne M. Myriel made almost no change in this order of things, which, as we see, he called 'the disposal of my household expenses'. The arrangement was accepted with absolute submission by Mlle Baptistine. To that devout woman M. Myriel was both her brother and her bishop, her friend in nature and her superior in the Church. Quite simply, she loved and venerated him. When he spoke she bowed her head, when he acted she sustained him. Only Mme Magloire grumbled a little. The bishop, as we have seen, had kept only a thousand francs for himself, which, with his sister's annuity, made a total of fifteen hundred francs a year. Upon this sum the two old women and the old man lived.

Nevertheless when a village curé came to Digne the bishop found means to entertain him, thanks to the strict economy of Mme Magloire and the shrewd management of Mlle Baptistine.

One day when he had been about three months in Digne the bishop remarked:

'And yet, with all this, I am still in difficulties.'

'I should think so!' cried Mme Magloire. 'Monseigneur has not even applied to the Department for an allowance to cover the cost of his carriage in the town and on his tours of the diocese. This was always granted to bishops in the old days.'

'Of course!' said the bishop. 'You are quite right, Madame Magloire.'

He made the application.

The Departmental Council, having weighed the matter, voted him an annual allowance of three thousand francs under the heading: 'Allotted to Monseigneur the Bishop for the purpose of his carriage and postal expenses and the cost of his pastoral journeys.'

This caused considerable outcry among the local citizenry and it moved a certain senator of the Empire, a former member of the Council of Five Hundred who had supported the 18 Brumaire and was now the holder of a princely senatorial seat near Digne, to write an indignant private letter to M. Bigot de Prémeneu* of which the following authentic extract may be quoted:

'Carriage expenses? What for, in a town of fewer than four thousand inhabitants? Postage and pastoral journeys? What is the use of these journeys? And what is the use of a vehicle for delivering letters in mountainous country with no roads? People go on horseback. The bridge over the Durance at Château-Arnoux can scarcely take an ox-cart. These priests are all the same, greedy and miserly. This one started with a show of virtue but now he's behaving like the rest. He has to have a carriage and a post-chaise. He wants all the luxuries of the old bishops. These informal priests! Affairs won't be properly managed, Monsieur le Comte, until the Emperor has rid us of these mountebanks. Down with the Pope!' [There was trouble with Rome at the time.] 'For my part, I am on the side of Caesar . . .' And so on.

Mme Magloire, on the other hand, was highly delighted.

'Good,' she said to Mlle Baptistine. 'Monseigneur started by thinking of others, but he has to think of himself in the end. He has attended to all his charities. Now there are three thousand francs for us – and high time!'

*A real person. He was one of the compilers of the *Code Civil* and Ministre de Cultes (religious affairs) under the Empire.

But that evening the bishop wrote the following note and handed it to his sister.

Carriage and Travel Expenses

Meat broth for the hospital patients	1500 francs
Maternity Society at Aix	250 francs
Maternity Society at Draguignan	250 francs
For foundling children	500 francs
For orphan children	500 francs
Total	3000 francs

Such was the personal budget of Monseigneur Myriel.

As for day-to-day charities, the dispensations, baptisms, prayers, consecration of churches and chapels, marriages and so forth, the bishop exacted funds for these from the rich, doing so the more rigorously since he passed the money on to the poor. Within a short time gifts of money were flowing in. Those who had and those who had not knocked at M. Myriel's door, the latter to seek the alms that the former had contributed. Within a year the bishop had become the treasurer of all charitable works and the cashier of all suffering. Considerable sums passed through his hands, but nothing could cause him to change his way of life or accept any trifle beyond his daily needs. Indeed, the reverse was the case. Since there is always more misery in the depths than compassion in the heights, everything was given, so to speak, before it was received. It was like water on parched land. However fast the money flowed in he never had enough; and then he robbed himself.

It being customary for bishops to preface their pastoral letters and orders with the full list of their baptismal names, the people of the region, from instinctive affection, elected to call him by the name which for them had the most meaning, Monseigneur Bienvenu. We shall follow their example and use this name when occasion arises. In any event, it pleased him. *Bienvenu* – or 'welcome'. 'It counteracts the Monseigneur,' he said.

We do not claim that the portrait we are making is the whole truth, only that it is a resemblance.

A hard office for a good bishop

Although he had converted his carriage into alms, the bishop did not on this account neglect his pastoral duties. Digne was a rugged diocese, with very little flat land, many mountains and, as we have seen, very few roads. It contained thirty-two curacies, forty-one vicarages, and two hundred and eighty-five chapels-of-ease and sub-curacies. To visit them all was a large undertaking, but the bishop accomplished it. He went on foot to near-by places, by carrier's cart to places on the plain, and by pack-mule into the hills. As a rule the two women accompanied him, but when the journey was too difficult he went alone.

He arrived one day at Senez, a former episcopal city, riding a donkey, his means at that moment being so scanty that he could afford no other conveyance. The mayor, welcoming him at the gates of the residence, watched with shocked eyes while he dismounted, and laughter arose from a few citizens who were standing by.

'Gentlemen,' said the bishop, 'I know what has outraged you. You find it arrogant in a simple priest that he should be mounted like Jesus Christ. Let me assure you that I do it from necessity, not from vanity.'

He was gentle and indulgent on these tours of office, preaching less than he talked. He treated no virtue as though it were beyond ordinary reach, nor did he use far-fetched reasoning and examples. To the people of a district which dealt harshly with its poor he would quote the example of their neighbours. 'Take the people of Briançon. They allow the needy, the widows and orphans, to cut their hay three days earlier than the rest. When their homes are in ruins they repair them for nothing. And so that is a region blessed by God. In the past hundred years they have not had a single murder.'

To villages over-intent upon yield and profit he said: 'Take the people of Embrun. If at harvest-time the father of a family is left single-handed, with his sons in the army and his daughters in service in the town, or if he is sick or disabled, the priest mentions the fact in his sermon; and on Sunday, after Mass, all the people of the village, men, women, and children, go to help him with his harvesting and carry the straw and grain into his barn.' To families at odds over questions of money and inheritance he said: 'Take the hill-people of Devoluy, a region so bleak that the nightingale is not heard there once in fifty years. When the father dies the sons go elsewhere to seek their fortune, leaving the property to the daughters so that they may find husbands.' In districts much given to litigation, where the farmers wasted their substance on official documents, he said: 'Take the peasants in the Queyras valley, three thousand souls. I tell you, it is like a little republic. They have no judge or bailiff. The mayor does everything. He apportions the taxes, from each according to his means; he resolves quarrels, divides patrimonies, delivers judgement, all without charge. He is obeyed because he is a just man among simple people.' And he also cited the example of Queyras in villages where there was no schoolmaster: 'Do you know what they do? Since a hamlet of ten or fifteen dwellings cannot afford a schoolmaster they have teachers paid by the valley as a whole who go from village to village, spending a week here and ten days there. These teachers also visit the fairs, as I myself have seen. You may recognize them by the quills stuck in their hatbands. Those who only teach reading wear a single quill, those who teach reading and arithmetic wear two quills, and the teachers of reading, arithmetic and Latin wear three. Those last are very learned men. But how shameful it is to be ignorant! You should do as they do in Queyras.'

That was how he talked, gravely and paternally, inventing parables when no example came to hand, going straight to the point with little phrase-making and frequent imagery, using Christ's own eloquence, persuaded and persuading.

IV

Works matching words

His conversation was friendly and light-hearted. He put himself on the level of the two old women who shared his life, and when he laughed it was the laughter of a schoolboy.

Mme Magloire was pleased to address him as Your Greatness. On one occasion he rose from his armchair to get a book which was on a top shelf. He was short in stature and could not reach it. 'Mme Magloire,' he said, 'will you be so good as to fetch a chair. My greatness does not extend so high.'

A distant connection, the Comtesse de Lo, seldom missed an

opportunity, when she was with him, of talking about what she called the 'hopes' of her three sons. She had several very aged relatives of whom her sons were the natural heirs. The youngest was due to inherit an income of a hundred thousand francs from a great-aunt; the second was the adopted heir of his uncle, a duke; and the oldest was direct heir to a peerage. As a rule the bishop listened in silence to these blameless and forgivable maternal effusions. But on one occasion he appeared more abstracted than usual. 'For Heaven's sake, Cousin,' said the lady in mild exasperation, 'what are you thinking about?' – 'I am thinking,' said the bishop, 'of the words uttered by, I believe, St Augustine – "Put your hope in Him who has no successor."'

On another occasion, upon receiving a letter informing him of the death of one of the local gentry which set forth in great detail the deceased's many titles of nobility and those of his family, he exclaimed: 'Death has a broad back! What a great load of honours it can be made to bear, and how assiduous are the minds of men that they can use even the tomb in the service of vanity.'

He had recourse at times to gentle raillery in which there was nearly always a serious note. During one Lent a youthful vicar came to preach in the cathedral at Digne and did so with some eloquence. His theme was charity. He urged the rich to give to the poor so that they might escape the torments of Hell, which he depicted in hideous terms, and attain to Paradise, which he made to sound altogether delightful. Among the congregation was a Monsieur Geborand, a wealthy and grasping retired merchant, who had made a fortune in the cloth-trade but had never been known to give anything to the poor. It was observed, after this sermon, that on Sundays he handed a single sou to the old beggar-women clustered outside the cathedral door. There were six of them to share it. Noting the event, the bishop smiled and said to his sister: 'Monsieur Geborand is buying a penny-worth of Paradise.'

He was not to be deterred in his labours for charity even by a direct refusal, and he found things to say which lingered in the mind. Among the company in a fashionable salon where he went to solicit alms was the Marquis de Champtercier, a rich, elderly miser who contrived to be both ultra-royalist and ultra-Voltairian. The type existed in those days. The bishop touched him on the arm and said, 'Monsieur le Marquis, you must indeed give me something.' The marquis turned away, saying curtly, 'Monseigneur, I have my own poor.' – 'Give *them* to me,' said the bishop.

He preached the following sermon in the cathedral:

'My brothers and friends, there are in France thirteen hundred and twenty thousand peasant cottages which have only three outlets, eighteen hundred and seventeen thousand which have only two, a door and one window, and three hundred and forty-six thousand which have only a door. This is due to something known as the tax on doors and windows. Consider the fate of poor families, old women and young children, living in those hovels, the fevers and other maladies! God gives air to mankind and the law sells it. I do not assail the law but I give thanks to God. In Isère, in Var, and in the upper and lower Alps the peasants do not even possess barrows but carry the dung on their backs. They have no candles but burn twigs and lengths of rope steeped in resin. That is what happens throughout the highlands of Dauphiné. They make bread every six months, baking it over a fire of dried dung. In winter they break the loaves with a hatchet and soak the bread for twenty-four hours before it can be eaten. My brothers, be merciful. Consider the sufferings of those around you.'

Having been born in Provence he had had no difficulty in familiarizing himself with the dialects of the Midi, whether of Languedoc or the lower Alps or Upper Dauphiné. This pleased the people and had greatly helped to bring him close to them. He was at home in the peasant's hut and in the mountains. He could expound great matters in the simplest terms, and speaking all tongues could find his way to all hearts.

For the rest, he was the same to all men, the fashionable world and the ordinary people. He judged nothing in haste, or without taking account of the circumstances. He said, 'Let me see how the fault arose.' Being, as he said with a smile, himself a former sinner, he lacked all sactimoniousness, and without self-righteous flourishes preached in forthright terms a doctrine which may be summed up as follows:

'The flesh is at once man's burden and his temptation. He bears it and yields to it. He must keep watch over it and restrain it, and obey it only in the last resort. Such obedience may be a fault, but it is a venial fault. It is a fall, but a fall on to the knees which may end in prayer. To be a saint is to be an exception; to be a true man is the rule. Err, fail, sin if you must, but be upright. To sin as little as possible is the law for men; to sin not at all is a dream for angels. All earthly things are subject to sin; it is like the force of gravity.'

Any ill-considered outburst of popular indignation would cause him to smile. 'It appears,' he would say, 'that this is a crime which everyone commits. See how outraged hypocrisy hurries to cover itself!'

He was indulgent to women and to the poor, oppressed by the weight of society. 'The faults of women, children and servants,' he said, 'and of the weak, the poor and the ignorant, are the faults of husbands, fathers and masters, and of the strong, the rich and the learned.' He also said: 'Teach the ignorant as much as you can. Society is to blame for not giving free education; it is responsible for the darkness it creates. The soul in darkness sins, but the real sinner is he who caused the darkness.'

As we can see, he had his own way of looking at things. I think he derived it from the Gospel.

He listened one day to a drawing-room discussion of a crime which was then under interrogation and was shortly to be tried. For love of a woman and the child she had borne him a wretched man, at the end of his resources, had coined false currency. Counterfeiting at that time was punishable by death. The woman had been arrested when attempting to pass the first coin the man had forged. She was detained, but there was no evidence except against her, and she alone could destroy her lover by testifying against him. She denied everything and persisted in her denial. The Public Prosecutor then advised a plan. By the cunning use of fragments of letters he persuaded the unhappy woman that her lover had been unfaithful to her, and in a fit of jealousy she divulged everything. The man was doomed. Both would be tried and he would be convicted. The tale was told, and everyone was in raptures over the artfulness of the Prosecutor, who had brought the truth to light and caused justice to be done by appealing to jealousy and the instinct of revenge. The bishop listened to it all in silence and finally asked:

'Where are this man and woman to be tried?'

'At the Assizes in Aix.'

'And where will the Prosecutor be tried?'

A tragic event occurred in Digne. A man was sentenced to death for murder. He was a man, neither wholly educated nor illiterate, who had been a fairground performer and public letter-writer. His trial had aroused great interest in the town. On the even of the day fixed for his execution the prison almoner fell ill. A priest was needed to solace the condemned man's last moments. The curé was sent for, but it seems that he refused to come, saying that it was no concern of his, that he had had nothing to do with the mountebank in question, that he was himself unwell and that in any case it was not his place. When this was reported to the bishop he said: 'The curé is right. It is not his place but mine.'

He went at once to the prison and to the 'mountebank's' cell, where he addressed him by name, took his hand and talked to him. He spent the rest of the day and the night with him, without food or sleep, praying to God for his soul and exhorting the man to have regard for it himself. He repeated the greatest truths, which are the simplest. He was the man's father, brother, friend; his bishop only to bless him. The man had been about to die in utter despair. Death to him was an abyss, and trembling upon that awful threshold he recoiled in horror. He was not so ignorant as to be wholly unmoved. The profound shock of his condemnation had in some sort pierced the veil which separates us from the mystery of things and which we call life. Peering beyond this world through those fateful rents he saw nothing but darkness. The bishop caused him to see light.

When they came for the man next day the bishop went with him showing himself to the crowd at the side of the fettered wretch, in his purple hood and with the episcopal cross hanging from his neck. He went with him in the tumbril and on to the scaffold. The man who had been so desolate the day before was now radiant. His soul was at peace and he hoped for God. The bishop kissed him and said when the knife was about to fall: 'Whom man kills God restores to life; whom the brothers pursue the Father redeems. Pray and believe and go onward into life. Your Father is there.' When he came down from the scaffold there was something in his gaze which caused the people to draw back. No one could have said which was the more striking, his pallor or his serenity. Returning to the humble abode which he smilingly called his palace, he said to his sister: 'I have been performing one of the duties of my office.'

Since the most sublime acts are often the least understood, there were people in the town who said it was all affectation. But this was drawing-room comment. The common people, who do not look for shabbiness where none exists, were deeply moved.

As for the bishop himself, the spectacle of the guillotine caused him a shock from which he was slow to recover.

A scaffold, when it is erected and prepared, has indeed a profoundly disturbing effect. We may remain more or less open-minded on the subject of the death penalty, indisposed to commit ourselves, so long as we have not seen a guillotine with our own eyes. But to do so is to be so shaken that we are obliged to take our stand for or against. Joseph de Maistre approved of the death penalty, Cesar de Beccaria abominated it. The guillotine is the ultimate expression of Law, and its name is vengeance; it is not neutral, nor does it allow us to remain neutral. He who sees it shudders in the most confounding dismay. All social questions achieve their finality around that blade. The scaffold is an image. It is not merely a framework, a machine, a lifeless mechanism of wood, iron, and rope. It is as though it were a being having its own dark purpose, as though the framework saw, the machine listened, the mechanism understood; as though that arrangement of wood and iron and rope expressed a will. In the hideous picture which its presence evokes it seems to be most terribly a part of what it does. It is the executioner's accomplice; it consumes, devouring flesh and drinking blood. It is a kind of monster created by the judge and the craftsman; a spectre seeming to live an awful life born of the death it deals.

This was the effect it had upon the bishop, and on the day following the execution, and for many days after, he seemed to be overwhelmed. The almost violent serenity of the fateful moment vanished: he was haunted by the ghost of social justice. Whereas ordinarily he returned from the performance of his duties with a glow of satisfaction, he seemed now to be assailed with a sense of guilt. There were times when he talked to himself, muttering gloomy monologues under his breath. This is a fragment that his sister overheard: 'I did not know that it was so monstrous. It is wrong to become so absorbed in Divine Law that one is no longer aware of human law. Death belongs only to God. What right have men to lay hands on a thing so unknown?'

Gradually those impressions faded and perhaps died away altogether. But it was observed that the bishop thenceforth avoided passing the place of executions.

M. Myriel could be summoned at any hour to the bedside of the sick and the dying. He did not forget that this was his first and greatest duty. Widowed and orphaned families had no need to send for him, he came of his own accord. He would sit for hours in silence with the man who had lost the wife he loved or the mother who had lost her child. But if he knew when to keep silent he also knew when to speak. The wisest of comforters, he did not seek to banish sorrow in forgetfulness but to ennoble and dignify it with hope. 'Take care how you view the dead,' he said. 'Do not think of that which rots. Look steadily and you will see the living light of your beloved in the bosom of Heaven.' He knew that faith gives health. He sought to counsel and soothe the despairing by pointing to the resigned, and to transform the grief which sees only a pit into the grief which sees a star.

V

How Monseigneur Bienvenu made his cassocks last too long

M. Myriel's private life was shaped by the same thoughts as his life in public. To anyone privileged to witness it at first hand, the self-imposed austerity of the Bishop of Digne was at once impressive and charming.

Like all old men and most thinkers, he slept little; but his brief slumbers were profound. In the morning, he spent an hour in meditation and then said Mass, either in the cathedral or in his oratory. Having done so he breakfasted on rye bread soaked in the milk of his own cows. Then he started work.

A bishop is a busy man. He has to see the clerk of the diocese every day, and on most days one or more of his vicars. He has to preside over meetings, grant dispensations, cast an eye over the flow of church publications, and attend to countless parochial affairs. He has to write pastoral letters, approve sermons, and resolve differences between curés and mayors, besides conducting a correspondence which is both clerical and administrative, with the State on one hand and the Holy See on the other. In short, he has a thousand matters to attend to.

Such free time as these occupations (as well as the daily offices and his breviary), allowed him, M. Myriel devoted to the needy and afflicted; and in the remaining time he worked. That is to say, he dug his garden or read and wrote, and for him both kinds of work bore the same name; both he called gardening. 'The spirit is a garden,' he said.

He dined at midday, a meal little different from his breakfast.

At about two o'clock, if the weather was fine, he would set out on foot through the countryside or the streets of the town, often visiting the humblest homes. He was to be seen walking alone with his head bowed in thought, leaning on his long stick, wrapped in a very warm quilted purple cloak, with purple stockings and heavy shoes, and wearing on his head the flat tricorn hat with gilt tassels hanging from its points.

There was a stir wherever he went, as though with his very passing he brought warmth and light. Children and old men came to the doorstep to greet him as they might greet the sunshine. Those in need were shown the way to his dwelling. He blessed and was blessed. Now and then he stopped to talk to the children and smile at their mothers. He visited the poor when he had money; when he had none he visited the rich.

Since he wore his cassocks until they were threadbare and did not wish the fact to be noticed, he never went into the town except in that padded cloak, which in summer was rather uncomfortable.

At half past eight in the evening he had supper with his sister while Mme Magloire stood over them waiting at table. No meal could be more frugal. But if one of his curés had been invited to supper Mme Magloire took advantage of the circumstance to prepare something more lavish, fish from the lakes or game from the hills. Any curé served as a pretext for a solid meal, and the bishop acquiesced in this. Otherwise the meal consisted of boiled vegetables and fried bread. They said in the town, 'When the bishop is not eating like a curé he eats like a Trappist monk.'

After supper he talked for half an hour with his sister and Mme Magloire and then withdrew to his own room to resume his writing, either on loose sheets of paper or in the margins of some folio volume. He was a man of letters and something of a scholar, and he has left behind him half a dozen manuscripts which are not without interest, including an essay on a line of Genesis – 'And the Spirit of God moved upon the face of the waters.' He contrasts this with three other versions: the Arabic, 'The winds of God blew'; that of Flavius Josephus, 'A wind from on high descended upon earth'; and finally the Chaldean version of the Rabbi Onkelos, 'A wind from God blew upon the face of the waters.' In another essay he examines the theological writings of Charles-Louis Hugo, Bishop of Ptolémaïs, a great-great-uncle of the present writer, in which he proves that a number of pamphlets published in the last century under the pseudonym of Barleycorn are to be attributed to this prelate.*

Sometimes while reading he would sink into a profound reverie from which he would emerge to scribble a few lines on the pages of whatever book he had in his hand. These jottings often had nothing to do with the book itself. We have before us a note written in the margin of a volume entitled, *Correspondance du lord Germain avec les généraux Clinton, Cornwallis et les amiraux de la station de l' Amérique. A Versailles, chez Poinçot, libraire, et à Paris, chez Pissot, libraire, quai des Augustins.*

The note is as follows:

O Thou which art.

Ecclesiastes names thee Almighty, the Maccabees name thee Creator, the Epistle to the Ephesians names thee Liberty, Baruch names thee Immensity, the Psalms name thee Wisdom and Truth, John names thee Light, the Book of Kings names thee Lord, Exodus names thee Providence, Leviticus Sanctity, Esdras Justice, creation names thee God, man names thee Father; but Solomon names thee Compassion, which is the most beautiful of all thy names.

At about nine o'clock the two women went upstairs to their rooms, leaving him alone on the ground floor until morning.

And here it is necessary that we should give an exact account of the dwelling of Monseigneur the Bishop of Digne.

VI

The guardian of his house

The house, as we have said, consisted of two floors with three rooms on each and an attic above them. Behind it was a quarter-acre of garden. The two women occupied the top floor and the bishop's quarters were below. The first of his three rooms, giving directly on to the street, served as the dining-room; the second was his bedroom and study, and the third his oratory. One could leave the oratory only by way of the bedroom, and the only way out of the bedroom was through the dining-room. At the far end of the oratory there was a screened alcove with a bed for the occasional guest. The bishop was accustomed to offer it to country curés whose personal or parish affairs brought them to Digne.

*Hugo's claim to be descended from the Bishop, who was in fact a bishop *in partibus*, appears to be unfounded. cf. E. Biré, *Victor Hugo avant 1830.*

The former hospital dispensary, a small building which had been added to the house, extending into the garden, had been converted into a kitchen and store-room. The garden also contained a shed, formerly the hospital kitchen, where the bishop kept two cows. Half of whatever milk they gave was sent every morning to the hospital. 'I pay my tithe,' he said.

His bedroom was large and difficult to heat in winter, and since logs were very dear in Digne he had had the notion of sealing off a part of the cowshed with a blank partition. It was here that he passed the very cold evenings. He called it his winter salon.

Like the dining-room, the winter salon was sparsely furnished, containing only a square whitewood table and four straw-seated chairs. The dining-room contained in addition an old sideboard painted with pink distemper. A similar sideboard, suitably draped with white cloths and imitation lace, served in the oratory as an altar.

Wealthy penitents and the devout ladies of Digne had more than once subscribed funds for providing the oratory with a handsome new altar. The bishop took the money and gave it to the poor. 'The soul of an unfortunate who thanks God for consolation,' he said, 'is the best of altars.'

There were two wicker prayer-stools in the oratory, and an arm-chair in the bedroom, also of wicker. When the bishop received half a dozen or more persons at a time – the prefect, officers from the garrison or students from the little seminary – chairs had to be fetched from the winter salon, and if necessary the armchair from the bedroom and the prayer-stools from the oratory. In this way seating for eleven visitors could be provided. Sometimes there were twelve, and on these occasions the bishop solved the problem by standing in front of the fire in winter, or in summer proposing that they should walk in the garden.

There was a chair in the screened alcove, but it had lost part of its straw seat and one of its legs, so that it had to be propped against the wall. Mlle Baptistine had in her bedroom a capacious wooden easy chair which had once been gilt and upholstered in flowered silk; but since this had had to be brought in through the window, on account of the narrowness of the stairs, it could not be used for general purposes. It had long been Mlle Baptistine's ambition to acquire a drawing-room armchair with tapered mahogany legs and yellow velvet upholstery with rosettes; but this would have cost at least five hundred francs, and in five years she had been able to save only forty-two francs ten sous, so in the end she had finally given up the idea. Do we ever realize our fondest dreams?

Nothing could have been more simple than the bishop's bedroom. A french window opposite the bed giving on to the garden; a narrow iron bedstead with a canopy of green serge, and beyond it, behind a curtain, an array of toilet articles betraying the fastidious habits of the one-time man of fashion. Two doors, one by the fireplace, leading to the oratory, and the other by the bookcase, leading to the dining-room. The shelves of the big, glass-fronted bookcase were filled. The fireplace, its wooden surround painted to resemble marble, was normally without a fire; it contained instead two ornamental fire-dogs, a form of episcopal luxury, embellished with flower-vases and foliations that had once been silver-gilt; and above the mantelpiece, where ordinarily a mirror is placed, there hung a once-silvered copper crucifix against a square of threadbare black velvet in a wooden frame that had lost its gilding. By the french window was a large table with an inkstand and a confusion of papers and thick tomes, and beside the table was the wicker armchair. A prayer-stool stood at the foot of the bed, borrowed from the oratory.

Two portraits in oval frames hung on the walls on either side of the bed. Small gilt inscriptions on the bare canvas surrounding the portraits indicated that they represented respectively the Abbé de Chaliot, Bishop of Saint-Claude, and the Abbé Tourteau, Vicar-General of Agde and Abbot of Grand-Champ, of the Cistercian order. The bishop had inherited these when he took over the room from the hospital patients, and had left them where they were. They were priests and presumably benefactors, two things entitling them to his regard. Otherwise all he knew about them was that they had received their appointments on the same day in April 1785, the one to his bishopric and the other to his living. He had made the discovery when Mme Magloire had taken down the portraits to dust them, the details being inscribed in faded ink on a small square of paper, yellowed with time and attached with sealing wafers to the back of the portrait of the Abbé de Grand-Champ.

The french window was covered by an aged curtain of some coarse material which had finally become so worn that Mme

Magloire had been obliged to put a large patch in it to save the cost of buying a new one. The patch was in the form of a cross, a fact upon which the bishop often remarked with pleasure.

All the rooms in the house, those on the ground floor as well as the upstairs rooms, were whitewashed like a barracks or hospital.

However, during the latter years, as we shall presently see, Mme Magloire discovered wall-paintings under the dismembered paper in Mlle Baptistine's room. This was accounted for by the fact that before becoming a hospital the house had been a place of assembly. The bedrooms had red-tiled floors, scrubbed every week, with straw mats beside the beds. For the rest, the house was maintained by the two women in a state of scrupulous cleanliness. This was the one luxury the bishop allowed. 'It is taking nothing from the poor,' he said.

But we may confess that of his former possessions he still retained a set of six silver knives and forks and a large silver soup-ladle which rejoiced the heart of Mme Magloire when they lay splendidly gleaming on the white tablecloth. And since we are depicting the Bishop of Digne as he was, we must add that he more than once remarked, 'I should find it hard to give up eating with silver.'

To this treasure must be added two massive silver candlesticks which he had inherited from a great-aunt. They held wax candles and stood as a rule on the bishop's mantelpiece; but when there was a guest, Mme Magloire lit the candles and placed them on the dining-table. In the bishop's room, at the head of the bed, was a small cupboard in which she locked the silver cutlery and ladle every night; but it must be added that the key was never removed.

The garden, somewhat the worse for the rather ugly buildings we have mentioned, was laid out in four intersecting paths round a drainage trap, and a fifth path ran round it flanking the white boundary wall. The paths enclosed four square plots bordered with box. Mme Magloire grew vegetables in three of these, and the bishop had planted flowers in the fourth. There were a few fruit trees. Mme Magloire once said teasingly to him: 'Monseigneur, you believe in making use of everything, but this fourth plot is wasted. Salads are more useful than flowers.' 'You are wrong,' replied the bishop. 'The beautiful is as useful as the useful.' Then, after a pause, he added: 'More so, perhaps.'

The fourth plot, divided into three or four beds, occupied nearly as much of the bishop's time as did his books. He would spend an hour or two there whenever he could, weeding, hoeing, and planting. He was not as hard on insect pests as a good gardener would have liked him to be. But then, he claimed no knowledge of botany, knew nothing of strains and genera and took no sides in the disputes between learned botanists. He did not study plants, he merely loved flowers. He had great respect for men of learning but even more respect for the ignorant, and without forfeiting either loyalty he watered his beds every summer evening with a green watering-can.

No door in the house could be locked. The dining-room door, which gave directly on to the cathedral close, had originally been as heavily equipped with locks and bolts as the door of a prison. The bishop had had all these removed so that by day or night the door was only latched and anyone could enter at any time. This had at first caused the two women great concern. 'Put bolts on your bedroom doors if you like,' he said to them. They came in the end to share his simple faith, or at least to behave as though they did, although Mme Magloire had moments of misgiving. As for the bishop, his view of the matter is conveyed by three lines which he wrote in the margin of a bible: 'This is the distinction: the doctor's door must never be shut; the priest's door must always be open.'

There is another note which he wrote in the margin of a work entitled, *A Philosophy of Medical Science*: 'Am I not as much a doctor as they? I too have my patients; in the first place, theirs, whom they call sick; and then my own, whom I call unfortunate.'

And he wrote elsewhere: 'Do not ask the name of the person who seeks a bed for the night. He who is reluctant to give his name is the one who most needs shelter.'

It happened one day that an estimable curé – I do not recall whether he was curé of Couloubroux or of Pompierry – having probably been prompted by Mme Magloire, asked Monseigneur whether it was not perhaps a little injudicious on his part to leave his door unlocked at all hours; and, in short, did he not fear lest some calamity might befall a house so unprotected? The bishop touched him gently on the shoulder and said, quoting the Psalms: 'Except the Lord keep the city, the watchman waketh but in vain.' Then he changed the subject.

It pleased him to say: 'There is priest's courage just as there is the courage of a colonel of dragoons . . . But,' he added, 'ours must be quiet.'

VII

Cravatte

Here an event falls naturally into place which cannot be omitted because of the especial light it throws on the character of the Bishop of Digne.

After the breaking-up of the robber band of Gaspard Bès, which had infested the gorges of Ollioules, one of Bès's lieutenants, Cravatte, escaped to the mountains. He hid for a time in the county of Nice with the few surviving members of the band, then moved to Piedmont and suddenly reappeared in France, in the region of Barcelonette. He and his companions were seen first in Jauziers and then in Tuiles. He hid in the caves of the Joug-de-l'Aigle and from there preyed upon hamlets and villages, moving down through the ravines of Ubaye and Ubayette. He even ventured as far as Embrun, where he broke into the cathedral one night and looted the sacristy. His maraudings alarmed the countryside. The gendarmerie pursued him, but he always escaped, sometimes by the use of force. He was an intrepid rogue.

It was during this reign of terror that the bishop arrived in the district on a tour of the diocese. He was met at Chastelar by the mayor, who urged him to turn back. Cravatte was in control of the hills as far as l'Arche and beyond. To go further would be dangerous, even with an escort, and it would mean risking the lives of three or four unfortunate gendarmes.

'Just so,' said the bishop. 'I intend to go without an escort.'

'Monseigneur,' cried the mayor, 'you must not even think of it!'

'I think so much of it that I refuse absolutely to have any gendarmes and I shall be leaving in an hour.'

'Alone?'

'Yes, alone.'

'Monseigneur, you cannot!'

'There is a humble commune in the mountains which I have not visited for three years,' said the bishop. 'The people are friends of mine, peaceable and honest shepherds who own no more than one in thirty of the goats they pasture. They spin brightly coloured woollen threads and play mountain airs on six-hole pipes. They need someone to talk to them from time to time about God. What would they think of a bishop who was afraid? What would they think of me if I did not go?'

'But the brigands, Monseigneur – if you should fall foul of them –'

'Just so,' said the bishop. 'Since you mention it, I may meet the brigands. They, too, must be in need of someone to speak to them of God.'

'But they are like a pack of wolves!'

'And perhaps that is why Jesus has appointed me to be their shepherd. Who can account for the ways of Providence?'

'They'll rob you.'

'I own nothing.'

'They may kill you.'

'An old priest mumbling his incantations? Why should they?'

'Merciful Heaven, Monseigneur – if you should meet them –'

'I shall ask them for alms for my poor.'

'Monseigneur, I beseech you not to go. You will be risking your life.'

'Is that really all, Monsieur le Maire?' said the bishop. 'I was not put into this world to preserve my life but to protect souls.'

There was nothing for it but to let him go. The tale of his obstinacy spread through the countryside, causing great alarm.

He left, accompanied only by a small boy who volunteered to act as his guide, having refused to allow his sister and Mme Magloire to go with him. They went on mules, meeting no one, and the bishop arrived safely at the hamlet of his friends the shepherds. He stayed there a fortnight, preaching, ministering, teaching, and moralizing. Before leaving he wished to have a ceremonial *Te Deum* sung, but when he discussed this with the curé he encountered a difficulty. There was no suitable church apparel. All the village could offer was its shabby sacristy and a few old chasubles trimmed with false braid.

'No matter,' said the bishop. 'Announce the *Te Deum* after the sermon. Something will turn up.'

Messengers were sent to the neighbouring churches, but the sum of all the treasures of those humble parishes was not enough to clothe a single cathedral cantor in a fitting manner.

And in this awkward situation a large chest arrived for the bishop, brought to the presbytery by two unknown horsemen who at once rode away. It was found to contain a cope of cloth-of-gold, a mitre ornamented with diamonds, an archbishop's cross, a magnificent crozier and the rest of the pontifical raiment stolen a month previously from the cathedral at Embrun. There was also a sheet of paper bearing the words: 'Cravatte to Monseigneur Bienvenu'.

'I said something would turn up,' commented the bishop. And he added, smiling: 'To him who is content with a curé's surplice God sends an archbishop's cope.'

'God, Monseigneur,' murmured the curé with a faint smile, '– or the devil?'

The bishop looked sternly at him and answered: 'God!'

When he returned to Chastelar people lined the roadside to see him. Mlle Baptistine and Mme Magloire were awaiting him at the presbytery, and he said to his sister: 'Was I not right? The poor priest went empty-handed to the poor people of the hills and comes back with his hands full. I set out with nothing but my trust in God and I have brought back the riches of a cathedral.'

And before they went to bed that night he said:

'We must never fear robbers or murderers. They are dangers from outside, small dangers. It is ourselves we have to fear. Prejudice is the real robber, and vice the real murderer. Why should we be troubled by a threat to our person or our pocket? What we have to beware of is the threat to our souls.'

He added, turning to his sister:

'A priest must never speak to protect himself against other men. Men do as God allows them to do. We may only pray to Him when we feel ourselves to be in danger, and we must pray, not for ourselves but for our brother, lest through us he fall into sin.'

However, episodes such as this occurred only rarely. We report those of which we have knowledge; but in general he spent his life doing the same things at the same time, and a month of his year resembled an hour of his day.

As to what became of the riches of Embrun Cathedral, it is a matter on which we prefer not to be questioned. They were very handsome objects, very tempting, very suitable for stealing for the good of the poor. Besides, they had already been stolen. Half the business had been done, and it only remained to alter the course of the theft, just to redirect it a little way. We will not comment ourselves on the matter; but later a somewhat cryptic note was found among the bishop's papers which may have had some bearing on it. It ran: 'The problem is to decide whether this should be returned to the cathedral or to the hospital.'

VIII

A philosopher in his cups

The senator of whom mention has already been made was a determined man who had pursued his career with a single-mindedness that ignored such hindrances as conscience, good faith, justice, and duty, achieving his ends without ever deviating from the path of his own interests. He was a former public attorney mellowed by success, a man without malice prepared at any time to do what he could for his sons and sons-in-law, his relatives and even his friends, having wisely elected to take the easy way through life and profit by every chance that offered. To do otherwise would have seemed to him absurd. He was intelligent and sufficiently well-educated to consider himself a disciple of Epicurus, although he probably owed more to such lesser writers as Pigault-Lebrun. He laughed as readily and amiably at the eternal truths as at the eccentricities of 'our excellent bishop', sometimes in the presence of the bishop himself.

It happened that on the occasion of some semi-official ceremony this senator, the Comte de —, and M. Myriel dined with the prefect. Over the dessert the senator, somewhat flushed with wine but still urbane, exclaimed:

'Let us talk, Monseigneur. It is hard for a senator and a bishop to look each other in the eye without winking. We are both oracles. I will confess to you that I have my own philosophy.'

'And rightly so,' said the bishop. 'A man's philosophy is the bed he lies on. Yours, Monsieur le Comte, is a bed of purple.'

'But let us talk like plain men.'

'Plain devils, if you would rather.'

'I will say at once that I do not regard writers such as the Marquis d'Argens, Pyrrho, Hobbes and M. Naigeon as charlatans. I have a row of philosophers on my shelves, in gilt-edged editions.'

'Like yourself, Monsieur le Comte.'

The senator continued: 'I detest Diderot. He's an ideologue, a demagogue, and a revolutionary who in his heart believes in God.

He's more bigoted than Voltaire. Voltaire made fun of Needham's attempt to reconcile the theory of spontaneous generation with the concept of God the Creator, and Voltaire was wrong, because Needham's eels prove that God is unnecessary. A drop of vinegar in a spoonful of dough replaces the *fiat lux*. Imagine the drop and the spoon to be that much larger and you have the world. Man is the eel. So where does the Eternal Father come in? My dear bishop, I find the Jehovah theory very tedious. It produces nothing but lean men with empty heads. I want none of the great All, which irritates me; I prefer the great Nothing, which leaves me untroubled. Between ourselves, and talking candidly as though you were my confessor, I will declare to you that I am a man of plain sense. I am not in love with your Jesus, who went about preaching renunciation and self-sacrifice – a miser's advice to beggars. Renunciation for what reason, sacrifice to what end? I have never heard of a wolf sacrificing itself for the good of another wolf. Let us stick to nature. We who are the top should have a higher philosophy. What is the use of being at the head of affairs, if you see no further than the end of the next man's nose? Let us live happily. Life is all we have. That man has any future life, above or below or anywhere else, is something that I flatly disbelieve. You urge upon me the need for sacrifice and renunciation. I am to ponder my every action, rack my brains with the problems of good and evil, justice and injustice, *fas* and *nefas*. Why? Because later I shall be called to account. And when? After my death. What fantasy! It will take a cunning judge to catch me after my death – a ghostly finger stirring a handful of dust. We must acknowledge the truth, we initiates who have peered under the skirts of Isis. There is neither good nor evil but only growth. We must look for reality, discard all else, get to the bottom of things, mustn't we? We need to have a nose for truth, to burrow in the earth for it and seize hold of it. To do so is glorious, it is to grow strong and rejoice. I stand four-square, my lord bishop. The immortality of man is a daydream, a soothing promise which you may believe if you choose. How pleasant to be Adam – to be pure spirit, an angel with blue wings on one's back! Was it not Tertullian who said that the blessed will travel from one star to another? Splendid. We are to be the grasshoppers of the firmament. And we are to see God. Well, well – what nonsense it all is. God is a grotesque humbug. I would not say that in print, mark you, but I will whisper it among friends over the wine. To renounce the things of this earth for Paradise is to throw away the substance for the shadow. To be the dupe of the Infinite – that doesn't suit me! I am nothing. I am Count Nothing, senator. Did I exist before my birth? No. Shall I exist after my death? No. What am I but an organized handful of dust? What am I to do on earth? I have a choice. I can suffer or enjoy. Where will suffering end? In oblivion, and I shall have suffered. Where will enjoyment end? Also in oblivion, but I shall have enjoyed. I have made my choice. One can eat or be eaten, and I would sooner eat. It is better to be the teeth than the grass. That's the way I look at it. In the end, whatever you do, the grave is waiting, the Pantheon for some of us, the same limbo for us all. *Finis.* Total liquidation, the vanishing point; death is dead, believe me. It makes me laugh, the idea that there may be someone waiting there with something to say to me. An old-wives' tale, a bogeyman for the kids, Jehovah for grown man. No, our tomorrow is only darkness. Beyond the tomb lie equal limbos, and it makes no difference whether you are Sardanapalus or Vincent de Paul. That's the truth of it. The only thing to do is live, use yourself while you have yourself. I have my philosophy, bishop, and my philosophers, but I do not let myself be fooled by make-believe. But that is not to say that there aren't some who need it, the poor, the under-fed, the down-and-outs. We give them myths to feed on, fairy-tales – the soul, immortality, Paradise, the stars . . . And they swallow it. They butter their dry bread with it. The man who has nothing else has God. It's better than nothing and I've no objection, but for myself I stick to realism. God is for the masses.'

The bishop clapped his hands.

'An admirable discourse!' he exclaimed. 'What a splendid thing that kind of materialism is. Not everyone can achieve it. But the man who has it can't be fooled; he isn't going to let himself be exiled like Cato, or stoned to death like Stephen, or burned alive like Joan of Arc. He has all the joys of irresponsibility, the feeling that he can encompass everything with an easy mind – places, sinecures, dignities, power however gained, profitable recantations, useful betrayals, comforting adjustments of conscience – and go to his grave having stomached them all. How pleasant for him! I am not rebuking you, Monsieur le Senateur; I cannot refrain from congratulating you. As you say, you great men have your own philosophy, subtle, refined, accessible only to the rich, suited to all occasions, an admirable seasoning for the pleasures of life. It is a philosophy distilled from the depths by those who specialize in such matters. But you are a good-hearted man, you do not grudge the masses their belief in God, any more than you grudge them their goose stuffed with chestnuts while you have your turkey and truffles.'

IX

A sister's account of her brother

To give an impression of the domestic life of the Bishop of Digne, and the way in which the two devoted women subordinated their actions, their thoughts, even their timorous feminine instincts to his habits and purposes, without his needing to express them in words, we cannot do better than transcribe a letter written by Mlle Baptistine to the Vicomtesse de Boischevron, her lifelong friend.

Digne, 16 December 18—

My dear Madame,

Not a day passes without our speaking of you. It is a habit, but now I have an added reason. In dusting and scrubbing the walls and ceiling, Mme Magloire made a discovery, and today our two bedrooms, with their old whitewashed wallpaper, would do no discredit even to a château as splendid as your own. Mme Magloire stripped away the paper and found something underneath. My sitting-room, in which there is no furniture since we use it only for hanging up the washing, is fifteen feet high and eighteen feet square. The ceiling, which was at one time painted gold, has beams like yours, but these were covered with canvas when the house was used as a hospital. There is also wainscoting dating from our grandmothers' time. But my bedroom is the one you should see. After stripping away ten layers of paper Mme Magloire came upon wall-paintings, which, if they are not very good, are at least tolerable. There is a picture of Telemachus receiving knightly honours from Minerva, and another of him in some garden of which I forget the name, but it is where the Roman ladies passed a single night. I cannot describe it all. I have Roman lords and ladies [here an illegible word] with their retainers. Mme Magloire has scrubbed it all clean and this summer she is going to repair the blemishes and re-varnish it, so that my room will be a positive museum. She also found two old wooden consoles in the attic. To have had them re-gilded would have cost six francs apiece and it is better to give the money to the poor; but anyway they are ugly and I would far rather have a round mahogany table.

I am as happy as ever. My brother is so good. He gives everything he has to the sick and needy. We never have enough. The winter is hard in these parts, and we have to do what we can for those in need.

At least we are fairly well warmed and lighted, and that is a great comfort.

My brother has his foibles. If he mentions them, it is to say that that is how a bishop should be. Would you believe it, our door is never locked. Anyone who chooses can walk straight into my brother's room. He is afraid of nothing, even at night. That is his kind of courage, he says.

He does not allow Mme Magloire and me to worry about him. He runs all kinds of risks and we are not supposed even to notice. One has to learn to understand him. He goes out in the rain, tramps through the puddles, travels in winter. He is not afraid of darkness or unsafe roads or chance encounters.

Last year he went alone into a part of the country where there were robbers. He would not take us with him. He was away a fortnight and we thought him dead, but he came back unharmed and said, 'Let me show you how I have been robbed,' and he opened a box containing all the jewels stolen from Embrun Cathedral, which the thieves had given him. I had gone with a few friends to meet him some miles along the road, and this time I could not help scolding him a little, although I did it only when the carriage was making a noise so that no one else could hear.

At one time I used to think, 'No danger will ever deter him, he's terrible.' But I have grown used to it. I make signs to Mme Magloire not to vex him. He runs what risks he pleases. I bear Mme Magloire off and go to my room and pray for him and then go calmly to sleep, knowing that if anything should happen to him it would be the end of me too and I should go to God with my brother and my bishop. Mme Magloire found it harder than I to accustom herself to what she calls his rashness. But now she has accepted the situation and we pray together and tremble together and go to sleep. If the devil walked into the house no one would prevent him. And after all, in this house what have we to fear? There is always Someone with us who is stronger. The devil may visit us, but God *lives* here.

And that is enough. My brother need no longer say a word to me. I understand him without words and we trust in Providence. That is how it must be with a man so great in spirit.

I asked him for the particulars you wanted concerning the family of Faux. As you are aware, he knows everything of this kind and remembers everything, for he is still a strong royalist. It seems that they are a very old Norman family from the region of Caen. There are records five hundred years old of a Raoul de Faux, a Jean de Faux and a Thomas de Faux, all gentlemen, of whom one was Seigneur de Rochefort. The last of the line was Guy-Etienne-Alexandre, who was a colonel and held a command in the Breton light cavalry. His daughter,

Marie-Louise, married Adrien-Charles, the son of Duc Louis de Gramont, colonel of the French Guards and lieutenant-general of the army. The name is spelt Faux, Fauq, or Faoucq.

I trust, dear Madame, that you will commend us to the prayers of your saintly relative, the cardinal. As for your dear Sylvanie, she was quite right not to waste the little time she spends with you in writing to me. It is enough for me to know that she is well and working as you would wish, and that she still loves me. I am happy to have news of her through you. My health is fairly good although I grow thinner every day. And now my paper is running out. A thousand affectionate thoughts.

   Baptistine.

P.S. Your sister-in-law is still here with her young family. Your great-nephew is charming. Do you know that he will soon be five? Yesterday he saw a horse wearing knee-pads and he asked, 'What's the matter with its knees?' His small brother drags an old broom round their apartment pretending it is a carriage and shouting, 'Hup!'

It will be seen from this letter that the two women, with that especial feminine genius which understands a man better than he understands himself, had learned to adapt themselves to the bishop's mode of being. Beneath that air of gentle candour that never belied itself, the Bishop of Digne performed great and sometimes gallant actions without seeming to be conscious of the fact. The women shivered but acquiesced. Mme Magloire might sometimes venture to remonstrate with him before the event, but never during or after it. Nothing, not so much as a gesture, was allowed to distract him while the action was in progress. At times, without his needing to say it or even perhaps being fully aware of it, such was his simplicity, they perceived that he was wholly the bishop and themselves no more than shadows in his house. They served him as the occasion required, and if the best obedience was to vanish from his sight they did so. With the admirable delicacy of instinct they knew that some forms of solicitude can be an encumbrance. And so, responsive to his nature if not fully understanding his thought, they did not seek to protect him even when they believed him to be at risk. They entrusted him to God.

As Baptistine said, her brother's end would be her own. Mme Magloire did not say it, but she knew it.

X

The bishop confronted by a strange light

Not long after the writing of the letter we have quoted, the bishop performed an act which, if the talk in the town is to be believed, was even more perilous than his excursion into the bandit country.

There was a man living in solitude not far from Digne whom we will call G—. Not to beat about the bush, he was an *ancien conventionnel*, that is to say, a former member of the Revolutionary Convention.

The narrow world of Digne referred to him with a kind of horror. A member of the Convention – think what that meant! It had been a world in which every man addressed his fellow as 'tu', and called him 'citizen'. This man was little better than a monster. He had not voted in fact for the death of the king, but in principle he had done so, so that he was a quasi-regicide and infamous. Why then had he not been brought to trial when the legitimate monarchy was restored? They might not have cut off his head – it is right that clemency should be exercised – but surely he should have been banished for life, if only to serve as an example. Besides which, he was an atheist, like all those people. And so on . . . Thus the geese cackled round the vulture.

But was G— really a vulture? He was, if one might judge by the wildness of his isolation.

Not having voted for the death of the king he had not figured in the decrees of exile and had been able to remain in France. He lived in a desolate valley about three-quarters of an hour from the town, with no road or habitation near it. Here, it was said, he tilled a plot of land and had contrived for himself a primitive dwelling like a beast's lair. No one went near him. Since he had gone to live there the pathway leading to the valley had vanished in the undergrowth. The place was known as *le maison du bourreau*, the hangman's house.

But the bishop, now and then glancing towards a clump of trees on the horizon which marked the edge of the valley, reflected, 'There lives a lonely soul.' Behind this thought lay another – 'I owe him a visit.'

It must be confessed, however, that the idea, natural enough at first glance, upon consideration seemed to him strange and impossible, even repellent. For in his heart the bishop shared the general feeling, and, without his fully realizing it, the former revolutionary inspired in him the kind of repugnance, bordering on hatred, which is best expressed by the word 'estrangement'. Should the shepherd recoil from the sick sheep? Assuredly not. But this was a villainous sheep. The bishop was in two minds. He started several times to visit the man but turned back.

Then one day it was learned in the town that the country boy who ran errands for G— had come in search of a doctor. The old monster was dying; he was partly paralysed and would not live through the night. 'A good thing too,' said some people. The bishop took his stick and putting on his cloak – partly to hide his worn cassock, but also because the evening breeze would be chilly – set out.

The sun was low on the horizon when he reached the unhallowed spot and realized, with a slight tremor, that he was near the beast's lair. He crossed over a ditch, negotiated a hedge, raised a barrier, entered an untidy garden and, advancing boldly across it, came in sight of the dwelling itself, half-hidden by tall shrubs.

It was a low-roofed, primitive cabin, small and clean, with a climbing vine fixed to the front. Seated by the door in an old wheelchair, a peasant's chair, was a white-haired man smiling at the sun, and standing beside him was the boy who did his errands, in the act of handing him a bowl of milk.

While the bishop stood regarding them the old man spoke.

'Thank you,' he said. 'That is all I want.' He turned his head from the sunset to look smiling at the boy.

The bishop moved forward and at the sound of his footsteps the old man looked towards him, his face expressing as much astonishment as a man is capable of feeling at the end of a long life.

'You are the first person to visit me in all the time I have been here,' he said. 'Who are you, Monsieur?'

'My name is Bienvenu Myriel,' replied the bishop.

'Bienvenu Myriel! I haven't heard the name. Is it you whom the people call Monseigneur Bienvenu?'

'It is.'

The old man said with a half-smile, 'In that case, you are my bishop.'

'More or less.'

'You are welcome, Monsieur.'

He held out his hand, but the bishop did not take it. He merely said:

'I am glad to see that I have been misinformed. You certainly don't look very ill.'

'I shall be cured of my affliction,' said the old man. He paused and said: 'I shall be dead in three hours.'

He went on: 'I know something of medicine. I know how the end comes. Yesterday only my feet were numb. This morning the chill had reached my knees and now I feel it extending to my waist. When it reaches my heart I shall cease to live. The sunset is beautiful, is it not? I asked the boy to wheel me out here so that I might have a last look at things. Please talk to me if you wish, it doesn't tire me. You did well to come to see a dying man. It is right that there should be a witness at such a moment. One has one's whims; I had hoped to live until the dawn, but I know that I have barely three hours. It will be dark, but what does that signify? Dying is a simple matter. No need of daylight. I shall die by the light of the stars.' He turned to the boy. 'Go and lie down. You're tired. You were up all night.'

The boy withdrew into the cabin, and the old man, gazing after him, murmured as though to himself:

'I shall die while he's asleep. Our two slumbers will go well together.'

The bishop was less moved than he felt he should have been. He could not feel the presence of God in this manner of dying. To tell the truth – for the inconsistencies of a noble spirit must be depicted with the rest – he who laughed so readily when addressed as Your Greatness was a little shocked at not being addressed as Monseigneur and half-inclined to say 'Citizen' in return. He was tempted to resort to the bluff familiarity which is common enough among doctors and priests but was not his own habit. When all was said, this man, this former member of the Convention, this representative of the people, had in his day been one of the great ones of the earth. Perhaps for the first time in his life the bishop was disposed to be stern.

But the representative of the people was regarding him with a diffident friendliness in which might have been discerned the humility proper to a man who knows that his end is near. The bishop, for his part, although as a rule he guarded himself against the display of inquisitive curiosity, which he held to be impertinent, could not prevent himself from studying the man with an attentiveness which, since it was not born of sympathy, would probably have caused his conscience to reproach him in the case of any other person. To him a revolutionary was little better than an outlaw and even beyond the law of charity.

Seated calmly and almost upright, his voice resonant, G— was one of those octogenarians who confound the physiologists. The Revolution knew many men of this kind, of a stature matching the time they lived in. One could feel the old man's capacity for endurance. Even now, with his end so near, he retained the appearance of health. In the clarity of his gaze, the firmness of his voice, and the vigorous movement of his shoulders, there was something that defied death. Azrael, the angel of the Muhammadan sepulchre, would have turned back, thinking he had come to the wrong door. G— seemed to be dying because he wished to die. There was a sense of liberation in his agony. Only his legs were motionless; it was here that the darkness had a hold on him. His feet were dead, but his head was still fully alive and he seemed in complete control of all his faculties. In that solemn moment he was like the king in the eastern fable, flesh above and marble below.

There was a stone by the doorway and the bishop seated himself upon it. He began his *exordium* without preliminaries.

'You are to be congratulated,' he said in a cold voice. 'At least you did not vote for the death of the king.'

The old man appeared to disregard the acid implications of the words 'at least'. He replied unsmilingly, meeting reproof with austerity.

'Do not go too far in your congratulations, Monsieur. I voted for the overthrow of a tyrant.'

'What do you mean?' asked the bishop.

'I mean that man is ruled by a tyrant whose name is Ignorance, and that is the tyrant I sought to overthrow. That is the tyrant which gave birth to monarchy, and monarchy is authority based on falsehood, whereas knowledge is authority based on truth. Man should be ruled by knowledge.'

'And by conscience,' said the bishop.

'They are the same thing. Conscience is the amount of inner knowledge that we possess.'

The bishop heard this with some astonishment. To him it was a new way of looking at things. The old revolutionary went on:

'In the case of Louis XVI, I voted against his death. I do not think I have the right to kill a man, but I believe it is my duty to abolish evil. I voted for the overthrow of the tyrant – that is to say, for an end to the prostitution of women, the enslavement of men, the dark night of the child. Those are the things I voted for in voting for the Republic. I voted for fraternity, for harmony, for a new dawn. I helped to bring about the downfall of prejudice and error, that their crumbling might let in light. We overturned the old world, we revolutionaries, and it was like the overthrow of a hothouse; from being a forcing-house of misery the world became a vessel of joy.'

'Not unmixed joy,' said the bishop.

'You may call it uncertain joy, and now, after the fateful return of the past that is called the Restoration, vanished joy. Our work, alas, was not completed. We destroyed the structure of the *ancien régime*, but we could not wholly destroy its thought. It is not enough to abolish abuses; custom must also be transformed. The mill was pulled down, but the wind still blows.'

'You destroyed. Destruction may be necessary, but I mistrust it when it is inspired by rage.'

'Justice has its anger, my lord Bishop, and the wrath of justice is an element of progress. Whatever else may be said of it, the French Revolution was the greatest step forward by mankind since the coming of Christ. It was unfinished, I agree, but still it was sublime. It released the untapped springs of society; it softened hearts, appeased, tranquillized, enlightened, and set flowing through the world the tides of civilization. It was good. The French Revolution was the anointing of humanity.'

The bishop could not refrain from murmuring: 'And 1793 – the Terror?'

The man of the Convention raised himself in his chair with an almost awesome solemnity and, as loudly as his dying state permitted, exclaimed:

'Ah, 1793. I thought we should come to that! The clouds had been gathering for fifteen hundred years and at last the storm broke. What you are condemning is a thunderclap.'

The bishop felt, perhaps without admitting it to himself, that these words had gone home. Nevertheless he put a good face on it.

'The judge speaks in the name of justice,' he said. 'The priest speaks in the name of pity, which is only a higher form of justice. A thunderclap must not make mistakes.' He looked steadily at the other. 'And Louis XVII?'

The dying man reached out a hand and took him by the arm.

'Louis XVII. What are you mourning? An innocent child? If so, I will weep with you. But if you are mourning a royal child I will ask you to consider. To me the case of the brother of Cartouche, an innocent child who was hanged by the armpits on the Place de Grève until he died, for no other crime than that he was the brother of Cartouche, is no less grievous than that of the grandson of Louis XV, an innocent child martyred in the Temple for the crime of being the grandson of Louis XV.'

'I do not care for that association of names,' said the bishop.

'Cartouche? Louis XV? To which do you object?'

There was a brief silence. The bishop was almost sorry he had come; yet he felt obscurely and strangely moved.

'Monsieur le Prêtre,' said the dying man, 'you do not care for the cruder aspects of truth. Christ cared. He drove the money-lenders from the temple. His scourge was a great teller of truths. When he said, "Suffer them to come unto me" he made no distinction between the children. He would have made no bones about associating the son of Barabbas with the son of Herod. Innocence wears its own crown, Monsieur; it needs no added dignity; it is as sublime in rags as in royal robes.'

'That is true,' said the bishop in a low voice.

'You have named Louis XVII. Let us understand one another. Are we weeping for all innocents, all martyrs, all children, whether low-born or of high estate? Then I weep with you. But, as I said, we must then go back far beyond '93 and Louis XVII. I will weep with you for the children of kings if you will weep with me for the children of the people.'

'I weep for them all.'

'But equally! And if the balance is to be tilted either way it must be on the side of the people, for they have suffered longer.'

There was another silence and it was the revolutionary who broke it. He raised himself on his elbow, pinching a fold of his cheek between his thumb and forefinger as one does mechanically in moments of questioning and judgement, and addressed the bishop with eyes so aflame with the intensity of his waning life that his words had the effect of an explosion.

'The people have suffered a long time, Monsieur. But that is not all. Who are you that you should question me and talk to me of Louis XVII? I do not know you. Since I came here I have lived alone in this place, never setting a foot outside it or seeing anyone except the boy who serves me. It is true that your name has reached me, confusedly, but, I may say, spoken not without respect. But that means nothing. A clever man has plenty of ways of winning the trust of simple people. I did not, for example, hear the sound of your carriage as you drove here; no doubt you left it a short distance away, perhaps at the fork in the road. I repeat, I do not know you. You tell me that you are a bishop, but that tells me nothing about your true self. I ask you again, who are you? You are a bishop, a Prince of the Church, a man richly provided for. The See of Digne, stipend fifteen thousand, expenses ten thousand, total, twenty-five thousand francs a year! You have your palace and your liveried retainers, your kitchens and your loaded table where water-fowl is served on Fridays, your carriage in which you journey in the name of Christ, who went barefoot. You are a prelate, amply supplied with earthly comforts, and like all prelates you rejoice in them. But to say that is to say too much or too little. It does not enlighten me as to your true worth, your essential value, now that you have come here, as I suppose, to bring me words of wisdom. To whom am I speaking? Who are you?'

The bishop bowed his head and murmured a line of the Psalms: '*Vermis sum* – But I am a worm and no man.'

'A worm in a carriage!' grunted the man of the people.

It was he who now wore a stern aspect and the bishop who was humble. The bishop said gently:

'Suppose it to be so. But you have still to explain to me how my carriage, which you say is waiting beyond the trees, my loaded table, the moorhen I eat on Fridays, my palace, my retainers, my twenty-five thousand francs income – you have still to explain how all this proves that compassion is not a virtue and clemency a duty, and that the year 1793 was not beyond all forgiveness.'

The old man passed a hand over his forehead as though to wipe away a mist.

'Before I answer you,' he said, 'I must ask your pardon. I have behaved badly, Monsieur. You are my guest and I have failed in courtesy. We are discussing my ideas, and I should answer you in terms of reason. Your wealth and privileges afford me an advantage in debate which it is tasteless to use. I shall not refer to them again.'

'I thank you,' said the bishop.

'You have asked me for an explanation. Where were we? You said, I think, that 1793 was unforgiveable.'

'Yes,' said the bishop. 'What have you to say to Marat applauding the guillotine?'

'And what have you to say to Bossuet singing the Te Deum when the dragoons savaged the Protestants?'

It was a rough answer, but it went home like a sword-thrust. The bishop was shaken, finding no reply, and at the same time he was irritated by the reference to Bossuet. The best minds have their blind spots and sometimes feel vaguely outraged by a lack of respect for logic.

The old man had begun to gasp, overtaken by the breathlessness of the dying; but although his voice had weakened there was no dimming of the clarity of his gaze.

'We may pursue the matter a little further. The Revolution, considered as a whole, was an immense human affirmation of which, alas, the year 1793 was a denial. You find it unforgiveable; but, Monsieur, what of the monarchy as a whole? Carrier was a criminal, but what would you call Montreval? Fouquier-Tinville was a villain, but what would you call Lamoignon-Baville? Maillard was abominable, but what of Saulx-Tavannes? Was Jourdain-Coupe-Tête any more a monster than the Marquis de Louvois? Monsieur, I grieve for Marie-Antoinette, an archduchess and a queen, but I grieve no less for the Huguenot woman, then nursing an infant, who under the great Louis was bound to a post, naked to the waist, while the child was held in front of her. Her breasts swelled with milk and her heart with anguish as the starving child cried to be fed and her gaoler said, "Recant!", offering her the choice between the death of her baby and the death of her conscience. What have you to say, Monsieur, to this torment of Tantalus inflicted on a mother? You must remember this: the Revolution had its reasons. Its fury will be absolved by the future. Its outcome is a better world. Out of its most dreadful acts there emerges an embrace for mankind. But I need not go on. I have too good a case. Besides, I'm dying.'

No longer gazing at the bishop, he summed up his thought in a few quiet words.

'The brutalities of progress are called revolutions. When they are over we realize this: that the human race has been roughly handled, but that it has advanced.'

He did not know, the man of the people, that one by one he had broken down the bishop's defences. But a last one remained, and from this supreme stronghold Monseigneur Bienvenu uttered words scarcely less harsh than those with which the interview had begun.

'Progress must believe in God. The good cannot be served by impiety. An atheist is an evil leader of the human race.'

The old man did not answer. A tremor shook him. He looked up at the sky and a tear formed slowly in his eye, to brim over and roll down his pale cheek. Still gazing upward and almost stammering, he murmured to himself:

'Thou who art Perfection! Thou who alone exist.'

The bishop was inexpressibly moved.

After a pause the old man pointed to the sky and said: 'The infinite has being. It is there. If infinity had no self then self would not be. But it is. Therefore it has a self. The self of infinity is God.'

He had spoken those last words in a clear voice and with a quiver of ecstasy, as though he saw some living presence. Then he closed his eyes. The effort had exhausted him. It was plain that in the course of a moment he had lived the few hours that remained to him. His last utterance had brought him very near to death.

The bishop saw that there was no time to lose. He had come there as a priest. His mood of extreme aloofness had changed by degrees to one of deep emotion. Gazing at the closed eyes and taking the old, cold, wrinkled hand in his, he leaned towards the dying man.

'This hour belongs to God,' he said. 'Do you not think it would be sad if we should have met in vain?'

The old man opened his eyes. There was a shadowed gravity upon his face.

'My lord bishop,' he said, speaking with a slowness that was perhaps due more to the dignity of the spirit than to failing strength, 'I have passed my life in meditation, study, and contemplation. I was sixty when my country summoned me to take part in her affairs. I obeyed the summons. There were abuses and I fought against them, tyrannies and I destroyed them, rights and principles and I asserted them. Our country was invaded and I defended it; France was threatened and I offered her my life. I was never rich; now I am poor. I was among the masters of the State, and the

Treasury vaults were so filled with wealth that we had to buttress the walls lest they collapse under the weight of gold and silver; but I dined in Poverty Street at twenty-two sous a head. I succoured the oppressed and consoled the suffering. I tore up the altar-cloths, it is true; but it was to bind our country's wounds. I have always striven for the advance of mankind towards the light, and sometimes I have resisted progress that was without mercy. I have on occasion protected my rightful adversaries, your fellow-priests. At Peteghem in Flanders, on the spot where the Merovingian kings once had their summer palace, there is an Urbanist convent, the Abbaye de Sainte-Claire en Beaulieu, which I saved from destruction in 1793. I have done my duty, and what good I could, so far as was in my power. And I have been hounded and persecuted, mocked and defamed, cursed and proscribed. I have long known that many people believe they have the right to despise me, and that for the ignorant crowd I wear the face of the damned. I have accepted the isolation of hatred, hating no one. Now at the age of eighty-six I am on the point of death. What do you ask of me?'

'Your blessing,' said the bishop, and fell on his knees.

When at length the bishop raised his head there was a look of grandeur on the old man's face. He had died.

The bishop returned home deeply absorbed in thought. He passed the night in prayer. When on the next day a few importunates sought to question him about the man of the people he merely pointed to the sky. Thereafter his tenderness and solicitude for the defenceless and suffering were doubled.

Any reference to 'that old scoundrel' caused him to lapse into a state of singular withdrawal. It would be impossible to say that the passing of that spirit in his presence, and the reflection of that lofty conscience upon his own, went for nothing in his own striving for perfection.

His 'pastoral visit' was, of course, a subject of considerable comment in local circles.

Was it the place of a bishop to be at the death-bed of a man like that, when clearly no conversion was to be looked for? Those revolutionaries are all apostates. So why had he gone? What business was it of his? He must have been very anxious to see a soul carried off by the devil.

A dowager, one of those ladies who mistake audacity for wit, rallied him as follows: 'We are all wondering, Monseigneur, when your lordship will be wearing a red revolutionary bonnet.'

'Red is an all-embracing colour,' said the bishop. 'How fortunate that those who despise it in a bonnet revere it in a hat.'

XI

A reservation

It would be a mistake to conclude from this that Monseigneur Bienvenu was a 'philosopher bishop' or a 'patriot priest'. His encounter, which could almost be called his communion, with the man of the people, left in him a kind of amazement which made him still more gentle. That was all.

Although no one could have been less concerned with politics, it is perhaps appropriate that at this point we should give some account of his attitude to the events of the day, supposing him ever to have adopted an attitude. We must therefore go back a few years.

Shortly after he was raised to the episcopacy the Emperor created him a Baron of the Empire, together with a number of other bishops. The arrest of the Pope, as we know, took place during the night of 5–6 July 1809. In consequence of this M. Myriel was summoned by Napoleon to attend the synod of French and Italian bishops convened in Paris. This council was held in Notre-Dame, assembling for the first time on 15 June 1811, under the presidency of Cardinal Fesch. M. Myriel was among the ninety-five bishops who were present. But he attended only one full assembly and three or four lesser meetings. It appears that, coming from his mountain diocese where he lived so close to nature and in such rustic simplicity, he brought to the illustrious gathering notions which had a damping effect. He very soon went back to Digne. When questioned about his prompt return he said: 'I made them uncomfortable. I brought a draught of outside air with me. It was as though someone had left the door open.'

He also remarked: 'What would you expect? Those gentlemen are princes. I'm nothing but a peasant bishop.'

The fact is that he incurred displeasure. Among his disconcerting utterances was one that he let fall one evening in the home of one of his most eminent colleagues: 'So many handsome clocks and carpets! So many rich liveries! It must be very embarrassing. I would not care to live with all this luxury around me, constantly reminding me that there are people who are cold and hungry. There are the poor! There are the poor!'

Let it be said in passing that the hatred of luxury is not a sensible hatred. It implies a hatred of the arts. But in a churchman, outside his rites and ceremonies, luxury is a defect. It suggests an attitude of mind in which there is little true charity. A wealthy priest is a contradiction. A priest should be close to the poor. But can a man live in daily and nightly contact with all the forms of distress and hardship without some of that wretchedness clinging to him like the dust of toil? Can we imagine a man at a brazier who does not feel the heat, a man working all day long at a furnace who never singes his hair, or blackens a fingernail, or has a drop of sweat or a speck of ash on his face? The first proof of charity in a priest, above all in a bishop, is poverty.

This was assuredly the view of the Bishop of Digne, but that is not to say that in certain ticklish matters he did not share what we may call the 'ideas of the century'. He took little part in the theological disputes of the time and expressed no opinion on questions affecting the relationship between Church and State; but if he had been obliged to declare himself he would, it seems, have been found to be more Ultramontane than Gallican. Since we are painting a portrait, and wish to conceal nothing, we must add that he was decidedly opposed to Napoleon in his decline. From 1813 onwards he supported or applauded every hostile demonstration. He refused to meet the Emperor when he passed through the diocese on his return from Elba and refrained from ordering public prayers for him during the Hundred Days.

In addition to his sister he had two brothers, one a general and the other a prefect, with both of whom he corresponded. For a time he was chilly towards the general because, holding a command in Provence, he had set out with a force of 1200 men in pursuit of Napoleon when he landed at Cannes, but had done so in a manner which suggested that he did not mean to overtake him. With the other brother, the former prefect, a good and worthy man who now lived in retirement in Paris, the bishop remained on affectionate terms.

Monseigneur Bienvenu, then, had his moments of partisanship like other men, his moments of bitterness and of illusion. The passions of the day did not leave that gentle spirit wholly undisturbed in its preoccupation with eternal things. Certainly a man such as he would have been better without political opinions. And here we must not be misunderstood; we are not confusing what are called political opinions with the belief in progress and the high patriotic, democratic, and human faith which in these days must be the basis of all large-minded thinking. Without going deeply into matters with which this book is only indirectly concerned, we may say this: it would have been better if Monseigneur Bienvenu had not been a monarchist and if his gaze had not for an instant been distracted from that serene contemplation in which, above the turbulence of human affairs, the pure rays of the three first principles, Truth, Justice, and Charity, are seen to shine.

While agreeing that it was not for any political purpose that God had created Monsiegneur Bienvenu, we would nevertheless have admired him had he, in the name of justice and liberty, pursued a course of high-minded and perilous resistance to Napoleon when the Emperor was at the height of his power. But what is admirable in the case of a rising star is less so when the star is setting. We can respect the struggle only when it is dangerous; and in any case, only those who fight from the beginning deserve the final victory. The man who did not speak out in the time of prosperity does better to keep silent in the time of adversity; only the assailant of success is the legitimate instrument of its downfall. For our own part, when Providence intervenes we bow our heads. The year 1812 was the beginning. The cowardly breaking of silence in 1813 by a hitherto acquiescent legislature now emboldened by disaster was a matter for disgust which it was shameful to applaud; and from the events of 1814 – the treacherous marshals, the Senate sinking into degradation, insulting what it had deified; idolatry turning its coat and spitting on its idol – it was a duty to avert our gaze. And in 1815, when final disaster was in the air and all France shuddered at its approach, when the shadow of Waterloo could be dimly discerned as it gathered over Napoleon, the agonized greeting extended by the Army and the people to the man condemned by Destiny was no subject for laughter. With every reservation made regarding the despot, a spirit such as that of the Bishop of Digne should surely not have failed to perceive all that was noble and touching in this embrace between a great nation and a great man on the edge of the abyss.

Except for this he was in all things just, true, fair-minded, intelligent, humble, and worthy; beneficent and benevolent, which is another beneficence. He was a priest, a sage and a man. And it must be said that even in that political stance of which we disapprove, and for which we have come near to condemning him, he was tolerant and magnanimous – more so, perhaps, than we who write. The commissionaire at the Town Hall had been put there by the Emperor. He was a sergeant of the Old Guard, a legionary of Austerlitz, as Bonapartist as the eagle itself. Now and then he rashly let fall remarks which the law of the day classed as seditious. Since the imperial profile had disappeared from the insignia of the Légion d'honneur he no longer turned out in full regalia, as he put it, so as to avoid wearing his medals. He had removed the cross Napoleon awarded him, leaving a gap on his tunic which he had no wish to fill. 'Better die,' he said, 'than wear three toads over my heart,' by which he meant the fleur-de-lis. Nor was he tactful in his outspoken references to Louis XVIII. 'Old Gout-in-English-gaiters,' he said; 'he can take himself and his side-whiskers to Prussia,' thus combining in a single anathema the two first objects of his abhorrence, Prussia and England. He said these things so often that he lost his job and found himself penniless with a wife and children. The bishop sent for him, scolded him gently, and engaged him as caretaker at the cathedral.

Monseigneur Bienvenu was a true pastor of his diocese, the friend of all men. In the nine years of his residence in Digne his gentle goodness had come to inspire a kind of filial devotion. Even his attitude to Napoleon had been accepted and as it were tacitly forgiven by the people, that warm-hearted, simple-minded flock who worshipped their Emperor but loved their bishop.

XII

The loneliness of Monseigneur Bienvenu

Nearly every bishop has his retinue of young priests, just as an army general has his gaggle of young officers. They are what St Francis de Sales has called 'the cubs', *les prêtres blancs-becs*. Every calling has its aspirants who cling to the skirts of authority; no power is without its votaries, no fortune without its court. Those with an eye to the future flutter round the illustrious present. Every bishop possessing any influence has a bevy of acolytes to run his errands and perform palace duties, eager thereby to win his lordship's regard. To stand well with the bishop is to set a foot on the ladder of promotion. Careers have to be considered, and the priesthood does not disdain sinecures.

The Church, like other walks of life, has its potentates. These are the fashionable bishops, well-endowed and urbane dignitaries, on excellent terms with the world, who doubtless know how to pray but also know how to lobby; men who do not scruple to constitute themselves the antechamber of a diocese, links between the sacristy and diplomacy, abbots rather than priests and prelates rather than bishops. Happy is he who has their ear. Being men of credit they can shower fat livings, prebends, archdeaconries, cathedral offices – steps on the road to higher preferment – upon the ambitious and the favoured, and upon the young who know how to please. In furthering their own interests they further those of their satellites; it is like a solar system in motion. They shed a glow of purple on their followers, and their prosperity, discreetly shared, is like bread scattered on the water. And in the background is Rome. The bishop who becomes an archbishop, the archbishop who becomes a cardinal, may carry others with him. There are secretarial appointments; there is the Rota, the Conclave, the pallium. From Lordship to Eminence is but a step, and between Eminence and Holiness there is only the wisp of smoke from a burnt voting-slip. Every tonsure may dream of a crown. The priest is the only man in our time who may legitimately become a king – and what a king, the highest of them all! So there is no greater hothouse of ambition than a seminary. Who shall say how many pink-cheeked choir-boys and youthful abbés share the day-dreams of the dairymaid Perrette, or how often ambition wears the guise of vocation, perhaps in all good faith?

But Monseigneur Bienvenu, humble, penurious, and retiring, was not among these potentates, a fact which was manifest in the total absence of young priests around him. In Paris, as we have seen, he had failed to please. No rosy future beckoned to the solitary old man, and no sprouting ambition unwisely sought to blossom in his shadow. His canons and parish vicars were excellent men, somewhat of the people as he was himself, immured as he was in the diocese with no access to higher preferment, resembling their bishop in all things except one, that they had reached the end of the road and he had achieved completeness. The impossibility of rising under Monseigneur Bienvenu was so apparent that the young priests he ordained secured introductions to the Archbishops of Aix or Auch and made off as soon as possible. For we must repeat, a man needs help. A saint addicted to excessive self-abnegation is a dangerous associate; he may infect you with poverty, and a stiffening of those joints which are needed for advancement – in word, with more renunciation than you care for – and so you flee the contagion. Hence the isolation of Monseigneur Bienvenu. We live in a squalid society. Success: that is the message seeping, drop by drop, down from the overriding corruption.

It may be remarked in passing that success is an ugly thing. Men are deceived by its false resemblances to merit. To the crowd, success wears almost the features of true mastery, and the greatest dupe of this counterfeit talent is History. Juvenal and Tacitus alone mistrust it. In these days an almost official philosophy has come to dwell in the house of Success, wear its livery, receive callers in its ante-chamber. Success in principle and for its own sake. Prosperity presupposes ability. Win a lottery-prize and you are a clever man. Winners are adulated. To be born with a caul is everything; luck is what matters. Be fortunate and you will be thought great. With a handful of tremendous exceptions which constitute the glory of a century, the popular esteem is singularly short-sighted. Gilt is as good as gold. No harm in being a chance arrival provided you arrive. The populace is an aged Narcissus which worships itself and applauds the commonplace. The tremendous qualities of a Moses, an Aeschylus, a Dante, a Michelangelo or a Napoleon are readily ascribed by the multitude to any man, in any sphere, who has got what he set out to get – the notary who becomes a deputy, the hack playwright who produces a mock-Corneille, the eunuch who acquires a harem, the journeyman-general who by accident wins the decisive battle of an epoch. The profiteer who supplies the army of the Sambre-et-Meuse with boot-soles of cardboard and earns himself an income of four hundred thousand a year; the huckster who espouses usury and brings her to bed of seven or eight millions; the preacher who becomes a bishop by loudly braying; the bailiff of a great estate who so enriches himself that on retirement he is made Minister of Finance – all this is what men call genius, just as they call a painted face beauty and a richly attired figure majesty. They confound the brilliance of the firmament with the star-shaped footprints of a duck in the mud.

XIII

What he believed

It is not for us to scrutinize the Bishop of Digne in terms of religious orthodoxy. A spirit such as his can inspire only respect. The truth of an upright man must be accepted on his own terms. Moreover, since natures vary, we must agree that all the beauties of human excellence may be fostered by faiths that we do not share.

As to the view he took of this or that dogma or mystery, these are secrets only to be revealed when the soul passes naked beyond the tomb. What we may assert with confidence is that for him no problem of faith was ever hypocritically resolved. The diamond is incorruptible. He believed as much as he could. *Credo in Patrem* was his constant cry, reinforced by the acts of his daily life which satisfied his conscience and assured him that he was true to God.

But what we are obliged to note is that, outside his faith and, so to speak, beyond it, the bishop overflowed with love. It was in this, *quia multum amavit*, that he was held to be weak by 'the sober-minded', by 'responsible citizens' and 'sensible people', those clichés of a tawdry world in which egotism takes its time from pedantry. What was this excess of love? It was a serene benevolence embracing all men and extending even beyond them. He lived disdaining nothing, indulgent to all God's creation. Even the best of men has in him a core of unconsidered callousness which he reserves for what is animal. The Bishop of Digne lacked this intolerance, which is nevertheless found in many priests. Although he did not go as far as the Brahmins, he had assuredly pondered the verse of Ecclesiastes which runs: 'Who knoweth the spirit of man that goeth upward, and the spirit of the beast that goeth downward to the earth?' Ugliness of aspect and deformities of instinct neither dismayed nor outraged him. He was moved by them and sometimes grieved, seeming to search, beneath the appearances of life, for a reason, an explanation or an excuse. He seemed to be asking God to rearrange things. He contemplated without anger, rather in the manner of a scholar deciphering a palimpsest, the chaos that still exists in nature, and his reflections sometimes drew from him strange utterances, as on one occasion when he was walking in his garden. He thought himself alone, but his sister was a few paces behind him. He stopped suddenly, staring at something on the ground. It was a very large spider, black, hairy, and repellent. She heard him say: 'The poor creature, it's not its fault.'

Why not record these almost sublime absurdities of goodness? They were childish indeed, but it was the childishness of St Francis of Assisi and Marcus Aurelius. He strained a muscle once in avoiding treading on an ant. Thus did he live. Sometimes he fell asleep in the garden, and never did he seem more worthy of veneration.

From the reports of Monseigneur Bienvenu's youth and early manhood it would seem that he had been a man of strong passions, even perhaps of violence. His universal compassion was due less to natural instinct, than to a profound conviction, a sum of thoughts that in the course of living had filtered through to his heart: for in the nature of a man, as in a rock, there may be channels hollowed by the dropping of water, and these can never be destroyed.

In 1815 he was seventy-five years old, but he looked no more than sixty. He was not tall but inclined to stoutness, and to combat this he walked a great deal, walking with a steady stride and with his back only very slightly bowed, a detail from which we draw no conclusions. Pope Gregory XVI, at the age of eighty, bore himself erect and smiling, but this did not prevent him from being a bad pope. Monseigneur Bienvenu had what is called a handsome presence, but such was his amiability that his looks were forgotten.

The childlike gaiety of his conversation was an especial grace that put all men at their ease. His whole being seemed to radiate happiness. The freshness of his colouring, and the unbroken row of white teeth which showed when he laughed, lent him that frank and approachable air which causes people to say of a youth, 'He's a nice lad,' and of the elderly, 'He's a sound man.' This, it will be recalled, was the impression he had made on Napoleon. It was the impression he made at a glance on any person seeing him for the first time. But to spend a few hours in his company and see him in a reflective mood was to witness the gradual transformation of the sound man into something altogether more imposing. The wide, grave forehead, rendered noble by the white hair, acquired an added nobility from meditation; majesty emanated from the goodness while still the goodness shone. To see this was to know something of the emotion one might experience on seeing an angel, smiling, slowly spread his wings while continuing to smile. It was to be imbued with a feeling of respect beyond words, and to feel oneself in the presence of a great spirit, tested and compassionate, whose thought was so all-embracing that it could be nothing else than sweet.

The days of his life, as we have seen, were filled with prayer, with the celebration of the offices, the giving of alms, the consoling of the afflicted, the tilling of his garden-plot; with brotherliness, frugality, hospitality, renunciation, trust, study and toil. Filled, indeed, is the correct word, for the bishop's days overflowed with goodness of thought and word and action. But the day was not complete for him if he was prevented by bad weather from spending an hour or two in his garden after the two women had retired to bed. It seemed to be a necessary ritual that he should prepare himself for sleep by meditating under the solemnity of the night sky. Sometimes, if they were awake, they would hear him at a late hour pacing up and down the paths. Peaceful in his solitude, adoring, matching the tranquillity of the heavens with the tranquillity of his own heartbeat, ravished in the shadows by the visible and invisible splendours of God, he opened his spirit to the thoughts coming from the Unknown. At those moments, when he offered up his heart in the hour when the night flowers offer up their scent, himself illumined in the bestarred night and unfolding in ecstasy amid the universal radiance of creation, he could not perhaps have said what took place in his spirit, what went out from him and what entered in: a mysterious transaction between the infinity of the soul and the infinity of the universe.

He pondered on the greatness and the living presence of God, on the mystery of eternity in the future and, even more strange, eternity in the past, on all the infinity manifest to his eyes and to his senses; and without seeking to comprehend the incomprehensible he contemplated these things. He did not scrutinize God but let his eyes be dazzled. He pondered on the sublime conjunction of atoms that gives matter its substance; that reveals forces in discovering them, creates the separate within the whole, proportion within immensity, countless numbers within infinity; and through light gives birth to beauty. This conjunction, this ceaseless joining and disjoining, is life and death.

Seated on a wooden bench with his back against a crumbling trellis he gazed at the stars through the gnarled and stunted outlines of his fruit trees. That quarter acre of land, with its poor growth and its encumbrance of buildings, was dear to him and sufficient.

What more could he need, this old man whose little leisure was divided between daytime gardening and night-time contemplation? Was not that narrow space with the sky its ceiling room enough for the worship of God in the most delicate of His works and in the most sublime? A garden to walk in and immensity to dream in – what more could he ask? A few flowers at his feet and above him the stars.

XIV

What he thought

A last word.

Since this account of him, particularly at the present time, and to use an expression currently in vogue, may have lent the Bishop of Digne a 'pantheistic' complexion, making it appear, to his discredit or otherwise, that he had evolved one of those personal philosophies, peculiar to our century, which sometimes grow in solitary minds and so possess them as to replace accepted religions, we must emphasize that no one who knew Monseigneur Bienvenu would have felt justified in supposing anything of the kind. It was the heart that inspired this man, and it was from its light that his wisdom proceeded.

No philosophical system; but many works. Abstruse speculation contains an element of vertigo, and there is nothing to suggest that he hazarded his reason in any apotheosis. The prophet may be bold, but a bishop must be cautious. He probably refrained on principle from looking too closely at those problems which are in some sort the reserve of towering and inconoclastic intellects. A sacred terror haunts the threshold of Enigma; the dark portals are flung wide, but there is a voice which warns the passer-by not to enter. Woe to him who ventures too far! Men of genius from the boundless depths of abstraction and pure speculation, situated as it were above dogma, propose their theories to God. Their prayers audaciously invite discussion. Their worship poses questions. That is personal religion, loaded with anxiety and responsibility for those who dare embark upon it.

There are no bounds to human thought. At its own risk and peril it analyses and explores its own bewilderment. One may almost say that in a kind of transcendent reaction it bewilders nature; the mysterious world around us gives back what it is given, and probably the contemplators are themselves contemplated. However this may be, there are men – but are they men? – who clearly discern beyond the horizon of dreaming the heights of the Absolute, who experience the terrible vision of the infinite mountain. Monseigneur Bienvenu was not one of these; he was not a man of genius. He would have mistrusted those sublimities whence certain men, and very great men such as Swedenborg and Pascal, have lapsed into madness. Such powerful thinking has its value; it is by these arduous roads that we approach perfection. But he took the short cut, the Holy Gospel.

He did not seek to assume the mantle of Elijah, to shed a light of the future upon the misty turmoil of events or resolve the prevailing light into a single flame; there was in him nothing of the prophet or the mystic. He was a simple soul who loved, and that was all.

That he expanded prayer to make of it a superhuman aspiration, this is probable. But we can no more pray too much than we can love too much; and if to pray outside the accepted texts is heresy, then St Teresa and St Jerome were also heretics.

His heart was given to all suffering and expiation. The world to him was like an immense malady. He sensed fever everywhere, sought out affliction and without seeking to answer the riddle did what he could to heal the wound. The awesome spectacle of things as they were enhanced his tenderness; he was concerned only to find for himself and inspire in others the best means of comfort and relief. The theme of all existing things was for that good and rare priest distress in need of consolation.

There are men who dig for gold; he dug for compassion. Poverty was his goldmine; and the universality of suffering a reason for the universality of charity. 'Love one another.' To him everything was contained in those words, his whole doctrine, and he asked no more. The senator to whom we have referred, the gentleman who thought himself a philosopher, once said to him: 'You see what the world is like, every man at war with every other, and victory to the strongest. Your "Love one another" is pure folly' – 'Well, if it is folly,' said Monseigneur without disputing the matter, 'then the soul must enclose itself within it like the pearl in the oyster.' Which is what he did. He enclosed himself in that folly and was wholly content to do so, putting aside the huge questions that fascinate and terrify, the endless vistas of abstraction, the chasms of metaphysics, all those depths which for the believer converge in God and for the atheist in limbo: destiny, good and evil, the conflict of man with man, the consciousness of men and the sleep-walking thought of animals, transformation by death and the recapitulation of lives in the tomb, the mysterious additions made by successive loves to the continuing self, the essence and the substance, the *Nihil* and the *Ens*, the soul, nature, liberty, necessity; problems sheer as precipices, sinister densities beckoning to the giants of the human intellect; abysses which a Lucretius, a Paul, or a Dante explore with blazing eyes, steadfastly turned towards the infinite, which seem to kindle the stars.

Monseigneur Bienvenu was simply a man who observed these mysteries from outside, not looking too closely, not stirring them with his finger or letting them oppress his mind, but in a spirit deeply imbued with reference for the hereafter.

BOOK TWO

THE OUTCAST

I
End of a day's journey

AT THE beginning of October 1815, and about an hour before
sunset, a man travelling on foot entered the town of Digne. The
few people who happened to be at their windows or doorways
observed him with a vague misgiving. It would have been hard to
find a traveller of more disreputable aspect. He was a man in the
prime of life, of medium height, broad-shouldered and robust, who
might have been in his late forties. A cap with a low leather peak
half hid his face, which was tanned by sun and weather and glistened
with sweat. His coarse yellow shirt, fastened at the neck with a small
metal clasp, gaped to reveal a hairy chest. He wore a scarf twisted
like a rope, threadbare duck trousers frayed at one knee and in
holes at the other, and a tattered grey jacket patched over one
elbow with a piece of green cloth sewn on with string. On his back
was a new and bulging soldier's knapsack and he carried a very
large, knotted stick. His stockingless feet were in hob-nailed shoes
and his beard was long. The dust and sweat of his day's journey
added a touch of squalor to his down-at-heel appearance. His head
was shorn but stubbly, having evidently not been shaved for some
days.

No one knew him. Presumably he was only passing through the
town, having come from the south, and possibly from the coast,
since he had entered by the road over which Napoleon had travelled
seven months previously on his way from Cannes to Paris. He
must have been walking all day, he seemed so tired. He was seen
to stop and drink at the public drinking-fountain at the far end of
the Boulevard Gassendi, on the outskirts of the town; but he was
clearly very thirsty because some children who followed him saw
him stop again, two hundred yards further on, at the fountain in
the market-place.

At the corner of the Rue Poichevert he turned left towards the
Town Hall, which he entered, emerging from it a quarter of an
hour later. A gendarme was seated outside the door on the stone
bench from which General Drouot, on 4 March, had read to the

startled populace Napoleon's famous Proclamation upon his landing in Golfe Juan. The stranger respectfully raised his cap. The gendarme did not acknowledge the salute but looked intently at him, watched him for some moments as he walked away, and then went into the building.

There was at that time a handsome inn in Digne bearing the sign of the Croix-de-Colbas. Its proprietor was a certain Jacquin Labarre, a man esteemed in the town because of his connection with another Labarre, proprietor of the inn of the Trois-Dauphins at Grenoble, who had served in the Guides. There had been many rumours concerning the Trois-Dauphins at the time of the Emperor's landing. It was said that General Bertrand had paid the inn a number of surreptitious visits in the previous January, disguised as a carter, and had bestowed medals on soldiers and fistfuls of coin on certain citizens. The truth is that Napoleon, arriving at Grenoble, had politely refused the mayor's offer of accommodation at the Prefecture saying that he was going to stop with a personal acquaintance, and had gone to the Trois-Dauphins. The reflected glory of the Trois-Dauphins Labarre extended over twenty-five leagues to the Labarre of the Croix-de-Colbas, who was referred to in the town as 'the cousin of the one in Grenoble'.

The stranger made for this inn, the best in the district, and entered by way of the kitchen, which opened directly on to the street. All the cooking-stoves were lighted and a fire burned brightly in the hearth. The innkeeper, who was also the cook, was busy among his pots and pans preparing a meal for a party of waggoners who could be heard loudly talking and laughing in the next room. As every traveller knows, no one fares better than the waggoner. A plump marmot, flanked by partridges and grouse, was turning on a long spit in front of the fire, and two large carp from the Lac de Lauzet and a trout from the Lac d'Alloz were cooking on the stove.

Hearing the door open the innkeeper said without looking up: 'What can I do for Monsieur?'

'A meal and a bed,' said the stranger.

'By all means –' but at this moment the innkeeper turned his head; after glancing at the visitor he added '– provided you can pay for it.'

'I have money,' said the stranger producing a shabby leather purse from his jacket pocket.

'In that case you're welcome.'

The man returned the purse to his pocket, dropped his knapsack on the floor by the door and, keeping hold of his stick, seated himself on a low stool by the fire. Digne is high in the hills and its October evenings are chilly. The innkeeper, still busy with his cooking, was none the less examining him.

'Will dinner soon be ready?' the man asked.

'Quite soon.'

While the stranger warmed himself, seated with his back turned to the room, the worthy innkeeper, Jacquin Labarre, got a pencil out of his pocket and tore a strip off a newspaper lying on a table by the window. He scribbled a line or two, folded the strip and handed it to a youngster who appeared to serve him as scullery-boy and personal attendant. He murmured a few words and the boy ran off in the direction of the Town Hall.

The stranger had seen nothing of this. He asked for the second time:

'Will dinner soon be ready?'

'Quite soon.'

The boy returned with the scrap of paper, and the innkeeper unfolded it with the promptness of someone who has been anxious for a reply. He read the message with care, then nodded his head and stood for a moment reflecting. Finally, he went over to the stranger, who appeared to be plunged in unhappy thought.

'I'm sorry, Monsieur. I can't have you here.'

The man swung round, half-rising to his feet.

'Why? Are you afraid I shan't pay? Do you want me to pay in advance? I tell you, I've got the money.'

'It isn't that.'

'Well, then?'

'You have the money, but –'

'But what?'

'But I haven't a room free.'

The stranger said calmly: 'Then put me in the stable.'

'I can't do that.'

'Why not?'

'The horses take up all the room.'

'Well then, a corner of the hay-loft. A truss of straw. We can see to that after dinner.'

'I can't offer you dinner.'

The words, spoken in a firm, deliberate tone, seemed to shake the stranger.

'But I'm dropping with hunger! I've been walking since day-break. I've covered a dozen leagues. I must have something to eat.'

'I've nothing to spare,' said the innkeeper.

The stranger uttered a short laugh and pointed to the spit and the stove.

'What's all that?'

'It's all reserved.'

'By whom?'

'By the waggoners.'

'How many are there?'

'Twelve.'

'There's enough there for twenty.'

'It's what they ordered and they paid in advance.'

The stranger sat down again and said without raising his voice:

'I'm at an inn and I'm hungry. I'm stopping here.'

The innkeeper then bent over him and said in a tone which caused him to start: 'Get out.'

The stranger at the moment was bent forward in the act of thrusting a few cinders back into the fire with the metal ferrule of his stick. He swung round sharply, but as he opened his mouth to reply the innkeeper, looking hard at him, went on in a low voice:

'That's enough talk. Do you want me to tell you who you are? Your name is Jean Valjean. And now do you want me to tell you *what* you are? I had my suspicions when you came in. I sent a note to the *Mairie* and this is the reply. Can you read?'

He held out the scrap of paper and after the stranger had looked at it he went on:

'I like to treat everyone politely. Kindly go away.'

The man rose, took up his knapsack and left.

He walked off seemingly at random along the main street, keeping close to the house fronts, his attitude one of dejected humilia-tion. He did not once look round. Had he done so he would have seen the proprietor of the Croix-de-Colbas standing in his doorway surrounded by a party of customers and passers-by, talking volubly and pointing towards him; and from the excited and hostile looks cast in his direction he would have realized that before long his arrival would be known throughout the town.

He saw nothing of this. A man crushed by misfortune does not look back, knowing only too well that ill-chance follows behind. He continued to walk blindly along streets unknown to him, for a time forgetful of his fatigue, such is the effect of despair. But he was suddenly conscious of an acute pang of hunger. It was growing dark. He looked about him, seeking some shelter for the night.

The better establishment was closed to him. What he sought now was the poorest of taverns, the humblest of lodgings for the poor. And as it happened a light shone at the end of the street; a torch of pine-twigs, hanging from a metal bracket, was visible against the pallor of the evening sky. He went towards it.

The place was the tavern at the end of the Rue de Chauffaut. The stranger paused for a moment at the window to peer inside at a low-ceilinged room lighted by a small table-lamp and the glow of a large fire. Some men were drinking while the host warmed himself at the fire, over which a stewpot bubbled hanging from a pot-hook.

There are two entrances to this tavern, which is also a species of hostelry, one giving on to the street and the other on to a small yard with a midden. The stranger did not venture to use the front entrance. He went into the yard, hesitated again, then diffidently raised the latch and pushed upon the door.

'Who's that?' asked the innkeeper.

'Someone looking for a meal and a bed.'

'Then come in. We can give you both.'

He entered and the heads turned to gaze at him as he stood between the light of the lamp and the light of the fire. They watched in silence while he unloosed his knapsack.

'There's a stew cooking,' the innkeeper said. 'Come and warm yourself, friend.'

The man sat down by the hearth, stretching out his tired feet to the blaze. A pleasant smell rose from the stewpot. What could be seen of his face under the low-peaked cap conveyed a vague impression of well-being mingled with that other poignant aspect which comes of habitual suffering. In other respects it was a strong face, vigorous and melancholy; and it contained a strange contradiction, appearing at first sight humble but then seeming masterful. The eyes under heavy brows shone like fire under a thicket.

But one of the company was a fish-merchant who on his way to the tavern had put his horse in Labarre's stable. As chance would have it, he had met this ill-favoured stranger that morning on the road between Bras d'Asse and some other village of which I forget the name. The man, who already seemed tired, had asked to be allowed to get up behind him, a request which the fishmonger had answered by digging his spurs into his horse. The fishmonger was one of the group which half an hour previously had clustered round Jacquin Labarre, and he had there told the story of this encounter. He now made a covert sign to the innkeeper, who went over to him. They exchanged a few words in an undertone while the stranger sat lost in thought.

Returning to his fireside, the host tapped the man on the shoulder and said:

'You must clear out of here.'

The stranger looked up and said gently: 'So you know?'

'Yes.'

'They turned me out of the other inn.'

'You're being turned out of this one.'

'But where am I to go?'

'Somewhere else.'

The man picked up his stick and knapsack and left.

Some boys who had followed him from the Croix-de-Colbas, and had evidently been waiting for him to emerge, flung stones at him as he did so. He swung round angrily brandishing his stick, and they scattered like a flock of birds.

He came to the prison. A bell-chain hung by the doorway and he pulled it. A panel in the door slid back.

'Monsieur,' said the man, removing his cap, 'will you be so kind as to let me in and give me lodging for the night?'

'This is a prison, not an inn,' said the voice of the door-keeper. 'If you want to be let in you must get yourself arrested.' The panel closed.

The stranger moved on into a narrow street where there were a great many gardens, some enclosed only by hedges, to give it a cheerful appearance. Among the gardens and hedges was a small, one-storeyed house with a lighted window. Peering through this window as he had done at the tavern he saw a large, whitewashed room containing a bed draped with printed calico, a cradle standing in a corner, a few wooden chairs and a double-barrelled shotgun hanging on the wall. A table was laid in the middle of the room, and the light from a brass lamp fell upon a cloth of coarse white linen, a pewter jug shining like silver and filled with wine, and a steaming earthenware tureen. A man of about forty with an open, amiable face was seated at the table dancing a small child on his knee while near to him sat a young woman suckling an infant. Father and child were laughing, while the mother smiled.

The stranger stayed for a moment thoughtfully contemplating this pleasant scene. Only he could have said what he was thinking. He may well have reflected that so happy a household might also be hospitable, and that where there was so much gaiety there might also be a little charity.

He tapped very gently on the window-pane but was not heard.

He tapped a second time and heard the wife say to her husband: 'I think there's someone knocking.'

'It's nothing,' said the man.

He tapped a third time, and now the husband rose, picked up the lamp and opened the door.

He was a tall man, part peasant, part craftsman, wearing a large leather apron attached over his left shoulder, in the bulge of which were a hammer, an old handkerchief, a powder-horn, and a variety of other objects, held in place by his belt, so that it constituted a loose pocket. He carried his head high, and his open shirt-front disclosed a powerful, untanned neck. He had thick eyebrows, bushy black side-whiskers, prominent eyes and, above all, that air of being in his own place which cannot be described in words.

'Forgive me, Monsieur,' said the stranger. 'If I pay you, will you give me a plate of soup and allow me to sleep in the shed in your garden? Will you do this, Monsieur? If I pay?'

'Who are you?' asked the master of the house.

'I have come from Puy-Moisson. I've been walking all day. Can you do this for me? If I pay?'

'I wouldn't refuse shelter to any decent man who can pay. But why don't you go to an inn?'

'There are no rooms.'

'What? But this isn't market-day. Have you tried Labarre?'

'Yes, I went there.'

'Well?'

The stranger said awkwardly: 'I don't know. He wouldn't have me.'

'What about the other place – Rue de Chauffaut?'

The stranger's embarrassment increased. He muttered: 'He wouldn't take me in either.'

A look of mistrust appeared on the peasant-face. The man's

gaze travelled slowly over the stranger and suddenly he exclaimed with a sort of shudder: 'Are you the man –?'

After a final glance he stepped rapidly backward, set the lamp on the table and took his gun down from the wall. At the words, 'Are you the man – ?', the woman had gathered the two children into her arms and now stood behind her husband, her bosom uncovered, staring with horrified eyes at the stranger while she murmured in the patois of the hill-country, '*Tsomaraude*, brigand'.

All this happened in less time than it takes to tell. After examining the stranger for a moment as though he were some kind of wild beast the master of the house returned to the door, gun in hand, and said:

'Clear out!'

'I beseech you,' said the stranger. 'A glass of water.'

'A bullet's what you'll get,' said the man.

He slammed the door and sounds of the shooting of bolts, the closing of shutters and the clang of an iron bar falling into its slot could be heard from outside.

Night was closing in and the cold alpine wind was blowing. By the last gleam of daylight the stranger saw, in one of the gardens flanking the lane, a sort of hut which looked as though it had been made of turfs. Clambering resolutely over a low wooden fence he went to examine it. It had a very low, narrow doorway and seemed to be one of those temporary shelters which road-workers put up. This was what he assumed it to be.

He was cold and famished. Hunger he was resigned to, but here at least was some protection against the cold. Places of this sort were not generally occupied at night. Lying flat on his stomach he wriggled inside. It was warm, and there was a bedding of straw. For a moment he lay motionless, too exhausted to move. Then, finding his knapsack uncomfortable, and since in any case it would serve him as a pillow, he began to unbuckle its straps. At this moment he heard a fierce sound of growling and, looking up, saw the head of a large bull-mastiff outlined against the faint light beyond the entrance.

The hut was a dog-kennel.

The man was himself vigorous and formidable. Grasping his stick and using the knapsack as a shield he fought his way out, not without further damage to his tattered clothes. He beat a retreat with his stick outthrust in the defensive posture known to fencers as *la rose couverte.* When at length, and not without difficulty, he had got back over the fence and found himself again in the lane, alone and shelterless, driven out of a dog-kennel, he sank rather than seated himself on a stone by the roadside, and it seems that a passer-by heard him cry aloud:

'I'm not even a dog!'

Presently he got up and walked on, leaving the town behind, hoping to find a tree or hayrick which would serve him for the night. He walked for some time with his head bowed, but eventually, when he felt himself to be remote from all human habitation, he paused to look about him. He was in a field and before him was a hillock covered with the stubble of the recent harvest, so that it looked like a shaven head.

The horizon was very dark, not only with the darkness of night but also with low cloud which seemed to emanate from the hillock itself and, rising, to fill the sky. At the same time, since the moon was not yet risen and there was still a last, faint glimmer of twilight, the clouds formed a pallid vault reflecting this light back to earth.

The earth was thus more brightly illumined than the heavens, producing a strangely sinister effect, and the sparse outline of the hillock loomed mistily and bleakly against a shadowed horizon. The whole scene was ugly, mean, desolate, and drab. There was no object in the field or on the hillock except a single misshapen tree rustling its branches a few yards from where the outcast stood.

Clearly he was a man largely lacking in those finer sensibilities which cause the spirit to respond to the mysteries of nature; nevertheless that prospect of sky and plain, the hillock and the tree, was so profoundly desolating that after standing a few moments in motionless contemplation he turned abruptly away. There are times when nature seems hostile.

He went back to Digne, of which the gates were now shut. In 1815 Digne was still enclosed by the walls and square towers which had sustained sieges during the wars of religion, although these have since been demolished. Passing through a breach in the ramparts he re-entered the town.

The time was about eight. Being unfamiliar with the streets he resumed his haphazard wanderings, passing by the Prefecture and the Seminary. As he crossed the cathedral square he shook his fist at the church.

There is a printing works at one corner of the square. It was here that the proclamations of the Emperor and the Imperial Guard to the army, brought from Elba and dictated by Napoleon himself, were first printed. Exhausted and with no further hope the outcast stretched himself on a stone bench by the doorway of this establishment.

An elderly lady who came out of the cathedral at this moment saw him lying there and asked, 'What are you doing?'

He answered roughly and angrily:

'My good woman, you can see what I'm doing. I'm sleeping here.'

The good woman, who indeed merited the designation, was the Marquise de R—.

'On this bench?' she asked.

'I've slept for nineteen years on a wooden mattress,' the man said. 'Now it's stone.'

'Were you a soldier?'

'Yes – a soldier.'

'Why don't you go to an inn?'

'Because I haven't any money.'

'Alas,' said Madame de R—, 'I have only four sous in my purse.'

'That's better than nothing.'

The man took the four sous and Madame de R— said:

'It's not enough to pay for lodging at an inn. But have you tried everything? You can't possibly spend the night here. You must be cold and hungry. Someone would surely take you in out of charity.'

'I've knocked at every door.'

'You really mean –?'

'I've been turned away everywhere.'

The lady touched his arm and pointed across the square to a small house beside the bishop's palace.

'Have you really knocked at every door?'

'Yes.'

'Have you knocked at that one?'

'No.'

'Then do.'

II

Prudence urged upon wisdom

That evening the Bishop of Digne, after returning from his customary walk through the town, had stayed late in his own room. He was busy with a large work on Christian Duty which, alas, was never completed. The book, which was to be a careful survey of all that the learned Fathers and Doctors have said upon this weighty matter, was to be divided in two parts, treating first the duties of the community as a whole and secondly of the duties of the individual according to the category to which he belonged. The duties of the community are major duties and St Matthew has resolved them into four: duty to God, duty to self, duty to one's neighbour, duty to all living creatures. As for the more particular duties, the bishop had found these defined and prescribed elsewhere. The duties of monarchs and their subjects were dealt with in the Epistle to the Romans; those of magistrates, wives, mothers, and young men by St Peter; those of husbands, fathers, children, and servants in the Epistle to the Ephesians; those of the Faithful in the Epistle to the Hebrews and those of virgins in the Epistle to the Corinthians. He was engaged in the laborious task of reassembling these prescriptions in a harmonious whole for the good of all men's souls.

At eight o'clock that evening he was still at work, writing rather uncomfortably on small slips of paper with a large volume open on his knees, when Mme Magloire entered as usual to get the silver cutlery out of the cupboard by the bed. A few minutes later the bishop, suspecting that the table was laid and that his sister might be waiting, closed his book and went into the dining-room. It was a rectangular room with a fireplace, a door giving directly on to the street, as we have said, and a window opening on to the garden.

Mme Magloire had just finished laying the table and was chatting with Mlle Baptistine before serving the meal. A lamp stood on the table, which was near the hearth where a fire was burning. The two women, both over sixty, may readily be pictured – Mme Magloire short, plump, and lively; Mlle Baptistine mild, slender, and fragile, a little taller than her brother, clad in a dress of the plum-coloured silk that had been fashionable in 1806, the year she had bought it in Paris, and which she had been wearing ever since. To borrow one of those popular expressions which have the merit that they say more in a word than can be achieved by a page of writing, Mme Magloire had the look of a peasant and Mlle Baptistine that of a lady. Mme Magloire wore a white cap with piping, a small gold cross at her neck (the only article of feminine jewellery in the house), a very white kerchief emerging from her dress of black homespun with its wide, short sleeves, which was tied at the waist with a green ribbon, and a stomacher of the same material fixed with two pins in front. On her feet she wore thick shoes and yellow stockings of the kind worn by the women of Marseilles. Mlle Baptistine's dress was cut in the 1806 pattern, high and narrow-waisted, with puffed shoulders, tabs, and buttons. She hid her grey hair under a curled peruke of the kind called *à l'enfant*. Mme Magloire had a look of bright intelligence and warmth of heart; the uneven corners of her mouth, with its upper lip thicker than the lower, gave an impression of imperious obstinacy. While the bishop remained silent she would address him with a forthright mingling of respect and familiarity, but directly he spoke she lapsed, like her mistress, into mute obedience. Mlle Baptistine talked very little, being content to obey and acquiesce. Even as a girl she had not been pretty, with her large, overprominent blue eyes and her long, pinched nose. She had been predestined to meekness, but faith, hope and charity, those virtues that enrich the soul, had raised meekness to saintliness. Nature had made her a lamb, religion had made her an angel of goodness.

Mlle Baptistine was later to tell the story of that night's events so often that there are persons still living who can recall its every detail. At the moment when the bishop entered the dining-room Mme Magloire was talking with some vehemence to her mistress about a matter which constantly occupied her mind and with which her master was well acquainted, namely, the fastening of the front door. It seemed that while she had been out shopping for the evening meal she had heard rumours. There was talk of a stranger in the town, a vagabond of forbidding aspect who must still be lurking in the streets, which made it inadvisable for anyone to be out late that night; the more so since the police service was not all it should be owing to bad blood between the prefect and the mayor, each of whom would be glad to make trouble for the other. In short the prudent citizen would do well to see after his own safety by shuttering and barricading his house and making sure that his front door was securely locked.

Mme Magloire laid particular stress on those last words, but the bishop, whose own room was rather cold, had sat down to warm himself by the fire and paid no attention. Accordingly she repeated them, and Mlle Baptistine, wishing to support her without vexing her brother, said cautiously:

'Brother, did you hear what Mme Magloire said?'

'Only vaguely,' said the bishop. He half turned with his hands on his knees and smiled at the old servant with the glow of firelight on his friendly, cheerful face. 'Well now, what is it? Do I understand that we are in some grave danger?'

Mme Magloire told the story again, instinctively elaborating it. The man was a gipsy, a ne'er-do-well, a dangerous beggar. He had tried to get a lodging with Jacquin Labarre, who had turned him away. He had arrived by way of the Boulevard Gassendi and had been seen wandering about the streets in the mist, a man with a knapsack and a terrible look on his face.

'Really?' said the bishop.

Encouraged by this show of interest, which suggested that the bishop shared something of her alarm, Mme Magloire continued triumphantly:

'Yes, Monseigneur, that kind of man. Something dreadful will happen tonight, everyone says so. When you think of the state of the police, and a town buried in the mountains like this with not a single lantern in the streets so that it's black as pitch when you go out . . . Well, what I say, and Mademoiselle agrees with me –'

'I am saying nothing,' murmured Mademoiselle. 'Whatever my brother does is right.'

Mme Magloire ignored the interruption.

'What we both say is that this house is not safe and that, if Monseigneur permits, I should go round to Paulin Musebois, the locksmith, and ask him to put back the bolts on the front door. We have them here, it wouldn't take him a minute. I say the door should be bolted, even if it's only for tonight, and anyway it's a shocking thing for the door to be simply on the latch so that any stranger can walk in, to say nothing of Monseigneur's habit of always inviting people in, even at midnight, gracious Heaven, they don't even need to ask, and when you think –'

At this moment there was a heavy knock on the door.

'Come in,' said the bishop.

III

The gallantry of absolute obedience

The door opened. It was flung widely open, as though in response to a vigorous and determined thrust. A man entered.

We know the man already. He stepped across the threshold and then stood motionless with the door still open behind him. His knapsack hung from his shoulder and his stick was in his hand. The firelight falling on his face disclosed an expression of exhaustion, desperation, and brutish defiance. He was an ugly and terrifying spectacle.

Mme Magloire was too startled even to exclaim. She stood trembling and open-mouthed. Mlle Baptistine half rose in alarm but then, as she turned towards her brother, her face recovered its customary tranquillity.

The bishop was calmly regarding the stranger. He opened his mouth to speak, but before he could do so the man, leaning on his stick with both hands and gazing round at the three elderly people, said in a harsh voice:

'Look. My name is Jean Valjean. I'm a convict on parole. I've done nineteen years in prison. They let me out four days ago and I'm on my way to Pontarlier. I've walked from Toulon in four days and today I covered a dozen leagues [about thirty miles]. When I reached this place I went to an inn and they turned me out because of my yellow ticket-of-leave which I'd shown at the *Mairie* as I'm obliged to do. I tried another inn and they told me to clear out. Nobody wants me anywhere. I tried the prison and the doorkeeper wouldn't open. I crawled into a dog-kennel and the dog bit me and drove me out just as if he were a man and knew who I was. I thought I'd sleep in a field under the stars, but there weren't any stars and it looked as though it was going to rain, and no God to stop it raining, so I came back here hoping to find a doorway to sleep in. I lay down on a bench in the square outside and a good woman pointed to your door and told me to knock on it. So I've knocked. What is this place? Is it an inn? I've got money. I've got one hundred and nine francs and fifteen sous, the money I earned by nineteen years' work in prison. I'm ready to pay, I don't care how much, I've got the money. I'm very tired, twelve leagues on foot, and I'm hungry. Will you let me stay?'

'Mme Magloire,' said the bishop, 'will you please lay another place.'

The man moved nearer to the light of the table-lamp, seeming not to understand.

'It's not like that,' he said. 'Weren't you listening? I'm a convict, a felon, I've served in the galleys.' He pulled a sheet of yellow paper out of his pocket and unfolded it. 'This is my ticket-of-leave – yellow, as you see. That's why everybody turns me away. Do you want to read it? I can read. There were classes in prison for anyone who wanted to learn. You can see what it says – "Jean Valjean, released convict, born in –" not that that matters "– served nineteen years, five years for robbery with violence, fourteen years for four attempts to escape – a very dangerous man." So there you are. Everybody kicks me out. Will you take me in? Is this an inn? Can you give me food and a bed for the night? Have you a stable?'

'Mme Magloire,' said the bishop, 'you must put clean sheets on the bed in the alcove.'

We have already described the absolute obedience of the two women. Mme Magloire went off without a word.

The bishop turned to the man.

'Sit down and warm yourself, Monsieur. Supper will very soon be ready, and the bed can be made up while you're having a meal.'

And now the man had really understood. His face, which had been so hard and sombre, was suddenly and remarkably transformed by an expression of amazement, incredulity and pleasure. He began to babble like a child.

'You really mean it? You'll let me stay? A convict – and you aren't turning me out! You called me "Monsieur". "Clear off, you dog," is what they mostly say. I thought you'd be bound to send me away, that's why I told you at once who I was. I'm grateful to the good lady who sent me here. Supper and a bed, with a mattress and sheets! It's nineteen years since I slept in a bed. Well, I've got the money, I'm ready to pay. May I ask your name, sir? I'll pay whatever you ask. You're a good man. You are an innkeeper, aren't you?'

'I'm a priest,' said the bishop, 'and this is where I live.'

'A priest! But a good priest. So you won't ask for payment. I suppose you're the curé of this great church. But of course! I'm stupid. I hadn't noticed your cap.'

He had put his knapsack and stick in a corner while he was speaking, and after returning the yellow document to his pocket he sat down. Mlle Baptistine was looking kindly at him.

'You're human, Monsieur le curé,' he went on. 'You don't despise people. A good priest is a fine thing. So I don't need to pay anything?'

'No,' said the bishop, 'keep your money. How much did you say – a hundred and nine francs?'

'And fifteen sous.'

'And how long did it take you to earn it?'

'Nineteen years.'

'Nineteen years!' The bishop sighed profoundly.

'I've still got it all,' the man said. 'All I've spent in these four days is twenty-five sous I earned by helping to unload some carts in Grasse. As you're a priest I may tell you that we had an almoner in the prison. And once I saw a bishop – a Monseigneur, as they say. He was from Marseilles. A bishop's a priest who's higher than the other priests, not that I've any need to tell you that, but for us it's all so strange, for men like me. He said mass at an altar in the prison yard and he had a sort of pointed hat on his head, gold, it glittered in the sun at midday. We were drawn up in ranks on three sides of the yard, with the guns pointing at us, fuses lighted. We couldn't see him very well. He talked, but he was too far off and we couldn't hear. That's what a bishop's like.'

The bishop had risen while he was speaking to shut the door, which had remained wide open. Mme Magloire came back into the room with the additional cutlery.

'Put them as near as possible to the fire, Mme Magloire,' the bishop said. He turned to his guest. 'The night wind is raw in the Alps. You must be cold, Monsieur.'

Each time he uttered the word 'Monsieur' in his mild, companionable voice the man's face lighted up. The courtesy, to the ex-convict, was like fresh water to a shipwrecked man. Ignominy thirsts for respect.

'This lamp doesn't give much light,' the bishop said.

Perceiving what he had in mind, Mme Magloire fetched the two silver candlesticks from his bedroom mantelpiece, lit them and set them on the table.

'Monsieur le curé,' said the man, 'you are very good. You don't despise me. You have taken me in and lighted your candles for me.

But I have not concealed from you where I come from and what I am.'

The bishop, seated at his side, laid a hand gently on his arm.

'You need have told me nothing. This house is not mine but Christ's. It does not ask a man his name but whether he is in need. You are in trouble, you are hungry and thirsty, and so you are welcome. You need not thank me for receiving you in my house. No one is at home here except those seeking shelter. Let me assure you, passer-by though you are, that this is more your home than mine. Everything in it is yours. Why should I ask your name? In any case I knew it before you told me.'

The man looked up with startled eyes. 'You know my name?'

'Of course,' said the bishop. 'Your name is brother.'

'Monsieur le curé,' the man cried, 'I was famished when I came in here. Now I scarcely know what I feel. Everything has changed.'

The bishop was regarding him. 'You have suffered a great deal,' he said.

'Well, yes – the red smock, the ball-and-chain, a plank to sleep on, heat, cold and hard labour, the galleys and the lash. The double-chain for a trifle, solitary for a single word. Chained even when you're sick in bed. And the dogs – well, they're better off than we were. Nineteen years of it. I'm forty-six. And now a yellow ticket. That's the story.'

'Yes. You have come from an unhappy place. But listen. There is more rejoicing in Heaven over the tears of one sinner who repents than over the white robes of a hundred who are virtuous. If you leave your place of suffering with hatred in your heart, and anger against men, you will be deserving of our pity; but if you leave with goodwill, in gentleness and peace, you will have risen above any of us.'

Mme Magloire had meanwhile dished up the meal, which consisted of a broth of water, oil, bread and salt with some scraps of bacon and mutton, figs, a fresh cheese, and a large loaf of rye bread. She had taken it upon herself to supplement the bishop's table-wine with a bottle of old wine from Mauves.

The bishop had recovered the cheerful expression of a man who is hospitable by nature. 'Supper is served,' he said gaily, and, as his custom was, he seated the guest at his right hand while Mlle Baptistine, naturally and unassumingly, took her place on his left.

The bishop said grace and himself served the broth. The man began to eat hungrily. But suddenly the bishop said:

'There seems to be something lacking on this table.'

Mme Magloire had, in fact, only laid places for three. But it was the custom of the house, when there was a guest, to set out the full set of silver cutlery for six persons, an innocent and childlike display of elegance, in that simple and austere household, which graced its poverty with dignity.

Again reading his thought Mme Magloire went out without speaking, and a minute later the rest of the set, laid for three additional guests, gleamed on the white tablecloth.

IV

The cheese-makers of Pontarlier

To convey some notion of what took place during that meal we cannot do better than quote part of a letter written by Mlle Baptistine to Mme de Boischevron in which she gives a detailed and artless account of the conversation between the bishop and the ex-convict.

... The man at first paid no attention to anyone. He ate as though he were starving. But after the broth he said:

'Monsieur le curé, all this is too good for me, but let me tell you that the waggoners, who would not let me share their meal, eat better than you.'

I may confess that this remark rather shocked me. But my brother replied:

'Their work is more tiring than mine.'

'No,' said the man. 'They have more money. I can see that you are poor. Perhaps you are not even a curé. Are you a curé? If God were just you would be that at least.'

'God is more than just,' said my brother, and he went on after a pause. 'I understand, Monsieur Jean Valjean, that you are on your way to Pontarlier.'

'On a route which I am under orders to follow.' This, I think, is what the man said. He continued: 'I have to start tomorrow at daybreak. It's a hard journey. The nights may be cold but the days are hot.'

'You are going to a good part of the country,' my brother said. 'My family was ruined in the Revolution and for a time I took refuge in the Franche-Comté where I got my living by manual labour. I was willing and I had no difficulty in finding work. There is plenty to be had. There are paper-mills, distilleries, oil-refineries, clockmakers, steel and copper mills, and at least twenty iron foundries, of which four, at Lods, Chatillon, Audincourt, and Beure, are very large.'

I think those are the places my brother named. He then turned to me and said:

'My dear, have we not relatives in the region?'

'We used to have,' I replied. 'Among others there was Monsieur de Lucenet, who was Captain of the Gates at Pontarlier under the *ancien régime.*'

'But we had no relatives left in '93,' said my brother. 'We had only our hands. I worked. In the region of Pontarlier, where you are going, Monsieur Valjean, there is a charming patriarchal industry consisting of the cheese-farms which they call *fruitières.*'

While encouraging the man to go on eating my brother described these Pontarlier *fruitières* to him in great detail. There are two kinds, those known as the *grosses granges*, the property of rich owners, with a herd of forty or fifty cows, which produce seven or eight thousand cheeses in a summer, and the *fruitières d'associations* formed by groups of the poorer peasants in the middle hills who share the cows and their produce and receive payment from a cheese-maker who is known as the *grurin*. The *grurin* takes three deliveries of milk a day and enters the quantities in a double register. Cheese-making begins towards the end of April, and the peasants take their cows up to the hill-pastures about the middle of June.

The man was reviving as he ate, and my brother encouraged him to drink the good Mauves wine which he himself does not drink because he says it costs too much. He told him about the cheese-making in the light and easy way with which you are familiar, breaking off occasionally to bring me into the conversation. He referred more than once to the excellent standing of the *grurin* as though he wished to convey to the man, without presuming directly to advise him, that this was a field of employment which he might do well to enter. One thing particularly struck me. I have told you the kind of man this was. Well, throughout the meal, and indeed throughout the evening, except for those few words at the beginning, my brother said nothing to remind him of what he was, nor did he tell him who he himself was. Clearly this was a possible occasion for a little sermonizing and for the bishop to make himself known to the malefactor in order to impress him. Another man, having him at his mercy, might have seized the opportunity to fortify his soul as well as his body with words of reproof and moral exhortation, or of sympathy mingled with the hope that he would mend his ways in the future. But my brother did not so much as ask the man where he was born. He did not ask his story. For the story must have included some account of his crimes and my brother clearly wished to avoid all reference to these. To the point, indeed, that when he was talking about the hill-people of Pontarlier and 'their pleasant labours high under heaven' and their contentment because they were innocent, he broke off abruptly as though fearing that he might say something to offend the man. Thinking it over afterwards, I believe I know what was in my brother's mind. He must have reflected that the man, this Jean Valjean, was sufficiently oppressed already with the burden of his wretchedness, and that it was better to distract his thoughts and make him feel, if only for a little while, that he was a man like any other. Was not this true charity? Is there not true evangelism in the delicacy which refrains from preaching and moralizing? To avoid probing an open wound, is not that the truest sympathy? This, I believe, was my brother's inmost thought. But I can also affirm that if this was his thought he gave no sign of it, even to me. From start to finish he was his ordinary self, and he dined with Jean Valjean precisely as he would have done with the provost or the curé of the parish.

Near the end of the meal, when we were at dessert, there was a knock at the door. It was Mme Gerbaud with her child in her arms. My brother kissed the child on the forehead and borrowed fifteen sous which I had handy and gave them to her. Valjean paid little attention to this. He had fallen silent and was looking very tired. When the old woman had left, my brother said grace, and then, turning to Valjean, he said, 'I'm sure you're ready for bed.' Mme Magloire quickly cleared the table. I realized that it was time for us to withdraw and leave the man to sleep, and we both went upstairs. But I sent Mme Magloire down a moment later with a goatskin rug from the Black Forest which I have in my room. The nights are bitterly cold and although it is old, more's the pity, and the hair is very worn, it would help to warm his bed. My brother bought it in Germany, at Tottlingen, near the source of the Danube, and also the little ivory-handled knife which I use at table.

Mme Magloire came back almost at once and we said our prayers in the room where we hang the washing to dry. Then each of us went to her own room without a word.

V

Quietude

Having bidden his sister good night Monseigneur Bienvenu picked up one of the two silver candlesticks and handed the other to his guest, saying, 'I will show you to your room, Monsieur.' The man followed him.

As we have seen, the arrangement of the rooms was such that to reach the oratory with its alcove, or to leave it, one had to go through the bishop's bedroom. They did so while Mme Magloire was in the act of replacing the silver in the cupboard by the bed, this being invariably the last thing she did before retiring.

The bishop showed his guest into the alcove, where the bed was newly made. The man put the candle on a small table.

'Sleep well,' said the bishop. 'Before you leave tomorrow you must have a bowl of warm milk from our cows.'

'Thank you, Monsieur l'abbé,' the man said.

And then, having uttered those peaceable words, suddenly and without warning he assumed a posture that would have horrified the two women had they been there to witness it. It is hard, even now, to say what impulse seized him at that moment. Did he intend to convey a warning or a threat, or was it simply a sort of instinctive movement incomprehensible even to himself? He swung round upon his elderly host, folded his arms, glared at him, and harshly exclaimed:

'This is wonderful! You're putting me to sleep in a bed next to your own.' He broke off to laugh, and there was a monstrous quality in his laughter. 'Have you thought what you're doing? How do you know I have never murdered anyone?'

The bishop replied quietly: 'That is God's affair.'

Then with his lips moving as though in prayer, or as though he were speaking to himself, he gravely raised his right hand, the first two fingers extended, and blessed the man, who did not bow his head in response; after which he turned and, without looking back, went to his own room.

When the alcove was occupied, a large curtain of serge was drawn across the oratory to hide the altar. The bishop knelt for a moment in front of this and said a short prayer.

A minute later he was in his garden, strolling and meditating, his mind and spirit absorbed in the contemplation of those mysteries which God reveals at night to eyes that remain open.

As for the man, he was so utterly exhausted that he could not even enjoy the luxury of clean white sheets. After blowing out the candle with his nostril, as convicts do, he stretched himself fully clad on the bed and sank instantly into a profound slumber.

Midnight was striking when the bishop returned to his room, and a few minutes later all the house was asleep.

Jean Valjean

In the small hours Jean Valjean awoke.

Jean Valjean came from a very poor peasant family in Brie. As a child he had not learnt to read. When he was old enough he had gone to work as a tree-pruner at Faverolles. His mother's name was Jeanne Mathieu and his father was Jean Valjean or Vlajean, the latter being probably a nickname, a contraction of 'voilà Jean'.

The boy was thoughtful without being melancholy, which is a characteristic of warm-hearted natures. In general he tended to be immature and rather unimpressive, at least in his outward aspect. He had lost both his parents when he was still very young. His mother had died of milk-fever, and his father, who was also a pruner, had been killed by a fall from a tree. His only living relative was a widowed sister older than himself who had seven children, boys and girls. She had housed and fed him while her husband was still alive, but the husband had died when the oldest child was eight and the youngest only one. Jean Valjean, who was then just twenty-four, had stepped into the breach and supported the sister who had cared for him. It had happened quite naturally, as a matter of plain duty, but with a certain surliness on the part of Valjean. All his youth had been spent in hard and ill-paid labour. He was never known to have a sweetheart, having had no time to fall in love.

He came home tired after work and ate his supper in silence. His sister, Mother Jeanne, would often take the best bits out of his bowl, the scrap of meat or whatever it might be, to give to one of the children. Seated with his head bowed and the long hair hiding his eyes, he would take no notice of this but would go on eating as though nothing had happened. Near the cottage where they lived, across the lane, was a farmhouse. The Valjean children, always ravenous, would borrow a jug of milk in their mother's name from the farmer's wife and drink it behind a hedge, snatching the jug from each other so greedily that they spilt milk on their clothes. Had their mother known she would have whipped them. But Valjean always paid, in his offhand, surly fashion, and they went unpunished.

His work as a tree-pruner brought him twenty-four sous a day during the season and at other times he worked as a harvester, cattleman, or at any other form of casual labour. He did what he could, and his sister also worked, but the seven children were a great burden. They were a sad little group, engulfed in poverty and always on the verge of destitution. And then came a particularly hard winter. Jean was out of work and there was no food in the house. Literally no bread – and seven children!

One Sunday night when Maubert Isabeau, the baker on the Place de l'Église in Faverolles, was getting ready for bed, he heard a sound of shattered glass from his barred shop-window. He reached the spot in time to see an arm thrust through a hole in the pane. The hand grasped a loaf and the thief made off at a run. Isabeau chased and caught him. He had thrown away the loaf, but his arm was bleeding. The thief was Jean Valjean.

This was in the year 1795. Valjean was tried in the local court for housebreaking and robbery. He possessed a shotgun which he used for other than legitimate purposes – he was something of a poacher – and this told against him. There is a legitimate prejudice against poachers who, like smugglers, are not far removed from brigandage. Nevertheless it may be remarked in passing that there is a wide gulf between men of this kind and the murderous criminals in the towns. The poacher works in the woods, and the smuggler in the mountains or on the sea. The towns make men ferocious because they make them corrupt. Mountains, sea, and forest make men reckless. They stir the wildness of men's nature, but do not necessarily destroy what is human.

Jean Valjean was found guilty. The Penal Code was explicit. There are terrible occasions in our civilization, those when the Law decrees the wrecking of a human life. It is a fateful moment when society draws back its skirts and consigns a sentient being to irrevocable abandonment. Jean Valjean was sentenced to five years hard labour.

On 22 April 1796, the victory of Montenotte was proclaimed in Paris, a victory won by the general commanding the army in Italy, referred to as Buona-Parte in the message addressed by the Directory to the Five Hundred, dated 2 Florial, Year IV. On the same day a large chain-gang was assembled at Bicêtre, of which Jean Valjean was one. A former turnkey at the prison, now aged nearly ninety, perfectly recalls the unhappy wretch who was chained at the end of the fourth row in the north corner of the prison yard. He was seated with the rest on the ground and seemed to understand nothing about his situation except that it was hideous. No doubt there was also a vague notion in his ignorant and untutored peasant mind that it was excessive. While heavy hammer-blows riveted the iron collar round his neck, he wept so bitterly that he could not speak except to mumble from time to time, 'I was a tree-pruner in Faverolles.' Still sobbing, he raised his right hand and lowered it in stages as though he were laying it upon seven heads of unequal height, a gesture designed to indicate that what he had done had been for the sake of seven children.

He was taken to Toulon, where he arrived, still chained by the neck, after a journey of twenty-seven days in a cart. Here he was clad in the red smock and everything that had been his life was blotted out, even to his name. He was no longer Jean Valjean, but No. 24601. As to what became of his sister and children, who knew or cared? What becomes of the leaves of a tree, sawed down at the root?

It is an old story. Those unhappy beings, God's creatures, left without support, guidance, or shelter, were scattered no one knows where. Each presumably went its own way, to become lost in that cold murk that envelops solitary destinies, the distressful shadows wherein disappear so many unfortunates in the sombre progress of mankind. They left the district. The church-tower of what had been their village, the hedgerows of what had been their countryside, forgot them; and after a few years' imprisonment even Jean Valjean forgot them. What had been an open wound was covered by a scar. That is all. During all the time he was in Toulon he only once had news of his sister. It was, I think, towards the end of his fourth year. I do not know how the news reached him. Someone who had known them in Faverolles had seen her. She was living in Paris, in a poor street near Saint-Sulpice, with only one of her children, the youngest, a little boy. Where were the other six? Perhaps she herself did not know. She was working as a folder and stitcher for a printer in the Rue de Sabot. She had to be there at six in the morning, well before daybreak in winter. There was a school in the same house where she took her seven-year-old boy. But since she started work at six and the school did not open until seven the child had to wait for an hour in the open air of the courtyard – in winter an hour of darkness. He was not allowed into the printer's shop because, they said, he got in the way. Passing workmen would see the poor little creature crouched half asleep on the cobbles, or huddled sleeping over his basket. On rainy days an old woman, the concierge, would take pity on him and let him into her den, which contained nothing but a truckle-bed, a spinning wheel, and two wooden chairs; and here the little boy would curl up in a corner, hugging the cat for warmth. At seven o'clock he went into school. This was what Jean Valjean learned, and the story brought a momentary blaze of light as though a window had been suddenly opened on the lives of those beings he had loved. Then it was closed again. He heard no more of them; he was destined never to see them again; and there will be no further mention of them in this tale.

Jean Valjean's turn to escape came towards the end of that fourth year. His fellow-prisoners helped him as was customary. He got away, and for two days drifted in freedom through the countryside: if to be tracked is freedom, to be constantly on the alert, to tremble at every sound, to be frightened of everything, a smoking chimney, a passing man, a barking dog, a galloping horse, a striking clock; to be frightened of the daylight because one can see, and of the darkness because one cannot; to be frightened of the road, the pathway, and the thicket; to be afraid to sleep. On the evening of the second day he was caught. He had neither eaten nor slept for thirty-six hours. The tribunal added three years to his sentence, making eight in all. His second turn came in the sixth year and again he used it, but with even less success. His absence was discovered at roll-call. The alarm-gun was fired, and that night the watch found him in the dockyard hiding under the keel of a vessel under construction. He fought against them, and for the crimes of attempted escape and resisting arrest the Code prescribed the penalty of an additional five years, two in double chains. Thirteen years. His third turn came in the tenth year, and again he tried and failed. For this he got another three years, making sixteen. It was in the thirteenth year, I believe, that he made his last attempt. He was out for only four hours, but they cost him another three years. Nineteen years altogether. He was released in October 1815, after being imprisoned in 1796 for having broken a window-pane and stolen a loaf of bread.

A brief parenthesis. This is the second time that the present writer, in his study of the penal system and the damning of men's souls by law, has found the theft of a loaf of bread to be the starting-point of the wrecking of a life. Claude Gueux stole a loaf, as did

Jean Valjean. English statistics have established that in London hunger is the direct cause of four robberies out of five.

Jean Valjean had gone to imprisonment weeping and trembling; he emerged impassive. He had gone despairing; he emerged grim-faced.

What had taken place in this man's soul?

VII
The inwardness of despair

We must try to answer the question. It is very necessary that society should look at these matters, since they are the work of society.

He was an untutored man, as we have said; but that is not to say that he was stupid. There was a spark of natural intelligence in him; and adversity, which sheds its own light, had fostered the light slowly dawning in his mind. Under the lash and in chains, on fatigue and in the solitary cell, under the burning Mediterranean sun and on the prisoner's plank bed, he withdrew into his own conscience and reflected.

Constituting himself judge and jury, he began by trying his own case.

He admitted that he was not an innocent man unjustly punished. He had committed an excessive and blameworthy act. The loaf of bread might not have been refused him if he had asked for it, and in any event it would have been better to wait, either for charity or for work. The argument, 'Can a man wait when he is half-starved' was not unanswerable, for the fact is that very few people literally die of hunger. Man is so constituted that he can endure long periods of suffering, both moral and physical, without dying of it. He should have had patience, and this would have been better even for the children. To attempt to take society by the throat, vulnerable creature that he was, and to suppose that he could escape from poverty through theft, had been an act of folly. In any case, the road leading to infamy was a bad road of escape. He admitted all this – in short, that he had done wrong.

But then he asked questions.

Was he the only one at fault in this fateful business? Was it not a serious matter that a man willing to work should have been without work and without food? And, admitting the offence, had not the punishment been ferocious and outrageous? Was not the law more at fault in the penalty it inflicted than he had been in the crime he committed? Had not the scales of justice been over-weighted on the side of expiation? And did not this weighting of the scales, far from effacing the crime, produce a quite different result, namely, a reversal of the situation, substituting for the original crime the crime of oppression, making the criminal a victim and the law his debtor, transferring justice to the side of him who had offended against it? Did not the penalty, aggravated by his attempts to escape, become in the end a sort of assault by the stronger on the weaker, a crime committed by society against the individual and repeated daily for nineteen years?

He asked himself whether human society had the right to impose upon its members, on the one hand its mindless improvidence and, on the other hand, its merciless providence; to grind a poor man between the millstones of need and excess – need of work and excess of punishment. Was it not monstrous that society should treat in this fashion precisely those least favoured in the distribution of wealth, which is a matter of chance, and therefore those most needing indulgence?

He asked these questions and, having answered them, passed judgement on society.

He condemned it to his hatred. He held it responsible for what he was undergoing and resolved that, if the chance occurred, he would not hesitate to call it to account. He concluded that there was no true balance between the wrong he had done and the wrong that was inflicted upon him, and that although his punishment might not be technically an injustice it was beyond question an iniquity.

Anger may be ill-considered and absurd; we may be mistakenly angered; but only when there is some deep-seated reason are we outraged. Jean Valjean was outraged.

Moreover society as a whole had done him nothing but injury. He had seen nothing of it but the sour face which it calls justice and shows only to those it castigates. Men had touched him only to hurt him; his only contact with them had been through blows. From the time of his childhood, and except for his mother and sister, he had never encountered a friendly word or a kindly look. During the years of suffering he reached the conclusion that life was a war in which he was one of the defeated. Hatred was his only weapon, and he resolved to sharpen it in prison and carry it with him when he left.

There was in Toulon a school conducted by monks which offered elementary instruction to those unfortunates who were willing to accept it. Valjean was among them. He went there when he was forty and learned to read, write, and calculate, with the feeling that to improve his mind was to fortify his hatred. There are circumstances in which education and enlightenment can become an extension of evil.

The sad fact must be recorded that having condemned society as the cause of his misfortune, he took it upon himself to pass judgement on the Providence which had created society, and this, too, he condemned. Thus during those nineteen years of torture and enslavement his spirit both grew and shrank. Light entered on one side and darkness on the other.

As we have seen, he was not bad by nature; he had been still virtuous when he was sent to prison. There he learned to condemn society and felt himself becoming evil; he condemned Providence and knew that he became impious.

It is difficult at this point not to pause for a moment to reflect.

Can human nature be ever wholly and radically transformed? Can the man whom God made good be made wicked by man? Can the soul be reshaped in its entirety by destiny and made evil because destiny is evil? Can the heart become misshapen and afflicted with ugly, incurable deformities under disproportionate misfortune, like a spinal column bent beneath a too low roof? Is there not in every human soul, and was there not in the soul of Jean Valjean, an essential spark, an element of the divine, indestructible in this world and immortal in the next, which goodness can preserve, nourish, and fan into glorious flame, and which evil can never quite extinguish?

These are weighty and obscure questions, to the last of which any psychologist would probably have answered no, had he seen Jean Valjean in Toulon during a rest period seated with arms crossed over a capstan-bar, the end of his chain thrust into his pocket to stop it dragging, a brooding galley-slave, sombre, silent, and vengeful, an outcast of the laws glaring in anger at men, one of the damned of civilization looking accusingly at Heaven.

There can be little doubt, and we may not pretend otherwise, that the observant psychologist would have seen in him a case of incurable abasement, a sick man for whom he might feel pity but for whom he could propose no remedy. He would have averted his gaze from the spiritual abysses he discerned and, like Dante at the gate of hell, have expunged from that life the word which God's finger writes on the brow of every man, the word Hope.

And what of Valjean himself? Was the spiritual state which we have depicted as plain to him as we have sought to make it to the reader? Had he any clear perception, after they were formed, or during their formation, of the elements of which his moral degradation was composed? Could a man so crude and untaught take any positive account of the process whereby, by gradual stages, his spirit had risen and sunk into those depths which through the years had come to constitute his moral horizon? We cannot venture to say so, and in fact we do not believe it. He was too ignorant to be lucid in his thoughts, even after so much hardship. There were times when he could not be sure of his own feelings. He lived in shadow, suffered in shadow, hated the shadows and may be said to have hated himself. He lived in darkness fumbling like a blind man, a man in a dream. Only occasionally was he overtaken by a burst of furious rage, rising within him or provoked from without, that was an overflow of suffering, a swift, searing flame illuminating all his soul and shedding its ugly light on everything that lay behind him and ahead, the chasms and sombre vistas of his destiny.

But these flashes passed, the darkness closed in again – and where was he? He did not know.

It is characteristic of this form of punishment, inspired by all that is pitiless, that is to say brutalizing, that gradually, by a process of mindless erosion, it turns a man into an animal, sometimes a ferocious one. Jean Valjean's repeated and obstinate efforts to escape are evidence of the effect of this legal chastisement on the human spirit. He would have made further hopeless attempts whenever the chance offered, without giving a thought to the consequences or to past experience. Like a caged wolf, he dashed madly for the door whenever he found it open. Instinct prompted him to run where reason would have bidden him stay: in the face of that overwhelming impulse, reason vanished. It was the animal that acted, and the added penalties inflicted on him when he was recaptured served only to increase its savagery.

A detail which we must not fail to mention is that in physical strength Jean Valjean far surpassed any other inmate of the prison. On fatigue duties, or hauling an anchor-chain or turning a capstan, he was worth four men. He could lift and carry enormous weights and on occasion did duty for the appliance known as a 'jack', in those days called an *orgueil*, from which the Rue Montorgueil, near the Paris *halles*, derives its name. Once when the balcony of the Toulon town-hall was being repaired, one of the admirable carya-tids by Puget which support it came loose and was in danger of falling. Valjean, who was on the spot, propped it up with his shoulder until help arrived.

His dexterity was even greater than his strength. There are prisoners, obsessed with the thought of escape, eternally envious of the birds and the flies, who make a positive cult of the physical sciences, daily performing a mysterious ritual of exercises. The climbing of a sheer surface, where scarcely any hand or foothold was to be discerned, was to Valjean a pastime. Given the angle of a wall and applying the thrust of his back and legs, with elbows and heels gripping the rough surface of the stone, he could climb three storeys as though by magic; he had even reached the prison roof.

He spoke seldom and never smiled. It took some extreme emotion to wring from him, perhaps once or twice in a year, the sour con-vict-chuckle that is like the laughter of demons. The sight of him suggested that he was continually absorbed in the contemplation of something terrible.

And so he was. With the hazy perception of an unformed nature and an overborne intelligence, he was confusedly aware of some-thing monstrous that oppressed him. Did he seek to look upward beyond the pallid half-light in which he crouched, it was to see, with mingled terror and rage, an endless structure rising above him, a dreadful piling-up of things, laws, prejudices, men and facts, whose shape he could not discern and whose mass appalled him, and which was nothing else than the huge pyramid that we call civilization. Here and there in the formless, swarming heap, near to him or at an inaccessible height, some detail would be thrown into sharp relief – the prison-warder with his truncheon, the gendarme with his sabre; above these the mitred bishop, and at the very top, like a sun, the Emperor radiantly crowned. Far from dispelling his own darkness, those distant splendours seemed only to intensify it. Life came and went above his head – laws, prejudices, facts, men and things – in the intricate and mysterious pattern God stamps on civilization, bearing down and crushing him with a placid cruelty and remorse-less indifference. Men fallen into the nethermost pit of adversity, lost in that limbo where the eyes do not follow, those outcasts of the law feel upon their necks the whole weight of society, so formidable to the outsider, so terrifying to the underdog. It was in this situation that Jean Valjean pondered, and what could his thoughts be?

What could they be but the thoughts of a grain of corn ground between millstones, if it were capable of thinking? All these things, reality charged with fantasy and fantasy laden with reality, ended by creating in him a frame of mind scarcely to be expressed in words. At times he would pause in his prison labours to stand reflective, and his reason, at once more mature and more disturbed, would recoil in disbelief. The things that happened to him seemed inconceivable, the world around him grotesque. He would say to himself: this is a dream, and stare at the warder standing a few feet away as though he were seeing a ghost – until suddenly the ghost dealt him a blow.

He was almost unconscious of the natural world. It would be nearly true to say of Jean Valjean that for him the sun did not exist, or any summer day, or clear skies or April dawns. Heaven alone knows what sullied light filtered through to his soul.

To sum up this account of him, so far as it can be done in concrete terms, we may say that in nineteen years Jean Valjean, the harmless tree-pruner of Faverolles and the sinister galley-slave of Toulon, thanks to the way imprisonment had shaped him, had become capable of two kinds of ill-deed: first the heedless, unpremeditated act executed in a blind fury, as some sort of a reprisal for the wrongs he had suffered; and secondly, the deliberate and considered crime, justified in his mind by the thoughts inspired by those wrongs. His calculated thinking passed through the three successive stages of reason, resolve and obstinacy which are only possible to natures of a certain kind. His impulses were governed by resentment, bitterness and a profound sense of injury which might vent itself even upon good and innocent people, if any such came his way. The beginning and the end of all his thought was hatred of human laws: a hatred which, if some providential happening does not arrest its growth, may swell in time into a hatred of all society, all mankind, all created things, becoming a savage and obsessive desire to inflict harm on no matter what or whom.

It will be seen that the yellow ticket he carried had some warrant for describing Jean Valjean as 'a very dangerous man'. Year by year, slowly but inexorably, his spirit had withered. Dry of heart and dry-eyed. During his nineteen years imprisonment he had not shed a tear.

VIII

Sea and shadow

Man overboard!

But the ship does not stop. The wind is blowing and the doom-laden vessel is set on a course from which it cannot depart. It sails on.

The man sinks and reappears, flings up his arms and shouts, but no one hears. The ship, heeling in the wind, is intent upon its business, and passengers and crew have lost sight of him, a pin-point in the immensity of the sea.

He calls despairingly, gazing in anguish after the receding sail as, ghostlike, it fades from view. A short time ago he was on board, a member of the crew busy on deck with the rest, a living being with his share of air and sunlight. What has become of him now? He slipped and fell, and this is the end.

He is adrift in the monstrous waters with only their turbulence beneath him, hideously enclosed by wave-crests shredded by the wind, smothered as they break over his head, tumbled from one to another, rising and sinking into unfathomable darkness where he seems to become a part of the abyss, his mouth filled with bitter resentment at this treacherous ocean that is so resolved to destroy him, this monster toying with his death. To him the sea has become the embodiment of hatred.

But he goes on swimming, still struggles despairingly for life, his strength dwindling as he battles against the inexhaustible. Above him he can see only the bleak pallor of the clouds. He is the witness in his death-throes of the immeasurable dementia of the sea, and, tormented by this madness, he hears sounds unknown to man that seem to come from some dreadful place beyond the bounds of earth. There are birds flying amid the clouds as angels soar over the distresses of mankind, but what can they do for him? They sing as they glide and hover, while he gasps for life.

He is lost between the infinities of sea and sky, the one a tomb, the other a shroud. Darkness is falling. He has swum for hours until his strength is at an end and the ship with its company of men has long since passed from sight. Solitary in the huge gulf of twilight he twists and turns, feeling the waves of the unknowable close in upon him. And for the last time he calls, but not to man. Where is God?

He calls to anyone or anything – he calls and calls but there is no reply, nothing on the face of the waters, nothing in the heavens. He calls to the sea and spray, but they are deaf; he calls to the winds, but they are answerable only to infinity. Around him dusk and solitude, the heedless tumult of wild waters; within him terror and exhaustion; below him the descent into nothingness. No foothold. He pictures his body adrift in that limitless dark. The chill numbs him. His hands open and close, clutching at nothing. Wind and tumult and useless stars. What can he do? Despair ends in resignation, exhaustion chooses death, and so at length he gives up the struggle and his body sinks for ever.

Such is the remorseless progression of human society, shedding lives and souls as it goes on its way. It is an ocean into which men sink who have been cast out by the law and consigned, with help most cruelly withheld, to moral death. The sea is the pitiless social darkness into which the penal system casts those it has condemned, an unfathomable waste of misery. The human soul, lost in those depths, may become a corpse. Who shall revive it?

IX

Fresh tribulations

When at the time of his leaving prison Jean Valjean heard the words, 'You are free,' the moment had seemed blinding and unbelievable, as though he were suddenly pierced by a shaft of light, the true light of living men. But this gleam swiftly faded. He had been dazzled by the idea of liberty. He had believed for an instant in a new life. He soon discovered the meaning of liberty when it is accompanied by a yellow ticket.

And with this came further disillusion. He had calculated that his savings during his imprisonment would amount to one hundred and seventy-one francs. It must be said in fairness that he had omitted to allow for Sundays and feast-days, days of enforced rest which reduced this total by about twenty-four francs. But there had been other deductions conforming to prison regulations, and the sum he received was one hundred and nine francs and fifteen sous.

He did not understand the reason for this and thought himself cheated – in plain language, robbed.

In Grasse, on the day after his release, he saw some men unloading bales of orange-blossom outside a scent-distillery. He volunteered his labour, and since the matter was urgent he was taken on. He was intelligent, strong, and adroit; he worked well and the foreman seemed content. While he was at work a passing gendarme noticed him and asked to see his papers. He had to show the yellow ticket, after which he went back to work. Earlier he had asked one of the other men the rate of pay for the day and had been told that it was thirty sous. In the evening, since he was obliged to move on next morning, he went to the foreman and asked for his wage. Without saying anything the man handed him twenty-five sous, and said when he protested, 'That's good enough for you.' He again protested and the foreman looked hard at him and said, 'Watch it or you'll be back inside.'

Again he felt that he had been robbed. Society had robbed him wholesale of a part of his savings; now it was the turn of the individual to rob him in detail. Release, he discovered, was not deliverance. A man may leave prison, but he is still condemned.

This was what had happened to him in Grasse. We know of his reception in Digne.

X

The man awakens

Jean Valjean awoke as the cathedral clock was striking two.

What had awakened him was an over-comfortable bed. He had not slept in a bed for twenty years, and although he had not taken off his clothes, the sensation was too unfamiliar not to disturb his sleep. Nevertheless he had slept for over four hours and recovered from his exhaustion. He was not accustomed to long hours of rest.

He opened his eyes and peered into the darkness, then closed them hoping to fall asleep again. But after a day of various emotions, when many thoughts have oppressed the mind, we may fall once asleep but not a second time. Sleep comes more readily than it returns. This was the case with Valjean. He could not get to sleep again and lay thinking.

He was in a state of great mental perturbation, assailed with a flood of old and new impressions which changed incessantly in shape, grew immeasurably, and suddenly vanished as though in a turgid stream. Many thoughts occurred to him, but there was one in particular that constantly returned, overshadowing the rest. It was the thought of the silver on the bishop's table.

Those silver knives and forks obsessed him. There they were, only a few yards away. He had seen Mme Magloire put them in the cupboard when he passed through the bishop's room, and he had noted the position of the cupboard, on the right as one entered from the dining-room. They were solid pieces of old silver and with the big ladle would fetch at least two hundred francs – twice what he had earned in nineteen years, although it was true that he would have got more if the authorities had not robbed him.

For a whole hour he remained in a state of indecision in which there was an element of conflict. The clock struck three. He opened his eyes again and sat up briskly, reaching out an arm to grope for the knapsack that he had let fall by the bedside. Then he swung his legs over and almost without knowing it found himself seated on the bed with his feet on the floor.

He remained for some time in this posture, a sinister figure to anyone seeing him thus seated in the darkness, the only wakeful person in that sleeping house. Suddenly he bent down, removed his shoes and laid them very quietly on the bedside mat. Then he returned to his state of pensive immobility.

The ugly thoughts jostled in his brain, came and went, bearing down on him like a physical weight; and at the same time, unaccountably, with the obstinate irrelevance of distracted meditation, he was thinking of something entirely different. One of his fellow-prisoners had been a man named Brevet who kept his trousers up with a single brace of knitted cotton. The check design of that brace repeatedly occurred to him.

He might have stayed like this until daybreak if the clock had not sounded again, striking the quarter or half-hour. It roused him as though it had been a signal.

He got to his feet and stood listening. The house was quite silent. He then moved cautiously towards the window, of which the outline was clearly discernible. The night was not very dark; there was a full moon intermittently hidden by large clouds scudding in the wind, creating out of doors an alternation of darkness and light, and indoors a sort of twilight, sufficient to move by, rising and dimming like the light from a basement window when people are passing outside. Having reached the window, Valjean examined it. It was not barred; it opened on to the garden and, after the local custom, was fastened only with a small latch. Cold air flooded the room when he opened it, and he quickly closed it again. He stared into the garden with the intent look of a man inspecting rather than seeing. It was enclosed in a low whitewashed wall, easy to climb. Beyond were trees spaced at regular intervals, indicating that the wall separated the garden from an avenue or planted lane.

Having concluded his survey he turned with an air of decision, went back into the alcove, picked up his knapsack and got something out of it which he laid on the bed. He put his shoes in one of the pockets, buckled the knapsack and strapped it on his back, put his cap on his head, pulling the peak low over his eyes, and groped for his stick, which he had stood in a corner by the window. Returning to the bed, he picked up the object he had placed there. It was a short iron bar, sharpened to a point at one end.

The darkness made it difficult to determine what purpose this piece of metal was designed to serve, whether it was intended for use as a lever or a bludgeon. By daylight it could have been seen to be an ordinary miner's spike. The convicts were sometimes put to work stone-quarrying in the hills behind Toulon, and it was not uncommon for them to be in possession of miners' tools. The spike of thick, solid metal was used for splitting rock.

Grasping it in his right hand and holding his breath, Valjean moved stealthily towards the door of the bishop's bedroom. He found it ajar. The bishop had not closed it.

XI
What he did

Valjean stood listening. There was no sound.

He gave the door a gentle push with one finger-tip, cautious as a cat planning to enter a room. It yielded soundlessly, opening a little wider. He paused, then pushed again.

The door still made no sound, and now it was wide enough open for him to pass through; but close by it was a small table set at an awkward angle which still blocked his passage. There was nothing for it but to open the door wider still. Summoning his resolution, he gave it a third and more vigorous push, and this time one of the hinges emitted a long and piercing squeak.

Jean Valjean shivered. The sound was as appalling to him as that of the Last Trump. In those first wild moments of dismay he could almost believe that the hinge had become endowed with supernatural life and was barking like a watchdog to warn the sleepers in the house. He sank quivering back on his heels, hearing the blood thunder in his temples while the noise of his breath was like wind roaring out of a cave. It seemed to him impossible that the dreadful din would not arouse the household as effectively as an earthquake. The door had given the alarm. The old man would start up, the old woman would scream, help would come running; within a quarter of an hour the town would be in an uproar and the gendarmes would be active. During those moments he thought he was lost.

He stayed where he was, stock still and not daring to move. Several minutes passed. The door was now wide open. He ventured to peer into the room. Nothing stirred. He listened and heard no sound of movement in the house. It seemed that the rusty hinge had not awakened anyone.

That peril was over, but although he was still in a state of great perturbation he did not turn back. He had not turned back even when he thought he was done for. His only thought was to get the business over quickly. He moved on into the bedroom.

It was perfectly quiet. Vague shapes were discernible which by daylight would have been seen to be papers scattered over a table, open folios, books piled on a stool, garments draped over a chair, a *prie-dieu*, now only visible as contrasts of light and shadow. Valjean moved cautiously forward, hearing from the far side of the room the quiet, steady breathing of the bishop. He came to an abrupt stop at the bedside, finding that he had reached it sooner than he expected.

Nature at times adds her own commentary to our actions with a kind of sombre and considered eloquence, as though she were bidding us reflect. For nearly half an hour the sky had been darkened by cloud. At the moment when Jean Valjean stopped by the bed the clouds were torn asunder as though by a deliberate act, and moonlight, flooding through the tall window, fell upon the bishop's face. He was sleeping peacefully. Because of the coldness of night in the lower Alps he wore a bed-jacket of brown wool which covered his arms to the wrists. His head lay back on the pillow in the abandonment of repose, and the hand wearing the episcopal ring, a hand responsible for so much that was good and well done, hung down outside the sheets. His face wore a look of serenity, hope, and beatitude, something more than a smile and little short of radiance, the reflection of light that was not to be seen. The spirits of the righteous in sleep commune with a mysterious heaven.

It was the light of this heaven that lay upon the bishop, a luminosity emanating from himself, the light of his own conscience. At the moment when the moon shone upon him, mingling with his inner light, he seemed in the soft half-dark to wear a halo. The brightness of the moon, the stillness of the garden, the quietness of the house, the deep repose of the hour, all this conferred a tranquil majesty upon the venerable white head now sunk in childlike sleep, an unconscious nobility approaching the divine.

Motionless in the shadow, gripping the spike in his hand, Jean Valjean stood gazing in a kind of terror at the old man. He had never before seen anything like this. On the moral plane there can be no more moving contrast than that between an uneasy conscience, bent upon a misdeed, and the unguarded slumber of innocence. In that solitary confrontation there was an element of the sublime of which Valjean was obscurely but strongly aware.

No one, not even himself, could have described his feeling. We have to imagine utmost violence in the presence of utmost gentleness. Nothing could have been discerned with certainty from his expression, which was one of haggard astonishment. He stood looking down and no one could have read his thoughts. That he was profoundly moved was evident, but what was the nature of his emotion?

He looked away from the bed. All that clearly emerged from his attitude and expression was that he was in a state of strange indecision, seemingly adrift between the two extremes of death on the one hand and salvation on the other – ready to shatter that skull or to kiss that hand.

After some moments he slowly raised his left arm and removed his cap; then, letting his arm sink as slowly as he had raised it, he resumed his attitude of contemplation, holding the cap in his left hand and the weapon in his right, the hair unruly on his wild head, while the bishop continued to sleep peacefully beneath his terrifying gaze. Above the mantelpiece the crucifix was dimly visible with its arms extended as though to both men, in benediction of the one and forgiveness of the other.

Valjean suddenly put his cap back on his head and without looking at the bishop moved quickly to the cupboard. He raised the spike, prepared to force the lock, but the key was in it. The first thing he saw when he opened the door was the basket of silver. He grabbed it, crossed the room with long strides regardless of precaution, re-entered the oratory, picked up his stick, opened the window, climbed over the sill, emptied the silver into his knapsack, threw away the basket, crossed the garden and, scrambling like a great cat over the wall, took to his heels.

XII

The bishop at work

At sunrise that morning Monsieur Bienvenu was in his garden. Mme Magloire came running out to him in great agitation.

'Monseigneur, monseigneur, do you know where the silver-basket is?'

'Yes,' said the bishop.

'Thank the Lord! I couldn't think what had happened to it.'

The bishop had just retrieved the basket from one of the flower-beds. He handed it to her saying, 'Here you are.'

'But it's empty!' she exclaimed. 'Where's the silver?'

'So it's the silver you're worrying about?' said the bishop. 'I can't tell you where that is.'

'Heaven save us, it has been stolen! That man who came last night!'

With the zeal of an elderly watchdog Mme Magloire ran into the oratory, peered into the alcove and came running back to her master, who was now bending sadly over a cochlearia that had been damaged by the basket when it fell.

'Monseigneur, the man's gone! The silver has been stolen!' She was looking about her as she spoke. The wall bore traces of the thief's departure, one of its coping-stones having been dislodged. 'That's the way he went – he climbed into the lane! The monster – he's gone off with our silver!'

The bishop after a moment's pause turned his grave eyes on her and said gently:

'In the first place, was it really ours?'

Mme Magloire stood dumbfounded. After a further silence the bishop went on:

'I think I was wrong to keep it so long. It belonged to the poor. And what was that man if not one of them?'

'Saints alive!' exclaimed Mme Magloire. 'It's not on my account or Mademoiselle's. But Monseigneur – what will Monseigneur eat with now?'

He looked at her in seeming astonishment. 'There is always pewter.'

'Pewter smells.'

'Well then, iron.'

'Iron has a taste.'

'Then,' said the bishop, 'wooden forks and spoons.'

A few minutes later he was breakfasting at the table where Jean Valjean had sat the night before and remarking cheerfully to his sister, who kept silent, and to Mme Magloire, who muttered under her breath, that no spoon or fork, even wooden ones, was needed for dipping bread into a bowl of milk.

'After all, what can you expect?' soliloquized Mme Magloire as she bustled to and fro. 'Taking in a man like that and putting him to sleep in the alcove. The mercy is we were only robbed. It makes me shudder!'

As the brother and sister were in the act of rising from the table a knock sounded on the door and the bishop called, 'Come in!'

The door opened to disclose a dramatic group. Three men were holding a fourth by the arms and neck. The three were gendarmes; the fourth was Jean Valjean.

A sergeant of gendarmes, who had been standing by the door and was evidently in charge of the party, entered the room and saluted.

'Monseigneur –' he began.

At this Valjean, who was looking crushed and woebegone, raised his head in stupefaction.

'Monseigneur . . .' he repeated. 'He isn't the curé?'

'Silence,' said one of the gendarmes. 'This is his lordship the Bishop.'

Monseigneur Bienvenu was meanwhile coming towards them as rapidly as his age allowed.

'So here you are!' he cried to Valjean. 'I'm delighted to see you. Had you forgotten that I gave you the candlesticks as well? They're silver like the rest, and worth a good two hundred francs. Did you forget to take them?'

Jean Valjean's eyes had widened. He was now staring at the old man with an expression no words can convey.

'Monseigneur,' said the sergeant, 'do I understand that this man was telling the truth? When we saw him he seemed to be on the run, and we thought we had better make sure. We found this silver in his knapsack and –'

'And he told you,' said the bishop, smiling, 'that it had been given him by an old priest with whom he stopped the night. I can see how it was. You felt bound to bring him here, but you were mistaken.'

'You mean,' said the sergeant, 'that we can let him go?'

'Certainly.'

The gendarmes released Valjean, who seemed to cringe. 'Am I really allowed to go?' he said, mumbling the words as if he were talking in his sleep.

'You heard, didn't you?' said a gendarme.

'But this time,' said the bishop, 'you must not forget your candlesticks.'

He fetched them from the mantelpiece and handed them to Valjean. The two women watched him do so without seeking by word or look to interfere. Valjean was trembling. He took the candlesticks mechanically and with a distracted air.

'And now,' said the bishop, 'go in peace. Incidentally, my friend, when next you come here you need not go through the garden. This door is never locked.' He turned to the gendarmes. 'Thank you, gentlemen.'

The gendarmes withdrew. Valjean stayed motionless as though he were on the verge of collapse. The bishop came up to him and said in a low voice:

'Do not forget, do not ever forget, that you have promised me to use the money to make yourself an honest man.'

Valjean, who did not recall having made any promise, was silent. The bishop had spoken the words slowly and deliberately. He concluded with a solemn emphasis:

'Jean Valjean, my brother, you no longer belong to what is evil but to what is good. I have bought your soul to save it from black thoughts and the spirit of perdition, and I give it to God.'

XIII
Petit-Gervais

Jean Valjean left the town as though he were still on the run. He plunged into the countryside, blindly following lanes and footpaths and not realizing that he was going in circles. Thus he spent the morning, without eating or feeling any sense of hunger. He was overwhelmed by new and strange sensations, among them a kind of anger, he did not know against whom. He could not have said if he was uplifted or humiliated. He had moments of strange tenderness which he resisted with all the hardness of heart which twenty years had brought him. His state of mind was physically exhausting. He perceived with dismay that the kind of dreadful calm instilled in him by injustice and misfortune had begun to crumble. What was to take its place? At moments he positively wished himself back in prison, and that these things had never happened to him; at least he would have been less distraught. Although it was late in the year there were still a few last flowers in the hedges whose scent as he passed recalled pictures of his childhood; and these memories, so long buried, were almost intolerable.

Thus he spent the day in a state of growing turmoil; and in the evening, when the sun had sunk so low that every pebble cast a shadow, he was seated on the ground by a thicket, in an expanse of russet plain that was totally deserted. Only the Alps were visible on the horizon; not so much as a village church-steeple was to be seen. He was then perhaps seven miles from Digne, and a footpath crossed the plain a few yards from the place where he sat.

Into his sombre meditations, which must have rendered his ragged appearance still more alarming to any passer-by, a lively sound intruded. A boy of about ten was coming along the footpath, singing as he came. He carried a *vielle*, a kind of small hurdy-gurdy, slung over his shoulder, and a box with his belongings on his back; one of those gay and harmless child vagrants, generally chimney-sweeps, who go from village to village with knees showing through the holes in their trousers. Now and then he paused, still singing, to play at 'bones' with the coins he was carrying, tossing them in the air and catching them on the back of his hand. They probably represented his entire fortune, and one was a piece of forty sous.

He stopped by the thicket to play his game without having

noticed Jean Valjean. Thus far he had caught all the coins, but this time he dropped the forty-sou piece, which rolled in the direction of Valjean, who promptly set his foot on it.

The boy had seen where it went. Without appearing in any way disconcerted, he went up to him.

The place was entirely solitary with no other soul in sight on the footpath or the plain, and no sound except the distant cry of a flock of birds passing high overhead. The boy stood with his back to the setting sun, which lighted his hair with threads of gold and cast a red glare on Valjean's brooding face.

'Monsieur,' said the boy with the childish trustfulness that is a mingling of innocence and ignorance, 'may I have my coin?'

'What's your name?' asked Valjean.

'Petit-Gervais, Monsieur.'

'Clear out,' said Valjean.

'Please, Monsieur,' said the child, 'may I have my money back?'

Jean Valjean lowered his head and did not reply.

'Please, Monsieur.'

Valjean was staring at the ground.

'My money!' the boy cried. 'My piece of silver. My coin!'

Valjean seemed not to hear him. The boy seized hold of his collar and shook him, while at the same time he tried to shift the heavy, iron-studded shoe covering his coin.

'I want my money, my forty-sou piece!'

He began to cry, and Jean Valjean, who was still seated, raised his head. His eyes were troubled. He stared with a sort of amazement at the child, then reached for his stick and cried in a terrifying voice, 'Who's there?'

'It's me, Monsieur. Petit-Gervais. Only me. Give me back my forty sous, if you please. Will you please move your foot?'

Then the boy grew angry, small as he was, and his tone became almost threatening.

'Move your foot, can't you! Are you going to move your foot?'

'Are you still there?' said Valjean, suddenly standing up but still keeping his foot on the coin. 'Damn you, clear out!'

The boy looked at him and was suddenly frightened. After a moment of stupefaction he turned and ran, without looking back or uttering a sound. Out of breath, he eventually came to a stop, and amid the tumult of his thoughts Valjean heard the sound of his distant sobbing. A minute later he had vanished from sight.

The sun had set. The shadows were closing about Jean Valjean. He had eaten nothing all day and was probably feverish. He remained standing in the same place, not having moved since the boy had run off. While his breath came slowly and unevenly his eyes were fixed on a spot some yards in front of him, as though he were wholly absorbed in contemplating a blue fragment of broken pottery lying in the grass. He shivered suddenly, conscious of the chill of evening.

He pulled down the peak of his cap, tried mechanically to fasten his shirt over his chest and then stooped to pick up his stick. In doing so his eye caught the glitter of the forty-sou piece, half buried by his foot in the earth.

It affected him like an electric shock. 'What's that?' he muttered under his breath. He stepped back a couple of paces and then stood still, unable to detach his gaze from that object shining in the dusk like an eye watching him. After some moments' pause he moved convulsively forward, snatched up the coin and then stood gazing to every point of the compass, quivering like a frightened animal in search of a hiding-place.

There was nothing to be seen. Night was falling, the plain was cold and empty and a purple mist was rising to obscure the twilight. He uttered an exclamation and began to walk rapidly in the direction taken by the boy. After going a hundred yards or so he stopped and stared again but still saw nothing. He shouted at the top of his voice:

'Petit-Gervais! Petit-Gervais!'

He waited, but there was no reply.

He was standing in the midst of gloom and desolation, surrounded by nothing but the dusk in which his gaze was lost and the silence in which his voice died away. A keen wind had begun to blow, endowing the objects around him with a kind of dismal life. Bushes waved their branches with a strange fury, as though they were threatening and pursuing.

He went on walking and then broke into a run, stopping now and then to cry out amid the solitude in a voice that was at once terrifying and despairing, 'Petit-Gervais! Petit-Gervais!' If the boy had heard he would certainly have hidden; but by now he was probably far away.

Valjean presently met a priest on horseback. He went up to him and asked:

'Monsieur le curé, have you seen a boy go by?'

'No,' said the priest.

'A boy called Petit-Gervais.'

'No. I've seen no one.'

Valjean produced two five-franc pieces and handed them to the priest.

'For your poor, Monsieur le curé . . . He was a boy of about ten with a box on his back, I think, and carrying a *vielle*. He was tramping, a chimney-sweep or something of the kind.'

'I haven't seen him.'

'Petit-Gervais his name was. Doesn't he come from one of the villages round here?'

'I think not,' said the priest. 'It sounds as though he was a stranger in these parts, a vagrant. We get them from time to time. We know nothing about them.'

With an almost savage gesture Valjean produced two more five-franc pieces and gave them to the priest. 'For your poor,' he said again. And then he cried out: 'Monsieur l'abbé, you must have me arrested. I'm a thief.'

The priest clapped his heels to his horse's flanks and rode off in terror.

Valjean continued to run in the same direction as before. He ran for a long time, calling as he went, but he saw no one else. Several times he turned aside to inspect a patch of shadow which might have been a person lying or crouching, but these turned out to be bushes or small boulders. Finally, at a place where three paths intersected, he stood still. Gazing into the distance he called for the last time, 'Petit-Gervais! Petit-Gervais!' and his voice sank without echo into the mist. He again murmured, 'Petit-Gervais,' so faintly that the words were scarcely audible, and this was his last attempt. His legs suddenly buckled under him as though some unseen power had struck him down with all the weight of his guilty conscience. He sank exhausted on to a piece of rock with his hands clutching his hair and his head between his knees, and he exclaimed, 'Vile wretch that I am!'

His heart overflowed and he wept, for the first time in nineteen years.

When he left the bishop's dwelling Jean Valjean, as we know, had been in a state of mind unlike anything he had ever experienced before and was quite unable to account for what was taking place within him. He had sought to harden his heart against the old man's saintly act and moving words. 'You have promised me to become an honest man. I am buying your soul. I am rescuing it from the spirit of perversity and giving it to God.' The words constantly returned to him and he sought to suppress them with arrogance, which in all of us is the stronghold of evil. Obscurely he perceived that the priest's forgiveness was the most formidable assault he had ever sustained; that if he resisted it his heart would be hardened once and for all, and that if he yielded he must renounce the hatred which the acts of men had implanted in him during so many years, and to which he clung. He saw dimly that this time he must either conquer or be conquered, and that the battle was now joined, a momentous and decisive battle between the evil in himself and the goodness in that other man.

Beset by these intimations, he reeled like a drunken man: but as, haggard-eyed, he went on his way, had he any clear notion of what must be the outcome for him of that episode in Digne? Did he truly understand all that it implied? Did any voice whisper to him that he was at a turning-point in his life, that henceforth there could be no middle way for him, that he must become either the best of men or the worst, rise even higher than the bishop himself or sink lower than the felon, reach supreme heights of goodness or become a monster of depravity?

We must again ask the question, did any dim understanding of all this enter his mind? It is true that misfortune sharpens the wits; but still it may be doubted whether Jean Valjean was in a condition to grasp so much. Such notions as occurred to him were glimpsed rather than clearly seen and did no more than plunge him into a state of agonized and almost intolerable confusion. The encounter with the bishop, immediately following his release from the black limbo of prison, had dazed him spiritually in the way that the eyes may be dazzled by the brilliance of daylight after a period of total darkness. The prospect now proposed to him, a life of goodness and purity, caused him to tremble with apprehension. He was truly at a loss. Like an owl overtaken by a sudden sunrise, he was blinded by the radiance of virtue.

What was certain, although he did not realize it, was that he was no longer the same man. Everything in him was changed. It was no longer in his power to behave as though the bishop had not spoken to him and touched his heart.

And it was in this state of disarray that he had encountered Petit-

Gervais and stolen his forty sous. Why had he done so? Assuredly he could not have answered the question. Had it been a last stirring of the evil generated in him by prison, a lingering impulse akin to what the physicists term latent energy? It had been that, and perhaps it had also been something less. In simple terms, it was not the man who had stolen; it was the animal which, from habit and instinct, had brutally set its foot on the coin while the man's intelligence wrestled with the new and dumbfounding thoughts that preoccupied it. When the man saw what the animal had done, Jean Valjean recoiled with a cry of horror.

The fact is – a strange phenomenon, only conceivable in the situation in which he found himself – that in robbing the boy he had committed an act of which he was no longer capable.

In any event, this last misdeed had a decisive effect upon him. It piercingly dispelled the chaos in his mind, separating light from darkness and working upon his spirit like a chemical reagent introduced into a turgid solution, which clarifies one element and precipitates another.

His immediate impulse, before taking time for thought, like a man clutching at a straw, had been to find the boy and return his money, and when he failed to do this he gave way to despair. In the moment when he uttered the words 'vile wretch', he had seen himself for what he was, being so far detached from himself as to see something that was like a ghost. What he saw was the flesh-and-blood man, stick in hand, clothing bedraggled, knapsack stuffed with stolen goods on his back, dark of face and darker still in thought, Jean Valjean the felon.

Excess of suffering, as we have seen, had made him in some sort a visionary. This was a vision. He truly saw that Jean Valjean, that evil countenance confronting him. At that moment he was near to asking who the man was, and he was appalled.

It was one of those moments of blinding and yet frighteningly calm insight when the thought goes so deep that it passes beyond reality. The tangible world is no longer seen; all that we see, as though from outside, is the world of our own spirit.

Thus he contemplated himself, as it were face to face, and there arose in his vision, at some mysterious depth, a sort of light resembling that of a torch. But as he looked more closely at this light growing in his consciousness he saw that it had a human form and that it was the bishop.

His mind's eye considered these two men now presented to him, the bishop and Jean Valjean. Only the first could have overshadowed the second. By a singular process special to this kind of ecstasy, as his trance continued the bishop grew and gained splendour in his eyes, while Jean Valjean shrank and faded. A moment came when Valjean was no more than a shadow, and then he vanished entirely. The bishop alone remained, flooding that unhappy soul with radiance.

Jean Valjean wept for a long time, sobbing convulsively with more than a woman's abandon, more than the anguish of a child. And as he wept a new day dawned in his spirit, a day both wonderful and terrible. He saw all things with a clarity that he had never known before – his past life, his first offence and long expiation, his outward coarsening and inward hardening, his release enriched with so many plans for revenge, the incident at the bishop's house, and this last abominable act, the robbing of a child, rendered the more shameful by the fact that it followed the bishop's forgiveness. He saw all this, the picture of his life, which was horrible, and of his own soul, hideous in its ugliness. Yet a new day had now dawned for that life and soul; and he seemed to see Satan bathed in the light of Paradise.

How long did he stay weeping? What did he then do and where did he go? We do not know. But it is said on that same night the stage-driver from Grenoble, passing through the cathedral square in Digne at three in the morning, saw in the shadows the figure of a man kneeling in an attitude of prayer outside the door of Monseigneur Bienvenu.

BOOK THREE

IN THE YEAR 1817

I

The year 1817

1817 WAS the year which Louis XVIII, with a royal aplomb not lacking in arrogance, called the twenty-second of his reign. It was the year in which M. Bruguière de Sorsum, the translator of Shakespeare, became celebrated. The hairdressing establishments, hoping for the return of powdered wigs and birds of paradise, broke out in a rash of azure and fleur-de-lis. It was the guileless period when Comte Lynch sat every Sunday as a churchwarden on the high bench in Saint-Germain-des-Prés, clad in the robes of a Peer of France, with his red ribbon and long nose and the stately bearing proper to a man who has performed a notable act. M. Lynch's notable act was as follows: on 12 March 1814, being then Mayor of Bordeaux, he had handed over the town a little too soon to the Duc d'Angoulême. Hence his peerage. It was the fashion in 1817 to engulf the heads of six- to eight-year-old boys in enormous fur hats with ear-flaps, which made them look like Eskimos. The French Army wore white uniforms in the Austrian fashion. Regiments were styled legions and instead of being numbered bore the names of *départements*. Napoleon was at St Helena, and since the English would not allow him any green cloth he had his old tunics turned. Pellegrini was singing, Mlle Bigottini was dancing, Potier was presiding at the Théâtre des Variètés and Mme Saqui had succeeded Forioso on the tight-rope. There were still Prussian troops in France. Legitimacy had asserted itself by cutting off first the hands and then the heads of Pleignier, Cabonneau, and Tolleron, convicted of having plotted to blow up the Tuileries. The Prince de Talleyrand, grand chamberlain, and the Abbé Louis, finance minister designate, exchanged the smiles of rewarded prescience, both having celebrated the Mass of the Federation held on the Champ de Mars on 14 July 1790, one as a bishop, the other as a deacon. In 1817 large wooden posts, painted blue and still bearing traces of gilt eagles and bees, lay rotting on the grass in that same Champ de Mars, some scorched by Austrian bivouac fires. They were what remained of the podium erected two years previously by order

of the Emperor for the ceremonial known as the Champ de Mai –
a celebration remarkable for the fact that it was held on the Champ
de Mars in the month of June. Two things were popular in the
year 1817, the selected edition of the works of Voltaire issued by
a certain Colonel Touquet and the 'Charter snuff-boxes', engraved with the People's Charter, designed by the same gentleman.
The latest Paris sensation was the murder committed by Dautun,
who had flung his brother's head into the pool in the Marché-
aux-fleurs. An official inquiry was opened into the loss of the
frigate *Méduse*, which was in due course to cover her captain
with shame and the painter Géricault with glory. Colonel Selves
went to Egypt, there to become a Moslem and assume the title of
Suleiman Pasha. The Ns were erased from the Louvre. The Pont
d'Austerlitz was swallowed up in the Jardin du Roi, a designation
embracing both the bridge and the Jardin des Plantes. Louis XVIII,
searching his Horace for instances of heroes who became emperors
and shoemakers who became heirs apparent, had two particular
cases in mind, Napoleon and Mathurin Bruneau, the cobbler whose
claim to be the Dauphin had won some support among the royalists
of Normandy. The Académie Française announced that the subject
of its essay award was 'The Happiness to be Derived from Scholar-
ship'.* An imitation Chateaubriand named Marchangy cropped up,
to be followed by an imitation Marchangy named d'Arlincourt. In
recognition of her masterpieces *Claire d'Albe* and *Malek-Adel*,
Mme Cottin was proclaimed the greatest writer of the age. The
Institut de France struck the name of Napoleon Bonaparte off its
rolls. By Royal Decree a naval college was established at Angoulême: since the Duc d'Angoulême was Grand Admiral of the Fleet,
clearly the town must be given the status of a seaport or the whole
principle of monarchy would be undermined. Mme de Stael died in
July. Political differences were still not unknown, the Café Lemblin,
in the Palais-Royal, favouring the Emperor as opposed to the
Café Valois which favoured the Bourbons. The newspapers had
shrunk, but if the format was diminished the freedom of expression
was tremendous. *Le Constitutionnel* was constitutional and *La
Minerve* spelt the name of Chateaubriand with a final 't', causing
much mirth among the citizenry at the expense of that great writer.

The suborned press showered insults on the persons exiled in
1815 – David was denied all talent, Arnault all wit, Carnot all

* Hugo himself competed for this award, receiving an honourable mention.

integrity; Soult had never won a battle and Napoleon had lost his genius. It is rare, as we know, for exiles to receive letters from their native country, since the police make it their particular duty to intercept them. David, who complained of this in a Belgian newspaper, was handsomely mocked in the Royalist press. Differences of terminology – 'regicides' as opposed to 'voters', 'enemies' instead of 'allies', 'Napoleon' for 'Buonaparte' – represented something more than a gulf between individuals. All sensible persons were agreed that King Louis XVIII, 'the immortal author of the Charter', had put an end for ever to the age of revolutions. The word 'Redivivus' was being carved on the pedestal in the garden by the Pont-Neuf destined for the statue of Henry VI. Plans were under discussion for the consolidation of the Monarchy, and in critical moments the right-wing leaders said, 'We must consult Bacol,' a deputy notable only for his ultra-monarchist views. But there was also a movement (cautiously approved by 'Monsieur', the king's brother) in favour of the Comte d'Artois; this was to become known as 'the waterside conspiracy' since the conspirators were accustomed to meet on the terrace of the Tuileries overlooking the Seine. Nor were other plots lacking. The Minister of Police was the Duc Decazes, a gentleman of moderately liberal views. Chateaubriand, clad in pyjama trousers and slippers, with a cap of Madras cotton on his grey head, stood every morning at his window in the Rue Saint-Dominique, peering into a mirror and cleaning his excellent teeth with a complete set of dentist's equipment while he dictated drafts of *La Monarchie selon la Charte* to his secretary, M. Pilorge. The leading critics rated Lafon higher than Talma. Charles Clodier was writing *Thérèse Aubert*. Divorce had been abolished. High-schools were called colleges, and the young collegians, their collars adorned with a golden fleur-de-lis, brawled over the Roi de Rome. The palace secret police complained to Her Royal Highness, Madame, about the portrait of her husband, the Duc d'Orléans, which was to be seen everywhere: the duke in his hussar uniform looked a great deal more imposing than the Duc de Berry in the uniform of the dragoons – a most uncomfortable circumstance. The City of Paris had the dome of the Invalides re-gilded at its own expense. The actor Picard – a member of the Academy, which Molière had never succeeded in becoming – was playing in *Les deux Philberts* at the Théâtre de l'Odéon, over the front of which the partly effaced words, 'Théâtre de l'Impératrice', could still be clearly discerned. It was generally agreed that M. Charles Loyson would become the genius of the century; envy, a sure sign of fame, was already beginning to assail him and the following line was written about him – '*Même quand Loyson vole, on sent qu'il a des pattes.*'* The philosopher Saint-Simon, largely unknown, was a celebrated Fourier in the Académie des Sciences whom posterity has forgotten and an unknown Fourtier living in an attic whom the future will remember. Byron was beginning to emerge: a footnote to a poem by Milleboye introduced him to France with the words 'a certain Lord Byron'. David of Angers was trying to shape marble. A contraption which reeked and spluttered was manoeuvring on the Seine between the Pont-Royal and the Pont-Louis-XV: a useless mechanical toy, an inventor's daydream observed with indifference by the Parisians – in fact, a steamboat. The aristocracy of the Faubourg Saint-Germain supported M. Delaveau for the post of Prefect of Police, because of his piety. Two leading surgeons quarrelled in the lecture-hall of the École de Médicine over the divinity of Christ, shaking their fists at each other. Cuvier, with one eye on Genesis and the other on the natural world, sought to placate religious bigotry by adapting fossils to the Scriptures and demonstrating the superiority of Moses to the mastodons. A man who, at the sight of the Comte d'Artois entering Notre-Dame, was so rash as to exclaim aloud, 'God, how I regret the day when I saw Bonaparte and Talma go arm-in-arm into the Bal-Sauvage!' was tried and sentenced to six months' imprisonment for sedition. But the traitors under Napoleon now came out of hiding. Men who had gone over to the enemy on the eve of battle cynically paraded their rewards and dignities; the deserters of Ligny and Quatre-Bras flaunted their monarchist allegiance with a brazenness that disregarded the injunction to be read on the walls of English public lavatories – 'Please adjust your dress before leaving.'

Such is a random, superficial picture of the year 1817, now largely forgotten. History discards nearly all these odds and ends and cannot do otherwise; the larger scene absorbs them. Nevertheless such details, which are wrongly called trifling – there are no trifles in the human story, no trifling leaves on the tree – are not without

*'Even when Loyson soars one feels that his feet are on earth.' The line is a parody, presumably by Hugo, of a line written by Antoine-Marin Lemierre before Loyson was born – '*Même quand l'oiseau marche on sent qu'il a des ailes.*' Charles Loyson, a young poet of great promise, died in 1820.

value. It is the lineaments of the years which form the countenance of the century.

And in that year of 1817 four young gentlemen of Paris played 'a merry prank'.

II
Double foursome

The four Parisians came, one from Toulouse, one from Limoges, the third from Cahors, and the fourth from Montauban; but they were students, and to say 'student' is to say 'Parisian'. To study in Paris is to belong to Paris.

They were unremarkable young men, average representatives of their kind, neither good nor bad, learned nor ignorant, brilliant nor doltish; handsome with the April lustre of their twenty-odd years. Four commonplace Oscars, for the Arthurs had not yet arrived. Ossian was still in vogue and the mode was Scandinavian and Caledonian. The pure English style was to come later, the first of the Arthurs, Wellington, having only just won the Battle of Waterloo.

The Oscars were named Felix Tholomyès, from Toulouse, Listolier from Cahors, Fameuil from Limoges, and Blachevelle from Montauban. Each, of course, had his mistress. Blachevelle loved Favourite, so-called because she had been in England: Listolier adored Dahlia, who had chosen a flower for her *nom de guerre*; Fameuil idolized Zéphine, short for Josephine; and Tholomyès had Fantine, called 'la Blonde' because of her golden hair.

Favourite, Dahlia, Zéphine, and Fantine were enchanting girls, scented and glowing, still with a flavour of the working-class since they had not altogether abandoned the use of their needles, distracted by love-affairs but with a last trace of the serenity of toil in their expressions, and in their hearts that seed of purity which in a woman survives her first fall from grace. One of the four, the youngest, was known as 'the baby'; and one was 'big sister'. Big sister was aged twenty-three. It must be said that the three older ones were more experienced, more heedless, and more versed in the ways of the world than Fantine la Blonde, who was encountering her first illusion.

Dahlia, Zéphine, and particularly Favourite could not have said as much. There had already been more than one episode in the tale of their love-affairs, and the Adolphe of Chapter One had become the Alphonse of Chapter Two and the Gustave of Chapter Three. Poverty and coquetry are fateful counsellors; the one complains and the other flatters, and both whisper in the ear of pretty working girls, defenceless creatures who cannot forbear to listen. Hence their disasters and the stones that are flung at them. They are swept off their feet by the prospect of all that is glorious and inaccessible.

Favourite, having been in England, was greatly admired by Zéphine and Dahlia. She had acquired a home of her own at a very early age. Her father, an elderly, coarse, and boastful teacher of mathematics, had never married but despite his years was still a womanizer. In his youth he had seen the skirts of a chambermaid caught up on a fender and the vison had caused him to fall in love. Favourite was the outcome. From time to time she saw her father, who nodded to her. One morning a wild-eyed elderly woman had entered her room saying, 'You don't know who I am? I'm your mother.' The woman had helped herself to food and drink, fetched a mattress and moved in. She was bad-tempered and devout. She never spoke to Favourite, stayed silent for hours on end, ate enough for four, and went downstairs to unbosom herself to the concierge, complaining about her daughter.

What had caused Dahlia to take up with Listolier, and perhaps with others, were her pretty pink fingernails. How could such nails be expected to do hard work? A girl wanting to remain virtuous must sacrifice her hands. As for Zéphine, she had won Fameuil's heart by her provocative and caressing way of saying, 'Oui, Monsieur'.

The young men were comrades and the girls were friends. Love-affairs of that kind always go hand-in-hand with that kind of friendship.

Virtue and philosophy are separate things, the proof of which is that, making due allowance for these irregular arrangements, Favourite, Zéphine, and Dahlia were philosophical, whereas Fantine was virtuous.

Virtuous, you may ask – but what of Tholomyès? Solomon would reply that love is a part of virtue. We will merely say that Fantine's was her first and only love, and she was wholly faithful. She was the only one of the four girls whom only one person addressed with the familiar *tu*.

She was one of those beings hatched, as it were, in the bosom of the people. Sprung from the nethermost depths of society, she bore the stigma of anonymity and the unknown. She had been born at Montreuil-sur-mer, but nothing was known of her parents. She was called Fantine because she had never been called anything else. At the time of her birth the Directory had been in power. She could have no family name since she had no family, and no baptismal name since at that time there had been no Church. She was called by the name bestowed on her by some passer-by who had seen her running barefoot in the streets, and she accepted it as she accepted the raindrops when they fell. La Petite Fantine – and that was all anyone knew about her. At the age of ten she had left the town and gone into service with a farming family in the neighbourhood. At fifteen she had gone to Paris 'to seek her fortune'. She was beautiful and had stayed pure as long as she could – a beautiful blonde with fine teeth. Gold and pearls were her dowry, but the gold was on her head and the pearls were in her mouth.

She worked in order to live, and presently fell in love, also in order to live, for the heart, too, has its hunger. She fell in love with Tholomyès.

For him it was a passing affair, for her the love of her life. The streets of the Latin quarter, swarming with students and grisettes, saw the beginning of the dream. In that maze on the hill of the Panthéon where so many knots have been tied and loosed, she fled for a long time to escape from Tholomyès, but always in such a fashion as to meet him again. There is a way of running which resembles pursuit. And so it happened.

Tholomyès, being the liveliest, was the guiding spirit of the small group formed by Blachevelle, Listolier, Fameuil, and himself.

He was an older student in the classic style. He was rich, with an income of four thousand francs, a matter of awestruck report on the Montagne Sainte-Geneviève. He was a thirty-year-old, ill-preserved rake, wrinkled and gap-toothed, with a bald patch of which he said unrepining, 'Tonsured at thirty, on one's knees at forty'. He had a poor digestion and a weakness in one eye; but his youth in its passing heightened his gaiety, replacing teeth with mockery, hair with lightheartedness, health with irony and adding a twinkle to the rheumy eye. He flourished in dilapidation; youth, retreating in good order, did so with laughter and high spirits. He had had a play refused by the Théâtre du Vaudeville, and now and then wrote indifferent verse. Moreover, he was superiorly sceptical of all things, which lent him great authority with lesser souls. In short, balding and ironical, he was the leader.

One day Tholomyès took the other three aside and said with an oracular flourish:

'For nearly a year Fantine, Dahlia, Zéphine, and Favourite have been asking us for a surprise and we have solemnly promised to give them one. They keep on about it, especially to me. Like the old women of Naples who exclaim to St Janvier, "Yellow Face, work your miracle!" they keep saying to me, "Tholomyès, when are you going to produce the surprise?" And in the meantime we have all had letters from our parents. We are harassed on both sides. I think the time has come. Let us now consider.'

Tholomyès then lowered his voice and what he said was so mirth-provoking that it drew a great burst of laughter from all four and caused Blachevelle to exclaim: 'That's a stupendous idea!'

The rest of the conference was lost in the smoke of an adjacent ale-house, but its outcome was a pleasure-party which took place on the following Sunday, the four young men and the four girls.

III

Four and four

It is not easy for us in these days to imagine what a country outing of students and grisettes was like forty-five years ago. Paris no longer has the same outskirts, and what might be termed the face of circum-Parisian life has wholly changed. Instead of the post-chaise we have the railway-carriage, and instead of the sailing-cutter the steamboat. We now talk of Fécamp as once we talked of Saint Cloud. Paris in 1862 is a town with all France for its suburbs.

The eight young people conscientiously indulged in all the rustic pastimes that were then available. It was the beginning of the holiday season, a warm, bright summer's day. The day before, Favourite, the only one who could write, had sent Tholomyès the following note in the name of the four girls, 'Early to rise for the great surprise!' – and they had got up at five that morning. They went by coach to Saint-Cloud, inspected the dry cascade exclaiming, 'How wonderful it must be when there's any water! breakfasted at the Tête-Noire, had fun tossing quoits by the big pond, climbed up to the

Lantern of Diogenes, bet macaroons on the gambling-wheel on the Pont de Sèvres, picked bunches of flowers at Puteaux, bought cream-puffs at Neuilly, ate apple-turnovers everywhere and were entirely happy.

The girls laughed and twittered like uncaged birds, now and then administering reproving taps to their young men. It was the morning intoxication of life, the unforgettable years, the trembling of the dragonfly's wing. Can you not remember it? Have you never walked through undergrowth thrusting the branches aside to protect the delightful head behind you, or slid down a damp slope with a girl clinging to your hand and protesting, 'Heavens, my new boots!' Let it be said that not even this trifling vexation troubled that happy company, although Favourite had said maternally when they set out, 'There are slugs on the paths. It's a sign of rain, my dears.'

All four girls were so enchantingly pretty. An elderly poet, seeing them go by under the chestnut-trees of Saint-Cloud at six that morning, exclaimed, 'There's one too many!' having in mind the three Graces. Favourite, the friend of Blachevelle and the eldest, being twenty-three, ran ahead under the branches, jumping ditches, skipping over bushes, leading the dance with the nimbleness of a dryad. Zéphine and Dahlia, whose looks were in some sort complementary, each enhancing the other, stayed close together, partly from coquetry and partly from friendship, and adopted English mannerisms. Melancholy was in vogue for women, as Byronism was later for men, and feminine hair was beginning to be only loosely curled. Zéphine and Dahlia wore theirs in tight rolls. Listolier and Fameuil, engaged in discussing their university professors, were describing to Fantine the dispute then in progress between M. Delvincourt and M. Blondeau, both of the Faculty of Law. Blachevelle was looking as though he had been expressly created for the purpose of carrying Favourite's shawl on Sundays.

Tholomyès, following behind, was still in charge. He was merry, but his leadership made itself felt; there was authority in his good-humour. His most notable garment was a pair of baggy nankeen trousers – elephant-legs as they were called – with understraps of copper mesh. He was carrying a handsome rattan cane and, since his audacity was boundless, he had in his mouth a strange object called a cigar. Nothing being sacred to him, he had taken up smoking.

'Tholomyès is extraordinary,' the others said in awe. 'Those trousers!'

As for Fantine, she was happiness itself. Those beautiful white teeth had evidently been intended most especially for laughter. She carried in her hand, more often than she wore it on her head, a straw bonnet with long white ribbons, and her thick golden locks, which so easily broke loose and were always having to be pinned up, might have been those of Galatea fleeing under the willows. Her lips were parted in delight. The corners of her mouth, sensually up-turned like an antique mask of Erigone, seemed to invite some bold advance, but long eyelashes cast their discreet downward shadow over this wantonness, as though to call it to order. Her clothing had a quality of song and flame. She was wearing a mauve dress of the gauzy material made in Barège, with bronze-leather bootees whose crossed laces disclosed white openwork stockings, and with a muslin bodice from Marseilles of which the name, *canezou* – a corruption of the words *quinze août*, as pronounced on the Canebière – denotes high summer and the warm south. The other three, less diffident, wore frankly low-necked dresses which, under their flowered hats, were both charming and provocative; but compared with this daring display, Fantine's *canezou* with its transparencies, its indiscretion and reticence, at once concealing and revealing, was a piquant triumph of modesty, and it may well be that the famous Court of Love presided over by the Vicomtesse de Cette with her sea-green eyes would have awarded it the prize for coquetry despite its intended restraint. What is most innocent is sometimes most calculating. These things happen.

Glowing of face and delicate in profile, eyes of deep blue with heavy lids, small, arched feet and admirably turned wrists and ankles, white skin with here and there an azure tracery of veins, firm, youth-ful cheeks, the sturdy, supple neck of an Aegean Juno and shoulders such as Coustou might have modelled with an enticing hollow between them visible through the gauze – such was Fantine, gaiety sobered by thoughtfulness, sculptural and exquisite, a statue to be guessed at beneath her draperies and a soul contained in the statue.

She was beautiful without being too aware of it. Those rare ob-servers, the worshippers of the beautiful who measure all things against perfection, would have discerned in this little working-girl, under her Parisian fripperies, a hint of antique harmony. The daughter of the shadows had breeding. She was graced with the two orders of beauty, style and rhythm. Style is the form of the ideal, rhythm is its movement.

We have said of Fantine that she was happiness itself; but she was also modesty. What the close observer might have perceived beneath the intoxication of youth, summer, and a love-affair, was an unconquerable reserve. She was always a little taken aback, and it is this innocent dismay which distinguishes Psyche from Venus. Her long, slender fingers were those of a vestal stirring the ash beneath the sacred flame with a rod of gold. Although, alas, she would have refused Tholomyès nothing, her expression in repose was above all virginal; a sort of dignity, earnest and almost austere, would at moments take possession of it, and it was strongly disconcerting to see her gaiety thus eclipsed in an abrupt withdrawal. In those moments of swift and sometimes emphatic gravity she was like a disdainful goddess. Her forehead, nose, and chin presented that balance of line, very different from the balance of proportion, which constitutes the harmony of a face; and in the eloquent interval separating the base of her nose from her upper lip she had that charming and scarcely perceptible fold which is the mysterious token of chastity, and which caused Barbarossa to fall in love with a Diana found in the ruins of Iconium.

Love, let us agree, may be a fault. Fantine's was the innocence that rides above it.

IV

Tholomyès sings a Spanish song

That day was flooded from beginning to end with sunshine. All Nature seemed on holiday. Scent rose up from the lawns of Saint-Cloud, leaves and branches fluttered in the river breeze, bees pillaged the clover, a riot of butterflies hovered over jasmine, milfoil, and wild oats, and the King of France's noble park was occupied by a host of vagabonds, the birds.

The four entranced couples were a part of all this magic, singing as they danced and ran, chasing butterflies, gathering wild flowers, wetting openwork stockings in the long grass, youthful, foolish, and kind, each exchanging a kiss now and then with any other, except Fantine, who was enclosed in her own shy dream and was in love. 'You've always got a look about you,' Favourite said.

These are life's delights. These momentary, happy pairings are a deep response to life and nature, a summons to warmth and light. There must once have been a good fairy who ordered the fields and trees expressly for young hearts, and thanks to her we have the eternal *école buisonnière*, that school for lovers under the sky which will endure as long as there are trees and novices. Hence the popularity of spring among thinkers. Nobleman and shop-boy, peer and peasant, the people of the Court and the people of the town, all are under the spell of that good fairy. They seek to find themselves in laughter, and there is a glow of discovery in the air, a miraculous transformation in the fact of loving. The lawyer's clerk becomes a god. The cries and chasings in the grass, the clasped waist, the murmur of half-spoken words that are a song of rapture, the cherry passed from mouth to mouth, these like a flame rising and sinking are the heaven of life. Girls sweetly give themselves and believe that it will last for ever. Philosophers, poets, and painters contemplate these ecstasies and cannot encompass them, so dazzled are they. 'The departure for Cythera' cries Watteau. Lancret, the painter of the middle-class, sees his people soaring skyward; Diderot opens his arms to all light loves, and d'Urfé brings in the druids.

After breakfasting, the four couples visited what was then called the King's Enclosure to see a plant newly arrived from India, of which we have forgotten the name but which was drawing all Paris to Saint-Cloud. It was a strange and charming tall-stemmed shrub whose dense tangle of threadlike branches bore no leaves but innumerable small white blossoms, so that it resembled a head of hair dusted with flowers. There was always an admiring crowd round it.

After this Tholomyès cried, 'I propose a donkey-ride,' and having bargained with a donkey-man they rode through Vanvres to Issy.

At Issy an incident occurred. The park, now part of the *bien national*, which at that time was owned by the army-caterer Bourguin, happened to be open. They went in through the wrought-iron gates and, after inspecting the statue of the anchorite in his grotto, ventured upon the mysteries of the famous hall of mirrors whose wanton distortions were worthy of a satyr become millionaire or a Turcaret turned into Priapus. Then they came to the great swing, slung between the chestnut-trees, which has been celebrated by the Abbé de Bernis. The girls were swung in turn amid laughter provoked by a billowing of skirts that would have delighted Greuze and which moved Tholomyès, who came from Toulouse and was partly Spanish, to deliver himself dolefully of an old Spanish song a *gallega*, doubtless inspired by some similar occasion.

> *Soy de Badajoz*
> *Amor me llama.*
> *Toda mi alma*
> *Es en mi ojos*
> *Porque enseñas*
> *A tus piernas.**

Only Fantine refused to let herself be swung.

'I don't like people to give themselves airs,' Favourite remarked rather sharply.

Having finished with the donkeys they took a boat along the Seine and walked from Passy up to the Barrière de l'Étoile. We may recall that they had been on their feet since five that morning, but there – 'There's no getting tired on a Sunday,' said Favourite. 'On Sundays tiredness doesn't happen.' At three o'clock they were sliding down the switchback, a singular structure then standing on the high ground round the Rue Beaujon, of which the rugged outline showed above the tops of the trees on the Champs-Élysées.

Now and then Favourite cried:

'But the surprise? When do we get the great surprise?'

'You must be patient,' said Tholomyès.

V

Chez Bombarda

Having exhausted the Russian Peaks and being by now a little weary, the thoughts of the party turned to dinner and they repaired to the Cabaret Bombarda, a branch establishment opened on the Champs-Élysées by the famous restaurateur, Bombarda, whose sign hung on the Rue de Rivoli at the corner of the Passage Delorme.

A big, ugly room with an alcove containing a bed at one end (the

*'I come from Badajoz. Love calls to me. All my soul is in my eyes because you are showing your legs.'

place was so full on a Sunday that they had to put up with this); two windows from which the embankment and the river could be seen through the elms; the radiant glow of August beyond the windows; two tables, one piled high with bouquets and male and female hats, and the other, at which the four pairs were seated, loaded with plates and dishes, bottles and glasses, jugs of beer and carafes of wine – little order on the table and some disorder below it, whence proceeded, in Molière's words, 'a great clatter of feet'. Such was the scene at about half past four that afternoon, with the sun beginning to set and the appetites to diminish.

The Champs-Élysées, filled with sunshine and people, was all glare and dust, those two constituents of glory. The Marly horses, neighing marble, reared in a golden haze. Carriages drove up and down. A squadron of the magnificent Gardes du Corps with a trumpeter at their head rode along the Avenue de Neuilly, and the white flag, touched with pink in the sunset, floated over the dome of the Tuileries. The Place de la Concorde, at that time re-named Place Louis XV, was thronged with strollers, many wearing the silver fleur-de-lis on a white ribbon, which in 1817 had still not disappeared from all buttonholes. Here and there clusters of little girls surrounded by applauding spectators sang the Bourbon ditty with its refrain, '*Rendez-nous notre père de Gand, Rendez-nous notre père*,' which had electrified the Hundred Days.

People from the working-class districts in their Sunday clothes, some wearing the bourgeois fleur-de-lis, were scattered over the open spaces, drinking, playing skittles, riding on the roundabouts. There were printer's apprentices in paper caps. There was laughter everywhere. It was a time of settled peace and royalist security. A confidential report to the King from the Prefect of Police, the Comte Anglès, on the Paris working population ended as follows: 'All things considered, Sire, there is nothing to be feared from these people. They are as heedless and indolent as cats. The lower orders in the provinces are restive, but not those in Paris. The men are all small in size. It would take two of them put together, Sire, to make one of your grenadiers. We have nothing to fear from the working people of the capital. What is remarkable is that their physical stature has further shrunk during the past fifty years and the people of the Paris suburbs are smaller than they were before the Revolution. They are not dangerous. An easy-going riff-raff, to sum up.'

No Prefect of Police believes that a cat can turn into a lion;

nevertheless the thing happens, and that is the miracle of the people of Paris. Moreover the cat, so despised by Comte Anglès, was held in reverence as the embodiment of liberty by the republics of antiquity; a bronze colossus of a cat stood in the main square at Corinth, as though it were complementary to the wingless Minerva of the Piraeus. The simple-minded Restoration police took a too rosy view of the Paris populace; it was not an 'easy-going riff-raff' as they thought. The Parisian is to the French what the Athenian was to the Greeks: no one sleeps better than he, no one is more openly frivolous and idle, no one appears more heedless. But this is misleading. He is given to every kind of listlessness, but when there is glory to be won he may be inspired with every kind of fury. Give him a pike and he will enact the tenth of August, a musket and you have Austerlitz. He was the springboard of Napoleon and the mainstay of Danton. At the cry of 'la patrie' he enrols, and at the call of liberty he tears up the pavements. Beware of him! His hair rising in anger assumes an epic quality, his shirt becomes a Grecian mantle, the first street uprising becomes a Caudine Fork. When the tocsin sounds the dweller in the back streets gains in stature, the little man assumes a terrible look and the breath from his narrow chest becomes a gale to change the skyline of the Alps. It is thanks to the little man of Paris that the Revolution, inspiring the armies, conquered Europe. He delights in song. Suit his song to his nature and you will understand. With just the 'Carmagnole' to sing he will only overthrow Louis XVI; but give him the 'Marseillaise' and he will liberate the world.

Having added this footnote to Comte Anglès's report we must return to our four couples, whose meal, as we have seen, was ending.

VI

I adore you

Table-talk and lovers' talk, both fleeting as air. Lovers' talk is the mist and table-talk the scent.

Fameuil and Dahlia were humming, Tholomyès was drinking, Zéphine was laughing, and Fantine was smiling. Listolier was blowing a wooden trumpet he had bought at Saint-Cloud. Gazing tenderly at her lover, Favourite said:

'Blachevelle, I adore you.'

This drew from him a question.

'What would you do, Favourite, if I stopped loving you?'

'Me?' she cried. 'You mustn't say such things, even as a joke! If you stopped loving me I'd come after you, I'd beat you, I'd scratch your eyes out, I'd have you arrested.'

While Blachevelle smiled the fatuous smile of gratified male vanity, she added: 'I'd scream the place down! I'd rouse the whole neighbourhood, you brute!'

Blachevelle by now was leaning back with his eyes closed in a simper of delight. Dahlia, who was still eating, murmured in an aside to Favourite:

'Are you really as fond of him as all that?'

'I can't stand him,' said Favourite in the same undertone, picking up her fork. 'He's mean. I like the boy over the way. Do you know the one I mean? You can see he's cut out to be an actor. I like actors. When he comes home in the evening his mother says, "Well, that's the end of peace for today; he'll start shouting till he's given me a headache" – because he goes up to the top of the house, right up to the attic with the rats, and he sings and recites and I don't know what so loud that you can hear him on the ground floor. He's earning twenty sous a day already, copying rubbish for a lawyer. His father was a chorister in Saint-Jacques-du-Haut-Pas. But he's really nice, and he adores me so much that one day when I was making batter for pancakes he said, "Mamselle, if you were to make your gloves into fritters I'd eat them." It takes a real artist to say a thing like that. He's sweet. I'm crazy about him. But I go on telling Blachevelle I adore him. I'm an awful liar, aren't I?'

Favourite was silent for a moment but then continued:

'I'm in a bad mood, Dahlia. Nothing but rain all this summer, and the wind gets on my nerves, it never seems to drop, and Blachevelle's really too mean for anything, and there are scarcely any peas to be had in the market and butter's so dear one doesn't know what to buy and – oh, well, I've got the spleen, as the English say. And to cap everything, here we are, dining in a room with a bed in it. I think life's disgusting!'

The wisdom of Tholomyès

Some members of the party were singing and others loudly talking. The room was in a state of uproar which Tholomyès now sought to abate.

'Let us talk with more reason and less speed,' he said. 'We must think if we wish to shine. Blurted conversation is an expense of spirit. Flowing beer gathers no head. Let us not be hasty, gentlemen, but mingle dignity with revelry, deliberation with appetite. *Festina lente.* Let us take a lesson from the spring. If it comes too soon it burns itself out – that is to say it freezes. Its excess of zeal destroys the peaches and apricots. And excess of zeal kills elegance and a good dinner. In this matter Grimod de la Reynière, the gourmet, was on the side of Talleyrand – "*Surtout, messieurs, pas trop de zèle.*" '

There was a chorus of protest from his audience.

'Leave us alone, Tholomyès,' said Blachevelle.

'Down with the tyrant!' cried Fameuil. 'It's Sunday.'

'And we're all sober,' said Listolier.

'My dear Tholomyès,' said Blachevelle, 'observe my state of calm.'

'You are the very marquis of calm,' said Tholomyès.

The Marquis of Montcalm was a prominent monarchist of the period. The pun, indifferent though it was, had the effect of a stone dropped into a pool: the frogs fell silent.

'Take comfort, my friends,' said Tholomyès in the cool tone of a leader reasserting his authority. 'Do not be too much impressed by a jest let fall in passing. Such trifles fallen from heaven are not necessarily deserving of respect. Puns are the droppings of the spirit in its flight. They may fall anywhere, and the spirit, having voided itself of a flippancy, rises into the blue. A white splash on a rock does not prevent the eagle from soaring. Not that I am a despiser of puns. I give them the credit they deserve, but no more. The loftiest spirits in mankind and perhaps beyond mankind, the most illustrious and delightful, have had resort to the play on words. Jesus made a pun about Peter, the Rock. Moses made a pun about Isaac, Aeschylus about Polynices, Cleopatra about Octavius. And we may note that without Cleopatra's pun, made before the Battle of Actium, no one would remember the town of Toryna, whose name is derived from a Greek word meaning a wooden spoon. But having conceded all this, let me return to my original matter. I repeat, dear brothers and sisters, *pas de ʒèle* – no clamour, no excess, even of gaiety, wit and merriment. Hear me, for I have the prudence of Amphiaraus and the baldness of Caesar. There must be a limit even to riddle-making – *modus in rebus* – and even to dining. Ladies you like apple-turnovers, but you must not over-indulge in them. Art and good sense must play their part even in the eating of apple-turnovers. Gluttony punishes the glutton. Indigestion was designed by God to impose morality on stomachs. And remember this: each of our passions, even that of love, has a stomach that must not be surfeited. We must write *finis* to all things at the proper time, exercise restraint when desire is still urgent, lock the door on appetite, put fantasy in the stocks and ourselves under arrest. The wise man is he who knows when the moment has come. Have faith in me, because I have read a little law, or so the examination results tell me, and can distinguish between what is explicit and what is implicit; because I have written a thesis in Latin on the methods of torture used in Rome at the time when Munatius Demens was Quaestor of Parricide; because it appears that I am shortly to be awarded my doctorate, from which it would seem that I am not wholly an imbecile. I urge you to be moderate in your desires, and as surely as my name is Félix Tholomyès this is wise counsel. Happy is he who when the hour strikes takes the heroic course and abdicates, like Sulla or Origen.'

Favourite had been listening with profound attention.

'Félix,' she said. 'Such a lovely name. It's Latin. It means happy.'

'My friends and brothers,' Tholomyès continued, 'do you wish to escape the pricks of desire, to dispense with the nuptial couch and defy love? It is easily done, and this is the prescription: lemonade and hard labour. You must exhaust yourselves in sleepless toil, drink tisanes of herbs and flowers, so limit your diet that you nearly starve, wear a hair shirt and take cold baths.'

'I'd sooner have a woman,' said Listolier.

'Woman!' exclaimed Tholomyès. 'Beware of woman! Woe to him who trusts himself to her inconstant heart. Woman is perfidious and devious. She hates the serpent as a professional rival. The serpent is in the house across the way.'

'Tholomyès, you're drunk,' cried Blachevelle.

'Perhaps I am.'

'Then at least be cheerful.'

'Very well.' And filling his glass, Tholomyès got to his feet.

'To the glory of wine! *Nunc te, Bacche, canam.* Forgive me, ladies, that's Spanish. The measure of a people is the measure of their wine. The *arroba* of Castille holds sixteen litres, the *cantaro* of Alicante twelve, the *almuda* of the Canaries twenty-five, the *cuatrin* of the Balearics twenty-six – and the jackboot of Tsar Peter thirty! All honour to the great Tsar, and to his boot which was greater still! Ladies, a word of friendly advice: change partners whenever you choose. It is proper that love should stray. The love-affair was never meant to be debased like an English charwoman with calloused knees, but to rove and flutter in gaiety of heart. To err is human, it is said; but I say that to err is to love. Ladies, I adore you all. Zéphine, Josephine, with your indignant expressions you would be enchanting if you were less reproving. And Favourite! One day when Blachevelle was crossing the gutter in the Rue Guérin-Boisseau he saw a girl in trim white stockings who showed her legs, and the sight so delighted him that he fell in love. Favourite, you have Grecian lips. There was a painter called Euphorion who was known as the painter of lips, and he alone would have been worthy to paint your mouth. And no one before you was worthy of the name of Favourite. You deserve to be awarded the apple, like Venus, and to eat it, like Eve. Just now you spoke of my name and I was touched. But names can be deceptive. My name is Félix but I am not happy. Words can be liars, we must not blindly believe what they say. In your place, Miss Dahlia, I would call myself Rose. A flower should be fragrant and a woman should have wit. Of Fantine I say nothing. She is a dreamer, a sensitive soul, a wraith shaped like a nymph with the downcast eyes of a nun who has drifted into the life of a grisette but takes refuge in illusion. She sings and prays, looks heavenward without much knowing what she sees or does, strays in a garden where there are more birds than exist in life. Take heed of what I say, Fantine – I, Tholomyès, am an illusion . . . But she is not even listening, lost in her golden-head dreams. Everything in her is freshness, softness, youth, and morning light. Dear Fantine, you should be called Marguerite or Pearl, you are a woman of the most splendid East . . . Ladies, a second counsel: do not marry. But why am I saying this? Why waste my breath? In the matter of marriage women are incorrigible, and nothing that wise men can say will prevent the stay-maker and the seamstress from dreaming of a husband loaded with diamonds. So be it: but, ladies, remember this – you eat too much sugar. If you have a fault it is that you are forever nibbling sweets. Your pretty white teeth crave sugar. But you must bear in mind that sugar is a salt; all salts are desiccating and sugar is the most desiccating of all. It heightens the rush of blood through the veins, leading to coagulation, to tubercles in the lung, to death. That is why diabetes leads to consumption. Therefore, ladies do not eat sugar, and live long . . . I turn now to the men. Gentlemen, make conquests. Be ruthless in robbing your comrade of his mistress. Thrust and parry – in love there is no friendship. Wherever there is a pretty woman there is open warfare, no quarter, war to the knife. A pretty woman is a *causus belli*; she is *flagrante delicto*. Petticoats have been the cause of every invasion in history. Woman is man's rightful prey, Romulus carried off the Sabine women, William of Normandy the Saxon women, Caesar the women of Rome. The man who is not loved preys like a vulture on the loves of other men, and for my part, to these unfortunates without a mistress I repeat the sublime proclamation of Bonaparte to the army of Italy: "Soldiers, you lack everything. The enemy has it." '

Tholomyès here paused for breath, and Blachevelle, supported by Listolier and Fameuil, broke into a nonsense-song, a topical catch with more rhyme than reason of the kind that springs up amid tobacco-smoke and is as swiftly blown away. The effect was to drive Tholomyès to higher flights. Draining his glass, he re-filled it and concluded his discourse as follows:

'Down with wisdom! Forget everything I have said. Let us be neither prudish nor prudent. I drink to merriment. Let us be merry and end our course on law with folly and with food. Indigestion and the Digest, Justinian the male principle and festivity the female. How splendid is creation, how filled with gaiety, the world glittering like a gem in the benefaction of summer, the blackbird pouring forth its un-fee'd song, the paths of the Luxembourg, the Rue Madame and the Avenue de l'Observatoire rich with the dreams of delicious nursemaids as they watch over the young. I would delight in the South American pampas if I had not the arcades of the Odéon. My soul flies out to virgin forests and savannahs. Everything is beautiful. The flies swarm in the sunlight and the humming-bird is born of the sun. Kiss me, Fantine.'

And absent-mindedly he kissed Favourite.

VIII

Death of a horse

'The food is better at Edon's than in this place,' said Zéphine.

'I prefer Bombarda,' said Blachevelle. 'The setting is more luxurious, more oriental. There are mirrors on the walls downstairs.'

'I'm more interested in what's on my plate,' said Favourite.

'But look at these knives, with their silver handles. They're bone at Edon's. Silver is worth more than bone.'

'Except to those who wear it on their chin,' said Tholomyès.

He was gazing out of the window at the dome of the Invalides. There was a brief pause.

'Tholomyès,' said Fameuil, 'Listolier and I have been disputing.'

'To dispute is excellent,' said Tholomyès. 'To quarrel is even better.'

'We were discussing a matter of philosophy. Which do you prefer – Descartes or Spinoza?'

'I prefer Desaugiers,' said Tholomyès. Desaugiers was a cabaret-singer.

Having thus pronounced judgement he continued:

'I am content to live. The world is not yet ended since we can still talk nonsense, and for this I give thanks to the immortal gods. We lie, but we laugh. We affirm, but we doubt. And that is admirable. The unexpected springs out of the syllogism. There are still people on earth who take pleasure in opening and closing that box of surprises, the paradox. The wine you are so peacefully drinking, ladies, is a Madeira from the Coural das Freiras vineyard, which is three hundred and seventeen fathoms above sea-level. Take heed of this as you drink. Three hundred and seventeen fathoms, and Monsieur Bombarda, that princely restauranteur, lets us have them for four francs fifty a litre.'

Fameuil attempted to interrupt.

'Tholomyès, your opinion is law. But do you think –'

Tholomyès brushed this aside.

'All honour to Bombarda! He would be the equal of Munophis of Elephanta if he could find me a dancing-girl, and of Thygelion of Cheroneus if he could bring me a hetaera. For believe me, ladies, there were Bombardas in Greece and Egypt, as Apuleius tells us. Alas, as Solomon said, there is nothing new under the sun, and as

Virgil said, *amor omnibus idem*, love is the same for all of us. Lisette goes off with her Louis in a boat at Saint-Cloud just as Aspasia embarked with Pericles in the fleet at Samos. Do you know who Aspasia was, ladies? She lived in an age when women were not supposed to possess souls, yet she had a soul that was both rose-pink and scarlet, hotter than flame and cooler than the dawn. She encompassed the two extremities of woman, she was the prostitute goddess, part Socrates, part Manon Lescaut. She was created for the service of Prometheus, should he desire a wanton.'

Being again in full spate Tholomyès might have been difficult to stop, but at that moment a horse fell in the street directly below their windows. It was a lean, aged mare, fit only for the knacker's yard, harnessed to a heavy cart. Exhaustion had brought it to a halt outside Bombarda's and it refused to go further. A crowd gathered. The carter, cursing loudly, applied his whip, whereupon the creature collapsed and could not be got to its feet again. The hubbub caused Tholomyès's audience to rise and go to the window.

'Poor horse,' sighed Fantine, and Dahlia exclaimed, 'Well, listen to her, making a fuss about a horse.'

But Favourite, taking advantage of the diversion, confronted Tholomyès with a resolute expression, arms crossed and head thrust back.

'Well,' she said, 'and what about the surprise?'

'Quite so,' said Tholomyès. 'The time has come. Gentlemen, it is time for us to surprise our ladies. Ladies, we must ask you to wait here for a few minutes.'

'It begins with a kiss,' said Blachevelle.

'On the forehead,' said Tholomyès.

Each solemnly kissed his mistress on the forehead; then the four young men moved in single file to the door, each with a finger to his lips.

Favourite clapped her hands as they went out.

'It's fun already,' she exclaimed.

'Don't be too long. We shall be waiting,' murmured Fantine.

Merry end to happiness

The girls, left to themselves, leaned in pairs on the two window-sills and chattered as they gazed down into the street. They saw the young men come out arm-in-arm and turn to wave gaily before disappearing in the dusty Sunday hubbub of the Champs-Élysées.

'Don't be long!' called Fantine.

'What do you think they'll bring us?' said Zéphine.

'Something nice, I'm sure,' said Dahlia.

'Me,' said Favourite, 'I hope it will be something in gold.'

Their attention was presently caught by a stir of activity at the water's edge which was visible through the trees. It was the hour of departure for mails and diligences, when nearly all the stage-coaches for the south and west passed by way of the Champs-Élysées, generally following the river embankment and leaving the town by the Passy gate. Great yellow- and black-painted vehicles with jingling harness drove by at short intervals, swaying under their canvas-covered load of travellers' luggage, packed with briefly glimpsed heads, grinding the cobblestones to dust and thundering past the crowd in a shower of sparks as though they were manned by furies. This commotion delighted the girls.

'Heavens, the noise!' said Favourite. 'They're like heaps of old iron trying to fly.'

One of these conveyances, of which they had only a glimpse through a thick cluster of elms, stopped for a moment and then drove on at a gallop. This surprised Fantine.

'Surely that's unusual,' she said. 'I thought the stage-coaches never stopped.'

Favourite made a gesture.

'Fantine is wonderful,' she said. 'I never cease to marvel. She's amazed by the most ordinary things. Listen, dear. Suppose I'm a passenger and I say to the driver, "I'm going on ahead. I'll be on the embankment, and you can pick me up as you pass." So the driver watches out for me and picks me up. It happens every day. My love, you know nothing about life.'

Some time passed in chatter of this kind and presently a thought struck Favourite.

'Well!' she said. 'What about this surprise?'

'Yes,' said Dahlia, 'the great surprise.'

'They're being very slow,' sighed Fantine.

As she finished sighing the waiter who had served their meal entered. He had something that looked like a letter in his hand.

'What's that?' asked Favourite.

'It was left behind by the gentlemen, to be handed to the ladies.'

'Then why didn't you bring it to us at once?'

Favourite snatched it from him and found that it was indeed a sealed letter.

'There's no address,' she said. 'But this is what is written outside: "Here is the Surprise." '

She hurriedly broke the seal, unfolded the sheet and read aloud (she was the one who could read):

Beloved mistresses!

Be it known to you that we have parents. The word is one that means little to you, but in the simple and honourable definition of the Code Civil it means fathers and mothers. And they are distressed, these excellent old people. They want us back. They call us prodigals and promise to kill the fatted calf upon our return. Being dutiful, we obey. When you read these lines five fiery horses will be taking us home to our papas and mammas. We are clearing out – going, going, gone – taking flight on the arms and wings of Laffitte and Caillard, those worthy coach-proprietors. The Toulouse coach is rescuing us from the primrose path which is yourselves, sweet loves. We are returning to the ways of society, duty and good behaviour at a steady trot of three leagues an hour. Our country requires that, like everyone else, we should become prefects, fathers of families, rural guards and Councillors of State. Honour us for our self-sacrifice. Weep for us a little and speedily replace us. If this letter rends your hearts, treat it in a like fashion. Adieu.

For nearly two years we have made you happy. Do not bear us ill-will.

Signed: Blachevelle
Fameuil
Listolier
Félix Tholomyès

Post-Scriptum. The dinner is paid for.

The four girls gazed at one another.

Favourite was the first to break the silence.

'All the same,' she said, 'it's a good joke.'

'It's very funny,' said Zéphine.

'I'm sure it was Blachevelle's idea,' said Favourite. 'It makes me quite in love with him. No sooner lost than loved. That's how things are.'

'No,' said Dahlia, 'it was Tholomyès's idea. It's typical.'

'In that case,' said Favourite, 'down with Blachevelle and long live Tholomyès!'

'Long live Tholomyès!' cried Dahlia and Zéphine and burst out laughing.

Fantine joined in the laughter; but when, an hour later, she was back in her room she wept bitterly. It was her first love, as we have said. She had given herself to Tholomyès as to a husband, and the poor girl had a child.

BOOK FOUR

TO TRUST IS SOMETIMES TO SURRENDER

I

A meeting between mothers

DURING THE first quarter of this century, in the village of Montfermeil not far from Paris, there existed a small tavern which has since disappeared. It was kept by a couple called Thénardier and was situated in the Ruelle du Boulanger. Nailed to the wall over the door was a board with a painted design depicting a soldier carrying another on his back, the latter clad in the starred and braided uniform of a general. Splashes of red paint represented blood, and the rest of the picture was filled with what was presumably the smoke of battle. Across the bottom ran the inscription: 'The Sergeant of Waterloo'.

Nothing is more commonplace than a cart or wagon outside a tavern, but the vehicle, or remains of a vehicle, which was to be seen outside the Sergeant of Waterloo on a certain spring evening in 1818 must surely have attracted the notice of a passing painter by its massive proportions. It was the fore-part of one of those drags used by foresters for carrying sawn timbers and tree-trunks, consisting of a massive iron pivot with an axle-shaft and two very large wheels. The general effect, resembling the gun-carriage of an enormous cannon, was lumbering and shapeless. Wheels, hubs, and shaft were smothered in a thick coating of yellow mud not unlike the plaster sometimes daubed on cathedrals. The woodwork was hidden under mud and the metalwork under rust, and from the axle there hung in loops a great chain that could have served to secure a criminal Goliath. It might have been designed for the harnessing of mastodons rather than the transport of timber; and it had a look of prison about it, superhuman fetters that could have been struck off the limbs of some monster. Homer might have associated it with Polyphemus, Shakespeare with Caliban.

What was it doing there? It served no purpose except to block the street until it mouldered into dust. Our ancient social order is filled with similar encumbrances, surviving for no other reason.

The lower part of the looped chain hung close to the ground, and seated on it as though it were a swing, forming a pretty group, were two little girls, the elder, aged about two and a half, holding the younger, aged eighteen months, in her arms. A shawl had been carefully tied to prevent them falling. Some mother, seeing that unsightly chain, had thought, 'What a nice toy for the children.'

The two children, who looked well cared-for, were clearly delighted with it. They were like roses on a scrap-heap, their eyes bright, their pink cheeks round with laughter. One was russet-haired, the other dark. The innocent faces shone with excitement, and the smaller of the two, with the chaste indecency of childhood, displayed a stretch of bare stomach. Above and around this picture of happiness loomed the piece of monstrous, mud-coated wreckage, its uncouth, twisted shape causing it to resemble the mouth of a cavern. The mother, a woman of no very attractive appearance but likeable at that moment, was seated a few yards away in the doorway of the tavern, swinging the children by pulling on a length of string, while at the same time she kept an eye on them with that protective watchfulness, half animal, half angelic, which is the quality of motherhood. With every movement the rusty links emitted a screech like a cry of protest; the children squealed with delight, the glow of sunset shone upon their rapture and nothing could have been more charming than this freak of chance that had turned an ugly monstrosity into a swing for cherubs.

While she swung the children, the mother was tunelessly singing a popular sentimental ditty of the moment. Her preoccupation with this, and with them, caused her to ignore what was going on in the street. But suddenly a voice spoke from close beside her.

'You have two very pretty children, Madame.'

The mother broke off her song and looked round. A young woman was standing near her. She too had a child which she held in her arms. She also had with her a large travelling-bag which looked very heavy.

The child was the most enchanting creature imaginable, a little girl of between two and three, the prettiness of whose attire matched that of the innkeeper's children. She wore a linen bonnet trimmed with Valenciennes lace, and a ribboned frock whose rumpled skirt disclosed a firm white dimpled thigh. She was apple-cheeked, pink, and healthy. Nothing could be seen of her closed eyes except that they were large with very long lashes. She was sleeping in her mother's arms with the perfect confidence of her age.

The mother, who seemed poor and unhappy, had the look of a

town worker reverting to her peasant state. She was young and perhaps pretty but the clothes she was wearing did not allow this to appear. A single lock of her seemingly abundant fair hair had escaped from beneath the tight, plain cap that she wore tied under her chin. A smile might have shown that she had fine teeth, but she did not smile; she looked indeed as though it were a long time since she had been dry-eyed. She was pale and evidently tired, and her gaze, as she glanced at her sleeping child, was one of intense solicitude. A large blue kerchief, like an invalid's shawl, draped the upper part of her body, with beneath it a calico dress and thick shoes, and over all a cloak of coarse wool. Her hands were rough and freckled, one forefinger pricked and calloused. It was Fantine.

It was Fantine, but scarcely to be recognized, although a closer examination would have shown that she still retained her beauty. But now a line of sadness, like the beginning of cynicism, ran down her right cheek. The airy garments, the gauzes and muslins, the gaiety and music, all this had vanished like the sparkle of hoarfrost from a tree, leaving only the blackened branches behind.

Ten months had elapsed since the 'merry prank', and it is not hard to imagine what had happened in that time.

After heedlessness had come the reckoning. Fantine had at once lost touch with Favourite, Zéphine, and Dahlia. The bond broken by the men had been cast aside by the women, and they would have been surprised a fortnight later if anyone had reminded them that they had once been friends, since now their friendship served no purpose. Fantine was left in solitude. Being abandoned by the father of her child – and such partings, alas, are irrevocable – she was thrown entirely on her own resources, having lost the habit of work and gained an aptitude for pleasure. The liaison with Tholomyès had caused her to despise her former calling; she had neglected the employments that had once been open to her and now had lost them. Nothing else was offered. She could scarcely read and could not write, having been taught as a child only to sign her name. She paid a letter-writer to write to Tholomyès, three letters in all, but he did not answer. She heard the street gossips murmur as they looked at her child, 'Does any man worry about these by-blows? They simply shrug their shoulders' – and her heart was hardened towards Tholomyès. What was she to do now, where was she to turn? She had done wrong, but she was essentially modest and virtuous. Perceiving the depth of degradation that threatened her, she had the fortitude to resist it. She resolved to return to her native town, Montreuil-sur-mer, where someone who knew her might give her work. It meant that she would have to conceal the evidence of her wrong-doing, and confusedly she foresaw another separation, even more heartrending than the first. But she held to her resolution. Fantine, as we shall see, possessed great courage in the face of life.

She had already renounced all personal adornment, wearing the plainest clothes and reserving her silks and laces for her daughter, her one remaining vanity and one which she held sacred. She sold all her possessions, which produced two hundred francs, but only eighty remained after her debts were paid. And on a fine spring morning she left Paris, a girl of twenty-two with her baby on her back. Those who saw them pass may well have pitied them. The girl had nothing in the world except her child, the child nothing except her mother. Fantine had breast-fed her, and this had weakened her chest, causing her to cough a little.

We shall have no further occasion to mention Monsieur Félix Tholomyès. It is enough to say that twenty years later, under King Louis-Philippe, he had become an influential, rich, and portly provincial attorney, a prudent voter and stern magistrate; but always a man of pleasure.

In the early afternoon, having travelled a part of the way at the cost of a few sous in one of the small public conveyances which then operated on the outskirts of Paris, Fantine reached Montfermeil and presently found herself in the Ruelle du Boulanger. Passing the Thénardiers' tavern, she had seen the two children on their improvised swing. There are sights which cast a spell, and for the young mother this was one of them. She stood gazing in enchantment, seeming to see in them the pointing finger of Providence itself. They were so evidently happy! Such was her delight that when the mother paused for breath between two lines of her song she could not refrain from murmuring:

'You have two very pretty children.'

The fiercest animals are disarmed by a tribute to their young. The mother thanked her and invited her to sit on the bench by the door while she herself remained seated on the step.

'My name is Thénardier,' she said. 'My husband and I keep this inn.'

This Madame Thénardier was robust, big-boned, and red-headed, a typical soldier's woman with the roughness characteristic of her kind, yet, oddly, with a hint of sentiment, a kind of mannish simper which she owed to her fondness for popular fiction, those fustian romances which cater for the fantasy of shop girls and tavern-wenches. She was still young, not more than thirty. Had she been standing upright, instead of sitting crouched in the doorway, her height and general look of a fair-ground wrestler might have alarmed the stranger and so shaken her confidence as to prevent the events to be related from taking place. Destinies may be decided by the fact that a person is seated and not standing.

Fantine told her story, altering it slightly. She was a working woman whose husband had died, and since she could not find work in Paris she was on her way to look for it in her own part of the country. She had left Paris on foot that morning, had travelled part of the way in a country omnibus and had walked from Villemomble to Montfermeil. Her little girl had walked a part of the way but was still very small; in the end she had had to pick her up, and the poor love had fallen asleep.

As she spoke these words she gave her daughter a most loving kiss, waking her up. The child opened wide eyes as blue as her mother's and gazing at the world saw what? – nothing and everything, with that intent, sometimes stern expression of small children which is among the marvels of their shining innocence, in contrast to our own sullied virtues. It is as though they know themselves to be angels and the rest of us only human. Then she laughed and, although her mother tried to restrain her, wriggled free with the irresistible vigour of a child who wants to be on the move. Seeing the other children on their swing she stopped short and put out her tongue in token of delight. Mme Thénardier lifted the little girls off the swing and said:

'Now you can all play together.'

Friendly relations are soon established at that age. In a matter of minutes the three were busily digging holes in the ground, to their great satisfaction. The newcomer had a self-assured gaiety which reflected her mother's devotion. She had found a scrap of wood to use as a spade and was energetically digging what might have been a mouse's grave – even a gravedigger's work is charming when done by a child.

The two women went on talking.

'What's your little girl's name?'

'Cosette.'

In fact, it was Euphrasie, but the mother had turned it into Cosette by the use of that touching alchemy of simple people which transforms Josef into Pepita and Françoise into Silette. It is a kind of linguistics which baffles the etymologist. We once knew a grandmother who contrived to turn Theodore into Gnon.

'How old is she?'

'Nearly three.'

The little girls were now grouped in a posture of dismay and excitement. Something had happened. They had uncovered a large worm and were at once frightened and ecstatic. Huddled together with their heads touching, they seemed to be enclosed in a halo.

'It's wonderful how quickly children get to know each other,' said Mme Thénardier. 'Look at them. They might all be sisters.'

This, no doubt, was the encouragement the other mother had been hoping for. Taking Mme Thénardier's hand, she turned to her and said:

'Will you look after my daughter for me?'

The Thénardier woman started slightly, expressing neither acceptance nor refusal. Fantine went on:

'I can't take her with me where I'm going. I have to find work, and it's not easy if you have a child. The people in those parts are so absurd. I think it was the hand of God that guided me here. When I saw your children, so happy and clean and pretty, I thought to myself, "That's a good mother." As you say, they would be like sisters. And besides, I shall soon come to fetch her. Will you look after her for me?'

'We shall have to think about it,' said Mme Thénardier.

'I could pay six francs a month.'

At this point a man's voice called from inside the house:

'Not less than seven, and six months in advance.'

'Six times seven makes forty-two,' said Mme Thénardier.

'Very well.'

'And another fifteen francs for extras,' called the man.

'Total, fifty-seven francs,' said the Thénardier woman, and while making the calculation she hummed a few bars of her song.

'You shall have them,' said Cosette's mother. 'I've got eighty francs. I shall still have enough to get me to my own country if I go on foot, and I'll find work and when I've saved a little money I'll come for her.'

The man's voice asked: 'Has she enough clothes?'

'That's my husband,' said Mme Thénardier.

'I guessed as much. Certainly she has enough clothes. She has a beautiful wardrobe, plenty of everything and silk dresses like a lady. They're all in my bag.'

'You'll have to let us have them,' said the man's voice.

'Well, naturally. Did you think I'd leave my daughter to go naked?'

The man's face appeared in the doorway. 'All right,' he said.

And so the bargain was concluded. Fantine stayed the night at the tavern, paid the money, left her daughter and the clothes, and set off next morning with a greatly lightened bag, expecting soon to return. It had happened quietly enough, but such partings are loaded with despair. A neighbour who saw her leave the town said later to Mme Thénardier:

'I've just seen a girl in the street sobbing as though her heart would break.'

The man Thénardier said to his wife: 'Well, that takes care of the bill that falls due tomorrow. I was fifty short. Do you realize I might have been summoned? That was a neat trap you set, you and the kids between you.'

'And not even meaning to,' said the lady.

I I

First sketch of two mean figures

A modest bag, but to the cat even the smallest mouse is better than none.

Who were these Thénardiers?

We may deal with them briefly for the present; the picture will be filled in later.

They belonged to that indeterminate layer of society, sandwiched between the middle and the lower classes, which consists of riff-raff who have risen in the world and more cultivated persons who have sunk, and which combines the worst qualities of both, having neither the generosity of the worker nor the respectable honesty of the bourgeois.

They were dwarfish natures capable of growing into monsters if ill-chance fostered the process. There was a seed of cruelty in the woman and of blackguardism in the man, and both were highly susceptible to the encroachments of evil. There are human creatures which, like crayfish, always retreat into shadow, going backwards rather than forwards through life, gaining in deformity with experience, going from bad to worse and sinking into even deeper darkness. The Thénardiers were of this kind.

The man especially was a problem for the physiognomist. There are men whom we instantly mistrust, sensing the void that encloses them. They are uneasy at their back and threatening in front. They contain an unknown element, so that one cannot answer for what they have done or will do. The shiftiness of their eyes betrays them. To hear them speak or see them move is to catch a glimpse of dingy secrets in the past and dark mystery in the future.

Thénardier, so he said, had been a soldier, a sergeant who, by his own account, had fought bravely in the 1815 campaign. We shall learn in due course what this amounted to. His tavern-sign bore witness to his feats of arms. He had painted it himself, being a Jack-of-all-trades who did everything badly.

It was the period when historical novels with classical settings, ranging from the works of Mademoiselle de Scudéri to those of Madame Barthélemy-Hadot, high-minded in tone but increasingly vulgar in content, were indulging the romantic tastes of Paris concierges and penetrating further afield. Madame Thénardier had just sufficient intelligence to read books of this kind, and she devoured them, soaking in them what little mind she possessed. Because of this she adopted an attitude of romantic subservience towards her husband, who was a ruffian with a gloss of education, at once crude and plausible, but an admirer of the sentimentalities of Pigault-Lebrun and rigidly conventional 'in matters of the fair sex', to use his own words. She was some fifteen years younger than her husband. When later the tearful novelette began to lose its vogue, and Richardson's Pamela was replaced by harridans, she became nothing but a spiteful woman who had revelled in silly fiction. But one cannot be unaffected by that sort of thing. One of its results was that her elder daughter was named Éponine. The younger, having narrowly escaped being called Gulnare, was christened Azelma.

It may be remarked in passing that this particular aspect of the strange period with which we are concerned, what may be termed the anarchy of baptismal names, was not wholly absurd or trivial. It was a social symptom as well as an offshoot of romantic fiction. Farm lads in the present day quite commonly bear such names as Arthur, Alfred and Alphonse, whereas the Vicomte (if vicomtes still exist) is named Thomas, Pierre or Jacques. This reversal whereby the 'elegant' name is bestowed on the rustic and the rustic name on the aristocrat is a manifestation of the spread of equality. The blowing of a new wind is to be felt, here as elsewhere, and behind the paradox we may discern an event of great and profound significance, the French Revolution.

III
The Lark

Mere lack of scruple does not ensure prosperity. The tavern was doing badly.

Thanks to their visitor's fifty-seven francs, Thénardier was able to honour his signature and escape a summons, but a month later they were again short of money. Mme Thénardier took Cosette's wardrobe to Paris and pawned it for sixty francs. When this was spent the couple came to regard her as a charity child and to treat her accordingly. Since she no longer had any clothes of her own she was dressed in the Thénardier children's discarded garments – that is to say, in rags. She was fed on the family leavings, a little better than the dog and rather worse than the cat. Indeed, the cat and dog were her companions, for she ate with them under the table from a wooden bowl like their own.

Fantine, as we shall see in due course, found employment in Montreuil-sur-mer and wrote a monthly letter – or, to be exact, had one written for her – asking for news of her daughter. The Thénardiers invariably replied that Cosette was in splendid health.

When the first six months expired, Fantine sent them the agreed monthly sum of seven francs, and she continued to do so each month. But by the end of the year Thénardier was saying, 'Handsome, isn't it? What's the good of seven francs?' He wrote demanding twelve, and Fantine, being persuaded that her child was happy and 'doing fine', meekly paid up.

There are natures which must compensate for love with hate. Because she doted on her own children, Mme Thénardier came to detest the outsider. It is sad to reflect that mother-love can have its ugly side. Small though the demands were which Cosette made upon her, she felt that they were at the expense of her own children, as though they were being robbed of part of the very air they breathed. Like many women of her kind, she had only a limited store of kindness and malice to bestow. Had it not been for Cosette, her daughters, adored though they were, would have come in for the lot. Thanks to the newcomer, they were spared the blows and only received the caresses. Cosette could scarcely move without bringing on herself a storm of violent and undeserved chastisement. This was the atmosphere she lived in, a gentle, defenceless little creature knowing nothing of the world or of God, constantly nagged at, slapped and punished and seeing in contrast two children like herself who were showered with affection.

Since Mme Thénardier ill-treated Cosette, Éponine and Azelma did the same, imitating their mother as children of that age commonly do.

Thus two years passed.

The village gossips said: 'Those Thénardiers are good people. They're not rich, but they're bringing up a pauper child who was planted on them.' It was believed that Cosette had been abandoned by her mother.

Meanwhile Thénardier, having by some devious means discovered that the child was probably illegitimate, had raised the price to fifteen francs. The *creature*, as he called her, was growing and never stopped eating, and he threatened to return her to her mother. 'She'd better not argue,' he said to his wife, 'or I'll dump the brat on her and give the show away. I've got to have more.' Fantine paid the fifteen francs.

The years went by, the child grew and so did her state of wretchedness. While she was still very small she had served as a scapegoat for the other two; but as she grew older – that is to say, by the time she was five – she became the household drudge.

At the age of five this may seem inconceivable, but alas it is true. Social oppression may begin at any age. Have we not recently witnessed the trial of a youth named Dumolard, an orphan turned thief who, according to the official report, being left destitute at the age of five, 'worked for his living and stole'?

Cosette was made to run errands, scrub floors, sweep the yard and the pavement, wash the dishes and even carry large burdens, and the Thénardiers felt this treatment to be the more justified since her mother, who was still in Montreuil, was no longer paying regularly. She was some months in arrears.

If Fantine had returned to Montfermeil at the end of three years she would not have known her daughter. The bright, pretty child she had left at the inn was now thin and pale-faced. She had a furtive air – 'sly', the Thénardiers said.

Ill-treatment had made her sullen and misery had made her ugly. Only the beauty of her eyes remained, and this was the more distressing because, being large, they mirrored a greater measure of unhappiness. It was heartrending to see her, a child not yet six, shivering in scanty, tattered garments, busy before daybreak on a winter's morning sweeping the pavement outside the house with a broom far too big for her small chapped hands.

She was known locally as *l'Alouette*, the Lark. The village people, with instinctive symbolism, had thought it a suitable name for the apprehensive, trembling little creature, scarcely more than a bird, who was always first up in that house and out of doors before dawn. But this was a lark that never sang.

BOOK FIVE

DEGRADATION

I

A tale of progress in the making of beads

MEANWHILE, WHAT of the mother who, as the people of Montfermeil supposed, had abandoned her child?

After leaving Cosette with the Thénardiers, Fantine had journeyed on to Montreuil-sur-mer. This, we may recall, was in the year 1818.

It was ten years since she had left the district, and in that time things had greatly changed. While she had been sinking into the depths of poverty, her native town had grown prosperous. During the past two years there had occurred one of those industrial developments which are major events in the life of a small community.

We must give some account of this matter, and indeed dwell upon it, since it is of some importance.

The traditional local industry of Montreuil-sur-mer was the manufacture of imitation English jet beads and the 'black glass' of Germany. Because of the cost of raw materials the industry had never been prosperous and its workers had been underpaid, but this situation had recently been transformed. Towards the end of 1815 a newcomer to the town had had the idea of substituting shellac for resin, and had also devised a simpler and less expensive form of clasp for such things as bracelets. These trifling changes amounted to a revolution. They greatly reduced costs, which in the first place enabled the trade to pay higher wages, and thus benefited the district. And they made it possible to reduce prices while increasing the manufacturer's profit. Three beneficial results; and in less than three years the innovator had grown rich, which is good, and had spread prosperity around him, which is better.

He was a stranger to the district. Nothing was known of his origins and little about how he started in life. He was said to have arrived in the town with very little money, a few hundred francs; and with this scanty capital, applied to the service of an ingenious idea and fostered with order and shrewdness, he had made a fortune for himself and for the community.

His clothes, his general appearance and his speech, when he came to Montreuil-sur-mer, had been those of a labourer. But it seems that on the December evening when he unobtrusively entered the town, with a pack on his back and a thorn stick in his hand, a serious fire had broken out in the Town Hall. Plunging into the flames he had, at the risk of his life, rescued two children whose father, as it turned out, was the Captain of Gendarmerie. So no one had asked to see his identity papers. He went by the name of Père Madeleine.

II

Madeleine

He was a man of about fifty, reserved in manner but good-hearted, and this was all that could be said about him.

Thanks to the rapid growth of the industry which he so admirably reorganized, Montreuil-sur-mer became a place of some consequence. Large orders came from Spain, which absorbs a great quantity of jet. Sales reached a scale almost rivalling those of London and Berlin, and Père Madeleine's profits were so great that in the second year he was able to build a new factory consisting of two large workshops, one for men and the other for women. The needy had only to apply, and they could be sure of finding employment and a living wage. Père Madeleine demanded goodwill from the men, pure morals from the women, and honesty from all. He separated the sexes so that the women could remain virtuous. In this he was inflexible, but it was the only matter in which he could be said to be intolerant; and since Montreuil-sur-mer was a garrison town, with ample opportunities for backsliding, his severity was the more justified. In general his coming had been providential for the whole region, once so stagnant, which now pulsed with the vigour of healthy industry. Unemployment and extreme poverty were forgotten. No pocket was so humble that it did not contain a little money, no dwelling so obscure that it did not shelter a little happiness.

Through the stir of activity of which he was the cause and centre, Père Madeleine, as we have said, had made a fortune for himself; but, strangely in a man of business, this did not seem to be his principal concern. He seemed to give far more thought to others than to himself. In 1820 he was known to have a credit of 635,000 francs at the banking-house of Laffitte; but, in addition to setting aside this sum, he had spent more than a million on the town and the poor.

The hospital was under-financed; he had endowed ten more beds. Montreuil was divided into an Upper and a Lower Town. The Lower Town, where he lived, had only one school, of which the ancient building was crumbling in ruins. He built two new schools, one for girls and the other for boys, and out of his own income doubled the meagre official salaries of the schoolmaster and mistress. To someone who expressed surprise at this he said, 'The first two servants of the State are the nurse and the teacher.' He established an old people's home, a thing then almost unknown in France, and a fund for the assistance of old and infirm workpeople. With the building of the new factory, a new residential area had sprung up around it in which there were a good many poor families, so he installed a free apothecary's shop.

At first the town gossips said of him, 'He's simply out to make money.' When it was found that he enriched the community before enriching himself they said, 'He has political ambitions.' This seemed the more likely since he was religious and attended church service, which was considered highly commendable at that time. He went to early mass every Sunday. The local deputy, always on his guard against competition, viewed this religious tendency with some apprehension. He had himself been a member of the *corps législatif* under the Empire, and he shared the religious views of an ex-Jesuit named Fouché, the Duke of Otranto, whose creature and friend he had been. In private he was amiably derisive of God. But when he learned that Madeleine, the wealthy manufacturer, went to seven o'clock mass, he scented a possible rival and resolved to outdo him. He engaged a Jesuit confessor and went to high mass and vespers. Political rivalry in those days was, almost literally, a race to the altar-steps. The poor, as well as God, benefited by the deputy's misgivings, for he also endowed two hospital beds – making twelve in all.

In 1819 it was rumoured in the town that on the recommendation of the prefect, and in consideration of his public services, the king was to nominate M. Madeleine mayor of Montreuil-sur-mer. Those who had declared him to be a political careerist seized upon this with the delight men always feel in exclaiming, 'I told you so.' The town was in a state of high excitement. And the rumour turned out to be correct. A few days later the nomination appeared in *Le Moniteur*. The next day M. Madeleine refused it.

During that same year, 1819, the products of Madeleine's new manufacturing process were displayed at the Industrial Exhibition, and acting on the jury's report the king appointed the inventor to be a *Chevalier* of the Légion d'honneur. This led to a new theory in the town – 'So that's what he was really after!' But M. Madeleine refused to accept the Grand Cross.

Decidedly the man was an enigma. The know-alls saved their faces by saying, 'Well anyway he's up to something.'

The district owed him a great deal and the poor owed him everything. He was so invaluable that he had to be honoured and so kindly that he had to be loved. His workpeople in particular adored him, and he accepted their adoration with a kind of grave melancholy. When it became known that he was extremely rich the 'society' of the town took notice of him, addressing him as Monsieur Madeleine; but his workpeople and the children still called him Père Madeleine, and it was this that drew from him his warmest smile. As he rose in the world, invitations were showered on him. 'Society' sought him out. The doors of Montreuil's most select drawing-rooms, which had of course been closed to the tradesman, were flung wide to welcome the millionaire. Frequent approaches were made to him, but he rejected them all.

And here the gossips were on firmer ground. He was, they said, an ignorant and uneducated man. No one knew where he came from. He would not know how to behave in polite society. It was not even certain that he could read.

When he was seen to be making money they had said, 'He's a business man.' When he scattered his money in charity they said, 'He's a careerist.' When he refused to accept honours they said, 'He's an adventurer.' When he rejected polite society they said, 'He's a peasant.'

By 1820, five years after his arrival in Montreuil-sur-mer, the services he had rendered were so outstanding, and public opinion was so unanimous, that the king again appointed him mayor of the town. Again he refused; but this time, faced by the prefect's rejection of his refusal, the insistence of the local dignitaries and the supplications of the people in the streets, he finally gave way. It was said that what had induced him to change his mind were the words shouted at him almost angrily by an old woman standing in her doorway – 'A good mayor is a useful person. How can you hold back when you have the chance to do good?'

This was the third stage of his rise in the world. 'Le père Madeleine' had become Monsieur Madeleine, and Monsieur Madeleine had become *Monsieur le Maire*.

III

Sums deposited with Laffitte

In other respects he remained as simple as on the day of his arrival. He was grey-haired and grave-eyed, with the tanned complexion of a working man and the thoughtful countenance of a philosopher. He ordinarily wore a broad-brimmed hat and a long tail-coat of broad-cloth buttoned to the chin. He performed his official duties as mayor, but otherwise kept himself to himself, speaking to few people, evading courtesies, exchanging brief greetings and hastily passing on, smiling to avoid the need for speech and giving alms to avoid the need for smiling. The women called him 'a kind old bear'. His greatest pleasure was to go for walks through the countryside.

He always took his meals alone, with a book at his elbow. He had a small but well-selected library. He loved books, those undemanding but faithful friends. It seemed that as his leisure increased with his growing fortune he made use of it to improve himself. His use of language became more refined, less uncouth, and more discriminating.

He often carried a shotgun on his walks but seldom used it. When he did so, however, he was a terrifyingly good marksman. He never killed a harmless animal or shot at a small bird.

Although he was no longer young it was said of him that he was immensely strong. He had a helping hand for whoever needed it, would hoist a fallen horse to its feet, put a shoulder to a bogged-down wheel, grasp the horns of an escaped bull. He always left home with a pocketful of small change and came back with it empty. When he walked through a village the ragged children ran after him in delight, swarming round him like flies.

He must at some time have lived in the country, for he possessed much recondite knowledge which he passed on to the peasants. He taught them how to destroy corn-moth by spraying the barn and soaking the cracks in the floor with a solution of common salt, and how to get rid of boll-weevil by hanging bunches of orviot in blossom on the walls and in the roofs of store-rooms and cottages. He had recipes against vetch and ground-ivy and other parasitic weeds that invade a cornfield. He protected a rabbit-enclosure against rats simply with the scent of a small Barbary pig which he installed in it.

On one occasion he watched a party of countryfolk busily engaged in pulling up nettles. Contemplating the uprooted and withering plants, he said: 'They're dead. But it would be a good thing if use were made of them. The young nettle is an excellent vegetable, and as it ages it develops fibres like those of hemp or flax. Nettle-cloth is as good as hemp-cloth. Chopped nettles can be fed to poultry and mashed nettles are good for cattle; nettle-seed mixed with their fodder gives the animals a glossy skin; the roots mixed with salt produce an admirable yellow dye. Moreover, nettles are a crop that can be harvested twice a year. And they need almost nothing – very little space and no husbanding or cultivation. Their only drawback is that the seed falls as it ripens and is difficult to harvest. With very little trouble nettles can be put to use; being neglected they become obnoxious and are therefore destroyed. How many men share the fate of the nettle!' After a moment of silence he added: 'My friends, remember this, there are no bad plants or bad men. There is only bad husbandry.'

The children loved him especially because he knew how to make fascinating toys out of straw and coconuts.

When he saw a church-door draped in black he entered, seeking out funerals as other men seek out christenings. Widowhood and the afflictions of others appealed to his strongly compassionate nature; he mingled with the mourners and the priests chanting round a coffin. It seemed that the words of the funeral psalms, with their vision of another world, were especially attuned to his thoughts. He listened with eyes uplifted, as though straining towards the mysteries of the infinite, to the sad voices singing on the threshold of the abyss of death.

He performed countless acts of kindness with as much precaution as though they were misdeeds. He would secretly enter a house after dark and go furtively up the stairs; and some poor devil, returning to his attic, would find that his door had been opened, and even forced, in his absence. His instant thought would be that he had been robbed, but then he would find nothing gone and a gold piece lying on the table. The 'miscreant' was Père Madeleine.

He was a friendly but sad figure. People said of him: 'A rich man who is not proud. A fortunate man who does not look happy.'

He was a man of mystery. It was said of him that he allowed no one to enter his bedroom, a real anchorite's cell furnished with winged hour-glasses and decorated with skulls and crossbones. This tale was repeated so often that certain elegant and audacious young ladies called upon him and asked, 'Monsieur le Maire, may we be allowed to see your bedroom? It is said to be like a cave.' He smiled and at once showed them in, putting them greatly out of countenance. It was a room with commonplace mahogany furniture, as ugly as such furniture generally is, and with cheap paper on the walls. They found nothing remarkable in it except two candlesticks of an antiquated design on the mantelpiece, which were presumably silver 'because they were stamped' – an observation very typical of the small-town mind.

But despite this, people went on saying that no one ever entered that room, and that it was like a tomb or a hermit's cave.

It was also rumoured that he had 'immense sums' on deposit with Laffitte, and that by a special arrangement these were held at his immediate disposal, so that he could walk into the bank whenever he chose and after signing a receipt walk out with two or three millions in his pocket. The reality of those 'two or three millions' was, as we have said, a sum of six hundred and thirty or forty thousand francs.

IV

Monsieur Madeleine in mourning

Early in 1821 the newspapers announced the passing of Monsieur Myriel, Bishop of Digne, 'known as Monseigneur Bienvenu', who had died in the odour of sanctity at the age of eighty-two. A detail may be added which the newspapers omitted to mention. For several years prior to his death the bishop had been blind but contented in his blindness, having his sister at his side.

We may remark in passing that to be blind and beloved may, in this world where nothing is perfect, be among the most strangely exquisite forms of happiness. To have a wife, daughter, or sister continually at call, a devoted being who is there because we have need of her and because she cannot live without us; to be able to measure her affection by the constancy of her presence and reflect,

'If she gives me all her time it is because I have all her heart'; to see the thought in default of the face, weigh fidelity in exclusion of the world, hear the rustle of a dress as though it were the rustling of wings, the comings and goings, the everyday speech, the snatch of song; to be conscious every minute of our own attraction, feeling the more powerful for our weakness, becoming in obscurity and through obscurity the star around which an angel gravitates – there are few felicities to equal this. The supreme happiness in life is the assurance of being loved; of being loved for oneself, even in spite of oneself; and this assurance the blind man possesses. In his affliction, to be served is to be caressed. Does he lack anything? No. Possessing love he is not deprived of light. A love, moreover, that is wholly pure. There can be no blindness where there is this certainty. Soul gropes for soul and finds it. And the found and proven soul is a woman. A hand sustains you, and it is hers; lips touch your forehead and they are her lips; the breathing at your side is her breath. To possess her every feeling from devotion to pity, to be never left in solitude, to have the support of that gentle frailty, that slender, unbreakable reed, to feel the touch of Providence in her hands and be able to clasp it in your arms, a palpable God – what happiness can be greater? The heart, that secret, celestial flower, mysteriously blossoms, and one would not exchange one's darkness for all light. The angel spirit is there, always there; if she moves away it is to return, she fades like a dream to reappear like reality. We feel the approaching warmth, and, with its coming, serenity, our gaiety and ecstasy overflow; we are radiant in our darkness. There are the countless small cares, those trifles that become huge in our void. The tenderest tones of the feminine voice are used for our comfort and replace the vanished world; they are a spiritual caress; seeing nothing we feel ourselves adored. It is a paradise in shadow.

This was the paradise from which Monseigneur Bienvenu passed to the other.

His death was reported in the local paper at Montreuil-sur-mer, and on the following day Monsieur Madeleine appeared clad in black with a band of crêpe round his hat. The matter was much discussed in the town since it seemed to throw a light on his background. 'He's in mourning for the Bishop of Digne,' said the drawing-rooms, and this redounded greatly to his credit, entitling him, for the moment, to a higher degree of consideration on the part of the aristocracy of Montreuil-sur-mer. The infinitesimal Faubourg Saint-Germain of the town was disposed to abandon its attitude of aloofness, since he appeared to be related to a bishop. Monsieur Madeleine was made aware of his promotion by an increase in the number of curtsies he received from the older ladies and smiles from the younger ones. One evening a dowager of that small circle, entitled by her ancient lineage to be inquisitive, ventured to question him. 'No doubt, Monsieur le Maire, the late Bishop of Digne was your cousin?'

'No, Madame.'

'But,' said the lady, 'you are in mourning for him.'

He replied: 'That is because in my youth I was a lackey in his family.'

It was also noted that whenever a vagrant boy appeared in the town looking for chimneys to sweep, the mayor sent for him, asked his name and gave him money. The word went round among the young 'Savoyards' and a great many of them came.

V

Flickers on the horizon

By degrees all opposition to him had died down. At first M. Madeleine had been subjected to the ill-report and calumny that by a sort of law afflict all those who become prominent; this had gradually dwindled into malicious anecdote and gossip which at length had ceased entirely. Respect and cordial esteem for him had grown until, in about 1821, the words Monsieur le Maire were spoken in Montreuil-sur-mer in much the same tone as the words Monseigneur l'Evêque had been spoken in Digne in 1815. People came from twenty miles around to consult Monsieur Madeleine. He resolved disputes, prevented law-suits, reconciled enemies. Every man trusted him to judge fairly, as though his guiding spirit were a book of natural law. It was like an epidemic of veneration spreading, in a matter of six or seven years, throughout the province.

One man only was wholly immune from the contagion and, regardless of what M. Madeleine did, refused to succumb to it as though from an unassailable instinct of wariness and distrust. It seems indeed that there exists in some men a genuinely animal instinct, pure and authentic as are all instincts, which determines their antipathies and sympathies, inexorably discriminating between one person and another without hesitation or afterthought, neither weakening nor contradicting itself; which is lucid within its own obscurity, infallible and overweening, rejecting every counsel of intelligence and every compromise of reason, and which, disdaining all outward appearances, secretly warns the man-dog of the presence of the man-cat, the man-fox of the presence of the man-lion.

It happened often that Monsieur Madeleine, walking amiably through the streets and receiving the affectionate greetings of his fellow-citizens, was observed by a tall man in a grey tail-coat carrying a heavy stick and wearing a low-brimmed hat. This person would watch him until he was out of sight, standing with arms crossed, slowly shaking his head and thrusting his lower lip against the upper until it reached his nose in a sort of purposeful grimace which seemed to say, 'Who is that man? I've seen him before. Anyway, he isn't fooling me.'

He was one of those people who, even glimpsed, make an immediate impression; there was an intensity about him that was almost a threat. His name was Javert and he belonged to the police.

In Montreuil-sur-mer he performed the distasteful but necessary duties of a police-inspector. He had not witnessed Madeleine's beginnings. When he took up his present post, which he owed to the influence of the Paris Prefect of Police, the manufacturer's fortune was already made and Père Madeleine had become Monsieur Madeleine.

Certain police officers have a particular cast of countenance in which primitive instincts are mingled with an air of authority. Javert had the air of authority, but without the primitive instincts.

It is our belief that if the soul were visible to the eye every member of the human species would be seen to correspond to some species of the animal world and a truth scarcely perceived by thinkers would be readily confirmed, namely, that from the oyster to the eagle, from the swine to the tiger, all animals are to be found in men and each of them exists in some man, sometimes several at a time.

Animals are nothing but the portrayal of our virtues and vices made manifest to our eyes, the visible reflections of our souls. God displays them to us to give us food for thought. But since they are no more than shadows, He has not made them educable in the full sense of the word – Why should He do so? Our souls, on the other hand, being realities with a purpose proper to themselves, have been endowed with intelligence, that is to say, the power to learn. Well-managed social education can extract from any human spirit, no matter of what kind, such usefulness as it contains.

This, of course, is to confine the matter within the limits of our visible earthly life, without prejudging the deeper question of the anterior and ulterior nature of creatures which are not men. The visible personality affords us no grounds for denying the existence of a latent personality. Having made this reservation, we may proceed.

Granted the supposition that in every man there is contained a species of the animal kingdom, we may at once place Inspector Javert. The Asturian peasants believe that in every wolf-litter there is a dog-whelp which the mother kills, because otherwise when it grows larger it will devour the rest of her young. Endow this dog with a human face, and you have Javert.

He had been born in prison, the son of a fortune-teller whose husband was in the galleys. As he grew older he came to believe that he was outside society with no prospect of ever entering it. But he noted that there were two classes of men whom society keeps inexorably at arm's length – those who prey upon it, and those who protect it. The only choice open to him was between those two. At the same time, he was a man with a profound instinct for correctitude, regularity, and probity, and with a consuming hatred for the vagabond order to which he himself belonged. He joined the police.

He did well. At the age of forty he was an inspector, having as a young man been a prison-warder in the Midi. But before going further let us look more closely at the human face which we have ascribed to Javert.

It consisted of a flat nose with two wide nostrils flanked by huge side-whiskers. A first glance at those two thickets enclosing two caverns was disconcerting. When Javert laughed, a rare and terrible occurrence, his thin lips parted to display not only his teeth but his gums, and a deep and savage furrow formed on either side of his nose as though on the muzzle of a beast of prey. Javert unsmiling was a bulldog; when he laughed he was a tiger. For the rest – a narrow brow and a large jaw, locks of hair concealing the forehead and falling over the eyebrows, permanent wrinkles between the eyes resembling a star of wrath, a dark gaze, a tight, formidable mouth, a look of fierce command.

His mental attitude was compounded of two very simple principles, admirable in themselves but which, by carrying them to extremes, he made almost evil – respect for authority and hatred of revolt against it. Theft, murder and every other crime were to him all forms of revolt. Everybody who played any part in the running of the State, from the First Minister to the *garde champêtre*, was invested in his eyes with a kind of mystical sanctity, and he felt nothing but contempt, aversion and disgust for those who, even if only once, transgressed beyond the bounds of law. His judgements were absolute, admitting no exceptions. He said on the one hand, 'The official cannot be wrong, the magistrate is always right,' and on the other hand, 'Those others are lost, no good can come of them.' He shared unreservedly the extreme views of those who attribute to human law some sort of power to damn or, if you prefer, to place on record the damned, and who set a river Styx at the entrance to society. He was stoical, earnest and austere, given to gloomy pondering, and like all fanatics, both humble and arrogant. His eyes were cold and piercing as a gimlet. His whole life was contained in two words, wakefulness and watchfulness. He drew a straight line through all that is most tortuous in this world. He possessed the conscience appropriate to his function, and his duties were his religion; he was a spy in the way that other men are priests. Woe to those who fell into his hands! He would have arrested his own father escaping from prison and denounced his mother for breaking parole, and he would have done it with a glow of conscious rectitude. His life was one of rigorous austerity, isolation, self-denial and chastity without distractions; a life of unswerving duty, with the police service playing the role that Sparta played for the Spartans – ceaseless alertness, fanatical honesty, the spy carved in marble, a mingling of Brutus and Vidocq.*

Javert's entire personality was that of the man who watches from concealment. The mystical school of Joseph de Maistre, which at that time was enriching the extreme monarchist journals with a high-flown cosmogony, would certainly have regarded him as a symbol.

* The ex-criminal who became chief of police and on whose Memoirs, published in 1828, Balzac based the character of Vautrin.

Normally, one could never see his forehead, hidden by his hat, his eyes buried beneath his eyebrows, his chin sunk in his cravat, his hands drawn up within his sleeves or the stick which he carried beneath his cloak. But when the time was ripe all this would spring out of hiding as though from an ambush, the narrow, bony forehead, the baleful glare, the menacing chin, the big hands and threatening cudgel.

In his rare leisure moments he read books, although he hated reading; which is to say that he was not wholly illiterate. The fact was now and then apparent in his speech. As we have said, he had no vices. When he was pleased with himself he allowed himself a pinch of snuff, his sole concession to human frailty.

It is small wonder that Javert was the terror of that class of people who are listed in the annual statistics of the Ministry of Justice as *Gens sans aveu*, persons without status. The mere mention of his name sufficed to scatter them; the sight of him petrified them. Such was this formidable man.

Javert had an eye constantly fixed on Monsieur Madeleine, an eye filled with suspicion and puzzlement. Madeleine had eventually become aware of this, but he seemed to regard it as a matter of no importance. He never questioned Javert, neither sought him out nor avoided him, and bore his heavy scrutiny without appearing to notice it, treating him, as he treated everyone, with an easy good-humour.

From certain words Javert had let fall it was evident that secretly, with the inquisitiveness of his kind which is as much a matter of instinct as of deliberate intent, he had studied all the traces of his earlier life which Monsieur Madeleine had left in other places. He seemed to know, and hinted as much, that someone had been making inquiries in another part of the country regarding a family that had disappeared. He was once heard to mutter to himself, 'I think I've got him.' But after that he was moodily silent. It seemed that the thread he had thought to grasp was broken.

For the rest, and the qualification is necessary for words that may otherwise bear too absolute a meaning, there can be nothing truly infallible in any human being, and instinct, of its nature, may be confused, misled, and perverted. Otherwise it would be superior to intelligence, and animals would be more enlightened than men.

Javert was plainly disconcerted by Monsieur Madeleine's ease and tranquillity of manner, but an occasion arose when his own strange demeanour attracted the notice of Monsieur Madeleine. What happened was as follows.

VI

Père Fauchelevent

Passing one morning through one of the unpaved alleys of the town Madeleine heard sounds of disturbance and saw a group of people gathered not far away. He found, on going up to them, that an old man known as Père Fauchelevent had been trapped beneath his cart after the horse had fallen.

Fauchelevent was one of the few people who at that time were still unfriendly to Monsieur Madeleine. A former law-scrivener, comparatively educated for a countryman, his business had already been going downhill when Madeleine arrived in the district. He had watched the rise of the humble day-labourer while he, a craftsman, was on the road to ruin, and, consumed with jealousy, had done what he could to injure Madeleine whenever the chance arose. Eventually he had gone bankrupt and being an elderly man without wife or family, possessing nothing but a horse and cart, he had since then earned his living as a carrier.

The horse had broken both hind-legs and could not get up. Fauchelevent was caught between the wheels. The manner of the fall was such that the whole weight of the heavily loaded cart was on his chest. Attempts had been made to drag him clear, but without success. An ill-judged, clumsy movement, a sudden pull of the cart, might crush him. There was no way of releasing him except by lifting the cart from below. Javert, who was already on the spot, had sent for a jack.

The crowd drew back respectfully as Madeleine approached. He at once asked if a jack was available and was told that someone had gone for one to the nearest smithy, but that it would take a quarter of an hour to bring it.

'A quarter of an hour!' exclaimed Madeleine.

It had rained hard the day before; the ground was very soft and the cart was sinking deeper into the mud, pressing more heavily on the old man's chest. In a matter of minutes his ribs might give way.

'This can't wait a quarter of an hour,' said Madeleine, turning to the men standing round.

'There's nothing else to be done.'

'But it'll be too late. Don't you see the cart's sinking deeper?'

'All the same –'

'Look,' said Madeleine. 'There's still room for a man to crawl under the cart and lift it on his back. In half a minute the old man can be pulled out. Is there anyone here with the muscle and the heart? I'm offering five louis d'or.'

No one moved.

'Ten,' said Madeleine.

The bystanders avoided his gaze. One of them muttered: 'He'd have to be devilish strong. He'd risk being crushed himself.'

'Come!' said Madeleine. 'Twenty.'

There was still no response.

'It's not that we don't want to,' a voice said.

Monsieur Madeleine turned and recognized Javert. He had not noticed him before.

'It's a question of strength,' Javert went on. 'You need to be tremendously strong to lift a load like that on your back.' With his eyes fixed upon Madeleine he said slowly: 'I have known only one man, Monsieur Madeleine, capable of doing what you ask.' Madeleine started. Still with his eyes upon him, Javert added casually: 'He was a convict.'

'Ah,' said Madeleine.

'In Toulon prison.'

Madeleine turned pale.

Meanwhile the cart was sinking and Père Fauchelevant was gasping and crying: 'I'm suffocating. My ribs are breaking. For God's sake, do something!'

Madeleine looked about him. 'Is there no one prepared to save this man's life for twenty louis d'or?'

No one moved. Javert repeated: 'I have known only one man capable of doing the work of a jack. The man I mentioned.'

'It's crushing me,' the old man cried.

Madeleine hesitated for another instant, met the vulture gaze of Javert, looked round at the motionless bystanders, and smiled sadly. Without a word he went on his knees and before anyone could speak was under the cart.

There was a moment of hideous uncertainty and silence. Madeleine, almost flat on his stomach beneath that terrifying weight, was seen to make two fruitless efforts to bring his elbows and knees together. A voice cried, 'Père Madeleine, come out of there!' Old

Fauchelevent himself cried: 'Go away, Monsieur Madeleine! I'm done for. Let me be or you'll be killed too.' Madeleine said nothing.

The onlookers stood breathless. The cart wheels were still sinking and it was already almost impossible for Madeleine to extricate himself.

Then suddenly the cart with its load was seen to rise slowly upward, its wheels half emerging from the quagmire. Crying in a stifled voice, 'Hurry up! Help me!' Madeleine made his supreme effort.

There was a sudden rush. The gallantry of a single man had lent strength and courage to all. The cart was lifted by ten pairs of arms and old Fauchelevent was saved.

Madeleine got to his feet. He was white although his face was running with sweat. His clothes were torn and caked with mud. The old man clasped him round the knees invoking the name of God. His own expression was an indescribable mingling of distress and triumph, and he gazed calmly back at Javert, who was still fixedly regarding him.

VII

Fauchelevent becomes a gardener in Paris

Fauchelevent had broken a knee-cap in his fall. Monsieur Madeleine had him taken to the infirmary, served by two Sisters of Mercy, which he had set up in his factory for the benefit of his workers. On the following morning the old man found a thousand-franc note on the bedside-table, with a note in Madeleine's handwriting – 'I am buying your horse and cart.' The cart was damaged and the horse was dead. Fauchelevent recovered, but with a permanently stiff knee. Acting on the advice of the sisters and the curé, Madeleine got him a job as gardener in a convent in the Saint-Antoine quarter of Paris.

Shortly after this Monsieur Madeleine was elected mayor, and when for the first time Javert saw him wearing the robes which vested him with full authority over the town, a tremor went through him like that of a hound which scents a wolf in sheep's clothing. Thereafter he avoided him whenever possible, and when his duties obliged him to have direct dealings with the mayor he addressed him in terms of the utmost formality.

In addition to the outward signs we have described of the prosperity brought to the town by Père Madeleine, there was a further indication which was not the less significant for being invisible. It was a sure sign. When people are in trouble, because work is short and trade is bad, the tax-payer uses every device to resist and evade payment, and the State is put to considerable expense to collect its dues. When on the other hand a region is prosperous and work abundant, taxes are easily paid and the cost of collecting them is small. It may be said, indeed, that the cost of tax-collection affords an infallible index of the poverty or wealth of a community. During a period of seven years this charge on the authorities in the Montreuil-sur-mer district had fallen by three-quarters, a fact to which the Minister of Finance, Monsieur de Villèle, made frequent reference.

Such was the state of affairs when Fantine returned to the town. No one remembered her, but fortunately the doors of Madeleine's factory were open. She found employment in the women's workshop. The work was new to her and she was not very good at it. Nor was the pay large but it sufficed to solve her problem; it brought her a living.

VIII

Madame Victurnien spends thirty-five francs in the cause of morality

When Fantine found that she could make ends meet she had a moment of rejoicing. To be able to live by honest toil was like a blessing from Heaven. Her natural readiness to work was genuinely revived. She bought a mirror, gazed with pleasure at her youth, her beautiful hair and white teeth, forgot a great many things, dreamed only of Cosette and her plans for the future, and was almost happy. She rented a small room and furnished it on credit against her future earnings – a survival of her disorderly habits.

Not being able to claim that she was married, she was careful to say nothing about her daughter. At first, as we have seen, she was meticulous in her payments to the Thénardiers. Since she could only sign her name she had resort to a public letter-writer. She sent frequent letters, and the fact was noted. It was whispered in the women's workshop that she 'gave herself airs'.

No one is more avidly curious about other people's doings than those persons whom they do not concern. Why is a certain gentleman only to be seen at dusk, and why is another always away on Thursdays? Why does so-and-so always go by the back streets? Why does a certain lady always dismiss her fiacre before reaching home, and why does she send out for note-paper when she has plenty already? And so on. There are people who are prepared to devote as much time and resources to the answering of these riddles as would suffice for a dozen good deeds; and quite gratuitously, with inquisitiveness its own reward. They will follow a person for days, keep watch at street corners and from doorways, at night, in cold and rain; they will bribe hall-porters, tip cab-drivers and lackeys, suborn chambermaids. And for what? For nothing. For the satisfaction of finding out, knowing and unravelling; from an itch to disclose. And it can happen that these broadcast secrets, mysteries exposed to the light of day, are the cause of disaster – duels, bankruptcies, ruined families, wrecked lives – to the delight of those who 'got to the bottom of it', from no personal interest, from instinct alone. It is a sad phenomenon.

There are persons whose malice is prompted by the sheer need to gossip. Their conversation – drawing-room chatter, antechamber asides – resembles a wide hearth of the kind that rapidly burns up logs. They need plenty of fuel, and their fuel is their neighbour.

So Fantine's doings were observed; besides which, some of the women were jealous of her golden hair and white teeth.

It was noted by the women in the workshop that at times she turned her head to wipe away a tear. They were moments when she was suddenly reminded of her child, and perhaps also of the man she had loved; the breaking of links with the past is a painful thing.

It was discovered that she sent at least two letters a month, always to the same address, paying the postage in advance. The name of her correspondent was also discovered – Monsieur Thénardier, inn-keeper at Montfermeil. The letter-writer, an elderly man who could not keep his mouth shut when his stomach was filled, was plied with wine in an ale-house, and so it became known that Fantine had a child. 'So that's the kind of woman she is!' A townswoman made the journey to Montfermeil, talked to Thénardier and on her return reported as follows: 'It cost me thirty-five francs but now I know everything. I've seen the child.'

The lady in question was a Madame Victurnien, an inflexible guardian of public morals. She was fifty-six and bore a countenance of mingled age and ugliness, with a shaky voice and a lively mind. Strange though it may seem, she had once been young. In the year '93 she had married a monk who had exchanged the tonsure for the red bonnet, going over from the Bernardins to the Jacobins. Dry, withered, acid, thorny, malicious, and venomous, she still lived on the memory of her departed monk, who had ruled her with a rod of iron. After the Restoration she had become a religious bigot, to the point that the priests had forgiven her her monk. She possessed a small property which she had ostentatiously bequeathed to a religious community, and she enjoyed the favour of the Bishop of Arras. This Madame Victurnien, then, went to Montfermeil and came back saying, 'I have seen the child.'

This was the month when Thénardier, having already raised the price from seven francs to twelve, raised it again to fifteen.

Fantine's case was hopeless. She could not leave the district because she owed money for her rent and furniture, a sum of about one hundred and fifty francs. She went and begged the workshop supervisor for money, who gave it to her but forthwith dismissed her; she had, in any case, been an indifferent worker. Overwhelmed by shame even more than by despair, she left the factory and took refuge in her room. Her fault was now known to everyone. She lacked the courage to plead her cause and did not venture to approach the mayor although she was advised to do so. The mayor, by way of the supervisor, had given her fifty francs because he was kind, and had sent her away because he was just. She accepted the verdict.

IX

Madame Victurnien's success

So the monk's widow had proved her worth.

As for Monsieur Madeleine, he knew nothing whatever about the matter. Life is made up of these confusions. On principle Madeleine almost never entered the women's workshop, having placed at its head an elderly spinster recommended to him by the curé. He had every confidence in his supervisor, a thoroughly respectable, honest woman, firm but fair-minded, imbued with the charity which is ready to give but possessing less of the charity which understands and pardons. He trusted her in everything. The best of men are often obliged to delegate their authority; and it was in the full assurance that she was acting rightly that the supervisor had tried the case of Fantine, given judgement and pronounced sentence. The fifty francs came from a fund which Monsieur Madeleine had placed at her disposal for the relief of employees in difficulties, and for which she was not required to account in detail.

Fantine tried to find work as a servant, but no one would take her. She could not leave the town. The second-hand dealer who had supplied her furniture – and such furniture! – said to her, 'If you do I'll have you arrested as a thief.' Her landlord, to whom she owed rent, said, 'You're young and pretty, you can pay.' She divided the fifty francs between them, returned three-quarters of the furniture, keeping only the bare essentials, and found herself without work or status, possessing nothing but a bed and still owing about a hundred francs.

She did piecework stitching of shirts for the soldiers of the garrison, which brought her in twelve sous a day. Her child cost ten sous. This was when she began to fall behind in her payments to the Thénardiers.

An old woman who lived in the house taught her the art of living in penury. There are two stages – living on little, and living on nothing. They are like two rooms, the first dark, the second pitch-black.

Fantine learned how to dispense entirely with a fire in winter, how to give up the tame bird which eats a handful of seed a day, how to turn a petticoat into a blanket and a blanket into a petticoat, and how to save candles by eating by the light from the window across the street. The rest of us have little notion of the use that a fragile being, grown old in privation and honesty, can make of a single sou. It becomes a talent in the end, one that Fantine acquired and with it a regrowth of courage.

She said to her neighbour: 'Well, what I say is, if I only sleep five hours a night and work the rest of the time I can just about earn enough to live on. And when you're unhappy you eat less. So what with work and not much food on the one hand, and grieving on the other, I can keep alive.'

To have had her child with her in her distress would have been happiness of a kind. She thought of sending for her. But was she to make her share her own destitution? And then, she owed money to Thénardier. How was that debt to be paid, and how pay the cost of the journey?

The old spinster who had instructed her in what may be termed the art of poverty was named Marguerite. She was truly devout, poor herself and charitable not only to the poor but also to the rich, just sufficiently educated to be able to sign her name 'Margueritte', and firm in her trust in God, which is the root of wisdom. There are many such virtuous souls in the depths who will one day rise higher; they are lives which have a tomorrow.

At first Fantine had been so overcome by shame that she had been afraid to leave the house. She felt in the streets that everyone looked at her; the heads turned but no one greeted her; and this ostracism pierced her like a keen wind, body and soul. In a small town the fallen woman is as it were exposed naked to the scorn and prying eyes of all-comers. In Paris she is at least unknown, and her anonymity is a garment. Fantine would have given all she possessed to be able to take refuge in Paris, but it was impossible. She had to learn to endure disdain as she learned to accustom herself to penury, and by degrees she did so. In two or three months she had shrugged off her shame and went about as though nothing had happened, pretending not to care. She came and went with her head held high and a bitter smile on her lips, and felt that she was becoming brazen.

Madame Victurnien, seeing her pass beneath her window and noting the wretched condition of the 'creature' who thanks to her public spirit had been 'put in her place', was highly gratified. The cruel of heart have their own black happiness.

Excess of work exhausted Fantine, and the small, dry cough from which she suffered grew worse. She said sometimes to Marguerite, 'Feel how hot my hands are.'

But in the mornings, combing with a broken comb the hair that flowed like silk over her shoulders, she still had moments of happy vanity.

X

Continued success of Madame Victurnien

Fantine had been dismissed at the end of the winter. She survived the summer, but then came the next winter, shorter days and shorter working hours. Winter! No warmth, no light, no midday, morning merging into evening, fog, twilight, and nothing to be clearly seen through the misted window. The sky had become a grating, the day a cellar, the sun a poor man at the door. The terrible winter season, which turns the rain from Heaven and the hearts of men to stone! Fantine's creditors were harassing her.

She could not earn enough and her debts grew. The Thénardiers bombarded her with letters, heartrending in tone and ominous in their exactions. They wrote to say that Cosette was obliged to go almost naked in the cold and that at least ten francs were needed to buy her a woollen dress. Receiving this letter, Fantine carried it crumpled in her hand throughout the day, and in the evening went to the barber at the corner of the street and withdrew her comb, letting her fair hair fall down to her waist.

'Such beautiful hair!' said the barber.

'What will you give me for it?' she asked.

'Ten francs.'

'Then cut it off.'

She bought a woollen dress and sent it to the Thénardiers, who were furious. The money was what they wanted. They gave the dress to their daughter Éponine, and the little lark, Cosette, went on shivering.

'My daughter's not cold any more,' thought Fantine. 'I have dressed her in my hair.' She wore small mob-caps to hide her shorn head and still looked pretty.

But a dark change was taking place within her. Now that she could no longer do up her hair she conceived a hatred for all mankind. She had long shared the universal veneration for Père Madeleine, but now, by dint of telling herself that he had dismissed her and was the cause of all her troubles, she came to hate him more than any man. When she passed the factory gates at the time when the workers were waiting to be let in she affected to sing and laugh derisively, which caused one old woman to remark, 'There's a wench that'll come to a bad end.'

In a spirit of defiance, and with fury in her heart, she took a lover, a chance acquaintance for whom she cared nothing. He was some sort of travelling musician, indolent and feckless. He beat her and finally left her, as repelled as she was herself.

But still she worshipped her child. The deeper she sank, the darker the shades that closed about her, the more radiant did that vision appear. 'Someday I'll be rich and have Cosette with me,' she said to herself, and this alone could cause her to smile. The cough did not get better and she had night sweats.

The following letter came from the Thénardiers:

'Cosette has caught the disease that is sweeping through the region, what they call a miliary fever. The medicine is very expensive. It is ruining us and we can no longer pay. If you do not send us forty francs within a week the child will die.'

This caused Fantine to burst into hysterical laughter, and she said to Marguerite:

'How wonderful! A mere forty francs! Two napoléons. Where do they expect me to get them? Are they mad?'

She re-read the letter standing by a window on the landing, and then, still laughing, ran downstairs and out into the street. To someone who asked what she found so funny she replied:

'A silly joke in a letter I've just had from some country people. They want forty francs from me, the poor, ignorant peasants!'

Crossing the market-square she saw a crowd gathered round a strangely shaped vehicle from which a man clad in red was addressing them. He was an itinerant dentist selling sets of false teeth, opiates, powders, and elixirs. Drawing closer, Fantine joined in the laughter at his oratory, in which slang for the common people was interlarded with highflown language for the well-to-do; and seeing her laugh, the dentist cried:

'You've got a fine set of teeth, my lass. If you'd care to sell me your two incisors I'll pay you a gold napoléon for each.'

'What are my incisors?'

'Your two top front teeth.'

'How horrible!' exclaimed Fantine.

'Two napoléons,' grumbled a toothless old woman standing near. 'She's in luck!'

Fantine fled, covering her ears to shut out the man's hoarse voice as he shouted after her:

'Think it over, my girl. Two napoléons are worth having. If you change your mind you'll find me this evening at the Tillac d'argent.'

Fantine ran home in a fury of indignation and told Marguerite what had happened.

'Would you believe it! The abominable man – how can they allow such creatures to travel round the country? He wanted to pull my two front teeth out. I should be hideous! Hair grows again, but not teeth. Oh, the monster! I'd sooner throw myself out of a top-storey window. He said he'd be at the Tillac d'argent this evening.'

'How much did he say he'd pay?' asked Marguerite.

'Two napoléons.'

'That's forty francs.'

'Yes,' said Fantine. 'That's forty francs.'

She went thoughtfully on with her work. After a quarter of an hour she stopped sewing and went on to the landing to re-read the Thénardiers' letter. She returned and said to Marguerite:

'What is this miliary fever? Have you heard of it?'

'Yes,' said the old woman. 'It's an illness.'

'Does it need a lot of medicine?'

'Yes, very strong medicine.'

'How do you get it?'

'It's just an illness that you catch.'

'And children catch it?'

'Especially children.'

'Do they die of it?'

'Very often,' said Marguerite.

Fantine left the room and went on to the landing to read the letter again. That evening she went out and was seen hurrying in the direction of the Rue de Paris, where the inns are.

When Marguerite entered Fantine's room next morning, doing so before daybreak because they always worked together and thus could share a candle, she found her seated cold and shivering on her bed. She had not been to bed. She was sitting with her bonnet on her knees, and the candle, which had been burning all night, was almost burned away.

Standing horror-stricken in the doorway, Marguerite cried:

'Heavens! You've used up a whole candle! What has happened?'

Fantine turned her cropped head towards her, and it seemed that she had aged ten years overnight.

'Lord preserve us!' cried Marguerite. 'What's the matter with you?'

'Nothing is the matter with me,' said Fantine. 'I'm happy. My baby isn't going to die of that dreadful disease for lack of medicine.'

She pointed to two napoléons that lay gleaming on the table.

'A fortune,' murmured Marguerite. 'A fortune! Where did you get them?'

'I earned them,' said Fantine.

She smiled as she said it, and the candle lighted her face. It was a bloodstained smile. There were flecks of blood at the corners of her mouth and a wide gap beneath her upper lip.

She sent the forty francs to Montfermeil.

Needless to say, the Thénardiers were lying. Cosette was not ill.

Fantine threw away her mirror. She had long since exchanged her small room on the second floor for an attic under the sloping roof, against the beams of which she constantly bumped her head. Paupers cannot reach the end of their abode, or of their destiny, except by crouching ever lower. She no longer possessed a bed but only a mattress on the floor, a tattered blanket and a rickety chair. A potted rose in one corner of the room had died of neglect. In another corner was a butter-tub which served as a water bucket; the water froze in winter, and its different levels were marked during long periods by rings of ice. She had lost all shame and was losing all personal pride. She wore soiled bonnets in the street and, from lack of time or from indifference, no longer mended her under-garments. As the heels of her stockings wore out she stuffed the stockings down into her shoes, a fact which was apparent from their wrinkles. She patched her old, worn stays with fragments of calico which tore at the least strain. The people to whom she owed money allowed her no peace, making scenes in the street and on the stairway. She spent whole nights in tears and brooding, her eyes overbright and with a constant pain in her back, at the top of her left shoulder-blade. She coughed a great deal. Profoundly hating Père Madeleine, she uttered no complaint against him. She stitched seventeen hours a day; but a contractor for prison labour, who was able to get the work done more cheaply, brought the free workers' daily wage down to nine sous. Nine sous for seventeen hours work! Her creditors became more insatiable than ever, the second-hand dealer, who had got back nearly all his furniture, never stopped badgering her. In God's name, what more could she do? Feeling hunted, she developed some of the instincts of a wild beast. And then Thénardier wrote to say that his patience was at an end and that if she did not send a hundred francs forthwith he would be obliged to turn Cosette out into the street, still convalescent after her grave illness, to fend for herself amid the rigours of the season and live or die as the case might be.

A hundred francs! In what calling was it possible to earn a hundred sous a day? There was only one. 'Well,' thought Fantine, 'I may as well sell the rest.'

She became a prostitute.

Christus nos liberavit

What is the true story of Fantine? It is the story of society's purchase of a slave. A slave purchased from poverty, hunger, cold, loneliness, defencelessness, destitution. A squalid bargain: a human soul for a hunk of bread. Poverty offers and society accepts.

Our society is governed by the precepts of Jesus Christ but is not yet imbued with them. We say that slavery has vanished from European civilization, but this is not true. Slavery still exists, but now it applies only to women and its name is prostitution.

It afflicts women, that is to say, it preys on grace, frailty, beauty, motherhood. It is not the least of man's shames.

At the sad point which our tale has now reached there is nothing left of the girl who was once Fantine. In becoming dirt, she has been turned to stone. To touch her is to feel a chill. She submits to and ignores the customer; she is the unmoving countenance of the dishonoured. Life and the social order have said their last word to her; everything has happened to her that can happen. She has known everything, borne and suffered everything, lost everything and shed her last tear. She is resigned with the resignation that resembles indifference as death resembles sleep. She no longer seeks to escape from anything, nor does she fear anything. Let the heavens fall, let the tides of the sea engulf her, and what can it matter, she has had her fill.

Or so she believes, but it is an error to suppose that we can ever exhaust Fate or reach the end of anything. What is the riddle of these countless scattered destinies, whither are they bound, why are they as they are?

He who knows the answer to this knows all things. He is alone. His name is God.

XII

The idleness of Monsieur Bamatabois

In every small town, and this was particularly so in Montreuil-sur-mer, there is a class of young men who squander an income of fifteen hundred francs in the provinces much as their peers in Paris squander an income of two hundred thousand. They belong to the great species of neuters, the geldings, parasites, nonentities who own a little land, a little silliness, and a little wit; who would look like clods in a fashionable salon but think themselves gentlemen in a tavern; who talk about 'my fields and my peasants', who boo actresses in the theatre to prove themselves men of taste, pick quarrels with the officers of the garrison to prove that they are men of spirit, shoot, smoke, yawn, drink, smell of tobacco, play billiards, watch the travellers descending from the stage-coach, live in the café, dine at the inn, own a dog which eats scraps under the table and a mistress who sets the dishes on top of it, watch their pennies, carry current fashions to the extreme, patronize the drama, despise women, wear out their old boots, copy London by way of Paris and Paris by way of Pont-à-Mousson, and grow old and feeble-minded having never worked or served any purpose or done any great harm.

Monsieur Félix Tholomyès, had he stayed in the provinces and never come to Paris, would have been one of these.

Richer, they would be called bucks or fops; poorer, they would be vagabonds. They are simply idlers, boring or bored or day-dreaming idlers, with a few wags among them.

At that period a fop sported a high collar, a spreading cravat, a watch with a fob, three superimposed waistcoats of different colours, the blue and the red being underneath, a high-waisted, olive-coloured, fish-tailed coat with a double row of silver buttons sewn close together and rising up to the shoulders, and trousers of a lighter olive adorned with pleats on either side, always an equal number ranging from one to eleven, this limit being never exceeded. To which may be added low boots with metal heelcaps, a narrow-brimmed tall hat, a very large cane and conversation sparkling with witticisms borrowed from Potier of the Théâtre des Variétés. Above all, spurs and a moustache. The moustache in those days was the hallmark of a civilian, the spurs were the mark of a pedestrian. The provincial fop wore longer spurs and a bushier moustache.

It was the period of the struggle of the South American republics against Spain, of Bolívar against Morillo. The narrow-brimmed hats, indicative of monarchist sympathies, were called *morillos*. Liberals wore broad-brimmed hats called *bolivars*.

Some eight or ten months after the events just recorded, on a snowy evening at the beginning of January 1824, one of these elegant idlers, a gentleman of orthodox opinions, for he was wearing a *morillo* and was in addition warmly clad in the sort of greatcoat that completed the fashionable costume in cold weather, was exercising his wit at the expense of a woman in a low-cut evening-gown with flowers in her hair who was prowling to and fro outside the officers' café.

The gentleman was smoking, this being highly fashionable. Each time the woman passed, he blew a cloud of smoke in her direction and favoured her with a fresh sally reflecting on her looks, her attire and anything else that occurred to him. The name of the gentleman was Monsieur Bamatabois. The woman, a sad and garish ghost coming and going through the snow, paid no attention to him, but with the sombre resignation of a soldier condemned to a flogging, continued her silent patrol, which every few minutes brought her within range of his sarcasms. Finding that he was producing no effect, the gentleman got to his feet, crept up behind her, scooped up a handful of snow and thrust it down her back between her bare shoulders. The woman uttered a cry and, turning, sprang at him like a tigress, ripping his face with her finger-nails and screaming at him in language that might have shocked an army sergeant. The stream of obscenities, uttered in a voice coarsened by cheap brandy, poured hideously out of a gap-toothed mouth. The woman was Fantine.

The noise brought the officers running out of the café. A circle of laughing, hooting, applauding spectators formed round this whirl-wind composed of two creatures whom it was difficult to recognize as a man and a woman, the man seeking to defend himself with his hat knocked off, the woman hitting, kicking, and screaming, frenzied and horrible.

Suddenly a tall man broke through the circle, seized the woman by her mud-stained satin corsage and said, 'You come along with me.' The woman looked round and was abruptly silent. Her eyes went glassy, and from being livid with fury she became pale and trembling with alarm. She had recognized Javert.

Monsieur Bamatabois took advantage of the interruption to hurry away.

XIII

At the police post

Thrusting aside the onlookers, Javert made rapidly for the police post on the far side of the square, dragging the unhappy woman with him. She made no resistance. Neither spoke a word. The spectators followed, hooting with delight. The utmost extremity of degradation is the obscene merriment to which it gives rise.

The police post was a low room, heated by a stove, with a barred, glass-panelled door opening on to the street. After entering with Fantine, Javert shut this door behind him, to the great disappointment of the sightseers, who stood on tiptoe and craned their necks in their effort to follow the proceedings. Curiosity is a form of gluttony: to see is to devour.

Fantine crouched down in a corner of the room, motionless and silent, huddled like a frightened animal. The duty-sergeant placed a lighted candle on the table. Javert seated himself at it, and getting a sheet of officially-stamped paper out of his pocket began to write.

Under present laws women of this class are wholly at the mercy of the police. The police can do with them what they like, punish them as they see fit and, if they choose, deprive them of those two sad possessions which they term their calling and their liberty. Javert was quite impassive, his sober expression betraying no emotion. But the fact is that he was gravely and deeply exercised in his mind. This was one of those cases where he must use his formidable discretionary powers without resort to any higher authority, but with all the scruples dictated by his own rigid conscience. His office chair at that moment was a seat of justice before which the case must be tried, judgement delivered, and sentence pronounced. He summoned all the powers of his mind, all his principles, to deal with this weighty matter, and the more he studied it the more outrageous did he find it. What he had witnessed was undeniably a crime. He had seen society, in the person of a landowner and voter, insulted and attacked in the street by a creature outside society. A prostitute had assaulted a citizen. He, Javert, had seen it with his own eyes. He wrote on in silence.

When he had finished writing he signed the document, folded it and, handing it to the duty-sergeant, said: 'Have this woman taken

183

to the gaol under guard.' He then turned to Fantine and said: 'You're getting six months.'

She uttered a cry of despair. 'Six months. Six months in prison, earning seven sous a day! But what about Cosette? What about my daughter? And I still owe more than a hundred francs to the Thénardiers, Monsieur l'inspecteur – did you know that?'

Without getting to her feet she dragged herself across the floor, muddied as it was by the boots of many men, shuffling hastily on her knees with her hands clasped.

'Monsieur Javert, I beg you to be merciful. It was not my fault. If you had seen how it started you would know. I swear by God it was not my fault. The gentleman, I don't know who he was, put snow down my back. Has anyone the right to put snow down a person's back when they're just walking past, doing no harm? It gave me a shock. I'm not very well, you see. And then he'd been saying unpleasant things to me, how ugly I was and about my having lost my teeth, as if I didn't know. I didn't answer, I just thought, well if it amuses him, and I walked quietly on and that was when he put the snow down my back. Monsieur Javert, is there no one who saw what happened and can tell you? I was wrong to lose my temper but when a thing like that happens, something ice-cold pushed down your back when you aren't expecting it, you forget yourself, you lose control. I shouldn't have damaged the gentleman's hat. But why did he have to run away? I'd have apologized – good God, I don't mind apologizing! Oh, let me off just this once, Monsieur Javert. I don't suppose you know, but all one can earn in prison is seven sous a day. It's not the Government's fault but that's all it is, seven sous, and I owe a hundred francs and if I don't pay my little girl will be turned out into the street. God help me, I can't have her with me, the life I lead. What will become of the poor mite? It's those people, those innkeepers, the Thénardiers, they aren't fair, they aren't reasonable, all they want is money. Don't send me to prison! They'll turn her out into the street, a child, at this time of year, mid-winter, you've got to think of that, Monsieur Javert. If she was older she could earn her living, but not at her age. I'm not really a bad woman. It isn't idleness or greed that has made me what I am. I drink eau-de-vie, but from sheer misery, not because I like it but it dulls the mind. If you'd looked in my wardrobe when things were going better for me you'd have seen that I wasn't just a light woman leading a disorderly life.

I had clean, decent linen, plenty of it. Have pity on me, Monsieur Javert!'

She crouched there with her bosom half-bared, hands clasped together, face wet with tears while the words poured out in a low, heartrending flow broken by that small, dry cough. The extremity of grief sheds its own awful radiance to transform even the most abject. At that moment, bending forward to press the hem of the policeman's greatcoat to her lips, Fantine was beautiful again. She might have melted a heart of stone, but nothing can melt a heart of wood.

'Well,' said Javert, 'I've listened to you. Is that all you have to say? Then off you go. You're getting six months, and the Eternal Father himself can't alter it.'

The solemn mention of the Eternal Father forced her to realize that the sentence was final. She collapsed on the floor moaning:

'Mercy!'

Javert turned his back on her and two policemen took her by the arms.

A few minutes previously a man had entered unobserved. Closing the door behind him he had remained with his back to it listening to Fantine's despairing plea. Now, while the men were trying to drag her to her feet, he emerged from the shadows and said:

'One moment, if you please.'

Javert looked round and saw that it was Monsieur Madeleine. Removing his hat, he bowed stiffly.

'I beg your pardon, Monsieur le maire.'

The words had a remarkable effect on Fantine. Rising instantly from the floor like a ghost emerging from the earth, she thrust aside the two men and, before they could stop her, had planted herself fiery-eyed in front of Madeleine.

'So you're the mayor, are you?'

She laughed and spat in his face.

Monsieur Madeleine wiped his cheek and said:

'Inspector Javert, this woman is to go free.'

Javert felt for a moment that he was going mad. He was beset by a confusion of the most violent emotions he had ever experienced in his life. To see a woman of the town spit in the face of the mayor was a thing so monstrous that even in his wildest imaginings he would not have dared to think it possible. And at the same time at the back of his mind he had an obscure sense of some kind of hideous connection between the woman and this man who was mayor which, to his horror, made the act intelligible. But when he saw the mayor, the magistrate, calmly wipe his face and heard him say that the woman was to go free, stupefaction overwhelmed him. Thought and words both failed him. He had passed beyond the bounds of amazement and could say nothing.

Fantine was no less astounded. Reaching out a bare arm, she clung to the nearest object available for her support – it was in fact the handle operating the damper of the stove – and staring about her began to talk in a low voice as though to herself.

'To go free! Not to spend six months in prison. But who said it? No one can have said it. I must have misheard. It couldn't have been that monster, the mayor. Did you say it, good Monsieur Javert, did you say that I was to go free? Look, I'll explain everything and then you will let me go. It was all the fault of that vile creature, the mayor. He dismissed me because of the things some of the women said. Wasn't that abominable, to turn away an honest working-girl? So then I couldn't earn enough, and that was the trouble. There's something the police should do, Monsieur Javert; they should prevent the prison contractors from injuring the poor. What I mean is this, you're earning twelve sous a day stitching shirts, and then it's cut down to nine and you can't earn enough to live on. So then you have to do what you can. I had Cosette to think of, so I was forced to become a bad woman. You do see, don't you, that it was that monster the mayor who was at the bottom of it all? And then I knocked the gentleman's hat off outside the officers' café, but he'd ruined my dress with his snow, and we girls, we only have one silk dress for evenings. Truly, I've never meant to harm anyone and I know plenty of women worse than me who are much better off. You did say, didn't you, Monsieur Javert, that I can go? You can ask people about me, you can ask my landlord, I'm paying regularly now, they'll tell you I'm honest ... Oh, I'm sorry, I moved the damper and the stove is smoking.'

Monsieur Madeleine had listened to this with deep attention. While she was speaking he had got out his purse, opened it and found that it was empty. Putting it back in his pocket he said:

'How much did you say you owed?'

Fantine, whose words had been addressed solely to Javert, swung round upon him.

'Am I talking to you?'

She said to the other men, 'You saw me spit in his face, didn't you?' and then to Madeleine, 'You brute of a mayor, you've come here to frighten me, but I'm not afraid of you. I'm only afraid of Monsieur Javert, good Monsieur Javert.'

She turned back to the inspector.

'The thing is, we've got to be fair, haven't we? I know you're fair, Monsieur Javert. After all, it didn't amount to anything. A man puts a little snow down a girl's back and it makes the officers laugh – well, they've got to have their fun and after all that's what we girls are for. But then you come along and it's your duty to keep order so you take away the girl who's making trouble, but then, thinking it over, and because you're kind, you decide to let me go, because of my little girl, because if I spend six months in prison I shouldn't be able to keep her alive. "But mind you don't come back, my wench!" you say to me. Oh, but I won't, Monsieur Javert, I won't; they can treat me how they like, I'll not do a thing! Only this time, you see, it hurt me, that lump of snow that I wasn't expecting, and so I lost my temper. I'm not very well, like I said, I cough a lot and it's as though I had a lump burning inside me. It's just here, you can feel for yourself, don't be afraid.'

She was no longer weeping and her voice was gentle. Taking Javert's large, rough hand she pressed it smiling against the whiteness of her throat. Then with sudden, rapid movements she repaired the disorder of her dress, shook out the folds of her skirt which had mounted almost to her knee, turned and marched to the door, saying with a friendly nod to the gendarmes:

'The inspector says I can go, so now I'm going.'

She had a hand on the latch and in another instant would have been in the street.

Until that moment Javert had stood motionless staring at the floor, a mere incident in the scene, like a statue that has not yet been put in place. But the sound of the latch aroused him from his stupor. He looked up sharply with that air of aggressive authority which is the more pronounced at the lower levels, the ferocity of a wild beast, which is atrocious in a small man.

'Sergeant,' he cried, 'can't you see the woman's walking out? Who said you could let her go?'

'I did,' said Madeleine.

At the sound of Javert's voice Fantine had started back, letting go the latch as though she had been caught in the act of stealing it.

When Madeleine spoke she turned to look at him, and from then on, without uttering a word and scarcely daring to draw breath, she gazed in turn from Madeleine to Javert and back, according to which of them was speaking.

Javert must clearly have been thrown quite off balance, as the saying is, for him to have barked at the sergeant as he had done after being instructed by the mayor to let Fantine go free. Had he positively forgotten that the mayor was present? Had he concluded in his own mind that it was impossible for anyone in authority to give such an order, and that the mayor had spoken in error? Or had he decided, in view of the monstrous happenings of the past hour, that the time had come when a supreme gesture must be made, when the bloodhound must turn magistrate, the police-officer assume the robes of justice, and that in this moment of utmost crisis, law and order, morality, government, the whole of society, were personified in himself, Javert?

Be that as it may, when Monsieur Madeleine spoke the words 'I did', police-inspector Javert was seen to turn towards him, pallid and blue-lipped, his whole body seized with a faint tremor, and with lowered eyes but in a firm voice he was heard to make the unprecedented reply:

'Monsieur le maire, that cannot be allowed.'

'Why not?' asked Monsieur Madeleine.

'The woman insulted a respectable citizen.'

'Listen to me, Inspector Javert,' Madeleine said in a calm, conciliatory voice. 'I know you to be an honourable man and I am very ready to explain my actions to you. This is the truth of the matter. I was crossing the square when you took the woman away. There were still people about and I asked what had happened. I heard the whole story. The respectable citizen was at fault, and by the letter of the law it was he who should have been arrested.'

Javert persisted: 'But she has insulted you too, the mayor of this town!'

'That is my affair,' said Madeleine. 'An insult to me may be said to be my property. I can do what I like with it.'

'If you'll forgive me, Monsieur le maire, the insult was not to yourself but to justice.'

'Conscience is the highest justice, Inspector Javert. I heard what the woman said. I know what I'm doing.'

'As for me, Monsieur le maire, I can't believe my ears.'

'Then you must be content to obey.'

'I have to do my duty. Duty requires me to send her to prison for six months.'

Monsieur Madeleine said gently: 'You must be quite clear about this. She will not serve a single day in prison.'

The peremptory words emboldened Javert to look Madeleine full in the face. He said, still in a tone of profound respect:

'It distresses me deeply to take issue with Monsieur le maire. Nothing of the kind has ever happened to me before. But I must venture to remind Monsieur le maire that I am acting within the terms of my authority. We will confine ourselves to the matter of the citizen, since Monsieur le maire prefers it. I was there. The woman flung herself on Monsieur Bamatabois, who is a citizen on the electoral roll and owner of the handsome house at the end of the esplanade, a three-storey stone house. Strange things happen in this world, but this is a matter of police regulations and comes within my province. I am holding the woman Fantine.'

At this Monsieur Madeleine folded his arms and said in a voice that had never before been heard in the town:

'The regulations you refer to are those affecting the Municipal Police. Under articles Nine, Eleven, Fifteen and Sixty-six of the Criminal Code I have authority over them. I order you to release this woman.'

Javert made a last effort.

'But, Monsieur le maire –'

'And let me also remind you of Article Eighty-one of the Law of 13 December 1799, dealing with arbitrary detention.'

'Allow me, Monsieur le maire –'

'That's enough.'

'But –'

'Kindly leave the post,' said Monsieur Madeleine.

Javert received this body-blow standing as rigidly as a Russian soldier. Bowing low to the mayor, he turned and left. Fantine moved away from the door to let him pass and stared at him in stupefaction as he did so.

She too had undergone a strange upheaval. She had found herself to be in some sort an object of dispute between two opposed powers. She had witnessed a conflict between two men who held her liberty in their hands, her very life and that of her child; one had sought to drag her deeper into darkness, the other to restore her to light. The two contestants, in the heightened vision of her terror, had seemed like giants, one speaking with the voice of a demon, the other in the tones of an angel. The angel had won, and what caused her to tremble from head to foot was the fact that this rescuing angel was the man she abhorred, the abominable mayor whom for so long she had regarded as the author of her troubles. He had saved her after she had most outrageously insulted him! Could she have been wrong? Must she now change her very heart? . . . She did not know and stood trembling, listening in turmoil, gazing with distracted eyes, and feeling with every word that Monsieur Madeleine spoke the knot of hatred dissolve within her, while a new feeling took its place, heartwarming and inexpressible, a sense of deliverance, trust, and love.

After Javert had gone, Monsieur Madeleine turned to her and spoke slowly and with difficulty, in the accents of an earnest man moved nearly to tears.

'I heard what you said. None of it was known to me, but I believe it to be true, I feel that it is true. I did not even know that you had left my employment. Why did you not appeal to me? No matter. I will pay your debts and arrange for your child to be brought here or else for you to go to her. You will live here or in Paris or where you choose. You need not work if you don't want to. I will see to it that you have what money you need. You will become honest again in being happy again. But let me assure you of this, that if it has all been as you say – and I do not doubt it – then you have never been anything but virtuous and chaste in the eyes of God. My poor girl!'

And this was more than Fantine could bear. To have Cosette! To escape from her present life. To be free and cared for, happy and honest, with Cosette. This prospect of paradise in the depths of her misery was too much for her. She could only gaze mutely at the man addressing her and utter little whimpering cries – oh – oh – oh . . . Her legs gave way beneath her; she fell on her knees before Monsieur Madeleine and before he could prevent it had taken his hand and pressed it to her lips.

Then she fainted.

BOOK SIX

JAVERT

I

The beginning of repose

MONSIEUR MADELEINE had Fantine taken to the factory infirmary where she was placed in the charge of the nursing sisters. She now had a raging fever and for part of the night was delirious, talking in a loud voice. Eventually, however, she fell asleep.

When she awoke about midday she heard the sound of breathing at her bedside, and drawing back the curtain, saw Monsieur Madeleine standing with his eyes fixed in an expression of anguished supplication on something above her head. Looking up, she saw that there was a crucifix nailed to the wall.

Monsieur Madeleine had been so transformed in the eyes of Fantine that now he seemed to her to be bathed in light. His lips were moving. She watched for a long time without venturing to interrupt him, but at length she asked timidly:

'What are you doing?'

He had been standing there for an hour waiting for her to awaken. He took her hand, felt her pulse and asked:

'How do you feel?'

'I'm feeling better. I've slept well. I'm sure I'm better. It was nothing serious.'

He then answered her question.

'I have been praying to the martyr above your head,' he said, and added in his thoughts, 'For the martyr at my side.'

He had spent the night and morning ascertaining the facts, and now he knew the whole tragic story of Fantine. He went on:

'You have suffered very greatly, my poor child, but you must not complain, for now you have your recompense. This is how men create saints, and it is useless to blame them because they cannot do otherwise. The hell you have endured is the doorway to Heaven, through which you had to pass.'

He sighed deeply. But she smiled up at him, that poignant smile lacking two teeth.

In the course of the same night Javert had written a letter, and had himself taken it to the post office that morning. It was a letter to Paris, addressed as follows: 'To Monsieur Chabouillet, secretary to the Prefect of Police'. The story of the scene in the police post had already become known, and the postmistress and certain other persons, seeing the letter and recognizing Javert's handwriting, concluded that he was sending in his resignation.

Monsieur Madeleine wrote at once to Thénardier. Fantine owed the couple a hundred and twenty francs. He sent them three hundred, instructing them to use the balance of this sum to bring the child immediately to Montreuil-sur-mer, where her mother lay ill.

Thénardier was amazed. 'By God,' he said, 'we aren't going to let the brat go, she's turned into a gold-mine. I can guess what has happened. Some rich joker has taken a fancy to the mother.'

He replied with a circumstantial demand for a total of over five hundred francs, substantiated by authentic bills from the doctor and apothecary who had attended Éponine and Azelma during long illnesses. Cosette, as we have said, had not been ill. It was simply a matter of changing the names, and he formally acknowledged receipt of the three hundred francs.

Monsieur Madeleine promptly sent an additional three hundred francs, requesting them to bring Cosette without delay.

'The devil we will!' said Thénardier.

Fantine, meanwhile, remained in the infirmary; she was not recovering.

The nursing sisters had at first treated her with dislike. Anyone who has seen the bas-reliefs at Rheims will recall the pouting lower lip of the wise virgins confronting the foolish virgins. The immemorial scorn of vestals for loose women is among the deepest instincts of respectable femininity, and in the case of the sisters it was enhanced by their religious vocation. But Fantine soon disarmed them with her humility and gentle manners, and their hearts were further touched by the fact that she was a mother. She said to them in a bout of fever: 'I have sinned, but when my child is restored to me it will be a sign that God has forgiven me. I could not have her with me while I was living a bad life because I could not have endured the look in her eyes. I was wicked for her sake, and that is why God has forgiven me. I shall feel God's blessing when she is here. I shall be strengthened by her innocence. She knows nothing of what has happened. She is truly an angel, dear sisters; at that age we have still not lost our wings.'

Monsieur Madeleine visited her twice daily, and she invariably asked, 'When shall I see Cosette?'

He would answer, 'Tomorrow, perhaps. She may be here at any moment,' and this would cause her face to light up.

But, as we have said, she was not getting better. Indeed, as the weeks passed her condition grew worse. The handful of snow rubbed on her bare back had, it seemed, dealt a shock to her system which caused the disease that had long been dormant within her to break out in a virulent form. The method of auscultation devised by Professor Laennec for the diagnosis and treatment of pulmonary disease was then coming into use, and the doctor examined her by this means.

'Well?' asked Monsieur Madeleine.

'Hasn't she got a child she wants to see?'

'Yes, a small daughter.'

'You'd better get her here as soon as possible.'

Madeleine was dismayed, but when Fantine asked what the doctor had said he forced himself to smile.

'He says we must get your daughter here as soon as possible, and then you'll get well.'

'He's right,' she said. 'Why are the Thénardiers keeping Cosette? But she will come, won't she? And then I shall be happy again.'

But the Thénardiers held on to Cosette, adducing a hundred dishonest reasons. She was not yet well enough to travel during the winter; there were still minor debts to be settled for which they were awaiting accounts; and so on.

'I shall have to send someone to fetch her,' said Madeleine. 'If necessary I'll go myself.'

He wrote the following letter at Fantine's dictation and then got her to sign it.

> Monsieur Thénardier,
>   You will hand Cosette over to the bearer.
> Everything owing will be paid.
>   I send you my regards.
>   Fantine

But at this point a most serious thing happened. Do what we may to shape the mysterious stuff of which our lives are composed, the dark threads of our destiny will always re-emerge.

The honesty of Javert

On a morning when Monsieur Madeleine was busy in his office, disposing of urgent business in case he should find it necessary to go to Montfermeil, he was informed that Inspector Javert wished to speak to him. The name affected him disagreeably. Since their encounter in the police post he had not seen Javert, who had been more careful than ever to avoid him.

'Show him in,' he said, and Javert entered.

Monsieur Madeleine stayed seated at his desk, pen in hand, intent on the report he was reading of certain minor infringements of the law. He received Javert with deliberate coldness, being unable to forget Fantine.

Javert respectfully saluted the mayor's back while the latter, without looking up, continued to make notes in the margin of the document in front of him. The inspector advanced a few steps into the room and then waited in silence.

An observer with some knowledge of Javert's character, one who had studied that barbarian in the service of civilization, that bizarre composite of Roman and Spartan, monk and army corporal, that spy incapable of falsehood, that Simon-pure watchdog; a physiognomist aware of his long-standing secret aversion for Madeleine and of the recent clash between them, would have been bound to ask, as he now looked at him, 'What has happened?' To anyone familiar with that upright, honourable, inflexible, and ruthless conscience it would have been apparent that Javert had passed through a serious personal crisis. There could be nothing in his soul that was not depicted on his countenance. Like all men of violence he was subject to abrupt changes of mood. Never had his demeanour been more strange or mystifying. He had bowed to Monsieur Madeleine on entering with an expression in which there was no rancour, anger, or defiance, and then, halting a few paces from his chair, he had stood rigidly upright in what was almost a parade-ground attitude, with the naïve, chilly uncouthness of a man who has never been gentle but always patient. Without speaking or moving, in true humility and silent resignation, calm, serious, with his hat in his hand and his eyes downcast, his posture midway between that of a soldier in the presence of his officer and a guilty person confronting his judge, he stood waiting until the mayor should see fit to notice him. All trace of the feelings and recollections one might have expected to see had vanished from that simple, rocklike countenance except for its look of sombre melancholy. His whole being expressed subjection and doggedness, a sort of gallantry in defeat.

At length the mayor put down his pen and half turned towards him.

'Well, Javert, what is it?'

Javert paused for a moment as though to collect his thoughts. Then he said in a sad and solemn voice that was not without ingenuousness:

'Monsieur le maire, a serious breach of discipline has been committed.'

'What breach?'

'An inferior member of the public service has shown the utmost disrespect for a magistrate. I have come, as in duty bound, to inform you of the fact.'

'Who is the offender?' asked Madeleine.

'Myself,' said Javert.

'You?'

'Yes.'

'And who is this magistrate who has been disrespectfully treated?'

'You are, Monsieur le maire.'

Monsieur Madeleine started up in his chair. Javert proceeded inexorably, with eyes still lowered.

'I have come, Monsieur le maire, to ask you to recommend to the authorities that I should be dismissed.'

The astonished Madeleine opened his mouth to speak, but Javert cut him short.

'You may say that I can resign, but that would not be enough. To resign is an honourable proceeding. I have committed an offence and I must be punished for it. I must be dismissed.' After a brief pause he added: 'Monsieur le maire, you treated me unjustly not long ago. This time you must deal with me justly.'

'But what in the world are you talking about?' cried Madeleine. 'In what way have you treated me with disrespect? What offence have you committed against me? What harm have you done me? You say you want to be relieved –'

'Dismissed,' said Javert.

'Very well, dismissed. I don't understand why.'

'I will explain, Monsieur le maire.'

Javert heaved a deep sigh and said in the same dispassionate, disconsolate voice:

'I was so furious after our dispute six weeks ago over that woman that I denounced you.'

'You denounced me?'

'To the Prefecture of Police in Paris.'

Monsieur Madeleine, who was not much more given to laughter than Javert himself, now laughed heartily.

'As a mayor who had encroached on the function of the police?'

'As an ex-convict.'

Madeleine's expression abruptly changed. Javert, who was still staring at the floor, continued:

'That is what I believed. I had had the idea for a long time. A certain facial resemblance, the inquiries you caused to be made in Faverolles, the great physical strength you displayed in the Fauchelevent episode, your skill as a marksman and your slight limp ... All trifles. Nevertheless I suspected you of being a man called Jean Valjean.'

'What name did you say?'

'Jean Valjean. He was a convict I saw twenty years ago, when I was a prison-warder at Toulon. It seems that after being released this Valjean committed a robbery at the house of a bishop and then robbed a small boy on the public highway. Efforts were made to re-arrest him, but he managed to get away, and there has been no trace of him for eight years. Well, I believed ... Anyway, that is what I did. In my resentment I denounced you to the Paris Prefecture.'

Monsieur Madeleine had returned to the documents on his desk. He asked in an entirely casual voice:

'And what did they say?'

'They said I was mad.'

'And?'

'And they were right.'

'I'm glad you realize it.'

'They must be right, since the real Jean Valjean has been found.'

The sheet of paper fell from Madeleine's hand. He looked hard at Javert and murmured expressionlessly, 'Indeed?'

'The facts are these,' said Javert. 'There was a man called Champmathieu living near the village of Ailly-le-Haut-Cloche. He was more or less destitute, one of those poor wretches of whom one wonders how they contrive to stay alive. Well, last autumn he was arrested for stealing cider apples. The evidence was clear enough. He had climbed a wall, broken branches off trees; he was even caught with some of the apples on him. So he was taken into custody. Up to that point it was no great matter, not much more than a case of petty larceny; but then things took an unexpected turn. The local lock-up was in bad repair, and so Champmathieu was transferred to the departmental prison at Arras. One of the prisoners at Arras was an old lag called Brevet who had been made a trusty for good conduct. The moment he set eyes on Champmathieu he exclaimed, "But I know this man. He's an ex-convict. We were in prison together in Toulon more than twenty years ago. His name's Jean Valjean." Champmathieu of course denied it, saying that he had never heard of Jean Valjean, but the matter had to be followed up. It was established that thirty years before, Champmathieu had been a tree-pruner in various parts of the country, but particularly in Faverolles. There was a very long interval, but the trail was picked up again in Auvergne and then in Paris, where he claims to have been a wheelwright and to have had a daughter who became a washerwoman, none of which is proved; and finally he turned up in these parts. Well now, what was Jean Valjean before he went to prison for theft? He was a tree-pruner. And where? In Faverolles. But that's not all. Valjean's baptismal name was Jean, and his mother's maiden name was Mathieu. It would be quite natural for him, when he came out of prison, to try to conceal his identity by adopting his mother's name and calling himself Jean Mathieu. He was in Auvergne, where the local accent turns *Jean* into *Chan* – Chan Mathieu – and from that it is a very short step to Champmathieu. I am sure you follow me, Monsieur le maire. Further inquiries were made in Faverolles but no trace could be discovered of Jean Valjean's family. Nothing unusual in that. Families of that class quite commonly vanish from sight – when they aren't mud they're dust. And after thirty years there was no one in the place who remembered Jean Valjean. So then they tried Toulon, and here they found two other convicts who had known him. They were men serving life-sentences, named Cochepaille and Chenildieu. They were brought to Arras and at once confirmed Brevet's statement that the so-called Champmathieu was Jean

Valjean. Same age, fifty-four, same build, same general appearance – in a word, the same man. The confrontation took place almost on the day when I posted my letter of denunciation to Paris. They wrote back saying that I was out of my wits and that Jean Valjean was in custody in Arras. I need not tell you the shock this gave me. I obtained permission to go to Arras to see this Champmathieu for myself . . .'

'And?' said Madeleine.

'Truth is truth, Monsieur le maire,' said Javert with the same sombre, implacable expression. 'I am forced to admit that that man is Jean Valjean. I, too, recognized him.'

Madeleine asked in a very low voice:

'You're sure?'

Javert gave a dry laugh of reluctant but absolute certainty.

'Oh, yes – I'm sure.' He was silent for some moments while mechanically he took a pinch of powdered wood from the blotting-bowl on the desk. 'Indeed, now that I have seen the real Jean Valjean I cannot imagine how I could have thought anything else. I must beg you to accept my profound apologies, Monsieur le maire.'

In addressing this humble request to the man who only a few weeks before had humiliated him in front of his own men, Javert, arrogant as he was, had assumed a simplicity and dignity of which he was quite unconscious. Madeleine's only reply was an abrupt question.

'And what does the man himself say?'

'Well, you see, it's a bad business, Monsieur le maire. If he's Valjean he's broken parole. To climb a wall and steal apples can be a mere escapade if it's a boy, or a minor offence in a grown man; but in the case of a convict on parole it's a crime – breaking and entering and all the rest of it, not just a case for the magistrates but for trial at the Assizes. And the penalty is not just a few days in gaol, but life imprisonment. And then there's the matter of the boy he robbed, the chimney-sweep, if, as I hope, he can be found. In fact, Valjean's in a hopeless position, or would be, if it were anyone but Jean Valjean. But he's a cunning fellow, and that's another thing that makes me sure this is he. Where another man would be screaming the place down, ranting and raving and swearing that he had never heard of Valjean, this one behaves as though he simply didn't understand – "My name's Champmathieu, and that is all I have to say" – a kind of mulish stupidity, which is much more effective. Oh, he's clever all right. But it won't work. The evidence is overwhelming – four people who recognize him. He's to be tried at Arras Assizes and I have been subpoena'd as a witness.'

Monsieur Madeleine had returned to the papers on his desk and was again poring over them and making notes with the air of a man with many things on his mind. He looked up at the inspector.

'Thank you, Javert. The details do not greatly interest me, and in any case we have business to attend to. I want you to go at once to the woman Buseaupied, who keeps a herb-stall on the corner of the Rue Saint-Saulve, and tell her that she must lodge a complaint against Pierre Chesnelong, the carrier, who nearly ran her and her daughter down. He's a reckless driver and it's time he was taught a lesson. Then there's Monsieur Charcelley, in the Rue Montre-de-Champigny, who complains that in heavy rain the water overflows out of his neighbour's gutter and floods his cellar. And there are reports of the contravention of police regulations in the Rue Gui-bourg, at the house of the widow Doris, and at the house of Madame Renée Le Bosse in the Rue du Garraud-Blanc. They want looking into. But I'm giving you a lot to do. You say you have to go to Arras. I take it that will not be for a week or so?'

'Sooner than that, Monsieur le maire. The case comes up tomorrow. I am catching the coach tonight.'

Monsieur Madeleine started slightly.

'How long will it take?'

'Certainly not more than a day. Sentence will be passed tomorrow evening at the latest, but I don't intend to wait for it, since there's no doubt what it will be. I shall leave directly I've given my evidence.'

'Good,' said Madeleine.

He made a gesture of dismissal, but Javert did not move.

'Forgive me, Monsieur le maire. I have to remind you of something.'

'Of what?'

'That I must be dismissed from the service.'

Monsieur Madeleine rose to his feet.

'Javert, you are an honourable man and I respect you highly. You are exaggerating your offence, which in any case is a matter that only concerns myself. You deserve to go up in the world, Javert, not down. I want you to stay in your present post.'

Javert confronted the mayor with a clear-eyed gaze in which there was the glint of a narrow conscience as rigid as it was upright. He said quietly:

'Monsieur le maire, I cannot agree to that.'

'I repeat,' said Madeleine, 'this is a matter that only affects me.'

But pursuing his own line of thought Javert continued:

'As to exaggerating, I have exaggerated nothing. This is how I see it. That I should have suspected you unjustly is not in itself important. It is our business to be suspicious, although we should be chary of suspecting our superiors. But you are a man of repute, a mayor, and a magistrate, and in a fit of anger and a spirit of revenge I denounced you, without evidence, as an ex-convict. That is very serious. I offended against authority in your person, and I am myself a representative of authority. If one of my subordinates had done this I should have said that he was unworthy to be a member of the service and have seen to it that he was dismissed. And so . . . Let me add one thing, Monsieur le maire. I have often been harsh in my life. I have treated others harshly, and it was right that I should do so. But if I were not now equally harsh with myself all my past acts would be unjustified. Am I to spare myself more than I spare others, to be the scourge of others and not of myself? It would be abominable and the people who talk about "that swine Javert" would be right. I do not wish for your indulgence, Monsieur le maire, I have been exasperated enough by your indulgence for others. I want none of it for myself. To me the kind of indulgence which consists in supporting a woman of the town against a respectable citizen, or a police officer against a mayor, or in any form the lower against the higher, this is false indulgence which undermines society. God knows, it's easy to be kind; the hard thing is to be just. If you had turned out to be what I suspected, Monsieur le maire, I should have shown you no kindness! I must treat myself as I would treat any other man. I have often thought, when I was showing no mercy to evil-doers, "Well, if ever you slip up you know what to expect." And now I have slipped, I have committed an offence, and there it is. It is right that I should be dismissed and broken. I still have my hands, I can work in the fields, it is no great matter. I must be made an example of, Monsieur le maire, for the good of the service. I request that Inspector Javert be dismissed.'

All this was said in a tone of high-flown humility and desperate conviction that endowed the strangely honest man with a bizarre greatness.

'Well,' said Monsieur Madeleine, 'we shall have to see.' And he held out his hand.

Javert started back, saying harshly: 'That is out of the question. A magistrate does not shake hands with an informer.' He repeated the words under his breath. 'An informer . . . When I abused my powers as a police officer I became nothing else.'

Bowing low he turned and made for the door; but here he paused and said, still with his eyes lowered:

'I shall continue to perform my duties, Monsieur le maire, until I have been replaced.'

He went out; and Monsieur Madeleine stood thoughtfully listening to the firm, decided footsteps as they died away down the corridor.

BOOK SEVEN

THE CHAMPMATHIEU AFFAIR

I

Sister Simplice

NOT ALL the events which follow became known in Montreuil-sur-mer, but the scanty report of them which reached the town created so great a stir that we are bound to describe them in detail. The reader will find among them two or three improbable circumstances which we record in the interest of truth.

During the afternoon following his interview with Javert, Monsieur Madeleine paid his customary visit to Fantine. Before doing so he asked to see Sister Simplice, one of the two nursing sisters of the order of St Lazarus who did duty in his infirmary, the other being Sister Perpetua.

Sister Perpetua was a plain countrywoman who had entered the service of God as she might have entered any other service, becoming a nun as she might become a cook. Such people are by no means rare, and the religious orders make no bones about accepting this raw material which can readily be shaped into a Capucine or an Ursuline. Their function is to do the rough work. The transition from farm-worker to Carmelite is an easy one, calling for no great effort; village and cloister share a common ground of ignorance which puts the countryman on a level with the monk. A few added folds turn the peasant smock into a cassock. Sister Perpetua, who came from Marines, near Pontoise, was a sturdy, patois-speaking, psalm-singing, grumbling servant of the Church who sugared the tisane according to her opinion of the sufferer, rebuked the sick and scolded the dying, almost flinging God in their faces, castigating their death-throes with angry, florid, honest and forthright prayers.

To compare Sister Simplice and her wax-like pallor with Sister Perpetua was like comparing a taper with a church candle. Vincent de Paul has beautifully depicted the Sister of Mercy in words that express both her freedom and her servitude. 'Their only convent is the sick-room, their only cell a hired lodging, their chapel the parish church, their cloister the streets of the town or the hospital ward, their discipline obedience, their shelter the fear of God and their veil, modesty.' This ideal was in Sister Simplice a living reality. No one knew her age; she had never been young and it seemed that she would never grow old. She was a calm and austere person – we can hardly say 'woman' – companionable but remote, who had never told a lie. She was so gentle as to seem fragile, but possessed a steely strength. She laid charmed fingers, slender and chaste, on the sufferer, and there was as it were a silence in her speech; she never spoke an unnecessary word and the sound of her voice would have graced a confessional or delighted a drawing-room. Her delicacy had adapted itself to the rough serge gown she wore, which served her as a constant reminder of Heaven. We must stress one particular. The fact that she never lied, had never spoken, for any reason or without reason, a word that was not strictly true, was the distinctive characteristic of Sister Simplice, the keynote of her virtue. Her unshakeable truthfulness had made her almost celebrated in the community, and Abbé Sicard refers to it in a letter to the deaf-mute Massieu. However honest and incorruptible the rest of us may be, our candour is always flawed by, here and there, some small, innocent falsehood. But it was not so with her. Can there be such a thing as a white lie, a little lie? The lie is the absolute of evil. There can be no small lie; who lies, lies wholly. The lie is the devil's own face. Satan has two names; he is Satan and he is Un-truth. That is what Sister Simplice believed, the belief she practised; and it was the source of the purity which shone from her, even from her lips and eyes. Her smile was pure and her gaze was pure; there was no cobweb or any grain of dust on the unsullied mirror of that conscience. Upon entering the order of St Vincent de Paul she had chosen the name Simplice in memory of the saint who had let her breasts be torn off rather than say she had been born at Segesta when her birthplace was Syracuse – a lie which would have saved her.[*]

Sister Simplice, when she entered the order, had two weaknesses which she gradually corrected: she liked sweets and she enjoyed getting letters. Her only reading was a book of Latin prayers in large print. She did not understand Latin, but she understood the book.

She had conceived an affection for Fantine, no doubt perceiving the virtue latent within her, and had taken her almost wholly in her own charge.

[*]This seems to be an invention of Hugo's. There is no mention of a St Simplice, or Simplicitas, in the *Acta Sanctorum.*

Monsieur Madeleine took Sister Simplice aside and recommended Fantine to her care in a tone so earnest that later she was to remember it. Then he went in to see Fantine.

Fantine awaited his daily visits as we await warmth and happiness. She said to the sisters: 'I'm only alive when the mayor is here.'

On this day she had a high fever. Directly she saw him she asked: 'And Cosette?'

He answered, smiling: 'Very soon.'

His manner towards her was normal except that he stayed an hour instead of his usual half-hour, much to her delight. He stressed to everyone concerned that she must go short of nothing, and at one moment his face was seen to grow very sombre. But this was explained when it became known that the doctor had murmured to him that she was sinking fast.

Then he returned to the *mairie* where his clerk saw him carefully studying a road-map of France that hung in his office. He pencilled some figures on a sheet of paper.

II

The perspicacity of Master Scaufflaire

From the *mairie*, Madeleine crossed the town to call upon a Fleming named Scaufflaer (French: Scaufflaire) who hired out horses and 'carriages if required'. The shortest way to his establishment was along a little-frequented street in which was the presbytery of Madeleine's own parish. The curé was said to be a worthy man and a wise counsellor. There was only one person in the street when Madeleine passed the presbytery, and this person happened to notice that after doing so he stopped, stood for a moment motionless and then, turning back, made for the presbytery door which had an iron knocker. He quickly seized hold of the knocker and raised it; but again he paused as though in thought and, after a few moments, instead of knocking, gently released it and continued on his way rather more rapidly than before.

He found Scaufflaire mending a piece of harness.

'Master Scaufflaire,' he asked, 'have you a good horse?'

'All my horses are good, Monsieur le maire,' answered the Fleming. 'What exactly do you mean?'

'I want a horse that can do twenty leagues in a day.'

'Twenty leagues! Harnessed to a chaise?'

'Yes.'

'And how much rest will it get at the end of it?'

'It will have to come back the next day.'

'The same distance?'

'Yes.'

'Love us and save us! A whole twenty leagues?'

Madeleine produced the scrap of paper on which he had jotted down the figures 5, 6, and 8½.

'Nineteen and a half, to be exact. Call it twenty.'

'Well, Monsieur le maire,' said the Fleming, 'I've got what you want, a small white horse from the Bas-Boulonnais, a wonderful animal. They tried to make him into a saddle-horse but he threw all his riders and no one could manage him. But I bought him and put him between shafts, and it turned out that that was what he wanted – gentle as a girl and goes like the wind, provided you don't try to get on his back. He'll pull but he won't carry. Everyone has their own ideas, and he seems to have got that one firmly in his head.'

'And he'll last the course?'

'Forty miles? He'll do it at a steady trot in under eight hours, provided –'

'Provided what?'

'Well, in the first place, he must have an hour's breather half-way, and you must keep an eye on him while he's eating to make sure the stable-boy doesn't steal the oats. The thing I've found, stopping at inns, is that more oats get drunk by the stable-boys than eaten by the horses.'

'I'll see to that.'

'Secondly – I take it the chaise is for yourself, Monsieur le maire, and that you know how to drive?'

'Yes.'

'You must travel alone and without baggage, to keep down the weight.'

'Certainly.'

'The charge will be thirty francs a day, including rest-days. I won't take a penny less, and you will pay for the animal's feed.'

Monsieur Madeleine got three napoleons out of his purse and laid them on the table.

'There's two days in advance.'

'One last thing,' said Master Scaufflaire, 'a chaise would be too heavy for this trip. I must ask Monsieur le maire to use my tilbury.'

'Very well.'

'Mark you, it's entirely open.'

'That doesn't matter.'

'Have you considered, Monsieur le maire, that this is winter and that the weather's extremely cold?' Madeleine made no reply to this, and the Fleming added: 'Or that it may rain?'

Monsieur Madeleine merely said:

'I want the horse and tilbury to be outside my door at four-thirty tomorrow morning.'

'Very well,' said Scaufflaire. He scratched with a finger-nail at a small stain on the surface of the table and said in the off-hand manner with which the Flemish disguise their perspicacity:

'It occurs to me, Monsieur le maire, that I still don't know exactly where you're going.'

He had been thinking of nothing else since the beginning of the interview, but for some reason had not ventured to put the question directly.

'Is this horse strong in the forelegs?' asked Madeleine.

'Yes, although you'll need to hold him up a little on the down-slopes. Will there be many down-slopes on this journey, Monsieur le maire?'

'Please be sure to have it round at my house punctually at half past four,' said Madeleine, and went out, leaving the Fleming 'flabbergasted', as he later said.

But a few minutes later the mayor returned, still with the same impenetrable, preoccupied manner.

'Monsieur Scaufflaire, what value do you put on your horse-and-tilbury, taking the two together?'

'Or rather, one in front of the other,' said the Fleming, attempting a joke.

'Well?'

'Do I understand that Monsieur le maire is proposing to buy them?'

'No, but I wish to insure you against possible loss or injury. You will repay the money when I bring them back. How much?'

'Five hundred francs, Monsieur le maire.'

'Here you are.'

Monsieur Madeleine laid a banknote on the table and again departed, this time not to return. Master Scaufflaire now bitterly regretted not having said a thousand. In fact, the horse and tilbury were worth about a hundred francs.

Scaufflaire called his wife and told her the story. Where the devil was the mayor going? They talked it over. 'He must be going to Paris,' the lady said. 'I don't think so,' said her husband. Madeleine had left behind the scrap of paper on which he had scribbled his figures. Scaufflaire studied it carefully. 'Five – six – eight and a half – they must be post-stages.' He looked at his wife. 'I've got it.' ... 'Where?' ... 'It's five leagues from here to Hesdin, six from Hesdin to Saint-Pol, and eight and a half from Saint-Pol to Arras. He's going to Arras.'

Monsieur Madeleine meanwhile was on his way home. This time he went a longer way round, as though deliberately avoiding the presbytery. He went up to his bedroom and shut himself in, which in itself was not unusual, for he often went to bed early. But the factory janitress, who was also his only servant, happening to notice that his light went out at eight-thirty, remarked to the cashier when he came in:

'Is the mayor not well? I thought he looked a little queer.'

The cashier occupied a room immediately below that of Monsieur Madeleine. Without paying much attention to what the janitress had said, he went to bed and to sleep. But towards midnight he was awakened by the sound of feet pacing up and down overhead, and he recognized the footsteps as those of Monsieur Madeleine. This was strange, for as a rule no sound came from Monsieur Madeleine's room until he rose in the morning. Then the cashier heard what sounded like the opening and shutting of a wardrobe, followed by the shifting of a piece of furniture. After this the footsteps started again. The cashier, now wide awake, sat up in bed and saw through his window a red glow from a lighted window reflected on the wall opposite. From its direction the light could only be coming from Monsieur Madeleine's room, and its constant flickering suggested that it was the light of a fire rather than of a lamp. There was no shadow cast by window-bars, which indicated that the window was wide open, and this, considering the coldness of the weather, was surprising. The cashier went back to sleep, but an hour or two later he woke again. The slow, steady footsteps were still pacing up and down above him.

The light was still reflected on the wall, but now it was pale and steady, like that of a lamp or candle. The window was still open.

We have now to relate what was happening in Monsieur Madeleine's room.

III

A tempest in a human skull

The reader will have realized that Monsieur Madeleine was indeed Jean Valjean.

We have already peered into the depths of that conscience and must now do so again, although we cannot do so without trembling. Nothing is more terrifying than contemplation of this kind. Nothing discernible to the eye of the spirit is more brilliant or obscure than man; nothing is more formidable, complex, mysterious, and infinite. There is a prospect greater than the sea, and it is the sky; there is a prospect greater than the sky, and it is the human soul.

To make a poem of the human conscience, even in terms of a single man and the least of men, would be to merge all epics in a single epic transcending all. Conscience is the labyrinth of illusion, desire, and pursuit, the furnace of dreams, the repository of thoughts of which we are ashamed; it is the pandemonium of sophistry, the battlefield of passions. To peer at certain moments into the withdrawn face of a human being in the act of reflection, to see something of what lies beyond their outward silence, is to discern struggle on a Homeric scale, conflicts of dragons and hydras, aerial hosts as in Milton, towering vistas as in Dante. The infinite space that each man carries within himself, wherein despairingly he contrasts the movements of his spirit with the acts of his life, is an overpowering thing.

Dante Alighieri found himself one day at a fateful doorway which he hesitated to enter. We too are confronted by such a doorway, and we too must hesitate but enter none the less.

There is little to be added to what the reader already knows about Jean Valjean, following his encounter with the boy, Petit-Gervais. Thereafter, as we have seen, he was a changed man, enacting in his life what the bishop had sought to make of him. It was more than a transformation; it was a transfiguration.

He contrived to vanish, sold the bishop's silver, keeping only the candlesticks as a reminder, and worked his way from town to town across France until eventually he came to Montreuil-sur-mer. Here he established himself in the manner we have described, rendered himself both unassailable and inaccessible, and, with a conscience darkened by his past but in the knowledge that the second half of his life was a repudiation of the first, settled down to live peaceably and hopefully with only two objects in mind – to conceal his true identity and sanctify his life, and to escape from men and find his way back to God.

The two considerations were so closely linked as to be inseparable in his mind, both so absorbing and overriding as to govern his every act. As a rule they worked harmoniously in his daily conduct, inclining him towards aloofness, making him benevolent and simple, both guiding him along the same path. But it happened occasionally that there was a clash between them, and on these occasions, as we have seen, the man known to Montreuil-sur-mer as Monsieur Madeleine did not hesitate to sacrifice the first consideration to the second – his personal security to his moral principles. Against all prudence he had kept the bishop's candlesticks and worn mourning for him; he sought out and questioned every vagabond boy who passed through the town; he had had inquiries made among the families in Faverolles, and he had saved the life of old Fauchelevent, regardless of Javert's penetrating eye. He had, it seems, concluded, after the manner of saints and sages, that his first duty was not to himself.

But no situation like the present had ever before arisen. Never had the two principles governing the life of this unfortunate man been brought so sharply into conflict. He had been made to realize this, still confusedly but profoundly, by the first words spoken by Javert when he entered his room. When the name he had sought to bury under so many layers of concealment was so unexpectedly uttered he had been completely stunned, dazed by the sinister quixotry of his destiny, and in his bewilderment he had known the tremor that precedes any great shock; he had bowed like an oak-tree at the approach of a tempest, or a soldier at the approach of an attack. He had felt the thunder-clouds massing above his head, and his first thought, as he listened to Javert, was to throw in his hand, to give himself up, get the man Champmathieu out of prison and take his place. It was a thought as piercing and agonizing as a knife-thrust in living flesh. But then it passed, and he said to himself, 'Steady – steady!' Repressing that first generous impulse, he recoiled from the heroic act.

Certainly it would have been a great thing if, following the bishop's solemn admonition, after the years of repentance and self-denial and in the full flood of a rehabilitation so well begun, he had not faltered even in the face of this fearful dilemma but had steadily pursued his course towards the abyss in the heart of which lay spiritual salvation; it would have been a great thing, but it did not happen. We must give a true account of what took place in his soul, and of nothing else. The first victor was the instinct of self-preservation. He hastily re-ordered his thoughts, controlled his emotions, took due note of the perilous proximity of Javert, postponed any final decision with a firmness inspired by terror, concentrated upon what had to be done and recovered his calm like a warrior retrieving his shield.

During the rest of the day he remained in that state of inward turmoil and outward serenity, taking only what may be termed 'safety precautions'. Everything was confusion in his mind, to the extent that he could see nothing clearly and could only have accounted for himself by saying that he had been dealt a stunning blow. He paid his customary visit to Fantine and prolonged it from kindness and with a feeling that he must lay particular injunctions on the sister in case he should be obliged to be absent. He had a vague notion that he should go to Arras, without being at all decided about it, telling himself that since he was exempt from all suspicion it could do no harm for him to go and see what happened; and so he hired the tilbury, in case he should need it.

He dined with a good appetite; but back in his bedroom he began to think.

He reviewed his situation and found it unbelievable, so much so that at one moment, prompted by an almost reasonless impulse, he got up from his chair and bolted the door. He was afraid of what might enter, barricading himself against the impossible.

The lamp worried him and he blew it out, afraid lest someone should see him.

Who?

Alas, what he sought to exclude and to stifle was already present in the room. It was his own conscience.

His conscience: that is to say, God.

But for a time he was able to lull himself into a sense of security. With the door bolted no one could lay hands on him, and with the light extinguished he was invisible. Seated in darkness with his elbows on the table and his head resting on his hands, he reflected.

'Where am I? Is this a dream? Did I really see Javert, and did he really say those things? This man Champmathieu, does he really look so like me? Is it conceivable? When I think how untroubled I was yesterday morning, how far from suspecting anything! What was I doing at that time? What does this whole business mean? What am I to do now?'

Such was his state of torment. His brain had lost the power to grasp the thoughts that sped like waves through it while he clutched his forehead in an effort to control them. It was a turmoil swamping his willpower and reason, from which nothing emerged except the sense of his own anguish as he sought in vain for clarity and resolve.

His head was burning. He got up and flung open the window. There were no stars in the sky. He came back and sat down again at the table.

The first hour passed in this fashion.

By degrees the thoughts began to crystallize in his mind and he was able to take a clearer view of his situation, not as a whole but in certain of its details. He perceived that, extraordinary and critical though it was, he was nevertheless entirely master of it.

This merely deepened his perplexity.

Apart from their strict underlying religious intention, his every act until that day had been for the purpose of digging a hole in which his real name might be buried. What he had most feared, in his moments of recollection and his wakeful nights, was to hear that name spoken. He had said to himself that the rebirth of that name would for him mean the end of everything, the destruction of the new life he had built, even – who could tell? – of the new soul he had fashioned. The thought alone, the very possibility, made him shudder. Had anyone told him that a day would come when the name, the hideous words 'Jean Valjean', would suddenly resound in his ears like a thunderclap, coming like a blaze of light out of darkness to tear aside the mystery in which he had disguised himself; and had they gone on to tell him that this would be no threat unless he chose to make it so, that the light would serve merely to deepen his disguise and that the worthy Monsieur Madeleine, being confronted with the ghost of Jean Valjean, might emerge from the encounter even more honoured and secure than before – had anyone said this to him he would have stared in amazement, thinking the words insane. Yet this was precisely what had happened, this heaping-up of impossibilities was a fact; God had allowed the fantasy to become reality.

As his mind cleared he became more precisely aware of his position. It was as though he had awakened out of sleep to find himself sliding down a slope in darkness, upright and shivering, struggling in vain to check his descent on the edge of a precipice. He saw clearly the figure of another man, a stranger, whom Destiny had mistaken for himself and was thrusting into that chasm. Someone had to go into the chasm, he or another, if it was to be sealed up.

He had only to let things take their course.

It came to this: that his place in prison was still vacant, rendered vacant by his robbery of the boy, that it was empty and awaiting him and would continue to claim him until he returned to it, and that this was inexorable. But now it seemed that he had found a substitute, the luckless Champmathieu. He could, if he chose, be in two places at once, a prisoner in the person of Champmathieu, and a member of society under the name of Madeleine, with nothing more to fear provided he allowed the brand of infamy to be set on Champmathieu's head, the stigma which, like a tombstone, once set in place can never be removed.

All this was so appalling and so strange that it caused in him the sort of upheaval that men experience only twice or thrice in a lifetime, a spiritual convulsion compounded of all the suspect elements in the heart, irony, triumph, desperation – something that may be termed an inward burst of laughter.

He suddenly re-lit his candle.

'After all,' he thought, 'what am I afraid of? Why do I have to sit here brooding? I'm safe at last. The one door through which the past might have entered to disrupt my life has now been closed, walled-up for good. The man who so nearly guessed the truth – who did guess it, by God! – Javert, the bloodhound sniffing at my heels, has been thrown completely off the scent. He has got his Jean Valjean and will trouble me no more. Very likely he will choose to leave the town and go elsewhere. And none of this is my doing. I had no part in it. So what is wrong? To look at me one might think that I had been overtaken by disaster. But after all, if another man is in trouble, that is not my fault. Providence has ordained it, and who am I to fly in the face of Providence? What more can I ask? The blessing I have most longed for during these years, the subject of my nightly dreams and prayers to Heaven, has now been granted me – perfect security! God has caused it to happen, and it is not for me to oppose the will of God. And why does God want it? So that I may continue as I have begun, to do good in the world and to set an example to other men, to let it be seen that the way of virtue and repentance is not divorced from happiness. I no longer understand why I was afraid to visit the curé, confess to him and ask his counsel, when clearly that is what he would have said to me – the matter has been settled, leave things as they are, let God have His way.'

Thus he reflected in the depths of his conscience, suspended, as it were, over his personal abyss. He got up and began to pace the room. 'No need to think about it any more,' he said. 'I have made up my mind.'

But he was far from happy.

We can no more prevent a thought returning to the mind than we can prevent the sea from rising on the foreshore. To the sailor it is the tide, to the uneasy conscience it is remorse. God moves the soul as He moves the oceans.

After a little while, despite himself, he resumed that sombre dialogue in which he was both speaker and audience, saying things he did not wish to say, hearing things he did not wish to hear, yielding to that mysterious power which said to him, 'Reflect', as two thousand years before it had said to another condemned man, 'Take up thy Cross!'

At that point, and in order that we may be fully understood, we must interpolate an observation.

It is certain that we talk to ourselves; there is no thinking person who has not done so. It may indeed be said that the *word* is never a more splendid mystery than when it travels in a man's mind from thought to conscience and back again to thought. The expressions frequently used in this chapter, such as 'He said', 'He exclaimed', are to be interpreted in this sense. We say and exclaim within ourselves without breaking silence, in a tumult wherein everything speaks except our mouth. The realities of the soul are none the less real for being invisible and impalpable.

He asked himself where he stood, and he questioned the 'decision' he had arrived at. He confessed to himself that what he had resolved upon – to let things take their course, to let God have his way – was quite simply outrageous. To acquiesce in this blunder on the part of destiny and men, to make no effort to prevent it, to endorse it by his silence, in short, to do nothing, was in fact to do *everything*: it was to descend to the most abject depths of criminal hypocrisy and cowardice.

For the first time in eight years the unhappy man had tasted the bitter flavour of an evil thought and an evil deed.

He spat it out in disgust.

He pursued his self-questioning, sternly demanding what he had meant when he said, 'My object is achieved.' Certainly his life had a purpose, but was it simply to hide himself, to outwit the police? Had everything he had done been for no better reason than this? Had he not had a greater purpose, the saving not of his life but of his soul, the resolve to become a good and honourable and upright man as the bishop required of him – had not that been his true and deepest intention? Now he talked of closing the door on the past when, God help him, he would be reopening the door by committing an infamous act, not merely that of a thief but of the most odious of thieves. He would be robbing a man of his life, his peace, his place in the sun, morally murdering him by condemning him to the living death that is called a convict prison. But if, on the other hand, he saved the man by repairing the blunder, by proclaiming himself Jean Valjean the felon, this would be to achieve his own true resurrection and firmly close the door on the hell from which he sought to escape. To return to it in appearance would be to escape from it in reality. This was what he must do, and without it he would have accomplished nothing, his life would be wasted, his repentance meaningless, and there would be nothing left for him to say except, 'Who cares?' He felt the presence of the bishop, more urgent than in life; he felt the old priest's eyes upon him and knew that henceforth Monsieur Madeleine the mayor, with all his virtues, would seem to him abominable, whereas Jean Valjean the felon would be admirable and pure. Other men would see the mask, but the bishop would see the face; others would see the life, but he would see the soul. So there was nothing for it but to go to Arras and rescue the false Jean Valjean by proclaiming the true one. The most heartrending of sacrifices, the most poignant of victories, the ultimate, irretrievable step – but it had to be done. It was his most melancholy destiny that he could achieve sanctity in the eyes of God only by returning to degradation in the eyes of men.

'Well then,' he said, 'let us decide upon it. Let us do our duty and save this man.'

Without knowing it he spoke the words aloud.

He turned to his account-books, checked them and saw that they were in order. He threw a sheaf of papers on the fire, the promissory notes of small tradesmen whom he knew to be in difficulties. He wrote and sealed a letter addressed to Monsieur Lafitte, banker, Rue d'Artois, Paris. Opening his desk he got out a wallet containing banknotes and the identity-card he had used in the year when he went to vote in the election.

Anyone watching him while he did these things would have discerned nothing of the heavy thoughts moving in his mind except that now and then his lips moved and now and then he stood fixedly regarding some object in the room as though it contained the answer to a question.

Having written the letter to M. Lafitte he put it in his pocket with the wallet and began to pace up and down again.

The tenor of his thoughts had not changed. Whichever way he looked, the course of duty glared at him as though the words were written in letters of fire – 'Stand up and say your name!'

And at the same time, as though they had assumed a tangible form, he saw the principles that had constituted the twofold rule of his life – to keep his name hidden, and to purify his soul. For the first time he saw them as wholly separate, and he saw the difference between them. He saw that whereas one must be good the other might turn to evil, that one spoke of dedication and the other of self-interest, that one proceeded from the light and the other from the dark.

He saw the conflict between them, and as the picture grew in his mind they took on huge proportions, so that he seemed to be witnessing within himself, amid the lights and shadows of that infinity of which we have spoken, a struggle between a goddess and a giantess. He was filled with terror, but it seemed to him that the good had gained the upper hand.

He perceived that this was the second turning-point in his spiritual life and in his destiny: the bishop had been the first, and the man Champmathieu marked the second. This was the uttermost crisis, the final trial of his fortitude.

His fevered state, which for a time had abated, was now rising again. A thousand thoughts crossed his mind, but still they reaffirmed his resolution.

He said to himself at one moment that perhaps he was taking the whole matter too seriously, that the man Champmathieu was perhaps not so important after all, and in any case he was a thief. But to this he replied that if the man had stolen a few apples it would entail no more than a month's prison sentence – a far step from the galleys. And who was to say for certain that he had stolen anything? The name of Jean Valjean seemed to render further proof unnecessary. Was not this how the king's prosecutors reasoned? A man is believed to be a thief because he is known to be a felon.

Then again the thought occurred to him that perhaps when he gave himself up, the nobility of the act would be taken into account, his honourable life during the past seven years, the good he had done, and that because of this he would be exonerated. But he quickly dismissed this thought, reflecting bitterly that the theft of those forty sous from Petit-Gervais would certainly be recalled, and that by this act he had become a recidivist, subject to hard-labour in perpetuity under the stringent terms of the law.

Setting aside all illusion, he sought to detach himself from earthly things and to find strength and consolation elsewhere. He told himself that he must do his duty and that perhaps he would be no more unhappy when he had done it than if he evaded it and allowed the honour and dignity, the high esteem, the wealth and popularity of Monsieur Madeleine to be rendered secretly shameful by a criminal act – and what sort of taste would that leave in his mouth? Whereas, if he made the sacrifice, all would be redeemed – the squalor of imprisonment, the suffering, the endless labour and ignominy – l y the assurance in his heart.

Finally he said to himself that in any event it was unavoidable. This was his destiny and he could not alter what had been ordained. The choice had been forced upon him between outward virtue and inward infamy, or outward degradation and purity of heart.

This play of melancholy thoughts did not lessen his courage but it wearied his brain. He began to think at random of irrelevant things. He was still pacing the room, with the blood beating violently at his temples. Midnight sounded, first from the parish church and then from the Town Hall. He counted the strokes, mentally comparing the two clocks, and this caused him to recall that a few days before he had seen in a second-hand shop an old clock bearing the name Antoine Albin de Romainville. He was cold. He stirred the fire, but it did not occur to him to shut the window.

He was falling into a state of apathy, and it cost him an effort to recall what he had been thinking about before midnight sounded. Finally he remembered. 'Yes,' he said, 'I have decided to give myself up.'

Then suddenly he thought of Fantine. 'That poor woman!' he exclaimed.

The abrupt recollection, coming as it were out of the blue, seemed to shed an entirely new light on his predicament. He exclaimed:

'But . . . ! I have been thinking of nothing but myself and my own peace of mind. I am to keep quiet or give myself up – stay hidden or save my soul – live on as a respected, despicable mayor or as a despised but honourable galley-slave. All this is pure egotism. What if I were to think of others, as our Christian duty requires?'

He began now to consider the consequences of his departure from the scene. The town and the whole region would suffer, the industry he had created, the workpeople, men and women and children, the old and needy, the many families who depended on him. He had come to a place that was moribund and made it prosperous, brought life to a desert. With his going that life would start to ebb, without him the place would sink and die. And did he owe nothing to Fantine, for whose sufferings he was in some degree responsible? He had promised to retrieve her child. If he failed in this, she too would surely die, and the Lord knew what would become of the child. All this would follow if he gave himself up. And what if he did not?

He paused on the question, seeming to hesitate for an instant and tremble; but then he resumed calmly:

'A man will go to life-imprisonment. But he was guilty of theft, no need to pretend otherwise. And I shall stay where I am, and that mother will be able to bring up her child. In ten years I shall have amassed ten millions and this will enrich the whole community. The money means nothing to me. The whole region will benefit – greater prosperity, new industries, more people. New villages will spring up where now there are only farms, and farms where now there is only waste land. Want will be abolished, and with it the crimes and vices that it causes. A rich and smiling land! And all this is to be sacrificed for what? For my personal gratification, for the sake of an heroic gesture, an act of melodrama. A woman is to die in hospital and her child on the streets, a whole community is to suffer, to save a man from a punishment which may or may not be excessive (he may well deserve it for something else; he is an old rascal anyway who cannot have long to live) – and in order that my private conscience may be appeased. But that is madness! If there is to be a weight on my conscience it is my own affair. My duty is to others, not to myself.'

He got up and again began to pace the room, feeling now that his conscience was at rest. Diamonds are to be found only in the darkness of the earth, and truth in the darkness of the mind. It seemed to him that having penetrated to those depths, having groped in the heart of darkness, he had found and grasped a diamond of truth that now lay gleaming in his hand.

'Yes,' he thought, 'this is the right course. There has to be a guiding principle. My mind is made up. I shall leave things as they are and there will be no more vacillation. I am Madeleine and will continue to be Madeleine, and as for the man who now bears the name of Valjean, so much the worse for him. I am no longer Valjean, I do not know him and he is no concern of mine. If another man has been inflicted with his name, that is the work of Chance, and Chance alone is responsible.' He looked at himself in the mirror over the mantelshelf. 'Oh, the relief of having decided! Already I feel a new man.'

He resumed his pacing of the room, but abruptly stopped, arrested by the thought that, now his decision had been taken, he must shirk none of its consequences. There were still objects concealed in that room which linked him with Jean Valjean and might bear witness against him if they were not destroyed.

Getting a small key out of his purse, he inserted it in a keyhole which was scarcely visible even to himself, so lost was it in the darker tints of the wallpaper. He opened the door of a cupboard, a sort of wardrobe built in between the projecting chimney and the corner of the room. The cupboard contained some rags of underclothing, a blue canvas smock, an old pair of trousers, a knapsack, and a stick with a ferrule at either end. Anyone who had seen Jean Valjean on his way through Digne in October 1815 would have recognized these things.

He had preserved them, with the silver candlesticks, as a reminder of the day when he had started life anew. But whereas he hid the prison relics, the bishop's candlesticks were openly displayed.

He looked furtively towards the door as though he feared that it might suddenly open, bolted though it was; then with a single, rapid movement, and without a glance at the relics which he had perilously guarded for so long, he tossed the whole bundle, rags, stick and knapsack, on to the fire. He closed the cupboard and as an added precaution, meaningless now that it was empty, moved a large piece of furniture in front of it to conceal the door.

In a very short time the room was lit up as the bundle burst into flame, while the thorn stick crackled, sending sparks far across the floor.

As the knapsack with its squalid contents disintegrated, something gleamed amid the embers. Closer examination would have shown that it was a coin – doubtless the forty-sou piece stolen from a small boy. But he was not looking at the fire. He had resumed his steady pacing of the room.

His eye was caught suddenly by the faint reflection of firelight in the silver candlesticks on the mantelpiece. 'Another reminder of Jean Valjean,' he thought. 'I must get rid of them.' And he took them down.

The fire was still hot enough to melt them into a shapeless lump of metal. For a moment he bent over it, warming himself with a genuine sense of comfort. 'How pleasant the heat is,' he thought. He stirred the embers with one of the candlesticks. In another minute both would have been on the fire.

But at that moment it seemed to him that he heard a voice speaking within him.

'Jean Valjean! Jean Valjean!'

The words filled him with terror, and the hair rose on his scalp.

'So be it,' said the voice. 'Finish what you have begun. Destroy the candlesticks, blot out the memory, forget the bishop, forget everything and think well of yourself. You have decided! An old man who understands nothing of what has happened, whose only crime may be that your name is now inflicted upon him, is to be sentenced in your place, condemned for the rest of his days to abjection and servitude. And you will remain an upright citizen, the respected and honoured Monsieur le maire. You will enrich the town, feed the poor, protect the orphan and live happy in the light of every man's esteem while another man wears the blue smock and the fetters which are rightly yours and bears your name in degradation. How fortunately things have turned out for you!'

The sweat had started on his brow and he stared haggardly into the flame. But the speaker in his heart had still not finished.

'Many voices will praise you, Jean Valjean, many will bless you, but there is one man who will not hear them and will curse you in his darkness. Take good heed! The blessings will fall away before they are heard in Heaven, and only the curse will reach God!'

The voice, weak at first and rising from the depths of his conscience, had gained in power until it rang in his ears, seeming now to come from somewhere outside himself, the last words so loud that he gazed round in terror and cried:

'Is someone there?' then answered the question with a foolish laugh: 'I'm being stupid. There can't be anyone.'

There was someone none the less, but it was not someone whom the human eye could see.

He put the candlesticks back on the mantlepiece, and the mournful regularity of his footsteps up and down the room disturbed the slumbers of the sleeper in the room below.

The act of walking both soothed and stimulated him. There are moments of crisis when we seek release in movement, as though to take council with any random object that meets our eye. But now it served only to heighten the consciousness of his predicament. The ironic chance that this man Champmathieu should have been mistaken for himself, and that this accident, which Providence seemed to have contrived for his salvation, must also cut the ground from beneath his feet! He had taken two decisions and now he recoiled from both, finding each unthinkable.

For a moment, and in utter despair, he envisaged the consequences of giving himself up, all he would be losing and what he would be getting in its place. He would be saying good-bye to a blameless and happy life, to honour, liberty, and every man's esteem. He would be free no longer to walk the fields, listen to birdsong, give pennies to the children. No look of warmth and gratitude would meet his gaze. He would leave the house he had built and this small room he lived in, which now seemed to him so pleasant; and the old concierge, his only servant, would no longer bring him his coffee in the morning. All this would go, and in its place would be the chaingang and the convict smock, the plank bed and the cell, all the horrors that he knew. At his age, after becoming what he now was! If he were still young ... But an old man, barefoot in iron-shod clogs, subject to insult and ill-usage, forced to show a leg morning and evening to the warder who inspected his fetters; a sight to be shown to the casual visitor, who would be told, 'That's the famous Jean Valjean, the one who was the Mayor of Montreuil-sur-mer'

. . . Fate, it seemed, could be as malignant as the human intelligence, as remorseless as the human heart!

Whichever way he turned, he faced the same alternatives – to cling to his paradise and become a devil, or become a saint by going back to hell. In God's name, what was he to do?

He was beset again with the mental agonies which for a time he had so painfully dispelled, and his thinking again became confused, lapsing into the apathetic sluggishness that is a part of despair. A name, Romainville, floated into his memory, and with it two lines of a song he had once heard. Romainville, he recalled, was a wood near Paris where young lovers went to gather lilac in April. He was lurching physically as well as spiritually, like an infant walking for the first time.

Struggling with this growing lassitude, he sought to bring some order into his thoughts, striving still to confront, and resolve for good and all, the dilemma which had brought him to this state of exhaustion: should he give himself up or keep silent? But he could see nothing clearly. The notions that flooded through his mind were becoming clouded, vanishing in smoke. One thing alone was plain to him, that whichever way he went something in him must inevitably die. Whether he turned right or left the end was a sepulchre, the death of one thing or the other, happiness or virtue. For the rest, all his uncertainties had returned. He was no further advanced than when he had begun.

Thus he strove in torment as another man had striven eighteen hundred years before him, the mysterious Being in whom were embodied all the saintliness and suffering of mankind. He too while the olive-leaves quivered around him, had again and again refused the terrible cup of darkness urged upon him beneath a sky filled with stars.

IV

Suffering in sleep

The clocks had struck three, and he had been pacing the room almost without pause for five hours, when at length he sank into his chair. He fell asleep and dreamed.

Like most dreams, this one was related to his situation only in its sense of heart-break and doom. Nevertheless it made so great an impression on him that later he wrote it down. His account of it is among the documents left behind after his death, and since the story of that night would be incomplete without it, we reproduce it here. It is the sombre fantasy of a sick soul.

The inscription on the envelope reads: 'What I dreamed that night'.

I was in the country, a vast, barren landscape where there seemed to be neither day nor night.

I was walking with my brother, the brother of my childhood years, of whom I may say I never think and whom I have almost forgotten.

We were talking and people passed us. We were talking about a woman, formerly a neighbour of ours, who when she was living in the same street always worked with her window open. As we talked about her we felt the chill of that open window.

There were no trees to be seen.

A man passed close to us. He was naked, the colour of ashes, and he was riding a horse the colour of earth. He was hairless, we could see his bare skull and the veins on his skull. He carried a wand in his hand, supple as a vine-twig and heavy as iron. He passed by and said nothing.

My brother said, 'Let us go by the sunken road.'

There was no shrub to be seen in the sunken road, nor any patch of moss. Everything was the colour of earth, even the sky. I said something as we walked along, and there was no reply. I found that my brother was no longer there.

I came to a village and thought when I saw it that it must be Romainville (why Romainville?).

The street by which I entered was deserted. I turned into a second street. At the corner of the two streets a man was standing with his back to the wall. I asked him, 'What is this place? Where am I?' He did not answer. I saw the open door of a house and went in.

There was no one in the first room. I went into the next. Behind the door of this room a man was standing with his back to the wall. I asked him: 'Whose house is this? Where am I?' He did not answer. The house had a garden.

I went into the garden. It was empty. Behind the first tree I found a man standing. I asked him: 'What garden is this? Where am I?' He did not answer.

I wandered through the village and perceived that it was a town. All the streets were deserted, all the doors were open. No living person passed along the streets or moved in the rooms or walked in the gardens. But at every street-corner, and behind every doorway and every tree, a man stood and was silent. I never saw more than one at a time. They watched me as I passed.

I left the town and walked on through the fields.

After a time I looked back and saw a large crowd coming behind me. I recognized all the men I had seen in the town. They bore themselves strangely. Without seeming to hurry they were walking faster than I. They made no sound as they walked. In a very little while they had caught up with me and surrounded me. The men's faces were the colour of earth.

The man whom I had first seen and questioned when I entered the town now said to me: 'Where are you going? Don't you know that you have been dead for a long time?'

I opened my mouth to reply, and found that there was no one there.

He awoke from his dream. He was very cold. A wind as chill as the wind at daybreak was causing the frame of the open window to creak in its hinges. The fire had gone out and the candle was nearly burnt down. The night was still black.

He got up and went to the window. There were still no stars in the sky.

From the window he could see the courtyard and the street. A sudden sharp sound caused him to look down. He saw two red stars below him, their rays oddly expanding and contracting in the darkness. 'No stars in the sky,' he thought, still bemused by his dream. 'They are on earth instead.'

This illusion was dispelled by a repetition of the sound, which woke him up completely. He saw that the two stars were the lamps of a carriage of which he could now distinguish the shape. It was a tilbury with a small white horse between the shafts, and the sound he had heard was that of the horse's hoofs on the cobbles.

'What is it doing here?' he wondered. 'Who can have called at this hour?'

At this moment there was a timid knock on the door. He shivered from head to foot and cried in a voice of fury:

'Who's there?'

'It's me, Monsieur le maire.'

He recognized the voice of the old woman, his servant.

'Well, what's the matter?'

'It will soon be five o'clock, Monsieur le maire.'

'Well?'

'The carriage is here.'

'What carriage?'

'The tilbury.'

'What tilbury?'

'Did not Monsieur le maire order a tilbury?'

'No,' he answered.

'The driver says he has brought it for you.'

'What driver?'

'Master Scaufflaire's driver.'

'Scaufflaire?' And suddenly a light dawned. 'Of course,' he said. 'Monsieur Scaufflaire.'

Had the old woman been able to see his expression at that moment she would have been frightened out of her wits.

There was a pause. He was staring stupidly at the candle, and, scraping up a little of the melted wax, he rolled it into a ball between his fingers. The old woman waited and at length ventured to raise her voice.

'Monsieur le maire, what am I to say to him?'

'Tell him to wait. I'm coming down.'

v

Spokes in the wheel

The postal service between Arras and Montreuil-sur-mer in those days still made use of small conveyances dating from the time of the Empire. They were two-wheel carts upholstered inside with rough leather, mounted on cylindrical springs and having two seats, one for the driver and one for a passenger. The wheels were fitted with those long, aggressive hubs that keep other vehicles at a distance and are still to be seen in Germany. The very large oblong mail-box was built into the back and painted black, while the trap itself was yellow.

We have nothing like them today. They had an oddly hump-backed appearance, and seen from far off, as they came into sight on the crest of a hill, they resembled the insects known, I think, as termites, which can pull a load much bigger than themselves. They travelled very fast. The post-cart which left Arras at one o'clock in the morning, having picked up the Paris mail, reached Montreuil-sur-mer a little before five.

As it approached the town that morning, coming down the slope from Hesdin, the post-cart clashed on a bend in the road with a small tilbury with a white horse which was being driven in the opposite direction by its sole occupant, a man in a greatcoat. The wheel of the tilbury received a heavy blow. The postman called to the driver to stop, but he took no notice and drove on at a fast trot.

'He's in a devil of a hurry,' the postman said.

Where was he going, this man in a hurry whose tribulations must surely have moved us to compassion? He could not have said. Why was he driving so fast? He did not know. He was driving blindly, he did not know where. To Arras, certainly; but perhaps to another place as well. He realized this at moments and shuddered.

He was driving through the darkness as though into an abyss. Something thrust him forward and something drew him on. His state of mind was such as no words can describe but all men will understand. Is there any man who, once at least in his life, has not found himself in that blackness of uncertainty? He had resolved nothing, decided nothing, settled nothing. Out of all his agonies of conscience no finality had emerged. More than ever he was back where he had started.

Why, then, was he going to Arras?

He repeated the arguments he had used when he hired the tilbury – that whatever the outcome it could do no harm for him to see with his own eyes and decide for himself; that it was even prudent, since he needed to know what took place; that no judgement could be formed except through firsthand observation and considered scrutiny; that distance made molehills into mountains, and when he set eyes on this Champmathieu, and saw him to be the worthless creature he doubtless was, he might well find it within his conscience to let him go to prison in his place. It was true that Javert would be there, as well as Brevet, Chenildieu, and Cochepaille, convicts who had known him in the past; but they would never recognize him in the Madeleine he now was. The thing was inconceivable. Even Javert had been completely misled. Suspicion and conjecture – than which nothing is more pig-headed – were entirely concentrated on Champmathieu.

So he was in no danger. This was a dark moment in his life, but one that he could live through. When all was said, his fate, however ugly it might prove to be, was in his own hands; he was its master. He clung to this thought.

In his heart he would have preferred not to go to Arras.

However he was going there, and he whipped up his horse, keeping it to the steady trot which covers seven or eight miles in an hour, but feeling something shrink within him as he drew nearer.

By daybreak he was in open country with Montreuil-sur-mer a good distance behind him. He watched the skyline grow light, and was aware, without observing it, of the chilly aspect of a winter's dawn. Morning, like evening, has its ghosts. He did not see them but was still conscious, as though by their physical presence, of the dark shapes of trees and hills making their mournful contribution to his violently agitated state of mind. Passing an occasional isolated house at the side of the road, he thought to himself, 'And there are people still sleeping!' The clop of the horse's hoofs, the jingle of harness and the clatter of the wheels over cobbles were a monotonous accompaniment to his thoughts – delightful sounds when we are in good spirits, but most dismal when we are melancholy.

It was broad daylight when he reached Hesdin, where he stopped at an inn to rest and feed his horse.

The horse, as Scaufflaire had said, was of the small, Boulonnais stock, overlarge in the head and belly and short in the neck, but with a broad chest and wide rump, stringy legs and sure feet; an unbeautiful breed, but healthy and robust. It had covered five leagues in two hours and there was no sweat on its flanks.

He did not get out of the tilbury. The stable-lad who brought the oats bent down suddenly to examine the left wheel and asked:

'Are you going far like this?'

He answered absently: 'Why?'

'Have you come far?' the boy asked.

'About five leagues.'

'Ah.'

'What does that "ah" mean?'

The boy took another close look at the wheel and then stood up.

'That wheel may have lasted for five leagues, but it certainly won't do more than another half league.'

He jumped down from the tilbury. 'Why do you say that, lad?'

'I say it's a marvel you've done as much as five leagues without going into the ditch. You can see for yourself.'

The wheel was, in fact, badly damaged. The clash with the post-cart had cracked two spokes and loosened the hub.

'Is there a wheelwright handy?' Madeleine asked.

'Certainly, Monsieur.'

'Will you be so good as to fetch him.'

'He's next door – hey, Maître Bourgaillard!'

Maître Bourgaillard, the wheelwright, was standing in his doorway. He came over to look at the wheel and pursed his lips like a surgeon over a broken leg.

'Can you repair it for me immediately?'

'Yes, Monsieur.'

'When shall I be able to leave?'

'Tomorrow.'

'Tomorrow?'

'It will take a good day's work. Is Monsieur in a great hurry?'

'A very great hurry. I must be on my way in an hour at the most.'

'Monsieur, that is impossible.'

'I'll pay whatever you ask.'

'It can't be done.'

'Well then, two hours.'

'It still can't be done. I shall have to make two new spokes and a hub. Monsieur will not be able to leave before tomorrow.'

'My business won't wait until tomorrow. If you can't repair the wheel, can you replace it?'

'How do you mean?'

'You're a wheelwright. Can you not sell me a new wheel? Then I could get on at once.'

'A single wheel? I haven't one that would fit. Wheels go in pairs, Monsieur. They have to match.'

'Then let me have a pair.'

'But all wheels don't fit all axles, Monsieur.'

'You can at least try.'

'It wouldn't do, Monsieur. I only have cartwheels to sell. We're small people in these parts.'

'Have you a gig for hire?'

The wheelwright had seen at a glance that the tilbury was hired. He shrugged his shoulders.

'You make a fine mess of the things you hire. I wouldn't let you have one even if I could.'

'Will you sell me one?'

'I haven't got one to sell.'

'Not a light carriage of any kind? I'm not particular.'

'This is a small village. All the same,' said the wheelwright, 'there's an old barouche which I house in my shed for a gentleman from the town who only uses it once in a month of Sundays. No reason why I shouldn't hire you that one provided the owner doesn't know. But it's a barouche, like I said. It needs two horses.'

'I'll hire post-horses.'

'Where would your honour be going?'

'To Arras.'

'And you want to arrive today?'

'I must.'

'It wouldn't do for you to arrive at four in the morning?'

'Certainly not.'

'Well, you see, when it comes to hiring post-horses ... Your honour has identity papers?'

'Yes.'

'Well, you can hire post-horses but you still won't get to Arras before tomorrow. This is a side-road and the stages are badly served. And it's the start of the ploughing season when the farmers need big teams. They get horses wherever they can, from the posts or anywhere else. You'd have to wait three or four hours at every stage. And you'd be going at a walk. There are a lot of hills.'

'Then I shall have to ride. Will you please unharness the tilbury. I take it someone can sell me a saddle.'

'Yes. But is this a saddle-horse?'

'Ah. It's as well you reminded me. It won't take a saddle.'

'In that case ...'

'Surely there's a horse in the village I can hire?'

'To go from here to Arras in one stretch? It would take a better horse than you'll find in these parts. You'd have to buy it in any case, because you aren't known round here. But you'd never get one, even if you offered a thousand francs.'

'Then what am I to do?'

'The only honest advice I can give you is to let me repair the wheel and go on tomorrow.'

'Tomorrow will be too late.'

'Well, I'm sorry.'

'Isn't there a mail that goes to Arras? When does it arrive here?'

'Tonight. The mails both travel at night, one up, one down.'

'And it will really take a whole day's work to repair this wheel?'

'A long one at that.'

'Even if you put two men on it?'

'Even if I put ten.'

'Can't you bind the spokes with twine?'

'Yes, perhaps; but that won't mend the hub. And the felloe's in bad shape.'

'Is there anyone in the town with carriages for hire?'

'No.'

'Is there another wheelwright?'

The stable-boy and Maître Bourgaillard both shook their heads. Madeleine felt a sense of overwhelming relief.

Clearly this was the work of Providence. It was by pure mischance that his wheel had been broken, a gesture on the part of Providence that at first he had ignored. He had done everything in his power to continue his journey, scrupulously examining every possibility. He had not let himself be put off by the season of the year, by fatigue, or by the cost. He had no cause to reproach himself. If he could get no further it was not his doing; Providence alone was to blame.

He drew a deep breath, able for the first time since Javert's visit to breathe freely, feeling that the iron band which for twenty hours had constricted his chest was now loosened. God was on his side and had declared the fact. He told himself that he had done his utmost and might now turn back with his conscience at rest.

If this conversation had taken place inside the inn, without being overheard, it is probable that the matter would have ended there, and that the long train of events which were to follow would never have occurred. But a conversation in a village street invariably attracts an audience. There are always people who want to hear. A group of spectators had gathered round them while he was questioning the wheelwright, among them a boy who slipped unnoticed out of the circle and broke into a run.

Just as Madeleine was finally making up his mind, this youngster returned, bringing with him an elderly woman.

'Monsieur,' she said, 'my boy tells me that you want to hire a gig.'

The harmless words, so inoffensively uttered, made him break into a cold sweat. The hand that had had him by the throat seemed to re-emerge from the darkness he thought he had left behind him, preparing to renew its grip.

He answered, 'That is true, Madame. I do wish to hire a gig.' And then he said quickly: 'But there isn't one to be had.'

'But there is,' the woman said.

'Where is it?' asked the wheelwright.

'In my yard.'

Madeleine trembled. The hand had seized him again.

The old woman did indeed possess a sort of gig with a wicker body which she kept under a lean-to shed in her yard. The stable-boy and the wheelwright, disconsolate at losing a customer, both vigorously decried it. It was a wreck, they said – a box mounted unsprung on its axle, with seats slung on leather straps – open to the weather – wheels rusted and rotten with damp – no more fit to take the road than the tilbury – the gentleman would be mad to trust himself to it – and so on . . .

All this was true, but decrepit though it was, the vehicle had both its wheels and might still get him to Arras.

He paid what was asked, left the tilbury to be repaired by the wheelwright, had the white horse harnessed to the gig, got in and continued on his way.

He confessed to himself as he started that a very short time before he had rejoiced in the thought that he need go no further: now he looked back on this rejoicing with a kind of anger, finding it absurd. Why take pleasure in retreat? After all, he had undertaken this journey of his own free will, no one had compelled him. And certainly nothing would come of it unless he decided otherwise.

As he was leaving Hesdin he heard a voice calling to him, 'Stop! Stop!' He pulled up sharply, with a gesture of convulsive eagerness akin to hope.

It was the boy, the old woman's servant.

'Monsieur, I'm the one who found the gig for you.'

'Well?'

'You haven't given me anything.'

Open-handed though he normally was, he found this demand excessive and almost nauseating.

'So that's what you want,' he said. 'You'll get nothing from me.'

He whipped up his horse and drove on.

He would have liked to make up the time he had lost in Hesdin. The little horse was sturdy and very willing, but the month was February, there had been rain and the roads were in a bad state. Moreover this gig was heavy and sluggish compared with the til-bury and there were a great many hills. It took him nearly four hours to reach Saint-Pol, a distance of perhaps fifteen miles.

He had the horse unharnessed and taken round to the stable at the first inn he came to, and, as he had promised Scaufflaire, he watched while it was fed. His thoughts were sombre and confused.

The innkeeper's wife came out to the stable.

'Is not Monsieur going to dine?'

'Why yes,' he said. 'In fact, I'm hungry.'

She was a woman with a fresh, cheerful face. He followed her into a low-ceilinged room with oilcloth on the tables.

'You must be quick,' he said. 'I have very little time.'

A plump Flemish maid hurriedly laid a place for him and he looked at her with a sense of reassurance.

'That's what's wrong with me,' he thought. 'I've had no breakfast.'

His meal was served. He snatched up a piece of bread, swallowed a mouthful, then put it down and ate no more. Turning to a carter at the next table he said:

'Why is the bread here so bitter?'

The man was German and did not understand.

An hour later he had left Saint-Pol and was heading for Tinques, which is some twelve miles from Arras.

What were his thoughts during this part of the journey? As in the morning he watched the passing of trees, thatched roofs, tilled fields, the changing vistas appearing at every bend in the road, an occupation soothing to the spirit that may almost take the place of thought. Nothing can be sadder or more profound than to see a thousand things for the first and last time. To journey is to be born and die each minute. Perhaps somewhere in the vague recesses of his mind he perceived parallels between this series of dissolving views and our human life. All the elements of life are in constant flight from us, with darkness and clarity intermingled, the vision and the eclipse; we look and hasten, reaching out our hands to clutch; every happening is a bend in the road . . . and suddenly we have grown old. We have a sense of shock and gathering darkness; ahead is a black doorway; the life that bore us is a flagging horse, and a veiled stranger is waiting in the shadows to unharness it.

Twilight was gathering when the children coming out of school in Tinques saw the traveller enter the village. These were indeed the shortest days in the year. He did not stop in Tinques, and as he was leaving it a roadmender looked up and said:

'That's a very tired horse.'

The poor beast could indeed only manage a walk.

'Are you going to Arras?' the man asked.

'Yes.'

'At the rate you're going you'll be a long time getting there.'

He reined in the horse and asked: 'How far is it?'

'A good seven leagues.'

'What! But the postal guide makes it five and a quarter.'

'Ah, but the road's up for repair. You'll find it closed a quarter of an hour from here. You'll have to go round. You turn left for Carency, you cross the river and then turn right when you get to Camblin. That's the Mont-Saint-Eloy road, which goes to Arras.'

'But it's getting dark. I shall lose my way.'

'You don't live in these parts?'

'No.'

'And it's all side-lanes. If you want my advice, Monsieur,' said the roadman, 'you'll go back to Tinques and stop the night. There's a good inn, and your horse is worn out. You can go on to Arras in the morning.'

'But I have to be there this evening.'

'Well, that's different. All the same, you'd better go to the inn and hire an extra horse. The lad in charge will see you through the lanes.'

He followed this advice and turned back. Half an hour later he drove briskly past the same spot with a sturdy additional horse. A stable-boy acting as postillion was seated on the shaft of the gig.

But more time had been lost and it was now quite dark. The going in the lanes was very bad. The gig lurched from one rut to the next, but he said to the boy: 'Keep up a trot and you'll get a double tip.'

Then, at a particularly heavy lurch, the cross-tree broke.

'I don't see how we can go on,' the lad said. 'I've nothing to harness my horse to. These lanes are terrible after dark. If you'll come back to Tinques for the night, Monsieur, we can be at Arras first thing in the morning.'

His reply was: 'Have you a hank of cord and a knife?'

'Yes.'

He cut a branch from the hedge and improvised a cross-tree. Another twenty minutes had been wasted, but they went on at a good pace.

The plain was misty with banks of fog drifting like smoke over the hilltops and whitish gleams amid the cloud. A wind from the sea set up a distant rumbling like the sound of someone moving furniture, a sense of awe filled the air, all life seemed to shiver in the darkness of the growing night.

The cold pierced through him. He had eaten nothing since the night before. And now he recalled another night-time journey, across the great plain on the outskirts of Digne. Eight years ago, and it might have been yesterday.

A distant church clock sounded and he asked:

'What time is it?'

'Seven, Monsieur. We shall be in Arras at eight, only three leagues more.'

Then for the first time, finding it strange that the thought had not already occurred to him, he reflected that perhaps all the effort he was making was useless. He did not even know what time the case was to be heard. He should at least have ascertained this. It was surely ridiculous to be rushing as he did without knowing whether he would get there in time. He began to make calculations. An assize court ordinarily began the day's session at nine in the morning. This case would certainly not occupy it for long. The theft of the apples was a very small matter. Then there was the question of identity, a few depositions to be heard, little or nothing for the advocates to say. By the time he arrived it would surely be all over!

The boy whipped up the horses. They had crossed the river and left Mont-Saint-Eloy behind.

The night was darker still.

VI

The testing of Sister Simplice

At that moment Fantine was in ecstasy.

She had passed a very restless night, coughing incessantly with a high fever; and she had had bad dreams. When the doctor called in the morning she was delirious. He had seemed much perturbed and had recommended that Monsieur Madeleine should be informed directly he returned.

Throughout the morning Fantine had been apathetic, saying very little and crumpling the bedclothes in her hand while under her breath she murmured figures which seemed to be calculations of distance. Her eyes were hollow and vacant, almost lifeless, but at moments they would light up and shine like stars. It would seem that as darkness approaches a light from Heaven shines for those who are about to leave the brightness of earth.

Each time Sister Simplice asked her how she felt she replied: 'Quite well. I long to see Monsieur Madeleine.'

When, a few months previously, Fantine had put aside the last shreds of her modesty, her shame, and her happiness, she had been the shadow of her former self; but now she was its ghost. Physical deterioration had completed the work of spiritual sickness. The woman of twenty-five had a wrinkled forehead and flaccid cheeks, pinched nostrils and loosened teeth, a sallow face, a bony neck and wasted limbs, and there were grey threads mingled with her fair hair. Disease is a great simulator of age.

The doctor came again at midday, gave certain instructions, asked if Monsieur Madeleine had visited her, and shook his head.

Monsieur Madeleine was in the habit of calling at three o'clock, and since punctuality is a part of kindness he was always punctual. By half past two Fantine was beginning to grow agitated. In the next twenty minutes she asked a dozen times to be told the time.

Three o'clock sounded and at the third stroke she sat upright, although ordinarily she had scarcely the strength to move. Her yellowed, wasted hands were tightly clasped and the sister heard her utter a sigh that was like the lifting of a great weight. She sat looking towards the door.

But no one entered. The door did not open.

She remained thus for a quarter of an hour, with her eyes fixed on the door, motionless, as though holding her breath. The sister was afraid to speak. The church clock struck the quarter and she sank back against the pillows. She said nothing but again began crumpling the sheet in her hands.

Half an hour passed, an hour, and no one came. Each time the clock struck Fantine sat up and looked towards the door, and then sank back again.

What was in her mind was plain enough, but she spoke no person's name, uttered no word of complaint or reproach. There was only her heartrending cough. It was as though a great shadow now oppressed her. Her cheeks had a livid pallor, her lips were blue. But at moments she smiled.

Five o'clock struck, and then the sister heard a very low and gentle murmur from her lips. 'But since I shall be going tomorrow, it is wrong of him not to come today.'

Sister Simplice was herself surprised that Monsieur Madeleine should be so late.

Fantine lay gazing at the sky from her bed. She seemed to be trying to remember something, and suddenly she began to sing in a voice no louder than a breath. She sang an old cradle-song with which she used to lull her baby daughter to sleep and which she had never once recalled in the five years since they had been separated. It was a song of gaiety and happiness, of loss and grieving, and she sang it so movingly as to cause even a hospital nurse to weep. Sister Simplice, hardened as she was to the cruelty of life, felt the tears rise in her eyes.

The clock struck six but Fantine did not seem to hear it. She seemed to be taking no more notice of her surroundings.

Sister Simplice sent a serving-girl round to the factory to ask if the mayor had returned and if he would soon be coming to the infirmary. The girl was back in a few minutes. Fantine continued to lie motionless, seemingly absorbed in the thoughts running through her mind.

The girl whispered to Sister Simplice that Monsieur le maire had driven off before six that morning, despite the cold, in a light carriage drawn by a white horse. He had gone quite alone, no one knew where. There were people who said that he had been seen on the road to Arras, and others claimed to have passed him on the Paris road. His manner when he left had been as kindly as usual. He had simply told the old woman not to expect him back that night.

While the two women were thus conversing in undertones with their backs turned towards her, Fantine, with the sudden feverish vitality which in certain illnesses lends an appearance of health to the enfeeblement of death, had risen to her knees on the bed and, supporting herself with her clenched fists on the mattress, was listening with her head thrust through the gap in the curtains. Suddenly she cried:

'You're talking about Monsieur Madeleine! Why are you whispering? What is he doing? Why hasn't he come?'

Her voice was so hoarse and rough that it might have been that of a man. The startled women swung round.

'Answer me!' cried Fantine.

The girl stammered: 'The concierge says he can't come today.'

'Lie down, my child,' said the sister. 'You must keep calm.'

Without obeying, Fantine said loudly, in a voice that was at once imperious and heartrending:

'He can't come? Why not? You know the reason. You were talking about it. I want to know.'

The girl whispered to the nun, 'Say he's at a Council meeting.'

Sister Simplice blushed faintly; she was being urged to tell a lie. On the other hand, she felt that to tell the truth would be to deal Fantine a blow which might have serious consequences in her present state. But her hesitation was soon over. Gazing gravely and compassionately at Fantine she said:

'The mayor has gone out of town.'

Fantine started up with shining eyes and sat back on her heels. There was a look of indescribable happiness on her ravaged face.

'He's gone out of town?' she cried. 'He's gone for Cosette!'

She raised her arms above her head, her expression radiant and her lips moving in a silent prayer. After a little pause she said:

'I'll lie down again. I'll do whatever I'm told. I behaved badly just now, I shouldn't have shouted at you. I know it's wrong to raise one's voice, I hope you will forgive me. I'm happy now. God is kind to me and Monsieur Madeleine is kind. He has gone to Montfermeil to fetch my little Cosette.'

She lay back, helped the sister to rearrange the pillows and kissed the small silver cross hanging from her neck which the sister had given her.

'You must rest, dear child,' Sister Simplice said. 'You mustn't talk any more.'

Fantine reached out hot hands whose feverish dampness caused the sister a pang.

'He's gone in the direction of Paris, but he won't need to go as far as that, Montfermeil is a little to the left before you get to Paris. When I asked him about Cosette yesterday he said, "Soon, soon" – do you remember? He wants to give me a surprise. He made me sign a letter for the Thénardiers. They'll have to give her up, won't they, now that they've been paid? People aren't allowed to keep a child when everything's been paid. Please, sister, don't try to stop me talking, I'm so happy, I feel so well, I shall see Cosette again. I'm even hungry. It's five years since I saw her. Oh, you don't know the hold a child can have on you! She'll be so angelic, you'll see. She had tiny pink fingers, she's going to have pretty hands, but of course then they were only baby hands. She's seven now, quite a big girl, almost grown up. I call her Cosette, her real name is Euphrasie. You know, this morning I was looking at the dust on the mantelshelf and somehow I had the idea that I should soon be seeing her again. It's wrong to go for years without seeing one's child. We have to remember that life doesn't last for ever. Oh, and it's so good of Monsieur Madeleine to have gone for her! The weather's very cold, isn't it? I hope at least he has a good warm overcoat. And they'll be here tomorrow, won't they? Tomorrow is the great day. You must remind me to put on my lace bonnet. It's a long way to Montfermeil. I came the whole way on foot, and it was hard. But the coaches go very fast. They'll be here tomorrow. How far is it to Montfermeil?'

The sister, who had no notion of distance, replied: 'I'm sure he'll be here tomorrow.'

'And I shall see Cosette! Tomorrow! Tomorrow! Oh, dear sister, I'm not ill any more. I'm beside myself with happiness. I could dance, if you asked me to.'

Anyone who had seen her a quarter of an hour earlier might well have been dumbfounded. Her face was flushed and glowing, her voice light and natural. From time to time she murmured to herself. A mother's rejoicing is near to that of a child.

'Well,' the sister said, 'now that you're happy you must be obedient and not talk any more.'

Fantine said softly, 'Yes, I must be good now that I'm getting my baby back,' and then lay motionless and silent, only gazing about her with wide, ecstatic eyes. The sister drew the bed-curtains, hoping that she would fall asleep.

The doctor called again between seven and eight, and hearing no sound tip-toed to the bedside; but when he drew back the curtains he saw by the night-light that she was gazing calmly up at him.

'They'll make up a little bed for her beside mine, won't they?' she said. 'As you see, there's just room.'

He thought she was delirious and taking Sister Simplice aside listened while she told him what she knew of the facts, namely that Monsieur Madeleine was to be away for a day or two, and that she had not thought it necessary to undeceive the patient, who assumed that he had gone to Montfermeil – and indeed it was possible that he had. The doctor nodded and went back to the bed.

'I can say good morning to her when she wakes up,' said Fantine. 'And at night I'll hear her breathing, the sweet lamb, and that will be a delight to me, because I don't sleep very well myself.'

'Give me your hand,' the doctor said.

She held it out and suddenly laughed. 'But of course! You don't know. I'm better, doctor. I'm going to get well. Cosette will be here tomorrow.'

The doctor found to his surprise that her condition had indeed improved. The tension was less and the pulse stronger. A surge of renewed life seemed to have revived her exhausted body.

'Didn't the sister tell you?' she said. 'The mayor himself has gone to fetch my little girl.'

He counselled silence and freedom from all disturbance, and pre-scribed quinine and a soothing potion in case she should become feverish again during the night. As he was leaving he said to Sister Simplice:

'There's a real improvement. If by great good fortune the mayor really does bring the child back – well, who can say? One hears of astonishing cases. Great happiness can sometimes work miracles. This is an organic disease and far advanced, but these things are wrapped in mystery. Perhaps we shall save her after all.'

VII

The traveller arrives and provides for his return

It was nearly eight when the gig passed under the gateway of the Hôtel de la Poste in Arras. The traveller got out, replying absently to the greetings of the inn servants; he sent away the extra horse and himself led the white horse round to the stable. Then he pushed open the door of a billiard-room on the ground floor and sat down at a small drinking-table. He had taken fourteen hours over a journey that he had hoped to make in six; but he could say in fairness to himself that the fault was not his, and in his heart he was not dis-pleased.

The landlady entered.

'Will Monsieur be stopping the night? Will he require dinner?' He shook his head.

'But the ostler says that your horse is tired out. It needs at least two days' rest.'

He considered. 'This is a posting-inn, I believe. There's a post office?'

'Yes, Monsieur.'

She took him to the office, where he learned that there was a place vacant on the mail leaving that night for Montreuil-sur-mer, the seat beside the mail-man. He reserved it and paid. The clerk warned him that it would leave punctually at one o'clock in the morning.

He left the inn and walked into the town. He did not know Arras and the streets were dark; nevertheless, he seemed reluctant to ask the way. He crossed the little river Crinchon and found himself in a maze of narrow streets. A man came by with a lantern, and after hesitating he approached him, but only after first looking round as though to ensure that his question would not be overheard.

'Monsieur, can you tell me the way to the Palais de Justice?'

'You are new to the town, Monsieur?' said the gentleman, who was elderly. 'I can take you there because, as it happens, that is where I am going myself – or rather to the Prefecture. The law-courts are at present under repair and the Prefecture is being used instead.'

'Is that where the assizes are held?'

'Yes. Before the Revolution the present Prefecture was the Bishop's Palace. Monsieur de Conzie, who was bishop in eighty-two, had a large hall built on to it. That is where cases are provisionally being heard.' As they walked along together, he added, 'Have you come to attend a trial? In that case you may be too late. As a rule the court rises at six.'

But when they reached the town square they found that the lights were still burning behind four tall windows in a large, gloomy building.

'You're in luck, Monsieur,' the gentleman said. 'Those are the windows of the assize court. They must be holding a late session, evidently some case has taken longer than was expected. Would it be the case you are interested in? A criminal trial, perhaps? Are you a witness?'

'No,' said the stranger, 'I have not come about any particular case, simply to speak to one of the attorneys.'

'Well, then,' said the gentleman, 'there is the door. You'll find a doorkeeper. You have only to go up the main stairway.'

A few minutes later Madeleine found himself in a crowded room where a number of persons in legal attire were clustered in separate groups, talking in low voices.

The sight of these groups of black-robed gentlemen murmuring together on the threshold of a court of law is always a chilling one. Little charity or compassion emerges from their talk, which is principally concerned with guessing which way the verdict will go. They are like clusters of buzzing insects absorbed in the construction of dark edifices of their own.

The room, which was spacious and lighted only with a single lamp, had been an antechamber in the days of the bishopric and was now being put to a similar use. Wide double doors, at that moment closed, separated it from the Great Hall where the assize court was in session.

The place was so dark that Madeleine did not hesitate to address the first lawyer he encountered.

'How is the case going, Monsieur?' he asked.

'It's over.'

'Over!'

The tone of his voice caused the lawyer to look at him.

'Excuse me, Monsieur – are you a relative?'

'No. I know no one here. And there was a conviction?'

'Naturally. Nothing else was possible.'

'What was the sentence?'

'Hard labour for life.'

Madeleine's next words were spoken in a voice so low that they could scarcely be heard.

'And the question of identity –?'

'Identity?' said the lawyer. 'But there was no question of identity. The case was perfectly straightforward. The woman had killed her child. The infanticide was proved, but the jury ruled out premeditation. She was condemned to life-imprisonment.'

'A woman!' said Madeleine.

'Of course. The woman Limosin. But what did you have in mind?'

'It doesn't matter. But if the case is over why are the lights still on?'

'They're trying another case. It started a couple of hours ago.'

'What case is that?'

'Another simple one. A recidivist, an ex-convict, charged with

240

theft. I forget the name. But a rascal, if ever I saw one. The mere look of him is enough to get him sent back to the galleys.'

'Would it be possible, Monsieur, for me to get into the court-room?'

'I very much doubt it. It's very crowded. But there is a temporary adjournment and perhaps some people will be leaving. You might manage when the court resumes.'

'Where does one go in?'

'Through that door.'

The lawyer left him. In the two or three minutes of that conversation Madeleine had been assailed by every conceivable emotion. The lawyer's casual words had pierced him like needles of ice and like shafts of fire. When he heard that the case was not yet over he had drawn a deep breath, but whether of relief or anguish he could not have said.

He drew near to several of the murmuring groups and listened to what they were saying.

The court had so much business before it that the presiding judge had decreed that these two relatively brief and simple cases should be disposed of on the one day. They had first taken the infanticide and were now dealing with the case of the ex-convict, the 'old lag'. He was charged with stealing apples, but this had not been proved. What had been proved, however, was that he had served a long term of imprisonment in Toulon, and this was what made the matter serious. The examination of the accused was completed and the depositions of the witnesses had been heard, but there remained the pleas of the prosecutor and the defending attorney, and it was unlikely that the business would be over before midnight. The prosecutor was a very capable advocate – he seldom failed to 'get his man' – and was, moreover, a person of refinement who wrote poetry.

An usher was standing by the door leading to the court-room. Madeleine asked him:

'Will this door soon be opened?'

'It won't be opened at all,' the usher said.

'Not even when the session is resumed? It's adjourned for the moment, isn't it?'

'They have just resumed, but the door won't be opened. The hall's already full.'

'You mean there's not a single place?'

'Not one. No one can be allowed in.' Then the usher added: 'As a matter of fact, there are one or two seats behind the president's chair, but these are reserved for persons holding public office.' After which he turned his back on him.

Madeleine withdrew and with a lowered head crossed the antechamber and started slowly down the stairway, pausing in deep preoccupation at every step. The violent inner conflict that had absorbed him since the previous evening was still unresolved; new aspects of the matter constantly occurred to him. When he reached the half-landing he leaned against the balustrade with his arms folded. Suddenly he unbuttoned his greatcoat, got out his pocketbook and a pencil, and by the light of the stairway lantern wrote hastily on a sheet of paper which he tore out of the pocket-book, 'M. Madeleine, Mayor of Montreuil-sur-mer.' He then ran up the stairs, thrust his way through the crowd in the antechamber, and handed the slip of paper to the usher, saying in an authoritative tone, 'Kindly take this to the presiding judge.'

The usher glanced at the paper and obeyed.

VIII

Admission by privilege

Without being aware of it the mayor of Montreuil-sur-mer had acquired a degree of celebrity. His high reputation in the Lower Boulonnais had spread beyond the borders of that region into the neighbouring departments. Apart from the service he had rendered the town by reviving the jet industry, there was not one of the 141 communes comprising the administrative district of Montreuil-sur-mer that did not owe him something. The manufacture of tulle at Boulogne, and the textile industries at Frévent and Boubers-sur-Canche had all benefited by his financial assistance. The name of Madeleine was everywhere held in high esteem, and towns such as Arras and Douai envied the fortunate small town of Montreuil-sur-mer.

The Councillor of the King's Court at Douai, who was presiding over the assize court at Arras, was therefore familiar with his name. When the usher, discreetly bending over his chair, handed him the slip of paper saying, 'The gentleman would like to be present at the hearing,' he at once nodded, scribbled a line on the bottom of the slip, and ordered him to be shown in.

The unhappy man himself had remained standing where the usher had left him, in the same oppressed attitude. The voice which now intruded on his thoughts was very different in tone from that of the haughty attendant who had turned his back on him a few minutes before. Bowing obsequiously, the usher said, 'If your honour would be so good as to follow me,' at the same time returning the slip of paper. Madeleine was near enough to the lamp to be able to read, 'The President of the Court presents his compliments to Monsieur Madeleine.' Crumpling the paper as though the words had left a bitter taste in his mouth, he followed the usher.

A minute or two later he was standing in a sombre, oak-panelled room lighted by two candles on a table with a green cloth. Before leaving him the usher had said, 'This is the judges' room. The door with the brass knob leads directly into the court-room. Monsieur will find himself behind the judge's chair.' The words were mingled in his mind with a vague recollection of passages and stairways along which they had passed.

He was now alone. This was the supreme moment. He strove to collect his thoughts and could not do so. It is precisely in those moments when we have most need to grasp the painful realities of life that our thoughts are most apt to lose their coherence. He was in the room where the judges retired to consult together and decide upon their verdict, and he gazed round it in a kind of apathy, the quiet, ominous room where so many lives had been shattered, where presently his own name would be spoken and his fate decided. He stared at the wall in inward contemplation, amazed that he should be the man standing in that room.

He had eaten nothing for twenty-four hours, he had been shaken by the jolting of the gig, but he felt none of this; he was not conscious of feeling anything.

Hanging on the wall was a framed letter written by Jean-Nicolas Pache, Mayor of Paris under the Revolution and author of the slogan, 'Liberty, Equality, Fraternity, or Death', in which Pache sent the local Commune a list of former ministers and deputies held under arrest in their homes. From the care with which Madeleine studied this letter, reading it several times, it might have been thought that he found it of particular interest. In fact, he was not aware of reading it; he was thinking about Fantine and the child Cosette.

Turning abstractedly away, his eyes fell on the brass handle of the door leading to the court-room. He had almost forgotten that door. He glanced casually at the handle and then his gaze returned to it, becoming wide and fixed, filled with a kind of terror. Beads of sweat formed on his scalp and rolled down his temples.

With a sudden start, that gesture of mingled authority and rebellion which says so plainly, 'Who says I must?', he turned away abruptly, crossed over to the door by which he had entered, opened it and went out. He found himself in a long, narrow passage with flights of steps, doorways, and several turns, lighted here and there by dim lamps like those in a sick-room – the passage along which he had come. He drew breath and stood listening. There was no sound to be heard, ahead of him or behind. He began to run as though he were pursued.

After turning several corners he paused again to listen. The same silence enclosed him, the same darkness. He was out of breath. He staggered and leaned against the stone wall, finding it cold to the touch. The sweat was chilled on his forehead. He shivered and stood upright.

And there, standing in shadow, shivering with cold and perhaps something else, he stayed considering. He had been thinking all that day and all the previous night. There was nothing left in him except a voice that said, 'Alas!'

A quarter of an hour passed. At length he bowed his head and sighed in anguish, and with his arms limply hanging, turned back. He walked slowly as though overpowered, as though someone had caught and seized him as he fled.

He re-entered the judges' room, and the first thing that caught his eye was the polished brass door-handle, shining like a baleful star. He stared at it as a lamb might stare at a beast of prey. He could not take his eyes off it. At intervals he moved a step nearer to the door.

Had he listened he would have heard a confused murmur of voices coming from the adjoining room; but he did not listen, and heard nothing.

Suddenly, and without knowing how it happened, he found himself standing at the door. He seized the handle with a convulsive movement and the door opened.

He was in the court-room.

IX
Place of decision

Closing the door mechanically behind him, he stood observing the scene.

This place, where the meticulous and solemn drama of criminal trial was being enacted in the presence of a crowded audience, was large and dimly lighted, filled at moments with the buzz of voices, and at moments profoundly silent. At the end where he was standing a number of bored-looking magistrates in robes were biting their nails or sitting with closed eyes. At the other end was a crowd of ragged spectators, lawyers in casual attitudes, and soldiers with hard, bold faces. Old and stained wainscoting, a grimy ceiling, tables draped with yellowed green baize, doors blackened with handprints, tavern lamps hanging from nails knocked into the woodwork and candles in brass candlesticks on the tables. Darkness, ugliness, and melancholy, but all pervaded with a sense of lofty austerity, a consciousness of the great human proceeding that we call law and the divine proceeding that is called justice.

No one paid any attention to him. All eyes were directed to a single point, a wooden bench with a small door behind it, set against one wall. The bench was lighted by candles and on it a man was seated, flanked by two gendarmes.

This was the man.

Madeleine had no need to seek him out. His eyes went instinctively towards him as though he had known in advance where he would be. And he seemed to be looking at himself grown old, not wholly similar in feature, but with the posture and general aspect, the unkempt hair, the wary, restless eyes, the smock – the man he had been when, with a heart filled with hatred and a mind burdened with the hideous memory of nineteen years' imprisonment, he had come to Digne.

He thought with a shudder, 'Oh, God, am I to become that again?'

The man, who was at least sixty and looked dull-witted and furtive, conveyed a general impression of coarseness.

Room had been made for Madeleine when he entered. The presiding judge had looked round, and realizing that this must be the mayor of Montreuil-sur-mer, had bowed his head in greeting. The advocate-general, whose official duties had several times brought him to the town, recognized Monsieur Madeleine and also saluted him. He was scarcely aware of these courtesies. He was staring about him, stupefied.

He had seen all this before, the judges, the clerk, the gendarmes, the crowd of curious, unfeeling faces. He had seen it twenty-seven years ago and now he was seeing it again, no longer a nightmare haunting his memory but the thing itself, gendarmes and judges, the assembly of flesh-and-blood humanity; he was reliving in dreadful truth, all that was most monstrous in his past. The past loomed like a gulf before him, and he closed his eyes in horror, crying in the depths of his soul, 'Never!'

And by a tragic freak of chance which so confounded his mind that he felt he must be going mad, he saw another man standing in his place, assumed by everyone to be Jean Valjean.

Everything was the same, the paraphernalia of the law, the lateness of the hour – even the faces of judges, gendarmes, and spectators seemed scarcely to have changed. Only one thing was different: a crucifix hung on the wall above the presiding judge's head, and this had been lacking in court-rooms at the time of his own trial. He had been tried in the absence of God.

There was a chair behind him and he sat down, terrified by the thought that someone might notice him. A pile of documents on the judge's table hid him from the court when he sat, so that he could observe without being seen. By degrees his wits returned to him and his sense of reality; he became calm enough to listen.

Among the jurymen was M. Bamatabois. Madeleine looked for Javert but could not see him, the witnesses' bench being hidden from his view by the clerk's table, and the hall, in any case, being poorly lighted.

He had entered at the moment when the accused man's advocate was concluding his speech for the defence, amid an attentive silence. The hearing had lasted three hours. For three hours the audience had watched a man, a stranger to the locality, an abject creature who was either profoundly stupid or profoundly cunning, crumble beneath the weight of a terrible probability. What was known of him? The witnesses who had been heard during the preliminary inquiry had been unanimous in their testimony, and other facts had emerged during the trial. The argument of the prosecution was as follows: 'The accused is not merely a petty thief who has been caught stealing fruit, but a highly dangerous ruffian, an ex-convict who has broken parole, a criminal named Jean Valjean who has long been sought by the law. Directly after being released from imprisonment in Toulon he committed a highway robbery with the use of force on the person of a boy named Petit-Gervais, a crime under Article 383 of the Penal Code for which we reserve the right to prosecute him when his identity has been legally established. He has now committed another theft. It is a case of recidivism. Convict him of this latest crime and he will in due course be tried for the earlier one' . . . The extent of the charge, and the unanimity of the witnesses, seemed to cause the accused astonishment more than any other emotion. He made negative gestures, or stared up at the ceiling, expressing himself with difficulty and replying awkwardly to the questions put to him; but his whole attitude was one of denial. He was like a half-wit in the presence of the keen minds arrayed against him, and like a foreigner in this society that had him in its grasp. And the case against him was growing steadily stronger, the likelihood of conviction steadily increasing, so that the spectators seemed more conscious of the fate that threatened him than he was himself. Even the possibility of a death-sentence, if his identity was established and he was convicted of the robbery of Petit-Gervais, could not be ruled out. What manner of man was he? What was the reason for his apparent indifference? Was it due to imbecility or to cunning? Did he understand too much, or nothing at all? These were the questions that puzzled the spectators and seemed to divide the jury. The affair was at once ugly and mystifying, its drama not just sombre but obscure.

The defending attorney had pleaded, not ineffectively, in that language of the provinces which has long been the eloquence of the court-room, formerly used by all advocates both in Paris and elsewhere, and now the classic mode, rarely heard except on the lips of speakers at the bar, who delight in its impressive sonority and rolling periods. It is a language in which a husband or wife is always a 'spouse', Paris 'the centre of art and civilization', the king 'the monarch', a bishop 'a saintly pontiff', a theatre 'a temple of Melpomene', a concert 'a musical occasion', newspaper errors 'imposture spreading its venom through the columns of a certain journal', and so on . . . Beginning with the theft of the apples, a matter difficult of treatment in lofty terms, the defending attorney argued that this was not conclusively proved. No one had seen his client (whom, as his advocate, he persisted in calling Champmathieu) climb the wall or break a branch off the tree. He had been caught in possession of the branch (which the speaker preferred to call 'the fruitful bough') but claimed that he had found it on the ground and picked it up. Where was the evidence to the contrary? Undoubtedly the wall had been climbed and a branch broken off, and no doubt the marauder had flung it away in panic. Certainly there had been a marauder, but what proof was there that it was Champmathieu? There was simply the fact that Champmathieu was an ex-convict. This his defender did not deny, since it appeared to be established. The accused had lived in Faverolles, he had been a tree-pruner, and the name Champmathieu might originally have been Jean Mathieu. All this was true, and moreover four witnesses had positively identified the man Champmathieu with the convict Jean Valjean. The defence had nothing to oppose to this except the man's own denial. But supposing him to be an ex-convict, did this prove that he had stolen the apples? It was at the best a presumption. Certainly the accused – and the defence must 'in good faith' concede as much – had adopted an unfortunate attitude. He had persisted in denying everything, not only the theft of the apples but also the fact that he had a prison record. It would have served him better to give way on the latter point, since the admission would certainly have rendered the court more disposed to lenience. He had been advised of this but had stubbornly refused to accept the advice, no doubt believing that by denying everything he could save everything. It was a grave error, but surely the man's lack of intelligence must be taken into account. He was clearly stupid. A long term of imprisonment and the vagabond life he had led since his release had further dulled his wits. Was he to be condemned for this? As to the matter of Petit-Gervais, since it did not enter into the present case the defence was not called upon to discuss it. The attorney concluded with a strong plea to the jury and the bench that if they were satisfied that the accused was Jean Valjean, he should be subjected only to the penalties applying to a released convict who has broken parole, not to the terrible chastisement inflicted on a recidivist felon.

The advocate-general then put the case for the prosecution with the florid vehemence that prosecuting attorneys are accustomed to use.

Complimenting the defending attorney on his 'good faith', he proceeded shrewdly to turn it to advantage. The defence appeared to accept that the accused was Jean Valjean, and since this was conceded to the prosecution it need not be further discussed. With an adroit change of subject the prosecutor launched into a thunderous attack on the immorality of writers of the romantic school, now becoming known to certain 'ultra' journals of the extreme right as the 'satanic school', to whose pernicious influence he attributed the misdeeds of Champmathieu, that is to say, Jean Valjean. Having exhausted this subject he came to Valjean himself. What kind of man was he? An outrageous villain, a monster of depravity, and so on ... The model for invective of this kind is to be found in the story told by Theramène in Racine's *Phèdre*, which does nothing for the play but has been of the greatest value to court-room orators, causing juries and spectators to 'shudder'. With an eye on the columns of the *Journal de la Préfecture*, the prosecutor worked up to a masterly peroration. This was the man, this vagabond whose life had been one of crime and whose term of imprisonment had done nothing to improve his character, as was evidenced by his assault on the boy Petit-Gervais – this was the man who, being caught on the public highway *in flagrante delicto*, had denied everything, the act of trespass, the theft and even his own name. Apart from the mass of corroborative evidence which need not here be cited, he had been recognized by four witnesses – by Javert, the incorruptible inspector of police, and by three of his former comrades in infamy, the felons Brevet, Chenildieu, and Cochepaille. And what had he to say to this overwhelming testimony? He simply denied it. The brazen impudence! Members of the jury, in the name of justice... And so on...

The accused had listened open-mouthed, in a sort of stupefaction not unmixed with awe. He was evidently amazed that any man could talk so fluently. In the more impassioned moments, when eloquence burst its bonds and the stream of epithets poured over him like a flood, he had gently wagged his head from side to side in the mute and melancholy protest which was all he had allowed himself throughout the trial. The spectators nearest him several times heard him murmur, 'This is what comes of not asking Monsieur Baloup.'

The prosecutor had drawn the jury's attention to this 'sullen attitude' which, he said, was evidently deliberate, not due to stupidity but to craftiness and cunning and the habit of evading the law, and which shed its own light on the 'profound perversity' of the accused. Reserving the case of Petit-Gervais for future consideration, he demanded the full penalty prescribed by the law, which, as matters then stood, was penal servitude for life.

The defending attorney, rising to make his concluding speech, began by congratulating the advocate-general on his 'admirable eloquence'. He went on to do his best, but weakly, evidently feeling that the ground had been cut from under his feet.

x
The accused

It was time for the case to be concluded. Ordering the accused to rise, the presiding judge put the formal question to him: 'Have you anything to add in your defence?'

The man stood twisting a grimy cap in his hands, seeming not to have heard. The judge repeated the question.

This time the man heard and seemed to understand. He started like someone awakening out of sleep, stared about him at the on-lookers, the gendarmes, his attorney, the jury and the judges, rested a huge fist on the wooden rail in front of his bench, and with his eyes fixed on the prosecutor began to speak. It was like an eruption, a flood of frantic, incoherent words jostling as they exploded from his mouth.

'I have this to say. I was a wheelwright in Paris and I worked for Monsieur Baloup. It was a hard life. A wheelwright always works out of doors, in a yard or an open shed, never a closed one, because he has to have room, you see. In winter you flap your arms to keep warm, but the bosses don't like that because it wastes time. It's rough, handling metal when there's ice between the cobbles, it wears a man out. You grow old before your time, you may be done for at forty. I was fifty-three and I found it very rough, and the other men, they're hard on you, "old bones" they say. All I got was thirty sous a day, less than the proper rate because I was old. My daughter was a washerwoman down by the river. She earned a bit that way and between the two of us we got along. It was hard on her too, bent over a washtub, soaked to the waist rain or shine and the wind cutting into you. Even if it's freezing you have to get the washing done – there are folk who haven't got many clothes, they're waiting for you to finish, so you have to keep at it or you'd lose customers. The tubs leak and you're soaked through to your petticoats. She worked at the Enfants-Rouges laundry as well, where there's water laid on. You don't wash at a tub but straight under the tap and rinse the things in a trough. At least it's indoors, so you're warmer, but there's all that steam from the hot water that hurts your eyes. She'd come back at seven dead tired and go straight to bed. Her husband used to beat her. She's dead now. We weren't very happy. She was a good girl, steady-going, never any fun. I remember one holiday, Mardi Gras it was, she went to bed at eight. That was our life. I'm telling the truth. You can ask anyone. Well, of course, it's silly to say that. Paris is like a swamp. Who ever heard of Père Champmathieu? But there's Monsieur Baloup. You can ask him. I don't know what else you expect me to say.'

He fell silent but remained standing. He had talked rapidly in a loud, harsh voice, hoarse and uncouth, and with a kind of exasperated simplicity. Once he had paused to nod to someone among the spectators. The string of random affirmations, coming jerkily like a series of hiccoughs, had each been accompanied by a gesture of his hand like that of a man cutting wood. When he had finished the audience burst out laughing. He gazed about him, not understanding, and then laughed himself.

This did him no good.

The presiding judge, a considerate and well-meaning man, then spoke.

He first reminded the jury that his Monsieur Baloup 'at one time a master wheelwright in Paris, for whom the accused claims to have worked' was not available as a witness: he had gone bankrupt and could not be found. Then, turning to the accused and advising him to listen carefully, he said: 'Your position is one which must cause you to think twice. You are the object of very serious suspicions. In your own interest I will ask you for the last time to give the court a plain answer to these questions. First, did you or did you not climb the wall of the Pierron smallholding, break a branch off a tree and steal the apples – in other words, commit the crime of theft with illegal entry? And secondly, are you or are you not the released convict, Jean Valjean?'

The accused shook his head in the manner of a man who understands and knows what he intends to say. Turning to face the judge, he opened his mouth and began:

'In the first place –'

But then he looked down at his cap and up at the ceiling and was silent.

'Listen to me,' the prosecutor said sternly. 'You refuse to answer questions, and your refusal in itself condemns you. It is apparent that your name is not Champmathieu. You are the convict Jean Valjean who at one time went by the name of Jean Mathieu, your mother's name, and you were born in Faverolles, where you were a tree-pruner. It is also clear that you stole the apples from the Pierron property. The jury cannot fail to draw this conclusion.'

The man had re-seated himself. But now he rose abruptly and cried:

'You're wicked, that's what you are! That's what I was trying to say, only I couldn't find the words. I'm one of those that don't eat every day. I was on my way on foot from Ailly where there were floods and the countryside swamped and nothing but mud and a few bushes at the roadside, and there was this branch with apples lying on the ground and I picked it up not meaning any harm. So I've spent three months in prison being chivvied and now you're all against me and telling me to answer your questions and the gendarme, who's all right, he keeps nudging me in the ribs and saying, "Go on – answer." But I don't know how to say things, I never had any schooling, I'm one of the poor. That's what you don't understand. I never stole anything, I just picked up something I found lying on the ground. You keep talking about Jean Valjean and Jean Mathieu. I don't know who they are. They're village people. I worked for Monsieur Baloup in the Boulevard de l'Hôpital and my name's Champmathieu. You're very clever, telling me where I was born, because it's more than I know. Not everyone has the luck to be born in a house. I think my father and mother were tramps, but I don't know for sure. When I was a kid they called me little Champmathieu and now I'm old Champmathieu. That's my baptismal name and you can make what you like of it. I've been in Auvergne and I've been in Faverolles, but can't a man go places without being a convict? I never stole anything. I'm Champmathieu and I worked for Monsieur Baloup and I lived in Paris. You make me tired with all your questions. Why does everyone have to pick on me?'

The prosecutor had remained standing. He now addressed the presiding judge.

'Monsieur le président, in view of the confused but shrewdly calculated denials on the part of the accused, who is trying to pass himself off as an idiot but will not succeed in doing so, I request the Court's permission to recall the witnesses Brevet, Cochepaille, and

Chenildieu and Inspector Javert, so that they may reaffirm their testimony identifying the prisoner with the convict Jean Valjean.'

'I must remind you,' said the president, 'that Inspector Javert is no longer in Court. With the Court's permission, and with the consent of both the prosecution and the defence, he has returned to his duties in Montreuil-sur-mer.'

'I stand corrected, Monsieur le président. In the absence of Inspector Javert I will remind the jury of what he said in this court a short time ago. Javert is a man highly respected for his personal probity and strict performance of his duties. His deposition was as follows: "I have no need to rely on circumstantial or material evidence in refuting the denials of the accused. I recognize him perfectly. His name is not Champmathieu. He is a highly dangerous ex-convict named Jean Valjean who was very reluctantly released at the end of his sentence. He had served nineteen years' hard labour for robbery with violence. He made five or six attempts to escape. Apart from the Petit-Gervais and Pierron robberies, I suspect him of having robbed his lordship the late Bishop of Digne. I saw him frequently when I was in the prison service in Toulon and, I repeat, I recognize him perfectly." '

This very positive affirmation appeared to make a deep impression on both the public and the jury. In the absence of Javert, the prosecutor demanded the recall of the three other witnesses so that they might again be formally questioned. The presiding judge gave the order and a minute later the prisoner Brevet was brought back into court escorted by a gendarme.

Brevet was clad in the black and grey smock of the central prisons. He was a man of about sixty whose appearance suggested both the man of affairs and the rogue, two things that sometimes go together. He had become some sort of turnkey in the prison to which his latest misdeeds had brought him, being, in the words of the authorities, 'a man who likes to make himself useful', and the almoner reported favourably on his religious beliefs. This, it must be remembered, was under the Restoration.

'Brevet,' said the president, 'you are under a shameful sentence and cannot give testimony on oath.' Brevet lowered his eyes. 'However, even a man thus degraded by the law may, in God's mercy, retain some sense of honesty and justice, and it is to this that I am appealing. If it still exists in you, as I trust it does, you will reflect very carefully before answering. You have to consider, on the one hand, the man whom your answer may destroy, and on the other hand the cause of justice which it may serve. This is a critical moment. You may have been mistaken ... The accused man will rise ... Brevet, look hard at the man in the dock and tell the Court if in all conscience you still recognize him as your former prison-mate, Jean Valjean.'

Brevet did as required and then said:

'Yes, Monsieur le président, I do. I was the first to recognize him and I stick to it. That is Jean Valjean, who came to Toulon in 1796 and went out in 1815. I went out a year later. He looks dull-witted now, but that is due to age; he looked crafty enough in prison. I positively recognize him.'

'You can sit down,' said the judge. 'The accused will remain standing.'

Chenildieu was then brought in, a convict under life-sentence as his red smock and green cap indicated, who had been fetched from Toulon to testify at this trial. He was a small man of about fifty with a yellow, wrinkled face and an impudent expression, whose physical aspect suggested some sort of nervous weakness but whose gaze contained a hint of immense will-power. His fellow-prisoners had nicknamed him 'Godless'. When the judge, addressing him in the same terms that he had used to Brevet, reminded him that his condition deprived him of the right to take the oath, he looked up and gazed sternly at the spectators; and when asked if he still recognized the accused he burst into laughter.

'How could I help recognizing him? We did five years on the same chain. What's the trouble, mate – you sulking?'

'Sit down,' said the judge.

Then came Cochepaille, also under life-sentence, a peasant from Lourdes who had become an outlaw in the Pyrenees. From pasturing sheep in the mountains he had drifted into brigandage, and in his general aspect he was no less ruffianly and even more stupid than the accused. He was one of those unfortunates shaped by nature to be wild animals and turned by society into gaolbirds.

The judge, with the same solemn invocation, put the same question to him and he answered promptly:

'It's Jean Valjean all right. We used to call him "Jean-the-crow-bar" on account of he was so strong.'

Each of the three affirmations, so clearly uttered in good faith, had drawn from the spectators a murmur of increasing volume and hostility towards the accused. The prisoner himself had listened to them with that air of astonishment which, according to the prosecution, was his principal weapon of defence. The gendarmes standing on either side of him heard him mutter after the first, 'Well, that's one!' After the second he said more loudly, and seemingly with a grim satisfaction, 'Fine!' And after the third he exclaimed, 'Famous!'

The judge looked at him.

'Prisoner at the bar, you have heard this testimony. What have you to say?'

He replied: 'I say it's famous!'

There was something like a roar from the audience, in which the jury came near to joining. The case was clearly hopeless.

'The ushers will call for silence,' said the presiding judge. 'I am about to pronounce sentence.'

But at this moment there was a movement behind the bench and a voice cried:

'Brevet, Chenildieu, and Cochepaille, I want you to look at me!'

All eyes turned in the direction of this voice, which was so grief-stricken, so terrible, that it chilled the hearts of all who heard it. A man who had been seated among the privileged spectators behind the judges had risen to his feet. Opening the gate in the low rail separating the bench from the body of the court, he strode to the centre of the court-room. The presiding judge, the prosecutor, Monsieur Bamatabois, and twenty others recognized him and exclaimed with one voice:

'Monsieur Madeleine!'

XI

Increased astonishment of Champmathieu

It was indeed he. The light from the clerk's lamp fell upon his face. He was holding his hat in his hand, his clothes were neat, his greatcoat carefully buttoned. He was very pale and trembled slightly. His hair, which had still been grey when he arrived in Arras, was now quite white. It had gone white during the hour that he had been in the court-room.

The profound sensation caused by his sudden appearance was followed by a bewildered silence. So great was the contrast between the anguish in the voice and the calm outward aspect of the man that it was hard to believe that it was he who had spoken. But the pause was only brief. Before the judge or prosecutor could speak, or any gendarme or usher make a movement, the man who was still known to everyone as Monsieur Madeleine advanced towards the three witnesses.

'Do you not recognize me?' he asked.

They shook their heads, staring at him in astonishment. The startled Cochepaille gave him a military salute. Monsieur Madeleine turned to face the court and said quietly:

'Gentlemen of the jury, you must acquit the accused. I must ask the court to order my arrest. I am the man you are looking for. I am Jean Valjean.'

No one breathed. The first stir of amazement was followed by a deathly stillness. The hall was seized with the kind of religious awe that grips a crowd in the presence of a great event, but the face of the presiding judge wore an expression of sympathy and sadness. After exchanging gestures with the prosecutor and a few low-spoken words with his fellow-judges, he addressed the court-room in a tone that everyone understood:

'Is there a doctor present?'

The prosecutor spoke.

'Gentlemen of the jury, this very strange and disturbing incident must inspire in us all sentiments which I have no need to express. We all know the mayor of Montreuil-sur-mer, the highly respected Monsieur Madeleine, at least by repute. If there is a doctor present I wish to associate myself with the bench in requesting him to attend to the gentleman, and see that he gets safely home.'

He seemed about to say more, but Madeleine himself cut him short, speaking in a voice of quiet authority. What follows are the words he used, the exact words, as they were recorded immediately after the trial and as they must linger in the minds of everyone who heard them, nearly forty years ago.

'I am grateful to you, Monsieur l'avocat général, but I am not mad, as you will see. You are on the point of committing a grave error, whereas I am performing an act of public duty. This man must be released. I am that wretched convict. What I now tell you is the truth, and it is sufficient for me that God is my witness. Here I am – you have only to take me. I did the best I could. I changed my name, I grew rich and became mayor; I sought to re-instate myself in the ranks of honest men. But it seems that it is not to be. I need not, at this point, tell you the whole story of my life, it will become known in due course. But it is true that I robbed the Bishop of Digne and the boy Petit-Gervais. You are right in supposing that Jean Valjean was a very evil wretch, although perhaps the fault was not wholly his. It is not for a man so lowly to remonstrate with Divine Providence or seek to advise society, but the degradation from which I sought to escape is none the less an evil thing. It is gaol that makes the gaolbird, and this is something that you must bear in mind. Before going to prison I was a peasant with very little intelligence, almost an idiot. It was prison that changed me. I had been stupid but I grew malignant, like a smouldering log that bursts into flame. Goodness and compassion saved me after brutality had come near to destroying me. But these are things that I cannot expect you to understand. You will find in the hearth in the place where I live the forty-sou piece I stole from Petit-Gervais. I have nothing to add. You have only to arrest me. But I see the advocate-general shake his head. You do not believe me, you think me mad. This greatly distresses me. At the least, an innocent man must not be convicted. It is a pity Javert is not here, for he would recognize me. These men say that they do not, but we shall see.'

The gentleness and melancholy of his voice was such as no words can convey. He turned to the three convicts.

'I recognize you, Brevet. Do you remember –' he paused for an instant, '– do you remember the braces you used to wear, with a check pattern?'

Brevet gave a start of surprise and stared at him wide-eyed. He went on:

'And you, Chenildieu. They called you "Godless" – it was the name you gave yourself. You have a bad scar on your right shoulder. You held it against a hot stove, trying to burn away the letters T.F.P. which were branded on it, but they are still visible. Is that not so?'

'It's the truth,' said Chenildieu.

He turned to Cochepaille.

'At the bend of your left arm, Cochepaille, there's a date in blue lettering tattooed with gunpowder. It is the date of the Emperor's landing at Cannes – 1 March 1815. Pull up your sleeve.'

Cochepaille did so, and a gendarme held a lantern so that its light fell on his bare arm. The date was there.

Madeleine then turned to face the court with a smile that still wrings the hearts of those who remember it, a smile of triumph and of utter despair.

'Now do you believe that I am Jean Valjean?'

There were no longer judges, lawyers, or gendarmes in the place, but only intent eyes and deeply troubled hearts. No man considered the part he might be called upon to play. The prosecutor forgot that he was there to prosecute, the presiding judge that he was there to pass sentence, the defender that he was there to defend. And, most strikingly, no question was raised, no legal authority invoked. It is the quality of awesome events that they seize upon the soul and make all men participants. Perhaps no one in that place was fully conscious of his own feelings, and certainly no one said to himself that he was witnessing the splendour of a great light; but all were dazzled by it.

That this was Jean Valjean could no longer be doubted. The truth was manifest. His pathetic appearance in itself sufficed to explain what seemed inexplicable a few minutes before. Without the need of further enlightenment every person in that assembly, as though by an electric impulse, instantly perceived the simple nobility of this action on the part of a man who was surrendering himself in order that another might not suffer in his place. Before this overwhelming fact all lesser questions were set aside. It was an impulse that soon passed but for the moment it was irresistible.

'I will trouble the Court no further,' said Jean Valjean. 'If I am not to be arrested at once I will leave. I have things to attend to. The Court knows who I am and where I am going, and can send for me when it chooses.'

He turned towards the door. No voice was raised, no arm outstretched to stay him. They stood aside to let him pass. He was invested at that moment with the hint of the divine which causes crowds to fall back in homage. He walked slowly. No one could say afterwards who had opened the door for him, but certainly it was open when he reached it. He turned and said to the prosecutor:

'Monsieur, I am at your disposal.'

Then he said to the assembly as a whole:

'You who are here present, you find me deserving of pity, do you not? For myself, when I consider what I came so near to doing, I think I am to be envied. But still I wish that none of this had happened.'

He went out and the door closed behind him as unobtrusively as it had opened.

It took the jury a very short time to acquit the man Champmathieu of the charge against him, and being at once released he went off in a state of total stupefaction, thinking all men mad and understanding nothing of what had transpired.

BOOK EIGHT

COUNTER-STROKE

I

In which mirror Monsieur Madeleine examines his hair

DAY WAS beginning to break. Fantine, after a restless night, but one filled with happy anticipation, had at length fallen asleep, and Sister Simplice had taken advantage of the fact to leave her bedside in order to prepare a new draught of quinine. She was bent over the array of bottles in the dispensary, obliged to peer closely at them in the misty dawn light, when suddenly she turned and uttered an exclamation. Monsieur Madeleine had silently entered the room.

'Monsieur le maire!'

He said in a low voice: 'How is she?'

'She seems better at the moment, but we've been very worried about her.'

Sister Simplice went on to tell him that Fantine had seemed to be sinking the day before but had recovered when she came to believe that he had gone to Montfermeil to fetch her child. She did not venture to question the mayor, but she saw from his expression that this was not the case.

'I'm glad,' he said. 'You were right not to undeceive her.'

'Perhaps so,' said the sister. 'But what are we to say to her now that you have come back without the child?'

He stood considering. 'God will guide me,' he said.

The light was growing and his face was more plainly visible. She looked at him suddenly and exclaimed:

'Merciful Heaven! Monsieur le maire, what has happened to you? Your hair is quite white.'

'White?'

She had no glass of her own. She searched in a case of instruments for the small hand-mirror which the doctor used to confirm that the dead had ceased to breathe. He took it and inspected himself and said, 'So!', but absently, as though he were thinking of other things. The sister's heart was chilled with the apprehension of events unknown to her.

He asked: 'May I see her?'

'Is Monsieur le maire not going to have her child brought here?' the sister asked, scarcely daring to put the question.

'Of course. But it will take two or three days.'

'If she does not see you until then she will imagine that you are still away. We can persuade her to be patient. And when the child is here she will naturally suppose that you have brought her. We shall not have to tell a lie.'

Again Monsieur Madeleine paused for thought, but then he said in his calm, firm voice:

'No, sister, I must see her now. I may perhaps have very little time.'

The sister seemed not to notice the word 'perhaps', which lent an enigmatic quality to this reply. She lowered her eyes and said respectfully:

'In that case, although she is resting, Monsieur le maire may go in.'

He said something about a door that closed badly, making a noise that might disturb her, and then, going into Fantine's room, drew back the bed-curtains. She was asleep, her breath coming in those painful gasps that are a part of her malady and rend the heart of a mother watching at the bedside of a dying child. But the laboured act of breathing scarcely troubled the serenity that had transformed her countenance, even in sleep. Her livid pallor was turned to a more gentle whiteness and there was a lustre on her cheeks. Her long, fair eyelashes, the one beauty that remained of her youth and innocence, fluttered slightly although her eyes were closed. Her whole being quivered as though at the unfolding of invisible wings making ready to spread and bear her upward. No one, seeing her, could have supposed that this was a case of desperate illness. She was more like a being about to take flight than one about to die.

When we reach out to pluck a flower the stem trembles, seeming both to shrink and to offer itself. The human body has something of this tremor at the moment when the mysterious hand of death reaches out to pluck a soul.

For some time Monsieur Madeleine stayed motionless at the bedside, looking from the sick woman to the crucifix above her head, as he had done two months before when he had come to visit her for the first time. They were in the same postures, she sleeping and he in prayer; but now her hair was grey and his was white.

The sister had not come in with him. He stood with a finger to his lips, as though there were someone present who must be enjoined to silence. And presently she opened her eyes, looked up at him, and said tranquilly, with a smile:

'And Cosette?'

II
Fantine is happy

She had made no gesture of surprise or delight; she was delight itself. The simple question had been uttered in a tone of such absolute trust and certainty, so complete an absence of misgiving, that he was at a loss. She went on:

'I knew you were here. I could see you even in my sleep. I have been seeing you for a long time, watching you all through the night. You were in a kind of radiance and there were heavenly figures hovering over you.'

He looked up at the crucifix.

'But where is Cosette? Why did you not sit her on my bed, ready for when I woke up?'

He murmured something in reply and afterwards could not remember what he had said. Fortunately the doctor had been summoned and now came to his rescue.

'You must keep calm, my child,' he said. 'Your little girl is here.'

Fantine's eyes shone with a brilliance that lighted all her face. She clasped her hands in a gesture expressing all that is most passionate and most humble in the act of prayer.

'Oh,' she cried, 'won't someone bring her in?'

With the touching self-deception of a mother she still thought of Cosette as a babe-in-arms.

'Not yet,' said the doctor. 'Not for the present. You're still feverish and the excitement would be bad for you. First you must get well.'

'But I am well! I'm perfectly well! How can you be so foolish? I want to see my baby!'

'You see how quickly you become agitated,' the doctor said. 'So long as you are in this state I cannot let you have your child. It is not enough to see her, you have to live for her. When you are calmer I will bring her to you myself.'

She hung her head. 'I beg your pardon, Monsieur le médicin. At one time I wouldn't have spoken like that, but so many bad things have happened to me that now I don't always know what I'm saying. I can understand that you don't want me to get over-excited, and I will wait if you say I must, but I swear to you that it would do me no harm to see my little girl. I can see her already, I've been seeing her all night. If you were to bring her to me now I would simply talk quietly to her, nothing more. It is not surprising, is it, that I should want to see her, now that she has been brought all the way from Montfermeil. But I'm not angry. I know I'm going to be happy. All through the night I saw brightness and smiling faces. You will bring Cosette to me when you think it right. I'm not feverish any more, I'm getting better and I feel sure that there is nothing seriously wrong with me: but I'll pretend to be ill and keep quite still to please the ladies here, and when they see how calm I am they'll say, "Now she can have her child." '

Madeleine had seated himself on a chair by the bed. She turned towards him, making a palpable effort to appear calm – 'to be good', as she termed it in the weakness of her sick state, which is like a return to childhood – so that they would make no difficulty about bringing Cosette to her. But she could not restrain herself from pouring out a flood of questions.

'Did you have a good journey, Monsieur le maire? It was so wonderfully kind of you to go for her. At least you can tell me how she is. Did she find the journey very tiring? She won't recognize me, alas; she'll have forgotten me after all this time. Children have short memories. They're like birds, living from one day to the next. Were her clothes in good order? Have the Thénardiers taken good care of her? Has she been properly fed? If you only knew how I worried about those things, the suffering they caused me at the time when I was penniless. But now all that is over and I'm happy. I so long to see her. Did you think her pretty, Monsieur le maire? She's beautiful, isn't she? You must have been very cold in the coach. Can she not be brought to me just for a moment, and then you can take her away at once. You're the mayor. Won't you do this for me?'

He took her hand. 'Cosette is beautiful,' he said. 'She's well and you will soon see her. But now you must rest. You've been talking too much, and you keep taking your arms out from under the bed-clothes, which makes you cough.'

Her speech had indeed been constantly interrupted by bursts of coughing. She made no further protest, fearing that her over-eager entreaty had already weakened the confidence she was trying to inspire. She went on more quietly:

'Montfermeil is a pretty place, isn't it? Visitors go there in the summer. Are the Thénardiers doing well? There aren't many people in those parts, and their tavern is a humble one.'

Monsieur Madeleine was still holding her hand while he gazed anxiously at her. There were things he had intended to say, but now he hesitated. The doctor had left and only Sister Simplice remained with them.

The silence that ensued was broken suddenly by a cry from Fantine.

'I can hear her! My darling, I can hear her!'

A child was playing in the yard, the daughter, perhaps, of one of the women who worked there. It was purely an accident, one of those chance happenings that are so often a part of the mysterious stage-management of scenes of tragedy. A little girl running up and down to keep warm, and laughing and singing as she ran. Children's games . . . Alas, is there any human occasion into which they do not enter?

'It's Cosette!' cried Fantine. 'I recognize her voice.'

The child ran off as casually as she had come, and her voice died away. Fantine lay for a time listening; then her expression darkened and Madeleine heard her murmur, 'How cruel of that doctor not to let me see her. But he has a cruel face.'

Presently, however, more hopeful thoughts returned and she lay talking to herself with her head relaxed on the pillow.

'We're going to be so happy. For one thing, we shall have a little garden, Monsieur Madeleine has promised, and that is where she'll play. She must have learnt her letters by now, and I'll teach her to spell. I'll watch while she skips across the grass chasing the butterflies. And presently she'll have her first communion. Now, when will that be?' She began to count on her fingers. 'One, two, three, four . . . She's seven now, so it will be in five years. She'll wear a white veil and openwork stockings, like a grown-up young lady . . . Oh, sister, I'm being so foolish, I'm thinking of my daughter's first communion!' And she laughed.

Madeleine had let go her hand and with eyes downcast was listening to her as one listens to the stir of wind in the trees, immersed in his own unfathomable thoughts. But suddenly she broke off, and her abrupt silence caused him to look at her. Her aspect was alarming.

She seemed scarcely to breathe. She had raised herself on her elbows, with one thin shoulder emerging from her nightgown. Her face, which a minute before had been radiant, was now white and she was staring with wide, startled eyes at some terrifying sight that, it seemed, had just appeared at the far end of the room.

'What is it, Fantine?' he asked. 'What's the matter?'

She did not answer but, still staring, touched him on the arm while with her other hand she pointed behind him.

He turned and saw Javert.

III

Javert is content

This is what had happened.

The clock had struck the half hour after midnight when Monsieur Madeleine left the assize court in Arras. He returned to the inn just in time to catch the mail, on which, we may recall, he had reserved a seat. His first act, upon reaching Montreuil-sur-mer at six in the morning was to post the letter he had written to M. Lafitte, the banker, after which he went to the infirmary to see Fantine.

Meanwhile, shortly after he left the assizes, the prosecutor, who was the first person in court to recover from the universal dismay, had risen to deplore this rash act on the part of the mayor of Montreuil-sur-mer, to declare that his own convictions were in no way altered by an incident which doubtless time would explain, and to demand the conviction of Champmathieu, who was unquestionably the real Jean Valjean. In this he was running counter to the general feeling of the public, the bench, and the jury. The defence lawyer had had little difficulty in showing that Madeleine's testimony completely demolished the case for the prosecution, to which he had added certain cogent, but not novel, observations on the subject of judicial error. The presiding judge supported him in his summing-up and within a few minutes Champmathieu was acquitted.

But the law needed a Jean Valjean, and if Champmathieu was not the man then it must be Madeleine. Directly the court adjourned the prosecutor closeted himself with the presiding judge and they conferred together 'of the necessity of seizing the person of the mayor of Montreuil-sur-mer'. The sentence, with its many 'ofs', is taken from the report written in his own hand to the office of the Public Prosecutor. The judge, now in a calmer frame of mind, made little objection. Justice had to take its course. It may be added that, although he was a good-hearted and reasonably intelligent man, the judge was a sturdy and indeed ardent royalist. It had shocked him to hear the mayor, referring to the landing at Cannes, use the word 'emperor' instead of 'Buonaparte'.

A warrant for Madeleine's arrest was promptly made out and sent by special messenger to Montreuil-sur-mer, for action by Inspector Javert.

Javert, as we know, had returned to Montreuil-sur-mer immediately after testifying. He was just getting up when the document reached him. The messenger, himself an experienced police officer, gave him a terse account of what had taken place after he left Arras. Javert's instructions were as follows:

'Inspector Javert will take into bodily custody Sieur Madeleine, mayor of Montreuil-sur-mer, who at today's hearing was formally identified as the released convict, Jean Valjean.'

Anyone not familiar with Javert who had seen him when he entered the infirmary, would have had no inkling of what was passing through his mind. His manner, as he walked with his customary deliberation up the steps, was calm and composed as usual, his grey hair immaculately combed. But anyone knowing him well, who had observed him more closely, would have been astonished. The buckle of his leather collar, instead of being at the back of his neck, was under his left ear. It was a portent.

Javert was a wholly consistent man who allowed no disorder to appear either in the performance of his duties or in his uniform, as methodical in his treatment of wrongdoers as he was meticulous in the buttoning of his tunic. If his collar buckle was maladjusted it could only mean that he was in a state of inward tension that may be compared to an earthquake.

He brought with him a corporal and four gendarmes whom he left in the courtyard while he asked the doorkeeper to direct him to Fantine's room. Since it was not unusual for men in uniform to wish to see the mayor, she did so without misgiving. Arrived at the room, he turned the handle, thrust open the door with the gentleness of a sick nurse or a police-spy, and entered.

Or, to be exact, he did not enter. He stood on the threshold with his cap on his head and his left hand thrust into his buttoned greatcoat. Protruding from beneath his arm was the metal head of his huge stick, the rest of which was hidden behind him. He remained like this unobserved for the better part of a minute, until Fantine suddenly pointed at him.

In the moment when the eyes of the two men met, Javert, without having moved or made the least gesture, became hideous. No human emotion can wear an aspect so terrible as that of jubilation. He had the face of a fiend who has found the victim he thought he had lost.

The certain knowledge that now at last he held Jean Valjean brought his whole soul into his eyes as the stirred depths came to the surface. The humiliation of having for a short time lost the scent and been led astray by Champmathieu was banished by the overweening delight of having guessed right in the first place, of knowing that instinct had not failed him. Delight was manifest in the arrogance of his bearing, in the ugly triumph that seemed to radiate from his narrow head, in the whole panoply of ugliness that intense gratification can induce.

Javert was in heaven. Without being fully conscious of the fact, but still with a sense of his importance and achievement, he was at that moment the personification of justice, light, and truth in their sublime task of stamping out evil. Behind him and around him, extending into infinite space, were authority and reason, the conscience of the law, the sentence passed, the public condemnation and all the stars in the firmament. He was the guardian of order, the lightning of justice, the vengeance of society, the mailed fist of the absolute, and he was bathed in glory. There was in his victory a vestige of defiance and conflict. Upright, arrogant and resplendent, he stood like the embodiment in a clear sky of the superhuman ferocity of the destroying angel, and the deed he was performing seemed to invest his clenched fist with the gleam of a fiery sword. He was setting his foot in righteous indignation upon crime, vice and rebellion, damnation, and hell, and was smiling with satisfaction as he did.

Yet in this outrageous St Michael there was a greatness that could not be gainsaid. He was terrible, but he was not ignoble. Integrity, sincerity, honesty, conviction, the sense of duty, these are qualities which, being misguided, may become hideous, but still they retain their greatness; amid the hideousness, the nobility proper to the human conscience still persists. They are virtues subject to a single vice, that of error. The merciless but honest rejoicing of a fanatic performing an atrocious act still has a melancholy claim to our respect. Without knowing it, Javert in his awful happiness was deserving of pity, like every ignorant man who triumphs. Nothing could have been more poignant or more heartrending than that countenance on which was inscribed all the evil in what is good.

IV

Authority reassumes its rights

Fantine had not set eyes on Javert since the day when the mayor had rescued her from him. Her sick mind understood nothing, but she did not doubt that he had come on her account. The sight of him was like a foretaste of death and she hid her face in her hands and cried:

'Monsieur Madeleine, save me!'

Jean Valjean (we shall henceforth call him by no other name) had risen to his feet. He said in the calmest of voices:

'Don't be afraid. He hasn't come for you.' And to Javert he said: 'I know what you're here for.'

Javert said: 'Then be quick about it.'

He spoke the words in savage haste, running them together in an unintelligible growl that scarcely resembled human speech. Disregarding the customary formalities, he made no official pronouncement, did not even produce the warrant. To him Jean Valjean was in some sort a mystical obsession, a shadowy opponent with whom he had wrestled for five years before at last overthrowing him. This arrest was not a beginning but an end. 'Be quick about it,' he said and did not move as he growled the words, fixing Valjean with the gaze, flung like a grappling-iron, with which he was accustomed to pull in offenders, the gaze which, two months earlier, had pierced Fantine to the marrow of her bones.

The terse utterance caused her to open her eyes; but with the mayor beside her what had she to fear?

Javert advanced into the room and barked: 'Well, are you coming?'

She looked in bewilderment about her. Only the sister and the mayor were present. Whom else could he be addressing in that peremptory tone except herself? And, trembling, she witnessed something unbelievable, so outrageous that never in her wildest delirium had she imagined it. She saw the policeman Javert seize the mayor by the collar, and the mayor meekly submit. It was as though the whole world had collapsed.

'Monsieur le maire!' she cried.

Javert uttered a hideous laugh, baring all his teeth. 'He isn't mayor any longer!'

Jean Valjean made no attempt to loosen the hand gripping his coat collar.

'Javert –' he said.

'Inspector, if you don't mind.'

'Inspector, I would like to have a word with you in private.'

'Speak up,' said Javert. 'People don't mutter when they talk to me.'

Jean Valjean said, still in an undertone: 'I want to ask you a favour.'

'I told you to speak up.'

'But this is for your ears alone.'

'I don't care what it is. I'm not listening.'

Jean Valjean turned towards him and said rapidly in a very low voice: 'Give me three days! Three days to fetch the unfortunate woman's child. I'll pay anything you like. You can come with me if you want to.'

'Are you joking?' said Javert. 'I didn't think you were so stupid. Three days to clear out! To fetch the woman's child, you say. That's rich!'

Fantine began to tremble. 'To fetch my child? But isn't she here? Sister, answer me – where is Cosette? I want to see her. Monsieur Madeleine –'

Javert stamped his foot. 'And now she's started! You hold your tongue, you slut! It's a fine state of affairs when gaolbirds become magistrates and whores are nursed like countesses. But we're going to put a stop to all that, and high time too!' He turned to regard Fantine, tightening his grip on Valjean. 'I tell you there's no Monsieur Madeleine here, no mayor either. There's no one but a criminal, a convict called Jean Valjean. That's the man I'm holding.'

Fantine sat upright, supporting herself on her rigid arms. Her eyes travelled from Valjean to Javert and then to the nun. She seemed about to speak, but only a whimper issued from her lips, while her teeth chattered. She reached out her arms in a gesture of anguish and with open hands groped like a person in the act of drowning. And suddenly she fell back against the pillow. Her head struck the head of the bed and then sank limply against her shoulder, the mouth open, the eyes wide and sightless.

She was dead.

Jean Valjean seized the hand gripping his collar and detached it as effortlessly as if it had been that of a child. He said to Javert:

'You have killed that woman.'

'That'll do,' Javert cried furiously. 'I didn't come here to argue. We've wasted enough time. The escort's waiting below. March, or I'll put the handcuffs on you.'

In a corner of the room was a dilapidated iron bedstead used occasionally by sisters on night-duty. Valjean went across to it and in an instant had broken up the rusty frame, a simple matter for a man of his strength. Then with one of the crossbars in his hand he stood confronting Javert, who retreated towards the door.

Armed with his metal cudgel, Valjean walked slowly to Fantine's bed; he looked round and said in a voice that was scarcely audible:

'I would advise you not to interfere with me at this moment.'

One thing is certain; Javert trembled.

He thought of going for the guard, but Valjean might use the chance to make a bolt for it. So grasping his stick by the thin end, he stayed leaning against the doorpost, not taking his eyes off his prisoner.

With an elbow on the knob at the head of the bed, and his chin resting on his hand, Jean Valjean stood contemplating Fantine's motionless form, silent and absorbed, clearly with no thought in his mind except for this life that had ended, his whole attitude one of inexpressible compassion. After some moments he bent towards her and spoke in a low voice.

What did he say to her? What could that man who was condemned say to that woman who was dead? What words did he use? No living person heard them. Did the dead hear them? There are touching illusions that are perhaps sublime realities. What is beyond doubt is that Sister Simplice, the only witness of the scene, often described how, at the moment when Valjean bent and spoke softly in Fantine's ear, she distinctly saw the dawning of a smile on the pallid lips and in the vacant eyes, wide in the astonishment of death.

Taking Fantine's head in both his hands, Valjean set it on the pillow, like a mother with her child; he retied the lace of her nightgown and tucked her hair under her cap. Then he closed her eyes.

One hand was hanging down beside the bed. He knelt and gently lifted it and touched it with his lips.

Then he rose and turned back to Javert.

'I am at your service,' he said.

V

A fitting grave

Javert consigned Jean Valjean to the town lock-up.

The arrest of Monsieur Madeleine created a sensation in Montreuil, indeed an extraordinary commotion. It is sad to have to record that at the mention of the word 'felon' nearly everyone deserted him. In a matter of hours all the good he had done was forgotten and he was simply 'the ex-convict'. In fairness it must be said that nothing was yet known of the events in Arras. Throughout the day, and at every gathering in the town, there were conversations like the following:

'Haven't you heard? He was a released convict' . . . 'Monsieur Madeleine? Impossible!' . . . 'But it's true. His name isn't Madeleine. It's something like Bejean or Bonjean. He's been arrested. He's in the town lock-up until they transfer him. He is to be tried at the assizes for a highway robbery he committed years' ago' . . . 'Well, I'm not surprised. I always though that man was too good to be true, the way he refused all decorations and handed out money to every rascal who asked for it. I always thought there was something queer about him.'

Such views were particularly prevalent in the drawing-rooms. One old lady, a subscriber to the monarchist journal *Le Drapeau blanc*, produced a comment of fathomless depth.

'So much the better. That'll teach the Bonapartists!'

Thus the ghost that had been known as Madeleine vanished from Montreuil-sur-mer. Only three or four persons in the whole town remained faithful to his memory, among them the old concierge who had served him.

On the evening of that day the devoted creature was seated in her porter's lodge, still bewildered and sadly pondering. The factory had been closed all day; the doors were bolted and the street deserted. There was no one on the premises but the two nuns, Sister Perpetua and Sister Simplice, who were keeping vigil at Fantine's bedside.

At the time when Monsieur Madeleine was accustomed to come the old woman got his key out of a drawer and made ready the taper in a stand which he used to light his way upstairs. She hung the key on the hook where he was accustomed to look for it, and placed the taper beside it, as though she were expecting him. Then she returned to her chair and her unhappy thoughts, having acted from force of habit, unconscious of what she was doing. It was not until an hour or two later that she suddenly exclaimed, 'Bless my soul! I've put his things ready for him.'

At this moment the window of her pigeon-hole was opened, and a hand reached for the key and lit the taper at her own lighted candle. She stared open-mouthed, stifling the cry that rose to her lips. The hand and coat-sleeve were unmistakably those of Monsieur Madeleine.

For a moment she could not speak, 'struck all of a heap' as she said later, but then she cried:

'God forgive me, Monsieur le maire, I thought you were –'

She could not finish the sentence and he did so for her.

'You thought I was in prison. So I was. I broke a window-bar, dropped down from a roof and here I am. I'm going up to my room. Will you please fetch Sister Simplice. No doubt she's in the infirmary.'

The old woman hurried off. He had uttered no word of warning, knowing that she would never betray him.

How he had managed to get into the courtyard without calling for the *porte cochère* to be opened is not known. He always carried a pass-key which opened any of the doors, but this must have been taken from him when he was searched in the prison. The point has never been cleared up. Climbing the stairs leading to his room, he left the taper on the topmost tread, cautiously opened his door, groped his way across the room and closed the shutters – a necessary precaution, since, as we know, his window could be seen from the street. Then he went back for the taper.

He glanced swiftly about him, at the table, the chair, and the bed, which had not been slept in for three nights. No trace remained of the disorder he had created three nights previously. The servant had 'done the room'. She had found amid the ashes in the hearth, and disposed neatly on the table, the charred, ferruled ends of his thorn stick and the forty-sou piece, now blackened by the fire.

Taking a sheet of paper, he wrote: 'Here are the remains of my thorn cudgel, and the coin stolen from Petit-Gervais to which I referred in the assize court,' and laid these objects on the paper so that they would be instantly seen by anyone entering the room. He got an old shirt out of a drawer and tore it into strips in which he wrapped the two silver candlesticks. He did all this without haste or agitation, gnawing meanwhile at a hunk of black bread, presumably prison bread which he had brought with him. The crumbs were found when later the police ransacked the room.

There was a soft knock on the door and Sister Simplice entered.

She was pale and red-eyed, and the candle she carried was shaking in her hand. The harsh blows of fate have this especial quality, that however self-perfected we may be, however disciplined, they draw from us the true essence of ourselves. The emotions of that day had turned the nun again into a woman. She had wept and she was trembling.

Jean Valjean had written another note. He handed it to her unfolded and said, 'I should be grateful, sister, if you would give this to the curé. You can read it.'

She read: 'I would ask Monsieur le curé to take charge of the money I am leaving here. He is to use it to pay the costs of my trial and the funeral expenses of the woman who died today. The rest is for the poor.'

The sister tried to speak but could do little more than stammer a few words. She did, however, manage to ask if he would like to see the dead woman for the last time.

'No,' he said. 'They're after me. They might arrest me at her bedside, and that would disturb her peace.'

He had scarcely finished speaking when they heard sounds from below, the tramping of feet and mingled with them the voice of the servant loudly protesting:

'I swear to you by God, Monsieur, that I have been here all day and all this evening, and that I have seen no one enter.'

A man said: 'But there's a light in his room.'

They recognized the voice of Javert.

The room was so arranged that the door, when it was fully opened, masked one corner. Jean Valjean blew out his light and slipped into this hiding-place. Sister Simplice went on her knees at the table.

The door opened and Javert entered.

There was a murmur of men's voices from the corridor, and the voice of the servant still raised in protest. The sister did not look up. She was praying. Her candle, standing on the mantelpiece, gave only a dim light.

At the sight of her Javert stood abashed.

It must be borne in mind that the core of Javert's being, the climate in which he lived, the very air he breathed, was respect for authority. He was all of a piece, admitting neither question nor compromise, and in his religious faith, as in all things, he was both superficial and rigidly orthodox. It goes without saying that for him the highest authority was that of the Church. A priest, in his eyes, was a soul incapable of error, a nun a creature incapable of sin. These were souls separated from the world by a wall with a single door which opened only to allow the passage of truth.

Seeing the sister, Javert's first impulse was to withdraw. But on the other hand he had a duty to perform which also admitted of no denial. So on second thoughts he stayed, resolved to hazard at least one question.

And there knelt Sister Simplice, who in all her life had never told a lie. Javert knew this and held her in especial veneration because of it.

'Sister,' he asked, 'are you the only person in this room?'

There ensued a terrible instant during which the trembling servant thought that she would faint. The sister looked up.

'Yes,' she said.

'Forgive me,' said Javert, 'if I ask you one thing more. Have you seen anyone this evening, a man? He has escaped from the prison and we are searching for him – the man called Jean Valjean. Have you seen him?'

'No,' replied the sister.

A second lie. She had lied twice, promptly and without hesitation, in an act of sacrifice.

'I apologize,' said Javert, and bowing deeply he withdrew.

Sister Simplice! The saintly woman has long since departed this life to join her brothers and sisters in the radiance of Heaven. May she be credited there for her falsehood!

Her denial was to Javert so conclusive that he did not even notice the fact that a taper, recently blown out, still stood smoking on the table.

An hour later a man on foot might have been seen amid the trees and mists, heading rapidly away from Montreuil-sur-mer in the direction of Paris. It was Jean Valjean. The testimony of two or three carters whom he passed on the road subsequently established that he was carrying a bundle and wearing a smock. Where he had obtained this was not certainly known, but an old workman had died in the hospital infirmary a few days before, and the smock may have been among the garments he left behind.

A last word about Fantine. We all have a common mother, the earth, and it was to this mother that she was restored.

The curé thought it well to retain, for the benefit of the poor, as much as possible of the money left behind by Jean Valjean. Perhaps he was right. After all, what were the persons directly concerned? – a criminal and a woman of the town. So he limited the funeral to the barest essentials, consigning Fantine to a pauper's grave in the free corner of the cemetery. Mercifully, God knows where to look for our souls. Her mortal remains were laid to rest, in company with other unconsidered bones, in a public grave resembling her own bed.

PART TWO
COSETTE

BOOK ONE
WATERLOO

I
Seen on the road from Nivelles

ON A FINE May morning last year (that is to say, in the year 1861) a traveller, the author of this tale, walked from Nivelles in the direction of La Hulpe. He followed a wide tree-lined road through a countryside where the small hills succeeded one another like waves of the sea. After passing Lillois and Bois-Seigneur-Isaac he saw to the west the belfry of Braine-l'Alleud, shaped like an inverted vase. He had left behind him a wood on the crest of a hill and, at a crossroad, a worm-eaten post inscribed, 'Former toll-gate No. 4', beside which was a drinking-place with the sign 'Au Quatre Vents. Échaleau, privately owned café'.

A little further on he came to a small valley with a stream running under small bridges built into the road embankment. The copse of bright-leaved trees which covered one side of this valley was dispersed on the other side amid fields, to dwindle in graceful disorder in the direction of Braine-l'Alleud. By the roadside, on his right was an inn with a four-wheel farm-wagon standing at its door, a bundle of hop-poles, a plough, a heap of brushwood, a lime-pit, and a ladder lying beside an old barn. A girl was working in a field in which a large yellow poster, probably to do with some local fair, flapped in the wind. Beyond the house was a rough pathway running past a duck-pond and vanishing amid thickets. He followed it.

After going a hundred yards and passing a fifteenth-century wall overhung by a steep tiled gable, he came to a wide, arched doorway, its square pillars in the formal style of Louis XIV adorned with carved medallions. A wall ran at a right angle to the austere façade encompassing this doorway, and on the patch of grass in front of it lay three abandoned harrows through which wild flowers were growing. The shabby double doors, one with a rusty knocker, were closed.

The sunshine was delightful, the foliage gently astir, more from the activity of birds than from the breeze. One gallant little bird, doubtless lovelorn, was singing his heart out at the top of a tall tree.

The traveller stooped to examine a depression on the ground, a fairly large circular crater near one of the stone door-pillars, and as he was doing so the door opened and a country-woman emerged. Seeing what he was looking at she said:

'That was made by a French cannon-ball.' She went on: 'And that hole up there in the door, that was made by a bullet from a *biscayen*, a gun firing canister-shot. It didn't go right through.'

'What is the name of this place?' the traveller asked.

'Hougomont,' she said.

The traveller walked on a little further and, gazing over hedges and between trees, saw on the skyline something resembling a lion.

He was on the battlefield of Waterloo.

II

Hougomont

Hougomont. It was a fateful place, the beginning of disaster, the first obstacle encountered at Waterloo by the great tree-feller of Europe whose name was Napoleon, the first knot to resist his axe.

It had been a manor house but is now only a farm. The origin of the name is *Hugomons*. The house was built by Hugo the squire of Somerel, he who endowed the sixth chaplaincy in the Abbey at Villiers.

The traveller pushed open the door, brushed past an old carriage standing in the porch and entered the courtyard. The first thing he noticed was a sixteenth-century doorway suggesting an arcade, of which the surrounding masonry had collapsed. Ruins often acquire the dignity of monuments. In the wall adjoining this arcade was an arched gateway with Henri IV keystones affording a view of trees in an orchard. Within the yard were a midden, some spades and mattocks, one or two carts, an old well-head with an iron super-structure, and a lively colt. There was also a chapel with a small belfry, and a pear-tree in blossom growing on a lattice on one side. This was the courtyard which Napoleon had sought to conquer, the plot of land whose possession might have given him the world. Hens were scratching in the dust. A low growl came from a large dog which was baring its teeth as though it represented the English.

The English in that place had fought most gallantly. For seven hours four companies of Guards under Cooke had defied the furious assault of an army.

Seen on the map, Hougomont with its yards and outbuildings forms a rough rectangle of which one corner has been lopped off. The south gate is at this corner, protected by a wall from which it can be covered at point-blank range. There are two main entrances, the south gate, which was the doorway of the original manor house, and the north gate, the entrance to the farm. Napoleon entrusted the assault to his brother Jerome. The divisions of Guilleminot, Foy, and Bachelu were flung against Hougomont; nearly the whole of Reille's corps was brought in, and the bullets of Kellermann's command spattered in vain against those heroic walls. They were never forced from the north and only breached from the south, without being taken.

The farm buildings occupy the southern flank of the main yard. A portion of the original north gate, shattered by the French, still hangs from the wall – four planks nailed to two cross-pieces bearing the scars of battle. This north gateway, in which a makeshift door has been installed, was like any other farm entrance, wide double doors attached directly to a wall made of stone in its lower part and brickwork above. The struggle for it was particularly violent, and the imprints of bloodstained hands were for a long time to be seen on the surrounding masonry. It was here that Bauduin was killed.

The fury of battle still lingers in that main yard; its horrors are still visible, its violence graven in stone, the life and death of yesterday. The breached and crumbling walls, their holes like gaping wounds, cry out in agony. It was more built-up in 1815 than it is today. Structures now demolished afforded buttresses and recesses, cover for the marksman.

The English had barricaded themselves within it; the French broke in but could not hold their ground. Beside the chapel is a shattered and gutted wing of the residence, all that remains of the manor house of Hougomont. The house itself served as a castle keep, the chapel as a strongpoint. It was a battle of extermination on both sides. The French, sniped at from all directions, from attic and cellar, from every window and peep-hole, every gap in the stone, brought faggots and set fire to buildings and men; musket fire was answered with flame.

Through the barred windows of the ruined wing of the house the remains of living-rooms are to be seen; a spiral staircase, pitted from top to bottom, looks like the interior of a broken shell. This stair-

case served two floors. The English, driven back upon it and clinging to the upper part, demolished the lower treads, and their broad
stone tiles still lie in a heap among the nettles. A dozen treads still
cling to the wall, the topmost carved with the design of a trident.
Three upper treads are solidly embedded; the rest of the staircase is
like a toothless jaw. Two old trees stand there, one dead, the other
damaged at the foot; but it still puts out leaves in April and since
1815 has grown up through the staircase.

The chapel was a scene of massacre. Its interior, now silent, gives
a strange impression. No mass has been said there since the carnage,
but the altar remains, a rough wooden altar against a backing of raw
stone. Four whitewashed walls, a door opposite the altar, two small
arched windows, a big wooden crucifix on the door and above it a
square air-vent blocked with a truss of straw, a shattered window-
frame on the ground – such is the chapel. Near the altar is fixed a
wooden statue of St Anne, dating from the fifteenth century, the
head of the Infant Jesus has been carried away by a bullet. The
French, dislodged from the chapel after holding it for a short time,
set fire to it. The place became a furnace; door and roof were burnt
down, but the wooden Christ was not burnt. The flames devoured
his feet, leaving only the charred stumps, but here they stopped. A
miracle, the country-people say. The beheaded Infant Jesus was less
fortunate than Christ.

The walls are covered with graffiti. Near the feet of the Christ one
may read the name Henguinez. And there are others – Conde de Rio
Maior; Marques y Marquesa de Almagro (Habana). There are
French names with exclamation marks, expressions of rage. The
walls were re-whitewashed in 1849, having been used for the exchange of national insults. It was by the door of the chapel that a
corpse was picked up still grasping an axe in its hand. The body was
that of sub-lieutenant Legros.

On the left, as one leaves the chapel, is a well, one of two in
the courtyard. But why has this one no bucket or hoisting-gear?
Why is water never drawn from it? Because it is filled with
skeletons.

The last person to draw water from this well was Guillaume Van
Kylsom, a peasant who lived in Hougomont, where he worked as a
gardener. His family fled on 18 June 1815, to take refuge in the
woods. For several days and nights the forest around the Abbey of
Villiers harboured the scattered local populace. Traces of their

makeshift encampments, such as half-burned tree-trunks, are still to be found amid the thickets.

Guillaume Van Kylsom, who had stayed at Hougomont 'to guard the house', hid in a cellar. The English found him there and by beating him with the flat of their sabres forced him into their service. They were thirsty and he fetched them water from the well. For many it was their last drink. The well from which so many of the dead had drunk was destined itself to die.

After the battle there was a pressing need to dispose of the corpses. Death tarnished victory in its own fashion, bringing pestilence on the heels of triumph. Typhus lurks in the shadow of glory. The well was a deep one, and so it became a tomb. Three hundred dead were flung into it, perhaps too hurriedly. Were they all dead? Legend says not, and that on the night following the burial voices were heard calling for help.

The well stands by itself in the middle of the yard, enclosed on three sides by walls of stone and brick resembling a square turret; there is a jagged hole in one of them, probably made by a shell. The fourth side is open, and it was here that the water was drawn. The turret had a roof, of which only the timbers remain. The metal brace on one wall is in the shape of a cross. Leaning over, one peers into a deep brick cylinder lost in darkness. Nettles grow at the foot of the walls.

The large blue flagstone which serves as an approach to all Belgian wells is lacking from this one. It has been replaced by half a dozen gnarled and knotted wooden trunks like huge bones. Bucket, chain, and windlass, are all gone; but the stone overflow-trough remains, and birds from the surrounding woods alight to drink from it after rain, and fly away.

Amid the ruins one building, the farmhouse, is still inhabited, its door open on to the courtyard. Beside the handsome gothic lock is a spoon-shaped iron handle sloping downwards. As a Hanoverian lieutenant named Wilda grasped this handle to take shelter in the house, a French sapper cut off his hand with an axe.

The gardener Van Kylsom, long since dead, was the grandfather of the family now living in the house. A grey-haired woman tells you: 'I was there. I was three years old. My sister, who was older, was frightened and she was crying. We were taken into the woods. I was in my mother's arms. We listened with our ears to the ground and I imitated the cannon-fire – boom, boom, boom.'

A gateway from the courtyard, as we have said, leads to the orchard. This is a terrible place.

It is divided into three parts, one may almost say, three acts. The first part is a garden, the second is the orchard proper, and the third part is a copse. The three parts are enclosed by the house and farm buildings on one side, a hedge on the left, a wall on the right, and at the far end another wall. The right-hand wall is brick and the far wall is stone. The garden, which slopes downwards and is planted with fruit bushes now overgrown with weeds, runs from a formal terrace with a balustrade of curved stone pillars. It was once a lord's garden in the French style preceding Lenôtre; today it is all ruin and brambles. The pillars were topped with stone globes like cannon-balls. Forty-three are still standing; the rest lie in the grass. Nearly all are scarred with musket-fire. One damaged pillar is leaning on its pedestal like a broken arm.

It was in this garden, which is on a lower level than the orchard, that six *voltigeurs* of the First Light Infantry, having penetrated thus far and being unable to get out, like trapped bears in a pit, did battle with two companies of Hanoverians, one of which was armed with carbines. The Hanoverians, ranged along the balustrade, were firing from above. The *voltigeurs*, returning fire from below, with no other cover than the gooseberry bushes, six gallant men against two hundred, took a quarter of an hour to die.

One goes up a few steps from the garden to the orchard. There in those few roods of land, fifteen hundred men fell in less than an hour. The wall, with its thirty-eight loopholes pierced at uneven heights by the English, looks ready to renew the battle. Two flat granite tombstones, marking English graves, lie under the sixteenth loophole. There are loopholes only in this southern wall, against which the main attack was directed. It is screened on the outside by a thick hedge, and the French, thinking they had only the hedge to contend with, burst through to come up against the wall with the English Guards entrenched behind it, thirty-eight loopholes blazing disciplined volleys, a storm of musketry that broke Soye's brigade. That was how Waterloo began.

Nevertheless the orchard was taken. Having no scaling ladders, the French clawed their way over the wall with their finger-nails and there was hand-to-hand fighting under the trees. All that grass was soaked in blood. A battalion from Nassau, seven hundred men, was wiped out. The far side of the wall, on which two of Kellermann's batteries concentrated, is pitted with grapeshot.

The orchard is as responsive as any other to the stir of May. It has its buttercups and daisies, the grass grows thick, farm horses graze there, washing-lines are strung between the trees, causing the visitor to bend his head. Walking through the greenery you stumble over mole-hills. There is a fallen, moss-grown tree-trunk against which Major Blackman lay dying, and under a tall tree near by the German General Duplat fell, a member of a French family exiled by the revocation of the Edict of Nantes. Close by it is a bent, sick apple-tree bandaged with straw and clay. Nearly all the apple-trees are dying of old age, and there is not one that does not bear the marks of musket or mortar-fire. The skeletons of dead trees abound in that orchard. Crows fly amid its branches, and beyond it is a copse filled with violets.

Bauduin killed, Foy wounded, fire, slaughter, carnage, a stream of English, German, and French blood furiously mingled, a well filled with corpses, the Nassau regiment and the Brunswick regiment wiped out, Duplat killed, Blackman killed, the English Guards savaged, twenty French battalions decimated out of Reille's corps of forty-three thousand, men done to death in that farm-plot of Hougomont with bullet and bayonet, fire and the sword: all this so that a yokel today may say to the traveller, 'For three francs, Monsieur, I will tell you the story of Waterloo.'

III

18 June 1815

We must use the privilege of the chronicler to turn back to the year 1815, to the period shortly preceding the events related in the first part of this book.

Had it not rained in the night of 17–18 June 1815, the future of Europe would have been different. A few drops of water, more or less, were what decided Napoleon's fate. Providence needed only a downpour of rain to make Waterloo the retort to Austerlitz. An unseasonably clouded sky sufficed to bring about the collapse of a world.

The Battle of Waterloo could not start until eleven-thirty because the ground was too wet. It had to dry out a little before the artillery could manoeuvre. And it was this that enabled Blücher to arrive in time.

Napoleon was an artillery officer and never forgot it. At the heart of this prodigious commander was the man who had reported to the Directory after the Battle of Aboukir, 'Some of our shot killed six men.' All his battle-plans were designed to suit the heavy armament. To bring the artillery to bear on the critical point, this to him was the key to victory. He treated the enemy general's strategy as though he were attacking a fortress, and he breached it. He pounded the weak points with grape-shot, and shaped and resolved battles with cannon-fire. His was a marksman's genius. To beat in the squares, pulverize the regiments, break the lines, maul and scatter the mass, this was the secret – ceaseless hammering – and it was done by the use of cannon. This formidable procedure, applied with genius, rendered him invincible for fifteen years, a dark master of the pugilism of war.

He relied more than ever on artillery in that June of 1815 because he had the advantage of numbers. Wellington had only 159 guns; Napoleon had 240.

Had the ground been dry, so that the artillery could move, the battle would have begun at six in the morning; it would have been over and done with by two, three hours before the Prussians could turn the scales.

How much of the blame for his defeat is to be attributed to Napoleon? Is the navigator necessarily responsible for the shipwreck?

Was Napoleon's undeniable physical decline at this stage accompanied by a weakening of his faculties? Had twenty years of warfare worn the blade as well as the scabbard, the soul as well as the body? Was the veteran becoming sadly manifest in the commander? In a word, was his genius fading, as many reputable historians believe, and was he frenziedly seeking to hide the fact from himself? Was he beginning to waver under chance setbacks, or – a grave weakness in a general – was he becoming careless of danger? Is there a point in the lives of men who may be termed the giants of action when their vision becomes clouded? Age is no threat to the great men of the mind. With the Dantes and the Michelangelos, to grow older is to grow: is it to shrink, in the case of the Hannibals and the Bonapartes? Had Napoleon lost his flair for victory? Was he no longer able to foresee the pitfall, to detect the trap, to discern the crumbling edge of the abyss; had he lost his instinct for averting disaster? He who had travelled all the roads to triumph, pointing the way with a lordly finger from his fiery chariot, was he now so locked in obsession as to lead his tumultuous following of legions over the precipice? Had he, at the age of forty-six, gone finally mad? Had this titanic coachman of destiny become no more than a breakneck driver?

We do not believe this.

His plan of battle, it is generally acknowledged, was masterly. It was to drive straight for the gap between the Allied forces and divide them in two, pushing the British towards Hal and the Prussians towards Tongres, and making of Wellington and Blücher two separate segments. Mont-Saint-Jean was to be carried and Brussels seized, the Germans flung back to the Rhine and the English into the sea. All this Napoleon intended to achieve by means of this battle; after which he would review the position.

It goes without saying that we do not claim to be writing a history of Waterloo. A critical moment in our tale is linked with the battle, but its history is not our concern. This has, in any case, been admirably recounted by Napoleon himself, from one point of view, and from other aspects by a galaxy of historians.

For our part, we leave to the experts their task, being ourselves no more than a remote observer, a traveller across the plain, scrutinizing that earth sodden with human blood and perhaps mistaking the appearance for the reality. We are not competent to deal in scholarly terms with a mass of facts in which, no doubt, there is an element of illusion, nor do we possess the military or strategic competence which would enable us to assess them professionally. It appears to us that a series of hazards dictated the course of events at Waterloo; and as for Destiny, that mysterious culprit, we judge it like those simple-minded judges, the common people.

IV

'A'

To form a clear idea of the Battle of Waterloo we have only to draw a capital A. The left leg of the A is the road from Nivelles, the right leg is the road from Genappe, and the cross is the sunken lane from Ohain to Braine-l'Alleud. The point of the A is Mont-Saint-Jean, where Wellington was. The foot of the left leg is Hougomont, where Reille and Jerome Bonaparte were, and the foot of the right leg is La-Belle-Alliance, Napoleon's headquarters. A little below the point where the cross of the A meets the right leg is La-Haie-Sainte; and the middle of the cross is the precise spot where the battle was decided. That is where the lion has been placed, an unwitting symbol of the supreme heroism of the Imperial Guard. The triangle formed by the upper part of the A is the plateau of Mont-Saint-Jean, the struggle for which was the essence of the battle.

The wings of the two armies extended to right and left of the roads from Genappe and Nivelles, d'Erlon facing Picton and Reille facing Hill. Beyond the apex of the A and the plateau of Mont-Saint-Jean lies the forest of Soignes.

As for the plain itself, imagine a wide rolling landscape, each successive fold dominating its predecessor, the whole rising to Mont-Saint-Jean and ending in the forest.

Two hostile armies on a field of battle are like two wrestlers, bodies interlocked, each seeking to throw the other. Everything is turned to account, the thicket becomes a strongpoint, the angle of a wall a buttress. Lacking any kind of shelter, a regiment may give ground; but a dip in the plain, an irregularity in the terrain, a convenient cross-road, a wood or a ravine, any of these may suffice to stay the feet of the colossus known as an army and prevent its retreat. He who abandons the field is beaten. Hence the necessity for the responsible commander to examine every feature of the countryside.

Both generals had carefully studied the plain of Mont-Saint-Jean, now called the plain of Waterloo. Wellington, with commendable foresight, had ridden over it the previous year, seeing in it a possible setting for a major battle. In the event he was the more favourably situated, the British army being on higher ground than the French.

To attempt a picture of Napoleon on that morning of 18 June, seated on his horse on the height of Rossomme with his field-glass in his hand, is scarcely necessary. Everyone is familiar with it, the calm profile under the small cocked hat of the College of Brienne, the green tunic with white facings, the grey top-coat hiding the epaulettes, the glimpse of red sash under the waistcoat, the leather breeches, the white horse with its cloth of purple velvet embroidered at the corners with a crowned N and an eagle, the cavalry boots worn over silk stockings, the silver spurs, the Marengo sword – this picture of the last Caesar lives in the memory of all men, acclaimed by some and reviled by others.

The figure has long been fully illumined, having emerged from the kind of legendary fog that emanates from most great men, and for a time hides the truth about them. Today history and broad daylight are one.

The daylight of history is merciless; it has the strange and magical quality that, although it is composed of light, and precisely because of this, it casts shadows where once only brilliance was to be seen, making of one man two images, each opposed to the other, so that the darkness of the despot counteracts the majesty of the leader. Thus the world arrives at a more balanced judgement. Babylon ravished diminishes Alexander, Rome in chains diminishes Caesar, Jerusalem sacked diminishes Titus. Tyranny follows the tyrant. It is grievous for a man to leave behind him a shadow in his own shape.

V

The fog of war

Everybody knows about the early stage of the battle, the tentative uncertain opening, dangerous for both armies but more so for the English than for the French.

It had rained all night and the ground was sodden with the downpour. Water lay in pools, in some places coming up to the axles of the ammunition-limbers and covering the lower harness with mud. If the crops of wheat and rye crushed under the wheels of the mass of vehicles had not partly filled in the ruts, all movement, particularly in the small valleys round Papelotte, would have been impossible.

The action was late in beginning. Napoleon, as we have said, was accustomed to keep the artillery under his direct command, using it like a pistol to be aimed at particular points in the battle, and for this it was necessary for the sun to come out and dry the ground so that the batteries could move at a gallop as required. But the sun did not shine. This was not Austerlitz. When the first gun was fired General Colville looked at his watch and noted that the time was eleven thirty-five.

The battle began with a furious assault – more furious, perhaps, than the Emperor intended – by the French left wing on Hougomont. At the same time Napoleon attacked in the centre, flinging Quiot's brigade against La-Haie-Sainte, while Ney thrust with the French right wing against the English left, occupying Papelotte.

The attack on Hougomont was partly a feint intended to induce Wellington to concentrate on that flank. The plan would have succeeded had not the four companies of English Guards and a detachment of Belgians from Perponcher's division clung so stubbornly to the position that Wellington needed only to reinforce them with four more companies of Guards and a battalion of Brunswickers.

The intention of the right-wing attack on Papelotte was to break the English left, cut the road to Brussels, thus barring the way to the Prussians, carry Mont-Saint-Jean, and force Wellington to fall back, first on Hougomont, then on Braine-l'Alleud and then on Hal. It was a clear-cut plan which largely succeeded. Papelotte and La-Haie-Sainte were both taken.

A detail may here be noted. The British infantry, especially Kempt's brigade, included a great many raw recruits. These young soldiers bore themselves gallantly against our own redoubtable infantry and despite their inexperience came out of the affair with honour. In particular they did excellent service as sharp-shooters. The sharp-shooter, being to some extent on his own, may be said to be his own commander. Novices though they were, these recruits had dash and showed themselves to possess something of the French capacity for improvisation. This did not altogether please Wellington.

After the fall of La-Haie-Sainte the battle hung in the balance. This middle phase, from midday until four o'clock, is indistinctly visible, shrouded in the fog of war. We have a glimpse of huge turmoil, a kaleidoscopic picture of outmoded military trappings, busbies, sabre-belts, crossed shoulder-straps, ammunition pouches, hussars' dolmans, wrinkled red riding-boots, heavy fringed shakos, the black tunics of Brunswick mingled with the scarlet of England, English soldiers with white-padded epaulettes, Hanoverian light horse in their narrow, red-plumed helmets, bare-kneed Scots in plaid and kilts, the white gaiters of our own grenadiers – isolated incidents rather than battle-lines, more suited to a painter such as Salvator Rosa than to an artillery commander such as Gribeauval.

There is an element of tempestuous convulsion in every battle – *quid obscurum, quid divinum* – and every historian, peering into the mêlée, can find what he looks for. Whatever the calculations of the generals, the clash of armed masses has unpredictable repercussions; each commander's plan shapes and distorts that of the other. One sector of the battlefield swallows up more combatants than another, just as water drains away more or less rapidly according to the nature of the soil. More men have to be sent to a particular point than was originally intended, the line writhes and wavers like a thread blowing in the wind. There is no logic in the flow of blood; the army fronts are like waves on the seashore, advancing and retreating regiments forming bays and headlands, impermanent as a shifting sand. Where there was infantry, artillery appears; artillery is replaced by cavalry; battalions are like puffs of smoke. At a given place there was a given object: look for it again and it is gone. The light shifts, the dark patches advance and retreat, a graveyard wind blows, driving and scattering the tragic multitude of men. All is movement and oscillation. The immobility of a mathematical plan or diagram may present a moment but never a day. To depict a battle we need a painter with chaos in his brush. Rembrandt is better than Van der Meulen; he who was accurate at noon is a liar by three o'clock. Geometry is misleading; only the tempest is true. And there comes a stage in every battle when it degenerates into hand-to-hand combat, dissolves in fragments, innumerable separate episodes concerning which Napoleon himself said that they belong more to regimental records than to the history of an army. Thus the historian has a right to summarize. He can do no more than grasp the broad outline. No narrator, be he never so conscientious, can fix the exact shape of that ugly cloud that is called a battle.

This, which is true of all great clashes between armies, applies particularly to Waterloo. Nevertheless there came a point, during the afternoon, when the shape of the battle was defined.

VI

Four o'clock in the afternoon

At about four o'clock Wellington's army was in serious trouble. The Prince of Orange was in command of the centre, with Hill commanding the right wing and Picton the left. The Prince, gallant and despairing, was calling upon his lowlanders, the men of Nassau and Brunswick, to stand fast. Hill, greatly weakened, was falling back upon Wellington and the reserve. Picton was dead, killed by a ball through the head at the moment when the colours of the French 105th regiment of the line had been captured by the English. For Wellington there were two critical points, Hougomont and La-Haie-Sainte. Hougomont was still holding out, but in flames. La-Haie-Sainte had fallen. Three thousand men had died in that farm. Of the German battalion which was among its defenders only five officers and forty-two men survived. The cavalry force of 1200 horses had lost half its strength, the Scots Greys and Ponsonby's heavy dragoons having been overwhelmed by Bro's lancers and Travers's cuirassiers. Most of its officers had fallen. Two infantry divisions, the fifth and sixth, had been virtually destroyed.

With Hougomont breached and La-Haie-Sainte captured, only one strong-point remained, the centre. This was still holding, and Wellington reinforced it, bringing in Hill, who was at Merbe-Braine and Chassé, who was at Braine-l'Alleud.

The English centre, slightly concave, very dense and compact, was in a strong position. It occupied the plateau of Mont-Saint-Jean, with the village behind it and a steep slope in front. At its back was a stone mansion, part of the state-owned domain of Nivelles, standing at the road-intersection, a sixteenth-century building of such solid construction that musket-fire ricocheted off it. The trees and thickets bordering the plateau had been pruned to create embrasures and loop-holes behind which the guns waited in ambush, and this work of concealment, an entirely legitimate stratagem of war, had been so skilfully carried out that Haxo, who had been sent by Napoleon to reconnoitre the enemy batteries, saw nothing and reported that there were no defence works other than the barricades on the road to Nivelles and Genappe. It was the time of year when the crops are in full growth, and a battalion of Kempt's brigade, armed with carbines, lay hidden in the standing corn.

In short, the Anglo-Dutch centre was well placed. What endangered its position was the forest of Soignes, a wide extent of woodland in its rear containing the marshes of Groenandel and Boitsfort. An army could not hope to carry out an orderly withdrawal over this rough terrain, where its units were bound to become separated and the artillery likely to be bogged down in the swamps. Many of the officers maintained – although it must be said that others disagreed with them – that retreat would become a rout.

Wellington reinforced the centre with one of Chassé's brigades, brought in from the right wing, one of Wincke's brigades, from the left, and Clinton's division. In support of his British contingent, consisting of Halkett's command, Mitchell's brigade, and Maitland's Guards, he brought in the Brunswick infantry, the Nassau contingent, Kielmansegge's Hanoverians, and Ompteda's Germans. Thus he had twenty-six battalions under his direct command. As Charras has said, 'The right wing was folded back behind the centre.' A very powerful battery occupied a fortified position on the site of what is now known as 'the Waterloo Museum'. In addition, concealed in a fold in the ground, Wellington had Somerset's Dragoon Guards, the other half of the justly renowned English cavalry. Ponsonby had been wiped out (he himself had been killed), but Somerset remained.

The battery, which might almost have been termed a redoubt if the work had been finished, was drawn up behind a low garden wall, hastily reinforced with sandbags, with a broad, open slope in front of it. There had been no time to complete its defence works.

Wellington, worried but impassive, had remained throughout the day seated on his horse in the same place, a little in front of the ancient mill of Mont-Saint-Jean, which still exists, and in the shade of an elm-tree which an Englishman, a vandal enthusiast, subsequently bought for 200 francs, cut down and took away. Wellington's bearing was one of icy heroism. The bullets whistled past him. Gordon, one of his aides, was killed at his side. Lord Hill demanded of him after a shell-burst, 'What are your orders, my lord, if you are killed?' ... 'Do what I'm doing,' Wellington replied, and he said tersely to Clinton, 'Hang on to the last man.' When things were clearly going badly he cried to the men of Talavera, Vitoria, and Salamanca, 'Don't yield an inch. Think of England!'

But at about four o'clock the English line wavered. There was suddenly nothing to be seen on the high ground of the plateau but the guns and gun-crews. The infantry regiments, unable to withstand the hail of French cannon and musketry fire, had taken refuge in the depression which the farm lane of Mont-Saint-Jean still crosses. There was a general movement of withdrawal. Wellington's battle line was crumbling. 'It's the beginning of the retreat!' Napoleon cried.

Napoleon is well-pleased

Although he was a sick man and troubled by a local ailment which made riding uncomfortable, the Emperor had never been in higher spirits than on that day. Since the morning his inscrutable countenance had worn a smile. The man of marble, the profound visionary, was blindly radiant on that day of 18 June 1815; the frowning commander of Austerlitz was happy at Waterloo. Thus does Destiny deceive us; our joys are shadows, the last laugh is God's.

'*Ridet Caesar, Pompieus flebit* – if Caesar laughs Pompey will weep,' said the men of the Fulminatrix legion. Pompey did not weep on this occasion, but it is certain that Caesar laughed.

It had seemed to Napoleon, since he and Bertrand had ridden after midnight through thunder and rain to the heights near Rossomme, thence to survey the line of English camp-fires lighting the horizon from Frischemont to Braine-l'Alleud, that the appointment with destiny fixed by him for the coming day on the field of Waterloo had been rightly determined. He had reined in his horse and sat for some time motionless gazing at the lightning and listening to the thunder; and, fatalist that he was, he had been heard to mutter the cryptic words, 'We are of one mind.' But Napoleon was mistaken. Destiny and he were no longer of one mind.

He had spent no time at all in sleep, every minute of that night bringing a new cause for satisfaction. He had made the round of the picket-lines, pausing here and there to talk to the men. At half past two, near the wood of Hougomont, he heard the sound of a marching column and for a moment had thought that Wellington was already withdrawing. 'It's the English rear-guard getting ready to clear out,' he said to Bertrand. 'I shall capture the six thousand English who have just landed at Ostend.' He was talking expansively, with the ardour he had shown when they disembarked in the Golfe Juan on 1 March, and pointing to a cheering peasant he exclaimed, 'There you are, Bertrand – a reinforcement already!' On this night of 17 June he mocked Wellington, saying, 'That Englishman needs a lesson.' The rain fell more heavily and there was a crash of thunder as he spoke.

At three-thirty that morning he lost one of his illusions. The officers sent out to reconnoitre reported that there was no movement in the enemy lines. Nothing was stirring, no camp-fires had been extinguished. Wellington's army was asleep; a profound silence reigned on earth while the skies resounded. At four o'clock a peasant was brought in who had acted as guide to an English cavalry column, probably Vivian's brigade, on its way to take up its position in the village of Ohain, on the extreme left. At five o'clock two Belgian deserters were brought in who said that the English army was awaiting battle. 'So much the better!' cried Napoleon. 'I'd sooner bowl them over than drive them back.'

At daybreak he dismounted on to the mud of the grass verge at the turn of the road from Plancenoit. He sent to Rossomme farm for a kitchen table and chair, and there seated himself, with a truss of straw for a footstool and a map of the battlefield spread out in front of him, saying to Soult, '*Joli échiquier*' – 'a nice chess-board!'

Owing to the rain and the state of the roads the commissariat convoys had not arrived; the soldiers had had little sleep and were wet and hungry; but this did not deter Napoleon from exclaiming blithely to Ney, 'Our chances are ninety in a hundred.' Breakfast was served to the Emperor at eight o'clock and he invited a number of his generals to join him. Over breakfast they discussed the fact that two nights previously Wellington had attended the Duchess of Richmond's ball in Brussels, and Soult, that rough warrior with the face of an archbishop, said, 'The real ball will be held today.' Napoleon laughed at Ney, who said, 'Wellington won't be such a fool as to wait for your majesty.' This was the kind of talk he enjoyed. 'He loved to tease,' said Fleury de Chaboulon. 'A lively humour was at the root of his nature,' said Gourgand; and Benjamin Constant said, 'He was full of jokes, more crude than witty.' This aspect of the great man deserves to be stressed. It was he who called his grenadiers 'grognards' and pinched their ears or tweaked their moustaches – 'He was always up to some game with us,' one of them said. During the mysterious return from Elba to France, when the French brig-of-war *Zephir* closed with the brig *Inconstant*, in which Napoleon was concealed, and asked for news of him, Napoleon himself, wearing the bee-embroidered hat with a white-and-purple cockade which he had devised in Elba, snatched up the speaking-trumpet and shouted, laughing: 'The Emperor is in excellent health.' The man who can laugh in this fashion feels himself to be in harmony with events. Napoleon had several bursts of laughter during that Waterloo breakfast. When the meal was over he was silent for a quarter of an hour; then two generals seated themselves on a truss of straw with writing-pads on their knee and he dictated the order of battle.

At nine o'clock, when the French army moved off in five columns, divisions in double lines, artillery between the brigades, bands at the head filling the air with the roll of drums and the clamour of trumpets, a powerful, vast, and joyous sea of helmets, sabres, and bayonets extended to the horizon, the Emperor was so moved that he twice cried: 'Magnificent! Magnificent!'

Incredible as it may seem, in the period between nine and ten-thirty the whole army took up its positions, being arrayed in six lines forming, in the Emperor's phrase, 'a pattern of six Vs'. In the profound lull preceding the storm, while he watched the deployment of the three batteries of twelve-centimetre guns detached from the three corps of Erlon, Reille, and Lobau with orders to open the attack by bombarding Mont-Saint-Jean at the intersection of the Nivelles and Genappe roads, the Emperor clapped Haxo on the shoulder, saying, 'Two dozen very pretty girls, General.'

Confident of the outcome, he had a smile of encouragement for the company of sappers from the First Corps, detailed to dig themselves in on Mont-Saint-Jean directly the village was taken. Only one momentary shadow marred the serenity of his mood. Over to his left, in the place where there is today a vast graveyard, he saw the Scots Greys drawn up on their splendid horses, and the sight drew from him an expression of regret – 'It's a pity,' he said.

Then he mounted his own horse and rode to a point a little in front of Rossomme. This narrow strip of grass to the right of the road from Genappe to Brussels was his second observation-post during the battle. (The third, which he went to at seven in the evening, was between La-Belle-Alliance and La-Haie-Sainte.) It is a terribly exposed place, a high, flat-topped mound which still exists, behind which the Imperial Guard was massed in a small depression in the plain. Bullets ricocheted up from the road surface, and as at Brienne the air above his head was filled with the whistle of grape-shot and musketry. The twisted remnants of shot and shell, rusted sabre-blades, and the like were later retrieved from almost the spot where his horse stood, and a few years ago a shell was dug up there with a damaged fuse and its explosive charge intact. It was here that the Emperor said to his guide, Lacoste, a hostile and terrified peasant, roped to the saddle of a hussar, who ducked at every salvo and tried to hide behind the horses, 'Idiot! You ought to be ashamed. Do you want to be shot in the back?' The writer of these lines, digging in the dusty earth of that hillock, himself found the neck of an exploded bomb eaten with the rust of forty-six years, and fragments of metal that broke like twigs in his hands.

The rolling countryside is no longer what it was on that June day when Napoleon and Wellington met. It has been disfigured for its own glorification, robbed of its natural contours to make a funeral monument, so that history, put out of countenance, can no longer recognize herself. Returning to Waterloo two years later, Wellington exclaimed: 'They have changed my battlefield!' Where the great pyramid of earth surmounted by a lion now stands there was a ridge with a negotiable slope on the side of the Nivelles road but what was almost an escarpment on the side of the Genappe road. Its height can be measured by the height of the two funeral mounds flanking the road from Genappe to Brussels, the one on the left the English memorial and that on the right the German. There is no French memorial. For France the whole plain is a graveyard. Thanks to the many thousand cartloads of earth which have made it into a pyramid 150 feet high and half a mile in circumference, the plateau of Mont-Saint-Jean is now accessible by a gentle incline; but on the day of the battle the approaches were much steeper, particularly on the side of La-Haie-Sainte – so much so that the English guns could not see the farm in the depths of the valley, the centre of the struggle. Moreover the heavy rainfall had ploughed gulleys in the steep slopes, adding mud to the difficulties of the ascent.

Along the crest of the ridge there ran a sort of trench, invisible to the observer at a distance, and this must be described.

Braine-l'Alleud and Ohain are Belgian villages about four miles apart, hidden from one another by the contours of the land and linked by a road that runs like a furrow through the rolling country-side, sometimes following the contours and sometimes buried between hills, so that at many points it is a ravine. In 1815, as now, the road crosses the plateau of Mont-Saint-Jean between the Genappe and Nivelles highways; but whereas it is now level with the surrounding land, it was then a sunken lane. Its two embankments have been removed to make the funeral mound. The greater part of the road was and still is embanked, sometimes to a depth of a dozen feet, with steep, overhanging sides which were liable to crumble under heavy rain. There were accidents. The road was so narrow at the approach to Braine-l'Alleud that in February 1637 a certain Monsieur Bernard Debrye, a Brussels merchant, was run over and killed by a farm-cart – a fact recorded by the stone cross standing near the cemetery. And it was so deep on the Mont-Saint-Jean plateau that a peasant named Mathieu Nicaise was killed by a land-slide in 1783; but the cross commemorating this event vanished in the clearance, and nothing of it now remains but its overturned pedestal on the grassy slope to the left of the lane running from La-Haie-Sainte to the Mont-Saint-Jean farm.

On the day of the battle nothing gave warning of this sunken lane flanking the ridge of Mont-Saint-Jean; a deep trench running along the escarpment, a hidden furrow in the earth, invisible and therefore terrible.

VIII

The Emperor questions the guide, Lacoste

So on that morning of Waterloo Napoleon was well content, and with reason. His plan of battle, as we have said, was admirable.

Nor did the many vicissitudes of the day dismay him: the holding of Hougomont, the stubborn resistance of La-Haie-Sainte; the death of Bauduin and wounding of Foy; the unexpected wall against which Soye's brigade was broken; the fatal negligence of Guille-minot, who had neither grenades nor powder bags; the bogging down of the batteries; the fifteen unescorted guns overturned by Uxbridge in a sunken lane; the relative ineffectiveness of explosives falling in the sodden earth of the English lines, so that grape-shot wasted itself in a shower of mud; Piré's failure at Braine-l'Alleud and the virtual wiping out of fifteen cavalry squadrons; the English right little shaken, and the left weakly assailed; Ney's strange blunder in advancing the four divisions of the First Corps *en masse* instead of in echelon, twenty-seven lines of two hundred men exposed to cannon-shot and rapid musket-fire, so that their attack was thrown into disorder, the supporting batteries on the flank uncovered, Bourgeois, Donzelot, and Durutte threatened and Quiot repulsed; Lieutenant Vieux, that Herculean product of the École Polytech-nique, wounded at the moment when he was breaking down the gate of La-Haie-Sainte with an axe under the plunging fire from the English fortifications barring the turn in the the road from Genappe to Brussels; Marcoquet's division caught between infantry and cavalry, mown down at point-blank range in a cornfield by Best and Pack, sabred by Ponsonby, and its battery of seven guns spiked; the Prince of Saxe-Weimar standing his ground against the Comte d'Erlon, Frischemont, and Smohain; the colours of the 105th and 45th line regiments captured; the Prussian Black Hussar captured by scouts of the flying column of *chasseurs* scouring the countryside between Wavre and Planchenoit, and the disturbing things this prisoner told them; Grouchy's late arrival; the fifteen hundred men killed in less than an hour in the orchard of Hougomont, and the eighteen hundred killed at La-Haie-Sainte in an even shorter time – all these stormy events, passing in the fog of battle beneath Napoleon's gaze, seemed scarcely to trouble him or cloud his aspect of imperial certainty. He was accustomed to see war as a whole, never casting up the columns of profit and loss. The figures mattered little to him provided they added up to the right total, which was victory. Early setbacks did not shake him, since he believed himself to be master of the conclusion. He could afford to wait; he was beyond question the equal of Destiny, to whom he seemed to say, 'You would not dare.'

A creature of light and dark, Napoleon believed himself to be protected in good and tolerated in evil. He had, or thought he had, a connivance on his side, one may almost say a complicity in the ordering of events akin to the invulnerability of the antique gods. Yet, with Beresina, Leipzig, and Fontainebleau behind him, he might well have had his doubts about Waterloo – as though a mysterious frown had appeared in the depths of the sky.

But when Wellington recoiled, Napoleon was thrilled. He watched the plateau of Mont-Saint-Jean being rapidly evacuated and the English battle-front disappear. It rallied but kept under cover. The Emperor rose in his stirrups with the light of victory in his eyes. He saw Wellington driven into the forest of Soignes and there destroyed, the final crushing of England by France; Crécy, Poitiers, Malplaquet, and Ramillies revenged. The man of Marengo would exact payment for Agincourt.

Contemplating this fateful prospect, he swept the field of battle for the last time with his glass. His Guard, drawn up with grounded arms on the lower slope behind him, watched him with an almost religious awe. He was intently studying the details of the terrain: slopes and ridges, the odd clump of trees, the barley-field, the foot-path, down to the last blade of grass. In particular he examined the

barriers of tree-trunks erected by the English across the two highways – the one on the Genappe road overlooking La-Haie-Sainte
and armed with two guns which were the only pieces of English
artillery bearing on the deepest sector of the battlefield, and the one
on the road to Nivelles, behind which gleamed the Dutch bayonets
of Chassé's brigade. Close by the latter stood the old, white-washed
Chapel of St Nicholas, on a bend in the lane running to Braine-
l'Alleud. Napoleon bent down and put a question to the guide,
Lacoste, who answered with a shake of his head – probably an act
of deliberate treachery.

Then the Emperor straightened up in the saddle and for a moment
sat pondering. Wellington had begun to withdraw: all that remained was to turn withdrawal into rout.

He turned abruptly and ordered a dispatch-rider to ride post-
haste to Paris with the news that the battle was won.*

He was the genius who commands thunder, and he had his
thunderbolt. He ordered the cuirassiers under Milhaud to take the
plateau of Mont-Saint-Jean.

IX

The unexpected

There were three thousand five hundred of them, extending over a
front of about a mile; twenty-six squadrons of big men on enormous
horses. Behind them, in support, were Lefebvre-Desnouettes's
division, a picked company of gendarmes, and the contingents of
the *chasseurs* and lancers of the Guard. They wore plumeless helmets and metal breastplates and carried cavalry muskets and long
sabres. The whole army had watched in admiration when they
moved into position at nine o'clock that morning, the dense column
with one artillery battery on its flank and another at its centre,
deploying in two ranks between the Genappe road and Frischemont to constitute the powerful and shrewdly placed second line
which, with Kellermann's cuirassiers on its left wing and Milhaud's
on its right, had so to speak two wings of iron.

The Emperor's aide-de-camp, Bertrand, brought them the order.
Ney drew his sword and placed himself at the head of the squadrons
as they went into action.

*This has been questioned. It seems that Grouchy may have misread
Napoleon's dispatch.

It was an awe-inspiring sight.

The great force of cavalry, sabres raised and standards fluttering, formed up in columns by divisions, moved as one man down the slope of the Belle-Alliance hill, vanished into the smoke of that fearsome valley where so many men had already fallen, emerged on the other side still in compact, orderly ranks and rode at a canter through a hail of fire up the muddy slope of the Mont-Saint-Jean plateau. They rode steadily, menacingly, imperturbably, the thunder of their horses resounding in the intervals of musket and cannon-fire. Being two divisions they were in two columns, Wathier's division on the right, Delord's on the left.

At a distance they resembled prodigious snakes of steel writhing across the battlefield and up towards the plateau. Nothing like it had been seen since the taking of the great Moskowa redoubt by the heavy cavalry. Murat was absent, but Ney was there. The great mass seemed to have become a monster with a single soul. The separate squadrons rose and fell like the rings of a serpent, disclosing gaps as now and then they became visible through the smoke in a confusion of helmets, cries, sabres, the heaving rumps of horses, amid the cannon and the trumpet-blast, a disciplined and dreadful tumult with breastplates gleaming like a serpent's scales.

These are tales that seem to belong to another age, legends of centaurs, titans with the heads of men and the bodies of horses galloping to the assault of Olympus, terrible, invulnerable, and sublime, both gods and beasts.

By a strange coincidence the attack of twenty-six squadrons was to be met by the same number of enemy battalions. Behind the ridge of the plateau and in the shadow of the masked battery, Wellington's infantry was formed up in thirteen squares, two battalions in each, the squares being arrayed in two lines of seven and six. Thirteen squares of motionless, resolute men waiting with levelled muskets for what was to come. They could not see their attackers, nor could the attackers see them. They could only hear the rising tide of men, the growing thunder of hooves, the jingle and the clatter of harness, the growl of a savage breath. There was a dreadful silence, and suddenly there appeared on the crest of the ridge a long line of uplifted arms brandishing sabres, helmets, trumpets, grey-moustached faces. With a cry of '*Vive l'empéreur!*' the cavalry, like the coming of an earthquake, swept on to the plateau.

And now a tragedy occurred. On the French right, and the English left, the head of the column of cuirassiers suddenly recoiled in indescribable confusion. Having surmounted the crest of the ridge, and as they broke into the full fury of their charge on the guns and the squares, the horsemen perceived that between themselves and the enemy there was a deep ditch – a grave. It was the sunken lane of Ohain.

What followed was appalling. This ravine, some fifteen feet deep between sheer banks, appeared suddenly at the feet of the leading horses, which reared and attempted to pull up but were thrust forward by those coming behind, so that horse and rider fell and slid helplessly down, to be followed by others. The column had become a projectile, and the explosive force generated for the destruction of the enemy was now its own destroyer. That hideous gulf could only be crossed when it was filled. Horses and men poured into it, pounding each other into a solid mass of flesh, and when the level of the dead and the living had risen high enough the rest of the column passed over. In this fashion a third of Dubois's brigade was lost.

It was the beginning of the defeat.

According to local tradition, which is clearly exaggerated, two thousand horses and fifteen hundred men perished in the sunken lane of Ohain. The figure probably includes bodies which were thrown into it later, on the day after the battle.

Before ordering the charge Napoleon had carefully surveyed the ground, but without seeing the lane, of which nothing was visible above the level of the plateau. But the sight of the white chapel standing at the bend of the Nivelles road had prompted him to put a question to the guide, Lacoste, presumably concerning the possibility of other obstacles. Lacoste had answered in the negative. It can almost be said that the shaking of a peasant's head was the cause of Napoleon's downfall.

But there are other considerations. To the question, was it possible for Napoleon to win this battle, our answer is, No. Because of Wellington? Because of Blücher? No. Because of God.

For Napoleon to have won Waterloo would have been counter to the tide of the nineteenth century. Other events were preparing in which he had no part to play, and their opposition to himself had long been apparent.

It was time for that great man to fall.

His excessive weight in human affairs was upsetting the balance; his huge stature overtopped mankind. That there should be so great a concentration of vitality, so large a world contained within the mind of a single man, must in the end have been fatal to civilization. The time had come for the Supreme Arbiter to decide. Probably a murmur of complaint had come from those principles and elements on which the ordering of all things, moral and material, depends. The reek of blood, the over-filled graveyard, the weeping mother, these are powerful arguments. When the earth is overcharged with suffering, a mysterious lament rising from the shadows is heard in the heights.

Napoleon had been impeached in Heaven and his fall decreed; he was troublesome to God.

Waterloo was not a battle but a change in the direction of the world.

X

The plateau of Mont-Saint-Jean

Simultaneously with the disclosure of the ravine the guns were unmasked. Sixty cannon and the musket-fire from thirteen squares ravaged the cuirassiers at point-blank range. The intrepid General Delord greeted his enemies with a military salute, and the charge of the cuirassiers continued without a pause. The disaster of the sunken lane had decimated but not dismayed them. They were men of the kind whose hearts grow larger as their numbers shrink.

Only Wathier's column had suffered. Delord's column, which Ney had caused to veer to the left, as though he suspected a trap, was still intact. Galloping *ventre à terre*, reins loose, pistol in hand and sabre between the teeth, the cuirassiers charged the English squares.

There are moments in battle when the souls of men so harden as to turn flesh to stone. Beneath this furious assault the English forces were unshaken. The mêlée was indescribable. The squares were attacked on all sides, ringed round with an inferno of assailants, and stayed immovable. The first row, kneeling, met the horsemen with their bayonets while the second row fired; and behind the second row the gunners of the light artillery reloaded. The ranks parted to allow the discharge of grape-shot and then re-closed. The cuirassiers' answer was to crush them, the huge horses trampling down the men and overleaping the bayonets to plunge gigantically within those living walls. The hail of fire ploughed gaps in the ranks of the cuirassiers and the cuirassiers forced breaches in the squares. The squares shrank in size as their numbers diminished, but they did not break, and they kept up a ceaseless fire against their assailants. The battle assumed a monstrous aspect, with the squares ceasing to be formations of men and becoming craters, the horsemen ceasing to be cavalry and becoming a tempest, every square a volcano enveloped in a thunder-cloud, lava defying the lightning.

The square on the extreme right, the most vulnerable of all being partly isolated, was almost annihilated in the first assault. It consisted of the 75th Highland regiment. Indifferent to the slaughter around him, the regimental piper, seated on a drum, continued to play airs that were the echo of his native forests, lakes, and hills. Those Scotsmen died remembering Ben Nevis as the Greeks had died remembering Argos – until a sabre-stroke, cutting down both bagpipe and the arm that held it, put an end to the lament.

The cuirassiers, relatively few in numbers and further weakened by the disaster of the sunken lane, were opposed to nearly the whole strength of Wellington's army, but they seemed to multiply, each man to possess the strength of ten. Certain of the Hanoverian battalions showed signs of giving ground, and seeing this Wellington bethought him of his own cavalry. If Napoleon at the same moment had thought of his infantry he would have won the battle. This oversight was his fatal error.

Suddenly the attacking cuirassiers found themselves under a twofold attack, the infantry squares in front of them and in their rear Somerset with his fourteen hundred dragoons. On his right was Dornberg with the German Light Horse, and on his left Trip with the Belgian heavy cavalry. The cuirassiers were thus attacked on all sides, but they were a whirlwind, their bravery beyond words. Only Englishmen of equal stature could confront Frenchmen such as these.

It was no longer a conflict of men but of shadows, furies, spirits exalted in a tempest of high courage amid the flashing of swords. Within minutes Somerset's fourteen hundred dragoons had been reduced to eight hundred, and Fuller, their lieutenant-colonel, was dead. Ney brought in Lefebvre-Desnouettes with his lancers and *chasseurs*. The Mont-Saint-Jean plateau was taken, re-taken, and taken again. The squares still held, surviving a dozen assaults. Ney had four horses killed under him. Half the cuirassiers were left dead or wounded on the plateau. The struggle lasted two hours.

The English army was profoundly shaken. There can be no doubt that had their first attack not been weakened by the tragedy of the sunken lane the cuirassiers would have broken the centre and gained the day. Clinton, who had seen Talavera and Badajoz, was amazed by that remarkable cavalry, and Wellington, more than half defeated, stoically murmured, 'Splendid!'

The cuirassiers broke seven squares out of the thirteen, captured or spiked sixty guns, and captured six regimental standards which were presented to the Emperor outside the Belle-Alliance farm by a party of three cuirassiers and three *chasseurs* of the Guard.

Wellington's position had decidedly worsened. That battle was like a duel between two grievously wounded men, each with the blood draining out of him, neither willing to yield. The question was, which would be the first to fall?

And still the struggle for the plateau continued. As to exactly how far the cuirassiers penetrated, no one can say, but it is known that the body of a cuirassier, with that of his horse, was found in the toll weighing-shed at the point where the four roads meet – those from Nivelles, Genappe, La Hulpe, and Brussels – having ridden right through the English lines. One of the men who carried the body away is still living at Mont-Saint-Jean, a man named Dehaze who was then eighteen.

Wellington knew that he was near to disaster. In a sense the cuirassiers had failed to achieve their objective, since they had not broken the English centre. Both sides were lodged on the plateau, but neither held it, and in fact the English still occupied the greater part. They had the village and its surrounding land, whereas Ney had only the ridge and its slopes. Both sides seemed to have taken root in that fateful soil.

But the weakness of the English seemed past remedy. Their losses had been appalling. Kempt, on the left wing, cried out for reinforcements, to which Wellington replied that there were none – 'they must fight till they drop'. And at almost the same moment, by a coincidence which illustrates the exhaustion of both armies, Ney was asking Napoleon for infantry and Napoleon was exclaiming: 'Where does he think I can get any? Does he expect me to manufacture them?'

Wellington's case was even worse. His infantry had been so badly mauled by the cuirassiers that in some sectors only a few men grouped round the colours marked the remains of a regiment. Battalions were commanded by captains or lieutenants, and indeed the list of senior officers killed or wounded on both sides was hideously long. Moreover Cumberland's Hanoverian Hussars, a whole regiment under their commander, Colonel Hacke (who was later court-martialled and cashiered), took to their heels and bolted into the forest of Soignes, spreading the news of disaster as far as Brussels. Baggage waggons, ammunition limbers, carts of wounded, seeing the French gain ground and draw near the forest, followed them; and the Dutch cried havoc. By the account of eye-witnesses still living, the train of fugitives stretched five miles and more in the direction of Brussels. So great was the panic that it reached the Prince de Condé at Malines and Louis XVIII at Ghent. Except for a small reserve stationed behind the field hospital set up in the Mont-Saint-Jean farm, and Vivian's and Vandeleur's brigades on his left wing, Wellington had no more cavalry, and a large number of his guns were out of action. These facts are reported by Siborne, and Pringle, somewhat exaggerating, claims that the Anglo-Dutch strength was reduced to 34,000 men. The Iron Duke remained calm but he was white-lipped. The Austrian and French military attachés, who were with the English headquarters staff, believed that the day was lost. At five o'clock Wellington looked at his watch and was heard to murmur: 'Blücher – or darkness.'

It was at about this moment that a line of bayonets came into view in the distance, twinkling on the heights round Frischemont.

This was the turning-point.

XI
The two guides

Napoleon's tragic miscalculation is known to everyone: he looked for Grouchy but it was Blücher who came – death instead of life. Destiny is shaped by moments such as this: with his eyes upon the throne of the world, he saw the shadow of St Helena.

If the shepherd boy who acted as guide to Bülow, Blücher's second-in-command, had advised him to come by the route above Frischemont, instead of by that below Planchenoit, the pattern of the nineteenth century might well have been different. Napoleon would have won Waterloo. Any other road, except the one below Planchenoit, would have brought the Prussian army to a ravine impassable by artillery, and Bülow would not have arrived in time. According to the Prussian General Muffling, a further hour's delay would have spelt disaster.

There had been much delay already. Bülow had bivouacked at Dion-le-Mont and set out at dawn, but he had been greatly hindered by the state of the road. Moreover, he had had to cross the river Dyle by the narrow bridge at Wavre. The French had set fire to the village street leading to the bridge, and since the ammunition waggons could not pass between the rows of burning houses they had to wait for the fire to be put out. It was not until noon that Bülow's advance-guard reached Chapelle-Saint-Lambert.

Had the battle begun two hours earlier it would have been over by four o'clock, and Blücher, too, would have fallen victim to Napoleon. Such are the immeasurable hazards of a Fatality beyond our grasp.

The Emperor, with his field-glass, was the first to see something on the horizon that fixed his attention. 'A sort of cloud,' he muttered. 'It looks to me like troops.' And turning to the Duke of Dalmatia he said: 'Soult, what can you see around Chapelle-Saint-Lambert?' Using his own glass the marshal replied: 'Four or five thousand men, Sire. It must be Grouchy.' All the glasses of the general staff were turned on this 'cloud', which remained motionless. Some officers thought that it was a halted column of men, but the majority believed it to be a grove of trees. The Emperor sent Domon's contingent of light cavalry to reconnoitre.

The fact is that Bülow had not moved because his advance-guard was weak. His orders were to concentrate his main force before joining battle. But at five o'clock, seeing Wellington's precarious state, Blücher ordered Bülow into the attack with the notable words: 'We must give the English a breather.'

Shortly afterwards, the divisions of Losthin, Hiller, Hacke, and Ryssel deployed ahead of Lobau's corps; Prince William of Prussia's cavalry debouched from the Bois de Paris, Planchenoit was in flames, and artillery fire began to reach as far as the ranks of the Imperial Guard drawn up behind Napoleon.

The Imperial Guard

We know the rest, the intervention of a third army and the transformation of the battle: eighty-six pieces of artillery bursting into sudden thunder, Pirch I overtaking Bülow, Zieten's cavalry led by Blücher in person, the French driven back in disorder under the combined English and Prussian fire as darkness began to fall. Disaster in front and disaster on the flank, and the Guard flung in in an attempt to stay the hideous collapse. Knowing they were about to die, the men shouted, '*Vive l'empereur!*' History knows no more poignant moment.

The sky had been overcast all day, but at eight o'clock that evening it cleared to allow the sinister red light of the setting sun to flood through the elms of the Nivelles road – the same sun that had risen at Austerlitz.

In this last crisis every battalion was commanded by a general. Friant, Michel, Roguet, Harlet, Porlet de Morvan, all were there. When the tall helmets of the grenadiers, adorned with the eagle badge, emerged from the mist of battle, steadfast, impeccably aligned, magnificent, the enemy felt the splendour of France and for an instant the victors hesitated. But Wellington cried, 'Up Guards and shoot straight!' and the red-coated Englishmen rose from their shelter behind hedges and poured out a withering volley that rent to shreds the tricolour and the eagles. Both sides charged and the last carnage began. The men of the Garde Impériale felt the army giving way around them in the disorder of total rout, the shouts of '*Vive l'empereur!*' turning to '*sauve qui peut*', and amid disaster on every side they continued to advance forward, dying with every step they took. No man hesitated, no soldier of the line but was the equal of his general in courage, no man flinched from suicide.

Ney, splendid in his acceptance of death, exposed himself to every hazard. He had a fifth horse killed under him. Foaming at the mouth, wild-eyed and running with sweat, his tunic unbuttoned, one epaulette half shorn away by a sabre stroke and his eagle-badge pierced by a bullet, bleeding and superb with a broken sword in his hand, he cried, 'This is how a Marshal of France dies on the field of battle!' But he did not die. Distraught and furious, he called to Drouet d'Erlon, 'Why haven't you got yourself killed?' And he cried amid the hail of bullets, 'Isn't there one for me? I'd like the whole lot in my belly!'* He was reserved for French bullets, unhappy man.

XIII
Catastrophe

In the rear of the Guard a grievous confusion prevailed.

The army was hastily falling back at every point – from Hougomont, La-Haie-Sainte, Papelotte, Planchenoit. The cry of treason was mingled with the cry of *sauve qui peut*. A disintegrating army is like the thawing of a glacier, a mindless, jostling commotion, total disruption. Ney found himself another horse and hatless and weaponless sought to make a stand on the Brussels road, striving to hold up both the English and the flying French, who swept past him crying '*Vive le maréchal Ney*' as they fled. He showered them with appeals and insults but was overborne. Two of Durutte's regiments were weaving this way and that, rebounding like shuttlecocks between the sabres of the Uhlans and the muskets of Wellington's infantry. Rout is the most hideous of all mêlées, with friends striking each other down in the effort to escape, formations losing all coherence and becoming the scattered foam of battle. Lobau on one wing and Reille on the other, both were swept away by that tide. Napoleon made vain efforts to set up a barrier with the last of the Guard and the commissariat detachments. Galloping along the lines of fleeing men he, too, besought, urged, threatened. It was all in vain. The gunners, unharnessing the horses from the guns, were using them to get away. Overturned guns and supply-waggons blocked the crowded roads, adding to the slaughter. The Prussian cavalry, newly arrived and unwearied, played havoc with the panic-stricken horde of men who, casting aside their weapons and ignoring their officers, sought to escape by way of roads, footpaths, bridges, fields, hills, and villages. An army of 40,000 men, the lions of France, become sheep for Zieten to slaughter at his leisure. That was the picture.

A last attempt at a stand was made at Genappe, where Lobau succeeded in rallying three hundred men. The entrance to the village was barricaded, but at the first blast of Prussian grape-shot, traces

*These words have been authenticated. Ney was executed on 7 October 1815, having been condemned to death by the French Chamber.

of which are still to be seen on the brickwork of a ruined building outside the village, the flight was resumed. It became atrocious. Blücher ordered that no man was to be spared, and Roguet set an example by announcing that he would shoot every grenadier who had taken a Prussian prisoner. Duhesme, the general commanding the Young Guard, caught in the doorway of a Genappe tavern, offered his sword to a Death's Head hussar in token of surrender; the hussar took it and then killed him. To the dishonour of old Blücher, victory was crowned with murder – let us punish, for we are history! The rout swept through Genappe, Quatre-Bras, Gosselies, Frasnes, Charleroi, Thuin, and did not stop till it reached the frontier – and this rabble of desperate men was the Grande Armée!

But was there no cause for this total collapse of an army whose gallantry had astonished the world? Yes. The shadow of a momentous justice lay over Waterloo. It was the day of destiny, when a force greater than mankind prevailed. Hence the terrified bowing of heads, the surrender of so many noble spirits. The conquerors of Europe were stricken with helplessness, unable to say or do anything as they felt the weight of that terrible Presence. *Hoc erat in fatis* – so was it written! On that day the course of mankind was altered. Waterloo was the hinge of the nineteenth century. A great man had to disappear in order that a great century might be born. One who is Unanswerable had taken the matter in hand, and thus the panic of so many heroes is explained. It was not merely a shadow that fell upon Waterloo but a thunderbolt; it was God himself.

At nightfall, in a field near Genappe, two officers, Bernard and Bertrand, came up with a haggard-eyed man who, having been borne thus far by the tide of defeat, had dismounted and, holding his horse by the bridle, was walking back alone in the direction of Waterloo. It was Napoleon, still trying to go forward, the giant somnambulist of a shattered dream.

XIV

The last square

A few squares of the French guards, as immobile in the rout as rocks in a torrent of water held out until nightfall. The coming of night meant the coming of death, and they waited unshakably for that double darkness to engulf them. Each individual regiment, sundered from the others and having no link with the army as a whole, died in its own way. They had taken up their last positions, some on the uplands of Rossomme, others on the plateau of Mont-Saint-Jean; here, abandoned but still formidable, they suffered their final agony, and Ulm, Wagram, Jena, and Friedland died with them.

By nine o'clock that evening only one square, at the foot of the plateau of the Mont-Saint-Jean, the slope scored by the hooves of the cuirassiers, was holding out against the concentrated artillery-fire of the victorious enemy. It was commanded by a little-known officer named Cambronne. With every burst of fire the square diminished but still it fought back, answering salvoes with rifle-fire, tightening its shrunken walls, while the fleeing men from other units, pausing to take breath, listened to the dwindling thunders of the battle amid the gathering night.

When finally only a handful of men was left, the heaped dead more numerous than the living, the flag in tatters, the ammunition-less muskets become no more than cudgels, a kind of superstitious awe assailed the victors and the English guns held their fire. There was a momentary pause. Those last defenders saw as though it were a gathering of spectres the dark figures of their enemy closing in on them, men on horseback and guns outlined against the fading pallor of the sky, and over all the giant death's-head which is the ghost that haunts all battlefields. They could hear the sound of the guns being reloaded and see the lighted fuses gleaming like the eyes of tigers in the dusk. In this final moment, when all was in suspense, one of the English generals, Colville or Maitland, called out to them, 'Brave Frenchmen, will you not surrender?' Cambronne answered, '*Merde!*'

XV
Cambronne

From respect for the decencies of language this word, perhaps the greatest ever uttered by a Frenchman, is not repeated in the history books; the sublime is banned from the record. At our risk and peril we have defied the ban. Amid the giants of that day there was one greater than all others, and it was Cambronne.

To speak the word and die, what can be greater than this? To accept death is to die, and it was not the fault of the man if, wounded, he nevertheless survived. The real victor of Waterloo was not the defeated Napoleon, or Wellington, who was so nearly defeated, or

Blücher, who scarcely fought; it was Cambronne. Thus to defy the lightnings is to be victorious.

To meet disaster in this fashion, challenging Fate itself, setting a springboard for the lion resurgent, hurling into the rainswept darkness that obscene retort that mocked the traitorous wall of Hougomont, the sunken lane of Ohain, the failure of Grouchy, the coming of Blücher; to incarnate irony at the mouth of the grave, staying erect when prostrate; to demolish the European coalition with a word, fling in the face of kings the *cloaca* known to the Caesars, make the crudest of words into the greatest by investing it with the splendour of France, insolently conclude Waterloo with *mardi-gras*, complete Leonidas with Rabelais, compress this victory in a single word that may not be spoken, losing the field but gaining history and at the end of carnage winning to one's side the hosts of laughter – this is sublime.

There they were, the kings of Europe, the triumphant generals, those thundering Jupiters, with a hundred thousand men and a million more behind them, with the gaping guns and the lighted fuses. They had trampled down the Imperial Guard and the Grande Armée; they had set their foot on Napoleon; and now there was only Cambronne, the earthworm who still outfaced them, searching for a word as one may reach for a sword. The word was spat out of his mouth. He hurled his scorn at that prodigious, mediocre victory, that victory without victors, feeling its impact but knowing its hollowness. He did more than spit: borne down by the weight of numbers and material circumstance, he expressed in a word the spirit that transcends those things, and the word meant excrement. Let us repeat it, to do this was to conquer.

The spirit of the greatest days visited that unknown man at that fateful moment. He found the word for Waterloo as Rouget de l'Isle had found the 'Marseillaise', in a breath of inspiration. The living breath passed through the ranks and the men shuddered and sang or uttered their death-cry. Cambronne's expression of giant contempt was hurled not merely at Europe in the name of the Empire, which would have been little enough: it was hurled at the past in the name of the Revolution; it was Danton speaking, Kléber bellowing defiance.

At the word an English voice gave the order to fire and the batteries flamed in a last, terrible belching of grape-shot. The hillside trembled. For a time the scene was obscured by a dense cloud of smoke touched here and there by the rays of the rising moon, and when this drifted away it could be seen that there was nothing left. That formidable remnant had been annihilated. The four walls of the living fortress lay shattered on the ground, with only here and there a movement among the bodies of the dead. Thus did the legions of France, greater than the legions of Rome, expire on the rain-soaked, blood-soaked earth of the Mont-Saint-Jean, amid the darkened corn, at the place where now the post-cart passes at four in the morning on its way to Nivelles, with Joseph the postman blithely whipping up his horse.

XVI

Quot libras in duce*

The Battle of Waterloo is an enigma as incomprehensible to the winners as to the loser. To Napoleon it was a panic; Blücher saw it simply as a matter of fire-power, and Wellington did not understand it at all. We have only to study the accounts, the confused reports, the contradictory views. The French General, Jomini, distinguishes four crucial moments; the German, Muffling, divides it into three stages. Lieutenant-Colonel Charras, whose views we do not always share, is alone in discerning the true nature of that collapse of the human intelligence at odds with divine hazard. All other historians are in some degree bewildered by it and grope in their bewilderment. It was a momentous day indeed, the collapse of a militarist monarchy which, to the amazement of kings, involved every kingdom in the overthrow of armed force and the defeat of war.

In an event of this nature, bearing the stamp of more than human necessity, the part played by man is negligible.

If we deny to Wellington and Blücher all credit for the victory of Waterloo, do we in any way detract from the greatness of England and Germany? No. The greatness of those countries is in no way affected by the happening at Waterloo. Peoples are great, thank Heaven, irrespective of the grim chances of the sword. Neither England nor Germany nor France can be contained in a scabbard. Overshadowing Blücher, in that epoch when Waterloo was no more than a clashing of sabres, was the Germany of Goethe, and overshadowing Wellington was the England of Byron. A huge upsurging of ideas is the keynote of our century, and England and

* Taken from the tenth Satire of Juvenal, referring specifically to Hannibal. Lit. 'How much does the General weigh?'

Germany each lends its own splendour to the light of the new dawn. They are illustrious because they think. The ennoblement which they bring to civilization is their own quality, born of themselves, not of any accident. Their increased greatness in the nineteenth century is not due to Waterloo. Only barbarian peoples are suddenly enhanced by victory, like streams swollen by a sudden downpour. Civilized peoples, particularly in our present age, neither rise nor sink according to the good or ill-fortune of a military leader. Their specific gravity in the human race is the result of something more than conflict. Their honour, thank God, their dignity, their genius and the light they shed, are not merely numbers drawn in the lottery of battle by those gamblers, the heroes and conquerors. Often the losing of a battle leads to the winning of progress. Less glory but greater liberty: the drum is silent and the voice of reason can be heard. It is a game of 'loser wins'. We must view Waterloo coolly in either aspect, rendering unto Chance what belongs to Chance and to God what belongs to God. It was not in the true sense a victory. It was a lucky throw of the dice.

A throw of the dice won by Europe and paid for by France – scarcely worth erecting the effigy of a lion to mark the spot.

It was the strangest encounter in history. Napoleon and Wellington were not enemies but opposites. Never has God, who delights in antitheses, contrived a more striking contrast or a more extraordinary confrontation. On the one side precision, foresight, shrewd calculation, cool tenacity, and military correctitude; reserves husbanded, the way of retreat ensured, advantage taken of the terrain; warfare ordered by the book with nothing left to chance. On the other side intuition, divination, military unorthodoxy, more than human instinct, the eye of the eagle that strikes with lightning swiftness, prodigious art mingled with reckless impetuosity; all the mysteries of an unfathomable nature, the sense of kinship with Destiny; river, plain, forest, and hill summoned and in some sort forced into compliance; the despot tyrannizing over the battlefield, faith in a star mingled with military science, enriching but also undermining it. Wellington was the technician of war, Napoleon was its Michelangelo; and this time genius was vanquished by rule-of-thumb.

Each side was awaiting someone, and it was the technician who calculated rightly. Napoleon awaited Grouchy, who did not come; Wellington awaited Blücher, who came.

Wellington represented the revenge of classic warfare. Napoleon in his dawn had met it in Italy and superbly beaten it. The old owl had fled the young hawk; the traditional concept had been not merely shattered but outraged. Who was this twenty-six-year-old Corsican, this magnificent ignoramus, who with everything against him and nothing for him, lacking supplies, munitions, guns, boots, almost lacking an army, had with a handful of men assailed the coalition of Europe and absurdly won impossible victories? Where did he spring from, this whirlwind madman who, without pausing for breath, with only the one force at his command, pulverized one after another the five armies of the Austrian Emperor, flinging Beaulieu back on Alvinzi, Wurmser on Beaulieu, Mélas on Wurmser, and Mack on Mélas. What was he, this upstart of war with the effrontery of a thunderbolt? The academic school of warfare disowned him while falling back before him. Out of this arose an implacable hatred of the old Caesarism for the new, of the orthodox sabre for the flaming sword, and of the conventional strategist for the genius. And on 18 June 1815, this hatred spoke the last word, inscribing above Lodi, Montebello, Montenotte, Mantua, Marengo, and Arcola the name of Waterloo. A triumph of mediocrity pleasing to the majority. Destiny permitted the irony. Napoleon in his decline encountered a youthful Wurmser: for to have another Wurmser we need only whiten Wellington's hair.

Waterloo was a battle of the first importance won by a commander of the second rank. What was most impressive in that battle was England – English steadfastness and resolution, English blood; and what was most superb in England was, with all respect, herself – not her commander but her men. Wellington, oddly ungrateful, declared in a letter to Lord Bathurst that his army – the army that fought on 18 June 1815 – was 'detestable'. What do the bones mouldering in the soil of Waterloo think of that?

England has been too modest in respect of Wellington; in overloading him with greatness she diminishes herself. He was heroic, but so were the men he commanded. He was tenacious – it was his signal quality, and we do not decry it – but the least of his footsoldiers and horsemen was as solid as himself. The iron soldier was the equal of the Iron Duke. And for our part our praises go to the army and the people of England. If any trophy is to be awarded it should go to them. The Waterloo Column in London would do greater justice if it raised to the heavens not the figure of a man but the image of a race.

But these words will not please the English. Despite their revolution of 1688, and our own of 1789, they still cherish their feudal illusions. They believe in heredity and hierarchy. They are a people unsurpassed in power and glory, but they still think of themselves as a nation, not as people. As people they willingly subordinate themselves, accepting a lord as a leader. The workman lets himself be despised, the soldier lets himself be flogged. We may recall that after the Battle of Inkerman a sergeant who had, it seems, saved the army could not be mentioned in dispatches by Lord Raglan because the English military hierarchy does not allow any man of less than commissioned rank to be named in a report.

What is wonderful in all battles on the scale of Waterloo is the part played in them by chance. The rain-sodden field, the sunken lane, the deafness of Grouchy, the guide who misled Napoleon and the guide who led Blücher aright – chance was marvellously skilful in its ordering of that débâcle.

It may be added that Waterloo was more a massacre than a battle. Of all set battles it was fought on the narrowest front in relation to the numbers of troops engaged. Napoleon's front was about three miles, Wellington's about two, and there were some 72,000 men on either side – hence the carnage. It has been estimated that at Austerlitz the French losses amounted to 14 per cent, the Russian to 30 per cent, and the Austrian to 44 per cent; and that at Wagram the French lost 13 per cent and the Austrians 14 per cent. At Waterloo the French losses were 56 per cent and the Allied losses 31 per cent, making a total for both armies of 41 per cent; 145,000 combatants, 60,000 dead.

The field of Waterloo today resembles any other stretch of country; it has the stillness of the earth which is the impassive nourisher of man. But at night a sort of visionary mist arises from it, and the traveller who chooses to look and listen, dreaming like Virgil on the field of Philippi, may catch the echoes of catastrophe. That monumental hillock with its nondescript lion vanishes, and the fearful event comes back to life. The battlefield recovers its reality, the lines of infantry wavering across the plain, the furious charges, the gleam of sabres and bayonets, the flame and thunder of cannon-fire. Like a groan emerging from the depths of a tomb the listener may hear the clamour of a ghostly conflict and see the shadowy forms of grenadiers and cuirassiers and the images of men departed – here Napoleon, there Wellington. All gone but still locked in combat, while the ditches run with blood, the trees shudder, the sound of fury rises to the sky and over those windblown heights – Mont-Saint-Jean, Hougomont, Frischemont, Papelotte, Planchenoit – the spectral armies whirl in mutual extermination.

XVII

Should we approve of Waterloo?

There exists a highly respectable school of liberal thought which does not deplore Waterloo. We are not of their number. To us Waterloo is the date of the confounding of liberty. It is strange that such a bird should have been hatched out of such an egg.

Waterloo, in terms of its ultimate significance, is the considered triumph of counter-revolution. It is Europe versus France, St Petersburg, Berlin, and Vienna versus Paris, the *status quo* versus the new order, the 15th of July 1789 attacked by way of the 20th of March 1815, the move to action-stations of monarchy against the indomitable upheaval of the French people. To subdue that great people which had been in a state of eruption for twenty-six years, such was its aim, an affirmation of solidarity between the Houses of Brunswick, Nassau, Romanoff, Hohenzollern, and Hapsburg, and the House of Bourbon. Waterloo was the assertion of the Divine Right of Kings. It is true that since the Empire had been a despotism, royalty was forced by a natural reaction to answer it with a degree of liberalism, and that a grudging constitutionalism emerged from Waterloo, to the great displeasure of the victors. The fact is that the Revolution, being wholly inevitable, could not be really destroyed. It re-emerged before Waterloo in the form of Bonaparte overthrowing old thrones, and after Waterloo in the person of Louis XVIII volunteering and submitting to the Charter. Bonaparte set an innkeeper's son on the throne of Naples and an ex-sergeant on the Swedish throne, proclaiming equality by the practice of inequality; Louis XVIII at Saint-Ouen endorsed the Declaration of the Rights of Man. To understand the nature of the Revolution we must call it 'progress'; and we may define progress by the word 'tomorrow'. Tomorrow irresistibly does its work, yesterday as today, and it always achieves its aims, although by strange means. It caused Wellington to make Foy, a plain soldier, into an orator: he fell wounded at Hougomont to re-emerge in parliament. That is the method of Progress, the craftsman to whom all tools are serviceable, the man who bestrode the Alps and the old, sick, well-intentioned monarch Louis XVIII, the conqueror and the gout invalid, one for use outside France, the other within. Waterloo put an end to the overthrow of European thrones by the sword, but the effect of this was to cause the work of revolution to proceed in another form. The day of the swordsmen was ended, the thinkers took their place. The tides of the century which Waterloo sought to stem flowed over the battlefield and still rose; that sinister victory was defeated by liberty.

To sum up, it is beyond question that the victor at Waterloo, the power behind Wellington which brought to his aid every field-marshal's baton in Europe (including, it is said, that of the Maréchal de France), which inspired the building of that mound of earth and bones on which was set the lion triumphant, which urged Blücher on to sabre the fleeing army, and which from the plateau of Mont-Saint-Jean hung over France like a bird of prey, this power was the counter-revolution. This was the power that murmured the infamous word 'dismemberment': but then, arrived at Paris, seeing the crater at its feet and realizing its peril, counter-revolution hastily revised its views and fell back upon babble about a charter.

We must read into Waterloo no more than it truly represented. There was no intention of liberty. The counter-revolution involuntarily turned liberal just as Napoleon, by a parallel phenomenon, involuntarily turned revolutionary. On 18 June 1815, that Robespierre-on-horseback was unseated.

XVIII
Revival of divine right

Dictatorship was ended, and with it a European system collapsed.

The Napoleonic empire dissolved in a darkness resembling the last days of Rome, and chaos loomed as in the time of the barbarians. But the barbarism of 1815, which must be called by its proper name of counter-revolution, was short-winded and soon stopped for lack of breath. The Empire, be it said, was mourned; tears were shed for it by heroic eyes. If glory be the sword turned sceptre, then the Empire was the embodiment of glory. It had diffused all the light that tyranny can shed, a sombre light, and worse, an obscure light which, compared with the true light of day, is darkness; and the ending of this darkness was like the ending of an eclipse.

Louis XVIII returned to Paris, and the dancing in the streets on 8 July effaced the enthusiasm of 20 March. The exile was back on the throne, a white banner flew from the Tuileries and the pinewood table from Hartwell was placed in front of the fleur-de-lis-embroidered chair of Louis XIV. Bouvines and Fontenoy were the happenings of yesterday, while Austerlitz had faded from sight. Altar and throne majestically clasped hands, and one of the least contested forms of nineteenth-century social health became established in France and throughout the Continent. Europe adopted the white cockade. The device *non pluribus impar*, 'not least among the many', reappeared in the stone sunburst decorating the barracks on the Quai d'Orsay. The Arc du Carrousel, with its tale of ill-famed victories, uncomfortable amid so much novelty and perhaps a little ashamed of Marengo and Arcola, saved its face with a statue of the Duc d'Angoulême. The cemetery of the Madeleine, the public graveyard in 1793, was covered over with marble and jasper, since within its dust lay the bones of Louis XVI and Marie Antoinette. A funeral monument rose amid the ramparts of Vincennes to commemorate the fact that the Duc d'Enghien had died in the month in which Napoleon had been crowned. Pope Pius VII, who had performed the ceremony, blessed the downfall as serenely as he had blessed the coronation. In the Palace of Schönbrunn, outside Vienna, there lingered the shadowy figure of a four-year-old boy whom it was seditious to refer to as the King of Rome. And all this happened – the kings returned to their thrones, the master of Europe was caged, the *ancien régime* became the new régime, and all the darkness and light in the world changed places – because on a summer afternoon a shepherd had said to a Prussian general in a wood, 'Go this way and not that way.'

That autumn of 1815 was like a melancholy spring. Old, poisonous realities changed their outward appearance, lies were wedded to the year 1789, divine right hid behind a charter, fictions became legal truths, prejudice, superstition, and moral dishonesty, taking Article 14 to heart, acquired the gloss of liberalism, all snakes sloughed their skins.

The stature of mankind had been at once heightened and diminished by Napoleon. The ideal, in that reign of splendid materialism, was given the strange name of ideology, a grave miscalculation on the part of the great man, making a mock of the future. But the people, that cannon-fodder that so loved the gunner, sought him everywhere. Where was he and what was he doing? 'Napoleon is dead,' a man shouted to a crippled survivor of Marengo and Waterloo . . . 'Him dead!' the soldier shouted back. 'That's how well you know him!' Imagination deified the fallen despot and for a long time after Waterloo the heart of Europe was overcast in the enormous emptiness left by his passing.

The kings took it upon themselves to fill this vacuum, and Europe used it for its own re-shaping. The *Belle Alliance* before Waterloo became the Holy Alliance.

Confronted by this reorganization of ancient Europe, the outlines of a new France began to emerge. The future which the Emperor had mocked made its appearance, bearing on its forehead the star of Liberty. Young eyes looked ardently towards it, but, a strange paradox, they were in love both with the future, which was Liberty, and with the past, which was Napoleon. The defeated gained stature in defeat and Bonaparte fallen appeared greater than Napoleon erect. England placed him in the charge of Hudston Lowe and France appointed Montchenu to keep an eye on him. His folded arms were the terror of thrones, and Alexander called him, 'My sleepless nights.' This fear was due to the force of revolution that was in him, and it explains and justifies Bonapartist liberalism. The exiled spirit still shook the old world and the kings reigned uneasily, seeing the rock of St Helena on the skyline.

That was Waterloo.

But in the eye of eternity what did it amount to? Tempest and thundercloud, the war and then the peace, not all that turmoil could for an instant trouble the gaze of the immense all-seeing eye wherein a grasshopper jumping from one blade of grass to the next equals the flight of an eagle between the towers of Notre-Dame.

XIX

The battlefield at night

Our story requires us to return to the battlefield.

The 18th of June 1815 was a night of full moon. The light favoured Blücher's savage pursuit of the routed army, disclosing the paths of its flight, putting the demoralized troops at the mercy of the ferocious Prussian cavalry and assisting the massacre; thus does night sometimes lend its countenance to disaster.

With the firing of the last shot the plain of Mont-Saint-Jean became deserted. The English moved into the French encampments, it being by custom an assertion of victory to sleep in the bed of the defeated. They set up their bivouacs beyond Rossomme. The Prussians careered onward on the heels of the retreat. Wellington sat down in the village of Waterloo to write his report to Lord Bathurst.

Never has the Virgilian *sic vos non vobis** been more applicable than it is to that village of Waterloo, which was a couple of miles distant from the scene of operations. Mont-Saint-Jean was bombarded; Hougomont, Papelotte, and Planchenoit were set afire; La-Haie-Sainte was carried by assault and La-Belle-Alliance was the meeting place of the victorious armies. Those names are scarcely remembered, whereas Waterloo, which played no part in the battle, has reaped all the glory.

We are not among those who sing the praises of war; we tell the truth about it when the need arises. War has tragic splendours which we have not sought to conceal, but it also has its especial squalors, among which is the prompt stripping of the bodies of the dead. The day following a battle always dawns on naked corpses.

Who are the despoilers, the tarnishers of victory, the furtive hands ransacking the pockets of glory? Certain philosophers, Voltaire among them, maintain that they are precisely the men who created the glory. The same men. The living rob the fallen; the hero of the day becomes the scavenger of the night; and surely he is entitled to do so, since he is responsible for the corpse he robs.

For our part, we do not believe it. We find it inconceivable that the same hands can gather laurels and drag the boots off the feet of the dead. True though it is that the victor is normally followed by the ghoul, we acquit the soldier, and especially the present-day, soldier, of this charge.

Every army has its camp-followers and it is to these that we must look, to the bat-like creatures, half-ruffian, half-servant, engendered by the twilight of war, wearers of uniform who do no fighting, malingerers, venomous cripples, sutlers riding in small carts, sometimes with their women, who steal what later they sell, beggars offering their services as guides, rogues and vagabonds of all kinds. These were what every army in the past – we do not speak of the present day – dragged in its train. No army and no country owned

* *Sic vos non vobis mellificatis apes* – thus do you make honey, but not for yourselves, O bees.

them; they spoke Italian and followed the Germans, or French and followed the English. Looting was born of looting. The abominable maxim 'live on the enemy' fostered the disease, which only strict discipline could quell. Certain military reputations are misleading; there are generals, even great ones, whose popularity it is not easy to account for. Turenne was adored by his men because he tolerated looting; evil condoned wears the mask of benevolence. The number of pillagers following in the wake of an army varied according to the severity of the commander. Hoche and Marceau had none; Wellington – we gladly do him that justice – had very few.

Nevertheless, the bodies of the dead were robbed during that night of 18–19 June. Wellington was uncompromising: any person caught in the act was to be shot forthwith. The looters preyed on one end of the battlefield while they were being executed at the other.

The moon shed a sinister light over the plain.

At about midnight a man prowled, or better, clambered, near the sunken lane of Ohain. From the look of him he was one such as we have described, neither English nor French, peasant nor soldier, less a man than a ghoul, drawn to the scene by the smell of the dead. Dressed in a sort of hooded cape, he moved warily and boldly, looking behind him as he advanced. As to who he was, the night probably knew him better than the day. He carried no bag but evidently had large pockets under his cape. Now and then he paused and after looking about him bent down and fumbled with what lay silent and motionless at his feet, then straightened and hurried on. His cautious posture and rapid, mysterious movements caused him to resemble the twilight beings that haunt ruins and in old Norman legends are known as *Alleurs*. Certain nocturnal stilt-birds of the marshes have a similar appearance.

An eye capable of penetrating the darkness might have discerned not far away from him, stationary and seemingly hidden behind the ruined building on the Nivelles road at the bend between Mont-Saint-Jean and Braine-l'Alleud, a small sutler's cart with a tarred wicker roof, to which was harnessed a half-starved horse browsing on nettles through its bit, and in which what seemed to be a female figure was seated on a pile of boxes and bundles. There was perhaps some connection between the cart and the prowler.

The night was wonderfully calm, without a cloud in the sky. In the meadows the branches of trees broken by gunfire but still hanging swayed gently in the breeze. A breath that was almost a sigh stirred the hedgerows, and a tremor ran over the grass like the passing of souls.

Distant sounds could be heard of patrols scouring the country-side and sentries in the English lines going their rounds. Hougomont and La-Haie-Sainte were still burning, casting a glare into the night from which the lights of the English campfires extended in a semicircle like a necklace of rubies.

We have told of the disaster of the sunken lane. All was now silence in that place where so many men had died. There was no longer any declivity. The wide, deep ditch was heaped to the brim, like an honest measure of barley, with the bodies of men and horses rising to the level of the ground on either side. On top were the bodies of the dead and at the bottom a river of blood which seeped through to the Nivelles road, where it formed a pool at the point where a barricade of trees had been erected, a place still shown to sightseers. It was here that the cuirassiers had met with disaster. The layer of the dead varied in depth according to the depth of the lane, and was less deep at the centre, over which Delord's division had passed.

This was the direction taken by our night prowler as he searched that immense hecatomb, peering at God knows what unspeakable sights and walking with his feet in blood.

He stopped suddenly. A few yards away, at a place where the bodies were less densely heaped, a hand protruded from the tangled mass of men and horses. The moonlight drew a gleam from something shining on one finger, a gold ring. The man bent down and for a moment crouched, and when he rose the ring was no longer there.

He did not rise to a standing position but stayed kneeling with his hands on the ground, in the posture of the jackal he resembled, while he looked cautiously about him. Finally, deciding that all was well, he got to his feet.

As he did so he started, feeling something tug him from behind. Swinging round, he saw that it was the hand he had robbed, which now clutched the hem of his cape.

An honest man would have been appalled, but this one laughed. 'Only the dead,' he said. 'Better a ghost than a gendarme.'

The hand relaxed its grip and fell back, having exhausted its strength.

'Is he alive after all?' the prowler wondered. 'Better see.'

Bending down again, he contrived to extricate the now unconscious body and drag it clear of its fellows. It was that of a cuirassier, an officer of fairly high rank; a gilt epaulette was visible above his breastplate. He wore no helmet and a sabre-cut had so disfigured his face that it was scarcely visible through the clotted blood. But he seemed to have no broken bones. By a fortunate chance, if the word fortunate may be used in this context, other bodies had formed an arch above him which had prevented him from being crushed. His eyes were closed. He wore on his breastplate the silver cross of the Légion d'honneur.

The prowler removed the cross, which vanished into one of the receptacles beneath his cape, and then, searching the officer's pockets, helped himself to a watch and a purse. While he was engaged in this act of mercy the officer opened his eyes, having been restored to consciousness by the roughness with which he was handled, the chill of the night and the fact that he could now breathe freely.

'Thank you,' he said weakly.

The prowler did not answer but looked up sharply, hearing a distant sound of footsteps, probably those of a patrol.

The officer murmured in the same dying voice:

'Who won the battle?'

'The English,' said the prowler.

'Look in my pockets,' the officer said. 'You'll find a purse and a watch.'

The prowler made a pretence of doing so and said: 'There's nothing there.'

'Then I have been robbed. I'm sorry. I wanted you to have them.'

The patrol was drawing nearer.

'Someone's coming,' said the prowler, starting to move away. The officer painfully raised his arm and held him back.

'You saved my life. Who are you?'

The prowler muttered hurriedly: 'I was in the French army like you. I've got to leave you. They'll shoot me if they catch me. I've saved your life. You must look after yourself now.'

'What's your rank?'

'Sergeant.'

'And your name?'

'Thénardier.'

'I shall not forget that name,' the officer said. 'And you must remember mine. My name is Pontmercy.'

BOOK TWO

THE SHIP *ORION*

I

No. 24601 becomes No. 9430

JEAN VALJEAN had been re-captured.

We may pass over the painful details and confine ourselves to reproducing two newspaper reports which appeared a few months after the events in Montreuil-sur-mer. The first, from the *Drapeau Blanc*, is dated 25 July 1823.

A district in the Pas-de-Calais has recently been the scene of a remarkable occurrence. A newcomer to the *département* named Madeleine had in the course of a few years, by the use of a new process, resuscitated an ancient local industry, the manufacture of jet beads and black glasswork. He made a fortune for himself and, it must be added, for the district, and in recognition of his public services was appointed mayor. The police presently discovered that this Monsieur Madeleine was none other than an ex-convict in breach of parole, sentenced for theft in 1796, whose name was Jean Valjean. He was re-imprisoned. It seems that before being arrested he contrived to withdraw from the banking house of M. Laffitte the sum of over half a million francs which he had placed there on deposit and which, it appears, he had acquired quite legitimately in the course of his trade. Where Jean Valjean concealed this money, before being sent back to the prison at Toulon, is not known.

The second report, which is rather more detailed, is taken from the *Journal de Paris* of the same date.

A released ex-convict named Jean Valjean was recently tried at the Assize Court of Var in circumstances worthy of attention. This rogue had succeeded in eluding the vigilance of the police. He had changed his name and contrived to get himself elected mayor of a small town in the north of the province where he had established an industrial enterprise of some importance. Eventually, thanks to the indefatigable zeal of the police authorities, he was exposed and arrested. He had a concubine, a woman of the town who died of shock on learning of his arrest. Thanks to his Herculean strength the villain was able to escape, but the police again laid hands on him in Paris three or four days later, when he was in the act of entering one of the small conveyances which run from the capital to the village of Montfermeil (Seine-et-Oise). It seems that he had profited by his period of liberty to withdraw a large sum of money deposited by him with one of our leading bankers, a sum of between six and seven hundred thousand francs. According to the prosecution he hid the money in a place known only to himself and the police have been unable to find it. However this may be, Jean Valjean was charged at the Assize Court of Var with an act of armed highway robbery committed some eight years ago on the person of one of those honest youngsters who, in the immortal lines of the Patriarch of Ferney,*

> ... De Savoie arrive tous les ans
> Et dont la main legèrement essuie
> Ces longs canaux engorgés par la suie.

The criminal offered no defence. It was proved by the able and eloquent prosecuting attorney that the robbery was carried out with accomplices and that Jean Valjean was a member of a robber band then operating in the Midi. Accordingly, on being found guilty he was sentenced to death. He refused to exercise his right of appeal, but the King, in his immense clemency, commuted the sentence to one of hard labour for life. Jean Valjean was consigned at once to Toulon prison.

We may recall that Jean Valjean was strict in his religious observances. This caused certain liberal organs, Le Constitutionnel among them, to declare that the commutation of the sentence represented a triumph for the clerical party.

On his return to prison Jean Valjean was given a new number. He became No. 9430.

We may add, before dismissing the subject, that with the departure of Monsieur Madeleine, prosperity also departed from Montreuil-sur-mer. Everything that he had foreseen during his night of feverish indecision came to pass. With his going the spirit of the town was lost, and there ensued that squalid battle for the proceeds of a great career, that fatal dismembering of a going concern, which is of daily occurrence in obscure human affairs but has only once attracted the notice of history, when it happened after the death of Alexander. Lieutenants crown themselves kings; foremen set up as factory-owners; jealous rivalries arise. Madeleine's large workshops were closed, the buildings fell in ruins and the workers were scattered. Some left the district, others found new

---

*Voltaire (in Le Pauvre Diable) is saying that he has more respect for the boys from Savoie 'whose hands skilfully clear those long channels blocked by soot' than for the so-called 'enlightened spirits' of the age.

work. Everything went forward on a small scale instead of on the grand scale, for gain instead of for the public good. Control at the centre gave place to cut-throat competition. Madeleine had inspired and directed everything, and without him it was every man for himself, conflict in place of the spirit of cooperation, malice in place of friendship, internecine hatreds in place of the founder's goodwill towards all men. The threads woven by Madeleine were twisted and broken; organization became slovenly, the quality of the product suffered, buyers lost confidence, orders fell away; and this led to lower wages, unemployment, and bankruptcy. And nothing was left over for the poor. It all vanished.

The State itself became aware that something had gone wrong. Less than four years after the assize court verdict, which transformed Madeleine into Jean Valjean for the benefit of the penal system, the cost of tax-collection had doubled in the district of Montreuil-sur-mer. Monsieur de Villèle drew the attention of the Assembly to the fact in February 1827.

II

Two lines of verse perhaps written by the Devil

Before going further we must describe in some detail a singular incident which took place at about that time in the neighbourhood of Montfermeil, and which may have a bearing on certain conjectures on the part of the authorities.

There lingers in the district of Montfermeil a very ancient superstition which is the more curious and precious inasmuch as popular superstitions in the vicinity of Paris are as rare as aloes in Siberia. We are among those who respect everything that achieves this degree of rarity. This, then, is the Montfermeil superstition. They believe that the Devil has from time immemorial made use of their forest for the concealment of his hoarded wealth. The local good-wives declare that it is not unusual to encounter at dusk in remote parts of the woods a black-avised man looking like a carter or butcher, shod in clogs and clad in homespun, who is instantly recognizable by the fact that he wears large horns in place of a hat. There are three courses to pursue when the encounter takes place. The first is to go up to the man and speak to him. One then finds that he is an ordinary countryman whose face is dark because of the failing light, engaged not in digging a hole but in cutting grass for his cows, and carrying a dung-fork on his back, the prongs of which, sticking up behind his head, seem in the dusk to be growing out of it. The person who thus approaches him goes home and dies within a week. The second course is to wait until the man has dug his hole, filled it in and gone away; one then hurries to the spot and digs up the 'treasure' which, of course, he has buried there. In this case one dies within a month. The third course is not to look at the man or go near him, but to make off at full speed – one then dies within a year.

Since all three courses have their drawbacks, the second, which at least holds out the prospect of wealth, if only for a month, is the one most generally adopted. But it appears that men who have been so intrepid as to open the hole and attempt to rob the Devil have found the operation singularly unprofitable. Such, at least, is the report of local tradition as summarized in the two cryptic lines of dog-Latin written by the bad monk, Tryphon, who was something of a sorcerer and is now buried at the Abbaye de Saint-Georges de Bocherville, near Rouen, where toads breed on his grave. The searcher is confronted by a heavy task, for the hole as a rule is very deep. He sweats and toils throughout the night – for this is work that can only be done at night – soaking his shirt, burning out his candle, breaking his shovel; and when at length he gets to the bottom of the hole, what treasure does he find? In the words of warning left by Tryphon:

> *Fodit, et in fossa thesauros condit opaca,*
> *As, nummos, lapides, cadaver, simulacra, nihilque.*

In other words, a penny-piece or perhaps a crown, a stone, a skeleton, a corpse, a spectral image folded in four like a sheet of paper in a wallet – or, sometimes, nothing at all. It appears that in our own time a powder-bag with bullets may also be found, or a greasy pack of cards obviously used by devils. Tryphon does not mention these latter items. He lived in the twelfth century, and the Devil, it seems, had not the wit to invent gunpowder before Francis Bacon, or playing cards before Charles VI. For the rest, whoever plays with the cards is certain to lose everything he possesses, and the powder has the characteristic that it makes the gun explode in its user's face.

Shortly after the authorities had come to the conclusion that Jean Valjean, during his few days' escape from captivity, had visited the district of Montfermeil, it was noticed in the village that an old road-mender named Boulatruelle had become strangely fascinated by the forest. He was a man who, it was understood, had served a prison sentence; he was kept under police observation, and since he could find no other work the municipality employed him at a reduced wage to mind the stretch of road between Gagny and Lagny.

Boulatruelle was not well thought of by the local people, being over-subservient, too humble, too ready to doff his cap to all and sundry, obsequious to the gendarmes and probably in league with the bands of footpads who lay in wait for travellers after dark. All that could be said in his favour was that he was given to drunkenness.

What had been observed was as follows:

For some time past Boulatruelle had taken to leaving his work of road-mending at an early hour and going off into the wood with his shovel. He was to be seen at dusk in the remotest clearings and the wildest places apparently searching for something and sometimes digging holes. Village women on their way through the wood at first mistook him for Beelzebub and then saw that he was Boulatruelle, which was scarcely more reassuring. He was evidently greatly put out by these encounters and made obvious efforts to conceal himself. His behaviour was altogether mysterious.

They said in the village: 'Clearly the Devil has made an appearance and Boulatruelle saw him and is now searching for his secret hoard.' The disciples of Voltaire wondered: 'Will Boulatruelle catch the Devil, or will the Devil catch Boulatruelle?' The old women frequently crossed themselves.

Eventually Boulatruelle ceased to scour the woods and returned to the orderly performance of his duties on the road. The subject was dropped.

But a few people remained interested, reflecting that, although there was probably no legendary treasure, there might yet be something behind the business, more substantial than supernatural banknotes, of which the road-mender had gleaned some knowledge. Foremost among these were the schoolmaster and the tavern-keeper, Thénardier, who made a point of being on friendly terms with everyone, even with Boulatruelle.

'He's been in prison, has he?' said Thénardier. 'Well, there's no saying who's been there or who's going.'

The schoolmaster remarked one evening that in the old days the law would have inquired more closely into Boulatruelle's doings in the woods, and that he would have been made to talk, by torture if necessary. If he had been put to the question by water he would not have held out for long.

'Then,' said Thénardier, 'let us put him to the question by wine.' So they had a party and plied the old man with drink. Boulatruelle drank enormously but said little, reconciling in a masterly degree the thirst of a toper with the discretion of a judge. At length, however, by dint of returning to the subject and seizing upon such hints as he let fall, Thénardier and the schoolmaster arrived at something like the following:

Early one morning, when Boulatruelle was passing through the wood on his way to work, he had seen a pick and shovel lying under a bush – 'hidden, as you might say'. He had supposed them to be the property of Père Six-Fours, the water-carrier, and had thought no more about it; but that evening, without himself being seen since he was hidden behind a tree-trunk, he had watched a certain individual leave the road and plunge into the thickest part of the wood – a person who had no connection with that part of the world' but whom he, Boulatruelle, had at one time known very well. Thénardier interpreted this as meaning 'a fellow-prisoner'. Boulatruelle had stubbornly refused to name names. The man had been carrying a square object which might have been a large box or a small chest. Such was Boulatruelle's astonishment that some minutes elapsed before he had the idea of following him, and by this time it was too late; the man had vanished into the undergrowth in the falling dusk and he could not catch up with him. So then he kept watch at the edge of the wood. There was a moon, he said. And after an hour or two the man reappeared, this time without the square object but carrying a pick and shovel. Boulatruelle had let him go without attempting to approach him, reflecting that the man was three times as strong as himself and armed with a pick, and would probably murder him if he found that he had been recognized. But the pick and shovel afforded a clue to what had been happening, which was confirmed when Boulatruelle went back to the thicket where he had seen them that morning, and found them gone. Evidently the man had been burying something, and since the box had been too small to contain a corpse Boulatruelle surmised that it must contain money.

Hence his researches. He had scoured the wood, inspecting every patch of ground that looked as though it might have been recently turned. But all in vain. He had found nothing.

So the subject ceased to interest the people of Montfermeil, except for a few goodwives who said: 'You can be sure the Gagny road-mender didn't make all that fuss for nothing. The Devil must certainly have been there.'

III
The broken shackle

Towards the end of October of that year of 1823 the ship-of-the-line *Orion*, which was later to be used as a training vessel but at that time was attached to the Mediterranean Squadron, put into Toulon dockyard for repairs after a spell of heavy weather.

Her entry, damaged as she was by the recent storm, did not go unnoticed, for she was flying a flag entitling her to an eleven-gun salute, which she duly returned, making twenty-two guns in all. It has been estimated that in ceremonial of this kind, salutes to royalty and other distinguished personages, the opening and closing of harbours, guns fired at daybreak and sunset from ships and fortresses throughout the civilized world, some 150,000 cannons are uselessly discharged every twenty-four hours. At six francs a time this amounts to 900,000 francs a day, or 300 millions a year. A detail in passing. Meanwhile the poor continue to die of hunger.

The year 1823 was known to the Restoration as 'the time of the Spanish war'. It was a war comprising many events in one and possessing many singular features. For the House of Bourbon it was a large-scale family affair, the French branch sustaining and defending the Madrid branch – that is to say, playing the part of elder brother. But the war was also a manifest return to our national tradition, complicated by a servile compliance with the wishes of the northern governments: the commander of the French forces, his Highness the Duc d'Angoulême, christened by the liberal sheets 'the hero of Andujar', contrived to display, within a triumphal posture somewhat contradicted by his pacific bearing, the very real age-old terrorism of the Holy Office at grips with the imaginary terrorism of the liberals and with the *sans-culottes*, now resuscitated, to the great dismay of dowagers, under the name of *descamisados* (shirtless). The war was monarchy resolutely opposing progress, described as 'anarchy'; it was a harsh assault on the principles of 1789 and a European cry of 'halt' to French ideas that were spreading throughout the world. It was under the generalship of the heir to the French throne, a young man of royal birth, the Prince de Carignan, later known as plain Charles-Albert, enlisted in this crusade of kings against peoples as a volunteer, and wearing an ordinary grenadier's uniform. The soldiers of the Empire again went to war, but under the white cockade, and saddened and eight years older. The tricolour flag was brandished abroad by a handful of Frenchmen, as the white flag had been waved at Coblentz thirty years before. Monks were to be found in our ranks; the spirit of liberty and progress was challenged by bayonets, and principles were mown down by gunfire. France destroyed by force of arms what she had created by force of spirit. For the rest – enemy leaders suborned, soldiers reluctant to fight, towns besieged by wealth, small military risk but always the danger of an explosion, as in the sudden invasion of a powder-factory; little bloodshed and little honour; disgrace for some and glory for no one ... Such was that war, instigated by princes descended from Louis XIV and conducted by generals taught by Napoleon, sadly lacking in the lustre of grand warfare or grand policy.

There were a few feats of arms that deserved to be taken seriously: the capture of the Trocadero, for example, was a well executed military operation. But in general, let us repeat it, the trumpets of that war sounded a hollow note and History has shared the disinclination of France to regard it as a triumph. There was a smell of corruption. Officers who should have put up a fight surrendered too easily, more generals were won over than battles won, and the victorious troops returned home humiliated. A degrading war, with the words Banque de France inscribed in the folds of the flag. Veterans of the war of 1808, who had witnessed the terrible death-throes of Saragossa, looked askance at citadels that so promptly opened their gates, and sighed for Palafox.*

A more important point, and one especially deserving of emphasis, is that besides affronting the military spirit of France the war outraged the spirit of democracy. It was an essay in enslavement in which the French soldier, born of democracy, was required to forge a yoke for others. A shameful contradiction. France's task is to arouse the soul of peoples, not to stifle it. From 1792 on, every

* Oudinot said: 'The thing that angers and perturbs me about this business is that those people think they've been fighting a war.'

revolution in Europe had been the French revolution. Liberty radiated from France, and this was a cosmic fact which only the blind failed to see – Napoleon himself had said it. So the war of 1823, an assault on the generous Spanish nation, was also an assault on the French revolution. The monstrous act committed by the French was committed under compulsion, for all the acts of armies, unless they be wars of liberation, are committed under compulsion. *Passive obedience* is the keynote. An army is a strange contrivance in which power is the sum of a vast total of impotence. That is the explanation of war, an outrage by humanity upon humanity in despite of humanity.

For the Bourbons the war of 1823 was a disaster. They mistook it for a success. They had no notion of the danger that lies in attempting to crush ideas by military order, and they carried naïveté to the point of believing that they had strengthened their position by introducing into it the immense weakness of a crime. The spirit of double-dealing pervaded their policy. The events of 1830 had their origin in 1823. The success of the Spanish campaign became a justification for other violent escapades aimed at re-establishing the divine right of kings. Having restored absolute monarchy in Spain, France might do the same for her own monarchs. They made the fatal blunder of mistaking the discipline of the soldier for the consent of the nation. These are the delusions that destroy thrones. It does not do to let the senses fall asleep, whether in the shade of the sacred tree or in the shadow of an army.

To return to the ship *Orion*.

She had formed part of the French naval squadron patrolling the Mediterranean during the war, until, as we have said, bad weather obliged her to put into Toulon for repairs. The presence of a ship-of-the-line in a seaport is something that always attracts a crowd of onlookers. She was a big ship, and the crowd loves bigness.

A ship-of-the-line is among the most splendid of all human challenges to the forces of nature, combining as it does what is most weighty with what is lightest, since its business is with all the forms of matter, solid, liquid, and fluid, and it has to deal with all three at once. It has eleven claws of iron to grip the seabed, and more wings and antennae than the most elaborate of insects to seize and hold the wind. The breath it exhales from its hundred and twenty guns is like a great blast of trumpets proudly defying the lightning. The ocean tries to confuse it with the terrifying similarity of its waves, but it has a mind of its own, the compass, pointing steadfastly to the north; and on the darkest night its lanterns replace the stars. Thus it opposes rope and canvas to the winds, wood to the waters, iron, copper, and lead to the rocks, light to darkness, and a needle to immensity.

To grasp the huge extent of the components constituting a ship-of-the-line we need only to visit one of the covered dockyards, six storeys high, in Brest or Toulon, where the ship in process of building is displayed to us, as it were, under glass. That huge beam of wood is a spar, and the seemingly endless column of timber lying on the dockside is the mainmast. From its bedding in the hull to its top in the clouds it is sixty fathoms high, and three feet thick at its base. An English mainmast rises two hundred and seventeen feet above the ship's water-line. The navy of our forefathers used rope hawsers for its anchor, but today we use chains, and the coiled chain of a single anchor is four feet high and twenty feet wide. As for the amount of timber needed – the ship is a floating forest.

And all this, be it noted, refers to the man-of-war of forty years ago, a sailing-ship. Steam, which was then in its infancy, has brought added marvels. In these days the ship combining sail and screw is propelled by three thousand square metres of canvas and an engine of two thousand five hundred horsepower. But, setting aside these modern wonders, the old ships sailed by Christopher Columbus and de Ruyter were among the greatest masterpieces of man, inexhaustible in power as the heavens are in breath, purposeful amid the vast confusion of waves over which they moved and which they dominated.

Nevertheless it can happen that a sixty-foot spar or towering mast may be snapped like a twig by the violence of a squall, that huge anchors may be twisted like fish-hooks, that even the roar of the great guns may be lost in the howl of the tempest, and all that strength and majesty forced to submit to powers that are greater still. That so much splendour can be reduced to impotence is awe-inspiring to the minds of men, and so it happens that every seaport contains a crowd of idlers come to gaze at those marvellous contrivances for war and seafaring, without clearly knowing why. And so it was that every day and all day the quays and jetties of Toulon swarmed with onlookers having no other business than to contemplate the ship *Orion*.

The *Orion* had been a sick ship for some time. In the course of a long spell at sea her lower hull had become so fouled with barnacles as to rob her of half her speed. She had been dry-docked for scraping the previous year, and had then gone to sea again. But the scraping had weakened her timber-fastenings, eventually causing planks to start so that she began to make water, and a violent equinoctial gale in the latitude of the Balearics had further damaged her hull on the port side. She had accordingly returned to Toulon.

She was moored near the Arsenal, being still in commission and under repair. Her hull was not damaged on the starboard side but a few upper strakes had been removed, as the custom was, to let the air in.

One morning the crowd of onlookers witnessed an accident.

The crew were taking the sails off her. The man loosening the starboard peak of the main-topsail suddenly lost his balance. A cry of alarm rose from the watching crowd as they saw him reel and slip, clutching the foot-rope as he fell, first with one hand and then with both; and there he hung, with the sea a hideous distance below him. The shock had set the foot-rope wildly swinging and he dangled from it like a stone in a sling.

To go to his help would be to run an appalling risk. No member of the crew, which consisted of local fishermen recently pressed into service, was disposed to attempt it. Meanwhile the man was becoming exhausted. His agonized face could not be seen, but the writhings of his body, the arms horribly stretched, clearly showed it. His efforts to hoist himself up served only to increase the swinging of the rope. He uttered no sound, seeking to conserve his strength. The crowd waited, expecting nothing except the moment when he would relax his hold, and heads were turned away in order not to see. There are occasions when a length of rope, a pole, or the branch of a tree is life itself, and it is a terrible thing to see a living being lose his grip and fall like a ripe fruit.

But suddenly a man was seen climbing the rigging with the agility of a wildcat. He wore a red smock, which meant that he was a convict, and a green cap, which meant that he was serving a life sentence. As he reached the topsail-yard a gust of wind carried his cap away, revealing a head of white hair; he was not a young man.

It was learned later that the man was one of a labour gang brought in from the prison. At the first alarm, and seeing the reluctance of the crew to risk their lives, he had gone to the officer of the watch and asked permission to try to save the luckless seaman. When this was granted he had broken the chain welded to the manacle round his ankle with a single blow of a hammer, and then, snatching up a coil of rope, had started up the shrouds. No one had been struck at the time by the remarkable ease with which the chain had been broken. This was only remembered after the event.

In a remarkably short time he had reached the topsail-yard. Here he paused for a moment, evidently reviewing the situation, and those few seconds were to the spectators like an eternity. Then a sigh went up as he was seen to run along the yard. Making the rope fast to its further end, he swarmed down it, and the spectators suffered the agony of seeing two men suspended over the void instead of one. It was like watching a spider grapple with a fly, except that here the spider was bringing life, not death. Not a sound was to be heard; the watchers held their breath as though fearing to add the least impulse to the breeze that was buffeting the two men.

The convict at length drew level with the seaman, only just in time, for in another minute he must have relaxed his grip. Hanging on with one hand, the convict used the other to lash the bight of the rope securely round the man's waist. Having done so he climbed back on to the yard and hauled the seaman up after him. He held him there for a moment to allow him to recover. Then, taking him in his arms, he walked with him along the yard to the masthead, whence he lowered him down to the cross-trees, where another member of the crew took charge of him.

And now the crowd burst into applause. Hardened prison-officers wept, women on the dockside embraced one another, and a cry of frenzied acclamation arose – 'That man must be set free!'

The man, meanwhile, was making it a point of duty to return promptly to his labours. In order to do so the more rapidly he slid down the rigging and ran along one of the lower yards, while all eyes were fixed upon him. And then, for one terrible moment, he was seen to hesitate and stagger, overtaken, perhaps, by the giddiness of exhaustion. A great cry went up from the crowd as he was seen to fall into the sea.

It was a perilous fall. The frigate *Algeciras* was moored close to the *Orion* and he had fallen into the gap between them. There was a danger that he might be trapped beneath one of the two hulls. Four men at once put out in a boat to rescue him, while the crowd cheered. But he did not come to the surface. He had vanished into the sea making scarcely a ripple, as though he had plunged into a vat of oil. The boat's crew sounded and dived in vain. The search continued until nightfall, but they did not even find his body.

Next day the local news-sheet contained the following item:

17 November 1823. Yesterday a convict working aboard the *Orion* fell into the sea and was drowned after rescuing a member of the crew. The body has not been recovered. It is assumed that it was caught in the piles under the Arsenal jetty. The man's prison registration-number was 9430 and his name was Jean Valjean.

BOOK THREE
FULFILMENT OF A PROMISE

I
The water situation at Montfermeil

MONTFERMEIL IS situated between Livry and Chelles, on the southern slopes of the high plateau separating the river Ourcq from the Marne. In these days it is a fair-sized town ornamented with stucco villas all the year round and with prosperous inhabitants on Sundays. In 1823 there were fewer villas and fewer contented citizens. It was then nothing but a woodland village with here and there a country house dating from the last century and distinguished by an air of opulence, wrought-iron balconies and tall windows whose small panes reflected different shades of green against the white of closed shutters. But Montfermeil itself remained a village still undiscovered by retired linen drapers and university professors, a peaceful and charming spot on a road that led nowhere. Life there was inexpensive and comfortable. The only problem, due to the height of the plateau on which it stood, was that of water.

Water had to be brought some distance. The end of the village nearest Gagny drew its supply from the beautiful pools in that part of the forest; but the other end, towards Chelles, which included the church, could only draw water from a small spring halfway down the slope near the Chelles road, about a quarter of an hour's walk from the village.

So the water supply was a matter of some concern to the households at that end of the village. The larger houses, the aristocracy, and the Thénardier tavern, all contributed a trifling daily sum towards the payment of a water-carrier, who by this means earned about eight sous a day. But he worked only until seven o'clock in the evening in summer and five o'clock in winter. After that, when darkness had fallen and the ground-floor shutters were closed, anyone who had run short must fetch water for himself or go without.

This was the nightmare of the little girl already known to the reader as Cosette. It will be recalled that Cosette was useful to the Thénardiers in two respects, as a means of extorting money from her mother and as a household drudge in her own person. That is why they kept her after the mother's payments had entirely ceased.

She was still useful as an unpaid servant, and it was she who was sent to fetch water when it was needed. Being terrified of going to the spring after dark, she took great care to see that the house was always well supplied.

Christmas 1823 was especially brilliant at Montfermeil. The beginning of the winter had been mild, without frost or snow. Parties of strolling players from Paris had been given leave by the mayor to set up their booths in the village street, and by permission of the same authority the stalls of travelling hucksters had been erected in the Place de l'Église and in the Ruelle du Boulanger, the lane in which, we may recall, the Thénardier tavern was situated. All this brought custom to the innkeepers of the town and a note of gaiety and excitement to its normally quiet life. We may add, in our capacity of faithful historian, that among the sights was a menagerie, attended by a band of ragged showmen come from Lord knows where, which included a hideous, red-crested vulture from Brazil, of a kind which was not acquired by the royal museum until 1845. The species is known to naturalists, I believe, as *Caracara polyborus*. Veterans of Napoleon's armies came to gaze at it with veneration, and the showmen claimed that its red cockade was a unique phenomenon devised by God for the sole benefit of their menagerie.

On Christmas Eve a group of men, carters and carriers, sat drinking in the low-ceilinged general room, lighted by four or five candles, of the Thénardier tavern. It was like any other tavern-room with its tables, pewter mugs, bottles, drinkers, smokers – little light and plenty of noise. But an indication of the year 1823 was afforded by the presence, on one of the tables, of two articles which were then fashionable in middle-class homes, a kaleidoscope and a magic-lantern. Mme Thénardier was attending to the joint which was roasting over a clear fire while her husband drank and talked politics with the customers.

Apart from politics, of which the main subjects were the war in Spain and the Duc d'Angoulême, there was local gossip of which the following is a sample:

'They've had a big wine harvest round Nanterre and Suresnes, a dozen casks where they only reckoned ten, the grapes were very juicy' . . . 'But they can't have been ripe?' . . . 'You don't wait for the grapes to ripen in those parts. If you do the wine ferments by the spring' . . . 'So it's a very light wine?' . . . 'Lighter than ours. You have to harvest it green' . . . And so on.

Or else it was a miller complaining.

'Can we be held responsible for what comes along in the sacks? You get all kinds of small seed which we haven't time to sift, so we just put it through the mill – charnel, fennel, hemp, fox-tail and God knows what besides, to say nothing of the grit you get in some corn, particularly from Brittany. I don't like milling that Breton stuff any more than a carpenter likes sawing a wooden beam with nails in it. The dust it makes! And then people complain about the flour, but it isn't our fault.'

In a window-seat a day-labourer and a farmer were fixing a price for hay-mowing in the spring.

'It doesn't matter about grass being damp,' the labourer was saying. 'It cuts all the better with the dew on it. But this grass of yours is difficult, monsieur. It's new-seeded and tender, which means it'll bend under the scythe.'

And so on.

Cosette was in her usual place, seated on the cross-bar under the kitchen table near the hearth. Clad in rags, her bare feet in wooden clogs, she was knitting woollen stockings for the Thénardier children by the light of the fire. A kitten was playing under the chairs and two fresh childish voices could be heard laughing and chattering in the next room, those of Éponine and Azelma. A leather strap hung from a nail in the wall near the hearth.

Occasionally the cry of a younger child, coming from somewhere in the house, made itself heard amid the hubbub of the tavern. This was the son born to Mme Thénardier during a previous winter – 'No knowing why,' she said. 'The cold weather, no doubt' – and whose age was now a little over three. His mother had nursed him but did not love him. 'Your son's squawking,' Thénardier said, when the noise became more persistent. 'Better go and see what he wants.' But the lady simply replied, 'He's a nuisance,' and he was left to go on screaming in the dark.

II

Completion of two portraits

Thus far this book has contained only an outline sketch of the Thénardiers. We must now look at them more closely.

Thénardier was now just over fifty and Mme Thénardier was nearly forty, which in a woman is the equivalent of fifty: so husband

and wife may be said to have been of the same age. The reader will perhaps have some recollection of Mme Thénardier as she was first described – tall, fair-haired, red-faced, fleshy, broad-shouldered, huge and active, resembling those monstrous women who parade themselves on fair grounds with paving-stones suspended from their hair. She did all the work of the house, beds, rooms, washing and cooking; she was the climate of the place, its fine and foul weather; she was the very devil; and her only assistant was Cosette, who was like a mouse in the service of an elephant. Everything trembled at the sound of her voice, window-panes, furniture, people. Her broad face was scattered with freckles like the holes in a cream-skimmer, and she had a slight beard. In short, a market-porter clad in women's clothes. She swore splendidly and boasted that she could crack a walnut with a blow of her fist. Had it not been for the romantic tales she read, which now and then caused the coy female to emerge surprisingly from the ogress, no one would ever have thought of her as a woman. She was like a drab grafted on to a fishwife. She talked like a gendarme, drank like a coachman, and treated Cosette like a gaoler. A single tooth protruded from her mouth when in repose.

Thénardier was a small, skinny, sallow-faced man, bony, angular and puny, who looked ill but enjoyed excellent health – that was where his deceptiveness began. He smiled constantly as a matter of precaution and was polite to all comers, even to the beggar whom he turned away from his door. He had the sharp stare of a weasel and the general aspect of a man of letters, in which he greatly resembled the portraits of the Abbé Delille. It pleased him to drink with his customers, but nobody had ever succeeded in getting him drunk. He smoked a large pipe and wore an apron over an old black jacket. He had literary pretensions and professed to follow the materialist philosophy, supporting his arguments with such names as Voltaire, Raynal, Parny and, oddly enough, St Augustine. He had, he said, a 'system'. For the rest, he was thoroughly crooked, a sanctimonious knave. The type is not unknown. It will be recalled that he claimed to have served in the army, and he took pleasure in describing how at Waterloo, being then a sergeant in the 6th or the 9th or some such regiment, he had defied single-handed a squadron of the Death's Head hussars and protected with his body a 'dangerously wounded general'. This was the reason for the garish inn-sign which had caused his establishment to be known locally as 'the tavern of the

Waterloo sergeant'. He was a liberal, both traditional and Bonapartist, and had subscribed to the settlement established in Texas for liberal and Bonapartist refugees which was known as the '*champ d'Asile*'. It was said in the village that he had studied for the priesthood.

Our own belief is that he had merely studied in Holland to be an innkeeper. In all probability he was a mongrel – a Fleming in Flanders, a Frenchman in Paris, a Belgian in Brussels – ready to wear whatever coat the occasion called for. We know what really happened at Waterloo. He was, as we see, given to exaggeration. A life of ebb and flow, without scruple and always with an eye to the main chance, these were the waters he swam in, and it is likely enough that in that troubled month of June 1815 he had been one of that tribe of sutlers and camp-followers of which we have already given some account, travelling in a ramshackle covered cart with wife and children, pilfering in one place and selling in another, and always intent on coming out on the winning side. At the end of that campaign, having, as he said, 'put a little something aside', he had set up in business in Montfermeil; but the 'something', which consisted of purses, watches, gold rings, and silver crosses harvested in the furrows of that corpse-strewn field, had not amounted to very much or got him very far.

There was a kind of stiffness in Thénardier's movements which recalled the barrack square when they were accompanied by an oath, and the seminary when accompanied by the sign of the cross. He was a smooth talker and liked to be considered erudite, but the schoolmaster had noted that he made 'howlers', and the bills which he presented to travellers, while elegantly penned, sometimes contained spelling mistakes. He was cunning, rapacious, indolent and shrewd, and by no means indifferent to maidservants, which was why his wife no longer kept any. She was a jealous giantess, believing the lean, yellow-faced little man to be infinitely desirable. Above all, Thénardier was wary and self-controlled, a cool-headed knave, which is the worst kind, since it contains so large an element of hypocrisy.

But that is not to say that he could not, on occasion, fly into a rage at least as great as those of his wife. It happened very rarely, but when it did, since in these moments he detested the whole human race (and he possessed a great store of hatred, being one of those who blame external circumstance for every mischance that befalls them and are always ready to visit upon their fellows the sum of their disappointments and frustrations), the fury would come foaming out of his mouth and eyes, and he was terrible. Woe to those who on such occasions fell foul of his wrath!

Apart from all this, Thénardier was highly observant, silent or talkative as circumstances required, and always perspicacious, with something of the look of a seaman wrinkling his eyes as he scans the horizon through his glass. A statesman, in short.

A new visitor to the tavern, seeing Mme Thénardier for the first time, invariably concluded that she was the real master of the house. It was a mistake. She was not even its mistress. Her husband was master and mistress both. She acted but he did the thinking. He controlled everything by a kind of invisible, unwearying magnetism. A word from him, even a gesture, sufficed and the monstrous woman obeyed. Without her giving much thought to the matter, Thénardier was to her a unique and superior being. She had the virtues of her failings; never would she have disagreed with her husband on any point of principle, and still less – the thing was unthinkable – would she have disputed any matter with him in public. Never would she have been guilty of that act so common to married women which parliamentarians call 'undermining the throne'. Although their union produced nothing that was good, there was a transcendent quality in Mme Thénardier's submission to her husband. That mountain of sound and flesh could be moved by the puny despot's little finger. Viewed in its grotesque physical aspect this may be seen as the manifestation of a universal law, the subjugation of matter by the spirit: for there are forms of ugliness which have their roots in abiding beauty. There was something unknowable in Thénardier, and it was this that accounted for his absolute domination over his wife. At moments she saw him as a lighted lamp, at other times felt him like a claw.

The formidable woman loved nothing but her children and feared no one but her husband. She was a mother because she was a female. But her mother-love was confined to her daughters; it did not, as we shall later see, extend to her son. As for the man, he had only one interest in life, which was to get rich.

In this he had failed. No stage worthy of his considerable talents had thus far opened to him. He was ruining himself in Montfermeil, if ruin is possible on that level. Established in Switzerland or the Pyrenees, he would have made a fortune. But an innkeeper has to live off the land in which he finds himself – the word 'innkeeper' being here applied to a particular individual and not to the class as a whole. In that year of 1823 Thénardier's urgent debts amounted to about 1500 francs, and he was a worried man.

Ironically enough he was one of those men who understand most thoroughly, and in the most modern terms, something that is a virtue among savage peoples and a commodity among the civilized – namely, hospitality. For the rest, he was a skilful poacher and renowned as a marksman. He had a cool, quiet laugh which was particularly dangerous.

His views on innkeeping escaped him now and then in flashes, professional aphorisms uttered as a rule for the benefit of his wife. 'An innkeeper's business,' he once said furiously and in a low voice, 'is to dispense to all comers food, rest, light, heat, dirty sheets, maidservants, fleas and smiles; to lure the passer-by, empty small purses and legitimately lighten large ones; to afford the travelling family respectful shelter and fleece the lot of them, men, women, and children; to reckon the cost of everything – the open window and the closed window, the chimney-corner, the armchair, the straight-backed chair, the stool, the settle, the feather-bed, the hair mattress, and the truss of straw; to know how much a mirror wears out in darkness and take this into account – and, by God, make the traveller pay for everything, down to the very flies his dog eats.'

They were an ugly and dreadful pair, the Thénardiers, a marriage of cunning and fury; but whereas the man calculated and manoeuvred, the woman gave no thought to absent creditors and cared nothing for yesterday or tomorrow, but lived vigorously and wholly in the moment.

And Cosette existed between the two of them, subject to pressure from either side like a creature that is at once ground between millstones and torn apart by pincers. Each had his own way of treating her. The blows she received came from the woman; the fact that she went barefoot in winter was due to the man. She ran upstairs and down, washed, swept, scrubbed and polished, drudged and gasped for breath, carried heavy burdens and performed arduous tasks, small though she was. There was no mercy to be expected from either mistress or master. The inn was a trap in which she was caught and held, her state of servitude the very pattern of oppression, herself the fly trembling and powerless in a spider's web.

The child endured and said nothing; but what goes on in the souls of those helpless creatures, newly arrived from God, when they find themselves thus flung naked into the world of men?

III

Men need wine and horses need water

Four new travellers had arrived and Cosette was a prey to gloomy misgivings. Although she was only eight, her life had been so hard that she viewed the world already with an old woman's eyes. Her face was bruised by a blow from Mme Thénardier, which caused that lady to remark, 'she looks a sight with that black eye'.

She was thinking as she sat under the table that the night was very dark, and that the jugs and pitchers in the bedrooms of the new arrivals had had to be filled, so that there was no more water in the house. There was some reassurance in the fact that not much water was drunk in the tavern. They had no lack of thirsty customers, but it was a thirst calling for wine, not water. Nevertheless she was given cause to tremble. Mme Thénardier lifted the lid of a cooking pot bubbling on the stove, then seized a glass and went over to the water-butt, while the little girl watched her in alarm. Only a thin trickle came when she turned the tap, half-filling the glass, and she exclaimed, 'Bother! We're out of water.'

There was a moment of silence while Cosette held her breath.

'Don't worry,' said Thénardier, looking at the half-filled glass. 'That'll be enough.'

Cosette went on with her work, but her heart was thumping. She counted the minutes as they dragged by, praying for it to be to-morrow morning. Every now and then a customer would put his head outside and say, 'It's black as pitch. You'd need to be a cat to get about without a lantern on a night like this,' and she would tremble afresh.

Then a travelling huckster who was stopping in the house came into the general room and said angrily:

'My horse hasn't been watered.'

'Indeed it has,' said Mme Thénardier.

'I tell you it hasn't, mistress,' the man said.

Cosette scrambled out from under the table.

'But he has, monsieur. I took him water myself, a whole bucket-ful, and I talked to him.'

This was not true. Cosette was lying.

'No higher than my knee and lies like a trooper!' the huckster cried. 'I tell you he hasn't, my girl. I know it for sure. When he's thirsty he snorts in a particular way.'

Cosette stuck to her guns, speaking in a voice so stifled with terror as to be scarcely audible.

'All the same, he has.'

'Look,' said the man angrily, 'there's not much in watering a horse, is there? Why not just do it?'

Cosette dived back under the table.

'Well, that's right,' said Mme Thénardier. 'If the horse hasn't been watered it ought to be. Where's the girl got to now?' She peered under the table and saw her crouched at the far end, almost under the drinkers' feet. 'Come out of there, you!'

Cosette crept out again.

'Now, Miss good-for-nothing, go and water that horse.'

'But, madame,' said Cosette faintly, 'there's no water left.'

Mme Thénardier's answer was to fling open the street door.

'Then go and get some,' she said.

Disconsolately Cosette fetched an empty bucket from a corner of the hearth. It was larger than herself, large enough for her to have sat in it. Mme Thénardier turned back to her stove and dipping in a wooden spoon tasted the contents of the pot.

'Plenty of water in the spring,' she muttered. 'No trouble at all. I think this could have done without the onions.'

She went over to a drawer in which she kept small change and other oddments.

'Here, Miss Toad,' she said. 'Here's a fifteen-sou piece. While you're about it you can get a large loaf at the baker's.'

Cosette took the coin without a word and put it carefully in the pocket of her apron. Then, with the bucket in her hand, she stood hesitating in the doorway, as though hoping someone would rescue her.

'Get a move on,' cried Mme Thénardier.

Cosette went out and the door closed behind her.

IV

The doll

The row of open-air stalls extended, as we have said, from the church as far as the Thénardiers' tavern. All were brightly lit to attract the custom of the village people who would presently be going to midnight mass. In the words of the Montfermeil schoolmaster, at that moment seated in the tavern, the numerous candles in their paper lanterns produced 'a magical effect'. But there was not a star to be seen in the sky.

The last of the stalls, exactly opposite the tavern door, dealt in bric-à-brac and glittered with trinkets, glasswork, and wonderful metal contrivances, and in the front, against a background of white drapery, the stallkeeper had set a large doll nearly two feet high, clad in a dress of pink crêpe, with a wreath of golden fronds on its head and with real hair and enamel eyes. This marvel had been on display all day, to the ravishment of all passers-by under the age of ten, without any Montfermeil mother having been rich enough, or lavish enough, to buy it for her child. Éponine and Azelma had spent hours gazing at it, and even Cosette had dared to glance at it now and then.

But now when she came out of the inn, tired and wretched though she was, she could not restrain herself from crossing the narrow street to examine that prodigious doll – 'the lady', as she called it. She stood entranced, not having seen it so close before. The stall to her was like a palace, and the doll was something more than a doll. It was a vision of delight and splendour, of wealth and happiness, flooding with a dreamlike radiance the squalor of her own bleak world. With the innocent and sad shrewdness of childhood, Cosette reckoned the distance separating the doll from herself. One would need to be a queen or at least a princess to own anything so magnificent. She considered the beautiful pink dress, the soft, fair hair, and thought, 'How happy that doll must be!' She could not tear herself away from the stall, and the more she gazed the more she marvelled. It was like Heaven. There were other dolls behind the big one, and these to her were fairies or angels, and the owner, pacing up and down at the back of the stall, was near to being the Eternal Father himself.

So enthralled was she that she quite forgot her errand until a harsh voice called her abruptly back to earth. 'Why, you slut, haven't you started yet? What do you think you're doing standing there? Just you wait – I'm coming after you.'

Mme Thénardier had happened to look out into the street. Cosette snatched up her bucket and ran.

V

Little girl alone

Since the Thénardier tavern was at the church end of the village, Cosette had to go for water to the woodland spring on the way to Chelles. Along the Ruelle du Boulanger and in the neighbourhood of the church the glare from the stalls lighted her way, but this light soon dwindled and then she was in darkness. She did what she could to allay her nervousness by rattling the bucket, which made a companionable sound. The darkness deepened as she went on. Not a soul was abroad in the streets except one woman who turned to stare at her as she went past, murmuring, 'What is a child doing out at this hour? Is it a phantom child?' Then, recognizing Cosette, she said, 'Why, it's the lark!'

Thus the little girl made her way through the tangle of narrow streets which mark the outskirts of Montfermeil on the Chelles side. While she still had houses or even bare walls on either side of her, she walked on bravely enough. Now and then the gleam of a candle showed through the cracks in a shutter, and this reminder of light and life, of human presence, sustained her courage. But her pace gradually slowed, and when she had passed the last house she came to a stop. To leave the lighted stalls behind had been hard enough; to leave the houses seemed impossible. She put down the bucket and stood slowly rubbing her head with the gesture common to frightened, bewildered children. She was no longer in the village but amid the surrounding fields, enclosed by empty blackness in which there were animals and perhaps evil spirits. She stood in despair, listening to the sounds of cattle and half-believing already that she could discern the flitting forms of ghosts. She picked up the bucket, rendered defiant by sheer terror – 'Well,' she thought, 'I'll simply say that there wasn't any water in the spring.' And she turned resolutely back towards the village.

But after going a little way she stopped again and again stood rubbing her head. She was thinking now of her mistress, the huge violent woman, anger blazing from her eyes. She looked despairingly about her. What was she to do? Ahead of her that formidable figure and behind her the shades of darkness and the woods. Mme Thénardier was the more real menace.

She turned again and this time broke into a run, running blindly and unhearing, pausing only for a moment to get her breath, and not ceasing to run until she had entered the wood.

By now she was on the verge of tears, surrounded by the night-time stirrings of the trees, as unable to think as she was to see. The night closed in upon her, all the immensity of darkness bearing down upon the tiny creature that she was.

The spring was only a few minutes' walk from the edge of the wood and Cosette was familiar with the path, having followed it often in daylight. So, being guided by habit, she did not lose her way. Looking to neither left nor right, for fear of seeing something in the undergrowth, she finally came to it.

It was a small, natural pool some two feet deep, carved by the flow of water in the clay soil, bordered by moss and fern, and edged with a few large stones. The stream rippled tranquilly as it flowed on beyond it.

Without pausing to rest, Cosette groped in the darkness for the small oak-tree growing by the pool which she was accustomed to use on these occasions. Seizing one of its branches, she clung to this while she leaned over and dropped her bucket into the water. Her state of nervous tension was such that she seemed to possess twice her normal strength; but it also accounted for the fact that she saw and heard nothing when, as she leaned forward, the fifteen-sou piece slipped out of her apron-pocket and fell into the water. She pulled up the bucket, nearly full, and set it down on the grass.

This done she found that she was exhausted. She would gladly have started back at once, but the effort of filling the bucket had been so great that she could scarcely move. She had to rest, and she sat down on the grass.

She shut her eyes and opened them again, not knowing why but feeling compelled to do so. The water trembling in the bucket was making rings like circles of pale fire. The sky above her was filled with dark clouds like huge puffs of smoke. The tragic masks of darkness seemed to be peering remotely down at her.

Jupiter hung in the sky, and she gazed distractedly up at that star which she did not know and which frightened her. The planet was, in fact, low on the horizon and passing through a thick layer of mist which lent it an uncanny, reddish tinge and so enlarged it that it looked like a luminous wound.

A cold wind was blowing over the land. There were no leaves rustling on the trees, and no reflected gleam, no play of light such as may be seen on a night in summer, relieved the darkness of the wood. The great bare branches rose ominously above her, and stunted, shapeless bushes rustled in the clearings, while the tall grasses writhed like so many eels beneath the wind and the long stems of brambles waved like tendrils seeking a prey. Dry wisps, borne on the wind, sped past as though they were flying in terror to escape pursuit. There was chill and melancholy everywhere.

Darkness afflicts the soul. Mankind needs light. To be cut off from the day is to know a shrinking of the heart. Where the eye sees darkness the spirit sees dismay. Even for the strongest there is apprehension in an eclipse, in the dead of night, in the blackness of a thunderclap. No man walks alone through the night-time forest without a tremor. Shadows and trees form two awe-inspiring layers in which a chimerical reality resides. The inconceivable appears with a spectral clarity almost at arm's length, and we see, floating in space or in our own mind, things as vague and intangible as the dreams of sleeping flowers. Wild shapes haunt the distance, the air we breathe is a black emptiness, we want to look back and are afraid. The hollows of night, all things grown stark, silent forms that vanish as we approach, the hint of unseen presences in the immensity of a tomblike silence, tree-trunks and overhanging branches and tall, quivering grass – against all this we have no defence; no man is so bold that he does not tremble and feel close to panic. There is something ugly at work, as though the very soul were becoming merged in darkness. And all this is inexpressibly terrible to a child. The dark forest is an apocalypse and the small wings of a child's soul flutter in anguish beneath its overhanging boughs.

Without knowing what was happening to her Cosette felt herself engulfed in the enormity of the natural world, not only terrified but seized with something worse than terror. She shuddered, and there are no words to describe the chill that pierced her to the heart. Her gaze had become distraught and she had a feeling that perhaps she would not be able to restrain herself from returning to that place tomorrow at the same hour.

As it were by instinct, to dispel this strange state of mind that she did not understand but which so demoralized her, she began to count aloud – one, two, three . . . and when she had got to ten she began again. This restored her sense of reality. She found that her hands, which had got wet when she drew the water, were very cold.

She stood up. She was still afraid, but now with a natural, panic fear which implanted only one thought in her mind, to get away, to run as fast as her legs would carry her out of the wood, past the fields, back to the world of houses and lighted windows. She looked down at the bucket. Such was her dread of her mistress that she dared not go without it. She seized the handle with both hands and found that it was all she could do to lift it.

She struggled with it for a dozen paces, but it was too full and too heavy and she was forced to put it down again. After resting for another moment she resumed the struggle and this time got a little further before she again had to stop. Then she went on. She walked bent forward like an old woman, with the weight of the bucket dragging on her thin arms and the metal handle biting into her small chilled hands, pausing frequently to rest; and each time she put the bucket down a little of the water slopped on to her bare legs. And this was happening to a child of eight in the woods at night, in winter, far from any human gaze. Only God was there to see, and perhaps her mother, alas, for there are things that rouse the dead in their graves.

She was breathing in painful gasps, sobbing under her breath, for such was her awe of Mme Thénardier that she dared not cry aloud even at that distance from her. To her the figure of her mistress was always present.

Her progress was very slow. Although she shortened her periods of rest and forced herself to go as far as possible after every pause she reckoned that it would take her over an hour to get back in this fashion to Montfermeil, and that Mme Thénardier would beat her when she arrived; and this was a further distress to be added to her terror of solitude and the night. She was nearly at the end of her strength, and still she had not got out of the wood. Coming to an old chestnut tree with which she was well acquainted, she made a last pause, longer than the previous ones, so that she might be properly rested, then bravely started again; but such was her despair that now she could not prevent herself from crying aloud – 'Oh, God help me! Please, dear God!'

And suddenly she found that the bucket no longer weighed anything. A hand that seemed enormous had reached down and grasped the handle. Looking up, she saw a burly, erect form beside her in the darkness. The man had come up behind her without her hearing him, and he had taken the bucket from her without speaking a word.

There are instincts which respond to all the chance meetings in life. The little girl was not afraid.

VI

The man in the yellow coat

During the afternoon of that same Christmas day in 1823 a man had spent some time walking up and down the most deserted stretch of the Boulevard de l'Hôpital, in Paris. He looked like someone in search of a lodging, and his preference seemed to be for the most humble houses in that down-at-heel outskirt of the Faubourg Saint-Marceau. As we shall presently see, he had in fact rented a room in that quarter.

In his clothes as in his whole bearing the man epitomized what may be termed the 'respectable beggar' – a combination of utmost poverty and extreme cleanliness. It is a rare mixture which inspires all sensitive persons with a twofold respect, for great need and great dignity. He was wearing a very old, carefully brushed tall hat, a threadbare tail-coat of a coarse ochre-yellow material – not an uncommon colour in those days – a long waistcoat with square pockets, black breeches turned grey at the knees, black woollen stockings and clumsy shoes with brass buckles. He might have been a former schoolteacher of good antecedents returned from emigration. His white hair, lined forehead, pallid lips and drawn, lifewearied countenance, all suggested that he must be well over sixty; but his firm, if slow, stride and the singular vigour of his movements put him at not more than fifty. The lines on his forehead were regular and would have predisposed any close observer in his favour. His upper lip had a curious fold which looked stern but was in fact humble. There was a hint of serene melancholy in his gaze. In his left hand he carried a small bundle wrapped in a cloth, and in his right a stout stick cut from a hedge. The stick had been carefully trimmed but did not look over-threatening; the knots had been smoothed and it had a knob that looked like coral but was fashioned of red wax. It was a cudgel that might pass for a walking-stick.

Few people go along that street, particularly in winter. The man seemed to avoid such as there were, although he made no particular show of doing so.

At that time King Louis XVIII was in the habit of driving nearly every day to Choisy-le-Roi, this being one of his favourite outings.

The royal coach with its escort was to be seen almost invariably at two o'clock galloping along the Boulevard de l'Hôpital. Such was its regularity that the poor people of the district had no need of watches. 'It's two o'clock,' they said. 'He's on his way back to the Tuileries.'

Some of them ran to watch him pass and others lined the roadway, for the passing of a king is an occasion. In any case, the comings and goings of Louis XVIII in the streets of Paris were always a matter of interest. They were speedy but impressive. The infirm monarch had a fondness for driving at a gallop; being unable to walk he liked to run – a cripple who would gladly have harnessed the lightning. Not wanting, but prepared to resist trouble, he drove with an escort of drawn sabres, the wheels of his great coach, with its lily-painted panels, thundering over the cobbles. There was only time to catch a glimpse of him. One saw in the righthand corner of the coach, against a background of white satin upholstery, a broad, firm, ruddy face, the forehead freshly powdered, a proud, hard, penetrating gaze, a cultivated smile, two large, plumed epaulettes on a bourgeois frockcoat, the Golden Fleece, the crosses of Saint Louis and the Légion d'honneur, the silver medallion of the Holy Spirit, and a wide blue sash over a large belly – that was the King. Outside Paris he carried his white-plumed hat on knees that were high-gaitered in the English fashion; but on entering the town he put the hat on his head, rarely bowing. He looked coldly at the people, and they returned the look in kind. The impression he had made upon his first visit to the Saint-Marceau quarter was summed up in the remark passed by an inhabitant of the quarter to his neighbour – 'So that fat man's the Government!'

This royal passage, then, was a daily incident in the life of the Boulevard de l'Hôpital; but the stroller in the yellow coat was evidently not an inhabitant of the quarter, and probably not even a Parisian, for he was unaware of what was happening. When at two o'clock the royal coach with its escort of silver-braided guards turned into the boulevard after rounding the Salpêtrière, he looked startled and even slightly apprehensive. There was no one but himself on the pavement. He hurriedly took refuge in a doorway, but this did not prevent the Duc d'Havre from noticing him. As commanding officer of the escort on that particular day, the Duc d'Havre was seated in the carriage facing the king. He leaned forward and said, 'That's an ugly-looking customer.' The police on duty also noticed the man, and one of them was ordered to follow him. But the man plunged into the small back streets and the policeman lost him in the gathering dusk, as was reported that same evening to the Comte d'Anglès, the Prefect of Police.

When he had shaken off his pursuer, the man in the yellow coat turned back, but not without looking round constantly to make sure that he was not followed. At a quarter past four, by which time it was dark, he passed the Porte-Saint-Martin theatre, where a play entitled *Les deux Forçats* [The Two Convicts] was being performed. Although he was walking fast, the announcement, lit by the flares outside the theatre, attracted his notice and he stopped to read it. Then he hurried on to the blind-alley of La Planchette and went into the Pewter Platter, the staging-inn for the Lagny coach, which was due to leave at half-past four. The horses were already harnessed and passengers were climbing the iron steps to the roof.

'Is there a vacant place?' the man asked.

'There's one, on the driver's seat next to me,' the coachman answered.

'I'll take it.'

'Then up you get.'

But having noted the passenger's shabby attire and scanty baggage the coachman demanded payment in advance.

'All the way to Lagny?' he asked.

'Yes,' said the traveller and paid the full fare.

They started off, and when they had passed the customs barrier the coachman tried to engage him in conversation, but he replied only with monosyllables. The coachman was reduced to whistling and swearing at his horses.

Presently the coachman turned up the collar of his greatcoat. It was cold, but the passenger did not seem to notice it. They passed through Gournay and Neuilly-sur-Marne, and at six o'clock they reached Chelles. Here the coachman stopped to give his horses a breather, pulling up outside the coaching inn established in the former buildings of the royal abbey.

'I'll get off here,' the man said, and seizing his stick and his bundle he jumped down from the coach. A minute later he had vanished; but he had not gone into the inn, and when, a few minutes later, the coach drove on he was not to be seen on the main street of Chelles.

'A man who doesn't come from these parts,' the coachman remarked to the inside passengers. 'I don't know him. He looked as though he hadn't got a sou, but he wasn't worrying about money. He paid the fare for Lagny, and then he gets off at Chelles. It's dark and all the houses are shuttered, he didn't go into the inn and still there's no sign of him. It's as though he'd been swallowed up in the earth.'

However, the man had not gone underground. After hurrying along the darkened main street he had turned left before reaching the church and taken the road to Montfermeil, seeming to be quite familiar with the locality. He was walking very fast, but hearing someone approach as he reached the crossing of the old tree-bordered lane that runs from Gagny to Lagny he dived into a ditch and waited until they were out of earshot. The precaution was scarcely necessary because, as we have said, it was a particularly dark December night, with scarcely a star in the sky.

This is the point where the slope of the hill begins. The man did not return to the Montfermeil road but, bearing to the right, strode rapidly across the fields until he reached the wood.

Once in the wood he slowed down and began to take careful note of the trees, advancing step by step as though he were rediscovering and following a path known only to himself. There was a moment when he paused uncertainly, seeming to have lost his way. Finally, by trial and error, he came to a clearing in which there was a large pile of whitish stones. Going rapidly up to these he peered at them closely in the misty darkness as though making some calculation. A few yards away there was a large tree covered with those gnarled excrescences that are the warts of vegetation; bending down, he ran his hand over them, seeming to identify or count them.

The tree was an ash, and near to it was a chestnut with a gash in its side which someone had repaired by nailing a band of zinc round the trunk. Standing on tip-toe, the man reached up and touched this band. Then he spent some time examining the ground between the chestnut and the pile of stones as though to discover whether the earth had been recently turned. Having done this he paused to get his bearings and continued on his way through the wood.

This was the man who had just met Cosette.

Making his way through the undergrowth in the direction of Montfermeil he had seen a small, shadowy figure gasping and wrestling with a burden which it was obliged constantly to put down. He saw as he drew nearer that it was a child with a very large bucket of water, so he came closer still and silently took hold of the bucket.

VII
Cosette and the stranger

Cosette was not afraid. The man spoke to her in a low, deep voice.

'Child, this is a very heavy thing for you to be carrying.'

She looked up and answered: 'Yes, monsieur.'

'Let me have it.'

She surrendered the bucket and they walked on together.

'It's certainly heavy,' he said with pursed lips. Then he asked: 'How old are you?'

'I'm eight, monsieur.'

'How far have you carried this?'

'From the spring back there.'

'And how far have you to go?'

'About a quarter of an hour from here.'

The man was silent for a moment, then he said sharply:

'But haven't you a mother?'

'I don't know,' the child replied; but before he could say anything further she went on: 'I don't think so. The others have, but I haven't.' And after a pause she added: 'I don't think I've ever had one.'

The man stopped walking. He put down the bucket and bending forward with his hands on the little girl's shoulders tried to make out her features. The thin, wan face was dimly visible in the faint light.

'What's your name?'

'Cosette.'

At this the man started violently. For a moment he continued to stare at her; then, taking his hands off her shoulders he picked up the bucket and they walked on. Presently he asked:

'Where do you live?'

'At Montfermeil, if you know where that is.'

'Is that where we're going?'

'Yes, monsieur.'

There was another pause.

'But who sent you out to fetch water at this time of night?'

'Madame Thénardier.'

The man's next words were spoken in a voice that he tried to make casual, but in which there was an odd tremor.

'What does she do, this Madame Thénardier?'

'She's my mistress. She keeps the inn.'

'An inn? Well, that's where I'll stop the night. You must show me the way.'

'It's where we're going,' Cosette said.

The man was now walking fast but she had no difficulty in keeping pace with him. She no longer felt tired. Now and then she glanced up at him with an expression of wonderful trust and assurance. No one had ever taught her to pray, but she had a sense of hope and happiness that seemed to be reaching up to Heaven.

Several minutes passed, and then the man said:

'Has Madame Thénardier no servants?'

'No, monsieur.'

'And you're all alone?'

'Yes.' After another pause she added: 'Well, there are the two children.'

'What children?'

'Ponine and Zelma.' She used her own version of their high-sounding names. 'They're Madame Thénardier's young ladies, her daughters, that is to say.'

'And what do they do?'

'Oh, they have lovely dolls and money-boxes. They can buy things. And they play games.'

'All day?'

'Yes.'

'And what do you do?'

'I work.'

'All day?'

She looked up at him with eyes now filled with tears that were hidden from him by the darkness.

'Yes, monsieur . . . Well, sometimes I play a little too, when I've finished my work and if they let me.'

'What do you play at?'

'Anything I can. They leave me to myself. But I haven't got many toys. Ponine and Zelma don't let me play with their dolls. All

I've got is a tiny lead sword about that long—' she put out her little finger.

'Which doesn't cut anything?'

'Oh, yes it does. It can cut lettuce-leaves and the heads off flies.'

They had reached the village and Cosette led the way through the streets. They passed the bakery, but she had forgotten about the loaf she was supposed to buy. The man had ceased to question her and was gloomily silent, but seeing the row of lighted stalls beyond the church he asked:

'Is there a fair on?'

'No, monsieur, but it's Christmas.'

As they approached the tavern she touched him timidly on the arm.

'Please, monsieur.'

'What is it, child?'

'We're nearly there.'

'Well?'

'May I have the bucket?'

'But why?'

'If madame sees someone carrying it for me she'll beat me.'

He gave her the bucket. A moment later they were at the tavern door.

VIII

Awkwardness of accommodating a poor man who may turn out to be rich

Cosette could not refrain from glancing at the splendid doll, which was still on display in the bric-à-brac stall. Then she knocked and the door was opened. Mme Thénardier appeared carrying a candle.

'So there you are, good-for-nothing. You've been long enough—fooling about, I suppose.'

'Madame,' said Cosette trembling, 'here is a gentleman who wants a room for the night.'

Madame Thénardier's glare was promptly replaced by the grimace of hospitality that is proper to innkeepers. She looked calculatingly at the stranger.

'This gentleman?'

'Yes, madame,' the man said, and raised a hand to his hat.

Well-to-do travellers are not ordinarily so polite. The gesture and her rapid inspection of the stranger's clothes and his bundle, wiped the smile from Mme Thenardier's face. She said coolly:

'Well, come in, my good fellow.'

The 'good fellow' did so. Mme Thénardier looked him over for the second time, taking especial note of his threadbare coat and slightly dented hat. She glanced inquiringly at her husband, who was still seated with the customers, and he responded with a wag of the forefinger and a pursing of the lips which said plainly: 'Not worth having'. Whereupon she exclaimed:

'I'm sorry. It seems the rooms are all full.'

'You can put me where you like,' the man said. 'In the hayloft or the stable. I'll pay the price of a room.'

'The price is forty sous.'

'Very well, forty sous.'

'All right. We'll see what we can do.'

'Forty sous,' a carter murmured to Mme Thénardier as she stepped aside. 'But the price is only twenty.'

'It's forty to him,' she replied in the same undertone. 'We don't take his sort for less.'

'Quite right,' her husband said. 'Disreputable customers do an establishment no good.'

The man meanwhile had deposited his stick and bundle on a bench and seated himself at a table where Cosette hurried to place a bottle of wine and a glass. The customer who had demanded water went to see to his horse. Cosette got back under the table with her knitting. After taking a sip of wine the man proceeded to study her with intent interest.

Cosette was plain. Had she been happier she might have been pretty. We have already given some account of her. She was thin and pale, and so small that although she was eight years old she looked no more than six. Her big eyes in their shadowed sockets seemed almost extinguished by the many tears they had shed. Her lips were drawn in the curve of habitual suffering that is to be seen on the faces of the condemned and the incurably sick. Her hands, as her mother had feared, were 'smothered with chilblains'. Because she was always shivering she had got into the habit of keeping her knees pressed tightly together. Her clothes were a collection of rags which would have been lamentable in summer and in winter were disgraceful – torn garments of cotton, with no wool anywhere. Here and there her skin was visible, and her many bruises bore witness to her mistress's attentions. Her bare legs were rough and red, and the hollow between her shoulder-blades was pathetic. Everything about her, her general attitude and bearing, her quavering and hesitant speech, her gaze, her silence, her every movement expressed a single impulse, that of fear.

Fear emanated from her so that she might be said to be enveloped in it. Fear caused her to draw her elbows in at her sides and her feet beneath her skirt, to take up as little room as possible and to draw no unnecessary breath; it had become, so to speak, the habit of her body, impossible of alteration except that it must grow worse. In the depths of her eyes there was the haggard gleam of terror.

So great was her fear that when she had come back soaked to the skin she had not dared to dry herself at the fire but had gone silently on with her work. She was eight years old, but her expression was ordinarily so apathetic, and sometimes so witless, that it seemed at moments that she must be turning into an idiot, or else a devil. Not only had she never been taught to pray, she had never set foot inside a church. 'When do I have the time?' Mme Thénardier demanded.

The man in the yellow coat continued to observe Cosette until suddenly Mme Thénardier exclaimed:

'Now I think of it, what about that loaf?'

Cosette, as she always did when the woman raised her voice, came hastily out from under the table. She had forgotten all about the loaf, and she now resorted to the time-honoured expedient of frightened children. She lied.

'The bakery was shut, madame.'

'You should have knocked.'

'I did knock but he didn't open.'

'Well, I shall find out tomorrow if that's true or not,' said Mme Thénardier. 'Heaven help you if it isn't. Meanwhile give me back the fifteen sous.'

Cosette plunged her hand into her apron-pocket and turned green. The coin was not there.

'Do you hear me?' said Mme Thénardier. 'I'm waiting.'

Cosette turned her pocket inside out but there was nothing in it. She had no notion what had become of the money. Words failed her and she stood petrified.

'So you've lost it, have you?' Mme Thénardier thundered. 'Or are you trying to steal it?' And she reached for the strap hanging above the chimney-piece.

The ominous gesture gave Cosette the strength to cry for mercy. 'Please, madame! Please!'

Mme Thénardier unhooked the strap.

While this was going on the man in the yellow coat had been feeling unobtrusively in his waistcoat pocket; in any case the other customers were too absorbed with their drink or cards to be interested in anything else.

Cosette was now huddled in the chimney-corner, trying frantically to hide or protect her half-naked limbs. Mme Thénardier raised her arm.

'Pardon me, madame,' the stranger said. 'I noticed something roll on the floor just now and I think it may have fallen out of the child's pocket. Perhaps I can find it.' He bent down as though to look. 'Yes, here it is.' And he held out a coin to Mme Thénardier.

'That's it,' the lady said, although it was not. It was a twenty-sou piece, but so much the better. Pocketing the coin, she contented herself with a final glare at Cosette, saying, 'All the same, mind it doesn't happen again.'

Cosette returned to what her mistress referred to as her 'nook', and her big eyes, fixed upon the stranger, shone with an expression hitherto unknown to them, mainly of innocent astonishment, but also with a kind of incredulous trust.

'By the way,' Mme Thénardier said to him, 'do you want any supper?'

He did not answer, seeming plunged in thought.

'Who the devil is this man?' she muttered to herself. 'Is he too poor to pay for a meal? Will he even settle for the room? Lucky he didn't think of stealing the money when he saw it on the floor.'

At this moment the door opened and Éponine and Azelma appeared.

They were two very pretty little girls with a look of the town rather than of the country, very charming, the one with glossy chestnut curls and the other with long dark plaits down her back, both of them lively and plump and clean with a glow of freshness and health that was pleasant to see. They were warmly clad but with a maternal skill which ensured that the thickness of the materials did not detract from their elegance. Winter was provided for but spring not forgotten. They brought brightness with them, and they entered like reigning beauties. There was assurance in their looks and gaiety, and in the noise they made. Their mother greeted them in a tone of mock-reproach overflowing with indulgence. 'So here you are, and high time too!'

She took them on her knee in turn, smoothed their hair, straightened their ribbons and set them down with a gentle maternal shake exclaiming, 'Such untidy moppets!' After which they went and sat in the chimney-corner, cooing over a doll which they shared between them. Cosette looked up now and then from her knitting and mournfully regarded them.

Éponine and Azelma, for their part, showed no interest in Cosette. She meant no more to them than if she had been the dog. The three little girls, the sum of their ages some twenty-four years, were already an embodiment of human society – envy on one side, indifference on the other. The doll the sisters were playing with was old and battered but it seemed nonetheless wonderful to Cosette, who had never had a doll of her own, a *real* doll, to use an expression which every child will understand.

But suddenly Mme Thénardier, busy about the room, caught sight of the child as she sat with her hands idle, watching the other two.

'Look at you!' she cried. 'Do you call that working? What you need, my girl, is a touch of the strap!'

Without rising from his chair the stranger turned towards her. 'Don't be too hard on her, madame,' he said with an almost timid smile. 'Let her play a little while.'

If the admonition had come from a traveller who had eaten his plate of mutton and washed it down with a couple of bottles of wine, and who did not look like the most undesirable of paupers, it would have amounted to a command. But that a man with a hat and coat like those he was wearing should express a desire of any kind was something that Mme Thénardier did not feel called upon to tolerate. She retorted sharply:

'The girl eats, doesn't she? So she's got to work. I don't feed her for nothing.'

'What exactly is she knitting?' the stranger asked in the same quiet voice which was so oddly at variance with his beggarly attire and powerful shoulders.

'Stockings, if you must know. Stockings for my daughters, who have scarcely any and will soon be going barefoot.'

The man glanced at Cosette's reddened feet.

'And when she's finished this pair of stockings?'

'It'll take her a good three or four days, the idle slut.'

'And what will they be worth when they're done?'

Mme Thénardier looked contemptuously at him.

'At least thirty sous.'

'Will you sell them to me for five francs?'

'Five francs!' exploded a customer who was listening. 'Five francs for a pair of stockings! Upon my word!'

Thénardier himself saw fit to intervene.

'If it is your humour, monsieur, you may have the stockings for five francs. We can refuse our customers nothing.'

'Cash down,' said madame in her terse fashion.

'Then I will buy them,' the man said, and getting a five-franc piece out of his pocket he laid it on the table. 'There's the money.' He turned to Cosette. 'You're working for me now, child. I want you to play a little, and rest.'

The customer was so startled by the sight of the five-franc piece that, deserting his glass, he came over to examine it.

'It's real, all right,' he announced. 'No question about it. It's a good 'un.'

Thénardier came up and put the coin calmly in his pouch. Mme Thénardier, deprived of speech, stood biting her lips and glaring. Cosette meanwhile was trembling. She ventured to ask:

'Madame, is it true? Am I really allowed to play?'

'Play for heaven's sake!' bellowed Mme Thénardier.

'Thank you, madame.' But although the words were addressed to her mistress, Cosette's whole heart went out to the stranger.

Thénardier returned to his seat. His wife went over and murmured in his ear:

'Who on earth can the man be?'

'I've known millionaires to wear coats no better than that,' he answered in a lordly tone.

Cosette had put aside her knitting but had not left her place. She always moved as little as possible. From a box on the floor behind her she produced some scraps of material and her tiny lead sword.

Éponine and Azelma had paid no attention to what was going on, being now absorbed in a highly important matter. They had caught hold of the kitten, letting their doll fall to the floor, and Éponine, the elder, was now dressing it in an assortment of red and blue rags, despite its struggles and mews of protest. While she performed this difficult operation, she was discoursing to her sister in the enchanting language of childhood, whose charm, like the splendour of a butterfly's wing, vanishes when one seeks to grasp it.

'It's much nicer than the other kind of doll because it really moves, and it squeaks and it's warm. I'm going to be a lady and this is going to be my baby that I'm bringing for you to see, and when you see that it's got a moustache you'll be very surprised, and when you see its ears and tail you'll be more surprised than ever, and you'll say, "Merciful Heavens!" and I'll say, "It's my little daughter, madame, and that's how she was born. Little girls are all like that nowadays." '

Azelma listened spellbound.

The drinkers meanwhile had burst into song, and with Thénardier assisting and applauding were making the room shake with their uproar.

Like birds building nests, so will children make dolls out of whatever comes to hand. While Éponine and Azelma were dressing the kitten, Cosette dressed her sword, and having done so rocked it in her arms and crooned a lullaby.

A doll is among the most pressing needs as well as the most charming instincts of feminine childhood. To care for it, adorn it, dress and undress it, give it lessons, scold it a little, put it to bed and sing it to sleep, pretend that the object is a living person – all the future of the woman resides in this. Dreaming and murmuring, tending, cossetting, sewing small garments, the child grows into girlhood, from girlhood into womanhood, from womanhood into wifehood, and the first baby is the successor of the last doll. A little girl without a doll is nearly as deprived and quite as unnatural as a woman without a child. So Cosette made her sword into a doll.

Mme Thénardier went back to the stranger, the 'yellow man' as she now thought of him. Upon reflection she had decided that her husband might be right and that he might turn out to be rich. The rich have the strangest whims!

She seated herself with her elbows on the table. 'Monsieur –' she began, and this form of address caused him to look up. Hitherto she had called him nothing but 'my good man' or 'fellow'.

'You see, monsieur,' she went on in a sanctimonious tone that was even more objectionable than her hectoring manner, 'I've nothing against the child being allowed to play, just for once, seeing that you've been so generous. But she has to work, you see, because she's got nothing of her own.'

'She's not your child?' the man said.

'Oh dear no! Just a pauper child we took in out of charity, and stupid into the bargain, probably water on the brain, you've only got to look at the size of her head. We do the best we can for her, but we aren't rich. We write letters, but there's been no reply for six months. It looks as though her mother must be dead.'

'Ah,' said the man, and sat pondering.

'Not that her mother amounted to much,' added Mme Thénardier. 'She abandoned the child.'

Cosette's eyes were intent upon her mistress, as though instinct had warned her that she was the subject of this conversation. She could not follow it entirely, being able to catch only a few words here and there. It came to an end when, upon the renewed insistence of his hostess, the 'yellow man', the millionaire, agreed to have something to eat.

'What would you like, monsieur?'

'Bread and cheese,' he said.

'So he's nothing but a pauper after all,' reflected Mme Thénardier.

The merry-makers, now three parts drunk, again broke into their ribald singing with renewed enthusiasm. It was a tasteful affair having to do with the Virgin and the Infant Jesus. Mme Thénardier, after fetching the bread and cheese, went over to join in the laughter. Cosette, under the table, was now staring wide-eyed at the fire, clasping her semblance of a doll in her arms. As she rocked it to and fro she crooned in a low voice, 'My mother's dead! My mother's dead! My mother's dead!'

But suddenly she broke off. She had noticed the Thénardier children's doll lying on the floor where they had left it when they captured the kitten. It was only a yard or two away from the kitchen table. Putting down her own makeshift doll, she looked round the room. Mme Thénardier was now talking in an undertone to her husband, the customers were eating, drinking, or singing, and Éponine and Azelma were busy with the kitten. Nobody was watching her. With a last cautious look round, she crawled out on hands and knees, seized the doll and a moment later was again under the table, but with her back now turned to the fire, and crouching to conceal the fact that she had the doll in her arms. The delight of having a real doll to play with was a rarity amounting to rapture. Only the stranger, now eating his modest meal, had noticed anything.

Cosette's rapture lasted only a few minutes. With all her precautions she had failed to notice that one of the doll's legs was sticking out so as to be visible from behind her. Azelma suddenly caught sight of a pink foot shining in the firelight. She nudged her sister and the two little girls sat staring in outraged amazement. Cosette had dared to take their doll!

Without letting go of the kitten, Éponine ran across to her mother and tugged at her skirt.

'Now what is it?' asked Mme Thénardier.

'Look,' said Éponine, and pointed to Cosette who, lost in the ecstasy of possession, was oblivious of all else.

Mme Thénardier's face assumed that particular expression, a mingling of the vile and the commonplace, which causes women of her kind to be known as harridans. Injured pride heightened her fury. Cosette had overstepped all bounds. She had dared to lay hands on what belonged to the daughters of the house. A Tsarina, seeing a peasant deck himself with the blue sash of her imperial son, could have appeared no more formidable.

In a voice hoarse with fury she cried:

'Cosette!'

Cosette swung round, trembling as though the earth were shaking under her feet.

'Cosette!' repeated Mme Thénardier.

Cosette laid the doll down with a gentle movement in which there was something like love as well as despair. Still looking at it, she clasped her hands and wrung them, a terrible thing to have to relate of a child. And then she did something that not all the cruel events of the day had forced her to do – not the errand in the woods, the heaviness of the bucket, the loss of the money, the sight of the strap or even the dire words Mme Thénardier had spoken about her mother. She burst into a flood of tears.

The stranger, meanwhile, had got to his feet.

'What's the matter?' he asked Mme Thénardier.

'Can't you see?' she answered, pointing to the *corpus delicti* now lying at Cosette's feet.

'I don't understand.'

'The brat has had the impudence to take my children's doll!'

'But what of it?' the stranger said. 'Why shouldn't she play with the doll?'

'She handled it,' pursued Mme Thénardier. 'She touched it with her filthy hands!'

Cosette sobbed more loudly than ever.

'Stop that noise!' the woman shouted.

The stranger turned abruptly towards the street door, opened it, and went out. Madame Thénardier took advantage of his sudden disappearance to administer a kick under the table which drew a cry from Cosette.

In a very short time the stranger was back, and now he was carrying the fabulous doll which during that day had been coveted by every child in the village. He set it upright in front of Cosette and said:

'Here – it's for you.'

During the hour or so that he had been in that place, lost in his thoughts, he must, it seems, have been obscurely aware of the bric-à-brac stall across the way, its profusion of offerings so brightly lighted that the glow was visible through the windows of the tavern.

Cosette looked up, as dazzled by his appearance with the doll as she might have been by a burst of sunshine. She heard the unbelievable words, 'It's for you' and stared, first at him, then at the doll, and then she slowly shrank back, withdrawing as far as she could under the table to huddle, silent and motionless, against the wall, scarcely daring to breathe.

Mme Thénardier, Éponine, and Azelma were standing like statues. The drinkers themselves had paused. A silence had fallen upon the room.

Mme Thénardier, thunderstruck, was again reduced to conjecture. What *was* this man? Was he a pauper or a millionaire? Or a combination of both, a criminal?

Over her husband's face passed the look of strained intensity that characterizes the human countenance when it is seized with a dominating passion. Glancing from the doll to the traveller, he seemed to sniff the man as he might have sniffed a hoarded treasure. But this lasted only an instant. He drew near his wife and murmured:

'That thing cost at least thirty francs. Don't be a fool. Crawl to him.'

Coarseness and innocence are alike in this, that they have no sense of contradiction.

'Well, Cosette,' said Mme Thénardier in the mildest of voices, 'aren't you going to take your doll?'

Cosette crept out of her retreat.

'The gentleman has given you a doll, dear child,' said Mme Thénardier. 'It's yours. You must play with it.'

Cosette gazed at the miraculous doll with a kind of terror. Her face was still wet with tears, but her eyes, like the sky at dawn, were beginning to glow with a strange new brightness. If someone had said to her out of the blue, 'Child, you are the Queen of France,' her feelings would have been little different from what they now were. And still she was afraid to touch the doll lest it exploded in thunder – a not unwarranted misgiving, with all the reasons she had for dreading her mistress's wrath. But her longing was even stronger. Drawing nearer to it, she looked up timidly and asked:

'May I really, madame?' No words can convey the mingling of anguish and ecstasy in her voice.

'But of course,' said Mme Thénardier. 'It's yours. The gentleman has given it to you.'

'Is it true, monsieur? Is it really true? Is the lady mine?'

The stranger seemed so near to tears that he could not speak. He nodded to Cosette and put the hand of 'the lady' in hers.

Cosette hastily withdrew her hand as though the lady's touch had burnt her. She stayed for a moment staring at the floor, and we have to record that during that moment she put out her tongue as far as it would go. Then she looked up and seized the doll.

'I shall call her Catherine,' she said.

It was a queer moment, the child's ragged garments enfolding the pink muslin finery of the doll.

'May I sit her on a chair, madame?'

'Of course, dear child,' said Mme Thénardier.

While Éponine and Azelma enviously looked on, Cosette sat Catherine on a chair and then herself sat on the floor, where she remained motionless and silent, simply looking at her.

'You must play with her, Cosette,' the stranger said.

'But I am playing,' she replied.

At that moment there was no one on earth whom Mme Thénardier detested more than she did this stranger who had descended upon Cosette like a visitant from another world. She had to keep herself in hand, but accustomed though she was to dissimulation in her constant striving to emulate her husband in all things, the effort to control her present feelings was almost too much for her. She hurriedly sent her daughters off to bed and then went so far as to ask the 'yellow man' for permission to send Cosette to bed as well, observing in motherly accents that the child had had a tiring day. Cosette departed with Catherine in her arms.

Mme Thénardier then crossed the room to where her husband was seated, and there relieved her feelings by pouring out a flood of words that were the more venomous because they had to be spoken in an undertone.

'That old lunatic, what's got into him, coming here and turning the place upside down, wanting the brat to play, giving her dolls – a forty-franc doll for a slut that I wouldn't give forty sous for! Next thing you know he'll be calling her "your Highness"! Is the man mad?'

'Well, but why shouldn't he spoil her if it amuses him?' retorted Thénardier. 'It suits you to make the child work, and it suits him to see her play. He's in his rights. The customer can do what he likes so long as he pays. What does it matter to you whether he's a ▪philanthropist or an imbecile? He's evidently got money.' Unanswerable words, coming from the master of the house, an innkeeper into the bargain.

The stranger meanwhile had returned to his attitude of meditation, sitting with an elbow on the table. The other customers, travelling salesmen and carriers, had drawn a little apart from him and were no longer singing. They were watching him with a kind of awed respect. A man so poorly clad who nevertheless produced crown pieces at the drop of a hat and bestowed princely gifts on a little creature in clogs, was a phenomenon deserving of notice.

Several hours went by. The midnight mass had been celebrated, the revelry was ended and the revellers departed; the room was now deserted and the fire had burnt low, but the stranger remained where he was, still in the same posture, only now and then shifting from one elbow to the other. Nothing more than that. Since Cosette's departure he had not spoken a word.

The Thénardiers lingered on, from precaution and also out of curiosity. 'Is he going to spend the night like this?' Mme Thénardier muttered. But when the clock struck two she admitted defeat. 'I'm going to bed,' she said to her husband. 'You can do what you like.' Thénardier seated himself at a corner table, lit a candle, and settled down to read the *Courrier français*. During the next hour or so he read the whole paper twice through, from the date on the first page to the name of the printer on the back, and still the stranger did not move.

Thénardier fidgeted, coughed, spat, blew his nose, and made his chair creak, all to no purpose. 'Is he asleep?' he wondered. The man was not asleep but it seemed that nothing could rouse him. Finally Thénardier took off his cap, went up to him and ventured to ask:

'Is monsieur not going to retire?'

He had chosen the word with care. 'Retire' sounded more respectful, less peremptory and familiar, than 'go to bed'. The phrase had the especial virtue that it would be reflected in to-morrow's bill. A room where one merely goes to bed costs twenty sous, but a room where one retires may cost twenty francs.

'Of course,' said the stranger. 'You're quite right. Where is your stable?'

'If monsieur will allow me,' said Thénardier smiling, 'I will lead the way.'

The man picked up his stick and his bundle. Candle in hand, Thénardier conducted him to a room on the first floor, a room of unexpected splendour with mahogany furniture and a red-curtained four-poster bed.

'But what's this?' the stranger asked.

'It was our wedding-chamber,' said Thénardier. 'My wife and I now sleep in another room. This one is not used more than three or four times in a year.'

'I should have been quite content in the stable,' the man said sharply.

Thénardier affected not to hear. He lighted two new wax candles standing on the mantelpiece. A fire was already burning in the hearth. Under a glass case on the mantelpiece was a woman's head-dress of silver thread and orange-blossom.

'What is that?' the stranger asked.

'It's my wife's bridal bonnet,' Thénardier said.

The stranger inspected it as though marvelling at this evidence that that female monster had once been a virgin. But in fact Thénardier was lying. When he had rented the house to turn it into a tavern he had left this room as it was, merely taking over the furniture and throwing in a secondhand bridal bonnet to do honour to his 'wife' and shed a lustre of respectability upon their establishment.

When the stranger looked round he found himself alone. Thénardier had silently withdrawn without saying good night, not wanting to treat with excessive friendliness a person whom he intended to fleece handsomely in the morning.

He found his wife in bed but not asleep. She looked up as he entered their bedroom and said:

'I suppose you know I'm going to get rid of Cosette tomorrow.'

'You're always in a hurry,' he replied coldly.

Nothing more was said, and a few minutes later their candle was blown out.

The stranger meanwhile, having disposed of his stick and bundle, was seated meditating in an armchair. Presently he took off his shoes, picked up one candle and blew out the other, opened the door and stood as though wondering which way to go. He walked along the passage to the stairs and heard the faint sound of a child's breathing. Following this sound he came to a sort of triangular recess, a doorless cupboard, under the stairs. Here, amid the jumble it contained of old baskets, boxes, and broken crockery, amid the dust and cobwebs, there was a bed – if a worn mattress, with straw bursting out of its seams, and a tattered blanket may be so described. There was no other covering. The mattress was on the floor and Cosette was asleep on it.

He stood looking at her.

Cosette was soundly asleep and fully dressed. She never undressed in winter because of the cold. The doll was clasped in her arms, its wide eyes gleaming in the candlelight. From time to time the little girl gave a deep sigh as though she were on the verge of waking, and then, with an almost convulsive movement, tightened her hold on the doll. One of her wooden shoes, but only one, lay beside the mattress.

An open door near Cosette's cubby-hole afforded a glimpse of a fair-sized room which was in darkness. The stranger went in.

At the far end, beyond a glass-paned door, he could see two small twin beds with very white coverlets. They were those of Azelma and Éponine, and they half-concealed an uncurtained wicker cradle containing the little boy whose wails had been heard throughout the evening.

The stranger surmised that this room communicated with that of the Thénardiers, and he was about to withdraw when his eye fell upon the fireplace. It was one of those vast inn hearths where, if there is any fire at all, it is always insufficient, so that the very sight of them is chilling. In the present case there was no fire, or even any ashes; but what had caught the stranger's eye were two small, elegant shoes which were not a pair, since they were of different sizes. He recalled the charming, age-old custom whereby on Christmas Eve children put a shoe in the hearth, hoping to find next morning that their good fairy had left a present in it. Éponine and Azelma had not neglected to do this, and bending down the stranger saw that the good fairy, that is to say their mother, had already been that way. A bright new ten-sou piece shone in each shoe.

He was again about to withdraw when he noticed something else. At some distance from these two shoes there was a third, a wooden clog of the crudest, ugliest kind, caked in ashes and dried mud. It was empty.

The stranger felt in his waistcoat pocket and put a gold coin in it, a louis d'or.

Then he went silently back to his room.

IX

Thénardier transacts business

A good two hours before daylight the next morning, Thénardier, seated pen in hand at a table in the general room, was composing the stranger's bill by the light of a candle, while his wife stood looking over his shoulder. Neither spoke. Their respective attitudes were, on the one side, one of intense calculation, and, on the other, awed respect for this lofty manifestation of the power of the human intellect. A bumping sound was to be heard in the distance. It was Cosette sweeping the stairs.

After a good quarter-of-an-hour's labour and a number of crossings out Thénardier produced the following masterpiece:

Bedroom No. 1

Supper	3 francs
Room	10 „
Candle	5 „
Fire	4 „
Service	1 „
Total	**23 francs**

The word 'service' was spelt 'serviss'.

'Twenty-three francs!' exclaimed the lady in a tone of rapture not unmingled with apprehension.

Like all great artists, Thénardier was not satisfied with his work. 'Pah!' he said, and it might have been Castlereagh drawing up France's bill at the Congress of Vienna.

'You're quite right, my dear,' his wife said, thinking of the doll given to Cosette in the presence of her daughters. 'It's fair. But it's a great deal. Do you think he'll pay?'

'He'll pay,' said her husband with his small, cold laugh.

The laugh was the expression of perfect assurance and authority. There was nothing more to be said, and his wife did not pursue the matter. She began to tidy the room while he paced up and down. After a silence he said:

'I owe a good fifteen hundred francs.'

He dropped on to the settle in the corner of the hearth and sat brooding with his feet in the warm ashes.

'While I think of it,' the woman said, 'you haven't forgotten, have you, that I'm turning Cosette out today? The sight of that doll makes me sick. I'd sooner be married to Louis XVIII than keep her here another minute.'

Thénardier was lighting his pipe. He said between puffs, 'Give the man his bill.' Then he got up and went out.

He had scarcely done so when the stranger entered, and instantly Thénardier reappeared behind him, standing in the half-open doorway, visible only to his wife.

The stranger was carrying his stick and bundle.

'Up so early!' said Mme Thénardier. 'Is monsieur leaving us already?'

She was twisting the bill awkwardly in her hands as she spoke,

373

her harsh face wearing an unaccustomed expression of diffidence or scruple. It was not easy to present a man who looked so obviously poor with a bill that size.

'Yes,' said the stranger in a preoccupied manner, 'I'm leaving.'

'Monsieur has no business to attend to in Montfermeil?'

'No, I'm only passing through. How much do I owe you, madame?'

Without answering, Mme Thénardier handed him the folded slip of paper. He glanced at it, but his thoughts were evidently elsewhere.

'Tell me, madame, are you doing well here in Montfermeil?'

'Fairly well,' said Madame Thénardier, for the moment astounded that the sight of the bill had not produced an immediate explosion. But then she resumed in a voice of extreme pathos. 'Times are very hard, monsieur, and we get so few visitors in these parts. This is poor country. If it weren't for an occasional rich and generous traveller like yourself, monsieur, I don't know how we'd manage. We have so many expenses. There's that child, for instance – you've no idea how much she costs.'

'What child?'

'Why, the one you saw last night, Cosette. "The lark", as the people round here call her. These stupid peasants with their nicknames. She's more like a bat than a lark. We don't ask for charity and we can't afford to give it. We earn very little and we're always having to pay out money. There's our licence and all the taxes, doors and windows and everything, monsieur knows what this government is like. And I have my own daughters to consider. I can't keep other people's children as well.'

The stranger hesitated and then said in a voice which he strove to make casual but which trembled slightly.

'Suppose I were to take her off your hands?'

'What – Cosette?'

'Yes.'

The woman's red, coarse face was illumined with a sudden, atrocious radiance.

'Why, monsieur, my dear monsieur, take her! Take her away, take charge of her, care for her, cosset her, pamper her, and may you be blessed by the Holy Virgin and all the saints in Paradise!'

'Well then, I will.'

'Truly? You mean to take her?'

'Yes.'

'And at once?'

'Certainly. Call her in here.'

'Cosette!' cried Mme Thénardier.

'In the meantime,' said the stranger, 'I might as well pay what I owe you. How much is it?'

He looked at the slip of paper and started slightly. 'Twenty-three francs!' Looking hard at his hostess, he repeated the amount in a tone that was half one of amazement and half a question.

But Mme Thénardier had had time to steel herself for the ordeal. She answered calmly:

'Certainly, monsieur – twenty-three francs.'

The stranger placed five five-franc pieces on the table.

'Well, go and fetch the child,' he said.

But at this moment Thénardier came right into the room saying: 'Monsieur owes twenty-six sous.'

'What!' exclaimed his wife.

'Twenty for the room,' said Thénardier coldly, 'and six for his supper. As for the child, that is something that I must discuss with the gentleman. Kindly leave us, my dear.'

Mme Thénardier had one of those flashes of enlightenment that are the reward of natural talent. Perceiving that the leading actor had now entered the stage she said nothing and withdrew.

When they were alone Thénardier invited the stranger to be seated but himself remained standing. His expression was now one of singular gentleness and simplicity.

'Monsieur,' he said. 'I must tell you at once that I adore that child.'

The stranger stared at him.

'What child?'

'It is strange how attached one can become,' Thénardier proceeded. 'What does money matter after all? Take back your hundred-sou pieces, monsieur. The child is what I care about.'

'What child are you talking about?' asked the stranger.

'Why, our little Cosette – aren't you proposing to take her away from us? Let me speak frankly, as between honourable men. I can't allow it, I should miss her too much. I've known her since she was a baby. It is true that she costs money and that she has her faults; it is true that we are not rich, and that I had to pay more than four hund-red francs for medicine for one of her illnesses. But we all have to do something in the service of God. She has neither father nor mother. I brought her up. I have food enough to feed her. I can't do without her. You know how it is with the affections. I'm a stupid fellow, I dare say, no sense at all, but I love the child and so does my wife, although she's a bit sharp-spoken at moments. It's just the same as if she were our own. I need to see her running about the house.'

The stranger was still gazing fixedly at him. He went on:

'You must forgive me, monsieur, but one does not hand over one's child to a passer-by. Am I not right? Although, of course, I'm not saying – you appear to be rich and have the look of an honest man – I'm not saying that if it were in her best interests . . . But I need to be certain as I am sure you will understand. Suppose, for instance, that I were to sacrifice my feelings and let her go, I wouldn't want to lose sight of her entirely. I should want to know where she was, so that I could visit her from time to time, just so that she'd know that her loving foster-father was still watching over her. There are things that are really not possible. I do not even know your name. If you were to take her off like this I should be left saying, "Where is she? What has happened to our dear Cosette, our little lark?" I must at least ask to see a scrap of paper, a passport or something.'

The stranger, without ceasing to regard him with eyes that seemed to pierce to his heart, said in a firm, incisive voice:

'Monsieur Thénardier, one does not need a passport to travel five leagues from Paris. If I take Cosette with me that will conclude the matter. You will not be told my name or my dwelling or where she will be. My intention is that she shall never again set eyes on you. I mean to break every connection with her present life. Do you agree to that – yes or no?'

Just as demons and evil spirits recognize by certain signs the presence of a higher God, so Thénardier realized that he had to do with a man of great moral strength. It was a matter of intuition; he understood it instantly and finally. Throughout the previous evening, while he had been drinking with the other customers, smoking, joining in the choruses, he had had his eye on the stranger, watching him like a cat and summing him up like a mathematician, spying on him both on principle and for the pleasure of doing so. Not a movement, not the least gesture on the part of the man in the yellow coat had escaped him. Even before the stranger had shown that he was interested in Cosette, Thénardier had guessed it. He had seen his gaze constantly return to her. What was the reason for his interest? Who was the man, and why, with a purse filled with money, was he so wretchedly clad? Exasperating questions to which Thénardier could find no answer, although he had pondered them throughout the night. The man could hardly be Cosette's father – was he perhaps her grandfather? But in that case why did he not say so? If one has a rightful claim one produces it. Evidently the man had no claim to Cosette. Then what was he? Thénardier had racked his brains, guessing at everything and understanding nothing. Nevertheless, when he had embarked on this interview, being persuaded that there was a secret which the stranger had reason for concealing, he had felt that he was in a strong position. The plain and forthright answer, showing the man of mystery to be so uncompromisingly mysterious, had taken the wind out of his sails. It was a quite unexpected development which threw his whole strategy in ruins. Summoning his wits, he hastily revised it. Thénardier was one of those men who can size up a situation at a glance. He felt that this was the moment for the straightforward approach, and like a great captain seizing the decisive instant that he alone has perceived, he promptly unmasked his batteries.

'Monsieur,' he said, 'I need fifteen hundred francs.'

The stranger got an old black leather wallet out of an inside pocket, extracted three banknotes and laid them on the table. He then pressed his large thumb on them and said:

'Fetch Cosette.'

What of Cosette meanwhile?

When she awoke that morning she had gone at once to look in her sabot and had found the gold coin. It was not a napoléon but one of the new twenty-franc pieces issued under the Restoration, with the imperial laurels replaced by a Prussian pigtail. Cosette was dazed, bemused by her changed fortunes. Although she did not know that this was a gold piece, never having seen one before, she stuffed it hastily in her pocket as though she had stolen it. But she knew very well that it was hers, she guessed where it had come from, and she had a feeling of delight that was also fear. She was delighted, but even more, she was bewildered. These lavish and beautiful gifts seemed to her not real. The doll and the gold piece both filled her with alarm; she trembled instinctively at so much splendour. Only the stranger did not frighten her, but, on the contrary, reassured her. Since the previous evening, amid all the surprises, even in her sleep her child's thoughts had been preoccupied with this man who looked old and poor and sad, and still was rich and kind. From the moment of their meeting in the wood, everything had changed for her. Less fortunate than the least of hedge-sparrows, Cosette had never known what it was to take refuge under a mother's wing. For five years, as far back as she could remember, she had shivered and trembled. She had been naked to the bitter wind of misfortune, but now it seemed to her that she was clothed. Her spirit had been chilled and now was warm. She was less frightened than she had been of her mistress. She was no longer alone; there was someone there.

She busied herself with her customary morning tasks, but the golden louis, hidden in the apron-pocket out of which the fifteen-sou piece had fallen the night before, was very much in her mind. She was afraid to touch it, but she spent whole minutes thinking about it, with, it must be said, her tongue sticking out. In the middle of sweeping the stairs she stood suddenly motionless, forgetful of the broom and the whole world, while she pictured that star shining in her pocket.

It was during one of these moments that Mme Thénardier came up to her, having been sent by her husband to fetch her. Strangely, she did not hit or even scold her.

'Cosette,' she said almost gently, 'you're to come at once.'

When Cosette appeared in the downstairs room the stranger undid his bundle. It contained a woollen dress, an apron, a camisole, a petticoat, a shawl, woollen stockings, a pair of shoes – all the clothing needed for an eight-year-old girl. Every article was black.

'Take these, child,' the stranger said, 'and get dressed as quickly as you can.'

Day was breaking when the people of Montfermeil, engaged in opening their shutters, saw a poorly clad man go along the Rue de Paris hand-in-hand with a little girl dressed in mourning who was carrying a large doll. They were walking in the direction of Livry. No one knew the man, and since she was no longer in rags a good many did not recognize Cosette.

Cosette was going away, she did not know with whom or whither. All she knew was that she was leaving the Thénardiers' house for good. No one had troubled to say good-bye to her, nor had she said good-bye to anyone. She left that place both hated and hating, a small, gentle creature in whom every natural instinct until that moment had been suppressed.

She walked gravely, gazing wide-eyed at the sky. She had put the golden louis in the pocket of her new apron, and now and then she peeped at it, afterwards looking up at the man beside her. She had a queer feeling, as though she had drawn close to God.

x
Who looks for better may find worse

Mme Thénardier, as her habit was, had left matters to her husband, expecting great things. After the stranger and Cosette had left he allowed a quarter of an hour to elapse before taking her aside and showing her the fifteen hundred francs.

'Is that all?' she said.

It was the first time in their association that she had ventured to criticize any of her lord's acts.

The blow went home.

'You're right,' he said, 'and I'm an idiot. Where's my hat?'

He folded the three banknotes, put them in his pocket and hurried out of the house, but he made the mistake of turning right instead of left. It was only after he had been told that the man and child had been seen going in the direction of Livry that he turned back that way, pressing on at his best speed and discoursing to himself as he went.

'The man must be a millionaire, yellow coat and all, and I'm a half-wit. First he handed over twenty sous, then five francs, then twenty-five and then fifteen hundred, all without a murmur. He'd have paid fifteen thousand! But I'll catch up with him.'

That bundle of clothes bought in readiness for the child, that was extraordinary. There was more than one secret here, and a man of sense does not let go of a mystery when he has caught sight of one. The secrets of the rich are like sponges steeped in gold: one has to know how to squeeze them. These thoughts were tumbling over in his mind – 'I'm a half-wit,' he said.

When, after leaving Montfermeil, you come to the bend in the road to Livry you can see it stretching for a great distance across the plain. Thénardier had reckoned that at this point he should be able to see the man and child ahead of him, but although he strained his eyes he could see nothing. Again he had to seek help, wasting more time, and was eventually told that they had gone in the direction of the woods near Gagny. He hurried that way. They had a good start, but the child must slow them up; besides, he knew the country well.

Suddenly he stopped and clapped a hand to his forehead like a man who has overlooked an essential detail and is ready to turn back.

'I should have brought my gun,' he said.

Thénardier was one of those two-sided men who may pass in a crowd and vanish without being recognized because chance has brought only one of their sides to light. It is the lot of many men to live in this half-submerged state. In normal, uneventful circumstances he had everything required to make him appear (we do not say, to *be*) what is commonly known as an honest tradesman, a good citizen. But at the same time, given the requisite conditions, the stimulus to his lower nature, he had all the makings of a thorough-paced villain. He was a tradesman harbouring a monster, and Satan must at times have crouched in a corner of whatever place he inhabited and admired his odious handiwork.

After a moment of reflection he concluded that to turn back now would only give them time to get away; so he pressed on with speed and with a purposefulness not far short of certainty, the keenness of a fox scenting a covey of partridges.

And when, after passing the ponds and obliquely crossing the large meadow to the right of the Avenue de Bellevue, he came to the grass walk which almost encircles the hill and skirts the vaulting of the old aqueduct of the Abbaye de Chelles, he saw, emerging from above a bush, a hat which had already given him much food for thought. The bush was a low one, and Thénardier surmised that the man and Cosette were seated just beyond it; although the child was too small to be seen he could see the head of her doll.

He had guessed rightly. They had sat down to allow Cosette to rest. Thénardier rounded the bush and suddenly confronted them.

'I beg your pardon, monsieur,' he said breathlessly. 'I am returning your fifteen hundred francs.' And he held out the three banknotes.

The man looked up.

'What does this mean?'

'It means, monsieur,' Thénardier said in a respectful tone, 'that I am taking Cosette back.'

Cosette shuddered and pressed herself against the man. He was looking Thénardier straight in the eyes. He repeated slowly, stressing every syllable:

'You are taking Cosette back?'

'Yes, monsieur. I've been thinking. I have no right to let you have her. I am a man of honour, monsieur. The child is not mine, she belongs to her mother. She was entrusted to my care by her mother and I can only return her to her mother. You will say, "But her mother is dead." That may be so. But in that case I can only hand the child over to a person bringing me a document signed by the mother saying that I am to hand the child over to that person. That is clearly essential.'

Without speaking the man put a hand in his pocket and Thénardier witnessed the reappearance of the wallet stuffed with banknotes. He quivered with delight. 'Stick to your guns, lad,' he thought. 'You're going to be bribed.'

Before opening the wallet the stranger glanced about him. The place was quite deserted, not a soul in sight. He opened the wallet, but instead of bringing out the sheaf of notes which Thénardier was looking for, he produced nothing but a sheet of paper which he unfolded and handed to him.

'You were right to ask for this,' he said. 'Please read it.'

Thénardier read:

> Montreuil-sur-mer
> 25 March 1823.
>
> Monsieur Thénardier,
>   You will hand Cosette over to the bearer.
> Everything owing will be paid.
>
>   I send you my regards,
>   Fantine.

'You recognize the signature?' the stranger said.

It was unmistakably Fantine's handwriting. Thénardier had no reply. He was filled with a violent, twofold resentment, at losing the handsome bribe he had been hoping for, and at having been defeated.

'You can keep the letter as your quittance,' the stranger said.

Thénardier retreated in good order.

'It's a well-forged signature,' he muttered between his teeth. 'However . . .' He made a last, despairing effort. 'Very well, monsieur, since you are the bearer of this letter. But it says that everything owing will be paid. That'll come to a great deal.'

The stranger got to his feet and said while he brushed the dust off his shabby sleeve:

'Monsieur Thénardier, the child's mother reckoned in January that she owed you a hundred and twenty francs. In February you sent her a bill for five hundred. You received three hundred at the end of February and another three hundred at the beginning of March. Nine months have passed since then, which at the agreed price of fifteen francs a month makes a total of one hundred and thirty-five francs. You had received a hundred francs in advance, leaving thirty-five still to be paid. I have today paid you fifteen hundred francs.'

Thénardier felt like a wolf with the jaws of a trap closing on him. 'Who is this devilish fellow?' he wondered. And he did what the wolf does. He made a spring. Brazen audacity had served him once already.

'Mister Don't-know-your-name,' he said, casting civility aside. 'Either you pay me another thousand crowns or I take Cosette back.'

The stranger said calmly:

'Come here, Cosette.'

He reached out his left hand to the child and with his right picked up the stick which was lying beside him on the grass. Thénardier became aware of the formidable nature of this cudgel with its heavy knob, and also of the loneliness of the spot. Without another word the stranger turned and, clasping Cosette by the hand, led her away into the wood, leaving the innkeeper, motionless and thunderstruck, to stare at his slightly bowed but massive shoulders and the size of his fists. From this he went on to consider his own puny frame – 'I was an utter dolt not to bring my gun,' he reflected, 'seeing that I was hunting.'

But still he did not give up. 'At least I'll find out where they're going,' he thought, and he began to follow them, the richer by two things – the letter signed 'Fantine', which was a joke against himself, and a consolation prize, the fifteen hundred francs.

The man was leading Cosette in the direction of Livry and Bondy. He was walking slowly with his head bowed in an attitude of pensive melancholy. The time of year, robbing the trees of their foliage, made it easy for Thénardier to keep them in sight while following at a safe distance. Nevertheless the man, looking round from time to time, presently noticed him. He at once drew Cosette into a coppice where they were less visible. 'The devil!' muttered Thénardier, and quickened his pace.

The density of the coppice obliged pursuer and pursued to draw closer together. At its thickest part the man again turned, and although Thénardier made what use he could of the undergrowth he could not prevent himself from being seen. The man looked uncertainly at him, then shook his head and went on. Thénardier continued to follow. After they had gone another two or three hundred paces the man again suddenly turned and again saw him. This time his gaze was so formidable that Thénardier decided it would be unwise to follow him further. He turned back.

XI
Reappearance of No. 9430

Jean Valjean had not died.

As we know, when he had fallen, or rather flung himself, into the sea he had been released from his shackles. He had swum under water to a moored vessel to which a boat was tied, and had hidden in the boat until nightfall. After dark he had taken to the sea again and swum along the coast to a place a short distance from Cap Brun. Here, since he did not lack money, he was able to buy clothes. There was a small drinking-place near Balaguier which specialized in supplying the needs of escaped convicts, a highly profitable sideline. Thereafter, like all fugitives seeking to escape the vigilance of the law and social mischance, Valjean had travelled a dark and circuitous road. He first found shelter in Les Pradeaux, near Beausset, and thence went to a village near Briançon in the Hautes-Alpes. It was a furtive, mole-like journey of which all the twists and turns are not known. Traces of him were later picked up at a village in the Pyrenees and in the neighbourhood of Périgueux. Eventually he reached Paris and thence had gone to Montfermeil.

His first act on reaching Paris had been to buy a complete set of mourning for an eight-year-old girl, after which he had rented a lodging. It will be recalled that on the occasion of his first escape from arrest he had paid a mysterious visit to Montfermeil, or to its environs, concerning which the police had certain theories. But he was still believed to be dead, and this was his greatest safeguard. Reading the report in a newspaper he had felt reassured and almost at peace, as though he had really died.

On the evening of the day when he rescued Cosette from the Thénardiers they returned together to Paris, entering the city after dark by the Monceaux barrier. Here he took a cab to the Esplanade de l'Observatoire, and then, with the little girl's hand in his, walked through deserted alleyways to the Boulevard de l'Hôpital.

It had been a strange day for Cosette, filled with extraordinary happenings. They had sat under hedges eating bread and cheese bought at remote inns, they had travelled by different conveyances but had also walked a good deal of the way. She had not complained, but she was very tired and Jean Valjean felt her hand tug more heavily at his as they walked. So he picked her up and set her on his back, and Cosette, without letting go of Catherine, laid her head on his shoulder and slept.

BOOK FOUR

THE GORBEAU TENEMENT

I

A vanishing quarter

A STROLLER forty years ago penetrating beyond the Salpêtrière, by way of the Boulevard de l'Hôpital as far as the Barrière d'Italie, would have come to a region where Paris seemed to disappear. It was not a wilderness, for there were inhabitants; not country, for there were streets and houses; not town, for the streets were rutted like country roads, and grass grew in them; nor was it a village, for the houses were too high. What, then was it? It was an inhabited place where there was no one, a deserted place where there was someone, a city boulevard, a Paris street, wilder by night than the forest, more melancholy by day than a graveyard. It was the ancient quarter of the horse-market, the Marché-aux-Chevaux.

Should he go beyond the crumbling walls of the market and even beyond the Rue du Petit-Banquier, past a courtyard enclosed in high walls, then an open space with stacks of tanner's bark looking like giant beaver-dams, then a timber-yard, then a long, ruined, moss-covered wall on which flowers grew in the spring, then a dismally decrepit building bearing the legend *Défense d'afficher*, our bold explorer, having ventured thus far into the unknown, would find himself in the Rue des Vignes-Saint-Michel. Here, close by a factory and between two garden walls, there stood in those days an ancient building which seemed at first sight to be no bigger than a cottage but was in fact as vast as a cathedral. Only one gabled end was visible from the street, and a single window. The rest was hidden, and it was all on one floor.

A detail which might have struck the observer was that whereas the door was only suited to a cottage, the window, had it been built of shaped stone instead of plastered cob, would have been worthy of a mansion. The door itself was nothing but a makeshift collection of planks held together by crudely cut crossbars. It opened directly on to a steep stairway as wide as itself, with high muddied treads, which from the street looked like a ladder vanishing into the darkness between two walls. At the top of the misshapen door-frame was a thin transverse beam in which a triangular aperture had been cut to allow the passage of light and air when the door was closed. On the inside of the door the figure 52 had been inscribed with an inked brush, but on the outside, above this aperture, was the figure 50, giving rise to some confusion. Where exactly was one? No. 50 on the outside, 52 inside. A few nondescript, dusty-coloured rags served as a curtain over the aperture.

The window was wide and lofty, with large panes and Venetian shutters; but the panes had been damaged in a variety of ways which were both concealed and made manifest by ingenious bandaging with strips of paper, and the shutters, unhinged and hanging loose, were more a threat to the passer-by than a protection to the inmates. A good many of the horizontal slats were missing and had been crudely replaced by boards nailed vertically: what had once been Venetian had ended up more like the conventional shutters.

This contrast in the same house between the squalid door and the respectable if dilapidated shutters had something of the effect of two ill-assorted beggars walking side-by-side, wholly different beneath their tattered garments, one having been a beggar all his life and the other having been once a gentleman.

The stairs led up to a huge building which looked like a converted warehouse. On either side of a long central corridor were a series of compartments of varying sizes, habitable at a pinch and more like cubicles than prison-cells. Such windows as they possessed looked out on to the waste land surrounding the house. The whole place was sepulchral – dark, gloomy, and unpleasant – pierced, according to whether the crevices were in the roof or the door, by chilly rays of sunlight or icy draughts. An interesting and picturesque feature of buildings of this kind is the enormous size of the spiders that infest them.

To the left of the door on the boulevard, at about shoulder height, a small walled-up window formed a recess piled with stones which children threw into it as they passed.

A part of this building has recently been demolished, but enough remains to show what it was originally like. The whole was probably not more than a century old – youth in the case of a church, but old age in the case of an ordinary house. It would seem that man's dwellings share his brevity and those of God His eternity.

The postmen called the tenement No. 50–52; but it was known in the neighbourhood as the house of Gorbeau. We must explain how this name originated.

The snappers-up of unconsidered trifles, who collect anecdotes as a botanist collects wild flowers and register unimportant dates in their memories, will know that round about the year 1770 there were two leading attorneys practising at the Palais du Châtelet, whose names respectively were Corbeau and Renard – Crow and Fox. The echo of La Fontaine's fable was too good to be overlooked, and scurrilous verses, parodying La Fontaine, went the rounds of the Palais.

The worthy practitioners, embarrassed by the innuendoes and ruffled in their dignity by the laughter that pursued them, resolved to change their names and applied to the King for permission to do so. The plea was presented to Louis XV on the day when two clerical dignitaries, one the Papal Nuncio and the other the Cardinal de la Roche-Aymon, both on their knees, had in the presence of His Majesty each placed a slipper on the naked foot of Madame Du Barry as she got out of bed. The King, still laughing, moved on from the bishops to the two attorneys who, by his indulgence, were permitted to make trifling alterations to their names. Maître Corbeau was given leave to add a tail to his initial letter, so that he became Gorbeau. Maître Renard was less fortunate, the only concession he obtained was leave to add a 'P' to his name, so that Renard the fox became Prenard the grasper, which was scarcely an improvement.

According to local tradition Maître Gorbeau had been the owner of No. 50–52 Boulevard de l'Hôpital and had, moreover, been responsible for its impressive window. Hence the name *la maison Gorbeau*.

Among the trees lining the boulevard there stands, outside No. 50–52, a tall, moribund elm; almost exactly opposite is the Rue de la Barrière des Gobelins, at that time an unsurfaced roadway in which there were no houses, planted with stunted trees that were green or mud-spattered according to the season, leading directly to the Paris wall. A smell of copper sulphate blew in waves from a near-by factory. The barrier was near by, for in 1823 the City wall still existed.

The barrier itself had macabre associations. It was on the road to Bicêtre, along which, under the Empire and Restoration, criminals condemned to death were brought into Paris on the day of their execution. It was also the scene of the crime known as the 'Fontaine-bleau barrier murder', of which the perpetrators were not discovered, an ugly mystery that has never been resolved. A little further on is the Rue Croulebarbe where Ulbach stabbed the goat-girl from Ivry in a thunderstorm, amid all the trappings of melo-drama. Still further on are the polled elms of the Barrière Saint-Jacques, masking the scaffold, that shabby and ignominious place of execution contrived by a bourgeois, shop-keeping society which sought to thrust capital punishment out of sight, being too pusillanimous to abolish it with magnanimity or to maintain it with authority.

Thirty-seven years ago, setting aside the Place Saint-Jacques, which seemed to have been expressly designed for its purpose and was always horrible, the most depressing spot in the whole dreary boulevard, and it is little more attractive today, was the site occupied by the tenement building, No. 50–52.

Respectable dwellings only began to appear some twenty-five years later. The place was utterly dismal. In addition to its own funereal aspect one was conscious of being between the Salpêtrière, part women's prison and part mad-house, of which the cupola was visible, and Bicêtre with its barrier – between the madness of women and the madness of men. As far as sight could reach there was nothing to be seen but slaughter-houses, the wall, and an occasional factory looking like a barracks or a monastery; shanties and heaps of rubble, strips of old wall black as shrouds and of new wall white as winding-sheets; trees in parallel rows, featureless edifices in long, cold lines, with the monotony of right-angles. No accident of terrain, not an architectural flourish, not a bend or curve: a glacial setting, rectilinear and hideous. Nothing chills the heart like sym-metry, for symmetry is ennui and ennui is at the heart of grief. Despair is a yawn. It is possible to conceive of something even more terrible than a hell of suffering, and that is a hell of boredom. If such a hell exists, that stretch of the Boulevard de l'Hôpital might have been the road leading to it.

But at nightfall, particularly in winter, at the time when the last light faded and the wind whipped the last brown leaves off the elms, when the darkness was at its deepest, unrelieved by stars, or when wind and moonlight pierced gaps in the clouds, the boulevard be-came suddenly frightening. Its straight lines seemed to merge and dissolve in shadow like stretches of infinity. The pedestrian was reminded of the gallows-tradition of that place, and its solitude, which had been the scene of so many crimes, was nightmarish. There seemed to be pitfalls hidden in the dark, every patch of deeper shadow was suspect, the spaces between the trees resembled graves. By day the place was ugly; in the evening it was melancholy; at night it was sinister.

On summer evenings old women might be seen seated under the trees on wooden benches half-rotted by the rain. They were much given to begging.

For the rest, the quarter, which looked more outmoded than antique, was already being transformed. Anyone wanting to see it as it had been needed to make haste, for every day brought some small change. The terminus of the Paris-Orléans railway line, situated only a short distance from the old faubourg, has for the past twenty years contributed to the process. Wherever a railway-station is built on the outskirts of a capital city it leads to the death of a suburb and the growth of the town. It would seem that around these centres of mass-movement, the powerful machines, the huge horses of civilization devouring coal and spewing flame, the polluted earth trembles and splits open to swallow up the ancient dwellings of men and allow new ones to appear.

Since the terminus of the Orléans line invaded the territory of the Salpêtrière, the ancient, narrow streets round the Fosses Saint-Victor and the Jardin des Plantes are being swept away by the stream of coaches, fiacres, and omnibuses which in the course of time have thrust back the houses on either side. These are phenomena which, however improbable they may seem, are nevertheless fact; and just as it may truly be said that the sun causes the southern aspects of city houses to vegetate and grow, so it is undeniable that the press of traffic widens the streets. The signs of a new life become manifest. In the most backward corners of that old, provincial quarter, paving stones made their appearance and sidewalks began to be built even before there were any walkers. On a memorable morning in July 1845, the smoke of tar-wagons was to be seen, and it may be said that on that day civilization reached the Rue Lourcine and Paris spread to the Faubourg Saint-Marceau.

11

Nest for owl and fledgling

Jean Valjean came to a stop outside the Gorbeau tenement. Like a bird of prey he had sought out the remotest spot he could find for the building of his nest. Still carrying Cosette, he got a sort of pass-key out of his waistcoat pocket, opened the door and, after closing it carefully behind him, climbed the stairs.

Arrived at the corridor, he produced another key with which he opened one of the doors. The room he entered, again at once closing the door, was a fair-sized garret furnished with a mattress on the floor, a table, a few chairs, and a lighted stove of which the glow was visible in one corner. A street-lamp on the boulevard cast a faint light into this drab interior. At the far end was a small inner room with a trestle-bed. Jean Valjean laid the child on this without waking her.

A candle stood in readiness on the table, together with flint and steel. After lighting it Valjean stood gazing at Cosette as he had done the night before, with an expression of devoted tenderness that was almost exaltation. With the perfect confidence that denotes the presence of either great strength or extreme weakness she had fallen asleep without knowing whom she was with, and she continued to sleep without knowing where she was. He bent and kissed her hand. Nine months previously he had kissed the hand of her mother, when she, too, had fallen asleep. The same, almost religious feeling, anguished and compassionate, pierced him to the heart. He went on his knees beside the bed.

The new day dawned with Cosette still sleeping, while the pallid beams of December sunshine, filtering through the garret window, traced long patterns of light and shadow on the ceiling. But suddenly the noise of a heavily-laden cart rumbling over the cobbles in the boulevard caused her to start up trembling.

'Yes, madame!' she cried. 'Yes. Yes. I'm coming!'

Still half-asleep, she scrambled out of bed and groped about her.

'Heavens, where's my broom?'

Then, with eyes fully opened, she saw the smiling face of Jean Valjean.

'Why, of course!' she exclaimed. 'It's all true! Good morning, monsieur.'

Children instantly and familiarly accept rejoicing and happiness because this is their natural element. Seeing Catherine at the foot of the bed, Cosette picked her up and, while she nursed her, showered Valjean with questions. Where were they? – Was Paris a very huge place? – Was Madame Thénardier a long way off? – Would she come after them? . . . And suddenly she exclaimed: 'How lovely it is here!'

It was the most squalid of garrets, but she felt free.

'Don't you want me to sweep the floor?' she presently asked.

'No,' said Jean Valjean. 'You're to enjoy yourself.'

Thus the day passed. Without caring that she understood nothing of what had occurred, Cosette was inexpressibly happy with her protector and her doll.

III

Misfortunes shared create happiness

At daybreak the next morning Jean Valjean again stood at Cosette's bedside waiting for her to awake.

Something quite new was taking place within him.

Valjean had never loved anything. For twenty-five years he had been alone in the world, never a father, a lover, husband, or friend. In prison he had been sullen, gloomy, chaste, ignorant, and ferocious. Nothing had ever touched the heart of that ex-convict. The feeling he had once had for his sister and her children had become so remote as to have vanished almost entirely. He had done what he could to find them and, failing, had dismissed them from his mind. Such is the way of human nature. The other affections of his youth, if there had been any, were wholly lost.

But when he had seen Cosette, snatched her up and borne her out of captivity, something had stirred within him. Everything in him that was passionate and capable of affection had been aroused and had flowed out to the child. To stand at her bedside watching while she slept was to experience a shiver of ecstasy. He discovered a mother's agonized tenderness without knowing what it was, for nothing is deeper or sweeter than the overwhelming impulse of a heart moved suddenly to love – a saddened, ageing heart made new!

But since he was fifty-five years old and Cosette only eight, all the loves that his life might have contained were now merged in a kind of splendour. This was the second of the two visions he had met with. The bishop had taught him the meaning of virtue; Cosette had now taught him the meaning of love. Their first days passed in this bemused state.

Cosette also became a different being, but without knowing it, poor child. She had been so young when her mother left her that she did not remember her. Like all children, like the tendrils of a vine reaching for something to cling to, she had looked for love, but she had not found it. They had all repulsed her, the Thénardiers, their children, and other children. There had been a dog which she had loved, but it had died. Apart from this, nothing had needed her and no one had wanted her. The sad fact was that at the age of eight her heart had been cold and untouched, not through any fault of hers or because she lacked the capacity to love, but because there had been no possibility of loving. But now, from the first day they were together, everything in her that could think and feel went out to this man. She experienced something that she had never known before, a sense of unfolding.

She did not think of Jean Valjean as being old and poor; she found him handsome, just as she found their garret pretty. Such were the effects of youth and happiness, in which change of scene and a new way of life also played their part. Nothing is more charming than the glow of happiness amid squalor. There is a rose-tinted attic in all our lives.

The gulf that nature had created between Valjean and Cosette, the gap of fifty years, was bridged by circumstance. The over-riding force of destiny united these two beings so sundered by the years and so akin in what they lacked. Each fulfilled the other, Cosette with her instinctive need of a father, Valjean with his instinctive need of a child. For them to meet was to find, and in the moment when their hands first touched, they joined. Seeing the other, each perceived the other's need. In the deepest sense of the words it may be said that in their isolation Jean Valjean had been a widower, as Cosette was an orphan; and in this sense he became her father. Her instant trust of him that evening in the wood, when his hand had clasped her own, was, after all, no delusion. The man's entry into the life of the child had truly been the coming of God . . .

Valjean had been careful in his choice of a refuge, and he seemed to have found one which afforded them absolute security. The room and inner-room which they occupied possessed the only window looking on to the boulevard, and since this was so they could not be overlooked by their neighbours, either within the house or across the way.

The lower part of No. 50–52, which was used as a storehouse by market-gardeners, had no communication with the single upper storey, being separated from it by a solid floor in which there was no trap or stairway, as it were the diaphragm of the building. The upper storey, as we have said, consisted of a number of rooms and a few attics. Of these only one was occupied, by an old woman who did Valjean's housework. The rest were empty.

It was this old woman, who went by the title of 'chief tenant' but in fact acted as caretaker, who had let the room to him on Christmas Eve. He had told her that he was a gentleman of private means, ruined by the failure of the Spanish loan, and that he proposed to live there with his granddaughter. He had paid six months in advance and instructed her to furnish the room and its inner chamber in the manner we have described, and it was she who had lit the stove and prepared everything for their arrival.

Weeks passed, and the two lived happily in their drab dwelling. Children sing at daybreak as naturally as the birds, and Cosette laughed, chattered, and sang throughout the day. It happened sometimes that Jean Valjean would take her small, red hand, still roughened by chilblains, and kiss it. More accustomed to being beaten, the poor child did not know what to make of this and was plunged in embarrassment. And at moments she grew serious and reflected on the black dress she wore. She was clad no longer in rags but in mourning, emerging from misery into life.

Valjean was teaching her to read and it sometimes occurred to him, as he listened to her spell out the words, that when he had taught himself to read in prison it had been with the idea of putting it to nefarious use. Instead of which, he was passing it on to a child. This brought a singularly gentle smile to his lips, and it led into wide fields of speculation. He had a sense that it was foreordained, that he was serving the purpose of a Being higher than man. To teach Cosette to read, to help her to be happy, this was becoming the mainspring of his life. He talked to her about her mother and taught her to say her prayers. She called him 'father', never any other name.

He was content to spend hours watching her and listening to her chatter as she dressed and undressed her doll. Life now seemed to him full of interest, the world seemed good and just; he harboured no grudge against any man, and saw no reason why he should not live to a ripe old age now that this child loved him. He saw a radiant future enchantingly lighted by Cosette. None of us is wholly free from egotism. There were moments when it pleased him to think that she would never be pretty.

This is a personal opinion, but to be wholly frank we must say that we can see no certainty that Jean Valjean, at the point he had reached when he came to love Cosette, would have been able to continue on the path of virtue without that moral support. He had been confronted by new aspects of the malice of men and the sufferings of society, limited aspects depicting only one side of the truth – the lot of women summed up in Fantine, public authority embodied in Javert. He had been sent back to prison, this time for a good deed. Renewed bitterness had assailed him, disgust and weariness, to the point that even the sacred memory of the bishop was perhaps at moments eclipsed. It must certainly have been reborn later, luminous and triumphant, but at that stage it was greatly diminished. Who can be sure that Jean Valjean had not been on the verge of losing heart and giving up the struggle? In loving he recovered his strength. But the truth is that he was no less vulnerable than Cosette. He protected her and she sustained him. Thanks to him she could go forward into life, and thanks to her he could continue virtuous. He was the child's support and she his mainstay. Sublime, unfathomable marvel of the balance of destiny!

IV

Matters observed by the chief tenant

As a precaution, Jean Valjean never left the house during the day. He walked for an hour or two every evening, sometimes alone but often with Cosette, choosing deserted side-streets, or going into churches after nightfall. The church he visited most often was Saint-Médard, which was the nearest. When he did not take Cosette she stayed with the old woman, the 'chief tenant'; but nothing delighted her more than to be allowed to go with him. They walked hand-in-hand and he talked quietly to her, enchanted by her gaiety.

The old woman cleaned and cooked and did their shopping. They lived modestly, always with a little fire but like people who are hard-pressed for money. Valjean had added nothing to the furnishings of their apartment, but he had replaced the glass-paned door of Cosette's inner room with a solid one.

He still wore his yellow coat, black breeches, and battered hat. The people of the neighbourhood supposed him to be very poor, and now and then, when he was out walking, a good-natured housewife would stop and offer him a sou. He accepted it, bowing. But it also sometimes happened that, encountering some poor wretch begging for charity, he would look cautiously about him, furtively thrust a coin into his hand, often silver, and then hurriedly walk on. This was unwise. He became known in the neighbourhood as 'the beggar who gives alms'.

The 'chief tenant', a soured old creature consumed with envious curiosity concerning her neighbours, took a great interest in Jean Valjean without his realizing it. She was hard of hearing, which made her talkative, and she had retained only two of her teeth, one on the upper jaw and one on the lower, which she constantly clicked together. She asked Cosette endless questions which the child could not answer, knowing nothing except that she came from Montfermeil. One day the old woman caught sight of Valjean entering one of the empty rooms on the corridor in what seemed to her a suspicious manner. She crept after him like a cat and watched through a chink in the door, which he had closed. No doubt as an added precaution, he was standing with his back to the doorway. She saw him reach into his pocket and take out a case containing scissors and thread. He then unstitched a part of the lining of his tail-coat and brought out a yellowed piece of paper which he unfolded. The old woman saw to her amazement that it was a thousand-franc note, only the second or third that she had seen in her whole life. She fled in great alarm.

A few minutes later Valjean came up to her and asked her to be so good as to change the note, saying that it was the quarterly instalment of his income which he had drawn the day before. Where had he drawn it? she wondered. He had not left the house until six, by which time the State savings bank would be closed. She set off on her errand turning the matter over in her mind, and the thousand-franc note, embroidered and multiplied, became the subject of many excited conversations among the housewives of the Rue des Vignes-Saint-Marcel.

It happened a few days later that Jean Valjean, in his shirt-sleeves, was sawing firewood in the corridor, while the old woman tidied his room. She was there alone, Cosette being in the corridor with Valjean. The yellow coat was hanging from a nail and the old woman examined it. The lining had been re-stitched. Prodding it carefully with her fingers she seemed to feel thicknesses of paper in the tails and lapels – undoubtedly more thousand-franc notes!

She also discovered that there were a great many things in the pockets, not only the scissors, needle and thread that she had already seen, but also a fat wallet, a very large clasp-knife and, highly suspect, several wigs of different colours. Every pocket in the coat seemed to contain some kind of provision against a possible emergency.

Meanwhile the winter was drawing to a close.

V

The sound of a dropped coin

There was a beggar with a pitch beside a condemned public well near the church of Saint-Médard on whom Jean Valjean bestowed alms, rarely passing the spot without giving him a few sous. Sometimes he talked to him. But there were those who said that the beggar was a police informer. He was a one-time beadle, aged seventy-five, who constantly intoned prayers.

On a certain evening Valjean went that way unaccompanied by Cosette. The beggar was in his usual place, hard by a street-lamp that had just been lighted, squatting as usual with his body bent forward, apparently praying. Valjean stopped and thrust the customary gift into his hand. As he did so the beggar looked up and gazed searchingly at him, then quickly bowed his head. It had happened in an instant, but it gave Valjean a shock. He seemed to have caught a glimpse, by the light of the street-lamp, not of the vacant, devotional countenance of the beggar, but of quite another face that was already known to him. It was like suddenly encountering a tiger in the dark. He stepped back, frozen with alarm, not knowing whether to stay or run, to speak or be silent, and stared at the beggar who, with his head now hidden beneath a tattered covering, seemed to have forgotten his existence. In that critical moment some instinct of self-preservation restrained Jean Valjean from speaking a word. The beggar looked precisely as usual, the same huddled figure, the same rags. 'I'm mad,' thought Valjean. 'I'm dreaming. The thing's impossible.' Nevertheless he returned home in a state of profound disquiet, scarcely daring to admit, even to himself, that the face he thought he had glimpsed was that of Javert.

Pondering the matter that night, he regretted not having spoken to the man so as to oblige him to raise his head again. The next evening he went back and found him there as usual. 'Good evening, old man,' he said resolutely and handed him a sou. The beggar looked up and said in a quavering voice, 'Thank you, thank you, kind sir.' It was unquestionably the old beadle.

Valjean was so entirely reassured that he could laugh at himself. 'How the deuce could I have mistaken him for Javert? I'm beginning to see things.' And he thought no more about it.

At about eight o'clock a few evenings later, when he was giving Cosette a reading-lesson in his room, he heard the street door of the house open and close. This was unusual. The old woman, the house's only other inhabitant, always went to bed at nightfall to save candles. Jean Valjean signed to Cosette to keep quiet. Someone was coming up the stairs. It was possible that the old woman, feeling unwell, had gone out to the apothecary. The footsteps on the stairs sounded like those of a man; but she wore heavy shoes, and nothing sounds more like the footsteps of a man than those of an old woman. Nevertheless, Valjean blew out his candle.

He sent Cosette to her room, telling her in a low voice to go quietly, and as he was in the act of kissing her on the forehead the footsteps ceased. Jean Valjean stayed silent and motionless, still seated in his chair with his back to the door and holding his breath. After a while, having heard nothing more, he turned cautiously round and saw through a crevice in the door a gleam of light that was like a sinister star in the surrounding darkness. Someone with a candle was outside.

Several minutes passed and then the light vanished. But there was no sound of footsteps, which suggested that the person listening at the door had removed his shoes. Valjean flung himself fully clad on his bed and did not close his eyes all night.

At daybreak, when he was on the verge of falling asleep, he was aroused by the creaking of a door along the corridor; then he heard footsteps sounding like those of the person who had climbed the stairs the night before. He leapt up and put an eye to his keyhole, which was a large one, hoping to catch a glimpse of the intruder. It was a man, as he had suspected, and this time he went past Valjean's room without stopping. The corridor was too dark for his face to be visible, but as he reached the top of the stairs he was silhouetted against the light coming from outside and Valjean had a full view of him from behind. He saw a tall man clad in a long tail-coat with a cudgel under his arm. A man with the formidable outline of Javert.

Valjean might have tried to get a better look at him through the window overlooking the boulevard, but this would have entailed opening the window, which he was afraid to do. Clearly the man had used a key to enter the house. But who had provided him with a key? What did it mean?

When the old woman came in at seven to do the room, Valjean looked hard at her but asked no questions. Her manner was unchanged. As she was sweeping the floor she said:

'Did monsieur hear someone come in last night?'

To a person of her age, living on that boulevard, eight o'clock was the same as midnight.

'Now you mention it, I did,' he answered casually. 'Who was it?'

'It was the new tenant. He has just moved in.'

'What is his name?'

'I don't exactly remember. A Monsieur Dumont or Daumont – something like that.'

'And what kind of man is he, this Monsieur Dumont?'

She looked at him with her small, foxy eyes and said:

'He's a rentier – like you.'

The words may have had no especial intention, but Valjean believed that the discerned one.

When the old woman had left, he made a roll of the coins he kept in a drawer, about a hundred francs, and put it in his pocket. Although he did this with care, so that the chink of money should not be heard, a five-franc piece fell out of his hand and rolled noisily across the floor.

At dusk he went downstairs and looked cautiously up and down the boulevard. It seemed to be entirely deserted, although there could be people hidden behind the trees.

He went upstairs again and said to Cosette, 'Come along.'

He took her hand and they left the house together.

BOOK FIVE

HUNT IN DARKNESS

I

Twists and turns

AT THIS point, in view of what follows and because of matters coming later in the story, a word of explanation is called for.

For some years past the author of this book, who regrets the necessity to speak of himself, has been absent from Paris. During this time the city has been transformed. A new city has arisen which to him is in some sort unknown. He has no need to say that he loves Paris, which is his spiritual home. But in the process of demolition and reconstruction, the Paris of his youth, of which he cherishes the memory, has become a Paris of the past. He must be allowed to talk of that Paris as though it still existed. It may well be that he will refer to a particular house in a particular street where today neither house nor street is to be found. The reader may verify such details if he thinks it worth the trouble. For the author's part, not knowing the new Paris, he writes of the one he knew and still treasures; it pleases him to suppose that something of it remains, and that not everything has vanished. Going about one's native land one is inclined to take many things for granted, roads and buildings, roofs, windows and doorways, the walls that shelter strangers, the house one has never entered, trees which are like other trees, pavements which are no more than cobblestones. But when we are distant from them we find that those things have become dear to us, a street, trees and roofs, blank walls, doors and windows; we have entered those houses without knowing it, we have left something of our heart in the very stonework. Those places we no longer see, perhaps will never see again but still remember, have acquired an aching charm; they return to us with the melancholy of ghosts, a hallowed vision and as it were the true face of France. We love and evoke them such as they were; and such as to us they still are, we cling to them and will not have them altered, for the face of our country is our mother's face.

The author, then, begs leave to treat of the past as though it were the present, and, asking the reader to make allowance for this, continues his tale.

Jean Valjean at once moved off the boulevard and into the side streets, constantly changing direction and now and then turning back to put any possible pursuer off the scent. It was the manoeuvre of the hunted stag, known to huntsmen as 'doubling in his tracks', which has the advantage, in country where a visible trail is left, that one set of tracks covers another.

The night was one of full moon, and this suited him. The moon, still low on the horizon, broke up the streets in patches of light and darkness. He could keep to the shadows and see what went on in the light. Perhaps he was too much inclined to ignore what might be lurking in the darkness; but nevertheless, in the network of deserted streets round the Rue de Poliveau, he felt reasonably sure that he was not being followed.

Cosette walked unquestioningly beside him. The hardships of the first six years of her life had taught her a passive stoicism. More-over, and we shall have occasion to refer to this again, she had grown accustomed to the idiosyncrasies of the man and the unex-pectedness of life in general, and she felt safe in his protection.

Jean Valjean knew no more than she where they were going, trusting to God as she trusted to himself. He, too, felt that his hand clasped that of a Being greater than himself, and it was as though some invisible presence were guiding him. But he had no clear idea of what he should do next, no considered plan. He was not even sure that the man he had seen was Javert, and if it were it did not follow that Javert had known him for Jean Valjean. Was he not disguised? Was he not believed to be dead? But strange things had happened in the past few hours and he could not disregard them. He was resolved never to return to the Gorbeau tenement. Like an animal driven from its lair he was looking for a temporary refuge, while he sought a safer lodging.

Their roundabout course brought them to the quarter of the Rue Mouffetard, as profoundly asleep at that hour as though this were the middle ages and the curfew still in force. They passed through a number of streets, the Rue Censier, the Rue Copeau, the Rue du Battoir-Saint-Victor, and the Rue du Puits-l'Ermite, in which there were lodging-houses, but none that suited Valjean. He could still not be sure, if after all he was being pursued, that he had wholly covered his tracks.

Eleven o'clock was sounding from the church of Saint-Étienne-du-Mont as they passed outside the police post in the Rue Pontoise, which was on the dark side of the street. A moment later the instinct to which we have referred prompted him to look back. He was in time to see, by the light of the lantern over the doorway of the post, the figures of three men moving in his direction, one of whom went into the building. The leader of the party looked to him decidedly suspect.

'Come, child,' he said to Cosette and hurriedly left the Rue Pontoise.

He made a detour, by-passing the Passage des Patriaches, which was closed at that hour, and following the Rue de l'Épée-de-Bois and the Rue de l'Arbalète, came to the Rue des Postes. Here, on what is now the site of the Collège Rollin, there was an open space at the junction of the Rue des Postes and the Rue Neuve-Sainte-Geneviève. (It goes without saying that the Rue Neuve-Sainte-Geneviève is far from being a new street, nor do post-carts travel along the Rue des Postes; in the thirteenth century it was a street of potters and its true name is Rue des Pots.)

The open space was bathed in moonlight and Valjean took refuge in a doorway, reckoning that if the men were still following him he could not fail to see them as they crossed over. And indeed, less than three minutes later they appeared. There were now four of them, tall men in brown tail-coats wearing round hats and carrying truncheons. No less sinister than their size and powerful build was their stealthy progress through that shadowed world. They were like ghosts disguised as citizens.

They stopped in the middle of the intersection and stood in a group as though consulting together. They seemed undecided. The one who appeared to be their leader turned and pointed energetically in the direction Valjean had taken, but another seemed equally convinced that they should go the opposite way. When the first man turned the moon shone full on his face, and Valjean now knew that it was Javert.

II

The Pont d'Austerlitz

This was the end of uncertainty for Jean Valjean but, fortunately for him, not for that of his pursuers. Their loss of time was his gain, and taking advantage of their indecision he left the doorway in which he had been hiding and retreated along the Rue des Postes in the direction of the Jardin des Plantes. Cosette was beginning to tire, so he picked her up and carried her. There was no one about and the street lamps had not been lighted because of the brightness of the moon.

Increasing his speed, he came in a few strides to the Poterie Goblet on the façade of which was still to be seen the ancient inscription proclaiming its wares – 'Jugs and jars, flower-pots, drain-pipes, tiles.' Passing the Rue de la Clef and the Fontaine Saint-Victor, he rounded the Jardin des Plantes by the streets at its lower end and so came to the river embankment. Here he turned to take stock of his position. The embankment, like the streets he had passed through, was deserted. He breathed again.

At the Pont d'Austerlitz, which in those days was still a toll-bridge, he went to the toll-collector's box and offered him a sou. 'Two sous,' said the war-veteran who kept the bridge. 'You're carrying a child who is able to walk. You must pay for two.'

He did so, annoyed at having thus drawn attention to himself. All flight should go unnoticed. A large cart came up at this moment, making like himself for the right bank of the river, and this was helpful to him; by walking beside it he could cross over in its shadow. Halfway across Cosette, whose legs were growing stiff, said that she would rather walk. He put her down and took her hand.

Across the river he saw timber yards a short distance to his right and decided to make for these. In order to reach them he had to cross a wide open space, but he did so without hesitation, believing that he had thrown his pursuers off the scent and was for the moment out of danger – pursued but not closely followed.

Between the walls of two of the yards there was a dark and narrow street, the Rue du Chemin-Vert-Saint-Antoine, which seemed to be exactly what he was looking for.

Before entering it, however, he turned and looked back. From where he stood he could see the whole length of the Pont d'Austerlitz. He saw four shadowy figures at the far end. They were coming away from the Jardin des Plantes, heading for the right bank.

So after all he had not lost them. Valjean quivered like a hunted animal finding the hounds still on its trail. One hope remained to him. It was possible that the four men had not reached the bridge in time to see him cross the open space hand-in-hand with Cosette. In that event, by following this narrow lane, he might find himself in a region of timber-yards or cultivated plots or waste-land where he would have a good chance of escaping them. The silent, narrow lane looked safe, so he entered it.

A vanished quarter

After some three hundred yards the lane forked. Valjean found himself confronted by the arms of a Y. Which to choose? Without hesitation he went to the right.

He did so because the left fork led in the general direction of the town, back to inhabited places, whereas the right led away from the town, towards open country.

He was no longer walking fast, being obliged by Cosette to go more slowly. He picked her up again and carried her, and she rested her head on his shoulder without speaking. He looked back from time to time, along the straight length of lane behind him. The first two or three times he did this he saw and heard nothing and, somewhat reassured, he continued on his way. But then, as he turned his head again, he seemed to detect a distant movement amid the shadows through which he had passed. He hurried on, more running than walking, hoping to come to a cross-road which would again enable him to put their pursuers off the track.

He came to a wall. It was not a wall which prevented all progress, being the boundary-wall of a lane crossing the end of the one he was following. Once again he had to decide between left and right.

He looked right. The new lane ran past a cluster of buildings which were either warehouses or barns and then came to a stop, ending in a high white wall that was clearly visible. To the left, however, it was open, debouching after a hundred yards or so into a wider street. Clearly he must go this way.

But as he was about to turn left he saw, standing at the end of the lane where it entered the street, a dark figure motionless as a statue. It seemed that a man had been posted there to bar his passage.

The part of Paris which Valjean had now reached, situated between the Faubourg Saint-Antoine and La Rapée, was one of those which have been completely transformed by recent developments, rendered hideous according to some people and improved according to others. The market-gardens, the timber-yards, and other old buildings have all gone, to be replaced by broad new streets, amphi-theatres, circuses, hippodromes, railway-stations, and a prison – progress accompanied by its corrective.

Half a century ago, in the language of common use, deriving so largely from tradition, which persists in referring to the Institut de France as 'les Quatre-Nations' and to the Opéra-comique as 'Fey-deau', this particular part of Paris was known as 'le Petit-Picpus'.* The Porte Saint-Jacques, the Porte Paris, the Barrière des Sergents, the Porcherons, La Galiote, Les Célestins, Les Capucins, Le Mail, La Bourbe, L'Arbre-de-Cracovie, La Petite-Pologne, Le Petit-Picpus, all these are names surviving from the old Paris into the new. Popular memory lives on the relics of the past.

Le Petit-Picpus, which scarcely existed and was never more than the approximation of a quarter, had something of the monkish aspect of a Spanish town. Its streets were poorly paved, its houses scattered. Except for the two or three streets with which we are concerned it was a region of walls and open spaces, without shops or vehicles, with only an occasional candle to be seen in a window and where all lights were extinguished after ten. Gardens, con-vents, timber-yards, and marshes; a few single-storeyed houses enclosed in walls as high as themselves.

Such was the quarter in the last century. It was roughly handled by the revolution, the aediles of the Republic having pulled down houses, run roads through it and established rubbish-dumps. Thirty years ago it began to disappear under the spread of new develop-ment, and today it has completely vanished. No present map of Paris contains any reference to Le Petit-Picpus, although it is clearly indicated on the 1727 map, published in Paris by Denis Thierry, Rue Saint-Jacques, and in Lyon by Jean Girin, Rue Mercière. Le Petit-Picpus centred around what we have called a Y of streets formed by the forking of the Rue du Chemin-Vert-Saint-Antoine, the left fork being the Petite Rue Picpus and the right the Rue Polonceau. What may be termed a cross-bar united the two arms of the fork, its name being the Rue Droit-Mur. The Rue Polonceau ended there, but the Rue Picpus went on in the direction of the Marché Lenoir. Whoever came from the Seine and reached the end of the Rue Polonceau had to his left the length of the Rue Droit-Mur, with its wall directly facing him, and to his right a

* An imaginary quarter broadly based by Hugo on the Quartier Saint-Victor.

short extension of the same street, with no outlet, known as the Cul-de-sac Genrot.

This was where Jean found himself.

Seeing the dark form at the corner of the Rue Droit-Mur and the Rue Picpus, he started back. There could be no doubt that the man was on the watch for him.

What was he to do? His retreat was cut off. The movement he had detected some distance behind him must mean that Javert was there with the rest of his party. Javert, evidently familiar with that maze of alleyways, had sent one of his men to cover the exit. Conjectures, so near to certainties, poured through Valjean's troubled mind like dust stirred by a gust of wind. He studied the Rue Picpus; that way a sentry stood on guard – the dark figure as he stared towards it was sharply silhouetted against the moonlit pavement. To go on was to fall foul of him; to go back was to fall into the hands of Javert. Valjean felt himself caught in a net that was slowly tightening. He looked despairingly up at the sky.

I V

Ways of escape

To understand what follows calls for a precise picture of the Rue Droit-Mur and in particular of the sharp turning which was on the walker's left as he entered this lane from the Rue Polonceau. The Rue Droit-Mur was almost entirely flanked on the right, as far as the Rue Picpus, by poor-looking houses; and on the left by a stark composite building made up of several sections which increased in height as they approached the Rue Picpus, so that the building was lofty at its far end but low at the end nearest the Rue Polonceau. Here, at the turning, it was nothing but a wall. But this wall did not exactly follow the line of the street; it was deeply recessed, so that anything within the recess was hidden from observers standing at a distance from it in the Rue Polonceau or the Rue Droit-Mur.

The wall on either side of this recess ran along the Rue Polonceau as far as a house bearing the number 49, and along the Rue Droit-Mur, where it was far shorter, to the building we have described, joining it under the gable and thus forming another re-entrant angle. This gabled façade was forbidding in appearance, having only one window, or rather, a pair of permanently closed vine-covered shutters.

The back of the recess was entirely filled by something that looked like a huge and crudely constructed doorway, a vast, shapeless assembly of perpendicular planks, those above wider than those below, the whole held together with long transverse strips of metal. At one side there was a *porte-cochère* of ordinary dimensions which had evidently been installed within the past fifty years. The branches of a lime tree hung over the wall, which at the Rue Polonceau end was covered with ivy.

To Jean Valjean, in his perilous situation, the apparent solitude and remoteness of the building had their attractions. He looked it over rapidly, feeling that if he could get inside he might be safe. Hope dawned in him.

Adjacent to all the windows on each floor of the central part of the building was the open mouth of an old leaden drain-pipe. These numerous pipes, all leading to a central conduit, formed a pattern not unlike that of a grape-vine trained up a farmhouse wall. This was the first thing that struck Valjean. Seating Cosette with her back to the wall, and telling her not to make a sound, he ran to the spot where the conduit reached the ground, thinking that perhaps the pipes might enable him to climb into the building. But the conduit was rotten with age and its fastenings far from secure; moreover all the windows were closely barred, even the dormer windows in the roof. In addition, the whole front of the house was bathed in moonlight, so that the observer at the end of the lane would certainly see him if he attempted the climb. And finally, would he be able to carry Cosette up the façade of a three-storey house?

He gave up this idea and crept back to the recess. Here at least he could not be seen, and it might be possible for him to force the door. The ivy-clad wall, above which the branches of the lime tree showed, must surely enclose a garden in which, despite the absence of foliage, they might be able to hide for the rest of the night.

Time was passing. He had to move fast. He tried the *porte-cochère* and discovered at once that it was fastened on both sides. The main door looked more hopeful. It was in a thoroughly dilapidated state, and the more vulnerable because of its great size; the planks were rotten and the iron bands holding them together, of which there were only three, were badly rusted. But when he came to examine it he found that this door was not a door at all; there were no hinges, no lock and no division at the centre. The iron bands ran without a break from one side to the other. Peering through the gaps between the planks, he could see roughly cemented stonework beyond them. He had to conclude, to his consternation, that what looked like a door was simply woodwork concealing a building. He might remove a plank, but then he would be faced by a wall.

V
Impossible by gas-light

At this moment a muffled, regular sound became audible in the distance. Valjean ventured to peer out of the recess. Some seven or eight soldiers in two files had just entered the far end of the Rue Polonceau. He caught the gleam of bayonets. They were coming his way.

The squad, at the head of which he could discern the tall figure of Javert, was advancing slowly and cautiously, and making frequent pauses, evidently to investigate every nook and cranny, every side-alley and doorway. This could only mean that Javert, having fallen in with a military patrol, had taken it under his command and that his own two men were marching in its ranks.

From the speed of their advance, and their constant pauses, Valjean reckoned that it would take them perhaps a quarter of an hour to reach the place where he was. It was an appalling thought. Those few minutes were all that separated him from the abyss which now yawned before him for the third time. But this time it meant more than prison; it meant the loss of Cosette, a life that would be a living death.

There was only one possible way out.

Jean Valjean had the singularity that he might be said to be doubly endowed, on the one side with the aspirations of a saint, on the other with the formidable talents of a criminal. He could draw on either as the case required.

It will be recalled that among his other gifts, acquired in the course of his numerous escapes from the prison in Toulon, he was a past master of the art of climbing walls without artificial aids, simply by muscular strength and dexterity, using back, shoulders, and knees in any angle or chimney, and profiting by any roughness of surface which might afford a toe- or finger-hold. By these means he could climb as high as six storeys if necessary. It was a talent which had caused the corner of the courtyard of the Conciergerie in Paris, whereby the condemned criminal, Battemolle, had escaped, to become famous.

Valjean considered the wall at the point where the branches of the lime tree were visible above it. It was about eighteen feet high. The lower part of the angle it made with the big building was filled by a triangular block of masonry probably designed to prevent this convenient corner from being put to insanitary use. Such preventive devices are common in Paris.

The block was about five feet high, and the distance from it to the top of the wall was not more than another fourteen feet. The wall was flat-topped, without spikes or other obstacle.

The problem was Cosette. He had no thought of abandoning her, but to carry her up to the top of the wall was impossible. A man needed all the strength he possessed for this kind of climb; the least added burden would upset his centre of gravity and bring him down.

A rope was what he needed, but he had none. How could he hope to procure one at midnight in the Rue Polonceau? If Jean Valjean had possessed a kingdom he would certainly have exchanged it at that moment for a rope.

Extreme situations bring flashes which may blind or inspire us. Looking frantically about him, Valjean noticed the lamp-bracket in the Cul-de-sac Genrot.

At that time there was no gas-lighting in the streets of Paris. Oil-lamps hanging from widely-spaced brackets were used, and these were lowered for lighting by means of a stout cord, the end of which ran into a grooved post. The reel on which the cord was wound was enclosed in an iron box to which the lamp-lighter had a key, and the cord itself was encased in metal up to a certain height.

With the energy of desperation, Valjean darted across the end of the Rue Polonceau into the cul-de-sac, broke open the box with his knife and an instant later had rejoined Cosette. He had his length of rope. Men in the utmost necessity can move wonderfully fast.

As we have said, the lamps had not been lit that night because of the brightness of the moon. The lamp in the Cul-de-sac Genrot was extinguished like the rest, and any passer-by would have been unlikely to notice that it was not in its proper place. But meanwhile the lateness of the hour, the darkness, the strangeness of their surroundings and the singular behaviour of Jean Valjean were beginning to distress Cosette. Any other child would long since have been in tears. She did no more than tug at his coat-tails. And the sound of the approaching patrol was growing steadily louder.

'I'm frightened, father,' she said. 'Who's that coming?'

'Quiet!' the hard-pressed man replied. 'It's Madame Thénardier.' She started convulsively and he went on: 'Don't talk. Leave everything to me. If you make a sound she'll hear you. She's coming to fetch you back.'

Then, without haste but without fumbling, with a cool precision that was the more remarkable in that Javert and the patrol might arrive at any moment, he removed his cravat, passed it round Cosette under her armpits, adjusting it carefully so that it would not hurt her, tied the ends to one end of his rope, using the knot which sailors call a bowline, took the other end of the rope between his teeth, removed his shoes and stockings and tossed them over the wall, climbed on to the block of masonry and thence climbed up the angle formed by the wall and the end of the building, doing so with as much ease and certainty as if he had had stair-treads under his elbows and heels. Within half a minute he was kneeling on top of the wall.

Cosette stared up at him in amazement, frozen to silence by the mention of Mme Thénardier. Then she heard his voice calling to her in a whisper.

'Stand with your back to the wall.' She did so. 'Don't make a sound and don't be afraid.'

She felt herself lifted off the ground. Before she had time to realize what was happening she too was on the wall. Jean Valjean seized hold of her and put her on his back. Grasping both her hands in one of his, he crawled on his stomach along the top of the wall until he reached the recess. As he had guessed, on the other side of the wood-work that had looked like a door there was a small building of which the sloping roof at its highest point was on a level with the wall. Fortunately the lime tree was very near, because the ground was considerably lower on this side than on the other. From where he crouched it looked a long way down.

He had just slipped down on to the roof of the buildings, but without letting go of the top of the wall, when a hubbub of voices announced the arrival of the patrol. Javert bellowed:

'Search the cul-de-sac! The Rue Droit-Mur and the Rue Picpus are both covered. I'll swear he's in the cul-de-sac!'

The soldiers dashed along the Cul-de-sac Genrot.

Jean Valjean let himself slide down the roof, still with Cosette on his back, and with the help of the lime tree dropped to the ground. Whether from terror or bravery, Cosette had not uttered a sound. Her hands were slightly grazed.

VI

Beginning of a puzzle

Jean Valjean found himself in a rather strange garden, one of those that seem made to be seen only in winter and by night. It was oblong in shape, with a poplar-walk along the far side, tall shrubs at the corners, and at the centre a cleared space in which a solitary, very large tree was to be seen, a few gnarled and stunted fruit-trees, vegetable-plots, a melon-patch with glass cloches gleaming in the moonlight and an old well-head. Here and there were stone benches seemingly covered with moss. The paths, which all ran straight, were bordered with small bushes and overgrown with moss and grass.

Valjean was standing beside the building whose roof he had used in his descent, with a pile of faggots at his side and, against the wall behind the faggots, a stone statue of which the face was so mutilated that it looked in the darkness like a shapeless mask. The building itself, which was in ruins, was divided into a number of small rooms, in one of which was a clutter of objects and apparently served as a storage shed.

The large building extending along the Rue Droit-Mur to the Petite Rue Picpus overlooked this garden in a double frontage forming a right-angle, its general appearance even more forbidding than on the street side. All the windows were barred and those on the upper storey were hooded like the windows of a prison. No light showed. One part of this double façade was buried in the shadow of the other, which lay like a black carpet over the garden.

No other house was to be seen. The end of the garden was lost in mist and darkness; but the tops of adjoining walls could be discerned, suggesting that there were cultivated plots of land beyond it, and the low roofs of the houses in the Rue Polonceau were also visible.

Any place more lonely and desolate it would have been hard to imagine. That the garden was deserted at that hour was understandable; but there was nothing about it to suggest that anyone ever walked there, even by day.

Jean Valjean's first act was to retrieve his shoes and stockings, after which he and Cosette entered the storage-shed. No fugitive ever feels wholly secure. With the thought of Mme Thénardier in her mind, the child's instinct was to hide. She clung to him trembling. Outside they could hear the noise of the patrol searching the cul-de-sac, the clatter of musket-butts on the cobbles, the voice of Javert calling to the man he had posted on guard and his stream of imprecations mingled with words that they did not catch.

Time passed and the commotion seemed to be receding. Valjean was still holding his breath. He had laid a hand gently over Cosette's mouth. Throughout this time the solitude in which they found themselves remained miraculously calm and wholly untroubled by the furious hubbub proceeding from so close at hand, as though the walls were built of the unheeding stones of which the Scriptures speak.

But suddenly, amid this profound tranquillity, a new sound arose, a sound both exquisite and divine, as ravishing to the senses as those other sounds were horrible. A hymn rose out of the shadows, an outburst of prayer and harmony in the dark and terrible silence of the night. The voices were those of women, blending the pure accents of virgins with the innocent tones of children, voices not of this earth, resembling the notes still ringing in the ears of the newly-born and those which reach the ears of the dying. The singing came from the gloomy edifice overlooking the garden. It was as though, while the howling of demons faded away in the distance, a chorus of angels had taken its place.

Cosette and Jean Valjean fell on their knees. They did not know the meaning of this or where they were, but both felt instinctively – man and child, penitent and innocent – that they must kneel. The singing had the strange quality that it did not rob the building of its apparent solitude, but was like a supernatural song issuing from an empty house.

While the singing continued Jean Valjean was bereft of thought, no longer conscious of the darkness but seeing a blue sky, feeling the spread of those wings that are a part of all of us. When it died down he could not have said whether it had lasted a long or a short time. The hour of ecstasy may be no more than an instant.

And now all was silence, nothing more to be heard in the street or in the garden. The threat and the reassurance, both had vanished. Only the stir of dried grass in the breeze made a soft and mournful sound.

VII
Continuation of the puzzle

A night breeze had risen, which suggested that it must be between one and two in the morning. Cosette was silent, and since she was sitting with her head against him, Valjean supposed that she had fallen asleep. But when he bent to look at her he saw that her eyes were wide open and staring with an expression that shocked him. She was shivering.

'Aren't you sleepy?' he asked.

'I'm cold . . .' And then after a moment she said: 'Is she still there?'

'Who?'

'Madame Thénardier.'

He had forgotten the means he had used to ensure her silence.

'No,' he said. 'She's gone. You have nothing to fear.'

She sighed as though a great weight had been lifted from her spirit.

The earth floor of the shed was damp, and the shed itself was open on all sides to the growing breeze. He took off his coat and wrapped her in it.

'Is that better?'

'Yes, father.'

'Lie down and wait for me. I'll be back very soon.'

Leaving the shed, he began to explore the outside of the large building in the hope of finding a better place of refuge. He came to doors but they were all locked, and all the ground-floor windows were barred. Crossing the interior angle of the building, he came to a row of arched windows beyond which was a faint light. Standing on tip-toe, he peered in at one of these. He was looking into a spacious room or hall, paved with large flagstones and broken with pillars, in which nothing was at first visible except masses of shadow and the dim glow of a night-light in one corner. The place was deserted and nothing moved in it. But after staring for some time he seemed to discern, lying on the stone floor, something that looked like a human form covered by a shroud. It was lying face down with its arms crossed in the posture of death; and a thin line trailing like a snake over the flags suggested that it had a rope round its neck. The misty half-darkness of the place added to the horror of this sight.

Jean Valjean was to say afterwards that in a life which had witnessed many terrors he had seen nothing more chilling to the blood than that inexplicable figure enacting some mysterious rite in those sombre surroundings. It was terrifying to suppose the figure dead; more terrifying still to suppose that it was alive.

Summoning his resolution, he pressed his face to the window-pane and remained there for what seemed to him a long time, seeking to discern in the figure some sign of life. But he saw no movement, and suddenly, being seized with a sense of inexpressible terror, he turned and ran. He ran back to the shed, not venturing to look round lest he see the figure bounding after him with waving arms. He was gasping by the time he reached the shed, his knees giving way and the sweat running down his back.

Where was he? Who could have imagined anything of the kind in a sort of sepulchre in the heart of Paris? What was this place of nocturnal mystery where angel voices cried out to the soul and, when it answered the summons, offered it a vision of horror, promising the radiance of Heaven and providing the blackness of the tomb? Yet it was a real house with a numbered doorway giving on to a street. It was not a dream. He had to touch the stones in order to convince himself of this.

The coldness of the night, its many stresses and anxieties and the present bewilderment of his mind, all this had rendered him feverish. He bent over Cosette and found that she was asleep.

VIII

The puzzle deepens

Cosette had fallen asleep with her head resting on a stone. He sat down beside her, and gradually, as he gazed at her, he grew calmer and recovered his wits.

He now clearly perceived the truth which was henceforth to be the centre of his life, namely, that while she was there, while he had her near him, he would need nothing except for her sake and fear nothing except on her account. He was not even conscious of feeling extremely cold, having taken off his coat to cover her.

He sat thinking, and only by degrees became aware of an odd sound that he had been unconsciously hearing for some time. It came from within the garden, the sound of a bell tinkling, faint but distinct, like a sheep-bell in the fields at night.

The sound caused him to turn his head, and, peering, he saw that there was someone else in the garden. A person, seemingly a man, was walking amid the rows of cloches on the melon-patch, pausing, stooping, and straightening with regular movements as though spreading something over the ground. He appeared to be limping.

Jean Valjean drew back with the instinctive recoil of the hunted, for whom all things are hostile and suspect. They fear daylight because it may cause them to be seen, and darkness because they may be taken by surprise. It was not long since the loneliness of the garden had caused him to shudder, but now he trembled because someone was there.

Turning abruptly from fanciful terrors to real ones, he reflected that perhaps Javert and his helpers were still in the vicinity, that very likely a man had been left to keep watch in the street, and that if this individual in the garden were to see him he would cry out and give the alarm. Taking the sleeping Cosette gently in his arms, he carried her behind a pile of old, disused furniture in the furthest corner of the shed. She did not stir.

He then resumed his observation of the man in the melon-patch. What was strange was that each of his movements was accompanied by this tinkle of a bell, which sounded more loudly when he was nearer, fainter as he moved away. If he made a rapid movement the tinkle became a tremolo; only when he was motionless was the bell silent. Clearly it was attached to him; but what *did* that mean? What kind of man was it who was 'belled' like a wether or a cow?

While he was wondering about this he felt Cosette's hands. They were ice-cold.

'Oh, God!' he exclaimed; and he said in a low voice, 'Cosette!' She did not open her eyes.

He shook her vigorously, but she did not wake.

'Is she dead?' he thought and stood upright, trembling from head to foot.

Appalling thoughts ran through his mind. There are times when the fears that assail us are like a regiment of furies beating at the walls of our brain. Where those we love are affected terror knows no bounds. He reflected that sleep in the open air may prove fatal on a cold night.

The child was lying motionless at his feet. He bent and listened to her breathing, which seemed to him so weak that at any moment it might cease.

How could he warm her? How revive her? He had no thought for anything but this.

He ran despairingly out of the shed. Whatever happened, within a quarter of an hour Cosette must be in a warm place and in bed.

IX

The man with the bell

He made straight for the man on the melon-patch, holding in his hand the roll of coins that had been in his waistcoat pocket. The man was bending down and did not see him. Valjean went up to him and said without preliminaries:

'A hundred francs!'

The man started and looked up.

'A hundred francs for you,' Valjean repeated, 'if you can give me shelter for tonight.'

The moonlight shone full on his tormented face.

'Why,' said the man, 'why, it's you, Père Madeleine!'

The sound of his own name, spoken at that hour and in that place by an unknown person, caused Valjean to start in utter amazement. He had been prepared for anything except this. The speaker was a bent and crippled old man clad in working garments, with a leather kneeling-pad on his left knee to which a fair sized bell was fixed. His face, which was in shadow, was not clearly visible. He took off his cap and burst into a torrent of quavering speech.

'In God's name how do you come to be here, Père Madeleine? How did you get in? It's as though you'd fallen from the sky, and that's no joke because if you fell from anywhere that's where it would be. But look at you, the clothes you're wearing – no necktie, no hat, no overcoat! You'd have scared the life out of me if I hadn't recognized you. But what's the meaning of it? Have even the saints gone crazy? How in the world did you get in?'

The words tumbled over one another in a stream of country volubility that was in no way disquieting, a mingling of bewilderment and innocent goodwill.

'Who are you, and what is this place?' Jean Valjean asked.

'What! Well, that's rich! I'm the man you put here, and this is the place you put me in. Do you mean to say you don't know me?'

'No. Nor do I understand how you know me.'

'You saved my life,' the old man said.

He turned, and the moonlight falling upon his face revealed the features of Fauchelevent, who had once been nearly crushed to death beneath a cart.

'Ah,' said Valjean. 'Yes. I know you now.'

'So I should hope,' the old man said reproachfully.

'But what are you doing out here at this hour?'

'I'm covering up my melons, d'you see.'

Fauchelevent still held in his hand the strip of straw matting which he had been in the act of spreading on the ground when Valjean had surprised him. He had been thus employed for some time, and it was this that accounted for the movements that Valjean had watched from the shed.

'I said to myself, well it's a fine, clear night and there's going to be a frost, so I might as well get my melons into their jackets.' He laughed. 'What's more, it's what you'd have done yourself in my place. But how do you come to be here?'

Finding himself known to the old man, at least by the name of Madeleine, Jean Valjean was still on his guard. He went on to question him in a strange reversal of roles, the midnight intruder become interrogator.

'What's that bell you're wearing on your knee?'

'That?' said Fauchelevent. 'That's to warn people off.'

'But why should anyone be warned off?'

The old man wagged his head and grinned.

'Bless you, there's nothing but women in this place, a lot of them young girls. It seems it might be dangerous for them to meet me. When they hear the bell they keep their distance.'

'But what is this place?'

'Go on, you must surely know.'

'I assure you I don't.'

'But seeing you got me the job here as gardener.'

'I still don't understand. You will have to tell me.'

'Why, then, it's the Convent of the Petit-Picpus.'

And then Valjean remembered. Chance, but it is better to say Providence, had led him to the very convent in the Saint-Antoine quarter where old Fauchelevent, crippled after his accident, had been engaged on his recommendation. That had happened two years ago. Valjean repeated, as though to himself, 'The Convent of the Petit-Picpus!'

'Now we've got that straight,' said Fauchelevent, 'perhaps you'll tell me, Père Madeleine, how the devil you managed to get in here? You may be a saint but you're also a man, and men aren't admitted.'

'But you're here.'

'I'm the only one.'

'All the same,' said Jean Valjean, 'I've got to stop here.'

'Lord preserve us!' exclaimed Fauchelevent.

Valjean drew close to him and said in a grave voice:

'Père Fauchelevent, I once saved your life.'

'I've just reminded you of it.'

'Well, now you can do as much for me.'

At this Fauchelevent clasped Jean Valjean's powerful hands in his own gnarled and wrinkled ones and for a moment was too moved for speech. Then he burst out:

'I thank God if I can repay something of what I owe you. To save your life! Monsieur le Maire, I am at your service!' His face was transfigured, and it was as though a light shone from it. 'What do you want me to do?'

'I'll tell you. Have you a room?'

'I have a sort of cottage beyond the ruins of the old convent. No one ever comes near it. There are three rooms.'

The cottage was in fact so well hidden beyond the ruins that Valjean had not noticed it.

'I must ask two things of you,' he said. 'First, that you will tell no one what you know about me. And secondly, that you will not seek to know more than you already do.'

'As you please. I know that you will do nothing dishonourable and that you have always been a God-fearing man, besides which, you got me my employment here. Your affairs are no business of mine. I am yours to command.'

'Thank you. Now I will ask you to come with me. We must fetch the child.'

'Ah,' said Fauchelevent. 'So there's a child.'

He followed Jean Valjean without another word, like a dog following its master.

Less than half an hour later Cosette, rosy once more in the

warmth of a good fire, was asleep in the old gardener's bed. Jean Valjean had put on his cravat and coat and retrieved the hat which he had thrown over the wall. While he was doing so Fauchelevent had removed his knee-pad with its bell, and it now decorated the wall, hanging on a nail by the fireside. The two men sat warming themselves with their elbows on a table on which Fauchelevent had set a morsel of cheese, bread, a bottle of wine, and two glasses. Laying a hand on Valjean's knee he said:

'So, Père Madeleine, you didn't recognize me at once. You save men's lives and then forget them. That's bad. They don't forget you. You are ungrateful, Père Madeleine!'

X

Which tells how Javert drew a blank

The events of which we have witnessed the reverse side, so to speak, had come about in a very simple fashion.

When Jean Valjean escaped from the prison in Montreuil-sur-mer, on the evening of the day when Javert arrested him at Fantine's bedside, the police had supposed that he would make for Paris. Paris is a whirlpool in which all things can be lost, sucked into that navel of the earth like flotsam into the navel of the sea. No forest can hide a man so well as its teeming streets, a fact well known to all kinds of fugitive. It is also known to the police, who scour Paris for what they have lost elsewhere. Javert was summoned to Paris to assist in the search for Valjean and had played an important part in his recapture. His zeal and energy on that occasion attracted the notice of M. Chapouillet, the secretary of the Prefecture under Comte Anglès. M. Chapouillet, who had interested himself in Javert in the past, had him transferred from Montreuil-sur-mer to Paris, where he rendered useful and, inappropriate though the word may appear in connection with such a calling, honourable service.

He thought no more about Jean Valjean (to a hound for ever on the scent, today's wolf causes yesterday's to be forgotten) until in December 1823 he saw his name in a newspaper. Javert was not a reader of newspapers, but as an ardent monarchist he was interested in the account of the landing of the 'prince generalissimo' at Bayonne. Having read this, he glanced over the rest of the paper and his eye fell on a paragraph at the bottom of a page reporting the death of the convict Jean Valjean. The statement was so positive that he had no reason to doubt it, and reflecting that it was a good riddance, he dismissed the matter from his mind.

Some time after his transfer a report was received in Paris from the Prefecture of Seine-et-Oise concerning the abduction of a child under peculiar circumstances in the commune of Montfermeil. The child, a girl of seven or eight, had been entrusted by her mother to a local innkeeper and had been 'stolen', in the words of the report, by a stranger. The child was named Cosette, and the mother was a woman named Fantine who had died in hospital, details not known. The report came Javert's way and it made him think.

He had not forgotten Fantine; nor had he forgotten that Jean Valjean had caused him to burst out laughing by asking for three days' respite so that he might go and fetch the woman's child. He recalled that Valjean had been arrested in the act of boarding the coach for Montfermeil. Moreover, there had been grounds for suspecting that this would not have been his first visit to Montfermeil and that he had been in the neighbourhood of the village on the previous day, although he had not been seen in the village itself. No one had understood at the time what had taken him to Montfermeil, but this was now clear to Javert. He had gone there for Fantine's child. And now the child had been abducted by a stranger. Could the stranger be Valjean? But Valjean was reported dead. Without saying anything to anyone Javert took the coach to Montfermeil.

He had gone there expecting enlightenment and had found only mystification.

In their first disappointment the Thénardiers had talked, and the story of 'the Lark's' disappearance had gone round the village. Various versions had circulated, culminating in the tale of abduction. Hence the police report. But after recovering from his sense of grievance Thénardier, with his admirable instinct of caution, had been quick to realize that it is never wise to attract the notice of Authority, and that a formal complaint about kidnapping would cause the eagle-eye of the Law to be turned upon himself and his many dubious transactions. The last thing an owl wants is to be examined by the light of a lamp. How, in particular, was he to account for the fifteen hundred francs he had accepted? He promptly changed his tune, put a gag on his wife, and expressed great astonishment when people talked as though the child had been stolen. He had been upset at the time by the speed with which she had been taken away; he would have liked, from sheer affection, to keep her a few days longer. But the gentleman who had come for her was her grandfather and it was only natural that he should want to have her. This was the story Javert heard when he arrived at Montfermeil. The 'grandfather', which was Thénardier's happy thought, eliminated Jean Valjean.

Nevertheless Javert tested the story with a few questions. Who was this grandfather and what was his name? Thénardier replied with perfect candour: 'He's a wealthy landowner. I saw his passport. I think his name is Monsieur Guillaume Lambert.' Lambert is a highly respectable name. Javert went back to Paris. 'Valjean is dead,' he said to himself, 'and I'm an ass.'

He was beginning to forget the whole affair when, in March 1824, a story reached him about an eccentric individual living in the parish of Saint-Médard who was known as 'the beggar who gives alms'. The man was said to be a person of independent means living with a small girl who knew nothing of their circumstances except that she herself came from Montfermeil. The name caused Javert to prick up his ears. An elderly beggar, a former beadle who was now a police-informer, supplied further details. The man was a very queer customer, never went out except at night, never spoke to anyone except occasionally to the poor, and never let anyone come near him. He wore a wretched old yellow overcoat which was probably worth millions because its lining was stuffed with banknotes . . . All this was decidedly interesting to Javert. In order to have a look at the queer customer he borrowed the ex-beadle's outer garments and the use of the pitch where he huddled every evening, intoning prayers and keeping his eyes open.

The 'suspect' duly appeared and gave the bogus mendicant money. Javert looked up as he did so, and Jean Valjean's shock when he thought he recognized the policeman was no greater than Javert's when he thought he recognized Jean Valjean. At the same time Javert realized that in the darkness he might have been mistaken. Valjean was officially dead. There was serious room for doubt, and Javert, scrupulous in all his dealings, did not lay hands on a man without being sure of his ground.

He followed his man to the Gorbeau tenement and got the old woman to talk, which was no difficult matter. She confirmed the detail of the overcoat lined with millions and told him about the thousand-franc note which she herself had handled. Javert rented a room in the tenement and occupied it that same evening. He listened at Valjean's door, hoping to hear the sound of his voice; but Valjean, seeing the light of his candle, foiled him by keeping silent.

Jean Valjean fled the next day; but the sound of the five-franc piece he let fall on the floor was overheard by the old woman, and hearing the chink of money she guessed that he intended to leave and hastened to warn Javert. When Valjean left the house that evening with Cosette, Javert was waiting for him, hidden with two men behind the trees along the boulevard.

Javert had applied to the Prefecture for full authorization but he had not disclosed the name of the person he hoped to arrest. He had kept this to himself for three reasons. First, because the least indiscretion might serve to warn Valjean; secondly, because to arrest an escaped convict who was believed to be dead, and whose record in the official files was that of a 'highly-dangerous criminal' would be a tremendous feather in his cap which would be resented by the old hands of the Paris police-force, who might try to rob him of the credit; and finally because Javert, being an artist, had a taste for the dramatic. He had no fondness for the kind of triumph that is robbed of its lustre by being proclaimed in advance. He liked to elaborate his masterpieces in secret and unveil them with a flourish.

He had followed Jean Valjean from tree to tree and from street-corner to street-corner, always keeping him in sight. Even in those moments when Valjean thought himself most safe Javert had had an eye on him.

Why, then, had he not at once arrested him? The reason is that he still had doubts.

We must remember that at that time the Paris police were not in a happy state, being much harassed by the free press. A number of arbitrary arrests, denounced in the newspapers, had led to questions in Parliament, and the Prefecture was nervous. To infringe the liberty of the subject was a serious matter. A major blunder on the part of a subordinate policeman might lead to his dismissal. It is not hard to imagine the effect of a news-item on the lines of the following, reproduced in twenty papers: 'Yesterday a white-headed grandfather, a respectable rentier out walking with his eight-year-old granddaughter, was arrested and taken to Police Headquarters as an escaped convict.'! . . . Besides which, we must repeat, Javert was a man of principle. To the voice of the Prefect was added the voice of his own conscience. He had genuine doubts. He had seen only Jean Valjean's back as he vanished into the darkness.

Valjean's acute anxiety and distress at this fresh disaster which had driven him to flight and forced him to seek haphazardly for a new place of refuge for Cosette and himself, his responsibility for the child and the necessity to accommodate his footsteps to hers, all this, without his realizing it, had so altered his gait, lending an impression of senility to his whole bearing, that even the police, in the person of Javert, could be misled by it. The impossibility of examining him closely, his shabby attire resembling that of an elderly schoolmaster, Thénardier's statement that he was the child's grandfather and finally his reported death, these were added elements of uncertainty.

Javert thought for a moment of going up to him and peremptorily demanding to see his papers. But if the man was not Jean Valjean, and not a respectable rentier either, then there was every likelihood that he was a villain deeply involved in the Paris underworld, possibly a dangerous gang-leader, at present keeping under cover for reasons of his own. In that case he would have contacts, accomplices, emergency hide-outs where he would eventually go to earth. His general behaviour and the circuitous route he was following suggested that he could scarcely be an honest citizen. To arrest him too soon might be to kill the goose that laid the golden eggs. What harm was there in waiting? Javert was confident that he would not escape.

So he continued tentatively to follow him until, some time later, by the light outside a tavern in the Rue Pontoise, he had a clear view of him and knew positively that this was Jean Valjean.

There is a kind of thrill known to only two creatures on earth – the mother who recovers her child and the tiger who recovers its prey. This was Javert's sensation at that moment. But simultaneously, being now assured that it was the formidable Jean Valjean, he realized that he had only two men with him, and he therefore applied to the police-post in the Rue Pontoise for assistance. Before grasping a stick of thorn we put on gloves.

This delay, and the pause at the Rollin crossroads to confer with his men, nearly caused him to lose the scent; but he quickly realized that Valjean would want to put the river between his pursuers and himself. He stood with his head bent, pointing like a hound, and then, with his customary sureness of instinct, made straight for the

Pont d'Austerlitz. A word with the toll-keeper told him what he wanted to know – 'Have you seen a man with a little girl?' . . . 'I charged him two sous.' Javert was on the bridge in time to see Valjean cross a moonlit space with Cosette. He saw him enter the Rue de Chemin-Vert-Saint-Antoine and at once he thought of the Cul-de-sac Genrot, which was a trap in itself, and the Rue Droit-Mur, of which the only other outlet was into the Petite Rue Picpus. Fanning out his beaters, in hunting parlance, he sent a man promptly by a roundabout route to close that end. Encountering a military patrol on its way back to the Arsenal, he commandeered it and took it along with him. In games of this sort the military are a trump card, and it is in any case axiomatic that in dealing with a wild boar one needs both the cunning of the hunter and a strong pack of hounds. Having thus completed his depositions, and knowing Valjean to be enclosed between the impasse on his right, the police agent on his left and the main party coming up behind him, Javert took a pinch of snuff.

Then, with a demonic and sensual pleasure, he settled down to enjoy himself. He *played* his man knowing that he had him, deliberately postponing the climax, granting him a last illusion of freedom, relishing the situation like a spider with a fly buzzing in its web or a cat letting a mouse run between its paws – the ecstasy of watching those last struggles! His net was shrewdly cast, he could close it when he chose, and Valjean, desperate and dangerous though he was, could not hope to resist the force arrayed against him.

So Javert moved slowly forward, methodically searching every nook and cranny of the street as though he were going through the pockets of a footpad. But when he reached the centre of his net he found that the fly had vanished. The impasse was empty, and the man posted at the end of the Rue Droit-Mur had seen no one.

Javert's fury of exasperation can be imagined. It happens sometimes that a stag breaks cover with the whole pack upon him and miraculously contrives to escape, leaving even the most experienced huntsman confounded. In one such situation Artonge exclaimed, 'It isn't a stag, it's a wizard!' Javert might well have said the same.

It is undeniable that Napoleon blundered in the Russian campaign, Alexander in the Indian war, Caesar in Africa, Cyrus in Scythia; nor was Javert guiltless of error in his campaign against Jean Valjean. He was wrong, perhaps, in hesitating to recognize him at the beginning: that first glance should have sufficed. He erred in not arresting him at once in the tenement, and again in the Rue Pontoise, when he had definitely recognized him. The conclave under the moon at the Rollin intersection was a mistake. To take counsel is prudent, but the huntsman must be on the alert when he is dealing with such wary animals as a wolf or a convict. In his over-anxiety to set his pack on the right scent Javert allowed his prey a moment of respite. Above all he was wrong when, having again sighted him, he allowed himself to indulge in the childish satisfaction of toying with a man of that calibre. He thought himself stronger than he was, able to play with a lion as though it were a mouse. And at the same time he under-rated his strength when he wasted precious times in seeking reinforcements. He was guilty of all these errors and yet he was one of the most shrewd and able detectives that ever lived – in the full sense of the hunting term, 'a wise hound'.

But who among us is perfect? Even the greatest strategists have their eclipses, and the greatest blunders, like the thickest ropes, are often compounded of a multitude of strands. Take the rope apart, separate it into the small threads that compose it, and you can break them one by one. You think, 'That is all there was!' But twist them all together and you have something tremendous – Attila hesitating between Marcians in the east and Valentinians in the west, Hannibal delaying too long in Capua, Danton slumbering in Arcis-sur-Aube.

Nevertheless, when he found that Jean Valjean had escaped him Javert did not lose his head. Convinced that his prey could not be far off, he posted watches, set up traps and ambushes, and scoured the district throughout the night. The first thing he noticed was the displaced street-lamp of which the cord had been cut. It was a valuable clue but a misleading one since it led him to concentrate the search on the Cul-de-sac Genrot. The blind-alley was partly enclosed by comparatively low walls flanking gardens beyond which lay wide stretches of uncultivated land. He concluded that Valjean must have gone that way, and the fact is that Valjean would probably have done so had he gone a little further into the blind alley, and he would then have been lost. Javert combed the gardens and wasteland like a man looking for a needle in a haystack.

At daybreak he left two capable men on watch and returned to Police Headquarters as shamefaced as the fox outwitted by a hen.

BOOK SIX

LE PETIT-PICPUS

I
Petite Rue Picpus, No. 62

NOTHING COULD have been more commonplace, half a century ago, than the *porte-cochère* of No. 62, Petite Rue Picpus. As a rule it stood invitingly half open, affording a view of two things, neither of them gloomy in themselves – a courtyard enclosed in vine-covered walls and the face of an indolent door-keeper. The tops of trees were to be seen beyond the further wall. When sunshine brightened the courtyard, or wine enlivened the door-keeper, it would have been hard for anyone passing this doorway not to derive from it a cheerful impression. Nevertheless the passer-by had had a glimpse of a most sombre place. The threshold might smile, but the house itself prayed and wept.

The visitor who succeeded in getting past the door-keeper (which was not easy and indeed for most people impossible, since there was a password which had to be known) was shown into a small vestibule affording access to a stairway so narrow that two persons could not pass on it. If, unintimidated by the wall-colouring of livid green above and chocolate below, one ventured up the stairs, one came, after passing two landings, still remorselessly accompanied by the green and chocolate, to a corridor. Stairway and corridor were lighted by two handsome windows, but the corridor turned a corner and was plunged into darkness. If, rounding this headland, one walked on a few paces, one came to a door which appeared the more mysterious in that it was not closed. Pushing it wide open, one found oneself in a very small room about six feet square, tiled, scrubbed, immaculate, and cold, with a wallpaper at fifteen sous the roll patterned with green flowers. Pallid daylight entered through a small-paned window occupying the whole of the lefthand wall. There was nothing to be seen or heard, not a footstep or a human sound. The walls were bare and the room was unfurnished, without even a chair.

In the wall facing the door there was a grille about a foot square composed of stout, intersecting iron bars forming squares – I had almost called them meshes – about an inch and a half across.

The green flowers of the wallpaper clustered round this grille, their orderly tranquillity in no way disturbed by its forbidding aspect. Even supposing a human creature to have been thin enough to wriggle through the aperture, the bars would have prevented it. Not only did the grille prevent the passage of a body, it prevented even the passage of the eyes, that is to say, of the spirit. Someone had evidently provided against this, for the bars of the grille were supplemented by a sheet of metal pierced with innumerable minute holes smaller than those in a milk-skimmer. There was an aperture at the bottom of this sheet exactly like the opening of a letter-box.

A bell-cord hung to the right of the grille, and the tinkling of the bell was followed by the sound of a voice disconcertingly close at hand.

'Who is there?'

It was a woman's voice, muted to the point of sadness.

And here again there was a magic password that had to be known. If the visitor did not know it the voice said no more, and the wall was silent as though nothing lay beyond it but the darkness of the tomb. But if the word was spoken the voice said:

'Turn to your right.'

In the wall facing the window there was a glass-paned door with a glass transom painted grey. Lifting the latch and passing through this doorway one had exactly the impression of entering a theatre-box protected by a metal grille, before the lights go up and the grille is lowered. It was indeed a kind of theatre-box, faintly illumined from behind by the light filtering through the panes of the door, a narrow place furnished with two old chairs and a worn straw mat – a theatre-box with a front at waist level on which was a sill of black wood. But unlike the gilded grilles at the Opéra this was a huge and hideous trellis of iron bars rigidly intertwined and fixed to the surrounding walls with fastenings as large as clenched fists.

As the eyes grew accustomed to the dim light and sought to peer beyond the grille, they found that they could penetrate no more than a few inches, their gaze being then arrested by a black shutter reinforced with crosspieces of yellow-painted wood. This shutter, composed of separate, narrow slats, covered the full extent of the grille. It was always closed.

After a few moments a woman's voice spoke from behind the shutter.

'I am here. What do you want of me?'

It was a known and loved voice, sometimes an adored voice. The sound of human breathing could scarcely be heard. It was as though a spirit were speaking from beyond the tomb.

If the visitor fulfilled certain conditions, which was rarely the case, a part of the shutter opened and the disembodied voice became an apparition. Insofar as the grille made it possible to see anything, a head appeared, of which only the mouth and chin were visible, the rest being covered by a black veil. One saw a black wimple and an indeterminate form enveloped in a black winding-sheet. The head spoke, but without looking directly at the visitor or ever smiling.

The light coming from behind the visitor was so disposed as faintly to illumine the figure beyond the grille, whereas the visitor remained in darkness. This was symbolical.

The draped figure was framed in a profound obscurity. One gazed intently, seeking to discern what else might lie beyond the aperture, but soon found that there was no more to be seen. There was nothing but darkness and shadow, a winter mist mingled with the vapours of the tomb, a sort of terrifying peace, silence that divulged nothing, not even a sigh, shadow that disclosed nothing, not even ghosts. One was gazing into the interior of a convent.

The melancholy and austere building was the Bernardine Convent of the Perpetual Adoration. The stage-box where the visitor was admitted was the parlour. The first voice which spoke was that of the sister in attendance, permanently seated, motionless and silent, on the other side of the wall at the square aperture, protected by the iron grille and the metal sheet with its countless holes, like a double vizor. The light filtering into the inner room came from the window looking out on to the world. None came from the convent itself. That sacred place was not to be viewed by profane eyes.*

Nevertheless things existed beyond that darkness. There were light and life within that semblance of death. Although the convent was the most strictly enclosed of all we shall seek to enter it, taking the reader with us, and, within the bounds of discretion, describe matters unseen by any chronicler and hitherto unrelated.

*The Order is a fictitious one, based on the Benedictine convent of the Perpetual Adoration of the Holy Sacrament in the Rue Neuve-Sainte-Geneviève (in what is now the 5th Arrondissement) and the Couvent Saint-Michel. There was also a Couvent des Dames du Sacré-Cœur et de l'Adoration Perpétuelle in the Saint-Antoine quarter. Hugo derived the exhaustive details which follow from ladies who had been inmates of these establishments.

The Order of Martin Verga

The convent, which by 1824 had existed for many years in the Petite Rue Picpus, was a Bernardine Community practising the discipline of Martin Verga. These Bernardine nuns were in consequence affiliated not to Clairvaux, like the Bernardine monks, but to Cîteaux, like the Benedictines. In other words, they were subject not to St Bernard but to St Benedict. As anyone will know who has looked into the archives, Martin Verga in 1425 founded a Bernardine-Benedictine congregation having its headquarters at Salamanca and an allied establishment at Alcala.

This congregation had put out shoots in every Catholic country in Europe, the grafting of one order on to another being a common practice in the Church of Rome. To take the case solely of the Benedictine Order which is here in question, and apart from the Discipline of Martin Verga, four other communities are affiliated to this one: two in Italy, those of Monte Cassino and Santa Giustina of Padua, and two in France, Cluny and St Maur; together with nine orders – Vallombrosa, Grammont, Celestines, Camaldaules, Carthusians, the Humiliati, the Olivetans, and the Silvestrans; and finally Cîteaux itself, the trunk from which the rest sprang, which is no more than an offshoot of St Benedict. Cîteaux dates from St Robert, Abbot of Molesme in the diocese of Langres in 1098. It was in 529 that the Devil, having retreated to the Desert of Subiaco (he was old: had he become a hermit?) was driven out of the former Temple of Apollo by St Benedict, then aged seventeen.

With the exception of the Carmelites, who go barefoot, wear a twig of osier at their throats and are never seated, the most severe rule is that of the Bernardine-Benedictines founded by Martin Verga. The nuns are clad in black with a wimple which, by St Benedict's express prescription, rises to the chin. A wide-sleeved robe of serge, a big woollen shawl, the wimple rising to the chin and cut square over the bosom, and a headband coming down to the eyes, such is their attire, all of it black except the headband, which is white. Novices wear the same garments, but in white. In addition the professing nuns have a rosary at their side.

The Bernardine-Benedictines of the Martin Verga order observe the practice of Perpetual Adoration, as do the Benedictine nuns known as the Dames du Saint-Sacrement, who at the beginning of this century had two houses in Paris, one in the Temple and the other in the Rue Neuve-Sainte-Geneviève. But in other respects the Petit-Picpus community was entirely separate. There were numerous differences of rule as of attire. The Bernardine-Benedictines in Petit-Picpus wore black wimples, whereas those of the other two communities were white; moreover, the nuns of the Temple and the Rue Neuve-Sainte-Geneviève wore a gilt or enamel crucifix some three inches long on their chests, while those of the Petit-Picpus did not. Their common observance of the Perpetual Adoration was the only link between the communities. It is not unknown for communities, similar in their approach to the mysteries of the childhood, life, and death of Jesus Christ and the Virgin, to be in other respects widely sundered from one another and even antagonistic, as was the case with the Oratoire d'Italie, founded in Florence by Philippe de Neri, and the Oratoire de France, founded in Paris by Pierre de Bérulle. The latter claimed precedence on the grounds that Philippe de Neri was merely a saint, whereas Bérulle was a cardinal.

To return to the harsh Spanish order of Martin Verga.

The nuns following this discipline practise austerity throughout the year, fasting in Lent and on numerous other days special to themselves; they rise from their first slumber at one in the morning to read their breviaries and chant matins until three, sleep between coarse woollen sheets on mattresses of straw, take no baths, light no fires, scourge themselves on Fridays, observe the rule of silence, only speaking among themselves during the recreation periods, which are very short, and wear hair shirts for six months of the year, from 14 September, the Exaltation of the Holy Cross, until Easter. These six months are indeed a modification of the original rule, which stipulated that hair shirts were to be worn throughout the year; but they were found to be intolerable in the heat of summer, causing fever and nervous spasms, and their use had to be restricted. Even so, when they resume the shirts on 14 September the nuns are feverish for several days. Obedience, poverty, chastity, permanent confinement within the walls: such are their vows, made more rigorous by the rules.

The prioress is elected for three years by the mothers of the order, called the *Mères Vocales*, the speaking mothers, because they have a voice on the chapter. She can only be twice re-elected, which limits her term of office to nine years.

The nuns never see the officiating priest, who is separated from them in the chapel by a curtain seven feet high. While he is in the pulpit they lower their veils. They are required always to talk in low voices and to walk with bowed heads and lowered eyes. Only one man is allowed to enter the convent, the archbishop of the diocese.

There is in fact one other man, the gardener. But he is always old, and in order that he may be always isolated in the garden, and the nuns have warning of his presence, a bell is fastened to his knee.

Their submission to the rule of the Prioress is absolute, canonical subjection in all its selflessness: as to the voice of Christ – *ut voci Christi* – at a gesture, the first sign – *ad nutum, ad primum signum* – instantly, with cheerfulness, with perseverance, with unquestioning blind obedience – *prompte, hilariter, perseveranter et caeca quadam obedientia* – like the file in the workman's hands – *quasi limam in manibus fabri* – empowered neither to read nor write without express permission – *legere vel scribere non addiscerit sine expressa superioris licentia.*

Each in turn makes what they call atonement. Atonement is the prayer for all sins, all errors, all disorders, violations, iniquities – all the crimes committed on earth. For twelve hours in succession, from four o'clock in the afternoon until four in the morning, the sister performing the act of atonement remains kneeling on the stones before the High Altar, her hands clasped and a rope round her neck. When her fatigue becomes unendurable she prostrates herself with her face to the earth and her arms crossed. This is her only relief. In this posture she prays for all the sinners in the universe. The act is noble to the point of sublimity.

Since it takes place before a pillar on which a candle burns it is termed either 'to make atonement' or 'to be on the block'. The nuns in their humility actually prefer the latter term, with its suggestion of castigation and abasement. This act of atonement is one demanding the whole spirit. The sister 'on the block' would not turn her head if the heavens were to fall.

In any event, there is always a sister on her knees before the High Altar. She kneels for an hour and is then relieved like a soldier on sentry-go. This is the Perpetual Adoration.

The prioresses and mothers nearly always bear names of a particular solemnity having to do not with saints and martyrs but with events in the life of Christ, such as Mother Nativity, Mother Conception, Mother Annunciation, Mother Passion. The names of saints, however, are not forbidden.

To anyone seeing them, only their mouths are visible. All have yellow teeth. No tooth-brush has ever entered the convent. The act of brushing the teeth is the topmost rung of a ladder of which the lowest rung is perdition.

They never say 'my' or 'mine'. They own nothing and may cherish nothing. Everything is 'ours' – our veil, our chaplet; if they were to speak of their shift they would say 'our shift'. Sometimes they become attached to some small object, a book of hours, a relic, a blessed medallion. When they find that they are beginning to cling to it they must give it up, recalling the words of St Theresa, to whom a great lady on the point of joining her order said: 'May I be allowed, Reverend Mother, to send for a copy of the Holy Bible which I greatly cherish?' ... 'Ah, you cherish something? In that case you cannot join us.'

None of them is allowed to shut herself away or to have any place or room of her own. They live in open cells. When two of them meet one will say, 'Praise and worship to the Holy Sacrament of the altar!', to which the other will reply, 'For ever!' The same words are spoken when one knocks at another's door: scarcely has she touched it than a soft voice on the other side is heard to say, 'For ever!'. Like all such practices, it becomes mechanical from force of habit, and sometimes the words 'For ever!' are spoken before there has been time to utter the preliminary sentence, which is after all rather long. The visitor upon entering says, 'Hail Mary!' and the other replies, 'Full of grace!' This is their form of good day, which is indeed 'full of grace'.

At every hour during the day the chapel bell sounds three additional strokes, and at this signal all of them – prioress, mothers, sisters, novices, postulants – interrupt what they are saying or doing or thinking to say together, 'At this hour of five' (or eight, or whatever the hour may be) '– and at all hours praised and worshipped be the Holy Sacrament of the altar!' This custom, which is designed to check the flow of thought and direct it back to God, is common to many communities, although the formula varies. In the community of the Infant Jesus, for example, they say: 'At this present hour, and at all hours, may the love of Jesus Christ glow in my heart.'

The Benedictine-Bernardine order of Martin Verga, cloistered fifty years ago in the convent of Petit-Picpus, chanted the offices to a grave psalmody that was pure plain-chant, and always at full voice throughout the service. Where there was a break in the missal they paused and murmured in low voices, 'Jesus-Mary-Joseph'. In the office for the dead the pitch was so low that women's voices could scarcely reach it. The effect was impressive and tragic.

The Petit-Picpus community caused a vault to be constructed under the High Altar which was intended to serve as their communal sepulchre. But the Government, it seems, would not allow bodies to be interred there. The dead have to be removed from the convent, and this greatly afflicts them as an infraction of their rule. As a small consolation they secured the right to be buried at a particular hour and in a particular corner of the ancient Vaugirard Cemetery, which was formerly owned by their community.

On Thursdays, the nuns heard Grand Mass, vespers and all the offices, precisely as on a Sunday. They scrupulously observed all the minor feast-days, scarcely known to the lay world, which the Church at one time lavished upon France and still does upon Spain and Italy. Their chapel attendances were interminable. As to the number and length of their prayers, we can best give an idea of this by quoting the ingenuous utterance of one of them – 'The prayers of the postulants are terrifying, those of the novices are worse, and those of the professed nuns are worst of all.'

Once a week the Chapter was convened, the prioress presiding and the mothers attending. Each sister in turn knelt on the stone and confessed aloud before them all the faults and sins she had committed during the week. The mothers conferred after each confession and prescribed the penance.

In addition to open confession, which was reserved for relatively serious matters, there was the practice known as 'la coulpe', derived from the Latin culpa, guilt. To perform 'la coulpe', was to prostrate oneself during the service at the feet of the prioress, and remain there until the latter (who was never referred to except as 'our mother') indicated by tapping on the wood of her stall that the sinner might rise to her feet. This act of penitence applied to very small matters – a broken glass, a torn veil, an instant's tardiness, a false note in the singing, any of these was enough. It was a spontaneous act, the culprit being her own judge of whether to perform it. On Sundays and feast-days four chantry-mothers sang the office at a large lectern with four singing-desks. One day one of these, in a psalm beginning with the word *Ecce*, sang instead the three notes C, B and G. For this slip, she endured a '*coulpe*' lasting throughout the service. What made her fault so terrible was that the chapter had laughed.

When any nun was summoned to the parlour, even the prioress herself, she lowered her veil in the manner described, so that only her mouth was visible. The prioress alone could communicate with outsiders, the rest being allowed to see only their nearest relatives, and that very rarely. When a person from beyond the walls desired to see a sister whom she had known and loved in the past, this was a matter of negotiation. In the case of a woman permission might be granted and they might talk through the closed shutters, which were opened only for a mother or sister. It goes without saying that permission was never granted to a man.

Such was the rule of St Benedict, rendered more harsh by Martin Verga.

III

Severities

The period of probation, or postulancy, lasted at least two years and often four; novitiate lasted another four years. It was rare for the final vows to be taken before the age of twenty-three or four. The Martin Verga order did not accept widows. They practised in their cells many forms of self-castigation of which they might not speak.

On the day when a novice took her final vows, clad in her richest garments with a chaplet of white roses on her elaborately dressed hair, she lay prostrate on the ground. A large black veil was cast over her and the office for the dead was sung. The nuns were divided into two files, one passing close to her and exclaiming in doleful accents, 'Our sister is dead!' to which the other file replied, 'Alive in Christ!'

At the time of our story a boarding-school formed part of the convent. It was a school for daughters of the nobility, most of them rich, bearing such names as Sainte-Aulaire and de Bélissen, and there was an English girl bearing the illustrious Catholic name of Talbot.

Instructed by the nuns, and isolated within those walls, these children were taught to abhor the world and the age in which they lived. One of them once said to the writer: 'The very sight of the cobbles in the street caused me to shiver from head to foot.' They were dressed in blue with a white coif and a bronze or enamel cross on their bosoms. On certain feast-days, in particular that of St Martha, they were allowed as a special favour to wear the dress of nuns and perform the offices and rites of St Benedict throughout the day. At first the nuns lent them their black garments, but this was held to be a profanation and the prioress forbade it, except in the case of novices. What is remarkable is that this practice, doubtless tolerated and encouraged in the convent in a secret spirit of proselytism, to give the children a foretaste of the religious life, was to them a real source of pleasure and recreation. They quite simply enjoyed it – 'It was something new, it made a change.' The innocence of childhood! – which, however, cannot make us worldlings understand the felicity of holding a sprinkler of holy water in the hand, or standing for hours on end chanting at a four-desk lectern.

Except in its most extreme practices, the pupils conformed to all the usages of the convent. There was one young lady who, even after leaving it and being married for several years, still had not broken herself of the habit of saying, 'For ever!' when someone knocked at her door. Like the nuns, the girls never saw their relations except in the parlour. Not even their mothers were allowed to embrace them. Indeed, strictness was carried so far that on one occasion, when a mother brought her three-year-old sister to visit one of the girls, the girl was reduced to tears because she was not allowed to kiss her. She begged that at least the child should be allowed to put a hand through the bars, but this, too, was refused, almost with indignation.

IV

Gaiety

Nevertheless those girls brought a touch of brightness to that sombre establishment.

At certain times youth sparkled amid the cloisters. The recreation bell sounded, a door creaked on its hinges and the birds said, 'Here come the children!' A wave of youth flooded over that garden laid out in the pattern of a cross. Glowing faces, smooth foreheads, innocent eyes alight with gaiety, every kind of dawn spread among the shadows. After the psalm-singing, the offices, the tolling of bells, came this hubbub of little girls, sweeter than the humming of bees. They played and called to one another, ran and clustered in groups; white teeth laughed and chattered in corners, while at a distance the veiled forms watched over them, shadows overseeing sunbeams; but what did it matter? – the radiance and the laughter were unabashed. Those melancholy walls had their moments of enchantment as, faintly illumined by the reflection of so much happiness, they looked down upon that soft commotion, like a shower of roses cast upon a place of mourning. The children romped beneath the eye of the nuns, their innocence untroubled by their immaculate gaze. Thanks to them the long hours of austerity were relieved by lighthearted interludes, little girls skipping while the big ones danced. Play and piety mingled in the convent, and nothing could have been more ravishing or sublime than this unfolding of young, fresh wings. Homer might have joined with Perrault in the laughter. There was youth enough in that shadowed garden – health, hubbub, excitement, happiness – to wipe the wrinkles off the faces of all the ancestral figures, whether of epic or of fairy-tale, dwellers upon thrones or under thatch, from Hecuba to Mother Goose.

Perhaps more than in any other place childish utterances were cherished of the kind that evoke laughter and a reminiscent sigh. Amid its gloom a five-year-old once said: 'Mother, a big girl has just told me that I shall only be here for another nine years and ten months. How lovely!'

And the following dialogue is recalled. A mother: 'Why are you crying, child?'

The child (aged six): 'I told Alix that I knew my French history. She says I don't know it, but I do.'

Alix (aged nine): 'No, she doesn't.'

The mother: 'What happened?'

Alix: 'She said to open the book anywhere and ask her the first question I came across, and she'd answer it.'

'Well?'

'Well, she couldn't answer it.'

'But what did you ask?'

'I opened the book anywhere, as she said, and I asked the first question I came to.'

'And what was it?'

'The question was: What happened next?'

Then there was the remark concerning a rather greedy parakeet, the property of a paying-guest at the convent: 'How well-mannered she is! She pecks at her food like a real lady.'

A confession was picked up off the floor, written in anticipation by a sinner aged seven: 'Father, I confess to avarice. I confess to adultery. I confess to having looked at gentlemen.'

The following tale was told on a grassy bank by pink six-year-old lips to a pair of wide blue eyes aged five:

'There were three little cocks who lived in a country full of flowers. They picked the flowers and put them in their pockets. Then they picked the leaves and they put those with their toys. There was a wolf in the country and a lot of woods. The wolf lived in the woods and he ate the little cocks.'

And then a poem:

> A blow was struck with a wooden stick.
> It was Punch beating the cat.
> This did not do the cat any good, it only hurt her.
> So a lady put Punch in prison.

The following is the heartrending utterance of a lost child, abandoned by her parents, who was being brought up in charity by the convent: 'Me, my mother wasn't there when I was born.'

There was a plump housekeeper who was to be seen bustling along the corridor with a bunch of keys. Her name was Sister Agatha. The really big girls (the ones over ten) called her Agathoclès – Agatha of the keys.

The refectory, a big rectangular room lighted by gothic windows on a level with the garden, was dark and damp and said by the children to be full of vermin. All the surroundings furnished their quota of small creatures, and each of its four corners had been given an appropriate name by the children – Spider Corner, Caterpillar Corner, Woodlouse Corner, and Cricket Corner. Cricket Corner was especially favoured because, being near the kitchen, it was warmer. These names had passed into general use, like the names of the four nations at the old Collège Mazarin, and the children belonged to the corner in which they sat. On one occasion the archbishop, on a pastoral visit, noticed a particularly pretty little fair-haired girl and asked another child who she was.

'She's a spider, Monseigneur.'

'Indeed! And that one there?'

'She's a cricket.'

'And that one?'

'She's a caterpillar.'

'Upon my word! And what are you?'

'I'm a woodlouse, Monseigneur.'

Every establishment of the kind has its particularities. The Château d'Écouen, for example, was converted under the Empire into a school for the orphan daughters of members of the Légion d'honneur. To determine the order of precedence in the procession of the Holy Sacrament they were divided into 'virgins' and 'flower-bearers'. There were also 'canopies' and 'censers', the former holding the cords of the canopy and the latter swinging censers as they passed in front of the High Altar. The flowers were retained as of right by the flower-bearers. Four 'virgins' led the procession. It was not uncommon, on the morning of the great day, to hear someone in the dormitory ask, 'Who are today's virgins?', and Madame Campan has quoted the words addressed by a seven-year-old, whose place was at the tail of the procession, to a big girl of sixteen who was at the front:

'Well, you're a virgin, but I'm not.'

V

Distractions

Over the door of the refectory there was inscribed in bold black letters the following child's prayer, known as the White Paternoster, of which the virtue was that it led the reader straight to Paradise.

'Little white Paternoster, whom God made, whom God spoke, whom God placed in Paradise, at night when I go to bed I find three angels by my bed, one at the foot and two at the head, with the good Virgin Mary in the middle, and she tells me to lie down and fear nothing. God is my father, the Virgin is my mother, the three apostles are my brothers and the three virgins are my sisters. The garment in which God was born covers my body; the cross of St Margaret is written on my breast. Madame the Virgin walked through the fields weeping for God and she met St John. "Monsieur St John, where have you come from?" . . . "I come from *Ave Salus*" . . . "And did you see God? Where is He?" . . . "He is in the Tree of the Cross with his feet hanging, his hands nailed and a little hat of white thorn on his head." He who repeats this three times at night and three times in the morning will gain Paradise in the end.'

In 1827 this characteristic prayer vanished under a triple-coating of whitewash. It must by now be fading from the memories of such of the children as are left, all of them old women today.

A big crucifix on the wall completed the decoration of the refectory, of which the only door opened on to the garden. Two narrow tables, with wooden benches on either side, extended in parallel the length of the room. The walls were white, the tables black, those two colours of mourning being the only contrast allowed in convents. The food was coarse, and even the children's diet was scanty, being restricted to a single dish of meat or salt fish with vegetables. They ate in silence under the eyes of the mother of the week, who now and then, if a fly ventured to buzz in defiance of the rules, opened and noisily clapped-to a wooden book. The silence was relieved by lives of the saints, read aloud by one of the older girls doing duty for the week at a small lectern standing under the crucifix. Set at intervals on the bare tables were earthenware bowls in which the children washed their platters and cutlery and into which they sometimes threw morsels of gristle or stale fish which they were unable to eat; for this they were punished. The bowls were called 'water puddles'.

Any child who broke silence was required to 'make a cross' with her tongue. And where did she do this? On the floor, by licking the stone flags. Dust, the end of all rejoicing, was the chastisement inflicted on the small pink tongue that had dared to wag.

There was a book in the convent of which only one copy had ever been printed and the reading of which was forbidden. It was the Rule of St Benedict, an arcanum which no profane eye might penetrate. The girls managed to get hold of it and read it avidly, in constant terror of being caught. They found little to reward them. A few incomprehensible pages on the sins of boys were what interested them most.

One of the garden paths was bordered by a few stunted fruit-trees. Despite strict supervision and severe penalties, they sometimes managed to pick up a windfall – a green apple, a rotting apricot, or a worm-eaten pear. And here I will quote a letter I have

in front of me, written by a former pupil, now the Duchesse de —
and one of the most elegant women in Paris.

'You hid your apple or pear as best you could. When you went
up to the dormitory to make your bed before supper you stuffed it
under your pillow to eat when you were in bed. Or if you couldn't
do that you ate it in the lavatory.' This was one of their greatest
delights.

On the occasion of another visit by the archbishop, one of the
girls, a Mademoiselle Bouchard who was related to the Montmo-
rencys, wagered that she would ask his Grace for a day's leave of
absence, a monstrous request in that austere community. The wager
was accepted although none of those who took part believed in it.
When the chance came, as the archbishop was inspecting the row of
children, Mlle Bouchard, to the consternation of her schoolfellows,
stepped forward and said, 'Monseigneur, I beg for a day's leave of
absence.' Mlle Bouchard was tall and pretty, with the most charming
of round, flushed faces. The archbishop, Monsieur de Quélen,
smiled and said: 'Only one day, child? It is surely not enough. I
grant you three days.' His Grace had spoken and the prioress was
powerless. It was an outrage to the convent but a triumph for the
girls of which we can only guess at the subsequent effects.

But the walls of the establishment were not so impenetrable that
echoes of the outside world, passion, drama and even romance,
could not sometimes creep in. The following is an authentic
incident which, although it has no bearing on our story, helps to
complete the general picture of the convent.

At about this time there was a mysterious visitor stopping at the
convent, not a nun but a lady who was treated with great respect
and who was known as Madame Albertine. Nothing was known of
her except that she was mad and was believed by the world to be
dead. It was rumoured that her present situation was due to certain
financial arrangements necessitated by a great marriage.

The lady, who was not more than thirty, dark-haired and handsome, was wont to gaze remotely about her with big, dark eyes.
Did she in fact see anything? She seemed to glide rather than walk,
she never spoke; it was doubtful if she even breathed, for her
nostrils were pinched and white as though she had drawn her last
breath. To touch her hand was like touching snow. She had a
strange, spectral grace and a chill enveloped her wherever she went.

Passing her one day in a corridor one of the sisters said to another: 'She might be dead.' The other replied: 'Perhaps she is.'

Countless tales were told about Madame Albertine, who was an object of intense curiosity. There was an enclosed stall in the chapel known as the Oeil-de-Bœuf because of its single, round opening, and it was here that she attended service. As a rule she occupied it alone, because the stall was on a higher level than the rest, making it possible for its occupant to see the preacher or officiating priest, which the nuns were forbidden to do. One day the sermon was preached by a young priest of very high rank. He was the Duc de Rohan, a peer of France who, as Prince de Léon, had been an officer in the Red Musketeers in 1815, and who died in 1833, a cardinal and Archbishop of Besançon. It was the first time M. de Rohan had preached in the convent. Madame Albertine as a rule followed the sermon and the office with perfect calm; but on this occasion, at the sight of M. de Rohan she half-rose from her seat and exclaimed aloud, in the silence of the chapel, 'What! Auguste!' Every head in the startled congregation was turned to gaze at her and the preacher looked up; but Madame Albertine had sunk back into her customary immobility. A breath of the outside world, a flicker of life, had touched that withdrawn and frozen face; then it had passed and the crazed woman became again a figure of death.

But those two words were the subject of endless speculation. 'What! Auguste!' – how much they must conceal! M. de Rohan's name was indeed Auguste. It was clear that Madame Albertine had moved in the highest circles and must herself be highly placed, since she had referred to so great a personage in such familiar terms. She must have some connection with him, perhaps a blood-relationship but certainly a close one, since she knew his childhood name.

Two very straitlaced duchesses, Mesdames de Choiseul and de Sérent, were regular visitors to the community, no doubt in virtue of their high social station, and they caused great alarm among the inmates. When the two old ladies swept past them the girls trembled and lowered their eyes.

M. de Rohan was also, without knowing it, an object of constant interest to the school-children. He had recently been made grand-vicar to the Archbishop of Paris, while awaiting his own bishopric, and he fell into the habit of coming quite frequently to officiate at the services in the Petit-Picpus chapel. The youthful recluses could not see him because of the curtains, but he had a soft, slightly hoarse voice which they learnt to recognize. He had been an army officer, and was said to be highly fastidious in his dress, his chestnut hair elaborately curled, a splendid silk sash about his waist, and his cassock most elegantly cut. He was particularly interesting to the sixteen-year-olds.

No sound from outside ordinarily reached the convent, but it happened one year that the notes of a flute were heard. This notable event is still remembered by that generation of boarders. The player was somewhere close at hand and the melody was always the same, a song now forgotten, '*Ma Zétalbé, viens régner sur mon âme*' – 'My Zétalbé, come reign in my heart!' It was heard several times a day. The girls listened entranced, the mothers were outraged, minds were distracted, punishments were showered. This went on for several months, and the girls all fell more or less in love with the unknown musician, each thinking of herself as Zétalbé. The sound came from the direction of the Rue Droit-Mur, and they would have risked anything, sacrificed anything, for a single glimpse of the 'young man with the flute' who played so deliciously. Several of them slipped through a service door during a rest period and crept up to the third floor, on the Droit-Mur side, in a vain attempt to see him. One went so far as to reach above her head and wave a handkerchief through the barred window. But two were even bolder. They contrived to climb on to the roof itself and at the risk of disaster had a sight of the 'young man'. He turned out to be an elderly gentleman, a former emigré now blind and destitute, playing in his attic to while away the time.

VI

The Little Convent

There were in the grounds of the Petit-Picpus three entirely separate buildings, the main convent, where the nuns lived, the boarding-house, and what was known as 'the Little Convent'. This was a lodging-house with its own garden inhabited by a collection of old nuns from other orders, the survivors of convents destroyed by the Revolution, and containing every shade of black, grey, and white, every variety and singularity of costume – a sort of patchwork convent, if the term may be allowed.

These unhappy exiles had been permitted under the Empire to take refuge with the Benedictine-Bernardines; the Government allowed them a small pension and the ladies of the Petit-Picpus had gladly received them. They were a strange confusion, each obeying her own Rule. The schoolgirls were sometimes allowed as a great treat to visit them, and so the memory of Mère Saint-Basile, Mère Sainte-Scolastique, and Mère Jacob among others, was impressed on certain youthful minds.

There was one among them who might be said to have been at home. This was a sister of the Order of Sainte-Aure, the only member of that order who had survived. At the beginning of the eighteenth century the ladies of Sainte-Aure had occupied this same house in the Petit-Picpus. The old nun in question, being too poor to wear the splendid costume of her order, which consisted of a white habit with a scarlet scapula, had piously dressed a doll in these garments, which she delighted to display and bequeathed to the establishment at her death. In 1824 one member of the order remained; today there is only the doll.

In addition to these devout mothers a few elderly society women had obtained the permission of the prioress, as had Madame Albertine, to retire to the Little Convent. Among them were Madame de Beaufort d'Hautpoul and Madame la Marquise Dufresne. There was another who was known in the convent only by the tremendous noise she made when blowing her nose. The girls christened her 'Madame Vacarmini', which may be translated 'thunderclap'.

Around the year 1820 Madame de Genlis, who was then editing a small periodical entitled *l'Intrépide*, asked leave to enter the convent as a resident guest, being recommended by the king's brother, the Duc d'Orléans. This caused a great stir in the hive, a quiver of apprehension, for Madame de Genlis had written novels; but she declared that she now detested them, and in any case she had embarked on a phase of fanatical devoutness. But she left after a few months, saying that there was not enough shade in the garden. The nuns were greatly relieved. Although very old, she still played the harp, and extremely well.

The convent chapel, which stood between the main convent and the school boarding-house and was designed to separate them, was of course shared by the whole community. Even the public was admitted by a kind of lepers' door from the street. But everything was done to ensure that the inmates would never set eyes on a face from outside. We have to imagine a church of which the main aisle has been bent by a giant hand, so that instead of extending beyond the altar it becomes a sort of gloomy cavern to the right of the priest, concealed behind the seven-foot curtains of which we have already spoken. Huddled together in the half-darkness on wooden stalls were the nuns of the choir on the left, schoolgirls and resident guests on the right, serving nuns and novices at the back – this is to give some impression of the community of the Petit-Picpus at divine service. The cavern, known as the choir, communicated with the cloisters by way of a passage. The chapel was lighted by windows on the garden side. At certain services which, by the rules of the order, were conducted in silence, the public was made aware of the presence of the nuns only by the creaking of stalls as they knelt or rose to their feet.

VII

Figures in the shadow

From 1819 to 1825 the prioress of Petit-Picpus was Mademoiselle de Blemeur, whose conventual name was Mère Innocente. She came of the family of Marguerite de Blemeur, who in the previous century had written a *Life of the Saints of the Order of St Benedict*. She was a woman in her sixties, short and plump, 'who sang like a cracked pot' according to the letter we have already quoted, but was in general an admirable person and the only cheerful member of the community, for which she was greatly loved. She inherited many of the qualities of her ancestress, being well-read, erudite, knowledgeable, widely versed in history and stuffed with Latin, Greek, and Hebrew – more like a monk than a nun.

The deputy-prioress was an aged and almost blind Spanish nun, Mère Cineres. There were sisters who had come from other orders, some who found the austerity intolerable, and one or two who were driven insane. There was a charmingly pretty girl of twenty-three, a descendant of the Chevalier Roze, whose conventual name was Mère Assomption. The sister in charge of the choir was Mère Sainte-Mechtilde, who liked to include in it a number of the schoolgirls. Ordinarily she selected a complete scale, that is to say, seven, aged from ten to sixteen. She made them sing standing, graded according to height, and the effect was like that of a reed pipe, a panpipe of angels. Among the serving sisters best loved by the girls were Sœur Sainte-Marthe, who was in her dotage, and Sœur Saint-Michel, whose long nose made them laugh.

All the nuns were indulgent to the children, reserving their severity for themselves. No fire was ever lit except in the girls' boarding-house, and their fare was refined compared with that of the nuns. They were tenderly cared for; but if a child addressed a nun in passing, the nun did not reply.

The effect of this rule of silence was that the faculty of speech was denied to humans and transferred to inanimate objects. At one moment it was the chapel bell that spoke, at another the gardener's bell. A particularly sonorous bell in the housekeeper's room, which was audible throughout the building, served as a kind of telegraph summoning the inmates to the performance of their hourly duties or notifying one in particular that she was wanted in the parlour. Each individual had a distinctive signal. That of the prioress was two strokes – one and one; that of the deputy-prioress one and two. A call of six-five was the summons to class, so familiar that the girls never talked of going into class but of 'going to six-five'. Four-four was the call of Madame de Genlis, which was very frequently heard – 'the devil with four horns', the more uncharitable said. Nineteen strokes heralded a great event, nothing less than the opening of the main door, a formidable, heavily-bolted sheet of metal which never turned on its hinges except to admit the archbishop.

Other than this dignitary and the gardener no man, as we have said, was allowed inside the convent proper. The schoolgirls, however, saw two others – the almoner, Abbé Banès, an old and ugly man whom they were able to observe through a grille in the choir, and the drawing-master, M. Ansiaux, who has been described as 'a terrible old hunchback'. It will be seen that the males were carefully selected.

Such was this singular establishment.

VIII

Post corda lapides

Having outlined its moral countenance it may be not inappropriate to depict in a few words its material aspect, of which the reader has already been given some impression.

The Convent of the Petit-Picpus-Saint-Antoine almost entirely filled the large irregular quadrilateral formed by four streets – the Rue Polonceau, the Rue Droit-Mur, the Petite Rue Picpus, and a now vanished alleyway which in old maps is called the Rue Aumarais. Its walls enclosed the area like a moat. The convent consisted of a number of buildings and a garden. The main building, taken as a whole, was a hybrid block of houses of which the ground plan, seen from above, resembled a gibbet. The upright of the gibbet occupied the whole stretch of the Rue Droit-Mur between the Petite Rue Picpus and the Rue Polonceau, the arm being a high, stark building with a barred façade on the Petite Rue Picpus and a *porte-cochère*, No. 62, at its extreme end. At about the centre of the frontage was a low, arched, crumbling doorway, filled with cobwebs, which was only opened for an hour or two on Sundays, and on the rare occasions when the coffin of a nun was taken out of the convent. This was the public entrance to the chapel. The supporting strut of the gibbet was a square room used for general purposes and called by the nuns 'the pantry'. The main building contained the cells of the mothers, the sisters, and the novices, and in the arm of the gibbet were the kitchen, the refectory, flanked by the cloister, and the chapel. The girls' boarding-house, which was not visible from outside, was situated between the doorway, No. 62, and the corner of the blind alley, Rue Aumarais. The rest of the quadrilateral consisted of the garden, which was on a lower level than the Rue Polonceau, so that the walls seen from inside were considerably higher than they appeared from the street. The garden, which was slightly concave, had a central knoll on which was a tall, slender pine-tree with four broad walks running from it as though from the boss of a shield, and disposed in pairs between these were eight lesser paths which, if the general plan had been circular, would have made the pattern resemble a cross superimposed on a wheel. The paths, all leading to the very irregular walls of the garden, were of unequal length. They were bordered by fruit bushes. At the end of one of the walks, flanked by poplars, were the ruins of the old convent, between the Rue Droit-Mur and the Little Convent, at the angle of the blind-alley. In front of the Little Convent was what was known as the 'little garden'. If we add to this a courtyard, a great many outcroppings and re-entrants formed by the internal irregularity of the buildings, and walls like those of a prison with nothing to be seen beyond them except the long black line of rooftops on the far side of the Rue Polonceau, we may form some idea of the Bernardine convent of Petit-Picpus as it existed forty-five years ago. It occupied the site of a tennis-court famous in the fourteenth and fifteenth centuries which had been known as 'the playground of eleven thousand devils'.

To conclude, those streets were among the oldest in Paris, even older than the names they then bore. The Rue Droit-Mur, for example, was once the Rue des Églantiers. God caused flowers to blossom before men shaped stone.

IX
A century under a wimple

Since we are discussing in some detail the life of a vanished convent and have presumed to throw open the doors of that sanctuary, we may venture to ask the reader to permit a further small digression, unrelated to the matter of this book but nevertheless of interest inasmuch as it reveals that even a convent may contain original characters.

Among the residents in the Little Convent was a centenarian lady who had come from the Abbaye de Fontevrault and who, before the Revolution, had belonged to the fashionable world. She talked a great deal about Monsieur de Miromesnil, who had been Keeper of the Seal under Louis XVI, and about a certain Madame Duplat, a judge's wife of whom she had been a close friend, neglecting no opportunity of bringing these names into her conversation. She told wonderful tales about Fontevrault, that it was like a small town and that there were streets within its walls.

She talked with a Picardy accent that charmed the schoolgirls. Every year she solemnly renewed her vows, saying to the priest, 'St Francis handed them down to St Julien, St Julien passed them on to St Eusebius, St Eusebius passed them on to St Procopius, etc., and now, father, I pass them on to you' – while the girls laughed, not up their sleeves but under their veils, stifled giggles of delight that caused the mothers to raise their eyebrows.

She told other tales. She said that when she was young the monks of St Bernard rivalled the Musketeers in the dissipated lives they led. The voice of a century spoke through her lips, but it was the eighteenth century. She described the custom in Champagne and Burgundy of the four wines. Before the Revolution, when a great personage, a Marshal of France, a prince or great lord, visited a town in either of these regions he was met by the town council bearing four goblets, each of which contained a different wine and bore a different inscription – *vin de singe, vin de lion, vin de mouton*, and *vin de cochon.* They represented the four stages of intoxication – gaiety, quarrelsomeness, dull-wittedness, and finally stupor.

She kept under lock and key a mysterious possession which she greatly valued. The Rule of Fontevrault allowed her to do so. She would shut herself in her room, which again was permitted by the Rule of her Order, and if she heard anyone approaching would lock the cupboard as quickly as her old hands could turn the key. When questioned about it she was silent, talkative though she was at other times, and proof against the most persistent curiosity. The matter was much discussed by idle tongues in the convent. What could the centenarian's treasure be – a sacred book, perhaps? – a unique chaplet? – a proven relic? . . . When the old lady died the cupboard was opened with what was, perhaps, unseemly haste. The object was found wrapped in linen as though it were a communion salver. It was a faience platter with a design of *putti* being pursued by apprentice apothecaries with huge syringes, a picture abounding in grimaces and comical postures. One of the charming *putti*, already spitted, was still struggling to escape, spreading his small wings and attempting to fly, while his pursuer crowed with satanic laughter. The moral was: love defeated by colic. The platter, a rare one it must be said, and one which may have furnished Molière with an idea, was still to be obtained as recently as September, 1845; a copy was on sale in an antique-shop on the Boulevard Beaumarchais.

This old lady never received a visitor from outside, because, she said, the parlour was too gloomy.

X

Origin of the Perpetual Adoration

That sepulchral parlour, which we have done our best to describe was unique in an austerity not to be found in other convents. In the parlour in the Rue du Temple, for example – admittedly the convent of another Order – the black shutters were replaced by a brown curtain and the room itself was a *salon* with a parquet floor, windows enclosed in muslin drapery, and walls hung with pictures, among them a Benedictine nun with her face uncovered, a flower-painting, and even a Turk's head. The garden of that particular convent contained what was said to be the largest and finest Spanish chestnut tree in all France, believed by the simple folk of the eighteenth century to be 'the father of all the chestnut trees in the kingdom'.

The Couvent du Temple, as we have said, was occupied by Benedictines of the Perpetual Adoration who were, however, quite different from those deriving from Cîteaux. The Order of the Perpetual Adoration is comparatively recent, having been founded only two centuries ago. In 1649 the Holy Sacrament was twice profaned within a few days in two separate Paris churches, those of Saint-Sulpice and Saint-Jean en Grève, an event as uncommon as it was outrageous, which shocked all the town. The Grand Prior and vicar of Saint-Germain-des-Près ordered a solemn procession of all his clergy at which the Papal Nuncio officiated. But this ceremony of expiation did not satisfy two worthy ladies, the Marquise de Boucs and the Countess de Chateauvieux. The outrage, although unrepeated, so preyed on their devout minds that they maintained that nothing less than a rule of 'Perpetual Adoration' in a woman's monastery could make sufficient atonement. The two ladies, one in 1652 and the other in 1653, furnished Mère Catherine de Bar, a Benedictine nun styled 'of the Holy Sacrament', with handsome endowments with which to found a Benedictine nunnery for this pious purpose. Permission was granted in the first instance by Monsieur de Metz, Abbot of Saint-Germain, with the proviso that 'no lady should be admitted to the order who did not bring with her a yearly income of 300 *livres*, entailing 6000 *livres* capital'. Thereafter letters patent were authorized by the king, and the whole, the abbatical charter and the royal licence, was registered at the Chamber of Accounts and with Parliament.

Such was the origin and legal basis of the establishment of the Benedictines of the Perpetual Adoration in Paris. Their first convent, 'newly built' by the endowments of Mesdames de Boucs and de Chateauvieux, was in the Rue Cassette.

As we see, this Order was quite distinct from the Benedictine Order known as the Cistercians. It was created by the Abbot of Saint-Germain-des-Prés, just as the Order of the Sacred Heart was created by the head of the Jesuit Order, and that of the Sisters of Charity by the head of the Order of St Lazarus.

It was also quite separate from the Bernardines of Petit-Picpus. In 1657 Pope Alexander VII had in a special bull authorized the Petit-Picpus Bernardines to practise Perpetual Adoration like the

Benedictines of the Holy Sacrament. But the two orders were none the less distinct.

XI
End of the Petit-Picpus

The dwindling of the Petit-Picpus convent began with the Restoration and was a part of the general decay of the order, which, like all religious orders, has been declining since the eighteenth century. Contemplation, like prayer, is a human necessity; but like everything touched by the Revolution it is destined to be transformed and, from being opposed to social progress, to become favourable to it.

The Petit-Picpus community rapidly shrank. By 1840 the Little Convent and the school had ceased to exist. There were no longer any very old women or young girls, the first being dead and the second fled away.

The discipline of the Perpetual Adoration is so harsh that it repels; vocations recoil from it and recruits are not forthcoming. In 1845 there were still a few groups of serving sisters but no chantry-nuns. Forty years ago the number was nearly a hundred, and fifteen years ago it was only twenty-eight. The prioress in 1847 was young, not yet forty, a sign that the choice was limited. As the number diminished the work of the community increased, the duties of each member becoming more arduous. The time was drawing near when there would be no more than a dozen bowed and labouring shoulders to sustain the heavy rule of St Benedict, a burden that grew no lighter, whether for the few or the many. A crushing burden, and so they died. Two, aged twenty-five and twenty-three, died while the author of this book was still living in Paris. It was because of this shrinkage that the convent was forced to give up the education of girls.

We could not have entered that extraordinary and little-known establishment except in the company of those who – to the profit of some, perhaps – are following the melancholy history of Jean Valjean. We have glanced at that community with its ancient practices that nowadays seem strangely novel. It was a walled garden. We have described it in detail but with respect, insofar as the detail and respect may be reconciled. If we have not understood everything, we have despised nothing. We are as far removed from the hosannas of Joseph de Maistre, who blessed the executioner, as from the gibes of Voltaire, who mocked the Crucifix: a lack of logic on Voltaire's part, be it said, for he would have defended Jesus as he defended Calas. To those who reject the superhuman incarnate what does the Crucifix represent? – the murder of wisdom.

In our nineteenth century the religious idea is undergoing a crisis. Certain things have been unlearnt, and this is good, provided other things are learnt. There must be no void in the human heart. Edifices may be pulled down, but only on condition that others are put in their place.

And in the meantime we must scrutinize the things that have vanished, needing to know if only to avoid them. Counterfeits of the past, under new names, may easily be mistaken for the future. The past, that ghostly traveller, is liable to forge his papers. We must be wary of the trap. The past has a face which is superstition, and a mask, which is hypocrisy. We must expose the face and tear off the mask.

Convents in general present a complex problem: the problem of civilization, which condemns them, and of liberty, which defends them.

[Book Seven: A Parenthesis, will be found as Appendix A, page 702].

BOOK EIGHT

CEMETERIES TAKE WHAT THEY ARE GIVEN

I

Which treats of the method of entering a convent

IT WAS into this establishment that Jean Valjean had fallen, in Fauchelevent's words, 'out of the sky'. After putting Cosette to bed he and Fauchelevent had a meal in front of a blazing fire and then, there being no other bed, they stretched out on bales of straw. Before closing his eyes Valjean said, 'I shall have to stay here,' and the words exercised Fauchelevent's mind for the rest of the night.

But the truth is that neither of them slept. Knowing now that Javert was on his trail Valjean realized that he and Cosette could not hope to hide anywhere in the town. Chance having brought him to the convent, his only thought was to remain there. In his situation it was at once the most dangerous and the safest place – most dangerous since no man might enter it, and to be discovered there would of itself cause him to be sent to prison; but safest because who would look for him there? The most unlikely hiding-place was the most secure.

Fauchelevent, for his part, was racking his brains. He began by saying to himself that the whole thing was beyond him. How had Monsieur Madeleine contrived to get in over that formidable wall and, what was more, bring a child with him? Who was the child, and where had they come from? Fauchelevent had heard no news of Montreuil-sur-mer since he had been in the convent, and he knew nothing of what had happened. Père Madeleine's manner discouraged questions, and he said to himself that in any case one does not question a saint. For him the great man had lost none of his greatness. Certain words that he had let fall, however, gave Fauchelevent the impression that he must have gone bankrupt owing to the hardness of the times, and was now running to escape his creditors; or perhaps he had been compromised in some political affair and must go into hiding. This latter thought did not displease the old man, who, like so many of our northern peasants, was at heart a Bonapartist. That Monsieur Madeleine should regard the convent as a place of refuge and wish to remain there was understandable; but the child remained a complete mystery. Faced by this element of the incomprehensible the old man lost himself in conjecture, seeing only one thing clearly, that the former mayor had saved his life. 'It's my turn,' he thought. 'He didn't waste any time thinking when he crawled under that cart to rescue me.' At all costs he must now come to his aid. Even if Monsieur Madeleine turned out to be a thief, even a murderer, he must still be saved, since he was also a saint.

But how contrive matters so that he could stay in the convent? Insuperable though the problem appeared, Fauchelevent refused to be daunted. The humble Picardy peasant, with no other resources than devotion, goodwill, and a store of peasant cunning which must now be made to serve a generous impulse, was steadfast in his resolve to outwit the defences of the convent and scale the rigid barriers of the Rule of St Benedict. Fauchelevent was an old man who all his life had been wholly self-centred but who now, at the end of his days, crippled, infirm and having no further interest in life, took pleasure in his sense of gratitude, and, having the chance to perform a good deed, clutched at it with the eagerness of a dying man offered a glass of some rare vintage which he has never previously tasted. Moreover the air he had breathed during his several years at the convent had so modified his character that a virtuous act of some kind had become for him a necessity.

So he determined to serve Monsieur Madeleine.

We have called him a humble Picardy peasant, and this is a true but incomplete description. We need now to look more closely at Père Fauchelevent. He was a peasant but he had been a law-scrivener, which lent sharp practice to his cunning and astuteness to his simplicity. Having for a variety of reasons failed in his business of scrivener he had sunk to the level of carter and casual labourer; but beneath the oaths and whiplashes inseparable, as it seems, from the handling of horses something of the scrivener still lingered. He had some natural intelligence and his language had become less uncouth than that of the ordinary peasant. He liked to discourse, which is rare among villagers, and people said of him, 'He talks almost like a gentleman.' In short Fauchelevent was what an earlier age would have termed half-burgess and half-villein, a mingling of citizen and rustic. Although harshly treated by the world and bearing the marks of this ill-usage, he was still a creature of impulse and spontaneity, qualities which prevent a man from being wholly bad. His faults and vices, such as they had been, were superficial, and in general his appearance was more prepossessing than otherwise. That aged forehead had none of the vertical wrinkles that betoken malice or stupidity.

At daybreak Père Fauchelevent, having deeply cogitated, opened his eyes and looked at Monsieur Madeleine who, seated on his truss of straw, was watching Cosette while she slept. He sat up and said:

'Well, here you are, but how are we going to arrange for you to be here?'

The question summed up the situation, arousing Jean Valjean from his preoccupations, and the two men took counsel together.

'To start with,' said Fauchelevent, 'you mustn't set foot outside this cottage, neither you nor the child. One glimpse of either of you in the garden will give us all away.'

'That is true.'

'The fact is, Monsieur Madeleine,' said Fauchelevent, 'you've arrived at a fortunate moment – or unfortunate, I should say. One of the ladies is very ill, said to be dying. The last rites are being performed, the forty-hour prayers, so the whole community has something on its mind and nobody is going to worry about us. A saint is departing this world. Well, of course, we're all saints here, the difference being that they call their dwellings cells and I call mine a shanty. There are prayers for the dying and prayers for the dead. So that means that for today we shan't be disturbed, but I can't answer for tomorrow.'

'In any case,' said Jean Valjean, 'this cottage is tucked away behind some sort of ruin. There are trees. Surely it can't be seen from the convent?'

'True, and the nuns never come near it. But there are the children.'

At this point Fauchelevent was interrupted by the single note of a bell. He broke off and signed to Valjean to listen. The bell sounded again.

'So she's dead,' he said. 'That's the death-knell. That bell will toll once a minute for the next twenty-four hours, until the body is taken out of the chapel. The children play in the garden. A ball has only to come bouncing this way and they'll be running after it, looking everywhere, although they know it isn't allowed. They're little imps, those children.'

'What children?'

'They'd spot you in no time, and you'd have the whole lot squealing, "There's a man!" But there's no danger of that today. There'll be no recreation period, nothing but prayers. Hark to that bell. Every minute, like I said.'

'I think I understand,' said Valjean. 'There's a boarding-school.' The thought had instantly crossed his mind that it might be a place for the education of Cosette.

'Little girls by the dozen,' said Fauchelevent. 'They'd run away squealing. A man in this place is like someone with the plague. That's why I have a bell tied to me, as though I were a wild animal.'

Jean Valjean was now plunged in thought, reflecting that this convent might be their salvation. He said aloud:

'The problem is to stay here.'

'No,' said Fauchelevent, 'the problem is to get out.'

Valjean started. 'To get out?'

'Yes, Monsieur. If you're to be admitted you must come from outside. You can't just be found here like this. For me, you've fallen from Heaven, but that's because I know you. The nuns expect people to come in through the door.'

Another bell now rang, sounding a more elaborate peal.

'Ah,' said Fauchelevent. 'That's to summon the mothers to the chapter. They always hold a chapter when someones dies. She died at daybreak, like people mostly do. But why can't you go out the way you came in? I don't want to ask questions, but how did you get in?'

Jean Valjean had turned pale. The thought of returning to that dreadful street caused him to shudder. It was like escaping from a tiger-infested forest and being advised to go back into it. He pictured the police swarming throughout the quarter, watchers and patrols all over the place, hands everywhere ready to seize him by the collar, with Javert presiding.

'Impossible,' he said. 'Père Fauchelevent, you must assume that I've fallen from the skies.'

'And I'm ready to believe it,' said Fauchelevent. 'No need to tell me anything. God picked you up to have a look at you and then let you go again. Only, He made a mistake. He should have put you in a monastery. There's another bell. That'll be for the porter to go to the Municipality to report the death, and they'll send a doctor to confirm it. All part of the ceremony of dying. The ladies don't like those visits. Doctors don't believe in anything. They lift up veils, and sometimes other things as well. But they've been very quick sending for the doctor this time. I wonder what's happened. That child of yours is still asleep. What's her name?'

'Cosette.'

'Is she really yours – as it might be, your granddaughter?'

'Yes.'

'There'll be no trouble getting her out of here. There's a service-door to the outside yard. I knock and the door-keeper opens. It'll just be old Fauchelevent going out with his gardener's hod on his back. You'll have to tell the little girl to keep quiet. She'll be inside the basket, hidden under a piece of sacking. I'll take her to a friend of mine, an old woman who keeps a fruit-shop in the Rue du Chemin-Vert. She's deaf and I'll have to shout, but I'll get her to understand that it's my niece and she's got to look after her until tomorrow. Then the child can come back here with you. Because I'll find some way of getting you in. I'll have to. But how are you going to get out?'

Jean Valjean shook his head.

'No one must see me, Père Fauchelevent. That is the essential thing. You will have to contrive something like Cosette's basket and piece of sacking.'

Fauchelevent scratched the lobe of his ear with the middle finger of his left hand, a sign of great perplexity. He was still pondering when the bell again rang.

'That'll be the doctor,' he said. 'He'll have a look and say, "She's dead all right." After the doctor has stamped the passport to paradise the undertaker sends round a coffin. If it's a mother, the mothers lay her out; and if it's a sister the sisters do it. And then I nail her up. That's part of my duties as gardener. A gardener is always something of a grave-digger. She's put in a small room by the chapel, with a door giving on to the street, and no man except the doctor is allowed in. Me and the pall-bearers, we don't count as men. That's where I nail up the coffin. The pall-bearers take her away, and gee-up, Dobbin, that's how we go to Heaven. They come with an empty box and take it away with something in it. And that's a burial. *De profundis.*'

A ray of sunshine flooding into the room fell upon Cosette's sleeping face, causing her lips to part as though she were drinking its light. Jean Valjean was gazing at her and no longer listening to

Fauchelevent. But the lack of an audience did not deter the old man. He droned tranquilly on.

'The grave will be in the Cimetière Vaugirard. They say they're going to do away with that old cemetery. It doesn't fit in with regulations, it wears uniform and it's going to be retired. A pity, because it's convenient. The grave-digger, Père Mestienne, is a friend of mine. The nuns from this convent have a special privilege, they're allowed to be taken there at nightfall. The Prefect issued a special order. But, lord, what a lot of things have happened since yesterday, Mother Crucifixion dead and Père Madeleine –'

'Buried alive,' said Jean Valjean, sadly smiling.

'Buried alive! Well, so you will be if you're here for good.'

The bell rang yet again, and this time Fauchelevent hastily took his own bell off its nail and strapped it to his knee.

'That's for me. The prioress wants me. There, I've gone and pricked myself with the buckle. You wait here, Monsieur Madeleine, and don't move till I come back. There's wine and bread and cheese if you're hungry.'

He went out muttering, 'I'm coming. I'm coming,' and Valjean saw him cross the garden as fast as his damaged leg allowed, glancing at his melon-patch as he passed. A few minutes later, having warned the nuns of his passing, he knocked gently on a door and a gentle voice replied, 'For ever. For ever.' – that is to say, 'Come in.'

The door was that of a small room adjoining the chapter-room which was used when the gardener was interviewed in connection with his duties. The prioress, seated on the only chair, was awaiting him.

II

Fauchelevent deals with a problem

To appear at once troubled and controlled in moments of crisis is the especial quality of certain characters and certain callings, notably priests and the members of religious communities. This double pre-occupation was apparent at the moment of Fauchelevent's entry in the aspect of the prioress, the charming and erudite and generally cheerful Mlle de Blemeur, Mère Innocente.

The gardener, with a respectful salutation, remained standing in the doorway. The prioress, who was telling her beads, looked up and said, 'Ah, it's you, Père Fauvent,' this being the abbreviation that was commonly used in the convent.

The old man bobbed and touched his forehead again.

'You sent for me, Reverend Mother.'

'I've something to say to you.'

'I too,' said Fauchelevent, with a boldness that secretly terrified him, 'have something to say to the Very Reverend Mother.'

'You have something to tell me?'

'A request.'

'Well, let me hear it.'

Old Fauchelevent, the one-time scrivener, was a peasant of the calculating kind. A shrewd show of ignorance can be effective; it disarms mistrust and it ensnares. During the period of a little more than two years that he had been in the convent Fauchelevent had become a part of the community. Solitary as he always was, busy about his garden, he had nothing else but curiosity to occupy his mind. The veiled women coming and going at a distance were to him like a fluttering of shadows, but by dint of observation and perspicacity he had endowed them with substance, bringing the spectral figures to life. He was like a deaf man who grows more long-sighted or a blind man whose hearing becomes acute. He had learnt to read the code of the bells and had reached the point where nothing was hidden from him in that silent, enigmatic place: the sphinx whispered her secrets in his ear. But knowing everything, Fauchelevent disclosed nothing. That was his especial skill. The convent thought him stupid, a great merit in religion. The mothers esteemed him highly, feeling that he was to be trusted. Moreover he was regular in his habits, never going outside the walls except for the obvious necessities of his garden. His discreet bearing counted greatly in his favour. However, he was in the confidence of two men: the porter, from whom he learned the proceedings of the chapter, and the grave-digger at the cemetery, who told him about the special interment rites. He might be said, in short, to view the nuns in a double light, with one eye on life and the other on death. But he did not abuse his knowledge and was valued accordingly. Old, crippled, seeing nothing and probably hard of hearing – such admirable qualities! It would be difficult to replace him.

And now, in the consciousness of his worth, he embarked at the invitation of the prioress upon a rambling and profound country discourse. He talked at length about age and infirmity, the increasing burden of his years, the size of the garden and the many tasks he had to perform, such as last night, for instance, when he had had to go out and straw the melons under the moon because of the danger of frost; and at length he came to the point, which was that he had a brother (the prioress started), not a young man (the prioress looked reassured) who, if permitted, would come to live with him and assist him, an excellent gardener who would serve the community better than he could himself; failing this, if his brother could not be accepted, feeling himself to be no longer equal to his task he would be compelled with the utmost regret to leave them. Finally, his brother had a granddaughter whom he wished to bring with him, a little girl who might be brought up under God by the community and who one day – who could tell? – might become a member of it.

When he had finished speaking the prioress ceased telling her beads and said:

'Would it be possible for you to obtain a stout iron crowbar by this evening?'

'For what purpose?'

'For use as a lever.'

'Yes, Reverend Mother,' said Fauchelevent.

Without saying any more the prioress rose and went into the next room, which was the chapter-hall, where the chantry mothers were doubtless assembled. Fauchelevent was left alone.

III

Mère Innocente

A quarter of an hour elapsed. The prioress returned and resumed her seat. Both speakers seemed preoccupied. We report as exactly as we can the conversation that ensued.

'Père Fauvent?'

'Reverend Mother?'

'You are familiar with the chapel?'

'I have a small recess where I hear Mass and the Offices.'

'And you have been in the choir in connection with your work?'

'Two or three times.'

'I want a stone to be lifted.'

'A heavy one?'

'The flagstone beside the altar.'

'The stone which closes the vault?'

'Yes.'

'That is a job for two men.'

'Mère Ascension, who is as strong as a man, will help you.'

'A woman is not the same as a man.'

'She's the only one. We all do what we can. Because Dom Mabillon has given us four hundred and seven epistles of St Bernard, and Merlonus Horstius only three hundred and sixty-seven, I do not for that reason despise Merlonus Horstius.'

'Nor I, Reverend Mother.'

'The merit lies in doing our best. A cloister is not a work-shop.'

'Nor is a woman a man. My brother's very strong.'

'Besides, you will have your crowbar.'

'That is the only kind of key for that kind of door.'

'There's a ring in the stone.'

'I'll slip the bar through it.'

'And it is set on a pivot.'

'Very well, Reverend Mother, I'll open the vault.'

'The four chantry mothers will be present.'

'And when the vault has been opened?'

'It will have to be closed again.'

'Will that be all?'

'No.'

'Tell me what else you want, Most Reverend Mother.'

'Fauvent, we trust you.'

'I am here to do your bidding.'

'And to keep silence.'

'Yes.'

'When the vault has been opened –'

'I'm to close it again.'

'But first there is something else . . .'

'Yes, Reverend Mother?'

'Something must be lowered into it.'

There was a moment of silence broken by the prioress after a slight pursing of her lower lip which seemed to denote hesitation.

'You know, do you not, Père Fauvent, that one of the mothers died this morning?'

'No.'

'You didn't hear the bell?'

'One hears nothing at the end of the garden.'

'Truly?'

'It's all I can do to hear my own bell.'

'She died at daybreak.'

'And then, the wind wasn't blowing my way.'

'It was Mère Crucifixion, of most blessed memory.'

The prioress was again silent while her lips moved as though in prayer. She went on:

'Three years ago Madame de Béthune, a Jansenist, was converted to orthodoxy, simply from having seen Mère Crucifixion at her devotions.'

'Ah, now I can hear the death-bell, Reverend Mother.'

'She has been taken into the mortuary chamber adjoining the chapel.'

'I know it.'

'No man other than yourself is allowed in that room, or should be allowed in it. Do not forget that. It would be a fine thing if a man were to enter the mortuary chamber!'

'More often!'

'What!'

'More often.'

'What did you say?'

'I said, more often.'

'More often than what?'

'I didn't say more often than anything, Reverend Mother. I just said, more often.'

'I don't understand. Why did you say it?'

'I was just agreeing with you, Reverend Mother.'

'But I didn't say, more often.'

'I know you didn't. I said it for you.'

At this moment the clock struck nine.

'At this hour of nine and at every hour praised and adored be the Holy Sacrament,' murmured the prioress.

'Amen,' said Fauchelevent.

The striking of the hour was fortunate. It put an end to the subject of 'more often', a tangle from which the prioress and he might never have extricated themselves. He mopped his forehead.

The prioress murmured a few more words, presumably of a devotional kind, and then resumed.

'During her lifetime Mère Crucifixion made conversions. Now that she is dead she will perform miracles.'

'She will perform miracles,' repeated Fauchelevent, falling into line and hoping not to get out of step.

'Our community has been greatly blessed in Mère Crucifixion. No doubt it is not given to everyone to die, like Cardinal de Bérulle, speaking the words of the Holy Mass. She did not attain to this happiness, but she died a most precious death. She was conscious to the last. She talked to us and to the angels. She laid upon us her last injunctions. If you possessed a little more faith, Père Fauvent, and had been there in her cell, she would have healed your leg by laying her hand on it. She was smiling. We felt that she was being resurrected in God. Paradise was present at her death.'

'Amen,' said Fauchelevent, thinking that this was the conclusion of a prayer. He waited in silence while the prioress told several of her beads.

'The wishes of the dead, Père Fauvent, must be respected. It is a matter in which I have consulted a number of ecclesiastics, pious men whose lives are given to the work of the Church, and who reap a rich harvest.'

'You know, Reverend Mother, you can hear the death-bell much better here than in the garden.'

'Besides, this is something more than a dead woman. She was a saint.'

'Like yourself, Reverend Mother.'

'For twenty years she slept in her coffin, having received the express permission of our Holy Father, Pope Pius VII.'

'The one who crowned the Emp— that is to say, Bonaparte.'

It was a surprising slip on the part of a man as astute as Fauchelevent, but fortunately the prioress, absorbed in her own thoughts, did not hear it. She went on:

'St Diodore, the Archbishop of Cappadocia, desired to have the single word, *Acarus*, which means an earthworm, inscribed on his tomb, and this was done. Is that not true?'

'Yes, Reverend Mother.'

'The blessed Mezzocane, Abbot of Aquila, desired to be buried under a gallows. This was done.'

'True.'

'St Terence, the Bishop of Ostia, at the mouth of the Tiber, desired that his tombstone should be engraved with the symbol denoting a parricide, in the hope that passers-by would spit on it. This was done. The wishes of the dead must be respected.'

'So be it.'

'The body of Bernard Guidonis, who was born in France near Roche-Abeille, was taken on his instructions, and in defiance of the King of Castille, to the Dominican church at Limoges, although Bernard Guidonis had been Bishop of Tuy, in Spain. Can this be denied? It is attested by Plantavit de la Fosse.'

'Then it must be true, Reverend Mother.'

More beads of the rosary were told.

'Père Fauvent, Mère Crucifixion will be buried in the coffin in which she slept for twenty years.'

'Quite right.'

'It will be a continuance of her sleep.'

'So that's the coffin I'm to nail up?'

'Yes.'

'And we won't bother about the one they bring in?'

'Exactly. The four chantry-mothers will help you.'

'To nail the coffin? But I don't need them.'

'No. To lower it.'

'To lower it? Where?'

'Into the vault.'

Fauchelevent started.

'The vault under the altar? But –'

'You will have a crowbar –'

'Yes, but –'

'The wishes of the dead must be respected. This was Mère Crucifixion's last wish, that her remains should not be consigned to profane ground, but that she should rest in death where she had prayed in life, under the altar in our chapel. She desired this of us – that is to say, she commanded it.'

'But it's forbidden.'

'Forbidden by man but sanctioned by God.'

'But what if it became known?'

'We trust you.'

'Me, I'm like a stone in the wall, but –'

'I have consulted with the Mothers of the Chapter, who are now assembled, and we have decided that Mère Crucifixion shall be buried according to her express desire. Think, Père Fauvent, of the miracles that may result from this! Think of the glory to our community under God! Miracles come from tombs.'

'But, Reverend Mother, if an agent from the Commission of Health –'

'St Benedict II defied Constantin Pogonat over a matter of burial.'

'– or the Commissioner of Police –'

'Chonodemaire, one of the seven German kings who joined the Gauls in the reign of Constantine, expressly acknowledged the right of members of religious orders to be buried in a place of religion, that is to say, under the altar –'

'– or an inspector from the Prefecture –'

'The world counts for nothing in the face of religion. Martin, the eleventh general of the Carthusians, gave his order this device: *Stat Crux dum volvitur orbis* – The Cross will remain while the world revolves.'

'Amen,' said Fauchelevent, happy to have his doubts set at rest, as they always were by the sound of Latin.

Any audience will suffice a person who has been too long silent. The orator Gymnastoras, being released from prison with his head stuffed with arguments and syllogisms, stopped at the first tree he came to and harangued it, doing his utmost to convert it to his views. Thus the prioress, normally confined within the barriers of silence and having words heaped up within her, rose to her feet and poured forth a torrent that was like the opening of a sluice-gate.

'I have Benedict at my right hand and Bernard at my left. Who was Bernard? He was the first Abbot of Clairvaux, and Fontaines in Burgundy is blessed inasmuch as it was his birthplace. His father was called Técelin and his mother was Alethea. He began at Cîteaux and ended at Clairvaux. He was ordained abbot by the Bishop of Châlon-sur-Saône, Guillaume de Champeaux. He instructed seven hundred novices and founded one hundred and sixty monasteries. He defeated Abelard at the Council of Rheims in 1140, and Pierre de Bruys and Henry his disciple, and a flock of black sheep known as the Apostolics. He confounded Arnaud de Bresce, pulverized the monk Raoul, slayer of Jews, dominated the Council of Rheims in 1148, and caused Gilbert de la Porée, Bishop of Poitiers, and Éon de l'Étoile to be condemned. He reconciled the differences of princes, enlightened King Louis the Young, counselled Pope Eugene III, ruled the Temple, preached the Crusade, and during his life performed two hundred and fifty miracles, as many as thirty-nine in a single day. Who was Benedict? He was the patriarch of Monte Cassino, the second founder of a monastic order, the Basil of the west. His order has produced forty popes, two hundred cardinals, fifty patriarchs, sixteen hundred archbishops, four thousand six hundred bishops, four emperors, twelve empresses, forty-six kings, forty-one queens, three thousand six hundred canonized saints, and it has endured for fourteen hundred years. Bernard on one side, and sanitation on the other; Benedict and the Inspector of Roadways! The State, the roads, the undertaker's parlour, regulations and administration – what have we to do with those things? No onlooker cares for the way we are treated. We have not even the right to consign our dust to the Lord. Your sanitation is a revolutionary invention. God is made subordinate to the Commissioner of Police – that is our present century! Silence, Fauvent!'

Fauchelevent had fidgeted in discomfort under this tirade. The prioress continued:

'The monasteries' right of sepulchre is not in doubt, only fanatics and misguided persons deny it. We live in times of terrible confusion. The world is ignorant of things that it should know and knows things that are better unknown. Men are gross and impious. There are people who do not distinguish between the great St Bernard and St Bernard of the Catholic Poor, a worthy cleric who lived in the thirteenth century. Some carry blasphemy to the point of likening the scaffold of Louis XVI to the Cross of Jesus Christ. But Louis XVI was only a king. We must be watchful for God! There are no longer right-minded and wrong-minded men. The name of Voltaire is known, but not the name of César de Bus: yet César de Bus is blessed and Voltaire is accursed. The late archbishop, Cardinal de Périgord, did not even know that Charles de Condren succeeded Bérulle, that François Bourgoin succeeded Condren, Jean-François Senault succeeded Bourgoin and was himself succeeded by the father of St Marthe, all generals of the Oratory. The name of Père Coton is remembered, not because he was one of the three founders of that Order but because he was the subject of an obscene allusion by the Huguenot king, Henri IV. St François de Sales endeared himself to worldly people by cheating at cards. And so they attack religion. Why? Because there have been bad priests, because Sagittaire, the Bishop of Gap, was the brother of Salone, Bishop of Embrun, and both were worshippers of Mammon.

What does that matter? Does it alter the fact that Martin de Tours was a saint who gave half his cloak to a poor man? The saints are persecuted, eyes are closed to truth, darkness is the daily wear. The most savage beasts are those that are blind. No one thinks seriously of Hell. Oh, the wickedness of the people! "In the name of the King" means, in these days, "In the name of the Revolution!" No man knows where his duty lies, to the living or to the dead. To die in sanctity is forbidden, burial is a civic matter. That is an outrage! St Léon II wrote two letters, one to Pierre Notaire and the other to the King of the Visigoths, disputing and rejecting the authority of the Exarch and the supremacy of the Emperor in this matter of the burial of the dead, and in the same matter Gautier, Bishop of Châlons, defied Otto, the Duke of Burgundy. The magistrature sustained them. In the old days the Chapter had a voice even in worldly affairs. The Abbé de Cîteaux, general of the Cistercian Order, was a hereditary member of the Parliament of Burgundy. We have always disposed of our dead as we saw fit. Is not the body of St Benedict himself in France, in the Abbaye de Fleury, called Saint-Benoit-sur-Loire, although he died in Italy, at Monte Cassino, in the year 543? All that is incontestable. I abhor schismatics and abominate heretics, but I will detest still more anyone who denies these things. We have only to read the works of Arnoul Wion, Gabriel Bucelin, Trithemus, Maurolicus, and Dom Luc d'Achery.'

The prioress sighed and then turned to Fauchelevent.

'Père Fauvent, is it agreed?'

'It is agreed, Reverend Mother.'

'We may rely upon you?'

'I shall obey. I am at the service of the convent.'

'That is well. You will close the coffin and the sisters will carry it into the chapel. The Office for the Dead will be held. Then they will return to the cloister, and between eleven and midnight you will come with your crowbar. Everything will take place in the greatest secrecy. Only the four chantry-mothers will be in the chapel, with Mère Ascension and yourself.'

'And the sister who is making atonement?'

'She will not turn her head.'

'But she'll hear.'

'She will not listen. Besides, what is known in the convent is not known to the world outside.'

There was a further pause. The prioress said:

'You will not wear your bell. There is no need for the sister making atonement to know that you are there.'

'If you please, Reverend Mother –'

'Yes?'

'Has the doctor been?'

'He will come at four o'clock. The bell has been rung to summon him. But you do not hear the bells?'

'I only listen for my own.'

'That is well.'

'I shall need a crowbar at least six feet long, Reverend Mother.'

'Where will you get one?'

'That will not be difficult in a place where there are so many iron bars. I have plenty at the bottom of the garden.'

'You are to come three-quarters of an hour before midnight. Don't forget.'

'Another thing, Reverend Mother.'

'Well?'

'If you have any other work of this kind, my brother is exceptionally strong.'

'You must do it as quickly as you can.'

'But I can't work fast. I'm getting old. That's why I need help. And I limp.'

'A limp is no sin. It may even be a blessing. The Emperor Henry II, who opposed the antipope Gregorius and restored Benedict VIII, was called by two other names, the Saint and the Cripple.'

'It's a great thing to have two,' murmured Fauchelevent, who was indeed a little hard of hearing.

'You had better allow a full hour, Père Fauvent. Be near the High Altar with your crowbar at eleven. The service will begin at midnight, and your work must be completed a good quarter-of-an-hour beforehand.'

'I will do everything in my power to prove my devotion to the community. That is understood. I'll nail the coffin, and at precisely eleven I shall be in the chapel. The chantry-mothers and Mère Ascension will also be there. Two men would be better still, but no matter, I shall have my crowbar. We will open the vault and lower the coffin and close the vault again. No traces will be left and the Government will suspect nothing. So it is all settled, Reverend Mother?'

'Not quite.'

'What else is there?'

'There will be the coffin that is brought in, an empty coffin. What are we to do with that, Père Fauvent?'

There was a pause while both considered this matter.

'It will be taken out and buried.'

'Empty?'

Another pause followed, and then Fauchelevent made a gesture dismissing that problem.

'Reverend Mother, I will nail both coffins. No one is allowed in that room except myself. I will cover the empty one with the pall.'

'But when the bearers carry it to the hearse, and when it is lowered into the grave, they will know by the weight that there is nothing in it.'

'The dev—' burst out Fauchelevent and checked himself as the prioress began to make the sign of the cross with her eyes upon him. He searched hastily for an expedient to cover his lapse.

'I'll put earth in the coffin, Reverend Mother – enough to make it feel as though there was a body.'

'Yes, that will do. Earth and the flesh are one. You will see to it, Père Fauvent?'

'Most certainly.'

The prioress's grave and troubled expression gave way to one of reassurance. She made a sign of dismissal, and Fauchelevent turned towards the door. But as he was about to leave the room she said gently:

'Père Fauvent, I am pleased with you. Tomorrow, after the burial, bring your brother to see me, and tell him to bring his granddaughter.'

IV

Stratagem of an ex-prisoner

The steps of a cripple are like the gropings of the half-blind; they do not quickly reach their destination. Moreover Fauchelevent was thinking. It took him nearly a quarter of an hour to return to the cottage. Cosette was awake and Jean Valjean had seated her by the fire. At the moment when Fauchelevent entered he was pointing to the gardener's hod hanging on the wall and saying:

'Listen carefully, my love. We have got to leave this place, but we shall come back here and be happy. The gardener will carry you out on his back in that basket. He will take you to a place where a lady will look after you until I come to fetch you. You must be very good and not say a word if you do not want Mme Thénardier to catch you.'

Cosette nodded gravely.

Valjean looked round at Fauchelevent.

'Well?'

'Everything's arranged and nothing is. I've got leave to take you to the prioress, but before I can bring you in you've got to go out. That's where the trouble lies. The child's easy enough provided she'll keep quiet.'

'I can answer for that.'

'But what about you, Père Madeleine?' Fauchelevent waited hopefully for an answer and finally burst out: 'Why on earth can't you go out the way you got in?'

Jean Valjean simply replied as he had done before:

'Impossible.'

'But in that case, how the dev— how the deuce are we to get you out?' Fauchelevent sat muttering, half to himself. 'There's another thing that worries me. I said I'd put earth in it, but that won't do. If it's packed tight it'll be too heavy, and if it's loose it'll shift about, it won't feel like a body. They'll suspect something.'

Valjean was staring at him, unable to follow any of this. The old man went on to explain the situation, the resolve of the Chapter that the dead nun should be interred in the chapel vault according to her wish and in defiance of regulations, the part which he was to play in the affair and the stratagem whereby he would present Valjean to the prioress as his brother and Cosette as his niece. But there remained this problem of the empty coffin.

'What coffin are you talking about?' asked Valjean.

'The municipal coffin. The doctor reports that a nun has died and the Municipality sends round a coffin, and the next day the pall-bearers come with a hearse and take her off to the cemetery. But if they lift an empty coffin they'll know there's nothing in it.'

'Then you must put something in it.'

'Another dead body? I haven't got one.'

'A living body.'

'What do you mean?'

'Me,' said Jean Valjean.

Fauchelevent, who was seated, rose up from his chair as though a fire-cracker had exploded beneath it.

'You!'

'Why not?' Valjean smiled one of his rare smiles which were like sunshine breaking through a winter's sky. 'When you told me that Mère Crucifixion had died I said, if you remember, that Père Madeleine was buried alive. That is what it will be.'

'In fact, you're just joking. You aren't serious.'

'But indeed I am. We are agreed that I must get out of here unseen. I said that you would have to find the equivalent of a hod and a piece of sacking. And there it is. The hod will be of pine and the sacking will be a black pall.'

'White. The nuns are always buried in white.'

'Well then, white.'

'You're no ordinary man, Père Madeleine.'

It was a device typical of the wild and foolhardy contrivances of prison inmates, but seeing it against the background of the disciplined and peaceful life of the convent Fauchelevent was as filled with amazement as if he had seen a heron fishing in the gutter in the Rue Saint-Denis.

'I have got to get out without being seen,' said Jean Valjean, 'and this is a way of doing it. But what happens exactly? Where will this empty coffin be?'

'In what is called the mortuary chamber, resting on trestles with a pall over it.'

'How long will it be?'

'Six feet.'

'Tell me about the mortuary chamber.'

'It's on the ground floor, with a barred window on to the garden, closed by shutters on the outside, and two doors, one to the chapel and the other to the street.'

'Have you the key to both doors?'

'No, only to the convent door. The porter has the other.'

'When does he unlock it?'

'Only to admit the pall-bearers to take away the coffin. When this has been done the door is locked again.'

'Who nails the coffin?'

'I do.'

'And you cover it with the pall?'

'Yes.'

'Will you be alone?'

'Yes. Except for the police doctor and the pall-bearers, no other man is allowed in the mortuary chamber. It's written on the wall.'

'Can you hide me in the chamber some time during the night when everyone's asleep?'

'Not in the chamber itself. But there's a closet where I keep my burial tools. I have a key to that.'

'What time will the hearse come tomorrow?'

'At about three in the afternoon. The body will be buried a little before nightfall in the Cimetière Vaugirard. It's some distance away.'

'So I shall have to hide all night and all tomorrow morning in your closet. I shall need food.'

'I can bring you some.'

'And you can nail me in the coffin at two.'

Fauchelevent sat back, cracking his finger-joints.

'It's impossible.'

'Nonsense. What is so difficult about putting a few nails in a coffin?'

What to Fauchelevent appeared inconceivable appeared to Valjean a simple matter. He had known worse things. Whoever has served a long prison sentence has learned the art of adapting his body to the means of escape. Flight, to the prisoner, is like the crisis in a grave illness that either kills or cures. A successful escape is a cure, and what will a man not do to be cured? To be carted away in a nailed box and kept in it for some hours husbanding one's breath, half-suffocating but not dying, all this was well within the dark powers of Jean Valjean. Indeed, the convict's expedient of a living man in a coffin has been used even by emperors. If we are to believe the monk Austin Castillejo, it was the means whereby Charles V, wishing to pay a last visit to La Plombe after his abdication, was taken into the Monastery of Saint-Just and out again.

Recovering his wits, Fauchelevent cried:

'But how are you to breathe? The thought appals me.'

'You have a brace-and-bit, I suppose, or a gimlet. You must bore a few small holes in the lid over my mouth. And you need not nail the lid too tightly.'

'All right. But what if you cough or sneeze?'

'An escaping prisoner does not cough or sneeze. We must make up our minds to it, Père Fauchelevent,' said Valjean. 'I must either be caught here or go out on that hearse.'

We all know the habit of cats of hesitating in an open doorway. Which of us has not said to a cat, 'Well, come in if you want to?' There are men who, in moments when a decision is called for, hover uncertainly like the cat, at the risk of being crushed by the closing of the door. These cautious spirits may run greater risks than those who are more daring. Fauchelevent was by nature one of them, but Valjean's imperturbability was too much for him. He muttered:

'Well, I suppose so. There's no other way.'

'What worries me,' said Valjean, 'is what will happen at the cemetery.'

'Well, at least that's no problem,' said Fauchelevent. 'If you can survive the coffin I can get you out of the grave. The grave-digger's an old wine-bibber of my acquaintance, Père Mestienne, a real soak. He'll be easy to handle. I can tell you what will happen. We'll get there just before dusk, three-quarters of an hour before the cemetery closes. The hearse takes you right to the grave with me walking behind, that being part of my job. I'll have a few tools in my pocket. They put a rope round the coffin and lower it into the grave, the priest says a few prayers, sprinkles holy water, makes the sign of the cross and then off they go, leaving me and Père Mestienne on our own, we're friends, you see. Well, perhaps he's drunk already, or perhaps he isn't. If he isn't I say to him, "Come and have a glass while the Bon Coing is still open." I get him properly soused, which won't take long because he's always halfway there; I leave him under the table and borrow his pass to the cemetery and come back alone. Or if he's drunk enough already I say, "You go on home and I'll do the job for you." Either way there'll be only me and I'll soon have you out of the grave.'

Jean Valjean reached out his hand and Fauchelevent clasped it with a touching display of peasant devotion.

'Then that is settled, Père Fauchelevent. We shall have no trouble.'

'Provided nothing goes wrong,' reflected Fauchelevent. 'But oh my Lord, if it does!'

Not even grave-diggers are immortal

On the following afternoon the rare pedestrians on the Boulevard du Maine removed their hats at the passing of an old-style hearse ornamented with skulls, crossbones, and falling tears. The coffin on the hearse was draped in a white pall embroidered with a black cross so large that it resembled a dead man with his arms hanging. It was followed by a draped carriage in which were a priest in his surplice and a choir-boy wearing a red cap. Two pall-bearers in uniforms of grey with black trimmings walked on either side of the hearse, and behind the carriage walked an old man with a limp, from the pocket of whose workman's overall there protruded the handle of a hammer, the blade of a chisel, and the double grip of a pair of pincers.

The procession was making for the Cimetière Vaugirard, which was exceptional among Paris cemeteries in that it had its own customs, besides having a main gateway and a smaller gate, known to the older inhabitants of the quarter who clung to old forms, as the carriage-gate and the foot-gate. As we have said, the Bernardine-Benedictines of the Petit-Picpus had secured the right to be buried in their own corner and at nightfall, the land having formerly belonged to their community. The grave-diggers, being thus obliged to work in the evening, and by darkness in winter, were required to observe special rules. At that time the Paris cemeteries closed at sundown, and the Cimetière Vaugirard had to conform to this regulation like the rest. The carriage-gate and the foot-gate stood side by side, and adjoining them was a small lodge, designed by the architect Perronet, which was the dwelling of the cemetery-keeper. Both wrought-iron gates were closed directly the sun sank behind the dome of the Invalides. If a grave-digger was still in the cemetery he could only get out by means of the special pass issued to him by the Municipality. There was a sort of letter-box in one of the shutters of the keeper's lodge. He thrust his card through this, and the keeper, hearing it drop, pulled the cord that opened the foot-gate. If he had forgotten to bring his card he shouted his name, and the keeper, who was sometimes in bed and asleep, got up and after identifying him opened the gate with his key. In this event the grave-digger paid a fine of fifteen francs.

These singularities, so jarring to administrative susceptibilities, brought about the official closing of the cemetery soon after 1830. It was succeeded by the Cimetière de Montparnasse, known as the Eastern Cemetery, but was in some sort perpetuated by the celebrated wine-house Au Bon Coing, of which the sign was a painting of a quince, and which stood on the fringe of the cemetery, with tables on one side and tombstones on the other.

At the time of which we write the Cimetière Vaugirard was already falling into disuse. Moss was invading it, and its flowers were vanishing. Respectable citizens had little desire to be buried there; it had a smell of pauperdom. Père-Lachaise, for example, was quite another matter; it was like mahogany furniture, a symbol of elegance. Vaugirard was an ancient enclosure laid out like an old French garden, with straight paths flanked by box and juniper and holly, old tombs under old yews and long grass.

The sun had still not set when the hearse and carriage entered the avenue leading to the cemetery gate, with Fauchelevent limping behind them. Fauchelevent was in a state of high delight. Everything had gone according to plan, the interment of Mère Crucifixion in the vault under the altar, the removal of Cosette, the introduction of Jean Valjean into the mortuary chamber and then into the empty coffin. The two conspiracies in which he had been involved, one with the nuns and the other with Monsieur Madeleine, one at the bidding of the convent and the other unknown to it, had both been carried through without a hitch. Valjean's massive calm was infectious. Fauchelevent no longer doubted their complete success. What remained to be done was trifling. He had helped the rubicund Père Mestienne, the grave-digger, to get drunk a dozen times in the past two years. He had Père Mestienne in his pocket; he could do what he liked with him, make him dance to whatever tune he chose. Fauchelevent had no misgivings. As they approached the gates he rubbed his big hands together, muttering, 'What a lark!'

The procession pulled up at the gates, where the burial-permit had to be shown. During the brief colloquy which ensued between the chief pall-bearer, representing the Municipality, and the keeper, a stranger joined the party, taking his place beside Fauchelevent. He was some sort of workman, clad in a smock with large pockets and carrying a pickaxe under his arm.

Fauchelevent looked at him in some surprise and asked:

'Who are you?'

The man replied: 'I'm the grave-digger.'

The effect on Fauchelevent was as though he had been hit by a cannon-ball.

'The grave-digger!'

'That's right.'

'But – but Père Mestienne is the grave-digger.'

'Used to be.'

'What do you mean?'

'He's dead.'

Fauchelevent had been prepared for anything except this, that a grave-digger should die. Yet the thing does happen, even grave-diggers die in the end. In digging the graves of others they prepare the way for their own.

Fauchelevent stared open-mouthed, finding scarcely the strength to stammer:

'It's impossible!'

'It's a fact.'

'But,' said Fauchelevent weakly, 'Père Mestienne has always been the grave-digger.'

'Not any more. After Napoleon, Louis XVIII. After Mestienne, Gribier. My name is Gribier.'

Fauchelevent gazed wanly at this Gribier. He was a tall, thin, sallow man with a face of flawless solemnity. He looked like a failed doctor who had taken up grave-digging. Fauchelevent burst out laughing.

'The things that happen! So Mestienne is dead, poor old Père Mestienne! But Père Lenoir is still alive. Do you know Père Lenoir? – the jug of wine on the counter, the flagon of good red Paris wine. Père Mestienne is dead and I grieve for him. He enjoyed life. But you too, comrade, you enjoy life. Don't you? We must have a glass together in a little while.'

The man replied: 'I've had schooling. I reached the fourth grade. I don't drink.'

The procession was again in motion, moving along the main avenue of the cemetery. Fauchelevent had fallen a little behind, limping as much from agitation as from infirmity. He was again examining the unexpected Gribier, who was one of those men who look old while still young and although slight of build are very strong.

'Comrade,' he said, and Gribier turned to look at him. 'I'm the grave-digger from the convent.'

'We are colleagues,' said Gribier.

Fauchelevent, untutored but very shrewd, had realized by now that he had a formidable character to deal with, a man of eloquence.

'So Père Mestienne is dead,' he murmured.

'Precisely. The good God consulted his files and found that it was the turn of Père Mestienne. He is quite dead.'

'The good God . . .' Fauchelevent repeated mechanically.

'The good God,' Gribier said with authority. 'To philosophers the Eternal Father, and to the Jacobins the Supreme Being.'

'But aren't we to get acquainted?' stammered Fauchelevent.

'We already know each other. You are a countryman and I am a Parisian.'

'You don't get to know a man until you've drunk with him. In emptying your glass you empty your heart. We must have a drink together. You can't refuse.'

'We must first attend to our business.'

Fauchelevent thought: 'I'm done for.'

They were now near the narrower pathway leading to the plot reserved for the nuns. Gribier said:

'Countryman, I have seven kids to feed. If they're to eat, I can't afford to drink.' He added with the impressiveness of a man who enjoys turning a phrase. 'Their hunger is the enemy of my thirst.'

The procession, rounding a clump of cypresses, was now on the narrower path. Its muddy state, following the winter rains, obliged the hearse to move more slowly. Fauchelevent drew closer to Gribier.

'There's a very good little Argenteuil wine . . .' he murmured.

'You must understand, villager,' said Gribier, 'that I should not by rights be a grave-digger. My father, who was a clerk, destined me for literature. But he had misfortunes. He lost money on the Bourse. I had to give up authorship. But I am still a public writer.'

'In fact, not really a grave-digger,' said Fauchevelent, grasping at this straw.

'The one does not interfere with the other. I'm a pluralist.'

This last word was beyond Fauchelevent. 'We must have a drink,' he repeated.

And here an observation is necessary. Fauchelevent had proposed a drink, but despite his anguished state he had failed to specify one particular, namely, who was to pay for it. In his dealings with Père Mestienne it was he who had proposed and the latter who had paid. Clearly in the changed circumstances an explicit offer should have been made, but the old peasant had instinctively left this matter – the proverbial moment of darkness, as Rabelais has called it – in suspense, the truth being that regardless of his terrors he did not at all wish to pay.

Gribier continued with a lofty smile:

'One has to eat. I agreed to take over the duties of Père Mestienne. When one has nearly completed one's studies one is a philosopher. I supplement the labour of the pen with the labour of the hand. I have my writer's stall in the market on the Rue de Sèvres – do you know it, the Marché aux Parapluies? All the kitchen-maids in the Croix-Rouge quarter come to me and I run up effusions for their sweethearts. In the morning I write love-letters and in the afternoon I dig graves. Such is life, countryman.'

The hearse ploughed on and Fauchelevent gazed distractedly about him with beads of sweat gathering on his forehead.

'However,' said Gribier, 'one cannot serve two mistresses. I shall have to choose between the pen and the shovel. The shovel blisters my hands.'

The procession came to a halt. The choir-boy got out of the carriage followed by the priest. One of the small front wheels of the hearse had risen slightly on a mound of earth beyond which was an open grave.

'What a lark!' repeated Fauchelevent in consternation.

VI

The narrow walls

Jean Valjean had so arranged himself in the coffin that he could breathe just enough. It is wonderful how far ease of mind may promote a sense of security. His plan was going well and had done so from the start. Like Fauchelevent he counted on Père Mestienne and he had no doubt of the outcome. Never had a more critical situation been met with more perfect calm.

The four walls of the coffin exuded a kind of terrible peace, as though Valjean's tranquillity partook in some sort of the repose of the dead. From within his confinement he could follow every stage of the tense drama in which his adversary was Death.

Shortly after Fauchelevent had nailed down the coffin-lid he had felt himself lifted up and then borne on wheels. The diminished jolting had told him when they had left the cobbles of the back streets and were on the smoother surface of the boulevards, and from the echo he had known when they were crossing the Pont d'Austerlitz. He had realized when they stopped for the first time that they were entering the cemetery, and when they stopped again he said to himself, 'We've reached the graveside.' The coffin jerked abruptly and there were scraping sounds which he guessed were made by ropes being passed round it. Suddenly he felt that he was standing on his head. The bearers and the grave-digger had failed to keep the coffin level and were lowering it head foremost into the grave. His momentary dizziness passed when he was motionless and again horizontal and knew that he was lying on the bottom.

He had a sensation of chill. A cool and solemn voice was raised above him intoning words of Latin which he could not understand, but uttering them so slowly and meticulously that he could distinguish every one.

'*Qui dormiunt in terrae pulvere, evigilabunt; alii in vitam aeternam, et alii in opprobrium, ut videant semper.*'

A boy's voice chanted:

'*De profundis.*'

The first voice said:

'*Requiem aeternam dona ei, Domine.*'

The boy replied:

'*Et lux perpetua luceat ei.*'

He heard what was like the sound of rain pattering on the lid of the coffin and knew that it was holy water. He thought: 'This will soon be over. A little patience. The priest will leave and Fauchelevent will take Mestienne off for a drink. Then he'll come back and let me out. An hour at the outside.'

The voice intoned, '*Requiescat in pace*', and the boy replied, '*Amen.*'

Jean Valjean, intently listening, presently heard the sound of departing footsteps. 'They're going away,' he thought. 'I'm alone.'

But then there was a sound above his head that was like the thunder of an avalanche. It was made by a spadeful of earth falling on the coffin-lid.

A second followed it and a third. The holes through which he breathed were being covered over.

A fourth spadeful fell.

There are things too strong for even the strongest man. Jean Valjean fainted.

VII
The missing card

The following scene had been enacted at the graveside.

When the hearse had left, followed by the priest and the choir-boy in the carriage, Fauchelevent, who had never taken his eyes off Gribier, saw him reach for his shovel, which was standing upright in the mound of earth. Fauchelevent then made the supreme sacrifice. Thrusting himself between the grave and the grave-digger, he folded his arms and said:

'I'll pay.'

Gribier looked at him in astonishment.

'What was that?'

'I said, I'll pay.'

'Pay what?'

'The wine.'

'What wine?'

'The Argenteuil.'

'Where is it, this Argenteuil?'

'At the Bon Coing.'

'Oh, go to the devil!' said Gribier, and tossed a spadeful of earth on the coffin.

The coffin gave back a hollow sound. Fauchelevent was now tottering on his feet, ready to fall into the grave himself. He cried in a strangled voice that was half a groan:

'But, comrade, before the Bon Coing closes!'

Ignoring this, Gribier drove his shovel into the mound of earth. Fauchelevent said again, 'I'm paying,' and clutched him by the arm. 'Listen, comrade, I'm the convent grave-digger and I've come to help you. But this is a job that can be done after dark. We should start by having a drink.' He clung to him despairingly, tormented by the thought, 'But even if we do have a drink, can I get him drunk?'

'Well, countryman,' said Gribier, 'all right, I'll have a drink with you, if you insist. But after the work is done, not before.'

He bent over his spade while Fauchelevent still sought to restrain him.

'But it's real Argenteuil, at six sous the carafe.'

'You're like a bell-ringer,' said Gribier. 'Ding-dong, ding-dong – always the same tune. Go away and leave me alone.'

He shovelled in the second spadeful of earth. Fauchelevent had now reached a state where he no longer knew what he was saying.

'But a drink – a drink! I've said I'll pay.'

'When we've put the baby to bed,' said Gribier, and down went the third spadeful. 'It's going to be cold tonight. We'd have the dead woman after us if we didn't cover her up properly.'

At this moment, as he was about to throw in the fourth spadeful, Fauchelevent's distracted gaze noted something. Gribier's side-pocket had gaped open as he was bending forward, and the old man had a glimpse of something white inside. As much light of inspiration as a Picardy peasant is capable of gleamed in Fauchelevent's eye. While Gribier was still bowed over his shovel he slipped a hand into the open pocket and deftly removed the contents.

The fourth spadeful went in, and Fauchelevent then said in a voice of the utmost calm:

'By the way, newcomer, have you got your card?'

Gribier turned to look at him.

'What card?'

'It's nearly sunset.'

'So the sun will have to put on his night-cap.'

'The gates will be shut.'

'And so?'

'So have you got your card?'

'Oh, that card.' Gribier felt in his pocket. He then felt in his other pocket, in every part of his garments. 'It seems I must have forgotten it.'

'Fifteen francs fine,' said Fauchelevent.

Gribier turned green, green being the pallor of sallow-faced men.

'May all the saints preserve us! Fifteen francs!'

'Three hundred-sou pieces.'

Gribier dropped his shovel.

This was Fauchelevent's moment.

'Come, come,' he said soothingly. 'No need to despair. No need to commit suicide and fill another grave. Fifteen francs is fifteen francs and I don't suppose you can afford it. But I'm an old hand. I know all the ins and outs. I'll tell you what you can do. One thing is certain, the sun's nearly set, it's touching the Invalides. The gates will be shut in five minutes.'

'That's true.'

'This is a good deep grave. You haven't time to fill it in and get out before they close.'

'True enough.'

'In which case, fifteen francs fine.'

'Fifteen francs.'

'But you've still got time to get out – where do you live?'

'Near the barrier, 87 Rue de Vaugirard. Fifteen minutes walk.'

'Well, you've still got time to get out if you go at once and hurry. You run along home and get your card, and the keeper will let you back in again and nothing to pay. So then you fill in the grave. Meanwhile I'll stay here and keep watch over the dead to make sure they don't get away.'

'That's very good of you, countryman.'

'Then off you go,' said Fauchelevent.

Gribier departed at a run and vanished behind the cypresses. Fauchelevent waited until the sound of his footsteps had died away, then bent over the grave and called:

'Père Madeleine!'

There was no reply.

Fauchelevent shivered. Tumbling rather than climbing down into the grave, he cried with his lips close to the head of the coffin:

'Are you there?'

Silence.

Trembling so much that he could scarcely breathe, Fauchelevent used his chisel and hammer to lever up the lid. The face of Jean Valjean shone whitely in the dusk, the eyes were closed.

Fauchelevent's hair rose on his head. He straightened himself and sagged weakly against the side of the grave, almost collapsing over the coffin. Jean Valjean lay motionless. He gazed down at him and murmured, 'He's dead!' Then he beat his breast with his clenched fists and cried, 'So this is how I save him!'

The poor old man burst into tears, talking aloud as he wept. It is a mistake to suppose that the monologue is unnatural. Strong emotion needs to find a voice.

'All because of Père Mestienne! Why did the old fool have to die just when no one expected it? He's responsible for this, and here's

Père Madeleine in his grave and nothing to be done. Where's the sense in that? He's dead, he's dead, and what about the little girl, what am I to do with her and what's the woman in the fruit-shop going to say? That a man like him should die like this – how can one believe in God? When I think of how he got me out from under my cart! Père Madeleine! He must have suffocated. I was afraid of it but he wouldn't believe me. A dirty trick for fate to play! He's dead, the best man that ever walked this earth. And there's the child. Well, I'm not going back to the convent, that's for sure, not after this. I'll stay with him. Two old men together, two crazy old men. But how did he get in in the first place? How did it all start? One shouldn't do these things. Père Madeleine! Monsieur le maire! But he can't hear. He can't get us out of this one!' And Fauchelevent tore his hair.

A distant sound of squeaking from beyond the trees told him that the cemetery gates were being closed.

He bent down again over Jean Valjean, and suddenly he started back, recoiling as far as the narrow walls of the grave would allow. Valjean's eyes were open and he was looking up at him.

The sight of death is terrible, but the sight of resurrection is scarcely less so. Fauchelevent was for a moment turned to stone, his face pale and drawn, not knowing whether he had to do with the living or the dead.

'I fell asleep,' said Jean Valjean and sat up.

'Holy Mother of Heaven!' cried Fauchelevent. 'How you frightened me!'

Rapture is the reflex of terror. He had nearly as much difficulty in recovering his wits as had Valjean.

'You're not dead after all! The strength there is in your spirit! I called and called to you and you came back. When I saw you there with your eyes shut I thought, that's it! He's suffocated! I was ready to go raving mad, fit for a strait-jacket. What would I have done if you'd been dead? What would that woman have thought of the little girl, a child dropped in her lap and the grandfather dead? Saints preserve us, what a story! And all the time you were alive!'

'I'm cold,' said Jean Valjean.

The words brought Fauchelevent back to earth and to the urgency of their situation. Although they were now in their right mind, both men were troubled by the desolate atmosphere of that place.

'Let's get out of here quickly,' Fauchelevent said. 'But first a drop of something.' And he got out the flask he had brought with him.

The flask completed what the fresh air had begun. After a gulp of *eau-de-vie* Valjean was himself again. He got out of the coffin and helped Fauchelevent to re-nail the lid; a minute later both men were standing beside the grave.

Fauchelevent's calm was now restored. They could take their time. The cemetery was closed and there was nothing to fear from Gribier, who must now be at home searching vainly for the card in Fauchelevent's pocket, without which he could not get in again. The old man took the spade and Valjean took the pick, and together they buried the empty coffin. When the grave was filled in he said:

'Now let's be off. I'll keep the shovel and you carry the pick.'

It was nearly dark.

Valjean had a slight difficulty in walking, confinement in the coffin having made him something near to a corpse. The rigidity of death had assailed him within those narrow walls; he had to shake off the chill of the grave.

'You're stiff,' said Fauchelevent. 'It's a pity I'm bow-legged. Otherwise we'd run.'

'Don't worry. I'll soon be in working order.'

They went back by the way the hearse had come. When they reached the gates and the keeper's lodge Fauchelevent dropped the grave-digger's card through the letter-box, the keeper pulled the cord, the foot-gate opened and they went out.

'How well it has all gone off,' said Fauchelevent. 'That was an excellent idea of yours, Père Madeleine.'

They passed through the Vaugirard barrier without the least trouble. In the neighbourhood of a cemetery a pick and shovel are a passport in themselves. The Rue de Vaugirard was deserted.

'Père Madeleine,' said Fauchelevent, studying the housefronts, 'your eyes are better than mine. Tell me when we get to No. 87.'

'We've just come to it,' said Valjean.

'There's no one about,' said Fauchelevent. 'Give me the pick and wait here a couple of minutes.'

He went into No. 87 and, guided by the instinct which takes a poor man to the attics, climbed to the top floor, where he knocked on a door. Gribier's voice called to him to come in.

Fauchelevent entered. The grave-digger's home was like all dwellings of the needy, a place of sparse and congested squalor. A packing-case, or it may have been a coffin, was used as a cupboard, a pail held the water-supply, a straw mattress served as a bed, and the floor took the place of table and chairs. Seated in a corner on a worn strip of carpet was a thin-faced woman surrounded by a huddle of children. The wretched place bore signs of a recent upheaval, as though it had been visited by its own private earthquake. Coverings had been stripped off, tattered garments scattered, a jug had been broken, the woman had been crying and the children had probably been beaten. It was evident that the grave-digger had been searching frantically for his card and blaming everyone for its loss. He had a look of desperation.

But Fauchelevent was too anxious to proclaim the happy ending to pay much attention to the regrettable aspects of his triumph. He marched in saying:

'I've brought back your pick and shovel.'

Gribier was staring at him in astonishment.

'It's you, countryman!'

'And you'll find your card at the keeper's lodge.'

'I don't understand,' said Gribier.

'Simple enough. The card must have fallen out of your pocket. I picked it up after you'd left. And then I filled in the grave. I've done the job for you, the keeper will give you back your card and you won't have to pay the fifteen francs. That's all.'

'Thank you, thank you, countryman!' cried Gribier, clasping him warmly by the hand. 'I'll pay for drinks next time.'

VIII

Successful interview

An hour later, when it was quite dark, the two men, with Cosette, knocked at the door of No. 62, Petite Rue Picpus.

They had fetched Cosette from the fruit-shop in the Rue du Chemin-Vert where Fauchelevent had taken her the evening before. Cosette had passed those twenty-four hours in a state of terrified bewilderment, understanding nothing and trembling so much that she had not once cried. Nor had she eaten or slept. The good-hearted woman of the shop had asked her countless questions to which the only reply was a mute, mournful stare. Cosette had told her nothing at all of what she had seen or heard during the past two days. She realized that something terrible had happened and was profoundly conscious of the need to 'be good'. Who does not know the effect of those words spoken in a certain tone of voice into a small, frightened ear? 'You mustn't say a word!' Fear is a deaf-mute. Moreover, no one can keep a secret better than a child. But when, after those miserable twenty-four hours, Jean Valjean returned to her, she welcomed him with such a cry of delight that any discerning person might have guessed the state she had been in.

Thus the twofold problem had been solved, of getting Valjean out of the convent and bringing him back again. The porter, who had his orders, unlocked the small service door leading from the outer yard to the garden, which twenty years ago was still to be seen from the street, in the wall facing the main door. They went through and made their way to the small inner parlour where on the previous day Fauchelevent had received his instructions from the prioress.

She was seated, rosary in hand, with the veiled figure of one of the chantry-mothers standing beside her. A single taper lighted the parlour, or made a pretence of lighting it.

The prioress examined Jean Valjean. Nothing is more penetrating than the gaze of a downcast eye. She asked:

'You are the brother?'

'Yes, Reverend Mother,' replied Fauchelevent.

'What is your name?'

Again it was Fauchelevent who replied.

'Ultime Fauchelevent.' He had had a brother of that name who had died.

'Where do you come from?'

Fauchelevent replied:

'From Picquigny, near Amiens.'

'How old are you?'

'Fifty.'

'And what is your trade?'

'Gardener.'

'Are you a good Christian?'

'All the family are good Christians.'

'This child belongs to you?'

'Yes, Reverend Mother.'

'You are her father?'

'Her grandfather.'

The chantry-mother murmured to the prioress:

'He answers well.'

In fact, Jean Valjean had not spoken a word.

The prioress was looking attentively at Cosette. She murmured to the chantry-mother:

'She'll be plain.'

The two women conferred softly for some minutes in the corner of the room. Then the prioress turned to Fauchelevent and said:

'Père Fauvent, you will have to get another knee-strap and bell. We shall now need two.'

So next morning two bells were to be heard tinkling in the garden, and the nuns could not resist the temptation to lift a corner of their veils. They saw two men working side by side under the trees. It was a tremendous happening, and a whisper broke the silence, 'There's an assistant-gardener.' To which the chantry-mothers added: 'He's the brother of Père Fauvent.'

In short, Jean Valjean with his knee-strap and bell was now installed as a recognized member of the establishment under the name of Ultime Fauchelevent.

What had principally decided the matter was the prioress's remark about Cosette, 'She will be plain.' Having reached this conclusion she took an instant liking to the little girl and made a place for her as a charity pupil in the school. And this was entirely logical. There may be no mirrors in a convent, but every woman is conscious of her appearance. The girl who knows herself to be pretty is less likely to become a nun, the sense of vocation varying inversely with the degree of beauty. So the plain ones are much preferred.

The affair greatly enhanced the standing of old Fauchelevent, who indeed had achieved a threefold success – with Jean Valjean, whom he had rescued and sheltered, with Gribier, who believed that he had saved him a fine, and with the convent, which thanks to him had defied Caesar in the service of God. There was now an occupied coffin in the Petit-Picpus vault and an empty one in the Cimetière Vaugirard, a breach of regulations which would have outraged Public Order had Public Order known about it. The convent's sense of obligation to Fauchelevent was great; he became the best of servants and the most treasured of gardeners. On the archbishop's next visit the prioress told his Grace the story, making it partly a confession and partly a boast. The archbishop related it, with approval but in confidence, to M. de Latil, confessor to

Monsieur, the king's brother. Indeed Fauchelevent's renown travelled as far as Rome. We have ourselves seen a letter written by the reigning pope, Leo XII, to one of his relatives, then serving under the papal nuncio in Paris, in which his Holiness says: 'It seems that in one of the Paris convents there is a most excellent gardener named Fauvan, a saintly man.' But none of this reached Fauchelevent in his cottage. He continued to hoe and graft and straw his melons in ignorance of his excellence and saintliness, no more conscious of fame than the pedigree bull whose picture appears in the *Illustrated London News* with the legend, 'Prize-winner at the Cattle Show'.

IX

Seclusion

Cosette in the convent continued to keep silent. She thought of herself, very naturally, as Jean Valjean's child. Knowing no more than this, there was no more for her to say. But in any event she would have said nothing. Nothing makes a child more secretive than unhappiness, and she had suffered so much that she was afraid of everything, of talking and almost of breathing. An incautious word had so often brought down an avalanche on her head! The time she had been with Valjean had not been long enough to give her a complete sense of security, but she quickly adapted herself to the convent. Her only regret was that she no longer had Catherine. This was something that she could not mention, although she did once say to Valjean, 'If I'd known I'd have brought her with me.'

As a pupil she had to wear the school uniform. Jean Valjean kept the clothes she discarded, the mourning garments he had brought her when he took her away from the Thénardiers, and which were still comparatively new. He packed them, the black dress, the woollen stockings and the shoes, together with a great deal of camphor and the other aromatics so plentiful in convents, in a small valise that he managed to procure, and this he kept on a chair by his bed, with the key always in his pocket. Cosette once asked him: 'Father, what is in that box that smells so nice?'

Old Fauchelevent, unconscious though he remained of his celebrity, was well rewarded for his good deed: in the first place, because it gave him great satisfaction; secondly because he had much less work to do; and thirdly because he was able to smoke three times as much as in the past, and with a particular relish, since it was Monsieur Madeleine who paid for the tobacco. But the nuns never adopted the name 'Ultime'; they referred to Valjean as 'the other Fauvent'.

Had those saintly ladies possessed the acuity of a Javert they might have been struck by the fact that whenever there was any errand to be run, outside the convent walls, it was always the old, crippled Fauvent who went, and never his brother. But, perhaps because eyes intent upon God are blind to earthly things, or perhaps because they were too interested in watching one another, they never noticed this.

It may be added that Jean Valjean was wise in his policy of lying low. Javert kept the district under close observation for an entire month. For Valjean the convent was an island in a hostile sea, his world was bounded by its walls. He saw enough of the sky to ensure his peace of mind and enough of Cosette to ensure his happiness. A new and tranquil life began for him.

He lived with Fauchelevent in the shanty at the bottom of the garden. The ramshackle building, which was still standing in 1845, consisted, as we have said, of three rooms with bare plaster walls. The largest of them was given to Monsieur Madeleine on the insistence of Fauchelevent, although Jean Valjean protested. The only adornment of this room, apart from the two nails on which hung his gardener's hod and his knee-strap, was a royalist bank-note for ten livres, issued in La Vendée in 1793 and nailed to the wall by Fauchelevent's predecessor, a former *chouan* who had died in the convent.

Valjean was an excellent gardener. Having started life as a tree-pruner he had no difficulty in returning to this trade. It will be recalled that he knew many secrets of country lore. The trees in the orchard were mostly of mixed strain; by pruning and grafting he greatly improved their yield.

Cosette was allowed to spend an hour with him every day, and since he was very much better company than the nuns, she adored him. She would come running to the cottage when the hour struck, filling it with her presence, and Valjean would glow with a pleasure heightened by the pleasure he gave her. It is a charming quality of the happiness we inspire in others that, far from being diminished like a reflection, it comes back to us enhanced. At times when she was playing with the other children he would watch them at a distance and he could always distinguish her laughter from the rest.

For she learned to laugh, and as she did so her whole appearance changed, its darkness was dispelled. Laughter is a sun that drives out winter from the human face. She was still not pretty but she was becoming a delightful little girl, capable of saying most sensible things in her soft, childish voice. When she went indoors at the end of the recreation period Valjean would gaze at the classroom windows, and he would get up at night to look at the windows of her dormitory.

God works in His own way. The convent itself, with Cosette, sustained and completed the transformation of Jean Valjean which the bishop had begun. It is certain that one of the paths of virtue leads to the sin of Pride, a bridge built by the devil himself. Jean Valjean had been tending in this direction when Providence brought him to Petit-Picpus. When he compared himself with the bishop he felt humble and unworthy; but as the years passed he had begun to compare himself with other men, and pride crept in. Perhaps, who knows, he would have lapsed again into hatred.

The convent had put a stop to this. It was his second place of confinement. In his youth, at what for him had been the beginning of life, and later, all too recently, he had known another, an ugly, terrible place whose harshness seemed to him an iniquitous distortion of justice, a crime on the part of the law. After prison, a convent: from being an inmate of the one he had become an observer of the other, and he scrupulously compared them in his mind.

At times, leaning on his spade, he would let his thoughts drift in meditation. He would recall the wretchedness of his former companions. They rose at dawn and worked till dark, such sleep as they were allowed being on plank-beds with the thinnest of mattresses in rooms warmed only during the harshest winter months. They wore hideous red caps and, as a concession, cotton trousers in the hot season and a woollen cloak in the cold. They drank no wine and were allowed meat only when on hard labour. They lived without names, were known only by numbers and to some extent turned into numbers themselves, eyes and voices lowered, hair cropped, subject to the lash and to constant humiliation.

Then his thoughts would turn to this other community. These women, too, had cropped hair, eyes and voices lowered, not in humiliation but under the mockery of the world, and their shoulders bore the marks not of the lash but of the scourging of their self-inflicted discipline. They too had discarded their worldly names, but in favour of others more austere. Never did they eat meat or drink wine, and they often went without food until evening. They were clad, not in red but in black woollen robes like shrouds, oppressive in summer and insufficient in winter, nothing added or subtracted according to the season, no comfort of linen in summer or wool in winter; and for six months in the year they wore hair-shirts which induced fever. They lived in unrelieved cold, in cells where no fire was ever lighted, and they slept, not on mattresses but on straw. Nor were they allowed to sleep in peace after the day's work but must rise out of the first warmth of slumber to pray in the ice-cold, gloomy chapel, kneeling on its stones. And each must take her share in the ritual of atonement, kneeling for twelve hours on end, or prostrate with her head on her crossed arms.

Those others had been men, these were women. The men had been criminals – thieves and murderers, bandits, fire-raisers, patricides. And what crime had these women committed? They had committed none.

On the one side, outrage, sacrilege, violence, all the forms that evil can take; on the other side perfect innocence almost risen above the world in a mysterious Assumption, holding to earth only through virtue and holding to Heaven through sanctity. On one side the whispered avowal of crimes committed; on the other side, the open confession of faults – such faults! – and such crimes! On the one side a stench, and on the other an ineffable perfume. On the one side a moral distemper, kept out of sight and isolated under the law, which slowly destroyed its victims; on the other side a chaste seclusion of souls inhabiting the same dwelling. There utter darkness and here shadow; but a shadow filled with light, a light filled with radiance.

Two places of slavery, but in the first a possible end, the legal limit of the sentence, the hope of escape; in the second perpetuity, with no other aspiration than, in the distant future, that light of liberty that men call death. In the first, only chains of metal, in the second the chains of faith.

And what came out of these places? From the first a vast malediction, a gnashing of teeth, in hatred, the evil of despair, a rage against all human kind, and a mockery of Heaven; from the second, blessedness and love. Yet in both places, so alike and so unlike, two sets of utterly different beings were accomplishing the same task, a work of expiation.

In the case of the first, Jean Valjean could understand this – personal expiation, expiation of oneself. But he was hard put to it to understand the second, being beyond reproach, beyond blemish, and he asked himself, trembling – expiation of what, and for what? The voice of his conscience answered him: the most godlike of human bounties, expiation on behalf of others.

Here we refrain from all personal reflections. We are simply the narrator, putting ourself in the place of Jean Valjean and seeking to convey what was in his thoughts. He was witness of the sublime height of self-abnegation, the highest possible peak of virtue – innocence which forgives the faults of men and expiates them in their stead; servitude accepted, suffering endured, torment sought after by souls that have not sinned in order to spare those that have; the love of mankind lost in the love of God, yet still preserved and suppliant; weak and gentle souls, bearing the affliction of those who are punished and smiling with those who are recompensed.

He thought of this and remembered that he had dared to pity himself! Often he would rise in the night and listen to the hymns of thanksgiving of those innocent beings bowed down by austerity, and the blood ran cold in his veins as he reflected that the voices of the justly chastised were raised only in blasphemy, and that he himself, no better than the rest, had shaken his fist at God.

Thinking of the events of his own life, he was moved to profound reflection, as though hearing the deep voice of Providence itself. The escapes, the barriers surmounted, the chances taken at the risk of death, the hard and difficult climb, the struggles to escape from one place of expiation which in the end had brought him to this other? Was not this an allegory of his life?

This house, too, was a prison, dismally resembling the one from which he had escaped, though it had been conceived with no such thought in mind. He was again confronted by locks and bars, but these protected angels. The high walls he had seen caging tigers here enclosed lambs. This was a place of expiation, but not of chastisement; yet it was more austere, more sombre and relentless than the other. These virgins were more harshly subdued than the convicts. A cold, rough wind, the wind that had frozen his youth, had blown through the nest of vultures; but the wind blowing through this dovecote was keener and more piercing still.

Why?

When he thought of these things his whole being was abased before the mystery of the Sublime. All pride left him; he looked unsparingly at himself, felt his weakness and often wept. Everything that had entered his life in the past six months brought him back to the saintly injunctions of the bishop, Cosette through love, the convent through humility.

Sometimes in the dark of evening, when the garden was deserted, he was to be seen on his knees on the pathway bordering the chapel, outside the window he had peered through on the night of his arrival and turned towards the place where he knew the sister who was making atonement would be prostrate in prayer. Thus kneeling to her, he too prayed. It seemed that he dared not kneel directly to God.

The things that now surrounded him, the peace of the garden, the scent of the flowers, the gaiety and laughter of the children, the grave simplicity of the nuns, the silence of the cloister, these things possessed his being until by degrees his very soul was informed with them, peace and silence and simplicity, the scent of flowers and of happiness. And he thought that at two critical moments in his life two of God's houses had taken him in, the first when all other doors were closed and human society rejected him, and the second when society was again his enemy and the prison gates were again open: without the first he would have drifted into a life of crime, without the second into a life of torment. His whole heart was melted in gratitude and his love was magnified.

Thus the years passed and Cosette grew into girlhood.

PART THREE
MARIUS

BOOK ONE

PARIS IN MICROCOSM

I
Parvulus

PARIS HAD her especial child and the woods have their especial bird. The bird is the sparrow, and the child is the street-urchin.

Paris and childhood, the heat of the furnace and the light of the dawn. Strike the two together and the spark you will draw from them is a small live person – *homuncio*, as Plautus would say.

A small, happy person. He does not eat every day but he goes to the play every evening if he chooses. He has no shirt to his back, no shoes on his feet, no roof over his head; like the flies, he does without these things. He is aged between seven and thirteen, lives in a gang, haunts the streets, sleeps in the open, wears a pair of his father's old trousers which come down to his heels, an old hat belonging to some other father which comes down below his ears, a single brace with a yellow border. He bustles about, keeps his eyes open, rummages everywhere, squanders time, hangs round the cafés, knows thieves and is familiar with trollops, talks argot, sings obscene ditties and has no evil in him. In his heart there is a pearl of innocence, and pearls do not dissolve in mud. While man is still a child God keeps him innocent.

If you ask the great city, 'Who is this person?,' she will answer, 'He's my child.'

II
Some of his characteristics

The Paris urchin is the dwarf born of a giantess.

Let us not exaggerate. This gutter-innocent may sometimes have a shirt, but if so only one; he may have boots, but they lack soles. He may have a dwelling, which he loves because there his mother awaits him; but he prefers the streets, because there he finds freedom. He has his own games and his own enmities, with hatred of the bourgeois at the bottom of them. He has his own metaphors: to die is 'to eat dandelion root'. He has his employments; he fetches cabs and lets down their steps, sweeps muddy crossings in the rain (making a *pont des arts*, as he terms it), repeats the latest official pronouncement for the benefit of the general public, cleans out the weeds that grow between paving-stones. He has his own money consisting of any scrap of worked metal picked up in public places. This strange currency, known to him as *loques*, is strictly valued and controlled in his child's bohemia.

He has his own fauna which he minutely scrutinizes in dark corners, all manner of insects, 'death's-head bugs', 'scavengers', and 'devils' – the last a species of black beetle with a menacing two-pronged tail. He has his fabulous monster, with a scaly stomach and horned back but neither a lizard nor a toad, a loathsome black and slimy creature inhabiting old chalk-pits and quarries which moves on its belly, sometimes slowly and sometimes fast, which utters no sound but is always on the watch, and is so terrible that no one has ever set eyes on it. He calls this 'le sourd', which may be interpreted as 'the soundless'. To search for *sourds* among the stones is a daring enterprise. Another amusement is to lift up a paving-stone and study the wood-lice. Every part of Paris is known to him for the interesting things that may be found there. There are earwigs in the timber-yards near the Ursulines, centipedes in the Pantheon, tad-poles in the ditches of the Champ de Mars.

When it comes to repartee the urchin is as gifted as Talleyrand, no less cynical but more honest. He has a talent for unpredictable mirth. He startles shopkeepers with sudden laughter, a ribaldry ranging from high comedy to farce.

A funeral passes, with a doctor among the mourners. 'Hey!'yells the urchin. 'When did the doctors start delivering their own work?' A grave-faced citizen among the onlookers, adorned with spectacles and a fob, swings round in a fury.

'Rascal, you pinched my wife!'

'What me, Monsieur? Search me!'

III

His pleasures

Of an evening, by virtue of the pennies he always manages to pick up, *homuncio* goes to the theatre, and in crossing the threshold he is transformed. The urchin becomes a god. A theatre is like a ship capsized with its hold uppermost; and this hold, the gallery, is the place of the gods. The god is to the urchin what the butterfly is to the grub, the same being borne on air. He has only to be there, radiating happiness with all his aptitude for enthusiasm and delight, the clapping of his hands like the beating of wings, for that congested ship's hold, squalid, foetid, hideous, and unhealthy, to become a Paradise.

Give a youngster what is superfluous, deprive him of what is needful, and you have an urchin.

The urchin does not lack literary instinct, but – it may be admitted with appropriate regrets – he has little classical bent. His nature is not that of an academic. To give an example, his admiration for that esteemed actress, Mademoiselle Mars, was tinged with irony. He called her Mademoiselle Huche, or, as it might be, Mademoiselle All Right.

He squeals, leers, reviles and quarrels, wears child's clothing under the tattered gown of a philosopher, fishes in the gutters, hunts in the sewers, haunts the street corners with his ribaldry, his laughter and his malice, whistles, sings, applauds, derides, finds without seeking, knows what he does not know, is at once a Spartan and a pickpocket, mad to the point of wisdom, lyrical to the point of lewdness, squatting on Olympus, wallowing in the mire and emerging decked with stars.

The Paris urchin is Rabelais in miniature. Little amazes him and still less impresses him. He scorns superstition, deflates exaggeration, laughs at mystery, sticks out his tongue at ghosts, brings pretension down to earth, caricatures the over-blown epic. Not because he is lacking in poetry, far from it; but for the solemn vision he substitutes his own irreverent fancy. Confronted by the giant Adamastor he would say, 'Blimey, a circus clown!'

IV

His uses

Paris begins with its strollers and ends with its street-urchins, two species produced by no other town. Passive acceptance content merely to look on, and inexhaustible enterprise; Respectability and Riot. In no other town are these so much a part of the natural scene. All monarchy is in the stroller, all anarchy in the urchin.

This pale-faced child of the Paris back streets lives and grows, gets all tied up and then finds his feet, in hardship, in the presence of social and human realities of which he is the perceptive witness. He thinks himself heedless but is not. He watches prepared to laugh, but prepared also for other things. You who are Prejudice, Abuse, Ignominy, Oppression, Iniquity, Despotism, Injustice, Fanaticism, beware of the wide-eyed urchin. He will grow up.

He is born of the rankest clay, but a handful of mud and a breath created Adam. It sufficed for a god to pass. A god has always passed by the urchin, Destiny is at work upon him, and the word, *gamin*, as we use it, contains the element of Chance. This pigmy shaped of common earth, ignorant, unlettered, uncouth, vulgar, mob-made, what will he grow into, an Ionian or a Boeotian? We must await the turning of the wheel, the spirit of Paris, the demon which creates both children of hazard and Men of Destiny, refining the potter's work, making an amphora out of a common jug.

V

His limits

The urchin loves the town but he also loves solitude, having in him something of the sage – *urbis amator*, like Fuscus, and *ruris amator*, like Flaccus.

To wander in contemplation, that is to say, to loiter, is for a philosopher an excellent way of passing the time, and particularly in that bastard countryside, ugly as a rule but fascinating for its twofold nature, which surrounds many large cities, and notably Paris. To observe those outskirts is to observe an amphibious world, trees giving way to rooftops, grass to pavements, furrowed fields to streets of shops, rutted lanes to human passions, murmurous nature to the clamour of mankind; and this is of extraordinary interest. Hence the fascination, for those of a thoughtful mind, of a stroll through unattractive regions to which only one adjective, *sad*, can be applied.

The writer of these lines was for many years an explorer of the outskirts of Paris, the gateways to the city, and they have left him with many memories. Patches of worn grass, stony paths, chalk and clay and rubble; the harsh monotony of fallow and untilled land; the early crops of market-gardeners seen suddenly in a sheltered place; the mingling of wilderness and order; the rough clearings where the drummers of the garrison parade, setting up a stuttering imitation of battle; places that are solitudes by day and the haunts of footpads, death-traps by night; the ramshackle windmill of which the sails still turn; the apparatus of a stone-quarry; the drinking-booth by the cemetery; the mysterious charm of high, shady walls cutting squarely into great stretches of wasteland bathed in sunshine and alive with butterflies – all these things attracted him.

Very few people know those singular places – la Glacière, la Canette, the hideous Grenelle wall pock-marked with cannon-fire, Mont-Parnasse, la Fosse-aux-Loups, les Aubiers on the bank of the Marne, Montsouris, la Tombe-Issoire, and the Pierre-Plate de Châtillon where there is a worked-out quarry now only used for growing mushrooms, with a trap-door of rotting planks leading into it. The countryside of Rome is one idea and the surroundings of Paris are another; to see no more than the prospect of fields, houses, and trees is to be confined to the surface, for all aspects of things are thoughts of God. The place where country merges into town is always impregnated with an underlying melancholy, nature and humankind join voices and local characteristics appear.

Anyone who has wandered as we have done in those solitudes on the outskirts of our suburbs, which may be termed the limbo of Paris, will have encountered here and there, in the most deserted spots and at the most unexpected moments, tumultuous groups of pale-faced, ragged, unwashed children, intent upon their own pursuits, amid the wild flowers in the shadow of a neglected hedge or a mouldering wall. They are the runaway children of the very poor, the outer boulevards their dwelling-place and this limbo their private domain. They are perpetual truants, artlessly singing their repertoire of scabrous songs, living their true life here, far from any supervision, in the gentle light of May or June; clustered in a circle round a hole in the ground into which they flip marbles with their thumb, quarrelling over farthings, rowdy, carefree, neglected, and happy. But at the sight of you they remember that they have business to transact and a living to earn; they offer to sell you an old woollen stocking filled with beetles, or a bunch of lilac. These little bands of children are among the charms, at once delightful and heart-breaking, of the outskirts of Paris.

And sometimes amid the cluster of boys there will be girls as well – their sisters, perhaps? – some of them quite big girls, lean and sun-burnt, freckle-faced, wearing headgear of grasses or poppies, gay, wild-looking and barefoot. One sees them eating cherries in the long grass, and in the evening one hears their laughter. These groups, seen bathed in the warm sun of midday, or half-seen in the dark, linger in the thoughts and memories of the wanderer.

Paris is the centre, its environs the circumference, of the whole world for these children. They never venture beyond, being no more able to leave the atmosphere of Paris than a fish is able to leave the water. For them nothing exists two leagues beyond the city gates. Ivry, Gentilly, Arcueil, Belleville, Aubervilliers, Menilmontant, Choisy-le-Roi, Billancourt, Meudon, Issy, Vanvres, Sèvres, Puteaux, Neuilly, Gennevilliers, Colombes, Romainville, Chatou, Asnières, Bougival, Nanterre, Enghien, Noisy-le-Sec, Nogent, Gournay, Drancy, Gonesse – these are the bounds of the Universe.

VI

A fragment of history

At the period of this tale, which after all is not very remote, there was not to be found, as there is today, a *sergent de ville* at the corner of every street (a benefaction we have no time to discuss.) Vagabond children were numerous in Paris. The statistics show that on an average 260 homeless children were rounded up every year in un-enclosed areas, on building sites and under the arches of the bridges. One of these rookeries, which is still famous, produced the 'swallows of the Pont d'Arcole'. This, it may be remarked, is the most disastrous of all social ills. All adult crime has its source in the vagabondage of the young.

Nevertheless we may except Paris, and in some degree, despite what we have said, the exception is justified. Whereas in every other great city the forgotten child becomes the deboshed man, and whereas nearly everywhere the child left to his own devices becomes rootless and immersed in open vice which destroys in him all conscience and sense of probity, the Paris urchin, we insist, however footloose and disreputable he may appear on the surface, remains in himself almost unspoiled. It is a magnificent phenomenon, splendidly manifest in the honesty of our popular revolutions, a kind of incorruptibility born of the instinct that resides in the air of Paris like salt in the waters of the ocean. To breathe Paris is to preserve one's soul.

But to say this is in no way to lessen the pang that assails us whenever we set eyes on one of those children who seem to trail behind them the shreds of a broken family. It is nothing very uncommon in our present state of civilization, incomplete as it still is, for disrupted households to disperse in darkness, no longer knowing what has become of the children, and leaving them on the public highways. Hence those obscure destinies. It is called, for the sad event has acquired a phrase of its own, 'being thrown on the Paris streets'.

Be it said in passing that abandoning children was not discouraged under the old monarchy. A touch of Egypt and Bohemia among the lower orders suited the book of those in high places. Hatred of popular education had become a dogma. What purpose was served by 'semi-literacy'? Such was the principle. But the vagabond child is the corollary of the unlettered child.

Moreover the monarchy sometimes needed children and scoured the streets for them. Louis XIV, to go back no further, had to build a fleet. It was a necessary measure, but consider what it entailed. No fleet of sailing vessels, dependent on the wind, could exist without attendant vessels propelled by other means to tow them to their moorings and link them with the shore. Oared galleys were to the fleet of those days what steam-tugs are to the fleet of today. But the galleys needed crews, that is to say, convicts, galley-slaves. Colbert, through the provincial governors and parliaments, created as many convicts as possible, and the magistrates gave him every assistance. The man who failed to raise his hat at the passing of a procession was judged to be a Huguenot and sent to the galleys. Any child found loitering in the streets, provided he was over the age of fifteen and homeless, went to the galleys. A great reign; a great century.

Under Louis XV children disappeared in Paris, kidnapped by the police for reasons that remain a mystery. Hideous tales were whispered of the King's 'purple baths'. Barbier refers naïvely to these matters. It happened sometimes that the press-gangs, or exempt-gangs, took children possessing parents, for want of others. The parents invoked the law, Parliament intervened – and who was hanged? Not the press-gangs but the parents.

Urchin classification

The street-urchins of Paris, the *gaminerie*, are almost a caste of which it may be said, 'not everyone can join'. The word itself, *gamin*, was printed for the first time in 1834, in a small work entitled *Claude Gueux*, thus passing from popular slang into the literary language. Its use occasioned some scandal, but it came to be accepted.

The attributes entitling a *gamin* to the esteem of his fellows are very varied. We know of one who was greatly honoured and admired because he had seen a man fall from the top of one of the towers of Notre Dame; another hero succeeded in getting into the back-yard where the statues intended for the dome of the Invalides were temporarily housed and had 'swiped' a bit of lead; a third had seen a coach overturn, and a fourth 'knew' a soldier who had nearly knocked out a citizen's eye. The first of these instances accounts for a characteristic flight of urchin-rhetoric: 'Coo, aren't I unlucky – never even seen anyone fall off a fifth floor!'

There is an old country jest that is not without eloquence. 'Père So-and-so, your wife has died of her illness. Why did you not send for the doctor?' ... 'What would you, Monsieur? The poor have to attend to their own dying.' But if this retort embodies all the sardonic acceptance of the peasantry, the free-thinking anarchy of the Paris urchin is certainly contained in the following. A condemned man on his way to the scaffold was listening in the tumbril to his confessor. An urchin yelled: 'He's talking to a sky-pilot, the dirty funk!'

A degree of audacity in religious matters improves the urchin's standing. To be strong-minded is important. To attend executions becomes a duty. You look at the guillotine and laugh. You give it all sorts of nicknames – 'The last course', 'the last mouthful', 'the grunter', 'old Mother Nowhere', and so on. To be sure of missing nothing you climb walls or trees, or on to balconies or roofs. The urchin is a born steeplejack, no more afraid of chimney-tops than a sailor is of a mast. No fair-ground equals La Grève, the place of execution, and Sanson, the executioner, and the Abbé Montès are the true celebrities. You hoot the victim to encourage him, and sometimes you admire him. The youthful Lacenaire* uttered the following prophetic words after watching the atrocious Dautun die bravely: 'I was jealous of him.' All the guillotine's victims are well-remembered, their memory handed down, their bearing, even to the clothes they wore.

A noteworthy accident is highly esteemed among the Paris urchins. Nothing inspires more respect than to have been severely injured, 'cut to the bone'. Nor is the clenched fist a trivial matter. 'Me, I'm tough,' is the commonest of boasts ... To be left-handed is to be envied, and a squint is a prized attribute.

VIII

Records the amiability of the late King

In summer he turns into a frog. As darkness falls in the evening he plunges head first into the Seine off the coal-barges and washer-women's boats by the Austerlitz and Jean bridges, shamelessly in-fringing the laws of decency and police regulations. But the police watch out for him, and this gives rise to a highly dramatic situation which on one occasion produced a memorable street-cry. The cry, which is one of warning from *gamin* to *gamin*, became celebrated round about 1830; it can be scanned like an Homeric couplet, its notation an echo of the antique *Evohe*, '*Ohé, Titi, ohéee! y a de la grippe, y a de la cogne, prends tes ʒardes et va-t'en, passe par l'égout !*'†

Sometimes this gadfly (he uses the word of himself) knows how to read; sometimes he can write, and he can always draw. By some mysterious process of mutual instruction he contrives to acquire all the talents most serviceable in public life: between 1815 and 1830 he imitated the cry of a turkey, and from 1830 to 1845 he drew a pear (the King's nickname) on the walls. One summer evening Louis-Philippe, returning home on foot, saw an undersized urchin strain-ing on tip-toe to draw an enormous pear on one of the pillars of the Neuilly gateway. With the amiability which he inherited from

---

* Pierre-François Lacenaire (1800–1835), poet, thief, and murderer, made the subject of a play by Théophile Gautier. Dautun was executed for the murder of his brother in 1814.

† Roughly: 'Ahoy, Titi, ahoy, ahoy, the coppers are coming, the law's on its way, pick up your duds and bolt through the sewers.'

Henri IV, the King helped him to finish it and then gave him a coin, a louis d'or. 'There's a pear on that too,' he said.

The *gamin* loves disorder, any kind of violent uproar. He abominates the priesthood. On one occasion an urchin was seen cocking a snook at the doorway of No. 69, Rue de l'Université. When asked why he did it he replied, 'A curé lives there.' The house is in fact the residence of the papal nuncio. But however Voltairian his attitude to religion, if he has the chance of becoming a choir-boy the *gamin* is quite likely to take it, in which case he decorously performs his duties. He has two consuming ambitions, never achieved: to overthrow the government and to get his trousers mended.

The *gamin* at his best knows every policeman in Paris and can name them all. He lists them on his fingers, studies their habits and files them away in his memory. He knows all about them. He will say unhesitatingly: 'So-and-so's a cheat ... So-and-so's a dirty swine ... So-and-so's great ... So-and-so's ridiculous ...' All the words have a special meaning for him. 'Old So-and-so thinks he owns the Pont-Neuf, he tries to stop people walking on the parapet. So-and-so likes pushing people around ...' And so on.

IX

The Ancient spirit of Gaul

There was something of the Paris *gamin* in Poquelin the clown who was born in les Halles, and something of him in Beaumarchais. *Gaminerie* is a manifestation of the Gallic spirit, good sense to which a certain pungency is sometimes added, like the alcohol in wine. And this may be carried to excess. If Homer nodded, Voltaire may be said to have played the urchin.

The *gamin* is respectful, sardonic, and insolent. He has bad teeth because he is underfed, and fine eyes because he has sharp wits. If Jehovah beckoned he would go scampering up the steps of Paradise. He fights with both hands and feet. He may grow in any direction. He plays in the gutter and rises above it in revolt, his audacity unchecked by musket-fire. The guttersnipe turns hero. Like the Theban boy he twists the lion's tail. He cries 'Aha!' among the trumpets like the war-horse in the book of Job. In an instant the urchin may be transformed into a giant.

In a word, he amuses himself because he is unhappy.

X
Ecce Paris, ecce homo

To sum up, the *gamin*, the urchin of present-day Paris, is like the *graeculus*, the 'little Greek', under Rome – a child population bearing on its brow the wrinkles of an ancient world. He is at once a national emblem and a disease. A disease that must be cured. How? By light. Light that makes whole. Light that enlightens.

All fruitful social impulses spring from knowledge, letters, the arts, and teaching. We must make whole men, *whole* men, by bringing light to them that they may bring us warmth. Sooner or later the splendid challenge of universal education will confront us with the authority of absolute truth; and those who govern under the scrutiny of the French Idea will then have to make this choice: Are we to have children of France or street-urchins of Paris, flames burning in the light of day or will-o'-the-wisps in shadow?

The *gamin* stands for Paris, and Paris stands for the world.

Paris is a sum total, the ceiling of the human race. The prodigious city is an epitome of dead and living manners and customs. To observe Paris is to review the whole course of history, filling the gaps with sky and stars. Paris has her Capitol, the Hôtel de Ville; her Parthenon, Notre-Dame; her Aventine Mount, the Faubourg Saint-Antoine; her Asinarium, the Sorbonne; her Pantheon which bears the same name; her Via Sacra, the Boulevard des Italiens; and her Tower of Babel, which is Public Opinion, drowning the voice of rhetoric in ridicule. Everything that is to be found elsewhere is to be found in Paris; she has her bumpkin, whom she calls *le Faraud*; her *transteverino*, whom she calls *le faubourien*; her native bearers, whom she calls market porters; her *lazzarone* whom she calls *le pègre*; and her own brand of cockney whom she calls *le gandin*. Her fishwife could hold her own with Euripides' herb-woman; the discobolus Vejanus lives again in Forioso the tightrope-walker; Theraponti-gonus Miles would go arm-in-arm with the grenadier Vadebon-coeur; Damasippus the second-hand dealer would loiter happily in the antique-shops; Vincennes would lay hands on Socrates, as some prison in Athens would have grabbed Diderot . . .

And so on. What is there that Paris does not possess? She has her prophets and her king-makers, her quacks, conjurers, and magicians. Rome put a courtesan on the throne and Paris put a grisette: but, when all is said, if Louis XV was not the equal of Claudius, Madame Du Barry was better than Messalina. Although Plutarch said that tyrants do not live to grow old, Rome under Sulla, as under Domitian, meekly bowed her head and watered her wine, and the waters of the Tiber, if we are to believe Varus Vibiscus, were like the waters of Lethe, they caused men to forget sedition. But Paris drinks a million litres of water a day and still sounds the tocsin when the need arises.

And with it all she is indulgent, royally accepting all things, easy-going in the realm of Venus, with callipygian leanings; ready to forgive where she is made to laugh, amused by ugliness, entertained by deformity, diverted by vice. Be comical and you will be accepted as a clown. Even hypocrisy, the supreme cynicism, does not revolt her; she is no more outraged by the posturing of Tartuffe than was Horace by the belching of Priapus. There is no aspect of the universal countenance that is not present in the face of Paris. The Bal Mabille may not be the polyhymnian dance on the Janiculum, but the shop-girl studies the actress in her finery as avidly as the procuress Staphyla studied the virgin Planesium. The Syrian hostess may have been more elegant than Mère Saguet in her Montparnasse restaurant, but you may find David d'Angers, Balzac, and Charlet seated together at a table in a Paris tavern. Paris reigns supreme and genius flowers within her. Adonais drives past with his twelve-wheel chariot of thunder and lightning; and Silenus rides in on his mule.

Paris is the world in miniature – Athens, Rome, Sybaris, Jerusalem, Pantin – all the civilizations, and all the barbarisms as well. She would be grieved if she had no guillotine.

A little of the Place de Grève is a good thing. What would the endless festivity amount to without that seasoning? Our laws have wisely provided it, and thanks to them the blade drips over the carnival.

XI

Mockery and rule

To Paris there are no bounds. No other city has held this dominance which sometimes derides what it subjugates. 'I seek but to please you, oh Athenians!' cried Alexander. Paris does more than make the law, she makes the fashion; and, more than the fashion, she makes the event. She can be foolish when the mood takes her, as it sometimes does. Then the world is foolish with her; and presently Paris opens her eyes and says, 'How silly I am!' and laughs in the face of humankind. The marvel of such a town! How wonderful that so much majesty is not troubled by its own parody, that the lips which today sound the summons to judgement will tomorrow play a tune on a jew's harp! Paris has a sovereign joviality. Her gaiety strikes like the lightning and her frolic brandishes a sceptre. Her hurricanes spring sometimes out of a grimace. Her explosions, her crises, her masterpieces, her prodigies, her epics reach to the ends of the earth, and so do her ribaldries. Her laughter is a volcanic outburst that bespatters the globe; her derision sears like flame. She thrusts her caricatures upon the nation as well as her ideals; the loftiest monuments of human civilization bow to her ironies and commemorate her gibes for all eternity. She is superb. She frees the world with her prodigious 14th July, and with her night of 4th August dissolves a thousand years of feudalism in three hours; she makes her logic the strong arm of the universal will; she reshapes herself in every form of the sublime and with her radiance lights the spirit of Washington, Kosciusko and Bolivar, of John Brown and Garibaldi. She is everywhere where the future dawns, in Boston in 1779, in Pesth in 1848, in Palermo in 1861, whispering the watchword, 'Liberty', in the ears of the American abolitionists at Harper's Ferry, and of the patriots of Ancona gathered in the shadows at the water's edge. It was her wind that bore Byron to his death at Missolonghi. She was the platform under the feet of Mirabeau, the crater under the feet of Robespierre. Her books, her theatre, her art, her science, her philosophy, these are the manuals of the human race – Pascal, Régnier, Corneille, Descartes, Rousseau, Voltaire, Molière for every century. She has made of her language the universal speech, and this speech has become the Word: it instils in every mind the idea of progress, and the liberating dogmas it has forged are the sword at the bedside of future generations; all heroes of the people in all countries since 1789 have been made of the spirit of her thinkers and poets. But none of this prevents her from playing the urchin. The huge genius that is Paris, while transforming the world with the light she sheds, can still charcoal the nose of Bouginier on the wall of the Temple of Theseus and write *Crédeville voleur* on the Pyramids.

Paris always shows her teeth, laughing when she does not scold.

Such is Paris. The smoke from her chimney-tops is the thinking of the world. A cluster of mud and stone if you like, but above all things a moral entity. She is more than great, she is immense. Why? Because she dares.

Daring is the price of progress. All splendid conquests are the prize of boldness, more or less. For the Revolution to happen it was not enough that Montesquieu predicted it, that Diderot preached it, that Beaumarchais announced it, that Condorcet planned it, that Arouet paved the way for it, that Rousseau dreamed of it – it needed Danton to dare it.

The cry, 'Boldness!', is a *Fiat Lux*. If mankind is to advance there must be installed permanently at the head of its columns proud instances of courage. Acts of daring light the pages of history and the soul of man. The sunrise is an act of daring. To venture, to defy, to persevere, to be true to one's self, to grapple with destiny, to dismay calamity by not being afraid of it, to challenge now unrighteous powers and now victory run wild, to stand fast and hold firm – these are the examples that the peoples need, the spark that electrifies them. The same formidable lightnings issue from the torch of Prometheus and the raucous bellow of Cambronne.

XII

The future latent in the people

As for the people of Paris, the man fully grown is still the urchin. To paint the child is to paint the town, which is why we have depicted this eagle in the guise of a sparrow.

It is above all in the back streets, let us be clear about this, that the real Parisian race is to be found, the pure stock, the true face; in the places where men work and suffer, for work and suffering are the two faces of man. There, in that ant-heap of the humble and unknown, the strangest types exist, from the stevedore of La Rapée to the horse-butcher of Montfaucon. *Fex Urbis*, 'the lees of the city', Cicero called them, and 'mob' was the word. Burke used mob, masses, crowd, public ... the words are easily said. But what does that matter? What does it matter if they go barefoot, or if they cannot read? Will you abandon them on that account, and make of their distress a curse? Cannot light penetrate to the masses? Light! Let us repeat it again and again – Light and more Light ... And then, who knows, opacity may be found to be transparent. Are not revolutions transformations? Let the philosophers continue to teach and enlighten, to think high and speak loud, turn gladly towards the sunrise, mingle in the market-place, proclaim the good news, dispense the alphabet, assert men's rights, sing the Marseillaise, foster enthusiasm, pluck the green shoots from the oaks. Turn the idea into a whirlwind. The crowd can be made sublime. We must learn to make use of that great furnace of principles and virtues which sparks and crackles and at moments bursts into flame. Those bare feet and arms, the rags, the ignorance, the abjection, the dark places, all may be enlisted in the service of the ideal. Peer through the heart of the people and you will discover the truth. The common sand that you tread underfoot, let it be cast into the furnace to boil and melt and it will become a crystal as splendid as that through which Galileo and Newton discovered the stars.

XIII
The boy Gavroche

Some eight or nine years after the events related in the second part of this tale there was to be seen on the Boulevard du Temple and in the streets around the Château-d'Eau a boy aged eleven or twelve who would have been an admirable embodiment of the *gamin* we have depicted except for the fact that, while the laughter of his years was on his lips, there was only darkness and emptiness in his heart. This youngster went round in a pair of man's trousers that did not come from his father, and a woman's blouse that did not come from his mother, castaway garments bestowed on him out of charity by comparative strangers. He had a father and mother nonetheless; but his father never gave him a thought and his mother disliked him. He was one of those children who are most to be pitied, those who possess parents but are still orphans. He was never happier than when he was in the streets, their very flagstones seeming to him less hard than his mother's heart.

He was a rowdy little boy, pale-faced, agile, alert and rascally, with a lively, sickly air. He darted here and there, sang, played pitch-and-toss, scratched in the gutters, stole now and then, but needlessly, like a cat or sparrow, laughed when he was called an urchin but was indignant when he was called a scamp. He had neither hearth nor home, nor any regular source of food; yet he was happy because he was free. By the time the poor have grown to man's estate they have nearly always been caught in the wheels of the social order and become shaped to its requirements; but while they are children their smallness saves them, they can escape through the smallest crevice.

Nevertheless, neglected though he was, it happened occasionally, two or three times a month, that the boy said to himself, 'I'll go and see Mamma.' So then he left the boulevards, the Cirque and the Porte Saint-Martin, headed for the river-embankment, crossed over and, passing through the working-class streets in the direction of the Salpêtrière, arrived eventually – where? At no other place than the house numbered 50–52 which is already known to the reader, the Gorbeau tenement.

At this particular time it happened that No. 50–52, which generally stood empty and eternally bore the notice 'Rooms to Let', was occupied by a number of people who, as is the common case in Paris, had no connection between them and no knowledge of one another. They all belonged to that indigent class which ranges from the lowest stratum of impoverished respectability down through every stage of pauperdom to that of the two beings who represent the nethermost rung of the social ladder, the crossing-sweeper and the *chiffonier*, the scavenger.

The 'chief tenant' had died since the days of Jean Valjean, and had been replaced by another exactly like her. As some philosopher has remarked, there is never any shortage of old women. The replacement was a Madame Bourgon and there was nothing remarkable about her life except the dynasty of three parrots who in succession had ruled over her heart.

The most squalid of all the present occupants of the tenement was a family of four, father and 1 other and two daughters, quite big girls, living together in the same garret, one of the cell-like rooms we have already described.

At first glance there was nothing remarkable about this family except its state of extreme destitution; the father, when he took the room, had given his name as Jondrette. But a short time after they had moved in – which, in the words of the chief tenant, 'was like the moving in of nothing at all' – he had said to the lady in question, who like her predecessor acted as door-keeper and swept the stairs, that if anyone should call asking for a Pole, an Italian, or possibly a Spaniard, he was the person they would be looking for.

This was the family of our lively barefoot urchin. He went there to be greeted by poverty and wretchedness, and, which was worse, never a smile, by hearts as chilly as the room itself. When he entered they asked where he had come from and he answered, 'off the streets'; when he left they asked where he was going and his answer was, 'back ot the streets'. His mother asked, 'Why did you come here?'

The boy had grown up in this absence of affection like the pallid weeds that grow in cellars. His situation caused him no particular distress and he blamed no one. The fact is that he had no idea how parents ought to behave.

But the mother loved his sisters.

We have omitted to mention that on the Boulevard du Temple the boy was known as Gavroche. Why Gavroche? Perhaps for the same reason that had caused his father to adopt the name of Jondrette. To tear up the roots seems to be instinctive with some families of the very poor.

The Jondrettes' garret in the Gorbeau tenement was at the far end of the corridor. The cell next to theirs was occupied by a penniless young man called Monsieur Marius.

It is with this Monsieur Marius that we are now concerned.

BOOK TWO

A GRAND BOURGEOIS

I

Ninety years and thirty-two teeth

THERE ARE still a few former inhabitants of the Rue Boucherat, the Rue de Normandie, and the Rue de Saintonge who remember a gentleman called Monsieur Gillenormand and take pleasure in recalling him. He was an old man when they were young, but for those who look back nostalgically at the confusion of shadows that we call the past his figure has not wholly vanished from that labyrinth of streets round the Temple which in the reign of Louis XIV were given the names of French provinces, just as in our own day the streets in the new Tivoli quarter have been given the names of European capitals; a development, it may be said, in which progress is made manifest.

M. Gillenormand, who was full of life in the year 1831, was one of those persons who have become interesting simply because they have lived a long time, and peculiar because whereas they were once like everyone else they are now like no one else. He was an idiosyncratic old gentleman and most decidedly a man belonging to another age, the complete picture of the somewhat aloof bourgeois of the eighteenth century, wearing his middle-class respectability with all the assurance of a marquis wearing his title. He was over ninety but still walked erect, talked loudly, saw clearly, took wine, ate, slept and snored. He possessed all his thirty-two teeth and wore spectacles only for reading. He was of an amorous disposition but declared that for ten years past he had positively and absolutely renounced women. He said that he could no longer please them, failing to add that it was because he was too old, but saying that it was because he was too poor. 'If I were not ruined,' he said, 'well . . . !' In fact, all that remained of his fortune was an income of about fifteen thousand francs, and he dreamed of inheriting an income of a hundred thousand and being again able to keep a mistress. He was not, as we see, one of those hypochondriacs like Monsieur de Voltaire, who spend their life dying; his was not the longevity of the cracked pot. The dashing old boy had always enjoyed good health. He was frivolous, quick-witted, and easily irritated, flying into a rage on the least provocation and generally against all reason. When contradicted he was liable to raise his stick and hit people, as they did in the *grand siècle*. He had an unmarried daughter of over fifty whom he shouted at and abused when he was in a temper and whom he would gladly have whipped, thinking of her as though she were a child of eight. He lustily abused his servants, using old-fashioned oaths. He had strange whims, allowing himself to be shaved daily by a barber who had once been mad and who detested him, being furiously jealous on account of his pretty and flirtatious wife. Monsieur Gillenormand had a high opinion of his own judgement in all things and considered himself extremely sagacious. 'The fact is,' he said, 'that I have unusual powers of discernment, so much so that if a flea bites me I can always tell what woman it came off.' The words most frequently on his lips were 'the person of refinement' and 'Nature'; but he did not use the latter in the sense generally accepted nowadays. When he brought it into his fireside discourse it was rather as follows – 'In order that civilization may have a bit of everything, Nature has even provided us with amusing specimens of barbarism. Europe has its tame samples of Asia and Africa. The cat is a drawing-room tiger and the lizard a pocket crocodile. The dancers at the Opéra are our rose-pink cannibals. They do not eat men but suck them dry, but rather, being sorceresses, they turn them into oysters and swallow them whole. The natives of the Carribees leave only the skeleton – they leave only the shell. That is the way we live now. We do not devour, we nibble; we do not exterminate, we scratch.'

II

The man and his dwelling

He lived in the Marais, at 6 Rue des Filles-du-Calvaire. The house was his property. It has since been pulled down and rebuilt, and no doubt has been given a new number in the process of re-numbering that has affected so many of the Paris streets. He occupied a vast ancient apartment on the ground floor, between the street and the gardens at the back, hung with Gobelin and Beauvais tapestries depicting pastoral scenes, details of which were repeated on the upholstery of the furniture. His bed was enclosed in a huge, nine-panelled screen of Coromandel lacquer, and the long curtains covering the windows fell in rich and ample folds. The garden immediately below his window was reached by a flight of steps up and down which the old man skipped in the most sprightly fashion. In addition to the library next to his bedroom he had a sitting-room in which he took great pride since it contained a magnificent straw tapestry with a fleur-de-lis design made in the prisons of Louis XIV, having been commissioned by Monsieur de Vivonne, the brother of Madame de Montespan and at that time Captain-General of the king's galleys, for his mistress. Monsieur Gillenormand had inherited this from an eccentric maternal great-aunt who lived to be a hundred. He had had two wives. His manners were midway between those of a courtier, which he had never been, and those of a man of law, which he might have become. He could be gay and confiding when he chose. In his youth he had been one of those men who are always deceived by their wives but never by their mistresses, because they are at once the most disagreeable of husbands and the most charming of lovers. He was a connoisseur of painting. There hung in his bedroom a wonderful portrait of some person unknown, painted by Jordaens with sweeping strokes of the brush and containing a mass of detail crammed in as though at random. His dress was in the style of neither Louis XV nor Louis XVI but rather that of the *incroyables* under the Directory. Up to that time he had still thought himself young and followed the fashion. His coat was of light cloth with broad lapels and long tails, and he wore knee-breeches and buckled shoes. He always had his hands in his pockets. He said roundly: 'The French Revolution was a load of scoundrels.'

III

Luc-Esprit

One night at the Opéra he had caught the eye simultaneously of two reigning beauties hymned by Voltaire, La Camargo, and La Sallé. Caught between these two fires he had beaten a heroic retreat in the direction of a dancing girl the same age as himself, an entirely undistinguished little creature named Nahenry with whom he was in love. But he abounded in romantic memories. 'La Guimard,' he would exclaim, 'how ravishing she was when last I saw her at Long-Champs, robed in exquisite sentiments, jewelled in hopefulness, clad in invitation to her very muff.' He had fond recollections of the waistcoats he had worn in his youth. 'I was as richly clad as a

Levantine Turk!' The Marquise de Boufflers, who saw him when he was twenty, described him as a charming rogue. He was outraged by the men now in power, finding them low-born and bourgeois. He read the daily papers, the 'newsprints' as he called them, with bursts of sardonic laughter. 'Corbière – Humann – Casimir Périer – and those are Ministers! Why not Monsieur Gillenormand, Minister? It would be farcical, but among those fools it would pass.' He made no bones about calling things by their proper or improper names, even in mixed company. He uttered obscenities and enormities with an elegant unconcern which was the permissiveness of his century. It may be remarked that that age of circumlocution in verse was also an age of crudity in prose. His godfather, predicting that he would be a man of genius, had bestowed on him the portentous baptismal names of Luc-Esprit.

IV

An aspirant centenarian

He had won prizes in his youth at the Collège in Moulins, the town of his birth, and the laurel-wreath had been placed on his head by no less a personage than the Duc de Nivernais, whom he called the Duc de Nevers. Nothing, not the Convention, the death of Louis XVI, Napoleon, or the return of the Bourbons, could efface the memory of that occasion. To him the Duc de Nevers was the great man of the century. 'Such a charming nobleman,' he said. 'So distinguished in his blue sash' . . . In Monsieur Gillenormand's eyes Catherine of Russia had atoned for the crime of the partition of Poland when she bought the secret of Bestuchef's gold for three thousand roubles. On this subject he was eloquent. 'The gold elixir, Bestuchef's yellow dye, General Lamotte's drops – in the eighteenth century those, at the price of a louis the half-ounce bottle, were the sovereign remedy for disasters in love, the panacea for the ills caused by Venus. Louis XVI sent the pope two hundred bottles.' He would have been beside himself if anyone had told him that this golden elixir was nothing but perchlorate of iron. Monsieur Gillenormand revered the Bourbons and held the year 1789 in horror. He never tired of relating how he had escaped the Terror, and the resourcefulness and ready wit he had needed to avoid having his head cut off. If any young man dared to praise the Republic in his hearing he turned purple in the face to the point of apoplexy.

Sometimes, referring to his age of ninety, he said, 'I trust I shan't see ninety-three again.' But at other times he proclaimed his intention of living to be a hundred.

V

Basque and Nicolette

He had theories, of which the following is one: 'If a man is a passionate lover of women but has a wife whom he does not greatly care for – plain, nagging, legitimate, conscious of her rights, steeped in the marriage code and sometimes jealous – he has only one way of dealing with the situation and securing his own peace of mind, and that is to hand the purse-strings over to her. In so doing he frees himself. The wife has something to keep her busy. She becomes addicted to the handling of banknotes until her fingers turn green; she watches over the farmers' stocks and building repairs, deals with bailiffs and lawyers, dictates to scriveners, pursues slow payers, draws up agreements, buys, sells, bargains and chaffers, passes judgement, interferes, arranges and disarranges. Even her blunders are a consolation to her, being her magisterial privilege. If her husband disdains her she has the satisfaction of ruining him.' Monsieur Gillenormand applied this theory in practice and it had become the story of his life. His second wife had so mismanaged his affairs that after her death he found that what remained of his fortune was only enough to provide him with a competence of fifteen thousand francs a year, three-quarters of the capital being invested in an annuity which would expire with him. He made this arrangement without hesitation, having no wish to leave anything behind him. Besides he had seen that patrimonies were a chancy business and might be confiscated as 'national property'; he had witnessed such machinations and had little fondness for the death-duty laws, the 'Grand-Livre de la Dette Publique'. 'All that has a smell of the Rue Quincampoix,' he said, referring to the financier John Law and the South Sea Bubble.

As we have said, the house in the Rue des Filles-du-Calvaire belonged to him. He had two servants, one male and one female. He gave them new names when they came to him, calling the men after their country of origin, Nîmois, Comtois, Poitevin or Picard. His latest valet was a plump, short-winded man of fifty-five incapable of running a dozen paces, and since he had been born in

Bayonne he called him Basque. As for the women, he called them all Nicolette (even La Magnon, of whom we shall hear more). When a haughty cook, a *cordon bleu* descended from a long line of concierges, presented herself he asked her what wages she expected. Thirty francs a month, was the answer. 'And what is your name?' ... 'Olympie' ... 'Well, I'll pay you fifty and your name will be Nicolette.'

VI

We meet La Magnon and her two children

With Monsieur Gillenormand suffering expressed itself in rage; unhappiness made him furious. He had all the prejudices and allowed himself every licence. The picture of himself which he liked to display for the sake of appearances and his private satisfaction was, as we have seen, that of the *vert-galant*, the ever-youthful lover. This, he said, was to have a 'royal reputation', and it was one which brought him unexpected blessings. A large basket, like an oyster hamper, was one day delivered at his house and found to contain a lusty, new-born male child, carefully swaddled and bawling its head off, of which a maid-servant whom he had dismissed six months previously claimed that he was the father. Since Monsieur Gillenormand was then eighty this caused an indignant outcry in his household. The audacity of it! Did the slut really suppose anyone would believe the story? But the old gentleman himself was not at all put out. Contemplating the bundle with a gratified smile, he exclaimed in ringing tones: 'What are you making a fuss about? What is so remarkable? You're simply showing your ignorance. The Duc d'Angoulême, Charles IX's bastard, was married at the age of eighty-five to a girl of fifteen. The Marquis d'Alluye, brother of the Cardinal de Sourdis, Archbishop of Bordeaux, when he was eighty-three had a son by a chambermaid of the wife of Monsieur Jacquin, a real love-child who became a Knight of Malta and a State Counsellor. One of the great men of our own century, the Abbé Tabaraud, was the son of a man of eighty-seven. These things are not unusual. You have only to read your Bible. Having said which I must declare that this young gentleman is not mine. However that is not his fault and he must still be looked after.' A handsome way of dealing with the situation. But the slut in question, the one called La Magnon, sent him a second present a year later, another boy. This was too much for Monsieur Gillenormand. He returned the two brats to their mother, undertaking to pay eight francs a month for their keep provided she did not do it again. He also said, 'I wish them to be properly cared for and I shall come to see them from time to time.' Which he did.

He had a brother in the priesthood who after being Rector of the Académie de Poitiers for thirty-three years had died at the age of seventy-nine. ('He died young,' said Monsieur Gillenormand.) The brother, whom he scarcely remembered, had been a peaceable skinflint who, being a priest, felt it his duty to give alms to such of the poor as he encountered; but the coins he gave them were always obsolete currency, and thus he found means of going to Hell by way of Paradise. As for their father, he had never stinted his alms but gave willingly and nobly. He had been benevolent, brusque, and charitable, and if he had been rich his way of life would have been magnificent. He liked everything concerning him to be done in the grand manner, even knavery. When he was cheated over an inheritance in a particularly crude and obvious fashion by a man of business he said solemnly: 'That is a disgusting way to behave. I am really ashamed of these shabby methods. Upon my soul, that is not the way a man of my sort should be plucked. I have been robbed like a traveller in the woods, but meanly robbed. *Sylvae sint consule dignae* – let the woods be worthy of a consul.'

Monsieur Gillenormand, as we have said, had had two wives and a daughter by each of them. The older daughter was still a spinster, but the younger had died at the age of thirty, having married a soldier of fortune who had served in the armies of the Republic and the Empire, been decorated at Austerlitz and promoted colonel at Waterloo. 'A disgrace to the family,' the old gentleman declared. He took a great deal of snuff, dusting his lace jabot with the back of his hand in a particularly elegant gesture. He had very little faith in God.

VII

A golden rule: never receive visitors except in the evening

Such was Monsieur Luc-Esprit Gillenormand, who had lost none of his hair, which was more grey than white and combed in fastidious ringlets. He was, when all is said, a gentleman worthy of esteem but belonging to the frivolity and greatness of the eighteenth century.

During the early years of the Restoration, Monsieur Gillenormand, who was still comparatively young (a mere seventy-four in 1814), had lived in the Faubourg Saint-Germain, in the Rue Servandoni by the Église Saint-Sulpice. He moved to the Marais only when he retired from society, well after his eightieth birthday.

His retirement was governed by certain fixed habits of which the first and most immutable was that his door was closed throughout the day. No caller, on no matter what business, was admitted to his presence until the evening. He dined at five and thereafter received visitors. Such was the fashion of his century, to which he resolutely clung. Daytime is vulgar, he said, and deserving only of closed shutters; the best people light their wits only when the heavens light their stars. He shut himself away from all men, even though it were the king himself, in the ancient elegance of his day.

VIII

Two, but not of a kind

We have mentioned Monsieur Gillenormand's daughters. There was a gap of ten years in their ages. In their youth there had been little resemblance between them, whether of looks or character; they were indeed as unlike sisters as possible. The younger was a delightful creature attracted towards everything that glitters, a lover of flowers, poetry and music, an ardent spirit soaring into boundless spaces who from her childhood had been in love with a romantic idea of heroism. The elder also had her daydream: what she saw on the horizon was something like a substantial contractor, perhaps a purveyor of military supplies, rich and splendidly stupid, the walking embodiment of a million francs. Or possibly a Prefect—and visions ran riot in her mind of official receptions with uniformed flunkeys at the door, magnificent balls, resounding speeches, and herself Madame la Préfète. The sisters, then, had this in common when they were girls, that each had her dream, each had wings, those of an angel in the one case and those of a goose in the other.

No ambition is ever wholly fulfilled, at least here on earth. No paradise becomes terrestrial in the age in which we live. The younger sister had married the man of her dreams, but she had died. The elder had never married at all.

At the time when she appears in our story she was an ageing pattern of virtue, an unshakeable prude with the sharpest nose and the dullest wits that ever a man came across. It was characteristic of her that outside her immediate family circle no one had discovered her Christian name; she was simply known as Mademoiselle Gillenormand the elder.

In the matter of prim hypocrisy Mlle Gillenormand could have given points to an English miss. She carried prudishness to the point of imbecility. Her life was haunted by a terrible memory: a man had once seen her garter.

This implacable modesty had increased with age. The front of her dress was never thick enough or high enough; she added pins and fastenings to places where no one would have thought of looking. It is the quality of prudishness that the less the fortress is threatened the more the garrison is strengthened. Nevertheless – and let who will explain this mystery of innocence – she accepted without displeasure the kisses of a young cavalry officer who was her great-nephew and whose name was Théodule. Except in this particular instance the label 'prude' which we have attached to her suited her entirely. Mlle Gillenormand was what may be termed a twilight spirit. Prudery is half a virtue, half a vice.

To prudishness she added religious bigotry, a suitable lining. She belonged to the Confrérie de la Vierge, wore a white veil on certain fast-days, mumbled special prayers, revered 'the Holy Blood', venerated 'the Sacred Heart', and passed hours in contemplation before a rococo Jesuit altar in a chapel closed to less privileged believers, letting her soul soar amid the small marble clouds and panels of gilded wood.

She had a chapel friend, an elderly virgin like herself named Mlle Vaubois, totally witless, compared with whom Mlle Gillenormand could feel herself to be an eagle of intelligence. Apart from the *agnus dei* and *ave Maria*, Mlle Vaubois's only interest was in the making of preserves. She was perfect of her kind, her mind a blank without a single flaw.

It may be added that in growing old Mlle Gillenormand had rather gained than lost. This is the case with passive natures. She had never been malicious, which is a negative form of goodness, and the years as they passed had smoothed off the asperities, bringing the softness of age. She was sad with an obscure sadness of which she herself did not know the secret. Her whole person expressed the stupor of a life that has ended without ever having begun.

She kept house for her father, and was to Monsieur Gillenormand what his sister had been to the old bishop, Monseigneur Bienvenu. These households consisting of an old man and an elderly daughter are not uncommon; they have a touching aspect, that of two weaknesses, each sustaining the other.

There was another member of the household besides those two, a little boy who always approached Monsieur Gillenormand in fear and trembling. Monsieur Gillenormand never addressed him except in harsh terms and sometimes with a raised stick: 'Come here, sir! Do you hear me, you young good-for-nothing? Answer me, can't you! Come here, you scamp, and let me look at you.' And so on. The fact is, he adored him.

The boy was his grandson, of whom we shall be hearing more.

BOOK THREE
GRANDFATHER AND GRANDSON

I
An old-time salon

WHEN MONSIEUR Gillenormand lived in the Rue Servandoni he had frequented a number of very distinguished salons. Bourgeois though he was, he was received. Indeed he was honoured and even sought after, for he possessed a twofold wit – the wit that was really his own, and the wit that others attributed to him. He went nowhere where he did not stand out. There are men who must attract notice at any price: where they cannot appear as oracles they must be clowns. But this was not Monsieur Gillenormand's style. His eminence in the royalist salons he visited made no demands on his self-respect. He was an oracle everywhere, outfacing such notables as Monsieur de Bonald and even Monsieur Bengy-Puy-Vallée.

In 1817, or thereabouts, he had invariably called on two after-noons a week at the home of a near neighbour, the Baronne de T—, a highly-respected lady whose husband had been French ambassa-dor in Berlin under Louis XVI. The late Baron de T—, who had been passionately interested in hypnosis and the phenomena of magnetism, had died in exile a ruined man, leaving nothing behind him except ten manuscript volumes, handsomely bound in morocco leather with gilt inscriptions, of a highly curious memoir concern-ing Friedrich Mesmer, his magnets and his healing séances. Madame de T— had thought it beneath her to publish these and subsisted on a small income that had somehow survived the wreck of their fortunes. She lived far removed from court circles – in a decidedly mixed world, as she said – a life of dignified poverty and isolation. But a few friends gathered twice a week round her widowed hearth, and there constituted a purely royalist salon. They drank tea and joined in loud laments, elegiac or dithyrambic according to the current set of the wind, concerning the times they lived in – the Charter, the Buonapartists, the debasement of the *cordon bleu* by its bestowal on persons of inferior rank, the Jacobin-ism of Louis XVIII – and in whispered hopes concerning Monsieur, who later became Charles X.

They were enchanted by the ribald ditties in which Napoleon

was referred to as Nicolas, or 'old Nick'. Duchesses and ladies of the utmost refinement took a delight in verses such as the following:

> Renfoncez dans vos culottes
> Le bout d'chemis' qui vous pend.
> Qu'on n' dis pas qu' les patriotes
> Ont arboré l'drapeau blanc!*

Execrable puns, harmless word-plays thought to be devastating, were much in vogue in these ultra-royalist coteries. Lists were compiled of the members of the Chamber of Peers – 'the abominably Jacobin chamber' – with the names appropriately distorted. From some innate desire to reverse the tide of fury they parodied the Revolution itself, and they had their own version of the revolutionary song.

> Ah! Ça ira, ça ira, ça ira!
> Les Buonapartist' à la lanterne!

Songs are like the guillotine, indifferently lopping off the heads of either side.

In the Fualdès affair, which occurred in 1816, they sided with Bastide and Jausion because Fualdès was a 'buonapartist'. They referred to the liberals as 'the brothers and friends' and there could have been no greater insult.

Like some church towers Mme de T—'s salon had two weathercocks, of whom one was Monsieur Gillenormand and the other the Comte de Lamothe-Valois. It was whispered of the latter in somewhat awed tones: 'You know who he is? He's the Lamothe of the Necklace Affair.' Partisans are singularly inconsistent.

We may add that among the bourgeoisie positions of honour are diminished by being too easy of access. One has to be careful whom one receives. Just as there is a loss of warmth in the presence of cold-natured persons, so there is a loss of esteem in the presence of persons who are despised. The old world considered itself to be above this law as it was above all others. Marigny, the brother of Mme Pompadour, had the entry to the Prince de Soubise *because* of the relationship, not in spite of it. Guillaume du Barry, who bestowed his name on the woman Vaubenier, was warmly received by the Maréchal de Richelieu. That world is like Olympus – even a thief is accepted in it if he is also a god.

---

*Roughly – 'Tuck the bottom of your shirt into your breeches. Never let it be said that patriots showed the white flag.'

There was nothing remarkable about the Comte de Lamothe-Valois, an old man of seventy-five in 1815, except his taciturn, portentous bearing, his cold, angular countenance, flawless manners, coat buttoned to his stock and the long legs encased in trousers the colour of burnt sienna which he invariably crossed when seated. His face was the same colour. Nevertheless he counted for something in that salon because of his 'celebrity' and also, strangely enough, because of the name of Valois.

As for Monsieur Gillenormand, he was valued for himself alone, a person of authority because he was authoritative. Without his habitual gaiety of manner being in any way affected, he contrived by his dignified bearing to give an impression of bourgeois honesty and high-mindedness. One is not the embodiment of a century for nothing. The passing of the years had endowed him with a halo of venerability.

Moreover his comments had often a decided ring of the old brigade. When, for example, the King of Prussia, having restored Louis XVIII, came to visit him informally under the name of Graf Ruppin, he was received by the descendant of Louis XIV rather as though he had been the Marquis of Brandenburg. Monsieur Gillenormand approved highly of this. 'All kings who are not the King of France,' he said, 'are mere provincials.' Again, someone asked in his presence what sentence had been passed on the editor of the *Courier français*. The reply was that he had been suspended. '*Suspendu,*' said Monsieur Gillenormand. 'The first syllable is one too many. He should be *pendu*' – that is to say, hanged. Remarks of this kind make reputations.

Monsieur Gillenormand as a rule visited Mme de T— accompanied by his tall, lean daughter, who was then over forty but looked fifty, and also by a pretty, bright-eyed little boy of seven who never entered that drawing-room without hearing the voices murmur around him, 'How good-looking he is. Poor child, what a shame.' This was the grandson we have already mentioned. He was referred to as 'poor child' because his father had been one of the 'brigands of the Loire', the name bestowed on Davout's army, which after the fall of Paris in 1815 had withdrawn beyond that river.

The brigand in question was the son-in-law we have also mentioned, whom Monsieur Gillenormand described as a disgrace to the family.

One of the red spectres of that time

Anyone walking through the little town of Vernon in those days, and crossing the beautiful stone bridge which, let us hope, will soon be replaced by some hideous construction of cables and girders, might have seen, if he looked down over the parapet, a man of about fifty wearing a leather cap, trousers and a jacket of grey homespun to which a faded ribbon had once been stitched, and wooden sabots. The man's skin was so sunburnt as to be almost black, his hair was almost white, and a deep scar ran from his forehead down over his sunken and prematurely aged cheek. He passed nearly all the day with a spade or hoe in his hands in one of the walled plots of land adjoining the bridge which form as it were a string of terraces along the left bank of the Seine, delightful enclosures filled with flowers which one might call gardens if they had been a great deal larger, or bouquets if they had been smaller. All these plots have the river on one side and a house on the other. In 1817 the man in the jacket and sabots occupied the humblest of the houses with the narrowest of the plots. He lived alone, in quiet solitude, except for a housekeeper who was neither young nor old, beautiful nor ugly, town- nor country-woman. The plot of ground which he called his garden was celebrated in the town for the beauty of the flowers he grew in it. Flowers were his sole occupation.

By dint of care and toil and watering he had added to the Creator's creation, having developed varieties of tulip and dahlia which Nature seemed to have overlooked. He was imaginative, having forestalled Soulange Bodin in the use of peat for the cultivation of certain rare shrubs from America and China. From daybreak in summer he was out on his garden-paths, weeding, clipping, hoeing and watering, busy amid his flowers with an air of gentle melancholy, sometimes passing an hour on end in motionless meditation listening to the song of a bird in a tree or the prattle of a child in a near-by house, or simply with his eyes intent on a drop of dew at the end of a blade of grass which the rays of the sun had turned into a jewel. He kept a scanty table and drank more milk than wine. A child could do what it liked with him and his housekeeper scolded him. He was shy to the point of unsociability, seldom going anywhere or seeing anyone except the poor who tapped on his window, and his curé, the Abbé Mabeuf, a good old man. But if any of the townspeople, or strangers for that matter, asked to see his tulips and roses he admitted them smiling. This was the 'brigand of the Loire'.

Any student of the military history of the period, memoirs, biographies, the *Moniteur* or the bulletins of the Grande Armée, might have been struck by the frequency with which the name of Georges Pontmercy occurred in them. As a young man Georges Pontmercy had been an infantryman in the Saintonge regiment, which after the Revolution formed part of the Army of the Rhine; for the old regiments under the monarchy still bore the names of their provinces and were not incorporated in brigades until 1794. Pontmercy fought at Spire, Worms, Neustadt, Turkheim, Alzey, and Mayence, where he was one of the two hundred composing Houchard's rearguard. He was one of the twelve men who held out against the entire corps of the Prince of Hesse behind the old ramparts of Andernach, only falling back when they were breached by enemy cannon-fire. He served under Kléber at Marchiennes and at Mont-Palissel where he had his arm broken by grapeshot. Then he was transferred to the Italian front, and he was one of the thirty grenadiers who defended the Col de Tende under Joubert. Joubert was promoted adjutant-general and Pontmercy became a sub-lieutenant. He was at Berthier's side under the cannonade at Lodi, after which Bonaparte said: 'Berthier was a gunner, a cavalryman, and a grenadier, all three.' He saw his old general, Joubert, fall at Novi at the moment when, with sword upraised, he was giving the order to charge. Having embarked with his company in a pinnace for transport from Genoa to a small port along the coast he sailed into a wasps'-nest of seven or eight English vessels. The Genoese captain wanted to push the guns overboard, hide the troops under the half-deck and pass himself off as a harmless merchantman; but Pontmercy hoisted the tricolour and sailed coolly through the fire of the British guns. Some fifty miles further on, his audacity increasing, he attacked and captured with his pinnace a large English transport bound with troops for Sicily and so heavily loaded with men and horses that she was down to the scuppers. In 1805 he was one of the Malher division which captured Gunzburg from the Archduke Ferdinand. At Wettingen, under a hail of bullets, he had consoled the last minutes of Colonel Maupetit, mortally wounded at the head of the 9th Dragoons. He had distinguished himself at

Austerlitz in that admirable march in echelon formation under enemy fire. When the cavalry of the Russian Imperial Guard over-ran a battalion of the 4th Regiment of the Line, Pontmercy had been one of the force that counter-attacked and threw back the Russians. The Emperor had awarded him a cross. Pontmercy had seen Wurmser taken prisoner in Mantua, Mélas in Alexandria and Mack in Ulm. He had been in the eighth corps of the Grande Armée which under Mortimer's command had captured Hamburg. Then he had transferred to the 55th Regiment of the Line, the former Flanders Regiment. He had been in the cemetery at Eylau where the heroic Captain Louis Hugo, uncle of the present writer, had for two hours held out against the utmost efforts of the enemy with a company of eighty-three men, and he was one of the three who had come out of that holocaust alive. He had fought at Friedland. He had seen Moscow, the Beresina, Lützen, Bautzen, Dresden, the Wachau, Leipzig and the mountain passes of Gelenhausen; later Montmirail, Château-Thierry, Craon, the banks of the Marne and the Aisne and the formidable entrenchments of Laon. At Arnay-le-Duc, being then a captain, he had sabred ten Cossacks and saved the life not of his general but of his corporal. He was blown up on that occasion and twenty-seven splinters were extracted from his left arm alone. Eight days before the capitulation of Paris he had exchanged with a comrade and joined the cavalry. To use an old expression, he was 'two-headed', that is to say, equally apt at handling the sabre or musket of a common soldier, or, as an officer, at commanding a squadron or battalion. It is this especial gift, perfected by training, which has brought certain specialist units into being, such as the dragoons, which are both horsemen and infantrymen. He had gone with Napoleon to Elba, and at Waterloo had commanded a squadron of cuirassiers in Dubois's brigade. It was he who had captured the Colours of the Luneburg battalion and, covered with blood, had flung the flag at Napoleon's feet, having sustained a sabre-cut across his face. The Emperor in high satisfaction had cried: 'You are hence-forth a colonel, a baron, and an officer of the Légion d'honneur.' To which Pontmercy had replied: 'I thank you, Sire, on behalf of my widow.' An hour later he had fallen in the sunken lane of Ohain . . . That was Georges Pontmercy, now a 'brigand of the Loire'.

We have heard something of his story. After being extricated by Thénardier from the sunken lane he had managed to rejoin the

French army and had eventually been conveyed in a series of ambulances to the Loire encampment. The Restoration had put him on half-pay and he was sent to live under surveillance at Vernon. King Louis XVIII, who chose to regard the events of the Hundred Days as non-happenings, had refused to recognize his rank as a colonel and officer of the Légion d'honneur or his title of baron. Nevertheless he missed no opportunity of signing himself 'Colonel Baron Pontmercy', and never went out without affixing the rosette of the Légion d'honneur to the old blue jacket which was the only one he possessed. The Procureur du Roi served him notice that he might be prosecuted for 'the illegal wearing of a decoration'. To the official bearing this missive he said with an acid smile, 'I don't know whether it is because I no longer understand French or you no longer speak it, but I don't understand a word.' He then went out eight days in succession wearing his rosette, but no one dared to interfere. When he received letters from official sources addressed to 'Major Pontmercy' he returned them unopened. Napoleon at the time was treating letters addressed by Sir Hudson Lowe to 'General Bonaparte' in the same fashion. Pontmercy had come to have the same bitter taste in his mouth as his Emperor. One morning, meeting the representative of the Public Prosecutor in the street, he went up to him and said: 'Monsieur, am I allowed to wear my scar?'

He had nothing but his very meagre major's half-pay, and the cottage he rented in Vernon was the smallest he had been able to find. He lived alone, as we have seen. He had found time, between two campaigns under the Empire, to marry Mlle Gillenormand. Her outraged parent had eventually consented to the match, saying with a sigh, 'Even the greatest families have to put up with it.' In 1815 Mme Pontmercy, in all respects an admirable wife and worthy of her husband, had died leaving one child. The boy might have been the consolation of Colonel Pontmercy's solitude, but his grandfather had imperiously claimed him, saying that otherwise he would disinherit him. The father had accepted this for his son's sake and had devoted himself to flowers.

For the rest, he had renounced everything, engaging in no movement or conspiracy, dividing his thoughts between the harmless things he did and the great things he had done – the growth of a carnation and the memory of Austerlitz.

M. Gillenormand had no dealings with his son-in-law. To him the colonel was a 'brigand', and to the colonel he was an old fool.

He never referred to the colonel except occasionally to make a mocking allusion to his 'barony'. It had been expressly agreed that the colonel would make no attempt to see or communicate with his son, on pain of the boy's being instantly turned out of the house and disinherited. To the Gillenormands Pontmercy was a leper, and they were resolved to bring up the child according to their own ideas. Perhaps the colonel was wrong to accept these conditions, but he did it for the best, believing himself to be the only sufferer. The child's expectations from his grandfather were small enough, but his aunt was another matter. Mlle Gillenormand had succeeded to a substantial fortune on her mother's side, and her sister's son was her natural heir.

The little boy, whose name was Marius, knew that he had a father, but that was all he knew. No one had told him more. However, the whisperings, the becks and nods and muttered asides in the society his grandfather frequented had made an impression on his child's mind, and being naturally disposed to accept the notions and opinions of the world around him, which were so to speak the air he breathed, he had come by degrees to think of his father with a sense of shame and with no desire to know him.

Thus he grew up; but every two or three months the colonel paid a surreptitious visit to Paris, like a convict breaking parole, and, hiding behind a pillar of the church of Saint-Sulpice at the hour when Aunt Gillenormand took Marius to Mass, was able to catch a glimpse of his son. He did so in fear and trembling lest the lady should see him. The battle-scarred warrior was frightened of the old maid.

It was to this circumstance that he owed his friendship with the curé of Vernon, Abbé Mabeuf.

This worthy priest was the brother of a churchwarden at Saint-Sulpice who had several times noticed a man staring at the little boy, a man with a scar on his cheek and tears in his eyes. The churchwarden had been struck by the fact that a man looking so much a man should have wept like a woman, and the face had stayed in his mind. One day when he was visiting his brother in Vernon he had come face to face with Colonel Pontmercy on the bridge and had recognized him. He had told the curé and they had found a pretext for calling on the colonel together. The visit had led to others. The colonel had at first been very reticent, but finally he had unbosomed himself and the curé and churchwarden had heard the story of how he had sacrificed his happiness for the sake of his son's future. As a result the curé conceived a great respect and affection for the colonel which the colonel returned. In any case, when both are honest and warm-hearted, no two men are more fitted to understand one another than an old priest and an old soldier. Indeed, they are the same man. One has served his country here below and the other serves his country in Heaven. There is no other difference.

Twice a year, on New Year's Day and the feast of St George, Marius wrote a letter to his father, dictated by his aunt, which might have been copied from a book on the art of letter-writing. This was all Monsieur Gillenormand would allow. The colonel replied with long, affectionate letters which the old man stuffed in his pocket without reading them.

III

R.I.P.

Mme de T—'s salon was all Marius knew of the world, the only opening that afforded him a view of life; a gloomy place and an opening that admitted more chill than warmth, more darkness than light. The boy, who was all high spirits when he entered that strange world, became quickly subdued and, which was even more foreign to his age, earnest-minded. Surrounded by those oppressive and idiosyncratic personalities, he looked about him in a kind of sober amazement which everything conspired to enhance. There were highly venerable elderly ladies in Mme de T—'s circle with names such as Mathan, Noé, Lévis which was pronounced Lévi, and Cambis, pronounced Cambyse. The aged countenances and biblical names were mingled in his mind with the Old Testament which he knew almost by heart. and when he contemplated them seated in a circle round a dying fire by the dim light of a green-shaded lamp, the stern profiles, the white or grey hair, the flowing skirts in the fashion of another age, their drab colours scarcely discernible, letting fall at rare intervals remarks that were at once majestic and astonishing, the little boy did so with startled eyes and with a feeling that these were not women but matriarchs and witches, not living beings but ghosts.

Mingled with the ghosts were a number of priests and noblemen, among the latter the Marquis de Sassenay, official secretary to the Duchesse de Berry, the Vicomte de Valroy who published mono-rhyming odes under the pseudonym of 'Charles-Antoine', the Prince de Beauffremont, still young but with greying hair and a lively and pretty wife whose low-cut dresses of red velvet with gold trimmings affronted the prevailing gloom, the Marquis de Coriolis d'Espinouse, celebrated for his mastery of 'measured politeness', the Comte d'Amendre with his amiable chin and the Chevalier de Port de Guy, mainstay of the Bibliothèque du Louvre, which was known as 'the king's study'. Monsieur de Port de Guy, who was bald and elderly rather than really old, was fond of recounting how in 1793, when he was sixteen, he had been imprisoned for subversion and manacled to the octogenarian Bishop of Mirepoix, also imprisoned for subversion but as a priest, whereas he himself had been charged as a soldier. This was at Toulon, and they had had the duty of going after dark to remove from the scaffold the heads and bodies of persons guillotined during the day. They had carried the bodies away on their backs, and their red convict smocks had acquired a thick caking of gore, damp at night but dry by the morning. Gruesome tales of this kind abounded in Mme de T—'s salon, where the reviling of Marat made it obligatory to sing the praises of Trestaillon, the leader of the White Terror in Nîmes. A few die-hard deputies met there to play a rubber of whist, and the Bailli de Ferrette, the former boon companion of the Comte d' Artois, looked in on his way to visit Monsieur de Talleyrand.

Among the priests may be mentioned the Abbé Halma, whose collaborator on *La Foudre* had once said to him, 'Bah! Who is there under the age of fifty? Only a few greenhorns!' There was also the papal nuncio, Monsignor Macchi, and two cardinals, Monsieur de la Luzerne and Monsieur de Clermont-Tonnerre. Cardinal de la Luzerne was a writer who was later to distinguish himself by having signed articles published in *Le Conservateur* side-by-side with those of Chateaubriand. Monsieur de Clermont-Tonnerre was Archbishop of Toulouse but paid frequent visits to Paris; a lively little old man who displayed red stockings under his hitched-up cassock and whose particular attributes were his detestation of the Encyclopedia and his passion for billiards. He had been introduced to Mme de T—'s salon by his closest friend, the former Bishop of Senlis, Monsieur de Roquelaure, who was noted for his tallness of stature and the assiduity of his work as a member of the Académie Française. These ecclesiastics, who for the most part were courtiers as well as churchmen, made their own contribution to the aristocratic tone of a salon which included five Peers of France. Nevertheless, since in this century the Revolution must make itself felt everywhere, that feudal gathering, as we have said, was dominated by a man of the middle-class, Monsieur Gillenormand.

The salon represented the essence and quintessence of 'white' reactionary Paris society. Prominent public figures, even those professedly royalist, were kept at arm's length, there being always an element of anarchy in current reputation. Chateaubriand, had he entered that drawing-room, would have been viewed with the utmost suspicion. Nevertheless a few royalists who had accepted the Republic were admitted on sufferance, among them Comte Beugnot, who had held a high position under the Empire.

Our present aristocratic salons bear no resemblance to that one. The Faubourg Saint-Germain of today has a smell of heresy. Our royalists have become democratic, and it is to their credit.

In Mme de T——'s superior world the most delicate and lofty sentiments prevailed, couched in terms of flowery politeness. Old forms that were the very spirit of the *ancien régime*, buried but still living, were unconsciously preserved, and some of these, particularly in the matter of language, would seem very odd today. The superficial student indeed might have mistaken for provincialisms what were merely survivals. A lady would be addressed as 'Madame la Générale', and even 'Madame la Colonelle' was not unknown. The charming Madame de Léon, no doubt recalling the Duchesses of Longueville and Chevreuse, preferred this form of address to her title of Princess, and the Marquise de Créquy was 'Madame la Colonelle'. That small world also adopted the habit, in private conversation with the king at the Tuileries, of addressing him in the third person as 'the king', the conventional 'your Majesty' having been 'debased by the Usurper'.

These were the terms in which men and events were judged. The age was mocked, which made it unnecessary to understand it. It was a circle of the blind leading the blind, each man sustaining the illusions of his fellow. The years following Coblenz were treated as though they had never happened. Just as Louis XVIII was, by the Grace of God, in the twenty-fifth year of his reign (the Charter of 1814 was officially issued in the *nineteenth* year of his reign, the Bonaparte interregnum being ignored), so might that little world of returned emigrés be said to be in the twenty-fifth year of their adolescence.

All was harmony; nothing was too much alive, a word was scarcely a breath, and a newspaper, like the salon itself, was a papyrus. There were young people, but they were partly dead. The liveries in the antechamber were faded. These totally outmoded persons were attended by servants of the same kind. Everything had an air of having lived a long time ago and of stubbornly holding out against the tomb. To conserve – conservation – conservative – the words constituted nearly their whole vocabulary. To be 'in good odour', that was the important consideration; and indeed aromatics played a significant part in the thinking of that world, their notions had a smell of vetiver. The masters were embalmed, and the valets stuffed with straw. A certain elderly marchioness, who had returned from emigration so penniless that she could only afford one maid, still talked about 'my people'.

In short, Mme de T—'s salon was 'ultra'. Since that word no longer has any meaning, although what it represents has perhaps not wholly disappeared, we must explain it.

To be 'ultra' is to go to the extreme. It is to attack the sceptre in the name of the throne and the mitre in the name of the altar; to abuse the cause one supports; to rush one's fences, outdo the executioner in the grilling of heretics, charge the idol with insufficient idolatry, insult by excessive adulation, find the pope insufficiently papist and the king insufficiently royalist. It is to denigrate the whiteness of alabaster or snow or the swan or the lily in the name of flawless whiteness; to be a partisan of causes to the point of becoming their enemy; to be so vehemently *for* as to be in fact *against*.

This spirit of 'ultraism' especially characterized the first phase of the Restoration. There has been nothing in history resembling that short period which began in 1814 and was ended in 1820 by the coming of Monsieur de Villèle, the statesman of the Right. Those six years were an extraordinary interlude, at once boisterous and bleak, gay and gloomy, lighted as though by the rays of a new dawn but at the same time overcast by the shadow of the great catastrophes still darkening the sky and only gradually receding into the past. In that mingling of light and dark a small world which was at once old and new, riotous and sad, youthful and senile, was rubbing its eyes. Nothing so resembles an awakening as a return. They eyed France with resentment, and France looked back at them with irony, old marquises like owls stalking the streets, returned emigrés and ghosts, '*ci-devant*' aristocrats amazed by everything, brave and noble gentlemen smiling to be back in France but also weeping, delighted to see their country again but in despair at not finding the monarchy they had known; the aristocracy of the crusader reviling the aristocracy of the Empire, that is to say, of the sword; historic clans who had lost all sense of history, descendants of the companions of Charlemagne disdaining the companions of Napoleon. Old insults were repaid; the sword of Fontenoy was a rusted mockery, the sword of Marengo odious and nothing but a sabre. The long-ago disowned yesterday. There was no longer any sense of what was great and what ridiculous. There was someone who called Bonaparte Scapin the clown ... That world is gone. Let us repeat it, nothing of that world remains. If, by recalling certain of its elements, we seek to reconstruct it, it seems as strange as the world before the flood. And indeed it has been swept away by a flood. It has vanished under two revolutions. What greater flood can there be than the flood of ideas? How quickly they submerge all that they set out to destroy, how rapidly do they create terrifying depths!

This, broadly, was the physiognomy of the 'ultra' salons in that distant and ingenuous age when Monsieur Martainville, the founder of the *Drapeau blanc*, was held to be a wittier man than Voltaire. They had their own literature and politics, devotedly absorbing the works of writers and publicists whose names are now forgotten. Napoleon was the irredeemable Ogre of Corsica. When later the Marquis de Buonaparté was allowed on to the stage of history as lieutenant-general of the king's armies, this was a concession to the changing spirit of the times.

They did not long retain their purity. As early as 1818 doctrinaires were beginning to appear among them, an unsettling development. These were royalists, in principle, but apologetically. Where the ultras proudly asserted their faith, the doctrinaires were a little ashamed of it. They were forthright but with silences, their political dogma appropriately tinged with irony; and they should have been successful. They made effective if excessive use of the white cravat and buttoned jacket. Their mistake, or their misfortune, was to put old heads on young shoulders. They posed as sages, hoping to leaven absolute, extremist principles with power exercised in moderation. They answered destructive liberalism with conservative liberalism, sometimes with rare intelligence. Their creed was as follows:

'Let us be grateful to monarchism. It has served us well. It has restored tradition, reverence, religion, and self-respect. It is loyal, brave, chivalrous, loving, and devoted. It dilutes, however reluctantly, the new-found greatness of the nation with the secular greatness of monarchy. It errs in not understanding the Revolution, the Empire, glory, liberty, new ideas, the younger generation, and the present century. But if it is mistaken in us, are we not sometimes mistaken in it? The Revolution, of which we are the heirs, should be aware of everything. The attack on monarchism is the reverse of liberalism. What a blunder and what blindness! Revolutionary France is lacking in respect for historic France, that is to say for its mother, for itself. The *noblesse* of the monarchy was treated after the 5th September as the *noblesse* of Empire was treated after the 8th July.* They were unjust to the Eagle and we are being unjust to the fleur-de-lis. It seems that something must always be condemned. But what purpose is served by tarnishing the crown of Louis XIV and abolishing the escutcheon of Henri IV? We laugh at Monsieur de Vaublanc, who removed the letter N from the Pont d'Iéna, but what he did was what we are now doing ourselves. Bouvines belongs to us, as does Marengo. The fleurs-de-lis are ours, and so is the N. These are our heritage. Why diminish it? We should no more disavow our country in the past than in the present. Why not accept all our history? Why not love all France?'

Thus did the doctrinaires criticize and defend monarchism, which was restive under criticism and furious at being defended.

The ultras represented the first phase of monarchism and the Congregation was characteristic of the second.

We may leave it at that. In the telling of this story the author has come upon this odd moment of contemporary history; he has been obliged to glance at it and to give some account of that vanished society. But he has done so rapidly and without bitterness or any thought of derision. He is attached to it by bonds of affectionate and respectful memory, since they relate to his mother. And it must be said that that small world had its own greatness. We may smile at it, but we cannot hate or despise it. It was the France of a bygone age.

Marius Pontmercy received the haphazard education of children

* The first of these dates, 5 September 1816, is that of the dissolution of the first Restoration parliament, the '*Chambre introuvable*'. The second is that of the second return of Louis XVIII in 1815.

of his class. When he grew too old for his Aunt Gillenormand, his grandfather entrusted him to a worthy tutor of unsullied classical innocence; thus his growing mind was subject first to a prude and then to a pedant. He did his years of high-school and read law at the university. He was a fanatical and austere royalist with little affection for his grandfather, whose frivolity and cynicism irked him, and with dark thoughts of his father. An ardent but reserved young man, high-minded, generous, proud, religious, impulsive; aloof to the point of asperity, uncompromising to the point of unsociability.

IV

Death of a brigand

The conclusion of Marius's classical studies coincided with the retirement of Monsieur Gillenormand from society. Bidding farewell to the Faubourg Saint-Germain and the salon of Mme de T—, the old gentleman withdrew to the Marais and his house in the Rue des Filles-du-Calvaire. In addition to the porter, his two servants were the housemaid Nicolette who succeded La Magnon, and the shortwinded Basque of whom mention has already been made.

In the year 1827, when Marius had just reached the age of seventeen, he came home one evening to find his grandfather awaiting him with a letter in his hand.

'Marius,' said Monsieur Gillenormand, 'you are to go to Vernon tomorrow.'

'Why?' asked Marius.

'To see your father.'

Marius trembled slightly. The last thing that had occurred to him was that he would ever be required to visit his father. Nothing could have been more unexpected, more surprising or, it must be said, more disagreeable to him. That their estrangement should be ended by enforced contact caused him no particular apprehension: it was simply tedious. Apart from his political reasons for disapproving of him, Marius was persuaded that his father – 'the swashbuckler', as Monsieur Gillenormand called him in his lighter moments – had no affection for him: why else should he have abandoned him to the care of others? Feeling himself unloved, he gave no affection in return; to him it was as simple as that.

He was so astonished that he asked no other question. His grandfather continued:

'It seems that he's ill. He wants to see you.'

There was a further pause.

'You'll have to start early,' Monsieur Gillenormand said. 'I understand there's a coach that leaves the Cour des Fontaines at six and gets there by evening. You'll have to catch that. He says it's urgent.'

He crumpled the letter and put it in his pocket. Marius might, in fact, have left that evening and been with his father next morning, for there was a night-coach to Rouen which left from the Rue du Bouloi and went by way of Vernon. But neither his grandfather nor he thought to inquire.

He reached Vernon at dusk next evening, when the candles were being lit, and asked the first person he met the way to the home of 'Monsieur Pontmercy'; for he took the Restoration view and did not think of his father as either a baron or a colonel. Arrived at the house, he rang the bell and a woman carrying a small lamp opened the door to him.

'Monsieur Pontmercy?' said Marius.

She looked at him without speaking.

'Is this where he lives?'

She nodded.

'May I speak to him?'

She shook her head.

'But I'm his son,' said Marius. 'He's expecting me.'

'Not any longer,' the woman said, and he saw that she was in tears.

She pointed to the door of a low-ceilinged room and he entered.

There were three men in the room, which was lighted by a tallow candle on the mantleshelf, one standing, one on his knees and the third, in his nightshirt, lying on the floor. The first two were the doctor and a priest; the third was the colonel.

He had been attacked by brainfever three days before and feeling that the attack was serious had written to Monsieur Gillenormand asking to see his son. He had grown worse, and that evening had risen from his bed, despite his housekeeper's efforts to restrain him, crying in delirium, 'My son is late. I must go to meet him.' He had collapsed in the antechamber and there had died. The doctor and the curé had been sent for, but both had arrived too late – like his son. By the dim light of the candle a tear was to be discerned on the colonel's pallid cheek. The eye from which it came was sightless, but the tear had not yet dried: it was the measure of his son's delay.

Marius stood looking down at this man whom he was seeing for the first and last time, the venerable, masculine face, the open eyes which saw nothing, the white hair, the once powerful limbs marked here and there with the furrows of old sabre-cuts and the red stars of bullet-wounds. He gazed at the huge scar imprinted by heroism on a face where God had imprinted kindness. He reflected that this man was his father and now was dead, and he was unmoved. The grief he felt was no greater than the grief he would have felt in the presence of any dead man.

Nevertheless an agony of mourning filled the room. The house-keeper was lamenting in a corner, the priest was praying and sobs were mingled with his prayers, the doctor was wiping his eyes; the very corpse was weeping.

The three of them in their affliction looked at Marius without speaking; he was a stranger. And Marius was ashamed at his lack of feeling. He had his hat in his hand, and he let it fall to the floor, to give the impression that grief had robbed him of the power to hold it. And then he despised himself for having done so. Was it his fault that he had not loved his father?

The colonel had left nothing. The sale of his possessions barely sufficed to cover the cost of the funeral. The housekeeper found a sheet of paper which she handed to Marius. It bore the following message, written in the colonel's hand.

For my son. The Emperor created me a baron on the field of Waterloo. Since the Restoration has refused me this title, paid for with my blood, my son will adopt it and bear it. It goes without saying that he will be worthy of it.

There was a further message on the other side.

My life was saved by a sergeant after Waterloo. His name was Thénardier. I believe that recently he kept a small inn in a village not far from Paris, Chelles or Montfermeil. If my son should find him he will do Thénardier every service in his power.

Not from any sense of duty towards his father, but from that vague respect for the wishes of the dead which is so strong in all men's hearts, Marius kept that missive.

Nothing else remained of the colonel. Monsieur Gillenormand

sold his sword and uniform to a secondhand dealer. The neighbours looted his garden of its rare flowers and the rest grew rank or died.

Marius spent only forty-eight hours in Vernon. Directly the funeral was over he returned to Paris and resumed his law studies, giving no more thought to his father than if he had never lived. The colonel was buried in two days and forgotten in three.

Marius wore a black band on his hat, and that was all.

V

How attendance at mass may create a revolutionary

Marius clung to the religious habits of his childhood. He went regularly to hear Mass at Saint-Sulpice, in the little lady-chapel where he had always sat with his aunt; but one day in a fit of absentmindedness he seated himself unthinkingly behind a pillar on a velvet-upholstered chair bearing the name of 'Monsieur Mabeuf, churchwarden'. The service had scarcely begun when an old man approached him and said:

'Monsieur, that is my place.'

Marius hastily moved and the old man took his seat. But at the end of the service he again approached him.

'You must forgive me for having disturbed you, Monsieur, and for now taking up a minute of your time. You must have thought me uncivil. I should like to explain.'

'There's no need at all,' said Marius.

'There is indeed. I would not wish to leave you with a bad impression of myself. I should like to tell you why I have a particular fondness for that place. It was from there that for some years, at intervals of two or three months, I watched an unhappy father who had no other opportunity of observing his son because he was debarred by a family compact from doing so. He came at the time when he knew the boy would be taken to Mass. The son had no idea that his father was there – indeed, he may not even have known that he had a father. The father concealed himself behind that pillar and watched the boy with tears in his eyes. He loved him deeply, as I could not help seeing. So the place has become as it were hallowed for me and it is there that I always hear Mass, preferring it to the churchwarden's bench where I am entitled to sit. I became acquainted with the unhappy man. There was a father-in-law and a wealthy aunt – and possibly other members of the family – who threatened to disinherit the boy if he had any contact with his parent. The father sacrificed himself for the sake of his son's future happiness. It was all to do with politics. Of course people must have political opinions, but there are some who go too far. The fact that a man fought at Waterloo does not make him a monster! It is not a sufficient reason for separating a father from his child. The gentleman was one of Bonaparte's colonels. He died, I believe, not long ago. He lived at Vernon, where my brother is curé. I forget his name – Pontmarie or Montpercy or something of the kind. He had a great scar on his face, from a sabre-cut.'

'The name is Pontmercy,' said Marius, who had turned pale.

'Yes, that's it! But did you know him?'

'He was my father,' Marius said.

The old churchwarden stared at him and exclaimed:

'So you're the child! Well, of course, you would be grown up by now. My dear lad, you had a father who greatly loved you.'

Marius offered the old man his arm and walked with him to his dwelling. The next day he said to his grandfather:

'Some friends and I are planning a shooting-party. Will you allow me to be away for three days?'

'Four if you like,' said Monsieur Gillenormand. 'Have a good time.' And winking at his daughter he murmured, 'Some wench, I'll be bound!'

VI

Outcome of a chance meeting

We shall see later where Marius went. He was away three days, and when he returned to Paris he went straight to the library of the School of Law and asked to see the file of the *Moniteur*.

He read the *Moniteur* and went on to read a number of histories of the Republic and the Empire, the *Memoirs from St Helena*, biographies, newsprints, official bulletins and proclamations, everything he could lay hands on. His first sight of his father's name in a Grande Armée bulletin put him in a fever of excitement for a week. He called upon generals under whom his father had served. He kept in touch with the churchwarden and learned from him something of his father's life in Vernon, his flowers and his solitude. In the end he formed a true picture of the gallant and gentle-hearted man, a mingling of a lion and lamb, who had been his father.

While this was going on, and it occupied all his leisure time and all his thoughts, he saw very little of his grandfather and aunt. He appeared at mealtimes but at other times he was not to be found. His aunt was aggrieved, but Monsieur Gillenormand chuckled, 'It's the time for wenching.' But he also remarked, 'I must say, I thought it was nothing but an escapade. It's beginning to look like a grand passion.'

It was certainly a passion.

Marius was beginning to worship his father. At the same time his ideas were undergoing a remarkable change, a transformation which took place in a series of stages. Since this story is the portrayal of a large number of the people of our time, we must look at these stages as they occurred.

The first effect upon him of his new insight into recent history was one of bewilderment.

Hitherto the Republic and the Empire had to him been words of ill-omen, the Republic a guillotine in the dusk, the Empire a sword in the night. But when he came to look closely into what he had supposed to be a chaos of darkness he found, with feelings of the utmost astonishment mingled with trepidation and delight, that it was a night filled with stars – Mirabeau, Vergniaud, Saint-Just, Robespierre, Camille Desmoulins, Danton, and then the rising of a sun which was Napoleon. He felt that he was losing his bearings and drew back, dazzled by so much brilliance. But collecting his wits after that first amazement and being able to contemplate the events with less abhorrence and the personalities with less apprehension, he came to see that these two groups of men and events might be resolved into two enormous facts, namely, that the Republic represented the sovereignty of civic rights transferred to the masses, and that the Empire represented the sovereignty of the French Idea, imposed upon Europe. The grand figure of the People was what emerged from the Revolution, and from the Empire there emerged the grand figure of France.

We have no need to dwell upon all that was disregarded in this summary and too-synthetic appraisal. We are tracing the gradual development of an unfolding mind. Progress does not happen overnight.

Marius now perceived that hitherto he had understood his

country no more than he had understood his father. He had known neither; as it were, he had deliberately closed his eyes. Now his eyes were opened and he was filled with admiration for the one and adoration for the other.

He was overwhelmed with sorrow at the thought that now there was no one except the dead to whom he could talk of what was in his mind. If God in His compassion had spared his father, how eagerly he would have gone to him, how ardently have cried: 'Father, I am here! I am your son! I think as you do!' How tenderly he would have clasped his hands and gazed at that scar, ready to kiss the hem of his garment. Why had he died so soon, before age or justice or his son's love could reach him? There was a constant sob of grief in Marius's heart, while at the same time he became more truly serious, more truly purposeful, more sure in his thinking and his faith. New lights were constantly dawning upon him, and it was as though a new being were taking shape within him. He was conscious of a sort of natural growth fostered in himself by these two discoveries, his father and his country.

It was as though a key had been placed in his hand and a door opened so that now he could interpret things that he had hated and account for things he had abhorred. He had a clear vision of the hand of Providence, human and divine, in great matters that he had been taught to abominate and great men he had been taught to revile. Thinking of the views he had held as recently as yesterday, which now seemed buried in the past, he was at once outraged and inclined to laugh.

The rehabilitation of his father led in the natural course of events to the rehabilitation of Napoleon; but this, it must be said, did not come easily to him.

He had been instilled from childhood with the views of the men of 1814. All the prejudices of the Restoration, its every interest and instinct, were directed towards the defamation of Napoleon, whom it execrated even more than it did Robespierre. It had cunningly exploited both the war-weariness of the nation and the hatred of the nation's mothers. Bonaparte had become a sort of fabulous monster, and to make him comprehensible to the simple minds of the people he had been depicted in every kind of terrifying guise, from the awe-inspiring and grandiose to the ugly and grotesque, as a Tiberius and as a buffoon. In referring to Bonaparte one might gnash one's teeth or explode with laughter, provided always that the basis was hatred.

Marius had never had any other conception of 'that man', and he clung to it with all the obstinacy of his nature. There was a stubborn being within him who abominated Napoleon.

But his study of recent history, above all documents and first-hand materials, caused the veil which had hidden Napoleon from Marius's eyes to be gradually dispelled. He began to perceive something immense, and to suspect that until then he had been as mistaken about Bonaparte as he had been about other matters. His vision grew daily clearer and, at first reluctantly but with a growing sense of exhilaration, as though drawn by an irresistible spell, he made the slow ascent from darkness to half-light and at length into the full blaze of enthusiasm.

There was a night when he sat alone at his desk by the open window of his small top-floor room, reading by the light of a candle, his thoughts interwoven with the impressions coming to him out of the dark infinity beyond the window, the starlit sky, the mysterious murmurs of the night. He was reading dispatches of the Grande Armée, those epic reports written on the field of battle, now and then coming upon a mention of his father and, constantly recurring, the name of the Emperor. All the greatness of the Empire was suddenly manifest as though a tide had risen within him. At moments he seemed to feel the nearness of his father's spirit and to hear his voice in his ear. He fell into a mystical trance, hearing the drums and trumpets, the thunder of gunfire, the steady tramp of marching men, and the distant gallop of horses. Looking upward he saw vast constellations shining in the immeasurable depths of the sky while great events took shape in the written words beneath his eyes. His heart was wrung. He was transported, breathless with revelation; and suddenly, not knowing what impulse prompted him, he got to his feet, leaned out of the window with arms outstretched, and gazing up into the silent immensity of the heavens cried, '*Vive l'Empereur!*'

For him this was the decisive moment. From that time on the Corsican Ogre, the Usurper, the tyrant, the monster who had been the lover of his sisters, the play-actor who took lessons from Talma, the poisoner of Jaffa, the tiger, the alien Bonaparte – all vanished, to be replaced in his thoughts by a remote and dazzling effulgence in which at an inaccessible height a marble Caesar shone. To his father the Emperor had been simply the beloved captain whom he revered and devotedly served; but to Marius he became more than this. He was the pre-ordained founder of the French power destined to succeed the Roman power in the domination of the world, the prodigious architect of a collapse, the successor of Charlemagne, Louis XI, Richelieu, Louis XIV and the revolutionary Committee of Public Safety, having his flaws, no doubt, his failings and even his crimes, since he was a man; but princely in his very failings, brilliant in his defects, powerful in his crimes. He was the Man of Destiny who had compelled all nations to acknowledge 'the great nation'. He was more even than this; he was France incarnate, conquering Europe with the sword and the world with the light he cast. Marius saw in Bonaparte the awesome spirit who would always arise on the frontier to safeguard the future: a despot, but issuing from a republic and summarizing a revolution. Napoleon became for him Man-and-People, as Jesus is Man-and-God.

As we can see, like all new converts to a religion, in the intoxication of his conversion he went too far. It was his nature to do so: being set upon a given slope it was nearly impossible for him to hold back. A fanatical ardour for the sword gained possession of him, bedevilling in his mind his ardour for the idea. He did not perceive that with his worship of the genius was indiscriminately mingled the worship of force: that is to say, that he was identifying himself with the two sides of his idol, the side which was brutal as well as the side which was divine. He erred in many other respects. He accepted everything. There are ways of falling into error while pursuing the truth. His was a kind of burning sincerity which made no distinctions. In the new course on which he was embarked, condemning the faults of the *ancien régime* in the measure that he extolled the glory of Napoleon, he disregarded all that might be said in its favour.

But however this might be, he had made an immense stride. Where once he had seen nothing but the fall of monarchy he now saw the rise of France. What had been for him a sunset was now a dawn. His whole direction was reversed.

All this took place in him without his family being aware of it. When in the course of his secret travail he had completely shed his former skin of a Bourbon-supporter and an ultra; when he had stripped away the aristocrat, the Jacobite and the royalist to become wholly a revolutionary, profoundly a democrat and very nearly a republican, he visited an engraver on the Quai des Orfèvres and ordered a hundred visiting-cards bearing the name 'Le Baron

Marius Pontmercy'. It was no more than a logical outcome of the change in him, in which everything gravitated around his father. But since he knew no one, and could not leave the cards with any hall-porter, he kept them in his pocket.

Another inevitable consequence was that as he drew nearer to his father, to the colonel's memory and to the things for which he had fought for twenty-five years, so he moved further away from his grandfather. As we have said, Monsieur Gillenormand's attitudes had for a long time jarred upon him. They were separated by all the disharmonies that must arise between a serious-minded young man and a frivolous old one. The gaiety of Gerontius affronts and exasperates the melancholy of Werther. Insofar as they had held the same political opinions and thought in the same general terms, Marius and his grandfather had met, as it were, on a bridge. But when this bridge collapsed the gulf between them was manifest. Marius was filled with resentment at the thought that Monsieur Gillenormand, for nonsensical reasons, had ruthlessly separated him from the colonel, depriving the father of his child and the child of its father. In his newfound reverence for his father he came almost to hate the old man.

But none of this was apparent. Only that he grew more and more reserved, spoke little at meals and was seldom at home. When his aunt reproached him with this he answered her gently, talking about study-courses, examinations, lectures, and so on. His grandfather stuck to his infallible diagnosis. 'The boy's in love. I know the symptoms.'

Now and then he went away for short periods.

'Where does he go?' his aunt wondered.

On one of these occasions, which were always short, he went to Montfermeil, obeying his father's injunction to look for the former Waterloo sergeant, the innkeeper Thénardier. But Thénardier had been sold up, the inn was closed and no one knew what had become of him. Marius's inquiries kept him away from home for four days.

'He's certainly got it badly,' said his grandfather.

They had a notion that he had taken to wearing on his chest, concealed under his shirt, something that hung by a black ribbon from his neck.

The 'wench'

Mention has been made of a cavalry-officer.

He was Monsieur Gillenormand's great-nephew, on his father's side, and his life was spent performing garrison duties in places remote from the family circle. Lieutenant Théodule Gillenormand had everything that was needed for a young man to be known as a fine officer. He had a 'girl's waist', a dashing way of carrying his sabre and a curled moustache. He very seldom came to Paris, so seldom that Marius had never met him. He was, as we may have said, Aunt Gillenormand's favourite, her preference being due to the fact that she almost never saw him. To see nothing of a person makes it possible to credit him with all the perfections.

One morning Mlle Gillenormand withdrew to her own room in a state of as much perturbation as her placid nature allowed. Marius had again applied to his grandfather for leave of absence. This had been granted, but the old gentleman had muttered in a frowning aside, 'He's getting worse than ever.' Mlle Gillenormand, greatly intrigued, had paused on the stairs to exclaim, 'It's really too much!' and had followed this with a question: 'Where in the world does he get to?' She suspected some more or less illicit romance, a woman veiled in secrecy, clandestine meetings, and she longed to know more. The hint of scandal is by no means abhorrent to such saintly natures.

To allay the undue excitement which these speculations aroused, she picked up her needle and settled down to one of those pieces of embroidery of which the design, under the Empire and the Restoration, consisted largely of carriage-wheels. A dull task and an absent-minded worker. She had been occupied with it for some time when the door opened and there stood Lieutenant Théodule, respectfully saluting her. She uttered a cry of delight. A woman may be elderly, prudish, devout and an aunt, but it is still pleasant to have a lancer walk into one's sitting room.

'You, Théodule!' she exclaimed.

'I'm passing through, aunt.'

'Well, come and kiss me.'

'There,' said Thèodule, doing so. Aunt Gillenormand went to her writing-desk.

'You'll stay at least for the week?'

'Alas, I must leave this evening.'

'Surely not.'

'There's no help for it.'

'Dear Théodule, do stay a little longer.'

'My heart says yes, but duty says no. It's quite simple. We're being transferred from Melun to Faillon and we have to go by way of Paris. So I thought, I'll look in and see my aunt.'

'Well, this is for your trouble,' and she pressed ten louis into his hand.

'For my pleasure, dear aunt.'

He kissed her again, and she had the pleasure of feeling her chest scratched by the braid of a military uniform.

'Are you riding with the rest of your regiment?'

'No. I wanted to see you so I got a special dispensation. My groom's taking my horse and I'm travelling by coach. And while I think of it, there's something I want to ask you.'

'Well?'

'It seems that my cousin, Marius Pontmercy, will also be on the coach.'

'How do you know that?' exclaimed Mlle Gillenormand, suddenly all eager curiosity.

'I saw his name on the list when I went to reserve my seat – Marius Pontmercy.'

'The wicked fellow!' his aunt cried. 'I'm afraid your cousin is not a well-conducted young man like you. So he's going to spend the night in a coach.'

'Just like me.'

'Yes, but with you it's duty, with him it's riotous living.'

'Dear me,' said Théodule.

At this point something remarkable happened to Mlle Gillenormand: she had an idea. Had she been a man she might well have clapped a hand to her forehead. She said urgently:

'It's true, is it not, that your cousin doesn't know you?'

'Yes. I've seen him, but he has never condescended to notice me.'

'And you'll be travelling on the same coach.'

'Him on top, me inside.'

'Where does the coach go?'

'To Andelys.'

'Is that where Marius is going?'

'Unless he gets off somewhere on the way, as I shall be doing. I have to change at Vernon for the Gaillon coach. I've no idea of Marius's destination.'

'Marius! Such an absurd name. How can anyone be called Marius? At least your name is Théodule.'

'I'd rather it was Alfred,' said the young man.

'Well, anyway, Théodule, I want you to listen to me.'

'Yes, aunt.'

'And pay great attention.'

'Yes.'

'The fact is, Marius is often away from home.'

'Ha!'

'He goes somewhere. He's sometimes away for several nights.'

'Is he indeed!'

'We want to know what is going on.'

Théodule replied with the calm of a seasoned warrior, 'A flutter, you can bank on it.' He added with a boisterous laugh, 'A wench, that's to say.'

'Exactly,' said his aunt, seeming to hear the voice of Monsieur Gillenormand and fortified in her own convictions by this repetition of the word 'wench'. 'And I want you to do us a favour. Follow Marius if you can. He doesn't know you, so there will be no difficulty. If it's a girl, try to catch sight of her and write and tell us all about her. Your grandfather will be greatly interested.'

Théodule had no particular fondness for work of this kind, but he was grateful for the ten louis and had a feeling that more might follow.

'Very well,' he said, 'I'll do my best.' And he reflected glumly: 'So I'm to play gooseberry.'

His aunt embraced him.

'You're not the sort to indulge in these escapades, dear Théodule. You're disciplined, you have principles and a sense of duty. You wouldn't leave your home to go gallivanting after some shameless hussy.'

Théodule grinned the grin of a pickpocket commended for honesty.

Marius, when he boarded the coach that evening, had no idea that he was being watched. As for the watchdog, his first act was to fall asleep, and he snored all night. At daybreak the guard roused the passengers who had to change at Vernon and Théodule remembered that this was where he got out. Then, as his wits returned, he remembered his aunt, the ten louis and his promise to keep an eye on his cousin. The thought made him laugh.

'He may have got out long ago,' he reflected as he buttoned his tunic. 'He could have got out at Poissy or Triel or Meulan or Mantes, if it wasn't Rolleboise or Pacy. What the devil am I going to write to the old girl?'

But at this moment he saw through the window a pair of black trousers descending from the top of the coach. It was Marius.

A peasant-girl with a basket of flowers had come up as the postilions changed horses and was urging the travellers to buy bouquets for their ladies. Marius bought an extravagant bunch of the best she had to offer.

'Upon my soul,' reflected Théodule, 'she must be a remarkably pretty woman if she's worth all that lot. I must certainly have a look at her.' And he proceeded to follow Marius, no longer because of his promise but from plain curiosity, like a hound hunting on its own account.

Marius paid no attention to him. One or two fashionably-clad women had got out of the coach, but he had not so much as glanced at them. He seemed to be unconscious of what was going on around him.

'He's in love, all right,' said Théodule.

Marius was making for the church.

'Better and better,' reflected Théodule. 'The church, of course. The best kind of rendez-vous is the one with a bit of religion in it. Nothing like a soulful glance under the noses of the saints!'

But when he reached the church Marius did not go inside but walked round it and vanished behind one of the buttresses.

'So they're meeting in the open,' thought Théodule. 'Well, let's have a look at the wench.'

He advanced cautiously round the buttress and then stopped dead in dismay.

Marius was kneeling on the grass with his face hidden in his hands. He had arranged his bunch of flowers. Close by where he knelt was a cross of black wood bearing the following name in white letters: COLONEL BARON PONTMERCY.

The 'wench' was a grave.

VIII
Marble meets granite

It was here that Marius had come the first time he left Paris and here that he came every time, when his grandfather said, 'He's on the rampage.'

Lieutenant Théodule was utterly taken aback by his discovery. He experienced a disagreeable and singular emotion which he was incapable of analysing, a mingling of respect for the dead and respect for a colonel. He withdrew, leaving Marius alone in the cemetery, and there was an element of military discipline in his withdrawal. Death had confronted him wearing officer's epaulettes and he came near to greeting it with a military salute. Not knowing what to write to his aunt, he decided to write nothing at all, and probably there would have been no sequel to his discovery had not the mysterious working of chance caused that incident in Vernon to be followed almost immediately by a repercussion in Paris.

Marius returned home in the early morning three days later, wearied by two sleepless nights of coach travel. He went straight up to his room, and feeling the need to refresh himself with an hour at the swimming school, went straight off to the baths, having only stopped to shed his top-coat and the black ribbon which he wore round his neck.

Monsieur Gillenormand, who like all elderly persons in good health had risen early, heard him come in. As nimbly as his old legs would allow, he hurried up to Marius's attic room meaning only to embrace him and perhaps, by adroit questioning, glean some notion of where he had been. But the youth moved faster than the octogenarian, and by the time he had climbed the stairs Marius was gone.

His bed had not been touched and the top-coat and black ribbon lay trustingly upon it.

'Better still,' said Monsieur Gillenormand.

A minute later he was in the drawing-room , where his daughter was busy with her cartwheel embroidery. He made a triumphal entry, bringing with him the top-coat and the ribbon.

'Victory!' he cried. 'Now we shall get to the bottom of the mystery. We shall put our finger on the spot. We shall plumb the riddle to its depths and spy out our cunning rascal's romance. I have the portrait.'

A small case of black shagreen, something like a medallion, was attached to the ribbon. The old man examined it for some moments without opening it, savouring it greedily and angrily like a starving beggar witnessing the serving of a rich meal that is not for him.

'It can only be a portrait, the sort of thing one wears on one's heart. How absurd they are! Probably some abominable strumpet, enough to make one shudder. The young have such bad taste these days.'

'Do open it, father,' the old maid said.

The case opened with a spring catch. They found nothing in it but a carefully folded sheet of paper.

'The old, old story!' cried Monsieur Gillenormand, bursting into laughter. 'Of course it's a love-letter.'

'We must read it!' his daughter cried.

She put on her glasses and they read it together. What they read was Colonel Pontmercy's dying message to his son.

The effect of this upon the old man and his daughter cannot be described. They were chilled as though by the presence of the dead. Neither spoke a word except that Monsieur Gillenormand muttered to himself, 'It's the bandit's handwriting, no doubt of that.'

The lady, after inspecting the document from every angle, replaced it in the case. At the same time something had fallen out of a pocket of the top-coat, a small, rectangular packet wrapped in blue paper. Mlle Gillenormand picked it up and undid it. It contained Marius's hundred visiting-cards. She handed one of them to her father, who read: Le Baron Marius Pontmercy.

The old man rang the bell for Nicolette. He picked up ribbon, case, and top-coat and tossed them into the middle of the room.

'Take those things away.'

A full hour passed in total silence. The old man and the old maid sat with their backs to each other thinking their separate thoughts, which were probably much the same. At length Mlle Gillenormand said:

'Pretty!'

A few minutes later Marius appeared, having just returned from the swimming-bath. Before he had even crossed the threshold his grandfather, who still had one of the visiting-cards in his hand, cried out in the sneering, bourgeois tone of voice which was so crushing in its effect:

'Well, well, well, well – so it seems you're a baron! My compliments. May I ask what this means?'

Marius flushed slightly.

'It means that I'm my father's son.'

Monsieur Gillnormand ceased to smile and said harshly:

'I am your father.'

'My father,' said Marius, speaking steadfastly with lowered eyes, 'was a humble, heroic man who gallantly served the Republic and France and was great in the greatest chapter in human history. He passed a quarter of a century under canvas, under cannon- and musket-fire by day and in snow and mud and rain at night. He captured two standards, received twenty wounds and died forgotten and neglected, having only one fault to his account, that he had given too much of his heart to two ingrates, his country and myself.'

This was more than Monsieur Gillenormand could endure. At the word 'republic' he had risen, or, to be more exact, leapt to his feet, and each successive word uttered by Marius had affected him, old royalist that he was, like the puff of a bellows on a brazier. His colour had mounted from grey to pink, from pink to scarlet and from scarlet to flame.

'Marius!' he thundered. 'Abominable boy. I know nothing of your father and do not want to know. But I know this, that all those people were villains and scoundrels, robbers and murderers. All of them, I tell you! Every one! I admit of no exceptions. Do you hear me? As for you, you are no more a baron than my slipper. The men who served Robespierre were villains and the men who served Bonaparte were knaves. They were renegades who betrayed – betrayed – betrayed their lawful king, and cowards who ran away from the Prussians and English at Waterloo! That is what I know. If your father was one of them, so much the worse. I know nothing of him. And that is that. I am your humble servant, Monsieur.'

Now it was Marius who was the brazier and his grandfather who was the bellows. The young man stood trembling in every limb while his senses reeled. He was the priest who sees his relics scattered to the winds, the fakir who sees his idol spat upon. That such things should be said in his presence was not to be borne, but what was he to do? His father had been grossly insulted, but the offender was his grandfather. How avenge the one without assailing the other? He could not insult his grandfather, but it was equally impossible for him to ignore the insult to his father. The hallowed grave on one side and white hairs on the other. He paused for some moments in furious indecision. Then, with his eyes fixed on the old man, he cried in a ringing voice:

'Down with the Bourbons and that fat pig Louis XVIII!'

Louis XVIII had been dead four years, but no matter.

The high colour drained out of the old man's face until his cheeks were as white as his hair. He turned towards the bust of the Duc de Berry and bowed deeply to it in a gesture of singular dignity. Then, twice, he silently paced the length of the room, from the hearth to the window and back, causing the parquet flooring to creak beneath his feet as though a figure of stone were moving over it. The second time he paused and bent over his daughter, who, like an elderly sheep, had witnessed the scene in stupefied consternation. He said with a smile that was almost calm:

'A baron like this gentleman and a bourgeois like myself cannot live under the same roof.'

Then, white and trembling, his forehead swelling in the terrible blaze of his wrath, he pointed a hand at Marius and cried:

'Clear out!'

Marius left the house.

On the following day Monsieur Gillenormand said to his daughter:

'You will send that blood-drinker sixty pistoles every six months, and you will never again utter his name in my presence.'

He had addressed her formally as *vous* instead of *tu*. Having a great accumulation of rage to get rid of, and no other outlet for it, he continued to do this for more than three months.

Marius had left the house in an equal fury which was aggravated by a particular circumstance, one of those trifling mishaps which complicate family dramas. The quarrel remains the same, but the sense of grievance is rendered more acute. In hastily gathering up his belongings from the floor of the salon at the old man's order, and carrying them up to his bedroom, Nicolette had dropped the black medallion containing the colonel's letter, probably somewhere in the darkness of the attic stairs. It could never be found. Marius was convinced that 'Monsieur Gillenormand' (whom thenceforward he never referred to in any other terms) had deliberately destroyed his father's 'testament'. Since he knew the words by heart there was no real loss, but the paper itself, the handwriting, that sacred relic, had been very dear to him.

He went off without saying where he was going, or knowing himself, with thirty francs in his pocket, his watch and a few clothes in an overnight bag. Hailing a cab, he had himself driven at random to the Latin quarter.

What was to become of Marius?

BOOK FOUR

THE ABC SOCIETY

I

A group which nearly became historic

BENEATH THE surface of that seemingly apathetic age there was a faint revolutionary stir. Gusts from the depths of '89 and '92 were again to be felt in the air. Youth, if we may be allowed the phrase, was on the move. Attitudes were changing, almost unconsciously, in accordance with the changing times. The compass needle swinging over its dial has its equivalent in men's souls. Everyone was preparing for a forward step. Royalists were becoming liberal, liberals were becoming democrats.

It was like a rising tide complicated by a thousand eddies. It is the nature of an eddy that it confuses things, hence the conjunction of oddly assorted ideas. Napoleon was venerated and, with him, liberty. We are describing a period in history, and these were its mirages. Opinions go through phases. Voltairian royalism, that weird variant, had a no less strange pendant – Bonapartist liberalism.

Other schools of thought were more sober-minded. There were those who looked for basic principles, those who stood for law. There was a passion for the Absolute, affording a glimpse of limitless achievement. The Absolute, by its very rigidity, sends spirits soaring heavenwards. Nothing excels dogma as a begetter of dreams: and nothing excels dreaming as a begetter of the future. Today's Utopia is the flesh and blood of tomorrow.

Advanced opinion was ambivalent. The mysterious beginnings of change threatened the established order, which was both suspect and crafty. In this lay a clear hint of revolution. The secret aims of power conflict fundamentally with the secret aims of the people. The incubation of revolt is the reply to the planning of coups d'état.

There did not yet exist in France such vast, widespread organizations as the German Tugendbund or the Italian Carbonari; but small, obscure cells were ramifying. The Cougourde was taking shape in Aix, and in Paris, along with similar bodies, there was the Society of the Friends of the ABC.

The ostensible purpose of the ABC Society was the education of children, but its real purpose was the elevation of men. The letters

ABC, as pronounced in French, make the word *abaissé*, that is to say, the under-dog, the people. The people were to assert themselves. To deride the pun would have been a mistake. A pun can be weighty in politics, as witness *Castratus ad castra*, which made of the eunuch Narses a Roman general, and 'You are Peter (the rock) and on this rock I will build my church.'

The ABC Society was small in numbers, no more than a secret society in embryo; we might almost call it a clique, if cliques gave birth to heroes. They had two meeting-places in Paris, the one a drinking-place called Corinthe, near Les Halles, of which there will be mention later on, and the other a small café on the Place Saint-Michel, the Café Musain. The first was handy for the workers, the second for the students.

The councils of the ABC Society were held as a rule in a back room at the Café Musain. The room, which was at some distance from the café proper, and separated from it by a long passage, had two windows and a door leading to an inconspicuous flight of steps down to the narrow Rue des Grès. Its frequenters smoked and drank, played cards and laughed, talking in loud voices about general matters and in low voices about particular ones. Nailed to the wall – a portent calculated to arouse the suspicions of any police agent – was an old map of France under the Republic.

Most of the members of the ABC Society were students having friendly relations with a number of workers. These are the names of the more important, those who have, to some extent, a place in history: Enjolras, Combeferre, Jean Prouvaire, Feuilly, Courfeyrac, Bahorel, Lesgle or Laigle, Joly, Grantaire. These young men formed a sort of family, united by friendship. All except Laigle came from the Midi.

They formed a remarkable group, one which has vanished into the limbo of the years that lie behind us, but at this point in our story it may be of value to shed some light on their youthful countenances before the reader follows them as they plunge into the shadow of a tragic adventure.

We have named Enjolras first, and the reason for this will be seen later. He was the only son of wealthy parents, a charming young man who was capable of being a terror. He was angelically good-looking, an untamed Antinous. From the thoughtfulness of his gaze one might have supposed that in some previous existence he had lived through all the turmoil of the Revolution. He was familiar with every detail of that great event; he had it in his blood as though he had been there. His was a nature at once scholarly and warlike, and this is rare in an adolescent. He was both thinker and man of action, a soldier of democracy in the short term and at the same time a priest of the ideal rising above the contemporary movement. He had deep eyes, their lids slightly reddened, a thick lower lip which readily curled in disdain, and a high forehead – a large expanse of forehead in a face like a wide stretch of sky on the horizon. In common with certain young men of the beginning of this century and the end of the last who achieved distinction early in life, he had the glow of over-vibrant youth, with a skin like a girl's but with moments of pallor. Grown to manhood, he still appeared a youth, his twenty-two years seeming no more than seventeen. He was austere, seeming not to be aware of the existence on earth of a creature called woman. His sole passion was for justice, his sole thought to overcome obstacles. On the Aventine hill he would have been Gracchus, in the Convention he would have been Saint-Just. He scarcely noticed a rose, was unconscious of the springtime and paid no heed to the singing of birds. The bared bosom of the nymph Evadne would have left him unmoved, and like Harmodius he had no use for flowers except to conceal a sword. He was austere in all his pleasures, chastely averting his eyes from everything that did not concern the republic, a marble lover of Liberty. His speech was harsh and intense, with a lyrical undertone, and given to un-expected flights of eloquence. It would have gone hard with any love-affair that sought to lead him astray. Had a grisette from the Place Cambrai or the Rue Saint-Jean-de-Beauvais, seeing that schoolboy face, the pageboy figure, the long, fair lashes over blue eyes, the hair ruffled in the breeze, the fresh lips and perfect teeth, been so taken with his beauty as to seek to thrust herself upon him, she would have encountered a cold, dismissive stare, like the opening of an abyss, which would have taught her not to confuse the Cherubini of Beaumarchais with the cherubim of Ezekiel.

At the side of Enjolras, who represented the logic of revolution, was Combeferre, representing its philosophy. The difference between logic and philosophy is that the one can decide upon war, whereas the other can only be fulfilled by peace. Combeferre supplemented and restrained Enjolras. He was less lofty but broader of mind. He sought to instil principles in terms of basic ideas, saying, 'Revolution, but civilization' and spreading wider horizons round the stern peaks of dogma. In all his thinking there was an element of the attainable and the practicable. Revolution with Combeferre was more breatheable than with Enjolras. Enjolras stood for its divine right, Combeferre for its natural right. The first went all the way with Robespierre, the second stopped at Condorcet. Combeferre lived closer than Enjolras to the life of everyday. Had it been given to these two young men to attain to the pages of history, the one would have been the man of principle, the other the man of wisdom. Enjolras was the more virile, but Combeferre was the more human – *homo* and *vir*, this was the distinction between them. Combeferre was as gentle as Enjolras was rigid, from innate purity. He respected the word 'citizen' but preferred the word 'man', and would gladly have called his fellows *hombre*, as the Spaniards do. He read everything, went to the theatre and attended public lectures, learning from Arago, the director of the Observatory, about the polarization of light and from Geoffrey Saint-Hilaire about the functions of the external and internal arteries, one of which serves the face and the other the brain. He was in touch with scientific developments, contrasted Saint-Simon with Fourier, deciphered hieroglyphics, broke up pebbles to study geology, could draw a silk-worm moth from memory, pointed out errors in the Dictionnaire de l'Académie, studied Puységur and Deleuze, vouched positively for nothing, not even the miracles, denied nothing, not even the existence of ghosts, browsed in the files of the *Moniteur*, and meditated. He declared that the future lay in the hands of the schoolmaster and was much concerned with the question of education. He believed that society should strive incessantly for the raising of intellectual and moral standards, the popularization of science, the dissemination of ideas and the enlightenment of the young, and he feared that the inadequacy of present methods, the poverty of literary teaching confined to the two or three centuries said to be 'classical', the tyrannical dogmatism of official pedants, their prejudices and rigid routines, would end by making our schools mere artificial forcing-houses. He was learned and a purist, precise, eclectic, hard-thinking, and at the same time imaginative 'to the point of fantasy', his friends said. He shared every dream for the future – the development of railways, the elimination of suffering by surgery, the fixing of pictures in a darkroom, the electric telegraph, the guided balloon. For the rest, he was undismayed by the barriers to human progress erected by superstition, despotism, and prejudice, being among those who believe that knowledge must always prevail in the end. Enjolras was a commander; Combeferre was a guide. One was moved to combat the former but to accompany the latter. This is not to say that Combeferre was incapable of fighting; he was ready if need be to assail an obstacle and attack it with violence. But it suited him better to make men aware of their destiny by persuasion and the use of reason and precept. Of the two extremes, he preferred enlightenment to conflagration. A bonfire will cast a glow, but why not await the rising of the sun? A volcano sheds a light, but the light of dawn is better. Combeferre perhaps preferred the white purity of the good to the savage splendour of the sublime. Light mingled with smoke, progress achieved by violence, these only partly satisfied his gentle, earnest soul. The sudden plunging of a nation into truth, the events of 1793, this frightened him; but he was even more repelled by apathy, in which he saw putrefaction and death. All in all, he preferred spray to mist, the torrent to the cloaca, Niagara to the Lac de Montfaucon. He wanted neither immobility nor over-haste. While his exuberant friends, chivalrously in love with the Absolute, extolled the splendid lottery of revolution, he was more disposed to let progress take its course, sane progress, cold-blooded perhaps but undefiled, methodical but irreproachable, phlegmatic but unshakeable. Combeferre would have prayed on his knees for the future to come in all simplicity, with nothing to trouble the vast, virtuous evolution of mankind. 'Good must be innocent,' he constantly said. And indeed, if it is the grandeur of revolution that, with eyes fixed on the blinding ideal, it flies like an eagle towards it with blood and flame in its talons, the beauty of progress resides in the fact that it is unsullied. Between Washington who represents the one and Danton who embodies the other, the difference is that between the angel with swan's wings and the angel with eagle's wings.

Jean Prouvaire was a shade more soft-hearted than Combeferre. He called himself Jehan, with the touch of fantasy that characterized the profound and widespread impulse of that time, which has given rise to our most necessary study of the middle ages. Jean Prouvaire was a lover; he cherished a pot of flowers, played the flute, wrote verses, loved the people, pitied women, wept over the lot of children, divided his faith equally between the future and God, and reproached the Revolution for having cut off an illustrious head, that of André Chénier. His voice, which was ordinarily soft, would suddenly become masterful. He was widely-read to the point of erudition and near to being an orientalist. Above all he was kind; and (a matter easily understandable by those who know how closely kindness is akin to greatness,) in poetry he favoured the grandiose. He knew Italian, Latin, Greek, and Hebrew, but the four languages served him for the reading of only four poets, Dante, Juvenal, Aeschylus, and Isaiah. In French he preferred Corneille to Racine and Agrippa d'Aubigné to Corneille. He loved to stroll through meadows of wild flowers and was scarcely less interested in the passage of the clouds than in the passage of events. There were two sides to his mind, the side of men and the side of God; he studied, or he meditated. During the day he pored over social questions – wages, capital, credit, marriage, religion, freedom of thought, freedom to love, education, the penal system, poverty, the right of free association, property, production and distribution, the riddle of the lowest stratum which spreads its shadow over the human ant-heap; and at night he contemplated the immensity of the heavens. Like Enjolras he was rich and an only son. He talked gently, bowed his head, smiled self-consciously, blushed for no reason, was awkward and extremely shy – and, for the rest, fearless.

Feuilly was a fan-maker, orphaned of both father and mother, who laboriously earned three francs a day and whose mind was obsessed with a single thought, to liberate the world. His other preoccupation was to educate himself, which he called self-liberation. He had taught himself to read and write, and everything he knew he had learned in solitude. He had a warm heart, an immense capacity for affection. Being an orphan he had adopted mankind as his parents. His country took the place of his mother. He hated to think that there should be any man without a country. With the profound instinct of a man of the people he cherished in his heart something that we now call the 'idea of nationality'. He read history precisely in order that his protest might be well-informed in this matter. In that youthful circle of Utopians, which was concerned principally with France, he stood for the world outside, specializing in Greece, Poland, Hungary, Romania, and Italy. The names cropped up constantly in his discourse, with or without reason, with the obstinacy of conscious rightness. The rape of Crete and Thessaly by Turkey, of Warsaw by Russia, of Venice by Austria, these things outraged him. Above all, the first partition of Poland in 1772 roused him to fury. There is no more powerful eloquence than that of indignation based on true conviction, and this was the power that he possessed. He never wearied of talking about that infamous event, a noble and gallant race subdued by treachery, a crime with three participants, a monstrous trap, the prototype and forerunner of all the shameful acts of oppression which had subsequently afflicted other nations, eliminating them, so to speak, in the moment of their birth. All contemporary social assassinations derive from the partition of Poland; it is a proposition of which all current political misdeeds are corollaries. Not a despot, not a traitor in the past near-century but in one way and another has paraphrased and endorsed that criminal act. When the history of modern betrayals is compiled, it will be first on the list. The Congress of Vienna examined it before committing its own crime. The 'tally-ho' was in 1772, the 'kill' in 1815. Such was Feuilly's thesis. The penniless workman had constituted himself the guardian of Justice, and Justice had rewarded him with a touch of greatness. The right, indeed, is indestructible. Warsaw can no more be Tartar than Venice can be Teutonic. Kings waste their energies in that contention, and lose their honour. Sooner or later the submerged nation rises again to the surface; Greece is still Greece and Italy, Italy. The struggle of the right against the deed persists for ever. The theft of a people can never be justified. These august swindles have no future. A nation cannot be shaped as though it were a pocket handkerchief.

Courfeyrac had a father who was addressed as Monsieur *de* Courfeyrac, a belief in that particle being one of the misconceptions of the Restoration bourgeoisie in the matter of aristocracy and titles of nobility. As we know, it has no real significance. But the bourgeoisie in the days of *La Minerve* esteemed it so highly that many who had legitimately borne it were constrained to abandon it, Monsieur de Constant de Rebecque becoming plain Benjamin Constant, and Monsieur de Lafayette plain Monsieur Lafayette. Not wishing to be behindhand, Courfeyrac called himself plain Courfeyrac.

Where Courfeyrac is concerned we might almost leave it at that, simply adding: for Courfeyrac read Tholomyès, the one-time lover of Fantine. He possessed that youthful ardour that may be termed the infernal beauty of the spirit. Later it fades like the grace and beauty of a kitten, becoming, on two legs, a bourgeois, and on four legs a tabby-cat. This is a type of individual that constantly recurs in seats of learning, as though its quality were handed down from generation to generation. Anyone listening to Courfeyrac in 1828 might have been hearing Tholomyès in 1817. Only, Courfeyrac was a decent young man. Despite their superficial resemblance, the difference between them was great. Inwardly they were poles apart. In the heart of Tholomyès there was a pander, in Courfeyrac a paladin.

Enjolras was the leader, Combeferre the guide and Courfeyrac the centre. The others shed more light, but he shed more warmth. He had, indeed, all the qualities of a centre, both roundness and radiation.

Bahorel had had a share in the bloody riot of June 1822, occasioned by the funeral of Lallemand, a student who had been killed in a liberal demonstration. Bahorel was a creature of good intentions but a dangerous ally, courageous, spendthrift, generous to the point of prodigality, voluble to the point of eloquence, bold to the point of audacity, the best possible material for the devil to work on, with opinions as crimson as his waistcoats. He was a born agitator: that is to say, he enjoyed nothing more than a quarrel except a rebellion, and nothing more than a rebellion except a revolution. He was always ready to smash a window, strip a street of its cobbles and then overthrow a government, just to see what would come of it – an eleventh-year student. He perceived the right but did not follow it. His motto was, 'No lawyers' and his coat-of-arms might have been a bedside table on which was a mortarboard. Whenever he passed the School of Law, which happened seldom, he buttoned his tail-coat, the top-coat having not yet been invented, as a precaution against contamination. He said of the school building, 'What a handsome old person!' and of the dean, Monsieur Delvincourt, 'What a noble monument!' His courses furnished him with matter for songs and his professors with subjects for caricature. He squandered a fairly large allowance in idleness, something of the order of three thousand francs. His family were farmers whom he had taught to respect their son. He said of them, 'They're peasants, not bourgeois. That's why they've got some sense.'

Bahorel, a creature of whims, frequented a number of cafés. The others had regular habits, he had none. He strolled. To err is human, to stroll is Parisian. But with all this he had an acute mind and was more given to thought than he appeared to be. He served as a link between the ABC Society and other groups, still not fully constituted, which were destined later to take shape.

In this conclave of youthful heads there was one which was bald.

The Marquis d'Avaray, whom Louis XVIII made a duke for having helped him into a hired cab on the day of his emigration, has related that when the king disembarked at Calais on his return to France in 1814, a man approached him with a petition. 'What is it you want?' the king asked. 'If it please your Majesty, a post-office' ... 'What's your name?' ... 'My name is L'Aigle.'

The king frowned, glanced at the written petition and saw that the name was spelt 'Lesgle'. This un-Napoleonic spelling amused him and he began to smile. 'The fact is, Sire,' said the man, 'that one of my forebears was a dog-minder who was nicknamed Lesgueules (the jowls). That is the origin of my name. Lesgueules has been shortened to Lesgle and corrupted to L'Aigle' ... This caused the king's smile to widen and later the man got his post-office. Whether by accident or design it was at Meaux (or 'Mots').

The bald member of the group was the son of this Lesgle, and he signed himself Laigle (de Meaux). His comrades rounded off the joke by calling him Bossuet.

Bossuet was a cheerful but unlucky young man, notable for the fact that he succeeded in nothing. On the other hand, he laughed at everything. He was bald at the age of twenty-five. His father had wound up with a house and land, but the son had promptly lost both in an ill-advised speculation. Nothing of his inheritance remained. He possessed learning and wit, but both miscarried. Nothing went right for him, everything failed him, all his undertakings went awry. If he tried to split logs he split his finger. If he acquired a mistress he rapidly discovered that he also had a new male friend. He was the constant victim of mischance, hence his merriment. He said, 'I spend my life walking under ladders.' Nothing surprised him, for he took these accidents for granted, smiling at the mockery of fate like someone who joins in the joke. He was poor, but his store of good humour was inexhaustible. He was always down to his last penny, but never to his last laugh. He greeted adversity like an old friend, patted disaster on the back, and was on first-name terms with fatality – 'Well, Old Man of the Sea!' This constant harassing had made him inventive. He was endlessly resourceful. Although he had no money he found the means, when he was in the mood, to squander 'fantastic sums'. On one occasion, so he said, he spent 'a hundred francs' on supper with a street-walker, and at the height of the orgy delivered himself of the resounding phrase, 'Daughter of five crowns, pull off my boots!'

Bossuet was slowly heading for the legal profession – reading law, that is to say, in the fashion of Bahorel. He had little in the way of lodging, sometimes none at all; he roosted with one friend or another but most often with Joly, a medical student two years younger than Bossuet.

Joly was a youthful *malade imaginaire*. Such medicine as he had learned had made him more a patient than a doctor. At twenty-three he considered himself a chronic invalid and he spent his life inspecting his tongue in the mirror. He maintained that man was subject to magnetism like a compass-needle, and placed his bed with its head pointing north and its feet south so that his circulation might not be affected by the attraction of the poles. He felt his pulse in thundery weather. For the rest, he was the gayest of them all. His youthful inconsistencies, exaggerated, morbid but light-hearted, blended harmoniously together to make an eccentric, agreeable young man to whom his comrades applied the English word 'jolly'. Joly had a habit of rubbing his nose with the knob of his cane, the sign of a sagacious mind.

All these young men, so diverse but who, when all is said, deserved to be taken seriously, had a religion in common: Progress. All were the direct descendants of the French Revolution, and even the most frivolous became serious at the mention of the year 1789. Their fathers in the flesh had been royalists, *feuillants*, doctrinaires of all kinds, but it made no odds. Those earlier contradictions meant nothing to this younger generation with the pure blood of principle coursing through its veins. They stood, without having passed through any intermediary stages, for uncompromising right and absolute duty. United and initiated, they were the underground portrayal of the ideal.

But amid these hot-blooded and passionate believers there was one sceptic, attracted to them, it would seem, by force of contrast. This was Grantaire, who ordinarily signed himself with the letter R – a play on the pronunciation of his name, *grand R* [or 'capital R']. Grantaire was a young man who made a point of believing in nothing. He was, however, one of those students who acquire a wide diversity of knowledge during their time in Paris. He knew that the best coffee was to be had at Lemblin's, that the best billiard-room was at the Café Voltaire, that the best rolls and nicest girls were to be found at the Ermitage on the Boulevard du Maine, excellent chicken at Mère Saguet's, bouillabaisse at the Barrière de la Cunette and a particularly good little white wine at the Barrière du Combat. He knew the best places for everything, besides being a boxer, gymnast and dancer, and skilled in the use of the singlestick. A great drinker into the bargain. He was astonishingly ugly, so much so that the prettiest boot-embroiderer of the day, Irma Boissy, was so revolted by his looks as to declare him to be impossible. But this in no way discouraged Grantaire, who gazed tenderly and fixedly at all women with an air of saying, 'If I chose', and strove to persuade his comrades that he was universally sought after.

Such words and phrases as 'rights of the people', 'rights of man', 'the social contract', 'the French Revolution', republic, democracy, humanity, civilization, religion, progress, came very near to meaning nothing whatever to Grantaire, who merely smiled at them. Scepticism, that dry-rot of the intellect, had left him without a whole thought in his head. He lived in irony, and his motto was, 'The only certainty is a full glass.' He was scornful of allegiance to any cause, as derisive of brother as of father, of the young Robespierre as of Loizerolles –'A fat lot of good it did them, getting killed.' He said of the crucifix, 'Well, that's one gallows that worked.' Womanizer, gambler, profligate and often drunk, he annoyed that circle of young dreamers by constantly humming a ditty in praise of Henri IV, which also extolled women and wine.

But, sceptic that he was, he had one fanatical devotion, not for an idea, a creed, an art or a science, but for a man – for Enjolras. Grantaire admired, loved, and venerated Enjolras. The anarchic questioner of all beliefs had attached himself to the most absolute of all that circle of believers. Enjolras had conquered him not by any force of reason but by character. It is a not uncommon phenomenon. The sceptic clinging to a believer is something as elementary as the law of complementary colours. We are drawn to what we lack. No one loves daylight more than a blind man. The dwarf adores the drum-major. The toad has its eyes upturned to Heaven, and for what? – to watch the flight of birds. Grantaire, earthbound in doubt, loved to watch Enjolras soaring in the upper air of faith. He needed Enjolras. Without being fully aware of it, or seeking to account for it to himself, he was charmed by that chaste, upright, inflexible, and candid nature. Instinctively he was attracted to his opposite. His flabby, incoherent, and shapeless thinking attached itself to Enjolras as to a spinal column. He was in any case a compound of apparently incompatible elements, at once ironical and friendly, affectionate beneath his seeming indifference. His mind could do without faith, but his heart could not do without friendship: a profound contradiction, for affection in itself is faith. Such was his nature. There are men who seem born to be two-sided. They are Pollux, Patrocles, Nisus, Ephestion. They can live only in union with the other who is their reverse side; their name is one of a pair, always preceded by the conjunction 'and'; their lives are not their own; they are the other side of a destiny which is not theirs. Grantaire was one of those, the reverse side of Enjolras. Truly the satellite of Enjolras, he formed one of that circle of young men, went everywhere with them and was only happy in their company. His delight was to see those figures moving amid the mists of wine, and they bore with him because of his good humour.

Enjolras, the believer, despised the sceptic and soberly deplored the drunkard. His attitude towards him was one of pitying disdain. Grantaire was an unwelcome Ephestion. But, roughly treated though he was by Enjolras, harshly repulsed and rejected, he always came back, saying of him: 'What a splendid statue!'

II

A funeral oration

On a certain afternoon which, as will be seen, has its bearing on the events previously related, Laigle de Meaux stood voluptuously propped in the dorway of the Café Musain, looking like a caryatid on holiday, idle except for his thoughts. He was gazing over the Place Saint-Michel. To stand with one's back against something upright is a manner of dozing on one's feet which is not displeasing to dreamers. Laigle de Meaux was musing without sorrow over a trifling misadventure which had befallen him two days previously at the School of Law, modifying his plans for the future, which were in any case sufficiently vague.

A state of reverie does not prevent a cab from passing or the dreamer from observing it. Through the mists of his meditations, Laigle de Meaux drowsily perceived a two-wheeled vehicle moving slowly round the Place as though uncertain of its destination. What was it looking for? Seated in the cab was a young man with a bulky travelling bag to which was affixed a card bearing in large black letters the name MARIUS PONTMERCY.

The sight of this name aroused Laigle. He straightened himself and called:

'Monsieur Marius Pontmercy?'

The cab stopped. The young man, who seemed also to have been plunged in thought, looked up.

'Eh?'

'You are Monsieur Marius Pontmercy?'

'Certainly.'

'I've been looking for you,' said Laigle de Meaux.

'What do you mean?' asked Marius, who had just left his grandfather's house and was now staring at someone he had never seen before. 'I don't know you.'

'I don't know you either,' said Laigle.

Marius frowned, thinking he had encountered a practical joker. He was not at that moment in the best of humours or prepared to put up with this kind of pleasantry in the open street. Laigle de Meaux was unabashed.

'Weren't you at Law School the day before yesterday?'

'Possibly.'

'You certainly were.'

'Are you a student?' asked Marius.

'Yes, monsieur, I am a student like yourself, and the day before yesterday I chanced to drop in at the school. One has these whims. The professor was calling the roll. As you know, they're particularly tiresome on these occasions. If you fail to answer after your name has been called three times it is struck off the list, and that means sixty francs down the drain.'

Marius was now listening with interest. Laigle proceeded:

'The professor was Blondeau. You know what he's like, with his pointed nose and spiteful nature. He delights in spotting absentees. He had craftily begun the roll-call at the letter P, and I wasn't paying attention because that isn't my initial. It was going quite well, no defaulters, all present and correct. But then he called "Marius Pontmercy" and there was no reply. He repeated it more loudly, looking hopeful, and when there was still no reply he picked up his pen. But I, monsieur, have bowels of compassion. I thought to myself, here is a good man about to be struck off, a living, breathing fellow-mortal who is unpunctual. Not a good student. Not a lead-bottomed student who studies, a Simon Pure pedant, bursting with art and letters, theology and erudition, cut and dried to the pattern prescribed by the Faculty. Here is a noble idler who enjoys life, who plays truant, who chases girls, who may at this very moment be in bed with my mistress. He must be saved! Down with Blondeau! And so, when Blondeau, having dipped his pen in the ink and gazing with beady eyes round the assembly repeated for the third time, "Marius Pontmercy," I answered, "Present!" In consequence of which you were not struck off.'

'Monsieur, I —' began Marius.

'But I was,' said Laigle de Meaux.

'But why?' asked Marius.

'It's quite simple. I had answered from near the podium, and then I moved towards the door to slip away. But he was staring fixedly at me, and with a diabolical cunning he switched back to the letter L, which is my initial. I come from Meaux and my name is Lesgle.'

'L'Aigle!' exclaimed Marius. 'The Eagle! What a splendid name.'

'So Blondeau called out the splendid name and I answered, "Present!" upon which, looking at me with a tigerish satisfaction, he smiled and said, "If you are Pontmercy you cannot be Lesgle," a remark uncomplimentary to yourself but grievous only to me. Having said which, he struck me off.'

'I'm mortified,' said Marius.

'Before going further,' said Laigle, 'I insist upon burying Blondeau with a few well-chosen phrases. We will suppose him to be dead. It would call for no great alteration in his skinniness, his pallor, his coldness, his stiffness or his smell. I pronounce the words, *Frudimini qui judicatis terram* – take note, oh judges of earth. Here lies Blondeau, Blondeau the nose, the willing ox of discipline, the slave of order, the destroying angel of the roll-call, who was upright, square, punctilious, inflexible, honest, and hideous. After which God will remove his name as he removed mine.'

'I'm most distressed . . .' said Marius.

'Young man,' said Laigle de Meaux, 'let this be a warning to you. In future be punctual.'

'I owe you a thousand apologies.'

'Do not expose your fellows to the risk of being struck off.'

'I'm really extremely sorry –'

Laigle burst out laughing.

'And I'm delighted. I was in danger of becoming a lawyer and this has saved me. After all, I shall not defend the widow or attack the orphan. No gown and no rostrum. I have been thrown out, and I owe it to you, Monsieur Pontmercy. I would like to pay you a visit of gratitude. Where do you live?'

'In this cab,' said Marius.

'A sign of wealth,' said Laigle calmly. 'I congratulate you. You have a lodging worth nine thousand francs a year.'

At this moment Courfeyrac emerged from the café. Marius was smiling sadly.

'I have had it for two hours and I would like to get out of it. The fact is, I don't know where to go.'

'Monsieur,' said Courfeyrac, 'come to the place where I live.'

'I should have the priority,' said Laigle, 'but I don't live any-where.'

'Dry up, Bossuet,' said Courfeyrac.

'Bossuet?' said Marius, 'I thought your name was Laigle.'

'A jest,' said Laigle. 'The eagle of words. They call me Bossuet.'

Courfeyrac got into the cab and directed the driver to the Hôtel de la Porte Saint-Jacques. By the evening Marius was installed in that hotel, in a room next to Courfeyrac's own.

III

Astonishment of Marius

Within a few days Marius and Courfeyrac were friends. Youth is a time of quick resilience and the rapid healing of wounds. Marius found that in company with Courfeyrac he could breathe freely, a sufficiently novel experience. Courfeyrac asked no questions, nor even thought of doing so. At that age the face tells everything and words are unnecessary. One can say of a young man that he has a speaking countenance. A single look, and we know him.

But one morning Courfeyrac did put a question to Marius. He asked abruptly:

'By the way, have you any political views?'

'Of course,' said Marius, slightly ruffled.

'Well, what are you?'

'I'm a Bonapartist democrat.'

'A wary compromise,' commented Courfeyrac.

The next day he took Marius to the Café Musain. Murmuring with a smile, 'I must introduce you to the revolution,' he led him into the back room used by the ABC Society and presented him to his friends with the single word, 'A novice'.

Marius had fallen into a hornet's nest of lively minds, albeit, taciturn and sober though he normally was, he was no less winged or capable of stinging than they. Being a solitary both by force of circumstances and inclination, and given to self-communion, he was at first somewhat dismayed by the tumult with which these young men assailed him, the hubbub of outspoken, unbridled thoughts, some so remote from his own thinking that he could not grasp them. He heard philosophy, literature, art, history, and religion discussed in terms that were quite new to him. New vistas were opened up, and since he could not get them in any perspective he was not sure that they were not visions of chaos. When he discarded his grandfather's views in favour of those of his father he had thought that his mind was made up; but now, in some perturbation and without wholly admitting it to himself, he began to suspect that this was not the case. His whole outlook began again to change; all his previous notions were called in question in a process of internal upheaval that he found almost painful. It seemed that his new friends held nothing sacred. No matter what the subject, it gave rise to forthright language that was disconcerting to his still-timid mind.

A theatre poster, announcing a new production of a stock repertory 'classic', came up for discussion, and Bahorel exclaimed, 'To hell with these old bourgeois tragedies!,' to which Combeferre replied:

'You're wrong, Bahorel. The bourgeoisie adore tragedies and they must be allowed to go on doing so. Costume-drama has its place in the scheme of things, and I am not one of those who in the name of Aeschylus deny it the right to exist. Nature contains its abortions, and its self-parodies. Take a beak that isn't a beak, wings that aren't wings, fins that aren't fins, paws that aren't paws, agonized squawks that make you want to laugh, and you have a duck. But if domestic poultry can exist side by side with real birds I see no reason why our "classic" tragedy should not exist side by side with the antique.'

It happened one day that Marius was strolling with Enjolras and

Courfeyrac along the Rue Jean-Jacques Rousseau. Courfeyrac took him by the arm.

'Do you see where we are? This is the former Rue Plâtrière, now named the Rue Jean-Jacques Rousseau after a curious household which lived here sixty years ago. Jean-Jacques and Thérèse. Children were born to them. Thérèse brought them forth and Jean-Jacques threw them out.'

Enjolras said sternly:

'I won't hear a word against Jean-Jacques. He is a man I revere. True, he disowned his children; but he adopted the people.'

None of the young men ever used the word 'Emperor'. Jean Prouvaire occasionally referred to Napoleon; the others all called him Bonaparte. Enjolras pronounced it *Buonaparte*.

IV

The back room at the Café Musain

One of the many conversations to which Marius listened, occasionally joining in, had a profoundly disturbing effect upon him.

It took place in the back room at the Café Musain on an evening when nearly all the members of the ABC Society were present. The big lamp had been ceremonially lighted. They had been talking casually of one thing and another, without excitement or uproar, each of them except Enjolras and Marius holding forth more or less at random. These gatherings of comrades can be tranquil occasions. Separate conversations were going on in all four corners of the room, words flung occasionally from one group to another.

No woman was allowed in that room except Louison, the scullery-maid, who passed through it now and then on her way to the kitchen, which they called the 'laboratory'.

Grantaire, who was decidedly drunk, was booming away in his own corner, arguing and refuting at the top of his voice. Suddenly he cried:

'I'm thirsty! I have a dream, brothers – that the great wine-tun of Heidelberg is seized with apoplexy and I am one of the leeches attached to it. I want to drink. I want to forget life. Life is the disgusting invention of God-knows-who. It doesn't last and it isn't worth anything. We twist our necks trying to stay alive. Life is a stage setting in which almost nothing is real. Happiness is an old canvas painted on one side. "All is vanity," said the preacher in

Ecclesiastes, and I agree with him, even if he never existed. Nothingness, not wanting to go naked, has clothed herself in vanity, which is the dressing-up of everything in big words. The kitchen becomes a laboratory, the dancer a professor of the dance, the fairground tumbler a gymnast, the boxer a pugilist, the apothecary a chemist, the wig-maker an artist, the house-botcher an architect, the jockey a sportsman, the wood-louse a pterygibranchiate. Vanity has an outside and an inside. The outside is the negro decked in beads, and the inside is the philosopher in rags. I weep for the one and laugh at the other. Our so-called honours and dignities, and even true dignity and honour, are generally an empty shell. Kings make a mock of human pride. Caligula made his horse a consul, Charles II knighted a sirloin of beef. Thus we may array ourselves between the Consul Incitatus and the most excellent Sir Sirloin. And the true worth of man is scarcely more admirable. Listen to any man praising his neighbour. White is the ferocious enemy of white; if the lily could speak, how it would tear the dove to shreds! A bigot talking of another bigot is as venomous as a snake. It is a pity that I am ignorant; I would tell you countless things if only I knew them. I have always had brains, but when I was at school I spent my time robbing orchards instead of poring over my books. So much for me. As for you others, I value you. I care nothing for your perfections, your excellences and good qualities. Every virtue flows over into vice. Prudence is the neighbour of miserliness, generosity of prodigality, bravery of bravado; excessive piety becomes sanctimoniousness; there are as many vices in virtue as holes in Diogenes's cloak. Which do we admire more, the killed or the killer, Caesar or Brutus? Generally it is the killer. Long live Brutus, who killed. That's virtue for you! Virtue perhaps, but madness as well. There are strange flaws in those great men. The Brutus who stabbed Caesar was in love with the statue of a little boy, the work of the Greek sculptor Strongylion who also carved the statue of the Amazon Eucnemon, renowned for the beauty of her legs, which Nero took with him on his travels. Strongylion left only those two statues, and they are a link between Brutus and Nero, each of whom loved one of them. History is one long repetition, each century plagiarizing the next. The battle of Marengo copies the battle of Pydna, and Clovis's victory at Tolbiac resembles Napoleon's victory at Austerlitz as closely as two drops of blood. I care nothing for victory. Nothing is more pointless than to win, the real triumph is to win over. But try to prove anything! We are content with success, which is mediocrity; and to conquer is misery. Alas, we meet everywhere with vanity and betrayal. Everything bows to success, even grammar. *Si volet usus*, if use ordains it, said Horace. So I scorn the human race. To come down from the whole to the part, am I to admire one particular people? Which people, may I ask? The Greeks? The Athenians, those Parisians of the ancient world, killed Phocion, as it might have been Coligny, and so toadied to their tyrants that Anacephores said of Pisistratus, "His urine attracts the bees." The most considerable man in Greece for fifty years was the grammarian, Philetas, who was so small and frail that he had to wear soles of lead to prevent himself being carried away by the wind. In the main square of Corinth there was a statue carved by Silanion and catalogued by Pliny. It was a statue of Episthates. And who was he? He was the wrestler who invented the cross-buttock. So much for the glory of Greece. Let us move on. Am I to admire England or France? Why France? Because of Paris? I have told you what I think of Athens. Why England? Because of London? I detest Carthage. And then London, the metropolis of luxury, is also the capital of poverty. Every year a hundred people die of hunger in the parish of Charing Cross alone. That's Albion. I may add, to put the lid on it, that I have seen an Englishwoman dancing with a crown of roses and blue spectacles. So to hell with England. But if I refuse to esteem John Bull should I therefore esteem Brother Jonathan? I have no fondness for that slave-owner. If we leave out "Time is money" what is left of England; and if we leave out "Cotton is king" what remains of America? Germany is lymphatic and Italy is bilious. Should we then love Russia? Voltaire did so, but he admired China as well. I will agree that there are beauties to be found in Russia, among others that of a strong despotism. But I feel sorry for the despots. Their health is precarious. One Alexis was beheaded, one Peter was stabbed, one Paul was strangled and another stamped to death by jackboots. Various Ivans have had their throats cut and several Nicholases and Basils have been poisoned. All of which suggests that the imperial residence of a Russian Tsar is a decidedly unhealthy place. All civilized people have one offering to propose for the admiration of the thinker: it is war. But warfare, civilized warfare, contains and summarizes every form of banditry, from brigandage on a mountain-pass to the marauding raids of the Comanche Indians in the American west.

Never mind, you may say to me, Europe is at least better than Asia. I will agree with you that Asia is a farce, but I do not see that we have much reason to deride the Grand Lama, we western peoples who have adopted into our modes and fashions all the complicated filth of majesty, from Queen Isabella's dirty chemise to the Dauphin's holed chair. Gentlemen of the human race, I say to hell with the lot of you. They drink the most beer in Brussels, the most eau-de-vie in Stockholm, the most chocolate in Madrid, the most gin in Amsterdam, the most wine in London, the most coffee in Constantinople and the most absinthe in Paris – and that is all we need to know. On the whole Paris comes off best. In Paris even the street scavengers are sybarites; Diogenes would have enjoyed being a scavenger in the Place Maubert as much as he enjoyed being a philosopher in the Piraeus. And here's something else you should know. The scavengers' drinking-places are called *bibines*. I salute all drinking-places, bars, bistros, cabarets, *guinguettes*, the *bibines* of the scavengers, and the caravenserais of caliphs. I am a voluptuary. I dine chez Richard at forty sous a head, but I must have a Persian carpet on which to roll Cleopatra naked. And here comes Cleopatra. Oh, it's you, Louison. How are you, my love?'

Then Grantaire, something more than drunk and pouring out words, seized hold of the scullery-wench and sought to drive her into his corner of the back room of the Café Musain. When Bossuet put out a hand to restrain him he became more voluble than ever.

'Hands off, Aigle de Meaux. You can do no good with Hippocratic gestures offering soothing potions. I refuse to be calmed. Besides, I am depressed. What can I say to you? Mankind is shoddy and misshapen. The butterfly is a success, but Man is a failure. God made a mess of that particular animal. A crowd is an assembly of ugliness and each member of it is a wretch. *Femme* rhymes with *infame* – woman with infamy. Yes, I am suffering from spleen, complicated by melancholy, nostalgia and hypochondria, and so I rant and rage and splutter and bore and irritate myself, and may God go to the devil.'

'Well, shut up in any case,' said Bossuet, who was discussing a point of law, up to the neck in a flood of legal terminology of which the following is a sample:

'For my part, although I'm scarcely a lawyer, at best only a half-taught amateur, this is what I maintain – that by Norman custom, a token sum should be paid to the lord at Michaelmas every year, subject to the rights of other title-holders whether by lease or copyhold or right of succession, whether mortgagors or mortgagees, holders of common or woodland rights –'

'Woodland rites,' sang Grantaire. 'Echo, sweet nymph of nowhere.'

On a quiet table near that of Grantaire there were arrayed a sheaf of paper, ink-well and pen, flanked by two glasses, in evidence of the fact that a stage-comedy was being roughed out. Its two compilers were talking in low voices with their heads close together.

'Better find some names first. When we've got the names they'll give us a plot.'

'That's true. You dictate and I'll write them down.'

'How about Monsieur Dorimon?'

'A rentier?'

'Undoubtedly. And with a daughter, Célestine.'

'Célestine. And then?'

'Colonel Sainval.'

'Sainval's too ordinary. Call him Valsin.'

Alongside the aspiring dramatists another couple, also taking advantage of the general hubbub to talk in low voices, were discussing a duel. An older man, aged thirty, was telling a youngster of eighteen about his prospective adversary.

'You'll have to watch out for yourself. He's a fine swordsman, no nonsense about him, no wasted passes, always on the attack, good wrists, quick reflexes and, damme, he's left-handed!'

In the corner opposite Grantaire, Joly and Bahorel were talking about their love-affairs over a game of dominoes.

'You're lucky,' said Joly. 'Your mistress is always laughing.'

'It's a mistake on her part,' said Bahorel. 'A mistress shouldn't laugh too much. It encourages you to be unfaithful. If she always looks happy your conscience doesn't trouble you, whereas if she looks miserable it does.'

'Wretch! A happy woman is a lovely thing. And you say you never quarrel.'

'That's because of the treaty we signed when we formed our little Holy Alliance. We drew a frontier and we never intrude on the other's territory. Hence the peace between us.'

'Peace,' said Joly, 'is happiness in process of digestion.'

'And what about you, Joly? How's your squabble going with Mamselle – you know who I mean.'

'She's still holding me off with cruel persistence.'

'And yet you look wan and thin enough to melt any girl's heart.'

'Alas.'

'If I were you, I'd ditch her.'

'That's easy to say.'

'And easy to do. Her name's Musichetta, isn't it?'

'Yes. But, my dear Bahorel, she's a wonderful girl, very literary, with small hands and feet, well dressed, fair complexion, dimples and eyes like a fortune-teller. I'm mad about her.'

'Then, my dear boy, you'll have to woo her. Be elegant and cut a dash. Get Staub the tailor to make you a pair of doeskin trousers, like Lucien de Rubempré in *Illusions perdues*. That would help.'

'But at what a cost!' cried Grantaire.

The third corner of the room was immersed in a discussion of poetry, pagan mythology as opposed to Christian mythology, with Jean Prouvaire taking the side of Olympus. Jean Prouvaire was diffident only in repose. When overtaken by excitement a sort of wild gaiety was mingled with his ardour and he became at once humorous and lyrical.

'We must not insult the antique gods,' he said. 'Perhaps they haven't left us after all. I can never feel that Jupiter is dead. You may say that they were all dreams; but even now, when the dreaming is over, all the great pagan myths are still with us. A mountain like Vignemale, for instance, with the outline of a fortress, still looks to me like the headdress of Cybele, and I have yet to be convinced that Pan doesn't come at night and blow through the hollow trunks of willows, covering the holes in turn with his hand . . .'

In the last corner they were talking politics, dissecting Louis XVIII's Charter, with Combeferre mildly defending it and Courfeyrac tearing it to shreds. They had a copy of the famous document in front of them, and he picked it up and brandished it, punctuating his discourse with the rustle of paper.

'In the first place, I've no use for kings. I'd like to see them abolished if only for economic reasons. A king is a parasite, and you don't get him for nothing. Have you any idea what they cost? At the death of François I the French national debt amounted to thirty thousand livres revenue; at the death of Louis XIV it was two milliard six hundred million, at twenty-six livres to the mark, which, according to Desmarest, was the equivalent of four milliard five hundred millions in 1760 and today would be the equivalent of twelve milliards. Secondly, with all respect to Combeferre, the *concession* of a charter is a dangerous way of doing things. To ease the transition, smooth the passage, damp the shock, slide the country imperceptibly from monarchy into democracy – all those are detestable proceedings. The people must never be led by the nose. Principles wilt and wither away in that constitutional fog. There must be no half-measures, no compromises, no concessions offered by the king to the people. Those offerings always include a Clause Fourteen, empowering the monarch to make special decrees "in the national interest" – giving with one hand and taking back with the other. I absolutely reject the Charter. It's nothing but a smoke-screen covering a lie. A nation which accepts it is abandoning its rights. Rights must be whole or they are nothing. The Charter – no!'

It was winter and two logs were crackling in the hearth. The temptation was more than Courfeyrac could resist. Crumpling the document, he tossed it on the fire, remarking dryly:

'So Louis XVIII's master-stroke goes up in flames!'

This was the tone of the gathering, sarcasm, jest and foolery, the thing that the French call wit and the English call humour, good taste and bad taste, good reasoning and bad, the tumult of talk volleyed from every corner of the room to echo like a cheerful cannonade above the talkers' heads.

V

Widening of the horizon

What is admirable in the clash of young minds is that no one can foresee the spark that sets off an explosion, or predict what kind of explosion it will be. A moment of light-heartedness produces a burst of laughter, and then, at the height of the merriment, a serious note is struck. A hasty word or an idle phrase may give the proceedings an entirely new turn, opening up unexplored fields. Chance is the conductor of those youthful symphonies.

A sudden thought pierced through the confusion of a talk to which Grantaire, Bahorel, Prouvaire, Bossuet, Combeferre, and Courfeyrac were all contributing. How does it happen that a single phrase may suddenly attract the notice of every person in a room?

As we have said, there is no knowing. In the midst of the hubbub Bossuet concluded whatever he had been saying to Combeferre by citing a date:

'18 June 1815 – Waterloo.'

At the mention of Waterloo, Marius, who had been leaning over his table with his chin resting on his hand and a glass of water beside him, suddenly looked up and gazed fixedly at the company.

'Strange, isn't it,' said Courfeyrac. 'I've always been struck by that number, 18. It is Bonaparte's fatal number. Put Louis in front of it, and Brumaire after it – Louis XVIII and 18 Brumaire – and you have the man's whole destiny, the end triggered by the beginning.'

Enjolras, who had hitherto been silent, now spoke.

'You should say, the crime matched by its expiation.'

The word 'crime' was more than Marius could accept, excited as he already was by the mention of Waterloo. He rose and walked slowly to the map of France hanging on the wall. In the bottom corner, in a separate compartment, was the map of Corsica.

'Corsica,' he said, pointing to it. 'A small island that made France great.'

It was as though a cold wind had blown. All conversation ceased and a feeling of expectancy filled the room. Enjolras, whose blue eyes seemed to be gazing into space, said without looking at Marius:

'France did not need Corsica to make her great. She is great because she is France.'

But Marius was not disposed to leave it at that. He turned to face Enjolras and spoke in a voice trembling with emotion.

'God forbid that I should seek to diminish France. But to associate her with Napoleon is not to diminish her. Let us be clear about that. I am a newcomer among you, and I must confess that you astonish me. Where do we all stand? Who are you, and who am I? Where do we stand about the Emperor? I've heard you call him Buonaparte, putting the accent on the "u" as the royalists do, and I may tell you that my grandfather goes even further and pronounces the final "e" as well. I think of you as young men, but where does your allegiance lie and what do you do about it? Whom do you admire if you do not admire the Emperor? What more do you want, what other great men, if that one is not good enough for you? He had everything. He was entire. He had in his brain the whole range of human faculties. He coded the laws like Justinian, was dictator like Caesar, and his conversation mingled the lightnings of Pascal with the thunderbolts of Tacitus. He made history and wrote it – his bulletins are epics. He combined the mathematics of Newton with the metaphors of Mahomet, and left behind him in the East words as great as the pyramids. At Tilsit he taught kingliness to emperors, at the Académie des Sciences he answered Laplace and in the Council of State he held his ground with Merlin. He infused soul into the calculations of some and the machinations of others. He was a lawyer among lawyers and an astronomer among astronomers. Like Cromwell, blowing out every other candle, he went to the Temple to bargain for a curtain-tassel. He saw everything and knew everything, which did not prevent him from rejoicing like the simplest of men over the cradle of his newborn son. And suddenly Europe found itself listening in terror to the march of armies, the thunder of artillery columns, the clouds of cavalry galloping like a tempest, the cries and the bugle-calls, the trembling of thrones while frontiers vanished from the map. They heard the sound of a superhuman blade being drawn from its sheath and they saw him towering on the horizon with flame in his hands and a dazzling light in his eyes, spreading amid the thunder his two great wings, the Grande Armée and the Vieille Garde, and they knew him for the Archangel of War!'

All were silent, and Enjolras bowed his head. Silence has always something of the effect of acquiescence or of the building of a wall. Scarcely pausing for breath, Marius continued with increasing vehemence.

'Let us be fair, my friends. What more splendid destiny could befall any nation than to be the Empire of such an Emperor, when the nation is France and its genius is added to the genius of such a man? To rise and prevail, to march in triumph from capital to capital, to make kings of grenadiers and decree the downfall of dynasties; to change the face of Europe at the pace of a cavalry-charge; to feel, when you are threatened, that the sword you hold is the sword of God; to follow Hannibal, Caesar, and Charlemagne in the person of one man; to be the nation whose every dawn is greeted with the tidings of a new victory; to awaken to the salvoes of gunfire from the Invalides, and live in the brilliance of imperishable names, Marengo, Arcole, Austerlitz, Iéna, Wagram! ... To make the French Empire the successor of Rome; to be the great nation that gave birth to the Grande Armée, sending its legions to the four corners of the world like a mountain sending forth its eagles; to be a nation ablaze with glory, sounding its titanic fanfare to echo down the corridors of history; to conquer the world twice over, by force of arms and by brilliance – all this is sublime! What can possibly be greater?'

'To be free,' said Combeferre.

And now it was Marius who bowed his head. The cool, incisive words had pierced like a swordthrust to the heart of his eloquence, and he felt his ardour evaporate. When at length he looked up, Combeferre was no longer there. Satisfied, no doubt, with that devastating reply, he had left the room, and the others had followed him, all save Enjolras, who, left alone with Marius, was now gravely regarding him. Marius, having by now somewhat recovered, did not yet consider himself beaten. Something of his fire remained, and would doubtless have been poured out in a further exordium to Enjolras had they not heard a voice in the passage outside. It was Combeferre, and this is the song he sang:

> If Caesar had offered me
> Glory and war
> For which I must abandon
> My mother's love
> I would say to great Caesar:
> 'Take back your sceptre and your chariot.
> I love my mother more, alas,
> I love my mother more.'

The wistful tenderness with which Combeferre sang it invested the little song with a strange grandeur. Marius was staring thoughtfully at the ceiling. He repeated, half-unconsciously, 'My mother? . . .'

And Enjolras laid a hand on his shoulder.

'Citizen,' he said, 'my mother is the Republic.'

VI

Domestic matters

That evening left Marius profoundly shaken and with a sense of obscure sadness, such a feeling as perhaps the earth knows when the ploughshare furrows it for the sowing of seed. It feels only the wound. The stirring of the seed and the joy of harvest come later.

Marius was filled with gloom. Having so lately found a faith, must he now renounce it? He told himself that he need not; he resolved not to doubt, and began despite himself to do so. To be torn between two creeds, one which one has not yet wholly abandoned and one which one has not yet embraced, this is intolerable; it is a half-light in which only a bat can be at ease. Marius, with his candid gaze, needed a true light; the twilight of doubt tormented him. However great his desire to stand firm and leave things as they were, he was inexorably compelled to go further; to reflect, to speculate, to prove. Where was his thinking to lead him? He greatly feared lest, having drawn so close to his father, he might now be drawn away from him, and the more he brooded the more did his perturbation grow. A barrier seemed to enclose him. He was in step neither with his grandfather nor with his friends, outrageous to the former and behind the times for the latter, and he had a sense of double isolation, both from the old and from the young. He gave up going to the Café Musain.

In his troubled state of mind, he gave little heed to certain prosaic aspects of life; but they were matters that could not be ignored. They brought themselves abruptly to his notice. The hotelkeeper came to his room and said:

'Monsieur Courfeyrac has vouched for you, has he not?'

'Yes.'

'But I need money.'

'Will you please ask Monsieur Courfeyrac if he can spare me a moment?'

Courfeyrac came to see him, and Marius told him what he had not thought of telling him until then, that for practical purposes he was alone in the world, having no parents.

'So what's to become of you?' asked Courfeyrac.

'I don't know,' said Marius.

'What are you going to do?'

'I don't know.'

'How much money have you?'

'Fifteen francs.'

'Do you want me to lend you some?'

'No – never.'

'Have you any clothes?'

'Only these.'

'Any jewellery?'

'A watch.'

'Silver?'

'Gold. Here it is.'

'I know a second-hand dealer who will take your tail-coat and spare pair of trousers.'

'Good.'

'That'll leave you with one pair of trousers, a waistcoat, a hat, and a jacket.'

'And my boots.'

'You mean you won't go barefoot? What luxury!'

'That ought to be enough.'

'And I know a clockmaker who will buy your watch.'

'That's good.'

'No, it isn't good. What will you do when the money's gone?'

'Whatever I have to do – anything honest.'

'Do you know English?'

'No.'

'German?'

'No.'

'That's a pity.'

'Why?'

'A friend of mine, a bookseller, is compiling a sort of encyclopedia. You might have translated articles for it, from English or German. It's badly paid work, but one can live on it.'

'Then I'll learn English and German.'

'And in the meantime?'

'I'll live on my clothes and my watch.'

The clothes fetched twenty francs and the watch forty-five francs.

'That's not bad,' said Marius when they got back to the hotel. 'With the fifteen francs I already have that makes eighty altogether.'

'And what about the hotel bill?' said Courfeyrac.

'Oh, lord, I'd clean forgotten!'

The bill came to seventy francs.

'The devil!' said Courfeyrac. 'So you're to live on five francs while you're learning English and five more while you're learning German. You'll either have to digest a language very quickly or make a hundred sous go a very long way.'

Meanwhile Aunt Gillenormand, who was at least a good soul in emergencies, had succeeded in discovering Marius's address. One morning he received a letter from her and a sealed package containing the 'sixty pistoles' his grandfather had authorized – that is to say, six hundred francs in gold. He returned the money with a graceful letter saying that he had found a means of livelihood which would supply him with all his needs. At the moment he had three francs in the world.

His aunt did not tell his grandfather of this, fearing to add to the old gentleman's fury. Besides which, he had told her never to mention that 'blood-drinker' again.

Marius left the Hôtel de la Porte Saint-Jacques, not wanting to run further into debt.

BOOK FIVE

THE VIRTUES OF MISFORTUNE

I
Marius penniless

LIFE BECAME very hard for Marius. To have eaten his clothes and
his watch was nothing; he had now to chew the cud of utmost necessity. It was a horrible time of days without food, nights without
sleep, evenings without light, a hearth without a fire, weeks without
work, and a future without hope; threadbare clothes, doors slammed
behind him because he had not paid the rent, the insolence of underlings, the scorn of neighbours, humiliation, loss of self-respect,
menial tasks performed, disgust, bitterness, and despair. Marius
learned to swallow all these things and to know what it was to have
nothing else to swallow. In that condition of life when a man has
most need of self-esteem because he lacks love, he felt himself
mocked because he was ill-clad, and ridiculous because he was
penniless. At the age when the heart of youth should be filled with a
lordly confidence his eyes were cast down to his worn boots and he
suffered all the slights and unjust abasement of extreme poverty: a
stern and terrible trial which brings the weak to infamy and the
strong to nobility; the crucible into which Destiny casts a man, to
make of him a ne'er-do-well or a demi-god.

For many great deeds are accomplished in times of squalid
struggle. There is a kind of stubborn, unrecognized courage which
in the lowest depths tenaciously resists the pressures of necessity
and ill-doing; there are noble and obscure triumphs observed by no
one, unacclaimed by any fanfare. Hardship, loneliness, and penury
are a battlefield which has its own heroes, sometimes greater than
those lauded in history. Strong and rare characters are thus created;
poverty, nearly always a foster-mother, may become a true mother;
distress may be the nursemaid of pride, and misfortune the milk that
nourishes great spirits.

There was a time in Marius's life when he swept his own landing,
bought a penn'orth of cheese from the grocer and waited until dusk
before going to the bakery to buy a small loaf which he took furtively away as though he had stolen it. He would sidle into the
neighbouring butcher's shop, elbowed by the chattering house-

wives – an awkward young man with books under his arm, at once timid and resentful, raising his hat obsequiously to the astonished butcher – and buy a mutton-chop wrapped in paper for six or seven sous. He would cook it himself and live on it sometimes for three days, first the lean, then the fat, and on the third day he would gnaw the bone.

Aunt Gillenormand tried more than once to come to his aid, sending him the sixty pistoles; but he always returned the money, saying that he did not need it.

He had been in mourning for his father when the upheaval in his life had occurred, and since then he had continued to wear black. But his clothes were gradually falling to pieces, and a day came when his jacket was no longer wearable, although he could still wear his trousers. In this emergency Courfeyrac, whom he had served in certain small ways, gave him an old jacket of his own. He had it turned at a cost of thirty sous so that it was as good as new. But it was made of green cloth. Accordingly he went out only after dark, when it looked black. Wishing still to go in mourning, he clad himself in darkness.

With all this he continued his law-studies and qualified as an advocate. Officially he shared Courfeyrac's chambers, which were presentable and contained a sufficient number of law-books, filled out with tattered novels, to constitute the library required by regulations. He had his letters sent to Courfeyrac's address.

When he had qualified he notified his grandfather of the fact in a formally worded letter that was, however, filled with dutiful respect. Monsieur Gillenormand's hands trembled as he read it, but having done so he tore it up and threw it in the wastepaper basket. A few days later his daughter overheard him talking aloud to himself in his room, a thing that always happened when he was in a highly agitated state. He was saying, 'If you weren't an imbecile you would realize that one can't be at the same time a baron and an advocate.'

II

Marius poor

Poverty is like everything else. In the end it becomes bearable. It acquires a pattern and comes to terms with itself. One vegetates – that is to say, continues to exist in a wretched sort of way that is just sufficient to sustain life. This is what happened to Marius Pont-mercy.

He had got over the worst and the road ahead of him looked somewhat smoother. By dint of hard work, courage, perseverance and resolution, he contrived to earn about seven hundred francs a year. He learned German and English, and thanks to Courfeyrac, who introduced him to his bookseller friend, he was able to fill the humble role of a literary 'devil'. He wrote prospectuses, translated newspaper articles, annotated new editions, helped to compile biographies and so on. The net result was an average income of seven hundred francs, on which he contrived to live, not too badly, in the manner which we will now describe.

He rented what passed for a room in the Gorbeau tenement at a price of thirty francs a year. Such furniture as it contained was his own. He paid the elderly 'chief tenant' three francs a month to sweep the floor and bring him a little hot water in the mornings, and an egg and a roll costing one sou. These constituted his breakfast, which fluctuated a few sous in price according to the price of eggs. At six in the evening he went down the Rue Saint-Jacques to dine *chez* Rousseau, opposite the print-dealer's on the corner of the Rue des Mathurins. He had no first course. His meal consisted of a portion of meat, at six sous, a half-portion of vegetables at three sous, and a dessert at three sous, with unlimited bread, costing another three sous. He drank no wine, but only water. When he paid at the desk, majestically occupied by Madame Rousseau, who in those days was already plump but still youthful, he gave the waiter a sou and Madame Rousseau gave him a smile. Then he left, having purchased for sixteen sous a dinner and a smile.

The Restaurant Rousseau, where so little wine was drunk and so much water, was a place of rest rather than stimulation. It no longer exists. Its proprietor was known as 'Rousseau *l'aquatique*', a play on the word *ruisseau*, meaning a stream.

So, breakfast for four sous and dinner for sixteen sous. His food cost him a franc a day, or 365 francs a year. Adding the thirty francs rent, the thirty-six for the old woman and something for minor expenses, Marius was fed, housed, and served for 450 francs a year. His outer clothing cost him a hundred francs a year, his linen and his laundry fifty francs each. The whole did not exceed 650 francs. He had fifty francs left, which made him rich, able occasionally to lend a friend ten francs. Courfeyrac had once borrowed sixty from him. The problem of heating was simplified by the fact that his room had no fireplace.

He always had two suits, an old one for everyday and a new one for special occasions. Both were black. He had only three shirts, one on his back, one in reserve, and one at the laundry. He replaced these when they wore out. They were generally frayed, for which reason he kept his jacket buttoned to the chin.

It took Marius some years to achieve this satisfactory state. They had been rough years, difficult to live through and surmount. He had never given up. He had suffered everything conceivable in the way of hardship and done everything except run into debt. He could pride himself on the fact that he had never owed anyone a sou. To him a debt was the beginning of slavery. He went so far as to say that a creditor is worse than a master; for a master owns only your physical presence, whereas a creditor owns your dignity and may affront it. Rather than borrow money he went without food. He had known many days of fasting. Realizing that all extremes meet, and that, if one is not on one's guard, material abasement may end in spiritual abasement, he set particular store by his pride. Words and gestures which in other circumstances he might have considered acts of ordinary politeness seemed to him to contain a hint of obsequiousness, and he recoiled from them. He offered nothing, fearing to be rebuffed. There was a kind of aloofness in his manner. He was withdrawn to the point of surliness.

In all his trials he was sustained and at times even exalted by a secret strength in himself. The soul aids the body and at moments uplifts it. It is the only bird that can endure a cage.

With the name of his father another name was imprinted in Marius's heart – the name of Thénardier. His naturally ardent and earnest temperament had caused him to invest with a sort of halo the man who, as he believed, had saved his father at Waterloo, the intrepid sergeant who had rescued him amid a hail of bullets. He never thought of his father without also thinking of that man, associating the two in an aura of almost religious veneration, a high altar for the one and a low altar for the other. His concern for Thénardier was heightened by the fact that he knew him to have been overtaken by misfortune. Since learning in Montfermeil of his bankruptcy and disappearance, he had done everything in his power to find him. He had scoured the region, visiting Chelles, Bouchy, Gourney, Nogent and Lagny, and the search, which had now gone on for three years, had cost him all the little money he could spare. No one had been able to give him news of Thénardier, and it was rumoured that he had left the country. His creditors had also been looking for him, no less assiduously than Marius, if for somewhat different reasons, but had not been able to run him to earth. This was the only debt Marius's father had bequeathed to him, and he held it to be a point of honour that he should pay it. 'My father lay dying on the field of battle,' he thought, 'and Thénardier rescued him amid the smoke and gunfire and carried him to safety on his back. And he owed my father nothing. How can I, who owe Thénardier so much, fail to seek him out in the trouble which has overtaken him and restore him to life. I must surely find him!' . . . Indeed, Marius would have given his right hand to find Thénardier, and would have shed his last drop of blood to rescue him from destitution. To find him and do him some signal service; to be able to say to him, 'You don't know me but I know you. Here I am – ask what you will of me' – this was Marius's most cherished and glorious dream.

III

Marius grown up

Marius was now twenty. It was three years since he had parted from his grandfather, and the situation between them remained unchanged.

They had not met or sought to be reconciled. A meeting would, it seemed, have served only to renew a quarrel in which neither would give way. If Marius was the irresistible force, old Gillenormand was the immovable object.

It must be said that Marius had misunderstood his grandfather. He had come to believe that Monsieur Gillenormand had never had any real fondness for him, that the forthright, sardonic old man who cursed and shouted and flourished his stick had never felt for him anything more than the harsh, casual affection of a stage stepfather. In this he was wrong. There are fathers who do not love their sons, but there has never been a grandfather who did not adore his grandson. The truth, as we have said, is that Monsieur Gillenormand idolized Marius; but he did so in his own fashion, to an accompaniment of chiding and even blows. The boy's departure had left a black emptiness in his heart. He had ordered that his name should never be spoken, and yet was sorry that the order was so faithfully obeyed. At first he had hoped that the youthful rebel, the Bonapartist and Jacobin, would come back. But the weeks passed, the months and years, and to the old man's grief he did not do so. 'What else could I have done but turn him out?' he asked himself; and then he wondered whether he would do the same thing if it were to be done again. His pride promptly answered yes, but his old head, shaking in the silence, mournfully answered no. He had periods of utter dejection, so greatly did he miss Marius. Old people need love as they need sunshine; it is warmth. For all his strength of character, something in him had been changed by Marius's absence. Not for anything in the world would he have reached out a hand towards 'that young monster'; but he suffered. He never asked after him but constantly thought of him. He continued to live in the Marais, more secluded than ever, still cheerful and forthright as he had always been, but now there was a note of harshness in his gaiety, as though it expressed both pain and anger, and his outbursts of fury were always succeeded by a fit of gloomy depression. He sometimes said to himself, 'If he were to come back, how I'd box his ears!'

As for his daughter, she was too shallow-minded to be capable of any deep affection. Marius became a remote and shadowy figure to her, and in the end she thought far less about him than about the cat or parrot which she doubtless possessed.

Old Gillenormand's unhappiness was rendered more acute by the fact that he contained it wholly within himself, never allowing it any outward expression; it was like one of those recently invented furnaces which consume their own smoke. It happened sometimes that an inquisitive acquaintance would ask after Marius – 'What is your grandson doing these days?' To which the old gentleman would reply, sighing if he was in melancholy mood, or shooting his cuffs if he wished to appear gay, 'The Baron Pontmercy is pursuing his career somewhere or other.'

And while the old man grieved, Marius congratulated himself. As with all brave hearts, misfortune had robbed him of bitterness. He thought of Monsieur Gillenormand only with kindness, but he had made up his mind that he could accept nothing from the man who had treated his father so badly. The rigours of his present life gratified and pleased him. He told himself with a kind of satisfaction that it was the least he deserved, an expiation; that otherwise he must have been punished in some other way, at some later date, for his unfilial indifference to his father; that it would have been unjust for his father to suffer everything and himself nothing. What were his own hardships and misfortunes, compared with the colonel's heroic life? It seemed to him that the only way he could emulate his father was by facing the trials of poverty as bravely as his father had faced the enemy, and he had no doubt that this was what the colonel had meant by the words, 'he will be worthy of it' – words which Marius could not wear on his breast, since the letter had been destroyed, but which he would wear forever in his heart.

And then, although he had been no more than a youth when his grandfather had turned him out, he was now a man. He felt like a man. Poverty, we must repeat, had been good for him. Poverty in youth, when it is mastered, has the sovereign quality that it concentrates the will-power upon striving and the spirit upon hope. By stripping our material existence to its essentials and exposing its drabness, it fosters in us an inexpressible longing for the ideal life. The well-to-do young man is offered a hundred dazzling and crude distractions – horses, hunting and gambling, rich food, tobacco, and all the rest – occupations for his baser nature at the expense of everything in him that is high-minded and sensitive. The poor young man struggles to stay alive; he contrives to eat, and his only solace is in dreaming. His only theatre is the free show that God provides, the sky and the stars, flowers and children, mankind whose sufferings he shares and the created world in which he is trying his wings. He lives so close to humanity that he sees its soul, so close to the divine creation that he sees God. He dreams and feels his own greatness; dreams again and feels tenderness. He progresses from the egotism of the man who suffers to the compassion of the man who meditates, and an admirable sentiment is born in him, of self-forgetfulness and feeling for others. Reflecting on the countless delights that nature showers on minds open to receive them, and denied to those whose minds are closed, he ends, a millionaire of the spirit, by pitying the millionaire of nothing but money. All hatred disappears from his heart as enlightenment grows in him. Indeed, is he really unhappy? No, he is not. A young man's poverty is never miserable. Any youngster, poor as he may be, with health and strength, a buoyant stride and clear eyes, hot-flowing blood, dark hair, fresh cheeks, white teeth and clean breath, is an object of envy to any aged emperor. And then, he gets up every morning to earn his livelihood, and while his hands are busily employed his backbone gains in pride and his mind gains in ideas. His day's work done, he returns to the delights of his contemplative life. He may live with feet enmeshed in affliction and frustration, hard-set on earth amid the brambles and sometimes deep in mud; but his head is in the stars. He is steadfast and serene, gentle, peaceable, alert, sober-minded, content with little, and benevolent; and he blesses God for having bestowed on him those two riches which the rich so often lack – work, which makes a man free, and thought, which makes him worthy of freedom.

This was the road which Marius had travelled, and, if the truth be told, he was now inclined a little too much to the side of contemplation. From the moment when he felt reasonably sure of earning a livelihood he had slowed down, finding it good to be poor and working the less to allow himself more time for musing. He sometimes spent whole days in reverie, plunged in dreams like a visionary in the debauch of an inward exaltation. He had settled the problem of his life in this fashion: to do as little material work as possible in order to work the more at immaterial things: in a word, to devote a few hours to practical affairs and squander the rest on the infinite. He failed to perceive, believing that he lacked nothing, that contemplation carried to this point becomes a form of sloth, and that, in contenting himself with having secured the bare essentials of life, he was relaxing too soon. It was clear that for a young man of his ardent and energetic nature this could be only a temporary state, and that upon his first encounter with the inevitable complexities of life Marius would wake up.

In the meantime, although he was now an advocate, contrary to what his grandfather supposed, he did not plead in the courts and engaged in no legal transactions. Day-dreaming had given him a distaste for the law. The thought of consorting with attorneys, hanging about the courts, chasing after briefs, was odious to him. Why take the trouble? He saw no reason to change his present way of life. His work as a bookseller and publisher's hack was not too demanding, and it sufficed for his needs.

One of the booksellers for whom he worked – it was, I believe, Monsieur Magimel – had offered him a permanent situation with lodging thrown in, regular work and a salary of fifteen hundred francs a year. The offer was attractive, but it would mean forfeiting his liberty. He would become a wage-slave, an employed man-of-letters. To Marius's way of thinking he would be both better and worse off, a gainer in petty comfort and a loser in dignity, exchanging a state of high-minded, unsullied poverty for one of dubious security, rather like a blind man becoming one-eyed. He refused.

His life was a lonely one, partly from his desire to remain uninvolved and also because, having been horrified by the circle presided over by Enjolras, he was not at all disposed to join it. They remained on friendly terms, ready to help one another when the need arose, but that was all. Marius had two real friends, a young man, Courfeyrac, and an old man, Monsieur Mabeuf, the churchwarden. Of the two he leaned rather towards the latter, to whom he owed the transformation in his life, the opening of his eyes which had caused him to know and love his father.

Yet in this matter Monsieur Mabeuf had been no more than the passive, unwitting instrument of providence. It was purely by chance that he had shed a light for Marius, doing so as unconsciously as the candle, not the bringer.

As for the upheaval which had taken place in Marius, this was something which Monsieur Mabeuf was quite incapable of understanding, still less of desiring or contriving. Since we are to meet him again later in the story it may be as well, at this point, to say a few words about him.

IV

Monsieur Mabeuf

When Monsieur Mabeuf said to Marius, 'Of course I approve of people holding political opinions,' he had been expressing his own attitude of mind. All political opinions came alike to him and he approved of them all without seeking to distinguish between them, like the Greeks, who referred to the Eumenides as 'beautiful, good, delightful' . . . asking only that they would leave them alone. His politics were confined to his passionate love of plants and, even more, of books. Like everyone else he had a label, since at that time nobody could live without one, but his 'ism' was of a non-committed kind: he was not a royalist, a Bonapartist, a chartist, an Orleanist, or an anarchist – simply a book-ist.

He could not understand why men should expend themselves in fury over such trivialities as the Charter, democracy, monarchy, republicanism and so forth when there were mosses, grasses, and shrubs for them to look at and folios and octavos for them to browse in. He was far from being idle; his passion for collecting books no more prevented him from reading them than did the study of botany prevent him from being a gardener. His friendship with Colonel Pontmercy had been based on the fact that what the colonel did for flowers, he did for fruit. He had produced a strain of pears as well-flavoured as the pears of Saint-Germain; and it is to him, it seems, that we owe the October *mirabelle* plum, which has become famous and is as well-liked as the summer *mirabelle*. He attended Mass more in a spirit of acquiescence than of devoutness, and also because, liking the faces of men but disliking the noise they made, Church was the only place where he could find them together and silent. Feeling that it was his duty to perform some civic function, he had become a churchwarden. For the rest, he had never succeeded in being as fond of any woman as he could be of a tulip-bulb, or of any man as of a manuscript. When he was well past sixty someone had asked him, 'Were you never married?' and he had answered, 'I forget.' And when it happened to him to exclaim (as who does not?), 'If only I were rich!' the thought was prompted, not, as in the case of Monsieur Gillenormand, by the sight of a pretty girl, but by the sight of a volume which he could not afford to buy.

He lived alone with an old housekeeper. He was somewhat gouty, and his rheumaticky fingers stiffened under the blankets when he was asleep. He had published a book with colour plates on *The Flora of the Cauteretz Region* which was well thought of and of which he owned the plates, selling the volume himself. Two or three purchasers a day called at his dwelling in the Rue Mézières, and this brought him in about two thousand francs a year, nearly his whole income. Poor though he was, he had contrived over the years, by patience and self-denial, to form a collection of rare books of all kinds. He never left home without a book under his arm, and often came back with two. The only adornment of the four-room ground-floor apartment, with a small garden, where he lived, was some framed dried grasses and a few engravings of Old Masters. The sight of a sabre or musket chilled his heart. He had never in his life gone near a cannon, not even at the Invalides. He had a reasonably good digestion, a brother who was a curé, white hair, no teeth in his head and no bite in his spirit, a slight tremor that pervaded his whole body, a Picardy accent, a childlike laugh, a readiness to take fright, and the general look of an old sheep. For the rest, he had no friendships or place of call among the living other than the establishment of an old bookseller near the Porte Saint-Jacques whose name was Royol. It was his ambition to produce a strain of indigo that would grow in France.

His housekeeper was another embodiment of innocence, an excellent, elderly virgin. Her tom-cat, Sultan, who might have mewed Allegri's 'Miserere' in the Sistine Chapel, satisfied all her emotional needs. She had never desired any man or been able to live without a cat. Like him, she had a moustache. Her pride was in her bonnets, which were always white. She passed her leisure hours after Sunday Mass counting the linen in her trunk and spreading out on her bed the dress materials which she bought but never had made into dresses. She knew how to read. Monsieur Mabeuf had nicknamed her Mère Plutarque.

Monsieur Mabeuf had taken a fancy to Marius because Marius, being young and gentle, warmed his old age without ruffling his diffidence. To the old a gentle youth is like sunshine without wind. At the time when Marius was immersed in military history, cannon-fire and counter-marches, all the prodigious battles in which his father had dealt and received tremendous sabre-cuts, he would go to call on Monsieur Mabeuf, who would talk to him about heroes as though they were flowers.

But when, in 1830, his brother the curé had died, Monsieur Mabeuf's whole life had been plunged in darkness. The bankruptcy of an attorney had led to a loss of ten thousand francs, the greater part of the capital that he and his brother had shared. The July Revolution caused a crisis in the book trade. The last thing to sell in any time of upheaval is a book on plants, and the sales of *The Flora of the Cauteretz Region* abruptly ceased. Weeks went by without a purchaser. Monsieur Mabeuf would start up hopefully at the sound of the bell only to be told sadly by Mère Plutarque, 'It's only the watercarrier, Monsieur' ... In short, a day came when Monsieur Mabeuf was obliged to leave the Rue Mézières, give up his post of churchwarden at Saint-Sulpice, and sell a part, not of his books but of his prints, those he valued the least. He moved to a small house on the Boulevard Montparnasse, which, however, he left at the end of the first quarter, for two reasons – first, because the rent of the ground-floor apartment and garden was three hundred francs, and two hundred was all he could afford; and secondly because, being adjacent to the Fatou shooting-gallery, he was troubled all day by the sound of pistol-shots, and this he found unendurable.

Taking with him his *Flora*, his plates, his dried grasses, books and portfolios, he removed to a small cottage near the Salpêtrière, in what was then the village of Austerlitz. Here, for fifty crowns, he acquired three rooms and a garden with a well, enclosed by a hedge. At the same time he sold the bulk of his furniture. On the day when he took up residence he was particularly cheerful and himself drove in the nails on which to hang his engravings and grasses. He spent the rest of the day digging the garden, and in the evening, seeing the look of gloom on Mère Plutarque's face, he patted her on the shoulder and said, smiling, 'Cheer up! We still have the indigo.'

Only two visitors, the bookseller from the Porte Saint-Jacques and Marius, ever called at his Austerlitz cottage – a name, be it said, of which the warlike flavour by no means pleased him.

In general, as we have already suggested, minds absorbed in wisdom or in folly, or in both at once as often happens, are little affected by the vicissitudes of daily life. Their personal destiny is a thing remote from them. Such detachment creates a state of acquiescence which, if it were the outcome of reflection, might be termed philosophical. But they submit to losses and reverses, even to physical decay, without being much aware of them. It is true that in the end there is an awakening, but it is late in coming. In the meantime they stand as it were aloof from the play of personal fortune and misfortune, pawns in a game of which they are detached spectators.

Thus it was that with the shadows deepening about him, with his hopes fading one after another, Monsieur Mabeuf had remained serene, rather childishly but profoundly so. His spiritual states resembled the swing of a pendulum. Once set in motion by an illusion, the swing continued for a long time, even after the illusion had vanished. A clock does not stop the moment one loses the key.

Monsieur Mabeuf had innocent pleasures, inexpensive and unexpected, bestowed on him by trifles. One day Mère Plutarque was reading a novel in a corner of the room. She read aloud, finding it easier in this way to understand what she was reading. To read aloud is to assure oneself that one is reading, and there are persons who read very loudly indeed, as though positively proclaiming the fact. She was reading in this fashion and Monsieur Mabeuf was half-listening but not really attending. The tale had to do with a dragoon officer and a village beauty, and she read:

'The beauty pouted and the dragoon ...' The French words were '*bouda*' and '*dragon*'.

Here she paused to wipe her glasses, and Monsieur Mabeuf, looking up, repeated:

'Buddha and the dragon ... Well, there is said to have been a dragon which lived in a cave and poured such torrents of flame from its nostrils that it scorched the sky. It had even set several stars on fire, and moreover it had tiger's claws. Buddha boldly entered its cave and converted it. That is a good book that you are reading, Mère Plutarque. There is no more charming legend.'

And he fell into a delicious abstraction.

V

Poverty and pennilessness

Marius had an affection for the simple-minded old man who was drifting by degrees into utter poverty, with a growing sense of perplexity but still with no feeling of dismay. He saw Courfeyrac from time to time, and he called on Monsieur Mabeuf; but only on rare occasions, once or twice a month.

Marius enjoyed going for long walks – along the outer boulevards or the Champ de Mars, or in the less frequented streets round the Luxembourg. He would spend long periods contemplating the market gardens – vegetable plots, poultry scratching amid the dung, a horse turning the wheel of a hoist. Strangers looked at him with surprise, and sometimes even with suspicion. But it was only an impecunious young man dreaming the hours away.

It was during one of these walks that he had discovered the Gorbeau tenement and, attracted by its cheapness and isolation, had rented a room there. He was known there only as Monsieur Marius.

A few retired officers, former comrades of his father, one or two generals among them, having learned of his existence occasionally invited him to their homes. He did not refuse these invitations, which gave him a chance to talk about his father. So from time to time he visited Comte Pajol, General Bellavesne, and General Fririon, at the Invalides. There was music and dancing. On these occasions he wore his better suit. But he went only on nights when the streets were dry, because he could not afford a cab and refused to show himself except with boots shining like mirrors. He sometimes remarked, but without bitterness: 'That is how things are. You may go to a polite salon with muddy garments but not with muddy boots. That is the sole requirement, the one thing that must be irreproachable – not your conscience.'

All passions except those of the heart are dissolved by reverie. Marius's political ardours had vanished, helped by the 1830 revolution, which had calmed and appeased him. He was the same young man, but without the fire, holding the same opinions but less vehemently. To be exact, he no longer had opinions, but only sympathies. The only party he belonged to was that of humanity. Among nations he preferred the French, within the nation he preferred the masses, and of the masses he preferred the women. It was they, above all, whom he pitied. He had come to prefer books to events and poets to heroes; and most particularly he preferred a book like Job to an event like Marengo. When after a day spent in meditation he returned home by the evening light of the boulevards, and saw through the branches of the trees the measureless space of the infinite, the nameless lights, the darkness and mystery, it seemed to him that all things that were not simply human were of very little account. He believed, and perhaps he was right, that he had penetrated to the heart of life and human philosophy, and he came to pay little attention to anything except the sky, which is the only thing that Truth can see from the bottom of her well.

But this did not prevent him from devising countless plans and projects for the future. A person able to look into Marius's heart, during that period of dreaming, would have marvelled at its purity. Indeed, if our earthly eyes possessed this power of seeing into the hearts of others, we would judge men far more surely by their dreams than by their thoughts. Thought must always contain an element of desire, but there is none in dreaming. The dream, which is wholly spontaneous, adopts and preserves, even in our utmost flights of fancy, the pattern of our spirit; nothing comes more truly from the very depths of the soul than those unconsidered and uncontrolled aspirations to the splendours of destiny. It is in these, much more than in our reasoned thoughts, that a man's true nature is to be found. Our imaginings are what most resemble us. Each of us dreams of the unknown and the impossible in his own way.

About halfway through that year of 1831 the old woman who ran errands for Marius told him that his neighbours in the tenement, a wretchedly poor family named Jondrette, were to be evicted. Marius, who spent so much of his time elsewhere, had scarcely realized that he had any neighbours.

'Why are they being turned out?' he asked.

'Because they're behind with their rent. They owe two quarters.'

'How much does it come to?'

'Twenty francs.'

Marius kept a reserve of thirty francs in a drawer.

'Here are twenty-five francs,' he said to the old woman. 'Pay the back rent and give the poor souls five francs for themselves. But don't tell them that the money comes from me.'

VI

The substitute

It so happened that Lieutenant Théodule's regiment was transferred to garrison duties in Paris, and the circumstance inspired Aunt Gillenormand with another idea. Her first idea had been to ask Théodule to spy on Marius; her second was to make him Marius's successor.

In any event, and more especially if Monsieur Gillenormand should feel the need of a young face about the house, these rays of morning light being grateful to old ruins, it was expedient that Marius should be replaced. 'It amounts to no more than changing a name in a book,' she reflected. For Marius read Théodule. A great-nephew was near enough to a grandson, and a lancer was surely as acceptable as a lawyer.

One morning when Monsieur Gillenormand was engaged in reading some such journal as *La Quotidienne*, his daughter entered the room and said in the mellowest of voices, for she was talking about her favourite:

'Father, Théodule is calling this morning to pay his respects.'

'And who is Théodule?'

'Your great-nephew.'

'Aha.'

The old gentleman returned to his reading, dismissing this unimportant great-nephew from his mind, and, as so often happened when he read the newspaper, was soon simmering with fury. The paper, which, it goes without saying, was of the royalist persuasion, announced without comment that on the following day one of those events was to take place which were then of daily occurrence in the life of Paris. The students from the faculties of Law and Medicine were to hold a meeting at twelve o'clock in the Place du Panthéon – 'for the purpose of discussion'. The subject of the meeting was one of the questions of the hour: that of the artillery of the Garde Nationale, and the dispute that had arisen between the Ministry of War and the Civil Militia over the guns parked in the courtyard of the Louvre. The students were having the temerity to debate this matter in public. It was nearly enough to bring Monsieur Gillenormand to boiling-point.

And Marius, being a student, would no doubt be taking part in the proceedings on the Place du Panthéon!

It was as the old gentleman was digesting this painful thought that Théodule, who had had the prudence to wear civilian clothes, was tactfully ushered in by Mlle Gillenormand. The lancer had reasoned as follows: 'The old druid hasn't put all his money into an annuity. It's worth dressing up from time to time, just to humour him.'

'Father,' said Mlle Gillenormand, 'here is your great-nephew Théodule.' And she murmured to the young man, 'Mind you agree with everything he says.'

She then withdrew. The lieutenant, unaccustomed to meeting persons of such antiquity, mumbled a greeting and performed an awkward gesture which started automatically as an army salute and finished up as a civilian bow.

'So it's you, is it? Well, sit down,' said the old man.

Having said this he forgot all about the visitor and resumed his train of thought. As Théodule seated himself he rose from his chair and began to pace the room, talking in a loud voice and fiddling with the watches in his two waistcoat pockets.

'That riff-raff holding a meeting in the Place du Panthéon! A bunch of young scallywags, God save us, only just out of the nursery! If you gave their noses a tweak milk would come out. And they're to debate in public! In God's name, what's the country coming to? Everything's going to the dogs! Civil militia! Civilians armed with cannon! And they'll be airing their views on the Garde Nationale! That's what Jacobinism leads to. And who else will be there, I ask you? I'll bet you a million to one there'll be no one else there except fugitives from justice and discharged convicts – republicans and gaolbirds, they're one and the same thing. Carnot asked, "Where do you want me to go, traitor?" and Fouché answered,

"Wherever you like, imbecile!" That's the republicans for you!'

'Quite right,' said Théodule.

Monsieur Gillenormand gave him a glance and continued:

'To think that that wretched youth should have had the impudence to join the rebels! Why did he leave my house? To become a republican. But in the first place the people don't want his republic, they don't want it, they've got enough sense to know that there have always been kings, and always will be, and that the people are simply the people. They laugh at his republic, the young idiot. Can there be any more horrible notion? To fall in love with Père Duchêne, think fondly of the guillotine, serenade the men of '93 – the young of today are so stupid one wants to spit on them! And they're all alike, no exceptions. You have only to breathe the air in the streets to be driven half insane. This nineteenth century is poisonous, full of young apes who think they amount to something because they've grown a goat's beard and left their parents in the lurch. If it's republican it's romantic. And what is this romanticism all about? I will tell you. It is about every imaginable lunacy. Last year they were all going to that play *Hernani.** Hernani* – I ask you! A mass of contradictions and abominations, and not even written in decent French. And cannons in the Louvre! That's the sort of thing that goes on nowadays.'

'You're perfectly right, uncle,' said Théodule.

'Cannons in the courtyard of a museum! Will you tell me what they're for? Do you want to bombard the Belvedere Apollo or blow up the Venus de Medici? The young men of today are all rascals, as useless as their Benjamin Constant. And when they're not scoundrels they're hobbledehoys. They do their best to make themselves unattractive, they dress badly, they're scared of women, they shy away from petticoats in a way that makes the girls laugh. Upon my word, I believe the poor little fools are afraid of love! They're uncouth, and on top of that they're stupid. They repeat music-hall jokes. They wear sack-coats, stableboys' waistcoats, coarse linen shirts, homespun trousers and boots of rough leather, and their talk is as coarse as their clothes. You could use their jargon to sole their slippers. And then they presume to have political opinions! They want to invent new systems, re-shape society, abolish the monarchy, do away with the law, rebuild the universe, turn everything upside-

*By Victor Hugo. Trs.

down and inside-out, and their idea of excitement is a sneaking glance at a washerwoman's legs as she's climbing on to her cart! Oh, Marius, Marius, poor young idiot! To be holding forth in public places, discussing, debating, *taking measures*! They call that "measures", God save us! Disorder reverting to childishness. Schoolboys debating on the Garde Nationale – you wouldn't get that among the Ojibways or the Cherokees. Those naked savages with heads like shuttlecocks, brandishing their tomahawks, are a lot less brutish than our young bachelors of arts. Rapscallions without two sous to rub together posing as men of learning and competence, propounding and arguing! It's the end of this wretched terrestrial globe. One final belch was needed and France has produced it. All right, my lads, go on debating! This state of affairs will continue as long as they can stand reading the papers under the arcade at the Odéon. It costs them one sou, and it robs them of whatever good sense and intelligence they possess, and of their heart and soul and spirit. They soak up that stuff, and good-bye to home and family. All the newspapers are a plague, even the *Drapeau blanc*. So there it is, my boy, and you can pride yourself on having plunged your old grandfather in despair!'

'Hear, hear!' said Théodule. Taking advantage of the pause while Monsieur Gillenormand got his breath, he added pontifically: 'All newspapers should be banned except the *Moniteur* and all books except the Army List.'

Monsieur Gillenormand proceeded:

'Like their man Sieyès, a regicide who ended up a senator, the way they all do. They start by calling everybody "citizen" and end up being called Monsieur le Comte. Pot-bellied counts who were once murderers! The philosopher Sieyès! In justice to myself I may say that I have never rated all their philosophizing any more highly than a clown's bladder. I once saw the senators going along the Quai Malaquais, in purple velvet cloaks embroidered with bees, and Henry IV hats. They were a dreadful sight, like a flock of monkeys in tiger-skins. I tell you, Citizens, that what you call progress is madness, your humanity a dream, your revolution a crime, your republic a monster, and that your young, virginal France comes out of a brothel. I say it to all of you, whether you're publicists, economists, jurists or greater experts in liberty, equality and fraternity than the blades of the guillotine. That's what I have to say to you, my good fellows!'

'Splendid!' cried the lieutenant. 'Every word of it is true!'

Monsieur Gillenormand paused on the verge of a gesture, turned, looked hard at the young man and said:

'You're a damned fool.'

BOOK SIX

CONJUNCTION OF TWO STARS

I

Birth of a nickname

MARIUS AT this time was a handsome young man with thick, very dark hair, a high, intelligent forehead, wide, sensitive nostrils, a frank, composed bearing and an expression that was at once high-minded, thoughtful, and ingenuous. His face, of which all the contours were rounded but still firm, had something of that German mildness that has invaded the French physiognomy by way of Alsace and Lorraine, and that absence of angles that set the Sicambri apart from other Romans, distinguishing the race of the lion from the race of the eagle. He had reached the time of life when the mind of a young man given to reflection is divided in almost equal proportions between depth and innocence. Faced by a difficult situation, he was likely to behave stupidly; but in a real emergency he could become magnificent. His manner was coolly courteous, reserved, and unforthcoming; but since his mouth was charming, with red lips and very white teeth, this air of aloofness was quite altered when he smiled. At moments, indeed, there was a striking contrast between the purity of his forehead and the sensual warmth of his smile. He had small but far-seeing eyes.

At the time of his utmost poverty he had seen girls look round at him as he passed and had fled from them in despair, believing that they were laughing at his shabby clothes, whereas the truth was that they were attracted by his good looks. This misconception had made him excessively shy. He had no girl of his own for the simple reason that he ran away from them all. Thus he continued to live in solitude – absurdly, as Courfeyrac said.

'You shouldn't be so high-falutin and stand-offish,' said Courfeyrac. 'Let me give you a word of advice, my lad. Don't be forever burying your nose in books. Give the girls a chance. They'd do you a lot of good, dear Marius. Always blushing and shying off the way you do, you'll end up a priest – or a hermit.' Courfeyrac had even been known on occasions to address him as 'Monsieur l'abbé'.

For a week after being lectured in this fashion Marius would avoid women more strenuously than ever, both young and old; he would also avoid Courfeyrac.

But among all the regiment of women there were two whom Marius did not seek to escape from or feel the need to defend himself against. Indeed, he would have been surprised to learn that they were women. The first was the hairy-chinned old body who did out his room, concerning whom Courfeyrac remarked, 'Seeing his cleaning-woman has a beard, Marius doesn't grow one of his own.' The other was a child whom he saw often but never really looked at.

During the past year or more Marius had noticed, on an alleyway in the Luxembourg garden, the one flanking the parapet of the tree-plantation, an elderly man and a very young girl, nearly always seated side by side on a bench at the more deserted end of the alleyway, near the Rue de l'Ouest. Whenever Marius's meditative strolls took him in that direction, and this happened very often, he was likely to see them. The man, who was perhaps sixty, had a grave and serious look, his robust, wearied aspect conveying the impression that he had been a soldier. Had he worn any kind of decoration Marius would have supposed him to be a half-pay officer. He looked good-natured but unapproachable, and he never returned the glance of a passer-by. He wore blue trousers, a blue tail-coat and a wide-brimmed hat which always seemed new, a black cravat and a Quaker shirt – that is to say, of dazzling whiteness but coarse material. A shop-girl passing near remarked to her friend, 'A nice, clean old widower'. His hair was very white.

The girl, when first Marius had noticed them, seated beside him on the bench which they seemed to have made their own property, was aged thirteen or fourteen. She was skinny to the point of ugliness, awkward and insignificant, although her eyes promised to be beautiful; but she gazed about her with a kind of unheeding assurance that he found displeasing. Her clothes were the mixture of too-old and too-young which is commonly seen on boarders at convent-schools – a badly cut dress of coarse black merino. They seemed to be father and daughter.

For a few days Marius was intrigued by this man who was not yet really old and the child who was not yet a person, but after this he ignored them. They, for their part, seemed not even to notice him. They sat peaceably together, the girl gaily chattering and the man saying little but glancing at her occasionally with a smile of profound fatherly affection.

Marius was in the habit of strolling the length of the alleyway where they sat, turning back along the same path, and often walking along it again. He did this several times a week. But although he saw the couple so frequently, no kind of salutation had ever been exchanged between them. The fact that they seemed to wish to avoid notice had, not unnaturally, aroused the interest of the students who occasionally strolled that way, the more studious after a lecture and others after a game of billiards. Courfeyrac, who belonged to the latter category, had scrutinized them, but finding the girl unattractive he made a point of passing rapidly by. Prompted by the girl's black clothes and the man's white hair, he had christened them 'Mlle Lanoire' and 'Monsieur Leblanc'. The names had become common currency among them. 'Monsieur Leblanc's on his usual bench,' the young men said, and Marius found it convenient to do the same.

For the purpose of our story we shall, for the present, follow their example.

Thus for the first year Marius saw them almost daily in the same place at the same time. He liked the look of the man but took no interest in the girl.

II

And there was light

But it happened in the second year, at precisely the point which our story has now reached, that Marius changed his itinerary, for no particular reason, and for some six months did not set foot in that alleyway. Then one day he went back there. It was a perfect summer morning, and he was as uplifted as we all are on a fine day, feeling his spirit respond to the song of birds around him and the brightness of the blue sky shining through the leaves.

He strolled along the alleyway, and there was the same couple, seated on the same bench. But as he drew near them he was struck by a change. The man was the same, but the girl was not. What he now saw was a tall and beautiful creature, endowed with all the charms and graces of womanhood at the precise moment when these are still mingled with the innocence of childhood, a moment of fragile purity only to be conveyed by the words, 'fifteen years old'. Soft chestnut hair flecked with gold, a forehead of marble, cheeks like rose-petals, a pale, sensitive skin, an exquisite mouth, its smiles like sunshine, like music, a head that Raphael might have used for the Virgin set on a neck that Jean Goujon might have bestowed on Venus. And finally, that nothing might be lacking in that ravishing countenance, a nose that was not beautiful but pretty, not straight or curved, Italian or Greek – a Parisian nose, which means one that is lively and sensitive, irregular and as nature made it, the despair of painters and the delight of poets.

Marius could not see her eyes, which were modestly veiled by her long, chestnut lashes; but this did not prevent her from smiling as she listened to what the white-haired man was saying, and nothing could have been more alluring than that smile from beneath lowered lids.

At the first glance Marius thought that it must be another girl altogether, perhaps the elder sister of the one he had previously seen. But when, following his former habit, he walked back along the alley and studied her more closely, he saw that it was the same. In six months the child had grown into a woman, that was all. It is the most commonplace of happenings. There comes a moment when the bud bursts overnight into flower and yesterday's little girl becomes a woman to entrap our hearts. This one had not merely grown but was transformed. Just as three April days may suffice for some trees to cover themselves with blossom, so six months had sufficed to clothe her with beauty. Her April had come.

Moreover, she was no longer a schoolgirl in a plush hat and woollen dress, with reddened hands and schoolgirl shoes. She had acquired taste as well as beauty and was now dressed with simple, unpretentious elegance. She was wearing a black silk dress, a cape of the same material, and a hat of white crepe. Her glove enhanced the slenderness of the hand that was playing with an ivory-handled parasol, and her silken slippers disclosed the smallness of her feet. Passing near her one was conscious of the pervasive, youthful fragrance that her whole being exhaled.

The man, however, was unchanged.

She looked up when Marius passed for the second time. Her eyes were a deep, azure blue, but their candid gaze was still that of a child. She glanced as casually at Marius as she might have done at an infant toddling under the trees or the urn on the stone balustrade behind her; and Marius walked on, his thoughts absorbed with other matters. He passed their bench several times without looking at her.

During the days that followed he resumed his customary walks in the Luxembourg, and, as usual, found the 'father and daughter' on their usual bench, but he paid them no attention. He thought no more about the girl now that she was beautiful than he had done when she was plain. He went that way simply from force of habit.

III

The workings of spring

It was a warm day, and the Luxembourg was bathed in sunshine and shadow. The sky was clear as though the angels had scrubbed it that morning, sparrows twittered in the chestnut trees and Marius, living and breathing but thinking of nothing in particular, wholly absorbed in being alive, went by their bench. The girl looked up at him and their eyes met.

What message was to be read in her eyes? Marius could not have said. Nothing and yet everything. A spark had passed between them.

She looked down and he continued on his way. What he had encountered was not the frank innocent gaze of a child. It was as though a door had suddenly opened and then had been as swiftly closed. There comes a day when every girl has this look in her eyes, and woe to him who encounters it!

That first gaze of a spirit that does not yet know itself is like the first glow of sunrise, the awakening of something radiant but still veiled. Nothing can convey the perilous charm of that unexpected gleam, shedding a sudden, hesitant light on present innocence and future passion. It is a kind of unresolved tenderness, chance-disclosed and expectant, a snare laid unwittingly by innocence, which captures a heart without intending or knowing what it does, a maid with the sudden gaze of a woman.

Rarely does it happen that a gaze such as this does not profoundly affect its victim. All purity and ardour is concentrated in that magical but fateful gleam which, more than the most calculated oglings of a coquette, has the power to implant in another heart the ominous flower, so loaded with fragrance and with poison, that is called love.

Returning to his garret that evening Marius considered the clothes he was wearing, and for the first time was conscious of the fact that he had the slovenliness, the bad taste and oafish stupidity to walk in the Luxembourg in his everyday clothes – a hat with a crumpled brim, clumsy working-man's boots, black trousers turning grey at the knees and a black jacket threadbare at the elbows.

IV
Beginning of a grave malady

The next day, attired in his new suit – new trousers, hat and boots, and even, prodigious luxury, a pair of gloves! – Marius set out at his accustomed hour for the Luxembourg. He met Courfeyrac on the way and pretended not to see him. Courfeyrac said later to his friends: 'I've just seen Marius's new hat and suit with Marius inside them. I suppose he was going to sit for an examination. He looked thoroughly silly.'

Arrived at the Luxembourg, Marius strolled round the pond and stared at the swans, then stood for a long time contemplating a statue with a hand blackened by mould and one hip missing. A plump middle-aged gentleman passed, holding a five-year-old boy by the hand. 'Avoid extremes, my son,' he was saying. 'Steer equally clear of despotism and anarchy.' Marius made a second tour of the pond, and then drifted in the direction of the alley, slowly and as it were reluctantly, as though he were at once impelled and inhibited from going there. But he was not conscious of this and supposed himself to be doing simply what he did every day.

Monsieur Leblanc and the girl were seated on their usual bench at the far end. Marius buttoned his jacket, pulled it down to make sure that it fitted snugly, glanced with some complacency at the sheen of his trousers and walked towards the bench with a slight swagger in which there was a hint of challenge and certainly a lurking thought of conquest. It may be said that he advanced upon it like Hannibal advancing upon Rome.

Except for this he was behaving quite in his customary manner, and his mind was still absorbed with his daily preoccupations. He was thinking about a text-book issued for the benefit of university students entitled *Manuel du Baccalauréat*, reflecting upon the ineptitude and lack of judgement shown by its compilers, who examined three of Racine's tragedies in their survey of literary masterpieces but only one of Molière's comedies. There was a slight singing in his ears. As he drew near the bench he again straightened his jacket, and he kept his eyes fixed on the girl, who seemed to fill all that end of the alleyway with a kind of blue haze.

But gradually his pace slowed, and when he was a short distance from the bench, but still by no means at the end of the alley, he came to a stop, turned and retraced his steps without having intended to do so or being consciously aware that he had not reached the end. The girl could scarcely have noticed him at that distance, or seen how handsome he looked in his best clothes. Nevertheless he held himself very straight in case anyone should be observing him from behind.

He walked to the far end of the alley and again turned back, this time coming nearer to the bench. In fact he got to within three trees of it but then found it almost impossible to go further, and for a moment he paused. It had seemed to him that the girl's face was turned towards him. With an extreme effort he overcame his hesitation and strode on, holding himself erect and looking neither to left nor right, his face flushed and a hand thrust into the opening of his jacket, like that of an elder statesman. His heart was pounding as he passed the bench. She was wearing the same silk dress she had worn the day before, and the same white hat. He heard the sound of an enchanting voice which could only be hers. She was talking quietly. She was exquisitely pretty. He felt this, although he made no attempt to look directly at her . . . 'She would certainly have some esteem for me,' he reflected, 'if she knew that I was the real author of the note on Marcos Obregon de la Ronda which Monsieur François de Neufchâteau included in the Introduction to his edition of *Gil Blas*, passing it off as his own work!'

He passed the bench, turned at the end of the alley and walked back again. This time he was very pale and his feeling was one of great perturbation. He went past the bench and the girl, and the notion that she might be watching him from behind made him tremble.

He did not go near them again but, further along the alleyway, he did something he had never done before. He sat down on a bench a short distance off and stayed there for some time, casting sidelong glances and reflecting in some recess of his mind that the person whose dress and hat he so greatly admired could scarcely fail to be impressed by the elegance of his own attire. Presently he rose and made as if to walk back again towards the bench, which was now enveloped in a sort of halo. But then he stood motionless.

For the first time, after fifteen months, it occurred to him that the gentleman accompanying the girl must surely have noticed him and must be finding his conduct somewhat odd. Also for the first time, it struck him that to have christened the gentleman 'Monsieur Leblanc', even in a private joke, showed a certain lack of respect.

He stood for some moments with his head bowed in thought, tracing a pattern in the dust with the stick he carried, then turned abruptly away from the bench and its occupants and went home.

He forgot to dine that evening, and only became aware of the fact when it was too late to go to the restaurant in the Rue Saint-Jacques. 'Ah well,' he thought, and chewed a crust of bread.

Before going to bed he brushed his jacket and folded his trousers with great care.

V

Shocks for Ma'am Bougon

On the following day Ma'am Bougon (this, which may be rendered as 'Ma Grumpy' was the name bestowed by Courfeyrac on the elderly door-keeper, 'chief lodger' and maid-of-all-work of the Gorbeau tenement; her real name was Madame Burgon, but, as we know, Courfeyrac was an iconoclast who respected nothing) noted to her intense astonishment that Monsieur Marius had again gone out in his best clothes.

He went to the Luxembourg but this time did not go further along the alley than the bench where he had sat the day before, whence he had a distinct but clear view of the white hat and black dress and, in particular, of the haze surrounding them. He remained there and did not go home until the garden was closed for the night. He had not noticed Monsieur Leblanc and his daughter leave, and presumed that they had done so by way of the gate on the Rue de l'Ouest. Thinking it over some weeks after the event, he could not remember where he had dined that night.

And the next day Ma'am Bougon was startled to see Marius again in his best suit.

'Three days running!' she exclaimed.

She tried to follow him, but he walked so fast, with such long strides, that it was a hopeless chase, a hippopotamus waddling after a chamois. She lost him in two minutes and returned home breathless and indignant, half suffocated by her asthma. 'Where's the sense in it?' she grumbled. 'Wearing his best every day and running people off their feet!'

Marius had gone to the Luxembourg. The girl and Monsieur Leblanc were there. He passed as close to them as he dared, while pretending to be deep in a book; but he still did not go very near, and presently he sat down on his own bench and for several hours contemplated the sparrows hopping in the alley, who seemed to be laughing at him.

Thus a fortnight passed. Marius no longer went to the Luxembourg to stroll but to seat himself always in the same place without ever asking the question, 'Why?' And every day he wore his best clothes.

Certainly she was wonderfully beautiful. All that could be said of her that was in any sense critical was that there seemed to be a contradiction between the look in her eyes, which tended to melancholy, and the brightness of her smile. This had a somewhat disconcerting effect, so that at moments her charming face was puzzling without ceasing to be delightful.

VI

Made captive

Towards the end of the second week, while Marius was seated in his usual place with an open book on his knee of which he had not read a page, he looked and suddenly quivered. Something had happened at the end of the alleyway. Monsieur Leblanc and his daughter had risen from their bench and were walking slowly in his direction. Marius shut his book, opened it again and made an effort to read it. He was still trembling while, as the halo drew nearer, he asked himself what attitude he should adopt. In a minute she would be within a few feet of him, treading the very dust that he so often trod, but the seconds dragged by like hours. He wanted to look impressive. It seemed to him that the gentleman was glancing his way in a somewhat irritated fashion. Was he going to address him? Marius lowered his head and did not look up again until they had drawn level with him. And as she passed the girl looked his way. She looked steadily at him with a soft pensive glance that caused him to tremble from head to foot. She seemed to be reproaching him for not having approached her in all this time, and to be saying, 'So now I've come to you.' He was dumbfounded by the play of light and shadow in her eyes.

He felt as though his head were on fire. The sheer ecstasy! She had come to him! And the way she had looked at him. He thought her more beautiful than ever, with a beauty that was at once feminine and angelic, that wholeness of beauty that had moved Petrarch to song and brought Dante to his knees. And at the same time he was horribly put out because his boots were dusty. He was sure that she had noticed his boots.

He gazed after her until she had vanished from sight, then got up and strode madly about the garden. In all likelihood he laughed at times and talked to himself aloud. He gazed so fondly at the children's nurses that each one thought he must be in love with her.

Finally he left the Luxembourg in the vague hope of seeing her in the street, but instead he ran into Courfeyrac under the Odéon arcade and promptly invited him to a meal. They dined *chez* Rousseau at a cost of six francs and a six-sou tip to the waiter. Marius ate like a starving man while babbling of anything that came into his head. 'Have you seen today's paper? That was a fine speech by Audry de Puyraveau' . . . He was head over heels in love.

After dinner he took Courfeyrac to the theatre. They saw Frédérick Lemaître at the Théâtre de la Porte-Saint-Martin playing in Robert Macaire's melodrama, *L'Auberge des Adrets*, and Marius was hugely entertained. But his conduct was increasingly strange. He refused, when they had left the theatre, to stare at the legs of a shopgirl skipping over a gutter, and was sternly disapproving when Courfeyrac said, 'I wouldn't mind adding her to my collection.'

Courfeyrac invited him to luncheon next day at the Café Voltaire, and he ate even more than he had done the previous evening. He was absent-minded and at the same time in a high state of exuberance, seeming to jump at any excuse to burst into laughter. He warmly embraced a young man from the country who was introduced to him. A circle of students had gathered round their table. After commenting on the state-salaried imbeciles who occupied professors' chairs at the Sorbonne, they went on to discuss the shortcomings and omissions of the compilers of dictionaries and in particular of Louis Quicherat. But Marius cut short the discussion by saying:

'All the same, it's very pleasant to have the Cross of the Légion d'honneur.'

'That's odd, coming from him,' murmured Courfeyrac in an aside to Jean Prouvaire.

'No,' said Jean Prouvaire. 'That's serious.'

It was indeed serious. Marius was in the first violent and entranced throes of a grand passion.

A single look had done it. When the charge is prepared and the fuse is laid nothing can be simpler. A glance is all the spark that is needed.

A woman's gaze is like a mechanical contrivance of a kind that seems harmless but in fact is deadly. We encounter it daily and give no thought to it – to the point, indeed, of ignoring its existence. We live untroubled lives until suddenly we find that we are caught. The machinery, the gaze, has laid hold of us, snatching at a loose end of thought, a momentary absence of mind, and we are lost. The machine swallows us up. We are in the grip of forces against which we struggle in vain, drawn from cog-wheel to cog-wheel, from agony to agony and torment to torment, our mind and spirit, fortune and future, our whole being; and according to whether we have fallen into the clutches of a base creature or a gentle heart we shall be disfigured by shame or transformed by worship.

VII
Confusion over the letter U

Solitude and detachment, pride, independence, a love of nature, the absence of regular employment, life lived for its own sake, the secret struggles of chastity and an overflowing goodwill towards all created things – all this had paved the way in Marius for the advent of what is known as passion. His feeling for his father had by degrees become a religion and like all religions had receded to the background of his mind. Something was needed to occupy the foreground, and what came to him was love.

A whole month went by during which he went daily to the Luxembourg. Nothing was allowed to deter him. 'He might be on sentry-go,' said Courfeyrac. He was in a state of constant rapture, knowing that the girl saw him.

Growing gradually bolder, he went nearer to the bench where she sat. But he did not walk directly in front of it. Partly from shyness, but also because, with the instinctive caution of lovers, he thought it prudent not to attract her father's notice. So with a Machiavellian cunning he took shelter behind trees and statues, posting himself so as to be visible as much as possible to her and as little as possible to the old gentleman. Sometimes he would stand for half an hour on end in the shadow of a Leonidas or a Spartacus, holding an open book over which he would discreetly glance at her, while she, for her part, turned her delightful head his way with a faint smile on her lips. While still talking calmly and naturally to her father, she would bestow on Marius all the dreams and secret fervours of her virgin gaze: a proceeding known to Eve from the day the world began, and to every woman from the day of her birth. While her lips spoke to the one, her eyes spoke to the other.

But it seemed that Monsieur Leblanc had begun to suspect what was happening, because quite often when Marius appeared he got to his feet and they strolled on. He exchanged their usual bench for one at the other end of the alleyway, evidently to see whether Marius would follow them there. Marius failed to understand and made the mistake of doing so. Then Monsieur Leblanc became irregular in his visits and did not always bring his daughter with him. When this happened Marius did not linger, which was another mistake.

Marius took no account of these portents. He had progressed by a natural transition from the stage of extreme caution to one of complete blindness. His passion was growing; he dreamed of his enchantress every night. Moreover an unexpected bounty had befallen him, casting oil on the flames and adding to the mist in his eyes. One evening he found a handkerchief lying on the bench which Monsieur Leblanc and his daughter had just left. It was a plain, unembroidered handkerchief, but white and of fine material, and it seemed to him to be impregnated with the most exquisite of scents. He snatched it up with rapture. It bore the initials U.F. At that time Marius knew nothing whatever about the girl, her name, her family, her dwelling-place; the two letters were a first clue on which he at once proceeded to erect a scaffolding of surmise. Clearly the U stood for her christian name – 'Ursula,' he thought. 'A delicious name!' He kissed the handkerchief, breathed its scent, wore it next to his heart by day and kept it under his pillow at night. 'I can feel her whole soul in it!' he told himself.

In fact, the handkerchief belonged to the old gentleman and had simply fallen out of his pocket.

Thereafter Marius never appeared in the Luxembourg without the handkerchief, pressing it to his lips or clasping it to his breast. The girl could make nothing of this and showed as much by her expression.

'Such modesty!' sighed Marius.

VIII

A puff of wind

Since we have used the word 'modesty' and are resolved to conceal nothing, we must now disclose that once, amid all his raptures, Marius was seriously displeased with his 'Ursula'. It was on a day when she and Monsieur Leblanc had left their bench and were strolling along the alley. A brisk breeze was blowing, bending the tops of the plane trees. Father and daughter, walking arm-in-arm, had passed by Marius's bench, and, as was to be expected of one in his desperate state, he had risen to his feet and was gazing after them

Suddenly a gust of wind livelier than the rest, and no doubt more officiously concerned with the business of the spring, blew across the alleyway from under the trees, setting the girl's dress in a delicious flutter, worthy of the nymphs of Virgil and the fauns of Theocritus, and swept up her skirts – those skirts more sacrosanct than the robes of Isis! – very nearly to the level of her garter. A beautifully shaped leg was revealed, and Marius, seeing it, was dismayed and furious. Nor was his sense of outrage lessened by the fact that with a startled movement she hastily smoothed down her skirt. It was true that no one else was there to see her, but supposing there had been someone! A dreadful thought, and her conduct was disgraceful! The poor child was, of course, in no way to blame; the wind was the only offender; but Marius, possessed by the Bartolo lurking in every Cherubino, was determined to disapprove and ready to be jealous of his own shadow. Thus it is that without justice or reason the extraordinary and bitter flame of jealousy of the flesh flares up in the heart of man. What is more, and setting aside this matter of jealousy, the sight of that charming leg had given him no pleasure; he would have been better pleased by a glimpse of any other woman's stocking.

When his 'Ursula' and Monsieur Leblanc, having reached the end of the alley, walked back past the bench on which he was seated, Marius gave her the most ferocious of frowns. The girl started slightly and her eyelids fluttered in a manner which plainly said, 'What's got into him?'

It was their first quarrel.

This exchange of glances was scarcely concluded when another person appeared in the alleyway. He was an old war-veteran, bowed and white-haired, wearing the uniform of Louis XV, the red oval badge with crossed swords, and the Saint-Louis cross awarded to soldiers, with an empty sleeve and a wooden leg. It seemed to Marius that he was looking extremely gratified, and, what is more, that as he limped by he glanced in his direction with a conspiratorial wink, as though they had shared some pleasurable experience. What had the old relic got to be so happy about? What link was there between that wooden leg and a certain other leg? Marius was now in a paroxysm of jealousy. 'He may have been there after all,' he reflected. 'He may have seen!' He wanted to strangle him.

But time heals all things. Marius's wrath abated, righteous though he held it to have been. He forgave her in the end; but it cost him an effort and he nursed his grievance for three whole days.

In spite of this, and also because of it, his infatuation increased.

IX
Disappearance

He had discovered, or thought he had, that her name was Ursula. But the appetite grows with loving. It was something to know her name, but it was not enough. In a few weeks he had exhausted that satisfaction and longed for more. He resolved to discover where she lived.

He had already made two blunders, the first in continuing to haunt them after they had changed their bench, and the second in leaving the garden whenever Monsieur Leblanc went there alone. Now he was guilty of a third and far greater one. He followed his 'Ursula'.

He found that she lived in the Rue de l'Ouest, in a modest-seeming house at the quiet end of the street. Thanks to this discovery he could add to the joy of seeing her in the Luxembourg the delight of following her home. But his appetite still grew. He had found out her name, or at least her first name, and a very charming one it was, and he knew where she lived; but now he wanted to know who she was.

One evening, having followed them to the house and seen them go in by the *porte cochère*, he went in after them and boldly addressed the porter.

'Was that the gentleman on the first floor, the one who has just come in?'

'No, Monsieur. He's the gentleman on the third floor.'

'The third floor front?'

'Well, but there is only the front. The whole house faces the street.'

'What kind of a gentleman is he?'

'A gentleman of private means. A good-hearted gentleman who does what he can for the poor, although he is not rich.'

'What is his name?' asked Marius.

The porter looked hard at him and asked:

'Is Monsieur connected with the police?'

This silenced Marius, but nevertheless he went off highly pleased with himself. He was making progress.

The next day Monsieur Leblanc and his daughter paid only a short visit to the Luxembourg, leaving early in the afternoon. Marius followed them home as usual; but when they reached the door Monsieur Leblanc, after standing aside to let the girl go in, turned and stared at him.

On the next day they did not come to the Luxembourg at all. After waiting until nightfall Marius walked to the house in the Rue de l'Ouest and saw lights behind the third-floor windows. He stayed there, strolling up and down, until the lights went out.

Again, on the following day, they did not appear in the Luxembourg, and again Marius kept watch under their windows. It was ten by the time their lights went out, and his dinner went by the board. Just as fever nourishes sickness, so does love sustain a lover.

A week passed in this fashion. Monsieur Leblanc and his daughter no longer came to the Luxembourg. Marius was plunged in melancholy conjecture. Fearing to keep watch on the house by daylight he relieved his anxieties by gazing up at the lighted windows after dark. Occasionally he saw a shadow pass in front of a lamp, and his heart beat faster.

But on the eighth day there was no light in the windows. Perhaps they had gone out for the evening. He waited, not merely until ten but until midnight and later. Still no light showed, and no one had entered the house. He left in a state of deep dejection.

On the morrow – for he was living now from tomorrow to to-morrow, and 'today' could be said scarcely to exist for him – on the morrow, having gone to the Luxembourg and, as he expected, failed to see them, he again went to the house as night was falling. And again there were no lights to be seen; the blinds were drawn and the third floor was in darkness.

Marius knocked at the *porte-cochère* and said to the porter:

'The gentleman on the third floor?'

'He's left,' the man said.

Marius reeled and asked feebly:

'When did he leave?'

'Yesterday.'

'Where has he gone?'

'I've no idea.'

'Didn't he leave an address?'

'No.'

The porter then recognized Marius. He glared at him and said:

'So it's you again! Well, you must certainly be a nark of some kind.'

BOOK SEVEN

PATRON-MINETTE

I
Mines and miners

ALL HUMAN societies have what is known to the theatre as an 'under-stage'. The social earth is everywhere mined and tunnelled, for better or for worse. There are higher and lower galleries, upper and lower strata in that subsoil which sometimes collapse under the weight of civilization, and which in our ignorance and indifference we tread underfoot. The Encyclopedia, in the last century, was a mine very near the surface. The catacombs, that dark cradle of primitive Christianity, lay waiting for the chance to explode under the Caesars and flood the world with light. For in the deepest shadow there is latent light. The volcano is filled with darkness capable of bursting into flame; lava at the start is black. Those catacombs where the first Mass was celebrated were not only the cellars of Rome, they were the under-stage of the world.

Beneath the social structure, that complex labyrinth, there are tunnellings of every kind. There are mines of religion and philosophy, politics, economics and revolution, galleries driven in the name of a theory or a principle, or mined in anger. Voices call from one gallery to the next. Utopias are born in these subterranean channels and spread their roots all ways. Sometimes they meet and fraternize. Rousseau offers his pickaxe to Diogenes, who lends his lantern in return. Calvin takes issue with Socin, the Italian heretic. But nothing can check or diminish the pressure of all these pertinacious activities, the huge concourse of energy seething in darkness, rising and falling and by slow degrees transforming the upper world from below and the outer world from within; a vast, secret turbulence. Society is scarcely aware of this process of burrowing which, leaving the surface untouched, gnaws at its entrails. So many different underground levels, different objectives, different harvests. And what comes of it all? The future.

The deeper one goes, the more unpredictable are the workers. At the level which social philosophy can recognize, good work is done; at a lower level it becomes doubtful, of questionable value; at the lowest level it is fearsome. There are depths to which the spirit of civilization cannot penetrate, a limit beyond which the air is not breatheable by men; and it is here that monsters may be born.

This descending ladder is a strange one, each of its rungs a platform where philosophy of some kind takes its stand and where its workers may be found, some divine and some misshapen. Below Hus there is Luther, below Luther Descartes, below Descartes Voltaire, below Voltaire Condorcet, below Condorcet Robespierre, below Robespierre Marat, below Marat Babeuf . . . and so on until, past the borderline separating the indistinct from the invisible, we are confusedly aware of shadowy figures that perhaps do not yet exist. Those belonging to yesterday are ghosts; those belonging to tomorrow are embryos. The mind's eye dimly perceives them. This conception of the future is a vision for philosophers. A foetal world in the womb of the state, unimaginable in shape.

Saint-Simon, Owen, and Fourier are also there, in divergent galleries. Indeed, although these underground pioneers are all linked by an invisible bond of which they are nearly always unaware, believing themselves to be isolated, their works are very different, the light shed by each being in conflict with that of the others. Their life and work may be uplifting or it may be tragic. Nevertheless, whatever the gulf between them, from the highest to the most obscure, the wisest to the most insane, they have this in common: they are all disinterested. Marat is as forgetful of self as was Jesus. They leave themselves wholly out of account, being concerned with something else. Their eyes are all intent upon one thing. They are searching for an Absolute. The greatest may have all Heaven in his eyes; but the least of them, no matter how confined, still has in his gaze a pale glimmer of the Infinite. So, no matter what he does, we must honour the man who bears this sign – a gleam of starlight in his eyes.

But there is another sign, that of the eye wholly without light.

It is here that evil has its source. Before the eye that sees nothing we must take heed and tremble. The social order has its black moles.

Below all those mines that we have spoken of, the many galleries, the huge complex of progressive or Utopian tunnellings, far deeper in the earth, lower than Marat, lower than Babeuf, far, far below all this and having no connection with those higher levels, there is the lowest level of all, the ultimate underworld. It is a terrible place, the pit of darkness, the stronghold of the blind. It is the threshold of the abyss.

The lowest level

Here disinterest vanishes and a demon is manifest – the spirit of each for himself. The sightless monster howls and scrabbles in the darkness. Anarchy lurks in that void.

The wild figures, half-animal, almost ghosts, that prowl in the darkness have no concern with universal progress, neither the thought nor the word is known to them, nothing is known to them but the fulfilment of their individual cravings. They are scarcely conscious, having within them a terrifying emptiness. They have two mothers, two foster-mothers, ignorance and poverty, a single guiding principle, that of necessity, and a single appetite, for all the satisfactions of the flesh. They are brutishly and fiercely voracious, not in the manner of a tyrant but of a tiger. By an inevitable process, by the fateful logic of darkness, the child nurtured in misery grows up to be a criminal, and what arises out of that lowest level of society is not the confused search for an Absolute but an affirmation of matter itself. The man becomes a beast of prey. Hunger and thirst are the point of departure and to be Satan is the final goal. It was from this cavern that Lacenaire, the poet and assassin, emerged.

We have glanced in previous chapters at a compartment on a higher level, the political, revolutionary, and philosophical world of the students. As we have seen, it is essentially a high-minded, upright, and honest world, capable of error certainly, and guilty of error, but deserving of respect since the error embraces heroism. The objective in that part of the mine may be summed up in a single word – progress. We must now peer more closely into the horror of this deepest depth.

There exists beneath the social structure – and, we must insist on this, it will continue to exist until ignorance has been done away with – a great cavern of evil. It is below all the other workings of the mine, and hostile to them all, infused with a hatred that admits of no exceptions. It knows no philosophers; its knives have never cut a pen; its darkness is utterly removed from the sublime dimness of the writing room. The blackened fists clenched beneath that stifling roof have never opened to turn the pages of a book or newspaper. The very revolutionaries on the higher level are aristocrats and exploiters to the denizens of that world, which has but a single aim, the destruction of everything.

Everything, including those higher levels which it execrates. In its hideous pullulation it undermines not merely the existing social order, but all philosophy and science, all law and human thought, civilization, progress, revolution itself. Its names are simply theft, prostitution, violence, assassination. It is darkness seeking chaos, walled-in with ignorance.

All the other levels seek to abolish it. That is what all their strivings amount to, their philosophy of progress, their contemplation of the Absolute no less than their striving to improve existing conditions. Do away with that cavern of ignorance and you destroy the burrowing mole which is crime. We can sum it up in very few words. The real threat to society is darkness.

Humanity is our common lot. All men are made of the same clay. There is no difference, at least here on earth, in the fate assigned to us. We come of the same void, inhabit the same flesh, are dissolved in the same ashes. But ignorance infecting the human substance turns it black, and that incurable blackness, gaining possession of the soul, becomes Evil.

III

Babet, Gueulemer, Claquesous, and Montparnasse

During the years 1830–35 a quartet of villains, Claquesous, Gueulemer, Babet, and Montparnasse, ruled the underworld of Paris.

Gueulemer was an unsung Hercules whose dwelling was the sewer under the Arche-Marion. He was six feet in height, with muscles of steel, a cavernous chest, the frame of a giant and a bird-brain. To see him was to think of the Farnese Hercules clad in cotton trousers and a velveteen jacket. With his monumental build he might have been a subduer of monsters, but he had found it simpler to become one himself. Something less than forty years of age, flat-footed, with close-cropped hair, shaggy cheeks and a small beard, it is not hard to picture the man. His muscles cried out for work, his stupidity would have none of it. He was a man of aimless strength and a casual murderer. In origin he was believed to be a Creole. Probably he had served for a time under Marshal Brune, having been a labourer in Avignon in 1855. It was after this that he took to crime.

The physical frailty of Babet was in sharp contrast to the burliness of Gueulemer. Babet was lean and cunning, transparent-seeming but unfathomable. One could see daylight between his bones but nothing in his eyes. He professed to be a chemist, had been a bartender *che*ʒ Bobèche and a clown in Bobino's circus; and he had played in vaudeville at Saint-Mihiel. He was a man of affectations, a fluent talker who underlined his smiles and put his gestures in inverted commas. His present trade was selling plaster busts of 'the Head of State' in the streets, in addition to which he drew teeth. He had exhibited freaks at fairs, and owned, besides a voice-trumpet, a caravan bearing the legend: 'Babet, dental artist, conducts scientific experiments on metals and metalloids, removes teeth, including stumps left behind by his colleagues. Price one tooth 1·50 frs., two teeth 2·00 frs., three teeth 2·50 frs. Do not miss this opportunity' (which meant, have as many out as possible). He had been married and had children, but did not know what had become of either wife or offspring, having mislaid them the way one mislays a handkerchief. He read the newspapers, which set him apart in the world he inhabited. Once, in the days when he and his family had been travelling the roads in their caravan, he had read a story in the *Messager* about a woman who had borne a child with a calf's head that seemed likely to live. 'Worth a fortune!' he had exclaimed. 'Catch my wife being clever enough to produce a child like that!' Eventually he had abandoned these pursuits to 'take on Paris' – his own expression.

As for Claquesous, he was darkness incarnate. He waited for nightfall before showing himself, creeping out of his hole at dusk and returning to it before daybreak. Nobody knew the whereabouts of this hole. Even after dark, in the company of his confederates, he evaded questions. Was his name really Claquesous? No, it was not. 'My name is, Mind-your-own-business,' he said. If anyone showed a light he put on a mask. He was a ventriloquist. Babet said, 'Claquesous is a night-bird with two voices.' He was mysterious, roving and frightening. No one knew if he had a real name, Claquesous being a nickname, or if he had a voice of his own, since his belly spoke more often than his mouth, or even if he had a face, since no one had ever seen anything but the mask. He vanished like a ghost and reappeared as though he had sprung out of the earth.

Finally, Montparnasse, a sorry creature. He was scarcely more than a child, a youth of under twenty with a pretty face, cherry-lips, glossy dark hair and the brightness of Springtime in his eyes. He had all the vices and aspired to all the crimes, feeding on evil an appetite that hungered always for worse. He was an urchin turned vagabond, a vagabond turned desperado, smooth, effeminate, graceful, strongly-built, pliant and ferocious. He wore his hat with the left-hand brim turned up to display a lock of hair, in the fashion of 1829. He lived by robbery with violence. His tail-coat was of excellent cut but frayed. Montparnasse was a fashion-plate living in squalor and committing murder, and the root cause of all his crimes was his desire to be well-dressed. The first wench who had praised his looks had instilled blackness in his heart, transforming Abel into Cain. Finding that he was handsome, he wanted to be elegant: but the highest elegance is idleness, and idleness in the poor is another name for crime. Few night-prowlers were as much feared as he. At the age of eighteen he had several murders to his credit; more than one dead body lay behind him, face down with arms outstretched in a pool of blood. Hair waved and pomaded, a slender waist, a woman's hips and the chest and shoulders of a Prussian officer, cravat meticulously tied, a flower in his button-hole, a murmur of women's admiration accompanying him and a blackjack in his pocket – such was this flower of the underworld.

IV

The gang

These four formed a single, Protean body, wriggling through the meshes of the law, evading the scrutiny of Vidocq 'in diverse guises, tree, flame and fountain', exchanging names and stratagems, vanishing into their own shadow, each the confidant and protector of the others, changing their outer aspect as one takes off a false nose at a masked ball, sometimes merging together to the point of being one person and at other times so multiplying themselves that they might be taken for a mob. They were not four men but a sort of four-headed monster preying wholesale on Paris, a monstrous embodiment of the evil lurking in the catacombs of society.

Thanks to their many and various enterprises, and their network of criminal contacts, Babet, Gueulemer, Claquesous, and Montparnasse had become in some sort the headquarters of villainy throughout the Département de la Seine. They were the setters of traps, the stabbers in the back. Persons desiring this kind of service, men with dark ambitions, applied to them. They put forward a project, and the foursome saw to it that it was carried out. They worked to specification, and were always able to find suitable assistants where additional manpower was needed, and provided the job covered the expense. Where the drama required a supporting cast they hired them, having at their disposal a company of small-time actors sufficient for any play.

They were accustomed to meet at nightfall, the time of their awakening, in the wasteland near the Salpêtrière. Here they took counsel together; with twelve hours of darkness ahead of them, they decided upon its use.

This four-man syndicate was known to the underworld by the name of '*Patron-Minette*'. In the old popular slang, which is fast disappearing, '*Patron-Minette*' meant 'morning' and '*Entre chien et loup*' meant 'evening'; no doubt the name was a reference to the conclusion of their labours, daybreak being the hour when ghosts vanish and thieves disperse. They were always referred to by this name. When the President of the Assize Court visited Lacenaire in gaol he mentioned a crime which Lacenaire denied having committed. 'Then who was it?' he asked. Lacenaire's reply was mystifying to the magistrate but intelligible to the police: 'It may have been Patron-Minette'.

One may sometimes deduce the nature of a play from the names of the characters; in the same way, one may get some idea of the nature of a gang. Here then are the names of the principal accomplices of Patron-Minette, names still to be found in the police archives:

Panchaud, alias Printanier, alias Bigrenaille.
Brujon (there was a dynasty of Brujons, of whom mention will be made later).
Boulatruelle, the road-mender whom we have already met.
Laveuve.
Finistère.
Homère Hogu, a black man.
Mardisoir.
Dépèche.
Fauntleroy, alias Bouguetière.
Glorieux, an ex-convict.
Barrecarrosse, alias Monsieur Dupont.
Lesplanade-du-Sud.

Poussagrive.

Carmagnolet.

Kruideniers, alias Bizarro.

Mangedentelle.

Les-pieds-en-l'air.

Demi-liard, or Deux-milliards.

Et cetera.

We may omit the rest, which were not the worst. Faces can be put to all those names. They stand, not only for individuals, but for types, each representing a variety of the misshapen fungi growing in the underworld of civilization.

Those persons, wary of letting their faces be seen, were not such as one passes in the street. In daytime, wearied by the wild happenings of the night, they slumbered in the abandoned lime-kilns and quarries of Montmartre and Montrouge, and sometimes in the sewers. They went to ground.

What has become of them? They still exist, as they have always done; and so long as society remains unchanged, they will continue to be what they are. One generation will succeed another, born in that cavern noxious with the fumes that society exudes. Ghostlike they return and are always the same, only bearing different names and clad in different skins. The individual passes, but the race survives.

They have the same skills. From pickpocket to cut-throat, the race preserves its purity. They can spot the purse in a pocket, and the watch; gold and silver have a special smell for them. There are innocent citizens of whom one might say that they are born to be robbed; they recognize these and patiently pursue them. At the sight of a foreigner or a newcomer from the provinces they quiver in anticipation like a spider in its web.

Those men, if one encounters them or simply sees them at midnight in a deserted boulevard, are terrifying. They seem to be not men at all, but figures composed of living mist: as though they were a part of the darkness, having no other existence, and have only momentarily detached themselves from it to live a few minutes of monstrous life.

What is needed to exorcize these evil spirits? Light, and still more light. No bat can face the dawn. We must flood that underworld with light.

BOOK EIGHT

THE NOXIOUS POOR

I

Looking for a girl in a hat, Marius encounters a man in a cap

SUMMER AND autumn passed, and winter came. Neither Monsieur Leblanc nor the girl had set foot in the Luxembourg. Marius had but one thought, which was to see that enchanting face again. He had searched endlessly and everywhere, but without success. He had ceased to be the hot-headed dreamer of dreams, the bold challenger of fate, the youthful builder of futures, his mind teeming with castles in the air. He was like a stray dog, plunged in black despair. His life had become meaningless. Work disgusted him, walking tired him, solitude bored him; the vast world of Nature, hitherto so filled for him with light and meaning, with wide horizons and wise counsels, had become an emptiness. Everything, it seemed, had disappeared.

He still meditated, for he could not do otherwise, but he took no pleasure in his thoughts. To every notion that occurred to him, every plan that entered his mind, he had the same answer: what use is it?

He took himself endlessly to task. Why had he followed her, when it was such happiness simply to look at her? And she had looked back at him – was not that tremendous in itself? She had seemed to like him, and what more could he ask? What more could there have been? He had been ridiculous, it was his own doing . . . And so on. Courfeyrac, to whom he said nothing since it was against his nature to do so, but who guessed a good deal, that being *his* nature, had at first congratulated him, if with some astonishment, on having fallen in love; but then, seeing his state of misery, he said: 'So you're human, like the rest of us. Well, let's go to the Chaumière.'

On one occasion, encouraged by the September sunshine, he had let himself be borne off to the Bal de Sceaux in company with Courfeyrac, Bossuet, and Grantaire. He had had a wild hope of seeing her there, but of course had not done so. 'All the same, it's a good place for finding lost women,' Grantaire had murmured to the others. Marius had left them to their own pursuits and had walked back, lonely, weary and sad-eyed, outraged by the noise and dust of the carriages of singing revellers that passed him in the night, and seeking to cool his fevered blood by breathing in the sharp scent of the walnut trees lining the road.

He relapsed more and more into solitude, aimless and apathetic, immersed in his private suffering, twisting and turning within the walls of his grief like a wolf in a cage, searching still for what he had lost and made dull-witted by love.

An incident occurred which greatly startled him. In one of the narrow streets off the Boulevard du Luxembourg he passed a man in workman's clothes wearing a peaked cap beneath which his very white hair was visible. Struck by the beauty of those white locks, Marius turned to look at him. The man was walking slowly as though preoccupied with a painful train of thought. And strangely, Marius seemed to recognize Monsieur Leblanc. The hair and profile were the same, as far as the cap allowed them to be seen, and his bearing in general was the same, except that he appeared more melancholy. But why the workman's clothes? What was the meaning of that? Was it an intentional disguise? Marius was greatly astonished. When he had recovered from his surprise his immediate thought was to follow him and see where he went. But he had left it too late. The stranger had already vanished down a side-street and he could not catch up with him. This episode preoccupied Marius for several days, but then he dismissed it from his mind, reflecting that, after all, he had probably been mistaken.

II

A find

Marius was still living in the Gorbeau tenement, indifferent to the people around him. As it happened, at that time the house was empty except for himself and the Jondrettes, the family of father, mother, and daughters whose rent he had once paid but to none of whom he had ever spoken. The other tenants had either gone elsewhere or died, or been turned out for non-payment of rent.

On one particular day that winter the sun shone for a little while during the afternoon; but it was 2 February, the ancient feast of Candlemas, when a treacherous sun, the precursor of six weeks' cold weather, had inspired Canon Mathieu Loensberg of Liège to write the following lines, which have deservedly become classic:

Qu'il luise ou qu'il luiserne,
L'ours rentre en sa caverne.

Which may be rendered:

> Whether it shines or pretends to shine,
> The bear retreats to his den.

Marius emerged from his own den as darkness was falling. It was time for dinner, and – such alas is the weakness of romantic passion – he had been forced to revert to the habit of dining. He left the house in time to hear Ma'am Bougon, who was sweeping the doorstep, deliver herself of the following memorable observation:

'So what's cheap in these days? Everything costs more. Nothing's cheap except toil and trouble, and you get those free of charge.'

Making for the Rue Saint-Jacques, Marius went slowly along the boulevard in the direction of the *barrière*, walking with his head bowed in thought. Suddenly he was jostled in the mist by two shabbily-dressed girls, breathlessly dashing in his direction as though they were running away from something, who bumped into him without seeing him. One was tall and thin, the other rather smaller. He had a glimpse of pale faces, dishevelled hair, tawdry bonnets, ragged skirts, and bare feet, and he caught a fragment of conversation as they passed.

The tall one was saying:

'The cops came along. They near as anything got me.'

The other said:

'I saw. I didn't half run for it.'

From which Marius gathered that, young as they were, they had had a brush with the gendarmes or the city police but had managed to escape.

He stood for a moment staring after them as they disappeared under the trees of the boulevard. Then, as he was about to continue on his way, he noticed a small, greyish object lying on the ground near him. He picked it up. It was a wrapping of sorts, evidently containing papers.

One of the girls must have dropped it as they passed. He turned and called after them but failed to make them hear, and so eventually, putting the package in his pocket, he went on to dinner. In a narrow street leading into the Rue Mouffetard he saw a child's coffin lying on three chairs, draped in black and lighted by a candle. The sight put him in mind of the two girls.

'Unhappy mothers!' he thought. 'If there is anything worse than to see one's children die it is to see them leading evil lives.'

Then dismissing these distracting shadows, and reverting to his own familiar griefs he fell to brooding again on his six months of love and happiness in the sunshine beneath the trees of the Luxembourg.

'How sad my life has become,' he reflected. 'I'm always running into young girls. Once they seemed angelic; now they are creatures of darkness.'

III

Letters

When he undressed that night he found the package in his pocket, having forgotten about it, and it occurred to him that it might contain the girls' address, or that of the owner if it was not they who had dropped it.

He undid the wrapping, which was not sealed, and found that it contained four letters, all addressed but also unsealed, and all smelling strongly of cheap tobacco.

The first was addressed to Madame la Marquise de Grucheray, No. —, the Square behind the Chambre des Députés. Since it might contain the clue he was looking for, Marius felt justified in reading it. It ran as follows:

Madame la Marquise,
The virtues of compasion and piety are the bonds that most closely bind sosiety. I beg you to turn your Christian eyes upon an unfortunate Spaniard, the victim of his loyalty and devotion to the sacred cause of legitimasy, for which cause he has shed his blood and devoted his whole fortune and is now in desperate need. He does not doubt that your noble self will come to his aid to preserve the unhappy life of a soldier of education and honour and many wounds, counting upon your humanity and the sympathy which Madame la Marquise is known to feel for his suffering countrymen. Their prayer will not go unheard and their gratitude will cherish her memory.

I have the honour to sign myself, Madame, with expresions of the deepest respect,
            Don Alvarez,
                Captain in the Spanish cavalry, royalist refugee in
                France, travelling for his country's sake but unable
                to get further through lack of funds.

630

No address followed the signature. Marius turned to the second letter, which was addressed to Madame la Contesse de Montvernet, 9, Rue Cassette.

Madame la Contesse,
I am the mother of six children, the last only eight months old, sick since my lying-in, diserted by my husband five months ago, in dredful poverty, not a penny in the world. I apeal to the charity of Madame la Contesse.

Yours obediantly,

Eve Balizard (wife and mother).

The third, like the others, was a begging-letter.

To Monsieur Pabourgeot, elector and wholesale milliner, Rue Saint-Denis, corner of the Rue aux Fers.
I venture to adress this letter to you to apeal for your favor and interest on behalf of a man of letters who has resently submited a play to the Théâtre-Français. The play is historical and takes place in Auvergne under the Empire. The style, I think, is natural and trenshant and, I believe, has some merit. There are verses for singing in four places. Comedy, drama and surprise are mingled with a variety of characters, with a flavor of romanticism throughout the plot which developes mysteriously with striking suprises in many brilliant scenes.
My principle aim is to satisfy the desire that progresively inspires the men of our century, namely, THE FASHION, that caprisious weather-cock which changes with every change in the wind. But in spite of the merits of my play I fear that jealousy and the greed of established authors may cause it to be rejected, for I am well aware of the way they treat newcomers.
Knowing your reputation, dear Sir, as an enlightened defender of the Arts I make bold to send my daughter to call on you. She will depict for you our parlous situation, lacking food and warmth in this winter season. When I say that I beg you will allow me to dedicate this play and all the other plays I hope to write to your esteemed self, this will prove how ernestly I desire to put myself under your protection and embelish my writings with your name. If you will condesend to honor me with even the smallest gift I will at once compose a poem in token of my gratitude. This poem, which I will endeavour to make as perfect as possible, will be submited to you before being inserted at the beginning of the play and spoken on the stage.

With my most respectful regards,

Genflot, man of letters.

P.S. Even as little as forty sous.
Excuse me sending my daughter and not coming myself. Alas, the insufficiency of my wardrobe prevents me going out.

The fourth letter was addressed to 'The Benevolent Gentleman outside the church of Saint-Jacques-du-Haut-Pas'.

Benevolent Sir,

If you will be so good as to acompany my daughter you will be the witnes of a shattered life and I will show you my certificates. This letter in itself will, I know, cause your generous spirit to be inspired with a sense of lively benevolense, for the truly philosophical are always a pray to strong emotions.

And you will agree, compasionate Sir, that only in the most cruel necesity will anyone take the painfull step of registering with the authorities, as though we were not free to suffer and die of starvation by ourselves while waiting for help in our distress. Fate is too cruel to some and too indulgent to others.

I await your visit or your gift, if you are so kind as to make me one, and beg you to acept the sentiments of profound respect with which I subscribe myself,

truly magnanimous Sir,

your most humble and obedient servant,

P. Fabantou, artist of the drama.

Having read the four letters, Marius found that he had not discovered what he wanted to know, since none bore the address of the writer. However, they were interesting in other respects. Although they purported to come from four different people, all were in the same handwriting, written on the same coarse, yellowed paper and impregnated with the same smell of tobacco. Moreover, although an attempt had clearly been made to vary the style, all contained similar spelling mistakes, the 'man of letters', Genflot, being no more exempt from these than the Spanish captain. It was impossible not to suppose that they were written by the same person.

But to attempt to solve this trifling mystery, which might have had the appearance of a practical joke if he had not come upon the package by accident, would be a waste of time. Marius was in too dejected a state to enter into the spirit of this diversion proposed to him by the streets of Paris, as though he were the blind man in a game of 'blind man's buff' with the four letters. There was nothing to indicate that they were the property of the two girls who had jostled him on the boulevard, and they were, in any event, evidently documents of no value. He wrapped them up again, tossed them into a corner and went to bed.

At about seven the next morning, by which time he had dressed and breakfasted and was trying to settle down to work, there was a tap on his door.

Since he had almost no possessions Marius was in the habit of leaving his door unlocked, except, as happened very occasionally, when he had urgent work to do. He left the key in the lock even when he went out. 'You'll be robbed,' Ma'am Bougon said. 'What of?' said Marius. But the fact remained that he had once been robbed of an old pair of boots, much to her satisfaction.

There was a second knock, as tentative as the first.

'Come in,' said Marius without looking up from the papers on his writing-table. 'What is it, Ma'am Bougon?'

But the voice that answered, saying, 'I beg your pardon, Monsieur,' was not that of Ma'am Bougon. It was more like the voice of a bronchitic old man, half-stifled, rendered husky as though by the drinking of spirits.

Marius looked up sharply and saw that his visitor was a girl.

IV

Rose of the underworld

A quite young girl was standing in the open doorway, facing the pallid light of the one small window in Marius's garret, which was opposite the door. She was a lean and delicate-looking creature, her shivering nakedness clad in nothing but a chemise and skirt. Her waistband was a piece of string, and another piece tied back her hair. Bony shoulders emerged from the chemise, and the face above them was sallow and flabby. The light fell upon reddened hands, a stringy neck, a loose, depraved mouth lacking several teeth, bleared eyes both bold and wary: in short, an ill-treated girl with the eyes of a grown woman; a blend of fifty and fifteen; one of those creatures, at once weak and repellent, who cause those who set eyes on them to shudder when they do not weep.

Marius had risen to his feet and was gazing in a sort of stupefaction at what might have been one of those figures of darkness that haunt our dreams. But what was tragic about the girl was that she had not been born ugly. She might even have been pretty as a child, and the grace proper to her age was still at odds with the repulsive premature ageing induced by loose living and poverty. A trace of beauty still lingered in the sixteen-year-old face, like pale sunlight fading beneath the massed clouds of a winter's dawn.

The face was not quite unfamiliar to Marius. He had a notion that he had seen her before.

'What can I do for you, Mademoiselle?'

She answered in her raucous voice:

'I've got a letter for you, Monsieur Marius.'

So she knew his name. But how did she come to know it?

Without awaiting any further invitation she walked in, looking about her with a pathetic boldness at the untidy room with its unmade bed. Long bare legs and bony knees were visible through the vents in her skirt, and she was shivering.

As he took the letter Marius noted that the large wafer sealing it was still damp. It could not have come very far. He read:

My warm-hearted neighbour, most estimable young man!

I have heard of the kindness you did me in paying my rent six months ago. I bless you for it. My elder daughter will tell you that for two days we have been without food, four of us, including my sick wife. If I am not deceived in my trust in humanity I venture to hope that your generous heart will be moved by our afliction and that you will relieve your feelings by again coming to my aid.

I am, with the expression of the high esteem we all owe to a benefactor of humanity,

Yours truly,
Jondrette.

P.S. My daughter is at your service, dear Monsieur Marius.

This missive threw an immediate light on the problem that had been perplexing Marius. All was now clear. It came from the same source as the other letters – the same handwriting, the same spelling, the same paper, even the same smell of rank tobacco. He now had five letters, all the work of one author. The Spanish Captain, the unhappy Mère Balizard, the dramatist Genflot, and the aged actor, Fabantou, all were Jondrette – if, indeed, that was his real name.

As we have said, during the time Marius had been living in the tenement he had paid little or no attention even to his nearest neighbours, his thoughts being elsewhere. Although he had more than once encountered members of the Jondrette family in the corridor or on the stairs, they had been to him no more than shadows of whom he had taken so little notice that he had failed to recognize the two daughters when they bumped into him on the boulevard; even now, in the shock of his pity and repugnance, he had difficulty in realizing that this must be one of them.

But now he saw it all. He realized that the business of his neighbour, Jondrette, was the writing of fraudulent begging letters under a variety of names to persons of supposed wealth and benevolence whose addresses he had managed to secure, and that these letters were delivered, at their own peril, by his daughters: for he had sunk so low that he treated the two young girls as counters in his gamble with life. To judge by the episode of the previous evening, their breathless flight and the words he had overheard, the girls were engaged in other sordid pursuits. What it came to was that in the heart of our society, as at present constituted, two unhappy mortals, neither children nor grown women, had been turned by extreme poverty into monsters at once depraved and innocent, drab creatures without name or age or sex, no longer capable of good or evil, deprived of all freedom, virtue, and responsibility; souls born yesterday and shrivelled today like flowers dropped in the street which lie fading in the mud until a cartwheel comes to crush them.

Meanwhile, while Marius watched her in painful astonishment, the girl was exploring the room like an audacious ghost, untroubled by her state of near nakedness in the ragged chemise which at moments slipped down almost to her waist. She moved chairs, examined the toilet-articles on the chest of drawers, fingered Marius's clothes and peered into corners.

'Well, fancy! You've got a mirror,' she said.

She was humming to herself as though she were alone, snatches of music-hall songs, cheerful ditties which her raucous, tuneless voice made dismal. But beneath this show of boldness there was a hint of unease and awkward constraint. Effrontery is an expression of shame. Nothing could have been more distressing than to see her fluttering about the room like a bird startled by the light or with a broken wing. It was plain that in other circumstances of background and education her natural, uninhibited gaiety might have made of her something sweet and charming. In the animal world no creature born to be a dove turns into a scavenger. This happens only among men.

Marius sat pondering while he watched her. She drew near to his writing-table.

'Books!' she said.

A light dawned in her clouded eyes. She announced, with the pride in attainment from which none of us is immune: 'I know how to read.'

Picking up a book that lay open on the table she read, without much difficulty:

'General Bauduin was ordered to seize and occupy, with the five battalions of his brigade, the Château de Hougomont, which is in the middle of the plain of Waterloo . . .'

She broke off and exclaimed:

'Waterloo! I know about that. It's an old battle. My father was there. My father was in the army. We're all real Bonapartists in our family. Waterloo was against the English.' She put the book down and took up a pen. 'I can write, too.' She dipped the pen in the ink and looked at Marius. 'You want to see? I'll write something to show you.'

Before he could say anything she had written on a blank sheet lying on the table: 'Watch out, the bogies are around.' She laid down the pen. 'No spelling mistakes. You can see for yourself. We've had some schooling, my sister and me. We haven't always been what we are now. We weren't brought up to be –'

But here she stopped and gazing with her dulled eyes at Marius she burst out laughing. In a tone in which the extreme of anguish was buried beneath the extreme of cynicism, she exclaimed, 'What the hell!'

She began to hum again and then said:

'Do you ever go to the theatre, Monsieur Marius? I do. I've a young brother who knows one or two actors and he gives me tickets. I don't like the gallery, the benches are uncomfortable and it's too crowded and there are people who smell nasty.'

She fell to examining Marius and said with a coy look:

'Do you know, Monsieur Marius, that you're a very handsome boy?'

The words prompted the same thought in both their minds, causing her to smile and him to blush. Drawing nearer, she laid a hand on his shoulder.

'You never notice me, Monsieur Marius, but I know you by sight. I see you on the stairs, and I've seen you visiting an old man called Père Mabeuf in the Austerlitz quarter when I've been that way. It suits you, you know, having your hair untidy.'

She was striving to make her voice soft but could only make it sound more guttural, and some of the words got lost in their passage from her throat to her lips, as on a piano with some of the notes missing. Marius drew gently away.

'I think, Mademoiselle,' he said with his accustomed cold gravity, 'that I have something belonging to you. Allow me to return it.'

He handed her the wrapping containing the four letters. She clapped her hands and cried:

'We looked for that everywhere!'

Seizing it eagerly, she began to unfold it, talking as she did so:

'Heavens, if you knew how we'd searched, my sister and me! And so you're the one who found it. On the boulevard, wasn't it? It must have been. We were running, and my sister went and dropped it, the silly kid, and when we got home we found it was gone. So because we didn't want to be beaten, because where's the sense in it, what earthly good does it do, it's simply stupid, we said we'd delivered the letters to the people they were written to and they hadn't coughed up anything. And here they are, the wretched letters. How did you know they were mine? Oh, of course, the handwriting. So you're the person we bumped into yesterday evening? It was too dark to see. I said to my sister, "Was it a gentleman?" and she said, "I think it was." '

By now she had fished out the letter addressed to 'The Benevolent Gentleman outside the church of Saint-Jacques-du-Haut-Pas'.

'Ah, this is for the old boy who goes to Mass. Well, it's nearly time so I'd better run along and catch him. Perhaps he'll give me enough for our dinner.' She burst out laughing again. 'And do you know what that will mean? It will be breakfast and dinner for yesterday and the day before – the first meal for three days. Well, who cares? If you don't like it you've got to lump it.'

This reminded Marius of why she had called upon him. He felt in his waistcoat pockets, while she went on talking as though she had forgotten his existence.

'Sometimes I go out at night and don't come home. Last winter, before coming here, we lived under the bridges. You had to huddle together not to freeze and it made my little sister cry. Water's dreadful, isn't it? Sometimes I wanted to drown myself, but then I thought, No, it's too cold. I go off on my own when I feel like it and sleep in a ditch, likely as not. You know, at night when I'm walking along the boulevards the trees look to me like pitchforks, and the houses, they're so tall and black, like the towers of Notre-Dame, and when you come to a strip of white wall it's like a patch of water. And the stars are like street lamps and you'd think they were smoking, and sometimes the wind blows them out and I'm always surprised, as though a horse had come and snorted in my ear; and although it's night-time I think I can hear street-organs and the rattle of looms, all kinds of things. And sometimes I think people are throwing stones at me and I run away and everything goes spinning round me. When you've had nothing to eat it's very queer.'

She was gazing absently at him. Marius, exploring his pockets, had now succeeded in retrieving a five-franc piece and sixteen sous, all the money he possessed at that moment. Enough for today's dinner, he reflected, and as for tomorrow, we'll hope for the best. So he kept the sixteen sous and offered her the five francs.

'The sun's come out at last!' she cried, eagerly accepting the coin; and as though the sun had power to release a torrent of the popular jargon that was her every day speech she declaimed:

'Well, if that isn't prime! Five jimmy-o'-goblins! Enough to stuff us for two days. You're a true nobleman, mister, and I tips my lid to you. Tripe and sausage and the tipple to wash it down for two whole blooming days.' Hitching up her chemise and making Marius a profound curtsey, she turned with a wave of her hand towards the door. 'Well, good day to you, mister, and your humble servant. I'll be getting back to the gaffer.'

On her way to the door she noticed a crust of stale bread gathering dust on the chest of drawers. She snatched it up and started to devour it.

'It's good, it's tough – something to get your teeth into!'
And she departed.

v

The peep-hole

Marius had lived through five years of penury and deprivation, sometimes of great hardship; but, as he perceived, he had never known the real meaning of poverty, utter destitution, until he encountered it in the person of that girl. To witness the abjection of men is not enough: one must also witness the abjection of women: and even this pales before the abjection of a child.

People reduced to the last extremity of need are also driven to the utmost limit of their resources, and woe to any defenceless person who comes their way. Work and wages, food and warmth, courage and goodwill – all this is lost to them. The daylight dwindles into shadow and darkness enters their hearts; and within this darkness man seizes upon the weakness of woman and child and forces them into ignominy. No horror is then excluded. Desperation is bounded only by the flimsiest of walls, all giving access to vice and crime.

Health and youth, honour and the sacred, savage delicacy of still-young flesh, truth of heart, virginity, modesty, those protective garments of the soul, all are put to the vilest of uses in the blind struggle for survival that must encounter, and submit to, every outrage. Fathers, mothers, sons, daughters, brothers, men and women alike merge into a composite, like a mineral alloy, in the murky promiscuity of sexes, relationships, ages, infamy and innocence. They huddle together, back to back, in a kind of spiritual hovel, exchanging glances of lamentable complicity. How pale they are, those unfortunates, how cold they are! They might be the inhabitants of a planet far more distant from the sun than our own.

To Marius the girl was in some sort an emissary of that underworld, disclosing a hideous aspect of its darkness. He was near to reproaching himself for his habit of abstraction and for the love-affair which until then had prevented him from giving a thought to his neighbours. The payment of their rent had been an automatic response, an impulse that might have occurred to anyone; he, Marius, should have done better. Only a thin partition separated him from that small cluster of lost souls groping in darkness and sundered from the living world; he had heard them living, or rather suffering, within a few yards of him – and he had paid no attention. All day and every day he had been conscious of their movements through the wall as they came and went and talked together, and he had not listened. Groans had been mingled with the words they spoke, but he had not heeded them. His thoughts had been elsewhere, squandered in dreams, infatuation, while these, his fellow-creatures and brothers in Christ, were slowly rotting beside him, abandoned to their agony. Indeed, it seemed to him that he was a part of their misfortune and had aggravated it. If they had had a different neighbour, one less self-absorbed and more concerned for others, a man of normal, charitable instincts, their desperate state would not have gone unnoticed, their distress-signals would have been heard, and perhaps they would have been rescued by now. Certainly they appeared utterly depraved, corrupt, vile and odious; but it is rare for those who have sunk so low not to be degraded in the process, and there comes a point, moreover, where the unfortunate and the infamous are grouped together, merged in a single, fateful word. They are *les misérables* – the outcasts, the underdogs. And who is to blame? Is it not the most fallen who have most need of charity?

While he thus lectured himself – for there were times when, like all truly honest persons, he was his own schoolmaster and took himself to task more sternly than he deserved – Marius was staring at the wall which separated him from the Jondrettes, as though by the act of doing so the warmth of his pitying gaze might be made to pass through it and comfort their distress. The wall was in fact no more than a lath-and-plaster partition with a few upright posts, through which, as we have said, every movement and sound of voices could be distinctly heard. Only a dreamer like Marius could have been unconscious of the fact. It was not papered on either side, so that its crude nakedness was apparent. Half-unconsciously Marius examined it while still pursuing his train of thought. Suddenly he stood up. In the upper part of the wall, near the ceiling, there was a triangular hole between three laths where the plaster had crumbled away. By standing on the chest of drawers one could see through it into the Jondrette's garret. Curiosity is, and must be, a part of compassion. The hole was like a Judas-window. It is lawful to take surreptitious note of misfortune for the purpose of relieving it. 'Let us see what these people are like,' said Marius, 'and how bad things really are.'

He got up on the chest of drawers, put his eye to the aperture and looked through.

VI

The beast in his lair

Cities, like forests, have their retreats in which the most evil and fearful of their denizens lurk in hiding. But whereas the dwellers in city dens are ferocious, malignant, and small – in a word, ugly – those in the forest lairs are fierce, wild, and generally large – that is to say, beautiful. All things considered, the animal den is preferable to the human den. A cave is better than a city slum.

What Marius was peering into was the latter.

Marius was poor and his own room was a barren place, but, as his poverty was high-minded so was his garret clean. The dwelling into which he looked was filthy, squalid, evil-smelling, and altogether noisome. Its only furnishings were a wicker chair, a rickety table, a few cracked dishes and, in opposite corners, two frowzy trucklebeds; its only lighting came through the grimy, cobwebbed panes of a small dormer-window which admitted just sufficient light to make the face of a man look like that of a ghost. The walls had a leprous appearance, being covered with cracks and scars like a human face disfigured by some repellent disease, oozing with damp, and inscribed here and there with crudely obscene drawings in charcoal.

Marius's room had a flooring of worn tiles; this place had no flooring other than the original rough-cast of the building, now blackened by the tread of feet; dust was, so to speak, incrusted in the rough surface, which was virgin soil only in the sense that it had never been touched by a broom, and it was littered with squalid garments and old worn footgear. For the rest, the room had a fire-place, on account of which it was rented for forty francs a year, and this open hearth housed a great variety of objects – a cooking-stove, a stew-pan, some sticks of firewood, rags hanging on nails, a bird-cage, ashes and even a small fire, of which the embers were sullenly smoking.

The generally repellent appearance of the garret was enhanced by the fact that it was large, a big, irregularly-shaped place of projections and recesses, nooks and crannies, the ups and downs of its attic roof, dark corners which looked as though they must harbour spiders big as a man's fist, cockroaches long as his foot, perhaps even human monstrosities.

The two beds were on either side of the fireplace, one by the door and the other by the window, both facing Marius. From his point of observation he could see, hanging on the wall in a black wooden frame, a coloured engraving at the foot of which, in large letters, were the words, THE DREAM. It depicted a sleeping woman with a sleeping child on her lap. Above them hovered an eagle in a cloud carrying a crown in its beak, and the woman was thrusting the crown away from the child's head, without, however, awakening. In the background was the figure of Napoleon enveloped in radiance and leaning against a pillar inscribed as follows:

MARINGO

AUSTERLITS

IENA

Below this picture something that looked like a wooden panel, taller than it was broad, and which appeared to have been wrenched off some building, stood leaning against the wall, presenting its rough, reverse side to the beholder, as though it, too, had some kind of daub painted on its other side and was waiting to be hung.

Seated at the table, on which Marius could see a pen, paper, and ink, was a man of about sixty, small, lean, sallow-faced, and haggard, with an expression of restless, venomous and wary cunning. A most unpleasant rogue. Lavater, the physiognomist, would have seen in him a combination of vulture and prosecuting attorney, one complementing the other, the man of legal trickery making the bird of prey ignoble, and the bird making the trickster repellent. He had a long, grey beard. He was clad above the waist in a woman's chemise, exposing a shaggy chest and arms covered with grey hair, and below the waist in muddied trousers and a pair of top-boots from which his toes protruded.

He was smoking a pipe (there might be no food in the place, but there was still tobacco!) and busily writing – doubtless a letter similar to those Marius had already seen. A battered volume lying on the table proclaimed by its russet binding that it was one of a standard edition of popular fiction issued for the use of public libraries. The title, printed in large capital letters, was: *God, the King, Honour and the Ladies* by Ducray-Dumeuil, 1814.

The man was talking while he wrote.

'Equality! There's no such blooming thing even when you're dead. You've only got to go to Père-Lachaise. The fine folk, anyone who can pay, they're up at the top, round the acacia alley, where it is paved. They can be driven there in hearses. But the small fry, the paupers, they're down at the bottom where there's no paving, no drains, nothing but mud. They stick 'em in there so they'll rot the quicker. If you want to visit their graves you walk in mud up to the knees.' He broke off to pound with his fist on the table, and said savagely: 'I'd like to eat the whole bloody lot!'

A burly woman who might have been aged forty or a hundred was squatting on bare heels by the fireplace. She, too, was clad only in chemise and a tattered skirt, patched with odd fragments of material and half-hidden beneath a coarse apron. Although she was in a crouching position she was evidently a very tall woman, a giant-ess by comparison with her husband. She had dingy russet hair, turning grey, which she constantly pushed back with a large, greasy stubby-fingered hand. A book lay open on the floor beside her, similar in format to the one on the table and probably another volume of the same romance.

On one of the truckle-beds a skinny, pale-faced child, almost naked, was seated with her legs dangling, seeming not to see or hear anything, or even to be alive. This was presumably the younger sister of the one who had called on Marius. At first sight she appeared to be no more than eleven or twelve, but a second glance showed that she was at least fifteen. It must be she who had said, 'I didn't half run for it!'

She was one of those children who, being at first retarded, sud-denly and rapidly mature, sickly human plants nurtured in poverty who have known neither childhood nor adolescence. At fifteen they look twelve years old, and at sixteen they look twenty, little girls one day and women the next, as though they were racing through life to be done with it the sooner. For the present, she still looked like a child.

There was nothing in the room to indicate that any work was ever done there, no tool or implement of any trade except a few dubious-looking metal objects lying in one corner. It was pervaded with the apathy that succeeds despair and precedes the death-agony, and Marius, looking down into it, found it more dreadful to contemplate than the grave itself, for it still harboured life and the living spirit. The garret and the cellar, those ditches sheltering the poorest dregs of humanity, are not the tomb but its antecham-ber; they are a vestibule where Death, closing in upon them, seems to parade his choicest terrors, as the rich display their greatest splendours at the entrance to their palaces.

The man had fallen silent, the woman had not spoken and the girl seemed not to be breathing. There was silence, broken only by the scratching of the pen, until the man exclaimed, without ceasing to write:

'Filth, filth, all is filth!'

This variation of the 'All is vanity' of the preacher drew a sigh from the woman.

'There, there, my dear, you mustn't get upset. It's beneath you to be writing to all these people.'

Bodies huddle close together in poverty as they do in cold, but hearts grow distant. To all appearances this woman must once have bestowed on the man all the love of which she was capable; but it was probable that the bickerings of daily life in the loathsome circumstances to which they were reduced had extinguished her love, leaving only its ashes. Nevertheless, as often happens, the forms of affection remained. She still addressed him as 'dear' and 'love', but they were words spoken with the lips, not from the heart.

He went on with his writing.

VII
Strategy and tactics

Marius, with a heavy heart, was about to get down from his post of observation when a sound caused him to stay where he was. The door opened abruptly and the elder girl came in.

She was wearing a pair of large men's shoes encrusted with the mud that had splashed over her ankles, and a tattered cloak which she had not worn when she visited Marius but had perhaps deliberately discarded, the better to win his compassion. Slamming the door behind her she paused to get her breath, for she had evidently been running, and then cried in triumph:

'He's coming!'

Her father and mother looked up at her, but the younger girl did not move.

'Who's coming?' the father asked.

'The old gent, the philanthropist from the Église Saint-Jacques.'

'He's really coming?'

'He's following me.'

'You're sure?'

'Of course I'm sure. He's coming in a fiacre.'

'A fiacre! Good God, he must be a Rothschild!'

The man had risen to his feet.

'But how can you be sure? If he's coming in a fiacre, how did you manage to get here ahead of him? Did he get the address right? Did you tell him it's the last door on the right at the end of the corridor? Let's hope he doesn't make any mistake. You found him in the church, did you? Did he read my letter? What did he say?'

'The way you go on!' said the girl. 'Well, look. I found him in

644

his usual place in the church, and I made him a bob and gave him your letter, and he read it and said, "Where do you live, child?" So I said, "I'll take you there, Monsieur," but he said no, his daughter had some shopping to do, if I'd give him the address he'd hire a cab and be here the same time as me. So I told him the address and he looked surprised. He sort of hesitated, but then he said, "Well, I'll come anyway." I saw him and his daughter leave the church and get into a fiacre, and I *did* tell him about it being the door at the end of the corridor.'

'That doesn't prove he's coming.'

'But I've just seen the fiacre in the Rue du Petit-Banquier. That's when I started to run.'

'How do you know it was the same fiacre?'

'Because I remembered the number.'

'What number?'

'440.'

'Good. You're a bright child.'

The girl gazed boldly at her father and looking down at her foot-gear said:

'Bright I may be, but I'm blessed if I'll wear these foul shoes again, they're unhealthy as well as filthy, and I don't know anything nastier than soles that flap and make a squelching noise with every step you take. I'd sooner go barefoot.'

'I don't blame you, my dear,' her father said with a gentleness of tone that was in marked contrast to her own sharpness. 'But they wouldn't let you inside a church. The poor have to have shoes. You can't visit God barefoot,' he added in a bitter aside, and then reverted to the main subject. 'But you're absolutely sure he's coming?'

'He's on my heels,' she said.

The man drew himself to his full height while a sort of radiance spread over his face.

'Wife,' he said, 'do you hear? The philanthropist is coming. Put out the fire!'

She stared at him bemusedly without moving. Darting with the nimbleness of an acrobat, he seized a broken jug standing on the mantelshelf and poured water on the embers. Then he said to the older girl:

'Strip that chair!'

She, too, failed to understand. Seizing the chair, he stripped it of its seat by thrusting a foot through the straw.

'Is it cold out?' he asked.

'Bitterly cold. It's snowing.'

He turned to the younger girl, seated on the bed by the window, and bellowed at her:

'Move, you idle slut. Can't you ever do anything? Get down to the end of the bed and smash a window-pane.'

She moved to the end of the bed and huddled there, shivering.

'Smash a window-pane?'

'You heard what I said.'

She stood up on the bed. By standing on tip-toe she could just reach the dormer window. In terrified obedience she punched it with her fist, and the pane broke and fell with a clatter to the floor.

'Good.' The man stood intently surveying the room like a general studying the field of a forthcoming battle. The woman, who had so far not uttered a word, now stood up and said in low slurred accents, as though she had difficulty in speaking:

'My dear, what is all this for?'

'Get into bed,' he answered.

The peremptory tone admitted of no dispute. She flung herself heavily on their bed. At that moment a sob was heard.

'Now what's the matter?' the man demanded.

The younger girl, without emerging from the darkness of the corner where she was now crouched, held up a bleeding arm. She had taken refuge by her mother's bed and was crying. It was the mother's turn to start upright.

'There – you see! All this silliness! She's cut herself breaking the window-pane.'

'Good. I thought she would.'

'What do you mean – good?'

'Shut up,' said the man. 'I've abolished the liberty of the press.' Tearing a strip off the woman's chemise he was wearing, he rapidly bandaged the child's wrist. 'Better and better,' he said. 'Now we've got a torn shirt as well.'

An icy breeze was blowing in, bringing with it a mist which spread through the room like cotton-wool unravelled by invisible fingers. Through the broken pane they could see the snow falling. The intense cold presaged by the Candlemas sunset was now upon them. Gazing about him to make sure that nothing had been overlooked, the man picked up a worn shovel and scattered dry ash over the wetted embers to hide them. Then, standing with his back to the fireplace, he announced:

'Now we're ready for the philanthropist.'

VIII
Light and squalor

The older girl reached out a hand to her father.

'Feel how cold I am,' she said.

'Rubbish,' he answered. 'I'm much colder than you.'

The woman burst out:

'Whatever it is, you're always worse off than anybody else!'

'Hold your tongue,' he said, and the look he gave her reduced her to silence.

A lull ensued. The older girl casually scraped mud off the hem of her cloak while the younger one continued to sob. Her mother had taken her head in her hands and was kissing her while she said in a low voice:

'It's nothing, darling. Don't cry. You'll make your father cross.'

'Not a bit of it,' the father said. 'Nothing of the kind. Cry as much as you like. Go on – cry!' He turned to his elder daughter. 'It's all very fine,' he said, 'but he still hasn't arrived. Suppose he doesn't come? I'll have put out the fire, knocked the bottom out of a chair, ripped up a chemise, and smashed a window all for nothing.'

'Besides hurting your child,' the mother said.

'This place is as cold as an ice-house. Suppose he doesn't come after all! He certainly doesn't mind keeping us waiting. He's probably thinking, "Let 'em wait – that's all they're fit for." Oh, God, how I hate them! I'd like to strangle the lot of 'em, the rich, the so-called charitable rich, living in clover and going to Mass, and dishing out sops and pious sentiments. They think they're our lords and masters and they come and patronize us and bring us their cast-off clothes and a few scraps to eat. Bastards! That isn't what I want. Money's what I want, and money's what they never give us. They say we'll just spend it on drink, that we're all sots and loafers. And what about them? Where did they spring from, for God's sake? Thieves, that's what they were, otherwise they'd never have got rich. I'd like to take the whole blasted works and stand it on its head. Perhaps everything would get smashed up, but at least it would mean that everybody would be in the same boat and we'd be that much to the good ... But what's he doing, this philanthropist of yours? Is he coming? Perhaps the old imbecile has forgotten the address. I don't mind betting –'

At this moment there was a light tap on the door. The man dashed to open it, bowing almost to the ground as he did so.

'Please come in, my dear sir! My noble benefactor, please enter, with your charming young lady.'

An elderly man and a young girl appeared in the doorway; and Marius, still at his peep-hole, was seized with a wonderment that it is beyond the power of words to describe.

It was She.

She! Everyone who has ever loved will feel the force of that small word. In the luminous mist that suddenly clouded his vision Marius could scarcely distinguish her features – the eyes, forehead, and mouth, the sweet face that had lighted his life for six months and then vanished, plunging him in darkness. And now the vision had reappeared – in this setting of unspeakable squalor!

He was trembling, his heart beating so wildly that his sight was troubled and he felt himself to be on the verge of tears. To be seeing her again after having searched for so long! It was as though he had lost his soul and now found it restored to him.

She was unchanged except that she seemed a little pale. Her face was enclosed in a hood of purple velvet, and she was wearing a black satin cloak and a long skirt beneath which a neat anklebone was visible. Her companion, as usual, was Monsieur Leblanc. On entering the room she had deposited a large parcel on the table.

The Jondrette woman, huddled on the bed behind the door, was glowering at the hood and the cloak and that delightful, happy face.

IX

Jondrette is near to weeping

The garret was so dark that to anyone coming from outside it was like entering a cavern. The newcomers therefore moved uncertainly, scarcely able to distinguish the objects around them, whereas they themselves were entirely visible to the denizens of the cavern, whose eyes were accustomed to the half-light. Monsieur Leblanc, with his kind, melancholy gaze turned to Jondrette, said:

'Monsieur, you will find a few things in the parcel – woollen stockings and blankets and suchlike.'

'Most noble sir, you overwhelm me,' said Jondrette, again bowing to the ground. But while the visitors were gazing about them, examining their lamentable surroundings, he muttered in a rapid aside to his elder daughter: 'What did I tell you? A bundle of clothes, nothing about money. They're all the same. Incidentally, the letter you gave the old fool – how was it signed?'

'Fabantou.'

'Ah, the dramatic artist.'

He had asked only just in time, for at this moment Monsieur Leblanc turned back to him and said uncertainly:

'I see that you are greatly to be pitied, Monsieur –' and he paused.

'Fabantou,' said Jondrette promptly.

'Ah, yes, Monsieur Fabantou.'

'An actor, Monsieur, who has had some success in his time.' And Jondrette, evidently considering that the moment had come to assert himself, proceeded in a voice that mingled the stridency of a fairground busker with the abjectness of a street-corner beggar. 'A former pupil of Talma, Monsieur, the great Talma himself! Fortune smiled upon me once, but now, alas, I am overwhelmed with misfortune. We are without food, Monsieur, and without heating. No warmth for my unhappy children. Our only chair without a seat. A broken window – in this weather! And my wife ill in bed.'

'Poor woman,' said Monsieur Leblanc.

'And our younger daughter injured,' said Jondrette.

The child, distracted by the newcomers, was so absorbed in contemplating the young lady that her sobs had ceased.

'Bawl, can't you?' muttered Jondrette under his breath, and, operating with the dexterity of a pickpocket, he gave her wrist a smart pinch. It drew a loud yell from her, and the lovely girl whom Marius had christened Ursula started forward.

'Oh, the poor child!' she exclaimed.

'You can see for yourself, dear young lady,' said Jondrette. 'Her wrist is bleeding. She had an accident in the machine-shop where she works at six sous an hour. They may have to cut off her arm.'

'Is that really so?' asked the old gentleman in consternation, and the daughter, taking it seriously, yelled louder than ever.

'Alas, I fear so,' her father said.

For some moments Jondrette had been gazing intently at the 'philanthropist', seeming to study his face while he talked, as though he were trying to remember something. Taking advantage of the fact that the visitors were now questioning the child about her injury, he darted to the side of his wife, who was huddled apathetically on her bed, and said in a whisper:

'Take a good look at this man.'

He then returned to Monsieur Leblanc and resumed his lament.

'You see how it is, Monsieur. The only rag of clothing I possess is this torn chemise belonging to my wife – in the middle of winter! I can't go out for lack of clothes. If I had a coat I'd go and see Mademoiselle Mars, who is an old and dear friend. Is she still living in the Rue de la Tour-des-Dames? We played together in the provinces, Monsieur. I shared in her triumphs. Célimène would come to my assistance, Monsieur! Elmira would lend Belisarius a helping hand! But I've nothing to wear and not a sou in the house. My wife sick, my child dangerously injured and not a sou. My wife has fits of giddiness. It's her time of life, and the nervous system has something to do with it. She needs treatment and so does my daughter, but who's to pay the doctor and the apothecary? I'd go on my knees for a penny-piece! And do you know, my sweet young lady, and you, my generous protector, who breathe the air of virtue and kindness and lend distinction to the church where my daughter sees you every day when she is at her devotions . . . Because I have taught my children religion, Monsieur. I have never wanted them to go on the stage. They have been strictly brought up, and no backsliding! I make no bones about that. The times I've lectured them on honour and virtue and morality. You have only to ask them. They know how to behave. They have a father to reckon with. They are not to be numbered among the unfortunates who because they have no family end by becoming public property – Mamselle Nobody who ends up Madame Anybody. There's none of that in the Fabantou family. They have been taught virtue and honesty and proper conduct and faith in God! . . . And do you know, most worthy sir, what is going to happen to us tomorrow? Tomorrow, the fourth of February, is the terrible day, the last day our landlord will allow us. If by this evening I have not paid in full we shall all be turned out – my sick wife and I, our elder daughter and our injured child – turned out into the street without shelter from the snow and rain! That is the position, Monsieur. I owe four quarters' rent, a whole year, making sixty francs!'

This was a blatant lie. The four quarters would have come to only forty francs, and he could not owe as many as four, since Marius, less than six months previously, had paid the two that were then outstanding. MonsieurLeblanc got a five-franc piece out of his pocket and laid it on the table; and Jondrette found a moment to whisper in his daughter's ear:

'See that? The bastard! What the devil's the good of five francs? It won't even pay for the chair and window-pane.'

Monsieur Leblanc meanwhile was taking off the brown overcoat he wore over his blue tail-coat. He laid it across the back of the chair and said:

'Five francs is all I have left on me at the moment, Monsieur Fabantou. But I'll take my daughter home and come back this evening. I think you said you need the money by this evening.'

Jondrette's face was suddenly and wonderfully illumined. He replied eagerly:

'Quite right, most worthy sir. I have to be at my landlord's by eight o'clock.'

'Then I'll come at six and I'll bring you the sixty francs.'

'My noble benefactor!' cried Jondrette. And he added in an aside to his wife: 'Are you looking at him?'

Taking his daughter's arm, Monsieur Leblanc turned towards the door.

'Until this evening, then.'

'Six o'clock,' said Jondrette.

'Six o'clock precisely.'

But as they were in the act of leaving the elder Jondrette girl exclaimed:

'Monsieur, you're forgetting your overcoat.'

Jondrette darted a blistering look at her, accompanied by a massive shrug of the shoulders. Monsieur Leblanc said smiling:

'I hadn't forgotten it. I'm leaving it here.'

'My protector!' cried Jondrette. 'My princely benefactor! I am moved to tears. Allow me to accompany you to your fiacre.'

'In that case you had better put the coat on,' said Monsieur Leblanc. 'It is really very cold.'

Jondrette required no further urging. He promptly wrapped himself in the coat. The visitors left the room together, with Jondrette leading the way.

X

The price of a public conveyance

Marius had missed nothing of the foregoing scene, and yet in a sense he had seen nothing. His eyes had been intent upon the girl, his heart had as it were enfolded her from the moment she entered the room; and throughout the time that she was there he had known the state of ecstasy that dulls everyday perception, concentrating his whole being upon a single matter. It was not a girl that he saw, but a glow of light enclosed in a satin cape and a fur hood. If some heavenly body had appeared in the room he could have been no more amazed.

He had watched her as she undid the parcel of clothes and blankets, following her every movement and seeking to hear her words as she gently questioned the ailing mother and bent compassionately over the injured child. He already knew her face and figure, her eyes and forehead and grace of movement, but he could not be quite sure that he had heard her voice, although he thought that once in the Luxembourg he had heard her speak a few words. He would have given years of his life to be able to hear everything she said, to be able to carry away some of that music in his heart, but nearly all was lost in the flourishings and trumpetings of Jondrette. He could only devour her with his eyes, scarcely able to believe that so exquisite a creature could be present amid the unspeakable inmates of that foul place, like a humming-bird in a nest of toads.

His only thought when she had departed was to go after her, to follow on her footsteps until at least he had found out where she lived and ran no risk of losing her again after this miraculous rediscovery. Jumping down from the chest of drawers, he snatched up his hat; but then on the verge of opening his door, he hesitated. The corridor was a long one, the stairs steep and narrow, and Jondrette was an indefatigable talker. Monsieur Leblanc would probably not yet have got back to his fiacre. If he should look round and see Marius in that house he might well take fright again, and again find the means of eluding him. What should he do? Should he wait a little? If he did so he might be too late to see where the fiacre went.

He hovered in perplexity, and at length, deciding that he must run the risk of being seen, he left his room.

The corridor was empty and so were the stairs. Hurrying down, he arrived on the boulevard just in time to see a fiacre turn the corner of the Rue du Petit-Banquier, heading back into Paris. He ran after it, and at the corner, saw it rapidly descending the Rue Mouffetard. It was already a long way ahead, and there seemed to be no way of overtaking it. Certainly he could not do so on foot, and in any case a person running madly after them would be bound to attract the notice of the occupants, and he would be recognized. But at this moment, by a rare and wonderful chance, he saw an empty hackney-cab going along the boulevard. Here was the solution of his problem, a means of following the fiacre swiftly and without the risk of being seen. Signalling to the driver, he called:

'One hour!'

Marius was without a necktie; he was wearing his shabby working jacket, from which several buttons were missing, and his shirt was torn. The cab stopped, but the driver, looking him over, reached out a hand with a grin, rubbing his thumb against his index-finger.

'Cash in advance,' he said.

Marius then remembered that he had only sixteen sous on him.

'How much?'

'Forty sous.'

'I'll pay you when you've brought me back.'

The cabby's only reply was to whistle derisively and whip up his horse.

Marius gazed miserably after him. For lack of twenty-four sous he was losing love and the hope of happiness, to be plunged again in darkness. After seeing a gleam of light he was again blind. He thought bitterly and with the utmost regret, be it said, of the five francs he had given that wretched girl. They might have saved him, rescued him from desolation, aimlessness, and solitude; instead of which, the bright thread of his destiny had again been broken and its darkest strands renewed. He went back to the tenement in despair.

He might have reflected that Monsieur Leblanc had promised to return that evening, and that this time he might be more successful in his efforts to track him down; but such was his state of dejection that the thought scarcely occurred to him.

As he was about to enter the house he saw Jondrette, enveloped in the 'philanthropist's' overcoat, standing beside the long, blank wall of the Rue de la Barrière des Gobelins in conversation with one of those sinister individuals known as 'gateway prowlers'; highly suspect figures, cryptic in their speech, who have a look of evil about them and who generally sleep by day, leading one to suppose that they do their work at night. The two men, standing motionless with their heads together under whirling snowflakes, formed a group which could not have failed to interest any guardian of the law, but which Marius scarcely noticed.

However, despite his melancholy preoccupations, the thought crossed his mind that the man Jondrette was talking to resembled a certain Panchaud, alias Printanier, alias Bigrenaille, who had been pointed out to him by Courfeyrac and was regarded in the quarter as a dangerous night-bird. His name has already appeared in our pages. He was destined later, from having figured in a number of criminal trials, to acquire considerable celebrity, although at this time he was still no more than an inconspicuous rogue. Today he is a folk-hero of the underworld, talked of in whispers in the night-haunts of criminals and in the exercise-yard at the prison of La Force. Indeed in this prison, from which in 1843 thirty prisoners achieved the unheard-of feat of escaping in broad daylight, doing so by way of the latrine sewer, the name of PANCHAUD may still be read, audaciously carved on a wall above the latrines during one of his previous attempts to escape. In 1832 the police already had their eye on him, but he had not yet made strides in his career.

XI

An offer of assistance

Marius went slowly up the tenement stairs; but as he walked along the corridor he saw that he was being followed by the elder Jondrette girl. The sight of her was now detestable to him, since she had had his five francs. There was no point in asking for them back; the fiacre had long since vanished from sight, and in any case she would not have returned them. Nor was there any point in asking her for the address of their visitors. Clearly she did not know this, since the letter signed Fabantou had been addressed simply to the gentleman at the Church of Saint-Jacques-du-Haut-Pas. He went into his garret, pushing the door to behind him.

But the door did not shut, and turning, he saw that a hand was holding it ajar.

'What is it?' he demanded.

It was the Jondrette girl. 'So it's you again,' said Marius almost harshly. 'What do you want now?'

She did not reply but stood thoughtfully regarding him, seeming to have lost all her earlier assurance. She had not entered the room, but was still standing in the half-light of the corridor.

'Can't you answer?' said Marius. 'What do you want of me?'

She looked at him with mournful eyes, in which however a faint light gleamed.

'Monsieur Marius,' she said, 'you seem upset. What is the matter?'

'With me?' asked Marius.

'Yes.'

'There's nothing the matter with me.'

'But there is.'

'Please leave me alone.' Marius tried again to shut the door, but she still held it open.

'You're making a mistake,' she said. 'You aren't rich, but you were generous this morning. Be kind now. You gave me money for food, now tell me what your trouble is. I can see you're unhappy about something, and I don't want you to be unhappy. Is there nothing I can do for you? You have only to say. I'm not asking for secrets, you have no need to tell me everything, but perhaps I can be useful. I help my father, so perhaps I can help you too. When it comes to delivering letters, knocking at doors, finding out an address or following someone, well, that's my job. You can tell me what you want, and perhaps there's someone I can talk to. Sometimes you go and talk to people and you find things out and everything's put right. You have only to say.'

He drew closer to her, a drowning man clutching at a straw.

'Well, listen, my dear –'

She interrupted him, her eyes suddenly glowing.

'Yes, talk to me nicely! That's much better.'

'Well, you brought that gentleman here, with his daughter. Do you know their address?'

'No.'

'Can you find out for me?'

The light had vanished from her face as swiftly as it had come.

'Is that what you want?'

'Yes.'

'Do you know them?'

'No.'

'In other words,' she said sharply, and with a hint of bitterness, 'you don't know *her*, and you want to?'

'Can you do it?' asked Marius.

'Get you the address of the beautiful young lady?'

The note of sarcasm irritated Marius.

'It doesn't matter which,' he said impatiently. 'The address of father and daughter. *Their* address.'

She looked hard at him.

'What will you give me?'

'Anything you want.'

'Anything?'

'Yes.'

'Then I'll get it.'

And abruptly she withdrew, closing the door behind her.

Marius dropped on to a chair and leaned forward with both elbows on his bed and his head in his hands, rendered almost giddy by the thought of all that had happened in so brief a time – the appearance of his divinity and her disappearance, and the undertaking this girl had just given him, which came as a ray of hope in his despair. But suddenly he started up.

The harsh voice of Jondrette was loudly raised next door, speaking words that instantly intrigued him.

'I tell you I'm sure. I recognized him.'

To whom else could he be referring, if not to Monsieur Leblanc? Was the mystery surrounding father and daughter to be resolved in this rough, unpredictable fashion? Without another thought Marius leapt rather than climbed on to the chest of drawers and again stood peering through his spy-hole into the Jondrettes' lair.

XII

Use made of a five-franc piece

Nothing had changed except that the woman and the two girls had undone the parcel and were now wearing stockings and vests. Two new blankets lay on the beds.

Jondrette, who had evidently just come in, was still gasping with the chill of the outside air. The girls were seated on the floor by the fireplace, the older binding up the younger one's hand. The woman was huddled on one of the beds staring in astonishment while her husband, with an extraordinary light in his eyes, strode up and down the room. She seemed dumbfounded by what he had been saying. She asked hesitantly:

'Really? Are you sure?'

'Of course I'm sure. It's eight years, but I recognized him all right. I spotted him at once. Do you mean to say you didn't?'

'No.'

'But I told you to have a good look at him – the general build of the man, and the face – he's scarcely aged in eight years, there are people who never seem to look any older, I don't know how they manage it – and then, the sound of his voice. He's better dressed, that's all. But, by God, I've got him now!' ... He broke off to address the two girls. 'Clear out, you two ... I'm surprised you didn't see it at once.'

The girls got submissively to their feet, and the mother murmured:

'With her cut hand?'

'The fresh air will do her good,' said Jondrette. 'Off you go.'

He was clearly not a man to be argued with. The girls obeyed. But as they reached the door Jondrette took the elder by the arm and said with particular emphasis:

'You're to be back here at exactly five o'clock. Both of you. I'm going to need you.'

Marius was by now even more keenly interested.

Left alone with his wife, Jondrette resumed his pacing of the room. He paused for a moment to tuck the chemise into his trouser-waist, and then, turning abruptly and confronting her with folded arms, he said:

'And I'll tell you another thing. That girl ...'

'The girl,' said his wife. 'Well, what of her?'

There could no longer be any doubt about whom they were talking. Marius was now in a state of feverish expectation, his whole being concentrated in his ears. But Jondrette had bent over the woman and was talking in a whisper. Straightening up, he concluded:

'That's who she is.'

'*Her?*' said the woman.

'Yes, her.'

No words can convey the tone of the woman's voice, in which stupefaction, hatred, and outrage were mingled with a monstrous ferocity. Her husband's whisper in her ear had had a startling effect on the gross creature lying on the bed: from being merely repulsive she had become hideous.

'Impossible!' she cried. 'Our daughters barefoot and not a dress to their name, and that one in satin and fur and ankle boots – two hundred francs' worth on her back and looking like a lady! You can't be right. For one thing, that brat was ugly and this one's not bad-looking, not bad at all. It can't be the same.'

'I tell you it is. You'll see.'

His absolute assurance caused the Jondrette woman to stare up at the ceiling, her broad, raddled face distorted. At that moment she appeared to Marius more formidable than her husband – a sow with the look of a tigress.

'That brat! And she comes here dressed like a lady and condescends to my daughters. I'd like to trample on her belly!'

Scrambling off the bed, she stood motionless for a moment, hair dishevelled, nostrils dilated, mouth half open while she thrust her clenched fists out behind her. Then she sank back on the bed. Her husband, paying no attention to this display, was again pacing the room. But after a brief silence he turned and faced her in his previous posture, with his arms folded.

'Do you want me to tell you something else?'

'What?'

He said in a low, tense voice:

'This is going to make our fortune.'

The woman stared at him as though wondering if he had taken leave of his senses.

'I've been a down-and-out long enough,' he went on, 'one of the starve-if-you-want-food-or-freeze-if-you-want-a-fire brigade. I'm tired of being one of the underdogs, a cur running with the pack. It doesn't amuse me any more, it isn't funny, I'm sick of God-almighty's jokes. I want to be able to eat my fill and drink my fill, guzzle to my heart's content and sleep it off, and never a stroke of work. I reckon it's my turn, by God! Before I die I want to know what it feels like to live like a millionaire.' He took another turn round the room and added: 'Me and certain others.'

'What does that mean?' she asked.

He nodded and winked and said in the voice of a street-hawker crying his wares:

'What does it mean? I'll tell you. It means –'

'Hush!' said the woman. 'Not so loud, if this is something other people aren't supposed to hear.'

'What other people? Him next door? I saw him go out a little while ago. Anyway, d'you think he'd be listening, Johnnie-head-in-air? I tell you, I saw him go out.'

He lowered his voice, but not enough to prevent Marius from hearing what he said. The fact that he missed nothing of what followed was in part due to the snowfall, which deadened the sound of vehicles passing along the boulevard.

'Listen,' Jondrette went on. 'I've got him, the rich philanthropist. It's in the bag. It's all arranged. I've been talking to people. He's coming at six, bringing the sixty francs. You heard the yarn I spun him, a year's rent and the landlord, when it isn't even quarter-day. He swallowed it, so he'll be here at six, when the fine fellow next door goes off to dine and old mother Burgon's out on a cleaning job. There won't be a soul in the place. Him next door doesn't ever get back before eleven. The girls will keep watch, you'll help us, and he'll cough up.'

'But supposing he doesn't?'

Jondrette made a gesture. 'We'll know what to do about it.'

For the first time Marius heard him laugh, a cold, soft laugh that made him shudder. Jondrette went to a cupboard and got out an old cap which he put on his head after brushing it with his sleeve.

'I've got to go out again. There are some other men I've got to see, real good 'uns. You'll see. It's a great game. I won't be long. You stay and keep house.' He stood in thought for a moment, with his hands in his trousers pockets, and then exclaimed: 'You know, it's a bit of luck he didn't recognize me. If he had he wouldn't be coming here again, not likely! It's the beard that saved me – my flowing, romantic beard!' He laughed once more and went over to the window. It was still snowing. 'Filthy weather,' he muttered, and drew the overcoat about him. 'It's too big for me, but no matter. It's a devilish good thing the old rascal left it or I shouldn't have been able to go out at all, and we'd have missed the chance. It's wonderful the way things work out.'

Pulling the cap down over his eyes, he left the room; but a moment later the door opened again and his crafty, savage face appeared round it.

'Something I meant to tell you. You're to have a charcoal fire going.'

He tossed his wife the five-franc piece the visitor had given him.

'A charcoal fire?' she repeated.

'That's right.'

'How much charcoal?'

'A good two bushels.'

'That'll cost thirty sous. I'll get something for supper with the rest.'

'Not on your life!'

'Why not?'

'I don't want you spending any more of the money. There's something I'll have to buy.'

'What's that?'

'Something . . . Is there an ironmonger's round here?'

'In the Rue Mouffetard.'

'Ah, yes, I know the place.'

'But how much is this thing going to cost?'

'Two or three francs.'

'That doesn't leave much for supper.'

'Then we must do without. We've something more important to think about.'

'Very well, love.'

The door closed again, and this time Marius heard Jondrette's footsteps go rapidly along the corridor and down the stairs.

The Saint-Médard clock struck one.

XIII

Marius acts

Despite his addiction to daydreaming Marius, as we know, was capable of firm and decided action. His solitary way of life, in developing his capacity for sympathy and compassion, had perhaps also made him more easy-going; but it had in no way diminished his capacity for outrage. He combined the benevolence of a Brahmin with the sternness of a judge: he might pity a toad, but he would set his foot on a viper. And what he had been peering into was a viper's nest, a den of monsters.

'These wretches must be dealt with,' he told himself.

None of the riddles that perplexed him had been answered; if anything they had become more mystifying. He had learnt nothing more about the girl in the Luxembourg and the gentleman whom he called Monsieur Leblanc except that Jondrette knew them. Only one thing was clear from the conversation he had overheard, and this was that some kind of trap was being prepared, the nature of which he did not know but which represented a serious threat to both of them, the girl in all likelihood and her father for certain. He had to thwart Jondrette's stratagems and destroy this spider's web.

He continued for a moment to watch the Jondrette woman. She had fetched an old iron brazier from a corner of the room and was doing something to it. He got down from the chest of drawers, moving with the utmost caution. Amid his dread of what was being prepared, and the horror with which the Jondrettes inspired him, was a glow of happiness at the thought that he might be able to serve his beloved.

But how? He could not warn the prospective victims since he did not know where to find them. They had appeared for a brief moment and then vanished into the huge labyrinth of Paris. He might mount guard outside the house at six o'clock that evening and warn Monsieur Leblanc when he arrived. But Jondrette and his friends would be likely to see him; the street would be deserted at that hour and they would be too many for him, able to carry him off or drive him away, leaving Monsieur Leblanc none the wiser.

One o'clock had struck. Marius had five hours in which to act. There was only one thing to be done. Changing into his good suit, he wrapped a scarf round his neck, put on his hat and stole out of the house as quietly as though he were walking barefoot on grass.

He turned out of the boulevard into the Rue du Petit-Banquier. A section of the street was flanked by a low wall, so low that in places he could have stepped over it, beyond which lay a patch of wasteland. Marius was passing by this wall, walking slowly in his preoccupation, his footsteps deadened by the snow, when he heard the sound of voices somewhere near him. He looked round, but the street was empty. It was broad daylight, but he could distinctly hear voices. It occurred to him to look over the wall.

Two men were seated in the snow with their backs to the wall, talking in undertones. Both were unknown to him. One was a bearded man in a smock and the other a long-haired man in tattered garments. The bearded man wore a Greek cap, the other was bare-headed and snowflakes glistened in his hair. By leaning over the wall above them Marius could hear what they were saying.

The long-haired man nudged the other in the ribs and said:
'With Patron-Minette it can't fail.'

'Think so?' said the bearded man.

'Sure as I'm sitting here. A carve-up of five hundred jimmys each, and the worst that can happen is a stretch of five or six years, ten at the outside.'

The other scratched his head under the Greek cap and said after reflection:

'Well, that's real money, no getting away from it.'

'I tell you, it can't miss,' said the hairy man. 'We'll have old Mister Whatsit properly sewn up.'

Then they went on to talk about a melodrama they had seen the night before at the Gaîté theatre, and Marius continued on his way.

It seemed to him that the words he had overheard, spoken by two men so strangely seated in the snow with their backs against a wall, might well have some connection with Jondrette's project. This, surely, must be the business they had been discussing.

Making for the Faubourg Saint-Marceau, he entered the first shop he came to and inquired the address of the nearest police-post. It was Number 14, Rue de Pontoise. He set out for it, and, foreseeing that he would have no dinner, stopped at a bakery on the way and bought a two-sou loaf of bread which he ate as he walked.

He reflected also that Providence must have its due. Had he not given the Jondrette girl his last five francs he would have followed Monsieur Leblanc's fiacre and thus would have known nothing of the plot being hatched by Jondrette, to which the old gentleman would have fallen a victim and probably his daughter as well.

XIV

A pair of punches

Arrived at Number 14, Rue de Pontoise, Marius went up to the first floor and asked to see the Superintendent of Police.

'The superintendent isn't here,' said the desk-clerk. 'There's an inspector sitting in for him. Is it urgent?'

'Yes,' said Marius.

He was shown into the superintendent's office. A tall man in a big greatcoat with a triple cape was standing on the other side of a metal grille with his back to a large stove and his coat-tails raised. He had a broad face, a thin, tight mouth, very bushy grey side-whiskers and keen eyes that seemed not merely to pierce but to explore. Indeed, he appeared little less ferocious and formidable than Jondrette; the hound can at times be as awkward a customer as the wolf.

'What do you want?' he asked with no attempt at civility.

'Are you the Commissaire de Police?'

'He's away. I'm acting for him.'

'This is a highly confidential matter.'

'Well, tell me about it.'

'And very urgent.'

'Then talk fast.'

His cool terseness was at once disconcerting and reassuring; he inspired both awe and confidence. Marius accordingly told his story in full, beginning with the statement that he was Marius Pontmercy, lawyer. A gentleman whom he knew only by sight was to be lured that evening into a trap. He had heard about the business because the man planning it occupied the room next to his own in the house where he lived. The villain in question was a man named Jondrette, but he would have accomplices, probably gateway prowlers, among them a certain Panchaud, also known as Printanier and as Bigrenaille. Jondrette's wife and two daughters were also involved. He, Marius, had no means of warning the victim because he did not even know his name. The trap was to be sprung at six o'clock that evening in a house in the most deserted part of the Boulevard de l'Hôpital, No. 50–52.

The mention of this number caused the inspector to look up sharply.

'Would it be the room at the end of the corridor?'

'Yes,' said Marius in surprise. 'Do you know the house?'

The inspector was silent for a moment, staring thoughtfully at the floor. 'It seems I do,' he said. And he went on, mumbling in his cravat and talking less to Marius than to himself. 'Looks like Patron-Minette's mixed up in it.'

The words struck Marius.

'Patron-Minette! I heard that name only a little while ago.'

He went on to repeat the conversation he had overheard in the Rue du Petit-Banquier. The inspector grunted.

'The hairy one was probably Brujon, and the one with the beard would be Demi-Liard, also known as Deux-Milliards. As for the injured party, I fancy . . . Damn, I've singed my coat. They always make these infernal stoves too hot . . . Number 50–52 – used to belong to Gorbeau.' He looked up at Marius. 'You only saw those two, the man with a beard and the hairy one?'

'And Panchaud, in the street, talking to Jondrette.'

'You haven't seen anything of a dressed-up youth, a sort of backstreet fop?'

'No.'

'Or a great hulk of a man who looks like the elephant in the Jardin des Plantes?'

'No.'

'Or a little crafty weasel of a man, who looks as though he might be an ex-convict?'

'No.'

'No, well – as for the fourth, it's not surprising you haven't seen him. Nobody ever does, not even his associates.'

'But who are all these people?' asked Marius.

'Besides,' said the inspector, ignoring the question, 'they don't go about in daylight.'

He was silent again, and then muttered:

'I know the place all right, number 50–52. Nowhere in it to hide, without those beauties spotting us, and then they'd call the show off. They're shy, you see; don't like an audience. We can't have that. I want to hear 'em sing and make 'em dance.'

Having concluded this monologue he looked hard at Marius.

'Would you be scared?'

'What of?'

'These men.'

'No more than you,' said Marius coolly. He was beginning to notice that this policeman never addressed him as sir.

The inspector continued to study him, and then said with a sort of sententious gravity:

'You talk like a brave man and an honest one. Courage does not fear crime, and honesty has no need to fear authority.'

Marius cut him short.

'All right. But what are you proposing?'

'The people living in that house have door-keys to let them in at night. I take it you have one?'

'Yes.'

'Have you got it with you?'

'Yes.'

'Then let me have it.'

Marius got out the key and handed it to him, saying as he did so:

'If you'll take my advice you won't go alone.'

The inspector bestowed on him the sort of glance Voltaire might have bestowed on a provincial academic who ventured to lecture him on poetry. Plunging with a single movement his two enormous hands into the capacious pockets of his greatcoat, he brought out two very small pistols of the kind known as *coups de poing*, or, 'punches'.

'Take these,' he said briskly. 'They're both loaded, two balls in each. Go back home and hide in your room so that they think you're out. Keep watch through that hole you spoke of. When they arrive, let them start their business, and when you think it's gone far enough fire a shot. Then I'll take charge. A single shot into the ceiling or anywhere. But not too soon, understand. They've got to start, there's got to be evidence. You're a lawyer. You know what I mean.'

Marius took the pistols and put them in a side-pocket of his jacket.

'They make a bulge like that, they show,' the inspector said. 'Better put them in your waist band.'

Marius did as he was told.

'And now there's no time to be lost. What time is it? Half past two. The party's at seven, you said?'

'Six,' said Marius.

'Well, that still gives me time, but only just. Don't forget what I told you. One pistol-shot.'

'I'll do it,' said Marius and turned to leave the room.

'One other thing,' the inspector said. 'If you should need me before then you'd better come here or send someone. The name's Javert.'

XV

Jondrette does his shopping

Shortly after this, at about three o'clock, Courfeyrac happened to walk along the Rue Mouffetard in company with Bossuet. The snow was falling more heavily than ever, and Bossuet was saying:

'To see all these snowflakes you'd think we were afflicted with a plague of white butterflies.' He broke off at the sight of a figure striding in a rather odd manner up the street in the direction of the barrier. 'Why, there's Marius!'

'So I see,' said Courfeyrac. 'Better not speak to him.'

'Why not?'

'Can't you see he's busy?'

'But what is he doing?'

'From the look of him, he's following someone.'

'It does look like that,' said Bossuet. 'But who?'

'Probably some poppet he's taken a fancy to.'

'I don't see any poppets anywhere,' said Bossuet. 'There isn't a wench in sight.'

Courfeyrac was staring.

'He's following a man!' he exclaimed.

It was a man in a cap, about twenty paces ahead of Marius. Although his back was turned to them they had a glimpse of a grey beard. The man was wearing a new overcoat very much too large for him and a pair of extremely ragged trousers spattered with mud.

Bossuet laughed. 'Who the devil would he be?'

'He must be a poet,' said Courfeyrac. 'Only a poet would go about in a tramp's trousers and a coat fit for a lord.'

'Let's follow the two of them and see where they go.'

'My dear Bossuet, Eagle of Words,' said Courfeyrac, 'what a great fathead you are! To follow a man who's following a man!'

They turned and went the other way.

Marius had seen Jondrette in the Rue Mouffetard and was following to see what he was up to. Jondrette hurried on unsuspecting. He turned out of the Rue Mouffetard, and Marius saw him go into one of the most ramshackle hovels in the Rue Gracieuse. He was there for about a quarter of an hour and then, returning to the Rue Mouffetard, he visited the ironmongery which at that time stood on the corner of the Rue Pierre-Lombard. A few minutes later he came out holding a large cold-chisel with a wooden handle which he proceeded to hide under his new coat. He turned left into the Rue du Petit-Gentilly and made rapidly for the Rue du Petit-Banquier. Marius did not follow him along this street, which was deserted as usual, but kept cautious watch from the corner. In this he was wise, because Jondrette, when he came to the low wall where Marius had heard the two men talking, looked round to make sure he was unobserved and then scrambled over the wall and disappeared.

The patch of wasteland beyond this wall adjoined the back yard

of a former dealer in hired conveyances, a man of unsavoury reputation who had been sold up but still kept a few old vehicles in his
shed.

Marius decided that he had better take advantage of Jondrette's
absence to get back to the tenement. It was growing late, and Ma'am
Bougon, when she went off to her work as a cleaning-woman, was
in the habit of locking the front door behind her. Since he had given
the inspector his key, he must be in before this happened.

Darkness was rapidly falling, and only a single gleam of light in
the black immensity of the heavens reflected the rays of the sun. It
was the moon rising red beyond the low cupola of the Salpêtrière.

Marius made all speed back to No. 50–52, and found the door still
open. He climbed the stairs on tip-toe and, keeping close to the wall,
crept along the corridor to his room. This corridor, it will be remembered, was flanked on either side by attics, all of them at that
moment empty and to let. Ma'am Bougon was in the habit of leaving their doors open. As he passed one of the supposedly empty cells
Marius had an impression of four motionless men's heads silhouetted for an instant against the faint light filtering through
the small window. He made no attempt to see more, not wishing
to be seen himself, and succeeded in reaching his room without
being either seen or heard. And just in time. A moment later he
heard Ma'am Bougon depart and the key turn in the lock of the
front door.

XVI

A snatch of song

Marius sat down on his bed. The time was about half past five – only
half an hour to go. He could hear the blood pounding in his veins
like the ticking of a clock in darkness. He thought of the forces
mustering in the shadows, the march of crime on the one side and
of justice on the other. He was not afraid, but he could not think
without a tremor of what was so soon to happen. As with all persons
plunged suddenly in an unforeseen adventure, the day's events had
for him a dreamlike quality, and he needed to finger the cold metal
of the pistols in his waistband to assure himself that he was not in
the grip of a nightmare.

It had stopped snowing. The moon, growing steadily brighter,
had now risen above the mist, and its rays, mingled with the white

reflection of the fallen snow, flooded his room with a cavernous light. A light was burning in the Jondrettes' lair. Marius could see through the hole in the partition a ruddy glow which looked to him like a blood-red eye. Certainly it did not look like the light of a candle. Otherwise nothing stirred in that room. No one moved or spoke or even breathed. It was locked in an icy silence so profound that, except for the light, one might have thought oneself beside a tomb.

Marius quietly took off his boots and thrust them under his bed. Several minutes passed. Then he heard the creaking of the street door. Heavy footsteps ascended the stairs and passed rapidly along the corridor, and the latch of the door next to his was noisily lifted. Jondrette had returned.

Voices were instantly raised. It seemed that they were all there but had kept quiet in the absence of the master, like wolf-cubs in the absence of the wolf.

'Here I am,' Jondrette said.

'Good evening, daddykins!' giggled the two girls.

'Well?' said his wife.

'Everything's fine,' said Jondrette, 'but my feet are frozen. I see you've got dressed. Good. You've got to look respectable.'

'I'm all ready to go out.'

'You won't forget what I told you? You'll do it right?'

'Don't worry.'

'You see –' began Jondrette, but he did not finish the sentence. Marius heard him drop some heavy object on the table, probably the chisel he had bought. 'Hello! Have you had something to eat?'

'Yes,' said the woman. 'I had three big potatoes and some salt. Seeing we had a fire, I baked them.'

'Good,' said Jondrette. 'Tomorrow I'll take you all out to dinner – roast duck and everything that goes with it. You'll dine like the king himself. Everything's fine.' He added in a lower voice, 'The trap's baited and the cats are waiting.' He then said, lower still: 'Put that in the fire.'

Marius heard the rasping sound of tongs or some other metal instrument being thrust into the charcoal.

'Did you grease the door-hinges so that they don't squeak?' asked Jondrette.

'Yes,' said the woman.

'What's the time?'

'Getting on for six. The half hour has struck at Saint-Médard.'

'Time for the girls to go on watch,' said Jondrette. 'Listen to me, you two.' A sound of whispering followed. Then he raised his voice again. 'Has Ma'am Bougon gone?'

'Yes,' said the woman.

'And you're sure he's not in next door?'

'He hasn't been in all day, and you know this is his dinner-time.'

'You're positive?'

'Quite.'

'All the same,' said Jondrette, 'no harm in having a look. You, girl – take the candle.'

Marius went down on hands and knees and slid silently under the bed. He had scarcely done so when light showed through the cracks in his door.

'He's out,' a voice called, and he recognized it as that of the older girl.

'Have you looked?' Jondrette asked.

'No, but his key's in the door, and that means he's out.'

'Go in all the same.'

The door opened and the girl entered carrying a candle. She looked much as she had done that morning, but even more garish in that light. She moved towards the bed, and Marius had a moment of acute alarm; but there was a mirror suspended on the wall near the bed, and this was what she was making for. She stood on tip-toe studying herself. A sudden clatter of metal against metal came from the next room.

She stood smoothing her hair with one hand while she smiled at herself in the glass and sang in her croaking voice:

> Our love was all too swiftly over,
> Happiness so soon is past.
> For one short week to have a lover!
> But true love should forever last,
> For ever, ever, ever last!

Marius lay trembling under the bed, thinking that she must surely hear the sound of his breathing.

She went over to the window and looked out, talking aloud to herself in the half-crazed way that was characteristic of her.

'How ugly Paris looks in a white shirt!'

She came back to the mirror and posed in front of it, examining herself front and three-quarter face. Her father's voice called:

'What are you doing?'

'I'm looking under the bed and the furniture,' she replied, still arranging her hair. 'There is no one here.'

'Then come back, for God's sake! Don't waste any more time.'

'All right, all right, I'm coming. There's never time for anything in this hole.'

She sang:

> You leave me to take the road to glory,
> But my heart will follow you all the way.

With a final glance at the mirror she went out, closing the door behind her. A moment later Marius heard the bare feet of the two girls going along the corridor while their father shouted after them:

'Now remember – one by the barrier and the other at the corner of the Rue du Petit-Banquier. Don't take your eyes off the door of the house, and if you see anything, get back here at the double. You've got a key.'

'A fine job!' the older girl called back. 'Keeping look-out barefoot in the snow.'

'Tomorrow you shall have fur-lined boots,' was the reply.

They went on down the stairs, and the sound of the front door closing indicated that they had gone out.

There was now no one left in the house except Marius and the Jondrette couple; and, presumably, the mysterious beings of whom he had caught a glimpse in the darkness of the unoccupied room.

XVII

Use made of Marius's five francs

Marius decided that it was time for him to return to his post of observation, and within an instant, moving with the suppleness of youth, he was back on the chest of drawers with his eye to the peep-hole.

The aspect of the Jondrette dwelling was singularly changed. He could now account for the strange light he had seen. A candle was burning in a tarnished candlestick, but this was not its source; the garret was flooded with the glare of a fair-sized brazier standing in the hearth and filled with glowing charcoal. The brazier itself was red hot, and the blue flame dancing on top of the charcoal helped him to discern the outline of the chisel bought by Jondrette in the Rue Pierre-Lombard, which had been thrust into it. In a corner by the door, as though put there for a specific purpose, were two piles of objects, one a heap of what looked like scrap-iron and the other a pile of rope. To an observer not knowing what was going on all this would have suggested two ideas, one very sinister and the other very simple. The den, thus illumined, looked more like a smithy than a gateway to the inferno; but Jondrette by the same light looked more like a demon than a blacksmith.

The heat of the brazier was so great that the candle, which stood on the table, was melting on the side nearest it. An antiquated copper dark-lantern, worthy of a Diogenes turned housebreaker, stood on the mantelshelf. The brazier was standing amid the cooling ashes of the hearth so that its smoke went up the chimney and did not drift into the room. The moon shining through the four small panes of the window mingled its whiteness with the ruddy glow that filled the garret, and to the poetic fancy of Marius, a dreamer even in this moment of action, it was like a thought of Heaven mingling with the ugly fantasies of earth. A faint draught from the broken window helped to dispel the fumes of burning charcoal.

The Jondrettes' garret, as the reader may recall from what has been said about the Gorbeau tenement, was admirably suited to acts of darkness and violence, a perfect setting for crime. It was the end room of the most isolated house in the least frequented boulevard in Paris. If ambushes had never existed, it was here that they might have been invented. The whole depth of the house and a row of un-occupied rooms separated this one from the boulevard, and its only window looked on to a wide expanse of open country broken by walls and fences.

Jondrette had lit his pipe and sat smoking on the seatless chair. His wife was talking to him in a low voice. If Marius had been Courfeyrac, that is to say, one of those young men who find humour in all things, the sight of her would have made him laugh. She was wearing a black hat with feathers not unlike those worn by the herald-at-arms at the coronation of Charles X, a vast tartan shawl, a woollen skirt and the men's shoes which her daughter had so des-pised earlier in the day. This was the get-up that had won her hus-band's approval, causing her to look 'respectable'. He himself was still wearing the overcoat bestowed on him by Monsieur Leblanc, and the contrast between this and his cotton trousers still presented the incongruity which Courfeyrac held to be the hall-mark of a poet. Suddenly he raised his voice:

'I've just thought of something. He'll be bound to come in a fiacre in this weather. Light the lantern and go downstairs with it and wait at the front door. Open the door directly you hear the cab draw up. Light him up the stairs, then run down again, pay off the cab, and send it away.'

'What about the money?'

Jondrette felt in his pocket and handed her a five-franc piece.

'Where does this come from?' she exclaimed.

'From him next door, this morning,' said Jondrette with dignity. Another thought struck him. 'You know something? We need two chairs.'

'What for?'

'To sit on.'

A shiver ran down Marius's spine as the woman said calmly:

'I'll get them from next door.'

She rose at once and left the room.

'Take the candle,' shouted Jondrette.

'It would only hamper me. I shall have two chairs to carry. There's moonlight enough.'

It was a physical impossibility for Marius to get down from the chest and under the bed in time. A hand groped heavily at his door, feeling for the handle, and then the door opened. Marius stayed where he was, rigid with dismay.

The woman entered. The dormer window allowed a narrow spread of moonlight to enter the room, framed by two wider spheres of darkness, one of which entirely covered the wall against which Marius was standing so that for practical purposes he was invisible. She looked about her without seeing him, picked up the two chairs, the only ones he possessed, and went out with them, leaving the door to swing noisily to behind her.

'Here they are,' she said, re-entering their own room.

'And here's the lantern,' said her husband. 'Now cut along downstairs.'

She hurried out again, leaving the man alone.

Jondrette placed the chairs on either side of the table, twisted the chisel in the burning charcoal and moved an old screen in front of the hearth to hide the brazier. Then he bent over the pile of rope as though inspecting it. Marius now realized that what he had supposed to be nothing but rope was in fact a well-made rope ladder with wooden rungs and two iron hooks to hang it by. Neither the ladder nor the several large implements, like bludgeons, among the scrap-iron in the other heap, had been in the room that morning. Jondrette must have brought them in during the afternoon, while Marius was out.

'They're metal-worker's tools,' thought Marius. Had he been better versed in these matters he would have recognized, among what he supposed to be ordinary workshop tools, certain more sinister implements used for the forcing of doors and locks, and others capable of cutting and splitting, burglars' chisels and jemmies.

The fireplace, and the table with the chairs on either side, were exactly opposite Marius. Now that the brazier was hidden the room was lighted only by the candle. The smallest objects, on the table or the mantelshelf, cast huge shadows, that of the broken water-jug covering half the wall behind it. The room was filled with a black and ominous calm, the forerunner of dreadful events.

Jondrette had let his pipe go out, in itself a sign of tension, and was again seated. The light of the candle threw into relief the sharp, bestial lines and hollows of his face. His eyebrows rose and fell and his right hand nervously opened and closed as though he were answering the last admonition of some counsellor within himself. In the course of this silent colloquy he abruptly pulled open the table drawer, got out a long table-knife and tested its edge with his finger. Then he put it back again and closed the drawer.

Marius got the pistol out of his right-hand fob pocket and cocked it, making a sharp click as he did so. Jondrette started and half rose from his chair.

'Who's there?' he called.

Marius held his breath, and after a moment Jondrette laughed, saying:

'I'm getting jumpy. Nothing but a board creaking.'

Marius kept the pistol in his hand.

XVIII

The two chairs

Of a sudden a distant, melancholy sound caused the windows to vibrate slightly. Six o'clock was striking at the church of Saint-Médard.

Jondrette noted each stroke with a nod of his head, and when the sixth had sounded he snuffed out the candle with his fingers. Then he began to pace the room, stood listening at the door, paced and listened again. 'So long as he comes!' he muttered, and returned to his chair. Scarcely had he seated himself than the door opened.

His wife stood in the corridor, her hideous grimace of welcome lighted from below by one of the apertures in the dark-lantern.

'Please to come in, Monsieur,' she said.

'My noble benefactor, enter!' cried Jondrette, hastily rising.

Monsieur Leblanc appeared. His serene bearing lent him a singular dignity. He placed four louis on the table.

'That is for your rent and urgent requirements, Monsieur Fabantou,' he said. 'We have to consider what else is needed.'

'May God reward you, most generous sir,' said Jondrette; and in a swift aside to his wife: 'Get rid of the cab.'

She vanished, and had reappeared by the time Jondrette with many bows and fulsome expressions of gratitude had seated Monsieur Leblanc on one of the chairs. She gave him a nod. The snow was so thick on the ground that the fiacre had made no sound in arriving or departing. Jondrette now took the chair facing Monsieur Leblanc.

If he is to gain a true impression of the scene that follows the reader must take into account the ice-cold night, the snow-covered spaces around the Salpêtrière shining whitely under the moon as though enveloped in a shroud, the street-lamps here and there relieving with a ruddy glow the desolate boulevards with their long lines of black elms, no moving figure to be seen within perhaps half a mile, and the Gorbeau tenement in its state of total silence, squalor, and darkness; and within the tenement, its shadows and its empty places, the large irregular garret lighted by a single candle with two men seated at the table, one serene of aspect and the other leering and dreadful, the woman hovering like a she-wolf in the background, and Marius, standing unseen on the other side of the partition with his eye to the aperture, intently following every word and every gesture with a pistol in his hand.

Marius's feeling was one of abhorrence but not of fear. Tightening his grip on the pistol-butt, he was reassured. 'I can stop the brute whenever I please,' he thought. The police were hidden somewhere close at hand, waiting for the summons to intervene. Moreover he was hopeful that this violent encounter between Monsieur Leblanc and Jondrette would throw some light on the things that he so longed to know.

XIX
The visitors

Monsieur Leblanc's first act when he was seated was to look round at the two empty beds. 'How is the hurt child?' he asked.

'Not well,' said Jondrette with a smile of mournful gratitude. 'She's in great pain. Her sister has taken her to the hospital to have the wound dressed. But you will be seeing them, my dear sir. They will be back soon.'

'Madame Fabantou seems to have recovered,' said Monsieur Leblanc, glancing at the weird attire of the Jondrette woman, who was standing between him and the door as though guarding the exit, in a posture of menace almost as if she was offering battle.

'She's desperately ill,' said Jondrette. 'But what is one to do? She has so much courage, you see. She's more than a woman – she's an ox.'

The elegant compliment drew a simper from the lady and she exclaimed coyly:

'You always flatter me, Monsieur Jondrette.'

'Jondrette?' said Monsieur Leblanc. 'I thought your name was Fabantou?'

'It's either,' said Jondrette promptly. 'Jondrette is my stage name.'

He gave his wife a look which Leblanc failed to notice and launched into a loud and unctuous discourse.

'We have always lived so happily together, my dear wife and I. Without that, what would become of us? We are so unfortunate, honoured sir. We have the will to work, we have the heart, but the work is not to be had. I do not know how the Government arranges these things, but I give you my word, my dear sir – and I am not a Jacobin or one of your half-baked democrats, although I wish them no harm – I give you my word that if I were a minister things would be very different. I will give you an example. I wanted my daughters to learn the packing trade. You will say, "What? A trade?" Yes, sir, a trade, a humble trade to earn an honest living. A sad decline, my noble benefactor. A degradation, considering what we once were. But alas, nothing remains to us of our former prosperity. Or rather, only one thing, a painting which I greatly value but which I shall have to part with if we are to live. For we have to live, do we not? We have to go on living.'

While Jondrette was thus holding forth with a seeming incoherence strangely at odds with his cool, calculating expression, Marius, looking beyond him, saw someone who had not been there before. A man had stolen into the room, moving so cautiously that the door-hinges had made no sound. He was wearing no shirt but a tattered waistcoat that gaped at every seam, loose corduroy trousers and ropesoled slippers; his bare arms were tattooed and his face was blackened. He was now seated with folded arms on the nearest bed, partly hidden behind the tall form of the Jondrette woman.

The kind of magnetic instinct that alerts our senses caused Monsieur Leblanc to notice him at almost the same moment as Marius, and he gave a start which Jondrette did not fail to perceive.

'You're looking at your overcoat,' he cried, drawing its folds more closely about him. 'The one you were so kind as to leave with me. It's a splendid fit, isn't it?'

'Who is that man?' asked Monsieur Leblanc.

'Him?' said Jondrette. 'He's a neighbour. Pay no attention to him.'

The neighbour had certainly an odd appearance. But chemical factories abound in the Faubourg Saint-Marceau, and it is not uncommon for factory-workers to have grimy faces. In any event, Monsieur Leblanc's attitude was still one of easy and untroubled confidence.

'I beg your pardon,' he said. 'What were you saying, Monsieur Fabantou?'

'I was telling you, my most noble patron,' said Jondrette, leaning forward with his elbows on the table and gazing tenderly at Monsieur Leblanc with eyes not unlike those of a boa-constrictor, 'that I have a picture for sale.'

A slight sound came from the door. A second man had entered and seated himself on the bed. Like the first he was bare-armed, and his face, too, was blackened with ink or soot. Although he had literally slid into the room, he had not been able to prevent Monsieur Leblanc from hearing him.

'Don't worry about them,' Jondrette said. 'They're just people living in the house. I was saying that I have a valuable picture. Perhaps you will allow me to show it to you.'

He rose and picking up the panel leaning against the wall turned it round and left it leaning there. The light of the candle was sufficient to show that it was indeed some sort of picture. Marius could make out none of the details because Jondrette was standing in the way. He had a brief glimpse of an ill-drawn figure crudely embellished with the garish colours of a fairground placard.

'What on earth is it?' asked Monsieur Leblanc.

'It is a masterpiece, my dear sir,' cried Jondrette. 'A picture of great price, and one which I cherish as I do my own daughters. It conjures up memories. But as I have said – and I cannot gainsay it – I have been reduced to such straits that I am forced to part with it!'

Perhaps by chance, or because he was growing uneasy, Monsieur Leblanc, while examining the picture, also glanced round. There were now four strangers present, three seated on the bed and one standing by the door, all bare-armed, motionless and with blackened faces. One of the three on the bed was half-lying with his back against the wall and his eyes closed, as though he were asleep. He was old, his white hair in horrid contrast to his daubed face. The other two seemed to be young men, one bearded and the other long-haired. None wore boots. Those not in slippers were barefoot.

Catching the direction of Monsieur Leblanc's glance, Jondrette said:

'They're friends of mine, all neighbours. They're furnacemen; they have dirty faces because they do dirty work. Don't worry about them, noble benefactor, but buy my picture. Have pity on my distress. I'll let you have it cheap. What do you consider it is worth?'

Monsieur Leblanc was looking closely at him, like a man now on his guard.

'It's an old inn-sign,' he said. 'It's worth about three francs.'

Jondrette said softly:

'Have you your wallet on you? I will accept a thousand crowns.'

Monsieur Leblanc rose, and standing with his back to the wall looked rapidly round the room. Jondrette was on his left, at the end nearest the window, and the woman and the four men were on his right near the door. The men did not stir, and seemed not even to see him. Jondrette continued to talk in a wailing voice, his gaze so distraught and his accents so pitiable that Monsieur Leblanc might have been pardoned for thinking that he had nothing more to deal with than a man driven out of his wits by misfortune.

'If you do not buy my picture, noble benefactor, then I shall have no recourse but to throw myself into the river. I wanted my daughters to learn the packing-trade, and rough packaging at that, foodstuffs and suchlike. But for that you need a solid edged table, with a flange, so that jars don't fall off it; you need all kinds of implements, a stove for heating glue to different temperatures according to the kind of material you're using, whether it's wood or metal or cardboard, cutters and shapers and pincers and stamps and lord knows what besides. And what do you earn by it? Four sous a day for four hours' work! And everything to be kept spotlessly clean. I ask you! Four sous a day. How is anyone to live on that?'

Jondrette was not looking at Monsieur Leblanc while he spoke. Monsieur Leblanc's eyes were fixed intently upon him, but Jondrette was watching the door. Marius, for his part, was gazing breathlessly from one to the other. Monsieur Leblanc seemed to be asking himself, 'Is the man mad?' Jondrette was babbling. He repeated several times, in varying accents of self-pity, 'Nothing left but to throw myself in the river . . . The other day I went down the steps by the Pont d'Austerlitz . . .'

But suddenly the dull eyes flamed; the little man drew himself up and became terrifying. Taking a step towards Monsieur Leblanc, he shouted:

'But never mind all that! Don't you know me?'

XX

The trap is sprung

The door of the garret was suddenly flung wide to admit three men in dark smocks wearing black paper masks. The first was thin and carried a long, iron-studded cudgel. The second, a species of colossus, was carrying a butcher's pole-axe. The third, a square-shouldered man, less lean than the first but less massive than the second, grasped a huge key stolen from some prison-door.

It seemed that this was what Jondrette had been awaiting. There was a rapid exchange of dialogue between him and the man with the cudgel.

'Is everything ready?' Jondrette asked.

'Yes,' the thin man replied.

'But where's Montparnasse?'

'The pretty boy stopped to chat to your daughter.'

'Which one?'

'The older.'

'The fiacre's ready?'

'Yes.'

'Two good horses?'

'First-rate.'

'And it's waiting where I said?'

'Yes.'

'Good,' said Jondrette.

Monsieur Leblanc had grown pale. He was looking about him in the manner of a man who now knows what he has to contend with, his head slowly turning as, in watchful astonishment but with no sign of fear, he considered the group of men confronting him. He was using the table as an improvised barricade. The man who a few moments before had looked like nothing but an amiable elderly gentleman had suddenly become a sort of athlete, his powerful hand grasping the back of his chair with a gesture that was at once formidable and surprising. His resolute courage in the face of danger was that of a nature to whom fortitude came as readily as goodness, as easily and as simply. The father of a beloved woman can never be wholly remote from us. Marius was filled with pride.

The three bare-armed ruffians whom Jondrette had described as furnace-men had meanwhile gone to the heap of scrap-iron. One had taken up a pair of shears, the second a pair of tongs, and the third a hammer; and now, without speaking a word, they stationed themselves in front of the door. The old man was still reclining on the bed, but with his eyes open. The Jondrette woman was seated beside him.

It seemed to Marius that the time was very near when he must give the alarm, and he raised his right hand with the pistol, pointing it upwards in the general direction of the corridor. Jondrette, having concluded his colloquy with the man with the cudgel, turned back to Monsieur Leblanc and repeated his question, this time accompanying the words with a low, sinister laugh.

'Don't you recognize me?'

Monsieur Leblanc looked steadily at him.

'No.'

Jondrette drew close to the table. Thrusting his fierce, angular countenance as near as he could bring it to the impassive face of Monsieur Leblanc, and crouching like a wild beast about to spring, he cried:

'My name isn't Fabantou or Jondrette either. My name is Thénardier! I'm the innkeeper from Montfermeil. Thénardier, d'you hear? Now do you recognize me?'

A slight quiver passed over Monsieur Leblanc's face, but he answered calmly and without raising his voice:

'No more than before.'

Marius did not hear this reply. His face at that moment, could anyone have observed him in the darkness, had grown haggard with stupefaction and dismay. At the sound of Thénardier's name he had trembled so violently as to have to lean against the partition for support, feeling a chill as though a sword-blade had been driven into his heart. His right arm, raised to fire the warning shot, sank slowly to his side, and when the name was repeated his nerveless fingers came near to letting it fall to the floor. Jondrette in disclosing his identity had not shaken Monsieur Leblanc, but he had shattered Marius. Monsieur Leblanc might not know the name, but Marius knew it. We must remember what it meant to him. His father's solemn injunction was written on his heart – 'A man called Thénardier saved my life. If my son should meet him he will do him every service in his power.' It had become for him an article of faith, a name linked with that of his father in his prayers. And now, here he was, Thénardier, the innkeeper of Montfermeil, his father's rescuer whom Marius had so long and vainly sought – a bandit, a monster in the act of committing an abominable crime, the nature of which was still not fully clear but which looked like murder. And the murder of whom, in God's name! . . . Could Fate have played any more scurvy trick than this? For four years Marius had been obsessed with the resolve to acquit the debt laid upon him by his father, to serve this man if he could find him; and now it seemed that instead he would be sending him to the gallows, to public execution on the Place Saint-Jacques, the man who had saved his father at the risk of his life! Yet how could he witness this infamy and not prevent it? – condemn the victim and spare the assassin? Could any debt be valid that was owed to such a man? . . . With his whole scheme of things collapsed about him, Marius stood and trembled. Everything depended on him; he held these people in the hollow of his hand. If he fired the warning shot Monsieur Leblanc would be saved and Thénardier destroyed; otherwise Monsieur Leblanc would be sacrificed and Thénardier would perhaps escape. One or the other must be on Marius's conscience. Was he to honour his father's last wishes, his own filial duty and solemn pledge, or permit the accomplishment of a crime? Two voices seemed to ring in his ears, that of the girl pleading for her father and that of the colonel commending Thénardier to his care. His senses were reeling and he felt his knees grow weak. Nor was there any time for thought, so furiously was the drama unfolding under his gaze. It was as though a whirlwind of which he had thought himself the master were carrying him away. He was on the point of fainting.

Meanwhile Thénardier, whom henceforth we shall call by no other name, was stalking up and down in a sort of frenzied triumph. Seizing the candlestick he banged it down on the mantelshelf with a gesture so violent that the candle was nearly extinguished and tallow splashed on the wall. Then, turning to Monsieur Leblanc, he spat at him.

'Your goose is cooked! You're spitted and roasted, my fine bird!'

He resumed his pacing, fulminating as he did so.

'So I've caught up with you at last, my noble philanthropist, my wealthy buyer of dolls! But you don't know me, eh? It wasn't you who came to my tavern in Montfermeil on Christmas Eve eight years ago and took away Fantine's brat, the Lark, so called? You weren't wearing a yellow coat, were you? You didn't come in with a parcel of clothes under your arm, just like you did this morning? Wife, are you listening? It seems he has a passion for calling on people with a bundle of stockings. He's a man of charity, you see. Perhaps you keep a clothes store, my generous millionaire, and give away your surplus stock to the poor? Charlatan! And so you don't know me! But I know you, all right. I recognized you the moment you shoved your face inside this door. Well, now you're going to learn that it isn't all that rosy, walking into a man's house which happens to be an inn, fooling him by being dressed like a tramp, taking away his domestic help and afterwards threatening him in the woods – you can't make it right by just bringing a few old hospital blankets and leaving an overcoat that doesn't fit! Scoundrel! Kidnapper!'

He paused, seeming to commune with himself as though the torrent of his fury had fallen into a sudden trough; and then, as though summing up the thoughts that were in his mind, he thumped with his fist on the table and cried:

'As though butter wouldn't melt in his mouth!'

He turned again to Monsieur Leblanc.

'You got the better of me once! You're the cause of all my troubles. For fifteen hundred francs you got hold of a girl who was mine and who certainly had rich connections; she'd brought me in money already, and I reckoned to live on her for the rest of my life. She might have made good my losses in that filthy dram-shop where they came to drink themselves senseless and where like the sot I was, I swallowed my own substance. By God, I wish all the wine drunk in that place had been poison! You must have thought I was a fine fool when you got away with the brat. You were the stronger that day in the forest. But now it's my turn. I hold the cards now, and you're done for, my beauty! It makes me laugh to think of it, the way you swallowed everything. I told you I was an actor, didn't I? And that I'd played with Mademoiselle Mars, whoever she may be, and that I had to settle up with my landlord by tomorrow, February the fourth! Poor imbecile, not even sense enough to know the date of quarterday! And the beggarly sixty francs he's brought me – too mean even to make it a hundred! And the high-minded sentiments! It made me laugh. I thought to myself, "All right, my beauty, I'll lick your boots this morning and cut your heart out tonight!"'

Thénardier stopped for lack of breath, his narrow chest heaving like a bellows. His eyes shone with the ignoble triumph of a weak, cruel, and cowardly nature which at last has the power to humble what it fears: a dwarf setting his foot on the head of Goliath; a jackal sinking its teeth into the flank of an ailing bull, too near death to be able to defend itself but still alive enough to suffer.

Monsieur Leblanc had made no attempt to interrupt him, but now that he had stopped of his own accord he said:

'I don't know what you're talking about. You seem to be under a delusion. I'm a poor man, very far indeed from being a millionaire. I don't know you. You're confusing me with someone else.'

'Ha!' bellowed Thénardier. 'You're sticking to that, are you, you old mountebank? You don't remember, eh? You've no idea who I am?'

'None,' said Monsieur Leblanc, with a cool courtesy that in the circumstances was singularly impressive. 'But I have a very good idea what you are. You're a scoundrel.'

As we all know, even the vilest creatures have their susceptibilities, even monsters are ticklish. The word 'scoundrel' caused the Thénardier woman to spring up off the bed. Thénardier snatched up a chair as though he meant to break it in pieces. 'Stay where you are!' he shouted to his wife, and again faced Monsieur Leblanc.

'A scoundrel, is it? That's what you rich call people like me. It's true I've failed in business, I'm in hiding, I've no money in my pocket – so that makes me a scoundrel. I haven't eaten for three days, so I'm a scoundrel! You keep yourselves warm with the best boots money can buy and fur-lined coats fit for an archbishop. You live in a first-floor apartment with a hall-porter, you stuff yourselves with truffles and asparagus at forty francs a bunch and green peas in January; and if you think the weather's cold you look in the paper to see what the temperature is by Chevalier's newfangled thermometer. But us, we're our own thermometers, we don't need to consult the newspaper to know how cold it is. We feel the blood freezing in our veins and we say, "There is no God!" And you come into the pig-sties we live in – pig-sties, that's what they are – and call us scoundrels. But as under-dogs, we're going to chew you up, we're going to make a meal of you! Let me tell you this, my fine-feathered millionaire, I was a man in a good way of business, once a licensed innkeeper, an elector, a respectable citizen – and I dare say that's more than you can say.' He turned to the group of men by the door and added, quivering: 'And he talks to me as though I was a pickpocket!'

In a fresh burst of fury, he turned back to Monsieur Leblanc.

'And here's something else for you, my noble philanthropist. I'm not just a nobody, a man without a name who goes about stealing children. I'm an ex-soldier of France. I should have had a medal. I fought at Waterloo, and I saved the life of a general called Count Something-or-other. He told me his name, but his infernal voice was so weak that I couldn't hear it. I'd have sooner had his name than his thanks, because it would have helped me to find him again. That picture I've just shown you, painted by David, the famous artist, do you know what it is? It's my portrait. He wanted to immortalize my feat of arms. I carried the general to safety on my back through the hail of musket-fire. That's the story. Not that the general ever did anything for me, he was no better than the rest of you. All the same, I saved his life and I've got documents to prove it. I'm a veteran of Waterloo, hell and damnation! And now that I've had the politeness to tell you, let's get this business over. I want money, a lot of money, the devil of a lot, or else by God, I'll do for you!'

Marius had had time to bring his feelings under some control, and he was still listening. There could no longer be the least doubt that this was the Thénardier of his father's message, and at the reference to the latter's ingratitude, which he was on the point of so fatally justifying, he flinched, for it added to his uncertainties. In all Thénardier's outpourings, the words and gestures, the fury blazing in his eyes; this explosion of an evil nature brazenly exposed, the mixture of bravado and abjectness, arrogance, pettiness, rage, absurdity; the hodge-podge of genuine distress, and lying sentiment, the shamelessness of a vicious man rejoicing in viciousness, the bare crudity of an ugly soul – in this eruption of all suffering and all hatred there was something which was hideous as evil itself and still as poignant as truth.

As the reader will have realized, the picture, supposedly by David, which he was asking Monsieur Leblanc to buy, was in fact nothing but the inn-sign he himself had painted, the sole relic he had preserved of his disaster in Montfermeil. Now that he was no longer standing in the way, Marius was able to study it, and he saw that the uncouth daub did indeed represent a battle, a man carrying another against a smoky background. Thénardier and Pontmercy, the gallant sergeant and the rescued officer. Marius was seized with a kind of delirium. The picture in some sort brought his father to life; it was no longer an inn-sign but a resurrection, the yawning of a tomb, the rising of a ghost. With throbbing temples Marius heard the sound of the guns at Waterloo, and it seemed to him that the bleeding figure of his father, so crudely depicted, had its eyes fixed upon him.

Thénardier had regained his breath.

'Well,' he said tersely, 'have you anything to say before we go to work on you?'

Monsieur Leblanc said nothing. Amid the ensuing silence a hoarse voice proclaimed:

'If there's any chopping to be done, I'm your man!'

A huge, unshaven, and grimy face loomed up by the doorway, the lips parted to display not teeth but a row of stumps. It was the face of the man with the pole-axe.

'Why have you taken your mask off?' Thénardier shouted furiously.

For some moments, as it seemed, Monsieur Leblanc had been following Thénardier's movements as, blind with rage and in the assurance that the door was guarded, and that there were nine of them to deal with a single unarmed man, he stamped up and down the room. In shouting at the man with the pole-axe he turned his back on the prisoner.

Monsieur Leblanc took instant advantage of this. Moving with astonishing speed, he thrust aside the table and chair and with a single bound had reached the window. It took him only a moment to open it and get a foot on the window-ledge. He was halfway through the window when six powerful hands laid hold of him and dragged him back. The three so-called furnace-men had flung themselves upon him. At the same moment the Thénardier woman grabbed him by the hair.

The commotion brought in the rest of the gang, who had been clustered in the corridor. The old man who had been lying on the bed, seemingly half-drunk, got up and staggered across the room with a roadmender's hammer. One of the furnace-men, whose smeared face was momentarily visible in the candle-light, and whom Marius now recognized as Panchaud (alias Printanier or Bigrenaille) was flourishing a species of bludgeon with an iron knob at either end.

It was too much for Marius. 'Forgive me, father,' he murmured and his finger sought the trigger. But as he was about to fire Thénardier cried:

'Don't hurt him!'

Far from enraging Thénardier, the prisoner's desperate bid to escape had sobered him. There were two men in Thénardier, the brute and the man of cunning. Until that moment, in the intoxication of his triumph, with the prey quiescent and seemingly at his mercy, the brute had prevailed; but now that the victim was showing signs of fight it was the man of cunning who took control.

'Don't hurt him,' he repeated, and in doing so unwittingly scored a success. Marius delayed the firing of the shot, which, with this new development, he no longer felt to be a matter of instant necessity. It might happen, after all, that some chance would occur to spare him the hideous alternatives of allowing the girl's father to perish or of destroying the saviour of his own father.

Meanwhile a prodigious struggle was in progress. Monsieur Leblanc had sent the old man reeling with a body-blow, and with further blows had felled two of his assailants to the ground. He was now kneeling with a knee on two other men, who lay groaning under the pressure as though it were that of a millstone. But the remaining four, gripping him by the arms and neck, prevented him from rising. Half victor and half vanquished, crushing some and stifled by others, vainly grappling with the men now piling upon him, Monsieur Leblanc vanished in the confusion of bodies like a boar under a baying pack of hounds.

Eventually they managed to drag him on to the bed nearest the window, treating him now with respect. The Thénardier woman had never loosed her grip of his hair.

'You get out of it,' Thénardier said. 'You'll tear your shawl.'

She obeyed instantly, growling like a she-wolf obeying its mate.

'You others,' said Thénardier, 'search him.'

Monsieur Leblanc made no further resistance. They searched him. He had nothing on him except a leather purse containing six francs and a handkerchief. Thénardier put the handkerchief in his pocket.

'No wallet?' he asked.

'No watch either,' said one of the men.

'It's what you'd expect,' said the masked man with the key, in a voice like that of a ventriloquist . . . 'He's an old hand.'

Thénardier, going across to the corner by the door, picked up a bundle of rope and tossed it to them.

'Tie him to the foot of the bed,' he said. He stood looking down at the old man, who was still lying motionless where he had been felled by Monsieur Leblanc's fist. 'Is Boulatruelle dead?'

'He's drunk, that's all,' said Bigrenaille.

'Shift him out of the way,' said Thénardier, and they rolled him over and dumped him by the heap of scrap-metal.

'Look, Babet, why did you bring so many people?' said Thénardier in an aside to the man with the cudgel. 'It's more than we need.'

'Couldn't be helped,' the other said. 'They all wanted to be in on it. Business is slack just now.'

The bed in question was something like a hospital bed, with four thick, roughly squared wooden bed-posts. Monsieur Leblanc still made no resistance. They roped him solidly, standing upright, to the post furthest from the window and nearest to the hearth.

When this was done Thénardier moved a chair and sat down almost facing him. The transformation in Thénardier was extraordinary. Within a few minutes his expression had changed from one of frenetic violence to a look of cool calculation. It was hard to believe that this politely smiling mouth was the same one that had been foaming in bestial frenzy so short a time before, and Marius, observing this sinister metamorphosis, felt the amazement of a man who sees a tiger transformed into an attorney.

'Monsieur . . .' Thénardier began. Breaking off, he waved away the men who were still holding Monsieur Leblanc. 'Move back a little. I want to talk to the gentleman.'

They withdrew towards the door, and he began again.

'Monsieur, you were foolish to try to jump out of the window. You might have broken your leg. Now, if you will allow me, we will discuss things quietly. But first I must tell you of something that has astonished me. Throughout this meeting you have not uttered a single cry.'

It was an undeniable fact, although Marius in his disturbed state had failed to notice it. The few words Monsieur Leblanc had spoken had been uttered without his having raised his voice. Even during the struggle by the window he had maintained a complete and singular silence.

'You might have shouted for help,' Thénardier went on. 'I should not have been surprised if you had. It's natural enough to do a bit of shouting when you find yourself surrounded by people whom you have cause to mistrust. We wouldn't have tried to prevent you. We wouldn't even have gagged you. And I'll tell you why. It's because this place is very sound-proof. There's nothing else to be said for it, but there is that. You could explode a bomb in this room, and to the nearest police post it would sound like a drunkard's snore. You could fire a cannon! So, you see, it's a handy place. But you didn't shout, and so much the better, I applaud your discretion. But shall I tell you the conclusion I draw from it? My dear sir, when anyone shouts for help who is most likely to answer? The police. And what comes after the police? – the law. So if you didn't shout it's because you are no more anxious to bring law and the police into the affair than we are ourselves. Which means – and I have long suspected this – that you have something to hide. The same applies to us. We have a common interest, and therefore we shall be able to come to terms.'

While he talked in this fashion, Thénardier, with his eyes intent upon Monsieur Leblanc, seemed to be seeking to bore into his very soul. In his choice of language, the crafty moderation, and the undertone of insolence, one might catch a glimpse of the man who by his own avowal had once 'studied to be a priest'.

And to Marius, now that he was aware of it, it must be said that the prisoner's strange conduct, his refusal to obey the natural impulse of any man in his situation, which amounted to a total disregard for his own safety, came as a painful shock. Thénardier's shrewd observation served only to intensify the fog of mystery surrounding the aloof, enigmatic figure whom Courfeyrac had christened 'Monsieur Leblanc'. But whatever he might be, as he stood there, bound with ropes and surrounded by a murderous gang, suspended as it were over a pit that seemed every minute to grow deeper, confronting with an equal impassiveness Thénardier's venomous fury and his cool argument, Marius could not help admiring the dignified melancholy of his countenance. His was clearly a spirit inaccessible to fear and incapable of dismay. He was one of those men who rise above the astonishment of desperate circumstance. Great though this crisis was, inevitable though disaster seemed, there was in his eyes nothing of the wild stare of the drowning man who sinks for the last time.

Rising casually to his feet, Thénardier went over to the fireplace and moved the screen, unmasking the glowing brazier in which the red-hot chisel was plainly discernible, its surface flecked with small points of light. Then he resumed his seat facing Monsieur Leblanc.

'To continue,' he said. 'We can come to terms. Let us do so amicably. I was wrong to fly into a rage in the way I did. I lost my head and talked extravagantly. I went too far. For example, I said that because you are a millionaire I intended to demand a great deal of money, an enormous amount. But that would not be reasonable. However rich you may be, you have expenses, as who has not? I have no wish to ruin you. I'm not a bloodsucker. I'm not one of those people who, because they have the upper hand, make ridiculous demands. I am prepared to meet you half-way and make concessions on my side. All I am asking is two hundred thousand francs.'

Monsieur Leblanc said nothing. Thénardier continued:

'As you see, I'm watering my wine to no small extent. I don't know the state of your fortune, but I do know that you have little regard for money and that a man as addicted to good works as yourself can certainly spare two hundred thousand francs for the father of a family in unhappy circumstances. You are a reasonable man yourself, and you will not suppose that I have gone to the trouble of organizing this affair – and all these gentlemen will agree that it is well contrived – simply in order to be able to drink cheap wine and eat scrag-end of veal for the rest of my life. Two hundred thousand is what it is worth, and I give you my word that once this trifle has been handed over our business will be concluded and you will have nothing more to fear. You will, of course, point out that you haven't got two hundred thousand francs on you. I am not so foolish as to have expected it. At the moment I am only asking one thing, that you will write a letter that I shall dictate.'

Here Thénardier paused. Speaking with particular emphasis and with a sidelong, smiling glance at the brazier, he said:

'I must warn you that it will not do for you to pretend you can't write.'

A Grand Inquisitor would have been envious of that smile.

Thénardier moved the table close to Monsieur Leblanc. He then got pen and ink and a sheet of paper out of the drawer, which he left open, revealing that it also contained a long-bladed knife. He thrust the paper towards Monsieur Leblanc.

'Now write,' he said.

For the first time the prisoner spoke.

'How do you expect me to write with my arms bound?'

'That's true,' said Thénardier. 'I apologize.' He turned to Bigrenaille. 'Untie the gentleman's right arm.'

The man did so, and when the prisoner's right hand was free Thénardier dipped the pen in the ink and passed it to him.

'You will please note, Monsieur, that you are completely at our mercy; but although no human power can save you, we should deeply regret having to proceed to unpleasant extremes. I do not know your name or your address, but I must warn you that you will remain bound until the messenger entrusted with the letter you are about to write has returned. I will now dictate.'

Monsieur Leblanc held the pen poised. 'My dear daughter –' Thénardier began, and at this the other started and stared at him. 'No,' said Thénardier. 'Better make it, My dearest daughter.' Monsieur Leblanc wrote accordingly, and he went on: 'You are to come at once.' Then he broke off. 'I suppose you address her as *tu*?'

'Who?' asked Monsieur Leblanc.

'The girl, of course,' said Thénardier. 'The child – the Lark.'

Monsieur Leblanc said without the least sign of emotion:

'I don't know what you're talking about.'

'Never mind,' said Thénardier and resumed his dictation: '. . . come at once. I need you very urgently. The bearer of this note will bring you to me. I shall be waiting. You have nothing to fear.' Again he changed his mind. 'No. Leave out that last sentence. It might make her suspicious. And now you must sign it. What is your name?'

The prisoner put down his pen and asked:

'Who is this letter for?'

'You know perfectly well. It's for the girl. I've already told you.'

It was apparent that Thénardier wished to avoid naming the girl. He had talked about 'the child' and 'the Lark', but, with the prudence of a wary man resolved to keep his secret from his accomplices, he had given her no precise name. To have done so would have been to deliver the whole business into their hands and tell them more than they needed to know. He repeated:

'Go on – sign it. What is your name?'

'Urbain Fabre,' the prisoner replied.

With a catlike movement Thénardier plunged his hand in his pocket and whipped out the handkerchief taken from Monsieur Leblanc. He held it up to the light of the candle, inspecting it for initials.

'U.F.,' he said. 'That's right. Urbain Fabre. Well, sign the letter U.F.'

The prisoner did so.

'And now give it to me. It needs two hands to fold it, so I'll attend to that myself. Good,' said Thénardier. 'Now you must address it – to Mademoiselle Fabre, at the place where you live. I know it isn't far from here, somewhere near Saint-Jacques-du-Haut-Pas, because that's where you attend Mass; but I don't know the street. I see you understand the position. You haven't lied to me about your name, so you won't do so about your address. Write it yourself.'

The prisoner reflected for a moment, then took up the pen and wrote:

'To Mademoiselle Fabre, care of Monsieur Urbain Fabre, 17 Rue Saint-Dominique-d'Enfer.'

Thénardier snatched up the letter with a sort of feverish excitement. 'Wife,' he called, and she hurried forward. 'Here it is. You know what you have to do. There's a fiacre down below. Get off at once and come back quick as you can.'

He turned to the man with the pole-axe.

'As you've taken your mask off you might as well go with her. Get up behind the fiacre. You know where it's waiting?'

'Yes,' said the man, and dropping his pole-axe in a corner, he followed the woman out of the room. Thrusting his head round the door, Thénardier shouted after her: 'Whatever you do, don't lose that letter. Remember it's worth two hundred thousand francs!'

'Don't worry,' her hoarse voice replied. 'I've pushed it down my front.'

In less than a minute they heard the cracking of a whip, which rapidly died away.

'Good,' grunted Thénardier. 'They aren't wasting any time. At that rate she'll be back in three-quarters of an hour.'

He moved one of the chairs and sat down with his arms folded and his muddy boots stretched out towards the brazier.

'My feet are cold,' he muttered.

Five members of the gang were now left in the room with Thénardier and the prisoner. The men, with their masks or black-smeared faces, might have been taken for coal-miners, Negroes or demons, according to taste, and they gave the impression that they treated crime as a business, going about it calmly, without anger or pity, indeed with a sort of boredom. They were huddled silently in a corner, like so many animals. Thénardier toasted his feet. The prisoner had relapsed into silence. A gloomy quiet had succeeded the furious hubbub of so short a time before. The candle, its tallow spreading like a mushroom, scarcely lighted the big garret; the brazier was dying down, and the heads of the men cast monstrous shadows on the walls and ceiling. No sound was to be heard except the breathing of the old drunkard, now fast asleep.

Marius waited in a state of anxiety which everything served to increase. The puzzle was more mystifying than ever. Who was the 'child' whom Thénardier had also called 'the Lark'? Was it his 'Ursula'? The prisoner had seemed quite unaffected by the mention of the Lark, and had answered in the most natural of voices, 'I don't know what you're talking about.' At least the riddle of the initials was now resolved. The U.F. stood for Urbain Fabre, and Ursula was not Ursula. This was the one thing that was clear to

Marius. He stayed at his observation-post, kept there by a sort of hideous fascination, almost incapable of movement or reflection, as though paralysed by the abominable things he had witnessed. He was waiting upon events, in any case, unable to collect his thoughts or decide what he should do.

'At least,' he reflected, 'if she is the Lark I shall know it, because the woman is going to bring her here. That will settle the matter. I will sacrifice my life to save her, if need be. Nothing shall prevent me.'

Nearly half an hour passed. Thénardier seemed lost in his own dark thoughts. The prisoner did not move. Nevertheless it seemed to Marius that now and then a slight, furtive sound came from his direction. But suddenly Thénardier turned to him.

'Monsieur Fabre,' he said, 'I may as well tell you this at once.'

Marius pricked up his ears. It sounded like the beginning of a disclosure.

'My wife will be back, we have only to wait. I believe the Lark is truly your daughter, and it's only right that you should have her. But listen. My wife will take her the letter. I told her to dress herself respectably, as you saw, so the young lady will have no misgivings about accompanying her. They will get into the fiacre, with my friend up at the back. But another cab will be waiting at a spot outside one of the gates with two excellent horses. The girl will be transferred to this, with my friend, and my wife will come back here to report that everything is in order. No one is going to harm your young lady. She'll be taken to a safe place and returned to you when the two hundred thousand francs has been paid. But if you should do anything to bring about my arrest, that will be unfortunate for the Lark. You understand?'

The prisoner said nothing. After a pause Thénardier concluded:

'You see, it's quite simple. Nothing bad will happen unless you bring it about. I'm only warning you.'

He paused again, and again the prisoner said nothing.

'As soon as my wife reports that the Lark is on her way,' said Thénardier, 'we will release you and you will be free to sleep in your own bed. As you see, we have no evil intentions.'

Marius was so appalled that his heart seemed to stop beating. The girl was not to be brought here but conveyed to some unknown destination! He could not seriously doubt who the girl was. And what was he to do? Fire the warning shot and deliver these villains into the hands of the police? But the man who had gone with the woman would still be free, and he would have the girl; and Marius recalled Thénardier's ominous words – 'that will be unfortunate for the Lark' ... It was not only his father's injunction that now made Marius hold his hand, but the danger that threatened his beloved.

The time dragged by. His dilemma seemed more hideous with every minute that passed. Marius reviewed the heart-rending possibilities, seeking desperately for a ray of hope and finding none, the tumult in his mind strangely contrasting with the funereal silence of the room.

At length the silence was broken by the sound of the house-door opening and closing. The prisoner stirred in his bonds.

'Here she is,' said Thénardier.

And a moment later the woman rushed into the room, flushed and breathless, her eyes glaring, banging her large hands against her thighs.

'It was a fake address!' she cried.

Her escort, following her in, picked up his pole-axe.

'A fake?' Thénardier repeated.

'There's no Monsieur Urbain Fabre at 17, Rue Saint-Dominique! They've never heard of him!' She spluttered and went on: 'The old man's been fooling you, Monsieur Thénardier. You're too good, that's the trouble. Me, I'd have carved his face up for a start, and if he still wouldn't talk I'd have roasted him until he told us where the girl is and how to get the money. But men haven't the sense of women. There's no Monsieur Fabre at Number 17. It's a big house with a courtyard and a door-keeper and everything, and I tipped him and talked to him and his wife, who is a fine-looking woman, and they know nothing about him.'

Marius breathed again. So the girl at least was safe – Ursula or the Lark, he no longer knew what to call her.

While his infuriated wife was vociferating, Thénardier had seated himself on the table. He sat there in silence for some moments, swinging his right leg and gazing with a savage satisfaction at the brazier. Then he turned to the prisoner and said slowly, and in a tone of singular ferocity:

'A false address. What did you expect to gain by that?'

'Time!' cried the prisoner in a ringing voice, and at the same moment he shook off the ropes that bound him. They had been cut. He was now only tied to the bed by one leg.

Before the other men had had time to realize what was happening he had reached out a hand to the brazier and then again stood upright. Thénardier, the woman, and the party of ruffians, clustered in stupefaction at the other end of the room, saw him defiantly facing them, holding the red-hot chisel by its wooden handle above his head.

It was revealed at the judicial inquiry into the affair at the Gorbeau tenement that the police, when they searched the garret, found a large coin which had been cut and worked in a particular fashion. It was one of those marvels of craftsmanship fashioned under cover of darkness, and for the purposes of darkness, with the patience engendered by imprisonment, and which are intended solely to serve as instruments of escape. These ugly and delicate products of immense skill are to the jeweller's art what the argot of the underworld is to poetry. There are Benvenuto Cellinis in the prisons, just as in our common slang there are Villons. The wretch determined to escape contrives, sometimes with no other tool than a worn knifeblade, to slice a copper coin in two thin sheets; he hollows them out without disturbing the design impressed on them, and then cuts a thread so that the two sheets can be screwed together, forming a box that he can open at will. Within the box a watchspring is concealed; and a watchspring, properly handled, will cut through a thick rope or an iron bar. The poor devil seems to possess nothing more than a penny piece, but he holds the key to liberty. The two halves of a coin of this kind were discovered under the bed by the window, and near them a tiny blue-steel saw which fitted inside. It is probable that the prisoner managed to conceal it in his hand while he was being searched and later unscrewed it when his hand was freed. He had used the saw to cut through the bonds, which would explain the slight sounds and furtive movements noticed by Marius; but he could not bend down for fear of giving himself away, and so had not been able to cut the rope binding his left leg.

The gang had recovered from this first surprise.

'Don't worry,' said Bigrenaille to Thénardier. 'He's still tied by one leg, and I guarantee he won't get out of that. I tied it myself.'

The prisoner now addressed them.

'You're a poor lot,' he said, 'but my own life is not much worth defending. As for making me talk – or making me write anything I don't want to write, or say anything I don't want to say ... Well, look!'

He drew up the sleeve covering his left arm and, holding it out, pressed the red-hot chisel against the bare skin.

The hiss of burnt flesh was audible, and a smell associated with torture-chambers spread through the room. Marius was sickened with horror, and even the ruffians gasped. But the expression of this remarkable elderly man scarcely altered. There was no hatred in the impassive gaze he directed at Thénardier, and no trace of physical agony in its serene nobility. In great and lofty natures the anguish of the flesh merely exalts the spirit, just as a soldiers' mutiny obliges the commander to show himself in his true colours.

'Poor fools,' he said, 'you need no more fear me than I fear you.' Withdrawing the chisel from his arm, he flung it through the open window, and the horrid implement vanished in the darkness, to fall hissing into the snow. 'Now you can do what you like with me.'

He was quite defenceless.

'Get hold of him,' said Thénardier.

Two of the men grasped him by the shoulders, and the masked man with a ventriloquist's voice took up his position in front of him, ready at the slightest movement to stun him with a blow of the huge key he carried.

Marius heard a sound of whispering immediately below him, so close to the partition that he could not see the speakers.

'There's only one thing for it –'

'Slit his throat!'

'That's it!'

Husband and wife were taking counsel together. Thénardier walked slowly over to the table and got out the knife.

Marius's hand was playing with the pistol-butt; his dilemma was now at its crisis. For an hour or more he had been tormented by the two voices of his conscience, one urging him to respect his father's wishes and the other insisting that he must save the prisoner. Both voices still clamoured within him, and his anguish was extreme. Until that moment he had clung to the faint hope that something would happen to reconcile those opposing impulses, but there had been nothing. Now the peril was imminent and he could delay no longer. Thénardier, knife in hand, stood hesitating a few paces from the prisoner.

Marius gazed wildly about him in the extremity of despair and suddenly he started. A brighter ray of moonlight, falling on the writing-table immediately behind him, shone upon a sheet of paper as though to bring it to his notice. It bore the sentence scrawled by the Thénardier girl that morning to prove that she could write. He could make out the bold, ill-written words:

'Watch out, the bogies are around.'

Instantly he saw what he must do. This was the solution of his problem, the means of saving both victim and assassin. Kneeling down, he reached for the paper. He softly detached a piece of plaster from the partition, wrapped the page round it, and flung it through the aperture so that it landed in the middle of the Thénardiers' room.

He was just in time. Thénardier, having overcome his last misgivings or scruples, was advancing upon the prisoner when he was checked by a sudden exclamation from his wife:

'Something fell!' she cried.

'What do you mean?'

She darted forward, picked up the small missive, and handed it to her husband.

'How did this get here?' he asked.

'How do you think? Through the window, of course!'

'That's right,' said Bigrenaille. 'I saw it.'

Thénardier hastily unfolded the paper and studied it by the light of the candle.

'It's Éponine's handwriting, by God!' He signed to his wife to read the message and said in a hoarse voice: 'Quick. The ladder. We'll leave the mouse in the trap and clear out!'

'Without cutting his throat?' his wife demanded.

'No time.'

'How do we go?' asked Bigrenaille.

'Through the window. If Ponine threw the message in that way it means that side of the house isn't guarded.'

The masked ventriloquist dropped his key and, raising his arms above his head, rapidly clapped his hands three times without speaking. It was a call to action. The men holding the prisoner let go of him; the rope ladder was swiftly unrolled and let down from the window, with its hooks secured to the window-ledge. The prisoner paid no attention to what was going on, seeming plunged in thought, or in prayer.

Directly the ladder was ready Thénardier called to his wife, 'Come on!' and made a dash for the window; but as he was about to climb through Bigrenaille grabbed him roughly by the collar.

'Not so fast, my old joker. We go first.'

'We go first,' the other men shouted.

'You're being childish,' said Thénardier. 'We're wasting time. They can't be far off.'

'Then,' said one of the men, 'we'll draw lots for who's to go first.'

'Are you crazy?' spluttered Thénardier. 'Are you raving mad? We've got the law on our heels and you want to stand round drawing lots out of a hat!'

'Perhaps you would like to borrow my hat,' said a voice from the doorway.

They swung round and saw that it was Javert. He stood there holding out his hat with a smile.

XXI
'*The best of the lot!*'

Javert had posted his men at nightfall and had taken up his own position behind the trees in the Rue de la Barrière-des-Gobelins, facing the Gorbeau tenement on the other side of the boulevard. He had intended to commence operations by 'pocketing' the two girls who were supposed to be on watch, but he had only succeeded in picking up Azelma. Éponine had deserted her post and they could not find her. Javert, waiting for the signal, had been considerably perturbed by the coming and going of the fiacre. Finally he lost patience, and being now convinced that he had uncovered a hornet's nest and that his luck was in – for he had recognized several of the men who entered the house – he had decided to go in without waiting for the pistol-shot, using Marius's key.

He had arrived at the crucial moment. The startled desperadoes snatched up the weapons they had just let fall and clustered together in readiness to defend themselves – seven men of terrifying aspect, armed with pole-axe and cudgel, shears, pincers and hammers, and Thénardier brandishing his knife. His wife had snatched up a huge slab of paving stone lying by the window which their daughters used as a stool.

Javert replaced his hat on his head and advanced two paces into the room with his stick under his arm and his sword still in its sheath.

'Take it easy,' he said. 'You can't escape through the window.

697

Better go out through the door, you'll find it less unhealthy. There are seven of you and fifteen of us. No point in turning it into a brawl. Let's all be sensible.'

Bigrenaille produced a pistol from under his smock and thrust it into Thénardier's hand, murmuring as he did so:

'That's Javert, a man I'm afraid to shoot at. Will you dare?'

'By God I will!' said Thénardier.

He levelled the weapon at Javert, who was not more than three paces away from him. Javert looked steadily at him and simply said:

'Better not. It won't fire anyway.'

Thénardier pulled the trigger. The pistol did not fire.

'What did I tell you?' said Javert.

Bigrenaille flung down the bludgeon he was carrying.

'You're the king of devils!' he cried. 'I give in.'

Javert looked round at the others.

'And the rest of you?'

They nodded.

'Good,' said Javert calmly. 'Now we're being sensible, like I said.'

'There's just one thing I ask,' said Bigrenaille, 'that I'll be allowed tobacco while I'm in solitary.'

'Agreed,' said Javert, and, turning, he shouted: 'You can come in now.'

A party consisting of *sergents de ville* armed with swords and policemen with truncheons entered the garret. They seized hold of the gangsters, and that dense assembly of bodies by the light of a single candle plunged the place in shadow.

'Handcuff the lot of them,' ordered Javert.

And as this was being done a voice which was not a man's, but was scarcely recognizable as that of a woman, shouted:

'Try to come near me!'

The Thénardier woman had taken up her stand in the corner by the window. She had shrugged off her shawl but still had on her hat. Her husband was crouched behind her, half-hidden by the cast-off shawl, and she was covering him with her body, standing with the paving-stone raised above her head like a giantess about to hurl a rock.

'Take care!' she cried.

They drew back towards the door, leaving a cleared space in the middle of the garret. The woman glanced at the men who had allowed themselves to be overpowered and muttered with an oath:

'Cowardly swine!'

Javert walked across the empty space while she glared at him.

'If you come any nearer I'll smash you!'

'A warrior,' said Javert, 'You bear yourself like a man, Mistress, but I have a woman's claws.' And he continued to advance.

Hair disordered and eyes blazing, she spread her legs, bent backwards and flung the slab of stone. Javert ducked and it passed over his head. It crashed against the wall, bringing down a shower of plaster, and rebounding, came to rest behind him. At the same moment Javert reached the couple. He clapped one heavy hand on the woman's shoulder and the other on her husband's head.

'Handcuffs!' he shouted.

The police in a body poured back into the room and within moments the order had been carried out. The woman, defeated at last, stared down at her manacled hands and those of her husband, and sank weeping to her knees.

'My daughters!' she cried.

'We've got them,' said Javert.

Meanwhile the police, having discovered the drunken man prostrate behind the door, were shaking him into life. He opened his eyes and stammered:

'Is it over, Jondrette?'

'Over and done with,' said Javert.

The handcuffed men, three with masks and three with blackened faces, still had the look of ghosts.

'Leave the masks on,' said Javert. Looking them over like Frederick the Great reviewing his troops at Potsdam, he greeted them in turn: 'Good evening to you, Bigrenaille – Brujon – Deux-Milliards . . .' And to the masked men, 'How nice to see you, Gueulemer – Babet – Claquesous.'

He then noticed the prisoner, who from the time the police had entered the room had stood with his head bowed and without speaking a word.

'Untie the gentleman,' he said. 'But no one's to leave until I give the order.'

After which he seated himself at the table, methodically wiped the pen and trimmed the candle, and taking a sheet of official paper from his pocket set to work on his preliminary report. But after writing the opening lines, which were no more than a routine formula, he looked up.

'Ask the gentleman to step forward.'

The police stared about them.

'Well, where is he?' Javert demanded.

He was gone. The prisoner – Monsieur Leblanc, Monsieur Urbain Fabre, the father of Ursula or the Lark – had disappeared.

The door was guarded, but the window was not. Directly his leg was untied, and while Javert was otherwise engaged, he had taken advantage of the confusion, the darkness, and the crowded state of the room to make his departure by that means. A man rushed to the window and looked out. There was no one to be seen. The rope-ladder was still swinging.

'Devil take it!' said Javert with tight lips. 'He must have been the best of the lot.'

XXII

The child who once cried in a tavern

On the evening following these events a youngster who seemed to have come from the Pont d'Austerlitz hurried along a narrow street in the direction of the Fontainebleau barrier. It was dark. The boy was pale and thin and wretchedly clad, wearing cotton trousers in that month of February, but he was singing at the top of his voice.

At the corner of the Rue du Petit-Banquier an old woman was ferreting in a garbage-heap by the light of a street lamp. The boy bumped into her and started back.

'Blimey, I thought it was an enormous – an ENORMOUS dog!' The emphasis he laid on the word as he sardonically repeated it is best conveyed by capital letters.

The old woman straightened up angrily.

'Little demon!' she shouted. 'If I hadn't been bending I know where I'd have put my foot.'

'Now then!' said the boy, already some way past her. 'Perhaps I wasn't all that wrong after all.'

The old woman, spluttering with indignation, seemed about to go after him, and the pale glow of the lamp fell upon her furious, wrinkled face with crowsfeet at the corners of the mouth. Her body was lost in shadow so that only the face was visible, and it was like a mask of decrepitude plucked out of the darkness by a beam of light. The boy considered her.

'Madame,' he said, 'does not possess the style of beauty that attracts me.'

He went on his way and again began to sing:

> The merry monarch, Coupdesabot,
> Was plump and very short, and so –

Here he broke off. He had arrived at the door of No. 50–52, and finding it locked he proceeded to kick it with a vigour more suited to the man's boots he was wearing than to his child's feet. The old woman caught up with him, shouting and gesticulating.

'Now what is it? What are you doing? Are you trying to break down the door?' He went on kicking and she screeched: 'That's no way to treat a respectable house!'

And suddenly she recognized him.

'So it's you, you little pest!'

'Why, it's the old dame,' said the boy. 'Good evening, Ma Bougon. I've come to call on my ancestors.'

The old woman responded with a grimace, unfortunately wasted in the darkness, which was a wonderful mixture of malice, decay, and ugliness.

'There's no one there, stupid.'

'Why, where's my father?'

'In prison – at La Force.'

'You don't say! And my mother?'

'She's in the Saint-Lazare.'

'Well, what about my sisters?'

'They're in the Madelonnettes.'

The boy scratched his head, stared at Ma'am Bougon, and whistled.

'Ah, well!'

Then he turned on his heels and she stood watching on the door-step while he disappeared beyond the black shapes of the elms shaking in the winter wind, his clear young voice again raised in song.

> The merry monarch Coupdesabot
> Was plump and very short, and so
> He went out shooting on a pair
> Of stilts to make the people stare,
> And spread his legs to let them through,
> And charged the customers *deux sous*.

PART FOUR

THE IDYLL IN THE RUE PLUMET
AND THE EPIC
OF THE RUE SAINT-DENIS

BOOK ONE

A FEW PAGES OF HISTORY

I
Well-tailored

THE YEARS 1831 and 1832, immediately succeeding the July Revolution, are among the most singular and striking in our history. These two years, in the setting of those that preceded and those that followed them, are like two mountains displaying the heights of revolution and also its precipitous depths. The social masses which are the base of civilization, the solid structure of superimposed and related interests, the secular outlines of France's ancient culture, all these constantly appear and disappear amid the storm-clouds of systems, passions and theories. These appearances and disappearances have been termed movement and resistance. At intervals one may catch a gleam of Truth, that daylight of the human soul.

This remarkable period is sufficiently distinct, and now sufficiently remote from us, for its main outlines to be discernible. We shall seek to depict them.

The Bourbon restoration had been one of those intermediate phases, difficult of definition, in which exhaustion and rumour, mutterings, slumber and tumult all are mingled, and which in fact denote the arrival of a great nation at a staging-point. Such periods are deceptive and baffle the policies of those seeking to exploit them. At the beginning the nation asks for nothing but repose; it has only one desire, which is for peace, and one aspiration, which is to be insignificant. In other words, it longs for tranquillity. We have had enough of great happenings, great risks, great adventures, and more than enough, God save us, of great men. We would exchange Caesar for Prusias and Napoleon for the Roi d'Yvetot – 'what a good little king he was', as Béranger sang. The march has gone on since dawn, and we are in the evening of a long, hard day. The first stage was with Mirabeau, the second with Robespierre and the third with Bonaparte. Now we are exhausted and each man seeks his bed.

What do they so urgently look for, the wearied devotions, the tired heroisms, the sated ambitions, the fortunes gained? They want a breathing-spell, and they have one. They take hold of peace tranquillity, and leisure, and are content. Yet certain facts emerge and call for notice by hammering on the door. They are facts born of revolution and war, living and breathing facts entitled to become part of the fabric of society, and which do so. But for the most part they are the under-officers and outriders whose business is to prepare lodgings for the commanders.

It is now that the political philosophers appear on the scene, while the weary demand rest and new-found facts demand guarantees. Guarantees are to facts what rest is to men.

That is what England demanded of the Stuarts after the Protector and what France demanded of the Bourbons after the Empire.

These guarantees are a necessity of the time. They have to be conceded. The princes 'offer', but it is the force of events that gives. This is a profound truth, necessary to know, which the Stuarts did not appreciate in 1660 and of which the Bourbons had not an inkling in 1814.

The predestined family which returned to France after the collapse of Napoleon was sufficiently naïve to believe that it was giving, and that what it had given it might take back; that the House of Bourbon possessed divine rights and that France possessed none; that the political concessions granted in the charter of Louis XVIII were no more than blossomings of the Divine Right, plucked by the House of Bourbon and graciously bestowed on the people until such time as it might please the king to reclaim them. But its very reluctance to concede them should have warned the House of Bourbon that the gift was not its own.

The Royal House was acrimonious in the nineteenth century. It pulled a wry face at every advance of the nation. To use a trivial word – that is to say, a commonplace and true one – it jibbed. The people saw this.

The Bourbons believed that they were strong because the Empire had been swept away before them like the changing of a stage-set. They did not perceive that they had been brought back in the same fashion. They did not see that they too were in the hands that had removed Napoleon.

They believed they had roots because they represented the past. They were wrong. They were a part of the past, but the whole past was France. The roots of French society were not in the Bourbons but in the nation. Those deep and vigorous roots were not the rights of a single family but the history of a people. They were everywhere, except under the throne.

The House of Bourbon was the illustrious and blood-stained core of France's history, but it was no longer the principal element in her destiny or the essential basis of her policies. The Bourbons were dispensable, they had been dispensed with for twenty-two years, the continuity had been broken. These were things they did not realize. How could they be expected to realize them, maintaining as they did that the events of 9 Thermidor had occurred in the reign of Louis XVII, and Marengo in the reign of Louis XVIII? Never since the beginning of history have princes been so blind in the face of facts, so unaware of the portion of Divine Authority which those facts embraced and enacted. Never has the earthly pretension which is called the right of kings so flatly denied the Right which comes from above.

It was a fatal blunder which prompted this family to lay hands on the guarantees 'offered' in 1814 – concessions, as they described them. A sad business. Those so-called concessions were our conquests, and what they called our encroachments were our rights.

When it thought the time was ripe, the Restoration, believing itself victorious over Bonaparte and enrooted in the nation – that is to say, believing itself to be both strong and deep – abruptly showed its face and chanced its arm. On a July morning it confronted France and, raising its voice, revoked both collective and individual rights, the sovereignty of the nation and the liberty of the citizen. In other words it denied to the nation that which made the nation, and to the citizen that which made the citizen.

This was the essence of those famous Acts which are called the Ordonnances de juillet.

The Restoration fell.

It was right that it should fall. Nevertheless it must be said that it had not been absolutely hostile to all forms of progress. Great things had been accomplished while the regime looked on.

Under the Restoration the nation had grown accustomed to calm discussion, which had not happened under the Republic, and to greatness in peace, which had not happened under the Empire. A free and strong France had provided a heartening example for the peoples of Europe. Revolution had spoken under Robespierre, and guns had spoken under Bonaparte: it was under Louis XVIII and Charles X that intellect made itself heard. The winds died down and the torch was re-lighted. The pure light of the spirit could be seen trembling on the serene heights, a glowing spectacle of use and delight. During a period of fifteen years great principles, long-familiar to the philosopher but novel to the statesman, were seen to be at work in peace and in the light of day: equality before the law, freedom of conscience, freedom of speech and of the press, careers open to all talents. So it was until 1830. The Bourbons were an instrument of civilization which broke in the hands of Providence.

The fall of the Bourbons was clothed with greatness, not on their side but on the side of the nation. They abandoned the throne solemnly but without authority. This descent into oblivion was not one of those grave occasions which linger as a sombre passage of history; it was enriched neither with the spectral calm of Charles I nor with the eagle-cry of Napoleon. They went away, and that was all. In putting off the crown they retained no lustre. They were dignified but not august, and in some degree they lacked the majesty of their misfortune. Charles X, causing a round table to be sawn square during the voyage from Cherbourg, seemed more concerned with the affront to etiquette than with the crumbling of the monarchy. This narrowness was saddening to the devoted men who loved their persons and the serious men who honoured their race. The people, on the other hand, were admirable. The nation, assailed with armed force by a sort of royal insurrection, was so conscious of its strength that it felt no anger. It defended its rights and, acting with restraint, put things in their proper place (the government within the law, the Bourbons, alas, in exile) and there it stopped. It removed the elderly king, Charles X, from under the canopy which had sheltered Louis XIV, and set him gently upon earth. It laid no hand on the royal persons except with sorrow and precaution. This was not the work of one man or of several men; it was the work of France, the whole of France; victorious France flushed with her victory who yet seemed to recall the words spoken by William of Vair after the Day of the Barricades in 1588: 'It is easy for those accustomed to hang upon the favours of the great, hopping, like birds on a tree, from evil to good fortune, to be bold in defying their prince in his adversity; but for myself, the fortunes of my kings will always be deserving of reverence, and especially in their affliction.'

The Bourbons took with them respect but not regret. As we have said, their misfortune was greater than themselves. They vanished from the scene.

The July Revolution at once found friends and enemies throughout the world. The former greeted it with enthusiasm and rejoicing, the latter averted their gaze, each according to his nature. The princes of Europe, like owls in the dawn, at first shut their eyes in wounded amazement, and opened them only to utter threats. Their fear was understandable, their wrath excusable. That strange revolution had been scarcely a conflict; it had not even done royalty the honour of treating it as an enemy and shedding its blood. In the eyes of despotism, always anxious for liberty to defame itself by its own acts, the grave defect of the July Revolution was that it was both formidable and gentle. And so nothing could be attempted or plotted against it. Even those who were most outraged, most wrathful, and most apprehensive, were obliged to salute it. However great our egotism and our anger, a mysterious respect is engendered by events in which we feel the working of a power higher than man.

The July Revolution was the triumph of Right over Fact, a thing of splendour. Right overthrowing the accepted Fact. Hence the brilliance of the July Revolution, and its clemency. Right triumphant has no need of violence. Right is justice and truth.

It is the quality of Right that it remains eternally beautiful and unsullied. However necessary Fact may appear to be, however acquiesced in at a given time, if it exists as Fact alone, embodying too little Right or none at all, it must inevitably, with the passing of time, become distorted and unnatural, even monstrous. If we wish to measure the degree of ugliness by which Fact can be overtaken, seen in the perspective of centuries, we have only to consider Machiavelli. Machiavelli was not an evil genius, a demon, or a wretched and cowardly writer; he was simply Fact. And not merely Italian Fact but European Fact, sixteenth-century Fact. Nevertheless he appears hideous, and is so, in the light of nineteenth-century morality.

The conflict between Right and Fact goes back to the dawn of human society. To bring it to an end, uniting the pure thought with human reality, peacefully causing Right to pervade Fact and Fact to be embedded in Right, this is the task of wise men.

But the work of the wise is one thing and the work of the merely clever is another.

The revolution of 1830 soon came to a stop.

Directly a revolution has run aground the clever tear its wreckage apart.

The clever, in our century, have chosen to designate themselves statesmen, so much so that the word has come into common use. But we have to remember that where there is only cleverness there is necessarily narrowness. To say, 'the clever ones' is to say, 'the mediocrities'; and in the same way to talk of 'statesmen' is sometimes to talk of betrayers.

If we are to believe the clever ones, revolutions such as the July Revolution are like severed arteries requiring instant ligature. Rights too loudly proclaimed become unsettling; and so, once righteousness has prevailed, the State must be strengthened. Liberty being safeguarded, power must be consolidated. Thus far the Wise do not quarrel with the Clever, but they begin to have misgivings. Two questions arise. In the first place, what is power? And secondly, where does it come from? The clever ones do not seem to hear these murmurs and continue their operations.

According to these politicians, who are apt at dissembling convenient myths under the guise of necessity, the first thing a nation needs after a revolution, if that nation forms part of a monarchic continent, is a ruling dynasty. Only then, they maintain, can peace be restored after a revolution – that is to say, time for the wounds to heal and the house to be repaired. The dynasty hides the scaffolding and affords cover for the ambulance.

But it is not always easy to create a dynasty. At a pinch any man of genius or even any soldier of fortune may be made into a king. Bonaparte is an instance of the first, and an instance of the second is Iturbide, the Mexican general who was proclaimed emperor in 1821, deposed in 1823, and shot the following year. But not any family can be established as a dynasty. For this some depth of ancestry is needed: the wrinkles of centuries cannot be improvised.

If we consider the matter from the point of view of a 'statesman' (making, of course, all due reservations), what are the characteristics of the king who is thrown up by a revolution? He may be, and it is desirable that he should be, himself a revolutionary – that is to say, a man who has played a part in the revolution and in so doing has committed or distinguished himself; a man who has himself wielded the axe or the sword.

But what are the characteristics needful for a dynasty? It must represent the nation in the sense that it is revolutionary at one remove, not from having committed any positive act, but from its acceptance of the idea. It must be informed with the past and thus historic, and also with the future and thus sympathetic.

This explains why the first revolutions were content to find a man, a Cromwell or a Napoleon, and why succeeding revolutions were obliged to find a family, a House of Brunswick or a House of Orléans. Royal houses are something like those Indian fig-trees whose branches droop down to the earth, take root and themselves become fig-trees: every branch may grow into a dynasty – provided always that it reaches down to the people.

Such is the theory of the clever ones.

So the great art is this: to endow success with something of the aspect of disaster, so that those who profit by it are also alarmed by it; to season advance with misgivings, widen the curve of transition to the point of slowing down progress, denounce and decry extremism, cut corners and finger-nails, cushion the triumph, damp down the assertion of rights, swaddle the giant mass of the people in blankets and put it hastily to bed, subject the superabundance of health to a restricted diet, treat Hercules like a convalescent, fetter principle with expediency, slake the thirst for the ideal with a soothing tisane and, in a word, put a screen round revolution to ensure that it does not succeed too well.

This was the theory applied in France in 1830, having been applied in England in 1688.

1830 was a revolution arrested in mid-course, halfway to achieving real progress, a mock-assertion of rights. But logic ignores the more-or-less as absolutely as the sun ignores candlelight.

And who is it who checks revolutions in mid-course? It is the bourgeoisie.

Why? Because the bourgeoisie represent satisfied demands. Yesterday there was appetite; today there is abundance; tomorrow there will be surfeit. The phenomenon of 1814 after Napoleon was repeated in 1830 after Charles X.

The attempt has been made, mistakenly, to treat the bourgeoisie as though they were a class. They are simply the satisfied section of the populace. The bourgeois is the man who now has leisure to take his ease; but an armchair is not a caste. By being in too much of a hurry to sit back, one may hinder the progress of the whole human race. This has often been the failing of the bourgeoisie. But they cannot be regarded as a class because of this failing. Self-interest is not confined to any one division of the social order.

To be just even to self-interest, the state of affairs aspired to after the shock of 1830 by that part of the nation known as the bourgeoisie was not one of total inertia, which is composed of indifference and indolence and contains an element of shame; it was not a state of slumber, presupposing forgetfulness, a world lost in dreams; it was simply a halt.

The word 'halt' has a twofold, almost contradictory meaning. An army on the march, that is to say, in movement, is ordered to halt, that is to say, to rest. The halt is to enable it to recover its energies. It is a state of armed, open-eyed rest, guarded by sentinels, a pause between the battle of yesterday and the battle of tomorrow. It is an in-between time, such as the period between 1830 and 1848, and for the word 'battle' we may substitute the word 'progress'.

So the bourgeoisie, like the statesmen, had need of a man who embodied the word 'halt'. A combination of 'although' and 'because'. A composite individual signifying both revolution and stability – in other words, affirming the present by formally reconciling the past with the future. And the man was there. He was Louis-Philippe of Orléans.

The vote of 221 deputies made Louis-Philippe king. Lafayette presided, extolling 'the best of republics'. The Paris Hôtel de Ville replaced Rheims Cathedral. This substitution of a half-throne for an entire throne was 'the achievement of 1830'.

When the clever ones had finished their work, the huge weakness of their solution became apparent. It had all been done without regard to the basic rights of the people. Absolute right cried out in protest; but then, an ominous thing, it withdrew into the shadows.

III

Louis-Philippe

Revolutions have vigorous arms and shrewd hands; they deal heavy blows but choose well. Even when unfinished, bastardized and doctored, reduced to the state of minor revolutions, like that of 1830, they still nearly always retain sufficient redeeming sanity not to come wholly to grief. A revolution is never an abdication.

But we must not overdo our praises; revolutions can go wrong, and grave mistakes have been made.

To return to 1830, it started on the right lines. In the establishment which restored order after the truncated revolution, the king himself was worth more than the institution of royalty. Louis-Philippe was an exceptional man.

The son of a father for whom history will surely find excuses, he was as deserving of esteem as his father was of blame. He was endowed with all the private and many of the public virtues. He was careful of his health, his fortune, his person and his personal affairs, conscious of the cost of a minute but not always of the price of a year. He was sober, steadfast, peaceable and patient, a friendly man and a good prince who slept only with his wife and kept lackeys in his palace whose business it was to display the conjugal bed to visitors, a necessary precaution in view of the flagrant illegitimacies that had occurred in the senior branch of the family. He knew every European language and also, which is less common, the language of every sectional interest, and spoke them all. An admirable representative of the 'middle class', he nevertheless rose above it and was in all respects superior to it, having the good sense, while very conscious of the royal blood in his veins, to value himself at his true worth, and very particular in the matter of his descent, declaring himself to be an Orléans and not a Bourbon. He was the loftiest of princes in the days when he was no more than a Serene Highness but became a *franc bourgeois* on the day he assumed the title of Majesty. Flowery of speech in public but concise in private; reportedly parsimonious, but this was not proved, and in fact he was one of those prudent persons who easily grow lavish where fancy or duty is involved; well-read but not very appreciative of literature; a gentleman but not a cavalier, simple, calm and strong-minded, adored by his family and his household; a fascinating talker; a statesman without illusions, inwardly cold, dominated by immediate necessity and always ruling by expediency, incapable of rancour or of gratitude, ruthless in exercising superiority over mediocrity, clever at frustrating by parliamentary majorities those mysterious undercurrents of opinion that threaten thrones. He was expansive and sometimes rash in his expansiveness, but remarkably adroit in his rashness; fertile in expedients, in postures and disguises, causing France to go in awe of Europe and Europe to go in awe of France. He undoubtedly loved his country but still preferred his family. He prized rulership more than authority, and authority more than dignity: an attitude having the serious drawback, being intent upon success, that it admits of deception and does not absolutely exclude baseness, but which has the advantage of preserving politics from violent reversals, the State from disruption and society from disaster. He was meticulous, correct, watchful, shrewd and indefatigable, sometimes contradicting and capable of repudiating himself. He dealt boldly with Austria at Ancona and stubbornly with England in Spain, bombarded Antwerp and compensated Pritchard. He sang the 'Marseillaise' with conviction. He was impervious to depression or lassitude, had no taste for beauty or idealism, no tendency to reckless generosity, utopianism, daydreaming, anger, personal vanity or fear. Indeed, he displayed every form of personal courage, as a general at Valmy and a common soldier at Jemmapes; he emerged smiling from eight attempts at regicide, had the fortitude of a grenadier and the moral courage of a philosopher. Nothing dismayed him except the possibility of a European collapse, and he had no fondness for major political adventures, being always ready to risk his life but never his work. He concealed his aims with the use of persuasion, seeking to be obeyed as a man of reason rather than as a king. He was observant but without intuition, little concerned with sensibilities but having a knowledge of men – that is to say, needing to see for himself in order to judge. He possessed a ready and penetrating good sense, practical wisdom, fluency of speech and a prodigious memory, upon which he constantly drew, in this respect resembling Caesar, Alexander, and Napoleon. He knew facts, details, dates and proper names, but ignored tendencies, passions, the diverse genius of the masses, the buried aspirations and hidden turbulence of souls – in a word, everything that may be termed the sub-conscious. He was accepted on the surface, but had little contact with the depths of France, maintaining his position by adroitness, governing too much and ruling too little, always his own prime-minister, excelling in the use of trivialities as an obstruction to the growth of great ideas. Mingled with his genuinely creative talent for civilization, order, and organization there was the spirit of pettifogging chicanery. The founder and advocate of a dynasty, he had in him something of a Charlemagne and something of an attorney. In short, as a lofty and original figure, a prince able to assert himself despite the misgivings of France, and to achieve power despite the jealousy of Europe, Louis-Philippe might be classed among the great men of his century and take his place among the great rulers of history if he had cared a little more for glory and had possessed as much feeling for grandeur as he had for expediency.

Louis-Philippe had been handsome as a young man and remained graceful in age. Although not always approved of by the nation as a whole, he was liked by the common people. He knew how to please, he had the gift of charm. Majesty was something that he lacked; the crown sat uneasily on him as king, and white hair did not suit him as an old man. His manners were those of the old regime, his behaviour that of the new, a blend of the aristocrat and the bourgeois that suited 1830. He was the embodiment of a period of transition, preserving the old forms of pronunciation and spelling in the service of new modes of thought. He wore the uniform of the Garde Nationale like Charles X and the sash of the Légion d'honneur like Napoleon.

He seldom went to chapel, and never hunted or went to the opera, being thus quite uninfluenced by clerics, masters-of-hounds and ballet-dancers, which had something to do with his bourgeois popularity. He kept no Court. He walked out with an umbrella under his arm, and this umbrella was for a long time a part of his image. He was interested in building, in gardening, and in medicine; he bled a postillion who had a fall from his horse, and would no more have been separated from his lancet than Henri III was from his dagger. The royalists laughed at this absurdity, saying that he was the first king who had ever shed blood in order to cure.

In the charges levelled by history against Louis-Philippe there is a distinction to be drawn. There were three types of charge, against royalty as such, against his reign, and against the king as an individual, and they belong in separate categories. The suppression of democratic rights, the sidetracking of progress, the violent repression of public demonstrations, the use of armed force to put down insurrection, the smothering of the real country by legal machinery and legality only half-enforced, with a privileged class of three hundred thousand – all these were the acts of royalty. The rejection of Belgium; the over-harsh conquest of Algeria, more barbarous than civilized, like the conquest of India by the English;

the bad faith at Abd-el-Kadir and Blaye; the suborning of Deutz and compensation of Pritchard – these were acts of the reign. And family politics rather than a national policy were the acts of the king.

As we see, when the charges are thus classified, those against the king are diminished. His great fault was that he was over-modest in the name of France.

Why was this?

Louis-Philippe was too fatherly a king. His settled aim, with which nothing might be allowed to interfere, of nursing a family in order to hatch out a dynasty, made him wary of all else; it induced in him an excess of caution quite unsuited to a nation with 14 July in its civic tradition and Austerlitz in its military history.

Apart from this, and setting aside those public duties which must always take precedence, there was Louis-Philippe's profound personal devotion to his family, which was entirely deserved. They were an admirable domestic group in which virtue went hand-in-hand with talent. One of his daughters, Marie d'Orléans, made a name for herself as an artist, as Charles d'Orléans did as a poet. Her soul is manifest in the statue which she named Joan of Arc. Two others of his sons drew from Metternich the following rhetorical tribute: 'They are young men such as one seldom sees and princes such as one never sees.'

Without distortion or exaggeration, that is the truth about Louis-Philippe.

To be by nature the '*prince égalité*', embodying in himself the contradiction between the Restoration and the Revolution; to possess those disturbing qualities of the revolutionary which in a ruler become reassuring – this was his good fortune in 1830. Never was the man more wholly suited to the event; the one partook of the other. Louis-Philippe was the mood of 1830 embodied in a man. Moreover he had this especial recommendation for the throne, that he was an exile. He had been persecuted, a wanderer and poor. He had lived by working. In Switzerland, that heir by apanage to the richest princedoms of France had sold an old horse to buy food. At Reichenau he had given lessons in mathematics while his sister Adelaide did embroidery and needlework. These things, in association with royal blood, won the hearts of the bourgeoisie. He had with his own hands destroyed the last iron cage at Mont Saint-Michel, built to the order of Louis XI and used by Louis XV. He was the comrade of Dumouriez and the friend of Lafayette; he had been a member of the Jacobin Club; Mirabeau had clapped him on the shoulder and Danton had addressed him as 'young man'. In 1793, when he was twenty-four, he had witnessed, from a back bench in the Convention, the trial of Louis XVI, so aptly named 'that poor tyrant'. The blind clairvoyance of the Revolution, shattering monarchy in the person of the king and the king with the institution of monarchy, almost unconscious of the living man crushed beneath the weight of the idea; the huge clamour of the tribunal-assembly; the harsh, questioning voice of public fury to which Capet could find no answer; the stupefied wagging of the royal head under that terrifying blast; the relative innocence of everyone involved in the catastrophe, those condemning no less than those condemned – he had seen all these things, he had witnessed that delirium. He had seen the centuries arraigned at the bar of the Convention, and behind the unhappy figure of Louis XVI, the chance-comer made scapegoat, he had seen the formidable shadow of the real accused, which was monarchy; and there lingered in his heart an awed respect for the huge justice of the people, nearly as impersonal as the justice of God.

The impression made on him by the Revolution was enormous. His memory was a living picture of those tremendous years, lived minute by minute. Once, in the presence of a witness whose word we cannot doubt, he recited from memory the names of all the members of the Constituent Assembly beginning with the letter A.

He was a king who believed in openness. During his reign the press was free and the law-courts were free, and there was freedom of conscience and of speech. The September laws were unequivocal. Though well aware of the destructive power of light shed upon the privileged, he allowed his throne to be fully exposed to public scrutiny, and posterity will credit him with this good faith.

Like all historic personages who have left the stage, Louis-Philippe now stands arraigned at the bar of public opinion, but his trial is still only that of the first instance. The time has not yet come when history, speaking freely and with a mature voice, will pass final judgement upon him. Even the austere and illustrious historian, Louis Blanc, has recently modified his first verdict. Louis-Philippe was elected by the approximation known as 'the 221' and the impulse of the year 1830 – that is to say, by a demi-parliament and a demi-revolution; and in any event, viewing him with the detachment proper to an historian, we may not pass judgement on him here without, as we have already seen, making certain reservations in the name of the absolute principle of democracy. By that absolute standard, and outside the two essential rights, in the first place that of the individual and in the second that of the people as a whole, all is usurpation. But what we can already say, subject to these reservations, is that all in all, and however we may view him, Louis-Philippe, judged as himself and in terms of human goodness, will be known, to adopt the language of ancient history, as one of the best princes who ever acceded to a throne.

What can be held against him except the throne itself? Dismissing the monarch, we are left with the man. And the man is good – good sometimes to the point of being admirable. Often, amid the heaviest perplexities, and after spending the day in battle with the diplomacy of a whole continent, he would return exhausted to his private apartments, and there, despite his fatigue, would sit up all night immersed in the details of a criminal trial, believing that, important though it was to hold his own against all Europe, it was still more important to save a solitary man from the executioner. He obstinately opposed his Keeper of the Seal and disputed every inch of the way the claims of the guillotine with the public prosecutors, those 'legal babblers' as he called them. The dossiers were sometimes piled high on his desk and he studied them all, finding it intolerable that he should neglect the case of any poor wretch condemned to death. On one occasion he said to the person we have already mentioned, 'I rescued seven last night.' During the early years of his reign the death-penalty was virtually abolished; the erection of a public scaffold was an outrage to the king. But, the execution-place of La Grève having vanished with the senior branch of his family, a bourgeois Grève was instituted under the name of the Barrière Saint-Jacques. The 'practical man' felt the need of a more-or-less legitimate guillotine, and this was one of the triumphs of Casimir Perier, who stood for the bigoted side of the bourgeoisie, over Louis-Philippe, who stood for their liberalism. He annotated the case of Beccaria with his own hand, and after the Fieschi plot he exclaimed, 'A pity I wasn't wounded! I could have pardoned him.' On another occasion, referring to the opposition of his ministers in the case of Barbès, one of the most noble figures of our time who was condemned to death in 1839 for his political activities, he wrote: '*Sa grâce est accordée, il ne me reste plus qu'à l'obtenir.*'*

For ourselves, in a tale wherein goodness is the pearl of rarest price, the man who was kind comes almost before the man who was great.

Since Louis-Philippe has been severely judged by some, and perhaps over-harshly by others, it is only proper that a man who knew him, and today is himself a ghost, should bear witness on his behalf at the bar of History. His testimony, such as it is, is clearly and above all else disinterested. An epitaph written by the dead is sincere; a shade can console another shade, and living in the same shadows has the right to praise. There is little risk that anyone will say of those two exiles, 'One flattered the other.'

IV
Flaws in the structure

At this moment, when our tale is about to plunge into the depths of one of those tragic clouds which obscure the beginning of Louis-Philippe's reign, there can be no equivocation; it is essential that this book should state its position in respect of the king.

Louis-Philippe had assumed the royal authority without violence, without any positive act on his part, through a revolutionary chance which clearly had little to do with the real aims of the revolution, and in which, as Duke of Orléans, he had taken no personal initiative. He had been born a prince and believed that he was elected king. He had not conferred the mandate on himself or attempted to seize it. It had been offered him and he had accepted it in the conviction, certainly mistaken, that the offer was in accordance with the law and that to accept it was his duty. He held it in good faith. In all conscience we must declare that Louis-Philippe did occupy the throne in good faith, that democracy assailed him in good faith, and that neither side is to blame for the violence engendered by the struggle. A clash of principles is like a clash of elements, ocean fighting on the side of water, tempest on the side of air. The king defended monarchy and democracy defended the

* 'His pardon is granted, it only remains for me to secure it.' The words may have been written to Hugo himself, who had sent the king a short poem pleading for Barbès. It is worth recalling that Hugo was living in exile when, long afterwards, he wrote this book.

people; what was relative, which is monarchy, resisted what was absolute, which is democracy. Society shed blood in the conflict, but the present sufferings of society may later become its salvation. In any event, it is not for us to attribute blame to those who did the fighting. The right in the matter was not a Colossus of Rhodes with a foot on either side, monarchist and republican; it was indivisible and wholly on one side; but those who erred did so sincerely. The blind can no more be blamed than the partisans of La Vendée can be dismissed as brigands. Violent as the tempest was, human irresponsibility had a share in it.

Let me complete this account.

The government of 1830 was in trouble from the start, born on one day and obliged on the morrow to do battle. Scarcely was it installed than it began to feel the undertow of dissident movements directed against the newly erected and still insecure structure. Resistance was born the day after its installation, perhaps even the day before. Hostility increased month by month, and from being passive became active.

The July Revolution, little liked by the monarchs outside France, was in France subject to a variety of interpretations. God makes known His will to mankind through the event, an obscure text, written in cryptic language, which men instantly seek to decipher, producing hurried makeshift renderings filled with errors, gaps and contradictions. Very few minds are capable of reading the divine language. The wisest, calmest and most far-sighted go slowly to work, but by the time they produce their rendering the job has long been done and twenty different versions are on sale in the market-place. Each interpretation gives birth to a political party, each contradiction to a political faction; and each party believes that it has the sole authentic gospel, each faction that it has its own light to shed.

Power itself is often no more than a faction. In all revolutions there are those who swim against the tide; they are the old political parties. To the old parties, wedded to the principle of heredity by Divine Right, it is legitimate to suppress revolution, since revolution is born of revolt. This is an error. The real party of revolt, in a democratic revolution, is not the people but the monarchy. Revolution is precisely the opposite of revolt. Every revolution, being a normal process, has its own legitimacy, sometimes dishonoured by false revolutionaries but which persists, even though sullied, and survives even though bloodstained. Revolutions are not born of chance but of necessity. A revolution is a return from the fictitious to the real. It happens because it had to happen.

Nevertheless the old legitimist parties assailed the 1830 revolution with all the venom engendered by false reasoning. Error provides excellent weapons. They attacked that revolution very shrewdly where it was most vulnerable, in the chink in its armour, its lack of logic; they attacked it for being monarchist. 'Revolution,' they cried to it, 'why this king?' Factions are blind men with a true aim.

The republicans uttered the same cry, but coming from them it was logical. What was blindness in the legitimists was clear-sightedness in the democrats. The 1830 revolution was bankrupt in the eyes of the people, and democracy bitterly reproached it with the fact. The July establishment was caught between two fires, that of the past and that of the future. It was the happening of a moment at grips with the centuries of monarchy on one side and enduring right on the other.

Moreover, in external affairs, being a revolution that had turned into a monarchy, the 1830 regime had to fall into line with the rest of Europe. Keeping the peace was an added complication. Harmony enforced for the wrong reasons may be more burdensome than war. Of this hidden conflict, always subdued but always stirring, was born a state of armed peace, that ruinous expedient of a civilization in itself suspect. The July Monarchy chafed, while accepting it, at the harness of a cabinet on European lines. Metternich would gladly have put it in leading-strings. Driven by the spirit of progress in France, it in its turn drove the reactionary monarchies of Europe. Being towed it was also a tower.

Meanwhile the internal problems piled up – pauperism, the proletariat, wages, education, the penal system, prostitution, the condition of women, riches, poverty, production, consumption, distribution, exchange, currency, credit, the rights of capital and labour – a fearsome burden.

Outside the political parties, as such, another stir became apparent. The democratic ferment found its echo in a philosophical ferment. The élite were as unsettled as the masses, differently but as greatly. While the theorists meditated, the ground beneath their feet – that is to say, the people – traversed by revolutionary currents, convulsively trembled as though with epilepsy. The thinkers, some isolated, some forming groups that were almost communities, pondered the questions of the hour, pacifically but deeply – dispassionate miners calmly driving their galleries in the depths of a volcano, scarcely disturbed by the deep rumblings or by glimpses of the furnace.

Their quietude was not the least noble aspect of that turbulent period. They left the question of rights to the politicians and concerned themselves with the question of happiness; what they looked for in society was the well-being of man. They endowed material problems, those of agriculture, industry, and commerce, with almost the dignity of a religion. In civilization as it comes to be shaped, a little by God and a great deal by man, interests coalesce, merge and amalgamate in such a fashion as to form a core of solid rock, following a law of dynamics patiently studied by the economists, those geologists of the body-politic. These men, grouped under a variety of labels, but who may be classified under the general heading of socialists, sought to pierce this rock and allow the living water of human felicity to gush forth from it.

This work extended to every field, from the question of capital punishment to the question of war, and to the Rights of Man proclaimed by the French Revolution they added the rights of women and children. It will not surprise the reader that, for a variety of reasons, we do not here proceed to a profound theoretical examination of the questions propounded by socialism. We will simply indicate what they were.

Problem One: the production of wealth.

Problem Two: its distribution.

Problem One embraces the question of labour and Problem Two that of wages, the first dealing with the use made of manpower and the second with the sharing of the amenities this manpower produces.

A proper use of manpower creates a strong economy, and a proper distribution of amenities leads to the happiness of the individual. Proper distribution does not imply an *equal* share but an *equitable* share. Equity is the essence of equality.

These two things combined – a strong economy and the happiness of the individual within it – lead to social prosperity, and social prosperity means a happy man, a free citizen, and a great nation.

England has solved the first of these problems. She is highly successful in creating wealth, but she distributes it badly. This half-solution brings her inevitably to the two extremes of monstrous wealth and monstrous poverty. All the amenities are enjoyed by the few and all the privations are suffered by the many, that is to say, the common people: privilege, favour, monopoly, feudalism, all these are produced by their labour. It is a false and dangerous state of affairs whereby the public wealth depends on private poverty and the greatness of the State is rooted in the sufferings of the individual: an ill-assorted greatness composed wholly of materialism, into which no moral element enters.

Communists and agrarian reformers believe they offer the solution to the second of these problems. They are mistaken. Their method of distribution kills production: equal sharing abolishes competition and, in consequence, labour. It is distribution carried out by a butcher, who kills what he distributes. It is impossible to accept these specious solutions. To destroy wealth is not to share it.

The two problems must be solved together if they are to be properly solved, and the two solutions must form part of a single whole.

To solve the first problem alone is to be either a Venice or an England. You will have artificial power like that of Venice or material power like that of England. You will be the bad rich man, and you will end in violence, as did Venice, or in bankruptcy, as England will do. And the world will leave you to die, because the world leaves everything to die that is based solely on egotism, everything that in the eyes of mankind does not represent a virtue or an idea.

It must be understood that in using the words Venice and England we are not talking about peoples but about social structures, oligarchies imposed upon nations, not the nations themselves. For nations we have always respect and sympathy. Venice the people will revive. England the aristocracy will fall; but England the nation is immortal. Having said this we may proceed.

Solve these two problems – encourage the rich and protect the poor; abolish pauperdom; put an end to the unjust exploitation of the weak by the strong and a bridle on the innate jealousy of the man who is on his way for the man who has arrived; achieve a fair and brotherly relationship between work and wages; associate compulsory free education with the bringing-up of the young, and make knowledge the criterion of manhood; develop minds while finding work for hands; become both a powerful nation and a family of contented people; democratize private property not by abolishing it but by making it universal, so that every citizen without exception is an owner, which is easier than people think – in a word, learn how to produce wealth and how to divide it, and you will have accomplished the union of material and moral greatness; you will be worthy to call yourself France.

This, apart from the aberrations of a few particular sects, was the message of socialism; this was what it searched for amid the facts, the plan that it proposed to men's minds. An admirable attempt, and one that we must revere.

It was problems such as this which so painfully afflicted Louis-Philippe: clashes of doctrine and the unforeseen necessity for statesmen to take account of the conflicting tendencies of all philosophies; the need to evolve a policy in tune with the old world and not too much in conflict with the revolutionary ideal; intimations of progress apparent beneath the turmoil; the parliamentary establishment and the man in the street; the need to compose the rivalries by which he was surrounded; his own faith in the revolution, and perhaps, finally, a sense of resignation born of the vague acceptance of an ultimate and higher right: his resolve to remain true to his own kin, his family feeling, a sincere respect for the people and his own honesty – these matters tormented Louis-Philippe and, steadfast and courageous though he was, at times overwhelmed him with the difficulty of being king.

He had a strong sense of the structure crumbling beneath him, but it was not a crumbling into dust, since France was more than ever France.

There were ominous threats on the horizon. A strange creeping shadow was gradually enveloping men, affairs and ideas, a shadow born of anger and renewed convictions. Things that had been hurriedly suppressed were again astir and in ferment. There was unrest in the air, a mingling of truths and sophistries which caused honest men at times to catch their breath and spirits to tremble in the general unease like leaves fluttering at the approach of a storm. Such was the tension that any chance-comer, even an unknown, might at moments strike a spark; but then the dusky obscurity closed in again. At intervals deep, sullen rumblings testified to the charge of thunder in the gathering clouds.

Scarcely twenty months after the July Revolution, the year 1832 opened with portents of imminent disaster. A distressed populace and underfed workers; the last Prince de Condé vanished into limbo; Brussels driving out the House of Nassau as Paris had driven out the Bourbons; Belgium offering herself to a French prince and handed over to an English prince; the Russian hatred of Tsar Nicholas; at our backs two southern demons, Ferdinand in Spain and Miguel in Portugal; the earth shaking in Italy; Metternich reaching out for Bologna and France dealing roughly with the Austrians at Ancona; the sinister sound in the north of a hammer renailing Poland in her coffin; angry eyes watching France from every corner of Europe; England, that suspect ally, ready to give a push to whatever was tottering and to fling herself upon anything ready to fall; the peerage sheltering behind Beccaria to protect four heads from the law; the fleur-de-lis scratched off the royal coach, and the cross wrenched off Notre-Dame; Lafayette diminished, Laffitte ruined; Benjamin Constant dead in poverty, Casimir Perier dead of the exhaustion of power; political sickness and social sickness declaring themselves simultaneously in the two capitals of the kingdom, the capital of intellect and the capital of labour – civil war in Paris and servile war in Lyons, and in both cities the same furnace-glow; the red glare of the crater reflected in the scowls of the people; the south fanatical, the west in turmoil; the Duchesse de Berry in La Vendée; plots, conspiracies, upheavals and finally cholera, adding to the growling mutter of ideas the dark tumult of events.

V

Facts making History which History ignores

By the end of April the whole situation had worsened. The ferment was coming to the boil. Since 1830 there had been small, sporadic uprisings, rapidly suppressed, but which broke out again: symptoms of the huge underlying unrest. Something terrible was brewing, and there were portents, still unclear but vaguely to be discerned, of possible revolution. France was watching Paris and Paris was watching the Faubourg Saint-Antoine.

The Faubourg Saint-Antoine, surreptitiously heated, was beginning to boil over. The taverns in the Rue de Charonne, odd though the adjectives may sound when applied to such places, were at once sober and tempestuous.

In these places the government was openly under attack, and the question of 'to fight or do nothing' was publicly debated. There were back-rooms where workers were made to swear 'that they would come out on to the streets at the first sound of the alarm and would fight, no matter how numerous their enemies'. When they had pledged themselves a man seated in a corner of the room would proclaim in a ringing voice, 'You have taken the oath! You have sworn!' Sometimes the proceedings took place in an upstairs room behind closed doors, and here the ceremony was almost masonic. The initiate was required to swear 'that he would serve the cause as he would serve his own father'. This was the formula.

In the downstairs rooms 'subversive' pamphlets were read – 'blackguarding the government', according to a secret report. Remarks such as the following were heard: 'I don't know the names of the leaders. We shall only be given two hours' notice on the day.' A workman said: 'There are three hundred of us. If we put in ten sous each that will be 150 francs for ball and powder.' Another said: 'I don't ask for six months or even two. We can be on level terms with the government in a fortnight. With 25,000 men we can stand up to them.' Another: 'I never get any sleep because I'm up all night making cartridges.' Now and then, 'well-dressed men, looking like bourgeois' appeared, causing 'some embarrassment' and 'seeming to be in positions of command'. They shook hands with 'the more important' and quickly departed, never staying longer than ten minutes. Significant remarks were exchanged in undertones. 'The plot is ripe, it's all prepared' . . . 'Everybody was muttering things like this,' in the words of a man who was present. Such was the state of excitement that one day a workman cried aloud in a café, 'We haven't the weapons!', to which one of his comrades replied, 'But the military have!' – unconsciously parodying Bonaparte's proclamation to the army in Italy. 'When it came to something very secret,' another agent's report said, 'they did not divulge it in those places.' It is hard to imagine what more they had to conceal, when so much was said.

Some meetings were held at regular intervals, and certain of these were confined to eight or ten men, always the same. Other meetings were open to all comers, and the rooms were so crowded that many had to stand. There were men who came from enthusiasm for the cause, and others 'because it was on their way to work'. As in the Revolution, there were ardent women who embraced all new-comers.

Other revealing facts came to light. A man walked into a café, had a drink and walked out again, saying to the proprietor: 'The revolution will pay.' Revolutionary agents were elected by vote in a café off the Rue de Charonne, the votes being collected in caps. One group of workers met on the premises of a fencing-master in the Rue de Cotte. There was a trophy on the wall consisting of wooden two-handed swords (*espadons*), singlesticks, bludgeons, and foils. One day the buttons were taken off the foils. One of the men said, 'There are twenty-five of us, but they don't reckon I'm worth anything. I'm just a cog in the machine.' He was Quénisset, later to become famous.

Small, significant trifles acquired a strange notoriety. A woman sweeping her doorstep said to another woman, 'We've been doing hard labour for a long time, making cartridges.' Posters appeared in the open street, appeals addressed to the Garde Nationale in the *départements*. One of these was signed, 'Burtot, wine-merchant'.

One day a man with a black beard and an Italian accent stood on a boundary-stone outside the door of a wine-shop in the Marché Lenoir and read out a striking document that seemed to have emanated from a secret source. Groups of people gathered and applauded. The passages which most stirred them have been recorded. 'Our doctrines are suppressed, our proclamations torn up, our billposters hounded and imprisoned . . . The recent collapse of the textile industry has converted many moderates . . . The future of the people is taking shape in our secret ranks . . . This is the choice that confronts us: action or reaction, revolution or counter-revolution. For no one in these days believes any longer in neutralism or inertia. For the people or against the people, that is the question, and there is no other . . . On the day we no longer suit you, destroy us; but until then, help us in what we are doing.' This was read out in broad daylight.

Other still more startling occurrences were, because of their very audacity, viewed with suspicion by the people. On 4 April 1832 a man climbed on to the boundary-stone at the corner of the Rue Sainte-Marguerite and proclaimed, 'I am a Babouviste!'; but they fancied that behind Babeuf lurked Gisquet, the Prefect of Police.

This particular speaker said, among other things:

'Down with property! The left-wing opposition is cowardly and treacherous. They preach revolution for effect. They call themselves democrats so as not to be beaten and royalists so as not to have to fight. The republicans are wolves in sheeps' clothing. Citizen workers, beware of the republicans!'

'Silence, citizen spy!' shouted a workman, and this brought the speech to an end.

There were strange episodes. One evening a workman near the canal met a 'well-dressed man' who said to him: 'Where are you going, citizen?' ... 'Monsieur,' the workman replied, 'I have not the pleasure of your acquaintance' ... 'But I know you well,' the man said. And he went on: 'Don't be afraid. I'm an agent of the committee. You're suspected of not being reliable. Let me warn you, if you give anything away, that you're being watched.' He then shook the workman by the hand and left him, saying: 'We shall meet again.'

Police agents reported scraps of conversation overheard not only in the cafés but in the street.

'Get yourself signed on quickly,' a weaver said to a cabinet-maker.

'Why?'

'There's going to be shooting.'

Two ragged pedestrians exchanged remarks reminiscent of the *jacquerie*:

'Who governs us?'

'Why, Monsieur Philippe.'

'No, it's the bourgeoisie.'

It would be wrong to suppose that we use that word *jacquerie* in any pejorative sense. The 'Jacques' were the poor, and right is on the side of the hungry.

A man was heard to say to another: 'We have a fine plan of campaign.'

Four men seated in a ditch at the Barrière-du-Trône crossroads were holding a muttered conversation of which the following sentence was overheard:

'They'll do their best not to let him go for any more walks in Paris.'

Who was the 'he'? An ominous riddle.

'The principal leaders', as they were called in the Faubourg, kept aloof. They were believed to meet in a café near the Pointe Sainte-Eustache, and a certain Auguste, president of the Tailors' Benefit Society in the Rue Mondétour, was said to be the link between them and the workers of the Faubourg Saint-Antoine. However, the identity of these leaders was never finally established, and no positive fact emerged to invalidate the lofty reply made later by one of the accused on trial by the Court of Peers in answer to the question:

'Who was your chief?'

'I knew of no chief, and recognized none.'

But all these were no more than words, suggestive but inconclusive, fragments of hearsay, remarks often without context. There were other portents.

A carpenter engaged in the erection of a wooden fence round the site of a house under construction picked up on the site a fragment of a torn letter on which he read the following: 'The committee must take steps to prevent the enlistment in its sections of recruits for other associations . . .' And further: 'We have learned that there are rifles, to the number of five or six thousand, at an armourer's shop in the Rue du Faubourg-Poissonnière (No. 5 bis). That section has no arms.'

This so startled the carpenter that he showed it to his comrades, and they found near to it another torn sheet of paper which was even more revealing. We reproduce the exact format for the sake of the document's historic interest.

Q	C	D	E	Learn this list by heart, then destroy it. All persons allowed to see it will do the same after you have given them their orders. Fraternal greetings. *L.* *u og a fe*

The persons in the secret learned only later what the four capital letters stood for – Quinturians, Centurians, Decurians, Éclaireurs (scouts). The letters *u og a fe* were a coded date – 15 April 1832. Under each of the capital letters were names with brief remarks appended. Thus: Q. Bannerel. 8 muskets. 83 cartridges. A safe man. – C. Boubière. 1 pistol. A pound of powder. – E. Teissier. 1 sabre. 1 ammunition pouch. Reliable. – Terreur. 8 muskets. Sturdy . . . And so on.

Finally a third sheet was found bearing, pencilled but still legible, a further and cryptic list of names. The loyal citizen into whose possession these documents came was familiar with their meaning. It seems that the names on the third list were the code-names (such as Kosciusko and Caius Gracchus) of all the sections of the Société des Droits de l'Homme in the fourth Paris *arrondissement*, with, in some cases, the name of the section-chief and an indication of his address. Today these hitherto unknown facts, which now are only a part of history, may be published. It may be added that this League of the Rights of Man appears to have been founded at a later date than that on which the pencilled list was found. At that stage, presumably, it was still in process of formation.

But on top of the spoken and written clues, concrete evidence was coming to light.

A raid on a second-hand dealer's shop in the Rue Popincourt unearthed, in the drawer of a commode, seven large sheets of grey paper, folded in four, containing twenty-six squares of similar paper folded in the form of cartridges, together with a card on which was written:

Saltpetre	12 ounces.
Sulphur	2 ounces.
Charcoal	$2\frac{1}{2}$ ounces.
Water	2 ounces.

The official report of the raid stated that the drawer had a strong smell of gunpowder.

A builder's labourer on his way home from work left, on a bench near the Pont d'Austerlitz, a small package which was handed in to the watch. It was found to contain two pamphlets signed Lahautière, a song entitled, 'Workers Unite' and a tin box filled with cartridges.

Children playing in the least frequented part of the boulevard between Père-Lachaise and the Barrière-du-Trône found in a ditch, under a pile of road-chippings and rubble, a bag containing a bullet-mould, a wooden form for making cartridges, a bowl in which there were grains of hunting-powder and a small metal cook-pot containing remnants of molten lead.

Police officers carrying out a surprise raid at five in the morning on the house of a man named Pardon (he later became head of the Barricade-Merry section, and was killed in the uprising of April

1834) found him standing by his bed making cartridges, one of which he had in his hand.

Two labourers were seen to meet after working hours outside a café in an alleyway near the Barrière Charenton. One passed the other a pistol, taking it from under his smock; but then, seeing that it was damp with sweat, he took it back and re-primed it. The men then separated.

A man named Gallais boasted of having a stock of 700 cartridges and 24 musket-flints.

The Government had word one day that firearms and 200,000 cartridges had been distributed in the faubourgs, and, a week later, a further 30,000 cartridges. The police, remarkably enough, were able to lay hands on none of this store. An intercepted letter contained the following passage: 'The day is not far distant when within four hours by the clock 80,000 citizens will be under arms.'

It was a state of open, one can almost say tranquil, ferment. The coming insurrection made its preparations calmly under the nose of the authorities. No singularity was lacking in this crisis that was still subterranean but already plainly manifest. Middle-class gentlemen discussed it amiably with work-people, inquiring after the progress of the uprising, much as they might have asked after the health of their wives.

A furniture-dealer in the Rue Moreau asked, 'Well, and when are you going to attack?', and another shopkeeper said, 'You'll be attacking soon. I know it. A month ago there were only 15,000 of you; today there are 25,000.' He offered his shotgun for sale, and his neighbour offered a small pistol at a price of seven francs.

The revolutionary fever was steadily rising, and no part of Paris, or of all France, was exempt. The tide was flowing everywhere. Secret societies, like a cancer in the human body, were spreading throughout the country. Out of the Society of Friends of the People, which was both open and secret, sprang the League of the Rights of Man, which, dating one of its Orders of the day 'Pluviôse, in the Fortieth Year of the Republic', was destined to survive court orders decreeing its dissolution, and which made no bones about calling its sections by such suggestive names as 'The Pikes', 'The Alarm Gun' and 'The Phrygian Bonnet'.

The League of the Rights of Man in its turn gave birth to the League of Action, composed of eager spirits who broke away in order to progress faster. Other new associations sought to lure members from the parent bodies, and section-leaders complained of this. There were the Société Gauloise and the Committee for the Organization of the Municipalities, also societies advocating the Liberty of the Press, the Liberty of the Individual, Popular Education, and one which opposed indirect taxation. There was the Society of Egalitarian Workers, which divided into three branches, Egalitarians, Communists, and Reformists. There was the Armée des Bastilles, a fighting force organized on military lines – units of four men under a corporal, ten under a sergeant, twenty under a second-lieutenant, and forty under a lieutenant – in which never more than five men knew one another, a system combining caution with audacity which seems to have owed something to Venetian models: its Central Committee controlled two branches, the Action branch and the main body of the Armée. A legitimist society, the Chevaliers de la Fidélité, tried to establish itself among these republican bodies, but it was denounced and repudiated.

The Paris societies overflowed into the larger provincial cities. Lyons, Nantes, Lille, and Marseilles had their League of the Rights of Man, among others. Aix had a revolutionary society known as the Cougourde. We have already used that word.

In Paris there was scarcely less uproar in the Faubourg Saint-Marceau than in the Faubourg Saint-Antoine, and the university schools were as agitated as the workers' quarters. A café in the Rue Saint-Hyacinthe, and the Estaminet des Sept-Billards, in the Rue des Mathurins-Saint-Jacques, were the students' headquarters. The Society of the Friends of ABC, which was affiliated with the 'Mutualists' in Angers and the Cougourde in Aix, met, as we have seen, at the Café Musain, but the same group also gathered at the cabaret-restaurant near the Rue Mondétour called Corinth. These meetings were secret, but others were entirely public, as may be gathered from the following extract from the cross-examination of a witness in one of the subsequent trials: 'Where was this meeting held?' ... 'In the Rue de la Paix' ... 'In whose house?' ... 'In the street' ... 'How many sections attended?' ... 'Only one' ... 'Which one?' ... 'The Manuel Section' ... 'Who was its leader?' ... 'I was' ... 'You are too young to have taken the grave decision to attack the Government. Where did your orders come from?' ... 'From the Central Committee.'

The army was being subverted at the same time as the civil population, as was later proved by the mutinies in Belfort, Lunéville, and Épinal. The insurrectionists counted on the support of several regiments of the line and on the Twentieth Light Infantry.

'Trees of liberty' – tall poles surmounted by a red bonnet – were erected in Burgundy and in a number of towns in the south.

This, broadly, was the situation, and nowhere was it more acute, or more openly manifest, than in the Faubourg Saint-Antoine, which was, so to say, its nerve centre. The ancient working-class quarter, crowded as an ant-heap and laborious, courageous and touchy as a hive of bees, simmered in the anticipation of a hoped-for upheaval, although its state of commotion in no way affected its daily work. It is hard to convey an impression of that lively and lowering countenance. Desperate hardship is concealed beneath the attic roofs of that quarter, and so are rare and ardent minds; and the moment of danger occurs when these two extremes, of poverty and intelligence, come together.

The Faubourg Saint-Antoine had other reasons for its feverish state. It was particularly affected by the economic crises, bankruptcies, strikes, unemployment, that are inseparable from any time of major political unrest. In a revolutionary period poverty is both a cause and an effect, aggravated by the very blows it strikes. Those proud, hard-working people, charged to the utmost with latent energies and always prompt to explode, exasperated, deep-rooted, undermined, seemed to be only awaiting the striking of a spark. Whenever there is thunder in the air, borne on the wind of events, we are bound to think of the Faubourg Saint-Antoine and the fateful chance which has set this powder-mill of suffering and political thought on the threshold of Paris.

The drinking-places of the quarter, so constantly referred to in this brief account, have acquired an historic notoriety. In troubled times their customers grow more drunk on words than on wine. A prophetic sense pervades them, an intimation of the future, exalting hearts and minds. They resemble those taverns on Mount Aventine built round the Sybil's cave and stirred by the sacred breath, where the tables were virtually tripods and one drank what Annius calls 'the Sybilline wine'.

The Faubourg Saint-Antoine is a people's stronghold. Times of revolutionary upheaval cause breaches in its walls through which the popular will, the sovereignty of the people, bursts out. That sovereignty may behave badly; it blunders, like all human action, but even in its blunderings, like the blind Cyclops, it remains great.

733

In 1793, according to whether the prevailing mood was good or evil, idealistic or fanatical, masses poured out of it which were heroic or simply barbarous. We must account for the latter word. What did they want, those violent men, ragged, bellowing and wild-eyed, who with clubs and pikes poured through the ancient streets of distracted Paris? They wanted to put an end to oppression, tyranny, and the sword; they wanted work for all men, education for their children, security for their wives, liberty, equality, fraternity, food enough to go round, freedom of thought, the Edenization of the world. In a word, they wanted Progress, that hallowed, good, and gentle thing, and they demanded it in a terrible fashion, with oaths on their lips and weapons in their hands. They were barbarous, yes; but barbarians in the cause of civilization.

They furiously proclaimed the right; they wanted to drive mankind into Paradise, even if it could only be done by terror. They looked like barbarians and were saviours. Wearing a mask of darkness, they clamoured for light.

And confronting these men, wild and terrible as we agree they were, but wild and terrible for good, there were men of quite another kind, smiling and adorned with ribbons and stars, silkstockinged, yellow-gloved and with polished boots; men who, seated round a velvet table-cloth by a marble fireplace, gently insisted on the preservation of the past, of the Middle Ages, of divine right, of bigotry, ignorance, enslavement, the deathpenalty and war, and who, talking in polished undertones, glorified the sword and the executioner's block. For our part, if we had to choose between the barbarians of civilization and those civilized upholders of barbarism we would choose the former.

But there is mercifully, another way. No desperate step is needed, whether forward or backward, neither despotism nor terrorism. What we seek is progress by gradual degrees.

God is looking to it. Gradualness is the whole policy of God.

VI
Enjolras and his lieutenants

At about this time, Enjolras, with an eye to possible contingencies, made a tactful survey of policy among his followers. While they were holding counsel in the Café Musain, he said, interlarding his words with a few cryptic but meaningful metaphors:

'It's just as well to know where one stands and whom one can count on. If one wants active fighters one has to create them; no harm in possessing weapons. People trying to pass are always more likely to be gored if there are oxen in the street. So let's take stock of our manpower. How many of us are there? No point in putting it off. Revolutionaries should always be in a hurry; progress has no time to waste. We must be ready for the unexpected and not let ourselves be caught out. It's a matter of reviewing all the stitches we've sewn and seeing if they'll hold, and it needs to be done at once. Courfeyrac, you can call on the polytechnic students, it's their free day. Today's Wednesday, isn't it? Feuilly, you can call on the workers at the Glacière. Combeferre has said he'll go to Picpus, there are a lot of good men there. Prouvaire, the stone-masons show signs of cooling off, you'd better find out how things are at the lodge in the Rue de Grenelle-Saint-Honoré. Joly can look in at the Dupuytren hospital and take the pulse of the medical students, and Bossuet can do the same with the law students at the Palais de Justice. I'll do the Cougourde.'

'And that's the lot,' said Courfeyrac.

'No.'

'What else is there?'

'Something very important.'

'What's that?' asked Combeferre.

'The Barrière du Maine,' said Enjolras.

He was silent for a moment, seeming plunged in thought, and then said:

'There are marble-workers at the Barrière du Maine, and painters and workers in the sculptors' studios. They're keen, on the whole, but inclined to blow hot and cold. I don't know what's got into them recently. They seem to have lost interest, they spend their whole time playing dominoes. It's important for someone to go and talk to them, and talk bluntly. Their place is the Café Richefeu and they're always there between twelve and one. It needs a puff of air to brighten up those embers. I was going to ask that dreamy character, Marius, but he doesn't come here any more. So I need someone for the Barrière du Maine, and I've no one to send.'

'There's me,' said Grantaire. 'I'm here.'

'You?'

'Why not?'

'You'll go out and preach republicanism, rouse up the half-hearted in the name of principle?'

'Why shouldn't I?'

'Would you be any good at it?'

'I'd quite like to try,' said Grantaire.

'But you don't believe in anything?'

'I believe in you.'

'Grantaire, do you really want to do me a service?'

'Anything you like – I'd black your boots.'

'Then keep out of our affairs. Stick to your absinthe.'

'That's ungrateful of you, Enjolras.'

'You really think you're man enough to go to the Barrière du Maine? You'd be capable of it?'

'I'm quite capable of walking along the Rue des Grès, up the Rue Monsieur-le-Prince to the Rue de Vaugirard, along the Rue d'Assas, across the Boulevard du Montparnasse and through the Barrière to the Café Richefeu. My boots are good enough.'

'How well do you know that lot at the Richefeu?'

'Not very well, but we're quite friendly.'

'What would you say to them?'

'Well, I'd talk to them about Robespierre and Danton and the principles of the Revolution.'

'*You* would?'

'Yes, me. Nobody does me justice. When I really go for something I'm tremendous. I've read Prudhomme and the *Contrat Social* and I know the Constitution of the Year Two by heart. "The liberty of the citizen ends where that of another citizen begins." Do you think I'm an ignoramus? I have an old *assignat* in my drawer. The Rights of Man, the Sovereignty of the people, I know the lot. I'm even a bit of an Hébertist. I can hold forth sublimely – for six hours on end, if need be, by the clock.'

'Be serious,' said Enjolras.

'I'm madly serious.'

Enjolras considered for a few moments, then made a gesture of decision.

'Very well, Grantaire,' he said soberly. 'I'll give you a trial. You shall go to the Barrière du Maine.'

Grantaire was living in a furnished room very near the café. He went out and was back in five minutes wearing a Robespierre waistcoat.

'Red,' he said, looking meaningfully at Enjolras. Smoothing the red points of the waistcoat with a firm hand, he bent towards him. 'Don't worry,' he said, and putting on his hat marched resolutely to the door.

A quarter of an hour later the back-room at the Café Musain was empty. All the 'Friends of ABC' had departed on their respective tasks. Enjolras, who had reserved the Cougourde d'Aix for himself, was the last to leave.

Those members of the Cougourde d'Aix who were in Paris were accustomed to meet in the Plaine d'Issy, in one of the abandoned quarries which are so numerous on that side of the city. While he was on his way there Enjolras reviewed the situation. The gravity of the times was apparent. When events which are the premonitory symptoms of social sickness stir ponderously into motion the least complication may impede them. It is a time of false starts and fresh beginnings. Enjolras had a sense of a splendid new dawn breaking through the clouds on the horizon. Who could tell? Perhaps the moment was very near when, inspiring thought, the people would assert their rights, and the Revolution, majestically regaining possession of France, would say to the world: 'More is to follow!' Enjolras was happy. The temperature was rising. He had, at that moment, a powder-train of friends scattered through Paris, and he was rehearsing in his mind an electrifying speech that would spark off the general explosion – a speech combining the depth and philosophic eloquence of Combeferre, the cosmopolitan ardours of Feuilly, the verve of Courfeyrac, the laughter of Bahorel, the melancholy of Jean Prouvaire, the knowledge of Joly, and the sarcasm of Bossuet. All of them working together. Surely the result must justify their labours. All was well. And this brought him to the thought of Grantaire. The Barrière du Maine was only a little off his way. Why should he not make a slight detour to look in at the Café Richefeu and see how he was getting on?

The clock-tower in the Rue de Vaugirard was striking when he thrust open the door of the café and, letting it swing to behind him, stood with folded arms in the doorway contemplating the crowded room filled with tables, men and tobacco-smoke.

Grantaire was seated opposite another man at a marble-topped table scattered with dominoes. He was banging on the marble with his fist, and this was what Enjolras overheard:

'Double six.'

'Four.'

'Blast! I can't go.'

'You'll have to pass. A two.'

'A six.'

And so on. Grantaire was wholly absorbed in the game.

BOOK TWO

ÉPONINE

I

The Field of the Lark

AFTER WITNESSING the unexpected outcome of the plot of which he had warned Javert, and directly after Javert had left the building, taking with him his prisoners in three fiacres, Marius himself slipped out. It was still only nine o'clock. Marius went to Courfeyrac, who was no longer the unshakeable inhabitant of the Latin Quarter but 'for political reasons' had gone to live in the Rue de la Verrerie, this being one of the quarters favoured by the insurrectionists at that time. 'I've come to lodge with you,' Marius said, and Courfeyrac pulled one of the two mattresses off his bed, spread it on the floor and said, 'You're welcome.'

At seven the next morning Marius returned to the tenement, paid his rent and what he owed Ma'am Bougon, had his books, his bed, his work-table, his chest of drawers, and his two chairs loaded on to a handcart, and departed leaving no address, so that when Javert came round during the morning to question him further about the previous night's affair he found no one there but Ma'am Bougon, who simply said, 'He's cleared out.'

Ma'am Bougon was convinced that Marius was in some way hand-in-glove with the criminals. 'Who'd have thought it?' she said to her friends in the quarter. 'A young man who looked as innocent as a newborn babe!'

Marius had two reasons for this prompt removal. In the first place, he now had a horror of that house in which he had encountered, at such close quarters, and in its most noisome and ferocious aspects, a form of social ugliness that was perhaps even more repulsive than the evil rich: namely, the evil poor. The second reason was that he did not want to be involved in the criminal proceedings which must surely ensue, when he would have been obliged to testify against Thénardier.

Javert assumed that the young man, whose name he had not noted, had taken fright and bolted, or possibly had not even gone back to his lodging at the time when the trap was sprung. He nevertheless endeavoured to find him, but without success.

Two months passed. Marius was still lodging with Courfeyrac. He learned from a friend at the law-courts that Thénardier was in solitary confinement, and every Monday he sent the clerk of the prison of La Force five francs for his benefit. Being now entirely out of funds, he had to borrow the sum from Courfeyrac. It was the first time in his life he had ever borrowed money, and these weekly subscriptions were an enigma both to Courfeyrac, who supplied them, and to Thénardier, who received them. 'Who on earth is the money going to?' wondered Courfeyrac, and 'Where on earth is it coming from?' wondered Thénardier.

Marius was deeply unhappy, his whole world in confusion and nothing good in prospect that he could see – once more blindly groping in the mystery that entangled him. He had had a brief, shadowy glimpse of the girl with whom he had fallen in love and the elderly man whom he presumed to be her father, those two unknown beings who were his sole interest and hope in life; and at the moment when he had thought to draw near them a puff of wind had borne them away like shadows. Not a spark of certainty or truth had emerged from the dreadful shock he had sustained, no possible basis of conjecture. He no longer even knew the girl's name, which he thought he had discovered. Certainly it was not Ursula, and 'the Lark' was only a nickname. And what was he to make of the man? Was he really hiding from the police? Recalling the white-haired workman he had seen near the Invalides, Marius now felt tolerably sure that he and Monsieur Leblanc were the same. Was he in the habit of disguising himself? He was both heroic and two-faced – why had he not shouted for help? Why had he run away? Was he in fact the girl's father? And finally, was he really the man Thénardier claimed to have recognized? . . . A string of unanswerable questions which, however, did nothing to diminish the angelic charm of the girl he had seen in the Luxembourg. Marius was in utter despair, his heart aflame and his eyes blinded, driven and drawn but unable to move. Everything was lost to him except love itself, even the instinctive perceptions of love. Ordinarily that flame which consumes us brings with it a hint of divination, something for the mind to work on. But Marius had none of these obscure inklings. He could not say to himself, '– if I were to go there, or try that? . . .' She must be somewhere, the girl who was no longer Ursula, but there was nothing to tell Marius where to look. His life could be summed up in very few words: absolute uncertainty and impenetrable fog. To see her again was his constant longing, but he had lost hope.

And to crown it all he was again in the grip of penury. Drawn close to him, hard on his heels, he felt that icy breath. For a long time now, in his state of torment, he had ceased to work. Nothing is more dangerous than to stop working. It is a habit that can soon be lost, one that is easily neglected and hard to resume. A measure of day-dreaming is a good thing, like a drug prudently used; it allays the sometimes virulent fever of the over-active mind, like a cool wind blowing through the brain to smooth the harshness of untrammelled thought; it bridges here and there the gaps, brings things into proportion and blunts the sharper angles. But too much submerges and drowns. Woe to the intellectual worker who allows himself to lapse wholly from positive thinking into day-dreaming. He thinks he can easily change back, and tells himself that it is all one. He is wrong! Thought is the work of the intellect, reverie is its self-indulgence. To substitute day-dreaming for thought is to confuse a poison with a source of nourishment.

This, as we may recall, was how it had been with Marius at the beginning, before love had come to plunge him wholly into that world of aimless and meaningless fantasies. A world in which we leave home only to go on dreaming elsewhere, indolently astray in a tumultuous but stagnant void. And the less we work the more do our needs increase. That is a law. A man in that dream state is naturally prodigal and compliant; the slackened spirit cannot keep a firm hold on life. There is good as well as bad in this, for if the slackening is perilous, generosity of spirit is healthy and sound. But the poor man who does not work, generous and high-minded as he may be, is lost. His resources dwindle while his necessities increase.

It is a slippery slope on to which the most honourable and strong-willed man may be drawn, no less than the weakest and most vicious; and it ends in one of two things, suicide or crime. Marius was slowly descending it, his eyes fixed on a figure that he could no longer see. This may sound strange, but it is true. The memory of an absent person shines in the deepest recesses of the heart, shining the more brightly the more wholly its object has vanished: a light on the horizon of the despairing, darkened spirit; a star gleaming in our inward night. This vision wholly occupied the mind of Marius, so that he could think of nothing else. In a remote way he was conscious of the fact that his older suit was becoming unwearable and the new one growing old, that his shirts and hat and boots were all wearing out; that is to say, that his very life was wearing out, so that he said to himself: 'If I could see her only once more before I die!'

He had but one consolation, that she had loved him, that her eyes had told him so, that although she did not know his name she knew his heart, and that perhaps, wherever she now was, in whatever undiscoverable place, she loved him still. Perhaps she even thought of him as constantly as he did of her. Sometimes, in those unaccountable moments known to every lover, when the heart feels a strange stirring of delight although there is no cause for anything but grief, he reflected: 'It is her own thoughts that are reaching me! ... And perhaps my thoughts are reaching her!'

Fancies such as these, which an instant later he brushed aside, nevertheless sufficed to kindle a glow in him which was something near to hope. Occasionally, and particularly in those night hours which most fill the dreamer with melancholy, he would write down in a notebook which he reserved wholly for that purpose the purest, most impersonal and loftiest of the meditations which love inspired in him. In this fashion he wrote to her.

But that is not to say that his reason was impaired. The reverse was true. He had lost the will to work and to pursue any positive aims, but he was more than ever clear-thinking and right-minded. He was calmly and realistically aware, if with a singular detachment, of what was going on around him, even of events and people for whom he cared nothing; he summed things up correctly, but with a sort of honest indifference, a frank lack of interest. His judgements, being almost absolved from hope, soared on a lofty plane.

Nothing escaped or deceived him in his present frame of mind; he saw into the depths of life, mankind and destiny. Happy is he, even though he suffers, whom God has endowed with a spirit worthy of both love and misfortune. Those for whom human affairs and the hearts of men have not been informed by this double light have seen and learned nothing. The state of the soul that loves and suffers is sublime.

So the days drifted by, bringing nothing new. It seemed to Marius only that the dark distance left for him to travel was rapidly growing shorter. He believed already that he could clearly see the threshold of the bottomless abyss. 'And shall I not see her even once more before I come to it?' he thought.

After walking up the Rue Saint-Jacques, by-passing the barrier and going some way along the former *boulevard intérieur*, one comes to the Rue de la Santé, then to the Glacière and finally, a little before the stream of Les Gobelins, to something like an open field which, in all the long, monotonous girdle of the outer boulevards of Paris, is the one place where Ruysdael might have cared to set up his easel. That indefinable something which we term charm is to be found there, in that green patch of grass strung with washing-lines and worn garments, in an old market-garden farmhouse built in the time of Louis XIII, with its tall roof eccentrically pierced with attic windows, and within the sound of laughter and women's voices. In the near distance are the Panthéon, the Tree of the Deaf Mutes, the Val-de-Grâce, black, squat, fantastical and magnificent; and somewhat lower, the staunch, square thrust of the towers of Notre-Dame. Because the place is worth seeing no one visits it; at the most a handcart or carter's waggon may pass by every quarter of an hour.

It happened, however, that Marius, in the course of one of his solitary walks, went that way, and that on this occasion there was a great rarity on the boulevard, another pedestrian. Vaguely struck by the picturesque look of the place, Marius turned to him and asked its name. 'It's called Lark's Field,' the stranger said; and he added: 'This is where Ulbach murdered the Ivry shepherdess.'

But after hearing the word 'lark' Marius had ceased to listen. In the state of dreaming there are sudden crystallizations that a word may suffice to bring about; the thoughts fix suddenly upon a single notion and nothing will dispel it. 'The lark' was the name which had replaced 'Ursula' in Marius's doleful musings. 'So this is her field,' he thought with the kind of irrational amazement proper to these fancies. 'Now I shall find out where she lives.'

It was absurd but irresistible. Every day thereafter he visited the Field of the Lark.

II

The hatching of crimes in the incubator of prison

Javert's triumph in the Gorbeau tenement had seemed complete but was not. In the first place, and it was his chief vexation, he had not laid hands on the victim of the plot. The prospective victim who escapes is even more suspect than the prospective murderer, and it seemed likely that this person, if he represented so rich a haul for the band of ruffians, must have been no less valuable a capture for the authorities.

Montparnasse had also escaped. They would have to wait for another chance to lay hands on that 'devil's playmate'. Montparnasse had in fact run into Éponine when she was keeping watch under the trees of the boulevard and had gone off with her, deciding that he was more in a mood to amuse himself with the daughter than play hired assassin for the father. It was a fortunate impulse and he was still at large. As for Éponine, Javert had picked her up later and she had gone to join her sister in the Madelonnette prison.

And finally, while the band were being conveyed from the tenement to the prison of La Force, one of its leading members, Claquesous, had got away. None of the police escort could say how it happened. He had simply vanished like a puff of smoke, handcuffed though he was, and all that could be said was that when they reached the prison he was no longer with them. It sounded like a fairy-tale – or perhaps it was something more sinister. Had he really melted like a snowflake into the shadows, or had he been assisted? Was he in fact one of those double-agents, much employed by the police in that unruly time, with one foot in the world of crime and one on the other side of the fence? Javert did not approve of these stratagems and would have nothing to do with them; but there were other police-officers in his section, his subordinates in rank but possibly more in touch with the workings of high authority, and Claquesous was so notable a villain that he would make an excellent informer. The thing was by no means impossible. However this might be, Claquesous had vanished and was not to be found, and Javert was more enraged than surprised.

As for Marius, 'that little nincompoop of a lawyer who had probably been scared out of his wits', and whose name Javert had forgotten, he was of trifling importance. In any event, a lawyer was easy to lay hands on – if, that is to say, he really was a lawyer.

The investigation had begun. The examining magistrate had thought it expedient to release one of the Patron-Minette gang from close confinement, hoping that he would talk. The one in question was Brujon, the long-haired man whose conversation Marius had overheard in the Rue du Petit-Banquier. He had been quartered in one of the prison yards, the Cour Charlemagne, where the warders were keeping an eye on him.

The name of Brujon is still remembered in La Force. In the hideous courtyard of the New Building, officially the Cour Saint-Bernard but known to the criminal world as the 'Lion's Den', on one of the foul, gangrenous walls reaching to the roof of the building, close by a rusty iron door, once that of the chapel of the ducal palace of La Force, which was later converted into a prisoners' dormitory, there was to be seen, as recently as twelve years ago, a crude drawing of a *bastille*, a prison-fortress, carved with a nail and bearing the name of the artist: BRUJON, 1811.

This Brujon of 1811 was the father of the Brujon of 1832.

The son, of whom we caught only a glimpse in the Gorbeau tenement, was an artful and decidedly capable young rogue whose general expression was one of innocent bewilderment. It was this look of innocence which had prompted the magistrate to release him from solitary, feeling that he might be of more value in the Cour Charlemagne than confined in a cell.

Criminals do not cease their activities because they have fallen into the hands of the law; they are not to be deterred by trifles. To be imprisoned for one crime does not prevent the planning of the next. They are like an artist with a picture hanging in the salon who nevertheless keeps busy in the studio.

Brujon seemed quite lost in prison. He was seen to stand about the courtyard for hours at a time, blankly contemplating the squalid list of canteen prices, which begins, 'Garlic, 62 centimes' and ends with 'Cigar, five centimes'. Or else he stood about shivering, with chattering teeth, saying that he had a fever and asking if any of the twenty-eight beds in the fever-ward was vacant.

But towards the end of February 1832, it transpired that the witless Brujon had dispatched three missives by prison messengers, sending them out not under his own name but under those of three of his fellow-prisoners. The three missives had cost him a total of fifty sous, a lavish expenditure which attracted the notice of the prison governor.

The matter was inquired into, and by consulting the record of such services posted up in the prisoners' common-room it was found that the sum had been divided as follows: three letters, one to the Panthéon, costing ten sous, one to the Val-de-Grâce, costing fifteen, and one to the Barrière de Grenelle, costing twenty-five sous, this last being the most expensive commission on the list. But it so happened that the Panthéon, the Val-de-Grâce, and the Barrière de Grenelle were the pitches of three of the most formidable 'barrier-prowlers', namely, Kruideniers alias Bizarro, Glorieux, a released convict, and Barrecarrosse, all of whom thus came under police observation, the presumption being that they were connected with Patron-Minette, two of whose leaders, Babet and Gueulemer, were now in custody. The three missives had been delivered, not to addresses but to persons waiting for them in the street, and it was believed that they had to do with a criminal enterprise in process of being planned. There were other reasons for suspecting this; the three men were accordingly arrested and it was assumed that Brujon's operation, whatever it was, had been nipped in the bud.

But about a week later one of the night warders, going his rounds on the ground-floor of the New Building, peered through the peep-hole in the door of Brujon's dormitory while he was slipping his time-disc into the box, known as the *boîte à marrons*, which was fixed to the wall outside every dormitory for that purpose, the system being designed to ensure that the warders performed their duties faithfully. He saw Brujon sitting up in bed and writing something by the dim light of the wall-lamp. He went in and Brujon was sent back to solitary for a month, but they were not able to discover what he had been writing. The police outside could not help them.

What is certain is that the next day a '*postillon*' was flung from the Cour Charlemagne into the Lions' Den, clearing the intervening five-storey building. A *postillon* is convict slang for a carefully kneaded lump of bread which is flung 'into Ireland', that is to say, over a prison roof from one courtyard into another, the term being of English origin, meaning from one country into another. Whoever picks up the missile will find a message inside it. If it is picked up by a prisoner, he passes it on to the person it is intended for; if by a warder – or by one of those secretly bribed prisoners known as 'sheep' in ordinary places of detention and 'foxes' in hard-labour prisons – it is handed in at the office and passed on to the police. On this occasion the *postillon* was delivered to the right address, although the addressee was at the time in a solitary-confinement cell. He was none other than Babet, one of the four leading spirits of Patron-Minette.

The message contained in the lump of bread was as follows:

'Babet. There's a job in the Rue Plumet. Garden with a wrought-iron gate.' This was what Brujon had written the previous night.

Although he was under close surveillance, Babet contrived to get the message passed from the La Force prison to that of the Salpêtrière, where a 'lady friend' of his was confined. The woman passed it on to an acquaintance of hers, a woman called Magnon who was being closely watched by the police but had not yet been arrested. This Magnon, of whom the reader has already heard, had a particular connection with the Thénardiers (to be described later) and by visiting Éponine could serve as a link between the Salpêtrière and Madelonnette prisons.

As it happened, the Thénardier daughters were released on the day she went to visit Éponine, the preliminary investigation into the affairs of their parents having disclosed insufficient evidence to warrant their detention. When Éponine came out, Magnon, who had been waiting at the prison gate, handed her Brujon's note and asked her to spy out the land. Éponine, accordingly, went to the Rue Plumet, located the wrought-iron gate and garden, and after a careful study of the house and its inhabitants called upon Magnon, who was living in the Rue Clocheperce. She gave her a 'biscuit', to be passed on to Babet's mistress in the Salpêtrière: the term, in the recondite jargon of the underworld, signifies 'no good'.

A few days later, when Babet and Brujon passed one another in a corridor of La Force, the one going to interrogation and the other coming away from it, Brujon asked, 'What about Rue P.?' and Babet answered, 'Biscuit.' Thus a criminal operation conceived by Brujon in the prison of La Force was still-born.

But the miscarriage, as we shall see, had results quite outside Brujon's intention. It happens often enough that, thinking to plan one event, we set in motion another.

III

Père Mabeuf's apparition

Marius no longer called upon anyone, but it happened now and then that he saw Père Mabeuf. While he had been slowly descending that melancholy stairway which may be termed the steps to the underground, since it leads to that place of darkness where life can be heard passing over one's head, Père Mabeuf, in his own fashion, had been making the same descent.

The sales of *Flora of Cauteretz* had wholly ceased; nor had the attempt to develop a new strain of indigo been successful. Monsieur Mabeuf's small garden in Austerlitz had the wrong exposure: all he could grow in it were a few rare plants which flourished in damp and shade. Nevertheless he had persisted. He had acquired a plot of land in the Jardin des Plantes, where the conditions were more favourable, in order to continue his experiments at his own expense, having raised the money by pawning the plates of his *Flora*. His luncheon was restricted to two eggs, one of which went to his elderly housekeeper, whose wages he had not paid for fifteen months, and often this was his only meal in the day. He no longer laughed his childlike laugh; he had grown morose and did not receive visitors. Marius was wise in not attempting to call on him. Occasionally they passed one another on the Boulevard de l'Hôpital when the old man was on his way to the Jardin des Plantes. They did not speak, but merely exchanged gloomy nods. It is the sad fact about poverty that the moment comes when it destroys relationships. They had been friends but now were merely on nodding terms.

Royol, the bookseller, was dead. Monsieur Mabeuf now had nothing but his own books, his garden, and his indigo plants, all that remained to him of happiness, pleasure in life and hope for the future. They enabled him to go on living. He said to himself: 'When I have grown my blue berries I shall be rich. I'll get the plates out of pawn and make my *Flora* fashionable again by dressing it up with humbug, newspaper advertisements and so forth; and I'll buy myself a copy of Pietro de Medino's *Art of Navigation*, the 1559 edition, with woodcuts – I know where I can get one.' In the meantime he worked all day on his indigo plot, returning home in the evening to water his garden and read his books. At this time Monsieur Mabeuf was very nearly eighty.

One evening he had a startling visitation.

He had returned home while it was still light. His housekeeper, Mère Plutarque, whose health was failing, was ill in bed. After dining off a bone on which a few scraps of meat remained and a piece of bread which he found on the kitchen table, Monsieur Mabeuf had gone to sit in the garden, on the old, overturned boundary-stone which served him as a garden bench. Close by this was a tumbledown wooden building of the kind commonly found in old orchard-gardens, with rabbit hutches on the ground floor and fruit-racks on its upper storey. There were no rabbits in the hutches but there were still a few apples on the racks, the last of the autumn crop.

Wearing his spectacles, Monsieur Mabeuf sat turning over the pages and re-reading passages of two books which delighted him and, which was more important at his age, greatly occupied his mind. The first of these was the famous treatise by Pierre de Lancre on *The Inconstancy of Demons* and the other was the discourse of Mutor de la Rubaudière on *The Devils of Vauvers and the Goblins of La Bièvre*. The latter was especially interesting to him because his own garden was one of those places believed in former times to be haunted by goblins. The sunset was beginning to cast a light on the upper half of things while it buried the lower half in darkness. While he read, glancing from time to time over the top of his book, Père Mabeuf was appraising his plants, among them a very fine rhododendron which was one of the consolations of his present life. They had had four dry days, wind and sun but not a drop of rain, and everywhere stems were wilting and buds drooping; everything needed to be watered, and the rhododendron was looking particularly sorry for itself. For Père Mabeuf plants were living beings. He had been working all day on his indigo plot and was tired out, but he got up nonetheless, put down his books on the bench and walked shakily to the well. He found, however, such was his state of exhaustion, that he had not the strength to pull up the bucket, and so he stood back, gazing wretchedly up at a sky that was now filling with stars.

The evening was one of those whose serenity allays the sufferings of man with a melancholy but timeless delight. The night promised to be as parched as the day had been. 'Stars everywhere,' the old man thought. 'And nowhere a cloud, not even a teardrop of rain.' His head sank on his breast, but then he looked up again. 'A tear of sympathy!' he prayed. 'A drop of dew.' Again he tried to raise the bucket but could not.

And at this moment a voice said:

'Père Mabeuf, would you like me to water your garden?'

At the same time there came a rustling like that of an animal in

749

the undergrowth, and from behind a shrub a tall, thin girl emerged who stood boldly confronting him, seeming less like a human being than a manifestation of the dusk.

Before Père Mabeuf, who as we know was timid by nature and easily alarmed, could say a word, this apparition, whose movements in the half-light had a sort of eerie abruptness, had drawn up the bucket and filled the watering-can. He watched while, bare-footed and clad in a ragged skirt, she bent over the flower-beds showering them with life; and the sound of water falling on the thirsty leaves was an enchantment to his ears. He felt that now the rhododendron was happy.

Having emptied the first bucketful, she drew a second and a third. She watered the whole garden. The sight of her striding along the paths, blackly silhouetted against the darkening sky with lanky arms outstretched under a tattered shawl, made him think of a large bat. When she had finished Père Mabeuf went up to her with tears in his eyes and laid a hand on her forehead.

'God will reward you,' he said. 'You must be an angel since you care for flowers.'

'I'm no angel,' she replied. 'I'm the devil, but it's all the same to me.'

Without heeding her words he exclaimed:

'How wretched it is that I'm too poor to be able to do anything for you!'

'But there is something you can do,' she said.

'What is it?'

'You can tell me where Monsieur Marius is living.'

He did not at first understand and stood with dim eyes gazing blankly at her.

'What Monsieur Marius?'

'The young man who used to come here.'

And now Monsieur Mabeuf had searched his memory.

'Ah, yes. I know who you mean. Monsieur Marius . . . You mean the Baron Marius Pontmercy, of course. He lives . . . or rather, he doesn't live there any more . . . I really don't know.' He had bent down while speaking to straighten a branch of the rhododendron. Still in this bowed position, he went on: 'But I can tell you this. He very often goes along the boulevard to a place in the neighbourhood of the Glacière, the Lark's Field. If you go that way you should have no difficulty in meeting him.'

When eventually Monsieur Mabeuf straightened himself he found that he was alone. The girl had disappeared. He was then genuinely a little apprehensive.

'Really,' he reflected, 'if my garden hadn't been watered I should think it was a spirit.'

Later, when he was in bed and on the verge of sleep, in that hazy moment when thought, like the fabulous bird that changes into a fish in order to cross the sea, takes on the form of dreaming in order to cross into slumber, this notion returned to him and he murmured confusedly:

'After all, it was very like what La Rubaudière tells us about goblins. Was it a goblin, perhaps?'

IV

The goblin appears to Marius

On a morning a few days after Monsieur Mabeuf received this strange visitation – it was a Monday, the day on which Marius was accustomed to borrow five francs from Courfeyrac for Thénardier – Marius, having put the money in his pocket, decided to 'go for a stroll' before leaving it at the prison, hoping that this would make him more disposed to settle down to work on his return. It was his invariable procedure. First thing in the morning he would seat himself at the writing-table contemplating a blank sheet of paper and the text he was supposed to be translating, which at that time was an account of the celebrated controversy between two German jurists, Gans and Savigny, on the subject of hereditary rights. He would read a few lines and struggle to write one of his own, and, finding himself unable to do so, seeing a sort of haze between himself and the paper, he would get up saying, 'I'll go for a stroll. Then I shall be more in the mood.' And he would go to the Field of the Lark, where the haze would be more pronounced than ever and his interest in Gans and Savigny proportionately less.

He would return home and again fail to work, being unable to bring order to his distracted thoughts. He would say to himself, 'I won't go out tomorrow. It stops me working.' And the next day he would go out as usual. His dwelling-place was more the Lark's Field than Courfeyrac's lodging. His real address should have been: Boulevard de la Santé, seventh tree after the Rue Croulebarbe.

On this particular morning he had deserted the seventh tree and was seated on a parapet overlooking the stream, the Rivière des Gobelins. Bright sunshine pierced the fresh, gleaming leaves of the trees. He sat thinking of *Her* until his thoughts, turning to re-proaches, rebounded upon himself, concentrating painfully on the indolence and spiritual paralysis that now possessed him, and the darkness that seemed to be thickening around him so that he could no longer see the sun.

And yet, amid the distressing incoherence of his meditations, which were not even a conscious process of thought, so far had he lost the will to action and the active sense of his despair; amid his melancholy self-absorption the stir of the outside world still reached him. He could hear, from either side of the little river, the sound of the Gobelins washerwomen pounding their linen in the stream, and above his head he could hear the birds singing and their wings fluttering in the elms – overhead the sounds of freedom, heedless happiness, winged leisure, and around him the sounds of daily work, joyous sounds which penetrated his abstraction, prompting him almost to conscious thought.

And suddenly, breaking in upon his state of tired ecstasy, a voice spoke, a voice known to him.

'Ah! There he is!'

He looked up and recognized the unhappy girl who had called upon him one morning, the elder Thénardier daughter, Éponine, whose name he had subsequently learned. Strangely, she appeared at once more impoverished and more attractive, two things which he would not have thought her capable of. She had progressed in two directions, both upwards and downwards. She was still barefoot and ragged as she had been on the day when she had marched so resolutely into his room, except that her rags were two months older, dirtier, their tatters more evident. She had the same hoarse voice, the same chapped, weather-beaten skin, the same bold and shiftless gaze, and added to these the apprehensive, vaguely pitiable expression that a spell in prison lends to the face of ordinary poverty. She had wisps of straw in her hair, not because, like Ophelia, she had gone mad, but because she had spent the night in a stable-loft. And with it all she had grown beautiful! Such is the miracle of youth.

She was contemplating Marius with a look of pleasure on her pale face and something that was almost a smile. For some moments she seemed unable to speak.

'So at last I've found you!' she finally said. 'Père Mabeuf was right. If you only knew how I've been looking for you. Did you know I've been in jug? Only for a fortnight and then they had to let me go because they'd got nothing against me and anyway I'm not old enough to be held responsible – two months under age. But if you knew how I've been searching – for six whole weeks. You aren't living in the tenement any more?'

'No,' said Marius.

'Well, I can understand that. Because of what happened. It's not nice, that sort of thing. So you've moved. But why are you wearing that shabby old hat? A young man like you ought to be nicely dressed. You know, Monsieur Marius – Père Mabeuf called you Baron Marius Something-or-other, but that's not right, is it? You can't be a baron. Barons are old. They go and sit in the Luxembourg, on the sunny side of the château, and read the *Quotidienne* at a sou a copy. I once had to give a letter to a baron like that – he must have been at least a hundred. Where are you living now?'

Marius did not answer.

'You've got a hole in your shirt,' she said. 'I'll mend it for you.' Her expression was changing. 'You don't seem very glad to see me.'

Marius still said nothing, and after a moment's pause she exclaimed:

'Well, I could make you look happy if I wanted to!'

'How?' said Marius. 'What do you mean?'

'You weren't so unfriendly last time.'

'I'm sorry. But what do you mean?'

She bit her lip and hesitated as though wrestling with some problem of her own. Finally she seemed to make up her mind.

'Oh well, it can't be helped. You look so miserable and I want you to be happy. But you must promise to smile. I want to hear you say, "Well done!" Poor Monsieur Marius! But you did promise, you know, that you'd give me anything I asked for.'

'Yes, yes! But tell me!'

She looked steadily at him.

'I've got the address.'

Marius had turned pale. His heart seemed to miss a beat.

'You mean –'

'The address you wanted me to find out. The young lady – you know . . .' She spoke the words with a deep sigh.

Marius jumped down from the parapet where he had been sitting and took her by the hand.

'You know it? You must take me there. You must tell me where it is. I'll give you anything you ask.'

'It's right on the other side of town. I shall have to take you. I don't know the number, but I know the house.' She withdrew her hand and said in a tone of sadness that would have wrung the heart of any beholder, but of which Marius in his flurry was quite unconscious: 'Oh, how excited you are!'

A thought had struck Marius and he frowned. He seized her by the arm.

'You must swear one thing.'

'Swear!' and she burst out laughing. 'You want *me* to swear!'

'Your father. You must promise – Éponine, you must swear to me that you'll never tell him where it is.'

She was gazing at him in astonishment.

'Éponine! How did you know that was my name?'

'Will you promise me?'

She seemed not to hear. 'But it's nice. I'm glad you've called me Éponine.'

He grasped her by both arms.

'For Heaven's sake, will you answer! Listen to what I'm saying. Swear that you won't pass this address on to your father.'

'My father . . .' she repeated. 'Oh, him. You needn't worry about him, he's in solitary. Anyway, what do I care about my father.'

'But you still haven't promised.'

'Well, let me go,' she cried, laughing, 'instead of shaking me like that! All right, I promise. What difference does it make to me? I'll say it. I swear I won't tell my father the address. Will that do?'

'Or anyone else?'

'Or anyone else.'

'Good,' said Marius. 'Now take me there.'

'This minute?'

'Yes, this minute.'

'Well, come along. Heavens,' she said, 'how delighted you are!' But after they had gone a little way she paused. 'You're keeping too close to me, Monsieur Marius. Let me walk on ahead and you must follow as though you didn't know me. It wouldn't do for a respectable young man like you to be seen in company with a woman of my kind.

No words can convey the pathos of that word 'woman', spoken by that child.

She walked a few paces and then stopped again. Marius caught up with her. She spoke out of the side of her mouth, not looking at him.

'By the way, you remember you promised me something?'

Marius felt in his pocket. All he had in the world was the five-franc piece intended for her father. He got it out and thrust it into her hand, and she opened her fingers and let the coin fall to the ground. She looked sombrely at him.

'I don't want your money,' she said.

BOOK THREE

THE HOUSE IN THE RUE PLUMET

I

The secret house

ROUND ABOUT the middle of the last century a Judge of the High Court and member of the Parliament of Paris, having a mistress and preferring to conceal the fact – for in those days great aristocrats were accustomed to parade their mistresses, but lesser mortals kept quiet about them – built himself a small house in the Faubourg Saint-Germain, in the unfrequented Rue Blomet, now the Rue Plumet.

The house was a two-storey villa, with two reception rooms and a kitchen on the ground-floor, two bedrooms and a sitting-room on the first floor, an attic under the roof and in the front a garden with a wide wrought-iron gate to the street. The garden was about an acre in extent, and this was all that could be seen from the street; but behind the villa there was a narrow courtyard, with, on its far side, a two-room cottage with a cellar, designed, if the need arose, to harbour a nurse and child. This cottage communicated, by a concealed door, with a very long, narrow, winding passageway, enclosed in high walls and open to the sky, so skilfully hidden that it seemed lost in the tangle of small-holdings of which it followed the many twists and turns, until eventually it emerged, by another concealed door, at the deserted end of the Rue de Babylone, in what was virtually another quarter, half-a-mile away.

This was the entrance used by the villa's original owner, so cunningly contrived that even had anyone troubled to follow him on his frequent visits to the Rue de Babylone, they could not have guessed that his ultimate destination was the Rue Blomet. By shrewd purchases of land the ingenious magistrate had gained possession of the whole area and was thus able to construct his secret passage without anyone being the wiser. When, later, he had divided up the land and sold it for vegetable-plots and the like, the new owners had supposed that their boundary-wall was also that of their neighbour on the other side, never suspecting that in fact there were two walls with a narrow, flagged footpath between them. Only the birds had observed this curiosity, which doubtless was the subject of much interested speculation among the sparrows and finches of a century ago.

The villa, built of stone in the style of Mansart and wainscoted and furnished in the manner of Watteau, rococo within and austere without, enclosed in a triple flowering hedge, was a blend of discretion, coyness, and solemnity such as befitted an amorous diversion of the magistrature. Both it and its passage have now vanished, but it was still standing fifteen years ago. In 1793 it was bought by a speculator who intended to pull it down, but being unable to complete the purchase he was forced into bankruptcy, so that in a sense it was the house that pulled down the speculator. Thereafter it remained uninhabited, crumbling slowly to ruins as any house does that has no human occupants to keep it alive. But it still had its original furnishings and was still offered for sale or rent, as the very rare passers-by along the Rue Plumet were informed by the faded billboard fixed in 1810 to the garden gate. And towards the end of the Restoration these same observers might have noted that the billboard had been taken down and that the ground-floor shutters were no longer closed. The house was again occupied, and the fact that there were double curtains in the windows suggested the presence of a woman.

In October 1829, a gentleman getting on in life had rented the property as it stood, including, of course, the cottage at the back of the villa and the passage leading to the Rue de Babylone, and had restored the two concealed doorways. As we say, the villa was already more or less furnished. The new tenant, having made good certain deficiencies, and put in hand repairs to the stairs and parquet flooring, the windows and the square tiling of the yard, had quietly moved in with a young girl and an elderly servant, more in the manner of an interloper than a man taking possession of his own house. The event had occasioned no gossip among the neighbours for the excellent reason that there were no neighbours.

This unobtrusive tenant was Jean Valjean, and the girl was Cosette. The servant was an unmarried woman named Toussaint whom Jean Valjean had saved from the workhouse, and who was old and provincial and talked with a stammer, three attributes which had predisposed him in her favour. He had rented the property under the name of Monsieur Fauchelevent, of private means. In the events that have already been related the reader will no doubt have been even more quick to recognize Jean Valjean than was Thénardier.

But why had Jean Valjean left the Petit-Picpus convent? What had happened?

The answer is that nothing had happened.

Jean Valjean, as we know, was happy at the convent, so much so that in the end it troubled his conscience. Seeing Cosette every day, and with the sense of paternal responsibility growing in him, he brooded over her spiritual well-being, saying to himself that she was his and that nothing could take her from him, that certainly she would become a nun, being surrounded by soft inducements to do so; that the convent must henceforth be the whole world for both of them, where he would grow old while she grew into woman-hood, until eventually he died and she grew old; and that, ecstatic thought, there would be no other separation between them. But as he thought about this he began to have misgivings, asking himself whether he was entitled to so much happiness, whether in fact it would not be gained at the expense of another person, a child, whereas he was already an old man; whether, in short, it was not an act of theft. He told himself that the child had a right to know something about the world before renouncing it; that to deny her in advance, without consulting her, all the joys of life on the pretext of sparing her its trials, to take advantage of her ignorance and isolated state to prompt her to adopt an artificial vocation, was to do outrage to a human being and tell a lie to God. It might be that eventually, realizing all this and finding that she regretted her vows, Cosette would come to hate him. It was this last thought, almost a selfish one and certainly less heroic than the others, that he found intoler-able. He resolved to leave the convent.

He resolved upon it, recognizing with despair that it must be done. There was no serious obstacle. Five years of retreat and dis-appearance within those four walls had dispelled all cause for alarm, so that he could now return to the world of men with an easy mind. He had aged and everything had changed. Who would now recognize him? Moreover the risk, at the worst, was only to himself, and he had no right to condemn Cosette to imprisonment in the convent because he himself had incurred a life-sentence. What did the risk matter, anyway, compared with his duty? Finally, there was nothing to prevent him from being prudent and taking pre-cautions. As for Cosette's education, it was now virtually complete.

Having made up his mind he awaited a favourable opportunity, and this soon came. Old Fauchelevent died.

Jean Valjean applied to the Prioress for an audience and told her that, his brother's death having brought him a modest legacy sufficient to enable him to live without working, he wished to leave the convent, taking his daughter with him; but since it was unjust that Cosette should have been brought up free of charge for five years without taking her vows, he begged the Reverend Mother to allow him to pay the community an indemnity of 5,000 francs. In this fashion he and Cosette departed from the Convent of the Perpetual Adoration.

When they did so he himself carried, not caring to entrust it to any other person, the small valise of which he had always kept the key in his possession. The little case had always intrigued Cosette because of the odour of embalming which emanated from it. We may add that thereafter Valjean was never separated from it. He kept it always in his bedroom, and it was the first and sometimes the only thing he took with him when he changed his abode. Cosette laughed at it, calling it 'the inseparable' and saying that it made her jealous.

For the rest, Valjean did not return to the outside world without profound apprehension. He discovered the house in the Rue Plumet and hid himself in it, going by the name of Ultime Fauchelevent. But at the same time he rented two apartments in Paris, partly so that he might not attract attention by always remaining in the same quarter, but also so as to have a place of retreat if he should need one and, above all, not be taken at a loss as he had been on the night when he had so miraculously escaped from Javert. Both apartments were modest and of poor appearance and were situated in widely separated parts of the town, one being in the Rue de l'Ouest and the other in the Rue de l'Homme-Armé.

Every now and then he would go to live in one or the other for a month or six weeks, taking Cosette with him but not their housekeeper, Toussaint. They were waited on by the porters of the two apartment-houses, and he let it be known that he was a gentleman of private means living outside Paris who found it convenient to keep a pied-à-terre for his use in the town. Thus this high-principled man had three homes in Paris for the purpose of evading the police.

Jean Valjean – Garde Nationale

Properly speaking, his home was in the Rue Plumet, and he had arranged matters as follows:

Cosette and the servant occupied the villa. The main bedroom with its painted pillars, the boudoir with its gilt mouldings, the late magistrate's salon hung with tapestries and furnished with huge armchairs – all these were hers; and she also had the garden. Valjean had installed in the bedroom a bed with a canopy of ancient damask in three colours and a very fine old Persian rug bought in the Rue du Figuier-Saint-Paul, but he had enlivened these austere antique splendours with gay and elegant furnishings suited to a young girl, a whatnot, a bookcase with gold-embossed volumes, a work-table inlaid with mother-of-pearl, a brightly decorated dressing-table, and a washstand of Japanese porcelain. Long damask curtains in three colours on a red background, matching the bed-canopy, draped the first-floor windows; and there were tapestry curtains on the ground floor. In winter Cosette's little house was heated from top to bottom. Valjean himself lived in the sort of porter's lodge across the yard, with a mattress on a truckle-bed, a plain wooden table, two rush-bottomed chairs, an earthenware water-jug, a few books on a shelf and never any fire. He dined with Cosette, and there was a loaf of black bread for him on the table. He had said to Toussaint when she first entered their employment, 'You must understand that Mademoiselle is the mistress of the house.' 'But w-what about you, Monsieur?' asked Toussaint in astonishment ... 'I am something better than the master – I am the father.'

Cosette had been taught the rudiments of housekeeping at the convent and she had charge of the household budget, which was extremely modest. Jean Valjean took her for a walk every day, always to the Luxembourg Garden and to its least frequented alleyway, and on Sundays they attended Mass, always at Saint-Jacques-du-Haut-Pas, since it was a long way from their home. That is a very poor neighbourhood and he was generous with alms, which made him well-known to the beggars haunting the church. This it was that had prompted Thénardier to address him as 'The benevolent gentleman of the Church of Saint-Jacques-du-Haut-Pas'. He liked to take Cosette with him when he visited the poor and the sick, but no visitor ever came to the house in the Rue

Plumet. Toussaint did the shopping and Valjean himself etched water from a near-by pump in the boulevard. Their store of wine and firewood was kept in a sort of semi-underground cellar near the Porte-de-Babylone door, of which the walls were carved in the semblance of a cave. It had served the late magistrate as a grotto: for without a grotto, in that time of follies and *petites-maisons*, no clandestine love-affair had been complete.

In the Rue de Babylone door there was a box designed for the reception of letters and newspapers; but since the present occupants of the villa were accustomed to receive neither, the only use of this former receptacle of *billets-doux* was for the reception of tax-demands and notices concerned with guard-duty. For Monsieur Fauchelevent, gentleman of private means, was a member of the Garde Nationale, not having been able to slip through the meshes of the census of 1831. The municipal inquiries undertaken at that time had penetrated even into the Petit-Picpus convent, a hallowed institution which had endowed Ultime Fauchelevent with an aura of respectability, so that when he left it he was considered worthy to join the Garde.

Accordingly, three or four times a year Jean Valjean donned his uniform and did his spell of duty – very readily, it may be said, because this was a trapping of orthodoxy which enabled him to mingle with the outside world without otherwise emerging from his solitude. Valjean had in fact just turned sixty, the age of legal exemption, but he did not look more than fifty and had no desire in any case to escape the sergeant-major or fail the Comte de Lobau. He had no standing in the community; he was concealing his true name and identity as well as his age; but, as we say, he was very willing to be a National Guard. His whole ambition was to appear like any other man who pays his taxes; his ideal was to be an angel in private and, in public, a respectable citizen.

One detail, however, must be noted. When Valjean went out with Cosette he dressed in the manner we have described and could easily be mistaken for a retired officer. But when he went out alone, which was generally at night, he always wore workman's clothes and a peaked cap which hid his face. Was this from caution or humility? It was from both. Cosette, accustomed by now to the strangeness of his life, scarcely noticed her father's eccentricities. As for Toussaint, she held him in veneration and approved of everything he did. When their butcher, having caught a glimpse of him, remarked, 'He's a queer customer, isn't he?' she answered, 'He's a s-saint.'

None of them ever used the door on the Rue de Babylone. Except for an occasional glimpse of them through the wrought-iron gate, it would have been difficult for anyone to guess that they lived in the Rue Plumet. That gate was always locked, and Valjean left the garden untended in order that it might not attract notice.

In this, perhaps, he was mistaken.

III

Of leaves and branches

This garden, left to its own devices for more than half a century, had become unusual and charming. Pedestrians of forty years ago stopped in the street to peer into it through the grille, having no notion of the secrets concealed behind its dense foliage. More than one dreamer in those days allowed his gaze and his thoughts to travel beyond the twisted bars of that ancient, padlocked gate hung between two moss-grown stone pillars and grotesquely crowned with a pattern of intricate arabesques.

There was an old stone bench in one corner, one or two lichen-covered statues, a few rotting remains of trellis-work that had blown off the wall; but there were no lawns or garden paths, and couch-grass grew everywhere. Gardeners had deserted it and Nature had taken charge, scattering it with an abundance of weeds, a fortunate thing to happen to any patch of poor soil. The gilly-flowers in bloom were splendid. Nothing in that garden hindered the thrust of things towards life, and the sacred process of growth found itself undisturbed. The trees leaned down to the brambles, and the brambles rose up into the trees; plants had climbed and branches had bent; creepers spreading on the ground had risen to join flowers blossoming in the air, and things stirred by the wind had stooped to the level of things lingering in the moss. Trunks and branches, leaves, twigs, husks, and thorns had mingled, married and cross-bred; vegetation in a close and deep embrace had cele-brated and performed, under the satisfied eye of the Creator, the holy mystery of its consanguinity, a symbol of human fraternity in that enclosure some three hundred feet square. It was no longer a garden but one huge thicket, that is to say, something as im-penetrable as a forest and as populous as a town, quivering like a bird's nest, dark as a cathedral, scented as a bouquet, solitary as a tomb, and as living as a crowd.

In the spring this giant thicket, untrammelled behind its iron gate and four walls, went on heat in the universal labour of seeding and growth, trembled in the warmth of the rising sun like an animal which breathes the scent of cosmic love and feels the April sap rise turbulent in its veins, and, shaking its tangled green mane, sprinkles over the damp earth, the crumbling statues, the steps of the villa, and even the empty street outside, a star-shower of blossom, of dew-like pearls, fruitfulness, beauty, life, rapture and fragrance. At midday a host of white butterflies hovered about it, and their fluttering in its shadows, like flakes of summer snow, was a heavenly sight. Under that gay canopy of verdure a host of innocent voices was raised, and what the twitter of birds neglected to say the buzz of insects supplied. In the evening a dreamlike haze rose up from it and enveloped it, a shroud of mist, a calm, celestial sadness covered it, and the intoxicating scent of honeysuckle and columbine emanated from it like an exquisite and subtle poison. The last calls could be heard of pigeon and wagtail nesting in the branches, and that secret intimacy of bird and tree could be felt: by day the flutter of wings rejoiced the leaves, and by night the leaves sheltered the wings.

In winter the house could just be seen through the bare, shivering tangle of the thicket. Instead of blossom and dewdrops there were the long, silvery trails of slugs winding over the thick carpet of dead leaves; but in any event, in all its aspects and in every season, that little enclosure breathed out an air of melancholy and contemplation, solitude and liberty, the absence of man and the presence of God. The rusty iron gate seemed to be saying: 'This garden belongs to me.'

It mattered little that the streets of Paris lay all around it, the classic, stately mansions of the Rue de Varenne no more than a stone's throw away, the dome of the Invalides very near and the Chamber of Deputies not far distant. Carriages might roll majestically along the Rue de Bourgogne and the Rue Saint-Dominique; yellow, brown, white and red omnibuses might pass at the nearby intersection; but the Rue Plumet remained deserted. The death of former house-owners, the passage of a revolution, the collapse of ancient fortunes, forty years of abandonment and neglect had restored to that favoured spot fern and hemlock, clover and foxglove, tall plants with pallid leaves, lizards, blindworms, beetles and all manner of insects, so that within those four walls there had risen from the depths of the earth an indescribable wildness and grandeur. Nature, which disdains the contrivances of men and gives her whole heart wherever she gives at all, whether in the ant-hill or the eagle's nest, had reproduced in this insignificant Paris garden the savage splendour of a virgin forest in the New World.

Nothing is truly small, as anyone knows who has peered into the secrets of Nature. Though philosophy may reach no final conclusion as to original cause or ultimate extent, the contemplative mind is moved to ecstasy by this merging of forces into unity. Everything works upon everything else.

The science of mathematics applies to the clouds; the radiance of starlight nourishes the rose; no thinker will dare to say that the scent of hawthorn is valueless to the constellations. Who can predict the course of a molecule? How do we know that the creation of worlds is not determined by the fall of grains of sand? Who can measure the action and counter-action between the infinitely great and the infinitely small, the play of causes in the depths of being, the cataclysms of creation? The cheese-mite has its worth; the smallest is large and the largest is small; everything balances within the laws of necessity, a terrifying vision for the mind. Between living things and objects there is a miraculous relationship; within that inexhaustible compass, from the sun to the grub, there is no room for disdain; each thing needs every other thing. Light does not carry the scents of earth into the upper air without knowing what it is doing with them; darkness confers the essence of the stars upon the sleeping flowers. Every bird that flies carries a shred of the infinite in its claws. The process of birth is the shedding of a meteorite or the peck of a hatching swallow on the shell of its egg; it is the coming of an earthworm or of Socrates, both equally important to the scheme of things. Where the telescope ends the microscope begins, and which has the wider vision? You may choose. A patch of mould is a galaxy of blossom; a nebula is an ant-heap of stars. There is the same affinity, if still more inconceivable, between the things of the mind and material things. Elements and principles are intermingled; they combine and marry and each increases and completes the other, so that the material and the moral world both are finally manifest. The phenomenon perpetually folds in upon itself. In the vast cosmic changes universal life comes and goes in unknown quantities, borne by the mysterious flow of invisible currents, making use of everything, wasting not a single sleeper's dream, sowing an animalcule here and shattering a star there, swaying and writhing, turning light into a force and thought into an element; disseminated yet indivisible, dissolving all things except that geometrical point, the self; reducing all things to the core which is the soul, and causing all things to flower into God; all activities from the highest to the humblest – harnessing the movements of the earth and the flight of an insect – to the secret workings of an illimitable mechanism; perhaps – who can say? – governing, if only by the universality of the law, the evolution of a comet in the heavens by the circling of infusoria in a drop of water. A machine made of spirit. A huge meshing of gears of which the first motive force is the gnat and the largest wheel the zodiac.

IV
The changed grille

It seemed that this garden, having been first created for the concealment of libertine mysteries, had deliberately transformed itself so as to render it suited to the harbouring of mysteries of a chaster kind. It no longer contained bowers or trim lawns, arbours or grottos, but was a place of magnificently ragged greenery that veiled it on all sides. Paphos, the town of Venus, had been turned into Eden, as though purged by some sort of repentance, and the coy retreat, so suspect in its purpose, had become a place of innocence and modesty. Nature had rescued it from the artifices of gallantry, filled it with shade and redesigned it for true love.

And in this solitude a ready heart was waiting. Love had only to show itself, and there to receive it was a temple, composed of verdure and grasses, birdsong, swaying branches, and soft shadow, and a spirit that was all tenderness and trust, candour, hopefulness, yearning, and illusion.

Cosette when she left the convent had been still not much more than a child, a little over fourteen and, as we have seen, at the 'awkward age'. Except for her eyes she was more plain than pretty. Although she had no feature that was ugly, she was uncouth and skinny, at once shy and over-bold – in a word, a big little girl.

Her education was concluded. That is to say, she had been instructed in religion, above all in the arts of devotion; also in history, or what passed for history in the convent, geography, grammar and the parts of speech, the Kings of France, a little music and drawing, and housekeeping. But she was ignorant of all other matters, which is both a charm and a peril. A young girl's mind must not be left too much in darkness or else too startling and too vivid imaginings may arise in it, as in a curtained room. She needs to be gently and cautiously enlightened, more by the reflection of reality than by its direct, harsh glare, a serviceable and gently austere half-light which dispels the terrors of youth and safeguards it against pitfalls. Only a mother's instinct, that intuitive blend of maiden recollection and womanly experience, can understand the composition and the shedding of that half-light; there is no substitute for this. In the forming of a young girl's soul not all the nuns in the world can take the place of a mother.

Cosette had had no mother, only a numerous assortment of mothers. As for Jean Valjean, with all his overflowing love and deep concern he was still no more than an elderly man who knew nothing at all.

But in this work of education, this most serious business of preparing a woman for life, how much wisdom is needed, how much skill in combating that state of profound ignorance that we call innocence! Nothing renders a girl more ripe for passion than a convent. It impels thought towards the unknown. The heart, turned in upon itself, shrinks, being unable to reach outwards, and probes more deeply, being unable to spread elsewhere. Hence the visions and fancies, the speculations, the tales invented and adventures secretly longed for, the castles of fantasy built solely in the mind, vacant and secret dwelling-places where passion may instal itself directly the door is opened. The convent is a prison which, if it is to confine the human heart, must endure for a lifetime.

Nothing could have been more delightful to Cosette when she left the convent, or more dangerous, than that house in the Rue Plumet.

It was at once the continuation of solitude and the beginning of freedom; an enclosed garden filled with a heady riot of nature; the same dream as in the convent, but with young men actually to be seen; a gate like the convent grille but giving on to the street.

Nevertheless, as we have said, when she came there Cosette was still a child. Jean Valjean made her a present of that untended garden. 'Do what you like with it,' he said. Cosette was at first amused by it. She explored the undergrowth and lifted stones in a search for 'little creatures', playing in the garden before she began to dream in it, loving it for the insects she found in the grass before she learned to love it for the stars shining through the branches above her head.

And then she wholeheartedly loved her father – that is to say, Jean Valjean – with an innocent, confiding love which made of him the most charming and desirable of companions. Monsieur Madeleine, we may recall, had read a great deal. Jean Valjean continued to do so, and had in consequence become an excellent talker, displaying the stored riches and eloquence of a humble and honest self-taught mind. His was a tough and gentle spirit, retaining just enough ruggedness to season its natural kindness. During their visits to the Luxembourg he discoursed upon whatever came into his head, drawing upon his wide reading and his past suffering. And Cosette listened while she gazed about her.

She adored him. She constantly sought him out. Where Jean Valjean was, there was contentment; and since he did not frequent the villa or the garden she was happier in the paved back-yard than in the blossoming enclosure, happier in the cottage with its rush-seated chairs than in her own tapestry-hung and richly furnished drawing-room. Jean Valjean would sometimes say, delighted at being thus pursued, 'Now run along and leave me in peace.'

She gently chided him, with that especial charm which graces the scolding of a devoted daughter.

'Father, it's cold in here. Why don't you have a carpet and a stove?'

'Dear child, there are so many people more deserving than I who have not even a roof over their heads.'

'Then why should I have a fire and everything else I want?'

'Because you're a woman and a child.'

'What nonsense! Do you mean that men ought to be cold and uncomfortable?'

'Some men.'

'Very well then. I shall come here so often that you'll *have* to have a fire.'

She also asked:

'Father, why do you eat that horrid bread?'

'For reasons, my dear.'

'Well, if you eat it, so shall I.'

So to prevent Cosette eating black bread Valjean changed to white.

Cosette had only vague recollections of her childhood. She prayed morning and night for the mother she had never known. The Thénardiers haunted her memory like figures in a nightmare. She remembered that one day, 'after dark', she had gone into the wood for water, in some place which she thought must have been far distant from Paris. It seemed to her that she had begun her life in a kind of limbo from which Jean Valjean had rescued her, and that childhood had been a time of beetles, snakes, and spiders. Drowsily meditating at night before she fell asleep, she concluded, since she had no positive reason to believe that she was Valjean's daughter and he her father, that her mother's soul had passed into him and come to live with her. Sometimes when he was seated she would rest her cheek on his white head and shed a silent tear upon it, thinking to herself, 'Perhaps after all this man is my mother!'

It sounds strange, but in her profound ignorance as a convent-bred child, and since in any case maternity is totally incomprehensible to virginity, she had come to believe that her mother had been almost non-existent. She did not even know her name, and when she asked Valjean he would not answer. If she repeated the question he merely smiled, and once, when she persisted, the smile was followed by a tear. Thus did Valjean by his silence hide the figure of Fantine in darkness. Was it from instinctive prudence, from respect for the dead, or from fear of surrendering that name to the hazards of any memory other than his own?

While Cosette had been still a child Valjean had talked to her readily enough about her mother, but now that she was a grown girl he found it impossible to do so. It seemed to him that he dared not. Whether because of Cosette herself, or because of Fantine, he experienced a kind of religious horror at the thought of introducing that shade into her thoughts, and of constituting the dead a third party of their lives. The more he held that shade in reverence, the more awesome did it seem. Thinking of Fantine he was compelled to silence as though amid her darkness he discerned the shape of a finger pressed to the lips. Could it be that all the shame of which Fantine was capable, which had been so savagely driven out of her by the events of her life, had furiously returned to mount fierce guard over her in death? We who have faith in death are not among those who would reject that mystical theory. Hence the impossibility he found in himself of uttering the name of Fantine, even to Cosette.

'Father, last night I saw my mother in a dream. She had two big wings. She must have come near to sainthood in her life.'

'Through martyrdom,' said Jean Valjean.

Otherwise Valjean was content. When he took Cosette out she hung proudly on his arm, happy with a full heart, and at the tokens of affection which she reserved so exclusively for himself and which he alone could inspire, his whole being was suffused with tenderness. In his rapture he told himself, poor man, that this was a state of things that would last as long as he lived; he told himself that he had not suffered enough to warrant such radiant happiness, and he thanked God from the depths of his heart for having caused him, unworthy wretch that he was, to be so loved by a creature so innocent.

V

The rose discovers that it is a weapon of war

One day Cosette, glancing in her mirror, exclaimed, 'Well!' It struck her that she was almost pretty, and the discovery threw her into a strange state of perturbation. Until that moment she had given no thought to her looks. She had seen herself in the glass but without really looking. She had been told so often that she was plain, and Jean Valjean was the only person who said, 'It's not true.' Despite this she had always considered herself plain, accustoming herself to the thought with the easy acceptance of childhood. And suddenly her mirror had confirmed what Jean Valjean said. She did not sleep that night. 'Suppose I were pretty?' she thought. 'How strange to be pretty!' She thought of girls whose looks had attracted notice in the convent, and she thought, 'Can I really be like them?'

The next day she carefully studied herself and had doubts. 'What can have got into me?' she thought. 'I'm quite ugly.' The fact was simply that she had slept badly; there were shadows under her eyes and her face was pale. It had caused her no great delight on the previous evening to think that she might be a beauty, but now she was sorry that she could not think it. She no longer looked in the glass and for more than two weeks tried to do her hair with her back to the mirror.

She was accustomed in the evenings to do embroidery, or some other kind of convent work, in the salon while Jean Valjean sat reading beside her. Looking up on one occasion, she was dismayed to find her father gazing at her with a troubled expression. And on another occasion when they were out together she thought she heard a man's voice behind her say, 'A pretty girl, but badly dressed' ... 'It can't be me,' she thought. 'I'm well dressed and ugly.' She was wearing her plush hat and woollen dress.

Finally, one day when she was in the garden she heard old Toussaint say: 'Has Monsieur noticed how pretty Mademoiselle is growing?' She did not hear her father's reply, but Toussaint's words filled her with amazement. She ran up to her bedroom and, for the first time in three months, looked hard at herself in the glass. She uttered a cry, delighted by what she saw.

She was beautiful as well as pretty; she could no longer doubt the testimony of Toussaint and her mirror. Her figure had filled out, her skin was finer, her hair more lustrous, and there was a new splendour in her blue eyes. The conviction of her beauty came to her in a single instant, like a burst of sunshine; besides, other people had noticed it, Toussaint had said so and the man in the street must, after all, have been talking about her. She ran downstairs and out into the garden feeling like a queen, seeing a golden sun stream through the branches, blossom on the bough, and hearing the song of birds, in a state of dizzy rapture.

Jean Valjean, for his part, had a sense of profound, indefinable unease. For some time he had been apprehensively watching this growing radiance of Cosette's beauty, a bright dawn to others but to himself a dawn of ill-omen. She had been beautiful for a long time without realizing it; but he had known it from the first, and the glow which enveloped her represented a threat in his possessive eyes. He saw it as a portent of change in their life together, a life so happy that any change could only be for the worse. He was a man who had endured all the forms of suffering and was still bleeding from the wounds inflicted upon him by life. He had been almost a villain and had become almost a saint; and after being chained with prison irons he was still fettered with a chain that was scarcely less onerous although invisible, that of his prison record. The law had never lost its claim on him. It might at any moment lay hands on him and drag him out of his honourable obscurity into the glare of public infamy. He accepted this, bore no resentment, wished all men well and asked nothing of Providence, of mankind or society or of the law, except one thing – that Cosette should love him.

That Cosette should continue to love him! That God would not prevent her child's heart from being and remaining wholly his! To be loved by Cosette was enough; it was rest and solace, the healing of all wounds, the only recompense and guerdon that he craved. It was all he wanted. Had any man asked him if he wished to be better off he would have answered, 'No.' Had God offered him Heaven itself he would have said, 'I should be the loser.'

Anything that might affect this situation, even ruffle the surface, caused him to tremble as at a portent of something new. He had never known much about the beauty of women, but he knew by instinct that it could be terrible. And across the gulf of his own age and ugliness, his past suffering and ignominy, he watched in dismay the superb and triumphant growth of beauty in the innocent features of this child. 'Such loveliness!' he thought. 'So what will become of me?'

It was in this that the difference lay between his devotion and that of a mother. What caused him anguish would have brought a mother delight.

The first signs of change were not slow to appear.

From the morrow of the day on which she had said to herself 'After all, I am beautiful!' Cosette began to give thought to her appearance. The words of that unknown man in the street, that unregarded oracle, 'Pretty, but badly dressed,' had implanted in her heart one of the two germs that fill the life of every woman, the germ of coquetry. The other germ is love.

Being now confident of her beauty, her woman's nature flowered within her. Wool and plush were thrust aside. Her father had never refused her anything. Instantly she knew all that there was to know about hats and gowns, cloaks, sleeves and slippers, the material that suits and the colour that matches: all that recondite lore that makes the women of Paris so alluring, so deep and so dangerous. The phrase 'divine charmer' was invented for the Parisienne.

In less than a month little Cosette, in her solitude off the Rue de Babylone, was not merely one of the prettiest women in Paris, which is saying a great deal, but one of the best dressed, which is saying even more. She wished that she could meet that man in the street again, just to 'show him' and hear what he had to say. The truth is that she was ravishing in all respects and wonderfully able to distinguish between a hat by Gérard and one by Herbaut. And Jean Valjean observed this transformation with the utmost misgiving. He who felt that he could never do more than crawl, or at the best walk, watched while Cosette grew wings.

It may be added that any woman glancing at Cosette would have known at once that she had no mother. There were small proprieties and particular conventions which she did not observe. A mother would have told her, for instance, that a young girl does not wear damask.

The first time Cosette went out in her dress and cape of black damask and her white crêpe hat, she clung to Jean Valjean's arm in a pink glow of pride. 'Do you like me like this?' she asked, and he answered in a tone that was almost surly, 'You're charming.'

During their walk he behaved much as usual, but when they were back home he asked:

'Are you never going to wear the other dress and hat again?'

They were in Cosette's bedroom. She turned to the wardrobe where her school clothes were hanging.

'Those old things! Father, what do you expect? Of course I shall never wear them again. With that monstrosity on my head I looked like a scarecrow!'

Jean Valjean sighed deeply.

From then on he found that Cosette, who had hitherto been quite content to stay at home, now constantly wanted to be taken out and about. What is the good, after all, of having a pretty face and delightful clothes if no one ever sees them? He also found that she had lost her fondness for the cottage and the back-yard. She now preferred the garden, and it did not displease her to stroll by the wrought-iron gate. Valjean, always the hunted man, never set foot in the garden. He stayed in the back-yard, like the dog.

Cosette, knowing herself to be beautiful, lost the grace of unawareness: an exquisite grace, for beauty enhanced by innocence is incomparable, and nothing is more enchanting than artless radiance that unwittingly holds the key to a paradise. But what she lost in this respect she gained in meditative charm. Her whole being, suffused with the joy of youth, innocence, and beauty, breathed a touching earnestness.

It was at this point that Marius, after a lapse of six months, again saw her in the Luxembourg.

VI

The battle begins

Cosette in her solitude, like Marius in his, was ready to be set alight. Fate, with its mysterious and inexorable patience, was slowly bringing together these two beings charged, like thunder-clouds, with electricity, with the latent forces of passion, and destined to meet and mingle in a look as clouds do in a lightning-flash.

So much has been made in love-stories of the power of a glance that we have ended by undervaluing it. We scarcely dare say in these days that two persons fell in love because their eyes met. Yet that is how one falls in love and in no other way. What remains is simply what remains, and it comes later. Nothing is more real than the shock two beings sustain when that spark flies between them.

At the moment when something in Cosette's gaze of which she was unaware so deeply troubled Marius, she herself was no less troubled by something in his eyes of which he was equally unconscious, and each sustained the same hurt and the same good.

She had noticed him long before and had studied him in the way a girl does, without seeming to look. She had thought him handsome when he still thought her plain, but since he took no notice of her she had felt no particular interest in him. Nevertheless she could not prevent herself from noting that he had good hair, fine eyes, white teeth, and a charming voice when he talked to his friends; that although he carried himself badly, if you cared to put it that way, he walked with a grace peculiar to himself; that he seemed to be not at all stupid; that his whole aspect was one of gentle simplicity and pride; and finally that he looked poor but honest.

On the day when their eyes met and at length exchanged those first wordless avowals that a glance haltingly conveys, Cosette did not at once understand. She returned pensively to the house in the Rue de l'Ouest where Jean Valjean, as his custom was, was spending six weeks; and when, next morning, she awoke and remembered the strange young man who after treating her for so long with perfect indifference seemed now disposed to take notice of her, she was by no means sure that she welcomed the change. If anything she was inclined to resent the condescension. With something like defiance astir within her she felt, with a childlike glee, that she was about to take her revenge. Knowing that she was beautiful she perceived, however indistinctly, that she was armed. Women play with their beauty like children with a knife, and sometimes cut themselves.

We may recall Marius's hesitation, his tremors and uncertainties. He stayed on his bench and did not venture to approach. And this provoked Cosette. She said to Valjean, 'Let us walk that way for a change.' Seeing that Marius did not come to her, she went to him. Every woman in these circumstances resembles Muhammad's mountain. And besides, although shyness is the first sign of true love in a youth, boldness is its token in a maid. This may seem strange, but nothing could be more simple. The sexes are drawing close, and in doing so each assumes the qualities of the other.

On that day Cosette's gaze drove Marius wild with delight, while his gaze left her trembling. He went away triumphant while she was filled with disquiet. From that day on they adored each other.

Cosette's first feeling was one of confused, profound melancholy. It seemed to her that overnight her soul had turned black, so that she could no longer recognize it. The whiteness of a young girl's soul, compound of chill and gaiety, resembles snow: it melts in the warmth of love, which is its sun.

Cosette did not know what love was. She had never heard the word spoken in an earthly sense. In the volumes of profane music which were admitted into the convent it was always replaced by some scarcely adequate synonym such as 'dove' or 'treasure trove', which had caused the older girls to puzzle over such cryptic lines as 'Ah, the delights of treasure trove' or 'Pity is akin to the dove'. But Cosette when she left had been still too young to ponder these riddles. She had, in short, no word to express what she was now feeling. Is one the less ill for not knowing the name of the disease?

She loved the more deeply because she did so in ignorance. She did not know if what had happened to her was good or bad, salutary or perilous, permitted or forbidden; she simply loved. She would have been greatly astonished if anyone had said to her: 'You don't sleep at nights? But that is against the rules. You don't eat? But that's very bad! You have palpitations of the heart? How disgraceful! You blush and turn pale at the sight of a figure in a black suit in a green arbour? But that is abominable!' She would have been bewildered and could only have replied: 'How can I be at fault in a matter in which I am powerless and about which I know nothing?'

And it happened that love had come to her in precisely the form that best suited her state of mind, in the form of worship at a distance, silent contemplation, the deification of an unknown. It was youth calling to youth, the night-time dream made manifest while still a dream, the longed-for ghost made flesh but still without a name, without a flaw and making no demands; in a word, the lover of fantasy given a shape but still remote. Any closer contact at that early stage would have frightened Cosette, half plunged as she still was in the mists of the convent. She had a child's terrors and all the terrors of a nun, and both still assailed her. The spirit of the convent, in which she had been bathed for five years, was only slowly evaporating from her person, and setting all the world outside aquiver. What she needed in this situation was not a lover or even a suitor but a vision. It was in this sense that she loved Marius, as something charming, dazzling and impossible. And since utmost innocence goes hand-in-hand with coquetry she smiled quite openly at him.

She looked forward throughout their walks to the moment when she would see Marius; she had a sense of inexpressible happiness; and she believed she was truly expressing all that was in her mind when she said to Jean Valjean: 'How delightful the Luxembourg Garden is!'

Those two young people were still sundered, each in their own darkness. They did not speak or exchange greetings. They did not know each other. They saw each other, and like stars separated by the measureless spaces of the sky, they lived on the sight of one another.

Thus did Cosette gradually grow into womanhood, beautiful and ardent, conscious of her beauty but ignorant of her love. And, for good measure, a coquette by reason of her innocence.

VII

Sickness and added sadness

All situations produce instinctive responses. Eternal Mother Nature obscurely warned Jean Valjean of the approach of Marius, and he trembled in the depths of his mind. He saw and knew nothing precise, but was yet fixedly conscious of an encroaching shadow, seeming to perceive something in process of growth and something in process of decline. Marius, no less on his guard, and warned according to God's immutable law by that same Mother Nature, did his best to hide from the 'father'. Nevertheless it happened now and then that Valjean caught a glimpse of him. Marius's demeanour was anything but natural, he was awkward in his concealments and clumsy in his boldness. He no longer walked casually past as he had once done, but stayed seated at a distance from them with a book which he pretended to read. For whose benefit was he pretending? At one time he had worn his everyday clothes but now he always wore his best. It looked even as though he had had his hair trimmed. His expression was strange and he wore gloves. In short, Jean Valjean took a hearty dislike to the young man.

Cosette, for her part, was giving nothing away. Without knowing precisely what was happening to her, she knew that something had happened and that it must be kept secret. But her sudden interest in clothes, coming at the same time as the young man's suddenly improved appearance, was a coincidence that struck Valjean. It was pure accident, no doubt – indeed, what could it be but accident? – but it was none the less ominous. For a long time he said nothing to her about the stranger, but eventually he could restrain himself no longer, and in a kind of desperation, like the tongue that explores an aching tooth, he remarked: 'That looks a very dull young man.'

A year previously Cosette, still an untroubled child, might have murmured, 'Well, I think he looks rather nice,' and a few years later, with the love of Marius rooted in her heart, she might have said, 'Dull and not worth looking at. I quite agree.' But at that particular moment in her life and in the present state of her feelings, she merely replied, with surpassing calm, 'You mean, that one over there?' as though she had never set eyes on him before. Which caused Jean Valjean to reflect on his own clumsiness. 'She'd never even noticed him,' he thought. 'And now I've pointed him out to her!'

The simplicity of the old and the cunning of the young! ... And there is another law applying to those youthful years of agitation and turmoil, those frantic struggles of first love against first impediments: it is that the girl never falls into any trap and the young man falls into all of them. Jean Valjean opened a secret campaign against Marius which Marius, in the spell of his youthful passion, quite failed to perceive. Valjean devised countless snares. He changed the time of their visits, changed the bench, came to the garden alone, dropped his handkerchief; and Marius was caught out every time. To every question-mark planted under his nose by

Valjean he responded with an ingenuous 'yes'. Meanwhile Cosette remained so solidly fenced in with apparent indifference and unshakeable calm that Valjean ended by concluding, 'The young fool's head over heels in love with her, but she doesn't even know he exists!'

Nevertheless he was acutely apprehensive. Cosette might at any moment fall in love. Do not these things always start with indifference? And on one occasion she let slip a word that frightened him. He rose to leave the bench, where they had been sitting for well over an hour, and she exclaimed: 'So soon?'

Still he did not discontinue their visits to the Luxembourg, not wishing to do anything out-of-the-way and fearing above all things to arouse her suspicions; but during those hours which were so sweet to the lovers, while Cosette covertly smiled at Marius, who in his state of entrancement saw nothing in the world except her smile, he darted fierce and threatening glances at the young man. He who had thought himself no longer capable of any malice now felt the return of an old, wild savagery, a stirring in the depths of a nature that once had harboured much wrath. What the devil did the infernal youth think he was up to, breaking in upon the life of Jean Valjean, prying, peering at his happiness, seeming to calculate his chances of making off with it?

'That's it,' thought Valjean. 'He's looking for an adventure, a love-affair. A love-affair! And I? I who have been the most wretched of men am to be made the most deprived. After living for sixty years on my knees, suffering everything that can be suffered, growing old without having ever been young, living without a family, without wife or children or friends; after leaving my blood on every stone and every thorn, on every milepost and every wall; after returning good for evil and kindness for cruelty; after making myself an honest man in spite of everything, repenting of my sins and forgiving those who have sinned against me – after all this, when at last I have received my reward, when I have got what I want and know that it is good and that I have deserved it – now it is to be snatched from me! I am to lose Cosette and with her my whole life, all the happiness I have ever had, simply because a young oaf chooses to come idling in the Luxembourg!'

At these moments a strange and sinister light shone in his eyes, not that of a man looking at a man, or an enemy facing an enemy, but of a watchdog confronting a thief.

We know what followed. Marius continued to act absurdly. He followed Cosette along the Rue de l'Ouest, and the next day he spoke to the porter, who spoke to Jean Valjean. 'There's a young man been asking about you, Monsieur.' It was on the day after this that Valjean gave Marius the cold glance which even he could not fail to notice, and a week later he moved out of the Rue de l'Ouest, swearing never again to set foot in that street or in the Luxembourg. They returned to the Rue Plumet.

Cosette uttered no complaint. She said nothing, asked no questions, seemed not to wish to know his reasons; she was at the stage when our greatest fear is of discovery and self-betrayal. Jean Valjean had had no experience of those particular troubles, the only attractive ones and the only ones he had never known. That is why he did not grasp the true gravity of Cosette's silence. But he did see that she was unhappy, and this perturbed him. It was a case of inexperience meeting with inexperience.

He tried once to sound her. He asked:

'Would you like to go to the Luxembourg?'

A flush rose on her pale cheek.

'Yes.'

They went there but Marius was not to be seen. Three months had passed, and he had given up going there. When on the following day Valjean again asked if she would like to go there Cosette said sadly and resignedly, 'No.'

He was shocked by her sadness and dismayed by her submissiveness. What was going on in her heart, that was so young but already so inscrutable? What changes were taking place? Sometimes instead of sleeping Valjean would sit for hours by his truckle-bed with his head in his hands; he would spend whole nights wondering what her thoughts might be, what they could possibly be. At these times his own thoughts went back despairingly to the convent, that sheltered Eden with its neglected blossoms and imprisoned virgins, where all scents and all aspirations rose straight to Heaven. How he now longed for it, that Paradise from which he had voluntarily exiled himself; how he now regretted the mood of self-abnegation and folly which had prompted him to bring Cosette out into the world! He was his own sacrificial offering, the victim of his own devotion, and he thought to himself as he sat pondering, 'What have I done?'

But none of this was disclosed to Cosette, never the least ill-humour or unkindness. For her he wore always the same gentle, smiling countenance. If there was any change to be discerned in him it took the form of greater devotion.

And Cosette languished. She missed Marius as she had rejoiced in the sight of him, in her own private fashion, without being fully aware of it. When Valjean changed the order of their daily walk, deep-seated feminine instinct suggested to her that if she displayed no particular interest in the Luxembourg Garden he would perhaps take her there again. But he seemed to accept her tacit consent, and as the weeks became months she regretted it. But too late. When at length they returned to the Luxembourg Marius was no longer there. It seemed that he had vanished from her life. That tale was over and there was nothing to be done. Could she hope ever to see him again? There was a weight in her heart that every day grew heavier, so that she no longer knew or cared whether it was winter or summer, rain or shine, whether the birds still sang, whether it was the season of primroses or dahlias, whether the Luxembourg was any different from the Tuileries, whether the laundry brought by the washerwoman was well or badly ironed, whether Toussaint had conscientiously done the day's shopping. She had become indifferent to all everyday matters, her mind occupied with a single thought, as she gazed about her with lack-lustre eyes that saw only the emptiness from which a presence had vanished.

But of this nothing was apparent to Jean Valjean except her pallor. Her manner towards him was unchanged. But the pallor worried him, and now and then he would ask, 'Are you not well?' and she would answer, 'I'm quite well, father.' Then there would come a pause, and feeling his own unhappiness she would ask, 'But you. Are you quite well?' and he would answer, 'There's nothing wrong with me.'

Thus those two beings, so exclusively and touchingly devoted, who had lived so long for each other alone, came to suffer side by side, each through the other, without ever speaking of the matter, without reproaches, each wearing a smile.

VIII

The chain-gang

Jean Valjean was the more unhappy of the two. Youth, whatever its griefs, still has its consolations. There were moments when he suffered to the point of becoming childish, and indeed it is the quality of suffering that it brings out the childish side of a man. He felt overwhelmingly that Cosette was escaping from him, and he sought to combat this, to keep his hold on her, by providing her with dazzling distractions. This notion, childish, as we have said, but at the same time doting, by its very childishness gave him some insight into the effect of gaudy trappings on a girl's imagination. It happened once that he saw a general in full uniform riding along the street, the Comte Coutard, military commander of Paris. He greatly envied that braided, ornate figure, and he thought to himself how splendid it would be to be dressed with a similar magnificence, how it would delight Cosette, so that when they strolled arm-in-arm past the gates of the Tuileries Palace, and the guard presented arms, she would be far too much impressed to take any interest in young men.

An unexpected shock came to dispel these pathetic fancies. They had formed the habit, since coming to live their solitary lives in the Rue Plumet, of going out to watch the sun rise, a quiet pleasure suited to those who are at the beginning of life and those who are approaching its end. To any lover of solitude, a stroll in the early morning is as good as a stroll after dark, with the added attraction of the brightness of nature. The streets are deserted and the birds in full song. Cosette, herself a bird, enjoyed getting up early. They planned these little outings the night before, he proposing and she agreeing. It was a conspiracy between them; they were out before daybreak and this was an especial pleasure to Cosette. Such harmless eccentricities delight the young.

Jean Valjean, as we know, had an especial fondness for unfrequented places, neglected nooks and corners. At this time there were many of these just beyond the Paris barriers, sparse fields that had been almost absorbed into the town, in which crops of stunted corn grew in summer and which, after reaping, looked more shaved than harvested. They were the places Valjean preferred, and Cosette did not dislike them. For him they represented solitude and for her, liberty. She could become a child again, run and frolic, leave her hat on Valjean's knees and fill it with bunches of wild flowers. She could watch the butterflies, although she never tried to catch them; tenderness and compassion are a part of loving, and a girl cherishing something equally fragile in her heart is mindful of the wings of butterflies. She made poppy-wreaths and put them on her head where, red-glowing in the sunshine, they set off her flushed face like a fiery crown.

They kept up this habit of early morning outings even after their lives had become overcast, and so it happened that, on an October morning, in the perfect serenity of the autumn of 1831, they found themselves at daybreak near the Barrière du Maine. It was the first flush of dawn, a still, magical moment, with a few stars yet to be seen in the pale depths of the sky, the earth still dark and a shiver running over the grass. A lark, seeming at one with the stars, was singing high in the heavens, and this voice of littleness, hymning the infinite, seemed to narrow its immensity. To the east the black mass of the Val-de-Grâce rose against a steel-bright sky, with the planet Venus shining above it like a soul escaped from darkness. Everywhere was silence and peace. Nothing stirred on the high road, and on the side-lanes only occasional labourers were to be glimpsed in passing on their way to work.

Jean Valjean had seated himself on a pile of logs at the side of a lane, by the gateway of a timber-yard. He was looking towards the high road, seated with his back to the sunrise, which he was ignoring, being absorbed in one of those moments of concentrated thought by which even the eyes are imprisoned, as though in enclosing walls. There are states of meditation which may be termed vertical: when one has plunged into their depths it takes time to return to the surface. Valjean was thinking about Cosette and the happiness which might be theirs if nothing came between them, about the light with which she filled his life, enabling his soul to breathe. He was almost happy in this daydream, while Cosette, standing beside him, watched the clouds turn pink. Suddenly she exclaimed:

'Father, I think something's coming.'

Valjean looked up. The high road leading to the Barrière du Maine is joined at a right angle by the inner boulevard. Sounds were coming from the point of intersection which at that hour were not easy to account for. A strange object appeared, turning the corner into the high road. It seemed to be moving in an orderly fashion, although by fits and starts, and it appeared to be some kind of conveyance, although its load was not distinguishable. There were horses and wheels, shouting voices and the cracking of whips. By degrees, as it emerged from the half-light, it could be seen to be a vehicle of sorts heading for the barrier near which Jean Valjean was sitting. It was followed by a second cart, similar in aspect, and by a third and fourth; altogether seven of these long carts rounded the corner, forming a tight procession with the horses' heads almost touching the back of the vehicle in front. Heads became visible, and here and there a gleam like that of a drawn sabre; there was a sound like the rattle of chains, and as the procession drew nearer, with sounds and outlines growing more distinct, it was like the approach of something in a dream. Bit by bit the details became clear, and the darkly silhouetted heads, bathed in the pallid glow of the rising sun, came to resemble the heads of corpses.

This is what it was. Of the seven vehicles proceeding in line along the high road the first six were of a singular design. They were like coopers' drays, long ladders on wheels with shafts at the forward end. Each of these drays, or ladders, was drawn by four horses in single file and their load consisted of tight clusters of men, twenty-four to each dray, seated in two rows of twelve, back to back with their legs dangling over the side; and the thing rattling at their backs was a chain, and the thing gleaming round their necks was a yoke or collar of iron. Each had his own collar, but the chain was shared by all of them, so that when they descended from the vehicle these parties of twenty-four men had to move in concert like a body with a single backbone, a sort of centipede. Pairs of men armed with muskets stood at the front and rear end of each vehicle, with their feet on the ends of the chain. The iron collars were square. The seventh vehicle, a large four-wheeled wagon with high sides but no roof, was drawn by six horses and carried a clattering load of iron cook-pots, stoves, and chains among which lay a few men with bound wrists and ankles who seemed to be ill. The sides of this wagon were constructed of rusty metal frames which looked as though they might once have served as whipping-blocks.

The procession, moving along the middle of the high road, was escorted on either side by a line of troops of infamous aspect wearing the three-cornered hats of soldiers under the Directory, dirty and bedraggled pensioners' tunics, tattered trousers, something between grey and blue, like those of funeral mutes, red epaulettes and yellow bandoliers; and they were armed with axes, muskets, and clubs. Mercenary soldiers bearing themselves with the abjectness of beggars and the truculence of prison-guards. The man who seemed to be their commander carried a horsewhip. These details, shrouded at first in the half-light, became steadily clearer as the light increased. At the front and rear of the procession rode parties of mounted gendarmes, grim-faced men with drawn sabres.

The procession was so long that by the time its head reached the barrier the last vehicle had only just turned into the high road. A crowd of spectators, sprung up in an instant as so commonly happens in Paris, had gathered on either side of the road to stand and stare. Voices could be heard of men calling to their mates to come and look, followed by the clatter of clogs as they came hurrying in from the fields.

The chained men in the drays, pallid in the chill of the morning, bore the lurching journey in silence. They were all clad in cotton trousers, with clogs on their bare feet. The rest of their attire was a dismally variegated picture of misery, a harlequinade in tatters, with shapeless headgear of felt or tarred cloth, while a few wore women's hats, or even baskets, on their heads and out-at-elbows workers' smocks or black jackets open to uncover hairy chests. Through the rents in their clothing tattoo-marks were visible – temples of love, bleeding hearts, cupids – and also the sores and blotches of disease. One or two had a rope slung from the side of the dray which supported their feet like a stirrup, and one was conveying a hard, black substance to his mouth which looked like rock but was in fact bread. Eyes were expressionless, apathetic or gleaming with an evil light. The men of the escort cursed them but drew not a murmur in reply. Now and then there was the sound of a cudgel thudding on shoulder-blades or on a head. Some of the prisoners yawned while their bodies lurched and swayed, heads knocked together and the chains rattled; others darted venomous looks. Some fists were clenched and others hung limply like the hands of dead men. A party of jeering children followed in the rear of the convoy.

Whatever else it was, this procession of carts was a most melancholy sight. It was certain that sooner or later, within an hour or a day, rain would fall, one shower succeeding another, and that with their miserable garments soaked the poor wretches would have no chance to get dry. Chilled to the bone, they would have no hope of getting warm; the chain would still hold them by the neck, their feet would still dangle in waterlogged clogs; and the thud of cudgels and the crack of whips would do nothing to still the chattering of their teeth. It was impossible to contemplate without a shiver these human creatures exposed like trees or stones to all the fury of the elements.

But suddenly the sun came out, a broad beam of light spread from the east and it was as though it set all those dishevelled heads on fire. Tongues were loosed, and there was an explosion of mocking laughter, oaths, and songs. The horizontal glow cut the picture in two, illuminating heads and torsos and leaving legs and the wheels of the carts in shadow. This was a terrible moment, for awareness returned to the faces like an unmasking of demons, wild spirits nakedly exposed. But lighted though it was, the picture was still one of darkness. Some of the livelier spirits had quills in their mouths through which they blew spittle at the spectators, for preference at the women. The dawn light threw their haggard faces into relief, not one that was not malformed by misery; and the effect was monstrous, as though the warmth of sunlight had been transformed into the cold brightness of a lightning-flash. The men in the first cart were bellowing the chorus of an old popular song, while the trees shivered and the respectable onlookers in the side-lanes listened with imbecile satisfaction to this rousing clamour of ghosts.

Every aspect of misery was to be seen in that procession, as though it were a depiction of chaos; every animal face was there represented, old men and youths, grey beards and hairless cheeks, cynical monstrosity, embittered resignation, savage leers, half-wit grins, gargoyles wearing caps, faces like those of girls with locks of hair straying over their temples, faces like those of children and the more horrible on that account, fleshless skeleton faces lacking only death. There was a Negro in the first cart who perhaps had been a slave and so was familiar with chains. All bore the stamp of ignominy, that dreadful leveller; all had reached that lowest depth of abasement where ignorance changed to witlessness is the equal of intelligence changed to despair. There was no choosing between these men who seemed, from their appearance, to be the scum of the underworld, and it was evident that whoever had organized this procession had made no attempt to distinguish between them. They had been chained together haphazard, probably in alphabetical order, and loaded haphazard on to the carts. But even horror assembled in groups acquires a common denominator, every aggregation of miseries results in a total: each of the separate chain-gangs had a character of its own, each cartload bore its own countenance. Besides the one that sang there was one that merely shouted, one that begged for money, one that ground its teeth, one that uttered threats, one that blasphemed, and the last was silent as the grave. Dante might have seen in them the seven circles of Hell on the move.

It was a march of the condemned on the way to torment, borne not on the flaming chariots of the Apocalypse but on the shabby tumbrils of the damned. One of the guards who had a hook on the end of his club gesticulated with it as though to plunge it into that heap of human garbage. Among the onlookers a woman with a five-year-old boy shook a warning finger at him and said: 'Perhaps that'll teach you to behave!' As the roar of singing and blasphemy increased the man who seemed to be in command of the escort cracked his whip, and at this signal a rain of blows fell on the passengers in the carts, some of whom bellowed while others foamed at the mouth, to the delight of the urchins swarming round the procession like flies round an open wound.

The look in Jean Valjean's eyes was dreadful to behold. They were eyes no longer, but had become those fathomless mirrors which in men who have known the depths of suffering may replace the conscious gaze, so that they no longer see reality but reflect the memory of past events. Valjean was not observing the present scene but was gripped by a vision. He wanted to jump to his feet and run, but could not move. There are times when the thing we see holds us paralysed. He stayed dazedly seated, wondering, in indescribable anguish, what was the meaning of this hideous spectacle and the pandemonium that accompanied it. And presently he clapped a hand to his forehead in a gesture of sudden recollection; he remembered that this was the convoy's usual itinerary, that it was accustomed to make this detour in order to avoid any encounter with royal personages, always possible on the road to Fontainebleau; and he remembered that he himself had passed through that barrier thirty-five years before.

Cosette was no less shaken, although for other reasons. She was staring in breathless bewilderment, scarcely able to believe her eyes. She cried:

'Father, what are those men?'

'Felons condemned to hard labour,' said Valjean.

'Where are they going?'

'To the galleys.'

At this moment the lashing and cudgelling reached its climax, with the flat of swords now being used. The prisoners, yielding to punishment, fell silent, glaring about them like captive wolves. Cosette was trembling. She asked:

'Father, are they still human?'

'Sometimes,' the wretched man replied.

It was in fact the chain-gang from Bicêtre, which was travelling by way of Le Mans to avoid Fontainebleau where the king was in residence. The detour lengthened the unspeakable journey by three or four days, but this was a small matter if thereby the royal susceptibilities could be spared.

Jean Valjean returned home deeply oppressed. The shock of encounters such as this may cause a profound revulsion of the spirit. So absorbed was he in his thoughts that he paid little attention, on their way home, to Cosette's further questions about what they had seen, and perhaps he did not even hear much of what she said. But that evening, when she was about to take leave of him and go to bed, he heard her murmur as though to herself: 'I believe if I were to meet a man like that in the street I should die of fright just from seeing him so close.'

It happened fortunately that on the next day some sort of official celebration was held in Paris, the occasion being marked by a military parade on the Champ de Mars, water-jousting on the Seine, fireworks, festivities and illuminations everywhere. Contrary to his general practice, Valjean took Cosette out to see the sights, hoping thus to efface from her mind the nightmare she had witnessed the previous day, and since the military review was the main event, and the wearing of uniforms was proper to the occasion, he wore his National Guard uniform, partly from an instinctive desire to escape notice. Their outing seemed to be successful. Cosette, who made a point of always seeking to please her father, and for whom in any case every show was a novelty, joined in the fun with the eager, lighthearted acceptance of youth, and gave no sign of despising that hotch-potch of organized rejoicing which is known as a 'public festival' – so much so that Valjean could feel that she had forgotten the previous day's events entirely.

But a few days later they happened to stand together on the steps leading to the garden, warming themselves in the sunshine of a fine morning. This was another departure from Valjean's general rule, and from Cosette's habit, in her unhappy state, of staying indoors.

Cosette was wearing a peignoir, one of those gauzy morning garments which adorn a girl like the mist surrounding a star, and, bathed in sunlight, her cheeks still rosy after a sound night's sleep, was playing with a daisy while her father tenderly watched her. Cosette knew nothing of the old children's game, 'He loves me ... he don't ... he'll have me ... he won't ...' – when had she had the chance to learn it? She was innocently and instinctively picking off the petals, not knowing that the daisy stands for a heart. If to those Graces a fourth could be added bearing the name of Melancholy, but smiling, she might well have played the role. Valjean watched her, fascinated by the contemplation of her slim fingers as she toyed with the little flower, forgetful of all else in the delight of her presence. A redbreast was chirruping on a branch above their heads. White clouds were sailing across the sky, so gaily that one might suppose they had only just been released from confinement. Cosette continued to play with the flower but absently, as though she were thinking of something else – surely it must be something charming. But suddenly, with the slow, graceful movement of a swan, her head turned on her shoulders and she asked:

'Father, that place, the galleys. What does it mean?'

BOOK FOUR

HELP FROM BELOW MAY BE
HELP FROM ABOVE

I

The outward wound and the inward healing

THUS BY degrees the shadows deepened over their life. There remained to them only one distraction, one which had once been a source of happiness – the feeding of the hungry and the gift of clothing to those who were cold. During those visits to the poor, on which Cosette often accompanied Jean Valjean, they regained something of the warmth that had formerly existed between them; and sometimes in the evening, after a successful day, when many needy persons had been succoured and many children's lives made brighter, Cosette could be almost gay. It was at this period that they visited the Jondrettes.

On the day following that visit Jean Valjean walked into the villa with his usual air of calm but with a large, inflamed, and suppurating wound resembling a burn on his left forearm, for which he accounted in an off-hand way. It led to his being confined to the house with a fever for more than a month. He refused to see a doctor, and when Cosette begged him to do so he said, 'Call a vet if you like.'

Cosette nursed him so devotedly and with such evident delight in serving him that all his former happiness was restored, the fears and misgivings all dispelled, and he reflected as he gazed at her, 'Oh, most fortunate wound!'

With her father ill Cosette recovered her fondness for the cottage at the back of the villa. She spent nearly all her time at his bedside, reading him the books he most enjoyed, which as a rule were books of travel. And Jean Valjean was a man reborn. The Luxembourg, the strange youth, Cosette's withdrawal – all these shades were banished: to the extent, indeed, that he was inclined to say to himself, 'I'm an old fool. I imagined it all.'

Such was his happiness that his discovery that the so-called Jondrettes were in reality the Thénardiers scarcely troubled him. He had made good his escape and covered his tracks, and what else mattered? If he thought of them at all it was to grieve for their abject state. They were now in prison, and therefore, he assumed, no longer able to harm anyone – but how lamentable a family!

As for the hideous spectacle at the Barrière du Maine, Cosette never referred to it.

Sister Sainte-Mechtilde, at the convent, had given Cosette music lessons. She had the voice of a small wild creature possessed of a soul, and sometimes in the evening, when she sat with the invalid in his cottage, she would sing poignant little songs that rejoiced Jean Valjean's heart.

Spring came, and the garden at that time of year was so delightful that he said to her, 'You never go in it, but I want you to' . . . 'Why then,' said Cosette, 'I will.'

So to humour her father she resumed her walks in the garden, but generally alone, for Valjean seldom entered it, as we know, probably because he was afraid of being seen through the gate.

Jean Valjean's wound, in short, brought about a great change. When Cosette saw that he was recovering and that he seemed happier, she herself had a sense of contentment of which she was scarcely aware, so gently and naturally did it come to her. This was in March. The winter was ending and the days were growing longer, and winter with its passing always takes with it something of our sorrows. Then came April, the dawn of summer, fresh as all dawns, and merry as childhood, if inclined to be fretful at times, like all young things. Nature in that month sheds rays of enchanted light which, from the sky and the clouds, from trees, meadows, and flowers, pierce to the heart of man.

Cosette was still too young not to be responsive to the magic of April. Insensibly, without her realizing it, the shadows lifted from her heart. Spring brings light to the sorrowing just as the midday sun does to the darkness of a cave. Cosette was no longer really unhappy, although she was scarcely aware of the change in her. When after breakfast she prevailed upon her father to spend a little time in the garden, and strolled up and down with him nursing his injured arm, she was unconscious of her happiness or of how often she laughed.

Jean Valjean watched in rapture as her cheeks regained the glow of health.

'Most fortunate wound!' he thought, and was positively grateful to the Thénardiers.

When he was fully recovered he resumed his habit of solitary night-time walks. It would be a mistake to suppose that one can wander in this fashion through the deserted districts of Paris without ever meeting with an adventure.

II
Mère Plutarque accounts for a phenomenon

It occurred one evening to the boy Gavroche that he had had nothing to eat all day. Nor, for that matter, had he had anything the day before. It was becoming tiresome, so he resolved to go in search of supper. He went on the prowl in the unfrequented regions beyond the Salpêtrière. This was where he thought he might be lucky. In places where there is no one about there are things to be found. He came to a small group of houses which he judged to be the village of Austerlitz.

On one of his previous excursions to those parts he had noticed an old garden, frequented by an old man and woman, in which there was a sizeable apple-tree and a tumbledown storage-shed which might well contain apples. An apple is a meal; it is a source of life. What had been Adam's downfall might be the saving of Gavroche. The garden was flanked by a lane that was otherwise bordered by thickets in default of houses. It had a hedge.

Gavroche located the lane, the garden, the apple-tree, and the shed, and he examined the hedge, which could easily be negotiated. The sun was setting and there was not so much as a cat in the lane; all things seemed propitious. But as Gavroche was starting to get through the hedge he heard the sound of a voice in the garden, and peering through he saw, within a few feet of the spot where he had intended to enter, a fallen stone serving as a garden bench on which was seated the old man belonging to the garden, with the old woman standing in front of him. Gavroche paused and listened.

'Monsieur Mabeuf!' the old woman said.

'Mabeuf! What a crazy name!' reflected Gavroche.

The old man made no response and the woman repeated:

'Monsieur Mabeuf!'

This time, still staring at the ground, the old man deigned to reply.

'Well, Mère Plutarque, what is it?'

'Plutarque – another crazy name,' reflected Gavroche.

'Monsieur Mabeuf,' the woman said in a voice which compelled the old man to listen, 'the landlord's complaining.'

'What about?'

'You owe three quarters' rent.'

'So in three months' time I shall owe four.'

'He says he's going to turn you out.'

'Then I shall have to go.'

'And the greengrocer says that until she's been paid she won't bring any more faggots. How are we going to heat the place this winter? We shall have no firewood.'

'There's always the sun.'

'And the butcher won't let us have any more meat.'

'I'm glad to hear it. Meat disagrees with me. It's too rich.'

'So what are we to live on?'

'On bread.'

'But it's the same with the baker, he won't give us any more credit either.'

'Ah, well.'

'So what are you going to eat?'

'We still have some apples.'

'But, Monsieur, we can't go on like this, without any money at all.'

'I have no money.'

The woman went off, leaving the old man to himself. He sat thinking. Gavroche was also thinking. It was now nearly dark.

The first result of Gavroche's thinking was that instead of scrambling through the hedge he crept into the middle of it at a point where the stems of the bushes were wide enough apart. 'A private bed-chamber,' he reflected. He was now almost directly behind the stone on which Père Mabeuf was seated, so close to him that he could hear the old man's breathing.

Here, for lack of supper, he settled down to sleep; but it was a catlike sleep with one eye open – Gavroche was always on the alert. The faint glow of the night sky cast its pallor on the earth, and the lane was like a white line drawn between two dark rows of undergrowth. And suddenly two figures appeared on the white line, one following at a short distance behind the other.

'Callers,' muttered Gavroche.

The first figure looked like that of a respectable elderly man, clad with the utmost simplicity and walking slowly because of his age, as though he were out for a stroll under the stars. The second figure, also male, was erect and slender. It was matching its pace to that of the first, but in a manner which suggested nimbleness and agility. There was something fierce and disquieting about this second figure, which nevertheless had a look of elegance – a well-shaped hat and a well-cut coat, probably of good cloth, which fitted tightly at the waist. Beneath the hat a youthful face was faintly discernible. There was a rose in the young man's mouth. Gavroche recognized him instantly. It was Montparnasse.

Gavroche crouched and watched, his bed-chamber an admirable post of observation. Clearly the second figure had designs upon the first, and that Montparnasse should be on the hunt at this hour, and in this place, was a fearsome thought. Gavroche's urchin heart went out to the elderly victim.

But what was he to do? For him to attempt to intervene would merely amuse Montparnasse – one weakling going to the rescue of another. There could be no escaping the fact that to that redoubtable eighteen-year-old cut-throat the two of them put together, an ageing man and a child, would be a couple of mouthfuls.

While Gavroche was still deliberating, the attack was launched, swift and ferocious as that of a tiger on a wild ass, or a spider on a fly. Montparnasse, tossing away his rose, flung himself upon his victim, seizing him from behind, and Gavroche could scarcely restrain a cry. A moment later one of the two men was on the ground, writhing and struggling with a knee like marble planted on his chest. But it was not at all what Gavroche had expected. The man on his back was Montparnasse, and the one on top was the elderly man, who had not only withstood the attack but had retaliated so drastically that in the twinkling of an eye the situation of victim and assailant had been reversed.

'What a splendid old boy!' thought Gavroche and could not refrain from clapping his hands; but although he was within a few yards of them the gesture was wasted, since both contestants were too intent upon their struggle.

There was presently a pause. Montparnasse lay motionless and for an instant Gavroche wondered if he were dead. The elderly man had not uttered a sound. He got to his feet and said:

'Get up.'

Montparnasse did so, but the other still had a grip on him.

Montparnasse had the abashed and furious look of a wolf savaged by a sheep. Gavroche, delighted by the turn of events, was watching with eyes and ears intent, and he was rewarded for his anxious sympathy by being able to catch most of the ensuing dialogue. The elderly man asked:

'How old are you?'

'I'm nineteen.'

'You're strong and healthy. Why don't you work?'

'It bores me.'

'What is your business in life?'

'Loafer.'

'Talk sense. Can I do anything to help you? What do you want to be?'

'A thief.'

There was another pause. The elderly man seemed plunged in thought; but although he stayed motionless he did not relax his hold on Montparnasse who, lithe and supple, was again kicking and struggling like an animal in a trap. His efforts were disregarded. The other kept him under control with the calm assurance of overwhelming strength. He thought for some time, and when at length he spoke it was to deliver a lecture, rendered the more solemn by the darkness that enshrouded them, which, although it was uttered in low tones, was spoken with such emphasis that Gavroche did not miss a word.

'My poor boy, sheer laziness has started you on the most arduous of careers. You call yourself a loafer, but you will have to work harder than most men. Have you ever seen a treadmill? It is a thing to beware of, a cunning and diabolical device; if it catches you by the coat-tails it will swallow you up. Another name for it is idleness. You should change your ways while there is still time. Otherwise you're done for; in a very little while you will be caught in the machinery, and then there's no more hope. No rest for the idler; nothing but the iron grip of incessant struggle. You don't want to earn your living honestly, do a job, fulfil a duty; the thought of being like other men bores you. But the end is the same. Work is the law of life, and to reject it as boredom is to submit to it as torment. Not wanting to be a workman you will become a slave. If work fails to get you with one hand it will get you with the other; you won't treat it as a friend, and so you will become its Negro slave. You flinch from the fatigues of honest men, and for this you will sweat like the damned; where other men sing you will groan, and their work, as you contemplate it from the depths, will look to you like rest. The ploughman and the harvester, the sailor and the blacksmith, they will be bathed for you in radiance like souls in Paradise. The splendid glow of a smith's furnace! The joy of leading a horse, of binding a sheaf of corn! The wonder of a ship sailing in freedom over the seas! But you, the idler, will toil and plod and suffer like an ox in the harness of Hell, when all you wanted to do was – nothing! Not a week will pass, not a day, without its overwhelming pressures; everything you do will cost an effort and every moment will see your muscles strained. What other men find light as a feather for you will have the heaviness of lead. The gentlest slope will seem steep and all life will be a matter of monstrous difficulty. The simplest acts, the very act of breathing, will be a labour to you, your very lungs will seem to have a crushing weight. To go in one direction rather than another will present you with a problem to be solved. The ordinary man when he wants to leave his home has only to open the door, and there he is, outside; but you will have to break through your own wall. What do ordinary people do when they want to go into the street? They simply walk downstairs. But you will have to tear up your sheets and make a rope of them, because you must go out by way of the window; and there you will be, dangling on your rope in darkness, rain or tempest; and if the rope proves too short your only course will be to drop. To drop at random from a doubtful height, and into what? Into whatever may chance to be below, into the unknown. Or you'll climb by way of a chimney, at the risk of getting burnt, or crawl through a sewer at the risk of drowning. I say nothing about the holes that must be covered up, the stones that must be removed and replaced, the plaster to be disposed of. You are confronted by a lock of which the householder has the key in his pocket, the work of a locksmith. If you want to break it you have to create a masterpiece. First you will take a large sou piece and cut it in two slices. As for the tools you use for this purpose, you will have to invent them. That's your affair. Then you will hollow the inside of the slices, taking care not to damage the outside of the coin, and cut a thread in the rims so that they can be screwed together without any trace being visible. To the world at large it will be nothing but a coin, but to you it will be a box in which you will carry a scrap of steel – a watch-spring in which you have cut teeth, making it into a saw.

And with this saw, coiled in a sou piece, you will cut through the bolt of a lock, the shank of a padlock, or the bars of your prison-cell and the fetter on your leg. And what will your reward be for working this miracle of art, skill, and patience if you are found to be its author? It will be prison. That is your future. Indolence and the life of pleasure – what snares they are! Can you not see that to decide to do nothing is the most wretched of all decisions? To live in idleness on the body politic is to be useless, that is to say harmful, and it can only end in misery. Woe to those who choose to be parasites, they become vermin! But you don't want to work. All you want is rich food and drink and a soft bed. You will end by drinking water, eating black bread, and sleeping on a bed of planks with fetters on your limbs, with the night cold piercing to your bones. You will break your chains and escape. All right – but you will crawl on your stomach through the undergrowth and live on grass like the beasts of the field. And you will be caught. After which you will spend years in an underground cell, chained to the wall, groping for the water-jug, gnawing crusts of bread that a dog would not touch, and maggoty beans – like a cockroach in a cellar! Have pity on yourself, my poor lad! You're still young. You were sucking at your mother's breast less than twenty years ago, and doubtless she is still alive. In her name I beseech you to listen to me. You want fine black cloth and glossy pumps, hair smoothly combed and scented; you want to be a gay dog and please the girls! But what you'll get is a shaven head, a red smock, and clogs. You want rings on your fingers, but you'll have one round your neck, and a cut of the whip if you so much as look at a woman. You'll start on that life at twenty and end at fifty. You'll start young and fresh, bright-eyed and white-toothed, and you'll end broken and bent, wrinkled, toothless and repellent, with white hair. My poor boy, you're on the wrong road. Sloth is a bad counsellor. Crime is the hardest of all work. Take my advice, don't be led into the drudgery of idleness. Rascality is a comfortless life; honesty is far less demanding. Now clear out and think about what I have said. Incidentally, what did you want of me? My purse, I suppose. Here it is.'

At length releasing his hold on Montparnasse, the elderly man handed him his purse, and Montparnasse, after weighing it for a moment in his hand, thrust it into the tail-pocket of his coat with as much care as if he had stolen it.

Having said his say, the elderly man turned away and went

calmly on with his walk. The reader will have no difficulty in guessing who he was.

'Old babbler!' muttered Montparnasse, and stood staring after him as he vanished in the gloom.

His momentary bemusement was unfortunate for him. While the stranger was disappearing in one direction, Gavroche was approaching from the other.

Gavroche had first glanced through the hedge to make sure that Père Mabeuf, who had presumably fallen asleep, was still in the same place. Then he scrambled out and crept towards where Montparnasse was still standing. Slipping his hand into the pocket of that handsome tail-coat, he deftly removed the purse, after which he slipped away like a lizard into the shadows. Montparnasse, who had no reason to be on his guard and in any case had been moved to thought, perhaps for the first time in his life, was quite unconscious of what had happened. Gavroche got back to the place where Père Mabeuf was sleeping, tossed the purse over the hedge and then made off at top speed.

The purse fell on Père Mabeuf's foot and awakened him. He picked it up and opened it in amazement. It had two compartments, in one of which was some small change while in the other there were six napoleons.

In high excitement Monsieur Mabeuf took it to his housekeeper. 'It must have fallen from Heaven,' said Mère Plutarque.

BOOK FIVE

OF WHICH THE END DOES NOT RESEMBLE THE BEGINNING

I

Solitude and the barracks

COSETTE'S STATE of unhappiness, so acute and poignant only a few months earlier, was growing less, even in her own despite. Youth and springtime, her love for her father, the brightness of birds and flowers, were by gradual degrees fostering in that young and virginal spirit something akin to forgetfulness. Did it mean that the fire was quite extinguished, or were the embers still glowing beneath a crust of ashes? The fact is that now she scarcely ever felt any sharp stab of pain. One day, recalling Marius, she thought, 'I don't even think of him!'

It was a few days after this that she observed, passing their garden gate, a handsome young cavalry officer with a wasp waist and a waxed moustache, fair hair and blue eyes, and with a sabre at his side, splendidly elegant in his uniform, a dashing, vainglorious figure, in all respects the opposite of Marius. He was smoking a cigar. Cosette supposed that he belonged to the regiment then quartered in the barracks in the Rue de Babylone.

She saw him again next day, and noted the time. After that – could it have been by accident? – she saw him almost daily as he sauntered past.

The young man's brother officers were not slow to detect that the overgrown garden behind that tiresome rococo gate harboured a good-looking wench who nearly always contrived to be on hand when the lieutenant (whom the reader has already met and whose name was Théodule Gillenormand) went that way.

'There's a girl who's got her eye on you,' they said. 'You ought to give her a glance.' To which he replied: 'Do you really think I've time to stare at all the girls who stare at me?'

This happened at precisely the time when Marius, in the depths of despair, was saying to himself, 'If I could see her just once more before I die!' If he had had his wish and seen Cosette gazing at the young lancer he would have died on the spot.

Which of them was to be blamed? Neither. Marius was one of

those who embrace sorrow and dwell in it; but Cosette was one of those who feel it deeply but recover.

Cosette, in any case, was going through that dangerous stage, fatal to womanhood left to its own devices, when the heart of a lonely girl resembles the tendrils of a vine which may attach itself, as chance dictates, to a marble column or an inn-sign. It is a brief, decisive phase, crucial for any motherless girl whether she be rich or poor, for riches are no defence against error. Misalliance may occur at any level, and the real misalliance is between souls. An unknown young man without birth or fortune may nevertheless be the marble pillar sustaining a temple of lofty sentiments and splendid thought, just as your opulent man of the world, if one looks not at his elegant exterior but at his inner nature, which is the special domain of women, may be no better than a witless wooden post, the resort of violent, drunken passions – an inn-sign, in short.

What was really the state of Cosette's heart? It was a state of passion assuaged or slumbering; of love in flux, limpid and gleaming, tremulous to a certain depth, but sombre below this. The picture of the handsome officer was reflected on the surface, but did a memory still linger in the deepest depths? Perhaps she herself did not know.

And then a singular incident occurred.

II

Cosette's alarm

During the first fortnight of April Jean Valjean went on a journey. As we know, it was a thing he occasionally did, at very long intervals. He would be away for a day or two, three at the most. No one knew where he went, not even Cosette; but on one occasion she had accompanied him in a fiacre as far as the corner of a small cul-de-sac bearing the name of the Impasse de la Planchette. Here he had got out and the fiacre had taken Cosette back to the Rue de Babylone. As a rule it was when the household was running short of money that he went on these excursions.

So Valjean was away, having said that he would be back in three days' time. Cosette spent the evening alone in the salon, and to relieve the monotony she sat down at her piano-organ and played and sang the chorus, 'Huntsmen astray in the woods!' from Weber's opera *Euryanthe*, which is perhaps the most beautiful piece of music ever composed. When she had finished she sat musing.

Suddenly she thought she heard the sound of footsteps in the garden.

It was ten o'clock. Her father was away and Toussaint was in bed. She went to one of the closed shutters and stood listening with her ear to it.

The footsteps sounded like those of a man walking very softly. Cosette ran up to her bedroom, opened the peep-hole in the shutter, and peered out. It was a night of full moon and everything was clearly visible.

There was no one to be seen. She opened the window. The garden was quite empty, and what little could be seen of the street was deserted as usual.

Cosette decided that she was mistaken and that the sound she thought she had heard had been simply an hallucination conjured up by Weber's dark, magnificent chorus, with its terrifying depths, evoking in the minds of its audience the magical forest in which can be heard the snapping of twigs beneath the restless feet of huntsmen half-seen in the dusk.

She thought no more about it; but then, Cosette was not nervous by nature. There was gipsy blood in her veins, that of a barefooted adventuress. We may recall that she was more like a lark than a dove. She had a wild but courageous heart.

At a somewhat earlier hour next day, when it was only beginning to grow dark, she went out into the garden. Intruding upon her random thoughts, she fancied that now and then she heard a sound like that of the previous night, as though someone were walking under the trees quite close to her; but she told herself that nothing more resembled the sound of footsteps in the grass than the sound of two branches rubbing together, and, in any case, she could see nothing.

She emerged from the 'shrubbery' and began to cross the small patch of grass between it and the steps of the villa. The moon, which was at her back, threw her shadow across the grass as she entered its light. And suddenly she stood still, terror-struck.

Beside her own shadow was another and singularly alarming one, a shadow wearing a round hat; it looked like that of a man walking a few paces behind her.

She stayed motionless for a moment, unable to cry out or even to turn her head. Finally, summoning all her courage, she looked round.

There was no one to be seen; and, looking down, she saw that the shadow had vanished. She went bravely back into the shrubbery and searched it, venturing even as far as the gate, but she found nothing.

She was truly alarmed. Could this be another hallucination, the second in two days? She might believe in one hallucination, but to believe in two was not so easy. And, most disturbing, it could not have been a ghost. Ghosts do not wear round hats. Jean Valjean returned home next day and she told him what had happened, expecting to be reassured and to hear him say lightly, 'You're a silly child.' But instead he looked troubled. 'It can't have been anything,' he said.

He made an excuse to leave her and went out into the garden, and she saw him carefully examining the gate.

She awoke during the night, and this time she was certain. She could distinctly hear the sound of footsteps beneath her window. She ran to the peep-hole in the shutter and looked out. A man was standing in the garden with a heavy cudgel in his hand. She was about to utter a cry when the moonlight fell upon his face. It was her father. She got back into bed thinking, 'He must be very worried!'

Jean Valjean passed all that night, and the two nights which followed, in the garden. She saw him through her peep-hole.

On the third night, at about one o'clock, when the moon was beginning to wane and rising later, she was awakened by a great burst of laughter and her father's voice calling to her, 'Cosette!' She sprang out of bed, put on her dressing-gown and opened the window. Her father was standing on the lawn.

'I woke you up to tell you everything's all right,' he said. 'Look. Here's your shadow in a round hat!'

He pointed to a shadow on the grass which did indeed look not unlike that of a man wearing a round hat. It was that of a cowled metal chimney belonging to a near-by house.

Cosette, too, began to laugh, with all her fears dispelled, and at breakfast next morning she was very gay on the subject of gardens haunted by the ghosts of chimney-stacks.

Jean Valjean recovered all his calm, and Cosette herself did not give much thought to the question of whether the chimney was really in the line of the shadow she had seen, or thought she had seen, or whether the moon was at the same point in the sky; nor did she question the singular behaviour of a chimney that beats a retreat when it is in danger of being caught – for the shadow had disappeared when she turned back to look for it, she was certain of that. She was quite convinced, and the notion that a stranger had entered their garden vanished from her thoughts.

But a few days later another incident occurred.

III

The remarks of Toussaint

There was a stone seat in the garden, close by the railing along the street, sheltered by a hedgerow from the gaze of the passer-by but so near to it that it might have been touched, at a pinch, by anyone reaching an arm through the railing and the hedge. Cosette was sitting on it one evening that April when Valjean was out. She was musing, overtaken by that feeling of sadness that assails us in the dusk and which perhaps arises – who can say? – from the mystery of the grave, of which we have intimations at that hour. Perhaps her mother, Fantine, lurked somewhere in the shadows.

The breeze was freshening. She got up and walked slowly round the garden, through the dew-soaked grass, reflecting idly, in her mood of melancholy abstraction, that she should wear thicker shoes when she went out at that time or she would catch cold.

She returned to the bench, but as she was in the act of sitting down she noticed, in the place where she had been sitting before, a fairly large stone which had not been there a few minutes earlier. She stood looking at it, and it occurred to her, since the stone could not have got there by itself, that it must have been placed there by someone reaching through the hedge. The thought startled her, and this time she was genuinely alarmed. There could be no doubt about the reality of the stone. She did not touch it, but ran back into the house without looking round and hurriedly closed and barred the shutters and bolted the front door. She said to Toussaint:

'Has my father come home?'

'Not yet, Mademoiselle.'

(We have mentioned that Toussaint had a stammer, and we hope to be forgiven for not constantly reproducing it. We dislike the musical notation of an infirmity.)

Valjean, with his fondness for solitary nocturnal walks, often did not return until late at night.

'You're always careful to see that the shutters are properly barred, are you not, Toussaint?' said Cosette. 'Especially on the garden side. And you put those little metal pegs in the rings?'

'Of course, Mademoiselle.'

It was a duty that Toussaint never neglected. Cosette was well aware of the fact, but she could not refrain from adding:

'This is a very lonely spot.'

'Well, that's the truth,' said Toussaint. 'We could be murdered in our beds before you could say knife, especially with Monsieur not sleeping in the villa. But you needn't worry; I lock the place up as though it were a prison. It's not a nice thing, two women alone in a house. Just imagine. You wake suddenly and there's a man in your room, and he tells you to hold your tongue while he cuts your throat! It isn't so much dying one's afraid of, because we've all got to come to that, but it's dreadful to think of being touched by those brutes. Besides which, their knives are probably blunt.'

'That will do,' said Cosette. 'Just make sure of our locks and bars.'

Terrified by this vividly improvised drama, and perhaps recalling her visions of a week or two before, Cosette was afraid to ask Toussaint to go out and look at the stone on the garden bench, from fear that if they opened the front door a party of villains would burst in. After locking and bolting every door and window in the house, and sending Toussaint to inspect the attics and cellars, she locked herself in her bedroom, peered under the bed and that night slept badly, haunted in her dreams by a stone the size of a mountain that was filled with caves.

But the next morning – it being the property of the sunrise to cause us to laugh at our terrors of the night, and our laughter being always proportionate to our fears – Cosette dismissed the whole thing, saying to herself: 'What was I thinking of? It's the same as those footsteps I thought I heard, and the shadow that was nothing but a chimney-stack. Am I turning into a frightened kitten?' And the sunlight, shining through the half-opened shutters and glowing redly through the curtains, so reassured her that she brushed it all away, even the stone. 'It didn't exist, any more than the man in the round hat. I simply imagined it.'

She dressed and ran out into the garden to the bench, and a shiver ran down her spine. The stone was still there.

But her alarm lasted only for a moment. What is terror after dark becomes merely curiosity by daylight. 'Well,' she thought. 'Let me see.'

The stone was quite large. She picked it up and saw that there was something underneath it. It was a white envelope, unaddressed and unsealed. But it was not empty. There was something that looked like a sheaf of folded paper inside. Cosette explored it with her fingers, with a feeling that was no longer one of fear or simple curiosity, but rather the dawning of a new apprehension. Extracting the contents, she found them to be a small paper-covered notebook of which every page was numbered and bore a few lines of very small and, she thought, very elegant handwriting. She looked for a name but found none; the writing was unsigned. For whom was it intended? Presumably for herself, since it had been deposited on her garden bench. Where had it come from? Seized with an over-powering fascination, she sought in vain to look away from the written pages fluttering in her hand, staring at the sky and at the street, at the acacias, bathed in sunshine, and at the pigeons flying over a near-by roof; but her gaze was drawn irresistibly back to the manuscript; she had to know what it had to say.

What follows is what she read.

IV

The heart beneath the stone

The reduction of the universe to the compass of a single being, and the extension of a single being until it reaches God – that is love.

Love is the salute of the angels to the stars.

How sad the heart is when rendered sad by love!

How great is the void created by the absence of the being who alone fills the world. How true it is that the beloved becomes God. It is understandable that God would grow jealous if the Father of All Things had not so evidently created all things for the soul, and the soul for love.

It needs no more than a smile, glimpsed beneath a hat of white crêpe adorned with lilac, for the soul to be transported into the palace of dreams.

God is behind all things, but all things conceal God. Objects are black and human creatures are opaque. To love a person is to render them transparent.

There are thoughts which are prayers. There are moments when, whatever the posture of the body, the soul is on its knees.

Separated lovers cheat absence by a thousand fancies which have their own reality. They are prevented from seeing one another and they cannot write; nevertheless they find countless mysterious ways of corresponding, by sending each other the song of birds, the scent of flowers, the laughter of children, the light of the sun, the sighing of the wind, and the gleam of the stars – all the beauties of creation. And why should they not? All the works of God are designed to serve love, and love has the power to charge all nature with its messages.

Oh, spring, you are a letter which I send her!

The future belongs far more to the heart than to the mind. Love is the one thing that can fill and fulfil eternity. The infinite calls for the inexhaustible.

Love partakes of the soul, being of the same nature. Like the soul, it is the divine spark, incorruptible, indivisible, imperishable. It is the fiery particle that dwells in us, immortal and infinite, which nothing can confine and nothing extinguish. We feel its glow in the marrow of our bones and see its brightness reaching to the depths of Heaven.

Oh, love, adoration, the rapture of two spirits which know each other, two hearts which are exchanged, two looks which interpenetrate! You will come to me, will you not, this happiness! To walk together in solitude! Blessed and radiant days! I have sometimes thought that now and then moments may be detached from the lives of angels to enrich the lives of men.

God can add nothing to the happiness of those who love except to make it unending. After a lifetime of love an eternity of love is indeed an increase; but to heighten the intensity, the ineffable happiness that love confers upon the spirit in this world, is an impossibility, even for God. God is the wholeness of Heaven; love is the wholeness of man.

We look up at a star for two reasons, because it shines and because it is impenetrable. But we have at our side a gentler radiance and a greater mystery, that of women.

Each of us, whoever he may be, has his breathing self. Lacking this, or lacking air, we suffocate. And then we die. To die for lack of love is terrible. It is the stifling of the soul.

When love has melted and merged two persons in a sublime and sacred unity, the secret of life has been revealed to them: they are no longer anything but the two aspects of a single destiny, the wings of a single spirit. To love is to soar!

On the day when a woman in passing sheds light for you as she goes, you are lost, you are in love. There is only one thing to be done, to fix your thoughts upon her so intently that she is compelled to think of you.

That which love begins can be completed only by God.

True love is plunged in despair or rapture by a lost glove or by a found handkerchief; but it needs eternity for all its devotion and its hopes. It is composed of both the infinitely great and the infinitely small.

If you are stone, be magnetic; if a plant, be sensitive; but if you are human be love.

Nothing satisfies love. We achieve happiness and long for Eden; we gain paradise and long for Heaven.
I say to you who love that all these things are contained in love. You must learn to find them. Love encompasses all Heaven, all contemplation, and, more than Heaven, physical delight.

'Does she still visit the Luxembourg?' ... 'No, Monsieur' ... 'It is in this church, is it not, that she attends Mass?' ... 'She does not come here any more' ... 'Does she still live in this house?' ... 'She has moved elsewhere' ... 'Where has she gone to live?' ... 'She did not say.'
How grievous not to know the address of one's soul!

Love has its childishness; other passions have pettiness. Shame on the passions that make us petty; honour to the one that makes us a child!

A strange thing has happened, do you know? I am in darkness. There is a person who, departing, took away the sun.

Oh, to lie side by isde in the same tomb and now and then caress with a finger-tip in the shades, that will do for my eternity!

You who suffer because you love, love still more. To die of love is to live by it.
Love! A dark and starry transfiguration is mingled with that torment. There is ecstasy in the agony.

Oh, the happiness of birds! It is because they have a nest that they have a song.
Love is a heavenly breath of the air of Paradise.

Deep hearts and wise minds accept life as God made it. It is a long trial, an incomprehensible preparation for an unknown destiny. This destiny, his true one, begins for man on the first stair within the tomb. Something appears to him, and he begins to perceive the finality. Take heed of that word, finality. The living see infinity; the finality may be seen only by the dead. In the meantime, love and suffer, hope and meditate. Woe, alas, to those who have loved only bodies, forms, appearances! Death will rob them of everything. Try to love souls, you will find them again.

I encountered in the street a penniless young man who was in love. His hat was old and his jacket worn, with holes at the elbows; water soaked through his shoes, but starlight flooded through his soul.

How wonderful it is to be loved, but how much greater to love! The heart becomes heroic through passion; it rejects everything that is not pure and arms itself with nothing that is not noble and great. An unworthy thought can no more take root in it than a nettle on a glacier. The lofty and serene spirit, immune from all base passion and emotion, prevailing over the clouds and shadows of this world, the follies, lies, hatreds, vanities and miseries, dwells in the azure of the sky and feels the deep and subterranean shifts of destiny no more than the mountain-peak feels the earthquake.

If there were no one who loved the sun would cease to shine.

V

Cosette after reading the letter

As she read this Cosette grew more and more thoughtful. Just as she finished it the young cavalry officer swaggered past the gate, this being his regular time. She thought him odious.

She turned back to the notebook, and now she found the handwriting delightful, always the same hand but in ink that varied in intensity, being sometimes dense black and sometimes pale, as happens when one writes over a period of days and adds water from time to time to the ink. It seemed that these were thoughts that had overflowed on to paper, a string of sighs set down at random, without order or selection or purpose. Cosette had never before read anything like it. The manuscript, in which she saw more clarity than obscurity, affected her like the opening of a closed door. Each of its enigmatic lines, shining with splendour in her eyes, kindled a new awareness in her heart. Her teachers at the convent had talked much of the soul but never of earthly love, rather as one might talk of the poker without mentioning the fire. These fifteen handwritten pages had abruptly but gently opened her eyes to the nature of all love and suffering, destiny, life, eternity, the beginning and the end, as though a hand, suddenly opening, had released a shaft of light. She could discern the author behind them, his passionate, generous, and candid nature, his great unhappiness and great hope, his captive heart and overflowing ecstasy. What was this manuscript if not a letter? A letter unaddressed, without name or date or signature, urgent, with no demands, a riddle composed of truths, a token of love to be delivered by a winged messenger and read by virgin eyes, an appointment to meet in some place not on earth, the love-letter of a ghost written to a vision. A calm but passionate unknown, who seemed ready to take refuge in death, had sent to his absent beloved the secret of human destiny, the key to life and love. He had written with a foot in the tomb and a finger in the sky. The lines, falling haphazard on the paper, were like raindrops falling from a soul.

And where did they come from? Who was their author? Cosette had not a moment's doubt. They could have come from only one person – from him.

The light of day was revived in her, everything was made good. She had a sense of inexpressible delight and anguish. It was he! He had been there, and it was his arm that had been thrust through the hedge! While she had been forgetful, he had searched and found her. But had she really forgotten him? Never! She was mad to have believed so, even for a moment. She had loved him from the first. The fire had been damped and had died down, but, as she now knew, it had only burned the more deeply in her, and now it had burst again into flame and the flame filled her whole being. The notebook was like a match flung by that other soul into her own, and she felt the fire break out again. She pored over the written words, thinking 'How well I know them! I have read it all before in his eyes.'

As she finished reading it for the third time Lieutenant Théodule reappeared beyond the gate, clicking his heels on the cobbles. Cosette was forced to look up. She now thought him fatuous, uncouth, impertinent, and altogether repellent, and she turned her head away indignantly, wishing she could throw something at him.

She went back into the house and up to her bedroom, to read the notebook yet again, learn it by heart, ponder on it. At length she kissed it and hid it in her bosom. The matter was decided. Cosette was again plunged in the anguished ecstasies of love; the infinity of Eden had opened for her once again.

She lived through that day in a state of bemusement, scarcely thinking, a thousand fancies tumbling through her head. She could guess at nothing, and the hopes amid her tremors were all vague; she dared be sure of nothing, but she would not reject anything. Pallors sped over her face, and shivers ran through her body. At moments she felt that she must be dreaming and asked herself, 'Can it be real?' But then she touched the notebook under her dress and pressing it to her heart felt its shape against her flesh. If Jean Valjean had seen her at those moments he would have trembled at the new look in her eyes. 'Oh, yes,' she thought. 'It can only be he; it comes to me from him!' And she thought that an intervention of the angels, some celestial chance, had restored him to her.

The wonders conjured up by love! The fantasies! That intervention of the angels, that celestial chance, was like the hunk of bread tossed from one inmate to another, from one courtyard to another, over the walls of the prison of La Force.

VI

No place for the aged

Jean Valjean went out that evening, and Cosette dressed up.

She did her hair in the way that suited her best and put on a gown that had been cut a little low at the neck so that it allowed the beginning of her bosom to be seen and was, as young ladies say, 'somewhat immodest'. It was not in the least immodest and more pretty than otherwise. She made these preparations without knowing why. Was she going anywhere? Was she expecing a visitor? No.

As evening fell she went into the garden. Toussaint was busy in the kitchen, which looked out on the back-yard. She walked under the trees, thrusting aside the branches now and then since some were very low. She came to the bench and found the stone still there.

She sat down and softly stroked it as though in gratitude. And suddenly she had that feeling that sometimes comes to us, of someone behind her. She looked round and started to her feet.

It was he.

He was bareheaded and he looked pale and thinner. His dark

clothing was scarcely visible in the dusk which cast a veil over his forehead and buried his eyes in shadow; beneath his incomparable sweetness of expression there was something of death and something of the night, and his face was faintly illumined with the light of the dying day and the suggestion of a soul in flight, as though he were still not a ghost but no longer a living man. He had dropped his hat, which lay in the bushes.

Cosette, near to fainting, did not utter a sound. She drew slowly away, because she felt herself drawn towards him. He did not move, but something emanated from him, a kind of warmth and sadness which must be in the eyes that she could not see.

In withdrawing Cosette found herself with her back to a tree, and she leaned against it. Without it she would have fallen.

Then he began to speak, in that voice that she had never heard before, speaking so softly that it was scarcely raised above the rustle of the leaves.

'Forgive me for being here. I have been in such distress, I could not go on living the way things were, and so I had to come. Did you read what I left on the bench? Do you perhaps recognize me? You mustn't be afraid. It's a long time ago, but do you remember the day when you first looked at me – in the Luxembourg, near the Gladiator? And the day when you walked past me? Those things happened on the 16th of June and the 2nd of July – nearly a year ago. After that I did not see you for a long time. I asked the woman who collects the chair-rents and she said she hadn't seen you. You were living in a new house in the Rue de l'Ouest, on the third floor. I found out, you see. I followed you. What else could I do? And then you disappeared. I thought I saw you once when I was reading the newspapers under the Odéon arcade and I ran after you, but it wasn't you, only someone wearing a hat like yours. I come here at night, but don't worry, no one sees me. I come and look up at your windows, and I walk very quietly so as not to disturb you. I was behind you the other evening when you looked round, and I hid and ran for it. Once I heard you singing and it made me very happy. Does it matter to you if I listen to you singing through the shutters? It can do you no harm. But you don't mind, do you? To me, you see, you're an angel. You must let me come sometimes. I think I'm going to die. If you knew how I adore you! Forgive me for talking like this, I don't know what I'm saying, perhaps I'm annoying you. Am I annoying you?'

'Mother!' she murmured, and sank down as though she herself were dying.

He caught her as she fell and clasped her tightly in his arms without knowing that he did so. He held her, trembling, feeling as though his head were filled with a mist in which lightnings flashed, feeling, in the tumult of his thoughts, that he was performing a religious rite that was also an act of profanation. For the rest, he felt no spark of physical desire for this enchanting girl whose body was now pressed so closely to his own. He was lost in love.

She took his hand and laid it against her heart, and he felt the shape of the notebook under her dress. He stammered:

'Then – you love me?'

She answered in a voice so low that it was scarcely to be heard: 'Of course! You know I do.' And she hid her russet head against the breast of the triumphant and marvelling young man.

He fell back on to the bench with her at his side. Neither could speak. The stars were beginning to show. How did it happen that their lips came together? How does it happen that birds sing, that snow melts, that the rose unfolds, that the dawn whitens behind the stark shapes of trees on the quivering summit of the hill? A kiss, and all was said.

Both were trembling. They looked at each other with eyes shining in the dusk, unconscious of the cool of the night, the chill of the stone bench, the dampness of the earth, the dew on the grass; they looked at each other, their hearts filled with their thoughts. Without knowing it, they had clasped hands.

She did not ask him, or even wonder, how he had contrived to get into the garden. It seemed to her so right that he should be there. From time to time their knees touched and both quivered. Now and then Cosette stammered a word, her soul trembling on her lips like a dewdrop on the petal of a flower.

And gradually they began to speak. Outpouring followed the silence which is fulfilment. The night was calm and splendid above their heads. Pure as disembodied spirits, they told each other about themselves, their dreams and their follies, their delights, their fantasies, their failings; how they had come to love each other at a distance, to long for each other, and their despair when they no longer saw each other. In an intimacy which nothing could ever make more perfect they told each other of all that was most secret and hidden in themselves, recounting, with an innocent trust in their illusions, everything that love and youth, and the vestiges of childhood that still clung to them, put into their heads. Two hearts were exchanged, so that when an hour had passed they were a youth enriched with the soul of a girl and a girl enriched with a young man's soul. Each pervaded, enchanted, and enraptured the other.

When they had finished, when everything had been said, she laid her head on his shoulder and asked:

'What is your name?'

'My name is Marius. And yours?'

'Cosette.'

BOOK SIX

THE BOY GAVROCHE

Scurvy trick played by the wind

SINCE 1823, while the tavern at Montfermeil was gradually sinking, not in the deeps of bankruptcy but in the sump of petty debt, the Thénardiers had had two more children, both boys, making five altogether, two girls and three boys. It was rather a lot. Mme Thénardier had rid herself of the last two, while they were still very young, in a singularly happy fashion.

'Rid herself' is the right way to put it. She was a woman possessing only a limited store of humanity, a phenomenon of which there are many instances. Like the Maréchale de la Mothe-Houdancourt, who mothered three duchesses, Mme Thénardier was a mother only to her daughters; her maternal instinct extended no further. Her hostility to mankind in general began with her sons, and it was here that her malice reached its peak. She detested the eldest, as we have seen, but she abominated the two others. Why? Because. The most terrible and unanswerable of reasons. 'Because I've no use for a litter of squalling brats,' she said. We must describe how the Thénardiers managed to get rid of their two youngest children and even make a profit out of them.

The woman Magnon, formerly the servant of Monsieur Gillenormand, of whom mention has already been made, had succeeded in getting her employer to support her two sons. She went to live on the Quai des Célestins, at the corner of the ancient Rue du Petit-Musc, of which the name does something to redeem its evil-smelling reputation. Some readers will recall the epidemic of croup which ravaged the riverside quarters of Paris thirty-five years ago and enabled medical science to experiment on a large scale with treatment by inhalation of alum, now superseded by the external application of iodine. Both La Magnon's sons were carried off by the epidemic at a tender age and on the same day – one in the morning and the other in the evening. It was a sad blow to their mother, for the children were valuable, each being worth eighty francs a month. The money was paid with meticulous regularity, on Monsieur Gillenormand's instructions, by his man of affairs, a retired lawyer's clerk living in the Rue du Roi-de-Sicile. The death of the children threatened to bring this happy state of affairs to an end, and La Magnon looked round for a way out of the difficulty. In the dark freemasonry of ill-doing of which she was a member all things are known, all secrets kept and each man helps his fellow. La Magnon needed two children and the Thénardiers had two to dispose of, of the same sex and age, a most fortunate coincidence. So the little Thénardiers became little Magnons, and La Magnon went to live in the Rue Clocheperce. In Paris to change the street in which one lives is to change one's identity.

Officialdom, not having been notified, raised no objection, and the transaction was carried out with the greatest ease. Mme Thénardier demanded a monthly rent of ten francs apiece for the two little boys, which La Magnon agreed to and, in fact, paid. It goes without saying that Monsieur Gillenormand kept up his payments. He visited the children every six months, but noticed no change. 'How like you they're growing, Monsieur!' said La Magnon.

Thénardier, with his usual adaptability, took advantage of the circumstance to turn himself into Jondrette. His two daughters and Gavroche had scarcely had time to notice that they had two small brothers. There is a level of poverty at which we are afflicted with a kind of indifference which causes all things to seem unreal: those closest to us become no more than shadows, scarcely distinguishable against the dark background of our daily life, and easily lost to view.

Nevertheless on the evening of the day on which she handed the boys over to La Magnon, with the firm resolve to be rid of them for ever, the Thénardier woman had, or pretended to have, a fit of conscience. She said to her husband, 'But it's abandoning our children!', to which he replied tersely and magisterially, 'Jean-Jacques Rousseau did even worse.' With her scruples thus disposed of, she became apprehensive: 'But suppose we have the police after us? Is it legal, what we've done, Monsieur Thénardier?' ... 'Of course it is, and anyway who's going to notice? Who worries about pauper children?'

La Magnon possessed what passed for elegance in her own sphere. She dressed with care. She shared her wretched but showily furnished apartment with a Frenchified Englishwoman who was a skilful thief. This Parisienne by adoption, who had wealthy contacts and a close connection with the diamonds of Mlle Mars, later became prominent in the police records. She was nicknamed 'Mamselle Miss'.

The two little boys had no reason to complain. Being worth eighty francs a head, they were carefully looked after, like any other valuable property – well-clad, well-fed, treated almost like little gentlemen – far better off under their false mother than under the real one. La Magnon, who aspired to gentility, used no coarse language in their presence.

Thus they lived for some years, and Thénardier began to envisage new possibilities. He said one day to La Magnon, when she brought him the monthly ten francs, 'Their "father" will have to see to their education.'

But suddenly the two unhappy children, hitherto well enough protected, even though it was by their misfortune, were flung neck and crop into real life and forced to start living it.

A mass-arrest of malefactors like that which had taken place in the Jondrettes' garret, which inevitably leads to further police investigation and imprisonments, is a disaster having wide repercussions in the criminal underworld. The downfall of the Thénardiers led to the downfall of La Magnon.

Shortly after La Magnon had passed the letter about the Rue Plumet on to Éponine, the police descended on the Rue Clocheperce. La Magnon and Mamselle Miss were arrested and the whole house, which harboured a number of suspicious characters, was searched. The two little boys were playing in a back-yard when this happened, and knew nothing about it. When they tried to go home they found the doors locked and the house empty. A cobbler, whose shop was across the street, called to them and gave them a written message from their 'mother'. It bore the address of Monsieur Barge, debt-collector, 8 Rue du Roi-de-Sicile – that is to say, Monsieur Gillenormand's man of affairs. 'You don't live here any more,' the cobbler said. 'You must go to this address. It's quite near, first turning on the left. Keep the paper in case you have to ask the way.'

They went off together, the older boy in the lead, clutching the scrap of paper. But he was cold, and his small, stiff fingers did not grip it tightly enough. A gust of wind along the Rue Clocheperce blew it out of his hand, and since it was growing dark he could not find it again.

After this they strayed at random through the streets.

In which the boy Gavroche profits by the great Napoleon

Springtime in Paris is often marred by harsh and bitter winds by which one is chilled if not quite frozen; they may spring up on the finest day, and their effect is like that of an icy draught blowing through a leaky window or ill-closed door into a warm room. It is as though the grim portals of winter had been left ajar. In the spring of 1832, the year of the first great European epidemic, these winds were more keen and piercing than ever; the door left ajar was not merely the door of winter but of the tomb: those gusts of wind were the breath of cholera. Their peculiarity, from a meteorological point of view, was that they did not exclude a high degree of electrical tension. There were frequent thunderstorms at that time.

On an evening when the wind was particularly vigorous, so much so that it might have been January, and the well-to-do had got out their winter overcoats, the boy Gavroche, shivering in his rags but still cheerful, stood gazing in apparent delight at a hairdresser's window in the neighbourhood of Orme-Saint-Gervais. He had somewhere acquired a woman's shawl, which he was using as a muffler. Ostensibly he was admiring the wax figure of a woman in a bridal gown, with a low-cut décolletée and a headdress of orange-blossom, which smiled at the populace as it slowly revolved on a stand between two lights; but the truth is that he was considering whether he might not 'lift' one or two of the cakes of soap in an open stall in the shop's doorway, thereafter to sell them at a sou apiece to a barber in another part of the town. He had often dined on one of those cakes of soap. It was a form of enterprise for which he had some talent and which he called 'trimming the trimmer'.

While he stood there with one eye on the revolving figure and the other on the array of soap he communed with himself in a low-voiced monologue as follows: 'Tuesday ... Was it Tuesday? ... It can't have been ... Well, but perhaps it was ... Yes, it was Tuesday.' The subject of the soliloquy is not known, but if it referred to the occasion of his last meal then that must have been three days ago, for the present day was Friday.

The barber, shaving a customer in his well-warmed shop, was keeping a sharp eye on this potential enemy, a frozen, impudent urchin with his hands plunged deep in his pockets but his wits plainly about him.

While Gavroche was studying the situation, glancing from the window to the Brown Windsor soap, two respectably clad small boys, both younger than himself, timidly opened the door and, entering the shop, asked for something in plaintive voices that sounded more like a sob than a plea. Both talked at once, and it was impossible to make out what they were saying because the voice of the younger was choked with misery and the teeth of the elder were chattering with cold. The barber turned furiously upon them and, still with his razor in his hand, thrust them back to the street exclaiming:

'Opening the door and letting the cold in for no reason!'

The children walked dolefully away, and now it was beginning to rain. Gavroche went after them.

'What's up with you two?' he demanded.

'We've nowhere to sleep,' the older boy said.

'Is that all?' said Gavroche. 'Well it's nothing to cry about. You aren't kittens.' And he went on, with a protective note under his air of lofty scorn. 'Come with me, moppets.'

They obeyed him instantly, as though he had been an archbishop, and both stopped crying. Gavroche led them up the Rue Saint-Antoine in the direction of the Bastille, but not without backward glances at the hairdresser's shop.

'That's a cold fish, that one,' he muttered. 'Probably English.'

A woman of the town, seeing them as they walked in single file with Gavroche at the head, gave a loud and disrespectful titter.

'Don't mention it, Miss Open-to-all,' said Gavroche.

But then he returned to the subject of the hairdresser.

'I got the wrong animal. He's not a fish but a snake. I'll get hold of a locksmith and tie a bell to his tail.'

The thought of the hairdresser had made him truculent. Crossing a gutter, they came up with a bearded caretaker, worthy to encounter Faust on the Brocken, with a broom in her hand.

'Madame,' he inquired, 'are you going to fly away on it?'

At the same time he splashed the freshly shined boots of a man who was passing.

'Young devil!' the man exclaimed furiously.

Gavroche stuck his chin out over the shawl.

'Monsieur has a complaint to make?'

'I'm complaining about you!'

'Sorry. No more complaints today. The office is closed.'

But further up the street he noticed, shivering in a doorway, a beggar girl of thirteen or fourteen whose skirts were so short that they left her knees uncovered. She was beginning to be too old to go about like that. These are the tricks that growing up plays. Skirts become too short when nakedness becomes indecent.

'Poor kid,' said Gavroche. 'She hasn't even got drawers on. Here, take this.'

He unwound the thick wool from around his neck and draped it over her skinny shoulders, and the muffler again became a shawl. The girl stared at him in astonishment, accepting the gift in silence. At the level of utmost poverty wits are too dulled to complain at misfortune or give thanks for a benefaction.

'Brrr!' said Gavroche, now shivering more than St Martin himself, who at least had kept half his cloak. And as though encouraged by the 'brrr' the rain came pouring down. Those black skies punish good deeds. 'And now what?' said Gavroche. 'Raining again. If it goes on like this I shall ask for my money back. All the same,' he went on, looking at the girl as she drew the shawl tightly about her, 'there's one person who can keep warm.' And he glared defiantly at the heavens. 'So that's one up to me!'

He walked on with the two little boys following closely behind him, and when they came to the barred window which was the sign of a baker's shop – for bread must be as rigorously protected as gold – he turned to them and said:

'Talking of which, have you kids had anything to eat?'

'Not since this morning, sir,' the elder boy replied.

'But haven't you any parents?' Gavroche demanded.

'Yes, sir, I beg your pardon, we have a father and mother, but we don't know where they are.'

'We've been walking for hours,' the elder boy went on. 'We've even looked in the gutters for something to eat, but we couldn't find anything.'

'I know,' said Gavroche. 'The dogs get everything.' He paused to consider and then said: 'So – the parents gone astray and no knowing what's become of them. That's bad, my children. It's a mistake to mislay grown-ups. Well, we've got to get a bite somewhere.'

He asked no further questions. To be homeless was no novelty in his life. But the elder of the two little boys, who had now almost entirely recovered the ready heedlessness of childhood, exclaimed:

'It's queer all the same. Mamma said she'd take us to get some box for the decorations of Palm Sunday.'

'My eye!' said Gavroche.

'Mamma's a lady and she lives with Mamselle Miss.'

'Does she now!' said Gavroche.

They were still standing outside the baker's shop, and for some moments he had been exploring the numerous recesses in his ragged attire. Finally he looked up with what he hoped was an air of calm satisfaction but which was really one of triumph.

'Don't worry, lads. This will do for supper for three.' And he brought a single sou out of one of his pockets.

Without giving them time to stare, he pushed them ahead of him into the shop and slapped the sou down on the counter, exclaiming:

'Baker's boy! Five centimes' worth of bread.'

The man behind the counter, who was in fact the baker himself, picked up a loaf and a knife.

'Three slices, boy,' said Gavroche, and added in a dignified manner, 'There are three of us.' Then, seeing that the baker, after a glance at the three diners, had selected a cheap loaf, he put a finger to his nose with a sniff as lordly as if it conveyed a pinch of Frederick the Great's snuff, and cried in outraged indignation:

'Wossat?'

Any reader who may be disposed to mistake this utterance for a word of Russian or Polish, or for one of those cries which the Mohawks or the Ojibasays address to one another across a river in the American far west, is hereby informed that it is an expression which he (the reader) commonly uses in place of the words, 'What is that?' The baker understood perfectly and replied:

'Why, it's bread, of course. Excellent second-class bread.'

'Meaning *larton brutal*, black bread, prison bread,' said Gavroche with cool disdain. 'What I want is white bread. The real, polished stuff. I'm in a spending mood.'

The baker could not restrain a smile, and while he cut the required loaf he surveyed his customers with an expression of sympathy, which outraged Gavroche.

'What do you think you're doing,' he demanded, 'looking us over like that?' The three of them laid end to end would have come to little more than six feet.

When the bread had been cut and the baker had pocketed his sou, Gavroche said to the two children, 'Well, sail in!' They stared in bewilderment and he burst out laughing. 'They're too small to know the language yet. Eat is what I mean.' He picked up two of the three slices, and thinking that the older boy was more deserving of his notice and should be encouraged to assuage his larger appetite, he handed him the larger of the two. 'Stop your gob with this.'

He kept the smallest slice for himself.

The little boys were ravenous, as was Gavroche. Standing there devouring the bread, they cluttered up the shop, and the owner, having got his money, was beginning to look sourly at them.

'Outside,' said Gavroche, and they continued on their way to the Bastille.

Now and then when they passed a lighted shop-window the smaller boy paused to look at the time by a gunmetal watch hanging on a string round his neck.

'A pampered chick,' reflected Gavroche; but then he muttered between his teeth: 'All the same, if I had brats I'd look after them better than that.'

By the time they had finished the bread they had come to the corner of the dismal Rue des Ballets, at the end of which the low, forbidding doorway of the prison of La Force is to be seen.

'Is that you, Gavroche?' a voice said.

'Is that you, Montparnasse?' said Gavroche.

The man who had spoken was indeed Montparnasse, concealed behind blue-tinted spectacles but perfectly recognizable to Gavroche.

'My word!' said Gavroche. 'A coat that fits like a poultice and blue goggles like a professor! Classy, that's what we are.'

'Not so bad,' said Montparnasse, and drew him away from the shop lights. The two little boys followed automatically, holding hands. When they were installed under the archway of a house entrance, out of earshot and sheltered from the rain, Montparnasse said:

'Know where I'm going?'

'To the gallows, like as not.'

'Idiot. I'm going to meet Babet.'

'So that's her name,' said Gavroche.

'Not her – him.'

'What – you mean Babet?'

'That's right.'

'But I thought he'd been jugged.'

'Yes, but he's skipped,' said Montparnasse, and he went on to describe how Babet, having been transferred to the Conciergerie, had escaped that same morning by slipping into the wrong file at the inspection parade. Gavroche greatly admired this act of cunning.

'What an artist!' he said.

'But that's not all,' said Montparnasse.

While he was listening to further details Gavroche had taken hold of the case Montparnasse was carrying. He tugged at the handle and the blade of a dagger came to light.

'Hey!' he said, hastily thrusting it back. 'So you're ready for action under the classy get-up!' Montparnasse winked. 'Are you expecting trouble with the cops?'

'You never know,' said Montparnasse airily. 'Just as well to be prepared.'

'Well, what exactly are you up to?'

'Things,' said Montparnasse, resuming his portentous manner. He then changed the subject. 'By the way, a queer thing happened to me the other day.'

'What was that?'

'A few days ago it was. I held up a respectable old gent and he handed me a sermon and his purse. I put it in my pocket, but when I looked for it a few minutes later there was nothing there.'

'Except the sermon,' said Gavroche.

'But what about you? What are you up to?'

'I'm going to put these kids to bed.'

'Put them to bed? Where?'

'In my place.'

'Where's that?'

'My home.'

'You mean you've got a lodging?'

'That's right.'

'Well, where is it?'

'It's in the elephant,' said Gavroche.

Montparnasse was not easily astonished, but this caused him to open his eyes.

'In the elephant?'

'That's right. The Bastille elephant. What's wrong with that?'

Montparnasse's face cleared and he looked approvingly at Gavroche.

'Of course,' he said. 'The elephant. What's it like?'

'Couldn't be better. Real comfort. No draughts like you get under the bridges.'

'But how do you get in?'

'I manage.'

'You mean there's a hole?'

'You bet. But you mustn't let on. It's between the front legs. The cops haven't spotted it.'

'So you climb up. Yes, I see.'

'It takes me about two seconds. But I'll have to find a ladder for these kids.'

Montparnasse glanced at them and laughed.

'How the devil did you come by them?'

'A barber made me a present of them,' said Gavroche simply.

Another thought had now occurred to Montparnasse. 'You recognized me pretty easily,' he muttered.

He got two small objects out of his pocket – two short lengths of quill bound with cotton – and inserted one in each nostril. They gave him a new nose.

'That changes you quite a bit,' said Gavroche. 'A great improvement. You should always wear them.'

Montparnasse was a good-looking youth but he could take a joke.

'Seriously,' he said, 'what's it like?'

His tone of voice had also changed. In the twinkling of an eye he had become a different person.

'Marvellous. How about giving us Punch and Judy?'

At this the two little boys, who had hitherto paid no attention to the conversation, being too busy picking their own noses, turned and looked hopefully up at Montparnasse; but the latter, unfortunately, had grown solemn. He laid a hand on Gavroche's shoulder and said gravely:

'I don't mind telling you, lad, that if I were in the market-place with my *dogue*, my *dague*, and my *digue* and you were so prodigal as to offer me ten sous I wouldn't mind digging for them. But this isn't Mardi Gras.'

This strange utterance had a remarkable effect on the boy. He turned and looked alertly about him, and seeing a policeman standing with his back to them not far away he uttered a grunt of enlightenment, quickly suppressed, and shook Montparnasse by the hand.

'Well, good night, I must take these kids along to my place. And by the way, if you need me some night that's where you'll find me. I live on the first floor. There's no hall-porter. Ask for Monsieur Gavroche.'

'Thanks,' said Montparnasse.

They then parted, Montparnasse making for the Grève and Gavroche for the Bastille. The younger of the two little boys, who was being pulled along by his brother, who was being pulled along by Gavroche, looked round several times for a last glimpse of the Punch and Judy man.

The clue to the cryptic utterance which had warned Gavroche of the presence of a policeman was contained in the repetition of the syllable 'dig', either within a word or as a link between two words, meaning, 'Watch out. We can't talk here.' It also contained an elegant literary allusion which escaped Gavroche. The words my '*dogue*', my '*dague*', and my '*digue*', meaning 'my dog, my dagger, and my woman', were slang of the Temple quarter, commonly used by fairground buskers and camp-followers in the *grand siècle*, when Molière wrote and Callot drew.

Twenty years ago there was still to be seen, in the south-east corner of the Place de la Bastille, near the canal-port dug out of the former moat of the prison-fortress, a weird monument which has vanished from the memory of present-day Parisians but which deserves to have left some trace of itself, for it sprang from the mind of a member of the Institute, none other than the Commander-in-Chief of the Army in Egypt.

We use the word 'monument', although in fact it was no more than a preliminary sketch; but a sketch on the grand scale, the prodigious corpse of a Napoleonic aspiration which successive adverse winds have borne further and further away from us until it has lapsed into history; but the sketch had a look of permanence which was in sharp contrast to its provisional nature. It was an elephant some forty feet high, constructed of wood and plaster, with a tower the size of a house on its back, that once had been roughly painted green but was now blackened by wind and weather. Outlined against the stars at night, in that open space, with its huge body and trunk, its crenellated tower, its four legs like temple columns, it was an astonishing and impressive spectacle. No one knew precisely what it meant. It was in some sort a symbol of the popular will, sombre, enigmatic, and immense; a sort of powerful and visible ghost confronting the invisible spectre of the Bastille.

Few strangers came to view the monster, and the people in the street scarcely glanced at it. It was crumbling to bits, the fallen plaster leaving great wounds in its flanks. The '*aediles*', to use the fashionable term, had forgotten about it since 1814. It stood gloomily in its corner, enclosed in a rotting wooden fence soiled by countless drunken cab-drivers, with cracks in its belly, a lath of wood protruding from its tail and tall grass growing between its feet; and since the ground level of the space around it had, by that gradual process common to the soil of all great cities, risen in the past thirty years, it seemed to be standing in a hollow, as though the earth were subsiding beneath it. It was crude, despised, repulsive, and defiant; unsightly to the fastidious, pitiful to the thinker, having about it a contradictory quality of garbage waiting to be swept away and majesty waiting to be beheaded.

As we have said, its aspect changed at night. Night is the true setting for all things that are ghosts. As darkness fell the venerable monster was transformed; amid the serenity of the gathering gloom it acquired a placid and awe-inspiring splendour. Being of the past it belonged to the night; and darkness befitted its nobility.

The ponderous, uncouth, almost misshapen monument, which was certainly majestic and endowed with a sort of savage and magnificent gravity, has since disappeared to make way for the sort of gigantic cooking-stove adorned with a chimney which has replaced the sombre fortress with its nine towers, rather as the era of the bourgeoisie has replaced feudalism. It is very proper that a cooking-stove should be the symbol of an epoch that derives its power from a cook-pot. This epoch will pass – indeed, is already passing. We are beginning to grasp the fact that although power can be contained in a boiler, mastery exists only in the brain: in other words, that it is ideas, not locomotives, that move the world. To harness locomotives to the ideas is good; but do not let us mistake the horse for the rider.

To return to the Place de la Bastille, the architect of the elephant achieved something greater in plaster, whereas the architect of the chimney-pot achieved something insignificant in bronze.

In 1832 the chimney-pot, that failed memorial to a failed revolution, grandiloquently baptized the July Column, was – and for our part we regret it – enveloped in a vast array of scaffolding and surrounded by a plank fence, which further isolated the elephant. It was to this deserted corner of the square, dimly lit by a distant streetlamp, that the urchin Gavroche brought the two 'kids'.

May we here break off our narrative to recall that we are dealing with a matter of fact, and that twenty years ago the magistrates tried the case of a child, charged with vagabondage and damaging a public monument, who had been found asleep inside the Elephant of the Bastille.

To proceed. When they reached the monster, Gavroche, conscious of the effect the very large may have on the very small, said reassuringly:

'Don't be afraid, young 'uns.'

He slipped into the enclosure through a gap in the surrounding fence and helped the little boys through. They followed him in silence, both somewhat apprehensive but trusting to this tattered Samaritan who had given them bread and promised them shelter for the night. There was a ladder lying along the fence, used by workmen in a nearby builder's yard. Gavroche hoisted it up with a remarkable display of energy and set it against one of the elephant's front legs. At the top a rough aperture in the creature's belly was visible. Gavroche pointed to this and to the ladder and said:

'Up you go, and inside!'

The little boys exchanged terrified glances.

'What! Mean to say you're scared?' exclaimed Gavroche. 'Well, I'll show you.'

Without deigning to use the ladder he shinned up the rough leg and in no time had reached the aperture, into which he disappeared like a lizard vanishing into a crevice. A moment later the little boys saw the white blur of his face peering down at them out of darkness.

'Well, come on up,' he called, 'and see how nice it is. You go first,' he added to the elder boy. 'I'll lend you a hand.'

The little boys nudged one another, at once scared and heartened; besides which, it was raining heavily. The elder decided to chance it, and at the sight of him on the ladder, while he himself was left alone between the beast's great feet, the younger came near to bursting into tears but did not dare. The elder boy climbed unsteadily while

Gavroche encouraged him with a flow of instructions like a fencing-master with a class, or a muleteer with a pack of mules.

'Don't be afraid. That's the way. Now your other foot. Now your hands. That's it. Well done!' Directly he came within reach Gavroche grabbed him by the arm and pulled him towards himself. 'Fine!' he said. The boy was through the entrance.

'Now wait here,' said Gavroche. 'Be so good as to take a seat, Monsieur.'

He slipped out again, slid down the elephant's leg with the nimbleness of a monkey, landed on his feet in the grass, picked up the five-year-old, set him halfway up the ladder, and climbed up behind him, calling to the older boy, 'I'll push, and when he gets to the top you pull!'

The younger boy was pushed, lugged, heaved, and bundled through the aperture almost before he knew where he was, and Gavroche, after kicking away the ladder so that it fell on the grass, clapped his hands and cried:

'We've done it, and long live General Lafayette!' After which outburst he said formally: 'Gentlemen, welcome to my abode.'

It was indeed the only home he had.

The unforeseen usefulness of the superfluous! The charity of great matters, the kindness of giants! That extravagant monument to the fantasy of an emperor had become the hide-out of an urchin. The pigmy was accepted and sheltered by the colossus. Citizens in their Sunday clothes passing the Elephant of the Bastille might glance at it in dull-eyed indifference saying, 'What use is it?' But it served to protect a homeless, parentless youngster against wind and hail and frost, to preserve him from the slumber in the mud which causes fever and the slumber in the snow which causes death. It housed the innocent rejected by society, and thus in some degree atoned for society's guilt, affording a retreat to one to whom all other doors were closed. It seemed indeed that the crumbling, scabby monster, neglected, despised, and forgotten, a sort of huge beggar crying in vain for the alms of a friendly look, had taken pity on that other beggar, the waif without shoes to his feet or a roof to his head, clad in rags, blowing on numbed fingers, living on such scraps as came his way. That was the use of the Bastille elephant. Napoleon's notion, disdained by men, had been adopted by God, and what could only have been pretentious had been made august. To complete his design the Emperor would have needed copper and marble, porphyry and gold; for God the structure of wood and plaster sufficed. The Emperor had a lordly dream: in that prodigious elephant, bearing its armoured tower and lashing its trunk, he had thought to embody the soul of the people: God had done something greater with it, He had made it a dwelling for a child.

The aperture by which Gavroche had entered was scarcely visible from outside, being, as we have said, hidden under the belly of the elephant and so narrow that only a cat or a small boy could have got through it.

'To start with,' said Gavroche, 'we must tell the doorkeeper that we are not at home.' And diving into the darkness with the ease of one familiar with his surroundings, he produced a plank with which to cover the hole.

He vanished again, and the little boys heard the hiss of a match-stick plunged in a bottle of phosphorus. The chemical match did not then exist: in those days the lighter invented by Fumade represented progress.

A sudden glow caused them to blink. Gavroche had lighted one of the lengths of string soaked in resin which are known as 'rats tails', and this, although it gave out more smoke than light, made the elephant's interior dimly visible.

Gavroche's two guests gazed about them with something of the feelings of a person inside the great wine-barrel of Heidelberg, or better, the feelings Jonah must have experienced when he found himself inside the whale. They were enclosed in what looked like a huge skeleton. A long beam overhead, to which massive side-members were attached at regular intervals, represented the back-bone and ribs, with plaster stalactites hanging from them like entrails; and everywhere there were great spiders' webs like dusty diaphragms. Here and there in the corners were patches of black that seemed to be alive and had changed their position with sudden, startled movements. The litter fallen from the back of the elephant on to its stomach had evened out the concavity of the latter, so that one could walk on it as though on a floor.

The younger of the little boys was clinging to his brother. He whispered:

'It's so dark!'

This drew an outburst from Gavroche. Their state of petrified alarm called for a sharp rebuke.

'What was that?' he demanded. 'Is somebody complaining?

Isn't this good enough for you? Perhaps you'd rather have the Tuileries? But I'm no royal lackey, let me tell you, so you might as well stop whimpering.'

A touch of roughness is salutary to weak nerves. The boys drew closer to Gavroche and, touched by the gesture of confidence, his manner changed.

'Lummox,' he said gently to the younger, 'it's outside that it's dark. It's raining outside, but not in here. The wind's blowing but here you don't feel it. There are mobs of people outside, but in here there's no one to bother you. And outside there isn't even a moon, but here we've got a light. What more do you want?'

They began to look less apprehensively about them, but Gavroche did not allow them much time to inspect the premises. 'This way,' he said, and thrust them towards what we have great pleasure in calling his bedchamber.

He had an excellent bed, complete with mattress and coverlet in a curtained sleeping-alcove. The mattress was a piece of straw matting and the coverlet a large blanket of rough wool, warm and almost new. The alcove was devised as follows:

Three thin upright posts, two in front and one at the back, were firmly embedded in the rubble of the floor – that is to say, of the elephant's stomach – and joined with cord at the top so as to form a pyramidal framework. Over this framework wire-netting was draped, carefully stretched and nailed here and there, so as to enclose the whole of it. An array of large stones held it down to the floor and ensured that nothing could get in. The netting, which took the place of curtains, was of the kind used in aviaries, so that Gavroche's bed was in fact in a cage. The general effect was like an Eskimo's tent.

Slightly moving one or two stones, Gavroche drew back two strips of netting and said to the little boys: 'Crawl in on hands and knees.' Having seen them inside, he followed them in, also crawling, and then replaced the stones to secure the entrance. The three of them lay down on the mattress. Small though the two boys were, neither could have stood upright in the cage.

Gavroche was still carrying the rat's tail. 'Silence, everyone,' he said. 'I'm going to dowse the glim.'

But the elder boy pointed to the netting and asked:

'Please, sir, what's that for?'

'To keep the rats out,' said Gavroche gravely, 'And now, silence.'

However, in consideration of their youth and inexperience, he deigned to give his guests a little added information.

'It comes out of the Jardin des Plantes, out of the zoo. They've got all kinds of stuff. You've only got to climb a wall or go in at a window and you can get anything you want.' While he was speaking he was folding the coverlet about the younger boy, who murmured drowsily, 'It's ever so warm.' He looked complacently at the coverlet.

'That comes out of the Jardin des Plantes too, out of the monkey-house.'

He drew the elder boy's attention to the mat on which they were lying, which was very thick and excellently made.

'I got that from the giraffe.'

After a pause he went on: 'The animals had all these things. I pinched them from them, but they didn't mind. I said they were for the elephant.'

Again he was silent and then he summed the matter up:

'You skip over walls and who cares about the government? That's the way it is.'

The little boys were gazing in awed admiration at this intrepid and resourceful adventurer who was a vagabond like themselves, a pauper as lonely and vulnerable as they, but who in their eyes appeared an almost supernatural being, a man of power with the leers and grimaces of a circus clown and the gentlest and most innocent of smiles.

'Please, sir,' said the elder shyly, 'aren't you afraid of the police?'

'We don't call them police,' said Gavroche tersely. 'We call them cops.'

The younger boy's eyes were still open although he was saying nothing. Since he was at the edge of the mat, with his brother in the middle, Gavroche solicitously reached across to make sure that he was properly covered and thrust a few old rags under his head to serve him as pillow. He turned back to the other boy.

'We're pretty well off here, eh?'

'It's wonderful,' the boy said, with a look of overflowing gratitude. As their soaked clothing dried both boys were beginning to feel warm.

'And now,' said Gavroche, 'perhaps you'll tell me what you two were crying about.' He jerked his thumb towards the younger. 'A kid his age, that's excusable; but a big chap like you, blubbering away like a calf, you ought to be ashamed.'

'Well,' protested the older boy, 'but we hadn't any home to go to.'

'You don't call it home,' said Gavroche. 'You call it your shack.'

'And we were scared of being out all night.'

'In the glim,' said Gavroche. 'Now, you listen to me. I don't want any more complaints. From now on I'm looking after you and we're going to have a fine time. You'll see. In the summer we'll go to La Glacière with Mavet, who's a mate of mine, and bathe in the river and run naked along the bank by the Austerlitz bridge, just to annoy the washerwomen. The things they shout at you, it's as good as a pantomime! And we'll go and see the human skeleton. There's one on the Champs-Élysées, a real, live man as thin as a skeleton. And I'll take you to the theatre, to the Frédérick-Lemaître. I get tickets, see, because I know the company. In fact, I acted in one of their plays. A gang of boys like me, we crawled about under a canvas to make it look like the sea. Maybe I'll be able to get you both a job. And we'll see the old Indians. Mark you, they aren't real Indians. They wear pink tights that wrinkle and you can see where they've been darned. And we'll go to the Opéra, we'll go into the gallery with the *claque*. It's a very good *claque* at the Opéra. I wouldn't want to go with the boulevard theatre *claques*. But at the Opéra some of them even pay, as much as twenty sous. But that's soft – the dummies, we call them. And we'll go and watch someone being guillotined, and you'll see the Public Executioner, Monsieur Sanson. He lives in the Rue des Marais and he has a letter-box in his door. You'll see! We'll have a high old time!'

At this moment a drop of wax fell on Gavroche's finger, bringing him back to earth.

'*Bigre!* The taper's burning down. We have to watch it. I can't afford more than a sou a month for lighting. When you turn in you go to sleep, you don't sit up reading the novels of Monsieur Paul de Kock. Besides which the light might show through the door and then we'd have the cops after us.'

'And anyway,' ventured the older boy, who alone was brave enough to speak to Gavroche, 'a drop of lighted wax on the straw might set the house on fire.'

'Burn down the shack,' said Gavroche. 'That's right. But not on a night like this.'

The storm had increased, and between the bursts of thunder they could hear the drumming of rain on the monster's back.

'It's coming down in bucketfuls,' said Gavroche. 'I like to hear it pouring down our house's legs. The winter's like another animal. It gives us all it's got, but it's wasting its time and trouble, it can't even wet us, and that makes it roar with fury, the old brute.'

This allusion to the thunder, of which Gavroche, like the nine-teenth-century philosopher he was, defied all the consequences, was followed by a particularly brilliant flash of lightning, so vivid that its reflection showed through the crevice in the elephant's belly. At the same time there was another clap of thunder, so loud that the little boys started up in dismay, nearly dislodging the wire netting. Gavroche burst out laughing.

'Easy does it, lads. Don't go breaking up the home. That was a fine old bang, wasn't it? Not one of your damp squibs. Well done, God! It was almost as good as the Théâtre de l'Ambigu.'

This said, he put the netting to rights, thrust the little boys gently back against the straw, pushed down their knees so that they were lying straight and went on:

'Well, as God has lit his candle I can blow out mine. We've got to sleep, my boys, being human. It's bad to go without sleep. It gives you the collywobbles. So snuggle down and I'll blow it out. Are you all right?'

'It's grand,' said the older boy. 'It feels as though I'd got feathers under my head.'

'Not your head,' said Gavroche. 'Your napper. Now let's hear you snore.' And he blew out the taper.

Scarcely was the light extinguished than a strange disturbance shook the netting in which the three children were enclosed, a multitude of small, metallic sounds, as though teeth and claws were worrying the wire, accompanied by small, piercing squeaks. The five-year-old boy, hearing this commotion above his head and petrified with alarm, nudged his brother, but the latter had already obeyed Gavroche's injunction to snore. Finally, when he could bear it no longer, he ventured to address Gavroche, in the lowest of voices and with bated breath.

'Monsieur . . .'

'Well?' said Gavroche with his eyes closed.

'What's that noise?'

'Rats,' said Gavroche, and turned on his side.

The rats, which bred by the thousand in the elephant's carcase and were the living patches of black of which we have spoken, had been kept at bay by the taper while it was alight, but directly that cavernous place, which was their stronghold, was plunged in darkness, and scenting what the excellent storyteller, Perrault, has called 'young flesh', they had swarmed over Gavroche's tent, and were trying to gnaw through the meshes of this new-style mosquito-net.

The little boy was still not happy.

'Monsieur,' he said again.

'Well!' said Gavroche.

'Please, what are rats?'

'A kind of mouse.'

This was fairly reassuring. The little boy had seen white mice and had not been afraid of them. Nonetheless he had another question.

'Monsieur . . .'

'Well?'

'Why don't you keep a cat?'

'I had one,' said Gavroche. 'I brought one in, but they ate it.'

This reply entirely undid the soothing effect of the previous one. The little boy began to tremble again, and the exchanges between him and Gavroche were resumed for the fourth time.

'Monsieur . . .'

'Now what?'

'Who was it who ate the cat?'

'The rats.'

'The mice?'

'Yes, the rats.'

Appalled by this thought of mice that ate cats, the little boy asked:

'But Monsieur, won't they eat us too?'

'Well, blow me!' said Gavroche. But the little boy was now in a state of extreme terror and he turned to him. 'Don't worry, they can't get in. And besides, I'm here. Here, take my hand. Now shut up and go to sleep.'

Reaching across the elder brother, Gavroche gave the younger one his hand, and the little boy clasped it and was comforted. Courage and strength are thus mysteriously transmitted. There was again silence, the sound of voices having frightened the rats away; they were back a few minutes later, but not all their squeakings and gnawings could disturb the three children, who by then were sound asleep.

The night hours passed. Darkness enveloped the immense Place de la Bastille, a winter's wind blew gustily to mingle with the rain, police patrols, peering into doorways, alleyways, the dark corners in search of nocturnal vagabonds, passed indifferently by the elephant. The monster stood motionless, eyes open in the darkness, as though meditating with satisfaction upon its good deed in sheltering three homeless children from the elements and from man.

To understand what follows the reader must recall that at that time the Bastille police-post was situated at the other end of the square, and that the officer on duty there could not see or hear anything that took place in the neighbourhood of the elephant. Towards the end of the last hour before dawn a man came running out of the Rue Saint-Antoine; he crossed the square, rounded the July Column, and, slipping through the palings, came to a stop under the elephant's belly. Had there been any light to see him by, the drenched state of his clothing would have suggested that he had spent the night in the open. Having reached the elephant – he uttered a strange, parrot-cry which is best conveyed by the word *kirikikioo*. He uttered it twice, and the second time it was answered by a clear, youthful voice which simply said:

'Right!'

A moment later the plank masking the hole was removed and Gavroche slid down the elephant's leg and dropped lightly at the man's side. The man was Montparnasse. As for the mysterious call, it was doubtless what had been implied by the words, 'Ask for Monsieur Gavroche.' Upon hearing it Gavroche had crawled out of his sleeping-tent, carefully replaced the netting, and hastened to answer the summons.

They nodded to each other in the darkness, and Montparnasse simply said:

'We need help. Come and lend a hand.'

'I'm ready,' said Gavroche, and asked no further explanation.

They headed for the Rue Saint-Antoine, by which Montparnasse had come, threading their way rapidly through the long file of carts which at that hour were making for the vegetable-market. The market-gardeners, crouched amid their lettuces and cabbages and swathed to the eyes in capes under the beating rain, paid no attention to them.

832

The hazards of an escape

This is what had happened at the prison of La Force during that night.

A plan of escape had been concerted between Babet, Brujon, Gueulemer, and Thénardier, although Thénardier was in solitary confinement. Babet had managed his own part of the business during the day, as we know from what Montparnasse had said to Gavroche. Montparnasse was to help from outside.

Brujon, having spent a month in a punishment-cell, had had time, first, to plait a rope, and secondly to evolve the plan. At one time a solitary-confinement cell consisted of stone walls, a stone ceiling, a tiled floor, a camp bed, a small, barred window, and a door reinforced with iron bands, the whole being known as a *cachot*. But the *cachot* was considered too severe. The cell now consists of an iron door, a barred window, a camp bed, a tiled floor, stone walls, and a stone ceiling, and is called a 'punishment-cell'. A faint light penetrates at mid-day. The drawback to these cells which, as we see, are not *cachots*, is that they leave men to their thoughts when they should be made to work.

Brujon had taken thought and got out of the punishment-cell with his rope. Since he was reputed to be highly dangerous he was transferred from the Cour Charlemagne to the New Building. Here he found, first Gueulemer and second a nail. The first meant crime and the second meant liberty.

Brujon, at whom we must now take a closer look, was, beneath his carefully calculated appearance of fragility and languor, a well-mannered, intelligent, thieving rogue with a disarming gaze and an abominable grin. The gaze was rehearsed, but the grin was natural. He had first concentrated on roof-tops, and had made strides in the business of robbing roofs and gutters of their lead by the process known as *gras-double*, or tripe-stripping.

What made that moment particularly favourable for a break-out was the fact that a part of the prison roof was being re-timbered and re-tiled. The Cour Saint-Bernard was no longer entirely cut off from the Cour Charlemagne and the Cour Saint-Louis. There were scaffolding and ladders; in other words, bridges and stairways for the use of the escaper.

The so-called New Building, which was in a state of lamentable decrepitude, was the prison's weakest point. Its walls had so crumbled under the effects of saltpetre that the dormitories had had to be lined with wooden panelling, because otherwise rubble was liable to fall on the sleepers in their beds. Despite its inadequacy, this New Building was where the most dangerous prisoners were housed, the 'hard cases', to use the prison term. The building contained four superimposed dormitories, with an attic above them known as the Bel-Air. A large chimney, probably a survival from the former kitchen of the Dukes of La Force, rose up from the ground floor, passing through the four dormitories like a flattened central column and emerging through the roof.

Gueulemer and Brujon were in the same dormitory, having been put as a precaution on the lowest floor. The heads of their beds, as it happened, were both against this chimney. Thénardier was exactly above them in the Bel-Air attic.

The stroller who pauses in the Rue Culture-Sainte-Catherine, at the gateway of the bath-house beyond the fire-station, will see a courtyard filled with flowers and bushes in tubs, at the far end of which is a small rotunda with two wings, painted white with green blinds – the pastoral dream of Jean-Jacques Rousseau. Not more than ten years ago it had at its back a tall, black wall, which was the outer wall of the prison of La Force. High though it was, this wall was over-topped by an even blacker roof rising behind it, that of the New Building, in which four barred dormer windows were to be seen. They were the windows of the Bel-Air attic dormitory, and the chimney rising above the roof was the one which passed through the lower dormitories.

The Bel-Air attic was a kind of sloping-roofed gallery partitioned by triple-grilles and metal-lined doors studded with huge nailheads. Entering it at the northern end one had the four windows on one's left, and on one's right, facing the windows, four fairly large square cages separated by narrow passage-ways and built of brickwork up to shoulder level and iron grilles reaching to the ceiling.

Thénardier had been confined in one of these cages since the night of 3 February. No one ever discovered how, and with what assistance, he managed to obtain and hide a bottle of the wine invented, it is said, by the prisoner Desrues, which contains a narcotic and was made famous by the gang known as the Endormeurs, the 'dopers'. There are in many prisons treacherous employees, thieves as well as gaolers, who sell a fraudulent loyalty to their masters and make their pickings on the side.

And so it happened that on the night when the boy Gavroche gave shelter to two forlorn children, Brujon and Gueulemer, knowing that Babet, who had escaped that morning, was waiting for them with Montparnasse in the street outside, rose softly from their beds and began to burrow into the chimney, using the nail that Brujon had acquired. The debris fell on Brujon's bed and made no sound. The noises of hail and thunder shook the doors on their hinges, filling the prison with an alarming but convenient din. Those of their fellow-inmates who were awakened pretended to be still asleep and did not interfere. Brujon was skilful and Gueulemer was powerful. Without any sound reaching the warder in the cell with a window looking into the dormitory, the chimney-flue was pierced, the chimney climbed, the grille at the top forced and the two redoubtable ruffians were out on the roof. The wind and rain were at their height and the roof was slippery. 'A fine night for a getaway,' said Brujon.

A gap six feet wide and eighty feet deep separated them from the outer wall, and below them they could discern the faint gleam of a guard's musket. They attached one end of the rope which Brujon had plaited to the bars of the metal grille, which they had twisted back, and flung the other end over the outer wall. Then, jumping the gap on to the top of the wall, they slid down the rope to the roof of a small building adjoining the bath-house, pulled the rope down after them, jumped over into the bath-house courtyard, crossed it and pushed open the porter's window, beside which hung the *cordon*. They pulled the *cordon*, opened the gate, and walked out into the street.

It was less than three-quarters of an hour since they had stood on their beds in the darkness, nail in hand and their plans all laid. Within a minute or so they had joined Babet and Montparnasse, who were lurking near by.

They had broken their rope in retrieving it, so that a part remained still attached to the grille at the top of the chimney; otherwise no harm was done except that they had very little skin left on their hands.

Thénardier had been warned of what was to happen, although it is not known how, and had stayed awake. At about one o'clock in the morning, the night being very dark, he had seen, through the window opposite his cage, two figures moving along the roof in the wind and rain. One of them stopped for an instant to look in at the window, and Thénardier recognized Brujon. It was all he needed to know.

Being registered as a dangerous criminal sentenced for attempted armed robbery, Thénardier was kept under close surveillance. A warder with a loaded musket, who was relieved every two hours, did sentry-duty outside his cage. The attic was lighted by a wall-lantern. The prisoner had fifty-pound irons on his legs. At four o'clock every afternoon a prison guard accompanied by two police dogs – this was still customary in those days – entered the cage, deposited a loaf of black bread on the floor by the bed, together with a jug of water and a bowl of thin broth with a few beans swimming in it, examined the prisoner's fetters and tapped on the bars of the cage. He and his dogs paid two further visits during the night.

Thénardier had obtained permission to keep a small iron spike which he used to skewer his bread to a crack in the wall – 'to keep it out of reach of the rats,' he said. Since he was under constant supervision this was not thought dangerous; but it was later recalled that one of the warders had remarked, 'It would be better if he had a wooden spike.'

At two in the morning the warder, a regular-army veteran, was relieved by a younger man, a conscript. Shortly afterwards the guard with the dogs paid his visit and noted nothing out of the way except the extreme youth and 'doltish air' of the new man. But two hours after this, at four o'clock, when it was the new man's turn to be relieved he was found prostrate and sleeping like a log outside Thénardier's cage. Thénardier was gone, and his broken leg-irons lay on the floor. There was a hole in the ceiling of the cage and another hole above it, in the roof of the building. A plank had been wrenched off the bed and presumably taken away, since it was not to be found. But a half-empty bottle was found containing the remains of the drugged wine that had put the soldier to sleep. His bayonet had disappeared.

At the time when the discovery was made Thénardier was thought to be well out of reach; but the truth is that although he was no longer in the New Building he was still in considerable danger. He had not yet made good his escape. After climbing out on to the roof he had found the length of rope attached to the grille protecting the chimney, but this broken remnant was far too short for him to be able to negotiate the outside wall as Brujon and Gueulemer had done.

Turning out of the Rue des Ballets into the Rue du Roi-de-Sicile, one comes almost immediately to a sort of squalid recess. A house occupied it in the last century of which only the back wall is still standing, a dingy pile of masonry rising to a height of three storeys, with buildings on either side. It contains two square windows, one of which is partly blocked by a worm-eaten beam of the wood that props up the wall. At one time one could see through these windows a further expanse of forbidding masonry, the outer wall of the prison.

The empty space left by the demolished house is half-filled by a fence of rotting planks reinforced by stone posts, and within this enclosure there is a small lean-to shed built against the remaining wall. There is a gate in the fence which, until a few years ago, was fastened only with a latch.

Thénardier reached the top of this wall at about three o'clock in the morning.

How had he got there? This is something that no one has ever been able to explain or understand. The lightning must have both hindered and helped him. Had he made use of the roof-menders' scaffolding and ladders to convey himself from roof-top to roof-top over the ill-assorted cluster of buildings, from the Cour Charlemagne to the Cour Saint-Louis, thence to the outer wall of the prison, and so, eventually, to the ruined wall? But there were so many gaps in this route as to make it seem impossible. Had he made the plank from his bed serve as a bridge from the attic to the outer wall, and then crawled on his stomach along that wall until he came to the ruin? But the top of the outer wall of the prison presented a very jagged outline, with steep ups and downs; it went down at the firemen's quarters and rose sharply at the bath-house; it was broken by intersections and was lower at the Hotel Lamoignon than over the Rue Pavée; there were sudden drops and right-angles. Taking all this into account, the exact manner of Thénardier's escape becomes inexplicable. Escape by either of these two routes was virtually impossible. Had Thénardier, actuated by that overwhelming passion for liberty that turns precipices into ditches, iron bars into wooden slats, an office clerk into an athlete, stupidity into instinct, instinct into intelligence and intelligence into genius, devised some quite other method? This has never been known.

There is in a prison escape an element of the miraculous that is not always realized. The man on the run, let us repeat, is a man inspired. There is starlight and lightning in the mysterious glow of flight, and the straining for liberty is no less remarkable than the soaring of the spirit to the sublime. To ask, of the escaped prisoner, how did he manage to achieve the impossible, is to ask, as we do of Corneille, 'When did he know *that he was dying*?'

However it may be, Thénardier, dripping with sweat and soaked with rain, clothes in shreds, hands skinned and knees and elbows bleeding reached the top of the ruined wall and lay stretched at full length along it, his strength exhausted. There was a drop of three storeys to the ground, and the rope he had with him was too short.

He lay there pale and helpless, all hope abandoned, still sheltered by the darkness but knowing that it would soon be light, expecting at any moment to hear the clock of the Church of Saint-Paul strike four, at which hour they would come to relieve the guard outside his cage and find him in a drugged slumber. He lay there contemplating in a kind of stupor the wet, dark surface gleaming faintly in the street lights at a terrible depth below him, the solid earth of liberty that could be his death. He was wondering if his three confederates had made good their escape, if they were awaiting him, if they would come to his aid. Excepting a police-patrol no one had gone along the street while he was there. Nearly all the market-gardeners from Montreuil, Charonne, Vincennes, and Bercy went to the market by way of the Rue Saint-Antoine.

Four o'clock struck, and he started. Very shortly afterwards the confused hubbub which accompanies the discovery of an escape broke out in the prison, the opening and slamming of doors, the screech of hinges, the thud of running feet, the voices hoarsely shouting; until finally the clatter of musket-butts on the paving of the courtyard sounded almost below him. Lights shone behind the barred windows of the dormitory and a torch moved along the attic roof of the New Building. The firemen from the near-by station had been summoned to assist, and their helmets, gleaming in torchlight under the rain, could be seen on the rooftops. At the same time he saw the first pallid glow of sunrise in the sky beyond the Bastille.

He was lying, incapable of movement, along a wall some ten inches wide, with a sheer drop on either side of him, dizzy at the possibility of falling and in horror at the certainty of capture, his thoughts swinging between these two alternatives like the pendulum of a clock – 'I'm dead if I fall and caught if I don't.' But suddenly he perceived amid the darkness of the street the figure of a man creep cautiously past the housefronts from the Rue Pavée and come to a stop in the recess, above which Thénardier was as it were suspended. He was joined by a second man moving with the same caution, then by a third and a fourth. When they were all together one of them opened the gate in the fence and they moved into the enclosure where the shed was – that is to say, almost directly below Thénardier. They had evidently chosen the recess as a place where they might confer without being seen by anyone in the street or by the sentry at the prison-gate, which was only a few yards away. In any case, the sentry was being kept in his box by the rain. Thénardier, unable to distinguish their faces, listened to what they said with the desperate attentiveness of a man at his last gasp. And suddenly he had a ray of hope. The men were talking *argot*, that is to say, thieves' slang.

One of them said, speaking in a low voice but quite clearly:

'*Décarrons. Qu'est-ce que nous maquillons icigo?* – We've got to clear out. What's the good of hanging about here?'

Another said:

'*Il lansquine à éteindre le riffe du rabouin. Et puis les coqueurs vont passer; il y a là un grivier qui porte gaffe, nous allons nous faire emballer icicaille.* – It's raining fit to dowse the fires of hell. Besides, the law will be along. There's a soldier on guard back there. We'll be copped if we stay here.'*

The two words, *icigo* and *icicaille*, both meaning *ici* (here), and of which the first belongs to barrier-slang and the second to the slang of the Temple, were highly enlightening to Thénardier. The first pointed to Brujon, who was a barrier-prowler, and the second to Babet, who among his many callings had once been a huckster in the Temple market. It was only in the Temple that the ancient slang of the Grand Siècle was still spoken, and Babet was the only one who spoke it perfectly. Without that *icicaille* Thénardier would not have recognized him, for he had entirely disguised his voice.

Another of the men said:

---

*Hugo himself added footnotes with translations in conventional French of these passages of *argot*, which are here reproduced as a sample of the cant. In the subsequent dialogue only his translations have been rendered into English. Trs.

'There's no hurry, we might as well wait a little. We can't be sure he won't need us.'

From this, which was in plain French, Thénardier recognized Montparnasse, who made it a point of pride to understand all the slangs and speak none of them.

The fourth man said nothing, but his huge shoulders were enough. Thénardier had no doubt that it was Gueulemer.

Brujon answered almost excitedly, but still keeping his voice low.

'What are you getting at? The innkeeper hasn't made it because he doesn't know how. He's an amateur. To weave a sound rope out of a blanket, bore holes in a door, cook up false papers, make skeleton keys, cut through leg-irons, hide everything and get away using the rope, it takes skill to do all that. You've got to know your business. The old fellow wasn't up to it.'

Babet added, speaking still in the recondite, classical *argot* used by Poulailler and Cartouche, which, compared with the coarse, lurid slang of Brujon, is like the language of Racine compared with that of André Chénier:

'He's probably been caught. He's nothing but a novice. He may have talked and given himself away. You can hear that shindy in the prison, can't you, Montparnasse? You can see the lights. He's been caught for certain. He'll be inside for another twenty years. I'm no coward, no one's ever said that of me; but there's nothing to be done and no sense in hanging about here until we're all in the bag. It's no use worrying, come along and we'll split a bottle or two of wine.'

'You can't leave a friend in the lurch,' muttered Montparnasse.

'I tell you he's caught,' repeated Brujon. 'He's sunk and there's nothing we can do. Let's clear out. I'm expecting to feel a hand on my shoulder any minute.'

Montparnasse continued to protest, but only weakly; the fact is that the four men, true to the code of loyalty among thieves, had spent the night hanging round the prison, regardless of the risk to themselves, hoping to see the form of Thénardier appear on top of some part of the wall. But it had been too much for them. The streets emptied by the pouring rain, themselves numbed with cold in their drenched clothes, the disturbing sounds issuing from within the prison, the time wasted, the police patrols, the waning of hope and growth of anxiety – all this prompted them to retreat. Even Montparnasse, who may have been especially beholden to Thénardier, being perhaps his unofficial son-in-law, was disposed to give way. In another moment they would have gone, and Thénardier on his wall groaned like the men of the *Medusa* on their raft when the ship they had sighted vanished over the horizon.

He dared not call out, since by doing so he might give himself away, but one resource was left to him. He fished out of his pocket the short length of rope he had detached from the grille over the chimney, and tossed it into the enclosure. It fell at the men's feet.

'That's my rope,' said Brujon.

'The innkeeper's up there,' said Montparnasse.

They looked up and Thénardier thrust his head into view.

'Quick,' said Montparnasse to Brujon. 'Have you got the rest of the rope?'

'Yes.'

'Tie the two bits together and chuck one end up to him. He'll have to fix it to the wall. There'll be enough for him to slide down.'

Thénardier ventured to speak.

'I'm numb with cold.'

'We'll soon get you warm.'

'I can't move.'

'You've only got to slide down. We'll catch you.'

'My hands are frozen.'

'Just tie the rope to the wall.'

'I couldn't do it.'

'One of us will have to go up,' said Montparnasse.

'Three storeys!' said Brujon.

An old plaster flue, part of a stove which at some time had burned in the shed, ran up the wall very near where Thénardier was lying. It has broken off since then, being very much the worse for wear, but traces of it are still to be seen. It was very thin.

'Someone could climb up by that,' said Montparnasse.

'That bit of piping?' said Babet. 'A grown man? You're crazy. Only a kid could do it.'

'That's right,' said Brujon. 'We need a boy. But where are we to find one?'

'I know where. I'll fetch him,' said Montparnasse.

Softly opening the gate and peering up and down the street to make sure that there was no one about, he closed it carefully behind him and set off at a run in the direction of the Bastille.

Some seven or eight minutes elapsed during which Babet, Brujon, and Gueulemer did not speak. Then the gate was opened again and Montparnasse reappeared, panting, with Gavroche at his side. The street was still deserted.

Gavroche stood calmly surveying the men with rainwater dripping from his hair.

'Well, lad,' said Gueulemer, 'can you do a man's job?'

Gavroche shrugged his shoulders and replied in the broadest *argot*:

'Kids like me are grown up and coves like you are kids.'

'He's got the gab all right!' said Brujon.

'So what do you want me to do?' asked Gavroche.

'Climb up that chimney-pipe,' said Montparnasse.

'Taking this rope with you,' said Babet.

'And tie it near the top of the wall,' said Brujon. 'To the crossbar of the window.'

'And then?' said Gavroche.

'That's all,' said Gueulemer.

Gavroche considered the rope, the flue, the wall, and the window and clicked his tongue in an expression of scorn at the simplicity of the task.

'There's a man up there,' said Montparnasse. 'You'll be saving him.'

'Will you do it?' asked Brujon.

'Don't be daft,' said Gavroche, as though the question were insulting, and he slipped off his shoes.

Gueulemer picked him up and set him on the roof of the shed, the planks of which sagged under his weight, then passed him the rope, which Brujon had re-tied during Montparnasse's absence. Gavroche went up to the flue, which ran through a hole in the lean-to roof; but as he was about to start his climb, Thénardier, seeing the approach of rescue and safety, peered down from the wall. The pallid light of dawn fell upon his sweat-dewed face, the white cheekbones, flat, barbarous nose and tangled grey beard, and Gavroche recognized him.

'Blow me,' he exclaimed, 'if it isn't my father! Well, no matter.'

Taking the rope between his teeth, he began to climb. He reached the top of the ruined wall and, sitting astride it, tied the rope securely to the upper crossbar of the window. Within a minute Thénardier was down in the street.

The moment his feet touched the ground, feeling himself out of danger, he lost all sense of fatigue, chill, and terror; the sufferings of the past hours vanished from his recollection like a puff of smoke, and that strange, ferocious intelligence was instantly alert and free, ready for further action. These are the first words he spoke:

'Well, so now who are we going to eat?'

No need to dwell upon the significance of that horridly lucid word, which meant to murder, to beat to death, to plunder – 'eat' in the literal sense of 'devour'.

'Let's get away fast,' said Brujon. 'Just a word and then we separate. There was a job that looked hopeful in the Rue Plumet, two women living alone in an isolated house in an empty street, with a rusty iron gate to the garden.'

'Well, what's wrong with it?' asked Thénardier.

'Your wench, Éponine, had a look round and she gave Magnon the "biscuit". There's nothing to be done there.'

'She's no fool,' said Thénardier. 'All the same, we ought to make sure.'

'Yes,' said Brujon. 'We might look it over.'

The men had paid no further heed to Gavroche, who during this conversation had seated himself on one of the stones supporting the fence. He waited a little longer, perhaps expecting his father to say something to him, then he pulled on his shoes and said:

'Is that all? You don't want me any more? Well, I've done the job, so I'll be going. I've got to see to those kids of mine.'

He then left them.

The five men left separately. When Gavroche had disappeared round the corner of the Rue des Ballets, Babet drew Thénardier aside and said:

'Did you look at that youngster?'

'What youngster?'

'The one who climbed the wall and brought you the rope.'

'Can't say I did much.'

'Well, I'm not sure, but I have an idea he's your son.'

'What!' said Thénardier. 'You don't say!'

And he departed.

[Book Seven: Argot, will be found as Appendix B at page 1243

BOOK EIGHT

ENCHANTMENT AND DESPAIR

I

Broad daylight

THE READER will have gathered that Éponine, having recognized the girl behind the wrought-iron gate in the Rue Plumet, whither she had been sent by Magnon, had begun by putting the ruffians off that particular house, and then had led Marius to it; and that Marius, after spending several days of ecstatic contemplation outside the gate, gripped by the force that draws iron to a magnet and the lover to the stones of his beloved's dwelling, had finally entered Cosette's garden much as Romeo had entered that of Juliet. It had indeed been less troublesome to him than to Romeo. Romeo had had to climb a wall, whereas Marius had needed only to force one of the rusty bars of the gate, which were already as loose in their sockets as an old man's teeth. He was slender and had had no diffiuclty in wriggling through; nor, since there was never anyone in the street and he went only after dark, did he run any risk of being seen.

Following that blessed and hallowed hour when a kiss had sealed the lovers' vows, he went there every evening. If at this moment in her life Cosette had had to do with an unscrupulous libertine, she would have been lost; for there are warm hearts whose instinct is to give, and she was one of those. Among the most great-hearted qualities of women is that of yielding. Love, when it holds absolute sway, afflicts modesty with a kind of blindness. The risks they run, those generous spirits! Often they give their hearts where we take only their bodies. That heart remains their own, for them to contemplate in shivering darkness. For with love there is no middle course: it destroys, or else it saves. All human destiny is contained in that dilemma, the choice between destruction and salvation, which is nowhere more implacably posed than in love. Love is life, or it is death. It is the cradle, but also the coffin. One and the same impulse moves the human heart to say yes or no. Of all things God has created it is the human heart that sheds the brightest light, and, alas, the blackest despair.

God decreed that the love which came to Cosette was a love that saves. During that month of May in the year 1832, in that wild garden with its dense tangle of undergrowth that grew daily more impenetrable and richly scented, two beings composed wholly of chastity and innocence, bathed in all the felicities under Heaven, nearer to the angels than to men, pure, truthful, intoxicated and enraptured, shone for each other in the gloom. To Cosette it seemed that Marius wore a crown, and to Marius Cosette bore a halo. They touched and gazed, held hands and clung together; but there was a gulf that they did not seek to cross, not because they feared it but because they ignored it. To Marius the purity of Cosette was a barrier, and to Cosette his steadfast self-restraint was a safeguard. The first kiss they had exchanged was also the last. Since then Marius had gone no further than to touch her hand with his lips, or her shawl, or a lock of her hair. To him she was an essence, rather than a woman. He breathed her in. She denied him nothing and he demanded nothing. She was happy and he was content. They existed in that state of ravishment which may be termed the enchantment of one soul by another, the ineffable first encounter of two virgin spirits in an idyllic world, two swans meeting on the Jungfrau.

In that first stage of their love, the stage when physical desire is wholly subdued beneath the omnipotence of spiritual ecstasy, Marius would have been more capable of going with a street-girl than of lifting the hem of Cosette's skirt, even to above her ankle. When on one occasion she bent down to pick something up and her corsage gaped to disclose the top of her bosom, he turned his head away.

What did take place, then, between those two? Nothing. They adored each other. The garden, when they met there after dark, seemed to them a living and consecrated place. Its blossoms opened to enrich them with their scent, and they poured out their hearts to the blossoms. A vigorous, carnal world of flowing sap surrounded those two innocents, and the words of love they spoke set up a quiver in the trees.

As to the words they spoke, they were breaths and nothing more, but breaths that set all Nature stirring. They were a magic which would have little meaning were they to be set down on paper, those murmurs destined to be borne away like puffs of smoke under the leaves. If we rob the words of lovers of the melody from the heart that accompanies them like a lyre, what remains is but the shadow. Is that really all? – mere childishness, things said and said again, triteness, foolishness and reasonless laughter? Yes that is all, but there is nothing on earth more exquisite or more profound. Those are the only things that are really worth saying and worth hearing, and the man who has never heard or uttered them is a bad man and a fool.

'You know . . .' said Cosette. (They addressed each other instinctively as '*tu*', neither knowing how this had come to pass.) 'You know, my real name is Euphrasia.'

'Euphrasia? But you're called Cosette.'

'Oh, that's just a silly name they gave me when I was a child. I'm really Euphrasia. Do you like Euphrasia?'

'Yes . . . But I don't think Cosette is silly.'

'Do you like it better than Euphrasia?'

'Well – yes.'

'Then so do I. You're quite right. It's a nice name. So you must always call me Cosette.'

And the smile accompanying the words made of that scrap of conversation an idyll worthy of a woodland in Heaven.

Another time, after looking hard at him she exclaimed:

'Allow me to tell you, Monsieur, that you're good-looking, you're very handsome, and you're clever, not a bit stupid, much more learned than I am. But I can match you in one thing – I love you!'

Marius in his rapture might have been hearing the melody of the spheres.

Then again, when he happened to cough, she gave him a little reproving pat and said: 'You're not to cough. No one is allowed to cough in my house without permission. It's naughty of you to cough and worry me. I want you to be well always, because if you aren't I shall be very unhappy.'

He said to her once: 'Do you know, at one time I thought your name was Ursula?' This thought kept them amused for the rest of the evening.

And during another conversation he suddenly exclaimed:

'Well, there was one time in the Luxembourg when I would have liked to break an army veteran's neck.'

But he did not go on with that story. He could not have done so without mentioning her garter, and this was out of the question. There was a whole world, that of the flesh, from which their innocent love recoiled with a kind of religious awe.

It was thus, and with nothing added, that Marius envisaged his life with Cosette – his coming every evening to the Rue Plumet, wriggling through that convenient gate, sitting beside her on the bench, the fold of his trouser mingling with the spread of her skirts while they watched the growing glitter of starlight through the trees, softly stroking her thumb-nail, addressing her as '*tu*', breathing with her the scent of the same flowers – all this was to continue indefinitely, to last for ever. Meanwhile the clouds drifted above their heads. When the wind blows it blows away more human dreams than clouds in the sky.

But that is not to say that this almost fiercely chaste love was wholly lacking in gallantry. No. To 'pay compliments' to the loved person is the first step on the way to caresses, tentative audacity trying out its wings. A compliment is something like a kiss through a veil. Physical fulfilment makes its presence known, while still remaining hidden. The heart draws back from this fulfilment in order to love the more. Marius's wooing, pervaded as it was with fantasy, was, so to speak, ethereal. The birds when they fly aloft in company with the angels must understand words such as he spoke. Yet there was life in them, manliness, all that was positive in Marius. They were words spoken in the grotto, the foreshadowing of those to be spoken in the alcove, lyrical effusions of mingled prose and poetry, soft flatteries, all love's most delicate refinements arranged in a scented and subtle bouquet, the ineffable murmur of heart to heart.

'How lovely you are!' sighed Marius. 'I scarcely dare look at you, and so I have to contemplate you at a distance. You are grace itself and my senses reel even at the sight of your slipper beneath the hem of your skirt. And the light that dawns when I catch a glimpse of what you are thinking! Such good sense. There are moments when you seem to me a figure in a dream. Go on talking and let me listen. Oh, Cosette, how strange and wonderful it is! I think I am a little mad. I so worship you. I study your feet with a magnifying glass and your soul with a telescope.'

To which she replied:

'I love you more with every minute that passes.'

Random conversations in which question and answer must take their chance, always returning to the subject of love, like those weighted dolls which always come upright.

Cosette's whole being expressed artlessness and ingenuousness, a white transparency, candour and light. One might say of her that she was light itself. She conveyed to the beholder a sense of April and daybreak; there was dew in her eyes. She was the condensation of dawn light in a woman's form.

It was natural that Marius should admire as well as adore her; but the truth is that the little schoolgirl, so newly shaped by the convent, talked with great sagacity and said many things that were both true and perceptive. Her very babblings had meaning. She saw clearly and was not easily deceived, being guided by the soft, infallible instinct of the feminine heart. Only women have this gift for saying things that are at once tender and profound. Tenderness and depth: all womanhood resides in these, and all Heaven.

In this state of utter felicity tears rose constantly to their eyes. A crushed insect, a feather fallen from a nest, a broken sprig of hawthorn, these things moved them to pity, and their rapture, always near to melancholy, found relief in tears. The sovereign manifestation of love is a sense of compassion that at times is well-nigh intolerable.

And with all this – for these contradictions form the lightning-play of love – they laughed constantly and unrestrainedly, so familiarly that they might have been a pair of boys at play. Yet even in hearts intoxicated with chastity Nature is always present, always in pursuit of her sublime, remorseless aims; and, however great the purity of souls, even in the most innocent of relationships the wonderful and mysterious difference is still to be felt which separates a pair of lovers from a pair of friends.

They adored each other; but still the permanent and the immutable subsist. We may love and laugh, pout, clasp hands, smile and exchange endearments, but that does not affect eternity. Two lovers hide in the dusk of evening, amid flowers and the twittering of birds, and enchant each other with their hearts shining in their eyes; but the stars in their courses still circle through infinite space.

II

The bemusement of perfect happiness

Thus, bathed in happiness, they lived untroubled by the world. They paid no heed to the epidemic of cholera which during that month ravaged Paris. They had told each other as much about themselves as they could, but it did not go very far beyond their names. Marius had told Cosette that he was an orphan, that his name was Marius Pontmercy, that he was a lawyer and that he got his living by working for publishers; that his father had been a colonel and a hero, and that he, Marius, had quarrelled with his grandfather, who was rich. He had also mentioned in passing that he was a baron, but this had made no impression on Cosette. Marius a baron? She had not understood, not knowing what the word meant. Marius was Marius. And on her side she had told him that she had been brought up in the Petit-Picpus convent, that her mother was dead, like his own, that her father was Monsieur Fauchelevent, that he was a good man who gave generously to the poor although he was poor himself, and that he denied himself everything while denying her nothing.

Strangely, to Marius in his present state of entrancement, all past events, even the most recent, seemed so misty and remote that he was quite satisfied with what Cosette told him. It did not occur to him even to mention the drama in the tenement, the Thénardiers, the burnt arm and the strange behaviour and remarkable disappearance of her father. All this had for the time being completely escaped his mind. He forgot in the evening what he had done in the morning, whether he had breakfasted, whether he had spoken to anyone. The trilling of birds deafened his ears to all other sounds; he was only really alive when he was with Cosette. And so, being in Heaven, it was easy for him to lose sight of earth. Both of them languorously bore the impalpable burden of unfleshly delights. It is thus that the sleep-walkers who are called lovers live.

Alas, who has not known that enchanted state? Why must the moment come when we emerge from that bliss, and why must life go on afterwards?

Loving is almost a substitute for thinking. Love is a burning forgetfulness of all other things. How shall we ask passion to be logical? Absolute logic is no more to be found in the human heart than you may find a perfect geometrical figure in the structure of the heavens. Nothing else existed for Cosette and Marius except Marius and Cosette. The world around them had vanished in a cloud. They lived in a golden moment, seeing nothing ahead of them and nothing behind. Marius was scarcely conscious of the fact that Cosette had a father; his wits were drugged with happiness. So what did they talk about, those lovers? They talked about flowers and swallows, sunset and moonrise, everything that to them was important; about everything and about nothing. The everything of lovers is a nothing. But as for her father, real life, the gang of ruffians, and the adventure in the attic – why bother to talk about all that? Was it even certain that that nightmare had really happened? They were together and they adored each other and that was all that concerned them. Other things did not exist. It is probable that the vanishing of Hell at our backs is inherent in the coming of Paradise. Have we really seen devils? – are there such things? – have we trembled and suffered? We no longer remember. They are lost in a rosy haze.

The two of them lived in that exalted state, in all the make-believe that is a part of nature, neither at the nadir nor at the zenith; somewhere between mankind and the angels; above the mire but below the upper air – in the clouds; scarcely flesh and blood, but spirit and ecstasy from head to foot; too exalted to walk on earth but still too human to disappear into the blue, suspended in life like molecules in solution that await precipitation; seemingly beyond the reach of fate; escaped from the rut of yesterday, today, tomorrow; marvelling, breathless and swaying, at moments light enough to fly off into infinite space, almost ready to vanish into eternity.

They drowsed wide-eyed in that cradled state, in the splendid lethargy of the real overwhelmed by the ideal. Such was Cosette's beauty that at moments Marius closed his eyes; and that is the best way to see the soul, with the eyes closed.

They did not ask where this was taking them; they felt that they had arrived. It is one of the strange demands of mankind that love must take them somewhere.

III

The first shadows

Jean Valjean suspected nothing.

Cosette, less given to dreaming than Marius, was gay, and that was enough to make him happy. The thoughts in Cosette's mind, her tender preoccupations, the picture of Marius that dwelt in her heart, all this in no way diminished the purity of her chaste and smiling countenance. She was at the age when a virgin girl bears her love like an angel carrying a lily. So Valjean was easy in his mind. And then when two lovers are in perfect harmony everything is easy to them; any third party who might disturb their love is kept in ignorance by those small concealments which are practised by all lovers. Thus, Cosette never opposed any wish of Valjean's. Did he want to go out? Yes, dear father. He would rather stay at home? Very well. He wanted to spend the evening with her? She was delighted. Since he always went to bed at ten, Marius on these occasions never entered the garden until after that hour, and after hearing Cosette open the door on to the terrace. It goes without saying that Marius never showed himself by daytime, and indeed Valjean had forgotten his existence. But it happened one morning that he remarked to Cosette: 'Your back's all white.' The evening before Marius, in a moment of rapture, had pressed her against the wall.

Old Toussaint, who went to bed early and only wanted to sleep once her work was done, was as ignorant as Valjean of what was going on.

Marius never set foot in the house. He and Cosette were accustomed to hide in a recess near the steps, where they could not be seen or heard from the street, and being seated were often content merely to clasp hands in silence while they gazed up at the branches of the trees. A thunderbolt might have fallen a few yards away without their noticing, so absorbed was each in the other. A state of limpid purity. Hours that were all white and nearly all the same. Love-affairs such as this are like a collection of lily-petals and doves' feathers.

The whole stretch of garden lay between them and the street. Every time Marius entered or left he carefully re-arranged the bars of the gate, so that the fact that they had been moved would not be noticed.

He left as a rule at midnight and walked back to Courfeyrac's lodging. Courfeyrac said to Bahorel:

'Would you believe it! Marius has taken to coming home at one in the morning!'

'Well, what of it?' said Bahorel. 'Still waters run deep.'

And sometimes Courfeyrac would fold his arms and say sternly to Marius:

'You're going off the rails, young fellow-me-lad.'

Courfeyrac, being of a practical turn of mind, did not take kindly to this glow of a secret paradise that surrounded Marius. He was not accustomed to undisclosed raptures. They bored him, and from time to time he would try to bring Marius down to earth. He said to him on one occasion:

'My dear fellow, you seem to me these days to be living on the moon, in the kingdom of dreams of which the capital is the City of Soap-Bubble. Be a good chap and tell me her name.'

But nothing would make Marius talk. Not even torture could have extracted from him the sacred syllables of the name, Cosette. True love is as radiant as the dawn and as silent as the tomb. But Courfeyrac perceived this change in Marius, seeing that his very secretiveness was radiant.

Throughout that mild month of May, Marius and Cosette discovered these tremendous sources of happiness: The happiness of quarrelling simply for the fun of making up; of discussing at length and in exhaustive detail persons in whom they took no interest whatever, which is one more proof that in the ravishing opera that is called love the libretto is of almost no importance. The happiness, for Marius, of listening to Cosette talk about frills and furbelows, and, for Cosette, of listening to Marius talk about politics. The happiness for both of them, while they sat with knee touching knee, of hearing the distant sound of traffic on the Rue de Babylone; looking upwards to speculate on the same star in the sky, or downwards to study the same glow-worm in the grass; of being silent together, which is even more delightful than to talk . . . And so on.

But meanwhile complications were looming.

One evening when Marius was on his way along the Boulevard des Invalides to keep their nightly rendezvous, walking as usual with his eyes on the ground, just as he was about to turn into the Rue Plumet a voice spoke to him.

'Good evening, Monsieur Marius.'

He looked up and saw Éponine.

The encounter gave him a shock. He had not given the girl a thought since the day she had led him to the Rue Plumet; he had not seen her again, and the memory of her had completely slipped his mind. He had every reason to be grateful to her; he owed his present happiness to her, and yet it embarrassed him to meet her.

It is a mistake to suppose that the state of being in love, be it never so happy and innocent, makes a man perfect. As we have seen, it simply makes him forgetful. If he forgets to be evil, he also forgets to be good. The sense of gratitude and obligation, the recollection of everyday essentials, all this tends to disappear. At any other time Marius would have treated Éponine quite differently; but absorbed as he was in the thought of Cosette he scarcely remembered that her full name was Éponine Thénardier, that she bore a name bequeathed to him by his father and one which, a few months earlier, he had longed to serve. We have to depict Marius as he was. Even the memory of his father had faded a little in the splendour of his love-affair.

He said awkwardly:

'Oh, it's you, Éponine.'

'Why do you speak to me in that cold way? Have I done something wrong?'

'No,' he said.

Certainly he had nothing against her – far from it. It was simply that, with all his warmth bestowed on Cosette he had none for Éponine.

He stayed silent and she burst out, 'But why –?' But then she stopped. It seemed that words had failed the once so brazen and heedless creature. She tried to smile but could not. She said 'Well...' and then again was wordless, standing with lowered eyes.

'Good night, Monsieur Marius,' she said abruptly, and left him.

IV

The watchdog

The next day was 3 June 1832, a date which must be set down because of the grave events now impending, that loomed like thunderclouds over Paris. Marius that evening was going the same way as on the previous evening, his head filled with the same thoughts and his heart charged with the same happiness, when he saw Éponine coming towards him past the trees on the boulevard. Two days in succession was too much. He turned sharply off the boulevard and made for the Rue Plumet by way of the Rue Monsieur.

This caused Éponine to follow him as far as the Rue Plumet, a thing which she had not previously done. Hitherto she had been content to watch him on his way along the boulevard without seeking to attract his notice. The previous evening was the first time she had ventured to speak to him.

So, without his knowing it, she followed him, and saw him slip through the wrought-iron gate into the garden. 'Well! He's going into the house!' she concluded, and, testing the bars of the gate, rapidly discovered his means of entry. 'Not for you, dearie,' she murmured sadly.

As though taking up guard duty, she sat down on the step at the point where the stone gatepost adjoined the neighbouring wall. It was a dark corner which hid her entirely. She stayed there for more than an hour without moving, her mind busy with its thoughts. At about ten o'clock one of the two or three persons accustomed to use the Rue Plumet, an elderly gentleman hastening to get away from that lonely and ill-famed street, heard a low resentful voice say, 'I shouldn't be surprised if he came here every night!' He looked round but could see no one, and, not daring to peer into the dark corner, hurried on in great alarm.

He did well to hurry, for a very short time afterwards six men entered the Rue Plumet. They came in single file, walking at some distance from one another and skirting the edge of the street like a scouting patrol. The first of them stopped at the wrought-iron gate, where he waited for the rest to catch up, until all six of them were gathered together.

They conferred in low voices.

'Sure this is the place?'

'Is there a dog?'

'I don't know. Anyway, I've brought something for it to eat.'

'Have you brought the gummed paper to do the window-pane?'

'Yes.'

'It's an old gate,' said a fifth man, speaking in a voice like that of a ventriloquist.

'So much the better. We can cut through the bars all the easier.'

The sixth man, who had not yet spoken, proceeded to examine the gate as Éponine had done an hour before and was not slow to discover the bar loosened by Marius. But as he was about to wrench it aside a hand emerging from the darkness seized him by the arm. He felt himself thrust backward and a husky voice said in a warning undertone, 'There's a dog!' The lanky figure of a girl rose up before him.

The man recoiled with the shock of the unexpected. He seemed to bristle, and nothing is more dismaying than the sight of a startled wild animal; their very fright is frightening. He drew back, exclaiming:

'Who the devil are you?'

'Your daughter.'

The man was Thénardier.

At this the five other men, Claquesous, Gueulemer, Babet, Montparnasse, and Brujon, gathered round them, moving silently, without haste and without speech, in the slow, deliberate manner that is proper to creatures of the night. They were equipped with a variety of sinister implements. Gueulemer had one of those curved crowbars that are known as jemmies.

'What are you doing here? What do you want? Have you gone crazy?' cried Thénardier, so far as anyone can be said to cry who is keeping his voice low. 'Have you come to try and put me off?'

Éponine laughed and flung her arms round his neck.

'I'm here because I'm here, dearest father. Aren't I even allowed to sit down in the street? You're the one who shouldn't be here. What's the use of coming here when it's no good? I told Magnon it was a biscuit. There's nothing to be got here. But you might at least kiss me. It's a long time since we saw each other. So you're out again?'

Thénardier grunted, trying to release himself from her arms:

'That's enough. You've kissed me. Yes, I'm not inside any more. And now, clear out.'

But Éponine still clung to him.

'But how did you do it? It was very clever of you to get out. You must tell me how you did it. And mother – where is she? You must tell me about mother.'

'She's all right,' said Thénardier. 'I don't know where she is. And now, clear out, can't you?'

'But I don't want to go,' said Éponine, pouting like a spoilt child. 'I haven't seen you for four months, and you want to send me away.' And she tightened her grip on him.

'This is getting silly,' said Babet.

'Hurry it up,' said Gueulemer. 'The cops'll be along.'

Éponine turned to the other men.

'Why, it's Monsieur Brujon! And Monsieur Babet. Good evening, Monsieur Claquesous. Don't you recognize me, Monsieur Gueulemer? And how are you, Montparnasse?'

'That's all right, they all know you,' said Thénardier. 'Well, you've said hallo, and now for God's sake go away and leave us in peace.'

'This is a time for foxes, not for hens,' said Montparnasse.

'You can see we've got a job to do,' said Babet.

Éponine took Montparnasse's hand.

'Careful,' he said. 'You'll cut yourself. My knife's open.'

'Montparnasse, my love,' said Éponine very sweetly, 'you must learn to trust people. Aren't I my father's daughter? Don't you remember, Monsieur Babet and Monsieur Gueulemer, that I was sent to look this place over?'

It is worthy of note that Éponine did not speak a word of *argot*. Since she had known Marius thieves' slang had become impossible for her. She pressed her thin, bony fingers into Gueulemer's rugged palm and went on:

'You know I'm not stupid. People generally believe me. I've been useful to you more than once. Well, I've found things out, and I swear there's nothing for you here. You'd be running risks for no reason.'

'Two women alone,' said Gueulemer.

'No. The people have left.'

'The candles haven't,' said Babet.

And he pointed through the tree-tops to a flickering light in the attic, where Toussaint, staying up later than usual, was hanging out washing to dry.

Éponine made a last effort.

'Anyway, they're very poor, nothing there of any value.'

'Go to the devil!' exclaimed Thénardier. 'When we've ransacked the house from top to bottom we'll know if there's anything worth having.'

He thrust her aside.

'Montparnasse, you're my friend,' said Éponine. 'You're a good lad. Don't go in!'

'Watch out you don't cut yourself,' said Montparnasse.

Thénardier spoke with the authority he knew how to assume.

'Off you go, girl, and leave the men to get on with their business.'

Éponine let go of Montparnasse's hand and said:

'So you're determined to break in!'

'That's right,' said the ventriloquist and chuckled.

'Well, I won't let you,' said Éponine.

She stood with her back to the gate, facing the six men, all armed to the teeth and looking like demons in the dark. She went on in a low, resolute voice:

'Listen to me. I mean this. If you try to get into the garden, if you so much as touch this gate, I'll scream the place down. I'll rouse the whole neighbourhood and have the lot of you pinched.'

'She will, too,' muttered Thénardier to Brujon and the ventriloquist.

Éponine nodded vigorously, adding, 'And my father for a start!'

Thénardier moved towards her.

'You keep your distance,' she said.

He drew back, furiously muttering, 'What's got into her?' And he spat the word at her: 'Bitch!'

She laughed derisively.

'Say what you like, you aren't going in. I'm not a dog's daughter but a wolf's. There are six of you, six men and I'm one woman, but I'm not afraid of you. You aren't going to break into this house, because I don't choose to let you. I'm the watchdog, and if you try it I'll bark. So you might as well be on your way. Go anywhere you like, but don't come here. I won't have it.'

She took a step towards them, and she was awe-inspiring. She laughed again.

'My God, do you think I'm scared? I'm used to starving in summer and freezing in winter. You poor fools, you think you can frighten any woman because you've got soft little sluts of mistresses who cower under the bedclothes when you talk rough. But I'm not scared.' She looked at her father. 'Not even of you.' With fiery eyes she glared round at the other men. 'What do I care if my body's picked up in the street tomorrow morning, beaten to death by my own father – or found in a year's time in the ditches round Saint-Cloud or the Île des Cygnes, along with the garbage and the dead dogs?'

She was interrupted by a fit of coughing, a hollow sound that came from the depths of her narrow, sickly chest.

'I've only got to yell, you know, and people will come running. There are six of you, but I'm the public.'

Thénardier again made a move towards her. 'Keep away!' she cried. He stopped and said mildly: 'All right, I won't come any nearer, but don't talk so loud. My girl, are you trying to prevent me working? After all, we have to earn our living. Have you no more feeling for your father?'

'You sicken me,' said Éponine.

'But we've got to eat.'

'I don't care if you starve.'

Having said which she sat down again on the step, humming the refrain of 'Ma grand'mère' by Béranger, the most renowned songwriter of the day:

857

Combien je regrette
Mon bras si dodu,
Ma jambe bien faite
*Et le temps perdu.**

She sat with her legs crossed, her elbow on her knee and her chin on her hand, swinging her foot with an air of indifference, the glow of a nearby street-lamp illuminating her posture and her profile. Through the rents in her tattered garment her thin shoulder-blades were to be seen. It would be hard to conceive a picture more determined or more surprising.

The six ruffians, disconcerted at being kept at bay by a girl, withdrew into the shadows and conferred together with furious shruggings of their shoulders, while she calmly but resolutely surveyed them.

'There must be some reason,' said Babet. 'D'you think she's fallen in love with the dog? But it would be a shame to pass it up. Two women and an old man who lives in the back-yard. There are good curtains in the windows. If you ask me, the man's a Jew. I reckon it's worth trying.'

'Well, you lot go in,' said Montparnasse. 'I'll stick with the girl, and if she gives so much as a squeak . . .' He flourished the knife which he kept up his sleeve.

Thénardier said nothing, seeming content to leave the decision to the others.

Brujon, who was something of an oracle, and who, as we know, was the original promoter of the enterprise, had not so far spoken. He seemed to be thinking. It was said of him that he would stop at nothing, and he was known to have looted a police post out of sheer bravado. Moreover, he made up poems and songs, and this caused him to be highly esteemed.

Babet now looked at him:

'Why aren't you saying anything?'

Brujon remained silent for some moments, and then, portentously wagging his head, spoke as follows:

'Well, listen. This morning I saw two sparrows fighting, and

*How sadly I miss
My smooth, round arm,
My well-turned leg
And the time that is gone.

this afternoon I bumped into a woman who abused me. Those are bad signs. Let's go.'

So they went away. Montparnasse muttered:

'All the same, if wanted, I was ready to give the girl a clout.'

'I wouldn't have,' said Babet. 'I don't hit women.'

At the bend of the street they paused to exchange a few cryptic words.

'Where are we going to sleep tonight?'

'Under the town.'

'Have you the key to the grating, Thénardier?'

'Maybe.'

Éponine, intently watching, saw them move off the way they had come. She got up and stole along behind them, keeping close to walls and housefronts until they reached the boulevard. Here they separated, and melted like shadows into the night.

v

Things of the night

With the departure of the robber band the Rue Plumet resumed its night-time aspect.

What had happened in that street would not have been unusual in a jungle. Trees and thickets, tangled branches, creepers and undergrowth live their own dark lives, witnessing amid their savage growth sudden manifestations of the life they cannot grasp. What lives on a higher plane than man peers down through the mist at what is lower, and things unknown by daylight encounter each other in the dark. Wild, bristling Nature takes fright at what it feels to be supernatural. The powers of darkness know each other and preserve a mysterious balance between them. Tooth and claw respect the intangible. Animals that drink blood, voracious appetites in search of prey, instinct equipped with jaws and talons, with no source or aim other than the belly, apprehensively sniff the shrouded spectral figure, stalking in filmy, fluttering garments, that seems to them imbued with a terrible dead life. Those brutish creatures, wholly material, instinctively fight shy of the measureless obscurity contained in any unknown being. A dark figure barring the way stops a wild animal in its tracks. What emerges from the burial-ground alarms and dismays that which emerges from the lair; the bloodthirsty fears the sinister; the wolf recoils from the ghoul.

VI

Marius gives Cosette his address

While that human watchdog was guarding the gate, and the six ruffians were giving in to a girl, Marius was with Cosette.

Never had the night been more starry and enchanting, the trees more tremulous, the scent of grass more pungent; never had the birds twittered more sweetly as they fell asleep amid the leaves, or the harmonies of a serene universe been more in tune with the unsung music of love; and never had Marius been more enraptured and entranced. But he had found Cosette unhappy. She had been weeping and her eyes were red. It was the first cloud in their clear sky.

His first words to her were, 'What's the matter?', and seated beside him on their bench by the steps into the villa she told him of her troubles.

'My father said this morning that I must be ready. He has business to attend to and we may have to leave this place.'

Marius trembled. At the end of life death is a departure; but at life's beginning a departure is a death.

In the past six weeks Marius, by gradual degrees, had been taking possession of Cosette: possession in ideal terms but deeply rooted. As we have said, in a first love it is the soul that is first captured, then the body; later the body comes before the soul, which may be forgotten altogether. Cynics may maintain that this is because the soul does not exist, but fortunately that sarcasm is a blasphemy. Marius possessed Cosette only in spirit; but his whole soul bound her jealously to him, and with overwhelming assurance. He possessed her smiles, the light of her blue eyes and the fragrance of her breath, the softness of her skin when he touched her hand, the magical grace of her neck, her every thought. They had vowed never to sleep without each dreaming of the other, and so he possessed all Cosette's dreams. His gaze dwelt endlessly on the small hairs on the nape of her neck, which sometimes he stirred with his breathing, and he told himself that there was not one of them that did not belong to him. He studied and adored the things she wore—ribbons, gloves, cuffs, slippers—seeing them as hallowed objects of which he was the proprietor. He thought of himself as the owner of the tortoiseshell comb in her hair, and went so far—such are the first stirrings of a growing sensuality—as to consider that there was not a tape in her garments, a stitch in her stockings, a fold in her corset, that did not belong to him. Seated beside Cosette he felt himself to be lord of his domain, master of his estate, near his ruler and his slave. It seemed to him, so deeply merged were their souls, that if they had tried to separate them they would not have been able to tell which part belonged to which . . . 'That bit's mine' . . . 'No, it's mine' . . . 'I'm sure you're wrong. That bit is me' . . . 'No. What you think is you is really me' . . . Marius was a part of Cosette, and Cosette was a part of Marius; he felt her life within him. To have Cosette, to possess her, this to him was no different from breathing. It was into this entranced state of absolute, virginal possession, this state of sovereignty, that the words, 'We may be going away,' suddenly fell; and it was the peremptory voice of reality warning him, 'Cosette is not yours!'

Marius suddenly woke up. For six weeks he had been living outside life. Now he was brought harshly back to earth.

He could not speak, but Cosette felt his hand grow cold. She asked, as he had done, 'What's the matter?' and he replied, so low that she could scarcely hear:

'I don't understand what you mean.'

'Father told me this morning that I must get ready,' she said. 'He said that he had to go on a journey and we would go together. He would give me his clothes to pack, and I must see to everything – a big trunk for me and a little one for him. It must all be ready within a week, and perhaps we should be going to England.'

'But that's monstrous!' cried Marius.

It is unquestionable that, to Marius at that moment, no act of despotic tyranny in the whole course of history, from Tiberius to Henry VIII, could rank with this in infamy – that Monsieur Fauchelevent should take his daughter to England because he had business there! He asked in a stifled voice:

'And when, precisely, will you be leaving?'

'He didn't say.'

'And when will you be coming back?'

'He didn't tell me that, either.'

Marius rose to his feet and said coldly:

'Cosette, are you going?'

She looked distractedly up at him.

'But –'

'Are you going to England?'

'Why are you being so cruel to me?'

'I'm simply asking if you're going.'

'But what else can I do?' she cried, wringing her hands.

'So you are going?'

'But if my father goes . . .'

Cosette reached for Marius's hand. 'Very well,' he said. 'Then I shall go away.'

Cosette felt the words, rather than understood them, and turned so pale that her face gleamed whitely in the darkness. She murmured:

'What do you mean?'

Marius looked away from her without answering; but then, looking back at her, he found that she was smiling. The smile of a woman one loves is discernible even in the dark.

'Marius, how silly we're being! I've got an idea.'

'What is it?'

'If we go you must come too. I'll tell you where, and you must meet me there, wherever it is.'

Marius was now fully awake. He had come down to earth with a bump.

'How can I possibly do that?' he cried. 'Are you crazy? It takes money to go to England, and I haven't any. I already owe Courfeyrac more than ten louis – he's a friend of mine. And I wear a hat that isn't worth three francs, and I've lost half the buttons off my jacket, and my cuffs are frayed and my boots leak. I haven't thought about things like that for six weeks. I haven't told you, Cosette, but I'm a pauper. You only see me at night and you give me your hand; if you saw me by daylight you'd give me alms. England! I can't even afford a passport.'

He got up and stood with his face pressed to the trunk of a tree with his arms above his head, unconscious of the roughness of the bark against his cheek and almost ready to collapse – a statue of despair. He stayed in this posture for a long time; depths such as these are timeless. Finally he turned, having heard a small, stifled sound behind him. Cosette was in tears.

He fell on his knees in front of her, and bending down, kissed the foot that showed beneath the hem of her skirt. She made no response. There are moments when, like a saddened and resigned goddess, a woman silently accepts the gestures of love.

'Don't cry,' he said.

'But if I've got to go away and you can't come too . . .'

'Do you love me?'

She answered him with the divine word that is never more moving than when spoken amid tears:

'I adore you.'

His voice as he spoke again was the gentlest of caresses.

'Then don't cry. Do that much for me – stop crying.'

'Do you love me?' she asked.

He took her hand.

'Cosette, I have never given anyone my word of honour because it frightens me to do so. I feel my father watching me. But I give you my most sacred word of honour that if you leave me I shall die.'

These words were uttered with so much quiet solemnity that she trembled, feeling chilled as though at a ghostly touch, terrifying but true. She stopped crying.

'Now listen,' he said. 'Don't expect me here tomorrow.'

'Why not?'

'Not until the day after.'

'But why?'

'You'll see.'

'A whole day without seeing you! But that's dreadful!'

'We must sacrifice a day for the sake of our whole lives.' And Marius murmured, half to himself: 'He won't change his habits. He never sees anyone except in the evening.'

'Who are you talking about?' asked Cosette.

'Never mind.'

'But what are you going to do?'

'Wait until the day after tomorrow.'

'Must I really?'

'Yes, Cosette.'

She took his head in her hands and, rising on tiptoe, sought to read his secret in his eyes.

'While I think of it,' said Marius, 'you must have my address in case you need it. I'm living with this friend of mine, Courfeyrac, at 16, Rue de la Verrerie.'

He got a penknife out of his pocket and scratched it on the plaster of the wall – 16, Rue de la Verrerie.

Cosette was intently watching him.

'Tell me what you're thinking. Marius, you're thinking of something. Tell me what it is, or how shall I sleep tonight?'

'I'm thinking this – that God can't possibly mean us to be separated. I shall be here the evening after tomorrow.'

'But what am I to do until then? It's all very well for you, you'll be out and about. You'll be doing things. Men are so lucky! But I shall be all alone. I shall be so wretched. Where are you going to morrow evening?'

'I'm going to try something.'

'Well, I'll pray for you to succeed and I'll never stop thinking about you. I'll ask no more questions because you don't want me to. You're the master. I'll spend tomorrow evening singing the music from *Euryanthe* that you like so much – you listened to it once outside the window. But you must be here in good time the day after tomorrow. I shall expect you at nine o'clock exactly. Oh, two whole days is such a long time! Do you hear me? At exactly nine o'clock I shall be waiting in the garden!'

'I shall be there.'

And without further speech, prompted by the same impulse, the electric current that unites lovers in their every thought, passionate even in their sorrow, they fell into each other's arms, unconscious that their lips were joined while their tear-filled eyes looked upward at the stars.

By the time Marius left the street was deserted. Éponine had just departed to follow the robber band as far as the boulevard.

While he had stood reflecting with his face against the tree-trunk, Marius had had an idea – one that alas he himself thought hopeless and impossible. He had taken a drastic decision.

VII

Old heart versus young heart

Monsieur Gillenormand had now passed his ninety-first year. He was still living with his daughter in the old house which he owned in the Rue des Filles-du-Calvaire. He was, we may recall, one of those veterans cast in the antique mould who await death upright, burdened but not softened by age, and whom even bitter disappointment cannot bend.

Nevertheless for some time Mlle Gillenormand had been saying, 'My father is failing.' He no longer cuffed his servants or so vigorously rapped the banister on the landing with his cane when Basque was slow in opening the door. His fury at the July Revolution had lasted barely six months, and his calm had been scarcely ruffled when in the *Moniteur* he had come upon that monstrous conjunction of words, 'Monsieur Humblot-Conte, Peer of France'. The truth is that the old man was filled with despair. He did not give way to it, he did not surrender, since it was not in his physical or moral nature to do so; but he was conscious of an inner weakening. For four years he had sturdily – that is the right word – awaited Marius's return, convinced that sooner or later the young scamp would knock at his door; but now there were melancholy moments when he reflected that if the boy did not come soon . . . It was not the approach of death that he found unbearable, but the thought that he might never see Marius again. Until quite recently this thought had never entered his head, but now it haunted and terrified him. Absence, as happens always in the case of true and natural feeling, had served only to increase his affection for the graceless boy who had deserted him. It is in the dark and cold December nights that we most ardently desire the sun. Monsieur Gillenormand, the grandfather, was wholly incapable – or thought he was – of making any move towards reconciliation with his grandson – 'I would rather die,' he thought. Although aware of no fault in himself, he thought of Marius with the profound tenderness and silent desolation of an old man on the threshold of the grave.

He was beginning to lose his teeth, which added to his unhappiness.

Without confessing it to himself, for the avowal would have made him furious and ashamed, Monsieur Gillenormand had never loved any of his mistresses as well as he loved Marius. He had had hung in his bedroom, facing the end of his bed so that it was the first thing he saw when he awoke, an old portrait of his other daughter, the one now dead who had become Madame Pontmercy, which had been painted when she was eighteen. He gazed at it constantly, and on one occasion remarked:

'I think he's like her.'

'Like my sister?' said Mlle Gillenormand. 'Yes, he is.'

'Like him, too,' the old man said.

Once, when he was sitting huddled with his knees together and his eyes half-closed in a posture of dejection, his daughter ventured to say:

'Father, are you still so angry with –' She broke off, afraid to say more.

'With whom?'

'With poor Marius.'

He looked up sharply, thumped with his old, wrinkled fist on the table, and cried in a voice ringing with fury:

'Poor Marius, indeed! That gentleman is a worthless scoundrel without heart or feeling or gratitude, a monster of conceit, a villainous rogue.' And he turned away his head so that she should not see the tears in his eyes.

Three days after this he broke a silence that had lasted four hours to say without preliminaries to his daughter:

'I have already requested Mademoiselle Gillenormand never to mention that subject agan.'

After this Aunt Gillenormand gave up the attempt, having arrived at the following conclusion – 'Father never greatly cared for my sister after she made a fool of herself. Clearly, he detests Marius.' By 'made a fool of herself' she meant marrying the colonel.

Apart from this, as the reader will have surmised, Mlle Gillenormand had failed in her attempt to find a substitute for Marius. Lieutenant Théodule had not brought it off. Monsieur Gillenormand had disdained him. The ravaged heart does not so readily accept palliatives. And for his part, Théodule, while interested in the possible inheritance, had disliked the business of ingratiating himself. The old man had bored the cavalry officer, and the cavalry officer had exasperated the old man. Théodule was cheerful but over-talkative, frivolous but commonplace, a high-liver but in shabby company; it was true that he had mistresses and that he talked about them, but he talked badly. All his virtues were flawed. Monsieur Gillenormand was outraged by his tales of casual encounters near the barracks in the Rue de Babylone. And then again, he sometimes turned up in uniform, his cap adorned with a tricolour cockade. This alone ruled him out. It had ended with the old gentleman saying to his daughter: 'I've had enough of Théodule. You can see him if you like, but I don't much care for peacetime warriors. I'm not sure that I don't prefer adventurers to men who simply wear a sword. The clash of blades in battle is a less depressing sound than the rattle of a scabbard on the pavement. And then, to parade oneself as a fighting man and be titivated like a woman, with a corset under one's *cuirasse*, is to be fatuous twice over. A real man avoids display as much as he does effeminacy. You can have your Théodule, he's neither one thing nor the other.'

His daughter's argument that Théodule was his great-nephew was unavailing. Monsieur Gillenormand, it seemed, was a grandfather to his finger-tips, but not in the least a great-uncle. Indeed, the comparison being forced on him, Théodule had served only to make him miss Marius the more.

An evening came – it was the 4th of June, but that did not prevent him from having a fire blazing in the hearth – when Monsieur Gillenormand, having dismissed his daughter, was alone in his room with its pastoral tapestries, seated in his armchair with his feet on the hob, half-enclosed in his nine-leafed screen, with two green-shaded candles on the table at his elbow and with a book in his hand which, however, he was not reading. According to his habit he was dressed in the fashion of the *incroyables* and looked like an old-style portrait of Garat, the Minister of Justice at the time of the execution of Louis XVI. This would have caused him to be stared at in the streets, but whenever he went out his daughter saw to it that he was enveloped in a sort of bishop's cloak which hid his costume. At home he never wore any sort of house-gown except in his bedroom. 'They make you look old,' he said.

He was thinking of Marius with both affection and bitterness, and, as usual, bitterness came uppermost. His exacerbated tenderness always ended by boiling up into anger. He was at the point where we seek to come to terms with a situation and to accept the worst. There was no reason, after all, why Marius should ever come back to him; if he had been going to do so he would have done so already. There was no more hope, and Monsieur Gillenormand was trying to resign himself to the idea that all was over, and that he must go to his grave without ever seeing 'that gentleman' again. But he could not do so; his whole being recoiled from the thought, his every instinct rejected it. 'What – never! He'll *never* come back? Never again?' His bald head had sunk on to his chest, and he was gazing with grievous, exasperated eyes into the fire.

And while this mood was on him his old man-servant Basque entered the room and asked:

'Will Monsieur receive Monsieur Marius?'

Monsieur Gillenormand started upright, ashen-faced and looking like a corpse revived by a galvanic shock. All the blood seemed to have been drained out of his body. He stammered:

'Monsieur – who?'

'I don't know,' said Basque, alarmed by his master's appearance.

'I haven't seen him. Nicolette says that a young man has called and I'm to tell you that it's Monsieur Marius.'

Monsieur Gillenormand said in a very low voice:

'Show him in.'

He waited, quivering, with his eyes fixed on the door until at length it opened and the young man entered. It was Marius.

He stood uncertainly in the doorway, as though waiting to be invited in. The shabbiness of his clothes was not apparent in the half-darkness of the room. Nothing of him was clearly visible but his face, which was calm and grave but strangely sad.

Monsieur Gillenormand, in the turmoil of his stupefaction and delight, was incapable for some moments of seeing anything but a sort of glimmer, as though he had been visited by an apparition. He was near to swooning. He saw Marius through a haze. But it was really he; it was Marius!

At last! After four years! When at length he was able to look him over he found him handsome, noble, distinguished, grown into a whole man, correct in bearing and agreeable in manner. He wanted to open his arms and summon him to his embrace; his whole being cried out to him ... until finally this surge of feeling found expression in words springing from the harsh underside of his nature, and he asked abruptly:

'What have you come for?'

Marius murmured in embarrassment:

'Monsieur ...'

Monsieur Gillenormand had wanted him to rush into his arms. He was vexed both with Marius and with himself. He felt that he had been too brusque and that Marius's response was too cold. It was an intolerable exasperation to him that he should be so tenderly moved inside and outwardly so hard. His bitterness revived. He cut Marius short, saying:

'Well, why are you here?'

The significance of that 'Well –' was, 'if you have not come to embrace me'. Marius stared at the old man's face, whose pallor gave it a look of marble.

'Have you come to apologize? Do you now see that you were wrong?'

Hard though the words sounded, they were intended to be helpful, to pave the way for the 'boy's' surrender. But Marius shivered.

He was being asked to disavow his father. He lowered his eyes, and said:

'No, Monsieur.'

'Well then,' the old man burst out in an access of pain and anger, 'what do you want of me?'

Marius clasped his hands, and moving a step towards him said in a low and trembling voice:

'Monsieur, I ask you to have pity on me.'

The words touched Monsieur Gillenormand. Had they been spoken sooner they would have melted him, but they came too late. The old man rose to his feet and stood white-lipped, leaning on his stick with his head swaying on his shoulders, but by his taller stature dominating Marius, whose eyes were still cast down.

'Pity indeed! A youth your age asking pity of a man aged ninety-one! You're beginning life and I'm leaving it. You go to the theatre, the dance, the café, the billiard-hall; you've got wits and looks to attract the women – while I huddle in midsummer spitting into the fire. You have all the riches that matter while I have all the poverty of age, infirmity, and loneliness. You have all your teeth and a sound digestion, a clear eye, health, strength, and gaiety and a good crop of dark hair, while I haven't even any white hairs left. I've lost my teeth, I'm losing the use of my legs and I'm losing my memory. I can't even remember the name of the streets round this house. Rue Charlot, Rue du Chaume, Rue Saint-Claude, I'm always muddling them up. That's the state I'm in. You have the whole world at your feet, bathed in sunshine, but for me there's nothing but darkness. You're in love, it goes without saying, but nobody on earth loves me. And then you come here asking for pity. That's something even Molière didn't think of. If it's the kind of joke you lawyers crack in the courts, I congratulate you! You're a waggish lot.' Then he said impatiently but more seriously, 'Well, and what is it you really want?'

'Monsieur,' said Marius, 'I know that I am not welcome here. I have come to ask for only one thing, and then I will go away at once.'

'You're a young fool,' the old man said. 'Who said you were to go away?'

It was the nearest he could get to the words that were in his heart – 'Ask my forgiveness! Fling yourself into my arms!' He realized that Marius was on the verge of leaving, driven away by the coldness of his reception; he knew all this and his unhappiness was sharpened by the knowledge; and since, with him, unhappiness was transformed instantly into rage, so did his harshness increase. He wanted Marius to understand, but Marius did not understand, and this made him more angry still.

'You deserted me, your grandfather! You left my house to go God knows where. You almost broke your aunt's heart. I've no doubt you found a bachelor life very much more pleasant – aping the young man-about-town, playing the fool, coming home at all hours, having a high old time. And not a word to us. You've run up debts, I suppose, without even asking me to pay them. You've joined in demonstrations, no doubt, behaved like a street hooligan. And now, after four years, you come back to me, and this is all you have to say!'

This rough attempt to evoke in Marius a display of affection simply had the effect of reducing him to silence. Monsieur Gillenormand folded his arms, a particularly lordly gesture as he used it, and concluded bitterly:

'Well, let's get to the point. You say you've come to ask for something. What is it?'

'Monsieur,' said Marius, with the expression of a man about to jump off a precipice, 'I have come to ask your consent to my marriage.'

Monsieur Gillenormand rang the bell and Basque appeared.

'Will you please ask my daughter to come here.'

The door was again opened a few moments later. Mlle Gillenormand showed herself in the doorway but did not enter the room. Marius was standing dumbly with his arms hanging, looking like a criminal. Monsier Gillenormand was pacing up and down. He glanced at his daughter and said:

'A trifling matter. Here, as you see, is Monsieur Marius. Bid him good day. He wants to get married. That's all. Now go away.'

The terse, harsh tone of the old man's utterance conveyed a strange fullness of emotion. Aunt Gillenormand darted a startled glance at Marius, seeming scarcely to recognize him, and then, without speaking or making any gesture, scuttled away from her father's fury like a dead leaf in a gale of wind. Monsieur Gillenormand resumed his place in front of the hearth.

'And so you want to get married – at the age of twenty-one.

You've arranged it all except for one trifling formality – my consent. Please be seated, Monsieur. There has been a revolution since I last had the privilege of seeing you, and the Jacobins came off best. You must have been highly gratified. No doubt you've become a republican since you became a baron. The two things go together. The republic adds savour to the barony, does it not? Were you awarded any July decorations? Did you help to take the Louvre, Monsieur? Quite near here, in the Rue Saint-Antoine, opposite the Rue des Nonnains-d'Hyères, there's a cannon ball lodged in the third storey of a house wall, bearing the inscription, 28 July 1830. You should go and look at it, it is most impressive. They do such charming things, these friends of yours. They're putting up a fountain, I believe, in place of the statue of the Duc de Berry. And so you want to get married? Would it be indiscreet to ask to whom?'

The old man paused, but before Marius could reply he burst out:

'So I suppose you've got some sort of position. Perhaps you've made a fortune. What do you earn as a lawyer?'

'Nothing,' said Marius in a voice of almost savage firmness and defiance.

'Nothing? So all you have to live on are the twelve hundred livres I allow you?'

Marius made no reply, and Monsieur Gillenormand went on:

'Well then, I take it the girl is rich.'

'No richer than I am.'

'You mean, she won't have a dowry?'

'No.'

'Expectations?'

'I think not.'

'Not a rag to her back! And what does her father do?'

'I don't know.'

'Well, what's her name?'

'Mademoiselle Fauchelevent.'

'Fauche – what?'

'Fauchelevent.'

'Pshaw!' said the old man.

'Monsieur!' cried Marius.

Monsieur Gillenormand cut him short, speaking in an aside to himself.

'So that's it. Twenty-one years old and no position, nothing but twelve hundred livres a year. Madame la Baronne Pontmercy will have to count her sous when she goes to market.'

'Monsieur,' cried Marius, in the distraction of seeing his last hope vanish, 'I beg of you, I beseech you in Heaven's name on my bended knees, to allow me to marry her!'

The old man uttered a shrill, anguished laugh which turned into a fit of coughing, then burst again into speech.

'So you said to yourself, "I'll have to go and see him, that old fossil, that old mountebank. It's too bad I'm not yet twenty-five. I wouldn't have to worry about him and his consent. As it is, I'll go there and crawl to him, and the old fool will be so happy to see me that he won't care who I marry. I haven't a sound pair of shoes and she hasn't a chemise to her back, but no matter. I'm proposing to throw away my career, my prospects, my youth, my whole life and plunge into poverty with a woman round my neck. That's what I intend to do, I'll tell him, and I'll ask his consent. And the old fossil will oblige ...." That's what you think, isn't it? Well, my lad, you can do what you please. Hamstring yourself, if you must. Marry your Pousselevent or Coupelevent or whatever her name is. But as for my consent, the answer is, never!'

'Grandfather –'

'Never!'

The tone in which the word was uttered robbed Marius of all hope. He rose and crossed the room slowly, swaying a little, with his head bowed, more like someone in the act of dying than someone merely taking his leave. Monsieur Gillenormand stood watching him, but then, when he was about to open the door, moving with jerky liveliness of a spoilt, imperious old man, he darted after him, seized him by the coat collar, dragged him vigorously back into the room, thrust him into an armchair and said:

'Tell me about it.'

It was the word 'grandfather' that had brought about the change in him. Marius stared in amazement. Monsieur Gillenormand's expression had become one of coarse, implicit bonhomie. The stern guardian had given way to the grandfather.

'Come on. Tell me all about your love-affairs. Don't be afraid to talk. Lord, what fools you young fellows are.'

'Grandfather ...' Marius said again, and the old man's face lighted up.

'That's it. Don't forget I'm your grandfather.'

There was so much bluff, fatherly indulgence in his manner that Marius, now suddenly transported from despair to hope, was quite bewildered. He was seated near the table and the light of the two candles, disclosing the dilapidated state of his attire, caused Monsieur Gillenormand to survey him with astonishment.

'You really are penniless, aren't you!' he said. 'You look like a tramp.' He pulled open a drawer and got out a purse which he put on the table. 'Here's a hundred louis. Buy yourself some clothes.'

'Oh, grandfather,' said Marius, 'if you knew how much I love her. The first time I saw her was in the Luxembourg, she was there every day. I didn't take much notice of her at first, but then – I don't know how it was – I fell in love with her. I was terribly unhappy, but in the end – well, now I see her every day at her home – her father doesn't know – we meet in the garden in the evening – and they're going away, he's going to take her to England. So when I heard this I thought to myself, I'll go and see my grandfather and tell him about it. Because otherwise I'll get ill, or go mad and throw myself in the river. I've got to marry her, I *must* marry her, or I shall go mad. Well, that's the whole truth. I don't think I've left anything out. She lives in a house in the Rue Plumet, with a garden and a wrought-iron gate. It's near the Invalides.'

Monsieur Gillenormand was seated radiantly beside him, adding zest to his delight in his presence and the sound of his voice with an occasional long pinch of snuff. But at the mention of the Rue Plumet he started, with his fingers to his nose, and let the snuff fall on his knees.

'The Rue Plumet? Wait a minute. Isn't there a barracks near there? That's it, your cousin Théodule – you know, the cavalry officer – he told me about her. In the Rue Plumet. It used to be the Rue Blomet. I remember perfectly – a girl in a garden with a wrought-iron gate in the Rue Plumet. Another Pamela. You have good taste, my boy. A pretty wench, from what I hear. I fancy that fool Théodule had his eye on her, but I don't know how far it went. Anyway, it doesn't matter, you can't believe a word he says, he's always boasting. My dear Marius, I think it entirely right that a young fellow like you should be in love. It's natural at your age. I'd far sooner have you in love with a wench than with revolution. I'd sooner have you crazy about a dancing partner, or twenty dancing partners, than about Monsieur de Robespierre. I'm bound to say that the only kind of *sans-culottes* I've ever cared for are the ones in skirts. A pretty wench is a pretty wench, and what's wrong with that? So she lets you in without her father knowing, does she? That's quite in order. I've had that kind of adventure myself, and more than once. But listen, you don't want to take it too seriously, you mustn't go asking for trouble – no drama, no talk of marriage or anything of that sort. You're a gay young blade, but you've got a head on your shoulders. You have your fun, but you don't marry. You come to see your grandfather, who's not a bad old boy at heart and always has a few louis stuffed away in a drawer, and you ask him to help you out. And grandfather says, "Why, that's easy!" Youth profits and age provides. I've been young, and one day you'll be old. Here you are, lad, and you'll pay it back to your own grandson. Two hundred pistoles. Have your fun, and what could be better? That's how it should be. You don't marry, but that needn't stop you – you understand?'

Marius, too shocked to be capable of speech, shook his head. The old man burst out laughing, winked an aged eyelid, tapped him on the knee and gazing conspiratorially at him said with an indulgent shrug of his shoulders:

'Why, you young nincompoop – make her your steady mistress!'

Marius turned pale. He had understood nothing of what his grandfather had said. The talk of the Rue Blomet, Pamela, the barracks, and the cavalry officer had been to him a meaningless rigmarole. None of it had anything to do with his lily-white Cosette. The old man had been babbling; but his babbling had ended in an admonition which Marius had understood: 'Make her your mistress!' The mere suggestion was an insult to Cosette, and it wounded her high-minded young lover like a swordthrust to his heart.

He rose, picked up his hat off the floor and walked firmly and resolutely towards the door. Here he turned, bowed deeply to his grandfather, straightened himself and said:

'Five years ago you insulted my father; today you have insulted my future wife. I shall ask nothing more of you, Monsieur. Farewell.'

Monsieur Gillenormand opened his mouth in stupefaction, reached out an arm and sought to get up from his chair; but before he could say anything the door had closed and Marius was gone.

The old man stayed motionless for some moments, unable to speak or breathe, as though a hand had clutched him by the throat.

Finally he struggled to his feet. He ran to the door, so far as his ninety-one years permitted him to run, opened it and cried:

'Help! Help!'

His daughter appeared, followed by the servants. He croaked pitifully:

'After him! Catch him! What have I done to him? He must be mad. He's going away again. Oh, my God, my God, this time he'll never come back!'

He ran to the window looking on to the street, opened it with aged, trembling hands and leaned out while Basque and Nicolette held him from behind.

'Marius!' he called. 'Marius! Marius!'

But Marius, turning the corner of the Rue Saint-Louis, was already out of earshot.

Monsieur Gillenormand clasped his hands to his head and with an anguished expression withdrew from the window. He sank into an armchair, breathless, speechless, and tearless, wagging his head and soundlessly moving his lips, with nothing more in his eyes or his heart than a blankness like the coming of night.

BOOK NINE

WHERE ARE THEY GOING?

Jean Valjean

AT ABOUT four o'clock on the afternoon of that same day, Jean Valjean had been seated alone on the shady side of one of the more isolated slopes of the Champ de Mars. From caution, from the desire for solitude, or simply because of one of those unconscious changes of habit which occur in all our lives, he now seldom went out with Cosette. He was wearing his workman's smock, grey linen trousers, and the long-peaked cap which hid his face. He was again on easy and happy terms with Cosette, his earlier anxieties having been put to rest; but during the past week or so other things had occurred to trouble him. One day as he walked along the boulevard he had seen Thénardier. Thanks to his disguise the latter had not recognized him, but since then he had seen him several times, often enough to convince him that Thénardier was now frequenting that part of the town. This had prompted him to take a major decision. Thénardier was the embodiment of all the dangers that threatened him.

Besides which, Paris was in an unsettled state, and for anyone with something to hide the present political unrest had the disadvantage that the police had become more than usually obtrusive, and might, in their search for agitators, light upon someone like Jean Valjean.

All these considerations troubled him. And something else had occurred to add to his unease, an unaccountable circumstance of which he had become aware only that morning. Rising early, before Cosette's shutters were opened, he had gone out into the garden and had suddenly noticed an address scratched on the wall, apparently with a nail – *16, Rue de la Verrerie.*

It was evidently recent. The letters stood out white against the dingy plaster, and there was fresh dust on the weeds at the foot of the wall. It might well have been done the previous night. Was it intended as a message for some third party, or was it a warning to himself? In any case it was certain that the garden had been broken into. Valjean was reminded of the other curious incidents that had disturbed the household. He pondered these matters, but said nothing to Cosette about this latest development, not wishing to alarm her.

The upshot was that, after due consideration, Jean Valjean had decided to leave Paris, and even France, and go to England. He had warned Cosette that he wanted to leave within a week. And now he sat on the grass in the Champ de Mars turning it all over in his mind – Thénardier, the police, the letters scratched on the wall, their prospective journey, and the difficulty of procuring a passport.

While he was thus engaged he saw, by the shadow cast by the sun, that someone was standing on the ridge of the slope at his back. He was about to turn when a scrap of folded paper fell on his knee, seeming to have been tossed over his head. Unfolding it, he read two words, pencilled in capital letters:

'CLEAR OUT.'

He got up quickly, but now there was no one on the slope. Looking about him he saw a queer figure, too tall for a child but too slight for a man, clad in a grey smock and drab-coloured corduroy trousers, scramble over the parapet and drop into the ditch encircling the Champ de Mars.

Valjean went home at once, his mind much exercised.

II

Marius

Marius dejectedly left his grandfather's house. He had gone there with only a gleam of hope; he left in utter despair.

The mention of a cavalry officer, his strutting cousin, Théodule, had made no impression on him, none whatever, as any student of the youthful human heart will readily understand. A playwright might have evolved complications arising out of this blunt disclosure from grandfather to grandson, but what the drama would have gained the truth would have lost. Marius was at the age when, in the matter of evil, we believe nothing; there comes a later age when we believe everything. Suspicions are nothing but wrinkles. Youth does not possess them. What overwhelms Othello leaves Candide untouched. As for suspecting Cosette, there were countless crimes which Marius could more easily have committed.

Taking refuge in the resource of the sore in heart, he wandered aimlessly through the streets, thinking of nothing that he could afterwards remember. At two in the morning he returned to Courfeyrac's lodging and flung himself fully dressed on his mattress. It was daylight before he fell into that state of troubled slumber in which the mind goes on working, and when he awoke he found that Courfeyrac, Enjolras, Feuilly, and Combeferre were all in the room, dressed for the street and seeming very agitated.

Courfeyrac asked him:

'Are you coming to the funeral of General Lamarque?'

For all they meant to him, the words might have been Chinese.

He went out some time after them, having put in his pocket the pistols Javert had loaned him on the occasion of the affair in February, which he had never returned. They were still loaded. It would be difficult to say what thought at the back of his mind prompted him to do this.

He roamed about all that day without knowing where he went. There were one or two showers of rain, but he did not notice them. He bought a roll at a baker's shop, thrust it in his pocket and forgot to eat it. It seems, even, that he bathed in the Seine without knowing that he did so. There are times when the head is on fire, and Marius was in that condition. He neither hoped for anything nor feared anything; this was what he had come to since the previous evening. He was waiting feverishly for the present evening, having only one clear thought in his mind, that at nine o'clock he would see Cosette. This last brief happiness was all that the future held for him; beyond it lay darkness. At moments, as he strayed along the frequented boulevards, it struck him that there was a strange hubbub in the town, and he emerged from his preoccupations to wonder, 'Are people fighting?'

At nightfall, at nine o'clock precisely in accordance with his promise, he was in the Rue Plumet, and as he drew near the wrought-iron gate he forgot all else. It was forty-eight hours since he had seen Cosette and now he was to see her again; all other thoughts were dispelled by this present rapture. Those minutes in which we live through centuries have the sovereign and admirable quality that at the time of their passing they wholly fill our hearts.

Marius slipped through the gate and hurried into the garden. Cosette was not in the place where ordinarily she awaited him. He crossed through the shrubbery and made for the recess by the steps. 'She'll be there,' he thought – but she was not there. Looking up he saw that all the shutters were closed. He explored the garden and found it empty. Returning to the house, half-crazed with love and grief and terror, like a householder returning home at an unpropitious moment, he banged with his fists on the shutters. He banged and banged again, regardless of the risk that a window might open to reveal the scowling face of her father demanding to know what he was about. This meant nothing to him compared with what he feared. He gave up banging and began to shout, 'Cosette! Cosette, where are you?' There was no reply. There was no one in the house or garden, no one anywhere.

Marius stared up with despairing eyes at the mournful dwelling, as dark and silent but more empty than a tomb. He looked at the stone bench where with Cosette he had passed so many enchanted hours. Finally he sat down on the steps, his heart swelling with tenderness and resolve. He blessed his love from the depths of his being, and said to himself that, now she was gone, there was nothing for him to do but die.

Suddenly he heard a voice calling through the trees, apparently from the street.

'Monsieur Marius!'

He looked up.

'Who's that?'

'Is that you, Monsieur Marius?'

'Yes.'

'Monsieur Marius, your friends are waiting for you at the barricade in the Rue de la Chanvrerie.'

The voice was not quite unfamiliar; it resembled the coarse, husky croak of Éponine. Marius ran to the gate, shifted the loose bar and, thrusting his head through, saw someone who looked like a youth vanish at a run into the darkness.

III

Monsieur Mabeuf

Jean Valjean's purse was of no service to Monsieur Mabeuf. His aged, childlike austerity had never encouraged gifts from Heaven nor was he disposed to admit that the stars could be transformed into louis d'or. Not knowing where the purse came from he took it to the local police post and left it there as an item of lost property to await a claimant. Needless to say, it was never claimed and did Monsieur Mabeuf no good.

For the rest, Monsieur Mabeuf continued on his downward course. His experiments with indigo were no more successful in the Jardin des Plantes than they had been in the Austerlitz garden. Last year he had owed his housekeeper her wages, this year he owed the rent. The pawnbroker had sold the plates of his *Flora* after thirteen months, and a tinker had made them into saucepans. Deprived of his plates, and unable even to finish off the incomplete sets of the *Flora* that he still possessed, he had sold the sheets of text and illustrations to a secondhand dealer at a knock-down price as 'remainders'. Nothing was now left to him of his life's work. He lived for a time on the proceeds of the sheets, and when he found that even this meagre nest-egg was nearly exhausted he gave up gardening and let his plot lie fallow. He had long ago given up the two eggs and occasional piece of beef on which he had once lived; his meals now consisted of bread and potatoes. He had sold the last of his furniture and everything he could spare in the way of clothes and bedding, also the majority of his books and engravings. But he still kept the most precious of his books, some of which, such as *La Concordance des Bibles*, by Pierre de Besse, and *Les Marguerites de la Marguerite* by Jean de la Haye, dedicated to the Queen of Navarre, were extremely rare. Monsieur Mabeuf never had a fire in his bedroom and went to bed when it grew dark to save candles. He seemed no longer to have neighbours; people avoided him when he went out and he was aware of this. The plight of a child concerns its mother and the plight of a young man may concern a girl; but the plight of an old man concerns no one, it is the most lonely of all despairs. Nevertheless Monsieur Mabeuf had not wholly lost his childlike serenity. His eyes still lighted up when they fell upon a book, and he could still smile while he pored over his edition of Diogenes Laertius, printed in 1644, which was the only copy extant. His glass-fronted bookcase was the only article of furniture he had retained, apart from bare essentials.

Mère Plutarque said to him one morning:

'I've no money to buy dinner.'

By 'dinner' she meant a small loaf and four or five potatoes.

'Can't you owe for it?' asked Monsieur Mabeuf.

'You know very well they won't let me.'

Monsieur Mabeuf opened the bookcase and spent a long time contemplating his books, each one in turn, like a parent compelled to sacrifice one of his children. Finally he snatched one off the shelf and went out with it under his arm. He returned two hours later with nothing under his arm and laid thirty sous on the table.

'That will do for dinner.'

But the same thing happened next day and the day after and every day. Monsieur Mabeuf went out with a book and came back with a trifling sum of money. Seeing that he was forced to sell, the second-hand bookseller paid him twenty sous for a volume he had bought for twenty francs, sometimes at the same establishment. Thus his library dwindled. He remarked now and then, 'After all, I'm eighty' – perhaps with a lingering thought that he would come to the end of his days before he came to the end of his books. His melancholy increased. But one day he had a triumph. He went off with a Robert Estienne which he sold for thirty-five sous on the Quai Malaquais and came back with a volume of Alde which he had bought for forty sous in the Rue des Grès. 'I owe five sous,' he said happily to Mère Plutarque. That day he had no dinner.

He was a member of the Société d'Horticulture. When his state of impoverishment became known the president of the society undertook to speak on his behalf to the Minister of Agriculture and Commerce. 'Why certainly!' said the minister. 'A worthy, harmless old man, a scholar, and a botanist – certainly we must do something for him.' Next day Monsieur Mabeuf received an invitation to dine at the minister's home, which, trembling with delight, he displayed to Mère Plutarque. 'We're saved!' he said. Arriving on the appointed evening, he noted that his ragged cravat, his rusty, old-fashioned jacket and his shoes, which had been polished with white of egg, greatly astonished the footmen. Nobody spoke to him, not even the minister. At about ten o'clock, still hoping for a word from someone, he heard the minister's wife, a handsome lady in a low-cut evening dress whom he had not ventured to approach, ask, 'Who is that old person?' He went home on foot, at midnight and in pouring rain, having sold a volume of Elzevir to pay for a fiacre to take him there.

He had fallen into the habit, before going to bed, of reading a few pages of his Diogenes Laertius, having sufficient knowledge of Greek to be able to savour the particulars of the version he possessed. This was now his only pleasure. A few weeks after the dinner-party Mère Plutarque fell suddenly ill. There is something even more distressing than the lack of means to buy a loaf of bread, from the baker, and that is to lack the means to buy drugs from the apothecary. The ailment grew worse, and the doctor prescribed a very expensive medicine. Monsieur Mabeuf went to his bookcase but it was now empty. The last volume had gone. All he had left was his Diogenes Laertius.

Monsieur Mabeuf put the unique volume under his arm and went out. This was on 4 June 1832. He went to Royol's successor in the Rue Saint-Jacques and came back with a hundred francs. He put the pile of five-franc pieces on his old servant's bedside table and retired to his bedroom without saying a word.

At dawn the next day he sat down on the overturned milestone which served him as a bench, and contemplated the still morning and his neglected garden. It rained now and then, but he did not seem to notice. During the afternoon he heard a strange commotion coming from the direction of the town, sounds that resembled rifle fire and the clamour of a vast crowd.

Monsieur Mabeuf looked up, and seeing a gardener passing on the other side of his hedge asked him what was happening. The gardener, with a spade over his shoulder, answered in the most unconcerned of voices:

'It's a riot.'

'What do you mean, a riot?'

'The people are fighting.'

'What about?'

'Blessed if I know,' said the gardener.

'Where is this happening?' asked Monsieur Mabeuf.

'Round by the Arsenal.'

Monsieur Mabeuf went into the house for his hat, looked round automatically for a book to tuck under his arm, found none, muttered, 'Oh, of course,' and set off for the town with a wild light in his eyes.

5 JUNE 1832

I

The outward aspect

OF WHAT does a revolt consist? Of everything and nothing, a spring slowly released, a fire suddenly breaking out, force operating at random, a passing breeze. The breeze stirs heads that think and minds that dream, spirits that suffer, passions that smoulder, wrongs crying out to be righted, and carries them away.

Whither?

Where chance may dictate. In defiance of the State and the laws, of the prosperity and insolence of other men.

Outraged convictions, embittered enthusiasms, hot indignation, suppressed instincts of aggression; gallant exaltation, blind warmth of heart, curiosity, a taste for change, a hankering after the unexpected; the impulse which makes us look with interest at the announcement of a new play, and the delight we take in those three knocks on the stage; vague dislikes, rancours, frustrations – the vanity that believes Fate is against us; discomforts, idle dreams, ambition hedged with obstacles; the hope that upheaval will provide an outlet; and finally, at the bottom of it all, the peat, the soil that catches fire – such are the elements of a revolt.

The greatest and the smallest; the beings on the fringe of life who wait upon chance, the footloose, men without convictions, hangers-on at the crossroads; those who sleep at nights in the desert of houses with no roof of their own other than the clouds in the sky; those who look to luck, not labour, for their daily bread; the unknown denizens of misery and squalor, bare-footed and bare-armed – all these belong to the revolt.

All those who cherish in their souls a secret grudge against some action of the State, or of life or destiny, are attracted to the revolt; and when it manifests itself they shiver and feel themselves uplifted by the tempest.

A revolt is a sort of whirlwind in the social atmosphere which swiftly forms in certain temperatures and, rising and travelling as it spins, uproots, crushes, and demolishes, bearing with it great and sickly spirits alike, strong men and weaklings, the tree-trunk and the wisp of straw. Woe to those it carries away no less than to those it seeks to destroy; it smashes one against the other.

It inspires those it lays hold of with extraordinary and mysterious powers, raising everyman to the level of events and making all men weapons of destruction; it makes a pebble into a cannon-ball, a labourer into a general.

If we accept the doctrine of certain exponents of political strategy, a weak revolt, from the point of view of those in power, is not undesirable: in principle any revolt strengthens the government it fails to overthrow. It tests the reliability of the army, unites the bourgeoisie, flexes the muscles of the police, and demonstrates the strength of the social framework. It is an exercise, almost a course of treatment. Power feels revived after a revolt, like a man after a massage.

But thirty years ago revolts were viewed differently.

There is in all matters a theoretical approach which calls itself 'common sense'. It is Molière's Philinte as opposed to his Alceste: the offer of compromise between what is true and what is false; discourse, admonition, rather patronizing extenuation which, because it is a mingling of blame and excess, supposes itself to be wisdom and is often no more than sophistry. A whole school of political thought, called 'moderate', springs from this approach. It is something between hot and cold – the tepid water. This school of thought, superficial but with simulated depth, analyses effects without looking to their cause, and with the loftiness of a pseudo-science rebukes the fever of the market-place.

This is what they say:

The riots which succeeded the achievement of 1830 robbed that great event of something of its purity. The July Revolution was a salutary blowing of the popular wind which instantly cleared the air. The subsequent rioting brought back the clouds, debasing a revolution that had been remarkable for its unanimity to the level of a brawl. In the July Revolution, as always when progress proceeds by jerks, there were hidden lesions; the rioting brought these to light. One could see that this or that thing had been broken. The July Revolution itself brought nothing but a feeling of deliverance; but after the riots one had a sense of catastrophe.

Any uprising causes the shops to shut and the funds to fall; it creates consternation on the Bourse, interferes with trade, causes bankruptcies; money runs short, the rich are apprehensive, public credit is shattered and industry thrown out of gear; capital is withheld and employment dwindles; there is insecurity everywhere, and countermeasures are adopted in every town. Hence the great fissures that arise. It has been estimated that the first day of the revolt cost France twenty million francs, the second forty, and the third sixty. Simply in financial terms, the three days' revolt cost a hundred and twenty million – that is to say, the equivalent of a lost naval battle ending in the destruction of sixty ships-of-the-line.

In the historical perspective, no doubt, the rioting was not without beauty: the war of the street barricades is no less grandiose and dramatic than war in the undergrowth, the one being inspired by the spirit of the town, the other by the spirit of the countryside. The riots threw a garish but splendid light on what is most particular to the character of Paris – hot-blooded devotion and tempestuous gaiety, students who proved that courage is a part of intelligence, the unshakeable Garde Nationale, the encampments of shopkeepers and fortifications of street-urchins, and the defiance of death displayed by the ordinary man in the street. The schools did battle with the soldiery. When all is said, between the combatants there was only a difference of age; they were of the same race; the young men who at twenty were ready to die for their ideas would at forty be ready to die for their families. The army, always unhappy in times of civil disturbance, opposed prudence to audacity. The riots, while they made manifest the reckless daring of the masses, stiffened the courage of the bourgeoisie.

All this is true, but did it justify the blood that was shed? And to the shedding of blood must be added the darkened future, the setback to progress, the disquiet of decent people, the despair of honest liberals, wounds inflicted by foreign absolutism on the revolution it had itself provoked, and the triumph of those defeated in 1830, who could now proclaim, 'We told you so!' It may be that Paris was aggrandized, but certainly France was diminished. Nor may we ignore – for everything must be taken into account – the massacres which too often dishonoured the forces of order grown ferocious in their repression of the spirit of liberty run mad. All in all, this revolt was a disaster.

Such is the summing up of that approximation of wisdom which the bourgeoisie, that approximation of the people, is all too ready to accept.

For our part we reject that over-flexible and, in consequence, over-convenient term 'revolt'. We seek to distinguish between popular movements. We do not ask if a revolt costs as much as a battle. In any case, why have a battle? This brings us to the question of war. Is external war less of a disaster than internal revolt? And is every insurrection a disaster? And what if the insurrection of 14 July did cost a hundred and twenty million? The installation of Philip V upon the throne of Spain cost France two milliards. Even had the cost been the same, we should prefer 14 July. Moreover, we do not accept those figures, which sound like argument but are simply words. Accepting the fact of a revolt, we seek to examine the thing itself. The doctrinaire attitude depicted above deals only with effects: we must look for the cause.

II
The root of the question

There is the street riot and the national insurrection: two expressions of anger, the one wrong and the other right. In democratic states, the only ones based on justice, it may happen that a minority usurps power; the nation as a whole rises, and in the necessary assertion of its rights it may have recourse to violence. In any matter affecting the collective sovereignty, the war of the whole against the part is an insurrection, and the war of the part against the whole is a form of mutiny: the Tuileries may be justly or unjustly assailed according to whether they harbour the King or the Assembly. The guns turned on the mob were wrong on 10 August and right on 14 Vendémiaire. It looks the same, but the basis is different: the Swiss guards were defending an unrighteous cause, Bonaparte a righteous one. What has been done in the free exercise of its sovereign powers by universal suffrage cannot be undone by an uprising in the street. The same is true of matters of pure civilization: the instinct of the crowd, which yesterday was clear-sighted, may tomorrow be befogged. The fury which was justified against Terray was absurd when directed against Turgot, since the one stood for privilege and the other for the reform of abuses.* The wrecking of machines, looting of warehouses, tearing up of railway lines, destruction of docks; mobs led astray, the denial of progress by the people's justice, Ramus murdered by his own students, the stoning of

*Both were Finance Ministers – Terray from 1769 to 1774, Turgot from 1774 to 1776.

Rousseau – all this is mob violence; it is Israel in revolt against Moses, Athens against Phocion, Rome against Scipio. But Paris rising against the Bastille – that is insurrection. His soldiers rising against Alexander, his sailors against Christopher Columbus, these are mere acts of mutiny. Alexander with the sword did for Asia what Columbus did for America with the compass – he opened up a world; and the gift of a new world to civilization is so great a spreading of light that resistance to it is culpable. Sometimes the mass counterfeits fidelity to itself. The mob betrays the people. Can anything be more strange, for example, than the action of the salt-makers who, after a long and bloody and wholly justified revolt, at the very moment of victory, when their cause was won, went over to the King in a counter-revolution against the popular uprising on their behalf. A sad triumph of ignorance! The salt-makers escaped the royal gallows, and, with the rope still round their necks, donned the white cockade. 'Down with the salt-tax!' became 'Long live the King!' The massacre of St Bartholomew's Eve, the September massacre, the massacre at Avignon (Coligny murdered in the first, Madame de Lamballe in the second, Marshal Brune in the third) – these were all acts of riot. The Vendée was a huge Catholic revolt.

The sound of righteousness in movement is clearly recognizable, and it does not always come from the tumult of an over-excited mob. There are insane outbursts of rage just as there are flawed bells: not all tocsins sound the true note. The clash of passion and ignorance is different from the shock of progress. Rise up by all means, but do so in order to grow. Show me which way you are going; true insurrection can only go forward. All other uprisings are evil. Every violent step backwards is mutiny, and to retreat is to do injury to the human cause. Insurrection is the furious assertion of truth, and the sparks struck by its flung paving-stones are righteous sparks. But the stones flung in mutiny stir up nothing but mud. Danton versus Louis XVI was insurrection, but Hébert versus Danton was mutiny.

Thus it is that if, as Lafayette said, insurrection is the most sacred of duties, sporadic revolt may be the most disastrous of blunders.

There is also the difference of temperature. Insurrection is often a volcano, revolt often a hedgerow fire.

Sometimes insurrection is resurrection.

Since the solution of all problems by universal suffrage is a wholly modern concept, and since history prior to it has for four thousand years been a tale of violated rights and the suffering of the masses, every period of history discloses such acts of protest as are within its means. There was no insurrection under the Caesars, but there was Juvenal, who wrote: '*Si natura negat, facit indignatio versum.*'* There was also Tacitus.

We need not speak of the exile in Patmos who mightily assailed the world as it was with a protest in the name of an ideal world, a huge, visionary satire, which cast upon Rome-that-was-Nineveh, Rome-that-was-Babylon, and Rome-that-was-Sodom the thunderous light of his *Revelation*. John on his rock is the Sphinx on its pedestal; he is beyond our understanding; he was a Jew and a Hebrew. But Tacitus, who wrote the *Annals*, was a Latin, and, better still, a Roman.

Since the rule of a Nero is black, it must be blackly depicted. The work of the graving-tool alone would be too weak; the lines must be drawn with the acid of a prose that bites deep.

Despots play their part in the works of thinkers. Fettered words are terrible words. The writer doubles and trebles the power of his writing when a ruler imposes silence on the people. Something emerges from that enforced silence, a mysterious fullness which filters through and becomes steely in the thought. Repression in history leads to conciseness in the historian, and the rocklike hardness of much celebrated prose is due to the tempering of the tyrant. The tyrant enforced upon the writer a condensation which is a gain in strength. The Ciceronian periods, scarcely adequate on the subject of Verres, would sound flowery applied to Caligula. Less roundness in the phrase produces more hitting power. Tacitus thinks with clenched fists. The honesty of a great spirit, fined down to justice and truth, is devastating.

It may be remarked in passing that Tacitus was not the historical contemporary of Caesar. His field was the Tiberii. Caesar and Tacitus are successive phenomena whose clash seems to have been mysteriously prevented by the Dramatist who down the centuries decrees entrances and exits. Both were great, and God spared their greatness by not bringing them into collision.† The passer of judgement assailing Caesar might have hit too hard and dealt unjustly with

*'Where talent is lacking, anger writes poetry.'

†Professor Guyard remarks that Hugo was here thinking of the first Napoleon (Caesar) and himself. He was the Tacitus of Napoleon III, that modern Tiberius.

him. God did not desire this. The great African and Spanish campaigns, the rooting out of the Silician pirates, the spread of civilization to Gaul, Britain, and Germany – those are the glories that crossed the Rubicon. There is a kind of delicacy in the divine justice, in its reluctance to let loose the redoubtable historian upon the illustrious usurper, preserving Caesar from Tacitus and allowing genius the benefit of extenuating circumstances.

Certainly despotism is always despotism, even under a despot of genius. There is corruption under the most illustrious of tyrants, but moral depravity is even more abominable under an ignoble tyrant. In those reigns nothing masks the shame, and the pointers of morals, a Tacitus or a Juvenal, can more usefully castigate the vileness that is indefensible in the eyes of men.

Rome had a fouler stench under Vitellius than under Sulla; under Claudius and Domitian there was a manner of baseness corresponding to the baseness of the tyrant. The institution of slavery is a direct product of despotism. A miasma arises from blunted consciences reflecting the mind of the master; public authorities are infamous, hearts shrunken, scruples dulled, souls like crawling slugs. So it was under Caracalla, under Commodus and Heliogabalus; but the Roman Senator under Caesar exhales only the rank odour proper to an eagle's eyrie. Hence the seemingly late appearance of a Tacitus or a Juvenal: it is when the evil is manifest that its denouncer shows himself.

But Juvenal and Tacitus, like Isaiah in the Old Testament and Dante in the Middle Ages, were individual men, whereas revolt and insurrection are the multitude, which is sometimes right and sometimes wrong.

Most commonly revolt is born of material circumstances; but insurrection is always a moral phenomenon. Revolt is Masaniello, who led the Neapolitan insurgents in 1647; but insurrection is Spartacus. Insurrection is a thing of the spirit, revolt is a thing of the stomach. John Citizen grows angry, and not always without cause. Where it is a question of famine, the street uprising – that of Buzançais, for example, in 1847 – has a real and moving validity. Nevertheless, it remains no more than an uprising. Why? Because although it has good reason it is wrong in method. It is ill-directed although right, violent although morally powerful; it hits out at random, thunders on like a blinded elephant, crushing everything in its path and leaving behind it the bodies of old men, women, and children. It sheds the blood of innocents, without knowing why. The feeding of the people is a rightful objective, but their massacre is a wrongful means.

All armed acts of protest, however warranted, even those of 10 August and 14 July, take the same course. First come the sound and fury, before the rightful cause emerges. Insurrection itself is no more than a street riot at the beginning, a stream that swells into a torrent. Ordinarily the stream flows into the ocean, which is revolution. But sometimes, pouring down from those mountain heights which dominate our moral horizon, justice, wisdom, reason, law, born of the pure source of idealism, after the long descent from rock to rock, after reflecting the heavens in the limpidity of its waters and being swollen by a hundred tributaries in its splendid show of triumph, the insurrection wastes itself eventually in some bourgeois quagmire, as if the river Rhine were to end in a marsh.

All that belongs to the past; the future is another matter. It is the particular virtue of universal suffrage that it cuts the ground from under the feet of violent revolt and, by giving insurrection the vote, disarms it. The elimination of war – warfare in the streets or warfare across frontiers – is the fruit of progress. Whatever may be happening today, peace is the meaning of tomorrow.

For the rest, whatever the difference may be between insurrection and revolt, the bourgeoisie are little aware of the distinction. For the bourgeois, both are sedition, rebellion pure and simple, a rebellion of the dog against its master which has to be restrained with chain and collar – until such time as the dog's head, vaguely discernible in the shadows, is found to have grown into the head of a lion. Whereupon the bourgeois cries, 'Long live the people!'

Having thus defined our terms we must ask, how will history assess the events of June 1832? Were they a revolt or an insurrection?

They were an insurrection.

It may happen, in the course of our account of that formidable convulsion, that we shall use words such as 'riot' and 'revolt', but this is to describe the facts on the surface, without losing sight of the distinction between revolt in appearance and insurrection in principle.

In its rapid explosion and melancholy suppression, the outburst of 1832 was possessed of such nobility that even those who regard it as no more than a riot cannot talk of it without respect. To them it is like a last echo of 1830. Over-heated imaginations, they maintain, do not cool in a day. Revolution does not come abruptly to an end. There must be a gradual aftermath, further rises and falls, before it settles down into a state of stability, like the lower slopes of a mountain merging into the plain. There are no Alps without their Jura, no Pyrenees without their Asturias.

That pathetic crisis in contemporary history which is known to latter-day Paris as 'the time of riots' was undoubtedly characteristic of the tempestuous occasions in the tale of the present century. We must add a last word before beginning our account of it.

The events to be related belong to that order of vivid and dramatic happenings which historians sometimes pass over for lack of time and space. But it is here, we must insist, that the reality of life is to be found, the stir and tremor of human beings. Small details are as it were the separate foliage of great events, lost to sight in the distant perspective of history. The so-called time of riots abounds in details such as these. And for reasons differing from those of history, the subsequent judicial investigations do not disclose everything, nor, perhaps, have they got to the bottom of everything. We propose to bring to light, amid the known and published details, things hitherto unknown, facts scattered by the forgetfulness of some men and the death of others. Most of the actors in that great drama have vanished; they fell silent upon the morrow; but we can truly say of what we have to relate, 'These are things which we saw.' We shall change certain names, for it is the function of history to chronicle, not to denounce; but we shall depict the truth. Confined within the bounds of the book we are writing, we shall deal with only one aspect and one incident, certainly the least known, of the events of 5 and 6 June 1832; but we shall do it in such a manner as to enable the reader to catch a glimpse, behind the dark curtain that we shall raise, of the true face of that terrible occurrence.

III

A burial and a rebirth

By the spring of 1832, although for three months cholera had chilled men's spirits and in some sort damped their state of unrest, Paris was more than ripe for an upheaval. The town was like a loaded gun, needing only a spark to set it off. The spark, in June 1832, was the death of General Lamarque.

Lamarque was a man of action and of high repute. Under the Empire and the Restoration he had possessed the two forms of courage required by those two epochs – courage on the battlefield and courage in the debating chamber. He was as eloquent as he had been brave: one sensed the swordthrust in his words. Like Foy, his predecessor, having staunchly borne the command he staunchly upheld the cause of liberty. He took his stand midway between the extremes of left and right, was esteemed by the people as a whole because he faced the hazards of the future, and by the crowd because he had loyally served the Emperor. With Counts Gérard and Brouet, he had been one of Napoleon's marshals *in petto* – that is to say, his possible successor in the military command. The treaties of 1815 had outraged him like a personal affront. He detested Wellington with a forthright hatred that pleased the masses; and for seventeen years, taking little note of subsequent events, Lamarque had mourned the tragedy of Waterloo. On his deathbed he had pressed to his heart the sword bestowed on him by his fellow officers of the Hundred Days, and he had died with the word *patrie* on his lips, as Napoleon had died with the word *armée*.

His death, which was not unexpected, had been feared by the people as a loss, and by the Government as a pretext. It was a day of national mourning, and, like all other bitterness, mourning may be transformed into revolt. That is what happened.

On the eve of 5 June, the day fixed for Lamarque's funeral, and on the morning of that day, the Faubourg Saint-Aintoine, through which the funeral procession was to pass, assumed a formidable aspect. The crowded network of streets became a hive of activity. Men were arming themselves with whatever they could lay hands on. There were joiners who snatched up the tools of their trade to 'break down doors', or converted them into daggers. One man in a state of bellicose fever had slept in his clothes for three nights. A carpenter named Lombier was accosted by a friend in the street who asked him where he was going. 'I haven't got a weapon,' said Lombier...'So?'...'I'm going to fetch a pair of dividers from my workshop' ... 'What will you do with them?' ... 'Blessed if I know' ... A man named Jacqueline, a carrier, accosted passing workmen with offers of a drink. Having stood them a glass of wine he asked, 'Have you got a job?' ... 'No' ... 'Well, go to Filspierre, between the Montreuil and the Charonne barriers. There's a job for you there.' There were weapons and ammunition at Filspierre's establishment. Certain recognized leaders 'did the round-up' – went from door to door collecting their followers. In cafés such as Barthélemy, near the Barrière du Trône, Capel, and the Petit-Chapeau, the drinkers inquired of one another, 'Where are you hiding your pistol?' . . . 'Under my jacket' . . . 'And you?' . . . 'Under my shirt' . . . There were whispering groups outside work-shops in the Rue Traversière and in the courtyard of the Maison-Brûlée. Among the most ardent of the agitators was a certain Mavot, who never stayed more than a week in any one job, being dismissed because the masters found 'one had to be constantly arguing with him'. He was killed the day after the funeral at the barricade in the Rue Ménilmontant. Pretot, who also died in the fighting, was his second-in-command; when asked what his aim was, he answered, 'Insurrection.' A group of workers gathered at the corner of the Rue de Bercy to await a man named Lemarin, the revolutionary agent for the Faubourg Saint-Marceau. Orders were issued almost publicly.

So on 5 June, on a day of alternating rain and sunshine, General Lamarque's funeral procession crossed Paris with full military ceremonial, somewhat swollen by special safety precautions. The escort consisted of two battalions of infantry with draped drums and reversed arms; ten thousand National Guards armed with sabres, and the National Guard batteries of artillery. The hearse was drawn by a team of young men. Invalided officers followed immediately behind it carrying branches of laurel. Then came a motley, excited, numerous crowd, representatives of the Amis du Peuple, the Schools of Law and Medicine, refugees from all nations bearing Spanish, Italian, German and Polish flags and banners of all kinds, children waving bunches of greenery, stonemasons and carpenters who were at that moment on strike, printers, recognizable by their paper caps – marching in pairs and in threes, shouting, nearly all carrying cudgels and a few armed with sabres, disorderly yet infused with a single spirit, both a mob and an organized body. The different groups had their own leaders. A man armed with a pair of pistols which he made no effort to conceal seemed to be inspecting them, and the files parted to make room for him. The streets leading to the boulevards, trees, balconies, and windows, all were packed with men, women and children anxiously watching. An armed crowd was on the march while an apprehensive crowd looked on.

Authority was also on the alert, with a hand on its sword-hilt. In the Place Louis XV were four mounted squadrons of carabineers, with muskets and musketoons loaded and full ammunition pouches, ready to go into action with trumpeters at their head; detachments of the Garde Municipale were drawn up in the streets of the Latin Quarter and in the Jardin des Plantes; there was a squadron of Dragoons in the Halle-aux-Vins; the 12th Light Infantry was divided between the Grève and the Bastille; the 6th Dragoons were on the Quai des Célestins and the courtyard of the Louvre was packed with artillery. The rest of the troops were held in reserve in barracks, to say nothing of the regiments on the outskirts of Paris. A disquieted government confronted the threatening multitude with 24,000 soldiers in the town itself and another 30,000 in the environs.

Rumours ran up and down the procession. There was talk of a legitimist conspiracy and of the Duc de Reichstadt, whom God had marked for death at the moment when the crowd was electing him to Empire (he died a few weeks later). Some person who has never been identified announced that when the time came two suborned works foremen would open the doors of an arms factory to admit the mob. The prevailing expression among the majority of the bareheaded spectators was one of mingled ardour and bewilderment, but here and there, amid that multitude so seized with violent but not ignoble emotion, the faces were to be seen of authentic evildoers, base mouths that talked of loot. There are certain kinds of civil disturbances that stir up the mud at the bottom of the pond, and any experienced police force is aware of the fact.

The procession moved slowly but feverishly along the boulevard from the mortuary chapel to the Bastille. The occasional showers of rain did nothing to deter the crowd. There were a number of incidents. While the coffin was borne round the Vendôme column stones were thrown at the Duc de Fitz-James, who was seen on a balcony with his hat on his head: the Gallic cock, emblem of the July Monarchy, was torn off a standard and trampled in the mud; a police sergeant was wounded with a swordthrust at the Porte Saint-Martin; a party from the École Polytechnique, the students of which had been confined to the school premises, broke out and joined the procession, to be greeted with cries of, 'Long live the École Polytechnique, long live the Republic!' At the Place de la Bastille long and impressive columns of interested spectators from the Faubourg Saint-Antoine added themselves to the procession, and signs of commotion became apparent. A man was heard to say to his neighbour, 'You see that fellow with the red beard? He's the one who'll give the order to shoot.' It seems that this red-bearded man, whose name was Quénisset, was some years later to be involved in another affair, the attempted assassination of the Dukes of Orléans and Aumale.

The hearse passed the Bastille, and, following the canal, crossed the small bridge and came to the esplanade of the Pont d'Austerlitz. Here it paused. A bird's-eye view of the procession at this moment would have displayed a comet with its head at the esplanade and its tail extending over the Quai Bourdon and along the boulevard, across the Place de la Bastille and on to the Porte Saint-Martin. A circle formed round the hearse, and the vast crowd fell silent. Lafayette delivered a farewell address to Lamarque. It was a moving and uplifting moment, with all heads bared and all hearts beating in sympathy. But suddenly a rider on horseback clad in black and carrying a red flag (some say that it was a pike surmounted by a red bonnet) appeared within the circle. Lafayette looked away, and General Exelmans left the procession.

The red flag unloosed a tempest and vanished in it. From the Boulevard Bourdon to the Pont d'Austerlitz a clamour arose from the multitude that was like the rising of a tide. Two tremendous cries were raised – 'Lamarque to the Panthéon!' and 'Lafayette to the Hôtel de Ville!' Two parties of young men, amid the applause of the crowd, harnessed themselves and began to drag Lamarque in his hearse across the Pont d'Austerlitz and Lafayette in a fiacre along the Quai Morland.

Meanwhile a detachment of the Cavalerie Municipale had appeared on the left bank and were barring the exit from the bridge, while on the right bank a detachment of dragoons moved along the Quai Morland. The young men dragging Lafayette's fiacre saw these as they debouched on to the *quai* and cried, 'Watch out! Dragoons!' The dragoons advanced grimly and purposefully at a walking pace and in silence, sabres sheathed, pistols in their holsters, musketoons in their rests.

Two hundred paces from the little bridge they halted. Lafayette's fiacre was moving towards them. They parted their ranks to let him through and then closed up behind him. At that moment the dragoons and the crowd were in direct contact. The women ran away in terror.

What happened in that fateful minute? No one will ever know. It was the dark moment when two clouds converge. Some people say that a bugle-call sounding the charge was heard from the direction of the Arsenal, others that a youth attacked one of the dragoons with a dagger. What is certain is that suddenly three shots were fired. The first killed the squadron commander, Cholet; the second killed a deaf old woman in the act of shutting her window in the Rue Coutrescarpe and the third singed an officer's epaulette. A woman cried, 'They're starting too soon!', and suddenly there appeared at the other end of the Quai Morland another squadron of dragoons which had been held in reserve. They galloped with bared sabres down the Rue Bassompierre and the Boulevard Bourdon, clearing a path in front of them.

And that is the whole story. The tempest was unleashed, stones fell like hail, volleys were fired and a mass of people rushed to the river and crossed that narrow arm of the Seine that has since been filled in. The builders' yards on the Île Louviers, that vast, ready-made fortress, bristled with combatants. Stakes were pulled up, pistols fired, a makeshift barricade erected. The young men who had been held up on the Pont d'Austerlitz now crossed the bridge at the double, dragging the hearse, and charged the Garde Municipale. The carabineers came up, the dragoons used their sabres, the crowd scattered in all directions while sounds of war echoed to the four corners of Paris. The cry, 'To arms' rang out and there were clashes everywhere. Fury fanned the uprising as the wind fans a forest fire.

IV

Earlier occasions

Nothing is more remarkable than the first stir of a popular uprising. Everything, everywhere happens at once. It was foreseen but is unprepared for; it springs up from pavements, falls from the clouds, looks in one place like an ordered campaign and in another like a spontaneous outburst. A chance-comer may place himself at the head of a section of the crowd and lead it where he chooses. This first phase is filled with terror mingled with a sort of terrible gaiety. There is rowdiness and the shops put up their shutters; people take to their heels; blows thunder on barred doors, and servants within enclosed courtyards can be heard gleefully exclaiming, 'There's going to be a bust-up!'

These are the things that happened in different parts of Paris within the first quarter of an hour.

In the Rue-Sainte-Croix-de-la-Bretonnerie a band of some twenty young men, bearded and long-haired, entered a café to re-emerge a minute later carrying a tri-colour flag still wrapped in crêpe, and having three armed men at their head, one carrying a sabre, the second a musket, and the third a pike.

In the Rue des Nonnains-d'Hyères a well-dressed citizen, bald and round-bellied, with a black beard, a bristling moustache and a loud voice, was openly offering cartridges to the passers-by.

Bare-armed men were parading the Rue Saint-Pierre-Montmartre with a black banner on which was inscribed in white letters the legend, 'Republic or Death', and in the Rue des Jeûneurs, the Rue de Cadran, the Rue Montorgueil, and the Rue Mendar there were groups waving flags bearing the word '*section*' and a number in letters of gold. One of these flags was red and blue, separated by a faint white stripe.

An arms factory on the Boulevard Saint-Martin was looted, as were three arms shops in the Rue Beaubourg, the Rue Michel-le-Comte, and the Rue du Temple. Within a few minutes the crowd had secured possession of 230 muskets, nearly all double-loaders, sixty-four sabres, and sixty-three pistols. Muskets and bayonets were distributed separately, that more men might be armed.

Young men armed with muskets took possession of apartments overlooking the Quai de la Grève for use as firing-posts. They rang the bell, walked in and set about making cartridges. A woman said afterwards: 'I didn't know they were cartridges until my husband told me.'

A party burst into a curio-shop in the Rue des Vieilles-Haudriettes and helped themselves to scimitars and other Turkish weapons.

The body of a builder's labourer, killed by a musket-ball, lay in the Rue de la Perle.

And on both banks of the river, on the boulevards, in the Latin Quarter and the quarter round Les Halles, breathless men – work-men, students, section-leaders – were reading out proclamations and shouting, 'To arms!' Street-lamps were being smashed, carriage sunharnessed, cobblestones torn up, trees uprooted, house-doors battered down, and piles of timber, paving-stones, barrels, and furniture built up into barricades.

The citizenry were forcibly enlisted. Houses were broken into and women forced to surrender any weapons belonging to their absent husbands, and a note of the proceeding was chalked on the door – 'Weapons handed over'. Some men even signed a formal receipt for a musket or sabre, saying, 'You can get it back tomorrow at the Mairie.' Isolated sentries and national guards on their way to their local headquarters were disarmed in the streets. Officers had their epaulettes ripped off. An officer of the Garde Nationale, being pursued by a band armed with cudgels and swords, was forced to take refuge in a house in the Rue du Cimetière-Saint-Nicolas from which he was not able to escape until dark and in disguise.

In the Saint-Jacques quarter students poured out of their lodging-houses up the Rue Saint-Hyacinthe to the Café du Progrès or down to the Café des Sept-Billards in the Rue des Mathurins. Here the young men distributed arms, standing on curbstones outside the doors. The timber-yard in the Rue Transnonain was looted to build barricades. Only in one place did the inhabitants resist, at the corner of the Rues Sainte-Avoye and Simon-le-Franc, where they pulled down a barricade. And in one place the insurgents gave ground. After firing on a detachment of the Garde Nationale they abandoned a half-constructed barricade in the Rue du Temple and fled along the Rue de la Corderie. The detachment found a red flag on the barricade, a bag of cartridges and 300 pistol bullets. They tore up the flag and bore off the fragments on the points of their bayonets.

All these incidents, here slowly related in succession, occurred almost simultaneously in separate parts of the town amid a vast tumult, like a string of lightning flashes in a single clap of thunder.

Within less than an hour twenty-seven barricades had sprung up in the quarter of Les Halles alone. At the centre was the famous House No. 50, which became the fortress of the workers' leader, Jeanne, and his 106 followers, and which, with the Saint-Merry barricade on one side and the Rue Maubuée barricade on the other, commanded three streets, the Rue des Arcis, the Rue Saint-Martin, and the Rue Aubry-le-Boucher, which faced it. Two barricades set at right angles ran from the Rue Montorgueil to the Grande-Truanderie, and from the Rue Geoffrey-Langevin to the Rue

Sainte-Avoye. No need to specify the countless barricades in twenty other quarters. There was one in the Rue Ménilmontant with a *porte cochère* lifted off its hinges and another within a hundred yards of the Préfecture de Police on which was an overturned coach.

A well-dressed man distributed money to the workers manning the barricade in the Rue des Ménétriers, and a mounted man rode up to the Rue Grenéta barricade and handed the leader something that looked like a roll of coins, saying, 'This is to cover expenses, wine, and so forth.' A fair-haired young man without a cravat went from one barricade to another passing on orders. Another, wearing a blue police cap and carrying a drawn sabre, was posting sentries. Within the barricades, cafés and porters' lodges were converted for use as guard-posts. In general the uprising conformed to accepted military procedure. The streets it made use of, narrow and with many twists and turns, were admirably chosen, particularly in the neighbourhood of Les Halles, where the network was more tangled than footpaths in a forest. It was said that the Société des Amis du Peuple had taken charge of operations in the Sainte-Avoye quarter. A man killed in the Rue du Ponceau was found to have on him a street-map of Paris.

But what had really taken charge of the uprising was a kind of wild exhilaration in the air. While rapidly building barricades, the insurgents had also seized nearly all the garrison-posts. In less than three hours, like a lighted powder-train, they had assailed and occupied, on the Right Bank, the Arsenal, the Mairie in the Place Royale, all the Marais, the Popincourt arms factory and all the streets round Les Halles; and on the Left Bank the Veterans' Barracks, the Place Maubert, the Deux-Moulins powder-factory and all the city barriers. By five o'clock in the evening they were masters of the Place de la Bastille, the Place de la Lingerie, and the Place des Blancs-Manteaux; their patrols were moving into the Place des Victoires and threatening the Banque de France, the Petits-Pères barracks, and the central Post Office. In a word, they held one third of Paris.

Everywhere battle had been joined on the largest scale, and through the disarming of soldiers, house-to-house requisitions and the looting of arms-shops, what had started as a brawl with brick-bats had become an engagement with musketry.

At about six o'clock that evening the Passage du Saumon had become a battlefield, with the insurgents at one end and the military at the other. An observer, the marvelling author of these lines, who had gone to witness the upheaval at first hand, found himself caught between two fires, with nothing but the half-pillars separating the shops to protect him from the bullets. He was pinned in this unhappy position for nearly half an hour.

Meanwhile, the drums were beating and the men of the Garde Nationale were putting on their uniforms, snatching up their arms, and pouring out of houses while the regiments of soldiers marched out of barracks. Opposite the Passage de l'Ancre a drummer-boy received a dagger-thrust, and another, in the Rue du Cygne, was assailed by some thirty youths who destroyed his drum and took away his sabre. Yet another was killed in the Rue Grenier-Saint-Lazare. Three officers died in the Rue Michel-le-Comte, and a number of wounded members of the Garde Municipale beat a retreat along the Rue des Lombards.

A detachment of the Garde Nationale found, outside the Cour Batave, a red flag bearing the inscription, 'Révolution républicaine No. 127'. Was it in fact a revolution?

The uprising had turned the centre of Paris into a vast, labyrinthine citadel. This was its focal point, and it was here that the matter had to be decided. The rest was mere skirmishing: and the proof that this was the real centre lay in the fact that thus far no fighting had gone on there.

The soldiers in certain regiments were of doubtful reliability, and this added to the terrifying uncertainty of the situation. They remembered the popular ovation with which, in July 1830, the neutrality of the 53rd regiment of the line had been rewarded. Two tried veterans of the great wars, Maréchal de Lobau and Général Bugeaud, were in command of the government forces, Bugeaud being subordinate to Lobau. Very large patrols consisting of detachments of regular soldiers flanked by entire companies of the Garde Nationale, and preceded by a Police Commissioner in ceremonial attire, set out to reconnoitre the streets held by the insurgents, while on their side the insurgents stationed outposts at the crossroads and audaciously sent out patrols beyond their barricades. Each side was probing the other. The Government, with an army at its disposal, was hesitant. It would soon be dark, and the Saint-Merry tocsin was beginning to sound.

The then Minister for War, Marshal Soult, who had fought at Austerlitz, was sombrely following the course of events. Oldstagers such as he, warriors accustomed to text-book manoeuvres and having no other guide than orthodox military tactics, are dismayed by the huge and formless blast of public anger. The wind of revolution is not easily controlled.

The suburban units of the Garde Nationale rallied hastily and in disorder. A battalion of the 12th Light Infantry arrived at the double from Saint-Denis; the 14th line regiment came in from Courbevoie; the École Militaire batteries had taken up their station in the Place du Carrousel and the guns were brought in from Vincennes.

The Tuileries were a solitude. Louis-Philippe was entirely calm.

V

The uniqueness of Paris

In the past two years, as we have said, Paris had witnessed more than one upheaval. Outside its rebellious districts nothing as a rule is more strangely untroubled than the face of Paris during an uprising. She very quickly adapts herself – 'After all, it's only a riot' – and Paris has too much else to do to let herself be disturbed by trifles. Only the largest of cities can offer this strange contrast between a state of civil war and a kind of unnatural tranquillity. Ordinarily, when the uprising begins, when the drums and the summons to arms are heard, the shopkeeper in another part of the town remarks to his neighbour, 'Seems there's trouble in the Rue Saint-Martin' ... or 'in the Faubourg Saint-Antoine' ... and he will very likely add unconcernedly, '– or somewhere that way'. And when later he hears the heartrending sound of musket-fire he comments, 'Seems to be hotting up.'

But then, if the trouble seems to be coming his way, he will hastily shut up shop and don his uniform – that is to say, safeguard his merchandise and risk his life.

There is shooting at a crossroads or in a street or alleyway, barricades are besieged, captured and recaptured, houses are pockmarked with bullets, blood flows, corpses litter the pavements – and two streets away one may hear the click of billiard-balls in a café. Curious onlookers laugh and gossip within a stone's throw of streets echoing with the sounds of war, theatres open their doors and present vaudeville, fiacres proceed along the street with parties on their way to dine, sometimes in the very quarter where the battle is in progress. In 1831 the firing stopped to allow a wedding to pass.

In the uprising of 12 May 1839, an old man in the Rue Saint-Martin, pulling a handcart adorned with a tricolour flag and containing bottles of some nondescript beverage, shuttled between the Government forces and the forces of anarchy, offering his wares impartially to either side.

Nothing could be more strange: and this is the peculiar characteristic of Paris uprisings, to be found in no other capital. For such things to happen, two qualities are requisite – the greatness of Paris and her gaiety. It calls for the city of Voltaire and of Napoleon.

But on this occasion, in the battle of 5 June 1832, the great city encountered something that was perhaps even greater than herself. She was stricken with fear. Everywhere, even in the remotest and most 'uninvolved' districts, closed windows and shutters were to be seen in broad daylight. Brave men reached for their weapons, and cowards hid. The heedless and preoccupied pedestrian vanished from the streets, many of which were as deserted as in the small hours of the night. Strange tales were told and terrifying rumours circulated – that *they* had captured the Banque de France – that there were six hundred of them in the Saint-Merry monastery alone, barricaded in the chapel – that the army was not to be trusted – that Armand Carrel had been to see Marshal Clauzel, one of Lamarque's pall-bearers, who had said, 'Find me one reliable regiment' – that Lafayette was ill but had nevertheless said to them, 'I'm on your side. I'll go wherever there's room for a chair' – that one had to be on one's guard against bands of pillagers who were looting isolated houses in the less frequented parts of the town (in this last one may discern the vivid imagination of the police, that Ann Radcliffe* of the government) – that a battery of artillery had been installed in the Rue Aubry-le-Boucher – that Lobau and Bugeaud had concocted a plan whereby four columns were to march upon the centre of the insurrection, coming respectively from the Bastille, the Porte Saint-Martin, the Place de la Grève and Les Halles – but on the other hand that the troops might evacuate Paris altogether and withdraw to the Champ de Mars – that no one knew what was going to happen, but the position was undoubtedly serious – that Marshal Soult's hesitation was disturbing – why did he not attack at once? The old lion was certainly very much perplexed, seeming to discern amid the confusion a monster hitherto unknown.

That evening the theatres did not open. The police patrols were

* Author of *The Mysteries of Udolpho*. Trs.

evidently on edge, searching pedestrians and arresting suspects. By nine o'clock more than eight hundred persons had been arrested and the prisons were full to bursting point, the Conciergerie in particular, where the long underground passage known as the 'Rue de Paris' was floored with bales of straw for the accommodation of the dense mass of prisoners whom Lagrange, the revolutionary from Lyon, was boldly haranguing. The rustling of so much straw, under so many bodies, was like the sound of a downpour. Elsewhere the prisoners were in the open air, huddled together in prison yards. There was apprehension everywhere, a tremulousness unusual to Paris.

People were barricading their houses, while wives and mothers waited anxiously for men who did not come home. Occasionally there was a distant rumble of cartwheels, and doorways echoed with a subdued tumult of voices reporting the latest developments – 'That was the cavalry ... there go the ammunition tenders ...' The sound of drums and bugle-calls, of sporadic firing; above all the dismal tolling of the Saint-Merry tocsin. The first thunder of cannon-fire was awaited. Armed men appeared at street corners and swiftly vanished, shouting, 'Go home!' Doors were hastily bolted while householders asked each other, 'Where will it end?' With every minute that passed Paris in the gathering dusk seemed more and more ominously tinged with the red glow of revolution.

THE STRAW IN THE WIND

I

The poetry of Gavroche

THE MOMENT when rebellion, arising out of the clash between civilians and the military in front of the Arsenal, enforced a backward movement of the crowd following the hearse, which, winding through the boulevards, brought its weight to bear, so to speak, on the head of the procession, was a moment of terrible recoil. The crowd broke ranks and scattered, some uttering bellicose cries, others in the pale terror of flight. The river of humanity filling the boulevards overflowed to left and right, breaking up into lesser streams along a hundred side streets with a sound like the bursting of a dam. At this moment a ragged small boy, coming down the Rue Ménilmontant with a sprig of flowering laburnun which he had picked on the heights of Belleville, noticed in a stall outside an antique shop an old cavalry pistol. Throwing away his flowers, he snatched it up, shouted to the proprietress, 'Missus, I'm borrowing your thingumajig!' and made off with it.

A few minutes later the terrified citizenry making their escape along the Rue Amelot and the Rue Basse found him flourishing his weapon and singing:

> Nothing to be seen at night,
> But in daytime all is bright
> And the gentlefolk turn pale
> At the writing on the wail.
> Do your duty, my fine lads,
> Blow away their silly hats!

Gavroche was going to war. Not until he reached the boulevard did he notice that the pistol had no hammer.

Where did they come from, that marching-song and the many other songs he sang? Who can say? Perhaps he made them up himself. Certainly he knew all the popular ditties of the day, to which he brought his own improvements. Ragamuffin that he was, he sang with the voice of Nature and the voice of Paris, mingling the song of the birds with the songs of the studio. He was well acquainted with art students, a tribe related to his own. He had, it seems, been for three months apprenticed to a printer. He had once run an errand for Monsieur Baour-Lormian, a Member of the Academy. In short, Gavroche was a lettered urchin.

But Gavroche still did not know that when on that stormy night he had offered the hospitality of his elephant to two homeless little boys he had been playing providence to his own brothers. Brothers rescued in the evening, father in the morning, that was how his night had been spent. After leaving the Rue des Ballets in the early hours he had hurried back to the elephant, from which he had skilfully extracted the two children; and after sharing with them the breakfast that he had somehow conjured up he had gone off on his own affairs, entrusting them to the mercy of the streets, his own foster-mother. His parting words had been: 'I'm leaving you now, in other words, buzzing off, or, as they say in polite circles, hooking it. You kids, if you can't find your mum and dad, come back here this evening and I'll fix you up with supper and a bed.' But the two children, whether because they had been picked up by a *sergeant de ville* and taken to the nearest police post, or kidnapped by some street performer, or had simply lost their way in the vast labyrinth of Paris, had not come back. Such disappearances are common enough at the lowest level of our society. Gavroche had not seen them again. In the ten or twelve weeks that had passed he had more than once scratched his head and wondered, 'Where the devil have my two kids got to?'

And now, still flourishing his pistol, he had arrived at the Pont-aux-Choux. He saw that only one shop in the street was open, and, which made the circumstance worthy of note, that this was a pastry-cook's. It was a heaven-sent opportunity to eat one last apple-puff before embarking upon new adventures. Gavroche tapped his clothing and turned out his trouser-pockets, and found nothing, not so much as a sou. He was tempted to cry out in vexation. It is a bitter thing to miss the most delicious of all confections.

He continued on his way, and two minutes later he was in the Rue Saint-Louis. Passing through the Rue du Parc-Royal, and feeling the need to console himself for the loss of the apple-puff, he allowed himself the huge satisfaction of pulling down theatre-posters in broad daylight. A little further on, coming upon a group of well-dressed citizens who looked to him like house-owners, he gesticulated and delivered himself of the following objurgation:

'A fine, plump lot they are, the well-to-do! They do themselves proud. They wallow in rich dinners. Ask them where their money goes and they can't tell you. They've eaten it, that's all – gone with the wind!'

II
Gavroche goes to war

To flourish a hammerless pistol in the public street is so splendid a gesture of defiance that Gavroche felt his spirits rising with every step he took. In the intervals of singing bursts of the 'Marseillaise' he discoursed as follows:

'All's well. My left foot's sore and I've got the rheumatics, but I'm feeling fine. The gentry have only to listen and I'll sing them revolutionary songs. Who cares for the coppers' narks, they're a lot of dirty dogs. Not that I've anything against dogs. But I wish my pistol had a hammer. I've come from the boulevard, mates, it's getting hot there, things are boiling up nicely. It's time to skim the pot. Forward, lads, and may the furrows run red with traitors' blood! I give my life to *la patrie*, and I shan't be seeing my best girl any more. No more Nini, but who cares? Let's make a fight of it – I've had enough of despotism.'

At this moment the horse of a trooper of the Garde Nationale fell in the street. Gavroche put down his pistol, helped the man up and helped him to get the horse on its feet. He then picked up the pistol and strode on.

All was peace and quiet in the Rue de Thorigny, and its indifferent calm, so proper to the Marais, was in marked contrast to the surrounding tumult. Four housewives were gossiping in a doorway. Scotland has its trios of weird sisters, but Paris has its foursomes of old biddies; and the 'thou shalt be King hereafter' flung at Macbeth on the blasted heath can have been no more ominous than the same words flung at Napoleon in the Rue Baudoyer. The hoarse croaking would have sounded much the same.

The ladies in the Rue de Thorigny were wholly intent upon their own affairs. Three were concierges and one was a *chiffonnière* (garbage-collector, rag-picker, and street-cleaner) with her hook and basket. Between them they seemed to represent the four extremities of age, which are decay, decrepitude, ruin and misery. The chiffonnière was humble. In that doorstep world it was she who made obeisance and the concierge who patronized, and this has to do with the accommodation arrived at between the exactions of the concierge and the compliance of the street-cleaner. There can be good will even in a broom. This chiffonnière was a grateful body, and fulsome in her smiles for the three concierges. Their talk was on the following lines:

'So you cat's still being a nuisance?'

'Well, you know what cats are, the natural enemies of dogs. It's the dogs that make the fuss.'

'Besides people.'

'And yet cat fleas don't get on to people.'

'Besides which, dogs are dangerous. I remember one year there were so many dogs that they had to write about it in the newspapers. It was the time when there were big sheep in the Tuileries, pulling the Roi de Rome in his little carriage. Do you remember the Roi de Rome?'

'The one I liked was the Duc de Bordeaux.'

'Well, I once saw Louis XVIII. I like Louis XVIII best.'

'The way the price of meat has gone up, Mme Patagon!'

'Don't talk of it! Butcher's shops are the limit, a perfect horror. All one can afford are the worst cuts.'

The chiffonnière remarked:

'My business is going from bad to worse. The rubbish heaps are worthless. Nobody gets rid of anything these days, they eat everything.'

'There are some who are worse off than you, Mme Vargoulème.'

'Well that's true,' said the chiffonnière deferentially. 'At least I have a regular position.' And yielding to the love of showing off that exists in all of us, she went on: 'When I got home this morning I cleared out my basket and did the sorting. I've got separate places for everything. Rags in a box, applecores in a bucket, linens in my cupboard, woollens in the chest of drawers, old papers on the window-sill, eatables in the cookpot, bits of glass in the fireplace, slippers behind the door, and bones under the bed.'

Gavroche, who had paused to listen, now inquired:

'Why are you old girls bothering with politics?'

He was met with a four-barrelled volley of abuse.

'Another of those ruffians!'

'What's that he's got in his paw? A pistol!'

'I ask you, a boy that age!'

'They're never happy except when they're going against the law.'

By way of reply Gavroche thumbed his nose with his fingers spread, and the chiffonnière exclaimed:

'Nasty little ragamuffin!'

The lady who answered to the name of Patagon clapped her hands together in outrage.

'There's going to be trouble, that's for sure. The errand boy next door, the one that's growing a beard, I've watched him go past every morning with his arm round a hussy in a pink cap, but this morning it was a musket he had under his arm. Mme Bacheux says there was a revolution last week in – in – well, where was it? – in Pontoise. And look at that little demon, carrying a pistol! It seems that the Rue des Célestins is full of cannons. Well, what do you expect, when the Government has to deal with rascals like him, always inventing new ways of upsetting everything, and just when things were quietening down after all the trouble we've had. Lord have mercy on us, when I think of that poor Queen that I saw go by in the tumbril! And what's more, it'll send up the price of tobacco. It's monstrous, that's what it is. Well anyway, I'll live to see you guillotined, my fine cocksparrow!'

'Your nose is running, old lady,' said Gavroche. 'Better wipe it.'

And he passed on. At the Rue Pavée the thought of the chiffonnière crossed his mind and he addressed her thus in fancy:

'You shouldn't abuse the revolutionaries, Mother Streetcorner. My pistol is on your side. It's to help you find more things worth eating in your basket.'

There was a sound of footsteps behind him, and he turned to see that Mme Patagon had followed and was shaking her fist at him.

'You're nothing but somebody's bastard!'

'As to that,' said Gavroche, 'I am profoundly indifferent.'

Shortly after this he passed the Hotel Lamoignon, to which he addressed a ringing appeal: 'On the way, lads – on to battle!'

Then he was seized with melancholy, and looking reproachfully at his pistol he said: 'I'm ready for action, but you won't act.'

He came upon a very thin dog and was moved to sympathy.

'Poor old fellow, you look like a barrel with all the hoops showing.'

He headed for the Orme-Saint-Gervais.

Righteous wrath of a barber

The worthy barber who had driven away the two little boys whom Gavroche had entertained in his elephant was at that moment engaged in shaving a veteran legionary who had served under Napoleon. After discussing the present disorders and the late General Lamarque, they had eventually arrived at the subject of the Emperor. From this had ensued a conversation which a sober citizen with a literary turn might have entitled, 'Dialogue between a Razor and a Sabre'.

'Monsieur,' said the barber, 'how was the Emperor as a horseman?'

'He didn't know how to fall. That's why he never did fall.'

'I'm sure he had very fine horses.'

'I studied the one he was riding the day he pinned the cross on me. It was a racy mare, all white, with ears set wide apart, deep withers, a narrow head with a black star, very long neck, good strong ribs and fetlocks, sloping shoulders and powerful hindquarters. A little over fifteen hands.'

'A pretty horse,' said the barber.

'Well, it belonged to His Majesty.'

The barber paused, feeling that after this dictum a momentary silence was called for. He then said:

'It's true, is it not, that the Emperor was only once wounded.'

'In the heel. At Ratisbon. I've never seen him so well turned out as he was that day – neat as a new pin.'

'But you, Monsieur, you must have been wounded many times.'

'Oh, nothing to speak of, a couple of sabre-cuts at Marengo, a ball in the right arm at Austerlitz and one in the left thigh at Iéna, a bayonet wound at Friedland, just there, and seven or eight lance wounds at Moskowa, all over the place they were. And at Lutzen I had a finger smashed by a shell-burst. Oh, and at Waterloo I got a bit of grape in the thigh. But that's all.'

'How splendid,' rhapsodized the barber, 'to die on the field of battle! I give you my word I'd sooner be killed by a cannon-ball in the belly than die slowly of illness in my bed, with doctors and medicines and all the rest of it.'

'You've got the right idea,' said the soldier.

He had scarcely spoken the words when there was a crash and

one of the window-panes lay shattered on the floor of the shop. The barber turned pale.

'Oh, my God!' he cried. 'There's one now.'

'One what?'

'A cannon-ball.'

'Think so?' said the soldier. 'Here it is.' And he stooped and picked up a large stone.

The barber got to the window just in time to see Gavroche making off at top speed towards the Marché Saint-Jean. With the thought of the two forlorn little boys in his mind, he had not been able to resist paying his respects to the barber.

'There, you see!' bellowed the barber, turning from white to crimson. 'They do damage just for the fun of it. What harm have I ever done that young devil?'

IV

The boy marvels at an old man

Gavroche, having arrived at the Marché Saint-Jean, where the police post had already been put out of action, proceeded to join forces with a party led by Enjolras, Courfeyrac, Combeferre and Feuilly. Nearly all were armed, Enjolras with a double-barrelled fowling-piece, Combeferre with two pistols in his belt and a National Guard musket bearing an old regimental number, Jean Prouvaire with an old cavalry musketoon, and Bahorel with a carbine, while Courfeyrac was brandishing an unsheathed sword-stick. Feuilly, with a naked sabre in his fist, was striding ahead shouting, 'Long live Poland!'

They had reached the Quai Morland hatless, collarless, breathless and soaked by the downpour, but starry-eyed, when Gavroche went calmly up to them.

'Where are you off to?'

'Join us,' said Courfeyrac.

Behind Feuilly was Bahorel, skipping rather than walking, a fish in the waters of insurrection. He had a crimson waistcoat and, as always, a ready tongue. The waistcoat startled an onlooker, who cried in alarm:

'Here come the Reds!'

'Red – reds!' repeated Bahorel. 'That's a fine thing to be frightened of, Mister. Speaking for myself, I'm not afraid of poppies, and little Red Ridinghood doesn't scare me out of my wits. Take my word for it, leave the fear of red to horned cattle.' He pointed to the most pacific of notices on a near-by wall, a dispensation on the part of the Archbishop of Paris to his flock, informing them that they might eat eggs in Lent. 'Flock!' he exclaimed. 'A polite way of saying geese.'

He tore down the placard and in doing so won the heart of Gavroche, who from that moment never took his eyes off him.

'You were wrong to do that,' Enjolras said to Bahorel. 'You should have left it alone. We've no quarrel with the Church. Don't waste your anger, save it for where it's needed.'

'It's all according to how you look at things,' said Bahorel. 'The clerical tone of voice annoys me. I want to be able to eat eggs without any by-your-leave. You're the cold zealot type, Enjolras, but I'm enjoying myself. And I'm not wasting anything, simply getting up steam. I tore down the placard because, by Hercules, I felt like it.'

The word 'Hercules' struck Gavroche, who was always anxious to learn.

'What does it mean?' he asked.

'It's the Latin for "thunder and lightning",' said Bahorel.

A tumultuous crowd was following them, composed of students, artists, youthful members of the Cougourde d'Aix, navvies and dock-labourers, armed with cudgels and bayonets, and a few, like Combeferre, with pistols in their belts. Among them was an old man who looked very old. He had no weapon and was trotting to keep up, although his expression was vague.

'Who's that?' asked Gavroche.

'Just an old man,' said Courfeyrac.

It was Monsieur Mabeuf.

V

The old man

We must relate what had happened.

Enjolras and his friends had been on the Boulevard Bourdon near the reserve warehouses, when the dragoons had charged, and Enjolras, Courfeyrac, and Combeferre had been among those who had gone off down the Rue Bassompierre, shouting, 'To the barricades!' On the Rue Lesdiguières they had encountered an old man wandering along the street.

What had attracted their notice was the fact that he was staggering as he walked, as though he were drunk. Moreover, although it had been raining all the morning and was now coming down harder than ever, he was carrying his hat in his hand. Courfeyrac recognized Monsieur Mabeuf, whom he had seen on several occasions when he had accompanied Marius to his door. Knowing the peaceable and more than timid nature of the old bibliophile he was horrified to find him there, hatless in the downpour and amid the tumult of charging cavalry and musket-shots. He had gone up to him and the following dialogue had ensued between them, the twenty-five-year-old rebel and the octogenarian:

'Monsieur Mabeuf, you must go home.'

'Why?'

'There's going to be fighting.'

'I don't mind.'

'Sabre-thrusts and bullets, Monsieur Mabeuf.'

'I don't mind.'

'Possibly cannon-fire.'

'Very well. And where are you going?'

'We're going to overthrow the Government.'

'Good.'

And the old man had joined their column. From then on he had not spoken a word, but his tread had grown firmer and when a workman had offered an arm for his support he had refused it with a shake of his head. He had advanced nearly to the front of the column, his movements those of a man on the march, his eyes those of a man in a dream.

'The old fire-eater!' one of the students exclaimed, and the word went round that he was a former member of the Convention, a regicide.

The column turned into the Rue de la Verrerie. Gavroche, now in the forefront, was singing some doggerel with the full strength of his lungs, so that his voice rang out like a trumpet-call.

> 'Now that the moon is risen high
> Into the forest let us fly,'
> Said Charlot to Charlotte.

Reinforcements

Their numbers were steadily increasing. They were joined in the Rue des Billettes by a tall, grey-haired man whose bold, vigorous appearance impressed Enjolras and his friends, although none of them knew him. Gavroche, still striding along at the head of the column, whistling, humming, and banging on shop-shutters with his hammerless pistol, had not noticed him.

They went past Courfeyrac's door in the Rue de la Verrerie. 'Good,' said Courfeyrac. 'I came out without my purse and I've lost my hat.' Leaving the party, he ran upstairs to his room, picked up his purse and an old hat, and also seized a large, square box about the size of a suitcase which was hidden under his dirty linen. As he hurried down again the concierge called to him:

'Monsieur de Courfeyrac!'

'Concierge, what is your name?' demanded Courfeyrac.

She was astonished.

'Why, you know it perfectly well. I'm the concierge, Mère Veuvain.'

'Well, if you insist on calling me Monsieur *de* Courfeyrac I shall have to call you Mère *de* Veuvain. And now, what is it you want?'

'There's someone waiting to see you.'

'Who is it?'

'I don't know.'

'Well, where is he?'

'In my lodge.'

'Damn!' said Courfeyrac.

'He's been waiting over an hour,' said the concierge.

At this moment a youth who seemed to be some sort of workman, slight of figure, pale-faced and freckled, wearing a torn smock and patched velveteen trousers, looking rather like a girl dressed in man's garments, came out of the lodge and said in a voice that was not in the least like that of a woman:

'I'm looking for Monsieur Marius.'

'He's not here.'

'Will he be back this evening?'

'I couldn't tell you. I certainly shan't be here myself,' said Courfeyrac.

The youth looked hard at him and asked:

'Why not?'

'Because I shan't.'

'Where are you going?'

'What's that got to do with you?'

'Would you like me to carry your box?'

'I'm going to the barricades.'

'Shall I come with you?'

'If you want to,' said Courfeyrac. 'The streets are open to everyone.'

He ran off to rejoin his friends, and when he had caught up with them gave two of them his box to carry. It was some time before he noticed that the youth had followed him.

A makeshift crowd does not always go where it first intended; it is borne on the wind, as we have said. They passed by Saint-Merry and presently, without quite knowing why, found themselves in the Rue Saint-Denis.

CORINTH

I

History of Corinth from its foundation

THE PARISIAN of today who enters the Rue Rambuteau from the direction of Les Halles and sees on his right, facing the Rue Mondétour, a basket-maker's shop bearing as its sign a basket shaped like the great Napoleon with the inscription, 'Napoleon all made of osier', can scarcely imagine the terrible events witnessed by that place a bare thirty years ago.

This was the site of the Rue de la Chanvrerie, spelt Chanverrerie in old documents, and of the celebrated tavern known as Corinthe.

The reader will recall what has been said about the barricade set up at this point, which was, however, overshadowed by the one at Saint-Merry. It is upon this Rue de la Chanverie barricade, the tale of which has now vanished from memory, that we hope to shed some light.

For the purpose of clarity we may revert to the method used in our account of the battle of Waterloo. Any person wishing to visualize with some degree of accuracy the situation of the buildings at that time standing round the Pointe Sainte-Eustache, to the northeast of Les Halles, at what is the entrance to the Rue Rambuteau, has only to imagine a letter N, with the Rue Saint-Denis at one end and Les Halles at the other, its two uprights being the Rue de la Grande-Truanderie and the Rue de la Chanvrerie, and the Rue de la Petite-Truanderie its diagonal line. The old Rue Mondétour cut sharply through all three lines, so that the relatively small rectangle between Les Halles and the Rue Saint-Denis on the one side and the Rue du Cygne and the Rue des Prêcheurs on the other, was divided into seven blocks of houses of different styles and sizes, seemingly set up at random and at all angles, and separated, like the blocks of stone in a builder's yard, by narrow passageways.

'Narrow passageways' is the best idea we can give of those dark, twisting alleys, running between tenements eight storeys high. The buildings themselves were so decrepit that in the Rue de la Chanvrerie and the Rue de la Petite-Truanderie they were buttressed by wooden beams running from one house-front to the one opposite.

The streets were extremely narrow and the central gutters wide, so that the pedestrian, walking along pavements that were always wet, passed shops like cellars, big, ironbound curbstones, over-large garbage heaps and doorways fortified with wrought-iron grilles. All this has now vanished to make way for the Rue Rambuteau.

The name 'Mondétour' or 'my detour' admirably depicts that labyrinth; and a little further on it was even better represented by the Rue Pirouette, which ran into the Rue Mondétour. The pedestrian going from the Rue Saint-Denis into the Rue de la Chanvrerie found the latter narrowing ahead of him as though he had entered a funnel. At the end of the short street he found his passage barred on the side of Les Halles by a block of tall houses, and might have thought himself in a blind alley if he had not discovered dark alleyways like trenches on either side affording him a way out. This was the Rue Mondétour, running from the Rue des Prêcheurs to the Rue du Cygne and the Rue de la Petite-Truanderie. At the end of this seeming blind alley, on the corner of the right-hand trench, there was a house much lower than the rest that formed a kind of break in the street.

It is in this house, only two storeys high, that three centuries ago a renowned tavern was light-heartedly installed, sounding a note of festivity on a site of which the poet, Théophile, has recorded:

> Here swings the awesome skeleton
> Of a sad lover who hanged himself.

Being well located, the tavern flourished and was handed down from father to son. In the days of Mathurin Régnier it was known as the Pot-aux-Roses, and, wordplay being fashionable at the time, its sign was a wooden post, or *poteau*, painted pink. In the last century the estimable Charles-Joseph Natoire, one of those masters of fantasy whose works are despised by our present-day realists, adorned the pink post with a bunch of Corinth grapes in celebration of the fact that he had on numerous occasions got mellow at the table where Régnier had got drunk. The delighted tavern-keeper had accordingly changed the name of his establishment and caused the words Au Raisin de Corinthe to be painted in gold across the top of the sign. Hence the name 'Corinth'. Nothing pleases the drinking man more than transitions of this kind, mental zig-zags appropriate to the lurching of his homeward-bound feet. The latest tavern-keeper of the dynasty, Père Hucheloup, had so far lost touch with ancient tradition as to have the post painted blue.

A ground-floor room with a bar and an upstairs room with a billiard-table, a spiral staircase through the ceiling, wine on the tables, smoke on the walls, candles in broad daylight – such was the tavern. A trapdoor in the lower room led to the cellar, and the Hucheloup apartment was on the upper storey, being reached by a flight of stairs that was more like a ladder than a stairway, its only entrance a curtained doorway in the ground-floor room. There were also two attics under the roof where the serving women were housed. The kitchen shared the ground floor with the main room.

Père Hucheloup may have been born to be a chemist; he was certainly a cook. People came to his establishment to eat as well as drink. He had invented one particular dish which was to be had nowhere else, consisting of stuffed carp, which he called *carpes au gras*. This was eaten by the light of a tallow candle or a lamp of the Louis XVI period on tables with nailed coverings of waxed muslin in lieu of tablecloths. People came from far and wide. Hucheloup had the notion one day of drawing the attention of the passer-by to his speciality. He dipped his brush in a pot of black paint, and, since his spelling was as original as his cooking, adorned his façade with the following striking announcement: 'CARPES HO GRAS.' A freak of heavy rainfall and hail one winter washed out the first S and the G, so that it read CARPE HO RAS. With the aid of wind and weather a plain gastronomic advertisement was thus transformed into the injunction of the poet Horace, '*Carpe horas*' – profit by the hours. From which it appeared that Père Hucheloup, although ignorant of French, had been a master of Latin, and that in seeking to abolish Lent he had become a philosopher. But it was also a plain invitation to step inside.

All that has since vanished. The Mondétour labyrinth was largely done away with in 1847, and probably none of it now remains. The Rue de la Chanvrerie and Corinth have vanished under the cobbles of the Rue Rambuteau.

Corinth, as we have said, was a meeting-place, if not a rallying-point, of Courfeyrac and his circle. Grantaire had discovered it. Having been beguiled first by the '*Carpe horas*' he had gone back for the '*Carpes au gras*', and to eat and drink and argue with his friends. The price was modest. They paid little and sometimes not at all, but were always welcome. Père Hucheloup was a kindly man.

He was also a tavern-keeper with a moustache and a quirky nature. He had a surly look, as though to overawe his regular customers, and he scowled at all comers, seeming more ready to quarrel than to serve them with soup. And yet, we must repeat, all were made welcome. His oddities had brought renown to his establishment, so that young men said to one another, 'Let's go and watch the old man huff and puff.' He had been a master-at-arms. But then suddenly he would explode with laughter; a thunderous voice and a good fellow. He was a comic spirit in gloomy guise; and his fondness for intimidating his guests was like those snuff-boxes that are shaped like pistols – the only detonation was a sneeze.

His wife, Mère Hucheloup, was bearded and extremely ugly.

Père Hucheloup died in 1830, taking with him the secret of the *carpes au gras*. His widow, scarcely to be consoled, continued to preside over the tavern. But the cooking degenerated and became lamentable, and the wine, which had always been poor, became even worse. Nevertheless, Courfeyrac and his friends still went there – 'From piety', as Bossuet said.

The widow Hucheloup was short-winded and ill-shaped but she had country memories and country speech. Her manner of telling a tale added a spice to her village and springtime recollections. Her greatest delight, she declared, had been to hear 'the redbreasts twittering in the bushes'.

The room on the upper floor housing the 'restaurant' was a long place cluttered with tables, benches, chairs, stools, and the ancient ricketty billiard-table. One reached it by way of the spiral staircase, which ended in a square hole in the corner, like a ship's hatchway. Lighted by a single narrow window and a lamp that was always kept burning, it had the look of a lumber-room. Every article of furniture with four legs behaved as though it had only three. The whitewashed walls were unadorned except for the following verse, dedicated to Mère Hucheloup:

> She startles at ten yards, at two you feel weak.
> There's a wart at the side of her pendulous beak:
> One is always afraid that if ever she blows it,
> It will come off and fall in her mouth ere she knows it.

This was inscribed in charcoal on the wall.

Mère Hucheloup, of whom this was a not unfaithful portrait,

spent her days passing unconcernedly in front of this legend. Two waitresses called Matelote and Gibelotte, who had never been known by any other name, helped with laying the tables, fetching the carafes of blue-tinted wine, and dishing up the various messes served to the customers in earthenware pots. Matelote, who was fat, flabby, red-haired and strident of voice, had been the favoured handmaiden of the late Père Hucheloup. Ugly she certainly was, as repulsive as any mythological monster; but, since the servant must always give way to the lady of the house, she was less ugly than Mère Hucheloup. Gibelotte, who was long and thin, pale with a lymphatic pallor, with dark-circled eyes and drooping lids, and was afflicted with what may be termed chronic exhaustion, was always first up in the morning and last to bed at night, gently and silently waiting upon everyone, even her fellow-waitress, and smiling drowsily in her fatigue.

There was a mirror over the bar-counter.

On the door of the restaurant were the words, written in chalk by Courfeyrac: 'Revel if you can and eat if you dare.'

II

Preliminary frolics

Laigle de Meaux, as we know, lodged more often with Joly than elsewhere. He perched there like a bird on a branch. The two friends lived, ate, and slept together, sharing everything, even the girl Musichetta from time to time. On the morning of 5 June they breakfasted at Corinth, Joly with a cold in the head that Laigle was also beginning to share. Laigle's clothes were the worse for wear, but Joly was neatly dressed. They entered the dining room on the first floor at about nine o'clock in the morning, to be welcomed by Matelote and Gibelotte.

'Oysters, cheese, and ham,' Laigle ordered as they sat down. The place was empty except for themselves, but as they were starting on their oysters a head appeared through the stairway hatch and Grantaire said:

'I was passing outside when I caught a delicious whiff of Brie, so here I am.'

Seeing that it was Grantaire, Gibelotte brought two more bottles of wine, making three in all.

'Are you going to drink both bottles?' Laigle asked.

'We're all ingenious, but you alone are ingenuous,' said Grantaire. 'Two bottles never hurt anyone.'

The others had begun by eating, but Grantaire began by drinking and one bottle was soon half empty.

'You must have a hole in your stomach,' said Laigle.

'You've certainly got one in your elbow,' said Grantaire, and having drained his glass he went on, 'My dear Laigle of the funeral oration, that's a very shabby jacket you're wearing.'

'I hope it is,' said Laigle. 'That's why we get on so well together, my jacket and I. It matches its creases with mine, moulds itself to my deformities, adapts itself to my every movements so that I only know it's there because it keeps me warm. Old clothes are like old friends. Have you just come from the boulevard?'

'No, I didn't come that way.'

'Joly and I saw the head of the procession go past.'

'It was a wonderful sight,' said Joly, speaking for the first time.

'And think how quiet this street is,' said Laigle. 'You'd never guess that Paris was being turned upside down. At one time, you know, it was all monasteries round here, monks of all descriptions, bearded and shaven, sandalled and barefooted, black and white, Franciscans, Capuchins, Carmelites, great, small and ancient Augustines . . . The place swarmed with them.'

'Don't talk to me about monks,' said Grantaire. 'The thought of those hair-shirts makes me itch.'

A moment later he uttered an exclamation of disgust.

'I've just swallowed a bad oyster! My hypochondria's starting again. Bad oysters and ugly waitresses, how I hate the human race! I came by way of the Rue Richelieu, past the big public library. The place is like a pile of oyster-shells. All those books, all that paper and ink, all those scribbled words. Somebody had to write them. Who was the idiot who said that man was a biped without a quill? And then I ran into a girl I know, a girl as lovely as a spring morning, worthy to be called April, and the little wretch was in a transport of delight because some poxed-up old banker has taken a fancy to her. The smell of money attracts women like the scent of lilac; they're like all the other cats, they don't care whether they're killing mice or birds. Two months ago that wench was living virtuously in an attic, sewing metal eye-holes into corsets, sleeping on a truckle-bed and living happily with a flower-pot for company. Now she's a banker's doxy. It seems it happened last night, and when I met her this morning she was jubilant. And what's so disgusting in that she's just as pretty as ever. Not a sign of high finance on her face. Roses are better or worse than women in this respect, that you can see when the grubs have been at them. There's no morality in this world. Look at our symbols – myrtle, the symbol of love, laurel, the symbol of war, the fatuous olive-branch, symbol of peace, the apple-tree, which nearly did for Adam with its pips, and the fig-leaf, the first forebear of the petticoat. As for right and justice, shall I tell you what they are? The Gauls wanted Clusium. Rome defended Clusium, asking what harm it had done them. Brennus replied, "The same harm that Alba did you, to say nothing of the Volscians and the Sabines. They were your neighbours; just as the Clusians are ours. Proximity means the same to us as it does to you. You seized Alba and we're taking Clusium." Rome would not allow it and so Brennus seized Rome, after which he cried, "*Vae victis!* – Woe to the conquered." That's right and justice for you. A world full of beasts of prey, a world full of eagles! It makes my flesh creep.'

Grantaire held out his glass to be refilled and then resumed his discourse, all three of them unconscious of the interruption.

'Brennus, who captured Rome, was an eagle. The banker who captures a grisette is an eagle of another kind, but one is as shameless as the other. So there is nothing for us to believe in. Drink is the only reality. It makes no odds what your opinions are – whether you're on the side of the skinny fowl, like the Canton d'Uri, or the plump fowl, like the Canton de Glaris – drink. You were talking about the boulevard and the procession and all that. So what of it? There's going to be another revolution. What astounds me is the clumsy means that God employs. He's always having to grease the wheels of events. There's a hitch, the machine isn't working, so quick, let's have a revolution! God's hands are always blackened with that particular grease. If I were he I'd do things more straight-forwardly. I wouldn't be for ever tinkering with the works; I'd keep the human race in order and string the facts together so that they made sense – no ifs and buts, and no miracles. The thing you call "progress" is driven by two motors, men and events. But unfortunately it happens now and then that something exceptional is called for. Whether it's men or events, the run-of-the-mill is not enough; you need geniuses in terms of men, and revolutions in terms of events. Huge accidents are the law, and the natural order of things can't do without them – and when you think of comets you can't help feeling that Heaven itself needs its star performers. God puts up a meteor when you least expect it, like a poster on a wall, or a weird star with an enormous tail attached to it for emphasis. And so Caesar dies. Brutus gives him a dagger-thrust and God sends a comet. Bingo! – And you have the aurora borealis or a revolution or a great man. You have the year '93 in capital letters, Napoleon the star and 1811 at the top of the bill. And a very fine poster it is, midnight blue and studded with tongues of fire. "This remarkable spectacle!" But watch out, you groundlings, because suddenly the whole thing's in ruins, the star and the drama as well. Good God, that's too much – and still it's not enough! These devices, snatched haphazard, they look magnificent but they're really feeble. The fact is Providence is simply playing tricks. What does a revolution prove? – simply that God's at his wits' end. He brings about a coup d'état because there's a break in continuity between the present and the future that He hasn't known how to mend. Which only confirms my theory about the unhappy state of Jehovah's fortunes. When I think of the unease up aloft and here below, the baseness and rascality and misery in Heaven and on earth, extending from the bird that can't find a grain of corn to me that can't find an income of a hundred thousand livres; when I think of human destiny, which is wearing very thin, even the destiny of kings, haunted by the rope like the hanged Prince de Condé; when I think of winter, which is nothing but a rift in the firmament through which the winds break loose, the shreds of cloud over the hilltops in the new blue of the morning – and dew-drops, those false pearls, and frost, that beauty powder, and mankind in disarray and events out of joint, and so many spots on the sun and so many craters in the moon and so much wretchedness everywhere – when I think of all this I can't help feeling that God is not rich. He has the appearance of riches, certainly, but I can feel his embarrassment. He gives us a revolution the way a bankrupt merchant gives a ball. We must not judge any god by appearances. I see a shoddy universe beyond the splendour of the sky. Creation itself is bankrupt, and that's why I'm a malcontent. Today is the fifth of June and it's almost dark; I've been waiting since early morning for the sun to shine. But it hasn't shone yet, and I'll bet you it won't shine all day – an oversight, no doubt, on the part of some underpaid subordinate. Yes, everything is badly managed, nothing fits with anything else, this old world is in a mess and I've joined the opposition. Everything's at odds, and the whole world is exasperating. It's like with children: those that ask don't get, and those that don't need, do. So I'm opting out. Besides, the sight of Laigle de Meaux's bald head afflicts me; it's humiliating to think that I'm the same age as that shiny pate. Well, I may criticize but I don't abuse. The world's what it is. I'm talking without malice, simply to relieve my mind. Be assured, Eternal Father, of my distinguished sentiments. Alas, by all the saints of Olympus and all the gods in Paradise, I was not born to be a Parisian – that is to say, to hover indefinitely, like a shuttlecock bouncing between two rackets, between the lookers-on and the activists. I was born to be a Turk and spend my days watching exquisite girls perform those lubricious oriental dances that are like the dreams of virtuous men; or a well-to-do countryman; or a gentleman of Venice attended by fair ladies; or a German princeling contributing half an infantry soldier to the German Confederation and occupying his spare time with drying his socks on his hedge, that is to say, his frontier. That's what I was really born for. I said a Turk, and I'm not gainsaying it. I don't know why people should be so against the Turks. There was good in Muhammad. The invention of the seraglio with houris and a paradise with odalisques is deserving of our respect. Let us not abuse Muhammadanism, the only creed that includes a hen-roost. I insist on drinking to it. This earth is a great imbecility. And now it seems the fools are going to fight one another, bash one another's heads in, in this month of high summer, when they might be out with a wench in the fields, breathing the scent of new-mown hay. Really people are too stupid. An old broken lantern that I saw the other day in an antique shop put a thought in my mind – it's time to bring light to the human race. And that thought has made me unhappy again. What good does it do to gulp down an oyster or a revolution? Again I'm growing dismal. This hideous old world. We struggle and fall destitute, we prostitute ourselves, we kill each other – and in the end we swallow it all!'

After this prolonged fit of eloquence Grantaire subsided in a fit of coughing, not undeserved.

'Talking about revolution,' said Joly, struggling with his stuffed-up nose, 'it seems that Barius – Marius – is head over heels in love.'

'Does anyone know who with?' asked Laigle.

'No.'

'Marius in love!' cried Grantaire. 'I can imagine Marius in a fog, and he has found himself a mist. He belongs to the tribe of poets, which is as good as saying that he's crazy. Marius and his Marie or Maria or Mariette, whatever she's called, they must be a rum pair of lovers. I can guess what it's like – rarefied ecstasies with kisses all forgotten, chastity on earth and couplings in the infinite. Two sensitive spirits sleeping together amid the stars.'

Grantaire was embarking on his second bottle, and perhaps his second harangue, when a newcomer appeared in the hatchway, a boy less than ten years old, ragged, very small, sallow and pug-faced but bright-eyed, thoroughly unkempt and soaked to the skin, but looking pleased with himself. Without hesitating, although plainly he knew none of them, he addressed Laigle de Meaux.

'Are you Monsieur Bossuet?'

'That's my nickname,' said Laigle. 'What do you want?'

'Well, listen, a tall, fair-haired cove on the boulevard asked me if I knew Mère Hucheloup. "You mean the one in the Rue Chanvrerie, the old man's widow?" I said. "That's right," he said. "I want you to go there and ask for Monsieur Bossuet. You're to give him this message, 'A-B-C.'" I reckon it's a joke someone's playing on you. He gave me ten sous.'

'Joly, lend me ten sous,' said Laigle. 'And you, too, Grantaire.' So the boy got another twenty sous.

'What's your name?' asked Laigle.

'Navet. I'm a pal of Gavroche.'

'You'd better stay with us,' said Laigle.

'And have some breakfast,' said Grantaire.

'I can't. I'm in the procession. I'm the one that shouts, "Down with Polignac!"'

And dragging one foot behind him, which is the most respectful of all salutations, the lad departed.

'That's a specimen of urchin pure and simple,' said Grantaire. 'There are a lot of varieties. There's the lawyer's *gamin*, known as a *saute-ruisseau*, the cook's *gamin*, or *marmiton*, the baker's *gamin*, or *mitron* –' he reeled off a long list, ending with '– royal *gamin*, or *dauphin*, and holy *gamin*, or *bambino*.'

Meanwhile Laigle was considering.

'A-B-C ... Meaning, Lamarque's burial.'

'And I suppose the tall fair-haired cove was Enjolras sending for you,' said Grantaire.

'Are we going?' asked Bossuet.

'It's raining,' said Joly. 'I swore to go through fire, but not water. I don't want to make my cold worse.'

'I'm staying here,' said Grantaire. 'Better a breakfast table than a hearse.'

'Very well, we stay where we are,' said Laigle. 'We might as well have some more to drink. Anyway, we can skip the funeral without skipping the insurrection.'

'I'm all in favour of that,' cried Joly.

'We're going on where 1830 left off,' said Laigle, rubbing his hands. 'The people are thoroughly worked up.'

'I care precious little about your revolution,' said Grantaire. 'I don't abominate this government – the Crown made homely with a cotton cap, the Sceptre ending in an umbrella. Come to think of him, in this weather Louis-Philippe can manifest his royalty in two ways, by waving his sceptre over the people and flourishing his umbrella at the gods.'

The room was dark, with dense clouds smothering the daylight. There was no one in the tavern or in the street, everyone having gone off to witness the happenings.

'It might be midnight,' said Bossuet. 'One can't see a thing. Gibelotte, fetch a light.'

Grantaire was sadly drinking.

'Enjolras despises me,' he murmured. 'He said to himself, "Joly's not well and Grantaire's sure to be drunk. I'll send the boy to Bossuet." If he'd come after me himself I'd have gone with him. To the devil with Enjolras, he can have his funeral.'

The matter being thus decided, the three of them stayed in the tavern. By two o'clock that afternoon their table was covered with empty bottles. Two candles were burning, one in a copper candlestick that was green all over and the other in the neck of a cracked carafe. Grantaire had tempted Joly and Bossuet to drink, and they had done something to restore his spirits.

But by midday Grantaire had gone beyond wine, that moderate source of dreaming. To the serious drinker wine is only an appetizer. In this matter of insobriety there is black as well as white magic, and wine is of the latter kind. Grantaire was an adventurous drinker. The black approach of real drunkenness, far from appalling, allured him. He had deserted the wine-bottle and gone on to the *chope*, the bottomless pit. Having neither opium nor hashish to hand, and wanting to befog his mind, he had had recourse to that terrible mixture of eau-de-vie, stout, and absinthe, which so utterly drugs the spirit. Those three ingredients are a dead weight on the soul, three darknesses in which the butterfly life of the mind is drowned; they create a vapour, tenuous yet with the membranous substance of a bat's wing, in which three furies lurk – Nightmare, Night, and Death, hovering over the slumbering Psyche.

Grantaire was still far from having reached that last stage; he was uproariously gay, and Bossuet and Joly were keeping up with him. They raised their glasses in a series of toasts, and to high-flown speech Grantaire added extravagance of gesture. Seated with dignity astride a chair, with his left hand on his knee, the arm akimbo, and his right hand holding his glass, he solemnly addressed the plump waitress, Matelote:

'Let the doors of the palace be flung wide! Let all men become members of the Académie Française and all have the right to embrace Madame Hucheloup. And let me drink!' Then he added, addressing Madame Hucheloup, 'Antique lady, hallowed by custom, draw near that I may gaze upon you.'

'Matelote and Gibelotte,' cried Joly, 'don't for Heaven's sake give Grantaire anything more to drink. He spends money like water. He has squandered two francs ninety-five centimes in reckless dissipation this morning alone.'

'Who is the person,' Grantaire intoned, 'who without my leave has plucked stars from the sky and set them on this table in the guise of candles?'

Bossuet, although very drunk, had remained calm. Seated on the ledge of the open window, with the rain beating on his back, he was gravely contemplating his friends.

But suddenly tumult broke out behind him, the sound of running feet and the cry of 'To arms!' Looking round he saw a party consisting of Enjolras, with a musket, Gavroche with his pistol, Feuilly with a sabre, Courfeyrac with a sword, Jean Prouvaire with a musketoon, Combeferre with a musket, and Bahorel with a carbine. They were proceeding along the Rue Saint-Denis, past the end of the Rue de la Chanvrerie, followed by an excited crowd.

The Rue de la Chanvrerie was short. Making a trumpet of his hands, Bossuet bellowed, 'Courfeyrac! Courfeyrac! Hoy!'

Courfeyrac heard the call and, seeing who it was, turned and advanced a few paces into the Rue de la Chanvrerie. His 'What do you want?' clashed with Bossuet's 'Where are you going?'

'To build a barricade,' shouted Courfeyrac.

'Why not here? This is a good place.'

'You're right, Laigle,' said Courfeyrac.

Beckoning to the others, he led them into the Rue de la Chanvrerie.

III

Darkness gathers about Grantaire

The place was indeed particularly suitable, with the side entrance from the street rapidly narrowing to the bottleneck constituted by Corinth, the Rue de Mondétour easily blocked on either side and direct, frontal attack impossible from the Rue Saint-Denis. Bossuet drunk had had the clear vision of a Hannibal sober.

Dismay gripped the whole street when the newcomers poured in. Casual loiterers took to their heels. In the twinkling of an eye doors were bolted and windows shuttered from one end to the other and from ground-floor to attic, and an old dame had rigged a mattress across her window as a protection against musket-fire. Only the tavern remained open, for the good reason that the party made straight for it. 'May the saints preserve us!' moaned Mère Hucheloup.

Bossuet had run down to greet Courfeyrac while Joly shouted to him from the window:

'Why haven't you got your umbrella? You'll catch cold like me.'

Within a few minutes twenty iron bars had been wrenched out of the tavern's window-grilles and street cobbles and paving-stones had been torn up over a distance of perhaps a dozen yards. A cart containing three barrels of lime, the property of a lime-merchant named Anceau, had been overturned by Gavroche and Bahorel, and the barrels had been surrounded by piles of paving-stones and flanked by empty wine-casks which Enjolras had brought up from Mère Hucheloup's cellar. Feuilly, with hands more accustomed to decorating the fragile blades of fans, had buttressed the whole with solid heaps of stone, procured no one knew where, and the large timbers used to prop up a near-by housefront had been laid across the casks. By the time Bossuet and Courfeyrac desisted from their labour half the street was blocked with a rampart higher than a man. Nothing can exceed the zeal of the populace when it is a matter of building up by pulling down.

The two waitresses had joined in the work, Gibelotte going to and fro with loads of rubble. Her weariness was equal to any task. She served paving-stones as she might have served bottles of wine, still looking half asleep.

An omnibus drawn by two white horses appeared at the end of the street. Climbing on the barricade, Bossuet ran after it, ordered the driver to pull up and the passengers to get out. After assisting the ladies to descend he dismissed the driver and brought the omnibus back with him, leading the horses. 'No omnibus,' he said, 'is allowed to pass Corinth. *Non licet omnibus adire Corinthum.*'

The horses were unharnessed and t urned loose along the Rue Mondétour, and the omnibus, pushed over on its side, made a useful addition to the barricade.

The distraught Mère Hucheloup had taken refuge on the upper floor, where she sat gazing wild-eyed at these proceedings and muttering about the end of the world. Joly deposited a kiss on her thick red neck and remarked to Grantaire: 'You know, I have always considered a woman's neck a thing of infinite delicacy.'

But Grantaire had now achieved the highest flights of dithyramb. When Matelote came upstairs he grabbed her round the waist and then bellowed with laughter out of the window.

'Matelote is ugly!' he shouted. 'Matelote is a dream of ugliness, a chimera! I will tell you the secret of her birth. A gothic Pygmalion carving cathedral gargoyles fell in love with one of them. He besought the God of Love to bring the stone to life, and that was Matelote. Look at her, everyone! She has hair the colour of lead-oxide, like Titian's mistress, and she's a good wench. I guarantee she'll fight well; there's a hero in every good wench. As for Mère Hucheloup, she's a sturdy old soul. Look at that moustache, in-herited from her husband; a real hussar, she is, and she'll fight too. These two alone will terrify the neighbourhood. Comrades, we're going to throw out the Government and that's the truth, as true as the fact that between margaric acid and formic acid there are fifteen intermediate acids. Not that I care a straw about that. My father always abominated me because I couldn't understand mathematics. The only things I understand are love and liberty. I'm good old Grantaire. Never having had any money I've never got into the way of having it and so I've never missed it; but if I'd been rich, no one else would have been poor. You'd have seen! This would be a far better world if the generous hearts had the fat purses. Think of Jesus Christ with Rothschild's fortune, the good he'd have done! Matelote, come and kiss me. You are sensual and shy. You have cheeks which call for a sister's kiss and lips which call for a lover.'

'Stow it, you wine-cask!' said Courfeyrac.

'I am High Magistrate and Master of Ceremonies!' proclaimed Grantaire.

Enjolras, who was standing on the barricade, musket in hand looked sternly round at him. Enjolras, as we know, was a Spartan and a puritan. He would have died with Leonidas at Thermopylae or massacred the garrison of Drogheda with Cromwell.

'Grantaire,' he called, 'go and sleep your wine off somewhere else. This is a place for intoxication but not for drunkenness. Don't dishonour the barricade.'

The sharp rebuke had a remarkable effect on Grantaire, as though he had received a douche of cold water. Suddenly he was sober. He sat down with his elbows on a table by the window, and looking with great sweetness at Enjolras called back:

'You know I believe in you.'

'Go away.'

'Let me sleep it off here.'

'Go and sleep somewhere else,' said Enjolras.

But Grantaire, still regarding him with troubled, gentle eyes, persisted:

'Let me sleep here, and if need be, die here.'

Enjolras looked scornfully at him.

'Grantaire, you're incapable of believing or thinking or willing or living or dying.'

'You'll see,' said Grantaire gravely. 'You'll see.'

He muttered a few more unintelligible words; then his head fell heavily on the table and – a not uncommon effect of the second stage of inebriety, into which Enjolras had so harshly thrust him – fell instantly asleep.

Efforts to console Mère Hucheloup

Bahorel, delighted with the barricade, exclaimed:

'Now the street's stripped for action. Doesn't it look fine!'

Courfeyrac, while partly demolishing the tavern, was doing his best to comfort the proprietress.

'Mère Hucheloup, weren't you complaining the other day that someone brought a charge against you because Gibelotte shook a rug out of the window?'

'That's true, Monsieur Courfeyrac . . . Saints preserve us, are you going to put that table on your horrible pile as well? . . . It was for the rug and a flower-pot that fell out of the attic window into the street. The Government fined me a hundred francs. Don't you think that is disgraceful?'

'Mère Hucheloup, we will avenge you.'

Mère Hucheloup seemed doubtful of the practical value of this vengeance, in which she resembled the Arab woman who complained to her father that her husband had smacked her face. 'You must pay him back, father – an affront for an affront' . . . 'Which cheek did he smack?' . . . 'The left' . . . The father thereupon smacked her right cheek. 'There you are. You can tell your husband that he chastised my daughter and I have chastised his wife.'

The rain had stopped and new recruits were arriving. Workmen brought in kegs of gunpowder under their overalls, a basket containing bottles of vitriol, some carnival torches and a hamper filled with fairy-lights 'left over from the king's birthday', a festival of fairly recent date, having taken place on 1 May.

These munitions were said to have come from a grocer named Pépin in the Faubourg Saint-Antoine. The single street-lamp in the Rue de la Chanvrerie was smashed, as were the lamps in surrounding streets

Enjolras, Combeferre, and Courfeyrac were directing all operations. A second barricade was going up at the same time, both barricades flanked by the Corinth tavern and set at right angles. The larger of the two blocked the Rue de la Chanvrerie, while the other blocked the Rue Mondétour on the Rue de la Cygne side. This second barricade was very narrow, being constructed only of barrels and paving-stones. They were manned by about fifty workers, some thirty of whom were equipped with muskets, having raided an armourer's shop on the way.

The rebels were an ill-assorted and motley crowd. One man, wearing a short, formal jacket, was armed with a cavalry sabre and two saddle-pistols; another, in his shirtsleeves, wore a billycock hat and had a powder-bag slung round his neck, and a third had made himself a breastplate of nine sheets of packing paper and carried a saddler's bradawl. One man was shouting, 'Let us die to the last man, bayonet in hand!' – as it happened, he had no bayonet. Another, clad in a frock-coat, was equipped with the belt and ammunition-pouch of the Garde Nationale, the latter stamped with the words, 'Public Order'. There were a good many muskets bearing regimental numbers, very few hats, no neckties, a great many bare arms and a few pikes – and their bearers were men of all ages and varieties, from pallid youths to burly, weather-beaten dock-labourers. All were working feverishly while at the same time they discussed their prospects – that help would arrive between two and three in the morning, that they could count on such-and-such a regiment, that the whole of Paris would rise – dire prediction mingled with a kind of bluff joviality. They might have been brothers, although they did not know one another's names. It is the ennobling quality of danger that it brings to light the fraternity of strangers.

A fire had been lighted in the kitchen, and pitchers, spoons, and forks, in short all the metal-ware in the establishment, were being melted down for casting into bullets. Drink was circulating everywhere. Percussion caps and small-shot were scattered amid wine glasses over the tables. In the upstairs room Mère Hucheloup, Matelote, and Gibelotte, variously affected by their state of alarm, the first dazed, the second breathless and the third, at last, wide awake, were tearing up old rags for dressings assisted by three of the rebels, three hairy and bearded stalwarts who worked with uncommon deftness and quite over-awed them.

The tall man whom Courfeyrac, Combeferre, and Enjolras had noticed when, uninvited, he joined their party at the corner of the Rue des Billettes, was doing useful work on the larger barricade. Gavroche was working on the smaller. As for the youth who had called at Courfeyrac's lodging asking for Marius, he had disappeared at about the time when the omnibus was overturned.

Gavroche, radiantly in his element, seemed to have constituted himself overseer. He bustled to and fro, pushing, pulling, laughing, and chattering as though it was his function to keep up everyone's spirits. What spurred him on, no doubt, was his state of homeless poverty; but what lent him wings was sheer delight. He was like a whirlwind, constantly to be seen and always to be heard, filling the air with the sound of his excited voice. His seeming ubiquity acted as a kind of goad; there was no pausing when he was by. The whole working-party felt him on its back. He disconcerted the dawdlers, roused the idlers, stimulated the weary, and exasperated the more thoughtful, amusing some and enraging others, exchanging banter with the students and epithets with the working-men; he was here, there, and everywhere, a gadfly buzzing about the lumbering revolutionary coach.

'Come on now, we want more paving-stones, more barrels, more of everything. Let's have a basket of rubble to stuff up that hole. This barricade's still not big enough, it's got to be higher. Shove everything on it, break up the house if necessary. Hullo, there's a glass-paned door!'

'So what are we going to do with a glass-paned door, my young lummox?' a workman demanded.

'Lummox yourself. A glass-paned door is a very good thing to have on a barricade – easy to attack, but not so easy to get past. Haven't you ever tried stealing apples over a wall with broken glass on top? Nothing like a bit of glass for cutting the soldiers' arms. The trouble is, you've no imagination, you lot.'

But what really worried Gavroche was his hammerless pistol. He went about exclaiming: 'A musket! I must have a musket! Why will no one give me a musket?'

'A musket at your age?' said Combeferre.

'And why not? I had one in 1830, when we kicked out Charles X.'

'When there are enough for all the men we'll start handing them out to the children,' said Enjolras, shrugging his shoulders.

Gavroche turned upon him and said with dignity:

'If you're killed before me I shall take yours.'

'Urchin!' said Enjolras.

'Greenhorn!' said Gavroche.

The sight of a dandified young man straying in bewilderment past the end of the street created a diversion. Gavroche shouted:

'Come and join us, mate! Aren't you ready to do a turn for your poor old country?'

The young man fled.

V

The preparations

The newspapers of the day, which reported that the 'almost unassailable' barricade in the Rue de la Chanvrerie reached the level of the second storey, were in error. The fact is that it was nowhere more than six or seven feet high, and so constructed that the defenders could shelter behind it or peer over it or climb on top of it by means of four piles of superimposed paving stones arranged to form a broad flight of steps. The outer side of the barricade, consisting of paving-stones and barrels reinforced by wooden beams and planks interlaced in the wheels of the cart and the overturned omnibus, had a bristling, unassailable appearance. A gap wide enough for a man to pass through had been left at the end furthest from the tavern to afford a means of exit. The shaft of the omnibus had been set upright and was held in position with ropes. It had a red flag affixed to it which fluttered over the barricade.

The small Mondétour barricade was not visible from that side, being concealed behind the tavern. Between them the two barricades constituted a formidable stronghold. Enjolras and Coufeyrac had not seen fit to barricade the other section of the Rue Mondétour, affording an outlet to Les Halles by way of the Rue des Prêcheurs, no doubt because they wished to preserve a means of communication with the outside world and considered that an attack by way of that tortuous alleyway was unlikely.

With the exception of this outlet, which might be technically termed a *boyau*, or communicating trench, and the narrow gap in the Rue de la Chanvrerie, the area enclosed by the two barricades, with the tavern forming a salient between them, was in the shape of an irregular quadrilateral, sealed on all sides. The distance between the main barricade and the tall houses behind it, facing the street, was about twenty yards, so that it could be said that the barricade was backed on to those houses, all of which were occupied but bolted and shuttered from top to bottom.

All this work was completed without interruption in less than an hour, and without the handful of intrepid defenders catching sight of a bearskin or bayonet. The few citizens who at that stage of the uprising ventured into the Rue Saint-Denis after glancing along the Rue de la Chanvrerie and seeing the barricade, went hurriedly on their way.

When both barricades were completed and the flag had been hoisted, a table was brought out of the tavern and Courfeyrac climbed on to it. Enjolras brought out the square box and Courfeyrac opened it. It was filled with cartridges, and at the sight of these even the stoutest hearts quivered and there was a momentary silence. Courfeyrac, smiling, proceeded to pass them out.

Every man was issued with thirty cartridges. Those who had brought powder with them set about making more, using the bullets that were being cast in the tavern. As for the barrel of powder, this was placed handy to the door and kept in reserve.

The roll of drums calling the forces of law and order to arms was sounding throughout Paris, but by now it had become a monotonous background noise to which no one paid any attention. It rose and fell, drawing nearer and receding, with a dismal regularity.

Together and without haste, with a solemn gravity, they charged muskets and carbines. Enjolras posted three sentinels outside the stronghold, in the Rue de la Chanvrerie, the Rue des Prêcheurs, and the Rue de la Petite-Truanderie. Then, with the work done, the weapons loaded and the orders given, alone in those gloomy, narrow streets where now there were no strollers, surrounded by silent houses in which there was no stir of human life, plunged in the gathering shadows of the dusk, amid a silence in which the approach of tragic and terrible events could be felt, isolated, armed, resolute and calm, they waited.

VI
Waiting

What did they do during those hours of waiting? We must tell of this, since this, too, is history.

While the men were busy making cartridges and the women busy with their bandages, while the lead for musket-balls was bubbling in a large cooking-pot on the stove, while armed look-outs kept guard on the barricades and Enjolras, whom nothing could distract, inspected his dispositions, Combeferre, Courfeyrac, Jean Prouvaire,

Feuilly, Bossuet, Joly, Bahorel, and a few others gathered together as though this were the most peaceful of student occasions, and, seated within a few feet of the defences they had built, with their loaded weapons leaning against their chairs, in a corner of the tavern which they had transformed into a fortress, these gallant young men, brothers in this supreme moment of their lives, recited love-poems.

Do you recall how life was kind
When youth and hope still filled our breast,
And we'd no other thought in mind
Than to be lovers and well-dressed?

When your age added in with mine
Made forty by our reckoning;
And, paupers, we did not repine,
For every winter's day was spring.

Brave days of modesty and pride,
When Paris was a lover's feast!
I brought you flowers at Eastertide,
And pricked my finger on your breast.

And men's eyes watched you with desire
When in the crowded streets we strolled.
Your beauty was a living fire
That had no thought of growing old;

No thought of strife and angry men,
Heads bowed beneath the tyrant's rod . . .
When first I kissed you, it was then,
Ah, then, thatI believed in God . . .

The time and place, the youthful recollections, the first stars showing in the sky, the funereal quiet of those deserted streets and the inexorable approach of desperate adventure, all this lent a touching pathos to the verses, and there were many of them, recited low-voiced in the dusk by Jean Prouvaire, who, as we know, was a poet.

Meanwhile, a fairy-light had been set on the small barricade, and on the larger one a wax torch of the kind that one sees on Mardi-Gras preceding carriages bearing masked revellers on their way to the ball. These torches, we may recall, had come from the Faubourg Saint-Antoine. The torch had been placed in a kind of enclosure made of paving-stones, which sheltered it on three sides from the wind, but left the fourth side open so that its light fell on the red flag. The street and the barricade remained in darkness, with nothing visible except that flag, lighted as though by a dark lantern, the rays of which lent to the crimson of the flag an ominous purple tinge.

The recruit from the Rue des Billettes

Night fell, but nothing happened. Only a confused, distant murmur was to be heard, broken occasionally by bursts of musket-fire, but these were rare, meagre, and remote. The prolonged pause was a sign that the Government was taking its time and assembling its forces. Those fifty men were awaiting the onslaught of sixty thousand.

Enjolras was seized with the impatience that afflicts strong characters on the threshold of great events. He went to look for Gavroche, who was now making cartridges in the downstairs room by the uncertain light of two candles set from precaution on the bar-counter because of the powder scattered over the tables. Their light was not visible from outside, and the rebels had also been at pains to ensure that there was no light on the upper floors.

Gavroche was very much preoccupied at that moment, but not precisely with cartridges. The man who had joined them in the Rue des Billettes had come into the downstairs room and seated himself at a table in the darkest corner. He had been issued with a large-bore musket, which was now propped between his knees. Until that moment Gavroche, his attention distracted by a thousand fascinating matters, had not so much as looked at him. He did so automatically when he entered the room, admiring the musket; but then, as the man sat down, he got to his feet. Anyone who had been watching the man until that moment might have noticed that he was observing everything around him, everything to do with the barricades and the rebel band, with a singular intentness; but from the moment when he entered the room he seemed to withdraw into himself and to take no further interest in what was going on. Gavroche, drawing nearer, walked round the detached and brooding figure with extreme caution, going on tiptoe like someone anxious not to awaken a sleeper. At the same time a series of expressions passed over his youthful countenance that was at once so impudent and so eager, so volatile and so profound, so gay and so heartrending, a series of grimaces like those of an aged man communing with himself – 'Rubbish! . . . It's not possible . . . I'm seeing things. I'm dreaming . . . Could it possibly be . . .? No, it can't be!' And Gavroche, rocking on his feet with his fists clenched in his pockets, head and neck wagging like the neck of a bird, expressed in an exaggerated pout all the sagacity of his lower lip. He was at once astounded, sceptical, convinced, and amazed; he had the look of a Chief Eunuch at the slave-market discovering a Venus among the offerings, or an art-lover coming upon a Raphael in a pile of discarded canvases. Every faculty was at work, the instinct that scents and the wits that contrive. Clearly something tremendous had happened to Gavroche.

And it was at this moment that Enjolras came up to him.

'You're small enough,' Enjolras said. 'You won't be noticed. I want you to slip out along the housefronts, out into the streets, and come back and tell me what's going on.'

Gavroche flung back his head.

'So we're good for something after all, us little 'uns. Well, that's fine. I'll do it. You trust the little 'uns, guv'nor, but keep an eye on the big 'uns. For instance, that one there.' He had lowered his voice as he nodded towards the man from the Rue des Billettes.

'What about him?'

'He's a police spy, a copper's nark.'

'You're sure?'

'He picked me up less than a fortnight ago by the Pont Royal, where I was having a stroll.'

Enjolras hurriedly left him and said a word in the ear of a dock-labourer who happened to be near. The man left the room and returned almost instantly with three others. The four men, four burly stevedores, grouped themselves unobtrusively round the table at which the man from the Rue des Billettes was seated, evidently ready to fling themselves upon him. Enjolras then went up to him and asked:

'Who are you?'

The abrupt question caused the man to start. Looking hard into Enjolras's eyes, he seemed to discern exactly what was in his mind, and smiling the most disdainful, unabashed, and resolute of smiles he answered:

'I see how it is . . . Yes, I am.'

'You're a police informer?'

937

'I'm a representative of the law.'

'And your name?'

'Javert.'

Enjolras nodded to the four men. Before Javert had time to move he was seized, overpowered, bound, and searched. A small round card was found on him, enclosed between two pieces of glass and bearing on one side the words 'Surveillance et Vigilance', and on the other the following particulars: 'Javert, Inspector of Police, aged 52' signed by the Prefect of Police of the time, M. Henri-Joseph Gisquet.

He also had a watch on him and a purse containing a few gold pieces. These were restored to him. But at the bottom of his watch-pocket was a scrap of paper in an envelope on which were his orders, written in the Prefect's own hand:

'Having fulfilled his political mission Inspector Javert will endeavour to confirm the truth of the report that the miscreants have places of resort on the right bank of the Seine, near the Pont d'Iéna.'

After being searched Javert was stood upright with his hands tied behind his back and bound to the wooden pillar in the centre of the room that had given the tavern its original name.

Gavroche, who had intently followed the proceedings, nodding his head in approval, now addressed Javert:

'So the mouse has caught the cat!'

Everything had happened so swiftly that it was all over before the news became known. Javert had not uttered a sound. Hearing what had happened, Courfeyrac, Bossuet, Joly, Combeferre, and some of the men on the barricades came trooping in. Javert, so securely lashed to the post that he could not move, confronted them with the cool serenity of a man who has never in his life told a lie.

'He's a police spy,' said Enjolras. And to Javert he said: 'You will be shot two minutes before the barricade falls.'

'Why not now?' Javert inquired with the utmost composure.

'We don't want to waste ammunition.'

'You could use a knife.'

'Policeman,' said the high-minded Enjolras, 'we are judges, not murderers.' He gestured to Gavroche. 'You! Get started. Do what I told you.'

'I'm off,' said Gavroche.

But at the door he paused.

'Anyway, let me have his musket. I'm leaving you the musician, but I'd like to have his trumpet.'

He made them a military salute and slipped happily through the gap in the large barricade.

VIII

Questions regarding a man called Le Cabuc

The tragic picture we are printing would be incomplete, the reader would not see in their true proportions those momentous hours of civic travail and revolutionary birth wherein confusion was mingled with noble striving, were we to omit from this summary account the incident of epic and savage horror which took place almost immediately after the departure of Gavroche.

Crowds gather and then, as we know, grow like rolling snow balls, attracting violent men who do not ask each other where they come from. Among those who joined the contingent led by Enjolras and the others, there was a man in worn labourer's clothes whose wild shouts and gestures were those of an uncontrolled drunkard. This man, who went by the name of Le Cabuc, but who was in reality quite unknown to the people who pretended to recognize him and who was either very drunk or pretending to be, had seated himself with several others at a table which they had dragged out of the tavern. While encouraging his companions to drink he seemed to be surveying the house at the back of the barricade, a five-storey house, looking along the street to the Rue Saint-Denis. Suddenly he cried:

'You know what, comrades? That house is the place to shoot from. With marksmen at all the windows, devil a soul could come along the street!'

'But the house is shut.'

'We can knock, can't we?'

'They won't open.'

'Then we'll break down the door.'

The door had a massive knocker. Le Cabuc went and hammered on it, without result. He knocked a second and a third time, but there was still no response.

'Is anyone in?' shouted Le Cabuc.

Silence.

So then he picked up a musket and hammered on the door with

the butt. It was an old-fashioned arched doorway, low and narrow, the door made solidly of oak, lined with sheet metal and reinforced with iron bands, a real fortress door. The blows of the musket-butt shook the house but left the door unshattered. However, they had evidently alarmed the inmates, because eventually a light showed and a small window on the third floor opened to disclose the grey head of a man who was presumably the doorkeeper.

'Messieurs,' he asked, 'What do you want?'

'Open the door!' shouted Le Cabuc.

'I'm not allowed to, Monsieur.'

'Do it all the same.'

'Out of the question.'

Le Cabuc levelled his musket, aiming at the man's head; but since he was standing in the street, and it was very dark, the door-keeper did not see him.

'Are you going to open, or aren't you?'

'No, Monsieur.'

'You refuse?'

'I do, my good –'

The sentence was cut short by the report of the musket. The ball took the old man under the chin and travelled through his neck, severing the jugular vein. He sank forward without a sound, and the candle he had been holding fell from his hand and went out. Nothing was now to be seen but a motionless head resting on the window-ledge and a rising wisp of smoke.

'There you are!' said Le Cabuc, grounding his musket on the cobbles.

Scarcely had he uttered the words than a hand fell on his shoulder, gripping it as tightly as an eagle's talon, and a voice said:

'On your knees!'

He turned to confront the white, cold face of Enjolras, who had a pistol in his other hand. He had been brought out at the sound of the shot.

'On your knees,' he repeated; and with an imperious gesture the slender youth of twenty, compelling the muscular broad-shouldered dock-worker to bend like a reed before him, forced him to kneel in the mud. Le Cabuc tried to resist, but seemed to be in the grip of a superhuman power. Enjolras, with his girlish face, his bare neck and untidy hair, had at that moment something of the look of an antique god. The dilated nostrils and glaring eyes conferred upon his implacable Greek countenance that expression of chaste and righteous anger which in the ancient world was the face of justice.

The men on the barricades had come hurrying to the scene and now stood silently a short distance away, finding it impossible to utter any word of protest at what was about to take place.

Le Cabuc, wholly subdued, made no further attempt to struggle. He was now trembling in every limb. Enjolras released his hold on him and got out his watch.

'Pull yourself together,' he said. 'Pray or ponder. You have one minute.'

'Mercy!' the murderer gasped, and then, with his head bowed, fell to muttering inarticulate profanities.

Enjolras did not take his eyes off his watch, and when the minute had passed he returned it to his pocket. He gripped Le Cabuc by the hair, and as the man knelt screaming pressed the muzzle of the pistol to his ear. Many of those hot-blooded men, who had so lightly engaged upon a desperate enterprise, turned away their heads.

The shot rang out, the murderer fell face down on the cobbles, and Enjolras, straightening, gazed sternly and assuredly about him. He thrust aside the body with his foot and said:

'Get rid of that.'

Three men picked it up, still twitching in its last death-throes, and flung it over the smaller barricade into the Rue Mondétour.

Enjolras stayed deep in thought, and who shall say what fearful shadows were massing behind his outward calm. Suddenly he raised his voice, and there was silence.

'Citizens,' said Enjolras, 'what that man did was abominable and what I have done is horrible. He killed, and that is why I killed. I was obliged to do it, for this rebellion must be disciplined. Murder is an even greater crime here than elsewhere. We are under the eyes of the revolution, priests of the republic, the tokens of a cause, and our actions must not be subject to calumny. Therefore I judged this man and condemned him to death. But at the same time, compelled to do what I did but also abhorring it, I have passed judgement on myself, and you will learn in due course what my sentence is.'

A quiver ran through his audience.

'We will share your fate,' cried Combeferre.

'It may be,' said Enjolras. 'I have more to say. In executing that man I bowed to necessity. But the necessity was a monster conceived in the old world, and its name is fatality. By the law of progress, this fatality must give way to fraternity. This is a bad moment for speaking the word "love"; nevertheless I do speak it, and glory in it. Love is the future. I have had resort to death, but I hate it. In the future, citizens, there will be no darkness or lightnings, no savage ignorance or blood-feuds. Since there will be no Satan there will be no Michael. No man will kill his fellow, the earth will be radiant, mankind will be moved by love. That time will come, citizens, the time of peace, light, and harmony, of joy and life. It will come. And the purpose of our death is to hasten its coming.'

Enjolras fell silent. His virgin lips closed, and he remained for some moments standing like a statue on the spot where he had shed blood, while his steadfast gaze subdued the murmur of voices about him. Jean Prouvaire and Combeferre silently clasped hands and, standing together at the corner of the barricade, gazed in admiration mingled with compassion at the stern-faced young man who was at once priest and executioner, shining like a crystal but unshakeable as a rock.

We may say here that when, after the business was over, the bodies were taken to the morgue and searched, a police-card was found on Le Cabuc. In 1848 the author of this work saw the special report on this episode delivered to the Prefect of Police in 1832.

It may be added that, according to a police surmise which seems to have been not without substance, Le Cabuc was Claquesous. The fact is that after the death of Le Cabuc nothing more was heard of Claquesous. He vanished without trace, seeming to have faded into invisibility. His life had been lived in shadow, his end was total darkness.

The band of rebels was still oppressed by that tragic trial, so rapidly conducted and so summarily concluded, when Courfeyrac caught sight of the slim young man who that morning had come to his lodging in search of Marius. This youth, who had a bold and heedless air, had come to rejoin them.

BOOK THIRTEEN

MARIUS ENTERS THE DARKNESS

I

From the Rue Plumet to the Quartier Saint-Denis

THE VOICE summoning Marius in the dusk to join the barricade on the Rue de la Chanvrerie, had sounded to him like the voice of Fate. He wished to die and here was the means; his knock on the door of the tomb was answered by a hand tendering him the key. There is a fascination in the melancholy inducements that darkness offers to the despairing. Marius parted the bars of the gate, as he had done so many times before, and leaving the garden behind him said, 'So be it!' Half-crazed with grief, with nothing clear or settled in his mind, unable to face the realities of life after those two intoxicated months of youthfulness and love, overwhelmed by the bewilderment of despair, his only thought was to put a rapid end to his misery. He set out at a brisk walk. As it happened, he was already armed, having Javert's pistols on him. The youth he thought he had discerned in the shadows had vanished.

He went from the Rue Plumet to the boulevard, crossed the Esplanade, the Pont des Invalides, the Champs-Élysées, and the Place Louis XV (both before and after this the Place de la Concorde) and so came to the Rue de Rivoli. The shops were open and women were shopping under the lights of the arcade or eating ices at the Café Laiter or cakes at the English pastry-cook's. But now and then a post-chaise set off at a gallop from the Hôtel des Princes or the Hôtel Meurice.

Marius went by way of the Passage Delorme into the Rue Saint-Honoré. Here the shops were shut. Shopkeepers were talking in their half-closed doorways, people were passing along the pavements, the street-lamps were lit and the houses were lighted as usual above the first floor. There was a detachment of cavalry in the Place du Palais-Royal.

But as he left the Palais-Royal behind him, following the Rue Saint-Honoré, Marius noted that there were fewer lighted windows. Doors were locked and there were no gossipers in the doorways. The street grew darker and the crowd more dense: for the number of people in the street had become a crowd – a crowd in which no one spoke, but from which a deep, heavy murmur arose. Around the Fontaine de l'Arbre-Sec there were 'rallying points', motionless groups of men detached from the ebb and flow of passers-by like rocks in a stream.

By the time it reached the end of the Rue des Prouvaires the crowd could move no more. It had become a solid, almost impenetrable mass of people talking in undertones. Scarcely any black coats and round hats were to be seen here. There were smocks and tradesmen's jackets, caps, sallow faces and bare heads of unkempt hair. This multitude swayed confusedly in the night mist, and its low-voiced muttering resembled a shudder. Although no man was walking there was nevertheless a sound of feet stamping in the mud. Beyond this concentration, in the Rue de Roule, the Rue des Prouvaires, and the further length of the Rue Saint-Honoré, not a lighted window was to be seen. The single lines of street-lamps were seen to dwindle along the street. The lamps in those days were like red stars slung on ropes which cast a pool of light like a great spider on the pavement. But these streets were not empty. Stacked muskets were to be seen in them, bayonets moving on sentry-go and bivouacking troops. No sightseer penetrated as far as this. All traffic had stopped. Here the crowd ended and the army began.

Marius was imbued with the pertinacity of a man who has ceased to hope. He had been summoned and he must go. He contrived to pass through the crowd and the army bivouacs, dodging sentries and patrols. By means of a detour he reached the Rue de Bethisy and made for Les Halles. At the end of the Rue des Bourdonnais the street-lamps ceased. After passing first through the zone of the crowd and then through the military zone he found himself in a zone that to him seemed terrible – not a civilian or a soldier, not a light; a place of solitary darkness. A chill assailed him. To turn into any street was like entering a cellar. But he continued on his way.

There was a sound of running footsteps passing close by him, whether those of a man or woman, of one person or more than one, he could not tell. They echoed and died away.

By twists and turns he arrived at an alley which he thought must be the Rue de la Poterie. Halfway along it he bumped into something which he found to be an overturned cask. His feet discovered puddles. There were potholes in the street and piles of loose paving stones. A barricade had been started and then abandoned. Climbing over this obstacle, he moved further down the street, feeling his way along the housefronts. A little further on he saw a blur of white which, when he drew nearer to it, turned out to be the two white horses unharnessed from the omnibus that morning by Bossuet. After straying all day about the streets they had come to rest in this place with the tired patience of animals that no more understand the ways of men than men understand the ways of Providence.

Marius went past them. As he entered a street which he thought must be the Rue du Contrat-Social there was the report of a musket, and the ball, fired at random from Heaven knew where, pierced a copper shaving bowl just above his head, hanging outside a barber's shop. That punctured shaving bowl was still to be seen in the Rue du Contrat-Social, near the pillars of Les Halles, in 1846.

It was at least a sign of life, but nothing else happened. Marius's journey was like a descent down a pitch-dark stairway. Nevertheless, he went on.

II
Paris – a bird's-eye view

Anyone capable at that moment of soaring over Paris on the wings of a bat or an owl would have had a dismal spectacle beneath his eyes.

The ancient quarter of Les Halles, intersected by the Rues Saint-Denis, Saint-Martin, and countless alleyways, which is like a town within a town, and which the insurgents had made their base and arms depot, would have looked to him like a huge patch of darkness in the centre of Paris, a black gulf. Owing to the breaking of street-lamps and the shuttering of windows, no light was to be seen there, nor was any sound of life or movement to be heard. The invisible guardian of the uprising, that is to say, darkness, was everywhere on duty and everywhere kept order. This is the necessary tactic of insurrection, to veil smallness of numbers in a vast obscurity and enhance the stature of every combatant by the possibilities which obscurity affords. At nightfall every window where a light showed had been visited by a musket-ball; the light had gone out, and sometimes the occupant had been killed. Now nothing stirred; nothing dwelt in the houses but fear, mourning, and amazement; nothing in the streets but a kind of awestruck horror. Not even the long rows of storeyed windows were visible, nor the jagged outline of house-tops and chimneys, nor the dim sheen of lights reflected on wet, muddy pavements. The eye looking from a height into that mass of shadow might have discerned here and there at remote intervals faint gleams of light throwing into relief the irregular shapes of singular constructions, like lanterns moving amid ruins; these were the barricades. The rest was a pool of utter darkness, misty and oppressive, above which rose the still, brooding outlines of the Tour Saint-Jacques, the Église Saint-Merry, and two or three others of those great edifices which man makes into giants and night turns into ghosts.

All round that silent, ominous labyrinth, in those quarters where the Paris traffic had not been brought to a standstill and where a few street-lamps still shone, the aerial observer might have perceived the metallic glitter of drawn swords and bayonets, the rumbling wheels of artillery and the silent gathering of battalions growing in numbers from one minute to the next – a formidable girdle slowly tightening around the uprising.

The besieged quarter was nothing but a sort of monstrous cavern, everything within it seeming motionless or slumbering, and the roads to it were all plunged in darkness, as we have seen.

A menacing darkness filled with traps and pitfalls, sinister to approach and more sinister still to penetrate, where those who entered trembled at the thought of those waiting to receive them, and those who waited dreaded those who must come. Invisible warriors crouched at every corner, deadly ambushes hidden in the depths of night. All uncertainty was ended. No other greeting was to be expected than the flash of a musket, no other encounter than the sudden, swift emergence of death; and no one to say whence or when it would come, only that it was certain. In that place designated for combat, the two sides were soon to come cautiously to grips – Government and insurrection, the Garde Nationale and the groups of workers, the bourgeoisie and the rebels. Each was under the same necessity, to end up dead or victorious. There was no other way. So far had things gone, so heavy was the darkness, that the most timid was filled with resolution and the boldest with fear. And for the rest, fury and fervour were equal on either side. On the one hand, to go forward was to die, but no man thought of going back; on the other, to stand fast was to die, but no man thought of flight.

It was necessary that on the next day the matter should be settled, that one side or the other should triumph, that the insurrection should become revolution or else a damp squib. The Government understood this as did the rebels; the humblest citizen knew it. Hence the feeling of anguish that pervaded the impenetrable darkness of that place where all was to be decided; the heightened tension pervading the silence from which so soon a disastrous clamour was to arise. Only one sound was to be heard, awesome as a death-rattle, sinister as a malediction, the tocsin of Saint-Merry. Nothing could have chilled the blood so surely as did the tolling of that desperate bell crying its lament into the night.

As often happens, Nature seemed to have matched herself to the undertakings of men. Nothing conflicted with the fateful harmonies of that set stage. No stars showed, and the scene was overhung with heavy cloud. A black sky brooded over the dead streets like a vast pall draping a vast tomb.

And while a battle that was still political was preparing in that place that had witnessed so many revolutionary acts; while the young people, the secret societies, and the schools, inspired by principle, and the middle-class inspired by self-interest, were advancing upon each other to clash and grapple; while each side hastened and sought the moment of crisis and decision – remote from all this and from the battlefield itself, in the deepest recesses of that ancient Paris of the poor and destitute which lay hidden beneath the brilliance of the rich and fortunate Paris, there was to be heard the sombre growling of the masses: a fearful and awe-inspiring voice in which were mingled the snarl of animals and the words of God, a terror to the faint-hearted and a warning to the wise, coming at once from the depths, like the roaring of a lion, and from the heights like the voice of thunder.

III

The extreme edge

Marius had reached Les Halles. Here everything was even quieter, darker and more immobile than in the surrounding streets, as though the icy peace of the tomb had risen up from the earth to spread beneath the sky. Nevertheless a glare was visible in the darkness, lighting the roofs of the houses separating the Rue de la Chanvrerie from Saint-Eustache. It was the torch that stood burning on the Corinth barricade. Marius, making his way towards it, was guided to the Marché-aux-Poirées, whence he could see the dark mouth of the Rue des Prêcheurs. He entered it, without being seen by the rebel sentry, who was at the far end. Feeling himself to be near his destination, he walked on with extreme caution and thus came to the turning into the short stretch of the Mondétour alleyway which, as we know, Enjolras had kept open as the channel of communication with the outside world. Reaching the corner, he peered into the alleyway past the house on his left.

Himself hidden in the shadow of the house, he saw, reflected on the cobbles, a faint glow coming from a small flickering light on top of what looked like a crudely constructed wall adjoining the tavern building, of which he could see a part; and, crouched in front of it, a number of men with muskets on their knees. This, within twenty yards of him, was the interior of the stronghold. The houses on his right hid the rest of the tavern, the larger barricade and the flag.

Marius had now only a step to go; whereupon the unhappy young man seated himself on a kerb-stone, folded his arms and fell to thinking about his father.

He was brooding on the heroic Colonel Pontmercy, that proud soldier who under the Republic had defended the frontiers of France and under Napoleon had reached the borders of Asia; who had seen Genoa, Alexandria, Milan, Turin, Madrid, Vienna, Dresden, Berlin, and Moscow, leaving on all the victorious battlefields of Europe drops of the same blood that flowed in Marius's veins; whose hair had turned prematurely white in a life of discipline and command; who lived with his sword-belt buckled, epaulettes falling over his breast, cockade blackened by powder, forehead creased by the weight of his helmet, in barrack-rooms, in encampments, under canvas, and in ambulances, and who after twenty years had returned from the wars with a scarred cheek and a smiling countenance, simple, tranquil, admirable, pure-hearted as a child, having done all that he could for France and nothing against her.

Marius said to himself that now it was his turn, his hour had sounded; that following his father he too must be bold and resolute, braving the musket-balls, baring his breast to the bayonets, shedding his blood seeking out the enemy and finding death if need be; that he too was going to war – but that his battlefield would be the streets, and it was a civil war that he would be fighting. It was civil war that opened like an abyss before him; it was into that abyss that he must fall.

And thinking of this he shivered.

He thought of his father's sword, which his grandfather had sold to a secondhand dealer and which he himself so sorely regretted. He told himself that it had done well, that chaste and gallant sword, to escape from him and take indignant refuge in oblivion; that it had taken flight because it had good sense and knew what the future held; that it had had a presentiment of this uprising, this war of gutters and paving-stones – volleys fired from loopholes in cellars, stabs in the back. Having known Marengo and Friedland it had no wish to visit the Rue de la Chanvrerie, and having served honourably with the father it was not minded to degrade itself with the son. Marius said to himself that if he had it with him now, if he had retrieved it from his dying parent's bedside to bear it with him into this dark brawl between Frenchmen and Frenchmen, the sword would have burnt his hand, flaming like a weapon of supernatural wrath. He said to himself that he was glad it was not there, that it was just and right that it had vanished, that the true guardian of his father's fame had been his grandfather, that it was better that the sword should have been auctioned, sold to a huckster, tossed on the scrap-heap rather than be buried in their country's flank . . . And Marius wept bitterly.

His plight was terrible, but what else could he do? To live without Cosette was impossible. Since she had left him, he could only die. Had he not sworn to her that he would die? She had left him knowing this; therefore his death must be agreeable to her. In any case, it was clear that she no longer loved him, since she had gone off in this fashion without a word of warning, without a letter, although she knew his address. Why go on living, what was there left for him to live for? And then, how could he now draw back, having come so far? To sniff at danger and then run away, peep into the barricade and go off trembling – 'I've had a look and that's enough. That's all I want. It's civil war, and I'm clearing out . . .!' To desert the friends who were awaiting him, who perhaps had need of him – a handful against an army! To fail in all things, love, friendship, and his pledged word, making patriotic sentiment the excuse for cowardice! This was unthinkable. If his father's ghost had seen him retreat he would have thrashed him with the flat of his sword crying, 'Coward, go forward!'

Marius had been sitting with his head bowed, while the argument surged this way and that. But suddenly he straightened as a splendid thought occurred to stiffen his resolve. There is a lucidity inspired by the nearness of the grave: to be close to death is to see clearly. The course on which he was perhaps on the verge of embarking seemed to him no longer shameful but splendid. The thought of street warfare was by some process of spiritual alchemy suddenly transformed in his mind. The questions he had been asking came crowding back, but they no longer troubled him. He had an answer to each one.

Why should his father be angry? Were there no circumstances in which rebellion acquired the dignity of a duty? How could it be degrading for the son of Colonel Pontmercy to play a part in the conflict that had now begun? This was not Montmirail or Champaubert but another matter entirely. It was a question, not of sacred soil but of a noble idea. The country might lament, but humanity would applaud. And indeed, would the country lament? France might bleed, but the cause of liberty would prosper, and in the triumph of liberty France would forget her wounds. And furthermore, looking at the matter still more broadly, why should there be any talk of civil war?

Civil war . . . What did the words mean? Was there any such thing as 'foreign war'? Was not all warfare between men warfare between brothers? Wars could only be defined by their aims. There were no 'foreign' or 'civil' wars, only wars that were just or unjust. Until the great universal concord could be arrived at, warfare, at least when it was the battle between the urgent future and the dragging past, might be unavoidable. How could such a war be condemned? War is not shameful, nor the sword-thrust a stab in the back, except when it serves to kill right and progress, reason, civilization, and truth. When this is war's purpose it makes no difference whether it is civil or foreign war – it is a crime. Outside the sacred cause of justice, what grounds has one kind of war for denigrating another? By what right does the sword of Washington despise the pike of Camille Desmoulins? Which is the greater – Leonidas fighting the foreign enemy or Timoleon slaying the tyrant who was his brother? One was a defender, the other a liberator. Are we to condemn every resort to arms that takes place within the citadel, without concerning ourselves with its aim? Then we must condemn Brutus and Coligny. Fighting in the undergrowth or in the streets – why not? That was the warfare of Ambiorix, of Artavelde, of Marnix, of Pelage. But Ambiorix fought against Rome,

Artavelde fought against France, Marnix against Spain, and Pelage against the Moors – all fought against foreigners. But monarchy is also a foreigner; oppression and divine right, both are foreigners. Despotism violates the moral frontier just as foreign invasion violates the geographical frontier. To drive out the tyrant or to drive out the English is in either case the reconquest of one's own territory. The moment comes when protest is not enough; reason must give way to action, and force ensure what thought has conceived. The Encyclopedia enlightens minds, but 10 August sets them in motion. After Aeschylus came Thrasybulus, and after Diderot came Danton. Multitudes are inclined to accept the existing master; their very mass creates apathy. Crowds lapse readily into compliance. They have to be stirred and driven, shaken by the very benefits conferred on them by deliverance, their eyes dazzled by truth, enlightenment forced on them with blows. They need to be a little shocked by their own salvation, and this it is that arouses them. Hence the necessity of fanfares and of wars. Great fighters have to arise, to stir nations with their audacity and shake loose the pitiful humanity buried in the shadow of Divine Right and Caesarian glory, of force and fanaticism, irresponsible power and absolute monarchy – the foolish mass that gazes open-mouthed at those dark and tawdry splendours. Down with the tyrant? But to whom are you referring? To Louis-Philippe? He was no more a tyrant than Louis XVI. Both were what history is accustomed to term 'good kings'. But principles cannot be fragmented: truth is the whole, and it does not admit of compromises. There can be no concessions, no indulgence for the man who must be removed. Louis XVI was a king by divine right. Louis-Philippe became king because he was a Bourbon: both in some degree represent the seizure of rights, and this world-wide usurpation must be contested. It is necessary, since France is for ever that which is beginning. When the ruler falls in France, he falls everywhere. In brief, what cause can be more just, what war more righteous, than that which restores social truth, restores liberty to its throne, restores their proper sovereignty to all men, displaces the purple from the head of France, reasserts the fullness of reason and equity, eliminates the seeds of antagonism by allowing each man to be himself, abolishes the hindrance to universal concord represented by monarcy and makes all mankind equal before the law? It is wars such as these that build peace. A vast citadel of prejudice, superstition, lies, exactions, abuses, violence and iniquity still looms over the world, enclosed within towers of hatred. It must be overthrown, its monstrous bulk reduced to rubble. To win Austerlitz is glorious; but to seize the Bastille is immense.

Every man has discovered in himself that the human spirit – and this is the miracle of its complex, ubiquitous unity – has the strange gift of being able to reason almost coldly in the most desperate extremity, so that in desolation and utmost despair, in the travail of our darkest meditation, we may still view our situation with detachment and weigh arguments. Logic enters our state of turmoil and the thread of syllogism runs unbroken through the tempest of our thought. This was Marius's state of mind.

Thinking these things, utterly downcast but resolute, still hesitant, and indeed trembling at the thought of what he was about to do, his gaze travelled over the interior of the barricade. The rebels were talking in low voices, not moving, and one could feel the unreal silence which denotes the last stage of expectancy. Above their heads, at a third-floor window, Marius could make out the form of what seemed to be a spectator or a witness, who was listening with a singular attention. It was the door-keeper killed by Le Cabuc. From below, by the light of the torch on the barricade, the figure was only dimly visible. Nothing could have been more eerie, in that flickering, uncertain light, than that head of tangled hair, the livid, motionless, astonished face, wide-eyed and open-mouthed, leaning over the street in a posture of intent curiosity. It was as though the man who was dead was contemplating those about to die. A long trail of blood from the head flowed in streaks down the wall as far as the first floor, where it stopped.

BOOK FOURTEEN

THE GREATNESS OF DESPAIR

I

The flag – Act One

STILL NOTHING had happened. The clock of Saint-Merry had struck ten, and Enjolras and Combeferre had seated themselves with their carbines near the narrow breach in the main barricade. They were not talking; both were listening with ears strained to catch the least, most distant sound of marching feet.

Suddenly the brooding silence was broken by the sound of a gay young voice, seeming to come from the Rue Saint-Denis, raised in an improvised ditty to the tune of '*Au clair de la lune*', and ending with a cockcrow:

> Save me if I swoon, mates,
> That old man, Bugeaud,
> He's not on the moon, mates,
> Though he's pretty slow.
> Cock-tails* on their caps, mates,
> Uniforms of blue,
> The troops are in our laps, mates –
> Cock-a-doodle-do!

'It's Gavroche,' said Enjolras, and he and Combeferre shook hands.

Running footsteps echoed down the empty street, a figure nimble as a circus clown scrambled over the omnibus and Gavroche, very much out of breath, leapt down from the barricade.

'They're coming! Where's my musket?'

An electric stir ran though the defenders and there was a sound of hands snatching up weapons.

'Would you like my carbine?' Enjolras asked.

'No, I want the big musket,' said Gavroche. He meant Javert's musket.

Two of the sentries had fallen back and re-entered the barricade almost at the same moment as Gavroche. They were the ones who had been posted at the end of the street and in the Petite-Truanderie.

---

*The Gallic cock was the emblem of the July Monarchy.

The sentry in the Rue des Prêcheurs was still at his post, which indicated that so far nothing was approaching from the direction of the bridges and the markets. The Rue de la Chanvrerie, of which only a short stretch was dimly visible in the light falling on the flag, looked to the defenders like a cavernous doorway opening into the mist.

Every man took up his action station. Forty-three defenders, among them Enjolras, Combeferre, Courfeyrac, Bossuet, Joly, Bahorel, and Gavroche, knelt behind the main barricade with muskets and carbines thrust through gaps between the paving-stones, alert and ready to fire. Six others, commanded by Feuilly, waited with loaded muskets at the windows on the two upper floors of the tavern.

A short time passed and then the tramp of marching feet, heavy, measured, and numerous, was clearly to be heard from the direction of Saint-Leu. The sound, faint at first but growing in volume, drew steadily nearer, approaching without a pause, with a calm, inexorable rhythm. Nothing else was to be heard; the mingled silence and sound recalled the entrance of the statue of the Commendatore in *Don Giovanni*; but that stony tread conveyed an impression of vastness, a suggestion not only of an army on the move but also of something spectral, the march of an unseen Legion. It drew nearer and nearer still, and then stopped. It was as though one could hear the breathing of many men at the end of the street. But still nothing was to be seen, except, in the depths of the murky darkness, a multitude of metallic gleams, needle-thin, scarcely perceptible and constantly in motion, like the phosphorescent threads that quiver beneath our eyelids in the first mists of sleep. They were bayonets and musket-barrels faintly illumined by the distant light of the torch.

There was a pause, as though both sides were waiting. Suddenly a voice called out of the darkness, the more awesome because no speaker was to be seen, so that it sounded like the voice of the darkness itself:

'Who's there?'

At the same time they heard the clicking of muskets being cocked.

Enjolras responded in lofty and resonant tones:

'The French Revolution!'

'Fire!' ordered the voice, and an instant glare of light shone upon the front of the houses as though a furnace-door had been swiftly opened and closed.

A hideous blow shook the barricade. The red flag fell. So heavy and concentrated was that volley that it carried away the flagstaff – that is to say, the tip of the shaft of the omnibus. Bullets ricocheting back off the houses behind them wounded several of the defenders. The effect of that first discharge was stupefying, its sheer weight enough to make the boldest man think twice. They were evidently confronted by, at the least, a whole regiment.

'Comrades,' shouted Courfeyrac, 'don't waste your powder. Wait till they show themselves before shooting back.'

'And first of all,' cried Enjolras, 'we must hoist the flag again.'

He picked it up from where it had fallen, right at his feet. At the same time they heard the rattle of ramrods in the muskets as the soldiers re-loaded.

'Who is brave enough?' demanded Enjolras. 'Who's going to put back the flag on the barricade?'

There was no reply. To climb on to the barricade at that moment, when the muskets were again being levelled, was simply to invite death. Enjolras himself trembled at the thought. He repeated:

'Does no one volunteer?'

II

The flag – Act Two

Since they had installed themselves in Corinth and set about building the barricade no one had paid any attention to Père Mabeuf. But he had not deserted the troop. He had found a seat behind the counter on the ground floor of the tavern, and here he had so to speak withdrawn into himself, seeming unaware of what was going on around him. Courfeyrac and others had spoken to him once or twice, warning him of the danger and advising him to get away, but he had seemed not to hear them. His lips moved when no one had spoken to him as though in reply to a question, but when anyone addressed him his lips were still and his eyes vacant. For some hours before the attack on the barricade he had remained seated in the same posture, with his fists clenched on his knees and his head bowed forward as though he were staring over a precipice. Nothing had caused him to change this attitude; it was as though his conscious self were not present within the barricades. After the rest had run out to take up their position only three persons were left in that ground-floor room – Javert, lashed to his pillar, the rebel with a drawn sabre who was mounting guard over him, and Monsieur Mabeuf. But the thunder of that first volley, the physical shock, seemed to bring him to life. He jumped up and crossed the room, and at the moment when Enjolras repeated the words, 'Does no one volunteer?' he showed himself in the doorway of the tavern.

His appearance created a stir among the defenders. Someone shouted:

'That's the Man of the Convention who voted for the King's death – the Representative of the People!'

Probably he did not hear.

Walking up to Enjolras, while the rebels made way for him with a sort of awe, he snatched the flag from the young man's startled hands, and, no one venturing to stop him, began slowly to mount the makeshift flight of paving-stones leading to the top of the barricade – an eighty-year-old man, his head swaying on his shoulders but his feet firm. So tragic and noble was the spectacle that the men around cried, 'Hats off!' Each step he took was terrifying to watch, the white hair, the shrunken face with its high, wrinkled forehead, the deep-set eyes, the open, astonished mouth, the old arms lifting the red flag on high, these things rose up out of the darkness, seeming to grow larger in the ruddy glare of the torch. It might have been the ghost of '93 arising from the tomb and bearing aloft the flag of Terror. When he reached the topmost step, a quivering, terrible ghost, and stood on the pile of rubble facing twelve hundred invisible muskets, facing death as though he were stronger than death, the whole dark barricade acquired a new and awe-inspiring supernatural dimension.

A silence fell, of the kind that only accompanies some prodigious event; and in the silence the old man flourished the red flag and cried:

'Long live the Revolution! Long live the Republic! Fraternity, Equality – and Death!'

Those behind the barricade heard a distant, rapid murmur like that of a hurried priest gabbling a prayer. It was probably the Commissioner of Police delivering the statutory warning from the other end of the street. The stentorian voice which had called to them before now shouted:

'Go away!'

Monsieur Mabeuf, white and haggard, eyes glowing with the wild light of madness, waved the flag and repeated:

'Long live the Republic!'

'Fire!' ordered the voice.

A second volley, like a charge of grapeshot, crashed into the barricade.

The old man tottered on his legs, attempted to recover, then let go the flag and fell backwards like a log, to lie full length on the ground with arms outstretched. Blood was pouring from him, and his sad, pale face seemed to be looking up to Heaven.

The rebels pressed forward, forgetful of their own safety, stirred by feelings loftier than man, and gazed with respectful awe at the dead body.

'They were gallant men, those regicides,' said Enjolras.

Courfeyrac drew close and whispered in his ear.

'This is between ourselves – I don't want to damp the enthusiasm – but no one was ever less of a regicide. I knew him. His name was Mabeuf. I don't know what got into him today. He was a brave old simpleton. Look at his expression.'

'A simpleton with the heart of a Brutus,' said Enjolras.

Then he raised his voice:

'Citizens, this is the example which our elders set the young. While we hesitated he volunteered. We drew back, but he went forward. This is the lesson which those who tremble with age teach those who tremble with fear. This old man is noble in the eyes of his country. He had a long life and a splendid death. Now we must safeguard his body, each of us must defend this dead old man as he would defend his living father, so that his presence among us makes our fortress unconquerable.'

A murmur of grim approval greeted these words.

Bending down, Enjolras lifted the old man's head and kissed him gently on the forehead. Then, handling him with the utmost tenderness, as though he feared to hurt him, he removed his coat and held it up so that all might see its bloodstained holes.

'This is our new flag,' he said.

III

Gavroche's musket

A long black shawl belonging to the Widow Hucheloup was draped over Père Mabeuf's body. Six men made a stretcher of their muskets and, with bared heads, bore him slowly and reverently into the tavern, where they laid him on the big table in the ground-floor room. Wholly intent upon the solemn nature of their task, they gave no thought to their own perilous situation.

When the body passed by Javert, who remained expressionless as ever, Enjolras said to him:

'You – it won't be long!'

Meanwhile Gavroche, who alone had stayed at his post keeping watch, thought he saw men moving stealthily towards the barricade. He shouted:

'Watch out!'

Courfeyrac, Enjolras, and the others came rushing out of the tavern. They were barely in time. A dense glitter of bayonets was now visible on the other side of the barricade. The tall forms of Municipal Guardsmen surged in, some climbing over the omnibus and others coming by way of the breach. Gavroche was forced to give ground, but he did not run away.

It was a critical instant, like the moment when floodwaters rise to the topmost level of an embankment and begin to seep over. In another minute the stronghold might have been taken.

Bahorel sprang towards the first man to enter and shot him at point-blank range; a second man killed him with a bayonet-thrust. Courfeyrac was felled by another man and called for help. The biggest of all the attackers, a giant of a man, bore down with his bayonet on Gavroche. Raising Javert's heavy musket, the boy took aim and pulled the trigger. Nothing happened. Javert had not loaded the musket. The Municipal Guardsman laughed and thrust at the youngster with his bayonet.

But before the bayonet could reach Gavroche the musket fell from the man's hands and he himself fell backwards with a bullet in his forehead. A second bullet took the man assailing Courfeyrac in the chest and laid him low.

Marius had entered the stronghold.

IV

The powder-keg

Crouched at the turning of the Rue Mondétour, Marius had witnessed the beginning of the battle, still irresolute and trembling. But he had not long been able to withstand that mysterious and everwhelming impulse that may be termed the call of the abyss.

The imminence of the peril – the death of Monsieur Mabeuf, that tragic enigma, the killing of Bahorel, Courfeyrac's call for help, the threat to Gavroche; friends to be rescued or avenged – all this had thrown hesitation to the winds. He had rushed into the mêlée with a pistol in either hand, and one had saved Gavroche, the other Courfeyrac.

Amid the din of musket-fire and the cries of the wounded the attackers had climbed on to the barricade, the top of which was now occupied by Municipal and Regional Guards and foot-soldiers of the line. They covered two thirds of its length but had not yet jumped down into the enclosure, seeming uncertain, as though they feared a trap. They hesitated, peering into the dark stronghold as they might have peered into a lion's den. The glare of the torch fell upon bayonets, bearskin caps and the upper part of menacing but apprehensive faces.

Marius was now weaponless, having flung away his discharged pistols; but he had seen the keg of powder near the door in the lower room of the tavern. While he was looking at it, a soldier levelled his musket at him, but as he was in the act of firing a hand was thrust over the muzzle, diverting it. The person who had flung himself forward was the young workman in corduroy trousers. The ball shattered his hand and perhaps entered his body, for he fell; but it did not touch Marius. It was an episode in misted darkness, half-seen rather than seen. Marius, on his way into the tavern, was scarcely aware of it. He had vaguely seen the musket levelled at him and the hand thrust out to block it, and he had heard the discharge. But at moments such as these, when events follow at breathless speed, we are not to be distracted from whatever purpose we have in mind. We plunge on blindly amid the fog around us.

The rebels, shaken but not panic-stricken, had rallied. Enjolras shouted, 'Steady! Don't fire at random!' In that first confusion they might indeed have hit each other. The greater number had retreated into the tavern, from the upper windows of which they dominated their assailants; but the most resolute, with Enjolras, Courfeyrac, Jean Prouvaire, and Combeferre, had taken up their stand with their backs to the house at the end of the street, where they stood confronting the soldiers and National Guardsmen on the barricade. All this had been accomplished without undue haste, with the strange and threatening gravity that precedes a set battle.

Muskets were levelled on both sides at point-blank range; they were so close that they could talk without shouting. At this point, when the spark was about to be struck, an officer in a stiff collar and large epaulettes raised his sword and said:

'Lay down your arms!'

'Fire!' ordered Enjolras.

The two volleys rang out simultaneously, and the scene was enveloped in thick, acrid smoke filled with the groans of the wounded and the dying. When it had cleared both sides could be seen, diminished but still in the same place, re-charging their weapons in silence. But suddenly a ringing voice cried:

'Clear out or I'll blow up the barricade!'

All heads were turned to stare in the direction of the voice.

Marius, seizing the powder-keg in the tavern, had taken advantage of the smoke-filled lull to slip along the barricade until he reached the structure of paving-stones in which the torch was fixed. To detach the torch and set the powder-keg in its place, thrusting aside the paving-stones, had taken him, urged on by a sort of terrible compulsion, only the time he needed to bend down and then stand upright; and now the men grouped at the other end of the barricade, officer's, soldiers, men of the National and Municipal Guard, stared in stupefaction at the figure holding the flaming torch over the opened keg while he repeated his challenge:

'Clear out or I'll blow up the whole place!'

First the octogenarian and then the youthful Marius: it was the revolution of the young following the ghost of the old!

'If you blow up the barricade,' a sergeant called, 'you'll blow up yourself as well!'

'And myself as well,' said Marius, and lowered the torch towards the keg.

But there was no longer anyone on the barricade. The attackers had made off in a disorderly stampede, leaving their dead and wounded behind, and were now vanishing into the darkness at the far end of the street. It was a rout, and the fortress had been relieved.

The last poem of Jean Prouvaire

His friends flocked round Marius, and Courfeyrac flung his arms about his neck.

'So you've come!' he cried.

'And welcome!' said Combeferre.

'At the right moment!' said Bossuet.

'I'd be dead otherwise,' said Courfeyrac.

'I'd have copped it too,' said Gavroche.

'Where is the leader?' Marius asked.

'You're now the leader,' Enjolras said.

Throughout that day Marius had had a furnace in his brain, but now it was a whirlwind, a tempest from outside himself that carried him away. He seemed to have been borne a huge distance outside life. The two radiant months of happiness ending abruptly in this inferno, the sight of Monsieur Mabeuf dying for the Republic, himself a rebel leader – all this was like an outrageous nightmare, so that it cost him an effort to realize that what was happening was real. He had not yet lived long enough to have discovered that nothing is more close at hand than the impossible, and that what must be looked for is always the unforeseen. He was observing his own drama as though it were a play he did not understand.

In his confused state of mind he did not recognize Javert, who, lashed to his pillar, had not turned a hair during the attack on the barricade and was observing the commotion around him with the resignation of a martyr and the detachment of a judge. Marius had not even noticed him.

The attackers made no further move. Although the sound of them could be heard at the far end of the street, they seemed disinclined to take the initiative, either because they were awaiting fresh orders, or because they were hoping for reinforcements before again assailing that formidable stronghold. The rebels had posted sentries, and the medical students among them were attending to the wounded.

All the tables had been taken out of the tavern except the two in use for the making of bandages and cartridges and the one on which Monsieur Mabeuf's body lay; they had been piled on to the barricade, being replaced in the downstairs room by mattresses from the beds of the Widow Hucheloup and her two waitresses. The wounded were laid on these mattresses. As for the three luckless women whose home was Corinth, no one knew what had become of them. They were eventually found huddled in the cellar.

A sad blow had damped the students' rejoicing at their temporary triumph. When the roll was called, one of them was found to be missing, one of the bravest and best, Jean Prouvaire. He was not to be found among the wounded or the dead. It seemed, then, that he must have been taken prisoner. Combeferre said to Enjolras:

'They've got our friend and we've got their agent. Are you really so set on the death of this spy?'

'Yes,' said Enjolras, 'but less than on the life of Jean Prouvaire.' They were talking in the downstairs room near Javert's pillar.

'Well then,' said Combeferre, 'I'll tie a handkerchief to my stick and go and bargain with them – their man in exchange for ours.'

'Wait,' said Enjolras, laying a hand on his. 'Listen!'

An ominous rattle of muskets had come from the other end of the street. A brave voice shouted:

'Long live France! Long live the future!'

It was the voice of Jean Prouvaire.

'They've shot him!' cried Combeferre.

Enjolras turned to Javert and said:

'Your friends have killed you as well.'

VI

The throes of death after the throes of life

It is a peculiarity of this type of warfare that the attack on a barricade is nearly always delivered from the front and that as a rule the attacker makes no attempt to outflank the defence, either because he fears an ambush or because he is reluctant to engage his forces in narrow, tortuous streets. The rebels' attention was therefore concentrated on the main barricade which was constantly threatened and where the battle would undoubtedly be resumed. However, Marius thought of the smaller barricade and went to inspect it. It was unguarded except by the lamp flickering on the paving-stones. The Mondétour alleyway, and the small streets running into it, the Petite-Truanderie and the Rue du Cygne, were entirely quiet.

As he was leaving, having concluded his inspection, he heard his own name faintly spoken in the darkness.

'Monsieur Marius!'

He started, recognizing the husky voice that two hours previously had called to him through the gate in the Rue Plumet. But now it was scarcely more than a whisper.

He looked about him, but, seeing no one, thought that he had imagined it, that it was no more than an hallucination to be added to the many extraordinary vicissitudes of that day. He started to move away from the barricade and the voice repeated:

'Monsieur Marius!'

This time he knew that he had heard it, but although he peered hard into the darkness he could see nothing.

'I'm at your feet,' the voice said.

Looking down, Marius saw a dark shape crawling over the cobbles towards him. The gleam of the lamp was enough to enable him to make out a smock, a pair of torn corduroy trousers, two bare feet and something that looked like a trail of blood. A white face was turned towards him and the voice asked:

'Don't you recognize me?'

'No.'

'Éponine.'

Marius bent hastily down and saw that it was indeed that unhappy girl, clad in a man's clothes.

'How do you come to be here? What are you doing?'

'I'm dying,' she said.

There are words and happenings which arouse even souls in the depths of despair. Marius cried, as though starting out of sleep:

'You're wounded! I'll carry you into the tavern. They'll dress your wound. Is it very bad? How am I to lift you without hurting you? Help, someone! But what are you doing here?'

He tried to get an arm underneath her to raise her up, and in doing so touched her hand. She uttered a weak cry.

'Did I hurt you?'

'A little.'

'But I only touched your hand.'

She lifted her hand for him to see, and he saw a hole in the centre of the palm.

'What happened?' he asked.

'A bullet went through it.'

'A bullet? But how?'

'Don't you remember a musket being aimed at you?'

'Yes, and a hand was clapped over it.'

'That was mine.'

Marius shuddered.

'What madness! You poor child! Still, if that's all, it might be worse. I'll get you to a bed and they'll bind you up. One doesn't die of a wounded hand.'

She murmured:

'The ball passed through my hand, but it came out through my back. It's no use trying to move me. I'll tell you how you can treat my wound better than any surgeon. Sit down on that stone, close beside me.'

Marius did so. She rested her head on his knee and said without looking at him:

'Oh, what happiness! What bliss! Now I don't feel any pain.'

For a moment she was silent, then with an effort she turned to look at Marius.

'You know, Monsieur Marius, it vexed me when you went into that garden. That was silly, because after all I'd shown you the way there, and anyway I should have known that a young gentleman like you –' She broke off, and passing from one unhappy thought to another, said with a touching smile: 'You think I'm ugly, don't you?' She went on: 'But now you're done for! No one will get out of this place alive. And I'm the one who brought you here! You're going to die. I was expecting it, and yet I put my hand over that musket barrel. How queer. But I wanted to die before you did. I dragged myself here when I got hurt, and nobody noticed. I've been waiting for you. I thought, "Won't he ever come?" I had to bite my smock, the pain was so bad. But now it's all right. Do you remember the time when I came into your room and looked at myself in your glass, and the day when I found you by the Lark's Field? So many birds were singing! It's not so very long ago. You offered me a hundred sous, and I said, "I don't want your money." Did you pick the coin up? I know you weren't rich. I didn't think of telling you to pick it up. It was a fine, sunny day not a bit cold. Do you remember, Monsieur Marius? Oh, I'm so, happy! We're all going to die.'

She was talking distractedly, in a manner that was grave and heartrending. The torn smock disclosed her naked bosom. While she spoke she pressed her injured hand to her breast, where there was another hole from which at that moment the blood spurted like wine from a newly tapped cask. Marius looked down at her in deep compassion, desolate creature that she was.

'Oh!' she cried suddenly. 'It's starting again. I can't breathe!'

At this moment the voice of Gavroche rang out in another burst of song like a cock-crow. He was sitting on a table loading his musket, and the song was a highly popular song of the moment:

> 'When Lafayette comes in sight,
> All the gendarmes take to flight –
> *Sauvons-nous! Sauvons-nous! Sauvons-nous! ...*'

Éponine had raised herself on one arm and was listening.

'That's him,' she said. She looked up at Marius. 'That's my brother. He mustn't see me. He'd scold.'

'Your brother?' Marius repeated, while in the bitterest and most painful depths of his heart he recalled the obligation to the Thénardier family laid upon him by his father. 'Whom do you mean?'

'The boy.'

'The one who's singing?'

'Yes.'

Marius made a movement.

'Oh, don't go!' she said. 'It won't be long.'

She was sitting almost upright, but her voice was very low and broken by hiccoughs. At moments she struggled for breath. Raising her face as near as she could to Marius's, she said, with a strange expression:

'Look, I can't cheat you. I have a letter for you in my pocket. I've had it since yesterday. I was asked to post it, but I didn't. I didn't want you to get it. But you might be angry with me when we meet again. Because we shall all meet again, shan't we? Take your letter.'

With a convulsive movement she seized Marius's hand with her own injured one, but without seeming to feel the pain, and guided it to her pocket.

'Take it,' she said.

Marius took out the letter, and she made a little gesture of satisfaction and acceptance.

'Now you must promise me something for my trouble...' She paused.

'What?' asked Marius.

'Do you promise?'

'Yes, I promise.'

'You must kiss me on the forehead after I'm dead ... I shall know.'

She let her head fall back on his knees; her lids fluttered, and then she was motionless. He thought that the sad soul had left her. But then, when he thought it was all over, she slowly opened her eyes that were now deep with the shadow of death, and said in a voice so sweet that it seemed already to come from another world:

'You know, Monsieur Marius, I think I was a little bit in love with you.'

She tried to smile, and died.

VII

Gavroche reckons distances

Marius kept his promise. He kissed the pale forehead, bedewed with an icy sweat. It was no act of infidelity to Cosette, but a deliberate, tender farewell to an unhappy spirit.

He had trembled as he took the letter Éponine had brought him. Instantly sensing its importance, he longed to read it. Such is the nature of man – scarcely had the poor girl closed her eyes than he wanted to open it. But first he laid her gently on the ground, feeling instinctively that he could not read it beside her dead body.

Going into the tavern, he unfolded it by the light of a candle. It was a short note, folded and wafered with feminine elegance, and addressed in a feminine hand to 'Monsieur Marius Pontmercy, *chez* M. Courfeyrac, No. 16, Rue de la Verrerie.' Breaking the seal he read:

My dearest,
    Alas, father insists that we must leave here at once. We go tonight to No.7, Rue de l'Homme-Armé, and in a week we shall be in England.
                        Cosette   4th June.

Such was the innocence of their love that Marius had not even known her handwriting.

What had happened may be briefly told: Éponine was responsible for everything. After the evening of 3 June she had had two things in mind: to frustrate the plan of her father and his friends for robbing the house in the Rue Plumet, and to separate Marius and Cosette. She had exchanged clothes with a youth who thought it amusing to go about dressed as a woman, while she dressed up as a man. It was she who, in the Champ de Mars, had given Jean Valjean the note warning him to change his address. Valjean had gone home and said to Cosette, 'We're moving this evening, with Toussaint, to the Rue de L'Homme-Armé, and next week we're going to London.' Cosette, shattered by this unexpected blow, had hurriedly written her letter to Marius. But how was it to be posted? She never went out alone and Toussaint, surprised by an errand of this nature, would certainly show the letter to her master. While she was debating the matter Cosette had caught sight of Éponine through the garden gate, wandering in her male attire up and down the street. Thinking she had to do with a young workman, she had called to the girl and given her five francs and the letter, asking her to take it at once to the address given. Éponine had put the letter in her pocket and the next day, the 5th, had gone to Courfeyrac's lodging, not to give him the letter but simply, as any jealous lover will understand, 'to have a look'. She had waited there for Marius, or anyway for Courfeyrac, still only 'having a look'; but when Courfeyrac told her that he and his friends were going to the barricade a sudden impulse had seized her – to plunge into that death, as she would have plunged into any other, and take Marius with her. She had followed Courfeyrac to find out where the barricade was situated, and then, since she was certain, having intercepted Cosette's letter, that Marius would go as usual to the Rue Plumet, she had gone there herself and passed on the summons, supposedly from his friend, which she had no doubt would lead him to join them. She had counted on Marius's despair at not finding Cosette, and in this had judged rightly. She had returned separately to the Rue de la Chanvrerie, and we know what had happened there. She had died in the tragic rapture of jealous hearts, who take the beloved with them into death, saying, 'No one else shall have him!'

Marius covered Cosette's letter with kisses. So she still loved him! He thought for a moment that now he must not die, but then he thought, 'She's going away!' She was going with her father to England, and his grandfather had refused to consent to their marriage. Nothing was changed in the fate that pursued them. Dreamers such as Marius have their moments of overwhelming despair, from which desperate courses ensue: the burden of life seems insupportable, and dying is soon over.

But he reflected that he had two duties to perform. He must tell Cosette of his death and send her a last message of farewell; and he must save that poor little boy, Éponine's brother and Thénardier's son, from the disaster that so nearly threatened them all.

He had his wallet on him, the same one which had contained the notebook in which he had written so many loving thoughts for Cosette. He got out a sheet of paper, and with a pencil wrote the following lines:

Our marriage was impossible. I went to my grandfather, and he refused his consent. I have no fortune; neither have you. I hurried to see you but you were no longer there. You remember the pledge I gave you. I shall keep it. I shall die. I love you. When you read this my soul will be very near at hand and smiling at you.

Having nothing with which to seal the letter he simply folded the paper in four and addressed it as follows: 'To Mademoiselle Cosette Fauchelevent, *chez* M. Fauchelevent, 7 Rue de l'Homme-Armé.'

Then after a moment's reflection he wrote on another sheet of paper:

'My name is Marius Pontmercy. My body is to be taken to the house of my grandfather, M. Gillenormand, 6 Rue des Filles-du-Calvaire, in the Marais.'

He returned the wallet to his jacket pocket and called to Gavroche.

'Will you do something for me?'

'Anything you like,' said Gavroche. 'Lord love us, if it weren't for you I'd have copped it.'

'You see this letter?'

'Yes.'

'I want you to deliver it. You must leave here at once' – at this Gavroche began to scratch his head – 'and take it to Mademoiselle Cosette at the address written on the outside – care of Monsieur Fauchelevent, number seven, Rue de l'Homme-Armé.'

'Yes, but look here,' said the valiant Gavroche, 'the barricade may be taken while I'm away.'

'The chances are that they won't attack again until daybreak, and the barricade won't fall until noon.'

The respite granted to the defenders did indeed give every sign of continuing. It was one of those lulls which commonly occur in night fighting, and which are always followed by an assault of redoubled fury.

'Well, then,' said Gavroche, 'why shouldn't I deliver the letter tomorrow morning?'

'It would be too late. By then all the streets round us will be guarded and you'd never get out. You must go at once.'

Gavroche had no reply to this. He continued to hesitate, unhappily scratching his head. But then, with one of those swift, birdlike movements that characterized him, he took the letter.

'Very well,' he said. And he went off at a run down the narrow Rue Mondétour.

The thought that had decided Gavroche was one that he did not disclose to Marius, for fear that he might raise objections. He had reflected that it was only just midnight, that the Rue de L'Homme-Armé was not far off, and that he could deliver the letter and be back in plenty of time.

BOOK FIFTEEN

IN THE RUE DE L'HOMME-ARMÉ

I
The treacherous blotter

WHAT IS the turmoil in a city compared with that of the human heart? Man the individual is a deeper being than man in the mass. Jean Valjean, at that moment, was in a state of appalling shock, with all his worst terrors realized. Like Paris itself he was trembling on the verge of a revolution that was both formidable and deep-seated. A few hours had sufficed to bring it about. His destiny and his conscience were both suddenly plunged in shadow. It might be said of him, as of Paris, that within him two principles were at war. The angel of light was about to grapple with the angel of darkness on the bridge over the abyss. Which would overthrow the other? Which would gain the day?

On the evening of that 5 June, Valjean, with Cosette and Toussaint, had removed to the Rue de l'Homme-Armé, and it was here that the unforeseen awaited him.

Cosette had not left the Rue Plumet without protest. For the first time in their life together her wishes and those of Jean Valjean had shown themselves to be separate matters which, if not wholly opposed, were at least contradictory. Objections on the one side had been met by inflexibility on the other. The abrupt warning to Valjean to change his abode, flung at him by a stranger, had so alarmed him as to make him overbearing. He had thought that his secret was discovered and that the police were after him. Cosette had been forced to give way.

They had arrived in tight-lipped silence at the Rue de l'Homme-Armé, each concerned with a personal problem, Valjean so perturbed that he did not perceive Cosette's distress, and Cosette so unhappy that she failed to discern his state of alarm.

Valjean had brought Toussaint with them, a thing he had never done on their previous removals. He foresaw that he might never go back to the Rue Plumet, and he could neither leave Toussaint behind not tell her his secret. In any event, he could trust her to be faithful. The start of betrayal, as between servant and master, is curiosity. But Toussaint, as though she had been born to be Valjean's servant, was quite incurious. She said in her stumbling peasant dialect, 'It's all one to me. I do my work, and the rest is no affair of mine.'

In their departure from the Rue Plumet, so hasty as to be almost flight, Jean Valjean had taken nothing with him except the cherished box of child's clothing which Cosette had nicknamed his 'inseparable'. A pile of luggage would have necessitated the services of a carrier, and a carrier is a witness. A fiacre had been summoned to the door in the Rue de Babylone, and they had driven off. It was only with difficulty that Toussaint had obtained permission to make up a few packages of clothes and toilet articles. Cosette had taken nothing but her letter-case and blotter. Valjean, as a further precaution, had arranged for them to leave at nightfall, which had allowed her time to write her letter to Marius. It was dark when they reached the Rue de l'Homme-Armé.

They went to bed in silence. The apartment in the Rue de l'Homme-Armé was on the second floor overlooking the courtyard at the back of the house, and consisted of two bedrooms, a living-room with a kitchen adjoining, and an attic room furnished with a truckle-bed, which fell to Toussaint. The living-room was also the entrance-lobby and it separated the two bedrooms. The apartment was equipped with all the necessary domestic paraphernalia.

Panic, such is human nature, may die down as irrationally as it arises. Scarcely had they reached their new dwelling than Valjean's alarm subsided until finally it had vanished altogether. There are places of which the calm communicates itself almost mechanically to the human spirit. The Rue de l'Homme-Armé is a small, unimportant street inhabited by peaceful citizens, so narrow that it is barred to vehicles at either end, silent amid the tumult of Paris, dark even in broad daylight, seemingly incapable of any emotion between its two rows of tall, century-old houses which keep themselves to themselves like the ancients they are. It is a street of placid forgetfulness, and Jean Valjean, breathing its odour of tranquillity, was caught by the contagion. How could anyone find him here?

His first act was to put the 'inseparable' beside his bed. He slept well. The night brings counsel, and, one may add, it soothes. He was almost light-hearted when he got up next morning. He found the living-room delightful, hideous though it was with its old round dining-table, the low sideboard with a mirror hanging on the wall above it, a worm-eaten armchair, and a few other chairs loaded with Toussaint's packages. A tear in one of these showed that it contained Valjean's National Guard uniform.

As for Cosette, she had asked Toussaint to bring her a cup of soup in her bedroom and she did not appear until the evening. At about five o'clock Toussaint, who had been busy all day putting things to rights, set a dish of cold chicken on the table and Cosette deigned to attend the meal, out of deference to her father.

This done, and saying that she had a headache, Cosette bade her father good night and went back to her bedroom. Valjean, having eaten a wing of chicken with a good appetite, sat with his elbows on the table, basking in his present security. He had been vaguely aware, while he was eating, of Toussaint's stammer as she tried to tell him the news – 'Monsieur, there's something happening. There's fighting in the town.' Absorbed in his own thoughts, he had paid no attention to this. In fact, he had not really listened. He got up presently and began to walk up and down the room, from the door to the window and back, feeling more and more at ease.

And with his growing serenity the thought of Cosette, his constant preoccupation, returned to him. Not that he was troubled by her headache, which he regarded as nothing but a trifling *crise de nerfs*, a girlish sulk that would wear off in a day or two; but he was thinking of her future, and, as always, with affectionate concern. After all, there seemed to be no reason why their happy life should not continue. There are times when all things look impossible, and times when all things look easy. For Valjean this was one of the latter occasions. As a rule they follow bad times as day follows night, by that law of succession and contrast which is at the heart of Nature, and which superficial minds call antithesis. In the placid street where he had taken refuge, Valjean shrugged off all the anxieties which for some time had been troubling him. From the very fact of having seen so many dark clouds, he now had glimpses of a clearer sky. To have left the Rue Plumet without difficulty or any untoward incident was in itself a gain.

It might well be prudent to leave France, if only for a few months and go to London. Well then, that was what they would do. What did it matter where they were provided they were together? Cosette was his only country, all that he needed for his happiness. The thought that perhaps he might not be all that Cosette needed for happiness, which at one time had caused him sleepless nights, did not now enter his mind. He was rid of all past troubles, in a state of brimming optimism. Cosette, being near him, seemed part of him – an optical illusion which everyone has experienced. He mentally planned their journey to England, endowing it with every imaginable comfort, and, in his day-dream, saw his happiness reborn no matter where they were.

But as he paced slowly up and down the room something suddenly caught his eye. He came face to face with the mirror hanging at an inclined angle over the sideboard, and, reflected in it, he read the following lines:

My dearest,

Alas, father insists that we must leave here at once. We go tonight to No. 7, Rue de l'Homme-Armé, and in a week we shall be in England.

Cosette 4th June.

Jean Valjean stood aghast.

Cosette when they arrived had put her blotting-book on the dresser, and in her distress had forgotten to remove it, leaving it open at the page on which she had blotted her letter to Marius, and the mirror, reflecting the reversed handwriting, had made it clearly legible. It was simple and it was devastating.

Valjean moved closer to the mirror. He re-read the lines without believing in their existence. They were like something seen in a lightning-flash, a hallucination. The thing was impossible; it could not be true.

Slowly his wits returned to him. He examined the blotter with a renewed sense of reality, studying the blotted lines which, in their reversed state, were a meaningless scrawl. He thought, 'But there's no sense in this, it's not handwriting,' and drew a deep breath of irrational relief. Which of us has not known these aberrations in moments of intense shock? The spirit does not give way to despair until it has exhausted every possibility of self-deception.

He stood staring stupidly at the blotter in his hand, almost ready to laugh at the hallucination which had so nearly deceived him. But then he looked again in the mirror and saw the words reflected in remorseless clarity. This was no illusion. The reflection of a fact is in itself a fact. This was Cosette's handwriting. He saw it all.

He trembled and, putting down the blotter, sank into the arm-chair by the sideboard, to sit there with his head lolling, his eyes dulled in utter dismay. He said to himself that there was no escape, the light of his world had gone out, since Cosette had written this to someone other than himself. But then he heard his own spirit, become again terrible, roar sullenly in the darkness. Try to rob a lion of its cub!

What is strange and sad is that at that time Marius had not received the letter. Fate had treacherously delivered it into Valjean's hands before Marius had seen it.

Until that moment no trial had been too much for Jean Valjean. He had endured hideous ordeals; no extremity of ill-fortune had been spared him; every utmost hardship, every vindictiveness and all the spite of which society was capable had been visited upon him. He had stood his ground unflinching, accepting, when he had to, the bitterest blows. He had sacrificed the inviolability he had gained as a man restored to life, surrendered his freedom, risked his neck, lost everything and suffered everything, and had remained tolerant and stoical to the point that at moments he seemed to have achieved the self-abnegation of a martyr. His conscience, fortified by so many battles with a malignant fate, had seemed unassailable. But anyone able to see into his heart would have been forced to admit that now he weakened.

Of all the torments he had suffered in his long trial by adversity, this was the worst. Never had the rack and thumbscrew been more shrewdly applied. He felt the stirring of forgotten sensibilities, the quiver of deep-buried nerves. Alas, the supreme ordeal – indeed, the one true ordeal – is the loss of the beloved.

It is true that the poor, ageing man loved Cosette only as a father; but, as we have already said, the emptiness of his life had caused this paternal love to embrace all others. He loved Cosette as his daughter, his mother, his sister; and since he had had neither mistress nor wife, since human nature is a creditor who accepts no compromise, that kind of love, too, was mingled with the others, confused and unrealized, pure with the purity of blindness, innocent, unconscious and sublime, less an emotion than an instinct, and less an instinct than a bond, impalpable, indefinable, but real. The true essence of love was threaded through his immense tenderness for Cosette like the seam of gold hidden unsullied beneath the mountainside.

We must recall the relationship between them that we have already described. No marriage between them was possible, not even a marriage of souls, and yet their destinies were assuredly joined. Except Cosette – that is to say, except a child – Jean Valjean had known nothing of the things that men love. No succession of loves and passions had coloured his life with those changing shades of green, fresh green followed by dark green, which we see in trees that have lived through a winter and men who have lived for more than fifty years. In short, as we have more than once emphasized, that inner fusion, that whole of which the sum was a lofty virtue, had resulted in making Jean Valjean a father to Cosette. A strange father compounded of the parent, son, brother and husband who all existed within him; a father in whom there was even something of the mother; a father who loved and worshipped Cosette, for whom she was light and dwelling-place, family, country, paradise.

So that now, when he realized that this was positively ended, that she was escaping from him, slipping through his fingers like water, like a mist; when he was confronted by the crushing evidence that another possessed her heart and was the end and purpose of her life, and that he was no more than the father, someone who no longer existed; when he could no longer doubt this, but was forced to say, 'She is going to leave me', the intensity of his pain was past enduring. To have done so much for it to end like this; to be no one, of no account! He was shaken throughout his being by a tempest of revolt, and he felt to the very roots of his hair an overweening re-birth of egotism – self bellowed from the depths of his emptiness.

There is such a thing as spiritual collapse. The thrust of a desperate certainty into a man cannot occur without the disruption of certain profound elements which are sometimes the man himself. Anguish, when it has reached this stage, becomes a panic-flight of all the powers of conscience. There are mortal crises from which few of us emerge in our right mind, with our sense of duty still intact. When the limit of suffering is overpassed the most impregnable virtue is plunged in disarray. Jean Valjean picked up the blotter again, and again convinced himself. As though turned to stone, he stood with eyes intent on those irrefutable lines, and such a darkness filled his mind as to make it seem that all his soul had crumbled.

He studied the revelation, and the exaggerations which his own imagination supplied, with an appearance of calm that in itself was frightening, for it is a dreadful thing when the calm of a man becomes the coldness of a statue. He measured this change effected by a remorseless destiny of which he had been quite unaware, re-calling his fears of the summer, so lightly dismissed. It was the same precipice, it had not changed; but now he was not standing at the edge, he was at the bottom. And, which was of all things most bitter and outrageous, he had fallen without knowing. The light of his life had vanished while he thought that the sun still shone.

His instinct spared him nothing. He recalled incidents, dates, certain flushes and pallors on Cosette's cheek, and he thought, 'That was he!' The lucid percipience of despair is like an arrow that never fails to find its target. His thoughts flew instantly to Marius. He did not know the name, but he promptly placed the man. He clearly saw, in the implacable revival of memory, the youthful stranger in the Luxembourg, the contemptible chaser of girls, the love-lorn idler, the fool, the cheat – for it is treachery to make eyes at a girl with a loving parent at her side.

Having decided in his mind that this young man was at the bottom of it all, Jean Valjean, the man who had redeemed himself, who had mastered his soul and with such painful effort resolved all life, hardship and suffering in love, turned his inward vision upon himself: and a ghost rose before his eyes – hatred.

Great suffering brings great weakness; it undermines the will to live. In youth it is perilous, but later it may be disastrous. For if despair is terrible when the blood is hot, the hair dark, the head still held high like the flame of a torch; when the thread of destiny has still to be unreeled and the heart may still beat faster with a worthy love; when there are still women and laughter and the whole wide world; when the force of life is undiminished – if despair even then is terrible, what must it be in age, when the years rush past with a growing pallor and through the dusk we begin to see the stars of eternity?

While he sat brooding Toussaint entered the room. Valjean turned to her and asked:

'Where is it happening? Do you know?'

She stared at him in bewilderment.

'I don't understand.'

'Didn't you say there was fighting going on somewhere?'

'Oh, I see,' said Toussaint. 'It's near Saint-Merry.'

There are actions which arise, without our knowing it, from the depths of our thought. No doubt it was owing to an impulse of this kind, of which he was scarcely conscious, that a few minutes later Valjean was out in the street. He was seated, bareheaded, on the kerbstone outside the house. He seemed to be listening.

Darkness had fallen.

A boy at war with street-lamps

How long did he stay there? What was the ebb and flow of his tragic meditation? Did he seek to recover himself? Was he so bowed down as to be broken, or could he still stand upright, finding within himself something still solid on which to set his feet? Probably he himself did not know.

The street was empty. The occasional apprehensive inhabitant, hurriedly returning home, scarcely noticed him. In times of peril it is every man for himself. The lamplighter, on his accustomed round, lit the lamp, which was just opposite the door of No. 7, and went his way. To anyone pausing to examine him in the half-light, Jean Valjean would not have seemed a living man. Seated on the kerbstone outside his door he was like a figure carved in ice. There is a frozen aspect of despair. Vague sounds of distant tumult, tocsins and fanfares, were to be heard, and mingled with these the clock of the Église de Saint-Paul, gravely and without haste striking the hour of eleven: for the tocsin is man, but the hour is God. The passing of time made no impression on Valjean; he did not move. But at about that time a sudden burst of firing sounded from the direction of the market, followed by a second, even more violent. Probably this was the attack on the Rue de Chanvrerie barricade which, as we know, Marius repulsed. The two volleys, their savagery seeming heightened by the outraged stillness of the night, caused Valjean to get to his feet and stand facing the direction from which the din had come: but then he sat down again, and, crossing his arms, let his chin sink slowly on to his chest while he resumed his inward debate.

The sound of footsteps caused him to raise his head. By the light of the street-lamp he saw a youthful figure approaching, pale-faced but glowing with life. Gavroche had arrived in the Rue de l'Homme-Armé.

He was gazing at the housefronts, apparently in search of a number. Although he could see Valjean he paid no attention to him. He stared up and then down, and, rising on tip-toe, rapped on doors and ground-floor windows. All were locked and barred. After trying five or six houses in vain he shrugged his shoulders and commented on the situation as follows:

'Well, blow me!'

Jean Valjean, who in his present state of mind would not have addressed or answered any other person, was irresistibly moved to question this lively small boy.

'Well, youngster, what are you up to?'

'What I'm after is that I'm hungry,' said Gavroche crisply; and he added, 'Youngster yourself.'

Valjean felt in his pocket and produced a five-franc piece. But Gavroche, skipping from one subject to another like the sparrow he was, had become aware of the street-lamp. He picked up a stone.

'You've still got lights burning in these parts,' he said. 'That's not right, mate. No discipline. I'll have to smash it.'

He flung the stone, and the lamp-glass fell with a clatter which caused the occupants of the near-by houses, huddled behind their curtains, to exclaim, 'It's '93 all over again!'

'There you are, you old street,' said Gavroche. 'Now you've got your nightcap on.' He turned to Valjean. 'What's that monstrous great building at the end of the street? The Archives, isn't it? You ought to pull down some of those pillars and make them into a barricade.'

Jean Valjean went towards him.

'Poor little chap,' he muttered. 'He's half-starved.' And he pressed the five-franc piece into his hand.

Startled by the size of the offering, Gavroche stared at the coin, charmed by its whiteness as it glimmered faintly in his hand. He had heard of five-franc pieces, he knew them by reputation, and he was delighted to see one at close quarters. Something worth looking at, he thought, and did so for some moments with pleasure. But then he held out the coin to Valjean, saying in a lordly fashion:

'Thank you, guv'nor, but I'd sooner smash street-lamps. Take back your bribe. It doesn't work with me.'

'Have you a mother?' Valjean asked.

'More than you have perhaps.'

'Then keep it and give it to her.'

Gavroche was melted by this. Besides, the man was hatless, and this predisposed him in his favour.

'You mean I can have it?' he said. 'It's not just to stop me smashing lamps?'

'Smash as many as you like.'

'You're all right,' said Gavroche. He put the coin in one of his

978

pockets, and with a growing assurance, asked: 'Do you live in this street?'

'Yes. Why?'

'Would you mind telling me which is Number Seven?'

'Why do you want to know?'

Gavroche was brought up short, feeling that he had already said too much. He ran a hand through his hair and said cryptically: 'Because.'

A thought occurred to Jean Valjean. Acute distress has these moments of lucidity. He asked:

'Have you brought me the letter I've been waiting for?'

'You?' said Gavroche. 'But you're not a woman.'

'A letter addressed to Mademoiselle Cosette.'

'Cosette,' muttered Gavroche. 'I think that's a rummy name.'

'Well then, I'm to give it to her. May I have it?'

'I take it you know that I've come from the barricades.'

'Of course . . .' said Valjean.

Gavroche fished in another pocket and got out the folded sheet of paper. He then gave a military salute.

'Confidential dispatch,' he said, 'from the Provisional Government.'

'Let me have it,' said Valjean.

Gavroche held the missive above his head.

'Don't go getting the idea that this is just a *billet doux*. It's addressed to a woman, but it's for the people. Our lot, we may be rebels, but we respect the weaker sex. We aren't like the fine world where it's all wolves chasing after geese.'

'Give it to me.'

'I'm bound to say,' said Gavroche, 'you look to me like a decent cove.'

'Quickly, please.'

'Well, here you are.' Gavroche handed over the letter. 'And hurry it up, Monsieur Chose. You mustn't keep Mamselle Chosette waiting.' He was pleased with this happy play on words.

'One thing,' said Jean Valjean. 'Should I take the reply to Saint-Merry?'

'If you did you'd be making what's called a floater,' said Gavroche. 'That letter comes from the barricade in the Rue de la Chanvrerie, to which I am now returning. Good night, citizen.'

Whereupon Gavroche departed – or, better, returned like a

homing pigeon to its nest. He sped away into the night with the swift certainty of a bullet, and the narrow Rue de l'Homme-Armé was again plunged in empty silence. In the twinkling of an eye the strange little boy, that creature of darkness and fantasy, had disappeared into the gloom amid the tall rows of houses, vanishing like a puff of smoke; and one might have thought that he had vanished for ever if, a minute after his departure, the indignant dwellers in the Rue du Chaume had not been startled by the crash of another street-lamp.

III

While Cosette and Toussaint sleep

Jean Valjean went back into the house with Marius's letter. As grateful for the darkness as an owl clutching its prey, he groped his way upstairs, gently opened his door and closed it behind him, and stood listening until he was assured that Cosette and Toussaint were asleep. Then, so greatly was his hand shaking, he made several vain attempts before extracting a spark from the Fumade tinder-box. His every action was like that of a thief in the night. Finally, with his candle lighted, he sat down at the table and unfolded the letter.

We cannot be said to read when in a state of violent emotion. Rather, we twist the paper in our hands, mutilating it as though it were an enemy, scoring it with the finger-nails of our anger or delight. Our eyes skip the beginning, hurrying on to the end. With a feverish acuteness we grasp the general sense, seize upon the main point and ignore the rest. In the letter written by Marius, Jean Valjean was conscious only of the following: 'I shall die ... When you read this my soul will be very near ...'

The effect of these words was to kindle in him a horrid exaltation, so that for a moment he was as it were dumbfounded by the sudden change of feeling in himself. He stared in a kind of drunken bemusement at the letter. There, beneath his eyes, was a marvel – the death of the hated person.

His triumph cried out hideously within him. So it was done with! His problem was solved, more rapidly than he had dared to hope. The individual who threatened his happiness was to vanish from the scene; and of his own free will. Without any action on the part of Jean Valjean, through no fault of his, this 'other man' was about to die, perhaps was already dead. Valjean's fevered mind made calculations. No, he was not yet dead. The letter was evidently intended to be read by Cosette tomorrow morning. Nothing had happened after those two bursts of musket fire between eleven and midnight. The real attack on the barricade would not begin until daylight. But it made no difference. Having joined in the battle the 'other man' was doomed to die, swept away in the stream of events ... Valjean felt that he was saved. Once again he would have Cosette to himself, without any rival, and their life together would continue as before. He had only to keep this letter in his pocket. Cosette would never know what had happened to that other man. 'I have only to let things take their course. There is no escape for the youth. If he is not yet dead he will certainly die. What happiness!'

But having assured himself of this, Valjean's gloom returned; and presently he went downstairs and roused the porter.

About an hour later he left the house again, clad in the full uniform of the National Guard and fully armed. The porter had had no difficulty in finding in the neighbourhood the means to complete his equipment. With a loaded musket and a pouch filled with cartridges he set off for Les Halles.

IV

Excess of zeal on the part of Gavroche

Gavroche, meanwhile, had been having an adventure. Having conscientiously shattered the street-lamp in the Rue du Chaume, he had passed on into the Rue des Vieilles-Haudriettes where, finding nothing worthy of his attention, he had seen fit to unburden himself of a lusty repertoire of song. The sleeping or terrified houses had been favoured with subversive ditties of which the following is a sample:

> The birds sit brooding in the trees
> Where distantly the river swirls
> Their chirping lingers on the breeze –
> But where are all the golden girls?

> Pierrot, my friend, you're on your knees,
> While through your head fair fortune whirls,
> And prayer perhaps may bring you ease –
> But where are all the golden girls?

> Toiling and buzzing like the bees
> You dream of houses decked with pearls,
> But I love Agnes and Louise –
> And where are all the golden girls? . . .

And so on . . . While he walked Gavroche was acting his song, for the weight of the refrain is in the gesture that accompanies it. His face, with its endless variety of expressions, writhed in a series of grimaces more fantastic and extraordinary than those of a torn cloth flying in the wind. Unhappily, since he was alone and in darkness, no one saw or could have seen him: and this wealth was scattered in vain.

But suddenly he stopped short – 'Away with sentiment,' he said.

His cat's eyes had discerned in the recess of a doorway what is known to painters as an ensemble – a composition, that is to say, of man and object. The object was a handcart, the man was an Auvergnat, a peasant from the Auvergne, lying asleep in it. The handles of the cart were resting on the pavement and the man's head was resting against the tail-board, so that he lay sloping downwards with his feet touching the ground. Gavroche, rich in worldly experience, at once knew what he had to deal with – a street carrier who had drunk rather too much and was now sleeping it off.

'So here's the use of a summer night,' reflected Gavroche. 'The Auvergnat is asleep in his cart. We requisition the cart for the service of the Republic and leave the Auvergnat to the Monarchy.' For it had instantly occurred to him that the cart would come in very handy on the barricade.

The man was snoring. Gavroche gently pulled the cart one way and the man the other by his feet, so that in a very short time the Auvergnat, undisturbed, was lying on the pavement. The cart was now free.

Gavroche, being always prepared for emergencies, was as always well equipped. He got out of his pocket a scrap of paper and a stub of red pencil pinched from a carpenter's shop, and wrote as follows:

French Republic
Received – one handcart.
(signed) GAVROCHE

He then put the receipt in the pocket of the snoring Auvergnat's waistcoat, grasped the handcart by the handles, and set off for the market at a run, pushing it with a glorious clatter in front of him.

This was dangerous, for there was a military post in the Imprimerie Royale, the royal printing-works. Gavroche did not think of this. The post was occupied by a section of the Garde Nationale from outside Paris. For some time there had been a certain restiveness in the section and heads had been raised from camp beds. The smashing of two street-lamps, followed by a song delivered at full lung-power, all this was rather surprising in unadventurous streets which were accustomed to put out their candles and go to bed at nightfall. For the past hour the urchin Gavroche had been setting up a stir in that peaceful neighbourhood that was like the buzzing of a fly in a bottle. The out-of-town sergeant was listening. But he was also waiting, being a prudent man.

The clatter of the handcart over the cobbles robbed him of all further excuse for delay, and he decided to go out and reconnoitre. '– there must be a whole gang of them,' he reflected. 'Gently does it.' Who could doubt that the Hydra of Anarchy had raised its head and was rampaging through the quarter? He ventured cautiously out of the post.

And Gavroche, pushing the handcart into the Rue des Vieilles-Haudriettes, found himself suddenly confronted by a uniform, a plumed helmet, and a musket. For the second time he was brought up short.

'So here we are,' he said. 'Authority in person. Good day to you.' Gavroche was never long put out of countenance.

'Where are you going, rascal?' barked the sergeant.

'Citizen,' said Gavroche, 'I haven't called you a bourgeois. Why should you insult me?'

'Where are you going, clown?'

'Monsieur,' said Gavroche, 'yesterday you were perhaps a man of wit, but today your wits have failed you.'

'I'm asking where you're going.'

'How politely you talk! You know, you don't look your age. You should sell your hair at a hundred francs apiece. That would net you five hundred francs.

'Where are you going? Where are you off to? What are you doing, you young scoundrel?'

'That's a very ugly word. Before you have another drink you should wash your mouth out.'

The sergeant levelled his musket.

'Will you or will you not tell me where you're going?'

'My lord General,' said Gavroche, 'I'm on my way to fetch the doctor for my wife, who's in labour.'

'To arms!' shouted the sergeant.

It is the hall-mark of great men that they can turn weaknesses into triumph. Gavroche summed up the situation at a glance. The hand-cart had got him into trouble and the handcart must get him out of it. As the sergeant bore down upon him, the cart, driven forward like a battering ram, took him in the stomach and he fell backwards into the gutter while his musket was discharged into the air. The sound of his shot brought his men rushing out of the post, and that first shot was followed by a ragged burst of firing, after which they reloaded and began again. This blind-man's-buff engagement lasted a quarter of an hour. The casualties were a number of window-panes.

Meanwhile, Gavroche, who had taken to his heels, pulled up half-a-dozen streets away and sat down on a kerbstone to get his breath. He raised his left hand to the level of his nose and jerked it forward three times, at the same time clapping the back of his head with his right hand – the sovereign gesture with which the Paris street-urchin sums up all French irony, and which is evidently efficacious, since it has endured for half a century.

But his triumph was damped by a sobering thought.

'It's all very fine,' he reflected. 'I'm laughing fit to split and having a high old time, but now I'm on the wrong road and I've got a long way to go. It won't do for me to get back too late.'

Running on he resumed his song, and the following stanza echoed through the sombre streets:

> We drain the wine-cup to the lees,
> And cheer the flag when it unfurls;
> And life and death are as you please –
> But where are all the golden girls?

The armed sortie from the post was not without a sequel. The handcart was captured and its drunken owner taken prisoner. The one was impounded and the other half-heartedly tried by court martial as an accomplice of the rebels. Thus did authority display its zeal in the protection of society.

Gavroche's adventure, now a part of the folk-lore of the Temple quarter, is among the most terrifying memories of aged citizens of the Marais, its title being 'Night attack on the post at the Imprimerie Royale'.

PART FIVE
JEAN VALJEAN

BOOK ONE
WAR WITHIN FOUR WALLS

I
Scylla and Charybdis

THE TWO barricades most likely to be recalled by the student of social disorder do not come within the period of this story. Both of them, each symbolic of a particular aspect of a redoubtable situation, were flung up during the insurrection of June 1848, the biggest street-war in history.

It sometimes happens in defiance of principle, regardless of liberty, equality and fraternity, universal suffrage, and the government of the whole by the whole, that an outcast sector of the populace, the riff-raff, rises up in its anguish and frustration, its miseries and privation, its fever, ignorance, darkness, and despair, to challenge the rest of society. The down-and-outs do battle with the common law: mobocracy rebels against Demos.

Those are melancholy occasions, for their dementia always contains an element of justice, and the conflict an element of suicide. The very words accepted as terms of abuse – down-and-outs, riff-raff, mobocracy – point, alas, rather to the faults of those who rule than to the sins of those who suffer, to the misdeeds of privilege rather than to those of the disinherited. For our own part, we can never utter those words without a feeling of grief and respect, for where history scrutinizes the facts to which they correspond it often finds greatness hand-in-hand with misery. Athens was a mobocracy: down-and-outs made Holland: the common people more than once saved Rome, and the rabble followed Jesus Christ.

There is no thinker who has not at times contemplated the splendour rising from below. It was of the rabble that St Jerome must surely have been thinking – the vagabond poor, the outcasts from which the apostles and martyrs sprang – when he uttered the words, *Fex urbis*, *lex orbis*, 'Dregs of the city, law of the world'.

The fury of the mob which suffers and bleeds, its violence running counter to the principles which bring it life, its assault upon the rule of law, these are popular upheavals which must be suppressed. The man of probity stands firm, and from very love of the people opposes them. But he deeply understands their reason, and does so with respect. It is one of those rare occasions when doing what we are in duty bound to do, we have a sense of misgiving which almost calls on us to stay our hand. We go on because we must but with uneasy conscience: duty is burdened with a heavy heart.

June 1848, let me hasten to say, was exceptional, an event which history finds it almost impossible to classify. All the words we have used must be discarded in respect of that extraordinary uprising, which embodied all the warranted apprehensions of labour demanding its rights. It had to be combated; this was necessary: for it was an attack on the Republic. But what, finally, was June 1848? It was a revolt of the populace against itself.

Where the theme is not lost sight of there can be no digression. We may therefore permit ourselves to direct the reader's attention to those two wholly unique strongholds which characterized that insurrection.

One barred the entrance to the Faubourg Saint-Antoine, and the other blocked the approach to the Faubourg du Temple. No one who beheld under that brilliant June sky those two formidable creations of civil war will ever forget them.

The Saint-Antoine barricade was enormous – some three storeys high and seven hundred feet in length. It ran from one end to the other of the vast mouth of the Faubourg – that is to say, across three streets. It was jagged, makeshift, and irregular, castellated like an immense medieval survival, buttressed with piles of rubble that were bastions in themselves, with bays and headlands and, in solid support, the two larger promontories formed by the houses at the end of the streets – a giant's causeway along one side of the famous Place de la Bastille that had witnessed 14 July. Nineteen lesser barricades were arrayed in depth along the street behind it. The sight of this barricade alone conveyed a sense of intolerable distress which had reached the point where suffering becomes disaster. Of what was it built? Of the material of three six-storey houses demolished for the purpose, some people said. Of the phenomenon of overwhelming anger, said others. It bore the lamentable aspect of all things built by hatred – a look of destruction. One might ask, 'Who built all that?'; but one might equally ask, 'Who destroyed all that?' Everything had gone on to it, doors, grilles, screens, bedroom furniture, wrecked cooking-stoves and pots and pans, piled up haphazard, the whole a composite of paving-stones and rubble, timbers, iron bars, broken window-panes, seatless chairs, rags, odds and ends of every kind – and curses. It was great and it was trivial, a chaotic parody of emptiness, a mingling of debris. Sisyphus had cast his rock upon it and Job his potsherd. In short it was terrible, an Acropolis of the destitute. Overturned carts protruded from its outer slope, axles pointing to the sky like scars on a rugged hillside: an omnibus, blithely hoisted by vigorous arms to its summit, as though the architects had sought to add impudence to terror, offered empty shafts to imaginary horses. The huge mass, jetsam of rebellion, was Pelion piled on the Ossa of all previous revolutions – 1793 on 1789, 9 Thermidor on 10 August, 18 Brumaire on 21 January, 1848 on 1830. The site was highly appropriate: it was a barricade worthy to appear on the place from which the grim prison had vanished. If the ocean built dykes, it was thus that it would build them: the fury of the tide itself was imprinted on that shapeless mound. And the tide was the mob. One seemed to behold riot turned to rubble. One seemed to hear, buzzing over that barricade as though it were their hive, the gigantic dark-bodied bees of violent progress. Was it a cluster of thickets, a bacchanalian orgy, or a fortress? Delirium seemed to have built it with the beating of its wings. There was something of the cloaca about it, and something of Olympus. One might see, in that hugger-mugger of desperation, roofing-ridges, fragments from garrets with their coloured wallpaper, window frames with panes intact set upright and defying cannon fire amid the rubble, uprooted fireplaces, wardrobes, tables, benches piled in clamouring disorder, a thousand beggarly objects disdained even by beggars, the expression of fury and nothingness. One might have said that it was the tattered clothing of the people – a clothing of wood, stone and iron – which the Faubourg Saint-Antoine had swept out of doors with a huge stroke of the broom, making of its poverty its protective barrier. Hunks of wood like chopping-blocks, brackets attached to wooden frames that looked like gibbets, wheels lying flat upon the rubble – all these lent to the anarchic edifice a recollection of tortures once suffered by the people The Saint-Antoine barricade used everything as a weapon, everything that civil war can hurl at the head of society. It was not a battle but a paroxysm. The fire-arms defending the stronghold, among which were a number of blunderbusses, poured out fragments of pottery, knuckle-bones, coat buttons, and even castors, dangerous missiles because of their metalwork. That barricade was a mad thing, flinging an inexpressible clamour into the sky. At moments when it defied the army, it was covered with bodies and with tempest, surmounted by a dense array of flaming heads. It was a thing of swarming activity, with a bristling fringe of muskets, sabres, cudgels, axes, pikes and bayonets. A huge red flag flapped in the wind. The shouting of orders was to be heard, warlike song, the roll of drums, the sobbing of women, and the dark raucous laughter of the half-starved. It was beyond reason and it was alive; and, as though from the back of some electric-coated animal, lightning crackled over it. The spirit of revolution cast its shadow over that mound, resonant with the voice of the people, which resembles the voice of God: a strange nobility emanated from it. It was a pile of garbage, and it was Sinai.

As we have said, it was raised in the name of the Revolution. But what was it fighting? It was fighting the Revolution. That barricade, which was chance, disorder, terror, misunderstanding and the unknown, was at war with the Constituent Assembly, the sovereignty of the people, universal suffrage, the nation and the Republic. It was the 'Carmagnole' defying the 'Marseillaise'. An insane but heroic defiance, for that ancient faubourg is a hero.

The faubourg and its stronghold sustained one another, the faubourg lending a shoulder to the stronghold and the stronghold bracing itself against the faubourg. The huge barricade was like a cliff against which the strategy of the generals from Africa was shattered. Its recesses and excrescences, its warts and swellings grinned, so to speak, and jeered through the smoke. Grapeshot vanished in its depths: shells were swallowed up in it; musket balls did no more than make small holes. What good does it do to bombard chaos? The soldiers, accustomed to the most fearful manifestations of war, were dismayed by this fortress that was like a wild beast, by its boar-like bristling and its mountainous size.

Some half a mile away, near the Château D'Eau where the Rue du Temple runs into the boulevard, the onlooker, if he was not afraid to risk his head by peering round the promontory formed by the Magasin Dallemagne, might see, far off, looking across the canal and along the streets rising up to the heights of Belleville, at the summit of the rise, a strange-looking wall about two storeys high, a sort of hyphen between the houses on either side – as though the street had folded in upon itself to shut itself off. This wall, built of paving-stones, was straight and perpendicular, as though it had been constructed with the aid of a T-square. It was, no doubt, lacking in cement, but, as with some Roman walls, this in no way impaired the rigidity of its structure. A view from above enabled one to ascertain its thickness: it was mathematically even from top to bottom. Its grey surface was pierced at regular intervals with almost invisible loopholes, like dark threads. The street bore every sign of being deserted: all doors and windows were closed. The wall erected across it, a motionless, silent barrier, had made of it a cul-de-sac in which no person was to be seen, no sound heard. Bathed in the dazzling June sunshine, it had the look of a sepulchre. This was the Faubourg du Temple barricade.

Coming to that place, and seeing that remarkable structure, even the boldest spirit was moved to ponder. It was immaculate in design, flawless in alignment, symmetrical, rectilinear and funereal, a thing of craftsmanship and darkness. One felt that its presiding spirit must be either a mathematician or a ghost: and, contemplating it, one spoke in a lowered voice.

When, as happened from time to time, someone ventured to enter that deserted stretch of road – a soldier or a representative of the people – there was a faint, shrill whistle, and he fell, either wounded or dead; or, if he escaped, a bullet buried itself in a shutter or housefront. Sometimes it was a burst of grapeshot, for the defenders had contrived to make two small cannon out of gas-piping blocked at one end with oakum and fire-clay. Nearly every bullet found its mark. There were corpses here and there and pools of blood. I remember seeing a butterfly flutter up and down that street. Summer does not abdicate.

The entrances to the houses in the neighbouring street were filled with wounded. One felt in that place the gaze of an unseen observer, as though the street itself were taking aim. Massed behind the hump of the narrow bridge across the canal, at the approach to the Faubourg du Temple, the attacking troops, grim-faced and wary, kept watch on that silent and impassive stronghold which spat death. Some crawled on their stomachs on to the hump, taking care that their tall helmets should not show.

The gallant Colonel Monteynard observed the barricade with a shuddering admiration. 'The way it's built!' he exclaimed. 'Not a stone out of line. It might be made of earthenware!' – and as he spoke the words, a bullet smashed the cross on his breast and he fell.

'The cowards!' men said. 'Why don't they show themselves? Why do they skulk in hiding?' ... That barricade at the Faubourg du Temple, defended by eighty men against ten thousand, held out for three days. On the fourth day, it was captured by the device of breaking through the adjoining houses and clambering over the roofs. Not one of the eighty 'cowards' attempted to escape. All were killed except their leader, Barthélemy, of whom we shall have more to say.

The Saint-Antoine barricade was a place of thunderous defiance, the one at the Temple a place of silence. The difference between these two strongholds was the difference between the savage and the sinister, the one a roaring open mouth, the other a mask. The huge, mysterious insurrection of June '48 was at once an outburst of fury and an enigma: in the first of these barricades the dragon was discernible; in the second, the sphinx.

The two strongholds were the work of two men, Cournet and Barthélemy, and each bore the image of the man responsible. Cournet of Saint-Antoine was a burly broad-shouldered man, red-faced, heavy-fisted, daring, and loyal, his gaze candid but awe-inspiring. He was intrepid, energetic, irascible and temperamental, the warmest of friends and the most formidable of enemies. War and conflict, the mêlée, were the air he breathed, they put him in high spirits. He had been a naval officer, and his voice and bearing had the flavour of sea and tempest – he brought the gale with him into battle. Except for genius there was in Cournet something of Danton, just as, except for divinity, there was in Danton something of Hercules.

Barthélemy, of the Temple, was thin and puny, sallow-faced and taciturn, a sort of tragic outcast who, having been beaten by a police officer, waited for the chance and killed him. He was sent to the galleys at the age of seventeen, and when he came out he built this barricade.

Later a terrible thing happened in London, where both men were in hiding. Barthélemy killed Cournet. It was a duel to the death, one of those mysterious affairs of passion in which French justice sees extenuating circumstances and English justice sees only the death penalty. Barthélemy was hanged. Thanks to the sombre ordering of society, that luckless man, who possessed a mind that was certainly resolute and perhaps great, by reason of material privation and moral darkness, began life in a French prison, and ended it on an English scaffold. Barthélemy at all times flew one flag only, and it was black.

II
What to do in a bottomless pit except talk?

Sixteen years are a useful period in the underground instruction of rebellion, and they were wiser in June 1848 than in June 1832. The barricade in the Rue de la Chanvrerie was nothing but a first outline, an embryo, compared with those we have been describing. Nevertheless, it was impressive for its time.

Under the eye of Enjolras, for Marius no longer took count of anything, the rebels made good use of the hours of darkness. The barricade was not merely repaired but strengthened, its height raised by two feet. Iron bars projected from between the paving-stones like couched lances. Fresh material had been brought in to add to the complexity of its outer face and it had been cunningly rebuilt so that on the one side it resembled a thicket and on the other side a wall. The stairway of paving-stones which made it possible to climb to the top, as on to the battlements of a fortress, had been restored. The whole area within the barricades had been tidied up, the ground-floor room of the tavern cleared and the kitchen converted into a first-aid post where all wounds had been dressed. More bullets had been cast and cartridges made. The weapons of the fallen had been redistributed, and the bodies of the dead removed. They were heaped in the Mondétour alleyway, still commanded by the rebels, of which the pavement had long been red with blood. Among the dead were four suburban National Guards. Enjolras had their uniforms laid aside.

Enjolras had advised everyone to get two hours sleep, and a hint from him amounted to a command. Nevertheless, only three or four obeyed it. Feuilly spent the two hours carving the words 'Long Live the People!' on the house facing the tavern. They were still there, carved with a nail on a beam, in 1848.

The three women had taken advantage of the darkness to vanish finally from the scene, which was a relief to the rebels. They were now hiding in a near-by house.

The majority of the casualties were still able and willing to fight;

but five badly wounded men lay on a bed of straw and mattresses in the kitchen, two of them National Guards. These latter were the first to be attended to.

No one remained in the downstairs room except Monsieur Mabeuf under his black shroud and Javert, lashed to his pillar.

'The house of the dead,' said Enjolras.

The table on which Monsieur Mabeuf lay was at the far end of the room, lighted by a single candle, its horizontal outline visible behind the pillar, so that the two figures, Javert upright and Mabeuf prone, vaguely suggested the form of a cross.

The shaft of the omnibus, damaged though it was by musket fire, was still sufficiently upright to fly a flag; and Enjolras who possessed the especial virtue of a leader, in that he always did what he said he would do, had attached the old man's bloodstained jacket to it.

No meal was possible, since there was neither bread nor meat. In the sixteen hours they had been there the fifty defenders of the barricade had devoured all the tavern's scanty store. There comes a point when every fortress that holds out becomes a raft of the *Medusa*. They had to put up with being hungry. It was on that Spartan day of 6 June that Jeanne, the commander of the Saint-Merry barricade, surrounded by supporters clamouring to be fed, retorted: 'What for? It is now three – by four o'clock we shall be dead.'

Since there was nothing to eat, Enjolras placed a ban on drinking, withholding wine altogether and rationing eau-de-vie. Fifteen hermetically sealed bottles were found in the cellar. Enjolras and Combeferre went down to inspect them, and Combeferre said when they came back:

'They must be some of Père Hucheloup's original stock. He started life as a grocer.

'Probably good wine,' said Bossuet. 'It's lucky Grantaire's still asleep. Otherwise we should have had a job protecting them.'

Despite murmurs of protest. Enjolras vetoed the fifteen bottles, and, to prevent anyone touching them, to make them as it were sacrosanct, he had them placed under Monsieur Mabeuf's table.

At two o'clock in the morning roll was called. There were thirty-seven of them.

Dawn was beginning to show, and the torch, replaced in its screen of paving-stones, had been extinguished. The interior of the stronghold, the small area of street which it enclosed, was still in shadow, and in that vaguely ominous first light it resembled the deck of a ship in distress. The dark forms of the defenders passed to and fro, while, overhanging the sombre redoubt, the housefronts and chimney-tops grew gradually distinct. The sky was in that state of fragile uncertainty which hovers between white and blue. Birds flew happily. The roof of the tall house at the back of the stronghold, which faced east, had a pinkish glow, and a morning breeze was stirring in the grey locks of the dead man in the third-storey window.

'I'm glad we've put out the torch,' Courfeyrac said to Feuilly. 'I didn't like the way it flared in the wind, as though it was afraid. A torch-flame resembles the wisdom of cowards: it gives a poor light because it trembles.'

Dawn rouses the spirits as it does the birds. Everyone was talking. Joly, seeing a cat exploring the gutter, was moved to philosophize.

'After all, what is a cat?' he demanded. 'It's a correction. Having created the mouse God said to himself, "That was silly of me!" and so he created the cat. The cat is the *erratum* of the mouse. Mouse and cat together represent the revised proofs of Creation.'

Combeferre was discoursing to a circle of students and workmen on the subject of the dead – Jean Prouvaire, Bahorel, Mabeuf, even Cabuc – and Enjolras's stern sadness.

'All those who have killed have suffered,' he said. 'Harmodius and Aristogeiton, Brutus, St Stephen, Cromwell, Charlotte Corday – all have had their moments of anguish. Our hearts are so sensitive, and human life is so great a mystery, that even after a civic murder, a liberating murder, if such exists, our feeling of remorse at having killed a man exceeds the joy of having served mankind.'

A minute later, such are the twists and turns of conversation, they had arrived, by way of the verse of Jean Prouvaire and a comparison of different translations of the Georgics, particularly of the passage describing the prodigies which heralded the death of Caesar, at the subject of Caesar himself, whence their discussion returned to Brutus.

'Caesar,' said Combeferre, 'was justly killed. Cicero was hard on him, but with reason. When Zoilus attacked Homer, Maevius attacked Virgil, Vise attacked Molière, Pope attacked Shakespeare and Fréron attacked Voltaire, these insults were merely in accord with the age-old law of envy and hatred: genius invites hostility. Great men are always more or less assailed. But Zoilus and Cicero are two birds of a different kind. Cicero did justice with the mind just as Brutus did justice with the sword. For my part, I condemn that latter kind of justice, but the ancient world accepted it. Caesar, in crossing the Rubicon, conferring, as though they came from himself, dignities which came from the people, and not rising to greet the Senate, performed, as Eutropius said, the acts of a king and almost of a tyrant – *regia ac paene tyrannica*. He was a great man, and so much the worse or so much the better – the lesson was the greater. His twenty-three wounds afflict me less than the spittle on the forehead of Christ. Caesar was stabbed to death by senators; Christ was mauled by underlings. In the greater outrage we perceive the God.'

Bossuet, dominating the talkers from the top of a heap of paving-stones and flourishing his carbine, cried:

'Oh Cydathenaeum! Oh Myrrhinus! Oh Probalinthus! Oh Graces of the Aeantides! Who will teach me to speak the lines of Homer like a Greek from Laurium or Edapteon?'

III

Light and shadow

Enjorlas made a tour of reconnaissance. He went out by the Mondétour alleyway, moving cautiously along the housefronts.

The rebels, be it said, were filled with hope. Their success in repelling the night attack had made them almost disdainful of the attack that must come with the dawn. They awaited it with confident smiles, no more doubtful of success than they were of their cause. Besides which, help must assuredly be on the way. They counted on this. With the gift of sanguine prophecy which is one of the strengths of the embattled French, they divided the coming day into three parts: at six o'clock in the morning a regiment which had been 'worked on' could come over to their side; at midday all Paris would rise in revolt, and by sundown the revolution would be accomplished. The tolling of the Saint-Merry tocsin, which had not ceased for a minute since the previous evening, was still to be heard, and this was evidence that the other stronghold, the big one commanded by Jeanne, was still holding out.

Heady prognostications of this ran from group to group in a kind of grim and gay murmur resembling the buzz of war in a hive of bees.

Enjolras returned from his cautious patrol of the surrounding darkness. He stood for a moment listening to this exuberance with arms folded and a hand pressed to his mouth. Then, cool and flushed with the gowing light of the morning, he said:

'The whole Paris army is involved. A third of it is concentrated on us, besides a contingent of the Garde Nationale. I made out the shakos of the Fifth Infantry of the line and the colours of the Sixth. We shall be attacked within the hour. As for the populace, they were excited enough yesterday but now they aren't stirring. We've nothing to hope for – not a single faubourg or a single regiment. They have failed us.'

The effect of these words on the gossiping groups was like that of rainfall on a swarm of bees. All were silent. There was a moment of inexpressible terror, overshadowed by the wings of death.

But it swiftly passed. A voice from one of the groups cried:

'All right, then we'll build the barricade up to twenty feet high, citizens, and defend it with our dead bodies. We'll show the world that if the people have deserted the republicans, the republicans have not deserted the people!'

The speech, releasing men from their private terror, was greeted with cheers.

No one can say who delivered it – some ordinary working man, one of the unnamed, random heroes who crop up in moments of human crisis and social evolution to speak decisive words, and then, having in a lightning flash given utterance to the spirit of the people and of God, relapse into anonymity. So much was it in tune with the mood of that 6 June 1832, that, at almost the same moment, defenders of the Saint-Merry stronghold raised their voices in a bellow that has gone down to history – 'No matter whether they come to our aid or not, we'll die to the last man!'

As we see, the two strongholds, separated though they were, were together in spirit.

IV

Five fewer; one more

After that unknown man, demanding that they should 'protest with their dead bodies', had voiced the resolution of them all there arose a roar of strange satisfaction, deadly in its impact but triumphant in tone.

'To the death! We'll all stay here.'

'Why all?' asked Enjolras.

'All of us – all!'

Enjolras said:

'It's a strong position. The barricade is sound. Thirty men can hold it. Why sacrifice forty?'

'Because no one wants to leave,' was the reply.

'Citizens,' cried Enjolras, with a hint of exasperation in his voice. 'The Republic is not so rich in men that it can afford to waste them. Heroics are wasteful. If it is the duty of some of us to leave, that duty should be carried out like any other.'

Enjolras, their acknowledged leader, possessed over his followers the kind of authority that is born of absolute conviction. Nevertheless, there were rebellious murmurs. A leader to his finger-tips, Enjolras stood his ground and demanded coolly:

'Will those who are afraid of our being no more than thirty kindly say so?'

The murmurs grew louder.

'Besides,' a voice said, 'it's all very well to talk about leaving, but we're surrounded.'

'Not on the side of Les Halles,' said Enjolras. 'The Rue Mondétour is clear. You can get to the Marché des Innocents by way of the Rue des Prêcheurs.'

'And there we'll be taken,' said another voice. 'They'll see a man in a smock and cap and they'll want to know where he comes from. They'll look at his hands, they'll smell powder, and he'll be shot.'

Without replying Enjolras touched Combeferre's shoulder and the two of them went into the tavern. They re-emerged a minute later, Enjolras carrying the four uniforms stripped off the bodies of the dead soldiers and Combeferre with their belts and helmets.

'Anyone can pass through the soldiers' ranks wearing these,' Enjolras said. 'They'll do for four of you.' He dropped the uniforms on the ground.

Their stoical audience still showed no sign of obeying, and Combeferre now addressed them:

'We must show a little pity,' he said. 'Don't you see what this means? It concerns the women. Have none of you any womenfolk, or any children? Have you or haven't you? What of the mothers rocking the cradles with their young around them? If there is one among you who has never seen a nursing breast let him raise his hand. You want to get yourself killed, and so do I, but I don't like the thought of women wringing their phantom hands over me. Die by all means, but do not cause others to die. The act of suicide we have resolved upon is sublime; but suicide is a private matter that admits of no extension, and when it is passed on to those nearest us it becomes murder. Think of small heads of fair hair, and old, white heads. Enjolras has just told me that on the fifth floor of a house at the corner of the Rue du Cygne he saw a candle burning and, silhouetted against the window-pane, the nodding head of an old woman who looked as though she had sat up waiting all night. If she is the mother of any one of you then he should hurry back to her and say, "Mother, here I am." He need not worry, the rest of us will do the job here. Those supporting a family by their labour have no right to sacrifice their lives – it is an act of desertion. Those of you who have daughters or sisters – have you thought of them? Who will feed them when you are dead? It is a terrible thing for a girl to go hungry. A man may beg, but a woman has to sell. Those charming creatures who are the delight of your life, the Jeannes or Lises or Mimis who fill your home with innocent gaiety and fragrance – are you to leave them to starve? What am I to say to you? There is a market in human flesh, and it is not your disembodied hands, fluttering over them, that will protect them from being drawn into it. Think of the streets, the shops outside which women go to and fro in low-cut gowns with their feet in the mud. Those women, too, were once chaste. Think of your sisters, those of you who have any. Prostitution, the police, the Saint-Lazare prison – that is what they will come to, those delicate, modest creatures, those marvels of gentleness and beauty. And you will no longer be there to protect them. You wanted to rescue the people from Royalty, and so you have handed your daughters over to the police. Take care, my friends; show compassion. Women, poor souls, are not much given to thinking. We pride ourselves on the fact that they are less educated than men. We prevent them from reading, from thinking, from concerning themselves with politics. Will you not also prevent them from going to the morgue tonight to identify your bodies? Those of you who have families must be sensible fellows and shake us by the hand and clear out leaving the rest of us to see this business through. I know it is not easy to run away. It's difficult. But the greater the difficulty the greater the merit. You say to yourself: "I've got a musket and here I am, and here I stay." It is easily said. But there is tomorrow, friends. You won't be living, but your families will. Think of their sufferings. Have you thought of what will happen to the rosy-cheeked, laughing, chattering infant that feels so warm in your embrace? I remember one such, no higher than my knee. The father died and some poor people took it in out of charity, but they had not enough to eat themselves. The child was always hungry. It never cried. It huddled near the cooking-stove, which was never lighted. The chimney had been patched with clay. The child with its small hands scratched out fragments of the clay and ate them. It breathed with difficulty; it was white-faced, with weak limbs and a swollen stomach. It said nothing and did not answer when it was spoken to. It was taken to the Necker hospital, which is where I saw it. I was a junior physician at that hospital. The child died. If there are parents among you, fathers who know the happiness of going for a walk on Sunday with a child clinging to his strong, protective hand, they should think of that dead child as though it were their own. I can see him now, that poor little boy, lying naked on the dissecting-table, with the ribs standing out under his skin like the furrows of a ploughed field. We found mud in his stomach and ashes in his teeth. Let us search our conscience and take counsel with our hearts. Statistics show that fifty-five per cent of abandoned children die. I repeat, we have the women to consider – mothers, girls and babies. Have I said anything about yourselves? I know very well what you are. I know that you are brave, and that your hearts are uplifted at the thought of shedding your lives in our great cause. I know that each of you feels that he has been chosen to die usefully and magnificently and that each wants his share in the triumph. That is splendid, but you are not alone in the world. You have to think of others. You must not be egoists.'

His audience gloomily bowed their heads.

Strange are the contradictions of the human heart, even in its noblest moments! Combeferre, who said these things, was not an orphan. He remembered other men's mothers, but not his own. He was himself one of the 'egoists'.

Marius, fasting and feverish, plunged from the heights of hope to the depths of despair and, seeing his personal shipwreck approach its end, was becoming ever more deeply sunk in that state of visionary stupor which precedes the fateful moment deliberately invited. A pyschologist might have studied in him the increasing symptoms of that classic condition well known to science, which bears the same relation to suffering as sensuality does to physical delight. Despair has its own ecstasies and Marius had reached them. He was witnessing events as though from outside, and the things going on around him seemed to him remote, a pattern to be conscious of, but of which the details were disregarded. He saw the figures of men coming and going in a haze, and heard the sound of voices speaking in a void.

But one thing troubled him. There was in his situation one thought that touched and aroused him. Although his only desire was to die, and nothing must be allowed to distract him from his purpose, the thought recurred to him in his desolate, befogged state, that this resolve must not prevent him from saving the life of some other person.

He suddenly spoke.

'Enjolras and Combeferre are right,' he said. 'I agree with them that there must be no unnecessary sacrifice. And there is no time to be lost. As Combeferre has said, some of you have families – mothers, wives, and children. Those men must leave at once.'

No man stirred.

'Married men and the supporters of families are to break ranks!' Marius repeated.

His authority was great. Enjolras was captain of the fortress, but Marius was its saviour.

'That is an order!' shouted Enjolras.

'I beseech you,' said Marius.

And then, stirred by Combeferre's address, shaken by Enjolras's order, and touched by Marius's plea, the heroic defenders began to denounce one another. 'That's right,' a youth said to another man. 'You're a father of a family. You must go' ... 'You're keeping your two sisters,' the older man replied. And the strangest of altercations broke out, as to who should not stay to be killed.

'Be quick,' said Courfeyrac. 'In another quarter of an hour it will be too late.'

'Citizens,' said Enjolras, 'this is the Republic, where universal suffrage prevails. You must decide by vote who is to go.'

He was obeyed. Within a few minutes five men had been selected and they stepped out of the ranks.

'Five!' exclaimed Marius. 'But there are only four uniforms.'

'Then,' said the five men, 'one of us must stay.'

And the noble-hearted dispute was resumed, as to which had the best reason for going.

'You have a wife who loves you ... You have an old mother ... You have neither father nor mother, but what about your three younger brothers? ... You're the father of five children ... You have a right to go on living; at seventeen you're too young to die ...'

Those great revolutionary barricades were gathering places of heroism. The improbable became natural, and no man surprised his fellow.

'Hurry up!' repeated Courfeyrac.

Someone shouted to Marius:

'You decide which one's to stay.'

'Yes,' said the five men. 'You choose and we'll obey.'

Marius had thought that he was no longer capable of any profound emotion, but at the idea that he should select a man for death he felt his blood run cold. He would have turned pale, had he not been pale already.

He moved forward and the five men, their eyes blazing with the fire that is the message of Thermopylae, greeted him with cries of 'Me! ... Me! ... Me! ...'

Marius, in his stupor, counted them. There were still five. Then he looked down at the four uniforms.

As he did so a fifth uniform was added to the heap, as though it had fallen from the clouds. The fifth man was saved!

Looking round, Marius recognized Monsieur Fauchelevent.

Jean Valjean had entered the stronghold.

Whether acting on information, or by instinct or chance, he had come by way of the Rue Mondétour, and, in his National Guard uniform, had had no difficulty in getting through. The rebel sentry posted in the alley had seen no reason to raise the alarm on account of a single man but had let him pass, reflecting that either he had come to join them or, at the worst, would be taken prisoner. In any event, the situation was too acute for the sentry to leave his post.

No one had noticed Valjean when he appeared, all eyes being intent on the five men and the four uniforms. Valjean had stood listening, and, grasping the situation, had silently stripped off his uniform and dropped it on the pile.

The sensation was enormous.

'Who is this man?' demanded Bossuet.

'At least,' said Combeferre, 'he's ready to save another man's life.'

Marius said authoritatively:

'I know him.'

This was enough for them. Enjolras turned to Jean Valjean.

'Citizen, you are welcome.' And he added. 'You know that we are about to die.'

Valjean, without replying, helped the man he had saved to put on his uniform.

V

The world as seen from the top of the barricade

Their situation, in that fateful hour and that inexorable place, found its ultimate and utmost expression in the supreme melancholy of Enjolras.

Enjolras embodied in himself the fullness of revolution. Yet he was incomplete, in so far as the absolute may be incomplete. There was in him too much of Saint-Just, too little of Anacharsis Clootz.* Nevertheless his thinking, in the ABC Society, had been to some extent influenced by the outlook of Combeferre. Gradually ridding himself of the narrow restrictions of dogma, he had begun to consider the wider aspect of progress, and had come to accept, as the final, magnificent goal of social evolution, the expansion of the great French Republic into the republic of all mankind. As for the immediate steps to be taken, since they were in a situation of violence he desired them to be violent; in this he was unshakeable, a follower of that epic, redoubtable school of thought which may be summed up in a date, the year 1793.

Enjolras was standing on the steps of the barricade with one arm resting on the muzzle of his carbine. He was thinking, quivering as though swayed in a breeze under the gallows – influenced by that place of death. A kind of dark fire smouldered in his absent, meditative eye. Suddenly he raised his head, and with his fair hair flowing back like that of the angel on his dark chariot of stars, or like a lion's mane, he cried:

'Citizens, can you conceive of the future? Streets in cities bathed

* A German visionary and follower of Hébert who went to the guillotine in 1794.

in light, green branches on the thresholds of the houses and all nations sisters, all men upright; old men blessing the young, and the past loving the present; thinkers wholly free to pursue their thought, and religious believers all equal before the law; Heaven itself the one religion, God its immediate priest and the conscience of mankind its altar. An end to hatred: the brotherhood of the workshop and the school; notoriety both punishment and reward; work for all men, justice for all men, and peace, an end to bloodshed and to war. To tame the natural world is the first step, and the second step is to achieve the ideal. Consider what progress has already been accomplished. The primitive races of mankind were terrified by the hydra that flew upon the water, by the dragon that belched fire, by the griffin, that aerial monster with the wings of an eagle and a tiger's claws – fearful creatures beyond the control of men. But man set his traps, the miraculous traps conceived by human intelligence, and in the end he captured them.

'We have tamed the hydra, and its new name is the steamship; we have tamed the dragon, and it is the locomotive; we have not yet tamed the griffin, but we have captured it and its name is the balloon. On the day when this Promethean task is completed and man has finally harnessed to his will the ancient triple chimera of the hydra, the dragon, and the griffin he will be the master of fire, air, and water, and he will have become to the rest of living Creation what the Gods of antiquity were to him. Have courage, citizens! We must go forward. But what are we aiming at? At government by knowledge, with the nature of things the only social force, natural law containing its penalties and sanctions within itself, and based on its evident truth: a dawn of truth corresponding to the laws of daylight. We are moving towards the union of nations and the unity of mankind. No more make-believers and no more parasites. Reality governed by truth, that is our aim. Civilization will hold its court in Europe and later will preside over all the continents in a Grand Parliament of Intelligence. History has already known something of the kind. The Amphictyonic League held two sessions a year, one at Delphi, the place of the Gods, and the other at Thermopylae, the place of heroes. Europe will have its Amphictyon, and presently the whole world. France carries this sublime future in her loins. It is here that the nineteenth century is being conceived. What Greece first essayed is worthy to be achieved by France. Listen to me, my friend Feuilly, sturdy workman that you are, man of the people and of all peoples. I honour you. You see clearly into the future, and see rightly. You knew neither father nor mother, Feuilly; you have made humanity your mother and justice your father. You are to die in this place, which is to say that you are to triumph. Citizens, no matter what happens today, in defeat no less than victory, we shall be making a revolution. Just as a great fire lights up all the town, so a revolution lights up all mankind. And what is the revolution that we shall make? I have already told you: it is the revolution of Truth. In terms of policy there is only one principle, the sovereignty of man over himself, and this sovereignty of me over me is called Liberty. Where two or more of these sovereignties are gathered together, that is where the State begins. But there can be no withdrawal from this association. Each sovereignty must concede some portion of itself to establish the common law, and the portion is the same for all. The common law is nothing but the protection of all men based on the rights of each, and the equivalent sacrifice that all men make is called Equality. The protection of all men by every man is Fraternity, and the point at which all these sovereignties intersect is called Society. Since this intersection is a meeting point, the point is a knot – hence what is called the "social bond". It is sometimes called the social contract, which comes to the same thing, since the word "contract" is etymologically based on the idea of drawing together. But equality, citizens, does not mean that all plants must grow to the same height – a society of tall grass and dwarf trees, a jostle of conflicting jealousies. It means, in civic terms, an equal outlet for all talents; in political terms, that all votes will carry the same weight; and in religious terms that all beliefs will enjoy equal rights. Equality has a means at its disposal – compulsory free education. The right to learn the alphabet, that is where we must start. Primary school made obligatory for everyone and secondary school available to everyone, that must be the law. And from those identical schools the egalitarian society will emerge. Yes, education! Light! – light – all things are born of light and all things return to it! Citizens, our nineteenth century is great, but the twentieth century will be *happy*. Nothing in it will resemble ancient history. Today's fears will all have been abolished – war and conquest, the clash of armed nations, the course of civilization dependent on royal marriages, the birth of hereditary tyrannies, nations partitioned by a congress or the collapse of a dynasty, religions beating their heads together like rams in the wilderness of the infinite. Men will no longer fear famine or exploitation, prostitution from want, destitution born of unemployment – or the scaffold, or the sword, or any other malice of chance in the tangle of events. One might almost say, indeed, that there will be no more events. Men will be happy. Mankind will fulfil its own laws as does the terrestrial globe, and harmony will be restored between the human souls and the heavens. The souls will circle about the Truth as the planets circle round the sun. I am speaking to you, friends, in a dark hour; but this is the hard price that must be paid for the future. A revolution is a toll-gate. But mankind will be liberated, uplifted and consoled. We here affirm it, on this barricade. Whence should the cry of love proceed, if not from the sacrificial altar? Brothers, this is the meeting place of those who reflect and those who suffer. This barricade is not a matter of rubble and paving-stone; it is built of two components, of ideas and of suffering. Here wretchedness and idealism come together. Day embraces night and says to her, "I shall die with you, and you will be reborn with me." It is of the embraces of despair that faith is born. Suffering brings death, but the idea brings immortality. That agony and immortality will be mingled and merged in one death. Brothers, we who die here will die in the radiance of the future. We go to a tomb flooded with the light of dawn.'

Enjolras fell silent rather than ceased to speak; his lips continued to move as though he were still speaking to himself, with the result that his audience continued to regard him, waiting to hear more. There was no applause, but much whispering. Words being but a breath, the stir of awakened minds is like the rustling of leaves.

VI

Marius and Javert

We must describe what was going on in Marius's mind.

His general situation we know. We have said already that the world for him had ceased to be real. He no longer grasped things clearly. He was moving, we must repeat, in the shadow of the great dark wings that spread over the dying. He felt that he was already in the grave, that he had crossed over to the other side, whence he could see the faces of the living only with the eyes of the dead.

How did Monsieur Fauchelevent come to be here? Why was he here? What had he come for? Marius did not ask himself these several questions. In any event, the quality of the state of despair being that we extend it to others besides ourselves, it seemed to him natural that everyone should have come there to die. But the thought of Cosette clutched at his heart.

Monsieur Fauchelevent did not speak to Marius or even look at him, and seemed not to have heard when Marius said, 'I know him.' This was a relief to Marius, and indeed, if the word can be used in such a context, it may be said to have pleased him. He had been always conscious of the impossibility of his addressing a word to this enigmatic figure who was to him both suspect and impressive. Besides, it was a very long time since he had seen him, and to anyone as shy and reserved as Marius this increased the impossibility.

The five selected men left the stronghold by way of the Rue Mondétour, looking precisely like members of the National Guard. One of them was weeping. Before leaving they embraced all those who were staying behind.

When the men restored to life had departed, the thoughts of Enjolras turned to the man condemned to death. He went into the tavern and asked:

'Do you want anything?'

Javert replied:

'When are you going to kill me?'

'You must wait. At the moment we need all our ammunition.'

'Then give me something to drink,' said Javert.

Enjolras brought him a glass of water, and, since his arms were bound, held it for him to drink.

'Is that all?' he asked.

'I'm not at all comfortable,' said Javert. 'It was scarcely kind to keep me lashed to this pillar all night. You can tie me up as much as you like, but you might at least let me lie on a table like that other fellow.' And he nodded in the direction of Monsieur Mabeuf.

It will be remembered that at the back of the ground-floor room there was a large table that had been used for the making of bullets and cartridges. Now that this was done, and the supply of powder used up, the table was no longer required. At Enjolras's order, four of the rebels released Javert from the pillar, a fifth holding a bayonet to his breast while they were untying him. Keeping his hands tied behind his back and holding him with a length of stout cord which permitted him to take a pace fifteen inches long, like a man mounting the scaffold, they walked him to the table and, stretching him out on it, tied him to it securely with a rope passed round his body. As a further precaution, to render any attempt at escape impossible, they passed a rope round his neck, ran the two ends between his legs and tied them to his wrists – the device known in prisons as the 'martingale'.

While they were doing this a man appeared in the doorway and stood staring with a singular fixity at Javert. The shadow he cast caused Javert to turn his head. He looked round and recognized Jean Valjean. He gave no sign of emotion. Coolly averting his gaze, he simply said, 'So here we are!'

VII

The situation deteriorates

The sky was growing rapidly lighter: but not a door or a window opened in the street. It was daybreak but not yet the hour of awakening. As we have said, the troops had been withdrawn from the far end of the Rue de la Chanvrerie, opposite the barricade; the street seemed clear, open to the public with a sinister tranquillity. The Rue Saint-Denis was as silent as the Avenue of the Sphinx at Thebes, with not a soul to be seen at the intersections now brightening in the reflected light of the dawn. Nothing is more dreary than this gathering of light in an empty street.

There was nothing to be seen but something to be heard. Mysterious movements were taking place some distance away. Clearly the crisis was imminent, and the sentries withdrew as they had done on the previous evening; but this time they all went.

The barricade was stronger than it had been at the first assault. After the departure of the five men it had been still further reinforced. Acting on the advice of the scout who was keeping an eye on the Halles area, Enjolras had taken a serious step. He had blocked the narrowest part of the Rue Mondétour, which until then had remained open, uprooting the paving-stones over a length of several more houses for the purpose. The stronghold, being now protected in front by the barricade across the Rue de la Chanvrerie, and on either flank by the barricades across the Rue du Cygne and the Rue Mondétour, had been rendered almost impregnable; but, on the other hand, it was totally enclosed. It had three fighting fronts but no outlet. 'A fortress, but also a mousetrap,' said Combeferre, chuckling. Enjolras had had some thirty paving-stones torn up for no reason, as Bossuet said, and piled up by the door of the tavern.

The silence in the direction from which the main attack was to be expected was now so ominous that Enjolras sent all his men to their action stations and a ration of eau-de-vie was distributed.

Nothing is more singular than a barricade preparing for an assault. Men take their places as though at the play, jostling and elbowing each other. Some make seats for themselves. The awkward corner is avoided, and the niche which may afford protection is occupied. Left-handed men are invaluable: they can fill places unsuited to the rest. Many men prefer to fight sitting down, to be able to kill and die in comfort. In the savage fighting of June 1848 a renowned marksman operating from a roof-terrace had an armchair of the Voltaire pattern brought up to him: he was caught by a discharge of grapeshot.

Directly the commander orders the men to action-stations all disorder ceases – the exchange of ribaldries, the gossiping groups, the groups of personal friends. Each man, seized with the common purpose, concentrates his thoughts on the enemy. A barricade not in immediate danger is chaos; but in the face of danger it is disciplined. Peril brings order.

When Enjolras, with his double-barrelled carbine, took up his position in the sort of redoubt he had reserved for himself, complete silence fell, broken only by a series of clicks along the wall as the men cocked their muskets.

For the rest, their state of mind was more proud and confident than ever. Extravagance of sacrifice is a stiffener of the spirit. They had nothing to hope for, but they had despair, that last resort which, as Virgil said, sometimes brings victory. Supreme resources may be born of supreme resolution. To plunge into the sea is sometimes to escape shipwreck; a coffin-lid may be a safety plank.

As on the previous evening, all eyes were intent on the end of the street, which was now bathed in daylight. They did not have long to wait. Sounds of movement were now clearly to be heard from the direction of Saint-Leu; but they were unlike the sounds that had preceded the first attack. There was a rattling of chains and a clatter of massive wheels over the cobbles – a sort of solemn commotion heralding the approach of more sinister ironmongery. And the old streets trembled, built as they were for the fruitful passage of commerce and ideas, not for the monstrous rumbling of engines of war. All eyes widened as the defenders stared through the barricade.

A piece of artillery came in sight.

It was being pushed by its gun-crew and was all ready stripped for action, with the front bogey-wheels removed. Two men supported the barrel, four were at the wheels, and the others followed, pulling the ammunition tender. A lighted fuse was visible.

'Fire,' shouted Enjolras.

The whole barricade flashed fire, and following the thunderous detonations a wave of smoke engulfed the gun and its crew. But when after some moments this cleared the men were seen to be hauling the gun into its position facing the barricade, working without haste, in correct, military fashion. Not one had been hit. The chief gunner, lowering the breech to get the range, was aiming the gun with the gravity of an astronomer adjusting a telescope.

'Well done the gunners!' cried Bossuet, and all the defenders clapped their hands.

In a matter of instants the gun was ready for action, its wheels straddling the gutter in the middle of the street, its formidable mouthpiece pointing at the barricade.

'Cheer up!' said Courfeyrac. 'This is where it gets rough. First the sparring and now the punch. The army is showing its fist. We are about to be seriously shaken. Musketry paves the way, but artillery does the job.'

'It's one of the new model bronze eight-pounders,' said Combeferre. 'If the proportion of tin to copper exceeds one tenth, the barrel's liable to get distorted. Too much tin weakens it, and the whole thing goes out of shape. Perhaps the best way of avoiding this would be to revert to the fourteenth-century practice of hooping – a series of steel rings, not welded to the barrel but encircling it at intervals from end to end. Meanwhile the fault has to be rectified as best it can. One can use a gauge to discover where the inside of the barrel bulges or narrows. But there's a better method, Gribeaural's "Moving Star".'

'They grooved cannon in the sixteenth century,' said Bossuet.

'Yes. It increased ballistic force but diminished accuracy. Besides, at short range the trajectory isn't level enough. There's too much of a curve for the projectile to be able to hit an intermediate object, which is necessary in battle, and the more so according to the proximity of the enemy and the rate of fire. The trouble with those grooved or rifled sixteenth-century cannon was due to the weakness of the charge, which itself was due to practical considerations such as the need to preserve the gun-mounting. In other words, the cannon, that lord of battle, can't do all it would like to do: its very strength is a weakness. A cannon-ball travels only at the speed of six hundred leagues an hour, whereas light travels at seventy thousand leagues a second – and that is the superiority of God over Napoleon.'

Enjolras meanwhile had ordered his men to reload, and the artillery men were loading their gun. The question was, however, would the barricade stand up to cannon-fire? Would it be breached? The discharge was awaited with tense anxiety.

The blow fell, accompanied by a roaring explosion; and a cheerful voice cried:

'I'm back!'

Gavroche had reappeared at the precise moment that the ball ploughed into the barricade, having come by way of the Rue du Cygne and scrambled over the small barrier confronting the maze of the Petite-Truanderie. His arrival made more impression than did the cannon-ball, which simply buried itself in the rubble, having done nothing worse than shatter a wheel of the omnibus and demolish the old Ancean handcart. Seeing which, the defenders burst out laughing.

'Carry on!' shouted Bossuet to the gunners.

VIII

The gunners show their worth

The defenders crowded round Gavroche, but he had no time to tell them anything. Marius, trembling, dragged him aside.

'Why have you come back here?'

'If it comes to that,' said Gavroche, 'why are you here at all?' And he surveyed Marius with his customary effrontery, his eyes widening with the glow of his own achievement.

'Who told you to come back?' Marius demanded sternly. 'Did you at least deliver my letter?'

Gavroche was feeling somewhat remorseful about that letter. In his haste to get back to the barricade he had got rid of it rather than delivered it. He was bound to admit to himself that he had behaved casually in bestowing it on an unknown man whose features he had not been able to distinguish. Certainly the man had been hatless, but that in itself was not enough. In short, he was not too pleased with himself in this matter, and he feared Marius's rebuke. So he took the easiest way out: he lied outrageously.

'Citizen, I gave the letter to the doorkeeper. The lady was asleep. She'll get it when she wakes up.'

Marius had sent the letter with two objects in mind, to bid farewell to Cosette and to save Gavroche. He had to content himself with having accomplished only one of them.

But the thought of the letter reminded him of the presence of Monsieur Fauchelevent in the stronghold, and it occurred to him that the two things might be connected. Pointing to Monsieur Fauchelevent, he asked:

'Do you know that man?'

'No,' said Gavroche.

It will be remembered that he had encountered Jean Valjean after dark. Marius's uneasy suspicions were dispelled. What did he know, after all, of Monsieur Fauchelevent's political opinions? He might be a convinced republican, which would account for his having come to join them.

Gavroche, meanwhile, at the other end of the barricade, was demanding, 'Where's my musket?' Courfeyrac had it given back to him. Gavroche went on to tell the 'comrades', as he called them, that they were now entirely surrounded. He had had great difficulty in getting back. A battalion of the line, based on the Petite-Truanderie, was keeping a watch round the Rue du Cygne, and the Rue des Prêcheurs, on the other side, was occupied by the Garde Municipale. The main strength of the army was facing them.

'And I authorize you to give them a boot up the backside,' said Gavroche, having concluded his report.

All this time Enjolras in his redoubt was watching and intently listening.

The enemy, evidently disappointed by the failure of their cannonball, had not fired the gun again. A company of infantry of the line had now moved into position at the end of the street, behind the gun. They were digging up the paving-stones and using them to build a low wall, a sort of breastwork not more than eighteen inches high, facing the barricade. At the left-hand end of this breastwork the head of another column of troops, massed along the Rue Saint-Denis, could be seen.

Enjolras caught a sound that he thought he recognized, the rattle of grape-canisters when they are taken out of the ammunition-tender. He saw the leader of the gun-crew readjust his aim, pointing the gun-muzzle slightly to the left. The crew reloaded the gun, and the leading gunner himself took the linstock and held it over the touch-hole.

'Heads down and get back to the wall,' shouted Enjolras. 'All of you down on your knees.'

The rebels, who had left their posts to listen to Gavroche, dashed frantically back, but the gun was fired before the order could be carried out, and they heard the hideous whistle of grape-shot. The gun was aimed at the narrow breach between the end of the barricade and the house wall. The bullets ricocheted off the wall, killing two men and wounding three. If it went on like that the barricade would cease to be tenable. It was not proof against grape-shot.

There was a murmur of dismay.

'We must not let that happen again,' said Enjolras.

He levelled his carbine at the leading gunner, who, bent over the breach of the gun, was finally adjusting its aim. He was a gunnery sergeant, a fair-haired, handsome young man with a gentle face and the look of intelligence appropriate to that formidable, predestined weapon which, by its very perfection of horror, must finally put an end to war.

Combeferre, at Enjolras's side, was staring at him.

'What a shame!' said Combeferre. 'How hideous this butchery is! Well, when there are no more kings there will be no more war-fare. You're aiming at that sergeant, Enjolras, but you're not look-ing at him. He looks a charming young man, and he is certainly brave. One can see that he thinks – these young artillery-men are highly educated. No doubt he has a family, a father and mother, and probably he's in love. He can't be more than twenty-five. He could be your brother.'

'He is,' said Enjolras.

'Yes,' said Combeferre, 'and mine too. We mustn't kill him.'

'We must. It has got to be done.' A tear rolled slowly down Enjolras's pallid cheek.

At the same moment he pressed the trigger. The young gunner spun round twice with arms extended and head flung back as though gasping for air, then fell sideways on to the gun and stayed motionless. Blood poured from the middle of his back, which was turned towards them.

His body had to be removed and a relief appointed in his place. It meant that a few minutes had been gained.

IX

Use of an old poacher's talent

Urgent views were exchanged along the barricade. The gun would soon fire again. They could not survive more than a quarter of an hour against grapeshot. Something had to be done to lessen its effect.

'Stuff that gap with a mattress,' ordered Enjolras.

'There isn't one to spare,' said Combeferre. 'The wounded are using them all.'

Jean Valjean, seated on a kerbstone at the corner of the tavern with his musket between his knees, had thus far kept aloof from the rest of the company and taken no part in the proceedings, seeming not to hear the remarks that were being made around him. Now, however, he got to his feet.

It will be recalled that when the party had entered the Rue de la Chanvrerie an old woman in one of the houses had rigged a mattress outside her window as a precaution against bullets. It was an attic window six storeys above ground, and the house was situated just outside the barricade. The mattress was suspended from two clothes-poles held by two cords running from nails driven into the woodwork of the window. The cords, at that distance, looked no thicker than a hair.

'Will someone lend me a double-barrelled carbine?' said Valjean.

Enjolras passed him his own, which he had just reloaded.

Jean Valjean took aim and fired, and one of the cords parted, leaving the mattress hanging by the other. He fired again, and the second cord whipped against the window. The mattress slid between the two poles and fell into the street.

There was a burst of applause from the defenders and someone cried:

'There's your mattress.'

'Yes,' said Combeferre, 'but who's going to fetch it?'

The mattress had fallen outside the barricade, into the no-man's-land between attackers and defenders. But the soldiers, infuriated by the death of their sergeant, were now lying on their stomachs behind the breastwork of paving-stones and keeping up a steady fire on the barricade while they waited for the gun to come into action again. The defenders had not been returning their fire because of the need to save ammunition. The bullets buried themselves harmlessly in the barricade; but the street in front of it was a place of hideous danger.

Jean Valjean went out through the breach, dashed through the hail of bullets, picked up the mattress and, carrying it on his back, brought it into the stronghold. He then used it to block the breach, fixing it against the house wall in a position where the gunners could not see it.

Then the defenders awaited the next salvo of grape, which was not slow in coming. The gun thundered out its charge of smallshot, but this time there was no ricochet. The mattress had had the desired effect; it had damped the spread of the bullets. The stronghold was spared this peril.

'Citizen,' said Enjolras to Jean Valjean, 'the Republic thanks you.'

Bossuet was laughing as he marvelled.

'How immoral that a mattress should prove so effective! A triumph of submissiveness over aggression! Glory be to the mattress, which neutralizes cannon!'

X
Dawn

It was at this moment that Cosette awakened.

Her bedroom was small, clean and modest, with a tall window giving on to the back courtyard of the house.

Cosette knew nothing of what was happening in Paris. She had retired to bed when Toussaint said, 'There seems to be trouble.' She had not slept for very long but she had slept soundly. She had had sweet dreams, which perhaps was due in part to the fact that the narrow bed was very white. A vision of Marius had appeared to her in a glow of light, and when she awoke with the sun in her eyes it was like the continuation of her dream.

Her first thoughts as she woke up were happy ones. She felt quite reassured. Like Jean Valjean a few hours before, she was experiencing that reaction of the spirit which rejects absolutely the thought of misfortune. She was filled with hope, without knowing why. Then she felt a clutching at her throat. It was three days since she had seen Marius. But she told herself that by now he must have got her letter, so that he knew where she was; and he was so clever that he was sure to find some means of reaching her. What was more, he would certainly come today, perhaps even this morning. Although it was now daylight, the sun was still low. It must be very early in the morning. But still she must get up, to be ready for Marius.

She knew now that she could not live without Marius, and this in itself was a sufficient reason for his coming. So much was certain. It was bad enough that she should have suffered for three days. Three days without Marius, which was horribly unkind of God. But at least she had survived it, that cruel joke played on her by Heaven, and today Marius would come, bringing good news. Such is youth! It quickly dries its tears and having no use for sorrow refuses to accept it. Youth is the future smiling at a stranger, which is itself. It is natural for youth to be happy. It seems that its very breath is made of happiness.

Moreover, Cosette could not exactly remember what Marius had told her about his enforced absence, which was to last only one day, or what explanation he had given her. We all know the artfulness with which a dropped coin hides itself, and the job we have to find it again. There are thoughts which play the same trick on us, rolling into a buried corner of our minds; and there it is, they've gone for ever, we can't put our finger on them. Cosette was decidedly vexed by the insufficiency of her memory. It was very wrong of her, and she felt guilty at having forgotten any words spoken by Marius.

She got out of bed and performed those two ablutions of the spirit and the body – her prayers and her toilet.

The reader may at a pinch be introduced into a marital bedchamber, but not into a young girl's bedroom. This is something that verse scarcely dares; to prose it is utterly forbidden. It is the interior of a bud not yet opened, whiteness in shadow, the secret resort of a closed lily not to be seen by man until it has been looked upon by the sun. A budding woman is sacred. The innocent bed with its coverlet tossed back, the enchanting semi-nudity that is afraid of itself, the white foot taking refuge in a slipper, the bosom that veils itself before a mirror as though the mirror were a watching eye, the chemise hastily pulled up to hide a shoulder from a piece of furniture that creaks as a carriage passes in the street, the ribbons, hooks and laces, the tremors, small shivers of cold and modesty, the exquisite shyness of every movement, the small, mothlike flutterings where there is nothing to be afraid of, the successive donning of garments as charming as the mists of dawn – such matters may not be dwelt upon; even to have hinted at them is too much.

The masculine gaze must display even more reverence at the rising of a girl from her bed than at the rising of a star; the very possibility that she can be touched should increase our respect. The down on a peach, the dust on a plum, the crystal gleam of snow, the powdered butterfly's wing, these are gross matters compared with the chastity that does not know that it is chaste. A virgin girl is a vision in a dream, not yet become a thing to be looked at. Her alcove is buried in the depths of the ideal. An indiscreet caress of the eyes is a ravishment of this intangible veil. Even a glance is a profanation. Therefore we shall depict nothing whatever of the soft commotion of Cosette's uprising. According to an eastern fable, the rose was white when God created it, but when, as it unfolded, it felt Adam's eyes upon it, it blushed in modesty and turned pink. We are among those who are moved to silence by young girls and flowers, finding them objects of veneration.

Cosette quickly dressed and did her hair – a simple matter in those days, when women did not pad out their tresses and ringlets, or insert any kind of framework. Then she opened her window and leaned out, hoping to be able to see a small length of street beyond the corner of the house, so that she could keep watch for Marius. But she could not do so. The back courtyard of the house was enclosed in high walls, beyond which were only gardens. She decided that they were hideous; for the first time in her life she found flowers ugly. The least glimpse of the street gutter would have suited her better. So she looked up at the sky, as though hoping that Marius might come that way.

And suddenly she burst into tears, not from any oversensibility but from disappointed hope and misery of her present situation. She had an obscure sense of disaster. It was in the air about her. She told herself that she could be sure of nothing, that to be lost to sight was to be wholly lost; and the thought that Marius might drop down from the heavens no longer seemed to her charming but most miserable. Then, such are these fantasies, calm returned to her and hopefulness, a sort of unwitting smile of trust in God.

Everyone was still in bed and a provincial silence reigned in the house. Not a shutter had been thrust open and the porter's lodge was still closed. Toussaint was not yet up, and Cosette naturally supposed that her father was asleep. She must have suffered greatly, and must still be unhappy, because she told herself that her father had been unkind; but she still relied on Marius. The extinction of that light was quite simply inconceivable. She began to pray. Now and then she heard the sound of thudding some distance away, and she thought it strange that people should be opening and slamming house-doors so early in the morning. In fact, this was the sound of cannon-fire from the barricades.

A few feet below Cosette's window, in the blackened cornice of the wall, there was a nest of house-martins. It stuck out a little beyond the cornice, so that she could see inside it. The mother-bird was there, with her wings spread over her brood, while the father flew back and forth bringing them food. The morning sun gilded that happy sight, that smiling instance of the glory of the morning. Cosette, with her hair in the sunshine and her mind filled with dreams, glowing inwardly with love and outwardly in the dawn, leaned mechanically further forward and, scarcely venturing to admit that she was also thinking of Marius, contemplated that family of birds, male and female, mother and children, with the sense of profound disturbance that a bird's nest imparts to a virgin girl.

XI

A musket-shot that does not miss but does not kill

The attackers kept up their fire, alternating musketry with grape-shot, but, it must be said, without doing any great damage. Only the upper part of the tavern suffered, the first-floor window and those in the attics gradually crumbling as they were riddled with grape and musket-balls. The men posted there had had to withdraw. In general, this is a tactic commonly used in attacking a street barricade: a steady fire is kept up to draw the fire of the insurgents, if they are so foolish as to return it. When they are seen to be running out of powder and shot the assault goes in. But Enjolras had not fallen into this trap. The fire was not returned.

At every volley Gavroche thrust his tongue into his cheek in a grimace of lofty disdain and Courfeyrac mocked the gunners – 'You might be scattering confetti, my good fellows.'

Inquisitiveness is as much present in battle as at a ball. Probably the muteness of the stronghold was beginning to perturb the attackers, causing them to fear some unforeseen development, so that they were consumed with the desire to know what was going on behind that impressive wall. The rebels suddenly perceived the gleam of a helmet on a near-by roof. A sapper had appeared, standing with his back to a tall chimney, having evidently been posted as a look-out. He could see straight down into the stronghold.

'That's tiresome,' said Enjolras.

Jean Valjean had returned Enjolras's carbine, but he had his musket. Without speaking he took aim at the sapper, and a moment later the helmet, struck by a bullet, clattered down into the street. The soldier hurriedly retreated.

Another look-out took his place, this time an officer. Valjean, having reloaded, fired again, and the officer's helmet went to join that of the first man. The officer was not stubborn; he, too, hastily withdrew. This time the point had been taken. No other observer appeared to spy on the fortress.

'Why did you fire at the helmet instead of killing the man?' Bossuet asked Valjean.

He did not reply.

XII

Disorder the upholder of order

Bossuet murmured to Combeferre:

'He didn't answer my question.'

'He's a man who does kindness with bullets,' said Combeferre.

Those readers with any recollection of that already distant epoch will know that the volunteer Garde Nationale from the districts surrounding Paris, always sturdily opposed to insurrection, were particularly ruthless and intrepid during those days of June 1832. Your honest cabaret proprietor in Pantin or Les Vertus or La

Cunette, seeing a threat to the prosperity of his establishment, was lion-hearted in the defence of his dance-floor, ready to risk his life to preserve the state of order in which he flourished. In those days which were both bourgeois and heroic, faced by concepts which had their knightly champions, private profit also had its paladins. Prosaic motives in no way detracted from the gallantry of their conduct. The shrinkage in the value of money caused bankers to sing the 'Marseillaise'. Blood was lyrically shed to safeguard the cash box, and the shop, that microcosm of the nation, was defended with a Spartan tenacity. It must be said that all this was extremely serious. Two sections of the populace were at war, pending the establishment of a balance between them.

Another sign of the times was the mingling of anarchy and governmentalism (the barbarous word then used by the orthodox). A mixture of order and indiscipline. The drums beat capriciously at the order of some hot-blooded colonel of the Garde Nationale; the order to fire was given by excited captains, and the men under them fought according to their own ideas and for their own purpose. In moments of crisis, the 'big days', instinct was more often consulted than the official leaders. There were freelance warriors in the ranks of order, fighters with the sword, like Fannicot, and fighters with the pen, like the journalist, Henri Fonfrède.

Civilization, of which the unhappy embodiment at that time was an aggregation of interests rather than a collection of principles, believing itself to be threatened raised a cry of alarm; and the individual, seeing himself as its centre, sought to defend it after his own fashion. Everyman took it upon himself to save society.

Zeal was sometimes carried to excess. A platoon of the Garde Nationale might constitute itself a court-martial and try and execute a captured rebel in five minutes. It was this kind of improvisation that had caused the death of Jean Prouvaire – a ferocious lynch-law with which neither side is entitled to reproach the other, for it was used by the republicans in America no less than by the monarchists in Europe. It was the source of many blunders. In one uprising, for example, a young poet named Paul-Aimé Garnier was chased across the Place Royale with bayonets at his back and had difficulty in escaping through the doorway of No. 6. He had been mistaken for a 'Saint-Simonien', a follower of the radical philosopher, Saint-Simon. The fact is that the book he was carrying under his arm was a volume of the memoirs of the Duc de Saint-Simon. A member of the Garde Nationale, seeing only the name, had clamoured for his death.*

On 6 June 1832, a suburban company of the Garde Nationale, commanded by the Captain Fannicot already referred to, allowed itself from pure self-indulgence to be decimated in the Rue de la Chanvrerie. The fact, singular as it is, was established by the judicial inquiry held after the 1832 insurrection. The zealous and hot-blooded captain, a *condottiere* of troops of the kind we have been describing, and a fanatical and insubordinate supporter of the Government, could not resist the temptation to open fire before the appointed time so as to overthrow the barricade single-handed – that is to say, with his own company. Exasperated by the hoisting of the red flag followed by an old coat which he took to be a black flag, he loudly criticized the authorities and army leaders, then in council, who had decided that the time for the final assault was not yet ripe, and, in the phrase made famous by one of them, were letting the insurrection 'stew in its own juice'. His own view was that the barricade itself was ripe, and since ripe fruit is ready to fall he put his theory to the test.

The men under his command were as hot-blooded as himself – 'wild men', as a witness described them. His company, which had been responsible for the shooting of Jean Prouvaire, was at the head of the battalion drawn up beyond the corner of the street. At the moment when it was least expected, the captain flung his men against the barricade. The attack, executed with more zeal than military skill, cost the Fannicot company dear. Before it had covered two-thirds of the Rue de la Chanvrerie it was met with a volley from all the defenders. The four boldest men, who were in the forefront, were shot at point-blank range and fell at the foot of the barricade, and the courageous mob of National Guards, men of the utmost bravery but lacking the steadiness of regular soldiers, fell back after some hesitation, leaving fifteen dead bodies in the street. That moment of hesitation gave the rebels time to reload, and a second, murderous volley caught them before they had got round the corner into safety. Indeed they were caught between two fires, because they also received a charge of grapeshot from the cannon, which went on firing, not having been ordered to stop. The bold

*This episode, described in *Choses vues* as having happened to Hugo himself in 1834, is here attributed to another person. The poet, Paul-Aimé Garnier, died in 1846.

but rash Fannicot was one of the casualties – killed, that is to say, by the forces of order.

The attack, which was more hot-headed than serious, annoyed Enjolras.

'The idiots!' he exclaimed. 'They're getting themselves killed and wasting our ammunition for no reason.'

Enjolras had spoken like the born rebel leader he was. Insurrection and repression fight with different weapons. Insurrection, with limited resources, can fire only so many shots and lose only so many men. An ammunition-pouch emptied, or a man killed, cannot be replaced. Repression, with the army at its disposal, has no need to spare men or, with its arsenals, to spare bullets; it has as many regiments as there are defenders on the barricades, and as many factories as the barricades have cartridge-cases. So these battles of one against a hundred must always end in the crushing of the rebels unless the spirit of revolution, spontaneously arising, casts its flaming sword into the balance. This can happen. And then it becomes a universal uprising, the very stones rise up, the strongholds of the populace teem with men, all Paris trembles; something more than human is unloosed and it is another 10 August or 29 July. A prodigious light shines, and the gaping jaws of force recoil; the lion which is the army comes face to face with the erect and tranquil figure of the prophet, which is France.

XIII
Passing gleams

All things are to be found in the chaos of sentiment and passions defending a barricade: there is gallantry, youth, honour, enthusiasm, idealism, conviction, the frenzy of the gambler and, above all, the fluctuations of hope.

One of these fluctuations, one of the vague surges of hope, suddenly, and at the most unforeseeable moment, ran through the defenders of the barricade in the Rue de la Chanvrerie.

'Listen!' shouted Enjolras, always on the alert. 'It sounds to me as though Paris were on the move.'

It is certain that for an hour or two on that morning of 6 June the insurrection gained a degree of impetus. The persistent summons of the Saint-Merry tocsin stirred latent impulses. Barricades went up in the Rue du Poirier and the Rue des Gravilliers. A young man with a carbine launched a single-handed attack on a cavalry squadron at the Porte Saint-Martin. Kneeling without cover on the boulevard, he aimed at, and killed, the squadron commander, saying when he had done so, 'Well, that's another who won't do us any more harm!' He was cut down with sabres. In the Rue Saint-Denis a woman fired at the National Guard from behind a Venetian blind, of which the slats were seen to tremble with every shot. A boy of fourteen was caught in the Rue de la Cossonerie with his pockets filled with cartridges. A regiment of cuirassiers, with General Cavaignac de Baragne at its head, was greeted as it entered the Rue Bertin-Poirée with a very lively and quite unexpected volley. In the Rue Planche-Mibray pots and pans and other domestic articles were flung at the troops from the roof-tops. A bad sign, this; and when it was reported to Marshal Soult, that Napoleonic veteran looked thoughtful, recalling an observation made by Suchet at Saragossa – 'When we get the old women emptying chamber-pots on our heads we're done for.'

These widespread portents, coming at a time when the uprising was thought to have been localized – manifestations of a growing anger, spurts of flame rising here and there out of the great mass of combustible material which is Paris – disquieted the army commander, and great haste was made to put out the fire before it spread. Accordingly the assault on the strongholds of Maubuée, de la Chanvrerie, and Saint-Merry was delayed until these lesser affairs had been dealt with, so that then only the three major outbreaks would remain and they could be crushed in a single operation. Preventive columns were sent through the fermenting streets, clearing the larger and probing the smaller ones to left and right, sometimes slowly and cautiously, sometimes at the double. The doors of houses from which shots had been fired were battered down while at the same time a cavalry operation cleared the gathering groups off the boulevards. The process was not soundless or free from the uproar that accompanies any clash between the army and the people. This was what Enjolras heard in the pauses between gun and musket-fire. Moreover, he saw wounded men on stretchers being carried past the end of the street, and he said to Courfeyrac, 'Those wounded don't come from here.'

But the hope did not last for long; the gleam was soon extinguished. Within half an hour the stir had died down as though it were a lightning-flash not followed by thunder, and the rebels again felt the weight of that pall of indifference that the people bestow on zealots whom they have abandoned. The general upheaval which had given signs of taking shape had been frustrated, and the attention of the Minister for War and the strategy of the generals could again be concentrated on the three or four strongholds remaining.

The sun had risen in the sky. A man called to Enjolras:

'We're hungry down here. Have we really got to die without getting a bite to eat?'

Crouched in his redoubt, with his eyes intent on the end of the street, Enjolras merely nodded.

XIV

In which we learn the name of Enjolras's mistress

Seated on a paving-stone near Enjolras, Courfeyrac continued to jeer at the cannon, and every passage of that sinister cloud of projectiles that is called grapeshot, accompanied by its monstrous din, drew from him an ironical comment.

'You're wearing yourself out, you poor old brute. You're getting hoarse. You're not thundering, only spluttering. It's breaking my heart.'

His remarks were greeted with laughter. He and Bossuet, whose valiant high spirits increased with danger, like Madame Scarron were substituting pleasantry for nourishment and, since wine was not to be had, spreading gaiety around them.

'I admire Enjolras,' said Bossuet. 'I marvel at his cool steadfastness. He lives alone, and this perhaps makes him unhappy; he resents the greatness which compels him to celibacy. We others have mistresses to rob us of our wits – make us brave, in other words. A man in love is like a tiger, and the least he can do is to fight like a lion. It's a way of getting our own back for the tricks the wenches play on us. Roland got himself killed to score off Angélique. All our heroism stems from our womenfolk. A man without a woman is like a pistol without a hammer; the woman sparks the charge. But Enjolras has no woman. He contrives to be brave without being in love. It's a very remarkable thing to be cold as ice and still as hot as fire.'

Enjolras seemed not to be listening, but anyone near enough might have heard him murmur the word *Patria*.

Bossuet was still laughing when Courfeyrac exclaimed: 'Here's another!' And in the voice of a ceremonial usher he announced: 'My lord Eight-Pounder!'

And indeed a second cannon had been brought into action. The gunners rapidly manoeuvred it into position alongside the first.

It was the beginning of the end.

A minute later both pieces fired together, accompanied by a volley of musketry from the supporting troops. Gunfire was also to be heard not far off. While the two guns were bombarding the stronghold in the Rue de la Chanvrerie, others, in the Rue Saint-Denis and the Rue Aubry-le-Boucher, were in action against the Saint-Merry redoubt, this simultaneous fire setting up an ominous echo.

Of the two pieces now battering the Rue de la Chanvrerie barricade, one was charged with grape, the other with ball. The one loaded with ball was aimed a little high so as to hit the upper edge of the barricade and fill the air with the splinters of paving-stones, the intention being to drive the defenders off the barricade itself and under cover. It was a preliminary to the main assault. Once the barricade had been cleared by cannon-fire, and musketry had driven the defenders away from the windows of the tavern, it would be possible for the attacking troops to advance along the street without being shot at, possibly without being seen, and over-run the barricade as they had done on the evening before, perhaps even taking it by surprise.

'We really must abate this nuisance,' said Enjolras, and he shouted: 'Open fire on the gunners.'

Everything was in readiness. The barricade, so long silent, burst furiously into flame, six or seven volleys following one another in a mingling of rage and joy. The street was filled with blinding smoke, but after a few minutes the bodies of two-thirds of the gunners could be dimly discerned, prostrate round the gun. Those still on their feet continued with rigid composure to serve the guns, but the rate of fire slackened.

'Good!' said Bossuet to Enjolras. 'A success.'

Enjolras shrugged his shoulders.

'Another quarter of an hour of that kind of success and we shan't have ten cartridges left.'

It seemed that Gavroche must have heard those words.

XV

Gavroche

Courfeyrac suddenly perceived someone crouched in the street just beyond the barricade. Gavroche, having fetched a basket from the tavern, had slipped out through the break and was calmly engaged in filling it with ammunition from the pouches of the men killed in the previous assault.

'What are you doing?' demanded Courfeyrac.

Gavroche looked up perkily.

'I'm filling my basket.'

'Haven't you ever heard of grapeshot?'

'So it's raining,' said Gavroche. 'So what?'

'Come back at once!'

'All in good time,' said Gavroche, and moved further along the street.

It will be remembered that Fannicot's retreating company had left a trail of dead behind them. Some twenty corpses were scattered over the length of the street, twenty ammunition pouches to be looted.

Smoke filled the street like a fog. Anyone who has seen low cloud at the bottom of a sheer mountain gorge will be able to picture it, that dense mist eddying and swirling between the two dark lines of tall houses. It slowly rose but was constantly renewed, a dark veil drawn over the face of the sun, so that the combatants at either end of the street, short though it was, could scarcely see each other.

This state of affairs, probably reckoned with and desired by the leaders of the assault, was very helpful to Gavroche. Under cover of the smoke, and thanks to his small size, he could move some distance into the street without being seen. He looted the first seven or eight pouches without being in much danger, creeping along on hands and knees, wriggling from one body to the next and emptying pouches and cartridge-belts like a monkey cracking nuts.

He was still not far from the barricade, but no one dared shout to him to come back for fear of drawing attention to him.

On one body, that of a corporal, he found a powder-flask.

'Handy in case of thirst,' he said and put it in his pocket.

As he moved further along the street the veil of smoke grew thinner, so that presently the soldiers of the line behind their breastwork and the men of the Garde Nationale clustered at the corner of the street were able to discern something moving in the haze. He was ransacking the pouch of a sergeant lying near a kerbstone when the body was hit by a bullet.

'Blazes!' said Gavroche. 'Now they're killing dead men.'

A second bullet struck a spark from the near-by cobbles and a third overturned his basket. Looking up, Gavroche saw that it had come from the street-corner. He got to his feet, and standing erect with his hands on his hips, his eyes fixed on the men of the Garde Nationale, he sang:

> They're ugly at Nanterre,
> It's the fault of Voltaire;
> And stupid at Palaiseau,
> All because of Rousseau.

Then he picked up his basket, retrieved the cartridges that had fallen out of it without losing one, and moved still nearer to the attackers to loot another pouch. A fourth bullet narrowly missed him. He sang:

> I'm no lawyer, I declare,
> It's the fault of Voltaire.
> I'm nothing but a sparrow
> All because of Rousseau.

A fifth bullet succeeded only in drawing another verse from him:

> There's joy in the air,
> Thanks to Voltaire;
> But misery below,
> So says Rousseau.

This went on for some time, a touching and heartrending scene. Gavroche, being shot at, mocked the shooters. He seemed to be thoroughly enjoying himself, a sparrow pecking at the bird-catchers. Every shot inspired him to another verse. They fired again and again at him and missed, and the soldiers and the men of the Garde Nationale laughed as they took aim. He leapt and dodged, ducked into doorways, vanished and reappeared, cocking a snook at the foe, and all the time continued to empty pouches and fill his basket. The rebels watched in breathless anxiety. The barricade trembled, and he sang. He was neither child nor man but a puckish sprite, a dwarf, it seemed, invulnerable in battle. The bullets pursued him, but he was more agile than they. The urchin played his game of hide-and-seek with death, and whenever the dread spectre appeared he tweaked its nose.

But at length a bullet caught him, better aimed or more treacherous than the rest. Gavroche was seen to stagger, and then he collapsed. A cry went up from the barricade. But there was an Antaeus concealed in that pygmy. A Paris urchin touching the pavement is a giant drawing strength from his mother earth. Gavroche had fallen only to rise again. He sat upright with blood streaming down his face, and raising his arms above his head and gazing in the direction of the shot, he again began to sing:

> I have fallen, I swear
> It's the fault of Voltaire,
> Or else this hard blow
> Has been dealt by —

He did not finish the verse. A second ball from the same musket cut him short. This time he fell face down and moved no more. His gallant soul had fled.

XVI
How a brother becomes a father

At that same moment two little boys in the Luxembourg Garden – for the eyes of the dramatist must be everywhere at once – were walking hand in hand. One was perhaps seven years old, the other about five. After being soaked by the downpour they were keeping to the sunnier paths, the elder leading the way. They were ragged and pale, with the look of lost birds. The younger said, 'I'm very hungry.'

The elder, who was developing a protective attitude, was holding his brother with his left hand while he clutched a stick in his right. The gardens were deserted, the gates having been closed as a precautionary measure in view of the uprising. The troops who had been encamped there during the night had left to go about their duties.

How, then, had those two children got there? They might have slipped through the half-open door of a police-post, or possibly have run away from a party of strolling players who had set up their booth nearby, at the Barrière de l'Enfer or on the Esplanade de l'Observatoire; or perhaps they had escaped the notice of the park-keepers at closing time the evening before, and spent the night in one of those sheltered corners where people sit and read their newspapers. In any event they were wandering at large and seemed unattached. To be astray and free is to be lost, which is what these children were.

They were the two little boys whom Gavroche had once sheltered, as the reader will remember – the Thénardier children, disposed of to La Magnon and attributed by that lady to Monsieur Gillenormand, and now become leaves fallen from those rootless branches, blown helter-skelter by the wind. Their clothes, which had been clean and neat in La Magnon's day, and had served to justify her in the eye of Monsieur Gillenormand, were now in tatters. In short, they had become a statistic, recorded by the police under the heading *Enfants Abandonnés* and picked up by them in the streets of Paris.

Only at a time of disorder could outcasts such as these have been found in a place like the Luxembourg; at any other time they would have been turned out. The children of the poor are not allowed in public gardens, although it might be thought that, like any other children, they have a right to flowers.

But there they were, thanks to the closed gates. They had slipped in, regardless of regulations, and had stayed there. The closing of the gates does not relieve the park attendants of their duties. Their supervision is supposed to be maintained, but it tends to grow lax. Besides which the attendants, infected by the disturbance, were more interested in events outside the gardens than in what was going on inside, and failed to notice the delinquents.

It had rained during the night and even a little in the morning; but June showers are no great matter. One scarcely remembers, on a day of radiant sunshine, that an hour ago there was a down-pour. The earth in summer dries as quickly as an infant's cheek. At the summer solstice the noonday sun is, so to speak, grasping. It envelops everything, applying a kind of suction to the earth, as though the sun itself were thirsty. A shower is a mere glass of water; any rainfall is instantly swallowed. The streaming morning becomes the delightful afternoon.

Nothing is more pleasant than greenery washed by the rain and dried by the sun into cleanliness and warmth. Gardens and meadows, with moisture at their roots and sunshine on their blossoms, become jars of incense, each giving out its scent. The world smiles and sings and bestows itself, and we feel a gentle intoxication. Springtime is a foretaste of paradise. The sun teaches men to endure.

At eleven o'clock on that morning of 6 June the Luxembourg, empty of people, was particularly charming. Lawns and flowerbeds mingled their colour and their fragrance, and the branches of trees seemed locked in an extravagant embrace in the warmth of the midday sun. Linnets were chirruping in the sycamores, sparrows flew rejoicing, woodpeckers assiduously tapped the trunks of the chestnut trees. The beds did dutiful obeisance to the legitimate royalty of the lily, the noblest of scents being that which comes from whiteness. Marie de Medici's old rooks were cawing in the tall trees, and the sun was gliding and crimsoning the tulips, which are simply every hue of flame made into flowers; and over the tulip beds darted the bees, like sparks from flames. All was grace and gaiety and there was no real threat in the shower that was approaching, which would be welcomed by honeysuckle and lily-of-the-valley and was causing the swallows to fly low. Any person there must have breathed happiness, security, innocence and benevolence. The thoughts falling from the sky were as soft as a child's hand that one bends down to kiss.

The statues under the trees, white and naked, were clad in garments of shadow dappled with light, goddesses in the tattered vesture of sunshine, its rags enclosing them on all sides. The earth around the big pond was already dried and almost scorched, and there was wind enough to cause little scurries of dust to arise. A few yellowed leaves, survivals from the autumn, fluttered gaily in pursuit of one another as though they were at play.

There was an inexpressible reassurance in this lavishness of light, this overflowing of life and sap, perfume and warmth. In the puffs of wind laden with love, the mingling of harmonies and reflections; in the lavish expense of the sun's gaze, that prodigious outpouring of liquid gold, one had a sense of inexhaustible abundance. And beyond it all, as though beyond a curtain of flames, one sensed the presence of God, that millionaire of the stars.

All had been washed clean, all the magnificence was immaculate so that an army veteran from the near-by barracks, looking through the railing, could proclaim, 'Nature's presenting arms in full-dress uniform'. And in the vast silence of contented Nature all Nature breakfasted. This was the hour. Creation took its seat at table, with a blue cloth in the heavens and a green cloth on earth, sunshine to light the feast. God served a universal repast, in which each creature found its rightful food – hempseed for the dove, millet for the chaffinch, worms for the robin, flowers for the bee, infusoria for the flies – and flies for the linnet. If to some extent one creature preyed upon another, that is a token of the mysterious mingling of bad with good; but no creature went hungry.

The two forlorn little boys had found their way to the pond, and, half-scared by the brilliant light, with the instinct of the poor and weak confronted by magnificence, even when it is impersonal, were crouched behind the swanhouse. Now and then a puff of wind brought distant sounds of tumult to their ears, shouting voices, the rattle of musketry and the heavy thud of cannon-fire. Smoke was rising above the house-tops in the direction of Les Halles; and a bell that sounded like a summons was tolling somewhere far away. The children paid little heed to this. From time to time the younger repeated in a mournful voice, 'I'm hungry.'

But at about the same time two other persons were approaching the pond. They were a gentleman nearing fifty and a six-year-old boy, evidently father and son. The boy was clutching a large bun.

In those days, certain near-by houses in the Rue Madame and the Rue d'Enfer had keys to the Luxembourg which their occupants could use when the gates were closed – a privilege that has since been abolished. No doubt this accounted for the presence of the new arrivals.

The two strays, seeing the 'quality' approach, tried to hide more securely.

The gentleman was of the middle-class, possibly the same one whom Marius, in the fever of love, had overheard in this very place counselling his child to avoid all excesses. He had a complacent, affable manner and a mouth which, since it never closed, was always smiling; a mechanical smile, the result of too much jaw and too little flesh, which displayed his teeth rather than his nature. The child, who had bitten into his bun but not finished it, looked over-fed. He was dressed in the uniform of the Garde Nationale, whereas his father was prudently wearing civilian attire.

Father and son stopped by the pond to look at its two swans, for which the gentleman seemed to have an especial admiration. He even resembled them, in the sense that he walked like them. At that moment, however, the swans were swimming, this being their principal talent, and they looked, and were, superb.

If the two ragamuffins had been near enough, and old enough to understand, they might have profited by the words of a citizen of solid worth.

'A wise man contents himself with little,' said the father. 'Look at me, my boy. I have no love of display. You'll never see me in robes of gold and precious stones. I leave such false adornments to persons of less regulated minds.'

Here there was a louder burst of sound from the direction of Les Halles, an uproar of voices and the tolling of a bell.

'What is that?' the boy asked.

'Saturnalia,' the sage replied. He had suddenly noticed the ragamuffins, huddled and motionless behind the green-painted shanty that housed the swans. 'And this is the beginning,' he said, adding after an impressive pause, 'Anarchy has entered the garden.'

His son, meanwhile, had taken a mouthful of his bun. He spat it out and suddenly burst into tears.

'What are you crying about?' the father asked.

'I'm not hungry,' the boy replied.

The father's smile expanded.

'One doesn't need to be hungry to eat a cake.'

'I don't like it. It's stale.'

'You don't want any more?'

'No.'

'Then throw it to our web-footed friends.'

The son hesitated. The fact that one does not want one's cake is not a reason for giving it away.

'Be generous,' said the father. 'We must always be kind to animals.'

Taking the bun, he tossed it into the pond. It fell not far from the edge, and the swans, who were plunging their heads in the middle of the pond, did not see it. The sage, fearing that it might be wasted, flapped his arms like a semaphore to attract their attention. Upon which, seeing something floating on the water, they proceeded slowly towards it, with the solemn stateliness that befits white creatures.

'You see?' said the sage, and delivered himself of a happy play on words: '*Les cygnes comprennent les signes.*'

There was another and still louder burst of tumult from that distant part of the town, and this time it sounded ominous. It can happen that one puff of wind may speak more authoritatively than another. This one clearly conveyed to the Luxembourg the roll of drums, the rat-a-tat of musketry, the bellow of voices, the thud of cannon, and the mournful tolling of the bell. Moreover at that moment a cloud obscured the sun.

The swans were still on their way.

'We must go home,' the father said. 'They're attacking the Tuileries.' He took his son's hand. 'It is no great distance from the Tuileries to the Luxembourg, no greater than the distance separating Royalty from the peerage.* There will be shooting.' He glanced up at the cloud. 'And perhaps it is going to rain as well. Even the heavens are taking a hand. We must hurry.'

'I want to see the swans eat my bun,' the little boy said.

'That would be imprudent,' the father said. And he led away his bourgeois offspring, who kept looking back until a clump of trees got in the way.

The bun was still floating on the surface of the pond, and now the two ragamuffins, as well as the swans, were approaching it, the younger with his eyes intent upon it and the elder with an eye on the retreating gentleman.

When father and son were out of sight the older boy flung himself down at the water's edge and, leaning over the stone rim of the pond as far as he dared, tried to fish out the bun with the stick he was holding in his right hand. The swans, seeing a rival, increased their speed and in doing so set up a ripple which helped the small fisherman. The bun was driven gently towards him, and by the time the swans arrived it was within reach of his stick. He swiftly drew it in, flourished his stick to frighten off the swans, then fished it out and got to his feet. The bun was soaked, but the boys were both hungry and thirsty. The elder boy divided it into two parts, one large and one small, and handing his brother the larger of the two said, 'There you are. Stop your gob with that.'

*The Palais du Luxembourg, at that time, was the hall of assembly of the French Senate or House of Peers.

XVII

Interlude

Marius had dashed out beyond the barricade with Combeferre behind him. But it was too late. Gavroche was dead. Combeferre brought back the basket of ammunition while Marius brought back the boy, reflecting sadly as he did so that he was repaying the service Thénardier had done his father, with the difference that his father had been still alive. When he returned to the stronghold with the body in his arms his face, like that of Gavroche, was covered with blood. A bullet had grazed his scalp without his noticing it.

Courfeyrac loosened his cravat and bandaged his forehead. Gavroche was laid on the table beside Monsieur Mabeuf, and the same black shawl sufficed to cover the bodies of the old man and the boy.

Combeferre doled out the captured cartridges – fifteen rounds to each man. But when he offered his share to Jean Valjean, who had not moved but was still seated motionless on his kerbstone, the latter shook his head.

'An eccentric fellow,' Combeferre muttered to Enjolras. 'He comes to join us but doesn't want to fight.'

'Which doesn't prevent him lending a hand,' said Enjolras.

'Heroes come in all shapes,' said Combeferre; and Courfeyrac, overhearing, remarked: 'He's a different kind from Père Mabeuf.'

It is worthy of note that the fire hammering the barricade scarcely troubled the defenders within the stronghold. Persons who have never experienced this kind of warfare can have no idea of the strange lulls which punctuate its more violent moments. Men move about, talking, jesting, even loitering. An acquaintance of the writer heard a combatant remark, in the middle of an attack with grapeshot, 'We might be at a school picnic.' The interior of this stronghold in the Rue de la Chanvrerie appeared, we must repeat, extremely calm. Every possible contingency and development had been, or was soon to be, experienced. From being critical the situation had become menacing, and before long, no doubt, it would become desperate. And as it worsened so did the heroism of the defenders glow more brightly, presided over by a dour-faced Enjolras, like a young Spartan devoting his drawn sword to the genius of Epidotas.

Combeferre, with an apron tied round him, was bandaging the

wounded. Bossuet and Feuilly were making more cartridges with the powder taken by Gavroche from the dead corporal, and Bossuet remarked to his companion, 'We shall soon be taking a trip to another world.' Courfeyrac was spreading out his entire arsenal on the small heap of paving-stones he had constructed for himself near Enjolras – his swordstick, his musket, two cavalry-pistols, and a pocket pistol – arranging them with the meticulous care of a girl tidying her workbox. Jean Valjean was silently contemplating the wall opposite him. A workman was tying a large straw hat belonging to Mère Hucheloup on his head – 'To guard against sunstroke,' he said. The young men of the Cougourde d'Aix were gaily chatting together, as though not to waste the chance of talking their native patois for the last time. Joly had got Mère Hucheloup's mirror down from the wall. Several men, having found some rather mouldy crusts of bread in a drawer, were avidly devouring them. Marius was worrying about what his father would have to say to him.

XVIII
The vulture becomes prey

We must lay stress on a psychological fact peculiar to the barricades. Nothing characteristic of this astonishing street warfare should be omitted.

Despite their strange aspect of interior calm, these strongholds have for those within them a kind of unreality. Civil war, wherein the fog of the unknown mingles with the flame of furious outburst, has always an apocalyptic quality; revolution is a sphinx, and he who has undergone the experience of fighting on the barricades may feel that he has lived through a dream.

What one experiences, as we have indicated in the case of Marius (and we shall see the consequences of this), is something at once greater and less than life. Emerging from the barricade, we are no longer fully conscious of what we have seen. We have done terrible things and do not know it. We have been caught up in a conflict of ideas endorsed with human faces, our heads bathed in the light of the future. There were corpses prostrate and ghosts walking erect. The hours were immeasurable, like the hours of eternity. We lived in death. Shadows passed before our eyes, and what were they? We saw bloodstained hands. It was a state of appalling deafness, but also of dreadful silence. There were open mouths that cried aloud, and open mouths that uttered no sound. We were enveloped in smoke, perhaps in darkness, seeming to touch the sinister exhalations of unknown depths. We see something red in a finger-nail, but we do not remember.

To return to the Rue de la Chanvrerie: suddenly, in between two volleys, they heard the striking of a clock.

'Midday,' said Combeferre.

Before it had finished striking Enjolras sprang to his feet and gave the following order in a ringing voice:

'Paving-stones are to be brought into the house to reinforce the first floor and attic window-sills. Half the men to stand by with muskets, the rest to bring in the paving-stones. There's not a minute to be lost.'

A squad of sappers with axes over their shoulders had appeared in battle-order at the end of the street. They could only be the head of a column, surely an attacking column, since the sappers, whose business was to break down the barricade, always preceded the soldiers who had to climb over it.

Enjolras's order was carried out with the precise haste that is proper to fighting ships and barricades, these being the two places whence escape is impossible. In less than a minute two-thirds of the paving-stones which Enjolras had caused to be piled in the Corinth doorway had been carried up to the first floor and the attic, and before another minute had passed they had been neatly disposed so as to block half the first-floor window and the attic windows. A few loopholes, carefully arranged by Feuilly, the chief architect, permitted the passage of the musket barrels. This precaution was the more easily carried out since there had been a lull in the firing of grapeshot. The two cannons were now trained on the middle of the barricade for the purpose of making a hole in it and, if possible, creating a breach through which the assault might pass.

When the paving-stones, that ultimate rampart, were in position, Enjolras had the bottles which he had placed under the table on which Mabeuf was lying taken up to the first floor.

'Who's to drink them?' Bossuet asked.

'The defenders,' said Enjolras.

The ground-floor window was then barricaded and the iron bars used to fasten the tavern door at night were placed in readiness.

The fortress was now completely prepared. The barricade was its outer rampart, and the tavern was its keep. Such paving-stones as remained were used to fill the gap in the barricade.

Since the defenders of a street barricade are always obliged to husband their ammunition, and the attackers are aware of this, the attackers go about their business with an irritating deliberation, taking their time and exposing themselves before the fighting starts, although more in appearance than in reality. The preparations for the attack are always carried out with a certain methodical slowness, after which comes the holocaust.

This delay enabled Enjolras to oversee and perfect everything. He felt that since men such as these were about to die, their death must be a masterpiece. He said to Marius: 'We are the two leaders. I shall give the last orders inside while you keep watch on the outside.'

Marius took up his post of observation on top of the barricade.

Enjolras had the door of the kitchen, which as we know was the casualty ward, nailed up.

'To keep the wounded from being hit by splinters,' he said.

He gave his last orders in the downstairs room, speaking tersely but in a profoundly calm voice. Feuilly took note of them and spoke for everyone.

'Axes to cut down the stairs should be ready on the first floor. Are they there?'

'Yes,' said Fleury.

'How many?'

'Two, and a pole-axe.'

'Good. We are twenty-six able-bodied defenders. How many muskets are there?'

'Thirty-four.'

'Eight more than we need. They should be loaded like the rest and kept handy. Sabres and pistols in men's belts. Twenty men on the barricade and six in the attic and on the first floor to fire through the loopholes. Not a man must be wasted. When the drum beats for the assault the twenty men down below must make a rush for the barricade. Those who get there first will have the best positions.'

Having thus made his plans, Enjolras turned to Javert.

'I haven't forgotten you,' he said. Putting a pistol on the table, he went on, 'The last man to leave this place will blow out this spy's brains.'

'Here?' someone asked.

'No. We don't want his body to be mixed up with our own. Anyone can get over the small barricade in the Rue Mondétour. It's only four feet high. The man's securely bound. He's to be taken there and executed.'

Only one man at that moment was more impassive than Enjolras; it was Javert himself.

At this point Jean Valjean intervened. He had been in the main group of defenders. He now left them and said to Enjolras:

'You're the leader, are you not?'

'Yes.'

'A short time ago you thanked me.'

'I thanked you in the name of the Republic. Two men saved the barricade – Marius Pontmercy and yourself.'

'Do you think I deserve a reward?'

'Certainly.'

'Then I will ask for one.'

'What is it?'

'That I may be allowed to blow that man's brains out.'

Javert looked up and, seeing Valjean, made a slight movement of his head.

'That's fair.'

Enjolras was reloading his carbine. He looked about him and asked:

'Does anyone object?'

There was silence and he turned to Valjean.

'All right. You can have the spy.'

Valjean took possession of Javert by seating himself on the end of the table. He picked up the pistol, and the sound of a click indicated that he had cocked it. But at almost the same instant there was a sound of trumpets.

'On guard!' cried Marius from the top of the barricade.

Javert laughed in the silent manner that was peculiar to himself. He looked coolly at the defenders.

'You're scarcely in any better case than I am.'

'Everybody out!' cried Enjolras.

The men rushed out, receiving in their backs, if we may be allowed the expression, Javert's parting words:

'It won't be long!'

XIX

The vengeance of Jean Valjean

When Jean Valjean was alone with Javert he undid the rope tied round the prisoner's body, of which the knot was under the table. He then signed to him to stand up. Javert obeyed with the indefinable smile which is the expression of captive supremacy. Valjean took him by the belt of his greatcoat, much as one takes an animal by its halter, and tugging him behind him led him out of the tavern, but slowly, because Javert, his legs stiff, could walk only with difficulty. Valjean had a pistol in his other hand.

Thus they crossed the interior of the stronghold, while its defenders, intent upon the coming attack, had their backs to them. Only Marius, at the end of the barricade, saw them pass, and that sinister pair, victim and executioner, reflected the sense of doom in his own spirit.

Jean Valjean with some difficulty helped Javert, bound as he was, to climb over the barricade leading to the Rue Mondétour, without, however, letting go of him for an instant. Having done so they were in the narrow alleyway, where the corner of the house hid them from the insurgents. The dead bodies dragged off the barricade formed a dreadful heap a few paces away, and among them was an ashen face, a pierced heart and the breast of a half-naked woman – Éponine.

Javert glanced sidelong at the dead body and murmured in a voice of profound calm:

'I think I know that girl.'

Then he turned to Valjean who, with the pistol under his arm, was regarding him in a manner which rendered the words, 'You know me, too,' unnecessary.

'Take your revenge,' said Javert.

Valjean got a clasp-knife out of his pocket and opened it.

'A knife-thrust!' exclaimed Javert. 'You're quite right. That suits you better.'

Jean Valjean cut the halter round Javert's neck, then the ropes binding his wrists and ankles; then, standing upright, he said:

'You're free to go.'

Javert was not easily taken aback but, with all his self-discipline, he could not conceal his amazement. He stared open-mouthed.

'I don't suppose I shall leave here alive,' Valjean went on. 'But if I do, I am lodging at No. 7, Rue de l'Homme-Armé, under the name of Fauchelevent.'

A swift tigerish grimace curled the corner of Javert's lip.

'Take care!' he said.

'Now go,' said Jean Valjean.

'Fauchelevent, you said? In the Rue de l'Homme-Armé?'

'Number seven.'

'Number seven,' repeated Javert.

He re-buttoned his greatcoat, straightened his shoulders, turned, and with folded arms, supporting his chin in one hand, he marched off in the direction of the market. Valjean stood watching him. After he had gone a few paces Javert turned and said:

'I find this embarrassing. I'd rather you killed me.'

He did not notice that he had ceased to address Valjean disrespectfully as *tu*.

'Clear out,' said Valjean.

Javert walked on slowly and a moment later had turned into the Rue des Prêcheurs. When he had vanished from sight Valjean fired the pistol into the air.

Then he went back into the stronghold and said, 'It's done.'

In the meantime the following had occurred.

Marius, more concerned with what was happening outside the stronghold, had paid little attention to the spy tied up in the obscure downstairs room of the tavern; but when he saw him in full daylight climbing over the barricade to his death, he recognized him. He suddenly recalled the police inspector in the Rue de Pontoise who had given him the two pistols which he had only recently used. Not only did he recall his face but he remembered his name.

The recollection was, however, hazy and uncertain, as were all his thoughts at that time. He did not put it to himself in the form of a positive statement but rather as a question. 'Is not that the police inspector who told me his name was Javert?' Perhaps there was still time to intercede in his favour, but first he must make sure that he was right. He turned to Enjolras, who had come from the other end of the barricade.

'What is the name of that man?'

'Which man?'

'The policeman. Do you know his name?'

'Of course. He told us.'

'Well, what is it?'

'Javert.'

Marius started forward, but at this moment there was the sound of a pistol-shot and Jean Valjean returned saying, 'It's done.'

A chill pierced Marius to the heart.

XX

The dead are right, but the living are not wrong

The death-throes of the stronghold were about to begin.

All things combined to create the tragic majesty of that supreme moment, a thousand mysterious shudders in the air, the breath of armed bodies of men moving along streets where they were not yet visible, the occasional galloping of cavalry, the heavy rumble of artillery on the move, musketry and cannon fire clashing in the labyrinth of Paris, the smoke of battle rising golden above the roofs, occasional distant cries that were vaguely terrible, the lightnings of danger everywhere, the Saint-Merry tocsin that now had the sound of a sob, the mildness of the season, the splendour of a sky filled with sun and cloud, the beauty of the day and the dreadful silence of the houses.

For since the previous evening the two rows of houses in the Rue de la Chanvrerie had become fiercely defiant ramparts, with bolted doors, windows, and shutters.

In those days, so different from our present time, when the hour had struck when the people wanted to have done with a situation that had gone on too long, a charter offered to them, or a body of law; when universal anger was suspended in the air, when the town acquiesced in the uprooting of its pavements, when insurrection won a smile from the bourgeois by whispering orders in their ear; in such times the citizen, penetrated with rebellion, as one might say, was the ally of the combatant, the private house fraternized with the improvised fortress into which it had been turned. But when the time was not ripe, when the insurrection was decidedly not agreed to, when the majority repudiated the movement, then there was no hope for the combatant; the town became a desert surrounding the revolt, hearts were frozen, all ways of escape were closed and the streets lay open to the army in its assault upon the barricades.

One cannot goad people into moving faster than they are prepared to go. Woe to him who tries to force their hands. A whole people does not let itself be driven. It leaves the insurrection to its own devices. The insurgent becomes a pestilence. The house is an escarpment, its door a refusal, its façade a closed wall. A wall that sees and hears and will have none of it. It might open its doors and save you, but it does not do so. The wall is a judge. It looks at you and passes sentence. How sombre are those barred houses! They seem dead, but are alive. Life in them, though it seems suspended, still persists. No one has emerged from them in twenty-four hours, but no one is missing. Within that rock people come and go, retire to bed and rise; they are a family, they eat and drink, and they are frightened, a terrible thing. Fear excuses that formidable inhospitableness, and it brings with it the extenuating circumstances of panic. Sometimes indeed, and this has been known, fear becomes passion, panic can turn into fury as prudence can turn into rage. Hence that profound expression, 'The fury of the moderates'. There can be a flare-up of terror from which, like a sinister smoke, anger arises ... 'What do those people want? They're never satisfied. They compromise peaceful men. As if we had not had enough of this sort of disorder! Why did they choose to come here? Well, they must get out of it as best they can, and so much the worse for them. It's their own doing, they'll only get what they deserve. It's no affair of ours. Look at our poor street, pocked with bullet-holes. They're a gang of ruffians. Mind you keep that door shut!' ... And the house acquires the semblance of a tomb. The insurgent crouches in deadly peril outside that door, seeing the guns and naked sabres. If he calls for help he knows that he is heard but that no one will answer; there are walls that might protect him, men who might save him – the walls have living ears, but the men have bowels of stone.

Whom shall we blame?

Nobody, and everybody.

The incomplete times in which we live.

It is always at its risk and peril that Utopia takes the form of Insurrection, substituting armed for reasoned protest, transforming Minerva into Pallas. The Utopia which grows impatient and becomes an uprising knows what awaits it; it nearly always happens too soon. So then it resigns itself, stoically accepting disaster in place of triumph. Without complaint it serves those who have disavowed it, even acquitting them, and its magnanimity lies in acceptance of desertion. It is indomitable in the face of obstacles and mild in the face of ingratitude.

In any case, is it ingratitude? Yes, in terms of the human species. No, in terms of the individual.

Progress in the life-style of man. The general life of the human race is called Progress, and so is its collective march. Progress advances, it makes the great human and earthly journey towards what is heavenly and divine; it has its pauses, when it rallies the stragglers, its stopping places when it meditates, contemplating some new and splendid promised land that has suddenly appeared on its horizon. It has its nights of slumber; and it is one of the poignant anxieties of the thinker to see the human spirit lost in shadow, and to grope in the darkness without being able to awake sleeping progress.

'Perhaps God is dead,' Gérard de Nerval once said to the writer of these lines, confusing progress with God and mistaking the pause in its movement for the death of the Supreme Being.

It is wrong to despair. Progress invariably reawakens, and indeed it may be said that she walks in her sleep, for she has grown. Seeing her again on her feet, we find that she is taller. To be always peaceful is no more a part of progress than it is of a river, which piles up rocks and creates barriers as it flows; these obstacles cause the water to froth and humanity to seethe. This leads to disturbance; but when the disturbance is over we realize that something has been gained. Until order, which is nothing less than universal peace, has been established, until harmony and unity prevail, the stages of progress will be marked by revolutions.

What, then, is Progress? We have just said it. It is the permanent life of all people. But it sometimes happens that the momentary life of individuals is opposed to the eternal life of the human race.

Let us admit the fact without bitterness: the individual has his separate interests and may legitimately seek to further and defend them; the present has its excusable quantity of egotisms; the life of the moment has its own rights and is not obliged to sacrifice itself incessantly for the future. The generation which now has its time upon earth is not obliged to shorten this time for the sake of generations – its equals, after all – which will later have their turn. 'I exist,' murmurs someone whose name is Everyone. 'I'm young and in love; I am old and I want rest; I work, I prosper, I do good business, I have houses to rent, money in State Securities; I am happy, I have a wife and children; I like all these things and I want to go on living, so leave me alone.' . . . There are moments when all this casts a deep chill on the large-minded pioneers of the human race.

Moreover Utopia, let us agree, emerges from its starry-eyed state when it goes to war. Being tomorrow's truth she borrows her method, which is war, from yesterday's lies. She is the future, but she acts like the past; she is the ideal, but she becomes the actuality, sullying her heroism with a violence for which it is right that she should be held responsible – tactical and expedient violence, against all principle, and for which she is inevitably punished. Utopia in rebellion defies the established military code: she shoots spies, executes traitors, destroys living beings and casts them into unknown shadow. She makes use of death, which is a grave matter. It seems that Utopia no longer believes in its own ideal, that irresistible and incorruptible force. She wields the sword. But no sword is simple; all are two-edged, and he who inflicts wounds with the one edge wounds himself with the other.

But subject to that reservation, made in all severity, it is impossible for us not to admire the glorious warriors of the future, the prophets of Utopia, whether they are successful or not. Even when they fail they are deserving of reverence, and perhaps it is in failure that they appear most noble. Victory, if it is in accord with progress, deserves the applause of mankind; but an heroic defeat deserves one's heartfelt sympathy. The one is magnificent, the other sublime. For ourselves, since we prefer martyrdom to success, John Brown is greater than Washington, Pisacane greater than Garibaldi.

It is necessary that someone should be on the side of the defeated. We are unjust to those great fighters for the future when they fail. We accuse revolutionaries of spreading terror. Every barricade seems to be an act of aggression. We stigmatize their theories, suspect their aims, mistrust their afterthoughts, and denounce their scruples. We reproach them with piling up a structure of misery and suffering, iniquities, grievances and despairs against the existing social order, and with dredging up shadows from the lowest depths as a pretext for conflict. We say to them: 'You are robbing Hell of its pavements!' To which they might reply: 'That is why our barricade is built of good intentions.'

Certainly the best solution is the one peacefully arrived at. We may agree, in short, that at the sight of paving-stones we think of the monster, and his good intentions are disquieting to society. But it is for society to save itself, and it is to its own good intentions that we appeal. No violent remedy is called for. To examine the evil with good-will, define it and then cure it – that is what we urge society to do.

However this may be, those men in all parts of the world who, with their eyes fixed upon France, struggle in the great cause with the inflexible logic of idealism, are deserving of honour. They offer their lives as a gift to Progress, they fulfil the will of Providence, they perform a religious rite. When the time comes, with as much indifference as an actor taking his cue in accordance with the divine scenario, they pass on into the tomb. They accept the hopeless battle and their own stoical disappearance, for the sake of the splendid and supreme universal outcome of the magnificent human movement which began with irresistible force on 14 July 1789. Those soldiers are priests. The French Revolution is a gesture of God.

For the rest, there are – and we must add this distinction to those already made in an earlier chapter – there are accepted insurrections which we call revolutions, and there are rejected revolutions which we call uprisings. An insurrection when it breaks out is an idea which submits itself to trial by the people. If the people turn down their thumbs then the idea is dead fruit, the insurrection has failed.

To go into battle on every pretext, and whenever Utopia desires it, is not the will of the people. Nations are not always and at every moment endowed with the temperament of heroes and martyrs. They are positive. In principle they find insurrection repugnant, first because it often leads to disaster, and secondly because its starting-point is always an abstract idea.

It is always for the ideal, the ideal alone – and this is splendid – that its devotees are prepared to sacrifice themselves. An insurrection is an outburst of enthusiasm. This enthusiasm may turn to rage, hence the recourse to arms. But every insurrection levelled at a government or a regime is aiming higher than this. We must insist, for example, that the leader of this insurrection of 1832, and most especially the youthful enthusiasts in the Rue de la Chanvrerie, were not precisely doing battle with Louis-Philippe. Most of them, in their conversation, did justice to the qualities of that king who was midway between monarchy and revolution; none hated him. But they were attacking in Louis-Philippe the younger branch of the divine right, precisely as they had attacked the older branch in Charles X; and, as we have said, what they were seeking to overthrow, in overthrowing monarchy in France, was the usurpation of man over man and of privilege over law throughout the world. Paris without a king signified a world without despots. That was how they reasoned. Their objective was a remote one, no doubt, perhaps vague, and one which receded as they strove to draw near it; but it was great.

That is how it is. And men sacrifice themselves for visions which for the sacrificed are nearly always illusions, but illusions, after all, in which all human certainties are mingled. The insurgent poeticizes and gilds the insurrection. He flings himself into the tragedy intoxicated with the thought of what he will achieve. And who can be sure that he will not succeed? We are small in numbers, with a whole army arrayed against us; but we are defenders of the right, of the natural law, the sovereignty of each man over himself which cannot possibly be renounced, of justice and truth, and if need be we will die like the Spartan three hundred. We do not think of Don Quixote but of Leonidas. We go forward and, being engaged in battle, do not retreat; we charge with our heads down, impelled by the hope of unimaginable victory, the revolution successful, progress set free, the human race made great, universal deliverance; or, at the worst, another Thermopylae.

These resorts to arms in the name of progress frequently fail, and we have said why. The crowd mistrusts the allurement of paladins. The masses, ponderous bodies that they are, and fragile on account of their very heaviness, fear adventure; and there is adventure in the ideal.

Moreover we must not forget that there are interests which have little sympathy with the ideal and the sentimental. Sometimes the stomach paralyses the heart.

It is the grandeur and the beauty of France that she is less concerned with the belly than other peoples; she slips readily into harness. She is the first to awaken, the last to fall asleep. She presses forward. She is a searcher.

All this depends on the fact that she is an artist. The ideal is nothing but the culmination of logic, just as beauty is the apex of truth. Artistic peoples are logical peoples. To love beauty is to seek for light. That is why the torch of Europe, which is civilization, was carried first by Greece, which passed it to Italy, which has passed it to France. Divine pioneering peoples – *Vitai lampada tradunt.*

What is admirable is that the poetry of a people is at the head of its progress. The quantity of civilization is measured by the quality of imagination. But a civilizing race must be a masculine race; it must be Corinth, not Sybaris. Those who become effeminate bastardize themselves. It is necessary to be neither a dilettante nor a virtuoso; but it is necessary to be an artist. In the matter of civilization one must not refine but sublimate. Subject to this condition, we endow mankind with the mastery of the ideal.

The modern ideal finds its prototype in art and its method in science. It is through science that we shall realize that sublime vision of poets: social beauty. We shall rebuild Eden in terms of $A + B$. At the stage which civilization has reached, the exact is a necessary element in what is splendid, and artistic feeling is not only served but completed by the scientific approach; the dream must know how to calculate. Art, which is the conqueror, must have as its point of stress science, which is the prime mover. The solidity of the mount is important. The modern spirit is composed of the genius of Greece mounted on the genius of India – Alexander on the elephant.

Races petrified in dogma or demoralized by wealth are unfitted for the conduct of civilization. Genuflexion before the idol or the golden crown weakens the muscles which march and the will-power which impels. Hieratic or mercantile preoccupations decrease the luminous quality of a people, narrow its horizon by lowering its level, and withhold from it that instinct, at once human and divine, which makes missionary nations. Babylon had no ideal, nor did Carthage. Athens and Rome had, and still, through all the darkness of centuries, they retain the glow of civilization.

France is a people of the same quality as Greece and Italy. She is Athenian in beauty and Roman in grandeur. Moreover, she is generous. She gives herself. More often than other peoples, she knows the mood of devotion and sacrifice. But it is a mood that comes and goes; and this is the great danger for those who seek to run when she is content to walk, and to walk when she wishes to stay still. France has her relapses into materialism, and at certain moments the ideas which obstruct the working of her splendid mind contain nothing that recalls her greatness but are rather of the dimensions of Missouri or some other southern state. What can be done about it? The giantess plays the dwarf; great France has her fantasies of smallness. That is all.

There is nothing to be said about that. Nations, like stars, are entitled to eclipse. All is well, provided the light returns and the eclipse does not become endless night. Dawn and resurrection are synonymous. The reappearance of the light is the same as the survival of the soul.

We may note the facts with calm. Death on the barricades or an exile's grave are, to those devoted to a cause, acceptable alternatives. The true name for devotion is disinterest. Let the deserted accept desertion and the exiled resign themselves to exile: we can only beseech the great people, when they withdraw, not to withdraw too far. They must not, on the pretext of returning to reason, advance too far on the downward path.

Matter exists, and the moment exists, as do the self-interest and the belly; but the belly must not be the sole source of wisdom. The life of the moment has its rights, and we admit them; but enduring life also has rights. Alas, to have climbed high does not preclude a fall. We see this in history more often than we would like. A nation is illustrious, it knows the taste of the ideal; then it lapses into squalor and finds this good. And if you ask why it has abandoned Socrates for Falstaff it replies: 'The truth is, I like statesmen.'

One last word before we return to battle.

A conflict like the one we are describing is nothing but a convulsive movement towards the ideal. Frustrated progress is sickly, and it is from this that these tragic epilepsies arise. We were bound to meet it on our journey, that affliction of progress, civil war. It is one of the fateful stages, both act and interval, in this play which centres upon a social outcast, and of which the real title is, *Progress*.

Progress!

That cry which we so often utter encompasses all our thought; and, at the point in the drama which we have now reached, the idea it contains having yet more than one trial to undergo, we may perhaps be allowed, if not to lift the veil, at least to let a clear light shine through it.

The book which the reader now holds in his hands, from one end to the other, as a whole and in its details, whatever gaps, exceptions, or weaknesses it may contain, treats of the advance from evil to good, from injustice to justice, from falsity to truth, from darkness to daylight, from blind appetite to conscience, from decay to life, from bestiality to duty, from Hell to Heaven, from limbo to God. Matter itself is the starting-point, and the point of arrival is the soul. Hydra at the beginning, an angel at the end.

XXI

The heroes

Suddenly a drum beat the charge.

The attack was a hurricane. During the night, under cover of darkness, the barricade had been stealthily approached. In the present broad daylight, and in that open street, there was no possibility of surprise: it was a matter of naked force, cannon-fire paving the way while the infantry rushed the barricade. Ferocity was now allied to skill. A powerful column of infantry of the line, broken at equal intervals by contingents of foot-soldiers from the national and municipal guards, and reinforced in depth by additional bodies of soldiery which could be heard but not seen, advanced at the double down the street, drums playing and trumpets sounding, bayonets fixed, sappers in the lead and, unshaken by the counter-fire, flung itself upon the barricade with the weight of a metal battering-ram against a wall.

The wall held.

The insurgents fired impetuously. The barricade under the assault had a crest of flashes like a lion's mane. The counter-attack was so violent that although at one moment it was submerged beneath the attackers, it shrugged off the soldiers as the lion shrugs off the dogs and was covered only as a cliff is covered with sea-foam, to re-emerge an instant later, sheer, black, and formidable.

The attacking column, forced to retreat, stayed massed in the street, exposed but terrible, and replied with a terrifying burst of musket-fire. Anyone who has witnessed a firework display will recall the pattern made by the cluster of rockets that is called a 'bouquet'. We must think of this bouquet as being not vertical but horizontal, with musket bullets or grapeshot at each of its points of fire, and carrying death in its patterned thunders. The barricade was subjected to this.

Determination was equal on either side. Bravery became almost barbarous and to it was added a sort of heroic ferocity beginning with the sacrifice of self. It was the time when members of the Garde Nationale fought like zouaves. The troops wanted to be done with it; the rebels wanted to fight. The acceptance of death in the fullness of youth and health turns daring into frenzy. Everyone in that mêlée was filled with the inspiration of a supreme moment. The street was littered with bodies.

Enjolras was at one end of the barricade, Marius at the other. Enjolras, who carried the whole affair in his head, was keeping under cover and reserving himself; three soldiers fell under his redoubt without even seeing him. Marius had no cover. He set himself up as a target. Half his body was exposed above the top of the barricade. There is no greater spendthrift than the miser who throws over the traces, and no man more terrible in action than a dreamer. Marius was formidable and reflective, engaged in the battle as though it was a dream, as it were a ghost firing a musket.

The defenders' ammunition was running low, but not their sarcasm. They still laughed, even amid that deadly whirlwind.

Courfeyrac was bare-headed.

'What have you done with your hat?' Bossuet asked.

'It was taken off by a cannon-ball,' Courfeyrac replied.

Or they said more serious things. Feuilly cried bitterly:

'What are we to make of the men' – and he cited well-known and even celebrated names, some belonging to the old army – 'who promised to join us and swore to assist us, who gave us their word of honour, who were to have been our leaders and who have deserted us?'

To which Combeferre replied with a melancholy smile:

'There are people who observe the rules of honour as we do the stars, from a very long way off.'

The ground within the barricade was so covered with used cartridge-cases that it might have been a snowstorm.

The attackers had the advantage of numbers; the rebels had the advantage of position. They were defending a wall whence they shot down at point-blank range the soldiers staggering amid their dead and wounded or enmeshed in the barricade itself. The barricade, constructed as it was and admirably buttressed, did indeed present one of those positions where a handful of men could defy a legion. Nevertheless, being constantly reinforced and expanding under the hail of bullets, the attacking column inexorably moved forward and now, little by little and step by step, but with certainty, the army was compressing the barricade like the screw of a wine-press.

The assaults continued one after another. The horror was steadily growing.

There ensued, on that heap of paving-stones in the Rue de la Chanvrerie, a struggle worthy of the ruins of Troy. That handful of haggard, ragged, and exhausted men, who had not eaten for twenty-four hours, who had not slept, who had only a few shots left to fire, so that they searched their empty pockets for cartridges, nearly all wounded, with head or arm swathed in rough, blackening bandages, having holes in their clothing through which the blood flowed, ill-armed with insufficient muskets and old, worn sabres, became Titans. The barricade was ten times assailed and climbed, but still it did not fall.

To form an idea of that conflict one must imagine a terrible pyre of courage set on fire and oneself watching the blaze. It was not a battle but the inside of a furnace; mouths breathed out fumes; faces were extraordinary, seeming no longer human but living flames; and it was awe-inspiring to watch those salamanders of battle move to and fro in the red haze. We shall not seek to depict the successive stages of the slaughter. Only an epic is entitled to fill twelve thousand lines with an account of battle. It might have been that Hell of Brahmanism, the most awful of the seventeen abysses, which the Veda calls 'the forest of swords'.

They fought body to body, hand to hand, with pistol-shots, sabre-thrusts, bare fists, from above and below, from all quarters, the roof of the house, the windows of the tavern, the vent-holes of the cellars into which some had slipped. They were one against sixty. The façade of Corinth, half pounded to rubble, was made hideous. The window, peppered with grapeshot, had lost both glass and framework and was nothing but a shapeless hole hastily blocked with paving-stones. Bossuet, Feuilly, Courfeyrac, Joly, all were killed; Combeferre, pierced by three bayonet thrusts while he was picking up a wounded soldier, had only time to look up to the sky before he died.

Marius, still fighting, was so covered with wounds, particularly on the head, that his face was smothered with blood as though he had a red scarf tied round it.

Enjolras alone was unscathed. When he was weaponless he reached to right or left and a blade of sorts was placed by a fellow rebel in his hand. Of four swords, one more than François I had had at Marignano, he had only the stump of one left.

Homer wrote: 'Diomed slays Axylus, the son of Teuthranis, who lived in happy Arisbe; Euryalus, the son of Mecisteus, destroys Dresos, Opheltios, Esepes, and that Pedasus whom the Naiad Abarbarea bore to the irreproachable Bucolion; Ulysses overthrows Pidutes of Percote, Antilochus, Ablerus; Polypaetes, Astyalus, Polydamas, Otus of Cyllend, Teucer and Aretaon. Meganthis dies beneath the pike-thrusts of Euripylus. Agamemnon, the king of heroes, fells Elatos, who was born in the fortified town washed by the rippling River Satnois.' In our old poems of battle Esplandian attacks with a two-forked flame the giant Marquis Swantibore, who defends himself by pelting the knight with the stones of towers he uproots. Ancient mural frescoes depict for us the dukes of Brittany and of Bourbon, armed and accoutred for battle, mounted and encountering each other, battle-axe in hand, visored with iron, shod with iron, gauntletted with iron, the one caparisoned with ermine, the other draped in blue; Brittany with a lion's head between the two horns of his crown, Bourbon adorned with a huge fleur-de-lys at his visor. But to be superb it is not necessary to flaunt, like Yvon, the ducal morion, or to carry in the hand a living flame, like Esplandian, or, like Phyles, the father of Polydamas, to have brought back a suit of armour from Ephyrae, the present of the king of Corinth; it is only necessary to give one's life for a conviction or for a loyalty. The simple-minded soldier, yesterday a peasant in La Beauce or Le Limousin, who strays, pigsticker at his side, round the children's nurses in the Luxembourg; the pale young student bent over a piece of anatomy or a book; a blond adolescent who trims his beard with scissors – infuse these with a sense of duty and plant them face to face in the Carrefour Boucherat or the blind alley Blanche Mibray, the one fighting for his flag, the other for his ideals, and both believing that they are fighting for their country, and you will find that the shadow cast by the country bumpkin and the aspirant doctor, in the epic field where mankind struggles, will be no less great than the shadow cast by Megaryon, the king of tiger-filled Lycia, in his struggle with the giant Ajax, the equal of the Gods.

XXII
Close quarters

When only two of the leaders were left alive, Marius and Enjolras at either end of the barricade, the centre, which for so long had been sustained by Courfeyrac, Joly, Bossuet, Feuilly, and Combeferre, gave way. The cannon-fire, without making an effective breach in the wall, had sufficiently damaged it. The top had been shot away, falling on either side, so that the debris formed two inclines, one within the stronghold and the other outside it, the one outside providing a ramp for the attackers.

A supreme assault was launched, and this time it succeeded. The mass of soldiery, bristling with bayonets and advancing at the double, was irresistible, and the dense front line of the attacking force appeared amid the smoke on the top of the barricade. This time all was over. The group of rebels defending the centre beat a hasty retreat.

And then in some of them the deeply implanted love of life was revived. Faced by that forest of muskets, several no longer wanted to die. It is a moment when the instinct of self-preservation cries out loud and the animal reappears in man. They were pressed against the six-storey house which formed the back of the stronghold. This house might be the saving of them. It was barricaded and, so to speak, walled in from top to bottom. Before the troops had penetrated into the stronghold, there was time for a door to open and close, only a moment was needed, and that door might be life itself to the handful of desperate men. Beyond the house lay streets, space, the possibility of flight. They began to hammer on the door with musket-butts, and to kick it, calling out and begging with clasped hands. But no one opened the door. From the window on the third floor the dead head looked down on them.

But Enjolras and Marius, and the seven or eight who rallied round them, gave the rest some protection. Enjolras had cried to the soldiers, 'Stand back!' and when an officer had refused to obey he had killed him. He stood now in the little interior courtyard of the stronghold, his back to the tavern, a sword in one hand, a carbine in the other, defending the door against the attackers and cried to his men, 'This is the only door.' Covering them with his body, defying a battalion single-handed, he let them pass behind him. They hastened to do so; and Enjolras, using his carbine as a cudgel to batter down the bayonets that threatened him, was the last to enter. There was a terrible moment, with the soldiers striving to force open the door and the rebels striving to close it. Finally it was closed with such violence that, as it was slammed to, it still bore, adhering to the woodwork, the severed finger of a soldier who had clutched it.

Marius had stayed outside. A ball had shattered his shoulder-blade. He felt himself grow dizzy and he fell. At this moment, when his eyes were already closed, he felt himself grasped by a vigorous hand, and in the moment before he sank into unconsciousness he had just time to think, mingled with the memory of Cosette, 'I'm taken prisoner. I shall be shot.'

Enjolras, not seeing Marius among those who had taken refuge in the tavern, thought the same. But it was a moment when there was no time to think of any death except one's own. Enjolras barred and double-bolted the door while a thunder of blows from musket-butts and the axes of the sappers descended on it from outside. Their attackers were now concentrating upon the door. The siege of the tavern had begun.

The soldiers were furiously angry. The death of the artillery sergeant had enraged them and, worse still, the rumour had gone round during the hours preceding the attack that the rebels were mutilating their prisoners, and that the headless body of a soldier lay in the tavern. Hideous rumours of this kind are a normal accompaniment of civil war, and it was a similar rumour which was later to lead to the disaster in the Rue Transnonain.

When the door was secured, Enjolras said to his fellows:
'We must sell our lives dearly.'

Then he went to the table on which the bodies of Mabeuf and Gavroche were lying. Two rigid, motionless forms, one large, one small, lay covered by a black cloth, and the two faces could be faintly discerned beneath the stiff folds of the shroud. A hand had escaped its coverings and hung down towards the floor. It was that of the old man.

Enjolras bent down and kissed the venerable hand as on the previous evening he had kissed the forehead. They were the only two kisses he had ever bestowed in his life.

In brief, the barricade had fought like a doorway of Thebes, and the tavern fought like a house in Saragossa. Those were obstinate defences. No quarter was given, no discussion was possible. Men are ready to die provided they also kill. When Suchet cried, 'Surrender!' Palafox replied, 'After the battle with firearms comes the battle with knives.' Nothing was lacking in the capture by assault of the Hucheloup tavern, neither the paving-stones rained down upon the besiegers from the upper window and roof, causing hideous injuries, nor shots fired from the cellars and attics, neither fury in the attack nor rage in the defence – nor finally, when the door gave way, the frantic dementia of slaughter. The attackers, rushing into the tavern, their feet entangled in the panels of the broken door, found not a single defender. The circular staircase, cut in halves with an axe, lay in the middle of the lower room, where a few wounded men were in process of dying. All those remaining alive were on the upper floor, and from here, by way of the hole in the ceiling which had been the entrance to the staircase, there came a terrible burst of fire. Those were the last cartridges. When they had been fired, and when the heroic defenders were left with neither powder nor shot, each seized two of the bottles set aside by Enjolras, of which we have spoken, and held back the attack with these most fragile cudgels. They were bottles of brandy. We are depicting these sombre aspects of the carnage as they happened. The besieged, alas, makes a weapon of everything. Greek fire did no dishonour to Archimedes, nor boiling pitch to Bayard. All forms of warfare are terror, and there is nothing to choose between them. The musketry of the attackers, although harassed and aiming upwards, was murderous. The edge of that hole in the ceiling was soon surrounded by dead heads from which hung long, streaming red threads. The din was indescribable; and a reeking cloud of smoke plunged the battle in darkness. Words are lacking to depict a horror that has reached this point. There were no longer men engaged in a struggle that was now infernal, no longer giants against Titans; it was nearer to Milton and Dante than to Homer. Demons attacked and spectres resisted. It was heroism become monstrous.

XXIII

Orestes fasting and Pylades drunk

Eventually, lending each other a back and making use of the remains of the staircase, climbing up the walls and clinging to the ceiling, and hacking down the last resistance at the edge of the hatchway, some twenty of the attackers, soldiers and National and

Municipal Guards, most of them suffering from wounds sustained in that final advance, blinded with their own blood, enraged and now savage, succeeded in reaching the upper room. Only one man in it was still on his feet – Enjolras. Without cartridges or a sword, his only weapon was the barrel of his carbine, the butt of which he had broken on the heads of the attackers. He had put the billiard-table between his assailants and himself, and had retreated to the corner of the room; but here, proud-eyed and erect, armed with nothing but that last fragment of a weapon, he was still sufficiently impressive for a space to be left around him. A voice cried:

'He's the leader. He's the one who killed the artilleryman. Well, he's set himself up for us. He's only got to stay there and we can shoot him on the spot.'

'Shoot me,' said Enjolras.

Flinging away the remains of the carbine and folding his arms, he offered them his breast.

The bold defiance of death is always moving. On the instant when Enjolras folded his arms, accepting his fate, the din of battle ceased in the room and chaos was succeeded by a sort of sepulchral solemnity. It seemed that the dignity of Enjolras, weaponless and motionless, weighed upon the tumult, and that this young man, the only one unwounded, proud, blood-spattered, charming, and disdainful as though he were invulnerable, impelled the sinister group to kill him with respect. His beauty, now enhanced by pride, was radiant, and as though he could be neither fatigued nor wounded, even after the appalling twenty-four hours which had passed, his cheeks were flushed with health. Perhaps it was to him that a witness was referring when later he said to the tribunal, 'There was one of the insurgents whom I heard called Apollo.' A National Guard who aimed his musket at Enjolras, lowered it and said: 'I feel as though I'd be shooting a flower.'

Twelve men formed up in the opposite corner of the room and silently charged their muskets.

A sergeant cried, 'Take aim!', but an officer intervened.

'Wait', he said.

He spoke to Enjolras:

'Would you like your eyes to be bandaged?'

'No.'

'It really was you who killed the artillery sergeant?'

'Yes.'

*

Grantaire had woken up a few moments previously.

As we may recall, he had been asleep since the previous day in the upper room of the tavern, seated on a chair and sprawled over a table.

He had been the perfect embodiment, in all its forcefulness, of the old expression, 'dead drunk'. The awesome mixture of absinthe, stout, and raw spirit had plunged him into a coma. Since his table was small and of no use to the defence, he had been left there. He was in his original posture, with his head resting on his arms, surrounded by glasses, tankards, and empty bottles, deep in the annihilating slumber of a hibernating bear or a bloated leech. Nothing had penetrated it, not the firing, nor the bullets and grape-shot that came in through the window, nor even the tremendous uproar of the final assault. Only the cannon had drawn an occasional snore from him; he seemed to be waiting for a ball to save him the trouble of waking up. Several dead bodies lay around him; and at first glance there was nothing to distinguish him from the truly dead.

It is not noise that awakens a drunken man, but silence. This is a singular fact that has often been observed. The collapse of every-thing around him had merely served to increase Grantaire's un-consciousness, as though it were a rocking cradle. But the pause induced by Enjolras came as a shock to his slumbers, the effect being that of a carriage drawn at a gallop which comes suddenly to a stop. The sleeper awoke. Grantaire sat up with a start, stretched his arms, rubbed his eyes, stared, yawned, and understood.

The ending of drunkenness is like the tearing down of a curtain. One sees, as a whole and at a single glance, everything that it concealed. Memory suddenly returns, and the drunkard who knows nothing of what has happened in the past twenty-four hours, has scarcely opened his eyes before he is aware of the situation. His thoughts return to him with a brisk lucidity; the non-being of drunkenness, a sort of fog that blinds the brain, vanishes to be replaced by an instant, clear grasp of things as they are.

The soldiers, intent upon Enjolras, had not even noticed Gran-taire, who had been slumbering in a corner, partly concealed from them by the billiard-table. The sergeant was about to repeat the order, 'Take aim!' when suddenly a loud voice cried:

'Long live the Republic! I'm one of them.'

Grantaire had risen to his feet.

The blazing light of the battle of which he had seen nothing, and in which he had taken no part, shone in the eyes of the transfigured sot. He repeated, 'Long live the Republic!' and walking steadily across the room took his stand beside Enjolras, confronting the muskets.

'Might as well kill two birds with one stone,' he said; and then, turning to Enjolras, he added gently: 'If you don't mind.'

Enjolras clasped his hand and smiled.

The smile had not ended when the volley rang out. Enjolras, pierced by eight shots, stayed leaning against the wall as though the bullets had nailed him there; only his head hung down. Grantaire collapsed at his feet.

Within a few minutes the soldiers had driven out the last of the rebels sheltering at the top of the house. They fired through a wooden lattice into the attic. There was fighting under the roof and bodies were flung out of windows, some of them still living. Two sappers who were trying to set the overturned omnibus upright were killed by carbine-shots from the attic. A man in a smock was flung out of it with a bayonet-thrust in his belly and lay groaning on the ground. A soldier and a rebel slid together down the sloping roof-tiles and, refusing to let go of each other, fell together in a fierce embrace. There was a similar struggle in the cellar – cries, shots, desperate exertion. Then silence. The stronghold was taken.

The soldiers began to search the surrounding houses and pursue the fugitives.

XXIV

Prisoner

Marius was indeed a prisoner, and of Jean Valjean. It was Valjean's hand that had grasped him as he fell, and whose grip he had felt before losing consciousness.

Valjean had taken no part in the battle other than in exposing himself to it. Had it not been for him, no one in those last desperate moments would have thought of the wounded. Thanks to him, present everywhere in the carnage like a providence, those who fell were picked up, carried into the tavern, and their wounds dressed. In the intervals he mended the barricade. But he did not strike a blow, even in self-defence. He silently assisted. And, as it happened, he had scarcely a scratch. The bullets would have none of him.

If he had had any thought of suicide when he entered that deadly place, he had failed in this. But we question whether he had thought of suicide, an irreligious act.

In the dense reek of battle Valjean had not seemed to see Marius; but the truth is that he had never taken his eyes off him. When a bullet laid Marius low, Valjean leapt forward with the agility of a tiger, seized him as though he were his prey, and carried him off.

The attack at that moment was so intensely concentrated upon Enjolras and the door of the tavern that no one saw Valjean carry Marius's unconscious form across the stronghold and vanish round the corner of the house. This, it will be remembered, made a sort of promontory in the street, affording shelter for a few square feet from bullets and also out of sight. In the same way there is sometimes one room in a blazing house that does not burn, or a quiet stretch of water behind an outcrop of land in a storm-lashed sea. It was in this retreat within the barricades that Éponine had died.

Here Jean Valjean stopped, lowered Marius to the ground, and with his back to the wall stood looking about him.

The situation was appalling. For perhaps two or three minutes this corner of wall might afford them shelter; but how to escape from the inferno? He remembered his torments eight years earlier in the Rue Polonceau, and how he had eventually got away; that had been difficult, but this time it seemed impossible. Facing him was that silent, implacable house that seemed to be inhabited only by a dead man leaning out of a window; to his right was the low barricade closing the Rue de la Petite-Truanderie, an obstacle easily surmounted; but beyond the barricade a row of bayonets was visible, those of the soldiers posted to block this way of escape. To climb the barricade would be to encounter a volley of musket-fire. And on Valjean's left was the field of battle. Death lurked round the corner.

It was a situation such as only a bird could have escaped from. But the matter had to be instantly decided, a device contrived, a plan made. The fight was going on within a few yards of him, and, by good fortune, it was concentrated on a single point, the door of the tavern; but if a single soldier had the idea of going round the house to attack it from the side all would be over.

Valjean looked at the house opposite, at the barricade and then at the ground, with the intentness of utmost extremity, as though he were seeking to dig a hole in it with his eyes.

As he looked something like a possibility emerged, as though the very intensity of his gaze had brought it to light. He saw, a few feet away, at the foot of that rigorously guarded lower barricade, half-hidden by tumbled paving-stones, an iron grille let into the street. Made of stout iron transverse bars, it was about two feet square. The stones surrounding it had been uprooted, so that it was, as it were, unsealed. Beneath the bars was a dark aperture, something like a chimney flue or a boiler cylinder. Valjean leapt forward, all his old experience of escape springing like inspiration into his mind. To shift the paving-stones, raise the grille, lift Marius's inert body on to his shoulder, and, charged with this burden, using elbows and knees, to climb down into this fortunately shallow well; to let the heavy grille fall shut behind him, over which the stones again tumbled, and find footing on a tile surface some ten feet underground – all this was done as though in delirium, with immense strength and hawklike speed. It took only a few minutes.

Valjean, with the still unconscious Marius, found himself in a long subterranean passage, a place of absolute peace, silence, and darkness. He was reminded of the time when he had fallen out of the street into the garden of the convent; but then it had been with Cosette.

Like a subdued echo above his head he could still hear the formidable uproar which accompanied the capture of the tavern.

BOOK TWO

THE ENTRAILS OF THE MONSTER

I

Land impoverished by the sea

PARIS POURS twenty-four million francs a year into the water. That is no metaphor. She does so by day and by night, thoughtlessly and to no purpose. She does so through her entrails, that is to say, her sewers. Twenty-five millions is the most modest of the approximate figures arrived at by statistical science.

After many experiments science today knows that the most fruitful and efficacious of all manures is human excrement. The Chinese, be it said to our shame, knew it before us. No Chinese peasant, according to Eckeberg, goes to the town without bringing back, at either end of his bamboo pole, two buckets filled with unmentionable matter; and it is thanks to this human manure that the Chinese earth is as fruitful as in the days of Abraham. The Chinese corn harvest amounts to 120 times the amount of seed. No guano is to be compared in fertility with the droppings of a town. A big city is the most powerful of dunging animals. To use the town to manure the country is to ensure prosperity. If our gold is so much waste, then, on the other hand, our waste is so much gold.

And what do we do with this golden dung? We throw it away. At great expense we send ships to the South Pole to collect the droppings of petrels and penguins, and the incalculable wealth we ourselves produce we throw back into the sea. The human and animal manure which is lost to the world because it is returned to the sea instead of to the land would suffice to feed all mankind. Do you know what all this is – the heaps of muck piled up on the streets during the night, the scavengers' carts and the foetid flow of sludge that the pavement hides from you? It is the flowering meadow, green grass, marjoram and thyme and sage, the lowing of contented cattle in the evening, the scented hay and the golden wheat, the bread on your table and the warm blood in your veins – health and joy and life. Such is the purpose of that mystery of creation which is transformation on earth and transfiguration in Heaven.

Return all that to the great crucible and you will reap abundance. The feeding of the fields becomes the feeding of men. You are free to lose that richness and to find me absurd into the bargain; that will be the high point of your ignorance.

It has been calculated that France alone through her rivers every year pours into the Atlantic half a milliard francs. You must note that those five hundred millions represent a quarter of our budget expenditure. Such is man's astuteness that he prefers to rid himself of this sum in the streams. It is the people's substance that is being carried away, in drops or in floods, the wretched vomit of our sewers into the rivers, and the huge vomit of the rivers into the sea. Each belch of our cloaca costs us a thousand francs, and the result is that the land is impoverished and the water made foul. Hunger lurks in the furrow and disease in the stream.

It is notorious, for example, that in recent years the Thames has been poisoning London. As for Paris, the outlet of most of the sewers has had to be brought below the last of the bridges.

A two-channel arrangement of locks and sluices, sucking in and pouring out, an elementary drainage system as simple as the human lung, such as is already functioning in some parts of England, would suffice to bring to our towns the pure water of the fields and to return to the fields the enriched water of the towns; and this very simple exchange would save us the five hundred millions which we fling away.

The present process does harm in seeking to do good. The intention is good, the result lamentable. We think to cleanse the town but weaken the population. A sewer is a mistake. When drainage, with its double function of restoring what it takes away, shall have replaced the sewer, which is mere impoverishment, then this, combined with a new social economy, will increase by a hundredfold the produce of the earth and the problem of poverty will be immeasurably lessened. Add to this the elimination of parasites, and the problem is solved.

Meanwhile wastage continues and public wealth flows into the river. Wastage is the word. Europe is exhausting itself to the point of ruin. As for France, we have named the figures. But since Paris amounts to one twenty-fifth of the total French population, and the Paris manure is the richest of all, to assess at twenty-five millions Paris's share in the annual loss of half a milliard is an underestimate. Those twenty-five millions, used for relief-work and for amenities, would double the splendour of Paris. The city wastes them in its sewers; so that one may say that the abundance of Paris, her festivities, her noble buildings, her elegance, luxury and magnificence, and the money that she squanders with both hands – all this is sewage.

It is in this fashion, in the blindness of a false political economy, that the well-being of the whole community is allowed to pour away. There should be nets at Saint-Cloud to trap the public wealth. Economically one may sum it up as follows: Paris is a leaky basket. This model capital city, of which every nation seeks to have a copy, this ideal metropolis, this noble stronghold of initiative, drive, and experiment, this centre and dwelling-place of minds, this nation-town and hive of the future, a composite of Babylon and Corinth, would, seen in this aspect, cause a peasant of Fo-Kian to shrug his shoulders.

To copy Paris is to invite ruin. And Paris, in this matter of immemorial and senseless waste, copies herself. There is nothing new in her ineptitude; it is not a youthful folly. The ancients behaved like the moderns. 'The cloaca of Rome,' wrote Liebig, 'absorbed all the well-being of the Roman peasant.' When the Roman countryside was ruined by the Roman sewer, Rome exhausted Italy, and when she had poured Italy through her drains she disposed of Sicily, then Sardinia, then Africa. The Roman sewer engulfed the world, sapping town and country alike. *Urbi et orbi* or the Eternal City, the bottomless drain.

In this, as in other matters, Rome set the example; and Paris follows it with the stupidity proper to intelligent towns. For the purpose of the operation she has beneath her another Paris, with its roads and intersections, its arteries and alleyways – the Paris of the sewers, a city of slime only lacking human kind.

We must avoid flattery, even of a great people. Where there is everything there is ignominy as well as sublimity: and if Paris contains Athens, the city of light, Tyre, the city of power, Sparta, the city of stern virtue, Nineveh, the city of prodigy, she also contains Lutetia, the city of mud. Moreover, the mark of her greatness is there also. The huge bilge of Paris achieves the strange feat that among men only a few, such as Machiavelli, Bacon, and Mirabeau, have achieved – an abjectness of grandeur.

The underside of Paris, if the eye could perceive it, would have the appearance of a vast sea-plant. A sponge has no more apertures and passageways than the patch of earth, six leagues around, on which the ancient city stands. Apart from the catacombs, the intricate network of gas-pipes and of piping that distributes fresh water to the street pumps, each a separate system, the sewers alone form a huge, dark labyrinth on either side of the river – a maze to which the only key is itself.

And here, in the foetid darkness, the rat is to be found, apparently the sole product of Paris's labour.

II

Ancient history of the sewer

If one thinks of Paris lifted up like a lid, the view of the sewers from above would resemble a great tree-trunk grafted on to the river. On the right bank the main sewer would be the trunk of the tree, its lesser channels being the branches and its dead ends the twigs.

This is a condensed and inexact simile, for the right-angle, which is characteristic of this form of underground ramification, is very rare in vegetable growths. One may form a more appropriate image by supposing that one is looking down on a grotesque jumble of eastern letters attached to each other haphazard, by their sides or their extremities.

Bilges and sewers played a great part in the Middle Ages, in the Bas-Empire and the Far East. Plague was born in them, despots died in them. The masses contemplated with an almost religious awe those hotbeds of putrescence, vast cradles of death. The Pit of Vermin at Benares was no less deep than the Pit of Lions at Babylon. Tiglath-Pilezar, according to the rabbinical books, swore by the vents of Nineveh. It is from the sewer of Münster that John of Leyden raised his false moon, and from the pit of Kekhscheb that Mokanna, the veiled prophet of Khorassan, raised his false sun.

The history of mankind is reflected in the history of cloaca. The Gemoniae depicted Rome. The sewer of Paris was a formidable ancient thing, both sepulchre and refuge. Crime, intelligence, social protest, liberty of conscience, thought and theft, everything that human laws pursue or have pursued has been hidden in it – the Maillotins in the fourteenth century, the Tire-laines in the fifteenth, the Huguenots in the sixteenth, the Illuminati in the seventeenth, the Chauffeurs in the eighteenth. A century ago the night-time dagger-thrust came out of it, the footpad in danger vanished into it. The forest had its caves, and Paris had its sewer. The *truanderie*, that Gallic gipsy band, accepted the sewer as a part of the Court of

Miracles, and at night, cunning and ferocious, crouched under the Maubué vomitoria as in a bedchamber.

It was natural that those whose daily work was in the alley Vide-Gousset or the Rue Coupe-Gorge should have this night-time dwelling in the culvert of the Chemin-vert bridge or the Hurepoix kennel. From these come a host of memories. All sorts of ghosts haunt those long, lonely corridors; foulness and miasma are everywhere, with here and there a vent-hole through which Villon from within converses with Rabelais without.

The sewer, in ancient Paris, is the resting-place of all failure and all effort. To political economy it is a detritus, and to social philosophy a residue. It is the conscience of the town where all things converge and clash. There is darkness here, but no secrets. Everything has its true or at least its definitive form. There is this to be said for the muck-heap, that it does not lie. Innocence dwells in it. The mask of Basil is there, the cardboard and the strings, accented with honest filth; and beside it, the false nose of Scapin. Every foulness of civilization, fallen into disuse, sinks into that ditch of truth wherein ends the huge social down-slide, to be swallowed, but to spread. It is a vast confusion. No false appearance, no white-washing, is possible; filth strips off its shirt in utter starkness, all illusions and mirages scattered, nothing left except what is, showing the ugly face of what ends. Reality and disappearance: here, a bottle-neck proclaims drunkenness, a basket-handle tells of home life; and there the apple-core that had literary opinions again becomes an apple-core. The face on the coin turns frankly green, the spittle of Caiaphas encounters the vomit of Falstaff, the gold piece from the gaming house rattles against the nail from which the suicide hung, a livid foetus is wrapped in the spangles which last Shrove Tuesday danced at the Opéra, a wig which passed judgement on men wallows near the decay which was the skirt of Margoton. It is more than fraternity, it is close intimacy. That which was painted is besmeared. The last veil is stripped away. A sewer is a cynic. It says everything.

This sincerity of filth pleases us and soothes the spirit. When one has spent one's time on earth suffering the windy outpourings which call themselves statesmanship, political wisdom, human justice, professional probity, the robes of incorruptibility, it is soothing to go into the sewer and see the mire which is appropriate to all this. And at the same time it teaches us. As we have said, history flows through the sewer. Saint Bartholomew seeps drop by drop through the paving-stones. The great assassinations, the political and religious butcheries, pass through that underworld of civilization with their bodies. To the thoughtful eye, all the murderers of history are there on their knees in that hideous penumbra, with a fragment of shroud for their apron, sadly washing out their offence. Louis XI is there with Tristan, François I with Duprat, Charles IX with his mother, Richelieu with Louis XIII; Louvois, Letellier, Hébert, and Maillard seek to efface the traces of their lives. One may hear the swish of spectral brooms and breathe the huge miasma of social catastrophe and see red reflections in the corners. A terrible water flows that has washed bloodstained hands.

The social observer should enter that darkness; it is a part of his laboratory. Philosophy is the microscope of thought, from which everything seeks to fly but nothing escapes. To compromise is useless: what side of oneself does one show by compromise; except what is shameful? Philosophy pursues evil with its unflinching gaze and does not allow it to escape into nothingness. Amid the vanishing and the shrinking it detects all things, reconstructing the purple from the shred of rag and the woman from the wisp. Through the cloaca it reconstructs the town, from the mire it recreates its customs; from the shard it deduces the amphora or the jug. From the impress of a fingernail on parchment it distinguishes between the Jewry of the Judengasse and that of the Ghetto. From what remains it rediscovers what has been, good, bad, false, true – the spot of blood in the palace, the inkspot in the cavern, the drop of grease in the brothel, the torments suffered, temptations encountered, orgies vomited up, the wrinkles of self-abasement, the traces of prostitution in souls rendered capable of it by their vileness, and on the smock of the Roman porter the elbow-mark of Messalina.

III

Bruneseau

The Paris sewer in the Middle Ages was a legend. In the sixteenth century Henri II attempted a sounding which failed. Less than a hundred years ago, as Mercier attests, the cloaca was left to itself, to make of itself what it could.

Such was ancient Paris, the victim of quarrels, indecisiveness, and false starts. For a long time it was stupid. Then the year '89 showed how sense comes to cities. But in the good old days the capital had little discernment; she did not know how to order her affairs either morally or materially, and could no more dispose of ordure than of abuses. Everything was difficult, everything raised questions. The sewerage itself was opposed to any discipline. A course could no more be laid down for it than could agreement be reached in the town; above was the unintelligible, below the inextricable; beneath the confusions of tongues lay the confusion of cellars, the labyrinth below Babel.

Sometimes the Paris sewer chose to overflow, as though that hidden Nile were suddenly angry. There were infamous sewer floods. That stomach of civilization digested badly; the cloaca at times flowed back into the town, giving Paris a taste of bile. These parallels of sewage and remorse had their virtue. They were warnings, very badly received it must be said. The town was angered by the audacity of its filth, and could not accept that its ordure should return; it must be better disposed of.

The flood of 1802 is within the memory of eighty-year-old Parisians. The mire formed a cross in the Place des Victoires, with its statue of Louis XIV. It entered the Rue Saint-Honoré by the two sewer mouths of the Champs-Élysées, the Rue Popincourt by the Chemin-Vert mouth, the Rue de la Roquette by the Rue de Sappe sewer. It covered the Rue des Champs-Élysées to a depth of thirty-five centimetres; and at midday, when the vomitorium of the Seine performed its function in reverse, it reached the Rue des Marais among other streets, covering a distance of a hundred and nine metres, only a few paces from the house where Racine had lived, respecting the poet more than it had the king. It attained its greatest depth in the Rue Saint-Pierre, where it rose three feet above the roof-gutters, and its greatest extent in the Rue Saint-Sabin, when it stretched over a distance of two hundred and thirty-eight metres.

At the beginning of this century the Paris sewer was still a place of mystery. Muck has never had a good name, but here it was a subject for alarm. Paris was confusedly aware that beneath her lay a dreadful hollow, resembling the monstrous bog of Thebes inhabited by worms fifteen feet long, and which might have served as a bath-tub for Behemoth. The great boots of the sewage workers never ventured beyond certain known points. It was still very near the time when the carts of the street-scavengers, from one of which Sainte-Foix had fraternized with the Marquis de Créqui, were simply emptied into the sewer. As for cleansing, this was left to the rain-storms, which obstructed more than they carried away. Rome invested her cloaca with a touch of poetry, calling it Gemoniae; Paris insulted hers, calling it the stench-hole. Science and superstition were agreed as to the horror. The stench-hole was as repellent to hygiene as to legend. Spectral figures emerged from the Mouffetard sewer, corpses had been flung into that of the Barillerie. Fagon attributed the terrible malignant fever of 1685 to the break in the Marais sewer, which until 1833 lay open in the Rue Saint-Louis, almost opposite the inn-sign of the Messager-Galant. The sewer-mouth in the Rue de la Mortellerie was famous for the plagues which spread from it: with the pointed bars of its grille resembling a row of teeth, it was like a dragon's mouth breathing hell upon men. Popular imagination credited that dark Parisian sink with a hideous endlessness. The idea of exploring it did not occur to the police. Who would have dared to sound those depths, to venture into that unknown? It was terrible. Nevertheless someone did venture. The cloaca found its Christopher Columbus.

On a day in 1805, during one of the Emperor's rare visits to Paris, the Minister of the Interior attended his *petit lever*. The rattle of sabres of those extraordinary soldiers of the Republic and the Empire could be heard in the Carrousel. There was an over-abundance of heroes at Napoleon's door – men from the Rhine, the Adige, and the Nile, comrades of Joubert, Desaix, Marceau, Hoche, and Kléber, men who had followed Bonaparte on the bridge at Lodi, who had accompanied Murat in the trenches of Mantua, who had preceded Lannes in the sunken road of Montebello. All the army, represented by a squad or a platoon, was there in that court-yard of the Tuileries, guarding Napoleon's rest. It was the splendid time when the Grande Armée had Marengo behind it and Austerlitz ahead of it . . . 'Sire,' said the Minister to Napoleon, 'yesterday I saw the bravest man in your Empire' . . . 'Who is he?' the Emperor asked. 'And what has he done?' . . . 'It is what he wants to do, Sire' . . . 'What is that?' . . . 'To explore the sewers of Paris.'

The man's name was Bruneseau.

Unknown details

The inspection took place. It was a formidable undertaking, a battle in darkness against pestilence and asphyxia. And also a voyage of discovery. One of the survivors, an intelligent workman who was then very young, later recalled certain details which Bruneseau had seen fit to omit from his report to the Prefect of Police as being unworthy of an official document. Methods of disinfection were at that time very rudimentary. Bruneseau had hardly entered the underground network when eight of his twenty workers refused to go further. The operation was complicated; it entailed cleaning and also measuring, noting the entry-points, counting the grilles and mouths, recording the branches with some indication of the current at various points, examining the different basins, determining the width and height of each corridor both from the floor of the sewer and in relation to the street surface. Progress was slow. It happened not infrequently that the ladders sank into three feet of slime. Lanterns flickered and died in the poisonous air, and from time to time a fainting man had to be carried out. There were pitfalls at certain places where the floor had collapsed and the sewer became a bottomless well; one man suddenly disappeared and they had great difficulty in rescuing him. On the advice of Fourcroy, the noted chemist, they lighted reasonably clear places with cages filled with oakum steeped in resin. The walls were here and there covered with shapeless fungi resembling tumours; the very stonework seemed diseased.

Bruneseau proceeded downstream in his survey. At the junction of two channels at the Grand Hurleur he detected on a jutting stone the date 1550, which indicated the limit reached by Philibert Delorme, charged by Henri II with inspecting the underground labyrinth of Paris. This stone was the token of the sixteenth century. Bruneseau found the handicraft of the seventeenth century in the Ponceau conduit and that of the Rue Vieille-du-Temple, vaulted over between 1600 and 1650, and of the eighteenth in the western section of the main canal, lined and vaulted over in 1740. The two vaults, especially the more recent, that of 1740, were more cracked and decrepit than the masonry of the ring sewer, dating from 1412, when the open stream of Ménilmontant was invested with the dignity of the main sewer of Paris – a promotion resembling that of a peasant who becomes the king's valet.

Here and there, notably under the Palais de Justice, dungeon cells were found built into the sewer. An iron collar hung in one of them. All were walled up. There were strange discoveries, among others the skeleton of a orang-utan that had vanished from the Jardin des Plantes in 1800, a disappearance probably connected with the famous appearance of the Devil in the Rue des Bernardins. The poor devil had been drowned in the sewer.

Under the long, vaulted corridor that ends at the Arche-Marion a rag-picker's hod was found in a state of perfect preservation. The slime everywhere, being bravely ransacked by the sewage workers, abounded in precious objects of jewellery and gold and silver, and coins. A giant filtering of the cloaca might have scraped up the wealth of centuries. At the junction of the Rue du Temple and the Rue Sainte-Avoye a strange copper medal was found, of Huguenot origin, having on one side a pig wearing a cardinal's hat and on the other a wolf in a tiara.

But the most surprising discovery was made at the entrance to the main sewer. This entrance had formerly been closed by a barred gate of which only the hinges remained. A dingy shred of material was attached to one of the hinges, having no doubt been caught on it as it floated by. Bruneseau examined it by the light of his lantern. It was of very fine cambric, and on its least worn part he discovered a heraldic coronet embroidered above the seven letters L A V B E S P. The coronet was that of a marquis, and the seven letters signified Laubespine. He realized that he was looking at a fragment of Marat's shroud. Marat in his youth, at the time when he was veterinary surgeon to the household of the Comte d'Artois, had had a love-affair, historically attested, with a great lady, of which a sheet was his only souvenir. On his death, since it was the only scrap of decent linen he possessed, he had been wrapped in it. Old women had dressed him for the grave, the tragic Ami du Peuple, in that relic of sensual delight.

Bruneseau left the rag there without destroying it, whether from contempt or respect who can say? Marat merited both. It was so imprinted with destiny that one might hesitate to touch it. Besides, the things of the tomb should be left where they choose to be. In short, it was a strange relic: a marquise had slept in it, Marat had rotted in it and it had crossed the Panthéon to end up with the sewer rats. The bed-chamber rag, of which Watteau might have exquisitely drawn the folds, had in the end been worthy of the dark gaze of Dante.

The total inspection of that unspeakable underside of Paris took seven years, from 1805 to 1812. While exploring, Bruneseau originated, planned, and carried out considerable construction work. In 1808 he lowered the Ponceau level, and, creating new channels everywhere, he drove the sewer in 1809 under the Rue Saint-Denis to the Fontaine des Innocents; in 1810 under the Rue Froidmanteau and the Salpêtrière; in 1811 under the Rue Neuve-des-Petits-Pères, the Rue du Mail, the Rue de l'Écharpe, and the Place Royale; in 1812 under the Rue de la Paix and the Chaussée d'Antin. At the same time he had the whole network disinfected. He was assisted from the second year by his son-in-law Nargaud.

Thus at the beginning of this century society cleansed its underside and performed the toilet of its sewer. So much at least was made clean.

Tortuous, fissured and unpaved, interspersed with quagmires, rising and falling, twisting and turning without reason, foetid and bathed in obscurity, with scars on its floor and gashes in its walls, altogether horrible – such, in retrospect, was the ancient sewer of Paris. Ramifications all ways, intersections, branches, crow's feet, blind alleys, salt-rimed vaults, reeking cesspits, poisonous ooze on the walls, drops falling from the roof, darkness: nothing could equal in horror that excremental crypt, Babylon's digestive system, a cavern pierced with roads, a vast molehill in which the mind seems to perceive, straying through the darkness amid the rot of what was once magnificence, that huge blind mole, the Past.

This, we repeat, was the sewer of former days.

V

Present progress

Today the sewer is clean, cold, straight, and correct, almost achieving that ideal which the English convey by the word 'respectable'. It is orthodox and sober, sedately in line, one might almost say, neat as a new pin – like a tradesman become Counsellor of State. One can see almost clearly in it. The filth is well-behaved. At first sight one might mistake it for one of those subterranean passages that aided the flight of princes in those good old days when 'the people loved their kings'. The present sewer is a good sewer, pure in style. The classic rectilinear alexandrine, having been driven out of poetry, seems to have taken refuge in architecture and to be part of the stonework of the long, shady, whitish vault. Every outlet is an arcade; the Rue de Rivoli has its counterpart in the cloaca. Moreover, if a geometrical line is to have a place anywhere, it is surely in the stercorary trench of a great city. The sewer today has a certain official aspect. Even the police reports of which it is sometimes the object treat it with some respect. Words referring to it in administrative language are lofty and dignified. What was once called a sluice is now a gallery, and a hole has become a clearing. Villon would no longer recognize his emergency lodgings. But the network still has its immemorial rodent population, more numerous than ever. Now and then a veteran rat will risk his neck at a sewer-window to survey the Parisians; but even these vermin are tame, being well content with their subterranean palace. Nothing is left of the cloaca's primitive ferocity. The rain, which once sullied it, now washes it. But we should not trust it too much on this account. Miasmas still infest it. It is more hypocritical than irreproachable. Despite the efforts of the police and the Health Commission, despite all attempts to purify it, it still exhales a vaguely suspect odour, like Tartuffe after confession.

We may agree then, when all is said, that cleaning is a tribute which the sewer pays to civilization; and since, in this respect, the conscience of Tartuffe is an advance on the Augean stable, so the Paris sewer is a step forward.

It is more than an advance, it is a transformation. Between the old and the present sewer a revolution has taken place. And who was responsible? The man whom everyone forgets, and whom we have named – Bruneseau.

VI

Future progress

The digging of the Paris sewer was no small matter. Ten centuries had worked at it without completing it, any more than they had completed Paris. It was a sort of dark, multi-armed polyp which grew with the city above it. When the city put out a street, the sewer stretched an arm. The old monarchy had constructed only twenty-three thousand metres of sewer: that was the point reached in Paris on 1 January 1806. From that time, to which we shall refer later, the work was effectively and energetically carried forward. Napoleon – the figures are curious – built 4,804 metres, Louis XVIII built 5,709, Charles X 10,836, Louis-Philippe 89,020, the Republic of 1848 23,381 and the present regime has built 70,500; in all, at this date, 226,610 metres, or 60 leagues of sewers, constitute the vast entrails of Paris. A dark network always in growth, unknown and enormous.

As we see, the underground labyrinth of Paris is today ten times what it was at the start of the century. It is hard to conceive of the perseverance and effort needed to bring it to its present state of relative perfection. It was with great difficulty that the monarchical authority, and the revolutionary in the last decade of the eighteenth century, succeeded in digging the five leagues of sewer which existed before 1806. Every kind of obstacle hindered the operation, some due to the nature of the ground, others to the prejudice of the working population of Paris. Paris is built on a site strangely opposed to pick and shovel, to all human management. Nothing is more difficult to penetrate than the geological formation on which is set the marvellous historical formation which is Paris; underground resistance is manifest whenever, and by whatever means, the attempt is made. There are liquid clays, live springs, rocks, and the deep sludgy pits known to science as *moutardes*. The pick advances laboriously through chalky strata alternating with seams of very fine clay, and layers of schist encrusted with oyster-shells, relics of the prehistoric ocean. Sometimes a stream destroys the beginning of a tunnel, drenching the workers; or a fall of rubble sweeps down like a cataract, shattering the stoutest roof-props. Only recently, when it became necessary to run a sewer under the Saint-Martin canal without emptying the canal or interfering with its use, a fissure developed in the canal bottom so that more water poured into the lower gallery than the pumps could handle; a diver had to find the fissure, which was in the neck of the great basin, and it was blocked only with difficulty. Elsewhere, near the Seine and even at some distance from the river, there are shifting sands in which a man may sink. There is also the danger of asphyxiation in the foul air and burial beneath falls of earth. There is a typhus, with which the workers become slowly infected. In our time, after four months of day and night labour principally designed to rid Paris of the pouring waters of Montmartre, and after constructing the Rue

Barre-du-Bec sewer some six metres underground, the foreman, Monnot, died. The engineer, Duleau, died after constructing 3,000 metres of sewer which included the formidable task of lowering the floor of the Notre-Dame-de-Nazareth cutting. No bulletins signalled these acts of bravery, more useful than any battlefield slaughter.

The Paris sewers in 1832 were very different from what they are today. Bruneseau had made a start, but it needed cholera to supply the impetus for the huge reconstruction which took place later. It is surprising to know, for example, that in 1821 a part of the ring sewer, known, as in Venice, as the Grand Canal, still lay open to the sky in the Rue des Gourdes. Not until 1823 did Paris find the 266,080 francs 6 centimes necessary to cover this disgrace. The three absorbent wells of the Combat, the Cunette, and Saint-Mande, with their ancillary outlets, date from only 1836. The intestinal canal of Paris has been rebuilt and, as we have said, increased more than tenfold in the last twenty-five years.

Thirty years ago, at the time of the insurrection of 5 and 6 June, it was still in many places almost the ancient sewer. A great many streets, now cambered, were then sunken. One often saw, at a point where the gutters of two streets met, large square grilles whose thick iron bars, burnished by the feet of pedestrians, were slippery for carts and dangerous for horses. And in 1832, in countless streets, the old gothic cloaca was still shamelessly manifest in great gaping blocks of stone.

In Paris in 1806 the figure was not much more than that for May 1663 — 5,328 fathoms. After Bruneseau, on 1 January 1832, it amounted to 40,300 metres. From 1806 to 1831 an annual average of 750 metres had been built; after which the figure rose to eight and even ten thousand a year, galleries built of cemented rubble on a foundation of concrete.

Apart from economic progress, the Paris sewer is part of an immense problem of public hygiene. Paris exists between two layers, of water and of air. The water layer, some distance underground but fed by two sources, is borne on the stratum of sandstone situated between chalk and jurassic limestone, and may be represented by a disc of some twenty-five leagues radius into which a host of rivers and streams seep. One may drink the mingled waters of Seine, Marne, Yonne, Oise, Aisne, Cher, Vienne, and Loire in a glass of water drawn from a well in Grenelle. The layer of water is healthy, coming first from the sky and then from the earth; the layer of air is unhealthy, for it comes from the sewer. All the miasmas of the cloaca are mingled with the breath of the town, hence its poor quality. It has been scientifically demonstrated that air taken from immediately above a dung-heap is purer than the air of Paris. In time, with the aid of progress, perfected mechanisms and fuller knowledge, the layer of water will be used to purify the layer of air – that is to say, to cleanse the sewer. By cleansing the sewer we mean the return of mire to the earth, of manure to the soil, and fertilizer to the fields. This simple fact will bring about a decrease in misery and increase in health for the whole community. As things are, the maladies of Paris spread some fifty leagues from the Louvre, taking this as the hub of the pestilential wheel.

It may be said that for ten centuries the sewer has been the disease of Paris, the evil in the city's blood. Popular instinct has never doubted it. The trade of sewage worker was more perilous and nearly as repugnant to the people as the trade of executioner, and held in abhorrence. High wages were needed to induce a mason to vanish into that foetid ooze. 'To go into the sewer is to go into the grave,' men said. All sorts of legends covered that colossal sink with horror, that dreadful place which bears the impress of the revolution of the earth and of men, in which the remains of every cataclysm is to be found, from the Flood to the death of Marat.

BOOK THREE

MIRE, BUT THE SOUL

I

The cloaca and its surprises

JEAN VALJEAN was in the Paris sewer. And here is another resemblance between Paris and the sea: as with the sea, the diver can vanish into it.

The change was unbelievable. In the very heart of the town, Valjean had left the town; in a matter of moments, the time to lift a lid and let it fall, he had passed from daylight into total darkness, from midday to midnight, from tumult to silence and the stillness of the tomb; and, by a chance even more prodigious than that in the Rue Polonceau, from utmost peril to absolute safety. He stayed for some moments listening, as though in a stupor. The trapdoor of salvation had suddenly opened beneath him. Celestial benevolence had in some sort caught him by betrayal; the wonderful ambushes of Providence!

Meanwhile the injured man did not move, and Valjean did not know whether his burden was living or dead.

His first sensation was one of utter blindness; he could see nothing. It seemed to him also that he had suddenly become deaf. He could hear nothing. The tempest of slaughter going on only a few feet above his head reached him only as a distant murmur. He could feel solid ground beneath his feet and that was all, but it was enough. He reached out one arm and then the other, touching the wall on either side, and perceived the narrowness of the passage; he slipped, and knew that the floor was wet. He cautiously advanced a foot, fearing a pitfall, and noted that the floor continued. A gust of foetid air told him where he was.

After some moments, as his eyes became adjusted, he began to see by the dim light of the hatchway by which he had entered. He could make out that the passage in which he had landed was walled up behind him. It was a dead-end. In front of him was another wall, a wall of darkness. The light from the hatchway died a few paces from where he stood, throwing a pallid gleam on a few feet of damp wall. Beyond was massive blackness, to enter which was to be swallowed up. Nevertheless it could and must be done, and with speed. Valjean reflected that the grille he had perceived might also be seen by the soldiers, who might come in search of him. There was no time to be lost. He had laid Marius on the ground; he picked him up and taking him on his shoulders marched resolutely into the darkness.

The truth is that they were less safe than Valjean supposed. Other dangers no less fearful, might await them. After the turbulence of battle came the cave of evil mists and pitfalls; after chaos, the cloaca. Valjean had moved from one circle of Hell into another. After walking fifty paces he had to stop. A question had arisen. The passage ran into another, so that now there were two ways he might go. Which to choose – left or right? How was he to steer in that black labyrinth? But the labyrinth, as we have said, provides a clue – its slope. Follow the downward slope and you must come to the river.

Jean Valjean instantly realized this. He thought that he was probably in the sewer of Les Halles, and that if he went left, following the slope, he would arrive within a quarter of an hour at some outlet to the Seine between the Pont-au-Change and the Pont-Neuf – appear, that is to say, in broad daylight in the most frequented part of Paris, perhaps even at a crossroads, to the stupefaction of the passers-by. Arrest would then be certain. It was better to press deeper into the labyrinthine darkness, trusting to chance to provide a way out. He moved upwards, turning to the right.

When he had turned the corner into the new passageway the distant light from the hatch vanished completely and he was again blind. He pressed on nonetheless, as rapidly as he could. Marius's arms were round his neck while his feet hung down behind. He held both arms with one hand, following the wall with the other. Marius's cheek was pressed against his own and stuck to it, since it was bleeding; he felt the warm stream trickling beneath his clothes. But the faint breathing in his ear was a sign of life. The passage he was now following was less narrow than the first, but he struggled painfully along it. Yesterday's rain had not yet drained away; it made a stream in the middle of the floor, and he had to keep close to the wall if he was not to have his feet in water. Thus he went darkly on, like some creature of the night.

But little by little, either because widely spaced openings let through a glimmer of light, or because his eyes had grown accustomed to the darkness, he recovered some degree of sight, so that he had a dim perception of the wall he was touching or the vaulted roof. The pupil dilates in darkness and in the end finds light, just as the soul dilates in misfortune and in the end finds God.

It was difficult to choose his path. The direction of the sewers in general follows that of the streets above them. At that time there were 2,200 streets in Paris; and one may picture a similar tangle below. The system of sewers existing at that time laid end to end would have had a length of eleven leagues. As we have said, the present network, thanks to the work of the past thirty years has a length of not less than sixty leagues.

Valjean started by making a mistake. He thought he was under the Rue Saint-Denis and it was unfortunate that he was not. There is an old stone sewer dating from Louis XIII under the Rue Saint-Denis, having only a single turn, under the former Cour des Miracles, and a single branch, the Saint-Martin sewer, of which the four arms intersect. But the Petite-Truanderie passage, of which the entrance is near the Corinth tavern, has never communicated with that under the Rue Saint-Denis; it runs into the Montmartre sewer, and this was the way Valjean had followed. Here there are endless chances of going astray, the Montmartre sewer being one of the most labyrinthine of all. Fortunately he had left behind him the Les Halles sewer, the plan of which is like a forest of ship's masts; but more than one perplexity lay ahead of him, more than one street corner (for streets are what they really are) offered itself in the darkness like a question mark. First, on his left, the huge Plâtrière sewer, a sort of Chinese puzzle, running with countless twists and turns under the Hotel des Postes and the cornmarket to the Seine; secondly, on his right, the Rue du Cadran with its three blind alleys; thirdly, again on the left, a sort of fork zig-zagging into the basin of the Louvre; and finally, on the right, the blind alley of the Rue des Jeûneurs, without counting small offshoots here and there – all this before he reached the ring sewer, which alone could take him to some place sufficiently far off to be safe.

Had Valjean known all this he would have realized, simply by feeling the wall, that he could not be under the Rue Saint-Denis. Instead of the old cut stone, the costly old-time architecture which had dignity even in its sewers, he would have felt cheap modern materials under his hand, bourgeois masonry; but he knew nothing of this. He went anxiously but calmly ahead, seeing and knowing nothing, trusting to chance, or to Providence.

And by degrees the horror grew upon him, the darkness pierced his soul. He was walking through a riddle. He had to pick his way, almost to invent it, without seeing it. Every step he took might be his last. Would he find a way out, and in time? Would this huge underground sponge with interstices of stone allow itself to be conquered? Would he come to some impenetrable place where Marius would bleed to death and he himself would die of hunger, leaving two skeletons in the darkness? He asked himself these questions and had no answer; he was Jonah in the body of the whale.

Suddenly he was startled. He perceived that he was no longer going uphill. The stream washed round the heels of his boots, instead of round the toes. The sewer was going downwards. Would he arrive suddenly at the Seine? The danger was great, but the danger of turning back was greater still. He pressed on.

He was not going towards the Seine. The ridge of sand on the right bank caused one of the streams to flow into the Seine, the other into the main sewer. The crest of the ridge follows a capricious line, its culminating point, where the streams separate, being beneath the Rue Sainte-Avoye and the Rue Montmartre. This was the point which Valjean had reached. He was on the right road moving towards the ring-sewer; but this he did not know.

Whenever he came to a branch he measured its dimensions with his hand, and if he found the opening less wide than the passage he was following he passed it, rightly considering that every smaller passageway must be a dead end. Thus he avoided the four-fold trap we have described.

A moment came when he realized that he had left behind the Paris petrified by the uprising and was under the Paris living its everyday life. There was a sound like distant steady thunder above his head, the sound of cartwheels. He had been walking for half an hour, according to his reckoning, without any thought of rest, only changing the hand with which he held Marius. The darkness was greater than ever, but this reassured him.

Suddenly he saw his own shadow, faintly visible on the floor of the passage in front of him. He was conscious of a dim light on the viscous walls. He looked back in stupefaction.

Behind him, at what seemed a great distance, there shone a dim, flickering light, as it were a star that was observing him. It was a police lantern, and within its glow some eight or ten moving figures were to be seen.

Explanation

On that morning a search of the sewers had been ordered, since it was considered that these might be used by the defeated rebels. Hidden Paris was to be ransacked while General Bugeaud cleared the open streets: a combined operation involving both the army and the police. Three squads of police agents and sewage men were exploring the underside of Paris, one the Right Bank, the second the Left Bank and the third the Cité. The police were armed with carbines, batons, swords and daggers. What Jean Valjean now saw was the lantern of the right-bank squad.

The squad had visited the curved passage and the three dead-ends under the Rue du Cadran. Valjean had passed them while they were in one of the dead-ends, which he found to be narrower than the main passageway. The police, emerging from the Cadran passageway, had thought they heard footsteps in the direction of the ring sewer. They were those of Valjean. The sergeant raised his lantern and they stared in his direction.

It was a bad moment for Valjean. Fortunately, although he could see the lantern, the lantern saw very little. It was light and he was in shadow, far from it and buried in darkness. He stopped, pressed against the wall. He did not know what was behind him. Sleeplessness, lack of food, and strong emotion had brought him to a state of hallucination. He saw a glow and moving forms, but did not know what they were.

When he ceased to move the sound ceased. The men listened and heard nothing, stared and saw nothing. They consulted together.

There was at this time an open space in the Montmartre sewer which has since been abolished because of the pool that formed in it when the heavy rains came down. The squad were able to assemble here. Valjean saw them form a sort of circle, heads close together. The outcome of their discussion was that they had heard nothing and there was no one there. To move towards the ring sewer would be a waste of time, and it would be better to make haste towards Saint-Merry where, if any rebel had escaped, he was more likely to be found.

The sergeant gave the order to go left towards the Seine. If they had divided into two parties and followed both directions Valjean would have been captured. It was as near as that. Probably, to guard against the possibility of an encounter with a number of rebels, they had been ordered not to separate. They turned away, leaving Valjean behind, but all he knew of it was the sudden vanishing of the lantern. For a long time he stayed motionless with his back to the wall, hearing the receding echo of that spectral patrol.

III

The man pursued

It must be said for the police of that time that even in the gravest circumstances they continued imperturbably to perform their duties. An uprising was not, in their view, a reason for giving villains a free hand, nor could society be neglected because the government was in danger. Ordinary duties were correctly carried out together with extraordinary ones. In the midst of an incalculable political event, and under the threat of revolution, without letting himself be distracted by all this, the policeman pursued the criminal.

This is precisely what happened on the Right Bank of the Seine on that afternoon of 6 June, a short way beyond the Pont des Invalides.

There is no bank there now. The aspect of the place has changed. But on that bank, some distance apart, two men seemed to be observing one another, one seeking to avoid the other. It was like a game of chess played remotely and in silence. Neither seemed in a hurry; both moved slowly as though each feared that by hastening he might speed up the other. As it were, an appetite in pursuit of a prey, without seeming to be acting with intent. The prey was wary and constantly alert. Due distance between tracker and tracked was preserved. The would-be escaper was a puny creature; the hunter a tall robust man, hard of aspect and probably of person.

The first, the weaker, sought to avoid the second, but he did so in a furious manner, and anyone looking closely at him would have seen in his eyes all the dark hostility of flight, the menace that resides in fear.

The river-bank was deserted. There were no strollers, nor even a boatman on any of the barges moored here and there. The men could best be seen from the opposite bank, and to anyone viewing them at that distance the first would have appeared a ragged, furtive creature, shivering under a thin smock, while the other had an aspect of officialdom, with the coat of authority buttoned close under his chin.

The reader would perhaps recognize the men, could he see them more closely. What was the second man seeking to do? Probably to clothe the first more warmly. When a man clothed by the State pursues a man clad in rags, it is to make him, too, a man clothed by the State. But the matter of colour is important. To be clad in blue is splendid; to be clad in red is disagreeable. There is a purple of the depths. It was probably this disagreeable purple that the first man was anxious to avoid.

If the other let him go on without attempting to lay hands on him, it was probably because he hoped to see him reach some significant spot – the delicate operation known as 'shadowing'. What makes this appear likely is that the uniformed man, seeing an empty fiacre pass along the quay, signalled to the driver, and the latter, evidently knowing with whom he had to deal, turned and kept pace with the two men. This was not noticed by the ragged fugitive.

The fiacre rolled past the trees of the Champs-Élysées, its driver being visible above the parapet, whip in hand. Among the secret instructions issued to the police is the following: 'Always have a vehicle handy, in case of need.'

Each manoeuvring with admirable strategy, the two men drew near a ramp running from the quay down to the bank, which enabled cab-drivers reaching Passy to water their horses. This has since been abolished in the name of symmetry. The horses go thirsty, but the eye is flattered.

It seemed likely that the man in the smock intended to climb this ramp and attempt to escape by the Champs-Élysées, a place abounding in trees but also in policemen. That part of the quay is very little distant from the house brought from Moret to Paris in 1824 by Colonel Brack, known as the house of François I. There is a guard-post very near it.

Surprisingly, the pursued man did not go up the ramp to the quay, but continued to move along the bank. His position was plainly becoming desperate. Apart from plunging into the Seine, what was he to do? He had no access to the quay other than the ramp or stairway, and he was near the spot, at the bend of the Seine towards the Pont d'Iéna, where the bank, growing ever more narrow, finally vanished underwater. There he would find himself trapped between the sheer wall on his right and the river on his left, with authority close behind him. It is true that the ending of the bank was concealed from him by a heap of rubble some seven or eight feet high, the remains of some demolition. But did he really hope to hide behind it? Surely not. The ingenuousness of thieves is not so great.

The heap of rubble formed a sort of hillock running from the water's edge to the quay wall. The fugitive reached this hillock and hurried round it, so that his pursuer could not see him. The latter, not seeing, was himself unseen; accordingly he abandoned all pretence and quickened his pace. He reached the heap and went round it, and then stood still in amazement. The man he was pursuing was not there! He had completely disappeared. Only some thirty feet of bank lay beyond the heap before it vanished into the river. The fugitive could not have plunged into the Seine or climbed on to the quay without being seen by his pursuer. What had become of him?

The man in the buttoned coat went to the extreme end of the bank and stood there reflecting, fists clenched and eyes gleaming. Suddenly he clapped a hand to his forehead. He had seen, at the point where the bank ended, a wide, low iron grille with a heavy lock and three massive hinges. It opened as much on to the river as on to the bank, and a dark stream flowed from it, running into the Seine.

Beyond the thick, rusty bars a dark vaulted corridor was to be seen. The man folded his arms and looked angrily at the grille. Since this served no purpose, he attempted to force it open, but it resisted all his shaking. It must certainly have been opened, although he had heard nothing, which was strange considering its rusty state. And it had been closed. This meant that whoever had opened it had done so not with a hook but with a key. The idea dawned suddenly on the pursuer and drew from him a roar of indignation:

'Upon my soul, a government key!'

Calming down immediately, he gave vent to his thoughts in a series of ironic monosyllables:

'Well! Well! Well! Well!'

Having said this, and hoping for he knew not what – to see the man emerge or other men arrive – he settled down by the heap of rubble to keep watch with the patience of a game-dog.

The driver of the fiacre, following all his movements, had come to a stop near the parapet above him. Foreseeing a long wait, he put nosebags on his horses. Occasional strollers from the Pont d'Iéna paused to observe those two motionless features of the landscape – the man on the bank and the fiacre on the quay.

IV

He too bears his cross

Jean Valjean had resumed his journey without again stopping. It became more and more laborious. The height of the passageway varies, being of an average five feet six inches; Valjean had to bend down to prevent Marius rubbing against the roof, and he had to feel his way constantly along the wall. The dampness of the stone and the slipperiness of the floor offered insecure hand- and foot-holds. He staggered in the horrid excrement of the town. The lights of vent-holes appeared only at long intervals, so pallid that what was sunlight might have been moonlight; all else was mist, miasma, and darkness. Valjean was both hungry and thirsty, especially thirsty, in that place of water where there was none to drink. Even his great strength, so little diminished with age, was beginning to flag, and the weight of his burden increased with his fatigue. He was carrying Marius so as best to allow him freedom to breathe. He felt the scuttle of rats between his feet, and one was so startled as to bite him. From time to time he was revived by a gust of fresh air from the vent-holes.

It was perhaps three o'clock in the afternoon when he reached the ring sewer. He was at first astonished by the suddenly increased width, finding himself in a passageway where his outstretched hands could not touch both walls nor his head the roof. This main sewer is in fact eight feet wide and seven feet high.

At the point where the Montmartre sewer joins the main sewer two other passageways form an intersection. Faced by four alternatives, a less sagacious man might have been undecided. Valjean took the widest way, the ring sewer. But here again the question arose – to go up or down? He felt that time was running out and that he must at all costs try to reach the Seine. That is to say, downward; and he turned to the left.

It was well that he did so, for the main sewer, being nothing but the former stream of Ménilmontant, ends, if one goes upwards, in a cul-de-sac, at the spring which was its original source. Had Valjean gone upwards he would finally have arrived, exhausted, at a blank wall. At a pinch, by turning back he might eventually have reached the Amelot sewer and thence, if he did not go astray in the maze beneath the Bastille, have come to the outlet to the Seine near the Arsenal. But for this he would have needed a detailed knowledge of the system, and, we must repeat, he knew nothing of it. Had he been asked where he was he could only have answered, 'In darkness.'

Instinct served him well. Descent was the way of safety. A little way beyond an effluent which probably came from the Madeleine, he stopped. A large hatchway, probably in the Rue d'Anjou, gave a light that was almost bright. With the gentleness of a man handling a wounded brother, Valjean laid Marius down at the edge of the sewer. Marius's bloodstained face in the pallid light of the hatchway was like a face of death. His eyes were closed, the hair plastered to his temples, his hands limp and dangling, and there was blood at the corners of his mouth. Gently thrusting inside his shirt, Valjean laid a hand on his chest and found that his heart was still beating. Tearing strips off his own shirt, he bandaged Marius's wounds as best he could.

Then, bending over the unconscious form in that dim light, he stared at him with inexpressible hatred.

He found two objects in Marius's clothing, the piece of bread left from the day before and his wallet. He ate the bread and, opening the wallet, found on the first page the lines Marius had written: 'My name is Marius Pontmercy. My body is to be taken to the house of my grandfather, M. Gillenormand, 6 Rue des Filles-du-Calvaire, in the Marais.'

Valjean pored over the message, memorizing the address; then he replaced the wallet in Marius's pocket. He had eaten and regained his strength. Taking Marius on his back with his head on his right shoulder, he resumed his downward path.

The main sewer, following the slope of the Ménilmontant valley, is nearly two leagues in length, and paved to a large extent; but the list of names with which we have enlightened the reader was not known to Valjean. He did not know what part of the town he was passing under or how far he had come. Only the increasing dimness of the occasional hatchways told him that the sun was setting, and the rumble of vehicles above his head had now almost ceased. He concluded that he was no longer under the centre of Paris but was nearing some outlying district where there were fewer streets and houses and, in consequence, fewer hatchways. He pressed on, feeling his way in the darkness, which suddenly became terrible.

<h2 style="text-align:center">V</h2>

<h3 style="text-align:center">The treachery of sand</h3>

He found that he was moving in water, and that what he had under his feet was not stone but sludge.

It happens sometimes on the sea coast that a man walking at low tide far out along the beach suddenly finds that he is moving with difficulty. The going is heavy beneath his feet, no longer sand but glue. The surface is dry, but every footprint fills with water. Yet all the beach wears the same aspect, so that the eye cannot distinguish between what is firm and what is not. The walker continues on his way, tending to move inland and feeling no disquiet. Why should he? But it is as though the heaviness of his feet increases with every step he takes. Suddenly he sinks several inches. He pauses, and looking down at his feet sees that they have disappeared. He picks up his feet and tries to turn back, but only sinks in deeper. The sand is over his ankles. He struggles and finds it reaching his calves. With indescribable terror he realizes that he is in a patch of shifting sand, where a man cannot walk any more than a fish can swim. He flings away whatever he is carrying, shedding his cargo like a vessel in distress. It is too late, the sand has reached his knees.

He shouts, waving hat or handkerchief, while the sand gains upon him. If the beach is deserted and there is no heroic rescuer at hand, then he is done for, destined to be swallowed up, condemned to that appalling burial which can be neither hastened nor delayed, which may take hours, dragging down a strong and healthy man the more remorselessly the more he struggles. He sees the world vanish from his gaze; sky, land, and sea. There is nothing he can do. The sand creeps up to his stomach, his chest. He waves his arms, shouts and groans in torment; the sand reaches his shoulders and neck, until nothing is left but staring eyes and a crying mouth that is suddenly silenced. Only an extended arm remains. The man is gone.

This fateful occurrence, still possible on some seashores, was also possible thirty years ago in the Paris sewer. During the work begun in 1833 the underground network was subject to sudden collapses, when in particularly friable stretches of soil the bottom, whether of paving stones as in the old sewers, or concrete, as in the new, gave way. There were crevasses composed of shifting sand from the seashore, neither earth nor water. Sometimes the depth was very great.

Terrible to die in such a fashion. Death may mitigate its horror with dignity; at the stake or in a shipwreck nobility is possible. But this suffocation in the sewer is unclean. It is humiliating. Filth is synonymous with shame; it is squalid and infamous. To die in a butt of Malmsey, like the Duke of Clarence, may pass; but to die in a pit of slime ... There is the darkness of Hell, the filth of evil; the dying man does not know whether he is to become a ghost or a toad.

Everywhere else the grave is sinister; here it is shapeless. The depth of these pits varied as did their length and density, according to the nature of the subsoil. Some were three or four feet in depth, others eight or ten; some had no bottom. The slime was almost solid in some places, almost liquid in others. A man might have taken a day to be swallowed up in the Lunière pit, a few minutes only in that of Phélippeaux, depending on the thickness of the slime. A child might be safe where a man would be lost. The first resource was to rid oneself of every burden, fling away one's bag of tools or whatever it might be; and this was what every sewage-man did when he felt the ground unsafe beneath his feet.

The pits were due to various causes: the friability of the earth, collapses at some lower level, heavy showers in summer, incessant rain in winter, long steady drizzle. Sometimes the weight of the houses broke the roof of a gallery or caused a floor to give way. The settling of the Panthéon, a quarter of a century ago, destroyed a part of the caves under the Mont Sainte-Geneviève. When such things happened the evil in some cases was manifest in cracks in the street, and could be quickly remedied. But it also happened that nothing was visible from above, in which case, woe to the sewage-men. Entering the collapsed place unawares, they might be lost. Such cases are entered in the records. There are a number of names, including that of one Blaise Poutrain, buried in a pit under the Rue Carème-Prenant.

There was also the youthful and charming Vicomte d'Escoubleau, one of the heroes of the siege of Lerida, which they assailed in silk stockings, violins leading the way. D'Escoubleau, surprised one night in the bed of his cousin the Duchesse de Sourdis, was drowned in a pit in the Beautrellis sewer, when he sought to escape from the Duke. Madame de Sourdis, learning the manner of his death, called for her smelling salts and was too busy inhaling them to weep. No love can survive such an event. Hero refuses to wash the corpse of Leander; Thisbe holds her nose before Pyramus, saying, 'Pooh!'.

VI
The pit

Jean Valjean had come to a pit. These were numerous under the Champs-Élysées, which because of its excessive fluidity did not lend itself to the work of construction and conservation. When in 1836 the old stone sewer beneath the Faubourg Saint-Honoré, where we find Valjean at this moment, was rebuilt, the shifting sand which runs from the Champs-Élysées to the Seine delayed the operation for six months, to the indignation of the surface dwellers, particularly those with private houses and carriages. The work was not only difficult but dangerous. It is true that there were four and a half months of rain, and the Seine was three times flooded.

The pit Valjean reached had been caused by the rain of the previous day. A depression in the flooring, insufficiently supported by the sand beneath, had led to a flood of rainwater, and the collapse of the floor had followed. The broken floor had subsided into the swamp, it was impossible to say over what distance. The darkness was greater here than anywhere else. It was a hole of mud in a cavern of night.

Valjean felt the surface slip away from under him, water on top, sludge beneath. He had to go on. Marius was at death's door and he himself exhausted. So he struggled on, and at first the bog did not seem unduly deep. But then it grew deeper – slime halfway up his legs and water above his knees. He had to keep Marius as best he could above the water, which had now reached his waist. The mire, thick enough to support a single man, evidently could not sustain two. Either of them might have passed through separately. Valjean went on, carrying what might already be a corpse.

The water reached his armpits and he felt himself sinking; it was all he could do to move. His own sturdiness that kept him upright was also an obstacle. Still carrying Marius, and by the use of unbelievable strength, he pressed on, sinking ever deeper. Only his head was now above water, and his two arms carrying Marius. In old paintings of the flood there is one of a mother carrying her child in this fashion.

He went on, tilting his face upwards so that he could continue to breathe. Anyone seeing him at that moment might have thought him a mask floating in the darkness. Dimly above him he could see the livid face of Marius. He made a last desperate effort, thrusting a foot forward, and it rested upon something solid – only just in time. He straightened and thrust with a kind of fury on this support, feeling that he had found the first step of a stairway back to life.

In fact this foothold, reached at the supreme moment, was the other end of the floor, which had sagged under the weight of water but without breaking. Well-built floors have this solidity; the floor still existed, and, climbing its further slope, Valjean was saved.

Emerging from the water, he stumbled on a stone and fell on his knees. This he thought proper, and he stayed in this posture for some time, his spirit absorbed in the thought of God. Then he stood upright, shivering and foul, bowed beneath his burden, dripping with mire; but with his soul filled with a strange lightness.

VII

Sometimes we fail with sucess in sight

He went on again. If he had not left his life in that pit, he seemed certainly to have left his strength there. The final effort had exhausted him. His weariness was now such that at every few paces he had to pause for breath. Once he had to sit down while he altered Marius's position, and he thought that he would never get up again. But if his strength was flagging his will was not, and he rose.

He went on despairingly, but almost quickly, and covered a hundred paces without looking up, almost without breathing, until suddenly he bumped into the wall. He had reached a turning without seeing it. Looking up, he saw in the far distance a light, and this was no cavern light, but the clear white light of day.

He saw the way of escape, and his feelings were those of a damned soul seeing the way out of Hell. He was no longer conscious of fatigue or of the weight of Marius; his muscles were revived, and he ran rather than walked. As he drew near to it he saw the outlet more plainly. It was a pointed arch, less high than the ceiling, which was growing gradually lower, and less wide than the passageway, which was narrowing. The tunnel ended in a bottleneck, logical enough in a prison but not in a sewer, and something which has now been corrected.

But when he reached it, Valjean stopped short. It was an outlet, but it offered no way out. The arch was closed with a stout grille, fastened with a huge, rusty lock. He could see the keyhole and the bolt securely in place – clearly it was double-locked. It was one of those prison locks that were common in Paris at that time. And beyond the grille was open air, daylight, the river and a strip of bank, very narrow but sufficient to escape by. All Paris, all liberty, lay beyond it; to the right, downstream, the Pont d'Iéna, to the left the Pont des Invalides. One of the most deserted spots in Paris, a good place to escape from after dark. Flies came and went through the grille.

The time was perhaps half past eight in the evening, and dusk was falling. Valjean set Marius down by the wall, where the floor was dry; then, going to the grille, he seized it with both hands. But his frantic shaking had no effect. He tried one bar after another hoping to find one less solid that might be used as a lever, or to break the lock. But no bar shifted. He had no lever, no possible purchase, no way of opening the gate.

Was this to be the end of it? He had not the strength to turn back, and could not, in any case, have struggled again through the pit from which he had so miraculously emerged. And could he hope to escape the police patrol for a second time? In any event, where was he to go? Another outlet might be similarly obstructed. Probably all outlets were closed in this way. By chance he had entered by one that was not, and in so doing had escaped into a prison. It was the end. All his efforts had been futile. God had rejected him.

Both men were caught in the great, grim cobweb of death, and Valjean felt the running feet of the deadly spider. He turned his back to the grille and sank on to the floor beside the motionless form of Marius, crouched rather than seated, his head sunk between his knees. There was no way out. It was the last extreme of anguish. Of whom did he think in that moment? Not of himself or of Marius. He thought of Cosette.

VIII

A fragment of torn clothing

While he was in this state of despair a hand was laid on his shoulder and a low voice said:

'We'll go halves.'

Valjean thought he was dreaming. He had not heard a sound. He looked up and saw a man standing beside him.

The man was clad in a smock. His feet were bare and he carried his shoes in his hand, having removed them so that he might approach Valjean in silence. Valjean did not hesitate. Unexpected though this meeting was, he knew the man instantly. It was Thénardier.

Despite his astonishment, Valjean was too accustomed to sudden emergencies, too weary and alert, to lose his self-possession. In any event his situation could not be made worse by the presence of Thénardier. There was a brief pause. Thénardier raised a hand to his forehead, knitting his brow and pursing his lips in the manner of a man seeking to recognize another. He failed to do so. Jean Valjean had his back to the light, and was anyway so begrimed and blood-stained that even in the brightest light he would have been unrecognizable. Thénardier, on the other hand, his face illumined by the light from the grille, faint though it was, was immediately known to Valjean, and this gave the latter a certain advantage in the dialogue that was to take place between them.

Valjean saw at once that Thénardier did not know him. The two men contemplated one another in the dim light, each taking the measure of the other. It was Thénardier who broke the silence.

'How are you going to get out?'

Valjean made no reply. Thénardier went on:

'No way of unlocking the door. But you've got to get away from here.'

'That's true.'

'So we'll go halves.'

'How do you mean?'

'You've killed a man. All right. I have a key.' Thénardier pointed at Marius and went on: 'I don't know you but I'm ready to help you. You must be a friend.'

Valjean began to understand. Thénardier supposed him to be a murderer.

'Listen, comrade,' Thénardier went on. 'You won't have killed that man without looking to see what he has in his pocket. Give me half and I'll unlock the door.' He produced a large key from under his smock. 'Want to see what a master key looks like? Here it is.'

Valjean 'stayed stupid', in Corneille's phrase, to the point of scarcely believing his ears. Providence had come to his rescue in a horrid guise, sending a good angel in the shape of Thénardier.

Thénardier fished in a large pocket concealed under his smock and brought out a length of rope which he offered to Valjean.

'I'll give you this as well.'

'What for?'

'And you'll need a stone. But you'll find plenty of those outside.'

'What am I to do with it?'

'Fool. You'll have to chuck the body in the river, and if it isn't tied to a stone it'll float.'

Valjean took the rope. We are all subject to such mechanical gestures. Thénardier snapped his fingers as a thought occurred to him.

'Come to that, how did you manage to get through the pit down there? I wouldn't have risked it. You smell foul.'

After a pause he went on:

'I keep asking questions and you're right not to answer. It's a preparation for the nasty quarter of an hour in court. And by not talking you don't risk talking too loud. Anyway, just because I can't see your face and don't know your name, that isn't to say I don't know what you are and what you want. I know, all right. You've done that cove in, and now you've got to get rid of him. Well, I'll help you. Helping a good man in trouble, that's my line.'

While professing to approve of Valjean's silence, he was evidently trying to get him to talk. He nudged his shoulder, seeking to see his profile, and exclaimed without raising his voice;

'Talking of that pit, you're a fine fool, aren't you? Why didn't you leave him there?'

Valjean remained silent. Thénardier tightened the rag that served him as a neck-tie, putting a finishing touch to his appearance of a capable, reliable man. He went on:

'Well, perhaps you were right. The workmen will be along tomorrow to fill in the pit. They'd find him, and bit by bit, one way or another, it would have been traced to you. Somebody must have come through the sewer. Who was it, and how did he get out? The police have their wits about them. The sewer would give you away. A discovery like that's uncommon, it attracts notice; not many people use the sewer for their business, while the river belongs to everyone. The river's the real drain. In a month's time your man is fished out at Saint-Cloud. So what does that prove? Nothing. A lump of carcass. And who killed him? Paris. No need for any inquiry. You were right.'

The more loquacious Thénardier became the more silent was Valjean. Thénardier again shook his shoulder.

'Well, now, let's settle up. I've shown you my key, let's see your money.'

Thénardier was haggard, wild, shabby, slightly threatening but friendly. And his manner was strangely equivocal. He did not seem quite at his ease, talking furtively in a low voice, and now and then putting a finger to his lips. It was hard to guess why. There were only the two of them. Valjean reflected that there might be other footpads hidden somewhere near, and that Thénardier did not want to share with them.

'Let's have it,' he said. 'How much did the chap have on him?'

Valjean searched his pockets. We may recall that he always carried money on him from the necessity of the hazardous life he lived. But this time he was caught short. In his preoccupation when he had donned his National Guard uniform the previous evening he had forgotten to take his wallet. He had only a little change in his waistcoat pocket, a mere thirty francs. He turned the muddy garment inside out and spread them on the floor – a louis d'or, two five-franc pieces and five or six sous.

'You didn't kill for much,' said Thénardier.

He began familiarly to pat Valjean's pockets and those of Marius, and Valjean, anxious to keep his back to the light, did not stop him. While searching Marius, Thénardier, with a pickpocket's adroitness, managed to tear off a fragment of material which he hid in his smock without Valjean's noticing; probably he thought that this would later help him to identify the murdered man and his murderer. But he found no more money.

'It's true,' he said. 'That's all there is.'

Forgetting what he had said about sharing, he took the lot. He hesitated over the sous, but on consideration took those as well.

'It's helping a cove on the cheap,' he said.

He again produced the key.

'Well, pal, you'd better go out. It's like a fair, you pay when you leave. You've paid.' And he laughed. In helping an unknown man to escape, was he disinterestedly concerned to save a murderer? We may doubt it.

After helping Valjean to lift Marius on to his shoulders he crept to the grille on his bare feet and peered out with a finger to his lips. Then he put the key in the lock. The bolt slid back and the gate opened without a sound; evidently the hinges were carefully oiled and it was used more often than one might think, presumably by some criminal gang, for which the sewer was a place of refuge.

Thénardier opened the gate just enough to allow Valjean to pass through, closed it after him, turned the key in the lock and then vanished into the darkness, as silently as if he walked on tiger's paws. An instant later the sinister agent of providence was invisible.

And Valjean was outside.

IX

Marius appears to be dead

He laid Marius on the bank. He was outside!

The darkness, stench, and horror were all behind him. He was bathed in pure, fresh air and surrounded by silence, the delicious silence of sunset in a clear sky. It was dusk; night was falling, the great liberator, the friend of all those needing darkness to escape from distress. The sky offered a prospect of immense calm; the river lapped at his feet with the sound of a kiss. There was a good-night murmur from the nests in the trees on the Champs-Élysées and a few stars faintly showed in the deepening blue of the sky. The evening bestowed on Jean Valjean all the tenderness of infinity, in that enchanting hour which says neither no nor yes, dark enough for distance to be lost, but light enough for nearness to be seen.

For some moments he was overwhelmed by this serenity, and forgetful of what had passed, all suffering lost in this drowsy glow of dark and light, where his spirit soared. He could not refrain from contemplating the huge chiaroscuro above him, and the majestic silence of the eternal sky moved him to ecstasy and prayer. Then, recalled to a sense of duty, he bent over Marius and sprinkled a few drops of water on his face from the hollow of his hand. Marius's eyelids did not move, but his open mouth still breathed.

Valjean was again about to dip his hand in the water when he had that familiar sense of someone behind him. He looked sharply round and found this to be the case. A tall man in a long coat, with folded arms and a cudgel in his right hand, was standing a few paces away. In the half-darkness it seemed a spectral figure; but Valjean recognized Javert.

The reader has doubtless guessed that the pursuer of Thénardier was Javert. After his unhoped-for escape from the rebel stronghold the inspector had gone to the Préfecture de Police, where he had reported to the prefect in person. He had then immediately returned to his duties, which entailed keeping watch on the right bank near the Champs-Élysées, a spot which for some time had been attracting the notice of the police. Seeing Thénardier, he had followed him. The rest we know.

We may also gather that the gate so obligingly opened for Valjean was a stratagem on the part of Thénardier. With the instinct of a hunted man, Thénardier had sensed that Javert was still there and he wanted to distract him. What could be better than to supply him with a murderer? Producing Valjean in his place, Thénardier would send the police off on another trail: Javert would be rewarded for his patience, and he himself, besides gaining thirty francs, would have a better chance of getting away.

Valjean had fallen out of the frying-pan into the fire. The two encounters, first with Thénardier and then Javert, caused him a severe shock.

Javert did not recognize Valjean, who, as we have said, looked quite unlike himself. Without unfolding his arms, but securely gripping his cudgel, he asked calmly:

'Who are you?'

'Myself.'

'Who is that?'

'Jean Valjean.'

Javert put the cudgel between his teeth and leaning forward clapped his hands on Valjean's shoulders, seizing them in a vice-like grip. Staring hard, he recognized him. Their faces were nearly touching. Javert's gaze was terrible. Jean Valjean stayed unresisting, like a lion consenting to the clutch of a lynx.

'Inspector Javert,' he said, 'you have got me. In any case, since this morning I have considered myself your prisoner. I did not give you my address in order to escape from you. But grant me one thing.'

Javert did not seem to hear. He was gazing intently at Valjean with an expression of wild surmise. Finally, releasing him, he took his cudgel again in his hand, and, as though in a dream, murmured:

'What are you doing here? Who is this man?'

'It is about him I wished to speak,' said Valjean. 'You may do what you like with me, but help me first to take him home. That is all I ask.'

Javert's face twitched, as always happened when someone thought him capable of making a concession. But he did not refuse. Bending down, he took a handkerchief from his pocket, soaked it in water, and bathed Marius's blood-stained forehead.

'He was at the barricade,' he muttered; 'the one called Marius.' First-class agent that he was, he had taken note of everything, even when he thought himself on the verge of death. He took Marius's wrist, feeling for his pulse.

'He's wounded,' said Valjean.

'He's dead,' said Javert.

'No. Not yet.'

'You brought him here from the barricade?' asked Javert. His state of preoccupation must have been great indeed for him not to have dwelt on that disquieting rescue, or even to have noted Valjean's failure to reply.

Jean Valjean, for his part, seemed to have only one thought in mind.

'He lives in the Marais, Rue des Filles-du-Calvaire,' he said, 'with a relative whose name I forget.' He felt in Marius's jacket, found the wallet, opened it at the written page and handed it to Javert.

There was still just light enough to read by, and Javert, in any case, had the eyes of a cat. He studied the words and grunted. 'Gillenormand, 6 Rue des Filles-du-Calvaire.' Then he shouted: 'Coachman!'

We may recall the fiacre which was waiting 'just in case'. In a very short time it had come down the ramp and Marius had been placed on the back seat, while Javert and Valjean sat in front. The fiacre drove off rapidly along the quay in the direction of the Bastille.

Leaving the quay it entered the streets, the coachman whipping up his horses. There was stony silence in the fiacre. Marius was prostrate in a corner, head drooping, arms and legs limp, as though he had only a coffin to look forward to. Valjean was a figure of shadow and Javert like a figure carved in stone. The dark interior of the fiacre, when it passed under a street lamp, was momentarily lighted and the three tragic figures were thrown into relief – the seeming corpse, the spectre, and the statue.

X

The prodigal returns to life

At every lurch a drop of blood fell from Marius's hair. It was quite dark when they reached 6 Rue des Filles-du-Calvaire. Javert got out first, and raising the heavy iron knocker, moulded in the ancient design of goat and satyr, knocked loudly. The door opened to disclose a yawning porter with a candle. Everyone was asleep. They retire early in the Marais, particularly in times of upheaval. That respectable old quarter, terrified of revolution, takes refuge in slumber like a child hiding its head under the sheets.

Jean Valjean and the coachman brought Marius from the fiacre, Valjean carrying him under the armpits and the coachman carrying him by the legs. As they did so Valjean thrust a hand under his torn clothes to feel his chest and make sure that his heart was still beating. It was in fact beating a little less feebly, as though the jolting of the fiacre had restored to it some degree of life.

Javert questioned the porter in a brisk, official tone.

'Anyone live here called Gillenormand?'

'Yes. What do you want of him?'

'We're bringing back his son.'

'His son?' exclaimed the porter in amazement.

'He's dead.'

Valjean, at whom the porter had been staring with horror as he stood, ragged and covered in mud in the background, shook his head. The porter seemed to understand neither of them.

'He was at the barricade,' said Javert, 'and here he is.'

'At the barricade!'

'He got himself killed. Go and wake his father.' The porter did not stir. 'Go on,' said Javert, and added: 'He'll be buried tomorrow.'

For Javert, the common incidents of the town were strictly classified, this being the basis of foresight and alertness, and every contingency had its place. Possible facts were, so to speak, in drawers from which they could be brought out as the case required, in varying quantities. Happenings in the street came under the headings of commotion, upheaval, carnival, funeral.

The porter awakened Basque. Basque awakened Nicolette, who awakened Aunt Gillenormand. They let the old man sleep on, thinking that he would know soon enough.

Marius was taken up to the first floor, without anyone in other parts of the house knowing what went on, and laid on an old settee in Monsieur Gillenormand's sitting-room. While Basque went in search of a doctor and Nicolette ransacked the linen cupboard, Valjean felt Javert's hand on his arm. He understood and went downstairs, with Javert close behind him. The porter watched them go as he had watched them arrive, with startled drowsiness. They got back into the fiacre, and the driver climbed on to his seat.

'Inspector,' said Valjean, 'grant me one last favour.'

'What is it?' Javert asked harshly.

'Let me go home for a minute. After that you can do what you like with me.'

Javert was silent for some moments, his chin sunk in the collar of his greatcoat. Then he pulled down the window in front of him.

'Drive to No. 7 Rue de l'Homme-Armé,' he said.

XI

Collapse of the absolute

Neither spoke a word during the journey.

What did Jean Valjean wish to do? He wished to finish what he had begun: to tell Cosette the news of Marius, give her perhaps some other useful information and, if possible, make certain final arrangements. Where he personally was concerned, all was over. He had been taken by Javert and had made no resistance. Another man in his place might have thought of the rope Thénardier had given him and the bars of the first prison cell he would enter; but since his encounter with the bishop there was in Valjean a profound religious abhorrence of any act of violence, even against himself. Suicide, that mysterious plunge into the unknown, which might entail some degree of death of the soul, was impossible for Jean Valjean.

At the entrance to the Rue de l'Homme-Armé, the fiacre stopped, since the street was too narrow to admit vehicles. Javert and Valjean got out. The coachman respectfully pointed out to Monsieur l'Inspecteur that the velvet upholstery of his cab was stained by the blood of the murdered man and the mud of his murderer, which is what he understood them to be. Bringing a notebook out of his pocket he requested the inspector to write a few words to this effect. Javert thrust the book aside.

'How much does it come to, including the time of waiting and the distance travelled?'

'I waited seven hours and a quarter,' the coachman replied, 'and my upholstery is new. It comes to eighty francs, Monsieur.'

Javert got four napoleons out of his pocket and dismissed him.

Valjean thought that Javert intended to escort him on foot to either the Blancs-Manteaux or the Archives police post, both of which were near at hand. They walked along the street which, as usual, was deserted. Valjean knocked on the door of No. 7 and it was opened.

'Go up,' said Javert. He had a strange expression, as though it cost him an effort to speak. 'I'll wait for you here.'

Valjean looked at him. This was little in accordance with his usual habits. But Javert now had an air of lofty confidence, that of a cat that allows a mouse a moment's respite; and since Valjean had resolved to give himself up and be done with it, this did not greatly surprise him. He entered the house, called 'It's me' to the porter, who had pulled the cord from his bed, and went upstairs.

On the first floor he paused. All Calvaries had their stations. The sash window was open. As in many old houses the staircase looked on to the street and was lighted at night by the street lamp immediately outside. Perhaps automatically, or simply to draw breath, Valjean thrust out his head. He looked down into the street, which was short and lighted from end to end by its single lamp. He gave a start of amazement. There was no one there.

Javert had gone.

XII

The grandfather

Basque and the porter had carried Marius, lying motionless on the settee, into the salon. The doctor had arrived and Aunt Gillenormand had got up. Aunt Gillenormand paced to and fro wringing her hands, incapable of doing more than say, 'Heavens, is it possible!' After the first shock she took a more philosophical view, to the point of saying, 'It was bound to end like this.' But she did not go so far as to say, 'I told you so', as is customary on these occasions.

At the doctor's orders a camp-bed was set up beside the settee. The doctor found that Marius's pulse was still beating, that he had no deep wound in his chest and that the blood at the corner of his lips came from the nasal cavity. He had him laid flat on the bed, without a pillow, his torso bare and his head on the same level as his body, to facilitate breathing. Seeing that he was to be undressed, Mlle Gillenormand withdrew and went to tell her beads in her own room.

There was no sign of internal injury. A bullet, diverted by his wallet, had inflicted an ugly gash along the ribs but had not gone deep, so that this was not dangerous. The long underground journey had completed the dislocation of the shattered shoulder-blade, and this was more serious. The arms had been slashed, but there was no injury to the face. The head, on the other hand, was covered with cuts, and it remained to be seen how deep they went, and whether they had penetrated the skull. What was serious was that they had caused unconsciousness of a kind from which one does not always recover. The haemorrhage had exhausted the patient; but there was no injury to the lower part of the body, which had been protected by the barricade.

Basque and Nicolette tore up rags for bandages. Lacking lint, the doctor temporarily staunched the wounds with wadding. Three candles burned on the bedside table, on which his instruments were spread. He washed Marius's face and hair with cold water, which rapidly turned red in the bowl.

The doctor looked despondent, now and then shaking his head as though in answer to himself. A doctor's voiceless dialogue is a bad omen for the patient. Suddenly, as he was gently touching the closed lids, the door of the room opened and a long, pale face appeared. It was the grandfather.

The fighting had greatly agitated and angered Monsieur Gillenormand. He had not been able to sleep the previous night, and had been in a fever all day. That night he had gone to bed early, ordering every door in the house to be locked, and had quickly fallen asleep. But old men sleep lightly. His bedroom was next to the salon, and despite all precautions the noise had awakened him. Seeing light under his door, he had got out of bed.

He stood in the doorway with a hand on the door-handle, his

head thrust forward, his body covered by a white bedgown that hung straight down without folds like a shroud, so that he looked like a ghost peering into a tomb. He saw the bed and the wax-white young man, eyes closed and mouth open, lips colourless, bared to the waist and covered with bright red scars.

He shook from head to foot with the tremor that afflicts old bones; his eyes, yellowed with age, had a glassy look, while his whole face took on the sharp contours of a skull. His arms sank to his sides as though a spring had been broken, and his stupefaction was manifest in the way he spread out his old, shaking fingers. His knees thrust forward, disclosing through the opening of his garment his skinny legs. He muttered:

'Marius!'

'He has just been brought here, Monsieur,' said Basque. 'He was on the barricade, and . . .'

'He's dead!' cried the old man in a terrible voice. 'The brigand!'

A sort of sepulchral transformation caused him to straighten up like a young man. 'You're the doctor?' he went on. 'Tell me one thing. Is he truly dead?'

The doctor, filled with anxiety, said nothing. Monsieur Gillenormand wrung his hands and burst into dreadful laughter.

'Dead! Dead on the barricade, in hatred of me! He did this against me, the bloodthirsty ruffian, and this is how he comes back to me. Misery of my life, he's dead!'

He went to the window, flung it wide as though he were stifling, and talked into the night:

'Gashed, slashed and done for, that's what he is now! He knew I was waiting for him, that his room was kept in readiness and his boyhood picture at my bedside. He knew he had only to return and I would be waiting at the fireside half mad with longing. You knew it. You had only to say, "Here I am," and you would be master of the house and I would obey you in all things, your old fool of a grandfather. You knew it and you said, "No, he's a royalist, I won't go." You went to the barricade instead and got yourself killed from sheer perversity. That is what is infamous! Well, sleep in peace. That is my word to you.'

The doctor, feeling that he had two patients to worry about, went to Monsieur Gillenormand and took his arm. The old man turned, and gazing at him with eyes that seemed to have grown larger, said quietly:

'Thank you, but I am calm, I am a man. I saw the death of Louis XVI, I can confront events. What is terrible is the thought that it is your newspapers that make all the trouble. Scribbles, orators, tribunes, debates, the rights of man, the freedom of the press – that's what your children are brought up on. Oh, Marius, it's abominable! Dead before me! The barricades! Doctor, you live in this quarter, I believe. Yes, I know you. I see you pass by in your cabriolet. I tell you, you are wrong to think that I am angry. To rage against death is folly. This was a child I brought up. I was old already, and he was small. He played in the Tuileries, and to save him from the keeper's wrath I filled in the holes that he dug with his spade. One day he cried, "Down with Louis XVIII!" and off he went. It is not my fault. He was pink and fair-haired. His mother is dead. Have you noticed that all small children are fair? Why is that? He was the son of one of the brigands of the Loire, but children are not responsible for their father's crimes. I remember when he was so high. He could not pronounce the letter "d". He talked like a little bird. I remember people turning to look at him, he was so beautiful, pretty as a picture. I talked sternly to him and flourished my stick, but he knew that it was only a joke. When he came to my room in the morning I might be grumpy, but it was as though the sun had come in. There is no defence against those little creatures. They take you and hold you and never let you go. The truth is that there was no one more lovely than that child. You talk of your Lafayettes, your revolutionaries – they kill me. It can't go on like this.'

He moved towards the still motionless Marius, to whom the doctor had returned, and again wrung his hands. His old lips moved mechanically, emitting disjointed words – 'Heartless! The rebel! The scoundrel!' – words loaded with reproach. By degrees coherence returned to him, but it seemed that he had scarcely strength to utter the words he spoke, so low and distant was his voice.

'It makes no difference, I too shall die. To think that in all Paris there was no wench to make that wretched boy happy! A young fool who went and fought instead of enjoying life. And for what? For a republic, instead of dancing, as a young man should do. What use is it to be twenty years old? A republic, what imbecility! Woe to the mothers who make pretty boys. So he's dead. Two funerals to go through the door of this house. So he did it for the glory of General Lamarque, that ranting swashbuckler – he got himself killed for the sake of a dead man. At twenty. It's enough to drive one mad. And never looking round to see what he was leaving behind. So now the old men have to die alone. Well, so much the better, it's what I hoped for, it will finish me off. I'm too old – a hundred, a thousand years old – I should have been dead long ago. This settles it. What good does it do to make him breathe ammonia and those other things you're trying on him? You're wasting your time, you fool of a doctor. He's well and truly dead. I should know, being dead myself. He hasn't done it by halves. Oh, this is a disgusting time, and that's what I think of you all, your ideas, your systems, your masters, your oracles, your learned doctors, your rascally writers and threadbare philosophers – and all the revolutions which for sixty years have startled the crows in the Tuileries! And since without pity you got yourself killed I shall not grieve for your death – do you hear me, murderer?'

At this moment Marius's eyes slowly opened and his gaze, in drowsy astonishment, rested upon Monsieur Gillenormand.

'Marius!' the old man cried. 'Marius, my child, my beloved son! You're living after all!'

And he fell fainting to the floor.

BOOK FOUR
JAVERT IN DISARRAY

JAVERT HAD walked slowly away from the Rue de l'Homme-Armé, walking for the first time in his life with his head bowed and, also for the first time, with his hands behind his back. Until then Javert had adopted of Napoleon's two attitudes only the one expressive of determination, arms folded over the chest; the attitude of indecision, hands behind the back, was unknown to him. Now a change had come over him; his whole person bore the imprint of uncertainty.

Walking through the silent streets, he took the shortest way to the Seine, finally arriving near the police-post in the Place du Châtelet, by the Pont Notre-Dame. Between the Pont Notre-Dame and the Pont-au-Change, on the one hand, and the Quai de la Mégisserie and the Quai aux Fleurs, the Seine forms a sort of pool traversed by a swift current. It is a place feared by boatmen. Nothing is more dangerous than that current, aggravated in those days by the piles of the bridges, which have since been done away with. The current speeds up formidably, swelling in waves which seem to be trying to sweep the bridges away. A man falling into the river at this point, even a strong swimmer, does not emerge.

Javert leaned with his elbows on the parapet, his chin resting on his hands. Something new, a revolution, a disaster, had occurred to him, and he had to think it over. He was suffering deeply. For some hours past he had ceased to be the simple creature he had been; his blinkered, one-track mind had been disturbed. There was a flaw in the crystal. He felt that his sense of duty was impaired, and he could not hide this from himself. When he had so unexpectedly encountered Jean Valjean on the edge of the river his feelings had been partly those of a wolf catching its prey and partly those of a dog finding its master.

He could see two ways ahead of him, and this appalled him, because hitherto he had never seen more than one straight line. And the paths led in opposite directions. One ruled out the other. Which was the true one?

To owe his life to a man wanted by the law and to pay the debt in equal terms; to have accepted the words, 'You may go,' and now to say, 'Go free,' this was to sacrifice duty to personal motive, while at the same time feeling that the personal motive had a wider and perhaps higher application; it was to betray society while keeping faith with his own conscience. That this dilemma should have come upon him was what so overwhelmed him. He was amazed that Valjean should have shown him mercy, and that he should have shown Valjean mercy in return.

And now what was he to do? It would be bad to arrest Valjean, bad also to let him go. In the first case an officer of the law would be sinking to the level of a criminal, and in the second the criminal would be rising above the law. There are occasions when we find ourselves with an abyss on either side, and this was one of them.

His trouble was that he was forced to reflect – the very strength of his feelings made this unavoidable. Reflection was something to which he was unused, and he found it singularly painful. There is in it always an element of conflict, and this irritated him. Reflection, on any subject outside the narrow circle of his duties, had always been to him a useless and wearisome procedure; but now, after to-day's happenings, it was torture. Yet he was obliged to study his shaken conscience and account for himself to himself.

What he had done made him shudder. Against all regulations, all social and legal organization, against the whole code he, Javert, had taken it upon himself to let a prisoner go. He had substituted private considerations for those of the community: was it not inexcusable? He trembled when he thought of this. What to do? Only one proper course lay open to him – to hurry back to the Rue de l'Homme-Armé and seize Valjean. He knew it well, but he could not do it.

Something prevented him. What was it? Could there be other things in life besides trials and sentences, authority and the police? Javert was in utter dismay. A condemned man to escape justice through his act! That these two men, the one meant to enforce, the other to submit to the law, should thus place themselves outside the law – was not this a dreadful thing? Jean Valjean, in defiance of society, would be free, and he, Javert, would continue to live at the government's expense. His thoughts grew blacker and blacker.

The thought of the rebel taken to the Rue des Filles-du-Calvaire might have occurred to him, but it did not. The lesser fault was lost in the greater. In any case, he was probably dead. It was the thought of Jean Valjean that oppressed and dismayed him. All the principles on which his estimate of man had been based were overthrown.

Valjean's generosity towards himself amazed him. Behind Valjean loomed the figure of Monsieur Madeleine, and they merged into one, into a figure deserving of veneration. Something dreadful was forcing its way into Javert's consciousness – admiration for a convicted felon. He shivered, but could not evade it. Try as he might, he had in his heart to admit the scoundrel's greatness. It was abhorrent. A benevolent evil-doer, a man who returned good for evil, a man near to the angels – Javert was forced to admit that this monstrosity could exist. He did not accept the fact without a struggle. He did not for a moment deny that the law was the law. What more simple than to enforce it? But when he sought to raise his hand to lay it on Valjean's shoulder an inner voice restrained him: 'You will deliver up your deliverer? Then go and find Pontius Pilate's bowl and wash your hands!' He felt himself diminished beside Jean Valjean.

But his greatest anguish was the loss of certainty. He had been torn up by the roots. The code he lived by was in fragments in his hand. He was confronted by scruples that were utterly strange to him. He could no longer live by his lifelong principles; he had entered a new strange world of humanity, mercy, gratitude and justice other than that of the law. He contemplated with horror the rising of a new sun – an owl required to see with eagle's eyes. He was forced to admit that kindness existed. The felon had been kind, and, a thing unheard of, so had he. Therefore he had failed himself. He felt himself to be a coward. Javert's ideal was to be more than human; to be above reproach. And he had failed.

All kinds of new questions arose in his mind, and the answers appalled him. Had the man performed a duty in showing him mercy? No, he had done something more. And he, in returning mercy, had denied his duty. So it seemed that there was something other than duty? Here all balance left him, the whole structure of his life collapsed; what was high was no more deserving of honour than what was low. Although instinctively he held the Church in respect, he regarded it as no more than an august part of the social order; and order was his dogma, and had hitherto sufficed him. The police force had been his true religion. He had a superior officer, Monsieur Gisquet; he had given no thought to that higher superior, which is God.

Now he became conscious of God and was troubled in spirit, thrown into disarray by that unexpected presence. He did not know how to treat this superior, knowing that the subordinate must always give way, never disobey or dispute orders, and that, faced by a superior with whom he does not agree, he can only resign. But how resign from God?

What it all came down to was that he was guilty of an unpardonable infraction of the rules. He had let a felon go. He felt that his life was in ruins. Authority was dead within him, and he had no reason to go on living.

To feel emotion was terrible. To be carved in stone, the very figure of chastisement, and to discover suddenly under the granite of our face something contradictory that is almost a heart. To return good for a good that hitherto one had held to be evil; to be of ice, and melt; to see a pincer become a hand with fingers that parted. To let go! The man of action had lost his way. He was forced to admit that infallibility is not always infallible, that there may be error in dogma, that society is not perfect, that a flaw in the unalterable is possible, that judges are men and even the law may do wrong. What was happening to Javert resembled the de-railing of a train – the straight line of the soul broken by the presence of God. God, the inwardness of man, the true conscience as opposed to the false; the eternal, splendid presence. Did he understand or fully realize this? No; and faced by the incomprehensibility he felt that his head must explode.

He was not so much transformed as a victim of this miracle. He submitted in exasperation, feeling that henceforth his very breath must fail. He was not used to confronting the unknown. Until now what had been above him had been plain and simple, clearly defined and exact. Authority . . . Javert had been conscious of nothing unknowable. The unexpected, the glimpse of chaos, these belonged to some unknown, recalcitrant, miserable world. But now, recoiling, he was appalled by a new manifestation – an abyss above him. It meant that he was wholly at a loss. In what was he to believe?

The chink in society's armour might be found by a wretched act of mercy. An honest servant of the law might find himself caught between two crimes, the crime of mercy and the crime of duty. Nothing any longer was certain in the duties laid upon him. It seemed that a one-time felon might rise again and in the end prove right. Was it conceivable? Were there then cases when the law, mumbling excuses, must bow to transfigured crime? Yes, there were! Javert saw, and not only could not deny it but himself shared in it. This was reality. It was abominable that true fact should wear so distorted a face. If facts did their duty they would simply reinforce the law. Facts were God-given. Did anarchy itself descend from Heaven?

So then – and in the extremity of his anguish everything that might have corrected this impression was lost, and society and human kind assumed a hideous aspect – then the settled verdict, the force of law, official wisdom, legal infallibility, all dogma on which social stability reposed, all was chaos; and he, Javert, the guardian of these things, was in utter disarray. Was this state of things to be borne? It was not. There were only two ways out. To go determinedly to Jean Valjean and return him to prison; or else . . .

Javert left the parapet and, now with his head held high, walked firmly to the police-post lighted by a lantern in the corner of the Place du Châtelet. He thrust open the door, showed the duty sergeant his card and sat down at a table on which were pens, inkstand and paper. It was something to be found in every police-post, fully equipped for the writing of reports. Javert settled down to write.

SOME NOTES FOR THE GOOD OF THE SERVICE

First: I beg Monsieur le Préfet to consider this.

Second: Prisoners returning from interrogation are made to take off their shoes and wait with their bare feet on the tiles. Many are coughing when they go back to prison. This leads to hospital expenses.

Third: Surveillance is well performed, with relief agents at regular distances; but in all important cases there should be at least two agents within sight of one another, able to come to each other's support.

Four: The special regulation at the Madelonnette prison, whereby prisoners are not allowed a chair even if they pay for it, is hard to justify.

Five: There are only two bars over the canteen counter at the Madelonnette, which enables the canteen-woman to touch the prisoners' hands.

Six: The prisoners called 'barkers' who summon prisoners to the parlour charge two sous for calling a man's name distinctly. This is robbery.

Seven: The prisoner who drops a thread in the weaving-room loses ten sous. This is an abuse on the part of the contractor, since the cloth is none the worse for it.

Eight: It is unsatisfactory that visitors to La Force should have to cross the Cour des Mômes to reach the Sainte-Marie-l'Égyptienne parlour.

Nine: Gendarmes in the courtyard of the Préfecture are often heard discussing Court proceedings. A gendarme should never repeat what he has heard in the course of his official duties.

Ten: Mme Henry is an excellent woman who keeps her canteen in good order. But it is wrong that a woman should be at the entrance to the secret cells. This is unworthy of the Conciergerie.

Having methodically written these lines without omitting a comma, Javert signed as follows:

'Javert, Inspector of the First Class, writing at the Place du Châtelet post.

'7 June 1832, at about one o'clock in the morning.'

He blotted and folded the sheet of paper, and addressing it to the Administration, left it on the table. He went out, and the barred, glass-paned door closed behind him.

Crossing the Place du Châtelet, he returned automatically to the spot he had left a quarter of an hour before and stood leaning with his elbows on the parapet as though he had never left it. It was the sepulchral moment that succeeds midnight, with the stars hidden by cloud and not a light to be seen in the houses of the Cité, not a passer-by, only the faint, distant gleam of a street-lamp and the shadowy outlines of Notre-Dame and the Palais de Justice.

The place where Javert stood, we may recall, was where the river flows in a dangerous rapid. He looked down. There was a sound of running water, but the river itself was not to be seen. What lay below him was a void, so that he might have been standing at the edge of infinity. He stayed motionless for some minutes, staring into nothingness. Abruptly he took off his hat and laid it on the parapet. A moment later a tall, dark figure, which a passer-by might have taken for a ghost, stood upright on the parapet. It leaned forward and dropped into the darkness.

There was a splash, and that was all.

BOOK FIVE

GRANDSON AND GRANDFATHER

I

We again see the tree with a zinc plate

SOME TIME after the events we have described Boulatruelle had a severe shock.

Boulatruelle was the Montfermeil road-mender whom we met in an earlier part of this tale. He was a man of many troubles, whose stone-breaking caused vexation to travellers on the road. But he cherished a dream. He believed in the treasure buried in the woods of Montfermeil and hoped to find it. In the meantime he picked the pockets of passers-by when he could.

But for the present he was being prudent. He had had a narrow escape, having been rounded up in the Jondrette garret with the other gangsters. Drunkenness had saved him, since it could not be proved that he had been there with criminal intent, and so he had been granted an acquittal, based on his undeniably drunken state. He had then returned to the woods and the road from Gagny to Lagny where under administrative supervision and in a subdued manner, warmed only by his fondness for wine, he had continued to break stones.

The shock was as follows. One morning just before daybreak, going as usual to work but perhaps a little more awake than on most days, he had seen among the trees the back view of a stranger who did not appear wholly unfamiliar. Drinker though he was, Boulatruelle had an excellent memory, a necessary weapon for anyone somewhat at odds with the law.

'Where the devil have I seen him?' he wondered, but could find no answer to the question. He considered the matter. The man was not local. He must have come on foot, since no public conveyance passed at that hour. He could not have come from any great distance, since he had no bundle or haversack. Perhaps he had come from Paris. But what was he doing there? Boulatruelle thought of the hidden treasure. Ransacking his memory, he recalled a similar encounter some years before. He had bowed his head while thinking, which was natural but unwise. When he looked up the man was no longer to be seen.

'By God I'll find him,' said Boulatruelle. 'I'll find out who he is and what he's up to. Can't have secrets in my woods.' He took up his pick, which was very sharp. 'Good for digging into the earth, or into a man.'

He set off in the general direction taken by the man. Before long he was helped by the growing daylight. Footprints here and there, crushed bushes and other indications, afforded him a rough trail, which, however, he lost. Pushing further into the wood, he climbed a small hillock and then had the idea of climbing a tree. Despite his age he was agile. There was a tall beech, and he climbed it as high as he could. From this eminence he saw the man, only to lose him again. The man had vanished into a clearing surrounded by tall trees. But Boulatruelle knew the clearing well because one of the trees was a chestnut that had been mended with a sheet of zinc nailed to the bark. Doubtless the heap of stones in the clearing is still there. There is nothing to equal the longevity of a heap of stones.

Boulatruelle almost fell out of the tree in his delight. He had run his man to earth, and doubtless the treasure as well. But to reach the clearing was not easy. Following the twisted paths, it took a quarter of an hour; but to go direct, forcing one's way through the toughest undergrowth, took twice as long. Boulatruelle made a mistake. For once in his life he took the straight line.

It was a laborious business. When, breathless, he reached the clearing some half an hour later, he found no one there. Only the heap of stones was there; no one had taken that away. But the man himself had vanished, no one could say in what direction. Worse still, behind the heap of stones and near the tree with its zinc plate, was a pile of earth, an abandoned pick-axe, and a hole.

The hole was empty.

'Scoundrel!' cried Boulatruelle, flinging up his arms.

II

From street warfare to domestic conflict

Marius lay for a long time between life and death, in a state of fever and delirium, endlessly repeating the name of Cosette. The extent of some of his wounds was serious because of the risk of gangrene, and every change in the weather caused the doctor anxiety.

'Above all,' he said, 'he must not be excited.' Dressings were difficult, sticking-plaster being unknown at that time. Nicolette tore up countless sheets, 'enough to cover the ceiling'. While the peril remained Monsieur Gillenormand, hovering distractedly at the bedside, was like Marius himself – neither dead nor alive.

Every day, and sometimes twice a day, a white-haired, well-dressed gentleman, according to the porter, came to ask for news of the sick man and brought with him a bundle of rags for bandages.

Finally, on 7 September, three months to the day after Marius had been brought to his grandfather's house, the doctor announced that he was out of danger. But because of the damage to his shoulder-blade he had to spend a further two months resting on a chaise-longue. There are always injuries which refuse to heal and cause great vexation to the sufferers, but on the other hand his long illness and convalescence saved Marius from the authorities. In France there is no anger, not even official, that six months do not extinguish; and uprisings, in the present state of society, are so much the fault of everyone, that it is better for eyes to be closed. We may add that Gisquet's inexcusable order, instructing doctors to denounce the wounded, outraged not only public opinion but that of the King himself, and this protected them. Apart from one or two who were captured in the fighting, they were not troubled; and so Marius was left in peace.

Monsieur Gillenormand at first went through every kind of torment, and then through every kind of rapture. It was with great difficulty that he was restrained from spending all his nights at the bedside. He insisted that his daughter should use the best linen in the house for the patient's bandages; but Mlle Gillenormand, prudent woman, contrived to save the best without his knowing. He personally supervised all the dressings, from which Mlle Gillenormand modestly withdrew, and when rotted flesh had to be scraped away he exclaimed in pain. Nothing was more touching than to see him tender the patient a cup of tisane with his old, shaking hand. He overwhelmed the doctor with questions, which he endlessly repeated. And on the day when the doctor announced that the danger was past, such was his happiness that he tipped the porter three louis. That night in his bedroom he danced a gavotte, snapping his fingers and singing a little song. Then he knelt down at a chair, and Basque, peeping through the partly open door, was sure that he was praying. Until then he had never believed in God.

His state of rapture grew as the patient's condition improved. He did absurd, extravagant things, such as running up and down stairs without knowing why. His neighbour, a pretty woman be it said, was astonished to receive a large bouquet from him, greatly to her husband's annoyance. He even tried to take Nicolette on his knee. He addressed Marius as 'Monsieur le Baron' and cried, 'Long live the Republic!' He watched over the prodigal like a mother, no longer thinking of himself. Marius had become the master of the house, and he, surrendering, was his grandson's grandson, the most venerable of children, such was his state of happiness. He was radiant and young, his white hair lending dignity to the warmth shining in his face.

As for Marius, during all his convalescence he had but one thought in mind, that of Cosette. When he ceased to be delirious he ceased to speak her name, but this was precisely because she meant so much to him. He did not know what had happened to her or to himself. Vague pictures lingered in his mind – Éponine, Gavroche, Mabeuf, the Thénardiers, and the friends who had been with him at the barricade. The appearance of Monsieur Fauchelevent in that sanguinary affair was a riddle to him. He did not know how he had come to be saved, and no one could tell him. All they could say was that he had been brought there in a fiacre. Past, present, and future, all were befogged in his mind. There was but one clear, fixed point: his resolve to find Cosette. In this he was unshakeable, regardless of what it might cost, or the demands he might have to make of his grandfather or of life.

He did not conceal the difficulties from himself. And we must stress one point: he was not won over or much moved by his grandfather's kindness, for one thing because he did not know of it all, and also because, in the wandering thoughts of a sick man, he saw in this new phenomenon an attempt to bring him to heel. He remained cool, and his grandfather's aged tenderness was wasted. He thought that all would be well while things remained as they were, but that any mention of Cosette would lead to a changed situation – the old quarrel revived. So he hardened his heart in advance. And with returning life his old grievances returned, so that the figure of Colonel Pontmercy came between him and his grandfather. He felt that he could not hope for kindness from one whose attitude to his father had been so harsh. With growing health he felt a kind of acrimony towards the old man, from which the latter suffered. Without giving any sign, Monsieur Gillenormand noted that Marius now never addressed him as 'father'. He did not, it is true, say 'Monsieur', but found ways of avoiding either.

Clearly a crisis was approaching. As nearly always happens, Marius skirmished before joining battle. It happened one morning that Monsieur Gillenormand, glancing at the newspaper, let fall a frivolously royalist remark on the Convention and Danton, Saint-Just and Robespierre.

'Those men of '93 were giants,' Marius said angrily.

The old man did not say another word, and Marius, never forgetting the inflexible grandparent of former years, saw in his silence a manifestation of deeply buried anger, and prepared himself for the struggle that must come. He was resolved that if Cosette were denied him he would strip the bandages off his wounds and refuse all food. His wounds were his armoury. He would have Cosette or die.

III

Marius attacks

One day while his daughter was tidying the room Monsieur Gillenormand bent over Marius's bed and said to him most tenderly:

'If I were you, dear Marius, I would begin to eat more meat than fish. A fried sole is excellent at the beginning of convalescence; but a good chop is what a man needs to put him on his feet.'

Marius, whose strength was now almost quite restored, sat up with clenched fists and glared at his grandfather.

'There is something I have to say to you.'

'What is it?'

'I want to get married.'

'But of course,' said the old man, laughing.

'How do you mean – of course?'

'That's understood. You shall have your little girl.'

Marius trembled with sheer amazement.

'You shall have her,' Monsieur Gillenormand repeated. 'She comes here every day in the shape of an elderly gentleman who asks for news of you. Since your injury she has spent her time weeping and making bandages. I know all about her. She lives at No. 7, Rue de l'Homme-Armé. You didn't think of that, did you? You thought to yourself, "I'll put it to him squarely, that old relic of the *ancien régime.* He was a beau once; he had his flutter and his wenches. He had his fun, and now we'll see." A battle, you thought, and you'd take the bull by the horns. So I suggest that you should eat a chop and you say you want to get married! What a jump! You thought there was bound to be an argument, not knowing what an old coward I am. You didn't expect to find your grandfather even sillier than yourself, too busy thinking of all the things you were going to say to me. But I'm not so foolish. I've made inquiries. I know that she's charming and good and that she adores you. If you had died there would have been three of us – her coffin and mine alongside your own. I had thought, when you were better, of simply bringing her to your bedside; but that's the sort of romantic situation that only happens in novels. What would your aunt have said? And the doctor? A pretty girl is no cure for fever. So there you are, and no need to say any more. I knew you did not care for me, and I thought, what can I do to make him love me? I thought, I can give him Cosette. You expected me to play the tyrant and ruin everything. Not a bit of it – Cosette is yours. Nothing could be better. Be so good as to get married, my dear sir. And be happy, my dear, dear boy.'

Having said which the old man burst into tears. He clasped Marius's head to his chest and they wept together.

'Father!' cried Marius.

'At last you love me!' the old man said.

There was a moment of supreme happiness during which neither could speak. Then the old man stammered:

'So at last you've said it – father.'

Marius gently disengaged his head.

'Father, now that I'm so much better I think I should be allowed to see her.'

'You shall. You shall see her tomorrow.'

'But father –'

'Well?'

'Why not today?'

'Well then, today. You have called me "father" three times and that has earned it. It is like the end of a poem by André Chénier, whose throat was cut by those vill— those giants of '93.'

Monsieur Gillenormand thought he had caught the trace of a frown on Marius's face, although the truth is that, his mind filled with thoughts of Cosette, Marius had not even heard him. Trembling at the thought that he might have blundered in that reference to the murderers of André Chénier, the old man hurriedly went out.

'Well, that was not the way to put it. There was nothing evil about those great men of the Revolution. They were heroes, not a doubt of it. But they found André Chénier troublesome, and so they had him guillo— I mean, they asked him in the public interest if he wouldn't mind . . .'

But he could find no way of ending the sentence. While his daughter smoothed Marius's pillows he ran out of the room as hurriedly as his age allowed, shut the door behind him, and, foaming with rage, found himself face to face with Basque. He seized him by the collar and cried:

'By all the gods, those villains murdered him!'

'Murdered who?'

'André Chénier.'

'Certainly, monsieur,' said the startled Basque.

IV

Mlle Gillenormand and Monsieur Fauchelevent

Cosette and Marius saw one another again. What it meant to them we shall not attempt to say. There are things beyond description, of which the sun is one.

All the household, including Basque and Nicolette, were assembled in Marius's room when she entered. She stood in the doorway, seeming enveloped in a glow of light. The old man, at that moment, had been about to blow his nose. He stopped short, gazing at Cosette over his handkerchief.

'Exquisite,' he cried and loudly blew.

Cosette was in Heaven, as dazed as a person can be by sheer happiness. She stood stammering, pale and pink, waiting to fling herself into Marius's arms, but not venturing to do so, afraid of thus showing her love to the world. We are pitiless to happy lovers, hampering them with our presence when they only want to be alone.

Standing behind Cosette was a white-haired man, grave but nevertheless smiling – a vaguely touching smile. It was 'Monsieur Fauchelevent' – that is to say, Jean Valjean. As the porter had said, he was very well dressed, entirely in new black garments, with a white cravat.

The porter was not within miles of discerning, in that respectable figure, the ragged, mud-smeared person who on 7 June had brought the unconscious Marius to the door. Nevertheless his porter's instinct was aroused, and he had not been able to refrain from saying to his wife, 'I don't know why it is, but I can't help feeling I've seen him somewhere before.'

Monsieur Fauchelevent was standing somewhat apart from the others. He had under his arm a package that looked like a volume wrapped in paper, the paper being greenish in colour and seeming damp.

'Does the gentleman always have a book under his arm?' Nicolette murmured to Mlle Gillenormand, who did not care for books.

'Why,' said Monsieur Gillenormand in the same low tone, 'he's a man of learning. So what is wrong with that? Monsieur Boulard, whom I used to know, never went anywhere without a book under his arm.'

Raising his voice and bowing, he said:

'Monsieur Tranchelevent . . .' He did not do it on purpose; but inattention to proper names was one of his aristocratic habits. 'Monsieur Tranchelevent, I have the honour, on behalf of my grandson, Baron Marius Pontmercy, to ask for your daughter's hand in marriage.'

Monsieur Tranchelevent bowed.

'Then that is settled,' said the old man, and turning to Marius and Cosette with arms upraised he said: 'My children, you are free to love one another.'

They did not need telling twice. The billing and cooing began. 'To see you again,' Cosette murmured, standing by the chaise-longue. 'To know that it is really you! Why did you go and fight? How dreadful! For four months I have felt that I was dead. How cruel of you, when I had done you no harm. You are forgiven, but you must never do it again. When I had the message asking me to come here I thought that I should die of joy. I have not even troubled to dress up. I must look terrible . . . But you don't say anything. Why do you let me do all the talking? We're still in the Rue de l'Homme-Armé. And your dreadful wound – I cried my eyes out. That anyone should suffer so much. Your grandfather looks very nice. No, don't try to stand up, it might be bad for you. Oh, I'm so happy, wild with happiness! Do you still love me? We live in the Rue de l'Homme-Armé. There's no garden. I've done nothing but make bandages, look at the blister on my finger, you bad man!' . . .

'Angel!' Marius said: the word that never wears out, the one most often used by lovers . . . And then, since there were others present, they fell silent, only touching each other's hand. Monsieur Gillenormand turned to the rest of the company and cried:

'Well talk, can't you! Make a little noise so that they can chatter in comfort!' He bent over them. 'And call each other *tu*. Don't be afraid.'

Aunt Gillenormand with a kind of amazement was observing the bright scene in her faded home. There was nothing shocked or envious in her gaze: it was that of an innocent creature of fifty-seven, a wasted life witnessing the triumph of love. Her father said to her:

'I told you this would happen to you . . .' He paused and went on after a moment's silence, '. . . to see the happiness of others.' Then he turned to Cosette. 'So sweetly pretty, like a painting by Greuze. And to think that she's to be all yours, you rascal! If I weren't fifteen years too old we'd fight a duel for her. Young lady, I am in love with you, and no wonder. What a charming wedding it will be! Saint-Denis du Saint-Sacrement is our parish, but I'll get a dispensation for you to be married in Saint-Paul, which is a nicer church, built by the Jesuits. The masterpiece of Jesuit architecture is at Namur, the church of Saint-Loup. You must go there when you're married. I am wholly on your side, Mademoiselle; all young ladies should get married, it's what they're for. Be fruitful and multiply. What can be better than that?' The old man skipped on his ninety-year-old heels and said to Marius: 'By the way – did you not have a close friend?

'There was Courfeyrac.'

'What's become of him?'

'He's dead.'

'Ah, well.'

He made Cosette sit down, sat beside them and took their four hands in his own.

'So enchanting, this Cosette, a true masterpiece. A young girl and a great lady. It's a pity she'll only be a baroness, she should be a marquise. Get it well into your heads, my children, that you are on the right road. Love is the folly of men and the wisdom of God. Love one another. But now I come to think of it, more than half of all I possess is tied up in an annuity. My poor children, what will you do after my death in twenty years' time?'

A quiet voice said: 'Mademoiselle Euphrasie Fauchelevent has six hundred thousand francs.'

It was Jean Valjean who had spoken. Hitherto he had not uttered a word, but had stood silently contemplating the happy group.

'And who is this Mademoiselle Euphrasie?' the old man asked.

'It's me,' said Cosette.

'Six hundred thousand?' exclaimed the old man.

'Less a few thousand francs,' said Valjean, and he put the parcel which Aunt Gillenormand had supposed to be a book on the table. Opening it he disclosed a bundle of banknotes, which, being counted, amounted to five hundred thousand-franc notes and one hundred and sixty-eight five-hundred-franc notes – in all, five hundred and eighty-four thousand francs.

'Well that's a very handsome book,' said Monsieur Gillenormand.

'Five hundred and eighy-four thousand francs,' murmured the aunt.

'That settles matters very nicely, does it not, Mlle Gillenormand?' the old man said. 'This young rogue of a Marius, he finds a millionairess in his dreamland. Trust the young people of nowadays. Students find girl-students worth six hundred thousand francs. Cherubino is a better man than Rothschild.'

'Five hundred and eighty-four thousand francs!' Mlle Gillenormand murmured again. 'As good as six hundred thousand!'

But as to Marius and Cosette, they were gazing into each other's eyes, scarcely aware of this trifle.

V

How to safeguard your money

No lengthy explanation is needed for the reader to understand that after the Champmathieu affair Jean Valjean had been able, during his brief escape, to come to Paris and withdraw from the Laffitte bank the money he had accumulated as Monsieur Madeleine. Fearing recapture, he had buried it in the clearing in the Montfermeil wood. The sum of 630,000 francs in banknotes was not bulky and could be put in a box; but to safeguard the box from damp he had put it in an oak chest filled with chestnut shavings. In this he had also put the bishop's candlesticks which he had taken from Montreuil-sur-mer. It was Valjean whom the road-mender, Boulatruelle, had seen. When he needed money Valjean had returned to the clearing, which accounts for the absences we have referred to; and when he knew Marius to be convalescent, foreseeing that the entire sum would come in useful, he had gone to retrieve it. This was the last time Boulatruelle had seen him. He had inherited his pickaxe.

The sum then remaining had amounted to 584,500 francs. Valjean had kept the five hundred for himself. 'We shall see how it works out,' he reflected.

The difference between this sum and the 630,000 francs withdrawn from Laffite represented the expenditure of ten years – from 1823 to 1833. The time in the convent had cost only 5,000 francs. Valjean had put the silver candlesticks on the mantelpiece, where they glittered to the great admiration of Toussaint.

For the rest, Valjean knew that he had nothing more to fear from Javert. It had been reported in the *Moniteur* that his drowned body had been found under a washerwoman's boat between the Pont au Change and the Pont Neuf. He had been a policeman with an irreproachable record, highly esteemed by his superiors, who concluded that he must have committed suicide while of unsound mind. 'Well,' reflected Jean Valjean, 'since he had me and let me go, that may well be true.'

VI

Two old gentlemen prepare for the happiness of Cosette

Preparations for the wedding were put in hand. The month was December and the doctor, being consulted, declared that it might take place in February. Several weeks of perfect bliss ensued, and Monsieur Gillenormand was far from being the least happy. He spent hours in the contemplation of Cosette.

'The sweet, pretty girl,' he said. 'So gentle and so good. Never have I seen so delightful a girl. Who could live anything but nobly with such a creature? Marius, my boy, you are a baron and you are rich. Don't, I beseech, you, waste your time lawyering.'

Cosette and Marius had been transported so rapidly from the depths to the heights that they would have been dazed had they not been dazzled.

'Do you understand it all?' he asked Cosette.

'No,' she replied. 'But I feel that God is watching over us.'

Jean Valjean arranged everything and made everything easy,

speeding Cosette's happiness with as much pleasure, or so it appeared, as she felt herself. Having been a mayor, he knew how to solve an awkward problem, that of Cosette's civic status. To reveal the truth about her origin might, who knows, have prevented the marriage. He endowed her with a dead family, which meant that no one could make demands on her. She was not his daughter but the daughter of another Fauchelevent. Two Fauchelevent brothers had worked as gardeners in the Petit-Picpus convent; and the fact was confirmed by the nuns, who, little interested in the matter of paternity, had never troubled to inquire which of them was her father. They willingly said what was wanted, a document was prepared and Cosette acquired the legal state of Mademoiselle Euphrasie Fauchelevent, an orphan. Jean Valjean, under the name of Fauchelevent, became her guardian and Monsieur Gillenormand her deputy guardian.

As for the money, it had been bequeathed to Cosette by a person who had preferred to remain anonymous. The original sum had been 594,000 francs; but of this 10,000 francs had been spent on little Euphrasie's education, 500 going to the convent. The legacy, held by a trustee, was to go to Cosette when she attained her majority or when she married. All of which, it will be seen, was highly acceptable, particularly since the sum involved exceeded half a million. There were one or two trifling oddities, but these passed unnoticed.

Cosette had to learn that she was not the daughter of the old man whom for so long she had addressed as father, and that another Fauchelevent was her real parent. At any other time she would have been greatly distressed, but in her present state of happiness this scarcely troubled her. She had Marius; and the coming of the young man made the older less important. And all her life she had been surrounded by mystery, so that this last change was not hard to accept. In any case she continued to call Jean Valjean 'father'.

She had taken a great liking to Monsieur Gillenormand, who showered presents on her. While Jean Valjean arranged her civic status, he attended to her trousseau, delighting in its magnificence. He gave her a dress of Binche lace which had come to him from his grandmother, saying that it was again becoming fashionable. 'Old styles are all the rage,' he said. 'The young women nowadays dress just as they did when I was young.' He rifled wardrobes filled with the belongings of his wives and mistresses; damask and moiré and painted Indian cloths, lacework from Genoa and Alençon, all kinds of elegant frivolity were lavished on the rapturous Cosette, whose soul soared skyward on Mechlin lace wings. It was a time of endless festivity in the Rue des Filles-du-Calvaire.

One day Marius, who with all his happiness enjoyed serious conversation, remarked for some reason that I do not recall:

'The men of the Revolution were so great that their deathless fame is already assured. Like Cato and Phocion they have become figures of antiquity.'

'Antiquity – antique moiré!' the old man cried. 'Marius, I thank you – just the idea I was looking for!' And the next day a magnificent dress of antique moiré the colour of tea was added to Cosette's wardrobe.

The old man drew morals from this finery.

'Love is all very well, but something more is needed. There must be extravagance in happiness, rapture must be spiced with superfluity. Let me have a milkmaid, but make her a duchess. Let me view an endless countryside from a colonnade of marble. Happiness unadorned is like unbuttered bread: one may eat it but one does not dine. I want the superfluous, the embellishment, the thing that serves no purpose. In Strasbourg Cathedral there is a clock the size of a three-storey house which condescends to tell you the time but does not seem to exist for that alone. Whatever hour it strikes, midday, the hour of the sun, or midnight, the hour of love, it seems to be giving you the sun and the stars, earth and ocean, kings, emperors and the twelve apostles, and a troop of little gilded men playing the trumpet – all this thrown in! How does a mere bare dial pointing the hours compare with that? The great clock of Strasbourg, and not just a Black Forest cuckoo-clock, is what suits me.'

Monsieur Gillenormand dwelt especially on the subject of festivity, invoking all the gaieties of the eighteenth century.

'You have lost the art in these days,' he cried. 'This nineteenth century is flat, lacking in excess, ignorant of what is rich and noble, insipid, colourless, and without form. Your bourgeois ideal is a chintz upholstered boudoir! But I can look back. On the day in 1787 when I saw the Duc du Rohan, who was Prince de Léon, and other peers of France drive to Longchamp, not in stately coaches but in chaises, I knew it was the beginning of the end. Look what follows. In these days people do business, play the market, make money and are rotten – smooth, neat, polished, irreproachable on the surface; but go deeper and you will raise a stench that would make a cow-hand hold his nose! You must not mind, Marius, if I talk like this. I say nothing against the people, but I have a bone to pick with the bourgeoisie. I am one myself, and that is how I know. There is so much that I regret – the elegance, the chivalry, the courtly manners, and the songs ... The bride's garter, which was akin to the girdle of Venus. What else caused the Trojan war, if not Helen's garter? Why else did Hector and Achilles deal each other mortal blows? Homer might have made the *Iliad* out of Cosette's garter, and put in an old babbler like me whom he would call Nestor. In the good old days, my friends, people married wisely – a good marriage contract followed by a good blow-out. One did oneself proud, sitting beside a pretty woman who did not unduly hide her bosom. Those laughing mouths, how gay they were! People set out to look pretty with make-up and embroidery. Your bourgeoise looked like a flower, your marquise like a statue. It was a great time, fastidious on the one hand and splendid on the other – and how we enjoyed ourselves! People nowadays are serious. The bourgeois is miserly and a prude. A wretched century – the Graces would be considered too lightly clad. Beauty is hidden as though it were ugliness. Everyone wears pantaloons since the Revolution, even the dancers. Songs are solemn, they have to have a message. People have to look important, and the result is that they all look insignificant. Listen, my children – joy is not simply joyous, it is great! Be gaily in love, and when you marry do so in all the fever and excitement of happiness. Decorum in church is proper, but when that's over – bang! A wedding should be royal and magical. I detest solemn weddings. That moment in life should be a flight to Heaven with the birds, even if next day you have to fall back to earth among the bourgeoisie and the frogs. There should be nothing meagre about that day. If I had my way it would be a day of enchantment, with violins in the trees, a sky of silver and blue, and the singing of nymphs and nereids, a chorus of naked girls. That is the programme I would like to see.'

Aunt Gillenormand viewed these matters with her customary placidity. She had had much to unsettle her in recent months – Marius fighting on the barricades, brought home more dead than alive, reconciled to his grandfather, engaged to be married to a pauper who turned out to be an heiress. The 600,000 francs were the culminating astonishment, after which she had reverted to her customary state of religious torpor, regularly attending Mass, telling her beads, murmuring *Aves* in one corner of the house while the words 'I love you' were being exchanged in another. There is a state of asceticism in which the benumbed spirit, remote from everything that we call living, is scarcely aware of any happening less catastrophic than an earthquake, nothing human, whether pleasant or unpleasant. 'It's like a bad cold in the head,' Monsieur Gillenormand said. 'You can't smell a thing, good or bad.'

It was the money that had decided the matter for her. Her father was so in the habit of ignoring her that he had not asked her whether he should give his consent to Marius's marriage, and this had ruffled her, although she had given no sign of it. She had thought to herself: 'Well, my father may decide about the marriage but I can decide about the means.' She was in fact rich, which her father was not. She had kept an open mind, but the probability is that if they had been poor she would have let them go on being poor – if her nephew chose to marry a pauper that was his affair. But a fortune of six hundred thousand francs is deserving of esteem, and since they no longer needed it she would undoubtedly leave them her own fortune.

It was arranged that the couple should live with Marius's grandfather. The old man insisted on giving up his bedroom, the best room in the house. 'It will make me young again,' he said. 'I have always wanted to have a honeymoon in that room.' He filled it with old, gay furniture and hung it with a remarkable material, golden flowers on a satin background, which he believed had come from Utrecht. 'The same as draped the bed of the Duchesse d'Anville à la Roche Guyon,' he said. And on the mantelpiece he put a little Saxon figurine holding a muff over her naked tummy. His library became Marius's advocate's office, this, as we know, being a legal requirement.

VII

Happiness and dreams

The lovers saw each other every day, Cosette coming with Monsieur Fauchelevent. 'It's not at all right,' said Mlle Gillenormand, 'for the lady to come to the gentleman.' But they had got into the habit during Marius's convalescence, and the greater comfort of the armchairs in the Rue des Filles-du-Calvaire, more suited to the tête-à-tête, had been an added inducement. Marius and Monsieur Fauchelevent saw one another but scarcely spoke, as though by tacit agreement. Every girl needs a chaperon, and so Cosette could not have come without him. Marius accepted him for this reason. They exchanged an occasional word on the political situation and once, when Marius asserted his conviction that education should be free and available to everyone, they found themselves in agreement and had a brief discussion. Marius found that although Monsieur Fauchelevent talked well, with an excellent command of language, there was something lacking in him. He was something less than a man of the world, and something more.

All sorts of questions concerning Monsieur Fauchelevent, who treated him with a cool civility, were at the back of Marius's mind. His illness had left a gap in his memory in which much had been lost. He found himself wondering whether he could really have seen that calm, sober man at the barricade. But no amount of happiness can prevent us from looking back into the past. There were moments when Marius, taking his head in his hands, recalled the death of Mabeuf, heard Gavroche singing amid the musket-fire and felt his lips pressed to Éponine's cold forehead. Enjolras, Courfeyrac, Jean Prouvaire – the figures of all his friends appeared to him and then vanished. Had they really existed, and where were they now? Was it true that they were all dead – all gone, except himself? All that had vanished like the fall of the curtain at the ending of a play. And was he himself the same man? He had been poor and now was rich, solitary and now he had a family, desolate and now he was to marry Cosette. He felt that he had passed through a tomb, black when he entered it but white when he emerged – and the others had remained in it. There were moments when those figures from the past crowded in upon him and filled his mind with darkness; then the thought of Cosette restored him to serenity. Nothing less than his present happiness could have washed out that disaster.

And Monsieur Fauchelevent had become almost one of those vanished figures. Seeing him quietly seated beside Cosette, Marius found it hard to believe that this was the man who had been with him at the barricade. That earlier Fauchelevent seemed rather a figment of his delirium. And there was a gap between them which Marius did not think of bridging. It is less rare than one may think for two men sharing a common experience to agree by tacit consent never to refer to it. Only once did Marius make the attempt. Bringing the Rue de la Chanvrerie into the conversation, he turned to Monsieur Fauchelevent and said:

'You know the street, do you not?'

'What street was that?'

'The Rue de la Chanvrerie.'

'I don't know the name of any such street,' replied Monsieur Fauchelevent with the greatest calm.

This reply, bearing simply on the name of the street, appeared to Marius more conclusive than it really was.

'I must have dreamed it,' he reflected. 'It was someone like him, but certainly not Monsieur Fauchelevent.'

VIII

Two men impossible to find

His state of rapture, great though it was, did not relieve Marius's mind of other preoccupations; and while the wedding preparations were going forward he subjected himself to scrupulous self-examination. He owed debts of gratitude both on his father's account and on his own. There was Thénardier, and there was the stranger who had brought him to Monsieur Gillenormand's house. He was resolved to find these two men, since otherwise they might cast a shadow on his life. Before moving joyously into the future he wanted to feel that he had paid due quittance to the past.

That Thénardier was a villain did not alter the fact that he had saved the life of Colonel Pontmercy. He was a rogue in the eyes of all the world except Marius. And Marius, not knowing what had really happened at Waterloo, was ignorant of the fact that although his father owed Thénardier his life, he owed him no gratitude. But the agents employed by Marius could find no trace of Thénardier. The woman had died in prison during the trial, and the man and his daughter Azelma, the sole survivors of that lamentable group, had vanished into obscurity.

The woman being dead, Boulatruelle acquitted, Claquesous vanished and the leading members of the gang having escaped from prison, the matter of the Gorbeau tenement conspiracy had been more or less abandoned. Two minor figures, Panchaud, known as Bigrenaille, and Demi-Liard, known as Deux Milliards, had been sentenced to ten years in the galleys, while their accomplices had been condemned in their absence to hard labour for life. Thénardier, as the instigator and leader, had been condemned to death, also in his absence. And that was all that was known of Thénardier.

As for that other man, the one who had saved Marius, the inquiries had at first produced some result but then had come to a dead end. The fiacre was found which had brought Marius to the Rue des Filles-du-Calvaire. The coachman declared that on the afternoon of 6 June, acting on the orders of a police agent, he had remained stationed on the Quai des Champs-Élysées from three o'clock until nightfall, and that about nine o'clock that evening the sewer-gate giving on to the river had opened and a man had come out carrying another man who seemed to be dead. The police agent had arrested the living man, and on his orders the cab-driver had 'taken the whole lot' to the Rue des Filles-du-Calvaire. He recognized Marius as the supposedly dead man. He had then driven the two other men to a spot near the Porte des Archives. And that was all he knew. Marius himself remembered nothing except that a strong hand had gripped him just as he was sinking unconscious to the ground at the barricade.

He was lost in conjecture. How had it happened that, having fallen in the Rue de la Chanvrerie, he had been picked up by a policeman on the bank of the Seine near the Pont des Invalides? Someone must have carried him there from the quarter of Les Halles, and how could he have done so except by way of the sewer? It was a wonderful act of devotion. This man, his saviour, was the man whom Marius sought, without discovering any trace of him. Although it had to be done with great discretion, he pursued his inquiries even as far as the Préfecture de Police, only to discover that they knew even less than the driver of the fiacre. They knew nothing of any arrest at the gate of the main sewer, and were inclined to think that the coachman had invented the story. A cabby looking for a tip is capable of anything, even of imagination. But Marius could no more doubt the truth of the story than he could doubt his own identity

The whole thing was wrapped in mystery. What had become of this man who had rescued him and then been arrested, presumably as a rebel? And what had become of the agent who had arrested him? Why had he kept silent? And how had the man escaped? Had he bribed the agent? Why had he not got in touch with Marius, who owed him so much? No one could tell him anything. Basque and Nicolette had had no eyes for anyone except their young master.

Only the porter with his candle had noticed the man and all he could say was, 'He was a terrible sight.' In the hope that they might provide him with some clue, Marius had kept the blood-stained garments in which he had been rescued. He made a queer discovery when he examined the jacket. A small piece was missing.

One evening when Marius was talking to Cosette and Jean Valjean about the mystery and his fruitless efforts to solve it, he became irritated by 'Monsieur Fauchelevent's' air of apparent indifference. He exclaimed almost angrily:

'Whoever he was, that man was sublime. Do you realize, Monsieur, what he did? He came to my rescue like an angel from Heaven. He plunged into the battle, picked me up, opened the sewer and then carried me for a league and a half through those appalling underground passages, bent double with a man on his back! And why did he do it? Simply to save a dying man. He said to himself, "There may be a chance for him, and so I must risk my life." He risked it twenty times over, with every step he took! And the proof is that no sooner had we left the sewer than he was arrested. And he did all this without any thought of reward. What was I to him? Simply a rebel. Oh, if all Cosette's money were mine.'

'It is yours,' Jean Valjean interrupted.

'I would give it all,' said Marius, 'to find that man!'

Jean Valjean was silent.

BOOK SIX

THE SLEEPLESS NIGHT

I

16 February 1833

THE NIGHT of 16 February was a blessed one, with a clear sky shading into darkness. It was the night of Marius and Cosette's wedding day.

The day itself had been delightful, not perhaps Monsieur Gillenormand's vision of cherubs and cupids fluttering above the heads of the bridal pair, but gentle and gay.

Wedding customs in 1833 were not what they are today. France had not yet borrowed from England the supreme refinement of abducting the bride, carrying her off from the church as though ashamed of her happiness like an escaping bankrupt or like rape in the manner of the Song of Songs. The chastity and propriety of whisking one's paradise into a post-chaise to consummate it in a tavern-bed at so much a night, mingling the most sacred of life's memories with a hired driver and tavern serving maids, was not yet understood in France.

In this second half of the nineteenth century in which we live the mayor in his robes and the priest in his chasuble are not enough. We must have the Longjumeau postilion in his blue waistcoat with brass buttons, his green leather breeches, waxed hat, whip and top boots. France has not yet carried elegance, like the English nobility, to the point of showering the bridal pair with worn-out slippers, in memory of Marlborough, who was assailed by an angry aunt at his wedding by way of wishing him luck. These are not yet a part of our wedding celebrations – but patience, they will doubtless come.

There was a strange belief in those days that a wedding was a quiet family affair, that a patriarchal banquet in no way marred its solemnity, that even an excess of gaiety, provided it was honest, did no harm to happiness, and finally that it was right and proper that the linking of two lives from which a family was to ensue should take place in the domestic nuptial chamber. In short, people were so shameless as to get married at home.

So the wedding reception took place, in this now outmoded

fashion, at the house of Monsieur Gillenormand. But there are formalities in these matters, banns to be read and so forth, and they could not be ready before the 16th. This, as it happened, was *Mardi gras*, to the perturbation of Aunt Gillenormand.

'*Mardi gras!*' exclaimed the old man. 'Well, why not? There's a proverb which says that no graceless child is ever born of a *Mardi gras* marriage. Do you want to put it off, Marius?'

'Certainly not,' said the young man.

'Very well then, the sixteenth it is.'

And so it was, regardless of public festivity. The day was a rainy one, as it happened, but there is always a patch of blue sky visible to lovers, although the rest of the world may see nothing but their umbrellas.

On the previous day Jean Valjean, in the presence of Monsieur Gillenormand, had handed Marius the 584,000 francs. The marriage deeds were very simple.

Since Valjean no longer needed Toussaint he had passed her on to Cosette, who had promoted her to the rank of lady's maid. As for Valjean himself, a handsome room in Monsieur Gillenormand's house had been expressly furnished for him, and Cosette had said so bewitchingly, 'Father, I beseech you!', that he had almost promised to live in it. But a few days before the wedding he had an accident, injuring his right thumb. It was a trifling matter, but it obliged him to wrap up his hand and keep his arm in a sling, which meant that he could not sign any documents. Monsieur Gillenormand, as deputy-guardian, had done so in his place.

We shall not take the reader to the mairie or the church ceremony, but will confine ourselves to recounting an incident, unperceived by the wedding party, which occurred on the way from the Rue des Filles-du-Calvaire to the church of Saint Paul.

At that time the northern end of the Rue Saint-Louis was being re-paved and there was a barrier across the Rue du Parc-Royal. This made it impossible for the wedding party to go the shortest way to the church; they had to go round by the boulevard. One of the wedding guests remarked that, being *Mardi gras*, there would be a great deal of traffic . . . 'Why?' asked Monsieur Gillenormand . . . 'Because of the masks' . . . 'Splendid,' said the old man. 'We'll go that way. These young folk are entering upon the serious business of life. It will do them good to start with a masquerade.'

So they went by way of the boulevard. The first carriage contained Cosette and Aunt Gillenormand, Monsieur Gillenormand and Jean Valjean; Marius, still kept separate from his bride as custom required, came in the second. Upon leaving the Rue des Filles-du-Calvaire they found themselves in a procession of vehicles stretching from the Madeleine to the Bastille and back. There were masks in abundance. Although it rained occasionally, Paillasse, Pantalon, and Gilles were not to be put off. Paris, in the happy humour of that winter of 1833, had put on the guise of Venice. We do not see a *Mardi gras* like that any more. Since everything is now an overblown carnival, carnivals no longer exist.

The side-streets, like the house windows, were thronged with spectators. Besides the masks there was the *Mardi gras* procession of vehicles, fiacres, hackney cabs, gigs, cabriolets, and others, kept so strictly in order by the police that they might have been running on rails. A person in one of those vehicles was both spectator and participant. The endless, parallel files of conveyances, going in opposite directions towards the Chaussée d'Antin and the Faubourg Saint-Antoine, were like rivers flowing up- and down-stream. Important vehicles bearing the quarterings of peers of France, or belonging to ambassadors, were allowed free passage in the middle of the road. England, too, cracked her whip in that scene of Parisian gaiety. My Lord Seymour, who had been endowed with a vulgar nickname, made a great show in his post-chaise. And also in the double file, escorted by gendarmes as conscientious as sheepdogs, were family barouches with grandmothers and aunts and charming clusters of children in fancy dress, six- and seven-year-old pierrots and pierrettes, very conscious of the dignity of taking part in this public ceremony.

Now and then there was a hold-up in one or other of the lines of vehicles, and they had to stop until the blockage was cleared. Then they went on again. The wedding party, heading in the direction of the Bastille, was on the right-hand side of the road. It was brought to a stop at the entrance to the Rue du Pont-aux-Choux, and the line going in the opposite direction stopped at almost the same moment. There was a carriage of masks in that line.

These carriages or, better, these cart-loads of masks are well known to the Parisians – so much so that if a *Mardi gras* or *mi-carême* were to go by without them people would say, 'There must be some reason. Probably the government's going to fall.' They are filled with clusters of Cassandras, Harlequins, and Columbines, figures of fantasy and mythology of every conceivable kind, and their tradition goes back to the early days of the monarchy. The household accounts of Louis XI include an item of 'twenty sous for three carts of masqueraders'. In these days they travel noisily in hired vans, inside and on top, twenty where there is room for six, girls seated on the men's knees, all laughing and screaming – hillocks of raucous merriment amid the crowds. But it is a gaiety too cynical to be honest. It exists simply to prove to the Parisians that this is a day of carnival.

There is a moral in those blowzy conveyances, a sort of protocol. One senses a mysterious affinity between public men and public women. How many infamous plots have been hatched beneath the semblance of gaiety, how often has prostitution served the purposes of espionage? It is sad that the crowds should be amused by what should outrage them, these manifestations of riotous vulgarity; but what is to be done? The insult to the public is exonerated by the public's laughter. The laughter of everyman is the accomplice of universal degradation. The populace, like all tyrants, must have its buffoons. Paris is the great, mad town whenever she is not the sublime city, and carnival is a part of politics. Paris, let us admit it, is very ready to be amused by what is ignoble. All she asks of her masters is – make squalor pleasant to look at. Rome was the same. She loved Nero, that monstrous exhibitionist.

As it happened, one of these bevies of masked men and women, in a big wagon, stopped on the left-hand side of the street at the moment when the wedding party stopped on the right.

'Hallo,' said one of the masks. 'A wedding.'

'A sham one,' said another. 'We're the real celebration.'

Too far off to converse with the wedding party, and in any case afraid of getting into trouble with the police, the two masks looked elsewhere. A moment later they and their companions had plenty to occupy them. The crowd began to howl and shower insults on them, and not all the extensive vocabulary they had picked up in the market-place could drown that lusty voice. There was a lurid exchange of abuse. Meanwhile two other members of the same company, one a Spaniard with an exaggerated nose and enormous black moustache, and the other a skinny young girl in a wolf-mask, had noticed the wedding party and were talking together amid the hubbub. It was a cold day, and the open cart was soaked with rain.

The girl in her low-necked dress coughed and shivered as she spoke. Their dialogue was as follows, the man speaking first:

'Hey!'

'Well?'

'See that old man?'

'Which?'

'The one in the first wedding coach, on our side.'

'The one with his arm in a sling?'

'That's him.'

'Well?'

'I'm sure I know him.'

'You do?'

'I'll take my oath on it. Can you see the bride if you stretch?'

'No.'

'Or the groom?'

'There isn't one, not in that carriage, unless it's the old man.'

'Try to see the bride. Crane your neck a bit more.'

'I still can't.'

'Well, never mind. There's something about that chap – I'll swear I've seen him somewhere.'

'And so what?'

'I dunno. Sometimes it comes in handy.'

'A fat lot I care.'

'I'll swear I know him.'

'Anything you say.'

'What the devil's he doing at a wedding?'

'Search me.'

'And where do that lot come from?'

'How do I know?'

'Well, look – there's something you can do.'

'What's that?'

'Get off the cart and follow them.'

'What for?'

'To find out who they are and where they're going. Hurry up, my girl. You're young.'

'I don't want to.'

'Why not?'

'I'm watched. I owe my day off to the cops. If I get off the cart they'll pick me up next instant. You know they will.'

'That's true. It's a nuisance. I'm interested in that fellow.'

'Anyone 'ud think you were a girl.'

'He's in the first carriage, the bride's carriage.'

'So?'

'That means he's the father.'

'There's other fathers.'

'Now listen – I can scarcely go anywhere unless I'm masked. That's all right for today, but there won't be any masks tomorrow. I'll have to keep under cover or I'm liable to be picked up. But you're free.'

'Not all that much.'

'More than I am, anyway. So you've got to try and find out where that wedding party was going, and who the people are and where they live.'

'Sounds easy, doesn't it? A wedding party going somewhere or other on *Mardi gras*. Like looking for a needle in a haystack!'

'All the same, you've got to try, Azelma, do you hear?'

Then the two lines resumed their progress in opposite directions, and the wagon of masks lost sight of the wedding party.

II

Jean Valjean still has his arm in a sling

To how many of us is it given to realize our dream? Perhaps the matter is decided by elections in Heaven, with the angels voting and all of us candidates. Cosette and Marius had been elected. Cosette at the church and the mairie was glowingly and dazzingly pretty. She had been dressed by Toussaint, with the help of Nicolette, in a dress of Binche lace with a white taffeta under-skirt, a veil of English stitching, a necklace of small pearls, and a crown of orange blossom, and she was dazzling in this whiteness, she might have been a virgin in process of being transformed into a goddess.

Marius's beautiful hair was lustrous and scented, but here and there beneath its thick locks the scars left by the wounds he had received on the barricade were still to be discerned.

Monsieur Gillenormand, proudly erect, his costume and his manners more than ever depicting the elegance of the days of Barras, escorted Cosette, replacing Jean Valjean, who could not give her his arm since he still wore it in a sling. Clad in black, he followed them smiling.

'Monsieur Fauchelevent,' the old man said to him, 'this is a great day. I decree happiness, the end of all grief and affliction. Nothing bad may be allowed to show itself. That in fact there are unhappy people is a disgrace to the blue of the sky. Evil does not come to the man who is good at heart. All human miseries have their capital and seat of government in Hell itself – in other words, those infernal Tuileries. But I'm not going to make a speech. I no longer have political opinions. All I want is for everyone to be rich and happy.'

When at length all the ceremonies were completed, at the mairie and at the church, when all the documents were signed, rings exchanged, and, hand-in-hand, he in black and she in white, the wedded couple emerged through the church doors between rows of admiring spectators to return to the carriage, Cosette could scarcely believe that it was all true. She looked at Marius, at the people, and at the sky, half afraid of waking out of a dream, and this look of doubtful amazement lent her an added charm. They returned home with Marius and Cosette seated side by side, while Monsieur Gillenormand and Jean Valjean sat facing them, Aunt Gillenormand being relegated to the second carriage. 'My children,' said the old gentleman, 'you are now a baron and baroness with thirty thousand francs a year.' And Cosette, leaning towards Marius, whispered angelically: 'It's true. My name is now the same as yours. I'm Madame You.'

Both were radiant in that supreme and unrepeatable moment, the union of youth and happiness. Between them they were less than forty years of age. It was the sublimation of marriage, and the two young creatures were like lilies. Cosette saw Marius in a haze of glory, and Marius saw Cosette as though on an altar; and somehow, behind these two visions, a mist for Cosette, a flame for Marius, there was the ideal and the real, the place of kisses and dreams, the marriage-bed.

All the tribulations they had gone through, the griefs, despairs and sleepless nights, all these added to the enchantment of the hour that was approaching, past sorrow was an embellishment of rapture, unhappiness an added glow to present delight. They were two hearts caught in the same spell, tinged with carnality in the case of Marius, of modest apprehension in the case of Cosette. 'We shall see our garden in the Rue Plumet again,' she whispered, while the fold of her dress flowed over his knee.

They returned to their house in the Rue des Filles-du-Calvaire, and triumphantly mounted the stairs up which Marius's unconscious form has been carried, months before. The poor, gathered at the doorway, received alms and blessed them. There were flowers everywhere, as many as there had been in the church; after the incense came the roses. They seemed to hear voices singing and felt Heaven in their hearts. And suddenly the clock struck. Marius gazed at Cosette's sweet bare arms and at the pink objects vaguely to be discerned beneath the lace of her corsage, and Cosette, seeing his eyes upon her, blushed a deep red.

Many old friends of the Gillenormand family had been invited, and they made much of Cosette, addressing her as Madame la Baronne. Théodule Gillenormand, now promoted captain, had come from Chartres, where he was stationed, to attend his cousin Pontmercy's wedding. Cosette did not recognize him; nor did he, the man of many light loves, recognize her. 'How right I was to take no notice of that tale of a cavalry officer,' old Monsieur Gillenormand murmured to himself. He pointed the joy of the occasion with a flow of maxims and aphorisms, in which Cosette supported him, spreading love and kindness as though it were a perfume around her. She talked with a particular tenderness to Jean Valjean, using inflections that recalled the innocent chatter of her childhood.

A banquet had been spread in the dining-room. Bright light is essential to great occasions. Dimness is unthinkable. It may be night outside, but there must be no shadows within. The dining-room was a scene of utmost gaiety. Hanging over the centre of the richly adorned table was a great Venetian chandelier with little birds of every colour perched among its candles. There were triple mirrors on the walls, and glass and crystal, porcelain, gold and silver shone and glittered. Gaps between the candelabra were filled with bouquets, so that wherever there was a candle there was a flower. In the ante-chamber three violins and a flute were softly playing Haydn quartets.

Jean Valjean was seated in a corner of the room by the open door, which almost hid him from sight. Just before they took their places at the table Cosette came over to him, and making a slow curtsey asked with a half-teasing tenderness:

'Dear Father, are you happy?'

'Yes,' he said. 'I'm happy.'

'Then why aren't you smiling?'

Valjean obediently smiled, and a moment later Basque announced that dinner was served.

The company proceeded into the dining-room led by Monsieur Gillenormand with Cosette on his arm and seated themselves in their pre-arranged places. There were armchairs on either side of the bride, one for the old gentleman and the other for Jean Valjean. But when they looked round for 'Monsieur Fauchelevent' they found that he was not there. Monsieur Gillenormand asked Basque if he knew what had become of him.

'Monsieur Fauchelevent requested me to say, monsieur, that his hand was paining him,' said Basque. 'He has therefore asked to be excused. He has gone out, but will be back tomorrow morning.'

This cast something of a chill upon the gathering, but fortunately Monsieur Gillenormand had high spirits enough for two. He said that Monsieur Fauchelevent had been quite right to go to bed early if he was in pain, slight though the injury was. This put everyone at their ease. Besides, what difference could a small patch of shadow make in such a wealth of light? Cosette and Marius were in one of those moments of bliss when they could be aware of nothing but happiness. And Monsieur Gillenormand had an idea.

'Since Monsieur Fauchelevent will not be with us,' he said, 'Marius shall occupy his chair. It should by rights go to his aunt, but I know she will not begrudge it him. Come and sit beside Cosette, Marius.'

Marius did as he was bidden, to the general applause; and so it fell out that Cosette, who had been momentarily distressed by Jean Valjean's absence, was made happy. She would not have regretted the absence of God himself, had Marius been there to take his place; and she laid her small, satin-clad foot upon his.

With the dessert Monsieur rose to his feet holding a glass of champagne (half-filled to allow for the shakiness of his ninety-two-year-old hand) and proposed the health of the young couple.

'You are obliged to listen to two sermons,' he said. 'The curé this morning and this evening the old grandfather. I will give you a piece of advice – adore one another. Be happy. There are no wiser creatures in all creation than the turtle-doves. The philosophers say, "Be moderate in your pleasures," but I say, enjoy them to the full. Go mad with pleasure and let the philosophers stuff their dull counsels down their throats. Can there be too much perfume in the world, too many rosebuds or green leaves or singing nightingales or breathless dawns? Can two people charm and delight one another too much, be too happy, too much alive? Moderate your pleasures – what nonsense it is! Down with the philosophers! Rapture is the true wisdom. Are we happy because we are good, or good because we are happy? I don't know. Life is made up of such riddles. What matters is to be happy without pretence; to be a blind worshipper of the sun. For what is the sun if not love, and what is love if not a woman! It is woman who is all-powerful. Is not Marius, that young demagogue, enslaved by the tyranny of that little Cosette? And gladly so! Woman! You may talk of Robespierre, but it is the woman who rules. That is the only kind of royalty I recognize. What was Adam except Eve's kingdom? What revolution did she need? Think of all the sceptres there have been – the royal sceptre surmounted by a fleur-de-lis, the imperial sceptre surmounted by a globe, Charlemagne's sceptre which was of iron, and that of Louis le Grand which was gold – and the Revolution took them between thumb and forefingers and squashed them flat! So much for sceptres; but show me a revolution against a little scented handkerchief – I should like to see that! What makes it so powerful when it is nothing but a scrap of material? Ah, well, we who belonged to the eighteenth century were just as foolish as you are. You needn't think you have changed the world just because you have discovered a cure for cholera and invented a dance called the cachucha. We still have to love women and there's no getting away from it. Love, women and kisses are a magic circle from which I defy you to escape, and for my part I wish I could get back into it. How many of you have seen the rising of the planet Venus, the great courtesan of the skies? A man can be in a fury, but when she appears he has to smile. We are all the same, we have our rages, but when a woman appears on the scene we're on our knees. Six months ago Marius was fighting, and today he has got married. It is well done, and he and Cosette are both right. You must live boldly each for the other, cling and caress, frantic only because you cannot do more. To love and be loved, that is the miracle of youth. Don't think I'm just inventing it. I too have had my dreams and sighs; I too have moonlight in my soul. Love is a child six thousand years old who should be wearing a long white beard. Compared with Cupid, Methuselah is the merest urchin. For sixty centuries men and women have settled their affairs by loving one another. The devil, who is cunning, elected to hate man; but man, more cunning still, chose to love woman, and in this way did more good than all the harm done by the devil. My children, love is an old invention but it is one that is always new. Make the most of it. You must be so close that when you are together you lack nothing, Cosette the sun for Marius and Marius the whole world for Cosette. Fine weather, for Cosette, must be her husband's smiles, and for Marius the rain should be his wife's tears. You have drawn the winning number in the lottery and you must treasure it. Each must be a religion to the other. We all have our own way of worshipping God, but the best of all, Heaven knows, is to love one's wife. Every lover is orthodox. The oath sworn by Henri IV puts sanctity somewhere between riot and drunkenness. I've no use for that oath, which makes no mention of women. They tell me I'm old, but it's wonderful how young I feel. I should like to hear the piping in the woods. Young folk who continue to be both beautiful and happy, these delight me. I would gladly marry again if anyone would have me. It is impossible to suppose that God made us for any other purpose than to enact all the fantasies and delights of love. That is what we believed when I was young, and how enchanting, how tender and gracious, the women were! I made my conquests! And so I say to you, love one another. If it weren't for love-making I don't know what use the spring would be, and for my part I would ask God to take away all the lovely things he has made for us – flowers and birds and pretty girls. My dear children, accept an old man's blessing!'

It was a gay, delightful evening, the tone being set by their host, who was so nearly a hundred years old. There was a little dancing and a great deal of laughter and happy commotion. But suddenly a silence fell. The newly married pair had disappeared. Shortly after midnight Monsieur Gillenormand's house became a temple.

And here we must pause. At the door of every bridal bedchamber an angel stands, smiling, with a finger to his lips.

There should be a radiance about houses such as this, the rapture they contain should somehow escape through their stones. Love is the sublime melting-pot in which man and woman are fused together, and this melting of two souls into one must stir the outer darkness. The lover is a priest, the ravished virgin a consenting, trembling sacrifice. If it were given to us to peer into a higher world, should we not see beneficent forms clustered over that glowing house; and would not the lovers, thinking themselves alone in their ecstasies, hear the flutter of wings? That small and secret bedchamber is wide open to Heaven. When two mouths, consecrated by love, draw close together in the act of creation it is impossible that this ineffable kiss does not cause a tremor among the stars.

This is the true felicity and there is no joy outside the ecstasy of love. The rest is tears. To love or to have loved is all-sufficing. We must not ask for more. No other pearl is to be found in the shadowed folds of life. To love is an accomplishment.

III

Inseparable

What had become of Jean Valjean?

After he had smiled at Cosette's gentle request, he had risen unnoticed and gone into the room next door, the same room into which, ragged and caked with mud, he had eight months earlier carried Monsieur Gillenormand's grandson. Its ancient woodwork was now decked with flowers, and the musicians were seated on the settee on which Marius had been laid. Basque was there, placing small bouquets on the dinner-plates. Valjean told him the reason for his departure and left.

The dining-room windows looked out on to the street, and Jean Valjean stood beneath them for a few moments listening to the sounds of the party behind him, the predominating voice of Monsieur Gillenormand, the violins, the laughter, the rattle of crockery and, distinguishable amid it all, the gentle happy voice of Cosette. Then he left the Rue des Filles-du-Calvaire and returned to the Rue de l'Homme-Armé.

He went by way of the Rue Saint-Louis and the Blancs-Manteaux, which, though rather longer, was the route he was accustomed to follow when walking between the two houses, to avoid the crowds and muddiness of the Rue Vieille-du-Temple. It was the way he had always come with Cosette, so he could take no other.

He arrived home, lit his candle, and went upstairs. The apartment was empty. Toussaint was not there and the sound of his footsteps was louder than usual. All the cupboards were empty and Cosette's bed was unmade, the pillow, without its lacy pillowslip, lying on a pile of folded blankets. All the feminine knick-knacks that had been Cosette's had been taken away, nothing remained in the room but its heavy furniture and bare walls. Toussaint's bed was also stripped. The only one that could be slept in was his own. He wandered from one room to another, shutting the cupboard doors. Then he went back to his own bedroom and put his candle on the table. He had taken his arm out of its sling and was using it as though it caused him no discomfort.

He went towards his bed, and as he did so his eye rested – was it by chance or was it intentional? – on the little black box that Cosette had called his 'inseparable'. When they had moved into the Rue de l'Homme-Armé he had placed it on a foot-stool beside his bed. He now got a key out of his pocket and opened it.

Slowly he took out the clothes in which Cosette had left Montfermeil, ten years before. First the little black dress, then the black scarf, then the stout child's shoes which Cosette could still have worn, so small were her feet, then the thick fustian camisole, the woollen petticoat, and, still bearing the impress of a small leg, two stockings scarcely longer than his hand. Everything was black, and it was he who had brought them when he took her from Montfermeil. He laid the garments on the bed, recalling that occasion. It had been a very cold December, and she had been shivering in rags, her small feet red from the clogs she wore. Her mother in her grave must have been happy to know that her daughter was in mourning, and that she was decently and warmly clad. He thought of those Montfermeil woods, through which they had walked together, the leafless trees, the absence of birds, the sunless sky; but still it had been delightful. He spread the garments on the bed and stood looking at them. She had been so little, carrying that big doll and with her golden louis in her apron pocket. She had laughed as they walked hand-in-hand, and he had become all the world to her.

Then the ageing white head sank forward, the stoical heart gave way and his face was buried in Cosette's garments. Anyone passing on the stairs at that moment would have heard the sound of dreadful sobbing.

IV

Undying faith

The fearful struggle, of which we have recorded more than one phase, had begun again. Jacob's battle with the angel lasted only one night; but how often had Jean Valjean been darkly joined in mortal conflict with his own conscience! A desperate struggle: his foot slipping at moments and, at others, the ground seeming to give way beneath his feet. How stubbornly his conscience had fought against him! How often had inexorable truth borne down like a great weight on his breast. How often, in that implacable light, had he begged for mercy – the light that the bishop had lit for him. How often had his rebellious spirit groaned beneath the knowledge of his plain duty. Opposition to God himself: self-inflicted wounds of whose bleeding he alone was conscious. Until finally, shaken, he had risen from despair above himself to say, 'Now it is settled. I may go in peace.' A melancholy peace!

But this night Valjean knew that the struggle had reached its climax. An agonizing question presented itself. Predestination does not always offer a straight road to the predestined; there are many twists and turns, forks and crossroads. Valjean had come to the most perilous of these. He had reached the ultimate intersection between good and evil and he saw it clearly. As had happened before, at critical moments of his life, two roads lay open to him, one seductive and the other terrifying. Which was he to take?

The road that appalled him was the one indicated by that mysterious finger that we always see when we try to peer into the darkness. Once more he was faced by the choice between the terrible haven and the alluring trap.

Is it true, then, that though the soul may be cured, destiny may not? Incurable destiny – how terrible a thing!

The question was this: how was he, Jean Valjean, to ensure the continued happiness of Cosette and Marius? It was he who had brought about that happiness, he who had forged it, and he could contemplate it with something of the satisfaction of the armourer who has worked well. They had each other, Marius and Cosette, and they were wealthy into the bargain; and all this was his doing.

But what was he now to do with it, this happiness that he had brought about? Should he take advantage of it, treat it as though it belonged to him? Cosette was another man's, but he still retained as much of her as he could ever possess. Could he not continue to be almost her father, respected as he had always been, able when he chose to enter her house? And could he, without saying a word, bring his past into that future, seat himself by that fireside as though it were his right? Could he greet them smiling with his tragic hands, and cross that innocent threshold casting behind him the infamous shadow of the law? Could he still keep silent?

One must have grown accustomed to the harsher face of destiny to be able to confront facts in all their hideous nakedness. Good and evil are behind the vigorous question-mark: 'Well,' demands the sphinx, 'what are you going to do?' Valjean, from long habit, looked it steadily in the eye. Pitilessly he considered the facts in all their aspects. Cosette, that exquisite creature, was his. lifeline. Was he to cling to it or let it go? If he clung to it, then he was safe; he could go on living. But if he let it go ... Then, the abyss.

Thus did he wrestle with himself, torn between conviction and desire. It was a relief to him that he had been able to weep. This may have calmed him, although the beginning had been fearful, a tempest fiercer than the one that had once driven him to Arras. But now he was brought to a stop. It is terrible, in the battle *à outrance* between self-will and duty, when we seek in vain for a way out, to find ourselves caught with our back to the wall. But there is no end to conscience, for this is God himself. It is a bottomless well into which one may fling the labour of a lifetime, liberty and country, peace of mind and happiness; but in the end one has to fling in one's heart. In the shades of the ancient hells there are pits like that.

Is it not permissible in the end to refuse? Cannot an endless bond be too much for human strength? Who would blame Sisyphus or Jean Valjean if at the last they said, 'That is enough.' The movement of matter is delimited by the forces to which it is subjected; may there not be a similar limitation on the movement of the soul? If perpetual motion is impossible, must we then insist upon perpetual devotion? The first step is nothing; it is the last which is difficult. Compared with Cosette's marriage and all that would ensue from it, what was the Champmathieu affair? What was the return to prison compared with entry into limbo? The first step downward may be obscured, but the second is pitch black. Why not this time look the other way?

Martyrdom is a sublimation, but a sublimation that corrodes. It is a torment that sanctifies. One may endure it at first, the pincers, the red-hot iron, but must not the tortured flesh give way in the end?

In the calm of exhaustion, Jean Valjean considered the two alternatives, the balance between light and dark. Was he to inflict his prison record on those two happy children, or accept the loss of his own soul? Was Cosette to be sacrificed, or himself?

His meditation lasted through the night. He remained until daylight in the same posture, seated and bent double on the bed, with fists clenched and arms out-flung like those of a man cut down from the cross. He was motionless as a corpse, while the thoughts flew and tumbled in his mind. Until suddenly he shuddered convulsively and pressed Cosette's garments to his lips. Only then did one see that he was alive.

One. Who was that one, when there was no one else there?

The One who is present in the shadows.

BOOK SEVEN

THE BITTER CUP

I

The seventh circle and the eighth heaven

THE DAY after a wedding is one of solitude. We respect the privacy of the newly-weds and perhaps their late arising. The hubbub of visits and congratulations does not begin until later. It was a little after midday when Basque, busily 'doing the antechamber', heard a tap on the door. There had been no ring, which showed discretion on that particular day. Basque opened and found Monsieur Fauche-levent. He showed him into the salon, which was still in a state of disorder.

'We're up late this morning, Monsieur,' said Basque.

'Is your master up?' asked Jean Valjean.

'How's monsieur's arm?' asked Basque.

'It's better. Is your master up?'

'Which master, the old or the new?'

'Monsieur Pontmercy.'

'Ah, Monsieur le Baron,' said Basque.

Titles are important to servants, upon whom something of their lustre is shed. Marius, as we know, was a militant republican and had fought to prove it; but despite himself he was a baron. The matter had caused something of a revolution in the family. It was now Monsieur Gillenormand who insisted upon the title and Marius who was disposed to ignore it; but since his father had written, 'My son will bear my title,' he obeyed. And then Cosette, in whom the woman was beginning to show, was delighted to be Madame la Baronne.

'I'll go and see,' said Basque. 'I'll tell him you're here.'

'No. Don't tell him that it's me. Tell him it is someone who wishes to speak to him in private, but don't mention my name.'

'Ah,' said Basque.

'I want to surprise him.'

'Ah,' said Basque again, as though this second 'ah' explained the first.

He went out, leaving Valjean alone.

The salon, as we have said, was in great disorder, almost as though anyone who happened to be listening could still have heard the echoes of last night's party. Flowers had fallen on the parquet floor, and burnt-out candles had draped the crystal lustre with stalactites of wax. Nothing was in its proper place. Three or four armchairs, grouped together in a corner, seemed to be still carrying on a conversation. But it was a gay disorder, for this had been a happy party. The sun had replaced the candles and shone bravely into the room.

Some minutes elapsed during which Jean Valjean remained motionless where Basque had left him. He was very pale. His eyes were so sunken with sleeplessness that they had almost disappeared, and his black coat had the tired creases of a garment that has been worn all night. He stood looking down at the glow of light cast by the sunshine on the floor.

The sound of the door opening caused him to look up. Marius entered, head up and face aglow with triumphant happiness. He, too, had not slept all night.

'Why, it's you, father!' he exclaimed. 'That silly fellow Basque chose to make a mystery of it. But you're early. It's only half past twelve and Cosette is still asleep.'

His use of the word 'father' was most felicitous. As we know, there had always been a certain constraint between them, ice to be broken or melted. Such was Marius's state of rapture that this no longer existed: 'Monsieur Fauchelevent' was father to him as he was to Cosette. He went on, the words pouring out of him:

'I'm so delighted to see you. We missed you so much last night. Is your hand better?' He did not wait for a reply. 'We've talked so much about you, Cosette and I. She's so fond of you. You haven't forgotten, I hope, that you have a room here. We don't want any more of the Rue de l'Homme-Armé. That ugly, squalid little street— how in the world did you ever come to live in it? But now you're coming here, and today, what's more, or you'll be in trouble with Cosette. I warn you, she means to have you here if she has to pull you by the nose! You've seen your room, it's very near our own, and it looks out over the garden. It's all in perfect order. Cosette put a big old velvet-upholstered armchair by the bedside, to open its arms to you, as she said. Every spring a nightingale nests in the acacias, you'll be hearing it in a couple of months. You'll have its nest on one side of you and ours on the other. It will sing in the night-time and Cosette will chatter in the daytime. She'll arrange your books for you and all your belongings. I understand there's a little valise that you particularly value, and I've thought of a special place for it. My grandfather has taken a great liking to you, and if you play whist that will make it perfect. And of course you'll take Cosette for walks when I'm working, just as you used to do, in the Luxembourg. We're absolutely determined to be very happy, and you're part of it, father, do you understand? Talking of which, you'll be lunching with us today?'

'Monsieur,' said Jean Valjean, 'I have something to tell you. I am an ex-convict.'

There are sounds that the mind cannot absorb although they are registered by the ear. Those words 'I am an ex-convict', emerging from the lips of Monsieur Fauchelevent and entering the ear of Marius, went beyond the limit. He knew that something had been said, but he could not grasp what it was. He stood open-mouthed.

And now he perceived what in his blissful state he had not noticed, that the man addressing him was in very bad shape. He was terribly pale.

Valjean took his arm out of the sling which still supported it, removed the bandage, and held his hand out to Marius.

'There's nothing wrong with my thumb,' he said. 'There never has been.' He went on: 'It was right that I should not attend your wedding party. I have kept in the background as much as possible. I invented this injury in order to avoid signing the marriage deeds, which might have nullified them.'

Marius stammered: 'But what does it mean?'

'It means,' said Valjean, 'that I have been in the galleys. I was imprisoned for nineteen years, first for theft and later as a recidivist. I am at present breaking parole.'

Marius might recoil in horror, might refuse to believe, but in the end he was forced to accept it. Indeed, as commonly happens, he went further. He shuddered as an appalling thought occurred to him.

'You must tell me everything – everything!' he cried. 'You are really Cosette's father!' And in horror he took a step backwards.

Jean Valjean raised his head with a gesture of such dignity that he seemed to grow in stature.

'In this you must believe me,' he said, 'although the sworn oaths of such as I are not accepted in any court of law. I swear to you before God, Monsieur Pontmercy, that I am not Cosette's father or in any way related to her. My name is not Fauchelevent but Jean Valjean. I am a peasant from Faverolles, where once I earned my living as a tree-pruner. You may be sure of that.'

'But what proof –?' stammered Marius.

'My word is the proof.'

Marius looked at him. He was melancholy but calm, with a kind of stony sincerity from which no lie could emerge. The truth was apparent in his very coldness.

'I believe you,' said Marius.

Jean Valjean bowed his head in acknowledgement.

'So what am I to Cosette?' he went on. 'Someone who came upon her quite by chance. Ten years ago I did not know that she existed. I love her certainly, as who would not? When one is growing old one has a fatherly feeling for all small children. You may perhaps be prepared to believe that I have something that can be called a heart. She was an orphan and she needed me. That is how I came to love her. Children are so defenceless that any man, even a man like me, may want to protect them. That is what I did for Cosette. Whether an act so trifling can be termed a good deed I do not know; but if it is, then let it be said that I did it. Let it be set down in extenuation. Now she has gone out of my life; our roads run in different directions. Besides, there is nothing more that I can do for her. She is Madame Pontmercy. Her life has changed, and she has gained by the change. As for the six hundred thousand francs, I will anticipate your question. It was a sum held for her in trust. As to how it came into my hands, that is quite unimportant. I have fulfilled my trust, and nothing more can be required of me. And I have concluded the matter by telling you my name. I have done so for my own sake, because I wanted you to know who I am.'

Jean Valjean looked steadily at Marius.

As for Marius, his thoughts were tumultuous and incoherent. We all have moments of bewilderment in which our wits seem to desert us; we say the first thing that comes into our head, although it is not the right thing. There are sudden revelations that cannot be endured, inducing a state of intoxication like that caused by a draught of some insidious wine. Marius was so stupefied that he talked almost as though Valjean had done him a deliberate injury.

'Why have you told me all this? Nobody forced you to. You could have kept it to yourself. You aren't being pursued, are you? No one has denounced you. You must have some reason of your own for blurting it out like this. Why have you done so? There must be more – something that you haven't told me. I want to know what it is.'

'My reason . . .' said Jean Valjean, in a voice so low that he might have been talking to himself. 'Why should an ex-convict proclaim himself to be an ex-convict? Well, it's a strange reason – a matter of honesty. There is a bond in my heart that cannot be broken, and such bonds become stronger as one grows older. Whatever may happen in one's life, they still hold. If I could have broken that bond, dishonoured it, all would have been well. I could simply have gone away. Coaches leave from the Rue Bouloi and you are happy, there was nothing to keep me. I tried to tear out that bond, but I could not do it without tearing out my heart as well. I thought to myself, since I cannot live anywhere else, I must stay here. You will think me a fool, and rightly. Why not just stay and say nothing? You have offered me a home. Cosette – but I should now call her Madame Pontmercy – loves me. Your grandfather would welcome me. We could live together as a happy, united family.'

But as he spoke that last word Jean Valjean's expression changed. He stood scowling at the floor as though he would like to kick a hole in it, and there was a new ring in his voice.

'A family! But I belong to no family, least of all yours. I am sundered from all mankind. There are moments when I wonder whether I ever had a father and mother. Everything ended for me with that child's marriage. She is happy with the man she loves, a worthy old man to watch over her, a comfortable home, servants, everything that makes for happiness; but I said to myself, "That is not for me." I might have lied and deceived you all by continuing to be "Monsieur Fauchelevent". I did it where she was concerned; but now it is a matter of my own conscience and I can do it no longer. That is my answer to you when you ask me why I have felt compelled to speak. Conscience is a strange thing. It would have been so easy to say nothing. I spent the whole night trying to persuade myself to do so. I did my utmost. I gave myself excellent reasons. But it was no use. I could not break that bond in my heart or silence the voice that speaks to me when I am alone. That is why I have come here to confess everything to you, or nearly everything. There is no point in telling you things that only concern myself. I have told you what matters, disclosed my secret to you, and, believe me, it was not easy to do. I had to wrestle with myself all night. You may believe me when I say that in concealing my real name I was harming no one. It was Fauchelevent himself who gave it me, in return for a service I had done him. I could have been very happy in the home you have offered me, keeping to my own corner, disturbing no one, content to be under the same roof as Cosette. To continue to be Monsieur Fauchelevent would have settled everything – except my conscience. No matter how great the happiness around me, my soul would have been in darkness. The circumstances of happiness are not enough, there must also be peace of mind. I should have been a figure of deceit, a shadow in your sunshine, sitting at your table with the thought that if you knew who and what I really was you would turn me out – the very servants would have exclaimed in horror! When we were alone together, your grandfather, you two children and myself, talking unconstrainedly, all seeming at our ease, one of us would have been a stranger, a dead man battening on the living; and condemned to this for the rest of his life! Does it not make you shudder? I should have been not only the most desolate of men but the most infamous, living the same lie day after day. Cheating you day after day, my beloved, trusting children! It is not so easy to keep silent when the silence is a lie. I should never have ceased to be sickened by my own treachery and cowardice. My "good morning" would have been a lie, and my "good night". I should have slept with the lie, eaten with it, returned Cosette's angelic smile with a grimace of the damned. And all for what? To be happy! But what right have I to happiness? I tell you, monsieur, I am an outcast from life.'

Jean Valjean paused. Marius had been listening without attempting to interrupt, for there are times when interruption is impossible. Valjean again lowered his voice, but now it contained a harsh note.

'You may ask why I should tell you this, if I have not been exposed and am not in any danger of pursuit. But I *have* been exposed, I *am* pursued – by myself! That is a pursuer that does not readily let go.' He gripped his coat collar and thrust it out towards Marius. 'Look at that fist,' he said. 'Don't you think it has a firm grip on that collar? That is what conscience is like. If you want to be happy you must have no sense of duty, because a sense of duty is implacable. To have it is to be punished, but it is also to be rewarded, for it thrusts you into a hell in which you feel the presence of God at your side. Your heart may be broken, but you are at peace with yourself.'

Then again his voice changed, containing a note of poignancy.

'This is not a matter of common sense, Monsieur Pontmercy. I am an honourable man. In debasing myself in your eyes I am raising myself in my own. Yes, an honourable man; but I should not be one if, through my fault, you continued to esteem me. That is the cross I bear, that any esteem I may win is falsely won; it is a thought that humiliates and shames me, that I can only win the respect of others at the cost of despising myself. So I have to take a stand. I am a felon acting according to his conscience. It may be a contradiction in terms, but what else can I do? I made a pact with myself and I am holding to it. There are chances that create duties. So many things, Monsieur Pontmercy, have happened to me in my life.'

Once again Jean Valjean paused. Then he resumed talking with an effort, as though the words left a bitter taste in his mouth.

'When a man is under a shadow of this kind he has no more right to inflict it upon others without their knowledge than he has to infect them with the plague. To draw near to the healthy, to touch them with hands that are secretly contagious, that is a shameful thing. Fauchelevent may have lent me his name, but I have no right to use it. A name is an identity. Although I was born a peasant, monsieur, I have done a little reading and thinking in my time; I have learnt the value of things. As you see, I can express myself fluently. I have done something to educate myself. To make use of a borrowed name is an act of dishonesty, as much a theft as to steal a purse or a watch. I cannot cheat decent people in that way – never, never, never! Better to suffer the tortures of the damned! And that is why I have told you all this.' He sighed and added a last word: 'Once I stole a loaf of bread to stay alive; but now I cannot steal a name in order to go on living.'

'Go on living!' cried Marius. 'Surely you don't need the name simply for that.'

'I know what it means to me,' said Valjean and nodded his head several times.

For a time there was silence. Both men were occupied with their own thoughts. Marius was seated by a table with his chin resting on his hand. Valjean had been pacing up and down. He stopped in front of a mirror and stood motionless, staring into it but seeing nothing. Then, as though replying to some observations of his own, he said:

'For the present, at least, I have a sense of relief.'

He began once more to pace the room. Then, seeing Marius's eyes upon him, he said:

'I drag my leg a little as I walk. Now you know why ... I ask you to consider this, monsieur. Let us suppose that I had said nothing but had come to live with you as Monsieur Fauchelevent, to share your daily lives, to walk with Madame Pontmercy in the Tuileries and the Place Royale, to be accepted as one of yourselves and then one day, when we are talking and laughing together, a voice cries "Jean Valjean!" and the terrible hand of the police descends on my shoulder and strips the mask away! ... What do you think of that?'

Marius had nothing to say.

'Now you know why I could not keep silent. But no matter. Be happy, be Cosette's guardian angel, live in the sun and do not worry about how an outcast goes about his duty. You are facing a wretched man, monsieur.'

Marius walked slowly across the room, holding out his hand. But he had to reach for Valjean's hand, which made no response, and it was like grasping a hand of marble.

'My grandfather has friends,' he said. 'I will get you a reprieve.'

'There is no need,' said Valjean. 'The fact that I am presumed dead is enough.' Releasing his hand from Marius's clasp he added, with an implacable dignity: 'All that matters is that I should do my duty. The only reprieve I need is that of my own conscience.'

At this moment the door at the other end of the salon was half-opened and Cosette's head peeped round it. Her hair was charmingly disordered and her eyes still heavy with sleep. With a movement like that of a bird peeping out of its nest she looked first at her husband and then at Jean Valjean, and exclaimed laughingly,

'I'm sure you've been talking politics. How absurd of you, when you might have been talking to me!'

Valjean started. Marius stammered, 'Cosette ...' and then was silent. They might have been two guilty men.

Cosette continued to gaze at them, her eyes shining.

'I've caught you out,' she said. 'I heard a few words that father Fauchelevent spoke just as I opened the door. Something about conscience and duty. Well, that's politics and I won't have it. Nobody's allowed to talk politics the day after a wedding.'

'You're mistaken,' said Marius. 'We were talking business. We were discussing how to invest your six hundred thousand francs.'

'Is that all?' said Cosette. 'Then I'm going to join you.' And she walked determinedly into the room.

She was wearing a voluminous white peignoir with wide sleeves which covered her from neck to toes. She looked herself over in a long mirror and then exclaimed in sheer delight.

'Once upon a time there was a king and queen ... Oh, I'm so happy!' After which she curtseyed to Marius and Valjean. 'And now I'm going to sit down with you. Luncheon is in half an hour. You can talk about anything you like and I won't interrupt. I'm a very good girl. I know men have to talk.'

Marius took her by the arm and said affectionately:

'We were talking business.'

'By the way,' said Cosette, 'when I opened my window I saw a flock of starlings in the garden – real ones, not masks. This is Ash Wednesday, but the birds can't be expected to know that.'

'I said we were talking business, dearest. Figures and that sort of thing. It would only bore you.'

'What a nice necktie you're wearing, Marius. You're looking very smart. No, it wouldn't bore me.'

'I'm sure it would.'

'No. I shan't understand, but I shall enjoy listening. When it's two people you love the words don't matter, the sound of their voices is enough. I just want to be with you, and so I'm going to stay.'

'My beloved Cosette, it's really impossible.'

'Impossible!'

'Yes.'

'Well,' said Cosette. 'And I was going to tell you such interesting things. For instance, that grandfather is still asleep and Aunt Gillenormand has gone to Mass, and father Fauchelevent's chimney is smoking and Nicolette has sent for the sweep, and she and Toussaint have quarrelled already because she teased Toussaint about her stammer. You see, you don't know a thing about what's going on. Impossible, is it? Well, you be careful, or I'll say "impossible" to you, and then where would you be! Darling Marius, please, please let me stay with you.'

'My sweet Cosette, I do promise you that we have to be alone.'

'But surely I don't count as just anyone.'

Jean Valjean had not spoken a word. She turned to him.

'In the first place, father, I must ask you to come and kiss me. Why haven't you been standing up for me? What sort of a father are you? Can't you see how unhappy I am? My husband beats me. So come and kiss me at once.'

Valjean moved towards her and she turned back to Marius.

'As for you, I'm frowning at you.'

Valjean had drawn close, and she offered him her forehead to kiss. But then she took a step back.

'Father, how pale you are! Is your hand still hurting you?'

'No, it's better,' said Valjean.

'Well, did you sleep badly?'

'No.'

'Are you feeling unhappy?'

'No.'

'Then kiss me. If you're well and happy I shan't scold you.'

Again she offered him her forehead, and he touched it with his lips.

'But you must smile.'

He did so, a spectral smile.

'And now you must take my side against my husband.'

'Cosette . . .' said Marius.

'Be cross with him. Tell him I can stay here. You can talk in front of me. You must think I'm very silly. Business indeed, investing money and all that nonsense – as if it were so difficult to understand! Men make mysteries out of nothing. I want to stay. I'm looking particularly pretty this morning, aren't I, Marius?'

She turned to him with a look of enchanting archness and it was as though a spark passed between them. The presence of a third party was unimportant.

'I love you,' said Marius.

'I adore you.'

And they fell into each other's arms.

'And now,' said Cosette smoothing her peignoir with a little smile of triumph, 'I'm staying.'

'My dear, no,' said Marius beseechingly. 'There's something we have got to settle.'

'It's still no?'

'I assure you, it's impossible.'

'Well, of course, when you talk to me in that solemn voice . . . Very well then, I'll go. Father, you didn't support me. You and my husband are both tyrants. I shall complain to grandfather. And if you think I'm going to come back and talk sweet nothings to you, you're very much mistaken. I shall wait for you to come to me, and you'll find that you'll very soon get bored without me. So now I'm going.'

She went out; but a moment later the door opened again and her glowing face reappeared peeping round it. 'I'm very cross with you both!' she said.

The door closed once more and the darkness returned. It was as though a ray of light had lost its way and flashed through a world of shadow.

Marius made sure that the door was firmly closed.

'Poor Cosette!' he murmured. 'When she hears . . .'

At these words Jean Valjean trembled in every limb and gazed frantically at Marius.

'Of course that's true. You'll tell Cosette. I hadn't thought of that. One has the strength to bear some things but not others. Monsieur, I beseech you to promise me not to tell her. Surely if you yourself know, that is enough. I might have told her of my own accord; I might have told everyone. But Cosette – she doesn't even know what it means. A felon, a man condemned for life to forced labour, a man who has been in the galleys. She would be appalled! Once she saw a convict chain-gang pass . . . Oh, my God!'

He sank into an armchair and buried his face in his hands. He made no sound, but the heaving of his shoulders showed that he was weeping. He was overtaken by a sort of convulsion and lay back in the chair as though he were unable to breathe, with his arms hanging limply at his sides. Marius saw his tear-stained face and heard his murmur, 'I wish I were dead.'

'Don't worry,' said Marius. 'I'll keep your secret.'

He went on in a voice that was perhaps less sympathetic than it should have been, conscious as he was of the new situation that had arisen and the huge gulf that lay between them:

'I am bound to speak of the trust money that you have so honourably and faithfully handed over. It was an act of probity for which you deserve to be rewarded. You yourself shall name the sum, and you need not hesitate to make it a large one.'

'I thank you, monsieur,' Valjean said gently. He sat thinking, mechanically rubbing thumb and forefinger together. 'Nearly everything is now settled, except for one last thing.'

'What is that?'

Making a supreme effort, Valjean said in a scarcely audible voice:

'You are the master. Do you think, now you know everything, that I should not see Cosette again?'

'I think it would be better,' Marius said coldly.

'Then I will not do so,' said Valjean, and getting up, he went to the door.

But with the door half opened he stood for a moment motionless, then closed it again and came back to Marius. He was now no longer pale but deathly white, and instead of tears in his eyes there was a sort of tragic flame. His voice had become strangely calm.

'Monsieur,' he said, 'if you will permit me I would like to come and see her. Believe me, I greatly desire to do so. If I had not wanted to go on seeing Cosette I should not have told you what I have; I should simply have gone away. But because I so wanted to go on seeing her, I was bound in honour to tell you everything. You understand, I am sure. She has been my constant companion for nine years. We lived first in that tenement, then at the convent and then not far from the Luxembourg, where you saw her for the first time. Later we moved to the Invalides quarter, to a house in the Rue Plumet with a garden and a wrought-iron gate. My own dwelling was in the backyard, where I could hear her play the piano. That has been my life. We were never separated during those nine years and a few months. She was like my own child. To go away and never see or speak to her again – to have nothing left to live for – that would be very hard. I wouldn't come often or stay for long. We could meet in that little room on the ground floor. I would be quite willing to come by the servants' entrance, but that would give rise to talk, and so it might be better for me to come by the ordinary way. Monsieur, if I cannot see her from time to time there will be nothing left for me in life, but it will be for you to decide how often. And there is another thing. We have to be careful. If I never came at all, that too would give rise to talk. It occurs to me that I might come in the evening, when it's beginning to grow dark.'

'You shall come every evening,' said Marius.

'Monsieur, you are very kind,' said Jean Valjean.

They shook hands. Happiness escorted despair to the door, and so they parted.

Questions that may be contained in a revelation

Marius was distracted. The lack of contact he had always felt for the man he had supposed to be Cosette's father was now explained . . . He had felt instinctively that Monsieur Fauchelevent was concealing something, and now he knew what it was. To have learned this secret in the midst of his happiness was like discovering a scorpion in a dove's nest. Was his happiness and that of Cosette henceforth to depend upon that man, was he to be accepted as a part of their marriage bond? Was there nothing more to be done? Was he linked to an ex-convict? It was a thought to make even angels shudder.

But then, as always happens, he began to wonder whether he himself were not also at fault. Had he been lacking in perspicacity and prudence, had he deliberately closed his eyes? Perhaps there was some truth in this; perhaps he had plunged impulsively into the love-affair with Cosette without paying sufficient attention to the circumstances of her life. He could even admit (and it is by admissions of this kind that life teaches us self-knowledge) that there was a visionary side of his nature, a kind of imaginative haziness that pervaded his whole being. We have more than once drawn attention to this. He remembered how during those six or seven rapturous weeks in the Rue Plumet he had not once referred to the drama in the Gorbeau tenement in which the victim had behaved so strangely. Why had he never asked her about it, or mentioned the Thénardiers, particularly on the day when he had met Éponine? He could not account for this, but he took note of it. Looking back coolly, he recalled the ecstasy of their falling in love, the absolute fusion of their souls, and the vague instinct which had impelled him to put that episode – in which, after all, he had played no part – out of his mind. In any event those few weeks had sped by like a dream; there had been no time to do anything except love one another. And what would have happened if he had told Cosette that story, naming Thénardier? If he had learned the truth about Jean Valjean? Would it have changed his feeling for Cosette, caused him to love her less? Assuredly not. So he had nothing to regret, no reason to reproach himself, and all was well. He had blindly followed the path he would have followed with eyes wide open. Love, in blinding him, had led to him to Paradise.

But that paradise now had its infernal aspect. The slight coolness that had existed between himself and the man whom he now knew as Jean Valjean contained an element of horror; pity as well, it must be said, and also amazement. That thief, that recidivist convict, had handed over the sum of six hundred thousand francs, all of which he might have kept for himself. Also, although nothing had obliged him to do so, he had revealed his secret, accepting both the humiliation and the risk. A false name is a safeguard to a condemned man. He might have lived out his life with a respectable family, but he had not yielded to that temptation, simply, it seemed, from motives of conscience. Whatever else Jean Valjean might be, he was assuredly a man of principle. It seemed that at some time or other a mysterious transformation must have taken place in him, since when his life had been changed. Such rectitude was not to be found in base motives; it was an indication of greatness of soul. And his sincerity could not be doubted; the very suffering his avowal had caused him, the painful meticulousness with which he had omitted no detail, was sufficient evidence. And here a contradiction occurred to Marius. About Monsieur Fauchelevent there had always been a hint of defiance; but in Jean Valjean it was trustfulness.

In his consideration of Jean Valjean, weighing one thing with another, Marius sought to achieve a balance. But it was like peering through a tempest. The more he strove to see him as a whole, as it were to penetrate to his heart, the more he lost him only to find again a figure in a mist. On the one hand there was his honourable handing over of the trust money, on the other hand the extraordinary affair in the Jondrette attic. Why had he slipped away when the police arrived, instead of staying to testify against his persecutors? Here at least the answer was not far to seek. He was a man wanted by the police. But then again, how had he come to be on the barricade and what was he doing there? As Marius now recalled, he had taken no active part in the fighting. At this question a ghost arose to supply an answer, Javert. Marius perfectly remembered Javert's bound form being taken outside by Valjean, and soon afterwards the sound of a pistol shot. So presumably there had been a personal vendetta between the two men and Valjean had gone there from motives of revenge. The fact that he had been late in arriving suggested that he had only just discovered that Javert had been taken prisoner. The Corsican vendetta had penetrated to certain sectors of the underworld where it was accepted as law; and there were men, more or less reformed, who, although they would be scrupulous in the matter of theft, would not be deterred from an act of vengeance. There seemed to be no doubt that Valjean had killed Javert.

A final question remained to which there was no reply, one that tortured Marius's mind. How had this long association with Cosette been formed? What strange fatality had brought them together? Were there links forged in Heaven with which it pleased God to join angels and demons, and could crime and innocence be united in some mysterious prison of the underworld? How was it to be explained? By what extraordinary conjunction of circumstances had it come about, the lamb attached to the wolf – or, still more inexplicable, the wolf attached to the lamb? For the wolf truly loved the lamb and for nine years had been the centre of the lamb's existence. Cosette's childhood and adolescence, her growth to womanhood, had taken place in the shadow of that monstrous devotion. And this gave rise to endless riddles. Considering Jean Valjean, Marius felt his mind reel. What was one to make of that extraordinary man?

The two symbolic figures in the book of Genesis are eternal. Until some deeper comprehension throws a new light upon our understanding of these things, human society will always be divided into two types of men, Abel and Cain, the higher and the lower. But what was one to make of this gentle-hearted Cain, the ruffian who had watched over Cosette, cherished her, protected her, seen to her education? What was it but a figure of darkness whose sole care had been to safeguard the rising of a star. And that was Jean Valjean's secret. It was also the secret of God.

At this twofold secret Marius recoiled, although the one half in some sort reassured him as to the other. God forges his own instruments, using what tools he needs. He is not responsible to Man. Jean Valjean had formed Cosette; in some degree he had shaped her soul. This was undeniable. Very well then, the craftsman might be deplorable but the result was admirable. God worked his miracle in his own way. He had created the exquisite Cosette and for the purpose had employed Jean Valjean, a strange collaboration. Are we to reproach him for this? Is it the first time dung has helped the spring to give birth to a rose?

Marius himself supplied the answers to these questions and he told himself that the answers were good. They were all points which he had not ventured to put to Valjean. But what further explanation did he need? Cosette was his; he adored her and she was utterly unsullied. What else mattered? The personal affairs of Jean Valjean were no concern of his. He concentrated on the words the unhappy man had spoken: 'I am not related to Cosette. Ten years ago I did not know that she existed.' As he said, he had been no more than an episode in her life, and now his part in it was over. It was for Marius henceforth to take care of her. Cosette had found her lover and husband, and, growing wings, had soared upward into Heaven, leaving the ugly, earthbound Jean Valjean behind.

Wherever Marius's thoughts led him, he always returned with a kind of horror to Valjean. Whatever the extenuating circumstances might be, there could be no escaping the fact that the man was a felon, a creature, that is to say, rejected by society, below the lowest rung of the social ladder, the lowest and the least of men. The law deprived men of his kind of all rights; and Marius, democrat though he was, was in this matter implacably on the side of the law. He was not, let us say, wholly progressive, able to distinguish between what has been written by Man and what was written by God, between what is law and what is right. He had not fully weighed these matters and was not repelled by the idea of revenge. He thought it natural that certain infractions of the law should be subject to lifelong punishment, and he accepted total ostracism as a normal social procedure. Until then, that was as far as he had gone, although it was certain that he would go further, being by nature well-disposed and instinctively progressive. But in the present state of his thinking he was bound to find Jean Valjean repulsive. A felon! The very word was like the voice of judgement. His reaction was to turn away his head. 'Get thee behind me . . .'

As to the questions which Marius had not put to Valjean, although they had all occurred to him – the Jondrette attic, the barricade, Javert – who can say where they might have led? The truth is that he had been afraid to ask them. It can happen to any of us, in a critical moment, that we may ask a question and then try not to hear the reply; and this is particularly so when love enters into the matter. It is not always wise to probe too deeply, most especially when we ourselves are affected. Who could say what the consequences to Cosette would have been of the answers to those questions, what infernal light would have been shed on her innocent life? The purest natures may be tainted by such revelations. So, rightly or wrongly, Marius had been afraid. He knew too much already. Desolated, he clasped Cosette in his arms and closed his eyes to Jean Valjean.

But, this being his attitude, it was agonizing to him that Cosette would still be in contact with the man. And thus he came near to reproaching himself for not having pressed his questions, which might have led him to a more drastic decision. He had been too magnanimous – in a word, too weak. He began to think that he had been wrong. He should have turned Valjean out of the house. He blamed himself for the wave of sentiment that had momentarily carried him away against his better judgement. He was displeased with himself.

And now what was he to do? The thought of Valjean's visits was repugnant; but here he checked himself, not wishing to probe too deeply into his own thoughts. He had made a promise, or been led into making a promise, and a promise must be kept, even, and indeed especially, a promise to a felon. In any event, his first duty was to Cosette.

This confusion of thought caused him to be greatly troubled in spirit, which was not easily hidden from Cosette. But love has its own cunning, and he managed. He asked her apparently casual questions, to which with innocent candour she unhesitatingly replied. Talking to her about her childhood and upbringing, he became more and more convinced that where she was concerned this one-time convict had been everything that was good, fatherly, and honourable. His first impulse had been the true one. The rank weed had cherished and protected the lily.

BOOK EIGHT

THE FADING LIGHT

I

The downstairs room

AT NIGHTFALL on the following day Jean Valjean knocked at the door of Monsieur Gillenormand's house and was received by Basque, who had evidently been told to expect him.

'Monsieur le Baron requested me to ask Monsieur whether he wished to go upstairs or would rather stay down here,' said Basque.

'I'll stay down here,' said Valjean.

Basque accordingly, treating the visitor with every sign of respect, showed him into the downstairs room. 'I will inform Madame,' he said.

The room on the ground floor was small and damp, with a low, arched ceiling, and was occasionally used as a cellar. It looked on to the street and was dimly lighted by a single barred window. Nor was it a room much visited by cleaners. Dust lay undisturbed and the spiders were untroubled. A large, blackened web, hung with the bodies of dead flies, covered one of the window-panes. A pile of empty bottles occupied one corner. Plaster was peeling off the yellow-painted wall. A fire had been lighted in the wooden fireplace at the far end, and two armchairs, placed on either side of a worn bedside rug which served as a carpet, were an indication that Valjean's preference for staying downstairs had been foreseen. The fire and the dingy window supplied the only light.

Jean Valjean was tired, having neither eaten nor slept for several days. He sank into one of the armchairs. Basque returned with a lighted candle and again withdrew. Valjean, seated with his chin sunk on his chest, gave no sign of having seen him. But suddenly he started to his feet, knowing that Cosette was standing behind him. He had not seen her enter, but he felt her presence. He turned and looked at her. She was enchantingly pretty. But it was not her beauty that he contemplated with that deeply penetrating gaze, but her soul.

'Well, of all things!' Cosette exclaimed. 'Father, I knew that you were a strange person, but I never expected this! Marius tells me that it is at your request that we're meeting down here.'

'That's quite true.'

'As I expected. Well, I warn you, there's going to be a scene. But let us start properly. Give me a kiss.' And she offered her cheek.

Valjean stayed motionless.

'So you don't move. The posture of a guilty man! Well, never mind, you're forgiven. The Lord told us to turn the other cheek, and here it is.'

She offered him her other cheek, but still he did not move. His feet seemed nailed to the floor.

'But this is serious,' said Cosette. 'What have I done to you? I'm at my wits' end. You owe it to me to make amends. You must dine with us.'

'I've dined already.'

'I don't believe you. I shall ask Monsieur Gillenormand to give you a good scolding. Grandfathers are the right people to keep fathers in order. So you're to come up to the salon with me this instant.'

'That's impossible.'

Cosette felt that she was losing ground. She stopped giving orders and resorted to questions.

'But why? And you have chosen the ugliest room in the house for us to meet in. This place is horrible.'

'*Tu sais* ...' But then, having addressed her with the familiar *tu*, Valjean corrected himself. '*Vous savez*, madame, that I'm peculiar. I have my whims.'

Cosette clapped her hands together.

'"Madame" and "*vous*"! Is this another whim? What in the world does it mean?'

Valjean bestowed on her a heartrending smile.

'You wanted to be "madame" and now you are.'

'But not to you, father.'

'You mustn't call me "father" any more.'

'What!'

'You must call me Monsieur Jean, or plain Jean, if you'd rather.'

'You mean that you're no longer my father? You'll be telling me next that I'm not Cosette! What in the world does it mean? What has happened? You won't live with us and you won't even come up to my sitting-room! It's like a revolution! But what have I done to you? What have I done wrong? There must be something.'

'There's nothing.'

'Well, then?'

'Everything is as it should be.'

'Why have you changed your name?'

'You've changed your own.' He gave her the same smile. 'Now that you're Madame Pontmercy surely I can be Monsieur Jean.'

'I simply don't understand. I think it's ridiculous. I shall ask my husband if you can be allowed to call yourself Monsieur Jean, and I hope he'll say no. You're upsetting me very much. It's all very well to have whims, but they mustn't hurt other people. You've no right to be cruel when you're really so kind.'

He made no reply. She seized his two hands and pressed them to her throat beneath her chin in a gesture of profound tenderness.

'Please, please be kind!' And she went on: 'And by that I mean, be nice and come here to live with us, and then we can go for walks together – there are birds here just as there are in the Rue Plumet. Don't set us guessing games but be like everyone else – live with us, have luncheon and dinner with us, be my father.'

He released his hands.

'You don't need a father any more. You have a husband.'

'What a thing to say,' Cosette exclaimed angrily. 'I don't need a father indeed! There's no sense in it!'

'If Toussaint were here,' said Jean Valjean, as though he were groping for any support, 'she'd be the first to agree that I've always had my peculiarities. There's nothing new in this. I have always liked my shady nook.'

'But it's cold in here and one can't see properly. And it's abominable of you to want to be Monsieur Jean, and I don't like you addressing me as *vous*.'

'On my way here,' said Valjean, 'I saw a piece of furniture in a shop in the Rue Saint-Louis. It was something I'd buy for myself if I were a pretty woman – a very nice dressing-table in the modern style, what is called rosewood, I think, with an inlay and drawers and a big mirror. It was very pretty.'

'You great bear!' said Cosette; and with the utmost fondness, with closed teeth and parted lips, she made a face at Valjean. 'I'm furious,' she said. 'Since yesterday you've all been making me cross. You won't take my side against Marius, and Marius won't take my side against you. I arrange a delightful room for you and it stays empty. I order a delicious dinner and you won't eat it. And my father, who is Monsieur Fauchelevent, wants to be called Monsieur Jean and insists on seeing me in a horrible damp cellar full of spiders and empty bottles. I know you're a peculiar person, but you should be indulgent to a newly married pair. You shouldn't start being peculiar at the very beginning. And you think you'll be happy in that horrible Rue de l'Homme-Armé, which I simply hated. What have you got against me? You're hurting me very much!' Then, becoming suddenly serious, she looked hard at him and asked: 'Are you cross with me because I'm happy?'

Unwitting innocence is sometimes more penetrating than cunning. The question, a simple one to Cosette, was a profound one to Jean Valjean. Thinking to administer a pinprick, she plucked at his heart. Valjean turned pale and for a moment said nothing. Then he murmured to himself:

'Her happiness was the sole object of my life. God can now give me leave of absence . . . Cosette, you are happy, and so my work is done.'

'You called me *tu*!' cried Cosette, and flung her arms round his neck.

He clasped her despairingly to his breast, and it was almost as though he had got her back again. The temptation was too great. Gently loosening her arms, he picked up his hat.

'Well?' said Cosette.

'I am leaving you, Madame. You are wanted elsewhere.' And from the doorway he said: 'I addressed you as *tu*. Please accept my apologies and assure your husband that it will not occur again.'

He went out, leaving her stupefied.

II

Further backslidings

Jean Valjean returned at the same time on the following evening. On this occasion Cosette asked no questions and did not complain about the room. She avoided addressing him either as 'father' or as 'Monsieur Jean', and she submitted to being addressed as 'Madame'. But she was less light-hearted than she had been. Indeed, she would have been sad, if sadness had been possible to her. Most probably she had had one of those conversations with Marius in which the man who is loved tells the beloved woman what he wants and she is content to obey. The curiosity of lovers does not extend far beyond their state of love.

The downstairs room had been put somewhat to rights. Basque had removed the bottles and Nicolette had dealt with the spiders. Valjean called every evening at the same time. He came every day, lacking the strength to take Marius's words otherwise than literally, and Marius arranged to be out when he came. The household accustomed itself to these novel proceedings on the part of Monsieur Fauchelevent, being encouraged to do so by Toussaint, who said, 'Monsieur has always been like this.' Monsieur Gillenormand summed the matter up by describing him as 'an original'. Besides, new arrangements are not easily accepted when one is in one's nineties; one has one's habits, and newcomers are not welcome. Monsieur Gillenormand was not sorry to be rid of Monsieur Fauchelevent. 'These originals are really quite common,' he said. 'They do the most extraordinary things for no reason at all. The Marquis de Canaples was even worse. He bought himself a palace and lived in the attic. Human beings are strange creatures.'

No one knew of the sinister background, and how could anyone have guessed it? There are marshes in India which behave in an extraordinary fashion, the waters becoming turbulent when there is no wind to stir them. The troubled surface is all one sees, not the hydra lurking beneath. Many men possess a secret monster, a despair that haunts their nights. They live ordinary lives, coming and going like other men. No one suspects the existence of a sharp-toothed parasite gnawing at their vitals which kills them in the end. The man is like a stagnant but deep pond, only an occasional unaccountable ripple troubles the surface. A bubble rises and bursts, a small thing but terrible: it is the breathing of the monster in the depths. The strange behaviour of some men, their habit of arriving when others are leaving, of haunting unfrequented places, seeking solitude, coming in by the side door, living poorly when they have money to spare – all such idiosyncrasies are baffling.

Several weeks went by in this fashion. By degrees Cosette grew accustomed to a new way of life, new acquaintances brought to her by marriage, visits, household responsibilities, important matters of this kind. But her real happiness was not expensive, consisting as it did of one thing only, to be alone with Marius. Whether she went out with him or stayed at home with him, this was her main preoccupation; and to walk out together, arm-in-arm in the sunshine, without concealment, openly facing the world in their own private solitude, this was a joy to both of them that never grew stale. Cosette had only one cause for vexation. Toussaint could not get on with Nicolette, and finally when it became clear that the two old maids had nothing in common, she left. Monsieur Gillenormand was in good health; Marius did occasional legal work; Aunt Gillenormand settled down with the newly married couple to live the unobtrusive life that sufficed her. Jean Valjean paid his daily visit.

The use of *vous* and 'Madame', and the fact that he was now Monsieur Jean, made him a different person to Cosette. The means he had used to detach her from him had proved successful. She was increasingly light-hearted but less tender. And still he felt that she loved him dearly. On one occasion she said abruptly to him: 'You used to be my father, but you aren't any more; you used to be my uncle, but you aren't any more; you used to be Monsieur Fauchelevent and now you're just plain Jean. Who are you really? I don't like this state of affairs. If I didn't know how good you are I should be afraid of you.'

He still lived in the Rue de l'Homme-Armé, being unable to bring himself to leave the quarter in which Cosette also lived. At first, when he came to see her, he stayed only a few minutes, but by degrees his visits grew longer. One day, she addressed him unthinkingly as 'father' and his sombre countenance was suddenly radiant. Then he said, 'You must call me Jean . . .' 'Of course,' she said, laughing, 'Monsieur Jean . . .' 'That's better,' he said and turned away his head so that she should not see the tears in his eyes.

III

They remember the garden in the Rue Plumet

That was the last time. From that moment all demonstrations of affection were banished between them – no more familiarities, no kiss of greeting, no use of that profoundly moving word, 'father'. Of his own free will he had relinquished all his happiness, and this was his final torment, that having in a single day lost Cosette as a whole, he had to go on losing her in detail. But the eye accustoms itself to a cellar-light. All in all, his daily glimpse of Cosette sufficed him. Those visits were the mainstay of his life. He would sit looking at her in silence, or would talk of incidents in the past, her childhood days and her little friends in the convent.

One afternoon (it was early in April, a warm day when the sun was bringing the world to life and there was a stir of awakening – budding leaves on the trees, primroses and dandelions beginning to show themselves in the grass of the garden outside their window) Marius said to Cosette, 'We said we would go back to our garden in the Rue Plumet. We mustn't be ungrateful,' – and off they went like swallows flying into the spring. That garden in the Rue Plumet had been for them the beginning of everything; it had harboured the springtime of their love. Since Jean Valjean had acquired the lease it was now the property of Cosette. They went there and, being there, forgot all else. When Valjean called at his accustomed hour Basque told him that Madame had gone out with Monsieur and they had not yet returned. Valjean sat down and waited, but when after another hour she still had not come he bowed his head and went away.

Cosette had so enjoyed their visit to the garden and reliving the past that the next day she could talk of nothing else. It did not occur to her that she had missed seeing Valjean.

'How did you go there?' Valjean asked her.

'We walked.'

'And how did you come back?'

'In a fiacre.'

For some time Valjean had been conscious of the rigidly economical fashion in which the young couple lived, and it perturbed him. He ventured upon a question.

'Why don't you have a carriage of your own? A coupé would cost you five hundred francs a month. You could easily afford it.'

'I don't know,' said Cosette.

'And then, Toussaint,' Valjean continued. 'She's gone but you haven't got anyone in her place. Why not?'

'Nicolette is quite enough.'

'But you ought to have your own maid.'

'I've got Marius.'

'And you ought to have a house of your own, with servants of your own and a carriage and a box at the opera. Nothing is too good for you. Why not take advantage of the fact that you're rich? Wealth can be a great source of happiness.'

Cosette made no reply.

Jean Valjean's visits did not grow shorter. On the contrary. When it is the heart that fails we do not pause on the downward path. In order to stay longer he talked about Marius, praising his many excellent qualities. It was a subject that never failed to enthral Cosette, and so time was forgotten, and he could allay the aching of his heart with more of her company. It happened more than once that Basque entered with the words, 'Monsieur Gillenormand has sent me to remind Madame la Baronne that dinner is served.'

On these occasions Valjean went thoughtfully home, wondering if there might be truth in the thought that had occurred to Marius, that he was a sort of chrysalis obstinately returning to visit its butterfly.

One evening he stayed even later than usual, and the next day he found that there was no fire burning in the hearth. 'Well, after all,' he thought, 'it's April and the weather is no longer cold.'

'Heavens, how cold it is in here,' Cosette exclaimed when she entered.

'Not at all,' said Valjean.

'Was it you who told Basque not to light the fire?'

'Yes. It will soon be May.'

'But we keep fires going until June, and in this cellar one wants one all the year round.'

'I didn't think a fire was necessary.'

'Another of your absurd ideas,' said Cosette.

The next evening there was a fire, but the two armchairs had been placed at the other end of the room, near the door. 'Now what does that mean?' Valjean wondered, and he restored the chairs to their original place.

But the lighting of the fire encouraged him, and that evening he stayed even longer than usual. When at length he rose to leave Cosette said:

'My husband said a queer thing to me yesterday.'

'What was that?'

'He said, "Cosette, we have an income of thirty thousand livres, twenty-seven thousand of yours and the three thousand my grandfather allows me" ... "Yes," I said, "that adds up to thirty" ... "Would you be brave enough to live on the three thousand?" he asked. I said I was ready to live on nothing at all provided I was with him; and then I asked, "Why do you say that?" ... "I just wanted to know," he said.'

Jean Valjean found nothing to say. Cosette had probably hoped for some sort of explanation, but he maintained a gloomy silence. He was so lost in thought that when he returned to the Rue de l'Homme-Armé he entered the house next door by mistake and did not realize what he had done until he had climbed two flights of stairs. His mind was filled with conjecture. It was evident that Marius had his doubts about the origin of those six hundred thousand francs and perhaps feared that they had come from some discreditable source – perhaps he had discovered that they had come from Valjean himself – and that he would sooner be poor with Cosette than live on tainted money.

In general Valjean had a vague sense that he was being rebuffed, and on the following evening this was brought forcibly home to him. The two armchairs had vanished. There was not a chair in the room.

'Why, what has happened?' Cosette exclaimed when she came in. 'Where have they got to?'

'I told Basque he could take them away,' Valjean replied, stammering slightly as he spoke.

'But why?'

'I shall only be staying a few minutes this evening.'

'Even so, there's no reason why we should stand up.'

'I think Basque needed the chairs for the salon.'

'What for?'

'Because you're expecting company, I suppose.'

'Nobody's coming.'

Valjean could think of nothing else to say. Cosette shrugged her shoulders.

'You told Basque to take the chairs away. And the other day you told him not to light the fire. You really are very peculiar.'

'Good-bye,' said Valjean. He did not say 'Good-bye, Cosette' but he had not the strength to say, 'Good-bye, Madame'.

He went off in despair, having now understood exactly what was happening, and the next evening he did not come at all.

Cosette did not notice this until the hour was past, and when she remarked upon it her thoughts were quickly distracted by a kiss from Marius.

On the following evening Jean Valjean again did not come.

Cosette was unperturbed. She slept soundly and scarcely gave the matter a thought until the next morning. She was so bathed in happiness! But then she sent Nicolette round to the Rue de l'Homme-Armé to inquire if 'Monsieur Jean' was well. Nicolette returned with the message that Monsieur Jean was quite well but was busy with his affairs. Madame would remember that he had sometimes had to go away for a few days. He would be doing so shortly, and would come to see her as soon as possible after he got back. In the meantime there was nothing to worry about.

Nicolette, when she called upon Monsieur Jean, had repeated her mistress's words, that 'Madame wished to know why Monsieur Jean had not come to see her the previous evening.'

'I have not been to see her for two evenings,' Jean Valjean said gently.

But Nicolette failed to notice this and did not report the remark to Cosette.

IV
Attraction and extinction

During the late spring and early summer of 1833 persons in the streets of the Marais, shopkeepers and loiterers in house doorways, noticed an elderly man decently clad in black who at about the same time every evening, when it was beginning to grow dark, left the Rue de l'Homme-Armé and walked to the Rue Saint-Louis. Having reached it he proceeded very slowly, seeming to see and hear nothing, his head thrust forward and his eyes intent upon a single object, which was the corner of the Rue des Filles-du-Calvaire. As he approached this point his eyes brightened with a glow of inward happiness, his lips moved as though he were talking to some unseen person and he smiled uncertainly. It was as though, while longing to reach his objective, he dreaded the moment when he would do so. When he was within a few houses of it his pace slowed to the point that he seemed scarcely to be moving at all; the swaying of his head and the intentness of his gaze put one in mind of a compass-needle searching for the pole. But however slow his progress, he had to get there in the end. Having reached the Rue des Filles-du-Calvaire, he stopped and trembled, and peered timidly round the corner into the street with the tragic expression of one who gazes into a forbidden paradise. Then the tear which had been slowly gathering in his eye became large enough to fall and roll down his cheek, sometimes reaching his mouth so that he tasted its bitterness. He would stay there for some minutes like a figure carved in stone and then slowly return by the way he had come, with the light in his eyes growing dimmer as the distance lengthened.

As time went on the elderly gentleman ceased to go as far as the corner of the Rue des Filles-du-Calvaire, and would stop and turn back half way along the Rue Saint-Louis; and one day he went only as far as the Rue Culture-Sainte-Catherine, from which point he had a distant view of the Rue des Filles-du-Calvaire. Then he shook his head, as though rejecting something, and turned back. Before long he did not go even as far as the Rue Saint-Louis, but stopped at the Rue Pavée. Then it was the Rue des Trois-Pavillons, and then the Rue des Blancs-Manteaux. His daily walk grew steadily shorter, like the pendulum of a clock that has not been re-wound and gradually ceases to swing. Every day he set out upon the same walk and perhaps was unaware of the fact that he constantly shortened it. His expression seemed to say, 'What is the use?' There was no longer any light in his eyes, nor did the tears gather as formerly. But his head was still thrust forward, painfully revealing the folds in his thin neck. Sometimes in bad weather he carried an umbrella, but he never opened it. The goodwives of the quarter said, 'He's simple,' and the children laughed as they followed him.

BOOK NINE

SUPREME SHADOW, SUPREME DAWN

I

Pity for the unhappy, but indulgence for the happy

To be happy is a terrible thing. How complacent we are, how self-sufficing. How easy it is, being possessed of the false side of life, which is happiness, to forget the real side, which is duty.

Yet it would be wrong to blame Marius. As we have said, before his marriage Marius asked no questions of Monsieur Fauchelevent, and since then he had been afraid to question Jean Valjean. He had regretted the promise which he had been induced to make and had said to himself more than once that he should not have made that concession to despair. And so he had by degrees excluded Valjean from his house and effaced him as far as possible from the thoughts of Cosette, deliberately intervening between them, but in such a way as to ensure that she would not realize what was happening. It was more than effacement; it was eclipse.

Marius was doing what he held to be right and necessary. He believed that in keeping Valjean at a distance, without harshness but also without weakness, he was acting upon serious grounds, some of which we already know and others of which we have still to learn. In the course of a law-suit in which he had been profession-ally involved he had met a former clerk in the Laffitte banking-house and had received from him certain information which he was unable to investigate further because of his promise of secrecy and Valjean's perilous situation. At the same time he believed that he had a serious duty to perform, namely, the restitution of six hundred thousand francs to some person whose identity he was seeking to discover as discreetly as possible. In the meantime he did not touch the money.

As for Cosette, she knew nothing of all these secrets; but she, too, was scarcely to be blamed. Marius's power over her was such that instinctively and almost automatically she did what he wanted. She sensed a 'feeling' on the part of Marius where Valjean was con-cerned, and without his having to say anything she blindly acqui-esced in it. Her obedience in this respect consisted in not remember-ing things that Marius had forgotten. It cost her no effort. Without her knowing why, or being in any way to blame, her spirit had become so merged in that of her husband that what was expunged from Marius's mind was also expunged from her own.

But we must not carry this too far. In the case of Jean Valjean her forgetfulness was only superficial. She was bemused rather than forgetful. In her heart she still loved the man whom for so long she had called father. But she loved her husband even more, and it was this that had somewhat disturbed the balance of her affections, causing her to lean to one side.

Occasionally she spoke of Jean Valjean, expressing astonishment at his absence. Marius reminded her that he had said he was going away. And this was true. He was in the habit of going away from time to time, although never for so long as this. Several times she sent Nicolette to the Rue de l'Homme-Armé to ask if 'Monsieur Jean' had returned. The answer, sent by Valjean himself, was always no. Cosette was not unduly perturbed, having only one need in life, and that was for Marius.

We may mention that Marius and Cosette had themselves been away. They had been to Vernon, where Marius had taken Cosette to his father's grave. Little by little Marius had detached Cosette from Jean Valjean, and she had allowed it to happen.

For the rest, what is sometimes over-severely described as the ingratitude of the young is not always so reprehensible as one may suppose. It is the ingratitude of Nature herself. Nature, as we have said elsewhere, always 'looks ahead'; she divides living creatures into those who are arriving and those who are leaving. Those leaving look towards darkness, and those arriving look towards light. Hence the gulf between them, fateful to the old, involuntary on the part of the young. The gulf, at first imperceptible, grows gradually wider, like the spreading branches of a tree. It is not the fault of the branches that, without detaching themselves from the trunk, they grow remote from it. Youth goes in search of joy and festivity, bright light and love. Age moves towards the end. They do not lose sight of one another, but there is no longer any closeness between them. Young folk feel the cooling of life; old people feel the chill of the grave. Let us not be too hard on the young.

Last flickers of a lamp without oil

One day Jean Valjean walked downstairs and a few paces along the street, then seated himself on a kerbstone, the same one on which Gavroche had found him on the night of 5 June. He stayed there a few minutes, then went upstairs again. It was the last swing of the pendulum. The next day he did not leave his room, and on the following day he did not leave his bed.

The concierge, who prepared his meagre repast, consisting of cabbage or a few potatoes with a little bacon, looked at the brown earthenware plate and exclaimed:

'But you ate nothing yesterday, my poor man.'

'Yes I did,' said Valjean.

'The plate's still full.'

'If you look at the water-jug you'll see that it's empty.'

'Well, that proves that you've had a drink, but not that you've eaten anything.'

'So perhaps all I wanted was water.'

'If you don't eat as well as drink it means that you've got a fever.'

'I'll eat something tomorrow.'

'Or next week, perhaps. Why put it off till tomorrow? And those new potatoes were so good.'

Valjean took the old woman's hand.

'I'll promise to eat them,' he said in his kindly voice.

'I'm not at all pleased with you,' she said.

Valjean saw no one except this old woman. There are streets in Paris along which no one passes and houses which no one enters, and he lived in one of them. While he had been in the habit of going out he had bought a small copper cross which he nailed to the wall facing his bed. A cross is always good to look at.

During the week that followed Valjean did not get out of bed. The concierge said to her husband: 'He doesn't get up and he doesn't eat anything. He isn't going to last long. He's very unhappy about something. I can't help feeling that his daughter has made a bad marriage.'

Her husband replied with lordly indifference:

'If he's rich enough he'd better send for the doctor; if he's too poor he can't afford to, and in that case he'll die.'

'But if he does send for the doctor?'

'He'll probably die anyway.'

The concierge was pulling up the blades of grass that had sprouted between the stones of what she called her own strip of pavement. She saw a local doctor passing the end of the street and took it upon herself to ask him to go upstairs.

'It's the second floor,' she said. 'He never gets out of bed and so the key's always in the door.'

When he came down the doctor said:

'The man's very ill indeed.'

'What's the matter with him?'

'Everything and nothing. From the look of him I would say that he has lost someone very dear to him. One can die of that.'

'What did he say to you?'

'He said he was quite well.'

'Will you come again, doctor?'

'Yes,' said the doctor. 'But he needs someone other than myself.'

III

The weight of a quill-pen

One evening Jean Valjean had difficulty in raising himself on his elbow. His pulse was so weak that he could not feel it; his breath came in short, faint gasps. He realized that he was weaker than he had ever been. And so, no doubt because he was impelled to do so by some over-riding consideration, he sat up with a great effort and got dressed. He put on his old workman's clothes. Now that he had given up going out he preferred them to any other. He had to pause several times to rest, and the business of getting his arms into the sleeves of his jacket caused sweat to drip from his forehead.

Now that he was alone he had moved his bed into the living-room in order to occupy as little of the apartment as possible. He opened the valise and, getting out Cosette's trousseau of small garments, spread them on the bed. The bishop's candlesticks were in their usual place on the mantelpiece; he got two wax candles out of a drawer and, putting them in the candlesticks, lighted them, although it was broad daylight. One may see candles lighted in rooms occupied by the dead. Every step he took, moving from one room to the other, exhausted him, and he had frequently to sit down and rest. It was not just a case of ordinary fatigue which uses up energy and recovers it; it was the last effort of which he was capable, exhausted life spending itself in an effort which it will not be able to repeat.

One of the chairs into which he sank was opposite the mirror, so disastrous for him and so providential for Marius, in which he had read the blotted handwriting of Cosette. He looked at himself in the mirror and did not recognize what he saw. He was eighty years old. Before Cosette's marriage he might have been taken for fifty. The wrinkles on his forehead were not the wrinkles of age but the mysterious stamp of death; one could see the impress of that inexorable finger. His cheeks sagged, and the colour of his skin was such as to make one feel that there was earth beneath it. The corners of his mouth drooped as in the masks that the ancients carved for the tombs of the dead. He was staring blankly in front of him, but with an expression of reproach, like one of those great figures of tragedy who rise in condemnation of some other man.

He was at the point, the last stage of despair, when pain is no longer active; the soul, as it were, has grown numb. It was growing dark. With great labour he dragged a table and chair close to the mantelpiece, and arranged writing materials on the table. Having done this he fainted, and upon recovering consciousness found that he was thirsty. Not being able to lift the water-jug to his lips, he tilted it painfully towards him and sipped from it. Then he turned towards the bed, and, still seated, for he could no longer stand, looked at the little black frock and the other garments that were so dear to him. He stayed looking at them for a long time, until with a shiver he realized that he was cold; then, leaning forward over the table lit by the bishop's candlesticks, he picked up his pen.

Since neither pen nor ink had been used for a considerable time, the quill was warped and the ink had dried. He had to get up and pour a few drops of water into the ink-pot, which he only managed to do with several pauses for rest, and he had to write with the reverse side of the quill. Now and then he wiped his forehead. His hand was shaking. Slowly he wrote the following lines:

Cosette, I bless you. There is something I must explain. Your husband was right to make me understand that I must go away. What he supposed was not altogether correct, but still he was right. He is a good man. You must go on loving him after I am dead. And you, Monsieur Pontmercy, you must go on loving my beloved child. Cosette, you will find figures on this paper if I have the strength to recall them. That is why I am writing to you, to assure you that the money is really yours. This is how it is. White jade comes from Norway, black jade from England, and black glass from Germany. Jade is lighter, more rare and more expensive. Imitations can be made in France as they can in Germany. You need a small mould two inches square and a spirit lamp to soften the wax. The wax used to be made of resin and lampblack, but I hit upon the idea of making it of lacquer and turpentine. It costs no more than thirty sous and it is much better. The buckles are made of purple glass fixed with wax in a black metal frame. The glass should be purple for metal frames and black for gold ornaments. A lot is sold in Spain, which is the country where . . .

And here the pen slipped from his fingers and he sank down, sobbing from the depths of his heart, with his head clasped in his hands.

'Alas, alas,' he cried within himself (those dreadful lamentations that are heard only by God), 'it's all over. I shall not see her again. It was a smile that came into my life and departed. I shall go into darkness without seeing her. If I could hear her voice, touch her dress, look at her just once more! To die is nothing, but it is terrible to die without seeing her. She would smile at me, she would say a word, and what harm would it do anyone? But it is all over and I am alone. God help me, I shall not see her again!'

At this moment there was a knock on the door.

IV
Marius receives a letter

That same day, or, more exactly, that same evening, Marius having withdrawn to his study after dinner to work on a brief, Basque brought him a letter, saying, 'The writer is waiting in the hall.' Cosette at the time was strolling with her grandfather-in-law in the garden.

A letter, like a person, can have a displeasing appearance – coarse paper, careless folding – the very sight of them can be unpleasant. This was such a letter. It smelt of tobacco. Nothing is more evocative than a smell. Marius remembered that tobacco, and looking at the superscription he read: 'To Monsieur le Baron Pontmerci, At his home'. The familiar smell of the tobacco reminded him of the handwriting, and in a sudden flash of divination he put certain things together: the smell of tobacco, the quality of the paper, the way it was folded, the pale watered ink – all this brought a picture to his mind, that of the Jondrette attic . . . By the strangest of chances, one of the two men for whom he had searched so diligently, thinking never to find him, had of his own accord come his way!

Eagerly unsealing the letter, he read:

Monsieur le baron,

If the Supreme Being had endowed me with talent I might be the Baron Thénard,* member of the Academy, but I am not. I simply bear the same name as his, and I shall be happy if this recommends me to your favor. Any kindness which you may do me will be resiprocated. I am in possession of a secret concerning a certain person. This person concerns you. I am keeping the secret for your ears alone, being desirus of being useful to you. I can provide you with the means of driving this person out of your house where he has no right to be, Madame la Baronne being a lady of noble birth. Virtue and crime cannot be allowed to go on living together any longer.

I await Monsieur le Baron's instructions,
Respectfully,

The letter was signed THÉNARD.

The signature was not wholly false, being merely a little abbreviated. But the style and orthography completed the picture. There could be no doubt whatever as to the writer's identity.

Marius's agitation was extreme. After his first surprise came a feeling of satisfaction. If he could now find the other man he sought, the one who had saved his life, all his troubles of conscience would be at an end. He went to his desk, got some banknotes out of a drawer, put them in his pocket, closed the drawer and then rang the bell. Basque appeared.

'Show the gentleman in,' said Marius.

'Monsieur Thénard,' Basque announced.

And now Marius had another surprise. The man who entered was completely unknown to him.

He was an elderly man with a big nose, his chin buried in his cravat, with green-tinted spectacles and grey hair smoothed and plastered down over his forehead like the wigs of coachmen to the English nobility. He was clad entirely in black, his garments being worn but clean, and a bunch of fobs hanging from his waistcoat

*Baron Thénard, a chemist, had been a member of the Académie des Sciences.

pocket suggested that he possessed a watch. He was carrying an old hat in his hand. He walked with a stoop, and the curve of his back made his bow upon entering all the deeper.

The first thing that struck Marius was that the suit he was wearing, although carefully buttoned, was too large and seemed to have been made for someone else. And here a brief digression becomes necessary.

There existed in those days in Paris, in a hovel near the Arsenal, an ingenious Jew whose business in life was transforming rogues into respectable men. Not for too long, since this might have made them uncomfortable. The change, which was simply one of appearance, lasted one or two days, at the rate of thirty sous a day, and was based on a set of clothes conforming as far as possible to accepted notions of propriety. The practitioner in question was called 'the Changer', this being the only name by which he was known to the denizens of the Paris underworld. He possessed a large stock, and the garments he hired out to his customers were more or less presentable. They covered all categories. From every hook in his establishment there hung, used and worn, a social status, that of a magistrate, banker, priest, retired army man, man of letters or statesman. He was in short the costumier of the great repertory theatre of Paris rascality, and his shop was the place whence every kind of crime emerged, and to which it returned. A ragged footpad went there, deposited his thirty sous, selected whatever clothes suited the particular project he had in mind, and came out looking another man. Next day the garments were faithfully returned; the Changer, who dealt exclusively with thieves, was himself never robbed. But the clothes he hired out had one drawback: they didn't fit. Anyone whose physical dimensions in any way departed from the normal was uncomfortable in them: he must not be too fat or too thin, the Changer catered only for the average. This created problems which his customers had to solve as best they could. The statesman's outfit, for example, would have been too large for Pitt and too small for Louis-Philippe. We may quote the note in the Changer's catalogue: 'Coat of black cloth, black knee-breeches, silk waistcoat, boots and linen' – to which was appended in the margin, 'former ambassador', together with an additional note which read: 'In a separate box a neatly frizzed wig, green-tinted spectacles, fobs and two quill-tubes an inch long wrapped in cotton-wool'. All this came from the same source, the 'former ambassador', and all was somewhat the worse for wear, with the seams whitening and a slit in one of the elbows. Moreover a button was missing from the breast of the jacket. This, however, was a detail, the statesman's hand being always laid upon his heart to cover the deficiency. Marius would at once have recognized this outfit had he been familiar with the seamy side of Paris life.

Marius's disappointment at finding himself confronted by a stranger turned to disgust as he examined the visitor more closely while the latter was exaggeratedly bowing.

'What do you want?' he asked sharply.

The visitor responded with a grimace which may be likened to the smile of a crocodile.

'I find it hard to believe that I have not already met Monsieur le Baron in society – at the house of Princess Bagration, perhaps, or of the Vicomte Dambray?' To pretend acquaintance with someone whom one has never met is always a shrewd move in the performance of a confidence trick.

Marius had listened attentively to the sound of the man's voice, and with a growing disappointment. He had a nasal intonation quite different from the thin, dry voice which Marius had expected.

'I know neither Madame Bagration nor Monsieur Dambray,' he said, frowning, 'and I have never visited either of them.'

Despite the terseness of his manner the visitor was not discouraged.

'Well, then, perhaps it was at the home of Chateaubriand. I am on the friendliest of terms with Chateaubriand. He quite often asks me in for a drink.'

Marius's frown grew darker.

'I don't know Monsieur de Chateaubriand either. Will you please come to the point. What can I do for you?'

The visitor bowed more deeply than ever.

'At least, Monsieur le Baron, do me the honour of listening to what I have to say. There is in America, in the region of Panama, a village called La Joya. It consists of a single house. A big, square, three-storey house built of bricks baked in the sun. Each side of the square is five hundred feet long, and each floor is set back twelve feet from the one below it, forming a sort of terrace which runs right round the building. There is an interior courtyard in which provisions and munitions are stored. There are no windows but only loopholes, no doors but only ladders – ladders leading from the ground to the first terrace, from the first to the second terrace and from the second to the third; ladders for climbing down into the courtyard. No doors to the rooms but only trap-doors; no stairways to the rooms but only ladders. At night the traps are closed and the ladders are drawn up, and loaded guns and carbines are installed at the loopholes. The place is a house by day and a fortress at night, with eight hundred inhabitants. That is the village. Why so many precautions, you may ask? Because it is situated in very dangerous country, full of cannibals. So why does anyone go there? Because it is a wonderful country in which gold is to be found.'

'Why are you telling me all this?' demanded Marius, who was becoming increasingly impatient.

'I am a wearied ex-diplomat, Monsieur le Baron. Our ancient civilization has become oppressive to me. I want to live among savage people.'

'And so?'

'Egotism, Monsieur le Baron, is the law of life. The day-labourer working in the fields looks round when the coach passes, but the peasant proprietor does not bother to do so. The poor man's dog barks at the rich and the rich man's dog barks at the poor. Everyone for himself. Self-interest is the object of all men and money is the loadstone.'

'I'm still waiting.'

'I want to settle in La Joya. There are three of us. I have a wife and a very beautiful daughter. It is a long journey and it costs a great deal. I need a little money.'

'What has that to do with me?'

Stretching his neck out of his cravat in a gesture proper to a vulture, the visitor smiled with redoubled ardour.

'Has Monsieur le Baron not read my letter?'

This was not far from the truth. The fact is that Marius had paid little attention to the contents of the letter, being more interested in the handwriting. In any case, a new thought had occurred to him. The man had mentioned a wife and daughter. Marius looked at him with a searching scrutiny that not even an examining magistrate could have bettered, but he only said, 'Go on.'

The visitor thrust his hands in his waistcoat pockets, raised his head, without, however, straightening his back, and returned Marius's gaze through the green-tinted spectacles.

'Very well, Monsieur le Baron, I will go on. I have a secret to sell you.'

'A secret which concerns me?'

'To some extent.'

'Well, what is it?'

'I will tell you the first part for nothing. You will, I think be interested.'

'Well?'

'Monsieur le Baron, you have living with you a thief and an assassin.'

Marius started.

'Not living with me,' he said.

Smoothing his hat with his sleeve, the visitor imperturbably continued:

'A thief and an assassin. Please note, Monsieur le Baron, that I am not talking about bygone transgressions that may have been cancelled out by process of law and repentance in the eyes of God, but of recent events, present happenings not yet known to the law. A man has insinuated himself into your confidence, almost into your family, under a false name. I will tell you his real name and I will tell you for nothing.'

'I'm listening.'

'His name is Jean Valjean.'

'I know that.'

'I will also tell you, also for nothing, what he is.'

'Please do.'

'He is an ex-convict.'

'I know that too.'

'You know it now that I have told you.'

'No. I knew it already.'

Marius's cool tone of voice and his apparent indifference to the information had their effect upon the visitor. He gave Marius a sidelong glance of fury which was rapidly extinguished; but brief though it was, it was not lost on Marius. There are looks like flame that can only come from beings of a certain kind; tinted glasses cannot hide them; they are like a glimpse of Hell.

The visitor smiled.

'I would not venture to contradict Monsieur le Baron. In any case you will see that I am well-informed. And what I now have to tell you is known to no one except myself. It concerns the fortune of

Madame la Baronne. It is a remarkable secret and it is for sale. I am offering it to you first of all, and at a low price – twenty thousand francs.'

'I know this secret already, just as I knew the others,' said Marius. The visitor thought it judicious to lower his price.

'Well, let us say ten thousand.'

'I repeat, you have nothing to tell me. I know what you're going to say.'

The visitor's expression changed.

'But I've got to eat, haven't I? Monsieur le Baron, this is an extraordinary secret. I will let you have it for twenty francs.'

'I tell you I know it already,' said Marius. 'Just as I knew the name of Jean Valjean and know your name.'

'Well, that's not difficult, seeing that I wrote it in my letter and have only just told you. It's Thénard.'

'You've left out the rest of it.'

'What's that?'

'Thénard*ier*.'

'Who might he be?'

In moments of peril the porcupine raises its quills, the beetle shams dead, and the infantry forms a square. This man laughed and airily flicked a speck of dust off his sleeve.

'You are also the workman Jondrette,' Marius went on, 'the actor Fabantou, the poet Genflot, the Spaniard Don Alvarez, and the widow Balizard.'

'The widow what?'

'At one time you kept a tavern at Montfermeil.'

'A tavern? Never!'

'And your real name is Thénardier.'

'I deny it.'

'And you're a thorough rogue. Here, take this.'

Marius got a banknote out of his pocket and tossed it in his face.

'Thank you, thank you, Monsieur le Baron!' The man bowed while he examined the note. 'Five hundred francs!' He murmured in an undertone, 'That's real money!' Then he said briskly: 'Well, we might as well be at our ease.'

And with remarkable adroitness he removed his disguise – the false nose, the tinted glasses and the two small tubes of quill which we mentioned just now and which figured in an earlier part of this tale* – stripping them away like a man taking off his hat. His eyes brightened, his uneven, knobbly and hideously wrinkled forehead was disclosed, and his nose was again a beak; in short, the avaricious, cunning countenance of the man of prey reappeared.

'Monsieur le Baron is infallible,' he said in a clear voice from which all trace of a nasal intonation had disappeared. 'I am Thénardier.'

And he straightened his back.

Thénardier was considerably taken aback and might even have been put out of countenance had this been possible for him. He had come there intending to astonish, and had himself been astonished. The fact that his humiliation had been rewarded with the sum of five hundred francs, which he had made no bones about accepting, had put the finishing touch to his amazement.

He was seeing this Baron Pontmercy for the first time in his life; nevertheless the baron had recognized him in spite of his disguise and seemed to know all about him. He seemed also to know all about Jean Valjean. Who on earth could he be, this almost beardless young man who was at once so icy and so generous, who knew all about everybody and treated rogues like a judge while at the same time paying them like a dupe? It must be borne in mind that although at one time Thénardier had been Marius's neighbour, he had never set eyes on him, a thing that happens often enough in Paris. He had written the letter we have just seen without having the least idea who he was. There was no connection in Thénardier's mind between the Marius occasionally referred to by his daughters and the present Baron Pontmercy. Nor did the name of Pontmercy mean anything to him because of the episode on the field of Waterloo, when he had heard only the two last syllables, which had not interested him since he had not supposed them to have any cash value.

For the rest, thanks to his daughter Azelma, whom he had put on the track of the bridal pair on 16 February, and thanks also to his own researches and his underworld connections, he had picked up a good many scraps of information. He had discovered, or perhaps guessed, who the man was whom he had encountered in the sewer, and from this it was a short step to finding out his name. He knew that the Baroness Pontmercy was Cosette; but as to this, he had

*The encounter between Gavroche and Montparnasse, Book Six, Chapter 2. Trs.

decided upon discretion. Who, after all, was Cosette? He himself did not precisely know. Thoughts of illegitimacy had occurred to him, since he had always regarded Fantine's story with suspicion, but what good would it do him to mention this? To be paid to keep silent? He had, or thought he had, something better than that to sell. It also occurred to him that to come to the Baron Pontmercy with the tale, unsupported by evidence, that his wife was a bastard would be to invite his boot on his backside.

To Thénardier's way of thinking his conversation with Marius had not yet really begun. He had been obliged to give a little ground, to modify his tactics, but nothing essential was lost and he was already the richer by five hundred francs. He had something important to say, and well-informed and well-equipped though the Baron Pontmercy was, he felt that he was in a strong position. To men of Thénardier's stamp, every conversation is a contest. How did he stand in the one which was now about to begin? He did not know whom he was talking to, but he knew what he was talking about. He rapidly surveyed his resources, and having admitted that he was Thénardier he waited.

Marius was also thinking. At last he had caught up with Thénardier. The man whom he had so long sought stood before him, and he could carry out the injunction laid upon him by his father. It was humiliating to know that the dead hero should have owed his life to a scoundrel and that the blank cheque he had left behind him had not hitherto been honoured. It seemed to Marius also, in his complex state of mind where Thénardier was concerned, that there were grounds for avenging his father for the misfortune of having been saved by such a man. In any event he was pleased. The time had at last come when he could rid his father's shade of this unworthy creditor, and it was as though he would be releasing his father's memory from a debtor's prison.

But apart from this he had another duty, namely, if possible to resolve the mystery of the source of Cosette's fortune. It was a matter in which Thénardier might be of some assistance.

Thénardier had carefully stowed the five-hundred-franc note in his pocket and was smiling almost tenderly at Marius. Marius broke the silence.

'Thénardier, I have told you your name. Do you want me also to tell you the secret you were proposing to sell me? I, too, have sources of information, and you may find that I know rather more than you do. Jean Valjean, as you say, is a murderer and a thief. He is a thief because he robbed a wealthy manufacturer, Monsieur Madeleine, whom he ruined. And he murdered the policeman, Javert.'

'I don't understand, Monsieur le Baron,' said Thénardier.

'I will explain. Round about 1822 there was a man living in the Pas-de-Calais who had at one time been in trouble with the law, but who, under the name of Monsieur Madeleine, had fully rehabilitated himself. He had become a man of probity and honour, and he had established a factory making objects of black glass which had brought prosperity to a whole town. It had also made his personal fortune, but this was as it were a secondary consideration. He looked after the poor, founded schools and hospitals, cared for the widow and the orphan – became in some sort the guardian angel of the region. He was elected mayor. A released convict who knew his background denounced him and took advantage of his arrest to draw from the Paris banking house of Laffitte – I have this from the chief cashier in person – a sum of over half a million francs belonging to Monsieur Madeleine, whose signature he forged. The released convict was Jean Valjean. As for the murder, Jean Valjean murdered the police agent, Javert. I know because I was there at the time.'

Thénardier darted at Marius the triumphant glance of a beaten man who finds that after all he has regained the ground he lost and victory is in sight. But his meek smile promptly returned. Abjectness, the humility of the inferior confronted by his superior, was a better card to play. He merely said:

'Monsieur le Baron, I think you are mistaken.'

'What!' exclaimed Marius. 'Are you denying what I've said? But those are facts!'

'They are incorrect. Monsieur le Baron has so far honoured me with his confidence that I feel it is my duty to tell him the truth. Truth and justice should come before all else. I do not like to hear a man unjustly accused. Jean Valjean did not rob Monsieur Madeleine, nor did he kill Javert.'

'How on earth do you make that out?'

'For two reasons. In the first place he did not rob Monsieur Madeleine because he himself is, or was, Monsieur Madeleine.'

'What in the world . . .?'

'And secondly he did not kill Javert because Javert killed himself. He committed suicide.'

'What!' cried Marius, beside himself with amazement. 'But what proof have you of this?'

'The police agent Javert,' said Thénardier, intoning the words as though they were a classical alexandrine, 'was found drowned under a boat moored near the Pont-au-Change.'

'Prove it!'

Thénardier fished in an inside pocket and got out a large envelope containing folded papers of different sizes.

'Here is my dossier,' he said calmly. He went on: 'Acting in your interests, Monsieur le Baron, I wished to discover the whole truth about Jean Valjean. When I tell you that he and Madeleine are one and the same, and that Javert was the only murderer of Javert, I can produce evidence to prove it, and not merely handwritten evidence – handwriting can be forged – but printed evidence.'

As he spoke Thénardier was getting copies of two newspapers out of the envelope, both faded and creased and smelling strongly of tobacco, but one of which seemed very much older than the other.

The reader knows of both these newspapers. The older of the two was the issue of the *Drapeau Blanc* dated 25 July 1823 in which Monsieur Madeleine and Jean Valjean were shown to be the same person. The more recent, the *Moniteur* of 15 June 1832, reported the suicide of Javert, adding that it followed Javert's verbal report to the Prefect of Police that, having been taken prisoner by the insurgents in the Rue de la Chanvrerie, he owed his life to the magnanimity of one of them, who had fired his pistol into the air.

There could be no doubting this evidence. The newspapers were unquestionably authentic. They had not been printed simply to support the testimony of Thénardier. Seeing how mistaken he had been, Marius uttered a cry of joy.

'Why, but then he's a splendid man! The fortune was really his! He's Madeleine, the benefactor of an entire region, and Jean Valjean, the saviour of Javert. He's a hero! He's a saint!'

'He's neither one nor the other,' said Thénardier. 'He's a murderer and a thief.' And he added in the tone of a man who begins to feel that he has the upper hand, 'Let us keep quite calm.'

The words murderer and thief, which Marius had thought disposed of, came like a cold douche.

'You mean there's more?' he said.

'Yes,' said Thénardier, 'there is more. Valjean did not rob Madeleine, but he is nonetheless a thief, and although he did not kill Javert he is nonetheless a murderer.'

'Are you talking about the wretched little crime he committed forty years ago, which, as your newspaper shows, has been fully expiated?' asked Marius.

'I'm talking about murder and theft, Monsieur le Baron, and I'm talking about facts. What I have now to tell you is something unpublished and quite unknown which may account for the fortune so cleverly bestowed on Madame la Baronne by Jean Valjean. I call it clever because it enabled him to buy his way into a respectable family, create a home for himself and obliterate his crime.'

'I might interrupt you at this point,' said Marius. 'But go on.'

'I shall tell you everything, Monsieur le Baron, and trust to your generosity for my reward. This secret is worth a large sum. You may ask why I have not gone to Valjean. The reason is very simple. There is nothing to be got out of him. He has handed all his money over to you, and since I need money for my voyage to La Joya, you are the person to whom I must apply. I am a little fatigued. Will you permit me to sit down?'

Marius nodded and sat down himself.

Thénardier seated himself in an upholstered armchair and replaced his papers in the envelope, remarking, as he re-folded the *Drapeau Blanc*, 'I had a job to get hold of this one.' He then sat back with his legs crossed, in the manner of a man sure of his facts, and embarked solemnly upon his narrative.

'On the sixth of June last year, Monsieur le Baron – that is to say, on the day of the uprising – a man was hiding in the Paris main sewer at the point between the Pont des Invalides and the Pont d'Iéna where it runs into the Seine.'

At this Marius drew his chair closer, and Thénardier proceeded with the assurance of an orator who feels that he has a firm hold on his audience.

'This man, who had a key to the sewer, had been obliged to go into hiding for reasons unconnected with politics. It was, I repeat, the day of the insurrection, and the time was about eight o'clock in the evening. Hearing the sound of approaching footsteps, the man took cover. Another man was in the sewer. This happened not far from the entrance, and there was sufficient light for the first man to recognize the second, who was walking bent double with a heavy burden on his back. The man was an ex-convict and his burden was a dead body. Clear proof of murder if ever there was one, and as for theft – well, one doesn't kill a man for nothing. He was going to drop the body in the river. A thing worth mentioning is that before reaching the sewer entrance he had to go through an appalling trough where he might have dumped the body; but if he had done so it would have been found by the sewage workers next day and that didn't suit him. He preferred to struggle through the pit with his burden, and it must have cost him an enormous effort. The risk he took was horrible and I am surprised that he came out of it alive.'

Marius's chair had drawn even closer. Thénardier paused for breath and went on:

'No need to tell you, Monsieur le Baron, that a sewer is not as wide as the Champs-Élysées. Two men occupying the same part of it are bound to meet. That is precisely what happened, and this second man said to the first: "You see what I'm carrying on my back? I've got to get out of here. You have a key. Hand it over." This ex-convict was a man of enormous strength. It was useless to refuse. Nevertheless the first man bargained, simply to gain time. He could see nothing of the dead man except that he was young and well-dressed, seemingly rich, and that his face was covered with blood. While they were talking the first contrived, without the murderer noticing, to rip off a small piece of the murdered man's coat. As evidence you understand, so as to be able to bring the crime home to the criminal. He then opened the sewer gate and let the man out with his burden on his back. After which he made himself scarce, not wanting to get mixed up in the affair, and in particular not wanting to be there when the murderer dropped his victim in the river. And now I think you will understand. The man carrying the corpse was Jean Valjean, and the man with the key was the person addressing you. As for the scrap of cloth –'

Thénardier concluded the sentence by pulling a muddy fragment from his pocket and holding it out, grasped between his two thumbs and forefingers.

Marius had risen to his feet, pale and scarcely able to breathe. He was staring at the scrap of cloth, and without taking his eyes off it he backed towards the wall and fumbled for the key in the door of a wardrobe. He opened the wardrobe and thrust in his arm without looking, still with his eyes fixed on the scrap of cloth which Thénardier was holding out.

'I have every reason to believe, Monsieur le Baron,' said

Thénardier, 'that the murdered man was a wealthy foreigner who had fallen into a trap set by Valjean when he had an enormous sum of money on his person.'

'I was the man,' cried Marius, 'and here is the coat I was wearing!' And he flung the bloodstained garment on the floor. Then, snatching the fragment of cloth from Thénardier, he bent over the coat and found the place from which it had been torn. It fitted exactly. Thénardier stood petrified, thinking, 'I'm done for!'

Marius rose up, trembling but radiant. He put a hand in his pocket and going furiously to Thénardier thrust a fist into his face, clutching a bundle of five-hundred and thousand-franc notes.

'You are an abominable liar and a scoundrel! You came here to accuse this man and you have cleared him; you wanted to destroy him and you have done the opposite. It's you who are the thief and the murderer! I saw you, Thénardier-Jondrette, in that foul garret in the Boulevard de l'Hôpital. I know enough about you to have you sent to gaol and further, if I wanted to. Here's a thousand francs for you, villain that you are!' He threw a thousand-franc note at him. 'And here's another five hundred, and now get out of here! What happened at Waterloo protects you.'

'Waterloo?' grunted Thénardier, pocketing the notes.

'Yes, you devil. You saved a colonel's life.'

'He was a general,' said Thénardier, looking up.

'He was a colonel. I wouldn't give a halfpenny for any general. And now get out and thank your lucky stars that I want to see no more of you. Here you are, here's another three thousand francs. Take them and go to America with your daughter, because your wife's dead, you lying rogue. What's more, I'll see to it that you get there, and when you do I'll see to it that you're credited with twenty thousand francs. Go and get yourself hanged somewhere else!'

'Monsieur le Baron,' said Thénardier, bowing to the ground, 'I am eternally grateful.'

And he left, having understood nothing, amazed and delighted by this manna from Heaven. We may briefly relate the end of his story. Two days after the scene we have described he set off for America under another name with his daughter Azelma and a letter of credit for twenty thousand francs to be drawn upon in New York. But Thénardier was incurable. He used the money to go into the slave-trade.

Directly he had left the house Marius ran into the garden, where Cosette was still strolling.

'Cosette!' he cried. 'Hurry! We must go at once. Basque, fetch a fiacre! Oh, God, he was the man who saved my life! We mustn't waste a minute. Put on your shawl.'

Cosette thought he had gone mad, and obeyed.

Marius could scarcely breathe. He pressed a hand to his heart to calm its beating. He strode up and down. He embraced Cosette. 'I'm such a fool!' he said. He was beside himself, seeing in Jean Valjean a figure of indescribable stature, supremely great and gently humble in his immensity, the convict transformed into Christ. Marius was so dazed that he could not tell exactly what he saw, only that it was great.

The fiacre arrived. He followed Cosette into it and ordered the driver to go to Number Seven, Rue de l'Homme-Armé.

'Oh, what happiness!' cried Cosette. 'I have been afraid to speak to you of the Rue de l'Homme-Armé. We're going to see Monsieur Jean.'

'Your father, Cosette. More than ever your father. Cosette, I have guessed something. You told me that you never received the letter I sent you by Gavroche. I know what happened. It was delivered to him, your father, and he came to the barricade to save me. It's his nature to save people. He spared Javert. He rescued me from that inferno and carried me on his back through the sewers, to bring me to you. Oh, I have been a monster of ingratitude! There was a deep trough, Cosette, where we might both have been drowned, and he carried me through it. I was unconscious, you see, and I didn't know what was happening. We're going to take him back with us, whether he likes it or not, and we'll never let him go again. Provided he's at home! Provided we can find him! I'll spend the rest of my life honouring him. It must have happened like that – Gavroche gave the letter to him instead of to you. And that explains everything. You do understand, don't you?'

Cosette did not understand a word.

'I'm sure you're right,' she said.

The fiacre continued on its way.

Night with day to follow

Jean Valjean looked round on hearing the knock on his door and feebly called 'Come in!'

The door opened and Cosette and Marius appeared. Cosette rushed into the room while Marius stood in the doorway.

'Cosette!' said Jean Valjean and sat upright in his chair, his face white and haggard, his arms extended and a glow of immense happiness in his eyes. Cosette fell into his arms. 'Father!' she cried.

Valjean was stammering broken words of welcome. Then he said, 'So you have forgiven me?' and, turning to Marius, who was screwing up his eyes to prevent the tears from falling, he said: 'And you too, you forgive me?'

Marius could not speak. 'Thank you,' said Valjean.

Cosette tossed her hat and shawl on to the bed, and seating herself on the old man's knees, she tenderly parted the locks of hair and kissed him on the forehead. Valjean was in a state of great bewilderment. Cosette, who had only a confused notion of what it was all about, embraced him again. Valjean stammered:

'One can be so stupid! I thought I should never see her again. Do you know, Monsieur Pontmercy, that at the moment when you entered the room I was saying to myself, "It's all over". There's the little dress she wore, there on the bed. I was the most miserable of men. That's what I was saying to myself at the very moment when you came upstairs – "I shall never see her again!" How idiotic it was! One forgets to trust in God. But I was so unhappy.'

For a moment he was unable to speak, but then he went on:

'I really did need to see Cosette for a little while every now and then. The heart must have something to live on. But I felt that I was not wanted, and I said to myself, "They don't need you, so stay in your own place. No one has the right to inflict themselves on other people." And now I'm seeing her again! Cosette, this is a very pretty dress you're wearing. Did your husband choose it? You don't mind, do you, Monsieur Pontmercy, if I address her as *tu*. It won't be for long.'

'Such a cruel father!' said Cosette. 'Where have you been? Why were you away so long? The other times it was only three or four days. I sent Nicolette, but they always told her you were away. When did you get back, and why didn't you let us know? Do you know, you've changed a great deal. How wicked of you! You've been ill and you never told us. Marius, take his hand and feel how cold it is.'

'Monsieur Pontmercy,' said Jean Valjean, 'have you really forgiven me?'

At the repetition of the words Marius broke down.

'Cosette, did you hear what he said? He asked me to forgive him! And do you know what he did? He saved my life and, even more, he gave me you! And then he sacrificed himself by withdrawing from our lives. He ran hideous risks for us and now he asks me to forgive him, graceless, pitiless clod that I have been! His courage, his saintliness, his selflessness are beyond all bounds. There is no price too high to pay for him.'

'You have no need to say all this,' murmured Jean Valjean.

'Why didn't you say it yourself?' demanded Marius, in a voice in which reproach was mingled with veneration. 'It's partly your fault. You save a man's life and then you don't tell him. Even worse, you pretended to confess to me and in doing so you defamed yourself.'

'I told you the truth,' said Valjean.

'No. The truth means the whole truth, not just part of it. Why didn't you tell me that you were Monsieur Madeleine and that you had spared Javert? Why didn't you tell me that I owed you my life?'

'Because I thought as you did. I thought you were right. It was better for me to break away. If you had known about the business of the sewer you might have made me stay with you. It would have upset everything.'

'What or whom would it have upset?' demanded Marius. 'Do you think we're going to allow you to stay here? We're going to take you with us. Good God, when I think that I only learnt all this by pure chance! You're coming with us. You're part of us. You're Cosette's father and mine. I won't allow you to spend another day in this horrible place.'

'Certainly I shan't be here tomorrow,' said Jean Valjean.

'And what does that mean? We shan't allow you to go on any more journeys. You aren't going to leave us again. You belong to us. We shan't let you go.'

'This time it's final,' said Cosette. 'We have a cab down below. I'm kidnapping you – if necessary, by force.'

Laughing, she went through the motions of picking up the old man in her arms.

'We've still kept your room for you. You can't think how pretty the garden is just now. The azaleas are coming on wonderfully, the paths are sanded with real sea sand, and there are little blue shells. You'll be able to eat my strawberries, I'm the one who waters them. And there won't be any more of this "Madame – Monsieur Jean" nonsense, we're a republic and we call each other *tu*, don't we, Marius? Everything will be different now. And oh, father, a most dreaful thing happened. There was a redbreast that had built its nest in a hole in the wall, and a horrid cat went and ate it. My darling redbreast, that used to look in at my window! It made me cry. I could have killed that cat. But now nobody's going to cry any more. We're all going to be happy. Grandfather will be so delighted when we bring you back with us. You shall have your own corner of the garden where you can grow anything you like and we shall see if your strawberries are as good as mine. And I'll do everything you say, and of course you'll have to obey me as well.'

Jean Valjean had listened without hearing. He had listened to the music of her voice rather than to the words, and one of those great tears which are the deep pearls of the soul brimmed in his eye. He murmured:

'This is the proof that God is good.'

'Dear father!' said Cosette.

'It is true,' said Jean Valjean, 'that it would be delightful for us all to live together. Those trees are filled with birds. I would stroll with Cosette. To be one of the living, people who greet each other in the morning and call to each other in the garden, that is a great happiness. We should see each other every day and would each cultivate our own corner, and she would give me her strawberries to eat and I would cut my roses for her. Yes, it would be delightful, only –' he broke off and said softly, 'well, it's a shame.'

The tear did not fall but lingered in his eye and he replaced it with a smile. Cosette took his two hands in hers.

'Your hands are so cold,' she said. 'Are you ill? Are you in pain?'

'No,' said Valjean. 'I'm not in pain. Only –' he broke off again.

'Only what?'

'I'm going to die in a little while.'

Cosette and Marius shuddered.

'To die!' exclaimed Marius.

'Yes, but that is not important,' said Jean Valjean. He drew breath, smiled and said: 'Cosette, go on talking. Your redbreast died. Go on talking about it. I want to hear your voice.'

Marius was gazing at him in stupefaction and Cosette uttered a piercing cry.

'Father! Father! You're going to live! You must live! I want you to live, do you understand?'

Jean Valjean looked up at her with adoring eyes.

'Very well, forbid me to die. Who knows, perhaps I shall obey. I was in the act of dying when you arrived. That stopped me. It was as though I were being reborn.'

'You're full of strength and life,' cried Marius. 'Do you think people die just like that? You have suffered greatly, but now your sufferings are over. I am the one to ask your forgiveness, and I do so on my knees. You must live, and you must live with us, and you must live for a long, long time. We're taking you back. Henceforth our every thought will be for your happiness.'

'You see?' said Cosette, in tears. 'Marius says you aren't to die.'

Jean Valjean continued to smile.

'If you take me back, Monsieur Pontmercy, will that make me any different from the man I am? No. God thinks as you and I do, and he has not changed his mind. It is better for me to go. Death is a very sensible arrangement. God knows better than we do what is good for us. That you should be happy, Marius Pontmercy and Cosette, that youth should marry with the morning, that you two children should have lilac and nightingales around you, that your life should be like a lawn bathed in sunshine and glowing with enchantment; and that I, who am no longer good for anything, should now die, that is surely right. We must be reasonable. There is nothing more left for me. I am well persuaded that my life is over. I had a fainting fit not long ago, and last night I drank all the water in the jug. Your husband is so good, Cosette. It is far better for you to be with him than with me.'

There was again a knock on the door and the doctor entered.

'Good day and good-bye, doctor,' said Valjean. 'These are my two children.'

Marius went up to him and spoke a single word – 'Monsieur?...' – but the the tone in which he said it made it an entire question. The doctor replied with a meaningful glance.

'Because things do not always please us,' said Valjean, 'that is no reason for reproaching God.'

There was a pause in which all were oppressed. Jean Valjean turned to Cosette as though he wished to carry her image with him into eternity. Even amid the shadows into which he had now sunk the sight of her could still raise him to ecstasy. The glow of her sweet face was reflected in his own. Even in the act of death there may be enchantment.

The doctor was feeling his pulse. 'You were what he needed,' he said to Cosette and Marius; and then in a whispered aside to Marius: 'Too late, I fear.'

Scarcely taking his eyes off Cosette, Valjean glanced serenely at Marius and the doctor. A low murmur escaped his lips.

'To die is nothing; but it is terrible not to live.'

Suddenly he stood up. These returns of strength are sometimes a sign of the final death-throes. He walked steadily to the wall, brushing aside Marius and the doctor, who sought to help him, and took down the little copper crucifix which was hanging there. Then he returned to his chair, moving like a man in the fullness of health, and, putting the crucifix on the table, said in a clear voice:

'He is the great martyr.'

Then his head fell forward while his fingers clutched at the stuff of his trousers over his knees. Cosette ran sobbing to hold him up, murmuring distractedly, 'Father, father, have we found you only to lose you?'

One may say of dying that it goes by fits and starts, now moving towards the grave and now turning back towards life. After that half-seizure Valjean regained strength, passed a hand over his forehead as though to brush away the shadows, and was almost entirely lucid. He seized a fold of Cosette's sleeve and kissed it.

'He's reviving!' cried Marius. 'Doctor, he's reviving!'

'You are both so good,' said Jean Valjean. 'I will tell you what has grieved me. What has grieved me, Monsieur Pontmercy, is that you have made no use of the money. It is truly your wife's money. Let me explain it to you, my children. I am glad you are here, if only for that reason. Black jade comes from England and white jade comes from Norway. It's all in this letter here. And I invented a new kind of fastening for bracelets which is prettier, better and cheaper. It made a great deal of money. Cosette's fortune is really and truly hers. I tell you this to put your minds at rest.'

The concierge had come upstairs and was looking through the half-open door. The doctor told her to go away, but he could not prevent the zealous woman from calling to the dying man:

'Do you want a priest?'

'I have one,' Jean Valjean replied; and he pointed upwards as though there were some other being present whom he alone could see. Indeed it is not improbable that the bishop was present in those last moments of his life. Cosette slipped a pillow behind his back. Valjean said:

'I beseech you, Monsieur Pontmercy, to have no misgivings. My life will have been wasted if you do not make use of the money that is truly Cosette's. I can assure you that our products were very good, rivalling what are known as the jewels of Berlin.'

When a person dear to us is about to die we fix him with an intent gaze that seeks to hold him back. They stood beside him in silent anguish, having no words to speak, Cosette clasping Marius by the hand.

Jean Valjean was visibly declining, sinking down towards that dark horizon. His breath was coming in gasps, punctured by slight groans. He had difficulty in moving his arms, and his feet were now quite motionless. But as the weakness of his body increased so his spirit grew in splendour, and the light of the unknown world was already visible in his eyes. His face became paler as he smiled. There was something other than life in it. His breath failed but his gaze grew deeper. He was a dead body which seemed to possess wings.

He signed to Cosette to come closer to him, then signed to Marius. It was the last moment of the last hour, and when he spoke it was in a voice so faint that it seemed to come from a long way off, as though there were a wall between them.

'Come close to me, both of you. I love you dearly. How sweet it is to die like this. And you love me too, dear Cosette. You'll weep for me a little, but not too much, I want you to have no great sorrows. You must enjoy life, my children. A thing I forgot to mention is that the buckles without tongues are more profitable than any other kind. They cost ten francs the gross to manufacture and sell at sixty. Excellent business, as you see, so there is really no reason, Monsieur Pontmercy, why you should be astonished at that sum of six hundred thousand francs. It is honest money. You can be rich with an easy mind. You must have a carriage and now and then a box at the theatre, and you, Cosette, must have beautiful dresses to dance in, and when you invite your friends to dinner. You must be happy. I am leaving the two candlesticks on the mantelpiece to Cosette. They are made of silver, but to me they are pure gold. I don't know whether the person who gave them to me is pleased as he looks down on me from above. I have done my best. You must not forget, my children, that I am one of the poor. You must bury me in any plot of ground that comes handy and put a stone to mark the spot. That is my wish. No name on the stone. If Cosette cares to visit it sometimes I shall be glad. And you too, Monsieur Pontmercy. I must confess that I have not always liked you, and I ask your forgiveness. She and you are now one person to me and I am very grateful. I know you are making Cosette happy. The greatest joy in my life has been to see her with rosy cheeks, and I have been grieved when she has looked pale. You will find in the chest of drawers a five-hundred-franc note. I haven't touched it. It is for the poor. Cosette, do you see your little dress there on the bed? Do you remember it? That was ten years ago. How time passes! We have been happy together. Now it is over. You must not weep, dear children, I shall not be far away. I shall watch over you from where I am. You need only to look when night has fallen and you will see me smile. Do you remember Montfermeil, Cosette? You were in the woods, and you were frightened. I helped you carry the bucket, do you remember? That was the first time I touched your poor hand. It was so cold! Your hands were red in those days, Mademoiselle, and now they are white. And do you remember that big doll? You called her Catherine, and you wished you could have taken her with you to the convent. You made me laugh at times, angel that you were. When it rained you floated straws in the gutter and watched to see which would win. Once I gave you a battledore of willow and a shuttlecock with yellow, blue and green feathers. I expect you have forgotten that. You were so enchanting when you were small. You hung cherries over your ears. All those things are in the past – the woods we walked through, the convent where we took refuge, your child's eyes and laughter, all shadows now. I believed that it all belonged to me, and that is where I was foolish. Those Thénardiers were wicked people, but we must forgive them. Cosette, the time has come for me to tell you your mother's name. It was Fantine. You must not forget it, Fantine, and you must bow your head whenever you speak it. She loved you greatly and she suffered greatly. She was as rich in sorrow as you are in happiness. That is how God evens things out. He watches us all from above and knows what he is doing amid his splendid stars. And now I must leave you, my children. Love one another always. There is nothing else that matters in this world except love. You will think sometimes of the old man who died in this place. Dearest Cosette, it was not my fault if lately I have not come to see you. It wrung my heart. I used to go to the end of your street. I must have looked a strange sight to the people who saw me. They must have thought me mad. One day I went without my hat . . . Children, my sight is failing. I had more to say, but no matter. Think of me sometimes. You are fortunate. I don't know what is happening to me, I can see a light. Come closer. I die happy. Bow your dear heads so that I may lay my hands on them.'

Cosette and Marius fell on their knees on either side of him, stifling their tears. His hands rested on their heads, and did not move again. He lay back with his head turned to the sky, and the light from the two candlesticks fell upon his face.

VI

The hidden grave

In the cemetery of Père Lachaise, not far from the communal grave and remote from the elegant quarter of that city of sepulchres which parades in the presence of eternity the hideous fashions of death, is a deserted corner near an old wall, and here, beneath a big yew tree, surrounded by mosses and dandelions, there is a stone. It is black and green, no more exempt than other stones from the encroachment of time, lichen and bird-droppings. There is no path near it, and people are reluctant to go that way because the grass is long and they are sure to get their feet wet. In sunny weather lizards visit it, there is a stir of grasses all around it and birds sing in the tree.

The stone is quite unadorned. It was carved strictly to serve its purpose, long enough and wide enough to cover a man. It bears no name.

But many years ago someone chalked four lines of verse on it which became gradually illegible under the influence of wind and weather and have now, no doubt, vanished entirely.

He sleeps. Although so much he was denied,
He lived; and when his dear love left him, died.
It happened of itself, in the calm way
That in the evening night-time follows day.

APPENDIX A

PART TWO: BOOK SEVEN:
A Parenthesis

I
The convent as an abstract idea

THIS BOOK is a drama in which the leading character is the Infinite.
Mankind takes second place.

That being so, since a convent lay upon our path we were obliged
to enter it. Why? Because the convent, which belongs to the West
as it does to the East, to antiquity as it does to the present time, to
Buddhism and Muhammadanism as it does to Christianity, is one of
the optical devices whereby man gains a glimpse of infinity.

This is not the place to pursue at unreasonable length certain lines
of thought; nevertheless, while wholly reserving our own views,
our reservations and even our resentments, we are bound to assert
that whenever we encounter the Infinite in man, however imperfect-
ly understood, we treat it with respect. Whether in the synagogue,
the mosque, the pagoda, or the wigwam, there is a hideous aspect
which we execrate and a sublime aspect which we venerate. So great
a subject for spiritual contemplation, such measureless dreaming –
the echo of God on the human wall!

II
The convent as historical fact

In the eyes of history, reason, and truth, monasticism stands condemned. Monasteries, when they are numerous in a country, are
clots in its circulatory system; they are encumbrances, centres of
indolence where there should be centres of labour. Monastic communities are to the social community as a whole what mistletoe is
to the oak or a verruca to the human body. Their prosperity and
well-being are the country's impoverishment. The monkish regime,
which was of value in the early stages of civilization, useful in
replacing brutality by spirituality, is harmful to the virility of a
nation. Moreover, when the discipline relaxes and enters upon its
stage of disorder, since it still sets an example it becomes harmful
for all the reasons that in its pure stage made it salutary.

Close confinement has had its day. The cloisters, useful for the early education of modern civilization, have hindered its growth and delayed its development. Considered as an institution and a means of education, the monasteries, which were good in the tenth century and of questionable value in the fifteenth, are deplorable in the nineteenth. The leprosy of monasticism has over the centuries devoured two great nations almost to the bone, Italy and Spain, one the light of Europe and the other its splendour, and at the present time those illustrious peoples are only beginning to recover, thanks to the sane and vigorous purification of 1789.

The convent, and in particular the ancient women's convent such as still existed at the beginning of the present century in Italy, Austria, and Spain, was one of the most sombre creations of the Middle Ages. Cloisters of that kind were the meeting-place of terrors. The Catholic convent, in the strict sense, was filled with the dark light of death.

The Spanish convent is especially funereal. Tower-like altars, high as cathedrals, rise up under gloomy vaults and domes scarcely visible in the shadowed light; huge white crucifixes hang on chains; ivory Christs stretch naked against ebony, bleeding rather than bloodstained, hideous and magnificent, elbows and knee-caps thrusting through the skin and flesh protruding from open wounds, figures crowned with thorns of silver and nailed with nails of gold, with drops of blood that are rubies on their foreheads and tears that are diamonds in their eyes. The diamonds and rubies seem to be liquid and cause weeping in the veiled forms in the darkness below, their bodies ravaged by sackcloth and the whip, their breasts crushed in wicker corsets, their knees bruised with prayer. They are women who believe themselves to be wives; ghosts who think themselves seraphim. Do they think, these women? Do they desire or love or live? No. Their nerves have turned to bone, and their bones to rock. Their veils are woven night, and the breath within them is like the breathing of death. The abbess, a spectral figure, both sanctifies and terrifies them. Immaculacy resides there, purity gone mad. Such are the old Spanish convents, haunts of a terrifying devotion, refuges of virgins, places without pity.

Catholic Spain was more Roman than Rome herself, and the Spanish convent was the Catholic convent par excellence. The archbishop, the chief eunuch of Heaven, imprisoned and spied upon that seraglio of souls set apart for God. The nun was the odalisque, the priest the eunuch. The rapt adōrers were selected in dreams and possessed by Christ, the beautiful youth who came down from the cross at night and filled the cell with ecstasy. High walls protected from all distractions the mystical Sultana whose Sultan had been crucified. Even a glance beyond the walls was an act of infidelity. The *in pace* replaced the leather sack. What in the East was flung into the sea, in the West was buried in the earth. The women on both sides wrung their hands, these destined for the waves, those for the grave; one lot was drowned, the other buried – a monstrous parallelism.

Worshippers of the past in the present day, being unable to deny these things, elect to smile at them. A strange and comfortable fashion has sprung up of obliterating the revelations of history, disparaging the commentaries of philosophy and evading all awkward facts and disturbing questions. 'Mere propaganda,' the wise men say, and the fools repeat it after them. Rousseau, Diderot, Voltaire, all were propagandists. I do not know who it was who recently discovered that Tacitus was a propagandist and Nero his victim, greatly to be pitied.

But facts are not so easily disposed of. The author of these lines has with his own eyes seen a relic of the Middle Ages some eight leagues from Brussels, easily visited by anyone: this is the entrance to the oubliettes of the Abbaye de Villers in the middle of a lawn which was the courtyard of the Abbey, and, at the edge of the river Dyle, four stone cells half in and half out of the water. They were *in pace* cells, each with the remains of an iron door, a latrine and a barred window, two feet above the level of the river on the outside and six feet above ground level inside. The river beyond the wall is four feet deep. The earth is always wet, and this wet earth was the *in pace* victim's bed. In one of these dungeons there is part of an iron collar fixed to the wall; in another there is a sort of square box composed of four slabs of granite, too short for anyone to lie down in it and too low for him to stand upright. The victim was put in it with a slab of stone on top. This thing exists. It can be seen and touched. But all this, the iron door, the barred window, the collar, the stone box, the flowing river, all is merely propaganda!

Conditions under which the past may be respected

Monasticism, as it existed in Spain and still exists in Tibet, is a wasting disease of civilization. It puts a stop to life. Quite simply, it depopulates. Claustration is castration. It has been the scourge of Europe. Add to this the violence so often inflicted on the conscience, the enforced vocations, feudalism depending on the monastery for its support, the older generation getting rid of surplus progeny in the cloister; and the savagery of which we have spoken, the *in pace*, the closed mouths and minds, so much intelligence condemned to the imprisonment of vows for life, the burial of living souls. No matter who you are, the thought of so much suffering and degradation must cause you to shudder at the sight of a veil or cassock, those two shrouds of human invention.

Nevertheless there are still places where, in spite of philosophy and progress, the cloistral spirit persists even in the nineteenth century, and a weird recrudescence of asceticism is even now astonishing the civilized world. This obstinate determination of old institutions to perpetuate themselves resembles the rancid scent which clings to your hair, the rotten fish which demands to be eaten, the tyranny of children's garments presuming to clothe a grown man, or the tenderness of corpses returning to embrace the living.

'Ingrate!' says the garment. 'I protected you in bad weather. Why do you now discard me?' ... 'I come from the open sea,' says the fish ... 'I was once a rose,' says the scent ... 'I loved you,' says the corpse ... 'I civilized you,' says the monastery. And to all this there is only one reply – 'Once upon a time.'

It seems strange that anyone should dream of the indefinite prolongation of institutions that have outlived their usefulness, of restoring dogmas now grown hollow, refurbishing shrines, restoring monasteries, reviving old superstitions and fanaticisms – in a word, of reviving monasticism and militarism, saving society by the multiplication of parasites and imposing the past on the present. Nevertheless there are those who advocate such procedures. These theorists, among them persons of intelligence, have a simple method: they cover the past with a veneer which they term social order, divine right, morality, the family, ancestral respect, ancient authority, sacred tradition, legitimacy, and religion; and this they ask honest men to accept. It is an argument well known to the ancients. They covered a black sacrificial heifer with chalk and called it white – *Bos cretatus*.

For our own part, we respect certain things belonging to the past and forgive all of it, provided it consents to stay dead. But if it tries to come alive we attack and seek to kill it.

Superstition, bigotry and prejudice, ghosts though they are, cling tenaciously to life; they are shades armed with tooth and claw. They must be grappled with unceasingly, for it is a fateful part of human destiny that it is condemned to wage perpetual war against ghosts. A shade is not easily taken by the throat and destroyed.

A monastery in France, in the middle of the nineteenth century, is like a school of owls blinking in the sunlight. The practice of rigid asceticism in the Paris of 1789, 1830 or 1848 – Rome flowering in the modern city – is an anachronism. In normal times one can dispel an anachronism merely by recalling the date; but these are not normal times.

We have to fight. We must fight, but at the same time we must distinguish. It is the essence of truth that it is never excessive. Why should it exaggerate? There is that which should be destroyed and that which should be simply illuminated and studied. How great is the force of benevolent and searching examination! We must not resort to the flame where only light is required.

Therefore, given the fact of the nineteenth century, we are opposed in principle to ascetic seclusion, whether in Asia or in Europe, in India or in Turkey. To speak of a monastery is to speak of a swamp. The tendency to putrescence is apparent, the stagnation is unhealthy, the fermentation renders the people feverish so that they waste away; and the spreading of such swamps becomes a plague of Egypt. We cannot think without horror of those countries where fakirs and bonzes, gurus, marabouts and dervishes swarm like the inmates of an ant-heap.

But when all this has been said there remains the question of religion. It is a matter possessing mysterious, almost terrifying aspects at which we may venture to look steadily.

The monastery viewed in the light of principle

Men join together and live together. They do so by virtue of the right of association. They shut themselves away by virtue of the right of every man to open or close his door. They do not go beyond the door by virtue of the right of all men to come and go as they please, which implies the right to stay at home.

And what do they do in this home? They talk in low voices and with lowered eyes, and they work. They renounce the world and the town, all sensuality, all pleasure, all vanity, all pride, all self-interest. They are clad in rough garments. Not one possesses any article of personal property. The man who was rich when he entered makes himself a pauper by giving all he has to the community. The man who was once a nobleman is the equal of the man who was once a peasant. All the cells are identical. All their occupants wear the same tonsure and the same clothes, eat the same food, sleep on the same straw, and die on the same ashes. The same sack on their body, the same cord round their waists. If it is decided to go bare-foot, all go barefoot. There may be a prince among them, but he is a shadow like the others. There are no more titles, even family names have disappeared. There are no Christian names. All submit to the equality of their baptismal names. They have dissolved the family of the flesh and constructed within their community the family of the spirit. They have no relations other than this assembly of men. They assist the poor and care for the sick. They elect those to whom they owe obedience. They call each other 'brother'.

At this point you may interject: 'But that is the ideal monastery!' It is sufficient that it should be a possible monastery for me to take it into account.

That is why in previous chapters I have talked of these establishments with respect. Disregarding the Middle Ages and Asia, and setting aside all historical and political considerations, I shall always consider the cloistered community, provided it is wholly voluntary and composed of those who freely consent, with a certain earnest attention and, in some respects, with deference. Where there is a community there is a commune, and where there is a commune there is the rule of law. The monastery is the outcome of the formula, Equality and Fraternity. But how splendid a thing is Liberty, and how great the transformation it effects! Only Liberty is needed to transform the monastery into a republic.

To proceed. The men or women enclosed within those walls are clad in the same fashion, are equals, and address each other as brother or sister. Very well; but do they do more than this?

Yes. They gaze into the gloom and kneel with clasped hands. What does this signify?

V

Prayer

They pray.

To whom?

To God.

To pray to God – what does it mean?

Does there exist an Infinity outside ourselves? Is that infinity One, immanent and permanent, necessarily having substance, since He is infinite and if He lacked matter He would be limited, necessarily possessing intelligence since He is infinite and, lacking intelligence, He would be in that sense finite. Does this Infinity inspire in us the idea of essence, while to ourselves we can only attribute the idea of existence? In other words, is He not the whole of which we are but the part?

At the same time, if there is infinity outside us is there not infinity within us? Are not these two infinities (a horrifying plural!) superimposed one upon the other, and is not the second infinity so to speak subjugated to the first, its mirror and its echo, an abyss that is concentric with another abyss? Is it not also intelligent? Does it not think, love and desire? If both infinities are intelligent, then each has in principle a Will, and there is an *I* in the higher infinity just as there is in the lower. That lower *I* is the soul, and the higher *I* is God. To establish in the mind a contact between the higher and the lower Infinities, this is to pray.

Nothing must be withdrawn from the human spirit; suppression is bad. We have to reform and transform. Certain of man's faculties are directed towards the Unknown – thought, reverie, prayer. The Unknown is an ocean; but what is conscience if not an ocean? It is the compass of the Unknown. Thought, reverie, prayer, these are great, mysterious radiations which we must respect. Whither do they penetrate, these majestic radiations of the soul? Into the darkness; that is to say, into the night.

It is the greatness of democracy that it denies and rejects nothing in humanity. Close by the Rights of Man, at the least set beside them, are the Rights of the Spirit.

To crush fanaticism and revere the Infinite, that is the law. It is not enough for us to prostrate ourselves under the tree which is Creation, and to contemplate its tremendous branches filled with stars. We have a duty to perform, to work upon the human soul, to defend the mystery against the miracle, to worship the incomprehensible while rejecting the absurd; to accept, in the inexplicable, only what is necessary; to dispel the superstitions that surround religion – to rid God of His maggots.

VI

The virtue of prayer

As to the methods of praying, all are good provided they are sincere. Read the book backwards, but strive towards the Infinite.

There is, as we know, a philosophy which denies the Infinite. There is also a pathological state which denies the existence of the sun: it is known as blindness. To treat a sense we lack as a source of truth is a truly blind effrontery. What is curious is the lofty and complacent air with which this groping philosophy disdains the philosophy which sees God. It is as though a mole were to exclaim, 'Really I'm sorry for them with their sun!'

As we know, there are illustrious and powerful atheists. These, brought to the truth by the power of their minds, are not quite convinced in their atheism; with them, it is little more than a matter of definition, and in any case, even if they do not believe in God, they are a proof of His existence, being themselves great spirits. We salute them as philosophers while wholly rejecting their philosophy.

What is also interesting is the use made of words. There is a school of metaphysics in the north, somewhat misty in its thinking, which thought to cause a revolution in human understanding by replacing the word Force with the word Will. But to say 'the plant wills' instead of 'the plant grows' would indeed be meaningful if one added 'the universe wills'. Why? Because it would follow that if the plant wills it has an ego; and if the Universe wills it must have a God.

For our part, although in contradistinction to this school of thought we reject nothing *a priori*, we find it more difficult to accept, as they do, the view that the plant has a will of its own than the view that the Universe has a will of its own, which they deny. To deny the will of the Infinite, that is to say, of God, is only possible if we deny the Infinite itself. We have demonstrated this.

The denial of the Infinite leads straight to nihilism. Everything becomes 'an idea conceived in the mind'. And with nihilism no discussion is possible, for the nihilist doubts the existence of the person he is talking to and is not even sure of his own existence. Even he may be no more than an idea conceived in his own mind. But what he does not realize is that he accepts the existence of everything he denies simply by uttering the word 'mind'.

In short, all roads are blocked to a philosophy which reduces everything to the word 'no'. To 'no' there is only one answer and that is 'yes'. Nihilism has no substance. There is no such thing as nothingness, and zero does not exist. Everything is something. Nothing is nothing. Man lives more by affirmation than by bread.

Merely to see and show is not enough. Philosophy must have an impetus, and its aim must be the improvement of man. Socrates must enter into Adam and produce Marcus Aurelius; in other words, cause the wise man to emerge from the happy man, and change Eden into a Lyceum. Knowledge should be a stimulus. What a sorry aim and sickly ambition it is merely to enjoy! The animal enjoys. To think, that is the real triumph of the spirit! To offer thought to slake the thirst of mankind, to give all men as an elixir the notion of God, to cause conscience to fraternize with knowledge and by this mysterious union render men just, that is the function of real philosophy. Morality is a flowering of truths. Contemplation leads to action. The Absolute must be practicable. The ideal must be practicable, capable of being eaten and drunk by the human spirit. It is the ideal which has the right to say: 'Take this which is my flesh and blood.' Wisdom is a holy communion; only if this is understood does it cease to be a sterile love of knowledge and become instead the one sovereign impulse of human brotherhood, while philosophy is raised to the status of religion.

Philosophy should not be merely a package composed of mystery so that it may be studied in comfort, a convenience for the satisfaction of the curious. For our part, deferring the development of our thought to another occasion, we will only say that we do not think of man as a starting point, nor our progress as the aim except in conjunction with the two forces of faith and love.

Progress is the aim: the ideal is the concept. And the Ideal is God.

Ideal, Absolute, Perfection, Infinite – all these words have the same meaning.

VII

Precautions to be taken in passing judgement

History and philosophy have certain duties to perform which are at the same time perpetual and quite simple; these are to combat the High Priest Caiaphas, in whose reign Christ was condemned to death, Dracon the judge, Trimalchio, who figures in the *Satiricon* of Petronius, and the Emperor Tiberius. This is clear and straightforward and presents no obscurity. But the right to live apart, even with all its discomforts and abuses, needs to be affirmed and tolerated. Monkishness is a human problem.

When we speak of monasteries, those resorts of error but of innocence, of misconception but of goodwill, of ignorance but of devotion, of torment but of martyrdom, we are bound nearly always to say both yes and no.

The monastery is a contradiction. Its aim is salvation, its method is sacrifice. It is the supreme egotism, and its outcome is supreme abnegation. One might indeed say that 'Abdicate that you may rule' is its motto.

The inmates of monasteries suffer to enjoy. They draw a bill of exchange on death, discounting the light of Heaven for darkness upon earth. They accept Hell as an advance upon their inheritance of Paradise. The taking of the veil or the frock is an act of suicide rewarded with eternity. It does not appear to us that this is a suitable subject for derision. Everything about it is serious, the good as well as the bad. The fair-minded man frowns but does not smile in mockery. Anger may be accepted, but not malice.

VIII

Faith and law

A few last words.

We condemn the Church when she is saturated with intrigue, we despise the spiritual life that is soured by the temporal, but we honour the thoughtful man wherever we find him. We salute those who kneel. Faith is necessary to man; woe to him who believes in nothing!

One is not idle because one is absorbed. There is both visible and invisible labour. To contemplate is to toil, to think is to do. The crossed arms work, the clasped hands act. The eyes upturned to Heaven are an act of creation. Thales remained immobile for four years.* He was the founder of philosophy. In our view cenobites are not idlers, nor are solitaries sluggards. To think of the Unknown is a serious matter. Without retracting anything that we have previously said, we believe that the thought of the grave should be constantly in the mind of the living. The Abbé de la Trappe, founder of the Trappist Order, furnished the reply to Horace – 'We all must die.'

To pervade one's life with a certain consciousness of its ending is the law of the wise man and also of the ascetic. It is here that these two come together. There is material growth, which we desire, and there is also moral grandeur, to which we cling. Thoughtless, hasty thinkers may ask:

'What is the use of those motionless figures crouched in the shadow of mystery? What purpose do they serve? What do they do?'

Alas, faced by the darkness that surrounds us all, and not knowing what the immense dispersal may make of us, we reply: 'There is perhaps no more sublime work than that performed by those motionless figures.' To which we add: 'And perhaps none more useful.' We need those who pray constantly to compensate for those who do not pray at all.

The whole question, for us, resides in the quantity of thought that is mingled with the prayer. It is a great thing that Leibnitz should pray; and that Voltaire should worship is wonderful. *Deo*

---

*Professor Guyard comments on this that Thales, the Ionic philosopher (636–546 BC), did at least live in solitude for four years. Trs.

erexit Voltaire – 'Voltaire built this to the glory of God' – is carved on the façade of the church at Ferney.

We are on the side of religion as opposed to religions, and we are among those who believe in the wretched inadequacy of sermons and the sublimity of prayer. For the rest, in the times in which we live – a moment in time which happily will not characterize the whole of the nineteenth century – this time when so many men have earthbowed heads and spirits scarcely loftier, when so many have no purpose other than pleasure and are wholly concerned with the shortlived, shapeless, material objects of life, anyone who cuts himself off from all this seems to us deserving of respect. The monastery is renunciation. The sacrifice which follows the wrong path is none the less a sacrifice. To make a duty of a stern error, this has its own greatness.

Considered of itself, in its ideal form, and surveying the truth impartially to embrace all its aspects, the monastery, and above all the women's convent – for in our society it is the women who suffer most, and in that exiled life of the cloister there is protestation – in the women's convent there is undeniably a certain majesty. That grey and dismal cloistered life of which we have given some outline is not in the true sense life at all, for it is not liberty; it is not the grave, for it is not completion; it is a strange place where, as from a mountain-peak, we contemplate on one side the limbo in which we dwell and on the other the limbo into which we shall enter: a narrow, misty frontier separating two worlds, illuminated and shadowed by both at once, where the enfeebled light of the world is mingled with the unknown light of death, a foreshadowing of the tomb.

For our own part, not believing in what those women believe, but living by faith as they do, we have never been able to contemplate, without a kind of tender religious awe, a sort of pity filled with envy, those devoted, trembling, and confiding creatures, humble and noble souls who dare to live at the very edge of mystery, to live suspended between a world which is closed to them and a Heaven which is not yet open, their faces turned towards a light which they cannot see, possessing simply the happiness of believing that they know where it is, yearning for the unknown, their eyes intent upon obscurity, kneeling motionless, lost, stupefied, and trembling, but at certain moments half exalted by the deep breathing of eternity.

PART FOUR: BOOK SEVEN:
Argot

I

Its origin

PIGRITIA IS a terrible word. It encompasses a world: *la pégre*, for which read robbery, and the hell which is *la pégrenne*, for which read hunger.

Thus idleness is a mother with two children: a son, who is robbery, and a daughter, who is hunger.

Where have we now got to? To argot.

What is argot? It is at once a nation and an idiom, robbery in its two aspects, the people and the language.

When, thirty-four years ago, the narrator of this grave and sombre history introduced into a work written with the same intention a thief who spoke argot, it was greeted with outrage and indignation – 'What! Argot! But that is the language of the underworld, of pickpockets and prisons, everything that is most abominable in society!' etc. etc. etc.

We have never understood this kind of objection.

Later two powerful novelists, the first a profound student of the human heart and the second a fearless friend of the common people, Balzac and Eugène Sue, having made criminals talk their natural language, as the author of *Le dernier jour d'un condamné* had done in 1828, were similarly castigated – 'Why do these writers inflict this revolting patois on us? Argot is a disgusting thing!'

No one would deny this. But when it comes to the probing of a wound, an abyss or a social phenomenon, can it be wrong to lead the way and penetrate to the heart of the matter? We had always thought this to be an act of courage, or at least a useful act, worthy of the sympathy that any performance of duty deserves. Why should not everything be explored and studied? Why stop halfway? To stop is the action of the plummet, not of the leadsman who operates it.

Certainly it is not an easy or an attractive task to peer into the lowest depths of the social order, the region where earth ends and mire begins; to burrow into the muck and capture and expose to the public view that debased idiom, that diseased vocabulary of which every word is like a scale of some monster of darkness and the swamp. Nothing can be more depressing than to expose, naked to the light of thought, the hideous growth of argot. Indeed it is like a sort of repellent animal intended to dwell in darkness which has been dragged out of its cloaca. One seems to see a horned and living creature viciously struggling to be restored to the place where it belongs. One word is like a claw, another like a sightless and bleeding eye; and there are phrases which clutch like the pincers of a crab. And all of it is alive with the hideous vitality of things that have organized themselves amid disorganization.

But since when has a horror been debarred from study? When has sickness driven the doctor away? Can one imagine a naturalist refusing to study a scorpion, a bat or a tarantula on the grounds that these things are too ugly? The thinker who turns his back on argot is like a surgeon who shrinks from a suppurating wound; he is a philologist reluctant to examine an aspect of language, a philosopher reluctant to scrutinize an aspect of humanity. For this must be said to those who are unaware of the fact: argot is both a literary phenomenon and a social consequence. The proper definition of the word is this: it is the language of poverty.

At this point we must pause. It can be argued that every trade and profession, one might almost say every accident in the social hierarchy and all forms of intelligence, have their argot, from the lawyer who wraps up an agreement in jargon of his own, the house agent who talks about 'extensive grounds' and 'modern conveniences', the butcher who talks about 'prime beef', to the actor who says, 'I was a flop.' The printer, the master-at-arms, the sportsman, the cobbler, the cavalry-officer all have their specialized language. At a pinch it can be claimed that the sailor who uses port and starboard for left and right is talking argot. There is an argot of the great and an argot of the little. That duchesses have their argot is proved by the following sentence from a letter written by a great lady at the time of the Restoration, *'Vous trouverez dans ces potains-là une foultitude de raisons pour que je me libertise.'* ('You will gather from this tittle-tattle a multitude of reasons why I am talking freely.') Twenty years ago there was a school of criticism which asserted that, 'Half Shakespeare is word-play and punning' – in other words, that he used argot. The poets and artists who label Monsieur de Montmorency a 'bourgeois' because he is not well versed in art and poetry are themselves talking argot. Classical scholars have their argot; mathematics, medicine, botany, all have their own language. The splendid language of the sea, resonance of the wind and the waves, the humming of the shrouds, the rolling of the ship, the roar of cannon, and the crash of the boarding-axe, all this is a superb and heroic argot that, compared with the barbaric argot of the underworld, is like a lion compared with a jackal.

All this is true, but whatever may be said in its favour this extension of the meaning of the word 'argot' is something that not everyone accepts. For our own part, we restrict the word to its old, precise meaning, and for us argot is simply argot. The true argot, argot par excellence (if those words may be used in this context), the immemorial argot which was a kingdom in itself, is, we must repeat, nothing but the ugly, restless, cunning, treacherous, profound and fatalistic language of the outcast and squalid underworld, the world of hunger and pauperism – *les misérables*. There exists, at the bottom of all abasement and misfortune, a last extreme which rebels and joins battle with the forces of law and respectability in a desperate struggle, waged partly by cunning and partly by violence, at once sick and ferocious, in which it attacks the prevailing social order with the pin-pricks of vice and the hammer-blows of crime. And for the purpose of this struggle the underworld has its own battle-language, which is argot.

To rescue from oblivion even a fragment of a language which men have used and which is in danger of being lost – that is to say, one of the elements, whether good or bad, which have shaped and complicated civilization – is to extend the scope of social observation and to serve civilization. It is a service rendered consciously or unconsciously by Plautus when he made a Phoenician talk to Carthaginian soldiers, and by Molière with his Levantine and the varieties of patois which he put into the mouths of so many of his characters. To this it may be replied that patois is a different thing – it is a language that has been used by a whole people or province. But what is argot? What purpose is served by 'rescuing' it? Our answer is simply that if there is one thing more deserving of study than the language spoken by a people or province it is the language spoken by misery; a language that has been spoken in France, for example, for more than four centuries: the language not merely of one particular misery, but of misery itself, all possible human misery.

Moreover we must insist upon the fact that the examination of social failings and deformities is ordained so that they may be recognized and cured, an inescapable task. The vocation of the historian of mores and ideas is no less strict than that of the historian of events. The latter deals with the surface of life, with battles and parliaments and the birth of princes, while the former is concerned with what goes on beneath the surface, among the people who work and wait upon the outcome of events, weary womenfolk and dying children, ignorance and prejudice, envy and secret rivalries between man and man, the vague tremors running through the mass of the impoverished, the unfortunate, and the infamous. He must descend in a spirit of both charity and severity to that secret region where the destitute are huddled together, those who bleed and those who strike, those who weep and those who curse, those who go hungry and those who devour, those who endure evil and those who cause it. Are the duties of the historians of hearts and souls less exacting than those of the historians of external fact? Has Dante less to say than Machiavelli? Is the under side of civilization less important than the upper side because it is darker and goes deeper? Can one know the mountain without also knowing the cave?

From the foregoing it might be inferred that a gulf exists between these two kinds of historian, but we have no such thought in mind. One cannot be a good historian of the outward, visible world without giving some thought to the hidden, private life of ordinary people; and on the other hand one cannot be a good historian of this inner life without taking into account outward events where these are relevant. They are two orders of fact which reflect each other, which are always linked and which sometimes provoke each other. All the features traced by providence on the surface of a nation have their sombre but distinct counterpart in the depths, and every stirring in the depths produces a tremor on the surface. True history being a composite of all things, the true historian must concern himself with all things. Mankind is not a circle with a single centre but an ellipse with two focal points of which facts are one and ideas the other.

Argot is nothing but a changing-room where language, having some evil end in view, adopts a disguise, reclothing itself with masked words and tattered metaphors, a process which renders it horrible.

It can scarcely be recognized. Is this really French, the great human language? It is ready to enter the stage, to put words into the mouth of crime, to act out the entire repertory of ill-doing. It no longer walks but shuffles, limps on a crutch that can be used as a club; it bears the name of vagrancy and has been daubed with make-up by ghostly dressers; it crawls and rears up its head, two characteristics of the reptile. It is prepared to play any part, made fraudulent by the forger, tainted by the poisoner, blackened by the soot of the incendiary; and the murderer has daubed it with red.

When, from the honest side of the fence, we listen on the fringe of society, we may hear the speech of those who are outside. We distinguish questions and answers. Without understanding it we catch a horrid murmur, resembling the human accent but nearer to growls than to words. That is argot. The words are misshapen, distorted by some kind of fantastic bestiality. We might be hearing the speech of hydras.

It is the unintelligible immersed in shadow; it grunts and whispers, adding enigma to the encircling gloom. Misfortune is dark and crime is darker still, and it is of these two darknesses put together that argot is composed. Obscurity is in the atmosphere, in the actions and in the voices: a dreadful toad-language which creeps and skips and monstrously moves in that vast fog of hunger, vice, lies, injustice, nakedness, asphyxia, and winter which is the bright noontide of the underworld.

Let us have compassion for those under chastisement. Alas, who are we ourselves? Who am I and who are you? Whence do we come and is it quite certain that we did nothing before we were born? This earth is not without some resemblance to a gaol. Who knows but that man is a victim of divine justice? Look closely at life. It is so constituted that one senses punishment everywhere.

Are you what is known as a happy man? Yet you experience sadness every day. Every day brings its major grief or its minor care. Yesterday you trembled for the health of someone dear to you, today you fear for your own; tomorrow it will be money trouble, the next day the slander of a calumniator, and on the day after that the misfortune of a friend; then there is the weather, or some possession broken or lost, or some pleasure which leaves you with an uneasy conscience; and another time it is the progress of public affairs. All this without counting the griefs of the heart. And so it goes on; as one cloud is dispelled another forms. Scarcely one day in a hundred consists of unbroken delight and sunshine. Yet you are one of the small number who are called happy! As for the rest of mankind, it is lost in stagnant night.

Thoughtful persons seldom speak of happiness or unhappiness. In this world, which is so plainly the antechamber of another, there are no happy men. The true division of humanity is between those who live in light and those who live in darkness. Our aim must be to diminish the number of the latter and increase the number of the former. That is why we demand education and knowledge. To learn to read is to light a fire; every syllable that is spelled out is a spark.

But to talk of light is not necessarily to talk of joy. One may suffer in the light; its excess burns. The flame is the enemy of the wing. To burn without ceasing to fly, that is the achievement of genius. When you have reached the stage of knowing and loving you will still suffer. The day is born in tears. The enlightened weep, if only for those still in darkness.

II

Roots

Argot is the language of the shadows.

Thought moves to its most sombre depths, social philosophy leads to the most poignant conclusions, when confronted by this enigmatic dialect which is at once blighted and rebellious. It is here that chastisement is visible; every syllable bears the brand. The words of this language of the people seem seared and shrivelled, as though by a red-hot iron; some, indeed, seem to be still smoking, and there are phrases which put one in mind of the swiftly bared and branded shoulder of a thief. Ideas are almost inexpressible in the language of the outlaw, of which the metaphors are sometimes so outrageous that one feels that they have worn manacles. But despite all this, and because of it, this strange patois is entitled to its place in that vast, impartial assemblage which finds room for a worn halfpenny as well as for a gold medal and which is known as literature. Argot, whether we like it or not, has its own grammar and its own poetry. If there are words so distorted that they sound like the muttering of uncouth mouths, there are others in which we catch the voice of Villon.

'*Mais où sont les neiges d'antan*' is a line of argot. Antan – *ante annum* – belongs to the argot of Thunes and signifies 'last year' and, by extension, 'the past'. It was possible thirty-five years ago, at the time of the departure of the great chain-gang of 1827, to read the following words scratched with a nail on the wall of one of the cells in Bicêtre prison by a leader of the Thunes mob condemned to the galleys: '*Les dabs d'antan trimaient siempre pour le pierre du Coëscne*', which means, 'The old-time kings always had themselves consecrated' – consecration, in this case, being the galleys

From the purely literary point of view few studies can be more interesting and fruitful than that of argot. It is a language within a language, a sort of sickly excrescence, an unhealthy graft producing a vegetation of its own, a parasite with roots in the old Gallic trunk whose sinister foliage covers half of the language. That is what one might term the first aspect, the vulgar aspect of argot. But for those who study the dialect as it should be studied, that is to say, in the way a geologist studies the earth, it is more like an alluvial deposit. Examining it one finds, buried beneath the old colloquial French, Provençal, Spanish, Italian, Levantine – that language of the Mediterranean ports – English, German, the French, Italian and Roman varieties of Romance, Latin and finally Basque and Celtic. A profound, weird conglomeration; a subterranean edifice erected by all outcasts. Each accursed race has contributed its layer, every heart and every suffering has added a stone. A host of souls, evil or low-born or rebellious, who have lived through life and passed on to eternity, are almost wholly present and in some sort still visible in the form of a monstrous word.

Do you wish for Spanish? The old Gothic argot is full of it: for example *boffette*, for which the French is *soufflet*, meaning a bellows, a puff of wind (blow) or a buffet, derived from *bofeton*; *vantarne* (later *vanterne*) meaning a window; *gat*, meaning cat, derived from *gato*; *acite*, oil, derived from *aceyte*. Or Italian? There is *spade*, sword, derived from *spada*; *carvel*, boat, derived from *carvella*. English? There is *bichot*, bishop; *raille*, a spy, derived from rascal; *pilche*, a case, derived from pilcher, a sheath. German? There is *caleur*, from the German *Kellner*, a waiter; *Herr*, the master, from *Herʒog*, the duke. Latin? *Franjir*, to break (Latin *frangere*); *affurer*, to steal (*fur*); *cadène*, a chain (*catena*). There is a word which appears in all the continental dialects with a sort of magical power and authority. It is the word *magnus* (great). In Scotland it becomes *mac*, meaning head of the clan,* such as Macfarlane or Macdonald; French argot turns it into *meck*, later *meg*, meaning God. Do you look for Basque? There is *gahisto*, the devil, derived from *gaiƺtoa*, evil; *sorgabon*, good night, derived from *gabon*, good evening. Celtic? There is *blavin*, handkerchief, derived from *blavet*, a spurt of water; *menesse*, woman (derogatory) derived from *meinec*, full of stones; *barant*, a stream, from *baranton*, fountain; *goffeur*, locksmith from *goff*, a smith; *guedouƺe*, death, which is derived from *guenn-du*, white-black. Finally, do you want history? Argot calls a crownpiece a *maltaise*, recalling the money which circulated in the Maltese galleys.

Apart from its philological origins, of which a few examples have been given, argot has other, more natural roots, emerging, so to speak, from the very spirit of man. First there is the actual creation of words, which is the mystery of all language – the depiction of objects by the use of words which, no one can say why or how, bear a countenance of their own. This is the primal basis of all language, what one might call the bedrock. Argot teems with such words, spontaneous words, created all of a piece no one can say where or by whom, words without etymology, analogy or derivation; solitary, barbaric, sometimes hideous words, which are nevertheless singularly expressive and which live. *Le taule*, the gaoler; *le sabri*, the forest; *taf*, meaning fear of flight; *le larbin*, the lackey; *pharos*, the general, prefect or minister; *le rabouin*, the devil. Nothing can be more strange than these words which both conceal and reveal. Some, such as *rabouin*, are at once grotesque and terrible, conveying the effect of a Cyclopean grimace.

Secondly, there is metaphor. The characteristic of a language that seeks both to say everything and to conceal everything is its abundance of imagery. Metaphor is a riddle behind which lurks the thief planning a robbery and the prisoner plotting an escape. No dialect is more rich in metaphor than argot – *devisser le coco*, to twist the neck; *tortiller*, to eat; *être gerbé*, to be judged; *un rat*, a stealer of bread; *il lansquine*, it is raining, an ancient, striking image which in some sort reveals its own date, relating the long, oblique lines of rainfall to the couched weapons of sixteenth-century pikemen, and also encompasses the popular saying, 'it's raining halberds'. Sometimes, as argot progresses from its first stage to the

*It should be noted, however, that 'mac' in Celtic means 'son'. (Note by Victor Hugo.)

second, words also pass from the savage, primitive stage to the metaphorical. The devil ceases to be *le rabouin* and becomes *le boulanger* (baker), 'he who puts in the oven'. It is more amusing but less impressive, something like Racine after Corneille, or Euripides after Aeschylus. And there are certain sentences of argot, belonging to both stages, which have a phantasmagoric quality. *Les sorgueurs vont sollicer des gails à la lune* (rustlers are going to steal horses tonight). This presents itself to the mind like a company of ghosts. One does not know what one is looking at.

Thirdly, there is expediency. Argot lives on the language, drawing upon it and making use of it as fancy directs, and sometimes, in case of need, arbitrarily and coarsely changing it. Sometimes, with ordinary words distorted in this fashion and interlarded with words of pure argot, it produces picturesque figures of speech in which one may find both original invention and metaphor. *Le cab jaspine, je marronne que la roulotte de Pantin trime dans le sabin* – 'The dog is barking, I suspect that the Paris coach is passing through the wood.' *Le dab est sinve, la dabuge est merloussière, la fée est bative* – 'The man (gentleman) is stupid, the wife is sly, the daughter is pretty.' Most frequently, in order to baffle any eavesdropper, argot simply adds an uncouth tail to the word, some such suffix as *aille, orgue, iergue* or *uche*. For example, *Vousiergue trouvaille bonorgue ce gigotmuche?* – 'Do you think this mutton's good?' A phrase addressed to a prison warder by a prisoner offering a sum of money for his escape. *Mar* is another suffix that has been recently added.

Argot, being the dialect of corruption, is itself soon corrupted. Moreover, as its purpose is always concealment, it changes as soon as it feels that it is being understood. Unlike every other form of vegetation, it is killed by any ray of light that falls upon it. So it is in a state of constant flux, evolving more in ten years than the everyday language does in ten centuries. *Larton* (bread) becomes *lartif*, *gail* (horse) becomes *gaye*, *fertanche* (straw) becomes *fertille*, *momignard* (child) becomes *momacque*, *les siques* (clothes) becomes *frusques*, *la chique* (church) becomes *l'égrugeoir*, *le colabre* (neck) becomes *le colas*. The devil is first *gahisto*, then *le rabouin* and then *le boulanger*; the priest is *le ratichon* and then *le sanglier*; the dagger is *le vingt-deux*, then *le surin* and then *le lingre*; the police are in turn *raliles, rousses, marchands de lacets, coqueurs* and *cognes*; the gaoler is *le taule, Charlot, l'atigeur*, and *le becquillard*. To fight in the seventeenth century was *se donner du tabac*; in the nineteenth, *se chiquer la gueule* – and there have been twenty different variants between those two. The words of argot are constantly in flight, like the men who use them.

But at the same time, and indeed because of this constant movement, old argot constantly re-emerges and becomes new. There are centres in which it survives. The Temple preserved the argot of the seventeenth century, and the argot of Thunes was preserved in Bicêtre when it was a prison. The old Thunes suffix of *anche* was heard in, for example, *Boyanches-tu?* (Want a drink?) and *il croyanche* (he believes). But constant change is nonetheless the rule.

If the philosopher decides to spare the time to examine this language that ceaselessly evaporates, he is led to painful but useful reflections. No study is more efficacious or fruitful in instruction. There is not a metaphor or etymological derivation of argot that does not contain a lesson

Among those people *battre* (to fight) means to sham – *on bat une maladie* (one shams an illness), for tricking is their strength. The idea of 'man' is inseparable from the idea of darkness. Night is *la sorgue*, and man is *l'orgue*: man is a derivation of night. They are accustomed to think of society as a climate that destroys them, and they talk of their freedom as other people talk of their health. A man who has been arrested is *un malade* (sick), and a man under sentence is *un mort* (dead).

What is most dreadful for the man enclosed within the walls of a prison is a sort of icy chastity: he calls the prison *le castus*. It is always the gayer side of life outside that he recalls when he is in that dismal place. He wears leg-irons but does not think of walking on his feet: he thinks of dancing; and if he manages to saw through his irons, dancing is his first thought and he calls the saw a *bastringue* (cheap dance-hall). A noun is *un centre* – a profound assimilation. A criminal has two heads, the one which thinks and plans, and the one which he loses on the block: he calls the first *la sorbonne* and the second *la tronche.** When a man has nothing left but rags on his body and viciousness in his heart, when he has sunk to the state of material and moral degradation which is summed up in the word *gueux*, he is then ripe for crime; he is like a well-sharpened, double-edged knife, one edge being his state of need and the other his depravity. Argot in this case does not call him *un gueux* but *un*

*La Sorbonne – the university of Paris. Tronche – commonplace slang, as it might be, 'nut'. Trs.

reguise (re-shaped). What is a gaol but a furnace of damnation, a Hell? The inmate calls himself *un fagot* (faggot). Finally, they call the prison *le collège*, a word which sums up the whole penitentiary system. And to the thief his prospective victims – you or I or any passer-by – are *le pantre*, from the Greek *pan*, meaning *everyone*.

Should you wish to know where the greater number of the prison-songs were born, those ditties which prison argot calls *lirlonfa*, the following is for your enlightenment.

There existed in the Châtelet in Paris a large, long cellar some eight feet below the level of the Seine. It possessed neither windows nor ventilators, its only outlet being by way of the door: men could enter it, but air could not. It had a vaulted stone ceiling and for floor ten inches of mud, the original tiling having disintegrated under the seeping of water. A massive beam ran from end to end of the cellar, eight feet above floor level, and from it, at regular intervals, hung chains three feet long ending in iron collars. It was here that men condemned to the galleys were housed before being sent on to Toulon. They hung here in darkness chained by the neck, unable to lie down because of the shortness of the chains, up to their knees in mud, legs soiled with their own excrement, unable to rest except by hanging on to the chains and, if they dozed off, constantly awakened by the stranglehold of the collar – and there were some who did not wake. In order to eat they had to use their feet to retrieve their portion of bread, which was dropped on the mud in front of them. How long were they left like this? One or two months, sometimes six months, in one case a year. They had been sentenced to the galleys for as little as poaching one of the king's hares. And what did they do in that hellish tomb? They did what can be done in a tomb – they died – and what can be done in Hell – they sang. Where there is no hope there is still song. In the sea round Malta when a galley was approaching one heard the sound of singing before one heard the sound of oars. The poacher Survincent, who survived that Châtelet cellar, said, 'It was the rhymes that kept me going.' Here it was that nearly all the argot ditties were born, including the melancholy refrain that was particular to the Montgomery galley – *Timaloumisaine, timoulamison.* Most of these songs were sad, but some were gay and one was tender:

> *Icicaille est le théâtre*
> *Du petit dardant.**

*This is the theatre of the little archer.

Do what you will, you cannot destroy that eternal remnant of the heart of man which is love.

In that world of dark deeds one keeps one's secrets. Secrecy is the privilege of everyman, the faith held in common which serves as the basis of union. To break secrecy is to rob every member of that savage community of something of himself. To inform is to *manger le morceau* (eat the piece) as though the informer had stolen something of the substance of his fellows and fed on the flesh of all of them.

What is *recevoir un soufflet* (to get your ears boxed)? The commonplace French expression is *voir trente-six chandelles* (to see thirty-six candles; English equivalent 'to see stars'). Argot here makes use of the word *camoufle*, which also means 'candle' and adds the 'et' from the word *soufflet*, establishing a new word on the academic level, and Ponlailler, saying, '*J'allume ma camoufle*' causes Voltaire to write, '*Langleviel la Baumelle mérite cent camouflets*' (Langleviel la Baumelle deserves to have his ears boxed a hundred times).

Burrowing into argot leads to countless discoveries. It leads us to the point of contact between respectable society and that of the outcasts; it is speech become a felon, and it is dismaying to find that the obscure workings of fate can so distort men's minds and bring them so low. The meagre thinking of the outcast! Will no one come to the rescue of the human souls lost in that darkness? Must they wait for ever for the liberating spirit, the rider upon the winds, the radiant champion of the future? Are they condemned for all time to listen in terror to the approach of the Monster of Evil, the dragon with foaming lips, while they remain without light or hope, a defenceless Andromeda, white and naked in the murk?

III

Argot that weeps and argot that laughs

As we see, argot as a whole, whether it is the dialect of four hundred years ago or that of today, is pervaded by a sombre symbolism which is at once an expression of grieving and of threatening. One may catch something of the old, wild sadness of those outlaws of the Cour des Miracles who played card-games of their own devising, some of which have come down to us. The eight of clubs, for example, was a big tree with eight large clover-leaves, a sort of fanciful representation of the forest; at the foot of the tree was a fire over which a hunter was roasting three hares on a spit, while behind, suspended over another fire, was a steaming pot from which a dog's head protruded. One may picture smugglers and counterfeiters seated round this idyllic and melancholy conception of their world as depicted on playing-cards. All the diverse expressions of thought in the kingdom of argot, whether song or jest or threat, had this quality of helpless despair. All the songs, of which some of the tunes have been retrieved, were heartrendingly piteous and humble. The thieving rabble, *le pègre*, was always *le pauvre pègre*, always the hare which hides, the mouse which scuttles, the bird which takes flight. It utters few but simple sighs, and one of its sighs has been preserved – '*Je n'entrave que le dail comment meck, le daron des orgues, peut atiger ses mômes et ses momignards et les locher criblant sans être atigé lui-même*' (I don't undertsand how God, the father of men, can torture his children and grandchildren and hear them cry without being tortured himself). The outcast, whenever he has a moment to think, makes himself small in the eye of the law and puny in the eye of society; he goes on his knees and begs for pity. One feels that he knows the fault is his own.

Towards the middle of the last century there was a change. Prison songs and thieves' refrains acquired as it were a flavour of jovial insolence. In nearly all the galley and prison songs of the eighteenth century there is a diabolical, enigmatic spirit of gaiety which puts one in mind of the dancing light cast by a will-o'-the-wisp in the forest.

> *Mirlababi, surlababo,*
> *Mirliton ribon ribette,*
> *Surlababi, mirlababo,*
> *Mirliton ribon ribo.*

This was being sung while a man's throat was being cut in a cellar or a corner of the woods.

It was symptomatic. In the eighteenth century the ancient melancholy of this oppressed class was dispelled. They began to laugh, mocking the powers that be. Louis XV was known as the 'Marquis de Pantin'. They were almost cheerful, glowing with a kind of lightness as though conscience no longer weighed upon them. Not merely did they perform acts of desperate daring, but they did so with a heedless audacity of spirit. It was an indication that they were losing the sense of their own criminality, finding among the thinkers of the day a kind of unwitting moral support, an indication that theft and robbery were beginning to infiltrate doctrine and current dogma, and thereby losing something of their ugliness while adding greatly to the ugliness of the latter. Finally it was an indication that, if nothing happened to prevent it, some tremendous event was on the way.

Let us pause for a moment. What are we now accusing – the eighteenth century? – its philosophy? By no means. The work of the eighteenth century was healthy and good. The encyclopaedists, led by Diderot, the physiocrats, led by Turgot, the philosophers, led by Voltaire, and the Utopians, led by Rousseau, these are four noble bodies. The immense advance of mankind towards enlightenment was due to them. They were the advance-guards of the human race moving towards the four cardinal points of progress, Diderot towards beauty, Turgot towards utility, Voltaire towards truth, and Rousseau towards justice. But at the side of the philosophers and below them came the sophists, a poisonous plant intertwined with healthy youth, hemlock in the virgin forest. While authority burned the great liberating books of the century on the steps of the Palais de Justice, writers now forgotten were publishing, with the king's sanction, books of a strangely subversive kind, avidly read by the outcasts. Some of these publications – patronized, astonishingly enough, by a prince – are to be found in the Bibliothèque Secrète, the Secret Library. These facts, profoundly significant though they were, passed unperceived. Sometimes it is the very obscurity of a fact that renders it dangerous. It is obscure because it is underground. Of all those writers, the one perhaps who had the most harmful effects on the masses was Restif de la Bretonne. Work of this kind, which was being produced all over Europe, did more damage in Germany than anywhere else. During a certain period, which is summarized by Schiller in his play, *Die Räuber*, theft and robbery were paraded under the guise of protest against property and work. They embraced certain specious, elementary notions, correct in appearance but absurd in reality, and, thus dissimulated and invested with names denoting abstract theories, permeated the mass of hard-working, honest people, without the knowledge of the rash chemists who had concocted the mixture and even of the masses who absorbed it. Hardship engenders anger; and while the well-to-do classes close their eyes – or slumber, which comes to the same thing – the less fortunate, taking their inspiration from any spirit of grievance or ill-will what happens to be lurking in the background, proceed to examine the social system. Examination in a spirit of hatred is a terrible thing!

From this, if the times are sufficiently awry, emerge those ferocious upheavals at one time known as *jacqueries*, compared with which purely political agitation is child's play, and which are not the struggle of the oppressed against the oppressor but rather the revolt of the deprived against the comfortably off. Everything then collapses, for *jacqueries* are the tremors of the people. This peril, which was perhaps imminent in Europe towards the end of the eighteenth century, was harshly averted by the French Revolution, that immense act of probity. The French Revolution, which was nothing but idealism in arms, broke out and with a single decisive gesture slammed the door on evil and opened the door to good. It posed the question, promulgated the truth, dispelled the fogs, cleansed the century, and crowned the people.

The nineteenth century has inherited and profited by its work, and today the social disaster which seemed to be foreshadowed is quite simply impossible. Only the blind still rage against it, and only fools are afraid of it. Revolution is the antidote to *jacquerie*!

Thanks to the Revolution, social conditions have changed and we have got the feudal and monarchic sicknesses out of our system. There is no longer anything medieval in our constitution. We have come past the time when those ugly interior convulsions burst into daylight, when we heard the muffled sound of stirring beneath our feet, when the surface of civilization was littered with molehills, when crevasses suddenly yawned and monstrous heads emerged from the earth.

Revolutionary feeling is a moral feeling. The feeling for what is right, once it has matured, develops a sense of duty. The law for every man is liberty, which ends, in Robespierre's admirable definition, where the liberty of others begins. Since 1789 the populace as a whole is expressed in the sublimated individual; no man is so poor that, having rights, he has not his place. The starving man feels in himself the honesty of France; the dignity of the citizen is an inner armour; the man who is free is scrupulous; he who votes rules. Hence the incorruptibility, the suppression of unhealthy aspirations, the eyes heroically averted from temptation. Revolutionary cleansing is such that on a day of liberation, a 14 July or a 10

August, there is no longer a populace. The first cry of the enlightened crowds as they grow in stature is, 'Death to thieves!' Progress is honourable; the Ideal and the Absolute do not pick pockets. It was the scavengers of the Faubourg Saint-Antoine who in 1848 escorted the carts filled with the treasures of the Tuileries; rags and tatters mounted guard over riches. In those carts there were chests, some half open, containing among a hundred dazzling adornments the ancient, diamond-studded crown of France surmounted by the royal carbuncle of regency, worth thirty millions. Those barefoot men preserved it.

So *jacquerie* is at an end. I am sorry for the clever men, haunted by an age-old fear which has found its last expression and now can only be serviceable in politics. The mainspring of the red spectre is broken, and everyone knows it. The scarecrow scares no longer. Birds perch on it, beetles nest in it and the bourgeois laughs at it.

IV

The two duties; to watch and hope

Does this mean then that all social dangers are over? Certainly not. There will be no more *jacqueries*, of this society can be assured; the blood will no longer rush to its head. But it has got to consider the way in which it breathes. Apoplexy is no longer a threat, but there is still consumption. Social consumption is simply poverty. One can die from wasting away as well as from being struck by lightning.

We never weary of repeating that we must before all else think of the disinherited, suffering masses, care for them, comfort and enlighten them, widen their horizon by bringing to them all forms of education. We must set them the example of toil, never of idleness, lessen the burden on the individual by increasing that borne by society as a whole, reduce poverty without reducing wealth, create great new fields of public activity, possess, like Briareus, a hundred hands to reach out to those who are in distress, use our collective power to set up workshops, schools, and laboratories open to men of all kinds, increase wages and decrease working hours, effect a balance between rights and possessions, that is to say, make the reward proportionate to the effort and the fulfilment to the need – in a word, derive more light and well-being from the social system for the benefit of the ignorant and oppressed. This is the first of fraternal obligations and of political necessities.

But all of this, we must emphasize, is no more than a beginning. The real question is, can work be the law without also being a right? We shall not pursue the matter, since this is not the place for it. But if the name for Nature is Providence, then the name for Society must be Provision.

Intellectual and moral growth is no less essential than material betterment. Knowledge is a viaticum; thought is a primary necessity; truth is as much a source of nourishment as corn. Argument lacking knowledge and wisdom grows thin. We must pity minds, no less than stomachs, that go unfilled. If there is anything more poignant than a body dying for lack of food it is a mind dying for lack of light.

All progress points in this direction, and the day is coming when we shall be amazed. As the state of the human race improves, its lowest layers will rise quite naturally above the zone of distress. The abolition of poverty will be achieved by a simple raising of the level. This is a blessed solution, and we shall be wrong to doubt it.

Certainly the influence of the past is very strong at the present time; it is reviving, and this rejuvenation of a corpse is surprising. It is on the march, and it seems to be winning – a dead thing yet a conqueror! It comes with its army of superstitions, its sword, which is despotism, its banner, which is ignorance, and in recent years it has won ten battles. It advances, laughs, and threatens; it is at our door. But we do not despair. Let us sell the field on which Hannibal is encamped. We who believe, what have we to fear? Ideas can no more flow backwards than can a river.

But those who do not welcome the future should consider this: in denying progress it is not the future that they condemn, but themselves. They are inoculating themselves with a fatal disease, the past. There is only one way of denying tomorrow, and that is to die.

The riddle will disclose its answer, the Sphinx will speak, the problem will be solved. The People, having burst their bonds in the eighteenth century, will complete their triumph in the nineteenth. Only a fool can doubt it. The coming achievement, the imminent achievement of universal well-being, is a phenomenon divinely preordained.

The immense pressure of events indicates that within a given time human society will be brought to its logical condition, that is to say, into equilibrium, which is the same as equity. A power comprising earth and Heaven emanates from humanity and directs it; it is a power that can work miracles, to which miraculous accomplishments are no more difficult than extraordinary deviations. Aided by the knowledge which comes from man, and the event which comes from another source, this power is undismayed by contradictions arising out of the problem it poses, which to the common mind seem impossibilities. It is no less adroit in producing solutions out of the conjunction of ideas than it is in producing lessons out of the juxtaposition of facts. One may expect anything of this mysterious power of progress which on one occasion caused East and West to meet in a sepulchre, and the Imams to treat with Bonaparte in the interior of the Great Pyramid.

Meanwhile there must be no pause, no hesitation, in the forward march of minds. Social philosophy is essentially the science of peace. Its purpose is, and its outcome should be, to dissipate anger by studying the reasons for antagonism. It scrutinizes and analyses, then reshapes. It proceeds by a process of reduction, eliminating the element of hatred.

That a society should be destroyed by the winds that assail human affairs is by no means unknown; history is filled with the shipwreck of nations and empires. The day comes when the hurricane, that unknown factor, bears custom, law, religion, everything away. One after another, the civilizations of India, the Chaldees, Persia, Assyria, and Egypt have perished, and we do not know why. We do not know the cause of these disasters. Could those societies have been saved? Were they at fault? Did they persist in some fatal vice which destroyed them? How great is the element of suicide in the death of a nation or a race? They are questions without answer. The condemned civilizations are lost in darkness. They were not seaworthy and so they sank and there is nothing more to be said. It is with a sort of horror that we peer into the depths of that sea which is the past, through the great waves of the centuries, at the huge wrecks which are Babylon, Nineveh, Tarsus, Thebes, and Rome. But if they are buried, we exist in the light of day. We are ignorant of the sickness of ancient civilizations, but we know the infirmities of our own. We are able everywhere to throw light upon it, to admire its beauties and lay bare its deformities. We probe it to see where it hurts, and when we have found the pain-centre our examination of the cause leads to the discovery of the remedy. Our civilization, the work of twenty centuries, is at once their monster and their prodigy; it is worth saving. And it will be saved.

To doctor it is to do a great deal; to enlighten it is to do still more. All the work of modern social philosophy should bear this end in mind. To auscultate civilization is the supreme duty of the thinker of today.

Let us repeat it, this auscultation is encouraging; and it is with emphasis on the note of encouragement that we wish to end these few pages of austere digression from our sombre narrative. Beneath social mortality we are conscious of human imperishability. The earth does not die because there are lesions on its body, craters and volcanoes out of which it pours its pus. The sickness of a nation does not kill Man.

Nevertheless, those who study the health of society must now and then shake their heads. Even the strongest-minded and most clear-thinking must have their moments of misgiving. Will the future ever arrive? The question seems almost justified when one considers the shadows looming ahead, the sombre confrontation of egoists and outcasts. On the side of the egoists, prejudice – that darkness of a rich education – appetite that grows with intoxication, the bemusement of prosperity which blunts the sense, the fear of suffering which in some cases goes so far as to hate all sufferers, and unshakeable complacency, the ego so inflated that it stifles the soul; and on the side of the outcasts, greed and envy, resentment at the happiness of others, the turmoil of the human animal in search of personal fulfilment, hearts filled with fog, misery, needs, and fatalism, and simple, impure ignorance.

Should we continue to look upwards? Is the light we can see in the sky one of those which will presently be extinguished? The ideal is terrifying to behold, lost as it is in the depths, small, isolated, a pin-point, brilliant but threatened on all sides by the dark forces that surround it: nevertheless, no more in danger than a star in the jaws of the clouds.